THREE GREAT NOVELS OF THE CIVIL WAR

THREE GREAT NOVELS OF THE CIVIL WAR

THE KILLER ANGELS
BY MICHAEL SHAARA

ANDERSONVILLE
BY MACKINLAY KANTOR

THE RED BADGE OF COURAGE
BY STEPHEN CRANE

EDITED BY MARC JAFFE

WINGS BOOKS
New York · Avenel, New Jersey

The editor wishes to thank his son-in-law, Robert F. Armistead, for supplying the original inspiration which resulted in this volume. Also thanks to Jeff Shaara for the biographical information on his father, Michael Shaara. Finally, as always, thanks to my wife, Vivienne Jaffe, for her guidance and constant support.

Copyright © 1994 by Random House Value Publishing, Inc.

This omnibus was originally published in separate volumes under the titles:
The Killer Angels, copyright © 1974 by Michael Shaara
Andersonville, copyright © 1955 by MacKinlay Kantor, copyright renewed © 1983 by Layne Shroder and Tim Kantor
The Red Badge of Courage by Stephen Crane

This edition contains the complete and unabridged texts of the original editions. They have been completely reset for this volume.

This 1994 edition is published by Wings Books,
distributed by Random House Value Publishing, Inc.,
40 Engelhard Avenue, Avenel, New Jersey 07001,
by arrangement with David McKay Company, Inc. for *The Killer Angels*; and Tim Kantor and Layne Kantor Shroder, the children of MacKinlay Kantor, the deceased author, for *Andersonville*.

Random House
New York • Toronto • London • Sydney • Auckland

Printed and bound in the United States of America

Library of Congress Cataloging-in-Publication Data

Three great novels of the Civil War / edited by Marc Jaffe.
     p.   cm.
    Contents: The killer angels / by Michael Shaara — Andersonville / by MacKinlay Kantor — The red badge of courage / by Stephen Crane.
    ISBN 0-517-12196-4
    1. United States—History—Civil War, 1861–1865—Fiction. 2. War stories, American. I. Jaffe, Marc. II. Shaara, Michael. Killer angels. III. Kantor, MacKinlay, 1904–1977. Andersonville. IV. Crane, Stephen, 1871–1900. Red badge of courage.
PS648.C54G74   1994
813.009'358—dc20   94-19298
                                                          CIP

8   7   6   5   4   3   2   1

CONTENTS

Fiction and the Civil War

The flow of words inspired by the Civil War began long before the guns fell silent at Appomattox. Along with journalism, there were poetry, fiction, diaries and letters, reaching from the most mundane to the brief, never-to-be forgotten sentences spoken by Abraham Lincoln at Gettysburg. The flow became a river, then almost a flood. By 1982, for example, one bibliography of books and articles about Gettysburg alone contained some 2,700 entries.

How significant was the part played by fiction in this current of writing and publication? The most important of all Civil War fiction—at least from the historical point of view—was Harriet Beecher Stowe's *Uncle Tom's Cabin,* published in 1852, years before the War. The novel was a sensation even in late twentieth-century terms, reaching a sale of 305,000 copies in the United States, and 2 1/2 million copies abroad (in English and translation) in its very first year of publication.

More than a mere bestseller, *Uncle Tom* was a political bombshell which, in the opinion of many, actually served as a precipitating factor in the conflict to come. From that point on, one can think of Civil War fiction as a series of singular milestones in literary history rather than a growing genre with a continuing popularity or even a core audience. Within a mere forty years after its appearance, for example, even Mrs. Stowe's classic was out of print.

Two post-Civil War writers identified with the South are clearly important for students of American literature, George W. Cable and Thomas Nelson Page, the latter because he set in motion the romanticized view of the wartime and antebellum plantation South, an image which reached its peak in *Gone With the Wind* in 1936. (In *Patriotic Gore,* the critic Edmund Wilson points out the "curious counterbalance" of the "enormous success" of *Uncle Tom's Cabin* and the Margaret Mitchell novel, appearing almost a century apart.)

In 1895 came another milestone, *The Red Badge of Courage.* It was important not only as a bestseller, but even more as part of the development of realistic fiction, taking the place of the florid Sir Walter Scott-inspired works which characterized the pre-Civil War years.

Not until the 1930s did the Civil War emerge again with real impact in popular literature—with *Gone With the Wind* and the novels of William Faulkner, particularly his magnificent *Absalom, Absalom.* From then on, a steady, though intermittent, presence of Civil War fiction appeared.

In 1955 came *Andersonville,* a bestseller and a Pulitzer Prize winner (and, interestingly and perhaps significantly, by comparison to *Uncle Tom,* very much in print forty years after its publication!). In the 1970s we see the publication of *The Killer Angels,* another Pulitzer Prize winner, and in the 1980s novels such as Toni Morrison's *Beloved* and Rosellen Brown's *Civil Wars.* Alongside these works arrived important popular fiction by writers like John Jakes and others, with a continuing surge of entertainment in mass-market paperback form.

The legacy of the Civil War is the nation we know today. Almost without exception the strands of glory and achievement, as well as social and political failure, can be traced back to that "irrepressible conflict." The three novels included in this volume provide not only memorable reading but a path of exploration of that past, perhaps more clearly marked than any other we could place before us.

It was not the last battle, as General Robert E. Lee had hoped. Far from it. But history has shown that Gettysburg was the critical battle of the Civil War, the one in which the stakes were the highest for both Gray and Blue. In the end, there was no clear victor; Lee's troops, those that remained after the slaughter, left the field and fought again. Meade's army licked its savage wounds, revived and ultimately prevailed. Gettysburg, though, was the great testing ground—of men and of issues, and became, therefore, an unsullied mirror for this nation's understanding of itself—in 1863, and even now.

A great battle deserves a great novel—and we have it in *The Killer Angels*. First of all, this is accurate history, military history, to be precise. It is, as the author says at the outset, based primarily on "the words of the men themselves, their letters and other documents." Unusual for a work of fiction, it even includes a series of eighteen clearly drawn battle maps, which serve almost as backdrops on a stage, to carry the reader through the often complex actions of company, brigade and army corps.

Yet with all this attention to factual accuracy, how fares the art of fiction in *The Killer Angels*? Are there heroes? Villains? Plot? Character? The conventions of narrative structure and conflict? Shaara attempts a bold experiment, almost a tour-de-force, and succeeds brilliantly.

The central presence in the novel is the battle itself—day by day. It begins from the point at which General Lee, already in Pennsylvania, is informed of the enemy's movements and decides on a course of action, and continues until the night of Friday, July 3rd, when the heavy rain came, "cleansing the earth . . . driving the blood deep into the earth, to grow it again with the roots toward Heaven." The author undertakes this chronology selectively, moving his point of view among no more than a half-dozen principal characters. He chooses the voices of Lee and Longstreet to focus on the fate of the army of the South. Toward the end, there is General Lewis Armistead, "a grave and courtly man, a soldier all his life," who "felt things more than anyone knew" despite a calm and martial bearing. He strongly sensed the darkness to come, yet drew his sword, pointed it at the smoke-bound Cemetery Ridge and called his brigade to battle with words that have rung down the years—"All right now boys, for your wives, your sweethearts, for Virginia!" It is Armistead's voice that carries the reader through perhaps the most poignant pages in the novel. His voice is as essential to the novel as is his death in Pickett's Charge, the closest the South was to reach to the taste of total victory throughout the entire war.

In a careful but disarming fashion, Shaara's chief Northern soldier is not a general, but Joshua Chamberlain, the thoughtful and intellectual colonel whose 20th Maine successfully defended Little Round Top and who survived to "become one of the most remarkable soldiers in American history," as well as governor of his home state and a controversial President of Bowdoin College in 1876.

The author sums it all up through Chamberlain, who observes evening fall over a field "like the gray floor of hell." Chamberlain knows he has been present at one of the great moments in history, and "he thought of Aristotle: pity and terror . . . so this is tragedy. Yes. He nodded. In the presence of real tragedy you feel

neither pain nor joy nor hatred, only a sense of enormous space and time suspended, the great doors open to black eternity, the rising across the terrible field
of that last enormous, unanswerable question."

For a green, young private like Stephen Crane's Henry Fleming in *The Red
Badge of Courage,* there is little time or inclination to place oneself in the great
sweep of history. War was a challenge and a lodestar; the far-off bugles sounded
the call to glory and the "breathless deeds" that test a boy's mettle. And so it
happened, though not at all as Fleming's farm-boy imagination made it out to be.
First came the boredom of months and months of drill and review, drill and
review; the only challenge was to try to keep warm.

At last comes a call to action, but to the men in the lines it was all chaos and
confusion. Artillery roars, bullets flick through leaves and branches; the wounded
cry out in torment. Henry watches his friend, tall Jim Conklin, fall like a tree, his
side looking as if "chewed by wolves"; and in the end he flees from his first
engagement. Time and events pass with a deadly swiftness; there is another engagement; the colonel orders a charge against the gray-clad enemy. Henry Fleming seizes the colors from a fallen comrade and rushes them to the front, "waving
his free arm in furious circles, the while shrieking mad calls and appeals. . . . He
himself felt the daring spirit of a savage religion—mad . . . capable of profound
sacrifices, a tremendous death."

After the successful attack comes Fleming's moment of contemplation of the
gritty memories of sins on the field of battle and the meaning of his survival; "His
eyes seemed to open to some new ways. . . . He felt a quiet manhood, nonassertive but a sturdy and strong blood. . . . He had been to touch the great death
and found that, after all, it was but the great death. He was a man."

The Red Badge of Courage was an immediate bestseller when it was published
in 1895, has been read by millions in the years since, and is required reading for
most high-school and college students today. It is such because it is very likely the
most perceptive and powerful exploration of the psychology of the individual in
combat, the essential nature of courage and cowardice. If, as Heraclitus said,
"War is the natural state of man," this is the most natural of novels, for it deals
solely with man and war—nothing else.

War, one must recall, is more than the thrust and parry of platoon or brigade
and the thunder of guns; it is more than the pride and sorrow of colonels and
generals or the fears and blind faith of teenage boys at the front. Far behind the
lines, war goes on, and a prison camp is perhaps an even more brutal crucible of
human nature than the heat of battle.

Andersonville is a story of the Civil War as it never has been told—before or
since its publication in 1955—only hinted at in some of the diaries and other
documents on which the novel is based. Like all the best of historical fiction, its
blend of fact and invention gives depth and drama to events of the past. Here, it
takes the reader to the very heart of one of the darkest episodes in all of American history, for some 14,000 Northern soldiers died in Andersonville prison, almost one-third of its population.

As the Southern planter Ira Claffey reflects, "Had Americans ever brought so
many Americans to death in such limited acreage before? . . . No great battle
was ever waged within the confines of a twenty-eight acre patch." Clearly, Mac-
Kinlay Kantor's great theme is the relationship of every man and woman to the
inexorable grasp of history. And American history provides no better exploration
for such a theme than the Civil War.

For the Claffeys of Georgia, the loss of three sons—killed in battle—is actually
a starting point; for the mother, a descent into memory; for daughter Lucy, a

thrust into the demands of everyday survival and the discovery of sexuality; for Ira, an ever-present reminder of his lonely responsibility for both blacks and whites on the plantation adjoining the infamous prison.

It is through Ira that the world of the wartime South is seen, at its best and worst; he serves as a kind of Greek chorus to the action and, at the very end, thinking of Pericles' famous funeral oration, he concludes that "he himself hold no desire or ambition, but this bruised collection of States must hold ambition, else this Nation was not fit for the sun to shine upon it. . . ."

There are other Southerners, brutal officers and men, many of them. Most significantly there is the familiar character out of history, Captain Henry Wirz, Swiss-born and accented, but "Southern" to the core, who is assigned the task of Superintendent of Andersonville. The twentieth-century echo here is not anachronistic, but carries special weight nonetheless, when Wirz is arrested after the surrender, saying plaintively, yet eagerly, "I carry out orders! They tell me to be superintendent of the stockade, so I serve. I *am* superintendent, I do my duty. . . ."

The Union prisoners run the gamut from the bestial to the angelic; their story is that of Everyprisoner. Their desire is to survive or to escape, and the strongest of body or spirit do both.

Kantor reserves his most powerful message, however, for an episode and a relationship neither inside the stockade, nor from remembered battles, nor the Georgia countryside in wartime. Two crippled young soldiers confront each other, the Northerner an escaped prisoner with only one arm, the Southerner devastated by the loss of a leg; their units had clashed, all unknowing, on that wheat field in Pennsylvania (Gettysburg again!). It is through their odd and painful reconciliation, a giving and a giving-up from one to the other, that we can see the way by which hatred is transmuted into love of one human being for another.

≡⁄≡

The Civil War has not loosed its grip on the American soul. Novels, as well as a wide spectrum of nonfiction works, continue to appear, and television and film have played an important role in recent years as an inspiration for renewed examination of what the War has meant to Americans. The novels which follow, however, have emerged and remain as landmarks. Taken together, they convey the experience of the War in the most profound way—through the reader's imagination. And like all great creative works, they go beyond surface content. *The Killer Angels* is a novel of command decision and its larger-than-life results. *The Red Badge of Courage* is a novel about the nature of bravery and cowardice— immediate and particular. *Andersonville* takes the widest view—human accountability on the scales of history.

Read then, and go forth to understand yourself and your legacy.

Marc Jaffe
Berlin, NY
July 15, 1994

THE KILLER
ANGELS

by
Michael Shaara

MICHAEL SHAARA was born in 1928 in Jersey City, New Jersey. After graduating from Rutgers University in 1951, he served as a paratrooper in the 82nd Airborne Division, was an amateur boxer and a police officer. In 1960 he became a professor of creative writing at Florida State University, where he won a faculty-wide award for excellence in teaching.

His writing career includes the publication of some 70 short stories, beginning in the early 1950s, in the heyday of such classic science fiction publications as *Astounding* and *Galaxy*. Subsequent stories were published in *The Saturday Evening Post, Playboy, Redbook, Cosmopolitan* and other magazines. His first novel, *The Broken Place,* was published in 1968. Other novels include *The Herald, The Noah Conspiracy* and *For Love of the Game* (published after his death).

Shaara's best known work is, of course, *The Killer Angels,* which won the Pulitzer Prize for fiction and has been a number one bestseller with over 1.2 million copies in print in its paperback edition alone. The novel has been a special inspiration to filmmakers. It is the basis for the monumental, four-hour film *Gettysburg,* released in 1994. Perhaps just as significant, Ken Burns, the renowned TV producer and director, has commented that reading *The Killer Angels* inspired him to begin work on his now-classic series, "The Civil War," and called it "a book that changed my life."

Michael Shaara died in 1988 at the age of 59. He is survived by his wife Helen, son Jeff, also a writer, and daughter Lila.

To Lila (old George)
. . . in whom I am well pleased

CONTENTS

MAPS

To the Reader

This is the story of the Battle of Gettysburg, told from the viewpoints of Robert E. Lee and James Longstreet and some of the other men who fought there.

Stephen Crane once said that he wrote *The Red Badge of Courage* because reading the cold history was not enough; he wanted to know what it was like to *be* there, what the weather was like, what men's faces looked like. In order to live it he had to write it. This book was written for much the same reason.

You may find it a different story from the one you learned in school. There have been many versions of that battle and that war. I have therefore avoided historical opinions and gone back primarily to the words of the men themselves, their letters and other documents. I have not consciously changed any fact. I have condensed some of the action, for the sake of clarity, and eliminated some minor characters, for brevity; but though I have often had to choose between conflicting viewpoints, I have not knowingly violated the action. I have changed some of the language. It was a naïve and sentimental time, and men spoke in windy phrases. I thought it necessary to update some of the words so that the religiosity and naïveté of the time, which were genuine, would not seem too quaint to the modern ear. I hope I will be forgiven that.

The interpretation of character is my own.

Michael Shaara

Harrisburg

Carlisle

Shippensburg

Chambersburg

Columbia

Lancaster

York

GETTYSBURG

Hanover

PENNSYLVANIA
MARYLAND

Hagerstown

Westminster

Frederick

BALTIMORE

Harpers Ferry

W. VA.

MARYLAND
VIRGINIA

Potomac River

WASHINGTON

Alexandria

Manassas Jct.

Chesapeake Bay

Susquehanna River

South Mountain

0 5 10 15 20
Miles

Route of Lee's Army, moving north
behind the mountains
Route of Stuart's Cavalry
Route of Union Army, moving north
out of Washington

SITUATION
June 1863

FOREWORD

JUNE 1863

I. The Armies

On June 15 the first troops of the Army of Northern Virginia, Robert E. Lee commanding, slip across the Potomac at Williamsport and begin the invasion of the North.

It is an army of seventy thousand men. They are rebels and volunteers. They are mostly unpaid and usually self-equipped. It is an army of remarkable unity, fighting for disunion. It is Anglo-Saxon and Protestant. Though there are many men who cannot read or write, they all speak English. They share common customs and a common faith and they have been consistently victorious against superior members. They have as solid a faith in their leader as any veteran army that ever marched. They move slowly north behind the Blue Ridge, using the mountains to screen their movements. Their main objective is to draw the Union Army out into the open where it can be destroyed. By the end of the month they are closing on Harrisburg, having spread panic and rage and despair through the North.

Late in June the Army of the Potomac, ever slow to move, turns north at last to begin the great pursuit which will end at Gettysburg. It is a strange new kind of army, a polyglot mass of vastly dissimilar men, fighting for union. There are strange accents and strange religions and many who do not speak English at all. Nothing like this army has been seen upon the planet. It is a collection of men from many different places who have seen much defeat and many commanders. They are volunteers: last of the great volunteer armies, for the draft is beginning that summer in the North. They have lost faith in their leaders but not in themselves. They think this will be the last battle, and they are glad that it is to be fought on their own home ground. They come up from the South, eighty thousand men, up the narrow roads that converge toward the blue mountains. The country through which they march is some of the most beautiful country in the Union.

It is the third summer of the war.

II. The Men

Robert Edward Lee. He is in his fifty-seventh year. Five feet ten inches tall but very short in the legs, so that when he rides a horse he seems much taller. Red-faced, like all the Lees, white-bearded, dressed in an old gray coat and a gray felt hat, without insignia, so that he is mistaken sometimes for an elderly major of dignity. An honest man, a gentleman. He has no "vices." He does not drink or smoke or gamble or chase women. He does not read novels or plays; he thinks they weaken the mind. He does not own slaves nor believe in slavery, but he does not believe that the Negro, "in the present stage of his development," can be considered the equal of the white man. He is a man in control. He does not lose his temper nor his faith; he never complains. He has been down that spring with the first assault of the heart disease which will eventually kill him. He believes absolutely in God. He loves Virginia above all, the mystic dirt of home. He is the most beloved man in either army.

He marches knowing that a letter has been prepared by Jefferson Davis, a letter which offers peace. It is to be placed on the desk of Abraham Lincoln the day after Lee has destroyed the Army of the Potomac somewhere north of Washington.

James Longstreet, Lieutenant General, forty-two. Lee's second in command. A large man, larger than Lee, full-bearded, blue-eyed, ominous, slow-talking, crude. He is one of the first of the new soldiers, the cold-eyed men who have sensed the birth of the new war of machines. He has invented a trench and a theory of defensive warfare, but in that courtly company few will listen. He is one of the few high officers in that army not from Virginia.

That winter, in Richmond, three of his children have died within a week, of a fever. Since that time he has withdrawn, no longer joins his men for the poker games he once loved, for which he was famous.

They call him "Old Pete" and sometimes "The Dutchman." His headquarters is always near Lee, and men remark upon the intimacy and some are jealous of it. He has opposed the invasion of Pennsylvania, but once the army is committed he no longer opposes. Yet he will speak his mind; he will always speak his mind. Lee calls him, with deep affection, "my old war horse." Since the death of Stonewall Jackson he has been Lee's right hand. He is a stubborn man.

George Pickett, Major General, thirty-eight. Gaudy and lovable, long-haired, perfumed. Last in his class at West Point, he makes up for a lack of wisdom with a lusty exuberance. In love with a girl half his age, a schoolgirl from Lynchburg named LaSalle Corbelle, to whom he has vowed ne'er to touch liquor. Received his appointment to West Point through the good offices of Abraham Lincoln, a personal friend, and no one now can insult Abe Lincoln in Pickett's presence, although Lincoln is not only the enemy but the absolute utterest enemy of all.

On the march toward Gettysburg Pickett's Virginia Division is by a trick of fate last in line. He worries constantly that he will miss the last great battle of the war.

Richard Ewell, Lieutenant General, forty-six. Egg-bald, one-legged, recently married. (He refers to his new wife absent-mindedly as "Mrs. Brown.") Eccentric, brilliant, chosen out of all Lee's officers to succeed to a portion of Stonewall Jackson's old command. But he has lost something along with the leg that a soldier sometimes loses with the big wounds. He approaches Gettysburg unsure of himself, in command of twenty thousand men.

Ambrose Powell Hill, Major General, thirty-seven. Has risen to command the other part of Jackson's old corps. A moody man, often competent, bad-tempered, wealthy, aspires to a place in Richmond society, frets and broods and fights with superiors. He wears a red shirt into battle. He should be a fine soldier, and sometimes is, but he is often ill for no apparent reason. He does not like to follow orders. At Gettysburg he will command a corps, and he will be sick again.

Lewis Armistead, Brigadier General, forty-six. Commander of one of George Pickett's brigades. They call him "Lo," which is short for Lothario, which is meant to be witty, for he is a shy and silent man, a widower. Descended from a martial family, he has a fighter's spirit, is known throughout the old army as the man who, while a cadet at the Point, was suspended for hitting Jubal Early in the head with a plate. Has developed over long years of service a deep affection for Winfield Scott Hancock, who fights now with the Union. Armistead looks forward to the reunion with Hancock, which will take place at Gettysburg.

Richard Brooke Garnett, Brigadier General, forty-four. Commands the second of Pickett's brigades. A dark-eyed, silent, tragic man. Followed Jackson in command of the old Stonewall Brigade; at Kernstown he has made the mistake of withdrawing his men from an impossible position. Jackson is outraged, orders a court-martial which never convenes. Jackson dies before Garnett, accused of cowardice, can clear his name and redeem his honor, the honor which no man who knows him has ever doubted. He comes to Gettysburg a tortured man, too ill to walk. He believes that Jackson deliberately lied. In that camp there is nothing more important than honor.

J. E. B. Stuart, Lieutenant General, thirty. The laughing banjo player, the superb leader of cavalry who has ridden rings around the Union Army. A fine soldier, whose reports are always accurate, but a man who loves to read about himself in the Richmond newspapers. His mission that month is to keep Lee informed of the movement of the Union Army. He fails.

Jubal Early, Major General, forty-six. Commander of one of Ewell's divisions. A dark, cold, icy man, bitter, alone. Left the Point to become a prosecuting attorney, to which he is well suited. A competent soldier, but a man who works with an eye to the future, a slippery man, a careful soldier; he will build his reputation whatever the cost. Dick Ewell defers to him. Longstreet despises him. Lee makes do with the material at hand. Lee calls him "my bad old man."

These men wore blue:

Joshua Lawrence Chamberlain, Colonel, thirty-four. He prefers to be called "Lawrence." A professor of rhetoric at Bowdoin College, sometimes professor of "Natural and Revealed Religion," successor to the chair of the famed Professor Stowe, husband to Harriet Beecher. Tall and rather handsome, attractive to women, somewhat boyish, a clean and charming person. An excellent student, Phi Beta Kappa, he speaks seven languages and has a beautiful singing voice, but he has wanted all his life to be a soldier. The College will not free him for war, but in the summer of 1862 he requests a sabbatical for study in Europe. When it is granted he proceeds not to France but to the office of the Governor of Maine, where he receives a commission in the 20th Regiment of Infantry, Maine Volunteers, and marches off to war with a vast faith in the brotherhood of man. Spends the long night at Fredericksburg piling corpses in front of himself to shield him from bullets. Comes to Gettysburg with that hard fragment of the Regiment which has survived. One week before the battle he is given command of the Regiment. His younger brother Thomas becomes his aide. Thomas too has yearned to be a soldier. The wishes of both men are to be granted on the dark rear slope of a small rocky hill called Little Round Top.

John Buford, Major General, thirty-seven. A cavalry soldier, restless and caged in the tamed and political East, who loves the great plains and the memory of snow. A man with an eye for the good ground, already badly wounded and not long to live, weary of stupidity and politics and bloody military greed. At Thorofare Gap he held against Longstreet for six hours, waiting for help that never came. Too good an officer for his own advancement, he rides a desk in Washington until luck puts him back in the field, where he is given two brigades of cavalry and told to trail Lee's army. He is first into Gettysburg, where he lifts up his eyes to the hills. He is a man who knows the value of ground.

John Reynolds, Major General, forty-two. Perhaps the finest soldier in the Union Army. Like Lee before him, a former commander of West Point, a courteous man, military, a marvelous horseman, another gentleman. His home is not far from Gettysburg. He has fallen in love late in life, but the girl is Catholic and Reynolds has not yet told his Protestant family, but he wears her ring on a chain around his neck, under his uniform. Early that month he is called to Washington, where he is offered command of the Army. But he has seen the military results of maneuvering by armchair commanders Halleck and Stanton, and he insists that the Army cannot be commanded from Washington, that he cannot accept command without a free hand. He therefore respectfully declines. The honor passes to George Meade, who is not even given the option but ordered to command. And thus it is John Reynolds, not Meade, who rides into Gettysburg on the morning of the First Day.

George Gordon Meade, Major General, forty-seven. Vain and bad-tempered, balding, full of self-pity. He takes command of the Army on a Sunday, June 28, two days before the battle. He wishes to hold a Grand Review, but there turns out not to be time. He plans a line of defense along Pipe Creek, far from Gettysburg, in the unreal hope that Lee will attack him on ground of his own choosing. No decision he makes at Gettysburg will be decisive, except perhaps the last.

Winfield Scott Hancock, Major General, thirty-nine. Armistead's old friend. A magnetic man with a beautiful wife. A painter of talent, a picture-book General. Has a tendency to gain weight, but at this moment he is still young and slim, still a superb presence, a man who arrives on the battlefield in spotlessly clean linen and never keeps his head down. In the fight to come he will be everywhere, and in the end he will be waiting for Lew Armistead at the top of Cemetery Hill.

All that month there is heat and wild rain. Cherries are ripening over all Pennsylvania, and the men gorge as they march. The civilians have fled and houses are dark. The armies move north through the heat and the dust.

"When men take up arms to set other men free, there is something sacred and holy in the warfare."

—Woodrow Wilson

"I hate the idea of causes, and if I had to choose between betraying my country and betraying my friend, I hope I should have the guts to betray my country."

—E. M. Forster

"With all my devotion to the Union and the feeling of loyalty and duty of an American citizen, I have not been able to raise my hand against my relatives, my children, my home. I have therefore resigned my commission in the Army. . . ."

—from a letter of
Robert E. Lee

Mr. Mason: How do you justify your acts?
John Brown: I think, my friend, you are guilty of a great wrong against God and humanity—I say it without wishing to be offensive—and it would be perfectly right for anyone to interfere with you so far as to free those you willfully and wickedly hold in bondage. I do not say this insultingly.
Mr. Mason: I understand that.

—from an interview with
John Brown after his
capture

Monday,
June 29, 1863

Mine eyes have seen the glory . . .

1

THE SPY

He rode into the dark of the woods and dismounted. He crawled upward on his belly over cool rocks out into the sunlight, and suddenly he was in the open and he could see for miles, and there was the whole vast army below him, filling the valley like a smoking river. It came out of a blue rainstorm in the east and overflowed the narrow valley road, coiling along a stream, narrowing and choking a white bridge, fading out into the yellowish dust of June but still visible on the farther road beyond the blue hills, spiked with flags and guidons like a great chopped bristly snake, the snake ending headless in a blue wall of summer rain.

The spy tucked himself behind a boulder and began counting flags. Must be twenty thousand men, visible all at once. Two whole Union Corps. He could make out the familiar black hats of the Iron Brigade, troops belonging to John Reynolds' First Corps. He looked at his watch, noted the time. They were coming very fast. The Army of the Potomac had never moved this fast. The day was murderously hot and there was no wind and the dust hung above the army like a yellow veil. He thought: there'll be some of them die of the heat today. But they are coming faster than they ever came before.

He slipped back down into the cool dark and rode slowly downhill toward the silent empty country to the north. With luck he could make the Southern line before nightfall. After nightfall it would be dangerous. But he must not seem to hurry. The horse was already tired. And yet there was the pressure of that great blue army behind him, building like water behind a cracking dam. He rode out into the open, into the land between the armies.

There were fat Dutch barns, prim German orchards. But there were no cattle in the fields and no horses, and houses everywhere were empty and dark. He was alone in the heat and the silence, and then it began to rain and he rode head down into monstrous lightning. All his life he had been afraid of lightning but he kept riding. He did not know where the Southern headquarters was but he knew it had to be somewhere near Chambersburg. He had smelled out the shape of Lee's army in all the rumors and bar talk and newspapers and hysteria he had drifted through all over eastern Pennsylvania, and on that day he was perhaps the only man alive who knew the positions of both armies. He carried the knowledge with a hot and lovely pride. Lee would be near Chambersburg, and wherever Lee was Longstreet would not be far away. So finding the headquarters was not the problem. The problem was riding through a picket line in the dark.

The rain grew worse. He could not even move in under a tree because of the lightning. He had to take care not to get lost. He rode quoting Shakespeare from memory, thinking of the picket line ahead somewhere in the dark. The sky opened and poured down on him and he rode on: *it will be rain tonight: let it come down.* That was a speech of murderers. He had been an actor once. He had no stature and a small voice and there were no big parts for him until the war came, and now he was the only one who knew how good he was. If only they could see him work, old cold Longstreet and the rest. But everyone hated spies. I come a single spy. Wet single spy. But *they* come in whole battalions. The rain began to ease off and he spurred the horse to a trot. *My kingdom for a horse.* Jolly good line. He went on, reciting *Henry the Fifth* aloud: "Once more into the breech . . ."

Late that afternoon he came to a crossroad and the sign of much cavalry having passed this way a few hours ago. His own way led north to Chambersburg, but he knew that Longstreet would have to know who these people were so close to his line. He debated a moment at the crossroads, knowing there was no time. A delay would cost him daylight. Yet he was a man of pride and the tracks drew him. Perhaps it was only Jeb Stuart. The spy thought hopefully, wistfully: if it's Stuart I can ask for an armed escort all the way home. He turned and followed the tracks. After a while he saw a farmhouse and a man standing out in a field, in a peach orchard, and he spurred that way. The man was small and bald with large round arms and spoke very bad English. The spy went into his act: a simple-minded farmer seeking a runaway wife, terrified of soldiers. The bald man regarded him sweatily, disgustedly, told him the soldiers just gone by were "plu" soldiers, Yankees. The spy asked: what town lies yonder? and the farmer told him Gettysburg, but the name meant nothing. The spy turned and spurred back to the crossroads. Yankee cavalry meant John Buford's column. Moving lickety-split. Where was Stuart? No escort now. He rode back again toward the blue hills. But the horse could not be pushed. He had to dismount and walk.

That was the last sign of Yankees. He was moving up across South Mountain; he was almost home. Beyond South Mountain was Lee and, of course, Longstreet. A strange friendship; grim and gambling Longstreet, formal and pious old Bobby Lee. The spy wondered at it, and then the rain began again, bringing more lightning but at least some cooler air, and he tucked himself in under his hat and went back to *Hamlet.* Old Jackson was dead. *Good night, sweet Prince, and flights of angels sing thee to thy rest . . .*

He rode into darkness. No longer any need to hurry. He left the roadway at last and moved out into a field away from the lightning and the trees and sat in the rain to eat a lonely supper, trying to make up his mind whether it was worth the risk of going on. He was very close; he could begin to feel them up ahead. There was no way of knowing when or where, but suddenly they would be there in the road, stepping phantomlike out of the trees wearing those sick eerie smiles, and other men with guns would suddenly appear all around him, prodding him in the back with hard steel barrels, as you prod an animal, and he would have to be lucky, because few men rode out at night on good and honest business, not now, this night, in this invaded country.

He rode slowly up the road, not really thinking, just moving, reluctant to stop. He was weary. Fragments of *Hamlet* flickered in his brain: *If it be not now, yet it will come. Ripeness is all.* Now *there's* a good part. A town ahead. A few lights. And then he struck the picket line.

There was a presence in the road, a liquid Southern voice. He saw them outlined in lightning, black ragged figures rising around him. A sudden lantern poured yellow light. He saw one bleak hawkish grinning face; hurriedly he mentioned Longstreet's name. With some you postured and with some you groveled and with some you were imperious. But you could do that only by daylight, when you could see the faces and gauge the reaction. And now he was too tired and cold. He sat and shuddered: an insignificant man on a pale and muddy horse. He turned out to be lucky. There was a patient sergeant with a long gray beard who put him under guard and sent him along up the dark road to Longstreet's head-quarters.

He was not safe even now, but he could begin to relax. He rode up the long road between picket fires, and he could hear them singing in the rain, chasing each other in the dark of the trees. A fat and happy army, roasting meat and fresh bread, telling stories in the dark. He began to fall asleep on the horse; he was home. But they did not like to see him sleep, and one of them woke him up to remind him, cheerily, that if there was no one up there who knew him, why, then, unfortunately, they'd have to hang him, and the soldier said it just to see the look on his face, and the spy shivered, wondering. Why do there have to be men like that, men who enjoy another man's dying?

Longstreet was not asleep. He lay on the cot watching the lightning flare in the door of the tent. It was very quiet in the grove and there was the sound of the raindrops continuing to fall from the trees although the rain had ended. When Sorrel touched him on the arm he was glad of it; he was thinking of his dead children.

"Sir? You asked to be awakened if Harrison came back."

"Yes." Longstreet got up quickly and put on the old blue robe and the carpet slippers. He was a very big man and he was full-bearded and wild-haired. He thought of the last time he'd seen the spy, back in Virginia, tiny man with a face like a weasel: "And where will your headquarters be, General, up there in Penn-sylvania? 'Tis a big state indeed." Him standing there with cold gold clutched in a dirty hand. And Longstreet had said icily, cheerily, "It will be where it will be. If you cannot find the headquarters of this whole army you cannot be much of a spy." And the spy had said stiffly, *"Scout,* sir. I am a scout. And I am a patriot, sir." Longstreet had grinned. We are all patriots. He stepped out into the light. He did not know what to expect. He had not really expected the spy to come back at all.

The little man was there: a soggy spectacle on a pale and spattered horse. He sat grinning wanly from under the floppy brim of a soaked and dripping hat. Lightning flared behind him; he touched his cap.

"Your servant, General. May I come down?"

Longstreet nodded. The guard backed off. Longstreet told Sorrel to get some coffee. The spy slithered down from the horse and stood grinning foolishly, shivering, mouth slack with fatigue.

"Well, sir—" the spy chuckled, teeth chattering—"you see, I was able to find you after all."

Longstreet sat at the camp table on a wet seat, extracted a cigar, lighted it. The spy sat floppily, mouth still open, breathing deeply.

"It has been a long day. I've ridden hard all this day."

"What have you got?"

"I came through the pickets at night, you know. That can be very touchy."

Longstreet nodded. He watched, he waited. Sorrel came with steaming coffee; the cup burned Longstreet's fingers. Sorrel sat, gazing curiously, distastefully at the spy.

The spy guzzled, then sniffed Longstreet's fragrant smoke. Wistfully: "I say, General, I don't suppose you've got another of those? Good Southern tobacco?"

"Directly," Longstreet said. "What have you got?"

"I've got the position of the Union Army."

Longstreet nodded, showing nothing. He had not known the Union Army was on the move, was within two hundred miles, was even this side of the Potomac, but he nodded and said nothing. The spy asked for a map and began pointing out the positions of the corps.

"They're coming in seven corps. I figure at least eighty thousand men, possibly as much as a hundred thousand. When they're all together they'll outnumber you, but they're not as strong as they were; the two-year enlistments are running out. The First Corps is here. The Eleventh is right behind it. John Reynolds is in command of the lead elements. I saw him at Taneytown this morning."

"Reynolds," Longstreet said.

"Yes, sir."

"You saw him yourself?"

The spy grinned, nodded, rubbed his nose, chuckled. "So close I could touch him. It was Reynolds all right."

"This morning. At Taneytown."

"Exactly. You didn't know any of that, now did you, General?" The spy bobbed his head with delight. "You didn't even know they was on the move, did ye? I thought not. You wouldn't be spread out so thin if you knowed they was comin'."

Longstreet looked at Sorrel. The aide shrugged silently. If this was true, there would have been some word. Longstreet's mind moved over it slowly. He said: "How did you know we were spread out?"

"I smelled it out." The spy grinned, foxlike, toothy. "Listen, General, I'm good at this business."

"Tell me what you know of our position."

"Well, now I can't be too exact on this, 'cause I aint scouted you myself, but I gather that you're spread from York up to Harrisburg and then back to Chambersburg, with the main body around Chambersburg and General Lee just 'round the bend."

It was exact. Longstreet thought: if this one knows it, *they* will know it. He said slowly, "We've had no word of Union movement."

The spy bobbed with joy. "I knew it. Thass why I hurried. Came through that picket line in the dark and all. I don't know if you realize, General—"

Sorrell said coldly, "Sir, don't you think, if this man's story was true, that we would have heard *something?*"

Sorrel did not approve of spies. The spy grimaced, blew. "You aint exactly on friendly ground no more, Major. This aint Virginia no more."

True, Longstreet thought. But there would have been something. Stuart? Longstreet said, "General Stuart's cavalry went out a few days back. He hasn't reported any movement."

The spy shrugged, exasperated, glooming at Sorrel. Sorrel turned his back, looked at his fingernails.

Longstreet said, "What have you heard of Stuart?"

"Not much. He's riding in the north somewhere. Stirring up headlines and fuss, but I never heard him do any real damage."

Longstreet said, "If the Union Army were as close as you say, one would think—"

"Well, I'm damned," the spy said, a small rage flaming. "I come through that picket line in the dark and all. Listen, General, I tell you this: I don't know what old Stuart is doing and I don't care, but I done my job and this is a fact. This here same afternoon of this here day I come on the tracks of Union cavalry thick as fleas, one whole brigade and maybe two, and them bluebellies weren't no four hours hard ride from this here now spot, and that, by God, is the Lord's truth."

He blew again, meditating. Then he added, by way of amendment, "Buford's column, I think it was. To be exact."

Longstreet thought: *can't* be true. But he was an instinctive man, and suddenly his brain knew and his own temper boiled. Jeb Stuart . . . was joyriding. God *damn* him. Longstreet turned to Sorrel.

"All right, Major. Send to General Lee. I guess we'll have to wake him up. Get my horse."

Sorrel started to say something, but he knew that you did not argue with Longstreet. He moved.

The spy said delightedly, "General Lee? Do I get to see General Lee? Well now." He stood up and took off the ridiculous hat and smoothed wet plastered hair across a balding skull. He glowed. Longstreet got the rest of the information and went back to his tent and dressed quickly.

If the spy was right the army was in great danger. They could be cut apart and cut off from home and destroyed in detail, piece by piece. If the spy was right, then Lee would have to turn, but the old man did not believe in spies nor in any information you had to pay for, had not approved of the money spent or even the idea behind it. And the old man had faith in Stuart, and why in God's name had Stuart sent nothing, not even a courier, because even Stuart wasn't fool enough to let the whole damned Army of the Potomac get this close without word, not one damned lonesome word. Longstreet went back out into the light. He had never believed in this invasion. Lee and Davis together had overruled him. He did not believe in offensive warfare when the enemy outnumbered you and outgunned you and would come looking for you anyway if you waited somewhere on your own ground. He had not argued since leaving home, but the invasion did not sit right in his craw; the whole scheme lay edgewise and raspy in his brain, and treading here on alien ground, he felt a cold wind blowing, a distant alarm. Only instinct. No facts as yet. The spy reminded him about the cigar. It was a short way through the night to Lee's headquarters, and they rode past low sputtering campfires with the spy puffing exuberant blue smoke like a happy furnace.

" 'Tis a happy army you've got here, General," the spy chatted with approval. "I felt it the moment I crossed the picket line. A happy army, eager for the fight. Singing and all. You can feel it in the air. Not like them bluebellies. A desperate tired lot. I tell you, General, this will be a factor. The bluebellies is almost done. Why, do you know what I see everywhere I go? Disgraceful, it is. On every street in every town, able-bodied men. Just *standing* there, by the thousands, reading them poor squeaky pitiful newspapers about this here mighty invasion and the last gasp of the Union and how every man must take up arms, haw." The spy guffawed. "Like a bunch of fat women at church. The war's almost over. You can feel it, General. The end is in the air."

Longstreet said nothing. He was beginning to think of what to do if the spy was right. If he could not get Lee to turn now there could be disaster. And yet if the Union Army was truly out in the open at last there was a great opportunity: a sudden move south, between Hooker and Washington, cut *them* off from Lincoln. Yes. Longstreet said, "What do you hear of Hooker? Where is he?"

The spy stopped, mouth sagging. "Oh by Jesus. Forgive me." He grimaced, shook his head. "I done forgot. There was an item in the newspaper this morning. Saying that Hooker was replaced. They gave the command to Meade, I think it was."

"George Meade?"

"Yes, sir. I think."

"You're sure?"

"Well, it was Meade the newspaper said, but you know them damn newspapers."

Longstreet thought: new factor. He spurred the horse, but he couldn't move fast because of the dark. Lee must listen. God bless the politicians. Reynolds was their best man. Why did they go to Meade? But I'm sorry to see Hooker go. Old Fighting Joe. Longstreet said, "It was Meade, then, and not Reynolds?"

"Rumor was that Reynolds was offered the job but wouldn't have it on a plate. That's what the paper said."

Old John's too smart to take it. Not with that idiot Halleck pulling the strings. But Meade? Fussy. Engineer. Careful. No genius for sure. But a new factor. A Pennsylvania man. He will know this country.

The spy chatted on amiably. He seemed to need to talk. He was saying, "Strange thing about it all, thing that bothers me is that when you do this job right nobody knows you're doing it, nobody ever watches you work, do you see? And sometimes I can't help but wish I had an audience. I've played some scenes, ah, General, but I've been lovely." The spy sighed, puffed, sighed again. "This current creation, now, is marvelous. I'm a poor half-witted farmer, do you see, terrified of soldiers, and me lovely young wife has run off with a drummer and I'm out a-scourin' the countryside for her, a sorrowful pitiful sight I am. And people lookin' down their noses and grinnin' behind me back and all the time tellin' me exactly what I want to know about who is where and how many and how long ago, and them not even knowin' they're doin' it, too busy feelin' contemptuous. There are many people, General, that don't give a damn for a human soul, do you know that? The strange thing is, after playing this poor fool farmer for a while I can't help but feel sorry for him. Because nobody cares."

They came to Lee's camp, in the grove just south of Chambersburg. By the time they got there Longstreet knew that the spy was telling the truth. Young Walter Taylor was up, annoyed, prissy, defending General Lee's night's rest even against Longstreet, who glowed once with the beginning of rage, and sent Taylor off to get the old man out of bed. They dismounted and waited. The spy sat under an awning, grinning with joy at the prospect of meeting Lee. Longstreet could not sit down. He disliked getting the old man up: Lee had not been well. But you could lose the war up here. Should have gone to Vicksburg. News from there very bad. It will fall, and after that . . . we must win here if we are to win at all, and we must do it soon. The rain touched him; he shivered. Too damn much rain would muck up the roads.

Lee came out into the light. The spy hopped to attention. Lee bowed slightly, stiffly.

"Gentlemen."

He stood bareheaded in the rain: regal, formal, a beautiful white-haired, white-bearded old man in a faded blue robe. He looked haggard. Longstreet thought: he looks older every time you see him. For a moment the spy was silent, enraptured, then he bowed suddenly from the waist, widely, formally, gracefully, plucking the floppy hat from the balding head and actually sweeping the ground with it, dandy, ridiculous, something off a stage somewhere designed for a king.

"General," the spy said grandly, *"à votre service."* He said something else in a strange and southern French. Longstreet was startled at the transformation.

Lee glanced at Longstreet: a silent question. Longstreet said, "Beg pardon, sir. I thought this urgent. The man has information."

Lee looked at the spy silently. His face showed nothing. Then he said formally, "Sir, you must excuse me, I do not know your name."

"The name is *Harrison,* sir, at present." The spy grinned toothily. "The name of an ex-President, ex-General. A small joke, sir. One must keep one's sense of humor."

Lee glanced again at Longstreet. Longstreet said, "The man has the position of the Union Army. He says they are very close. I have a map."

He moved to the map table, under the awning. The spy followed with reproach. Lee came slowly to the table, watching the man. After a moment he said to Harrison, "I understand that you are General Longstreet's"—a slight pause— "'scout.'" Lee would not use the word *spy*. "I believe we saw you last back in Virginia."

"That's a fact," the spy worshipped. "I been kind of circulatin' since, amongst the bluebellies, and I tell you, General, sir, that it's an honor and a priv—"

Longstreet said, "He claims their lead elements are here. He says there is a column of strong Union cavalry not four hours off."

Lee looked at the map. Then he sat down and looked more closely. Longstreet gave the positions, the spy fluttering mothlike behind him with numbers and names and dates. Lee listened without expression.

Longstreet finished. "He estimates perhaps one hundred thousand men."

Lee nodded. But estimates meant nothing. He sat for a moment staring at the map and then bowed his head slightly. Longstreet thought: he doesn't believe. Then Lee raised his eyes and regarded the spy.

"You appear to have ridden hard. Have you come a long way?"

"Sir, I sure have."

"And you came through the picket line after dark?"

"Yes, sir—" the spy's head bobbed—"I did indeed."

"We are in your debt." Lee stared at the map. "Thank you. Now I'm sure General Longstreet will see to your accommodations."

The spy was dismissed, had sense enough to know it. He rose reluctantly. He said, "It has been my pleasure, sir, to have served such a man as yourself. God bless you, sir."

Lee thanked him again. Longstreet instructed Sorrel to see that the man was fed and given a tent for the night and to be kept where Longstreet could find him if he needed him, which meant: keep an eye on him. The spy went out into the dark. Longstreet and Lee sat alone at the table in the rain.

Lee said softly, "Do you believe this man?"

"No choice."

"I suppose not." Lee rubbed his eyes, leaned forward on the table. With his right hand he held the muscle of his left arm. He shook his head slowly. "Am I to move on the word of a paid spy?"

"Can't afford not to."

"There should have been something from Stuart."

"There should have been."

"Stuart would not have left us blind."

"He's joyriding again," Longstreet said. "This time you ought to stomp him. Really stomp him."

Lee shook his head. "Stuart would not leave us blind."

"We've got to turn," Longstreet said. His heart was beating strongly. It was bad to see the indomitable old man weak and hatless in the early morning, something soft in his eyes, pain in his face, the right hand rubbing the pain in the arm. Longstreet said, "We can't risk it. If we don't concentrate they'll chop us up."

Lee said nothing. After a moment Longstreet told him about Meade. Lee said, "They should have gone to Reynolds."

"Thought so too. I think he turned it down."

Lee nodded. He smiled slightly. "I would have preferred to continue against General Hooker."

Longstreet grinned. "Me too."

"Meade will be . . . cautious. It will take him some time to take command, to organize a staff. I think . . . perhaps we should move quickly. There may be an opportunity here."

"Yes. If we swing in behind him and cut him off from Washington . . ."

"If your man is correct."

"We'll find out."

Lee bent toward the map. The mountains rose like a rounded wall between them and the Union Army. There was one gap east of Chambersburg and beyond that all the roads came together, weblike, at a small town. Lee put his finger on the map.

"What town is that?"

Longstreet looked. "Gettysburg," he said.

Lee nodded. "Well—" he was squinting—"I see no reason to delay. It's their army I'm after, not their towns." He followed the roads with his finger, all converging on that one small town. "I think we should concentrate in this direction. This road junction will be useful."

"Yes," Longstreet said.

Lee looked up with black diamond eyes. "We'll move at first light."

Longstreet felt a lovely thrill. Trust the old man to move. "Yes, sir."

Lee started to rise. A short while ago he had fallen from a horse onto his hands, and when he pushed himself up from the table Longstreet saw him wince. Longstreet thought: go to sleep and let me do it. Give the order and I'll do it all. He said, "I regret the need to wake you, sir."

Lee looked past him into the soft blowing dark. The rain had ended. A light wind was moving in the tops of the pines—cool sweet air, gentle and clean. Lee took a deep breath.

"A good time of night. I have always liked this time of night."

"Yes."

"Well." Lee glanced once almost shyly at Longstreet's face, then looked away. They stood for a moment in awkward silence. They had been together for a long time in war and they had grown very close, but Lee was ever formal and Longstreet was inarticulate, so they stood for a long moment side by side without speaking, not looking at each other, listening to the raindrops fall in the leaves. But the silent moment was enough. After a while Lee said slowly, "When this is over, I shall miss it very much."

"Yes."

"I do not mean the fighting."

"No."

"Well," Lee said. He looked to the sky. "It is all in God's hands."

They said good night. Longstreet watched the old man back to his tent. Then he mounted and rode alone back to his camp to begin the turning of the army, all the wagons and all the guns, down the narrow mountain road that led to Gettysburg. It was still a long dark hour till dawn. He sat alone on his horse in the night and he could feel the army asleep around him, all those young hearts beating in the dark. They would need their rest now. He sat alone to await the dawn, and let them sleep a little longer.

2

CHAMBERLAIN

He dreamed of Maine and ice black water; he awoke to a murderous sun. A voice calling: "Colonel, darlin'." He squinted: the whiskery face of Buster Kilrain.

"Colonel, darlin', I hate to be a-wakin' ye, but there's a message here ye ought to be seein'."

Chamberlain had slept on the ground; he rolled to a sitting position. Light boiled in through the tent flap. Chamberlain closed his eyes.

"And how are ye feelin' this mornin', Colonel, me lad?"

Chamberlain ran his tongue around his mouth. He said briefly, dryly, "Ak."

"We're about to be havin' guests, sir, or I wouldn't be wakin' ye."

Chamberlain looked up through bleary eyes. He had walked eighty miles in four days through the hottest weather he had ever known and he had gone down with sunstroke. He felt eerie fragility, like a piece of thin glass in a high hot wind. He saw a wooden canteen, held in the big hand of Kilrain, cold drops of water on varnished sides. He drank. The world focused.

". . . one hundred and twenty men," Kilrain said.

Chamberlain peered at him.

"They should be arriving any moment," Kilrain said. He was squatting easily, comfortably, in the opening of the tent, the light flaming behind him.

"Who?" Chamberlain said.

"They are sending us some mutineers," Kilrain said with fatherly patience. "One hundred and twenty men from the old Second Maine, which has been disbanded."

"Mutineers?"

"Ay. What happened was that the enlistment of the old Second ran out and they were all sent home except one hundred and twenty, which had foolishly signed *three*-year papers, and so they all had one year to go, only *they* all thought they was signing to fight with the Second, and Second only, and so they mutinied. One hundred and twenty. Are you all right, Colonel?"

Chamberlain nodded vaguely.

"Well, these poor fellers did not want to fight no more, naturally, being Maine men of a certain intelligence, and refused, only nobody will send them home, and nobody knew what to do with them, until they thought of *us*, being as we are the other Maine regiment here in the army. There's a message here signed by Meade himself. That's the new General we got now, sir, if you can keep track as they go by. The message says they'll be sent here this morning and they are to fight, and if they don't fight you can feel free to shoot them."

"Shoot?"

"Ay."

"Let me see." Chamberlain read painfully. His head felt very strange indeed, but he was coming awake into the morning as from a long way away and he could begin to hear the bugles out across the fields. Late to get moving today. Thank God. Somebody gave us an extra hour. Bless him. He read: . . . *you are therefore authorized to shoot any man who refuses to do his duty.* Shoot?

He said, "These are all *Maine* men?"

"Yes, sir. Fine big fellers. I've seen them. Loggin' men. You may remember there was a bit of a brawl some months back, during the mud march? These fellers were famous for their fists."

Chamberlain said, "One hundred and twenty."

"Yes, sir."

"Somebody's crazy."

"Yes, sir."

"How many men do we now have in this Regiment?"

"Ah, somewhat less than two hundred and fifty, sir, as of yesterday. Countin' the officers."

"How do I take care of a hundred and twenty mutinous men?"

"Yes, sir," Kilrain sympathized. "Well, you'll have to talk to them, sir."

Chamberlain sat for a long moment silently trying to function. He was thirty-four years old, and on this day one year ago he had been a professor of rhetoric at Bowdoin College. He had no idea what to do. But it was time to go out into the sun. He crawled forward through the tent flap and stood up, blinking, swaying, one hand against the bole of a tree. He was a tall man, somewhat picturesque. He wore stolen blue cavalry trousers and a three-foot sword, and the clothes he wore he had not taken off for a week. He had a grave, boyish dignity, that clean-eyed, scrubbed-brain, naïve look of the happy professor.

Kilrain, a white-haired man with the build of an ape, looked up at him with fatherly joy. "If ye'll ride the *horse* today, Colonel, which the Lord hath provided, instead of walkin' in the dust with the others fools, ye'll be all right—if ye wear the hat. It's the *walkin'*, do you see, that does the great harm."

"*You* walked," Chamberlain said grumpily, thinking: shoot them? *Maine* men? How can I shoot Maine men? I'll never be able to go home.

"Ah, but, Colonel, darlin', I've been in the infantry since before you was born. It's them first few thousand miles. After that, a man gets a limber to his feet."

"Hey, Lawrence. How you doin'?"

Younger brother, Tom Chamberlain, bright-faced, high-voiced, a new lieutenant, worshipful. The heat had not seemed to touch him. Chamberlain nodded. Tom said critically, "You lookin' kinda peaked. Why don't you ride the horse?"

Chamberlain gloomed. But the day was not as bright as it had seemed through the opening of the tent. He looked upward with relief toward a darkening sky. The troops were moving in the fields, but there had been no order to march. The wagons were not yet loaded. He thought: God bless the delay. His mind was beginning to function. All down the road and all through the trees the troops were moving, cooking, the thousands of troop and thousands of wagons of the Fifth Corps, Army of the Potomac, of which Chamberlain's Twentieth Maine was a minor fragment. But far down the road there was motion.

Kilrain said, "There they come."

Chamberlain squinted. Then he saw troops on the road, a long way off.

The line of men came slowly up the road. There were guards with fixed bayonets. Chamberlain could see the men shuffling, strange pathetic spectacle, dusty, dirty, ragged men, heads down, faces down: it reminded him of a history-book picture of impressed seamen in the last war with England. But these men would have to march all day, in the heat. Chamberlain thought: not possible.

Tom was meditating. "Gosh, Lawrence. There's almost as many men there as we got in the whole regiment. How we going to guard them?"

Chamberlain said nothing. He was thinking: How do you force a man to fight—for freedom? The idiocy of it jarred him. Think on it later. Must do something now.

There was an officer, a captain, at the head of the column. The Captain turned them in off the road and herded them into an open space in the field near the Regimental flag. The men of the Regiment, busy with coffee, stood up to watch. The Captain had a loud voice and used obscene words. He assembled the men in two long ragged lines and called them to attention, but they ignored him. One slumped to the ground, more exhaustion than mutiny. A guard came forward and yelled and probed with a bayonet, but abruptly several more men sat down and then they all did, and the Captain began yelling, but the guards stood grinning confusedly, foolishly, having gone as far as they would go, unwilling to push further unless the men here showed some threat, and the men seemed beyond threat, merely enormously weary. Chamberlain took it all in as he moved toward the Captain. He put his hands behind his back and came forward slowly, studiously. The Captain pulled off dirty gloves and shook his head with contempt, glowering up at Chamberlain.

"Looking for the commanding officer, Twentieth Maine."

"You've found him," Chamberlain said.

"That's him all right." Tom's voice, behind him, very proud. Chamberlain suppressed a smile.

"You Chamberlain?" The Captain stared at him grimly, insolently, showing what he thought of Maine men.

Chamberlain did not answer for a long moment, looking into the man's eyes until the eyes suddenly blinked and dropped, and then Chamberlain said softly, "*Colonel* Chamberlain to you."

The Captain stood still for a moment, then slowly came to attention, slowly saluted. Chamberlain did not return it. He looked past the Captain at the men, most of whom had their heads down. But there were eyes on him. He looked back and forth down the line, looking for a familiar face. That would help. But there was no one he knew.

"Captain Brewer, sir. Ah. One-eighteen Pennsylvania." The Captain tugged in his coat front, produced a sheaf of papers. "If you're the commanding officer, sir, then I present you with these here prisoners." He handed the papers. Chamberlain took them, glanced down, handed them back to Tom. The Captain said, "You're welcome to 'em, God knows. Had to use the bayonet to get 'em moving. You got to sign for 'em, Colonel."

Chamberlain said over his shoulder, "Sign it, Tom." To the Captain he said, "You're relieved, Captain."

The Captain nodded, pulling on the dirty gloves. "You're authorized to use whatever force necessary, Colonel." He said that loudly, for effect. "If you have to shoot 'em, why, you go right ahead. Won't nobody say nothin'."

"You're relieved, Captain," Chamberlain said. He walked past the Captain, closer to the men, who did not move, who did not seem to notice him. One of the guards stiffened as Chamberlain approached, looked past him to his captain. Chamberlain said, "You men can leave now. We don't need any guards."

He stood in front of the men, ignoring the guards. They began to move off. Chamberlain stood for a moment looking down. Some of the faces turned up.

There was hunger and exhaustion and occasional hatred. Chamberlain said, "My name is Chamberlain. I'm Colonel, Twentieth Maine."

Some of them did not even raise their heads. He waited another moment. Then he said, "When did you eat last?"

More heads came up. There was no answer. Then a man in the front row said huskily, in a whiskey voice, "We're hungry, Colonel."

Another man said, "They been tryin' to break us by not feedin' us." Chamberlain looked: a scarred man, hatless, hair plastered thinly on the scalp like strands of black seaweed. The man said, "We ain't broke yet."

Chamberlain nodded. A hard case. But we'll begin with food. He said. "They just told us you were coming a little while ago. I've told the cook to butcher a steer. Hope you like it near to raw; not much time to cook." Eyes opened wide. He could begin to see the hunger on the faces, like the yellow shine of sickness. He said, "We've got a ways to go today and you'll be coming with us, so you better eat hearty. We're all set for you back in the trees." He saw Glazier Estabrook standing huge-armed and peaceful in the shade of a nearby tree. "Glazier," Chamberlain said, "you show these men where to go. You fellas eat up and then I'll come over and hear what you have to say."

No man moved. Chamberlain turned away. He did not know what he would do if they did not choose to move. He heard a voice: "Colonel?"

He turned. The scarred man was standing.

"Colonel, we got grievances. The men elected me to talk for 'em."

"Right." Chamberlain nodded. "You come on with me and talk. The rest of you fellas go eat." He beckoned to the scarred man and waved to Glazier Estabrook. He turned again, not waiting for the men to move off, not sure they would go, began to walk purposefully toward the blessed dark, wondering again how big a guard detail it would take, thinking he might wind up with more men out of action than in, and also: what are you going to say? Good big boys they are. Seen their share of action.

"Gosh, Lawrence," Tom Chamberlain said.

"Smile," Chamberlain said cheerily, "and don't call me Lawrence. Are they moving?" He stopped and glanced pleasantly backward, saw with delight that the men were up and moving toward the trees, toward food. He grinned, plucked a book from his jacket, handed it to Tom.

"Here. This is Casey's *Manual of Infantry Tactics.* You study it, maybe someday you'll make a soldier." He smiled at the scarred man, extended a hand. "What's your name?"

The man stopped, looked at him for a long cold second. The hand seemed to come up against gravity, against his will. Automatic courtesy: Chamberlain was relying on it.

"I'm not usually that informal," Chamberlain said with the same light, calm, pleasant manner that he had developed when talking to particularly rebellious students who had come in with a grievance and who hadn't yet learned that the soft answer turneth away wrath. *Some* wrath. "But I suppose somebody ought to welcome you to the Regiment."

The man said, "I don't feel too kindly, Colonel."

Chamberlain nodded. He went on inside the tent, the scarred man following, and sat down on a camp stool, letting the man stand. He invited the man to have coffee, which the man declined, and then listened silently to the man's story.

The scarred man spoke calmly and coldly, looking straight into Chamberlain's eyes. A good stubborn man. There was a bit of the lawyer about him: he used chunky phrases about law and justice. But he had heavy hands with thick muscular fingers and black fingernails and there was a look of power to him, a coiled tight set to the way he stood, balanced, ugly, slightly contemptuous, but watchful, trying to gauge Chamberlain's strength.

Chamberlain said, "I see."

"I been in eleven different engagements, Colonel. How many you been in?"

"Not that many," Chamberlain said.

"I done my share. We all have. Most of us—" he gestured out the tent flap into the morning glare—"there's some of them no damn good but most of them been all the way there and back. Damn good men. Shouldn't ought to use them this way. Looky here." He pulled up a pants leg. Chamberlain saw a purple gash, white scar tissue. The man let the pants leg fall. Chamberlain said nothing. The man looked at his face, seemed suddenly embarrassed, realized he had gone too far. For the first time he was uncertain. But he repeated, "I done my share."

Chamberlain nodded. The man was relaxing slowly. It was warm in the tent; he opened his shirt. Chamberlain said, "What's your name?"

"Bucklin. Joseph Bucklin."

"Where you from?"

"Bangor."

"Don't know any Bucklins. Farmer?"

"Fishermen."

Former Sergeant Kilrain put his head in the tent. "Colonel, there's a courier comin'."

Chamberlain nodded. Bucklin said, "I'm tired, Colonel. You know what I mean? I'm tired. I've had all of this army and all of these officers, this damned Hooker and this goddamned idiot Meade, all of them, the whole bloody lousy rotten mess of sick-brained pot-bellied scabheads that aint fit to lead a johnny detail, aint fit to pour pee outen a boot with instructions on the heel. I'm tired. We are good men and we had our own good flag and these goddamned idiots use us like we was cows or dogs or even worse. We aint gonna win this war. We can't win no how because of these lame-brained bastards from West Point, these goddamned gentlemen, these *officers*. Only one officer knew what he was doin: McClellan, and look what happened to *him*. I just as soon go home and let them damn Johnnies go home and the hell with it."

He let it go, out of breath. He had obviously been waiting to say that to some officer for a long time. Chamberlain said, "I get your point."

Kilrain announced, "Courier, sir."

Chamberlain rose, excused himself, stepped out into the sunlight. A bright-cheeked lieutenant, just dismounted, saluted him briskly.

"Colonel Chamberlain, sir, Colonel Vincent wishes to inform you that the corps is moving out at once and that you are instructed to take the advance. The Twentieth Maine has been assigned to the first position in line. You will send out flankers and advance guards."

"My compliments to the Colonel." Chamberlain saluted, turned to Kilrain and Ellis Spear, who had come up. "You heard him, boys. Get the Regiment up. Sound the *General,* strike the tents." Back inside the tent, he said cheerfully to Bucklin, "We're moving out. You better hurry up your eating. Tell your men I'll be over in a minute. I'll think on what you said."

Bucklin slipped by him, went away. Chamberlain thought: we're first in line.

"Kilrain."

The former sergeant was back.

"Sir."

"Where we headed?"

"West, sir. Pennsylvania somewhere. That's all I know."

"Listen, Buster. You're a private now and I'm not supposed to keep you at headquarters in that rank. If you want to go on back to the ranks, you just say so, because I feel obligated—well, you don't have to be here, but listen, I need you."

"Then I'll be stayin', Colonel, laddie." Kilrain grinned.

"But you know I can't promote you. Not after that episode with the bottle. Did you have to pick an officer?"

Kilrain grinned. "I was not aware of rank, sir, at the time. And he was the target which happened to present itself."

"Buster, you haven't got a bottle about?"

"Is the Colonel in need of a drink, sir?"

"I meant . . . forget it. All right, Buster, move 'em out."

Kilrain saluted, grinning, and withdrew. The only professional in the regiment. The drinking would kill him. Well. He would die happy. Now. What do I say to *them?*

Tom came in, saluted.

"The men from the Second Maine are being fed, sir."

"Don't call me sir."

"Well, Lawrence, Great God A-Mighty—"

"You just be careful of the name business in front of the men. Listen, we don't want anybody to think there's favoritism."

Tom put on the wounded look, face of the ruptured deer.

"General Meade has his *son* as his adjutant."

"That's different. Generals can do anything. Nothing quite so much like God on earth as a general on a battlefield." The tent was coming down about his head; he stepped outside to avoid the collapse. The General and God was a nice parallel. They have your future in their hands and they have all power and know all. He grinned, thinking of Meade surrounded by his angelic staff: Dan Butterfield, wild Dan Sickles. But *what do I say?*

"Lawrence, what you goin' to do?"

Chamberlain shook his head. The regiment was up and moving.

"God, you can't shoot them. You do that, you'll never go back to Maine when the war's over."

"I know that." Chamberlain meditated. "Wonder if *they* do?"

He heard a flare of bugles, looked down the road toward Union Mills. The next regiment, the 83rd Pennsylvania, was up and forming. He saw wagons and ambulances moving out into the road. He could feel again the yellow heat. Must remember to cover up. More susceptible to sunstroke now. Can't afford a foggy head. He began to walk slowly toward the grove of trees.

Kilrain says tell the truth.

Which is?

Fight. Or we'll shoot you.

Not true. I won't shoot anybody.

He walked slowly out into the sunlight. He thought: but the truth is much more than that. Truth is too personal. Don't know if I can express it. He paused in the heat. Strange thing. You would die for it without further question, but you had a hard time talking about it. He shook his head. I'll wave no more flags for home. No tears for Mother. Nobody ever died for apple pie.

He walked slowly toward the dark grove. He had a complicated brain and there were things going on back there from time to time that he only dimly understood, so he relied on his instincts, but he was learning all the time. The faith itself was simple: he believed in the dignity of man. His ancestors were Huguenots, refugees of a chained and bloody Europe. He had learned their stories in the cradle. He had grown up believing in America and the individual and it was a stronger faith than his faith in God. This was the land where no man had to bow. In this place at last a man could stand up free of the past, free of tradition and blood ties and the curse of royalty and become what he wished to become. This was the first place on earth where the man mattered more than the state. True freedom had begun here and it would spread eventually over all the earth. But it had begun *here*. The fact of slavery upon this incredibly beautiful new clean earth was appalling, but more even than that was the horror of old Europe, the curse of nobility, which the South was transplanting to new soil. They were forming a new aristocracy, a new breed of glittering men, and Chamberlain had come to crush it. But he was fighting for the dignity of man and in that way he was fighting for himself. If men were equal in America, all these former Poles and English and Czechs and blacks, then they were equal everywhere, and there was really no such thing as foreigner; there were only free men and slaves. And so it was not even patriotism but a new faith. The Frenchman may fight for France, but the American fights for mankind, for freedom; for the people, not the land.

Yet the words had been used too often and the fragments that came to Chamberlain now were weak. A man who has been shot at is a new realist, and what do you say to a realist when the war is a war of ideals? He thought finally. Well, I owe them the truth at least. Might's well begin with that.

The Regiment had begun to form. Chamberlain thought: At least it'll be a short speech. He walked slowly toward the prisoners.

Glazier Estabrook was standing guard, leaning patiently on his rifle. He was a thick little man of about forty. Except for Kilrain he was the oldest man in the Regiment, the strongest man Chamberlain had ever seen. He waved happily as Chamberlain came up but went on leaning on the rifle. He pointed at one of the prisoners.

"Hey, Colonel, you know who this is? This here is Dan Burns fom Orono. I know his daddy. Daddy's a preacher. You really ought to hear him. Best damn cusser I ever heard. Knows more fine swear words than any man in Maine, I bet. Hee."

Chamberlain smiled. But the Burns boy was looking at him with no expression. Chamberlain said, "You fellas gather round."

He stood in the shade, waited while they closed in silently, watchfully around him. In the background the tents were coming down, the wagons were hitching, but some of the men of the Regiment had come out to watch and listen. Some of the men here were still chewing. But they were quiet, attentive.

Chamberlain waited a moment longer. Now it was quiet in the grove and the clink of the wagons was sharp in the distance. Chamberlain said, "I've been talking with Bucklin. He's told me your problem."

Some of the men grumbled. Chamberlain heard no words clearly. He went on speaking softly so that they would have to quiet to hear him.

"I don't know what I can do about it. I'll do what I can. I'll look into it as soon as possible. But there's nothing I can do today. We're moving out in a few minutes and we'll be marching all day and we may be in a big fight before nightfall. But as soon as I can, I'll do what I can."

They were silent, watching him. Chamberlain began to relax. He had made many speeches and he had a gift for it. He did not know what it was, but when he spoke most men stopped to listen. Fanny said it was something in his voice. He hoped it was there now.

"I've been ordered to take you men with me. I've been told that if you don't come I can shoot you. Well, you know I won't do that. Not Maine men. I won't shoot any man who doesn't want this fight. Maybe someone else will, but I won't. So that's that."

He paused again. There was nothing on their faces to lead him.

"Here's the situation. I've been ordered to take you along, and that's what I'm going to do. Under guard if necessary. But you can have your rifles if you want them. The whole Reb army is up the road a ways waiting for us and this is no time for an argument like this. I tell you this: we sure can use you. We're down below half strength and we need you, no doubt of that. But whether you fight or not is up to you. Whether you come along, well, you're coming."

Tom had come up with Chamberlain's horse. Over the heads of the prisoners Chamberlain could see the Regiment falling into line out in the flaming road. He took a deep breath.

"Well, I don't want to preach to you. You know who we are and what we're doing here. But if you're going to fight alongside us there's a few things I want you to know."

He bowed his head, not looking at eyes. He folded his hands together.

"This Regiment was formed last fall, back in Maine. There were a thousand of us then. There's not three hundred of us now." He glanced up briefly. "But what is left is choice."

He was embarrassed. He spoke very slowly, staring at the ground.

"Some of us volunteered to fight for Union. Some came in mainly because we were bored at home and this looked like it might be fun. Some came because we were ashamed not to. Many of us came . . . because it was the right thing to do. All of us have seen men die. Most of us never saw a black man back home. We think on that, too. But freedom . . . is not just a word."

He looked up into the sky, over silent faces.

"This is a different kind of army. If you look at history you'll see men fight for pay, or women, or some other kind of loot. They fight for land, or because a king makes them, or just because they like killing. But we're here for something new. I don't . . . this hasn't happened much in the history of the world. We're an army going out to set other men free."

He bent down, scratched the black dirt into his fingers. He was beginning to warm to it; the words were beginning to flow. No one in front of him was moving. He said, "This is free ground. All the way from here to the Pacific Ocean. No man has to bow. No man born to royalty. Here we judge you by what *you* do, not by what your father was. Here you can be *something*. Here's a place to build a home. It isn't the land—there's always more land. It's the idea that we all have value, you and me, we're worth something more than the dirt. I never saw dirt I'd die for, but I'm not asking you to come join us and fight for dirt. What we're all fighting for, in the end, is each other."

Once he started talking he broke right through the embarrassment and there was suddenly no longer a barrier there. The words came out of him in a clear river, and he felt himself silent and suspended in the grove listening to himself speak, carried outside himself and looking back down on the silent faces and himself speaking, and he felt the power in him, the power of his cause. For an instant he could see black castles in the air; he could create centuries of screaming, eons of torture. Then he was back in sunlit Pennsylvania. The bugles were blowing and he was done.

He had nothing else to say. No one moved. He felt the embarrassment return. He was suddenly enormously tired. The faces were staring up at him like white stones. Some heads were down. He said, "Didn't mean to preach. Sorry. But I thought . . . you should know who we are." He had forgotten how tiring it was just to speak. "Well, this is still the army, but you're as free as I can make you. Go ahead and talk for a while. If you want your rifles for this fight you'll have them back and nothing else will be said. If you won't join us you'll come along under guard. When this is over I'll do what I can to see that you get fair treatment. Now we have to move out." He stopped, looked at them. The faces showed nothing. He said slowly, "I think if we lose this fight the war will be over. So if you choose to come with us I'll be personally grateful. Well. We have to move out."

He turned, left silence behind him. Tom came up with the horse—a pale-gray lightfooted animal. Tom's face was shiny red.

"My Lawrence, you sure talk pretty."

Chamberlain grunted. He was really tired. Rest a moment. He paused with his hands on the saddle horn. There was a new vague doubt stirring in his brain. Something troubled him; he did not know why.

"You ride today, Lawrence. You look weary."

Chamberlain nodded. Ellis Spear was up. He was Chamberlain's ranking officer, an ex-teacher from Wiscasset who was impressed with Chamberlain's professorship. A shy man, formal, but very competent. He gestured toward the prisoners.

"Colonel, what do you suggest we do with them?"

"Give them a moment. Some of them may be willing to fight. Tom, you go back and see what they say. We'll have to march them under guard. Don't know what else to do. I'm not going to shoot them. We can't leave them here."

The Regiment had formed out in the road, the color bearers in front. Chamberlain mounted, put on the wide-brimmed hat with the emblem of the infantry, began walking his horse slowly across the field toward the road. The uneasiness still troubled him. He had missed something, he did not know what. Well, he was an instinctive man; the mind would tell him sooner or later. Perhaps it was only that when you try to put it into words you cannot express it truly, it never sounds as you dream it. But then . . . you were asking them to die.

Ellis Speer was saying, "How far are we from Pennsylvania, Colonel, you have any idea?"

"Better than twenty miles." Chamberlain squinted upward. "Going to be another hot day."

He moved to the head of the column. The troops were moving slowly, patiently, setting themselves for the long march. After a moment Tom came riding up. His face was delighted. Chamberlain said, "How many are going to join us?"

Tom grinned hugely. "Would you believe it? All but six."

"How many?"

"I counted, by actual count, one hundred and fourteen."

"Well." Chamberlain rubbed his nose, astounded.

Tom said, still grinning, "Brother, you did real good."

"They're all marching together?"

"Right. Glazier's got the six hardheads in tow."

"Well, get all the names and start assigning them to different companies. I don't want them bunched up, spread them out. See about their arms."

"Yes, sir, Colonel, sir."

Chamberlain reached the head of the column. The road ahead was long and straight, rising toward a ridge of trees. He turned in his saddle, looked back, saw the entire Fifth Corps forming behind him. He thought: 120 new men. Hardly noticeable in such a mass. And yet . . . he felt a moment of huge joy. He called for road guards and skirmishers and the Twentieth Maine began to move toward Gettysburg.

3

BUFORD

The land west of Gettysburg is a series of ridges, like waves in the earth. The first Rebel infantry came in that way, down the narrow gray road from the mountain gap. At noon they were in sight of the town. It was a small neat place: white board houses, rail fences, all in order, one white church steeple. The soldiers coming over the last ridge by the Lutheran Seminary could see across the town to the hills beyond and a winding gray road coming up from the south, and as the first gray troops entered the town there was motion on that southern road: a blur, blue movement, blue cavalry. They came on slowly around the last bend, a long blue smoking snake, spiked with guns and flags. The soldiers looked at each other across vacant fields. The day was very hot; the sky was a steamy haze. Someone lifted a gun and fired, but the range was too long. The streets of Gettysburg were deserted.

Just beyond the town there were two hills. One was wooded and green; the other was flat, topped by a cemetery. The Union commander, a tall blond sun-burned man named John Buford, rode up the long slope to the top of the hill, into the cemetery. He stopped by a stone wall, looked down across flat open ground, lovely clear field of fire. He could see all the way across the town and the ridges to the blue mountains beyond, a darkening sky. On the far side of the town there was a red brick building, the stately Seminary, topped with a white cupola. The road by the building was jammed with Rebel troops. Buford counted half a dozen flags. He had thought it was only a raiding party. Now he sensed power behind it, a road flowing with troops all the way back to the mountains.

The first blue brigade had stopped on the road below, by a red barn. The commander of that brigade, Bill Gamble, came up the hill on a muddy horse, trailed by a small cloud of aides, gazed westward with watery eyes. He wheezed, wiping his nose.

"By God, that's infantry."

Buford put the glasses to his eyes. He saw one man on a black horse, waving a plumed hat: an officer. The Rebel troops had stopped. Buford looked around, searching for other movement. He saw a squad of blue troopers, his own men, riding down into deserted streets. Still no sound of gunfire.

Gamble said, "That's one whole brigade. At least one brigade."

"Do you see any cavalry?"

Gamble swept the horizon, shook his head.

Strange. Infantry moving alone in enemy country. Blind. Very strange.

Gamble sneezed violently, wiped his nose on his coat, swore, wheezed. His nose had been running all that day. He pointed back along the ridge beyond the cemetery.

"If you want to fight here, sir, this sure is lovely ground. We tuck in here behind this stone wall and I'd be proud to defend it. Best damn ground I've seen all day."

Buford said, "It is that." But he had only two brigades. He was only a scout. The big infantry was a long day's march behind him. But Gamble was right: it was lovely ground.

"By God, I think they're pulling back."

Buford looked. The gray troops had turned; they had begun to withdraw back up the road. Slowly, very slowly. He could see back-turned faces, feel the cold defiance. But he felt himself loosen, begin to breathe.

"Now that's damned strange." Gamble sniffled. "What do you make of that?"

Buford shook his head. He rode slowly along the stone wall, suspending judgment. There was no wind at all; it was exactly noon. It was very quiet among the gravestones. Superb ground. He thought: they must have orders not to fight. Which means they don't know who we are or how many. Which means they have no cavalry, no eyes. He stopped by a white angel, arm uplifted, a stony sadness. For five days Buford had been tracking Lee's army, shadowing it from a long way off as you track a big cat. But now the cat had turned.

Buford said aloud, "He's coming this way."

"Sir?"

"Lee's turned. That's the main body."

"You think so?" Gamble mused, wriggling his nose. "Could be. But I would have sworn he was headed for Harrisburg."

"He was," Buford said. An idea was blowing in his brain. But there was time to think, time to breathe, and he was a patient man. He sat watching the Rebs withdraw, then he said, "Move your brigades into town. That will make the good citizens happy. I'm going to go have a look."

He hopped the stone wall, rode down the long slope. He owed a message to Reynolds, back with the infantry, but that could wait until he was sure. He was old army cavalry, Kentucky-born, raised in the Indian wars; he was slow, he was careful, but he sensed something happening, a breathless something in his chest. He rode down through the town and out the road the Rebs had taken. There was no one in the streets, not even dogs, but he saw white faces at windows, a fluttering of curtains. There were no cows anywhere, or chickens, or horses. Reb raiding parties had peeled the land. He rode up toward the brick building with the cupola and topped a crest. Off in the distance there was another rise; he could see the Reb column withdrawing into a blue west. He saw the lone officer, much closer now, sitting regally on horseback, outlined against a darkening sky. The man was looking his way, with glasses. Buford waved. You never knew what old friend was out there. The Reb officer took off his hat, bowed formally. Buford grimaced: a gentleman. A soldier fired at very long range. Buford saw his staff people duck, but he did not hear the bullet. He thought: they'll be back in the morning. Lee's concentrating this way. Only one road down through the mountains; have to come this way. They will all converge here. In the morning.

He turned in his stirrups, looked back at the high ground, the cemetery. The hills rose like watchtowers. All that morning he had seen nothing but flat ground. When the Rebs came in, in the morning, they would move into those hills. And Reynolds would not be here in time.

Gamble rode up, saluting. Tom Devin, the other brigade commander, arrived with a cheery grin. Gamble was sober sane; Devin was more the barroom type.

SITUATION
NOON
June 30

Oak Hill

CASHTOWN ROAD

MUMMASBURG ROAD

CARLISLE ROAD

HAGERSTOWN ROAD

SEMINARY

GETTYSBURG

YORK PIKE

Willoughby Run

Seminary Ridge

BUFORD

Cemetery Hill

Culp's Hill

HANOVER ROAD

BUFORD

EMMITSBURG ROAD

Cemetery Ridge

BALTIMORE PIKE

Rock Creek

Devil's Den

TANEYTOWN ROAD

Little Round Top

Big Round Top

Don Pitcher

Buford enters Gettysburg from the south
Confederate troops withdraw

Buford walked the horse back and forth along the rise. He said aloud, "I wonder where their calvalry is."

Devin laughed. "The way old Stuart gets around, he could be having dinner in Philadelphia."

Buford was not listening. He said abruptly, "Get your patrol out. Scout this bunch in front of us, but scout up north. They'll be coming in that way, from Carlisle. We've got a bit of light yet. I want to know before sundown. I think Lee's turned. He's coming this way. If I'm right there'll be a lot of troops up the northern road too. Hop to it."

They moved. Buford wrote a message to John Reynolds, back with the lead infantry:

> *Have occupied Gettysburg. Contacted large party of Reb infantry. I think they are coming this way. Expect they will be here in force in the morning.*

The word would go from Reynolds to Meade. With any luck at all Meade would read it before midnight. From there it would go by wire to Washington. But some of Stuart's cavalry had cut the wires and they might not be patched yet, so Washington would be in the dark and screaming its head off. God, that miserable Halleck. Buford took a deep breath. The great joy of the cavalry was to be so far away, out in the clean air, the open spaces, away from those damned councils. There were some moments, like now, when he felt no superior presence at all. Buford shook his head. He had been badly wounded in the winter, and possibly as you got older you had less patience instead of more. But he felt the beautiful absence of a commander, a silence above him, a windy freedom.

The last Reb infantry walked away over the last rise. The Reb officer stood alone for a moment, then waved again and withdrew. The ridge was bare.

Buford sniffed: distant rain. The land around him was hot and dry and the dust of the horses was blowing steadily up from the south as the wind began to pick up, and he could see a darkness in the mountains, black sky, a blaze of lightning. A squadron of Gamble's cavalry moved slowly up the road. Buford turned again in the saddle, looked back again at the high ground. He shook his head once quickly. No orders: you are only a scout.

Devin rode back, asking for instructions as to where to place his brigade. He had a cheery boyish face, curly yellow hair. He had much more courage than wisdom. Buford said abruptly, accusing, "You know what's going to happen in the morning?"

"Sir?"

"The whole damn Reb army's going to be here in the morning. They'll move right through town and occupy those damned hills—" Buford pointed angrily— "because one thing Lee ain't is a fool, and when our people get here Lee will have the high ground and there'll be the devil to pay."

Devin's eyes were wide. Buford turned. The moods were getting out of hand. He was no man for war councils, or teaching either, and no sense in brooding to junior officers—but he saw it all with such metal brilliance: Meade will come in slowly, cautiously, new to command, wary of reputation. But they'll be on his back from Washington, wires hot with messages: attack, attack. So he will set up a ring around the hills and when Lee's all nicely dug in behind fat rocks Meade will finally attack, if he can coordinate the army, straight up the hillside, out in the open in that gorgeous field of fire, and we will attack valiantly and be butchered valiantly, and afterward men will thump their chests and say what a brave charge it was.

GETTYSBURG

The vision was brutally clear: he had to wonder at the clarity of it. Few things in a soldier's life were so clear as this, so black-line etched that he could actually see the blue troops for one long bloody moment, going up the long slope to the stony top as if it were already done and a memory already, an odd, set, stony quality to it, as if tomorrow had occurred and there was nothing you could do about it, the way you sometimes feel before a foolish attack, knowing it will fail but you cannot stop it or even run away but must even take part and help it fail. But never this clearly. There was always some hope. Never this detail. But if we withdraw—there is no good ground south of here. *This* is the place to fight.

Devin was watching him warily. Buford was an odd man. When he rode off there by himself he liked to talk to himself and you could see his lips moving. He had been too long out in the plains.

He looked at Devin, finally saw him. He said abruptly, "No orders yet. Tell your men to dismount and eat. Rest. Get some rest."

He rode slowly away to inspect the ground in front of him, between him and the Rebels. If we made a stand here, how long do you think we could hold? Long enough for John Reynolds to get here with the infantry? How long would that take? Will Reynolds hurry? Reynolds is a good man. But he might not understand the situation. How do you make him understand? At this distance. But if you hold, you at least give him time to see the ground. But how long can you hold against Lee's whole army? If it is the whole army. These are two very good brigades; you built them yourself. Suppose you sacrifice them and Reynolds is late? For Reynolds will be late. They're always late.

Think on it, John.

There's time, there's time.

The land was long ridges, with streams down in the dark hollows. Dismounted, along a ridge, with all night to dig in, the boys could hold for a while. Good boys. Buford had taught them to fight dismounted, the way they did out west, and the hell with this Stuart business, this glorious Murat charge. Try that against an Indian, that glorious charge, saber a-shining, and he'd drop behind a rock or a stump and shoot your glorious head off as you went by. No, Buford had reformed his boys. He had thrown away the silly sabers and the damned dragoon pistols and given them the new repeating carbines, and though there were only 2,500 of them they could dig in behind a fence and hold *anybody* for a while.

But could they hold long enough?

Wherever he rode he could look back at the hills, dominant as castles. He was becoming steadily more nervous. Easy enough to pull out: the job is done. But he was a professional. Damned few of them in this army. And he would not live forever.

Rain clouds blotted the western sun. The blue mountains were gone. Gamble's first scouts rode back to report that the Rebs had gone into camp just down the road, about three miles out of Gettysburg. Buford rode out far enough to see the pickets for himself, then he rode back toward the green hills. He stopped by the Seminary and had a cup of coffee. The staff left him alone. After that he deployed the brigades.

He had made no plans, but it didn't hurt to prepare. He told Gamble to dismount and dig in along the crest of the ridge just past the seminary, facing the Rebs who would come down that road. He posted Devin in the same way, across the road from the north. Three men in line, every fourth man to fall back with the horses. He watched to see that it was done. They were weary men and they dug silently and there was no music. He heard an officer grumbling. The damned fool wanted to charge the Reb picket line. Buford let loose a black glare. But it was a good line. It would hold for a while, even old Bobby Lee. If John Reynolds got up early in the morning.

It was darker now, still very quiet. No need to make the decision yet. They could always pull out at the last minute. He grinned to himself, and the staff noticed his face and relaxed momentarily. Buford thought: one good thing about cavalry, you can always leave in a hell of a hurry.

Buford turned and rode back through the town, anxious for news from his scouts. People were moving in the streets. He collected a small following of happy boys, one small ragged girl with a beautiful, delicate face. He smiled down, but in the square ahead he saw a crowd, a speaker, a circle of portly men. He turned quickly away. He was no good with civilians. There was something about the mayors of towns that troubled him. They were too fat and they talked too much and they did not think twice of asking a man to die for them. Much of the east troubled Buford. A fat country. Too many people talked too much. The newspapers lied. But the women . . . Yes, the women.

He rode by one porch and there was a woman in a dress of rose, white lace at the throat, a tall blond woman with a face of soft beauty, so lovely that Buford slowed the horse, staring, before taking off his hat. She stood by a vined column, gazing at him; she smiled. There was an old man in the front yard, very old and thin and weak; he hobbled forward, glaring with feeble, toothless rage. "They's Johnny Rebs eva-where, eva-where!" Buford bowed and moved on, turned to look back at the beautiful woman, who stood there watching him.

"Go back and say hello, General."

A coaxing voice, a grinning tone: lean Sergeant Corse, a bowlegged aide. Buford smiled, shook his head.

"Widow woman, I betcha."

Buford turned away, headed toward the cemetery.

"If ye'd like me to ride back, General, I'm sure an interduction could be arranged."

Buford chuckled. "Not tonight, Sergeant."

"The General could use a di-version. Beggin' yer pardon, General. But ye'r too shy a lad, for yer age. Ye work too hard. These here now quiet towns, now, nothin' ever happens here, and the ladies would be so delighted to see you, an important adventurous man such as you, who has seen the world, now, ye'd be doin' 'em a gracious favor, just wi' yer presence."

Buford smiled. "I'm about as shy as a howitzer."

"And similarly graceful. Begging yer pardon."

"Zackly." Buford began the slow ride up the hill to the cemetery.

"Ah," the Sergeant said sadly, "but she was a lovely lass."

"She was that."

The Sergeant brightened. "Well, then if the General does not mind, I may just ride on over there meself, later on, after supper, that is, if the General has no objections." He pushed the glasses back up on his nose, straightened his hat, tucked in his collar.

Buford said, "No objections, Sergeant."

"Ah. Um."

Buford looked.

"And, ah, what time would the General be having supper, now?"

Buford looked at the staff, saw bright hopeful eyes. The hint finally got to him. They could not eat until he had eaten. They trailed him wherever he went, like a pennant; he was so used to their presence he did not notice their hunger. He was rarely hungry himself these days.

The Sergeant said woefully, "The folks in this here town have been after us for food. The Rebs didn't leave them much. The General ought to eat what we got while we got it, because the boys is givin' it away." He glared reproachfully at the other officers.

"Sorry," Buford said. He pointed to the cemetery. "I'll eat right here. A little dried beef. You gentlemen have some supper."

They rode on into the cemetery. He dismounted at last, first time in hours, sat down on stone in silent pain. He thought: body not much good but the mind works well. Two young lieutenants sat down near him, chewing on corn dodgers. He squinted; he did not remember their names. He could remember if he had to, duty of a good officer; he could fish in the memory for the names and pull them up out of the darkness, after a while, but though he was kind to young lieutenants he had learned a long time ago it was not wise to get to know them. One of these had wispy yellow hair, red freckles, he had a strange resemblance to an ear of corn. The other was buck-toothed. Buford suddenly remembered: the buck-toothed boy is a college boy, very bright, very well educated. Buford nodded. The Lieutenants nodded. They thought he was a genuis. He had thrown away the book of cavalry doctrine and they loved him for it. At Thorofare Gap he had held against Longstreet, 3,000 men against 25,000, for six hours, sending off appeal after appeal for help which never came. The Lieutenants admired him greatly, and he could sometimes overhear them quoting his discoveries: *your great fat horse is transportation, that's all he is, with no more place on a modern battlefield than a great fat elephant.* He turned from eager eyes, remembering the cries for help that never came. That time it was General Pope. Now it was General Meade. Make no plans.

He sat watching the lights come on in Gettysburg. The soldiers bordered the town along the west and the north in two long fire-speckled fences—a lovely sight in the gathering dusk. The last light of June burned in the west. He had one marvelous smoke—a dreamy cigar. Tomorrow he will come, old Bob Lee himself, down that western road, on a gray horse. And with him will come about seventy thousand men.

One of the Lieutenants was reading a newspaper. Buford saw rippled black headlines: CITIZENS OF PENNSYLVANIA: PREPARE TO DEFEND YOUR HOMES! A call for militia. He smiled. Militia would not stop old Bobby Lee. We have good old George Meade.

Now now. Have faith. He might be very good.

The hell he is.

Buford peered quickly around, not knowing if he had said that out loud. Damned bad habit. But the Lieutenants were chatting. Buford looked past them to the silent town. Pretty country. But too neat, too tidy. No feel of space, of size, a great starry roof overhead, a great wind blowing. Well. You are not a natural Easterner, that's for sure. Extraordinary to think of war here. Not the country for it. Too neat. Not enough room. He saw again the white angel. He thought: damn good ground.

He sat on a rail fence, watching the night come over Gettysburg. There was no word from the patrols. He went around reading the gravestones, many Dutch names, ghostly sentinels, tipped his hat in respect, thought of his own death, tested his body, still sound, still trustable through a long night, but weaker, notice-ably weaker, the heart uneven, the breath failing. But there was at least one good fight left. Perhaps I'll make it here. His mind wandered. He wondered what it would be like to lose the war. Could you ever travel in the South again? Probably not for a while. But they had great fishing there. Black bass rising in flat black water: *ah.* Shame to go there again, to foreign ground. Strange sense of enormous loss. Buford did not hate. He was a professional. The only ones who even irritated him were the cavaliers, the high-bred, feathery, courtly ones who spoke like Englishmen and treated a man like dirt. But they were mostly damn fools, not men enough to hate. But it would be a great shame if you could never go south any more, for the fishing, for the warmth in winter. Thought once of retiring there. If I get that old.

Out of the dark: Devin.

"Sir, the scouts are in. You were right, sir. Lee's coming this way all right."

Buford focused. "What have you got?"

"Those troops we ran into today were A. P. Hill. His whole Corps is back up the road between here and Cashtown. Longstreet's Corps is right behind him. Ewell's Corps is coming down from the north. They were right in front of Harrisburg but they've turned back. They're concentrating in this direction."

Buford nodded. He said absently, "Lee's trying to get around us, between us and Washington. And won't that charm the Senate?"

He sat down to write the message to Reynolds, on a gravestone, by lantern light. His hand stopped of itself. His brain sent nothing. He sat motionless, pencil poised, staring at the blank paper.

He held good ground before and sent off appeals, and help never came. He was very low on faith. It was a kind of gray sickness; it weakened the hands. He stood up and walked to the stone fence. It wasn't the dying. He had seen men die all his life, and death was the luck of the chance, the price you eventually paid. What was worse was the stupidity. The appalling sick stupidity that was so bad you thought sometimes you would go suddenly, violently, completely insane just having to watch it. It was a deadly thing to be thinking on. Job to be done here. And all of it turns on faith.

The faces were staring at him, all the bright apple faces. He shuddered with vague anger. If Reynolds says he will come, Reynolds will come. An honorable man. I hope to God. Buford was angry, violently angry. But he sat down and wrote the message.

He was in possession of good ground at Gettysburg. If Reynolds came quick, first thing in the morning, Buford could hold it. If not, the Rebs would take it and there was no ground near that was any good. Buford did not know how long his two brigades could hold. Urgent reply.

It was too formal. He struggled to make clear. He stared at it for a long while and then sealed it slowly, thinking, well, we aren't truly committed, we can still run, and gave the message to the buck-toothed lieutenant, who took it delightedly off into the night, although he'd been in the saddle all that day.

Buford felt the pain of old wounds, a sudden vast need for sleep. Now it was up to Reynolds. He said to Devin, "How many guns have we got?"

"Sir? Ah, we have, ah, one battery, sir, is all. Six guns. Calef's Battery, that is, sir."

"Post them out along that west road. The Cashtown road."

Buford tried to think of something else to do but it was all suspended again, a breezy vacancy. Rest until Reynolds sends the word. He sat down once more, back against a gravestone, and began to drift slowly away, turning his mind away as you shift a field of vision with your glasses, moving to focus on higher ground. He remembered a snowstorm. Young lieutenant delivering military mail: days alone across an enormous white plain. Lovely to remember: riding, delivering mail. He dreamed. The wound began to hurt. He woke to the Sergeant, bowlegged Corse: the man dragged drearily by on a spattered horse, raised disgusted eyes.

"The husband, by God, is an *undertaker.*"

He rode mournfully off. The sound of music began to drift up the hill from Gettysburg. A preacher from the Seminary began a low, insistent, theological argument with a young lieutenant, back and forth, back and forth, the staff listening with admiration at the lovely words. The staff began to bed down for the night. It was near midnight when the buck-toothed boy came back from Reynolds, panting down from a lathered horse. Buford read: *General Buford: Hold your ground. I will come in the morning as early as possible. John Reynolds.*

Buford nodded. All right. If you say so. The officers were up and gathering. Buford said to the buck-toothed boy, "Did he say anything else?"

"No sir. He was very busy."

"How far back is he?"

"Not ten miles, sir, I don't think."

"Well," Buford said. He faced the staff: the eager, the wary. "We're going to hold here in the morning." He paused, still fuzzy-brained. "We'll try to hold long enough for General Reynolds to come up with some infantry. I want to save the high ground, if we can."

There was a breathy silence, some toothy grins, as if he had announced a party.

"I think they'll be attacking us at dawn. We ought to be able to stop them for a couple of hours."

At Thorofare Gap we held for six. But that was better ground.

Devin was glowing. "Hell, General, we can hold them all the long damned day, as the feller says."

Buford frowned. He said slowly, "I don't know how long will be necessary. It may be a long time. We can force them to deploy, anyway, and that will take up time. Also, that's a narrow road Lee's coming down, and if we stack them up back there they'll be a while getting untracked. But the point is to hold long enough for the infantry. If we hang onto these hills, we have a good chance to win the fight that's coming. Understood?"

He had excited them. They were young enough to be eager for this. He felt a certain breathless quality himself. He ordered a good feed for the night, no point now in saving food. They moved out to give their orders. Buford rode out once more, in the dark, to the picket line.

He posted the lead pickets himself, not far from the Rebel line. There were four men along the bridge: New York and Illinois, two of them very young. They were popeyed to be so near the Rebs. Closer than anybody in the whole dang army.

Buford said, "They should come in just at about first light. Keep a clear eye. Stay in there long enough to get a good look, then shoot and run. Give us a good warning, but fire only a few rounds. Don't wait too long before you pull out."

A corporal said stiffly, "Yes, sir, General, sir." He broke into a giggle. Buford heard a boy say, *"Now aint you glad you jined the calvry?"*

Buford rode back to the Seminary. He made his headquarters there. In the morning he would have a good view from the cupola. He dismounted and sat down to rest. It was very quiet. He closed his eyes and he could see fields of snow, miles and miles of Wyoming snow, and white mountains in the distance, all clean and incredibly still, and no man anywhere and no motion.

4

LONGSTREET

In Longstreet's camp, they were teaching the Englishman to play poker. They had spread a blanket near a fire and hung a lantern on a tree and they sat around the blanket slapping bugs in the dark, surrounded by campfires, laughter and music. The Englishman was a naturally funny man. He was very thin and perpetually astonished and somewhat gap-toothed, and his manner of talking alone was enough to convulse them, and he enjoyed it. His name was Fremantle—Lieutenant Colonel Arthur Lyon Fremantle—late of Her Majesty's Coldstream Guards, observing for the Queen. There were several other foreigners in the group and they followed Longstreet's headquarters like a small shoal of colorful fish. They were gathered around the blanket now, watching Fremantle perform, and everyone was laughing except the Prussian, Scheiber, a stocky man in a stained white suit, who was annoyed that no one could speak German.

Longstreet sat with his back against a tree, waiting. His fame as a poker player was legendary but he had not played in a long time, not since the deaths of his children, and he did not feel like it now; but he liked to sit in the darkness and watch, passing the time silently, a small distance away, a member of it all warmed by the fire but still not involved in it, not having to talk.

What bothered him most was the blindness. Jeb Stuart had not returned. The army had moved all day in enemy country and they had not even known what was around the next bend. Harrison's news was growing old: the Union Army was on the move. Longstreet had sent the spy back into Gettysburg to see what he could find, but Gettysburg was almost thirty miles away and he had not yet returned. Longstreet dreamed, storing up energy, knowing the fight was coming and resting deliberately, relaxing the muscles, feeling himself loose upon the earth and filling with strength slowly, as the lungs fill with clean air. He was a patient man; he could outwait the dawn. He saw a star fall: a pale cold spark in the eastern sky. Lovely sight. He remembered, counting stars at midnight in a pasture: a girl. The girl thought they were messages from God. Longstreet grinned: she loves me, she loves me not.

"Sir?"

He looked up—a slender, haughty face: G. Moxley Sorrel, Longstreet's chief of staff. Longstreet said, "Major."

"I'm just back from General Lee's headquarters, sir. The General has retired for the night. Everything going nicely, sir. General Lee says we should all be concentrated around Gettysburg tomorrow evening."

"Nothing from Stuart?"

"No, sir. But some of General Hill's troops went into Gettysburg this afternoon and claim they saw Union cavalry there."

THE
FIRST DAY
-DAWN-
Buford's Defensive Position
West of Gettysburg

Longstreet looked up sharply. Sorrel went on: "They had orders not to engage, so they withdrew. General Hill thinks they were mistaken. He says it must be militia. He's going back in force in the morning."

"Who saw cavalry? What officer?"

"Ah, Johnston Pettigrew, I believe, sir."

"The scholar? Fella from North Carolina?"

"Ah, yes, sir. I think so, sir."

"*Blue* cavalry?"

"Yes, sir."

"Why doesn't Hill believe him? Does Hill have other information?"

"No, sir. Ah, I would say, sir, judging from what I heard, that General Hill thinks that, ah, Pettigrew is not a professional and tends to be overexcited and perhaps to exaggerate a bit."

"Um." Longstreet rubbed his face. If there was infantry coming, as Harrison had said, there would be cavalry in front of it.

"What does General Lee say?"

"The General, ah, defers to General Hill's judgment, I believe."

Longstreet grimaced. He thought: we have other cavalry. Why doesn't the old man send for a look? Tell you why: he can't believe Stuart would let him down.

"Have you any orders, sir?" Sorrel was gazing longingly toward the poker game.

"No."

"The men are anxious to have you join the game, sir. As you once did."

"Not tonight, Major."

Sorrel bowed. "Yes, sir. Oh, by the way, sir, General Pickett sends his compliments and states that he will be dropping by later this evening for a chat."

Longstreet nodded. There'll be a complaint from old George. But good to see him. Sorrel moved off into a burst of laughter, a cloud of lovely tobacco. Longstreet sat brooding.

There was an odor of trouble, an indefinable wrong. It was like playing chess and making a bad move and not knowing why but knowing instinctively that it was a bad move. The instincts were yelling. As they used to do long ago at night in Indian country. He gazed out into the black. The stars were obscured. It was the blindness that bothered him. Cavalry in Gettysburg? Harrison would know.

"Sir?"

He looked up again. In soft light: Fremantle.

"Beg your pardon, sir. Most humbly, sir. I'm not disturbing you?"

"Um," Longstreet said. But there was something about the man, prepared for flight, that made Longstreet grin. He was a scrawny man, toothy, with a pipelike neck and a monstrous Adam's apple. He looked like a popeyed bird who had just swallowed something large and sticky and triangular. He was wearing a tall gray hat and a remarkable coat with very wide shoulders, like wings.

He said cheerily, "If I am disturbing you at all, sir, my most humble apologies. But your fame, sir, as a practitioner of poker, is such that one comes to you for advice. I hope you don't mind."

"Not 't'all," Longstreet said. Sometimes when you were around Englishmen there was this ridiculous tendency to imitate them. Longstreet restrained himself. But he grinned.

"What I wanted to ask you, sir, is this. I gather that you are the authority in these matters, and I learned long ago, sir, that in affairs of this kind it is always wisest to go directly, *straightway*, may I say, to the top."

Longstreet waited. Fremantle relaxed slightly, conspiratorially, stroked a handlebar mustache.

"I am most curious, General, as to your attitude toward a subtle subject: the inside straight. On what occasion, or rather, under what circumstance, does one draw to an inside straight? In your opinion. Your response will be kept confidential, of course."

"Never," Longstreet said.

Fremantle nodded gravely, listening. There was nothing else. After a moment he inquired, "Never?"

"Never."

Fremantle thought upon it. "You mean *never*," he concluded.

Longstreet nodded.

"Quite," Fremantle said. He drew back, brooding, then drew himself up. "Indeed," he said. "Well, thank you, sir. Your most humble servant. My apologies for the disturbance."

"Not 't'all."

"I leave you to more important things." He bowed, backed off, paused, looked up. "Never?" he said wistfully.

"Never," Longstreet said.

"Oh. Well, right-ho." Fremantle went away.

Longstreet turned to the dark. A strange and lacey race. Talk like ladies, fight like wildcats. There had long been talk of England coming in on the side of the South. But Longstreet did not think they would come. They will come when we don't need them, like the bank offering money when you're no longer in debt.

A cluster of yells: he looked up. A group of horsemen were riding into camp. One plumed rider waved a feathered hat: that would be George Pickett. At a distance he looked like a French king, all curls and feathers. Longstreet grinned unconsciously. Pickett rode into the firelight, bronze-curled and lovely, hair down to his shoulders, regal and gorgeous on a stately mount. He gestured to the staff, someone pointed toward Longstreet. Pickett rode this way, bowing. Men were grinning, lighting up as he passed; Longstreet could see a train of officers behind him. He had brought along all three of his brigade commanders: Armistead, Garnett and Kemper. They rode toward Longstreet like ships through a gleeful surf, Pickett bowing from side to side. Someone offered a bottle. Pickett raised a scornful hand. He had sworn to dear Sallie ne'er to touch liquor. Longstreet shook his head admiringly. The foreigners were clustering.

Pickett stopped before Longstreet and saluted grandly. "General Pickett presents his compliments, sir, and requests permission to parley with the Commanding General, *s'il vous plaît*."

Longstreet said, "Howdy, George."

Beyond Pickett's shoulder Lew Armistead grinned hello, touching his hat. Longstreet had known them all for twenty years and more. They had served together in the Mexican War and in the old 6th Infantry out in California. They had been under fire together, and as long as he lived Longstreet would never forget the sight of Pickett with the flag going over the wall in the smoke and flame of Chapultepec. Pickett had not aged a moment since. Longstreet thought: my permanent boy. It was more a family than an army. But the formalities had to be observed. He saluted. Pickett hopped out of the saddle, ringlets aflutter as he jumped. Longstreet whiffed a pungent odor.

"Good Lord, George, what's that smell?"

"That's me," Pickett said proudly. "Ain't it lovely?"

Armistead dismounted, chuckling. "He got it off a dead Frenchman. Evening, Pete."

"Woo," Longstreet said. "I bet the Frenchman smelled better."

Pickett was offended. "I did not either get it off a Frenchman. I bought it in a store in Richmond." He meditated. "Did have a French name, now that I think on it. But *Sallie* likes it." This concluded the matter. Pickett glowed and primped, grinning. He was used to kidding and fond of it. Dick Garnett was dismounting slowly. Longstreet caught the look of pain in his eyes. He was favoring a leg. He had that same soft gray look in his face, his eyes. Too tired, much too tired.

Longstreet extended a hand. "How are you, Dick?"

"Fine, General, just fine." But the handclasp had no vitality. Lew Armistead was watching with care.

Longstreet said easily, "Sorry I had to assign you to old smelly George. Hope you have a strong stomach."

"General," Garnett said formally, gracefully, "you must know how much I appreciate the opportunity."

There was a second of silence. Garnett had withdrawn the old Stonewall Brigade without orders. Jackson had accused him of cowardice. Now Jackson was dead, and Garnett's honor was compromised, and he had not recovered from the stain, and in his company there were many men who would never let him recover. Yet Longstreet knew the quality of the man, and he said slowly, carefully, "Dick, I consider it a damned fine piece of luck for me when you became available for this command."

Garnett took a deep breath, then nodded once quickly, looking past Longstreet into the dark. Lew Armistead draped a casual arm across his shoulders.

"Dick's been eating too many cherries. He's got the Old Soldier's Disease."

Garnett smiled weakly. "Sure do." He rubbed his stomach. "Got to learn to fight from the squatting position."

Armistead grinned. "I know what's wrong with you. You been standing downwind of ole George. You got to learn to watch them fumes."

A circle had gathered at a respectful distance. One of these was Fremantle, of Her Majesty's Coldstream Guards, wide-hatted. Adam's-appled. Pickett was regarding him with curiosity.

Longstreet remembered his manners. "Oh, excuse me, Colonel. Allow me to present our George Pickett. Our loveliest general. General Pickett, Colonel Fremantle of the Coldstream Guards."

Pickett bowed low in the classic fashion, sweeping the ground with the plumed hat.

"The fame of your regiment, sir, has preceded you."

"General Pickett is our ranking strategist," Longstreet said. "We refer all the deeper questions to George."

"They do," Pickett admitted, nodding. "They do indeed."

"General Pickett's record at West Point is still the talk of the army."

Armistead hawed.

"It is unbecoming to a soldier, all this book-learning," Pickett said haughtily.

"It aint *gentlemanly,* George," Armistead corrected.

"Nor that either," Pickett agreed.

"He finished last in his class," Longstreet explained. "Dead last. Which is quite a feat, if you consider his classmates."

"The Yankees got all the smart ones," Pickett said placidly, "and look where it got them."

Fremantle stood grinning vaguely, not quite sure how to take all this. Lew

Armistead came forward and bowed silently, delicately, old courtly Lo, giving it a touch of elegance. He did not extend a hand, knowing the British custom. He said, "Good evening, Colonel. Lo Armistead. The 'Lo' is short for Lothario. Let me welcome you to 'Lee's Miserables.' The Coldstream Guards? Weren't you fellas over here in the discussion betwixt us of 1812? I seem to remember my daddy telling me about . . . No, it was the Black Watch. The kilted fellas, that's who it was."

Fremantle said, "Lee's Miserables?"

"A joke," Longstreet said patiently. "Somebody read Victor Hugo—believe it or not I have officers who read—and ever since then we've been Lee's Miserables."

Fremantle was still in the dark. Longstreet said, "Victor Hugo. French writer. Novel. *Les Miserables.*"

Fremantle brightened. Then he smiled. Then he chuckled. "Oh that's very good. Oh, I say that's very good indeed, Haw."

Pickett said formally. "Allow me to introduce my commanders. The elderly one here is Lewis Armistead. The 'Lothario' is a bit of a joke, as you can see. But we are democratic. We do not hold his great age against him. We carry him to the battle, and we aim him and turn him loose. His is what we in this country call an 'Old Family'—" Armistead said briefly, "Oh God"—"although doubtless you English would consider him still an immigrant. There have been Armisteads in all our wars, and maybe we better change the subject, because it is likely that old Lo's grandaddy took a pot-shot at your grandaddy, but anyway, we had to let him in this war to keep the string going, do you see? Age and all."

"Creak," Armistead said.

"The next one here is Dick Garnett. Ah, Richard Brooke Garnett."

Garnett bowed. Pickett said, "Old Dick is a good lad, but sickly. Ah well—" Pickett made a sad face—"some of us are born puny, and others are blessed with great natural strength. It is all God's will. Sit down, Dick. Now this next one here—" he indicated stoic Jim Kemper—"this one is not even a soldier, so watch him. Note the shifty beady eye? He's a politician. Only reason he's here is to gather votes come next election."

Kemper stepped forward, hand extended warily. He had been speaker of the Virginia House and he was not fond of foreigners. Fremantle took the hand with forced good will. Kemper said brusquely, "Look here now, Colonel. Been wondering when you people were going to get out and break that damned Yankee blockade. How about that?"

Fremantle apologized, grinning foolishly. Now the Prussian was here and the Austrian, Ross. A crowd was forming. Pickett went on to introduce some of his staff: Beau Harrison, his IG, and Jim Crocker. Crocker was moodily sentimental, already a bit drunk. He was returning now after an absence of thirteen years to his old alma mater, Pennsylvania College, in Gettysburg. Someone suggested they drink to that, but Pickett reminded one and all soulfully of his oath to Sallie, schoolgirl Sallie, who was half his age, and that brought up a round of ribald kidding that should have insulted Pickett but didn't. He glowed in the midst of it, hairy, happy. Fremantle looked on, never quite certain what was kidding and what wasn't. He produced some brandy; Armistead came up with a flask; Kemper had a bottle of his own. Longstreet thought: *careful.* He sat off to one side, withdrawing, had one long hot swig from Armistead's flask, disciplined himself not to take another, withdrew against the trunk of a cool tree, letting the night come over him, listening to them talk, reminiscing. He knew enough to stay out of it. The presence of the commander always a damper. But after a few moments Pickett detached himself from the group and came to Longstreet.

"General? A few words?"

"Sure, George. Fire."

"By George you're looking well, sir. Must say, never saw you looking better."

"You look lovely too, George." Longstreet liked this man. He was not overwhelmingly bright, but he was a fighter. Longstreet was always careful to give him exact instructions and to follow him to make sure he knew what to do, but once pointed, George could be relied on. A lovely adventurous boy, thirty-eight years old and never to grow older, fond of adventure and romance and all the bright sparkles of youth. Longstreet said happily, "What can I do for you, George?"

"Well, sir, now I don't mean this as a reflection upon *you*, sir. But well, you know, sir, my Division, my Virginia boys, we weren't at Chancellorsville."

"No."

"Well, you know we were assigned away on some piddling affair, and we weren't at Fredericksburg either; we were off again doing some other piddling thing, and now they've taken two of my brigades, Corse and Jenkins, and sent them off to guard Richmond—*Richmond*, for the love of God—and *now*, General, do you know where I'm placed in line of march? *Last*, sir, that's where. Exactly last. I bring up the damned rear. Beg pardon."

Longstreet sighed.

Pickett said, "Well, I tell you, sir, frankly, my boys are beginning to wonder at the attitude of the high command toward my Division. My boys—"

"George," Longstreet said.

"Sir, I must—" Pickett noted Longstreet's face. "Now, I don't mean to imply *this* command. Not you, sir. I was just hoping you would talk to somebody."

"George." Longstreet paused, then he said patiently, "Would you like us to move the whole army out of the way and let you go first?"

Pickett brightened. That seemed a good idea. Another look at Longstreet's face.

"I only meant, sir, that we haven't—"

"I know, George. Listen, there's no plot. It's just the way things fell out. I have three divisions, right? There's you, and there's Hood and McLaws. And where I go you go. Right? And my HQ is near the Old Man, and the Old Man chooses to be here, and that's the way it is. We sent your two brigades to Richmond because we figured they were Virginia boys and that was proper. But look at it this way: if the army has to turn and fight its way out of here, you'll be exactly *first* in line."

Pickett thought on that.

"That's possible?"

"Yup."

"Well," Pickett mused. At that moment Lew Armistead came up. Pickett said wistfully, "Well, I had to speak on it, sir. You understand. No offense?"

"None."

"Well then. But I mean, the whole war could be damn well over soon, beg pardon, and my boys would have missed it. And these are Virginians, sir, and have a certain pride." It occurred to him that Longstreet not being a Virginian, he might have given another insult.

But Longstreet said, "I know I can count on you, George, when the time comes. And it'll come, it'll come."

Armistead broke in, "Sorry to interrupt, but they're calling for George at the poker table." He bowed. "Your fame, sir, has preceded you."

Pickett excused himself, watchful of Longstreet. Pickett was always saying something to irritate somebody, and he rarely knew why, so his method was simply to apologize in general from time to time and to let people know he meant well and then shove off and hope for the best. He apologized and departed, curls ajiggle.

Armistead looked after him. "Hope he brought some money with him." He turned back to Longstreet, smiling. "How goes it, Pete?"

"Passing well, passing well." An old soldier's joke, vaguely obscene. It had once been funny. Touched now with memories, sentimental songs. Longstreet thought: he's really quite gray. Has reached that time when a man ages rapidly, older with each passing moment. Old Lothario. Longstreet was touched. Armistead had his eyes turned away, following Pickett.

"I gather that George was trying to get us up front where we could get shot. Correct? Thought so. Well, must say, if you've got to do all this damn marching at my age there ought to be some action some time. Although—" he held up a hand —"I don't complain, I don't complain." He sat, letting a knee creak. "Getting rickety."

Longstreet looked: firelight soft on a weary face. Armistead was tired. Longstreet watched him, gauging. Armistead noticed.

"I'm all right, Pete."

"Course."

"No, really. I . . ." He stopped in mid-sentence. "I am getting a little old for it. To tell the truth. It, ah . . ." He shrugged. "It isn't as much fun when your feet hurt. Ooo." He rubbed his calf. He looked away from Longstreet's eyes. "These are damn good cherries they grow around here. Wonder if they'd grow back home."

Laughter broke from Pickett's group. A cloud passed over the moon. Armistead had something on his mind. Longstreet waited. Harrison had to be back soon. Armistead said, "I hear you have some word of the Union Army."

"Right." Longstreet thought: Hancock.

"Have you heard anything of old Win?"

"Yep. He's got the Second Corps, headed this way. We should be running into him one of these days." Longstreet felt a small jealousy. Armistead and Hancock. He could see them together—graceful Lo, dashing and confident Hancock. They had been closer than brothers before the war. A rare friendship. And now Hancock was coming this way with an enemy corps.

Armistead said, "Never thought it would last this long." He was staring off into the dark.

"Me neither. I was thinking on that last night. The day of the one-battle war is over, I think. It used to be that you went out to fight in the morning and by sundown the issue was decided and the king was dead and the war was usually over. But now . . ." He grunted, shaking his head. "Now it goes on and on. War has changed, Lewis. They all expect one smashing victory. Waterloo and all that. But I think that kind of war is over. We have trenches now. And it's a different thing, you know, to ask a man to fight from a trench. Any man can charge briefly in the morning. But to ask a man to fight from a trench, day after day . . ."

"Guess you're right," Armistead said. But he was not interested, and Longstreet, who loved to talk tactics and strategy, let it go. After a moment Armistead said, "Wouldn't mind seeing old Win again. One more time."

"Why don't you?"

"You wouldn't mind?"

"Hell no."

"Really? I mean, well, Pete, do you think it would be *proper?*"

"Sure. If the chance comes, just get a messenger and a flag of truce and go on over. Nothing to it."

"I sure would like just to talk to him again," Armistead said. He leaned back, closing his eyes. "Last time was in California. When the war was beginning. Night before we left there was a party."

Long time ago, another world. And then Longstreet thought of his children, that Christmas, that terrible Christmas, and turned his mind away. There was a silence.

Armistead said, "Oh, by the way, Pete, how's your wife? Been meaning to ask."

"Fine." He said it automatically. But she was not fine. He felt a spasm of pain like a blast of sudden cold, saw the patient high-boned Indian face, that beautiful woman, indelible suffering. Children never die: they live on in the brain forever. After a moment he realized that Armistead was watching him.

"If you want me to leave, Pete."

"No." Longstreet shook his head quickly.

"Well, then, I think I'll just set a spell and pass the time of day. Don't get to see much of you any more." He smiled: a touch of shyness. He was five years older than Longstreet, and now he was the junior officer, but he was one of the rare ones who was genuinely glad to see another man advance. In some of them there was a hunger for rank—in Jubal Early it was a disease—but Armistead had grown past the hunger, if he ever had it at all. He was an honest man, open as the sunrise, cut from the same pattern as Lee: old family, Virginia gentleman, man of honor, man of duty. He was one of the men who would hold ground if it could be held; he would die for a word. He was a man to depend on, and there was this truth about war: it taught you the men you could depend on.

He was saying, "I tell you one thing you don't have to worry on, and that's our Division. I never saw troops anywhere so ready for a brawl. And they're not just kids, either. Most of them are veterans and they'll know what to do. But the morale is simply amazing. Really is. Never saw anything like it in the old army. They're off on a Holy War. The Crusades must have been a little like this. Wish I'd a been there. Seen old Richard and the rest."

Longstreet said, "They never took Jerusalem."

Armistead squinted.

"It takes a bit more than morale," Longstreet said.

"Oh sure." But Longstreet was always gloomy. "Well, anyhow, I've never seen anything like this. The Old Man's accomplishment. Incredible. His presence is everywhere. They hush when he passes, like an angel of the Lord. You ever see anything like it?"

"No."

"Remember what they said when he took command? Called him Old Granny. Hee." Armistead chuckled. "Man, what damn fools we are."

"There's talk of making him President, after the war."

"They are?" Armistead considered it. "Do you suppose he'd take it?"

"No, I don't think he would take it. But, I don't know. I like to think of him in charge. One honest man."

"A Holy War," Longstreet said. He shook his head. He did not think much of the Cause. He was a professional: the Cause was Victory. It came to him in the night sometimes with a sudden appalling shock that the boys he was fighting were boys he had grown up with. The war had come as a nightmare in which you chose your nightmare side. Once chosen, you put your head down and went on to win. He thought: shut up. But he said:

"You've heard it often enough: one of our boys can lick any ten of them, that nonsense."

"Well."

"Well, you've fought with those boys over there, you've commanded them." He gestured vaguely east. "You know damn well they can fight. You should have seen them come up that hill at Fredericksburg, listen." He gestured vaguely, tightly, losing command of the words. "Well, Lo, you know we are dying one at a time and there aren't enough of us and we die just as dead as anybody, and a boy from back home aint a better soldier than a boy from Minnesota or anywhere else just because he's from back home."

Armistead nodded carefully. "Well, sure." He paused watchfully. "Of course I know that. But then, on the other hand, we sure do stomp them consistently, now don't we, Pete? We . . . I don't know, but I feel we're something special. I do. We're good, and we know it. It may just be the Old Man and a few other leaders like you. Well, I don't know what it is. But I tell you, I believe in it, and I don't think we're overconfident."

Longstreet nodded. Let it go. But Armistead sat up.

"Another thing, Peter, long as the subject is up. I've been thinking on your theories of defensive war, and look, Pete, if you don't mind the opinion of an aging military genius, just this once? Technically, by God, you're probably right. Hell, you're undoubtedly right. This may be a time for defensive war. But, Pete, this aint the *army* for it. We aren't bred for the defense. And the Old Man, Lord, if ever there was a man not suited for slow dull defense, it's old R.E."

Longstreet said, "But he's a *soldier.*"

"Exactly. And so are you. But the Old Man is just plain, well, too *proud.* Listen, do you remember when he was assigned to the defense of Richmond and he started digging trenches, you remember what they started calling him?"

"The King of Spades." God, the Richmond newspapers. "Right. And you could see how hurt he was. Most people would be. Stain on the old honor. Now, Pete, you're wise enough not to give a damn about things like that. But Old Robert, now, he's from the old school, and I'll bet you right now he can't wait to get them out in the open somewhere where he can hit them face to face. And you know every soldier in the army feels the same way, and it's one of the reasons why the morale here is so good and the Union morale is so bad, and isn't that a fact?"

Longstreet said nothing. It was all probably true. And yet there was danger in it; there was even something dangerous in Lee. Longstreet said, "He promised me he would stay on the defensive. He said he would look for a good defensive position and let them try to hit us."

"He did?"

"He did."

"Well, maybe. But I tell you, Pete, it aint natural to him."

"And it is to me?"

Armistead cocked his head to one side. Then he smiled, shook his head, and reached out abruptly to slap Longstreet's knee.

"Well, might's well be blunt, old soul, and to hell with the social graces. Truth is, Peter, that you are by nature the stubbornest human being, nor mule either, nor even *army* mule, that I personally have ever known, or ever hope to know, and my hat is off to you for it, because you are also the best damn *defensive* soldier I ever saw, by miles and miles and miles, and that's a fact. Now—" he started to rise —"I'll get a-movin', back to my virtuous bed."

Longstreet grunted, found himself blushing. He rose, went silently with Armistead toward the crowd around Pickett. Moxley Sorrel was on his feet, pounding his palm with a clenched fist. The Englishman, Fremantle, was listening open-mouthed. The Prussian, Scheiber, was smiling in a nasty sort of way. Longstreet caught the conclusion of Sorrel's sentence.

". . . know that government derives its power from the consent of the governed. Every government, everywhere. And, sir, let me make this plain: *We do not consent. We will never consent.*"

They stood up as Longstreet approached. Sorrel's face was flushed. Jim Kemper was not finished with the argument, Longstreet or no. To Fremantle he went on: "You must tell them, and make it plain, that what we are fighting for is our freedom from the rule of what is to us a foreign government. That's *all* we want and that's what this war is all about. We established this country in the first place with strong state governments just for that reason, to avoid a central tyranny—"

"Oh Lord," Armistead said, "the Cause."

Fremantle rose, trying to face Longstreet and continue to listen politely to Kemper at the same moment. Pickett suggested with authority that it was growing quite late and that his officers should get back to their separate commands. There were polite farewells and kind words, and Longstreet walked Pickett and Armistead to their horses. Kemper was still saying firm, hard, noble things to Sorrel and Sorrel was agreeing absolutely—mongrelizing, money-grubbing Yankees—and Longstreet said, "What happened?"

Pickett answered obligingly, unconcerned, "Well, Jim Kemper kept needling our English friend about why they didn't come and join in with us, it being in their interest and all, and the Englishman said that it was a very touchy subject, since most Englishmen figured the war was all about, ah, *slavery,* and then old Kemper got a bit outraged and had to explain to him how wrong he was, and Sorrel and some others joined in, but no harm done."

"Damn fool," Kemper said. "He *still* thinks it's about slavery."

"Actually," Pickett said gravely, "I think my analogy of the club was best. I mean, it's as if we all joined a gentlemen's club, and then the members of the club started sticking their noses into our private lives, and then we up and resigned, and then they tell us we don't have the right to resign. I think that's a fair analogy, hey, Pete?"

Longstreet shrugged. They all stood for a moment agreeing with each other, Longstreet saying nothing. After a while they were mounted, still chatting about what a shame it was that so many people seemed to think it was slavery that brought on the war, when all it was really was a question of the Constitution. Longstreet took the reins of Pickett's horse.

"George, the army is concentrating toward Gettysburg. Hill is going in in the morning and we'll follow, and Ewell is coming down from the north. Tomorrow night we'll all be together."

"Oh, very good." Pickett was delighted. He was looking forward to parties and music.

Longstreet said, "I think that sometime in the next few days there's going to be a big fight. I want you to do everything necessary to get your boys ready."

"Sir, they're ready now."

"Well, do what you can. The little things. See to the water. Once the army is gathered in one place all the wells will run dry. See to it, George."

"I will, I will."

Longstreet thought: don't be so damn motherly.

"Well, then. I'll see you tomorrow night."

They said their good nights. Armistead waved farewell.

"If you happen to run across Jubal Early, Peter, tell him for me to go to hell."

They rode off into the dark. The moon was down; the night sky was filled with stars. Longstreet stood for a moment alone. Some good men there. Lo had said, "Best defensive soldier." From Lewis, a compliment. And yet, is it really my nature? Or is it only the simple reality?

Might as well argue with stars.

The fires were dying one by one. Longstreet went back to his place by the camp table. The tall silent aide from Texas, T. J. Goree, had curled up in a bedroll, always near, to be used at a moment's notice. For "The Cause." So many good men. Longstreet waited alone, saw one falling star, reminding him once more of the girl in a field a long time ago.

Harrison came back long after midnight. He brought the news of Union cavalry in Gettysburg. Longstreet sent the word to Lee's headquarters, but the Old Man had gone to sleep and Major Taylor did not think it important enough to wake him. General Hill had insisted, after all, that the reports of cavalry in Gettysburg were foolish.

Longstreet waited for an answer, but no answer came. He lay for a long while awake, but there was gathering cloud and he saw no more falling stars.

Just before dawn the rain began: fine misty rain blowing cold and clean in soft mountain air. Buford's pickets saw the dawn come high in the sky, a gray blush, a bleak rose. A boy from Illinois climbed a tree. There was mist across Marsh Creek, ever whiter in the growing light. The boy from Illinois stared and felt his heart beating and saw movement. A blur in the mist, an unfurled flag. Then the dark figures, row on row: skirmishers. Long, long rows, like walking trees, coming up toward him out of the mist. He had a long paralyzed moment which he would remember until the end of his life. Then he raised the rifle and laid it across the limb of the tree and aimed generally toward the breast of a tall figure in the front of the line, waited, let the cold rain fall, misting his vision, cleared his eyes, waited, prayed, and pressed the trigger.

CARLISLE

RODES

EWELL

EARLY

Shippensburg

CHAMBERS-
BURG   JOHNSON
          A.P.   HILL
HOOD   McLAWS   ANDERSON   PENDER HETH
LONGSTREET   Mummasburg
PICKETT
                          Cashtown   BUFORD

                                     GETTYSBURG   SYKES V

                                                HANOVER
                    REYNOLDS I   SLOCUM XII
                                                    STUART
                    HOWARD XI   SICKLES III
                                            Littlestown
          PENNSYLVANIA
          MARYLAND
Leitersburg   HANCOCK II

                                    SEDGWICK VI

                           Monocacy

                           River

SITUATION
-EVENING-
June 30

0   5   10
         Miles

FREDERICK

WEDNESDAY,
JULY 1, 1863
THE FIRST DAY

. . . of the coming of the Lord

1

LEE

He came out of the tent into a fine cold rain. The troops were already up and moving out on the misty road beyond the trees. Some of them saw the white head and came to the fence to stare at him. The ground rocked. Lee floated, clutched the tent. Got up too quickly. Must move slowly, with care. Bryan came out of the mist, bearing steaming coffee in a metal cup. Lee took it in pained hands, drank, felt the heat soak down through him like hot liquid sunshine. The dizziness passed. There was fog flat and low in the treetops, like a soft roof. The rain was clean on his face. He walked slowly to the rail where the horses were tethered: gentle Traveler, skittish Lucy Long. Stuart had not come back in the night. If Stuart had come they would have wakened him. He said good morning to the beautiful gray horse, the great soft eyes, said a silent prayer. He thought: tonight we'll all be together.

Troops were gathering along the rail fence, looking in at him. He heard a man cry a raucous greeting. Another man shushed him in anger. Lee turned, bowed slightly, waved a stiff arm. There was a cluster of sloppy salutes, broad wet grins under dripping hats. A bareheaded boy stood in reverent silence, black hat clutched to his breast. An officer moved down the fence, hustling the men away.

Lee took a deep breath, testing his chest: a windblown vacancy, a breathless pain. He had a sense of enormous unnatural fragility, like hollow glass. He sat silently on a rail, letting the velvet nose nuzzle him. Not much pain this morning. Praise God. He had fallen from his horse on his hands and the hands still hurt him but the pain in the chest was not bad at all. But it was not the pain that troubled him; it was a sick gray emptiness he knew too well, that sense of a hole clear through him like the blasted vacancy in the air behind a shell burst, an enormous emptiness. The thing about the heart was that you could not coax it or force it, as you could any other disease. Will power meant nothing. The great cold message had come in the spring, and Lee carried it inside him every moment of every day and all through the nights—that endless, breathless, inconsolable alarm: *there is not much time, beware, prepare.*

"Sir?"

Lee looked up. Young Walter Taylor. Lee came slowly awake, back to the misty world. Taylor stood in the rain with inky papers—a cool boy of twenty-four, already a major.

"Good morning, sir. Trust you slept well?"

The clear black eyes were concerned. Lee nodded. Taylor was a slim and cocky boy. Behind Lee's back he called him "The Great Tycoon." He did not know that Lee knew it. He had a delicate face, sensitive nostrils. He said cheerily, "Nothing from General Stuart, sir."

Lee nodded.

"Not a thing, sir. We can't even pick up any rumors. But we mustn't fret now, sir." A consoling tone. "They haven't got anybody can catch General Stuart."

Lee turned to the beautiful horse. He had a sudden rushing sensation of human frailty, death like a blowing wind: Jackson was gone, Stuart would go, like leaves from autumn trees. Matter of time.

Taylor said airily, "Sir, I would assume that if we haven't heard from the general it is obviously because he has nothing to report."

"Perhaps," Lee said.

"After all, sir, Longstreet's man is a paid spy. And an *actor* to boot." Taylor pursed his lips primly, flicked water from a gray cuff.

Lee said, "If I do not hear from General Stuart by this evening I will have to send for him."

"Yes, sir."

"We'll send the Maryland people. They'll be familiar with the ground."

"Very good, sir." Taylor shifted wet papers. "Message here from General Hill, sir."

"Yes."

"The General wishes to inform you that he is going into Gettysburg this morning with his lead Division." Taylor squinted upward at a lightening sky, "I expect he's already under way. He advises me that there is a shoe factory in the town and his men intend to, ah, requisition some footgear." Taylor grinned.

"General Ewell is moving down from the north?"

"Yes, sir. The rain may slow things somewhat. But General Ewell expects to be in the Cashtown area by noon."

Lee nodded. Taylor peered distastefully at another paper.

"Ah, there is a report here, sir, of Union cavalry in Gettysburg, but General Hill discounts it."

"Cavalry?"

"Yes, sir. General Pettigrew claims he saw them yesterday afternoon. General Hill says he was, ah, overeager. General Hill says he expects no opposition but perhaps some local militia, with shotguns and such."

Taylor grinned cheerily. Lee remembered Longstreet's spy. If it is Union cavalry, there will be infantry close behind it. Lee said, "Who is Hill's head commander?"

"Ah, that will be General Heth, sir."

Harry Heth. Studious. Reliable. Lee said, "General Hill knows I want no fight until this army is concentrated."

"Sir, he does."

"That must be clear."

"I believe it is, sir."

Lee felt a thump, a flutter in his chest. It was as if the heart was turning over. He put his hand there, passed one small breathless moment. It happened often: no pain, just a soft deep flutter. Taylor was eyeing him placidly. He had no fear of the Army of the Potomac.

"Will the General have breakfast?"

Lee shook his head.

"We have flapjacks in small mountains, sir. You must try them, sir. Fresh butter and bacon and wagons of hams, apple butter, ripe cherries. Never seen anything like it, sir. You really ought to pitch in. Courtesy of mine host, the great state of Pennsylvania. Nothing like it since the war began. Marvelous what it does for

N

CARLISLE

Shippensburg

EWELL

CHAMBERS-
BURG

LONGSTREET

Mummasburg

Cashtown

HILL

GETTYSBURG

South

PENNSYLVANIA
MARYLAND

Leitersburg

HAGERSTOWN

Monocacy River

DAWN
July 1

0   5   10
Miles

FREDERICK

morale. Never saw the men happier. Napoleon knew a thing or two, what? For a Frenchman?"

Lee said, "Later." There was no hunger in the glassy chest. Want to see Longstreet. Up ahead, in the mist, A. P. Hill probes toward Gettysburg like a blind hand. Hill was new to command. One-legged Ewell was new to command. Both had replaced Stonewall Jackson, who was perhaps irreplaceable. Now there was only Longstreet, and a thumping heart. Lee said, "We will move the headquarters forward today, this morning."

"Yes, sir. Sir, ah, there are a number of civilians to see you."

Lee turned sharply. "Trouble with our soldiers?"

"Oh no, sir. No problem there. The men are behaving very well, very well indeed. Oh yes, sir. But, ah, there are some local women who claim we've taken all their food, and although they don't complain of our having paid for it all in the good dear coin of the mighty state of Virginia—" Taylor grinned—"they *do* object to starving. I must say that Ewell's raiding parties seem to have been thorough. At any rate, the ladies seek your assistance. Rather massive ladies, most of them, but one or two have charm."

"See to it, Major."

"Of course, sir. Except, ah, sir, the old gentleman, he's been waiting all night to see you."

"Old gentleman?"

"Well, sir, we conscripted his horse. At your orders, as you know. I explained that to the old man, fortunes of war and all that, but the old gentleman insists that the horse is blind, and can be of no use to us, and is an old friend."

Lee sighed. "A blind horse?"

"Yes, sir. I didn't want to trouble you, sir, but your orders were strict on this point."

"Give him the horse, Major."

"Yes, sir." Taylor nodded.

"We must be charitable with these people, Major. We have enough enemies."

"Oh yes, sir." Taylor made a slight bow. "The men have the strictest orders. But I must say, sir, that those orders would be easier to follow had the Yankees shown charity when they were back in Virginia."

"Major," Lee said slowly, "we will behave ourselves."

Taylor recognized the tone. "Yes, sir," he said.

Lee rested against the rail fence. He noticed at last a struggling band: "Bonny Blue Flag." A brave but tinny sound. He bowed in that direction, raised his coffee cup in tribute. A tall thin soldier waved a feathered hat: the music bounced away. Lee said, "I would like to see General Longstreet. My compliments, and ask him to ride with me this morning, if he is not otherwise occupied."

"Breakfast, sir?"

"In a moment, Major."

Taylor saluted formally, moved off. Lee sat for a moment alone, gazing eastward. Cavalry. If Longstreet's spy was right, then there could truly be cavalry in Gettysburg and masses of infantry right behind. We drift blindly toward a great collision. Peace, until night. He rubbed the left arm. Must show no pain, no weakness here. The strength now is in Longstreet. Trust to him.

He saw the old gentleman, who thanked him with tears for the return of the blind horse. A Pennsylvania woman flirted, asked for his autograph. He gave it, amazed, wondering what good it would do her in this country. He met with his aides: angry Marshall, graybearded Venable. Marshall was furious with the absent

Stuart, was ready to draw up court-martial papers. Lee said nothing. The courteous Venable drew him politely away.

"Sir, I have a request to make."

"Yes."

Venable: a courtly man, a man of patience. He said, "Could you speak to Dorsey Pender, sir? He's had a letter from his wife."

Lee remembered: beautiful woman on a golden horse, riding with Pender on the banks of the Rappahannock. Lovely sight, a sunset sky.

"Mrs. Pender is, ah, a pious woman, and she believes that now that we have invaded Pennsylvania we are in the wrong, and God has forsaken us—you know how these people reason, sir—and she says she cannot pray for him."

Lee shook his head. God protect us from our loving friends. He saw for one small moment the tragic face of his own frail wife, that unhappy woman, the stone strong face of his mother. Venable said, "I think a talk might help Pender, sir. Another man would shake it off, but he's . . . taken it badly. Says he cannot pray himself." Venable paused. "I know there are others who feel that way."

Lee nodded. Venable said, "It was easier in Virginia, sir. On our home ground."

"I know."

"Will you speak to him, sir?"

"Yes," Lee said.

"Very good, sir. I know it will help him, sir."

Lee said, "I once swore to defend this ground." He looked out across the misty grove. "No matter. No matter. We end the war as best we can." He put his hand to his chest. "Napoleon once said, 'The logical end to defensive warfare is surrender.' You might tell him that."

"Yes, sir. Thank you very much, sir."

Venable went away. Lee felt a deeper spasm, like a black stain. I swore to defend. Now I invade. A soldier, no theologian. God, let it be over soon. While there's time to play with grandchildren. It came too late. Fame came too late. I would have enjoyed it, if I were a younger man.

He moved back to the map table. The guilt stayed with him, ineradicable, like the silent alarm in the fragile chest. Swore to defend. Misty matters. Get on with the fight. He looked down at the map. The roads all converged, weblike, to Gettysburg. And where's the spider? Nine roads in all. Message from Ewell: his troops were on the move, would be coming down into Gettysburg from the north. Lee looked at his watch: eight o'clock. The rain had stopped, the mist was blowing off. He thought: good. Too much rain would muck up the roads. The first sun broke through, yellow and warm through steaming tree leaves, broad bright light blazed across the map table. Lee began to come slowly awake, blinking in the blaze of morning.

Out on the road the troops were moving in a great mottled stream: Longstreet's First Corps, the backbone of the army, moving up behind Powell Hill. The barefoot, sunburned, thin and grinning army, joyful, unbeatable, already immortal. And then through the trees the familiar form: big man on a black horse, great round shoulders, head thick as a stump: James Longstreet.

It was reassuring just to look at him, riding slowly forward into the sunlight on the black Irish stallion: Dutch Longstreet, old Pete. He was riding along in a cloud of visitors, bright-clad foreigners, observers from Europe, plumes and feathers and helmeted horsemen, reporters from Richmond, the solemn members of Longstreet's staff. He separated from the group and rode to Lee's tent and the motley bright cloud remained respectfully distant. Lee rose with unconscious joy.

"General."

"Mornin'."

Longstreet touched his cap, came heavily down from the horse. He was taller than Lee, head like a boulder, full-bearded, long-haired, always a bit sloppy, gloomy, shocked his staff by going into battle once wearing carpet slippers. Never cared much for appearance, gave an impression of ominous bad-tempered strength and a kind of slow, even, stubborn, unquenchable anger: a soft voice, a ragged mouth. He talked very slowly and sometimes had trouble finding the right word, and the first impression of him around that gay and courtly camp was that he was rather dull-witted and not much fun. He was not a Virginian. But he was a magnificent soldier. With Jackson gone he was the rock of the army, and Lee felt a new clutching in his chest, looking at him, thinking that this was one man you could not afford to lose. Longstreet smiled his ragged smile, grumbled, jerked a finger over his shoulder.

"Her Majesty's forces in the New World passed a restful night."

Lee looked, saw the ludicrous man in the lustrous hat and the wide gray coat. The man made a sweeping, quixotic bow, nearly falling from the horse. Colonel Fremantle was up. Lee gave a formal bow, smiling inwardly.

Longstreet observed with sloe-eyed surprise. "After a while, you know, he actually begins to grow on you."

"You're keeping him entertained?"

"Not exactly. He's got his heart set on a cavalry charge. Drawn sabers, all that glorious French business. He was horrified when I had to tell him we didn't use the British square."

Lee smiled.

"But he's a likable fella." Longstreet took off his hat, scratched his head. "Can't say he's learning much. But he seems to like us, all right. He says you have a great reputation in Europe."

Lee said, "There'll be no help from there."

"No."

"President Davis has hope."

"Well, I guess that won't do him any harm to hope."

"At least we'll be good hosts." Lee felt a sudden strength. It came out of Longstreet like sunlight. Lee said happily, "And how are *you* this morning, General?"

"Me?" Longstreet blinked. "I'm all right." He paused, cocked his head to one side, stared at the old man.

Lee said happily, "You must take care of yourself."

Longstreet was mystified. No one ever asked him how he felt. His health was legendary, he never tired.

Lee said diplomatically, "The Old Soldier's illness is going around."

"It's the damned cherries," Longstreet gloomed. "Too many raw cherries."

Lee nodded. Then he said softly, "General, in the fight that's coming, I want you to stay back from the main line."

Longstreet looked at him, expressionless. Black eyes glistened, bright and hard under hairy eyebrows. Impossible to tell what he was thinking.

Lee said, "You are only veteran commander."

Longstreet nodded.

"If I should become once again indisposed," Lee said.

"God forbid." Longstreet stared. "And how are *you?*"

Lee smiled, waved a depracating hand. "I am well, very well. Thank God. But there is always . . . a possibility. And now Jackson is gone, and we must all do more than before. And I do not know if Hill or Ewell are ready for command, but I know that you . . ."

He paused. Hard to speak in this fashion. Longstreet was staring with cold silent eyes. Lee said sternly, "You have a very bad habit, General, of going too far forward."

Longstreet said, "You cannot lead from behind."

"Well. Let me put it plainly. I cannot spare you."

Longstreet stood silent for a moment. He bowed slightly, then he grinned. "True," he said.

"You will oblige me?"

"My pleasure," Longstreet said.

Lee rubbed his nose, looked down at the table. "Now, let us look to the day. Nothing will happen today. But we have an opportunity, I believe."

"Nothing from Stuart?"

Lee shook his head. Longstreet grumbled, "The Federals are closing in."

"I have no new information."

"When Stuart comes back, if he does come back—which he will eventually, if only just to read the Richmond newspapers—you ought to court-martial him."

"And will that make him a better soldier?"

Longstreet paused. He said, "All right. What will?"

"Reproach, I think. I must let him know how badly he has let us down."

Longstreet chuckled. He shook his head, gazing at Lee. "Yes, by George. Maybe. Reproach from *you*. Yes." Longstreet grinned widely. "Might do the job. But me . . . I'm not good at that."

"Different men, different methods. Docile men make very poor soldiers."

Longstreet grinned wryly. "An army of temperamentals. It isn't an army, it's a gentlemen's club. My God. Remember when old Powell Hill wanted to fight me a duel, right in the middle of the war?"

"And you ignored him. You did exactly right."

"Yep. He might have shot me."

Lee smiled. His heart rolled again, a soft sudden thump, leaving him breathless. Longstreet was grinning, staring off toward the road, did not notice. Lee said, "One new item. I have confirmed some of your man Harrison's information. The new commander is definitely George Meade, not Reynolds. The news is carried in the local newspapers."

Longstreet reached inside his coat, extracted a fat cigar.

"You can trust my man, I think. I sent him into Gettysburg last night. He said he saw two brigades of Union cavalry there."

"Last night?"

"I sent you a report."

Lee felt a tightening in his chest. He put his hand to his arm. He said slowly, "General Hill reports only militia."

"It's cavalry, I think." Longstreet chewed, spat.

Where there is cavalry there will be infantry close behind.

"Whose troops?"

"John Buford."

Longstreet meditated.

"Meade's coming fast. Looks like he's trying to get behind us."

"Yes." Lee thought: the direction does not matter. Fight him wherever he is. Lee said, "We have an opportunity."

Longstreet chewed, nodded, grinned. "Yep. Objective was to get him out of Washington and in the open. Now he's out. Now all we have to do is swing round between him and Washington and get astride some nice thick rocks and make him come to us, and we've got him in the open."

Take the defensive. Not again. Lee shook his head. He pointed to Gettysburg.

"He has been forcing the march. The weather has been unusually hot. He will arrive strung out and tired, piece by piece. If we concentrate we can hit him as he comes up. If we ruin one or two corps we can even the odds."

He was again breathless, but he bent over the map. Longstreet said nothing.

"He's new to command," Lee said. "It will take him some days to pick up the reins. His information will be poor, he will have staff problems."

"Yes, and he will have Washington on his back, urging him to throw us out of Pennsylvania. He has to fight. We don't."

Lee put his hand to his eyes. He was fuzzy-brained. Longstreet loved the defense. But all the bright theories so rarely worked. Instinct said: hit hard, hit quick, hit everything. But he listened. Then he said slowly, "That move will be what Meade expects."

"Yes. Because he fears it."

Lee turned away from the table. He wanted no argument now. He had been down this road before, and Longstreet was immovable, and there was no point in argument when you did not even know where the enemy was. Yet it was good counsel. Trust Longstreet to tell the truth. Lee looked up and there was Traveler, led by a black groom. The staff had gathered, the tents were down. Time to move. Lee took a deep, delighted breath.

"Now, General," he said, "let's go see what George Meade intends."

They moved out into the open, into the warm sunlight. It was becoming a marvelous day. Out on the road the army flowed endlessly eastward, pouring toward the great fight. Lee smelled the superb wetness of clean mountain air. He said, "General, will you ride with me?"

Longstreet bowed. "My pleasure."

Lee mounted in pain, but the hot sun would heal the old bones. They rode out into a space in the great gray bristling stream. Another band played; men were shouting. It was lovely country. They rode through soft green rounded hills, a sunny morn, a splendid air, moving toward adventure as rode the plumed knights of old. Far back in the woods there was still fog in the trees, caught in the branches like fragments of white summer, and Lee remembered:

> *Bow down Thy Heavens, O Lord, and come down,*
> *Touch the mountains, and they shall smoke.*

He closed his eyes. Blessed be the Lord my strength, which teacheth my fingers to fight and my hands to war. Amen.

They rode several miles before they heard the first thunder.

Lee reined to a stop. Silence. Motion of ragged white clouds. He said, "Did you hear that?"

Longstreet, who was slightly deaf, shook his head.

"It might have been thunder." But Lee waited. Then it came: low, distant thumping. Ominous: angry. Longstreet said grimly, bright-eyes, angered, "I don't hear too well any more."

"That was artillery," Lee said. Longstreet gazed at him with black marble eyes. "You don't think . . ." Lee began, then stopped. "I'd better ride forward," he said. Longstreet nodded. Lee looked at his watch. Not quite ten in the morning. He left Longstreet and rode toward the sound of the guns.

2

BUFORD

Just before dawn Buford rode down the line himself, waking them up, all the boyish faces. Then he climbed the ladder into the white cupola and sat listening to the rain, watching the light come. The air was cool and wet and delicious to breathe: a slow, fine, soaking rain, a farmer's rain, gentle on the roof. The light came slowly: there were great trees out in the mist. Then the guns began.

A single shot. He sat up. Another. Two more widely spaced. Then a small volley, a spattering. A long silence: several seconds. He stared at white air, the rounded tops of smoky trees. Men were moving out in the open below him. An officer paused on horseback in the road. The firing began again, Rebel guns, farther off, but not many. Buford was cold. He shuddered, waited.

The first attack was very short: a ragged fire. Buford nodded, listening. "Yes. Tried to brush us off. Got a bloody nose. Now he'll get angry, all puffed up like a partridge. Now he'll form up a line and try us for real, and he'll hit the main line." The mist was lifting slowly, the rain was slackening, but Buford could not see the line. He felt the attack come and turned his face toward the sound of the guns, judging the size of the attack by the width of the sound, and he sat grinning alone in the cupola, while the Rebel troops pushed his line and drew back, bloody, and tried again in another place, the firing spreading all down the line like a popping fuse, and then there was another long silence, and Buford could feel them reforming again, beginning for the first time to take this seriously. The next assault would be organized. He looked at his watch. Reynolds should be awake by now. They will have eaten their breakfast now, the infantry, and maybe they're on the march.

There was a silence. He climbed down out of the cupola. The staff waited whitefaced under dripping trees. Buford asked for coffee. He went back inside the Seminary and waited for the firing to begin again before sending his first word to Reynolds. It took longer than he expected. If whoever was out there attacking him had any brains he would probe this position first and find out what he was attacking. Buford listened for the scattered fire of patrols coming in, moving along his flanks, outlining him, but there was nothing. A long silence, then a massed assault. Buford grinned, baring fangs. Damn fool. He's got a brigade in position, that's all. He's hitting me with one brigade, and I'm dug in. Lovely, lovely.

He wrote to Reynolds: "Rebel infantry attacked at dawn. Am holding west of Gettysburg, expecting relief. John Buford."

The fire was hotting up. He heard the first cannon: Calef's Battery opening up down the road, grinned again. No Reb cannon to reply: not yet. He sent the messenger off into the mist, climbed again into the cupola.

The light was much clearer. He saw speckles of yellow fire through the mist:

SITUATION
9:00 A.M., July 1
Buford's Defense

winking guns. The road ran black through misty fields. He saw one black cannon spout red fire at the limits of his vision. On the far side of the road there was a deep railroad cut—an unfinished railroad; he had not noticed it before. He saw horsemen moving behind the line. Then he heard that ripply sound that raised the hair, that high thin scream from far away coming out of the mist unbodied and terrible, inhuman. It got inside him for a suspended second. The scream of a flood of charging men: the Rebel yell.

It died in massive fire. There was still no cannon on the other side. Calef's Battery blasted the mist, thunder among the lighter fire. The assault began to die away.

The wounded were beginning to come back off the line. Buford went down from the cupola, restless, found Bill Gamble in the field by Calef's Battery, checking ammunition. There was blood on his left sleeve. His nose was still running. He grinned wetly at Buford.

"Hey, General. That was quite a scrap."

"How are your losses?"

"Not bad. Not bad at all. We were dug in pretty good. We got 'em right out in the open. Really got a twist on 'em. Arrogant people, you know that? Came right at us. Listen, we got some prisoners. I talked to 'em. They're Harry Heth's Division, of Hill's Corps. That's what I've got in front of me."

Buford nodded. Gamble was talking very quickly, head moving in jerky twitches.

"Sir, as I remember, Heth's got near ten thousand men. They're all within sound of the fight, back that road, between here and Cashtown."

Buford squinted. The rain had quit but the sky was still low and gray. He could see a long way off through the trees, and there were ragged bodies in the fields, groups of men digging, cutting trees for cover.

Gamble said, "Sir, he'll be back with all ten thousand."

"It'll take him a while to deploy," Buford said.

"Yes, but he's got Hill's whole Corps behind him. Maybe twenty-five thousand. And Longstreet behind that. And Ewell in the north."

"I know."

"Thing is this. When John Reynolds gets here, he won't have the whole army with him, only a part of it. Point is—" he sniffled, wiped his nose—"as I see it, the Rebs will be here this afternoon with everything they've got."

Buford said nothing. Gamble sniffed cheerily.

"Just thought I'd mention it. Now, what you want me to do here?"

Buford thought: if it was a mistake, God help us.

"Heth will be back in a bit," Buford said. "If he's got any brains at all, and he's not stupid, he'll know by now that he's got a brigade in front of him. Don't think he'll wait to get his whole Division in line. That would take half the morning."

"He doesn't need his whole Division."

"Right. Does Devin report any activity on his front?"

"Not a thing."

"All right. I'll have Devin pull some of his people out and leave a cover in the north and have him dig in alongside, lengthening your line. When Heth comes back he'll run into two brigades. That should hold him until Reynolds gets here."

"Right," Gamble said. He peered up at the sky. "Glad the rain is gone. Don't want anything to slow up Reynolds."

"Take care of yourself."

"You know me: the soul of caution."

Buford moved off toward the north. He sent a second message to Reynolds.

He pulled Devin out of line in the north and brought him in alongside Gamble: two thousand men facing west. All that while whenever he came near the line he could see enemy troops moving in the fields across the way, spreading out as they came down the road, like a gray river spreading where it reaches the sea. If Heth was efficient and deliberate he had the power to come straight through like an avalanche. Buford could hear the artillery coming into place on the far side, heard the spattering of rifle fire from probing patrols. He looked at his watch; it was after eight. Reynolds had to be on the road. The infantry had to be coming. He rode back and forth along the line, watched Devin's men digging in, heard bullets clip leaves above him as snipers crawled closer. *We cannot hold ten thousand. Not for very long.* If Heth attacks in force he will roll right over us, and we lose the two brigades and the high ground too, and it will have been my fault. And the road in the north is open; they can come in there and they'll be behind us, on our flank.

There was nothing he could do about that; he had no more troops. But he pulled a squad out of Devin's line and put the young Lieutenant with corn-silk hair in charge and gave him orders.

"Son, you ride on out that road to the north about five miles. You squat across some high ground, where you can see. First sign you get of enemy coming down that road, you ride like hell this way and tell me. Understand?"

The squad galloped off. A cannon shell burst in the air nearby, raining fragments in the wet leaves around him. The first Reb cannon were in position, limbering up easily, casually, getting the range. Now Buford had a little time to think. It all depends on how fast Reynolds comes. It all depends on how many men he's got with him and how fast Lee is moving this way. Nothing to do but fight now and hold this line. But he kept looking at his watch. There ought to be some word. He galloped back to the Seminary and climbed the cupola and gazed back to that southern road, but there was nothing there. A short while after that he saw the enemy come out in the open, line after line, heard the guns open up, dozens of guns, watched his own line disappear in smoke. The big attack had come.

Gamble was down. The first report was very bad, and Buford rode over and took command, but it was only concussion and Gamble was back on his feet in a few moments, ragged and dirty. There was a breakthrough on the right but some junior officers patched it. Lone infantry began bending around the right flank. Buford mounted some men and drove them off. There were moments in smoke when he could not see and thought the line was going; one time when a shell burst very close and left him deaf and still and floating, like a bloody cloud.

On the right there was another breakthrough, hand-to-hand fighting. He rode that way, leaping wounded, but it had been repulsed when he got there. One by one Calef's guns were being silenced. No one had yet broken away, no one was running, but Buford could feel them giving, like a dam. He rode back to the Seminary, looked down the road. Nothing. Not much more time. He felt the beginning of an awful anger, an unbearable sadness, suppressed it. He rode back to the line. The fire was weakening. He stood irresolute in the road. An aide suggested he go to cover. He listened. The Rebs were pulling back, forming to come again. But the Reb cannon were pounding, pounding. He heard the great whirring of fragments in the air, saw air bursts in bright electric sparks. He rode slowly along the smoking line, looking at the faces. The brigades were wrecked. There was not much ammunition. They were down in the dirt firing slowly, carefully from behind splintery trees, piled gray rails, mounds of raw dirt. They had maybe half an hour.

Pull out before then. Save something. He rode back toward the Seminary. He climbed the cupola, looked out across the field of war. Wreckage everywhere, mounded bodies, smoking earth, naked stumps of trees. He could see a long way now, above the rolling smoke which had replaced the mist, and the road coming down from the far-off mountains was packed with soldiers, thousands of soldiers, sunlight glittering on jeweled guns. He looked toward the south—and there was Reynolds.

He was coming at a gallop across the fields to the south, a line of aides strung out behind him, cutting across the field to save time. No mistaking him: matchless rider gliding over rail fences in parade-ground precision, effortless motion, always a superb rider. Buford blinked, wiped his face, thanked God. But the road behind Reynolds was empty.

The General rode into the yard below, dismounted. Buford waited in the cupola, weariness suddenly beginning to get to him in waves. In a moment Reynolds was up the ladder.

"Good morning, John."

An immaculate man, tidy as a photograph, soft-voiced, almost elegant. Buford put out a hand.

"General, I'm damned glad to see you."

Reynolds stepped up for a look. Buford explained the position. In all his life he had never been so happy to see anybody. But where was the infantry? Reynolds swung, pointed a gloved hand.

The blue line had come around the bend. Buford saw with a slight shock the first column of infantry, the lovely flags. Reynolds said softly, "That's the First Corps. The Eleventh is right behind it."

Buford watched them come. He leaned against the side of the cupola. Reynolds had turned, was surveying the hills to the south. There was a set, hard, formal look to him, but a happiness in his eyes. Buford thought: he has brains to see.

Reynolds said, "Good job, John."

"Thank you."

"This is going to be very interesting."

"Yes," Buford said.

"They seem to be forming for another assault. That's Harry Heth, isn't it? Very good. He'll come in here thinking he's up against two very tired cavalry brigades, and instead he'll be hitting two corps of fresh Union infantry." Reynolds smiled slightly. "Poor Harry," he said.

"Yes, sir," Buford said.

"You can start pulling your boys out. As soon as we set up. Well done. Well done indeed. You can put them out on my flanks. Keep an eye on that north road. I expect Dick Ewell to be coming in shortly."

"Yes, sir."

They went down out of the cupola. Reynolds mounted a beautiful black horse. Buford came out into the open, saw his staff tidying itself up, combing hair, buttoning buttons. Shells were falling on the ridge nearby and bullets were slicing leaves, but Reynolds sat astride the horse in a motionless calm, looking out toward the fight, picture of a soldier, painted against the trees. Reynolds called in one of his officers. He said slowly, somewhat delicately, pronouncing each word in turn, evenly, machinelike, "Captain, I want you to ride as fast as you can to General Meade. Tell him the enemy is advancing in strong force and that I am afraid they will get the heights beyond the town before I can. We will fight them here inch by inch, through the town if necessary, barricading the streets. We will delay them as long as possible. I am sending messages to all my commanders to come to this place with all possible speed. Repeat that."

The Captain did, and was gone. Reynolds sent messages to other commanders: Doubleday, Sickles. Then he said, to Buford, "I think I'll move over and hurry the boys along."

"Obliged," Buford said.

"Not at all." He wheeled the horse gracefully, still something of that elegant quality of display in the fluid motion, and rode off. In the direction he took Buford heard music. A blue band was playing. Buford issued his own orders. The great weight was off him. Now it belonged to Reynolds. And there was no regret. Through most of his life he had resented the appearance of higher command. Now it came to save him. A new thing. He did not mind at all. Must be the age. Well, you have gone to the limit, lad. You have reached your own personal end.

Tom Devin was up. He was annoyed to be pulled out. Buford looked at him, shook his head. In a moment Reynolds was back, leading blue troops at double time through the fields, tearing down rail fences as they came. Buford's heart was stirred: the Black Hats, Simon Cutler's Iron Brigade, best troops in the Union Army. An omen. They began to move out onto the road by the Seminary, regiment after regiment, moving with veteran gloom, veteran silence, steady men, not many boys. One man was eating cherries hurriedly from a mess tin; another had a banjo on his back which was bothering him, and he swung it around to cover his front and banged the man in front of him, who complained, to peculiar laughter. One man asked one of Buford's aides loudly which way was the war and offered to go the other way, and an officer turned and began sending them into line along the crest Gamble had held. Then Reynolds was back.

The Rebel shells were beginning to pass overhead. They had seen new troops coming and some of the fire was falling now on Gettysburg. Reynolds summoned another aide.

"Lieutenant, get on into town and tell these people to stay in off the streets. There's liable to be a fair-sized dispute here today, and give anyone you meet my compliments, along with my suggestion that every person stay indoors, in cellars if possible, and out of harm's way. Especially children." He peered at the aide. "Joe, how do you see with those things on?" The aide wore glasses that were very muddy. He took them and tried to clean them and smeared them with jittery fingers. A shell hit a treetop across the road and splinters flickered through the grove and spattered against the brick wall. Reynolds said pleasantly, "Gentlemen, let's place the troops."

He motioned to Buford. They rode out into the road. Buford felt a certain dreamy calm. Reynolds, like Lee before him, had once commanded the Point. There was a professional air to him, the teacher approaching the class, utterly in command of his subject. Reynolds said, "Now, John, he's got a good fifteen thousand men out there, wouldn't you say?"

"Yes. Be a lot more in a little while."

"Yes. Well, between us we can put almost twenty thousand in the field in the next half hour. We're in very good shape, I think."

"For a while," Buford said.

Reynolds nodded.

He turned in his saddle, looked back toward the hills. "Isn't that lovely ground?" he said.

"I thought so."

"Keep at it, John. Someday, if you're spared, you may make a soldier." He bowed his head once slightly. It came over Buford like a sunrise that he had just received Reynolds' greatest compliment. At that moment it mattered very much. "Now," Reynolds said, "let's go surprise Harry Heth."

They rode out together, placing the troops. The First Corps moved into line on the left. The Eleventh Corps moved in behind them, swung out to the right. Through all that the Reb cannon were firing steadily and smoke was filling up the hollow between the armies and no one could see the motion of the troops. The Eleventh was still not in line when the new Reb attack came rolling up out of the smoke. Reynolds moved off to the left, close to the line. Buford heard music, an eerie sound like a joyful wind, began to recognize it: "The Campbells Are Coming." He recognized Rufus Dawes and the Sixth Wisconsin moving up, more Wisconsin men behind them, deploying in line of skirmishers and firing already as they moved up, the line beginning to go fluid as the first Reb troops poured over a partly deserted crest, and met the shock of waves of new troops coming up from the south.

Buford got one last glimpse of Reynolds. He was out in the open, waving his hat, pointing to a grove of trees. A moment later Buford looked that way and the horse was bare-backed. He did not believe it. He broke off and rode to see. Reynolds lay in the dirt road, the aides bending over him. When Buford got there the thick stain had already puddled the dirt beneath his head. His eyes were open, half asleep, his face pleasant and composed, a soft smile. Buford knelt. He was dead. An aide, a young sergeant, was crying. Buford backed away. They put a blanket over him. Off to the left there was massive firing. There was a moment of silence around them. Buford said, "Take him out of here."

He backed off. Across the road a woman was chasing a wild-haired child. A soldier ran past her and caught the child and gave it to her. Buford went to a great shade tree and stood in the dark for a moment. Too good a man, Reynolds. Much too good a man. Buford wandered slowly back out into the light. It was very hot now; he could feel sweat all down his face.

A detail from a New York regiment carried Reynolds away, under a blanket. Buford's aides came to him, back to the shepherd. There were no orders to give.

The battle went on without a commander. The men fought where Reynolds had placed them. Buford slowly withdrew his cavalry, as Reynolds had ordered. All the rest of that morning gray Rebel troops came pouring down that narrow road. No messages came. The line continued to hold. There did not seem to be anyone in command, but the line held. After a while Buford mounted what was left of his cavalry and rode slowly out that road to the north. He could not hold for long, but he could hold for a little while, and the yellow-haired lieutenant was out there alone.

3

LEE

They had stripped the rails from both sides of the road, to widen the passage, and some of the men were marching in the fields.

The road was already going to dust and the dust was rising, and there was nothing to see ahead but troops in the dust toiling upward toward the crest of a divide. The bands played as he went by. He nodded, touching his cap, head cocked, listening, searching beyond the music and the noise of rolling wagons and steely clinking of sabers and guns for the distant roll of artillery which was always there, beyond the hills. They came to a narrow pass: rocky country, dark gorges, heavily wooded. He thought: if there is a repulse, this will be good country to defend. Longstreet could bring up his people and hold this place and we would shelter the army back in the mountains.

He began almost to expect it. He had seen retreat. There would be clots of men out in the fields, out far from the road, moving back the other way, men with gray stubborn faces who would not listen. Then there would be the wounded. But here they would block the road. No room to maneuver. If Longstreet's spy was right and there had been masses of cavalry ahead, what the blue cavalry could do to his packed troops . . .

Lee knew that he was worrying too much, recognized it, put a stop to it. He bowed his head and prayed once quickly, then was able to relax and compose himself. He rode up into the pass and the country began to flatten out, to go down toward Cashtown. The day was hazy and he could not see far ahead. He began to pass empty houses, dark doors, dark windows. The people had fled. He entered Cashtown and there at the crossroads, mounted, watching the troops pass, was Powell Hill.

Hill was sitting with his hat down over his eyes, slouching in the saddle, a pasty illness in his face. He smiled a ghostly smile, drew himself up, saluted, waved toward a brick house just off the road.

Lee said, "General, you don't look well."

"Momentary indisposition." Hill grinned weakly. "Touch of the Old Soldier's Disease. Would you like to go indoors, sir?"

Lee turned to Taylor. "We will establish temporary headquarters here. All dispatches to this place." To Hill he said, "What artillery is that?"

Hill shook his head, looked away from Lee's eyes. "I don't know, sir. I sent forward for information a while back. Harry Heth is ahead. He has instructions not to force a major action. I told him myself, this morning."

"You have no word from him?"

"No, sir." Hill was not comfortable. Lee said nothing. They went to the brick house. There was a woman at the gate to whom Lee was introduced. Near her stood a small boy in very short pants, sucking his thumb. Lee was offered coffee.

Lee said to Hill, "I must know what's happening ahead."

"Sir, I'll go myself."

Hill was up abruptly, giving instructions to aides. Lee started to object, said nothing. Hill was a nervous, volatile, brilliant man. He had been a superb division commander, but now he commanded a corps, and it was a brutal military truth that there were men who were marvelous with a regiment but could not handle a brigade, and men who were superb with a division but incapable of leading a corps. No way of predicting it. One could only have faith in character. But to be ill, on this day—very bad luck. Lee watched him. He seemed well enough to ride. Good. Hill was gone.

Lee began work on a plan of withdrawal. Moments later Walter Taylor was in with General Anderson, who had just come into town to look for Hill. Anderson's Division, of Hill's Corps, was stacking up on the road south of town, moving in behind Pender and Heth. Anderson had come to find out about the sound of the guns. He knew nothing. Sitting in the house was galling. Lee was becoming agitated. Anderson sat by, hat in hand, watchfully.

THE
FIRST DAY
-11:00 A.M.-
After the death of Reynolds,
Heth attacks Doubleday's
I Corps

Lee said abruptly, impulsively, "I cannot imagine what's become of Stuart. I've heard *nothing*. You understand, I know nothing of what's in front of me. It may be the entire Federal army."

He stopped, controlled himself. But he could wait no longer. He called for Traveler and moved on out of Cashtown, toward Gettysburg.

Now he could begin to hear rifle fire, the small sounds of infantry. He touched his chest, feeling a stuffiness there. So it was more than a duel of artillery. Yet Heth was not a fool. Heth would have reasons. Suspend judgment. But Jackson is not here. Ewell and Hill are new at their commands; all in God's hands. But there was pain in his chest, pain in the left arm. He could see smoke ahead, a long white cloud, low, like fog, on the horizon. The troops around him were eager, bright-faced; the bands were playing. He came out into a field and saw men deploying, moving out on both sides of the road, cutting away the fences: Pender's Division. He put his binoculars to his eyes. Troops were running in a dark grove of trees. Taylor said that Gettysburg was just ahead.

Lee rode left up a flat grassy rise. Below him there was a planted field, rows of low green bush, rolling toward a creek, broken by one low rail fence and a few thick clumps of trees. Beyond the stream there was a rise and atop the rise was a large red building with a white cupola. To the left was an open railroad cut, unfinished, a white wound in the earth. There was smoke around the building. A battery of artillery was firing from there. Lee saw blue hills to the south, in the haze, but now, sweeping the glasses, he could begin to see the lines of fire, could sense by the blots of smoke and the pattern of sound what had happened, was happening, begin piecing it together.

Heth's Division had formed on a front about a mile, had obviously been re-pulsed. The Union infantry was firing back from a line at least as long as Heth's. There did not seem to be many cannon, but there were many rifles. Was this the whole Union force or only an advance detachment? Ewell was off to the north; Longstreet was miles away. What had Heth gotten himself into?

The fire from Heth's front was slowing. His troops were not moving. Lee could see many wounded, wagons under trees, clusters of men drifting back through a field to the right. Aides began coming up with messages. Taylor had gone to look for Heth. Lee was thinking: how do we disengage? how do we fall back? where do we hold until Longstreet comes up?

He sent a message to Ewell to advance with all possible speed. He sent a note to Longstreet telling him that the Union infantry had arrived in force. But he knew Longstreet could do nothing; there were two divisions in his way. Lee looked at his watch: well after two o'clock. Darkness a long way away. No way of knowing where the rest of Meade's army was. Possibly moving to the south, to get between Lee and Washington.

And here, at last, was Harry Heth.

He rode up spattering dust, jerking at the horse with unnatural motions, a square-faced man, a gentle face. He blinked, saluting, wiping sweat from his eyes. He had never been impulsive, like Hill; there was even at this moment something grave and perplexed about him, a studious bewilderment. He had been the old army's leading authority on the rifle; he had written a manual. But he had gotten into a fight against orders and there was a blankness in his eyes, vacancy and shame. Lee thought: *he does not know what's happening.*

Heth coughed. "Sir, beg to report."

"Yes."

"Very strange, sir. Situation very confused."

"What happened?"

Lee's eyes were wide and very dark. Heth said painfully, "Sir, I moved in this morning as directed. I thought it was only a few militia. But it was dismounted cavalry. John Buford. Well, there weren't all that many and it was only cavalry, so I just decided to push on it. The boys wouldn't hold back. I thought we shouldn't ought to be stopped by a few dismounted cavalry. But they made a good fight. I didn't expect . . . They really put up a scrap."

"Yes." Lee was watching his eyes.

Heth grimaced, blowing. "Well, sir, they wouldn't leave. My boys got the dander up. We deployed the whole division and went after them. We just about had them running and then all of a sudden I see us moving in on infantry. They got infantry support up from the south. The boys got pushed back. Then we re-formed and tried again, couldn't stop there, sir, but there's more infantry now, I don't know how many. But I don't know what else we could have done. Sir, I'm sorry. But it started out as a minor scrap with a few militia and the next thing I know I'm tangling with half the Union army."

"Who are they?"

"Sir?"

Lee was watching the fight, which was now relatively quiet. The smoke was clearing, blowing toward the north. He could see blue troops moving in the trees on the Union right, moving out on the flank. He looked north, but he could see nothing beyond the ridge. The blue troops seemed to be pulling back that way, retreating, reforming. Strange. The battery up by the cupola had stopped firing. Riding up through the haze: Dorsey Pender. Letter from a pious wife.

To Heth Lee said, "What units have you engaged?"

"The cavalry was Buford, sir. Two brigades. They really fought. Then there was the First Corps, the black hats, John Reynolds' old corps. Then there was another corps, but we still haven't got it identified."

At Lee's shoulder, Taylor said quietly, insistently, "General, you are in range of the enemy batteries."

Lee said, "It's quiet now." He looked once more at Heth; his anger died. No time for blame. But there *must* be information.

Taylor insisted, "You gentlemen are standing together. May I suggest that you move at least to the shelter of the trees?"

There was a sudden fire on the left, a burst in the north. Lee felt an acute spasm of real anger. He clutched his chest. *I know nothing.*

Heth said, "I'd better look to my flank." He moved away. A rider came up—a courier from Rodes.

"General Rodes' compliments, sir. I have the honor to inform you that the General has joined the engagement with his entire division and is attacking the Union right. He begs me to inform you that General Early is behind him and will be on the field within the hour. Do you have any instructions, sir?"

Lee felt a thrill of delight, mixed with alarm. Rodes had come in right on the Union flank; the blue troops were turning to meet a new threat. And Early was close behind. A flank assault, already begun. Lee sat staring north. No way to tell. He could order forward the entire army. Heth was here and Pender. Rodes' attack might almost have been planned.

But he did not know how many Federals were ahead. Rodes might be attacking half the Union army. Another Sharpsburg. And yet, and yet, I cannot call him back; he is already committed. Lee said, "Nothing for now. Wait here."

He turned to Taylor. "I want all possible knowledge of the enemy strength. Ride forward yourself and observe. And be careful."

Taylor saluted formally and rode off, the grin breaking across his face just as he turned. Lee turned and began heading back toward the road. Now Heth was back.

"Sir, Rodes is heavily engaged. Shall I attack?"

Lee shook his head, then said loudly, "No." He rode on, then he said over his shoulder, "We are not yet prepared for a full engagement. Longstreet is not up."

Heth said, "There aren't that many of the enemy, sir."

"What are your casualties?"

"Moderate, sir. There's been some fighting. But Pender is in position. Together, sir, we could sweep them."

Lee waited. It did not feel right. There was something heavy and dark and tight about the day, riding stiffly in the broad barren field, in harsh sunlight. The firing in the north was mounting. Batteries of artillery had opened up.

"Who is commanding there?" Lee pointed to the hills beyond the town.

Heth blinked, suddenly remembering. "Sir, I'd forgotten. We have word that General Reynolds was killed."

Lee turned. "John Reynolds?"

"Yes, sir. Prisoners state he was killed this morning. I believe Doubleday has succeeded him."

"Are you sure?"

"The news seems reliable."

"I'm sorry," Lee said. His mind flashed a vision of Reynolds. A neat trim man. A gentleman, a friend. Lee shook his head. It was queer to be so strange and tight in the mind. He seemed unable to think clearly. Reynolds dead. Gone. Doubleday behind him. Doubleday an unknown quantity, but certainly nothing spectacular. But Reynolds' First Corps was solid. What to do?

"I can support Rodes, sir," Heth said.

Lee looked at him. *He knows he has brought this on; he wants to fight now to retrieve it. His answer is to fight, not to think; to fight, pure and simple.* Lee rode slowly forward, nearing the trees ahead alongside the road. *You can depend on the troops, but can you count on the generals? Why has Rodes attacked? Will Hill fight well, or Rodes either? What I need is Longstreet and he is not here. A mistake to bring him up last.*

Another courier. "General Early has arrived, begs to report that he is attacking to the north of General Rodes."

Lee stopped, looked north. It was working almost like a plan. It was possible to see Intention in it. The Union formed to face him and fought well and now was being flanked from the north, simply because Lee's men had orders to come to Gettysburg, and they were coming in almost behind the Union defenses. Lee felt a sharpness in the air. His blood was rising. He had tried to be discreet, but it was all happening without him, without one decision; it was all in God's hands. And yet he could leave it alone himself no longer. Rodes and Early were attacking; Heth and Pender were waiting here in front of him. Lee's instinct sensed opportunity. *Let us go in together, as God has decreed a fight here.*

He swung to Heth. "General, you may attack."

To Pender he said the same. He gave no further directions. The generals would know what to do now. With that word it was out of his hands. It had never really been in his hands at all. And yet his was the responsibility.

He rode forward to the rise ahead, across the small creek. Now he had a clearer view. Pender's Division was on the move; he heard the great scream of the massed Rebel yells. Now batteries were in position behind him, beginning to open up on the woods near the cupola. Lee ducked his head as the shot whickered over him. He did not like to stand in front of artillery. Some of the artillery was moving forward. Rifle fire was breaking out. The wind shifted; he was enveloped in smoke. Marshall's face appeared, an incoherent message. Lee tried to find some place to watch the assault. Pender's whole force was streaming forward across the fields, into the woods. Lee saw flags floating through white smoke, disembodied, like walking sticks. Shell bursts were appearing in the air, white flakes, round puffs. One blossomed near. There was Marshall again. Lee heard fragments split the air near him. He moved into a grove of trees: oak, chestnut. There was a white house nearby, a white rail fence, a dead horse lying in a black mound in the sun.

He waited in the grove, listening to the enormous sound of war. Eventually he sat, resting himself against the bole of a tree. It was dark and cool back in here out of the sun. Men were dying up ahead. He took off his hat, ran his fingers through his hair, felt his life beating in his chest. The fight went on. Lee thought for the first time that day of his son. Rooney, wounded, lying not far from here. He closed his eyes, prayed for his boy, for all of them. He put his hand down on black dirt, was reminded: Pennsylvania. I am the invader.

Once more the Rebel yell—inhuman screaming of the onrushing dead. Another unit was going. He rose and went forward, trying to see, but no point in that. There was too much smoke. Yet it might help if he was seen. He moved up out of the grove of trees, onto the road. The road ahead was crowded with wounded. There were men lying under wagons, out of the sun, most of them semi-naked, covered with bandages, blood. He saw another dead horse, a splintered wagon; the severed forefoot of a horse lay near him in gray dust. Smoke was pouring down the road as from a great furnace. He moved forward; his staff followed him. Here was A. P. Hill.

Hill said, white-faced, "Very hard going. Heth is down."

Lee looked at him, waiting.

"Wounded in the head. I don't know how serious. But the Division is moving. Pender is on the flank. But the Yankees are fighting well. I don't recall them fighting this well before."

Hill seemed peculiarly calm, vacant, as if he was not wholly present. He was a handsome man who had a great deal of money but was not "society" and was overly aware of it and very touchy about it.

Lee said, "Let me know General Heth's condition as soon as possible."

Lee sat down against a rail fence. A band came by, playing an incoherent song, fifes and bugles. The sky was overcast with blowing white smoke, the smell of hot guns, of blasted earth, the sweet smell of splintery trees. Lee was in the way, in the road; men were gathering around him, calling to him. He saw a house, an empty front porch. He moved toward that way and stared down toward the smoke. Firing was intense. He sent couriers to Early and Rodes to advise them of his new headquarters and to ask for progress. He had no idea of the whereabouts of Ewell, who was supposed to be in command over there and who probably knew less of what was happening than Lee did. Longstreet was right: command was too loose. But no time for that now.

A courier from Early: The enemy was falling back. Lee could hear an officer near him erupt in a high scream. "They're runnin', Great God Amighty, they're runnin'!"

Lee looked down the smoky street, saw a man helping another man along the road, saw masses of men moving vaguely through a field, saw flashes of artillery. The fire seemed to be slowing down. There were many men yelling. A lieutenant came down the road, pointing back toward the smoke, yelling wildly that someone was hurt.

A. P. Hill said, at Lee's elbow, "General Heth's surgeon has examined him, sir. He says he ought to be all right, but he will be out of action for a while."

"Where is he?"

"In a house over this way." Hill pointed.

"You will take good care of him, of course. And, General, see to yourself. You can do no more good now. I want you to rest."

Hill said softly, calmly, vacantly, "I'm fine, General, just fine."

But he looked as if he were about to faint. Lee was thinking: if Longstreet were only here. How many in the Union Army? If the First Corps is here and the Eleventh, the rest must not be far behind. He heard more men yelling. In the street he saw officers waving their hats, grinning enormous grins. Victory? A rider came up, from Pender. A young man with a marvelous wide mustache said, "General Pender begs to report the enemy is falling back." Officers threw hats in the air. Lee smiled, could not be heard. One man touched him, another patted his back. He raised his glasses and looked to the clearing smoke.

He turned to Marshall. "I'll go forward."

Traveler was at the rail outside. Lee mounted and rode. Men were cheering him now, touching the horse as he went by. He tried to control his face. The wounded were everywhere. Some of them were Union boys, looking at him insensibly as he went by. A courier from Early: a rout on the left flank. The Union Eleventh Corps was running. More cheers. Lee closed his eyes once briefly. God's will. *My trust in Thee. Oh Lord, bless You and thank You.*

He moved forward to the rise ahead, across a small creek. Taylor said, "This must be Willoughby Run." Lee halted at the crest. Now he could see; the land lay before him wreathed in smoky ridges. Half a mile away lay the town, white board buildings, dirt roads. Beyond it was a high hill that rose above a series of ridges running off to the east. Blue troops were pouring back through the town, moving up the sides of the hill. The couriers were right: they were retreating. Victory. Lee put his glasses to his eyes, felt his hands tremble, focused, saw: Union artillery forming on the high hill, men digging. The fight was not over. Must not let those men occupy the high ground. Lee turned. To Taylor he said, "Find Hill's chief of artillery, tell him I want fire placed on that hill. I don't want it occupied. What word do you have from Ewell? And send General Hill to me."

Taylor moved off. Lee was thinking: we must continue the assault. The blue troops are on the move; now we must keep them moving. But Heth is down. He looked for Pender's courier, informed him to tell General Pender to continue the assault. But Early and Rodes were closer, on the left. If they only kept moving. The guns on the high hill were beginning to fire.

Here was Powell Hill, looking worse. He said, "The men have done all they can do. Heth's division is exhausted. Pender says he has had the hardest fighting of the war."

Lee studied him, looked away, back to the hill above Gettysburg. Hill may be sick but Pender was trustworthy. If Pender had doubts . . .

Taylor arrived. "General Ewell is with General Early, sir. We are in communication."

"Good," Lee said. "Deliver this message in person. Tell General Ewell the Federal troops are retreating in confusion. It is only necessary to push those people to get possession of those heights. Of course, I do not know his situation, and I do not want him to engage a superior force, but I do want him to take that hill, if he thinks practicable, as soon as possible. Remind him that Longstreet is not yet up."

Taylor repeated the message, rode off. Beyond that hill Lee could begin to feel

THE
FIRST DAY
3:00–4:00 P.M.
Concerted attack of Ewell's Corps
on Howard's flank, with Heth
and Pender attacking
Doubleday

the weight of the Union Army, the massive blue force pouring his way. What kind of soldier would Meade turn out to be? We must not give him the high ground. Lee looked southeast, saw two rounded hills. We might swing around that way. They have marched quicker than I expected. Thank the Lord for Longstreet's spy.

He heard more cheering, to the rear, looked, saw Longstreet. Moving forward slowly, calmly, like a black rock, grinning hungrily through the black beard. Lee flushed with pleasure. Longstreet dismounted, extended a hand.

"Congratulations, General. Wish I could have been here."

Lee took the hand warmly. "Come here, I want you to see this." He waved toward the field ahead, the hill beyond Gettysburg.

An officer near him said, "General Lee, it's Second Manassas all over again!"

"Not quite," Lee said cheerily, "not quite." He was delighted to have Longstreet here. Now through the streets Johnson's Division was moving, Longstreet's people could not be far behind. With every step of a soldier, with every tick of the clock, the army was gaining safety, closer to victory, closer to the dream of independence.

Longstreet studied the field. After a moment he said, "We were lucky."

"It couldn't have worked better if we had planned it."

Longstreet nodded. Lee explained the position that Ewell had orders to move to the left and take that hill. Longstreet studied the hill* while Lee spoke. After a moment he said, "Fine. But this is fine. This is almost perfect." He turned to Lee. "They're right where we want them. All we have to do is swing around that way—" he pointed toward Washington—"and get between them and Lincoln and find some good high ground, and they'll have to hit us, they'll have to, and we'll have them, General, we'll have them!"

His eyes were flashing; he was as excited as Lee had ever seen him. Lee said, amazed, "You mean you want me to *disengage?*"

"Of course." Longstreet seemed surprised. "You certainly don't mean—sir, I have been under the impression that it would be our strategy to conduct a defensive campaign, wherever possible, in order to keep this army intact."

"Granted. But the situation has changed."

"In what way?"

"We cannot disengage. We have already pushed them back. How can we move off in the face of the enemy?"

Longstreet pointed. "Very simply. Around to the right. He will occupy those heights and wait to see what we are going to do. He always has. Meade is new to the command. He will not move quickly."

Lee put his hand to his face. He looked toward the hill and saw the broken Union corps falling back up the slope. He felt only one urge: to press on and get it done. He said nothing, turning away. There was a messenger from General Ewell. Lee recognized the man, Captain James Power Smith, Ewell's aide. The Captain was delighted to see the Commanding General.

Ewell's message was cautious: "General Ewell says he will direct Early and Rodes to move forward, but he requests support of General Hill on his right. He says that there is a strong Union position south of the town which should be taken at once."

Lee asked which position Ewell meant. He handed Smith the glasses. Smith said the position was beyond the one in front, at the top of which there was a cemetery.

---

* Cemetery Hill.

Lee looked at his watch. It was almost five o'clock. Still two hours of daylight. He said to Longstreet, "General, how far away is your lead division?"

"McLaws. About six miles. He is beyond Johnson's train of wagons."

Lee shook his head. To Smith he said, "I have no force to attack the hill. General Hill's Corps has had hard fighting. Tell General Ewell to take that hill if at all possible. Have you seen Major Taylor?"

"No, sir."

"You must just have passed him."

Lee sent Smith away. He remembered: he had ordered artillery to fire on the hill, but none was firing. He sent to find out why. He began to realize he was really very tired. But if a strong Union force was on a hill to the south . . . but without Longstreet's Corps a general assault was impossible. Where was the artillery? Where was Hill? Why had Early and Rodes stopped their attacks? He could see the town below choked with soldiers, horses, but there was no advance.

He turned, saw Longstreet watching him. He had the look of a man suppressing his thoughts. Lee said, "Say it, General."

"We shouldn't have attacked here, General. Heth had his orders."

Lee waved a hand. "I know that. But we have pushed them back."

"In the morning we will be outnumbered."

Lee shrugged. Numbers were meaningless. "Had I paid attention to numbers, General . . ." Lee left the rest unsaid.

Longstreet said, "If we moved south, toward Washington, we could fight on ground of our choosing."

"The enemy is *here*, General. We did not want the fight, but the fight is here. What if I ask this army to retreat?"

"They will do as you order."

Lee shook his head again. He was growing weary of this. Why didn't Ewell's assault begin? A cautious commander, new to his command. And A. P. Hill is sick. Yet we won. The soldiers won. Lee pointed toward the hill.

"They will probably retreat. Or Ewell will push them off. But if Meade is there tomorrow, I will attack him."

"If Meade is there," Longstreet said implacably, "it is because he wants you to attack him."

That was enough. Lee thought: docile men do not make good soldiers. He said nothing. Longstreet could see the conversation was at an end. He said, "I'll bring my boys up as soon as I can."

Lee nodded. As Longstreet was going, Lee said, "General."

"Yes, sir?"

"Your spy was correct in his reports. Had it not been for that report, this army might have been destroyed in detail. I thank you."

Longstreet nodded. If the compliment pleased him, he did not show it. He moved off.

Lee stood alone, troubled. He had had enough of defensive war. The King of Spades. Let us attack, and let it be done. I am extraordinarily tired. You are an old man. And if something happens to you?

He picked up the glasses, waiting for Ewell's attack. No attack began.

Harrisburg

CARLISLE

Shippensburg

Susquehanna River

Mountain

To
Chambersburg

Cashtown

York

South

GETTYSBURG

Hanover

CHAMBERLAIN

PENNSYLVANIA
MARYLAND

Emmitsburg

Union Mills

Manchester

N

Big Pipe Cr.

Union Town

Westminster

Monocacy River

FREDERICK

Route led by
Chamberlain's 20th Maine,
Vth Corps, Union Army,
Union Mills to
Gettysburg, July 1

0   5   10
Miles

BALTIMORE

4

CHAMBERLAIN

Chamberlain rode slowly forward, into the western sun. It was soft green country, a land of orchards and good big barns. Here and there along the road people came out to see the troups go by and there were a few cheers, but most of the people were silent and glum, not hostile, apprehensive. The sight was depressing. Some of them were selling food to the troops. One farmer had a stand offering cold milk for sale, at outrageous prices, and after Chamberlain was past there was a scuffle and some of the men requisitioned the milk and told him to charge it to the U.S. Guvmint. Chamberlain heard but did not look back. It was beginning to be very hot, and Chamberlain closed his eyes to let the salt sweat gather in the corner of his eyelids and wiped it away and rode with his eyes closed, himself tucked away back in the dark under his hat. When he opened his eyes again the day was violently bright and very dusty, and so he rode half asleep, eyes partly closed, dreaming.

At noon they reached the Pennsylvania border. Now there were more people and they were much more friendly and the band behind struck up "Yankee Doodle." Now the farmers began to hand out free food; Chamberlain smelled fresh bread baking. A very pretty young girl with long blond hair rushed up to him and pressed a warm cake into his hand and he was embarrassed. The regiment greeted the girl with cheers. It was good to be first in line. No dust ahead. Chamberlain swiveled in the saddle and looked back down the road, and there down in the dust like a huge blue snake came the whole Fifth Corps along the winding road, some men on horses riding high in black hats, among the tilting flags. More bands were playing. Chamberlain wiped sweat from his eyes.

It was time to dismount. A good officer rode as little as possible. He got down from the horse and began to march along in the dust, in the heat. Near him he could hear Tom Chamberlain talking to one of the new men from the Second Maine, explaining the ways of this regiment. Tom was proud but not too proud. The Second Maine had seen more action. Chamberlain thought of Tom and his mind wandered back to Maine: young Tom lost, in the dark of the winter, a long search, Mother crying, we never found him, he survived out there and came back himself, a grinning kid with a bright red nose, never once afraid . . .

"One of the things you get to know," Tom Chamberlain was saying, "is that this here brigade has got its own special bugle call. You ever hear tell of Dan Butterfield?"

"General Butterfield what was with Hooker?"

"Right. Same man. Well, he used to be our brigade commander."

"They say he was a pistol. No man like him for having a good time." He gave a lewd wink, suggestion of coarseness.

"Well, I don't know about that, but he liked to write bugle calls. Trouble with this army is too many bugle calls. Call for artillery and infantry and get up and eat and retreat and all that, and it got a mite confusin', so Ole Dan Butterfield wrote a call for this here Brigade, special. If there is an order for this Brigade, well, somebody else would be blowing his blame bugle and we'd think it was for us only it wasn't, but we would follow the order anyway, and next thing you know we'd be in trouble."

"That happened to us once," the Maine man said. "Half the Regiment charged and the other half retreated. You had your choice." He chuckled. "Seems a good system, come to think on it."

"Well, in this Brigade we got a special call. You hear that call and you know the next call is for you. Goes like this:

"We call it 'Dan Butterfield,' just like this: 'Dan, Dan, Dan, Butterfield, Butter-field.' "

The Maine man said glumly, "In the middle of a fight I'm supposed to remember *that?*"

"It's easy if you remember." He sang it again: "Dan, Dan, Dan, Butterfield."

"Um," the Maine man said.

"Ole Butterfield wrote a lot of bugle calls. You know Butterfield's Lullaby?"

"Butterfield's what?"

Tom hummed a few bars of what was still known as Butterfield's Lullaby but which the army would later know as "Taps" and which now had no connotation of death, which simply meant rest for the night, rest after a long day in the dust and the sun, with the bugles blaring, and Joshua Chamberlain, listening, thought of the sound of Butterfield's Lullaby coming out of the dark, through a tent flap, with the campfires burning warm and red in the night, and Chamberlain thought: you can grow to love it.

Amazing. Chamberlain let his eyes close down to the slits, retreating within himself. He had learned that you could sleep on your feet on the long marches. You set your feet to going and after a while they went by themselves and you sort of turned your attention away and your feet went on walking painlessly, almost without feeling, and gradually you closed down your eyes so that all you could see were the heels of the man in front of you, one heel, other heel, one heel, other heel, and so you moved on dreamily in the heat and the dust, closing your eyes against the sweat, head down and gradually darkening, so you actually slept with the sight of the heels in front of you, one heel, other heel, and often when the man in front of you stopped you bumped into him. There were no heels today, but there was the horse he led by the reins. He did not know the name of this horse. He did not bother anymore; the horses were all dead too soon. Yet you learn to love it.

Isn't that amazing? Long marches and no rest, up very early in the morning and asleep late in the rain, and there's a marvelous excitement to it, a joy to wake in the morning and feel the army all around you and see the campfires in the morning and smell the coffee . . .

. . . awake all night in front of Fredericksburg. We attacked in the afternoon, just at dusk, and the stone wall was aflame from one end to the other, too much smoke, couldn't see, the attack failed, couldn't withdraw, lay there all night in the dark, in the cold among the wounded and dying. Piled-up bodies in front of you to catch the bullets, using the dead for a shield; remember the sound? Of bullets in dead bodies? Like a shot into a rotten leg, a wet thick leg. All a man is: wet leg of blood. Remember the flap of a torn curtain in a blasted window, fragment-whispering in that awful breeze: *never, forever, never, forever.*

You have a professor's mind. But that is the way it sounded.

Never. Forever.

Love that too?

Not love it. Not quite. And yet, I was never so alive.

Maine . . . is silent and cold.

Maine in the winter: air is darker, the sky is a deeper dark. A darkness comes with winter that these Southern people don't know. Snow falls so much earlier and in the winter you can walk in a snowfield among bushes, and visitors don't know that the bushes are the tops of tall pines, and you're standing in thirty feet of snow. Visitors. Once long ago visitors in the dead of winter: a preacher preaching hell-fire. Scared the fool out of me. And I resented it and Pa said I was right.

Pa.

When he thought of the old man he could see him suddenly in a field in the spring, trying to move a gray boulder. He always knew instinctively the ones you could move, even though the greater part was buried in the earth, and he expected you to move the rock and not discuss it. A hard and silent man, an honest man, a noble man. Little humor but sometimes the door opened and you saw the warmth within a long way off, a certain sadness, a slow, remote, unfathomable quality as if the man wanted to be closer to the world but did not know how. Once Chamberlain had a speech memorized from Shakespeare and gave it proudly, the old man listening but not looking, and Chamberlain remembered it still: "What a piece of work is man . . . in action how like an angel!" And the old man, grinning, had scratched his head and then said stiffly, "Well, boy, if he's an angel, he's sure a murderin' angel." And Chamberlain had gone on to school to make an oration on the subject: Man, the Killer Angel. And when the old man heard about it he was very proud, and Chamberlain felt very good remembering it. The old man was proud of his son, the Colonel. Of infantry. What would he have thought of the speech this morning? Home and Mother. Mother wanted me to be a parson. Vincent picked me, *me,* to lead the Regiment. Folks back home will know by now. Commander of the Regiment. Why *me?* What did Vincent see?

He turned his mind away from that. Think on it when the time comes. You think too much beforehand and you get too self-conscious and tight and you don't function well. He knew that he was an instinctive man, not a planner, and he did best when he fell back on instinct. Think of music now and singing. Pass the time with a bit of harmony. Hum songs, and rest.

But it was very hot.

Could use some Maine cool now.

Home. One place is just like another, really. Maybe not. But truth is it's just all rock and dirt and people are roughly the same. I was born up there but I'm no stranger here. Have always felt at home everywhere, even in Virginia, where they hate me. Everywhere you go there's nothing but the same rock and dirt and houses and people and deer and birds. They give it all names, but I'm at home everywhere. Odd thing: unpatriotic. I was at home in England. I would be at home in the desert. In Afghanistan or far Typee. All mine, it all belongs to me. My world.

Tom Chamberlain was saying, "You should have seen the *last* commander, Old Ames. He was the worst, I mean to tell you, the triple-toed half-wound, spotted mule *worst.*"

"Where was you boys at Chancellorsville?"

"Well now." A painful subject. Joshua Chamberlain opened his eyes.

"The fact is," Tom said gloomily, "we was not engaged."

"Well now, a lot of us wa'nt engaged. That there Hooker, I hear he froze right up like a pond in the dark."

"Well, we had us a misfortune." Tom turned eyes sad as a trout. He was a lean, happy, excitable man who had turned out to be calm and serene in combat. Soldiering was beginning to intrigue him.

"The thing was, damn, we had these here 'noculations. You ever been 'noculated?"

The man swore earnestly. Tom nodded. "Well, then, you know. Only thing was, we wound up sick, half the dang regiment. And come time for the fight at Chancellorsville our Surgeon Major—that's a stumble-fingered man named Wormy Monroe—he up and reported us unfit for combat. So they went ahead and sent us back to mind the dang telegraph wires. We wasn't allowed to 'sociate with nobody. Old Lawrence there he went on up and argued, but wouldn't nobody come near us. It was like he was carrying the plague. Lawrence said hang it, we ought to be the first ones in, we'd probably give the Rebs a disease and be more useful than any other outfit in the whole army. Matter of fact, way things turned, we probably would've been more use than most of them people. Anyway we wasn't in it."

The Maine man was chuckling. Chamberlain thought: would have thought mountain men were tougher than city boys. But mountain men get all the diseases. City boys get immune as they grow up. We were a thousand strong when we left Maine.

Gallant six hundred . . . Half a league, half a league . . .

It was quieter now. No one was talking. Sound of troops at route step, shuffle in the dust, dull clink of mess kits, a band in the distance, tinny, forlorn, raw call of a cow in the sunlight. A voice in his ear, a hand on his arm.

"Colonel, sir—" exasperated—"beg the Colonel's pardon, but would the Colonel do us all a favor and get back on the damned horse?"

Colonel opened his eyes into the glare, saw: Tozier. Color Sergeant Tozier. A huge man with a huge nose, sweat bubbling all over his face. "I'll tell you, sir, be a damn site easier handlin' these here new recruits if the officers would act like they got sense, sir."

Chamberlain blinked, wiped at his sweat. Some of the men were watching with that odd soft look on their faces that still surprised Chamberlain. He started to say something, shook his head. Tozier was right. He mounted the horse.

Tozier said, "How are you, sir?"

Chamberlain nodded, grinned weakly.

"We don't need no more new commanding officers," Tozier said. "Here you, Lieutenant, keep an eye on the Colonel."

Tom said, "Yes, sir." Tozier departed. Chamberlain thought: good thing old Ames didn't see him. My boys. Ames shaped them. But they're mine. Year ago they held meetings to decide what to do; if they disagreed with an officer, they stopped and argued. Can't conduct an army as a town meeting.

They were coming into Hanover. Out in a field dead bodies lay in untidy rows. The arms were up above the heads, the clothes were scattered, shoes were missing. The hair of some was flickering in the wind and they looked alive. Chamberlain learned: Stuart had been through here and there'd been a brush. The sight of dead men awakened them all.

A clear day, very hot. Wind swinging to the south. Buzzards ahead. As they rode ladies waved handkerchiefs, a band played the "Star-Spangled Banner." Chamberlain wondered: will the people here let the buzzards have them? Or will they bury them, Stuart's men?

The people of Hanover were delighted to see them. Now as they got closer to the Rebels people seemed much happier everywhere. Happiness seemed to increase in direct proportion to how close you were. When we actually get there, Chamberlain thought, it will be easy to tell: the men will be kissing you.

Chamberlain rode upright through town. On the far side he slumped again. For a short while Colonel Vincent came up to ride with him. Vincent was the new brigade commander—a very handsome man with thick sideburns, from the 83rd Pennsylvania. He had a good reputation and he had the air of a man who knew what he was doing. But Chamberlain had seen that air before. Hooker had it. And if ever there was a man who did not know what he was doing . . .

Vincent had heard about the 114 volunteers. He was impressed. He thought that things were looking up. The army was ready for a fight. That in itself was an impressive fact, after all that had happened. He showed Chamberlain the new brigade flag: triangular, white, with a blue border, a red Maltese Cross in the center. The man looked at it without interest. It meant nothing much, as yet. Vincent rode back. The man from the Second Maine said sadly, "You ever hear about *our* flag? It cost twelve hundred dollars."

But the men were tired. There was silence again. Chamberlain saw a rider going to the rear, a blue courier. Then there was the first wagon, then another. There was fighting at Gettysburg. Off against the horizon he could see a haze, a dark haze, as of dirt stirred into the air.

Nothing to do now but rest on the march. The troops became very still. It was darker now. The land around them was hilly and green, turning slowly gold, then hazy purple. It was a beautiful afternoon. At dark, word came forward to go into bivouac. Vincent came up and stopped the column, and the men moved gratefully out into a field, carrying the rails of the fences with them for evening fires. They had marched more than twenty miles again; it was now a hundred miles in five days. Now for the first time the new Maine men heard the call: Dan, Dan, Dan, Butterfield! Butterfield!

And then down the road came more riders, rushing to the rear on lathered horses. Chamberlain looked up to watch them go, sensing alarm. He could feel the Gray army beyond the hills. A moment later there came the bugle call: Dan, Dan, Dan, Butterfield, Butterfield, then forward.

A universal groan. No rest now. The rattle of the rails being dropped, a general cursing. Chamberlain reformed the regiment out in the road. Dispatch from Vincent: Move out.

Word of what had happened moved slowly down the column, but it was a long while before word came down to Chamberlain. By that time it was well after dark and the moon was rising, yellow in hazy air, huge in the trees, gazing like one single vacant eye, and Vincent rode up.

Two Corps had been engaged at Gettysburg and had been driven off. The First Corps had done well, but the Eleventh, those Dutchmen, had run again, as they did at Chancellorsville. Now the First was holding and screaming back for reinforcements. John Reynolds was hurt, possibly killed. Proceed with all possible speed.

Chamberlain did not protest. In the darkness he could feel his strength rising, coming over him in the cooler air of evening. Not far to Gettysburg now. He could hear no guns. But now along the roadway there were people rushing out, people lining the rail fences, anxious, overjoyed. From houses back off away from the road there was a waving of flags, a fluttering of white handkerchiefs; women lifted lamps at the windows. There were many healthy-looking young men lining the road and some of the men from Maine grumbled. But the rest were too tired. Chamberlain saw some staggering, then one fell out. He collapsed in a clatter of falling rifle, of mess tins rattling in the dust. He was pulled aside. Chamberlain arranged a detail to pick up fallen men.

On and on. Now it was much darker and the moon was high, and then ahead there was an officer, a staff officer, sitting on a black horse. He rode out to meet Chamberlain as he passed.

"Colonel, tell your men. General McClellan has assumed command of the army."

Chamberlain did not have to spread the word. It went down the ranks like a wind in wheat. Some of the men cheered hoarsely. One man fired a rifle, and then Tozier talked to him. For a long moment Chamberlain believed it. McClellan was back. God bless old Lincoln. The only general of the whole mess who knew what he was doing. But then the troops moved on and the moon went behind a cloud and Chamberlain knew that it could not be true.

But the men marched believing they were behind McClellan. He was the only general Chamberlain had ever seen who was truly loved. The Rebs loved Lee, no doubt of that. And we loved Mac. Chamberlain thought: two things an officer must do, to lead men. This from old Ames, who never cared about love: *You must care for your men's welfare. You must show physical courage.*

Well, Chamberlain thought, there's no McClellan. There's only Meade, whom none of these people know, let alone like, and he'll be cautious. So I've taken care, as best I can, of their welfare. Now tomorrow we'll see about the courage.

Now there were the wounded, the stragglers. Men limped back, sat out in the fields making fires, sulked along eastward, out in the dark. Now there were rumors: a terrible defeat, someone had blundered, two hundred thousand Rebs, the Eleventh Corps had deserted. Chamberlain ordered his men to close up and keep moving and not to talk. Damn the rumors. You never knew what was true until days or weeks or even months afterwards. He called close up, close up, first order he had given since morning, and then shortly after that the order came to stop, at last.

It was almost midnight. There were clouds again and it was very dark, but Chamberlain could see a hill in front of him and masses of troops and tents ahead. The Twentieth Maine went off the road and most went to sleep without fires, some without pitching tents, for the night was warm and without a wind. Chamberlain asked a passing courier: how far to Gettysburg? and the man pointed back over his shoulder. You're there, Colonel, you're there.

Chamberlain lay down to rest. It was just after midnight. He wondered if McClellan would really be back. He prayed for a leader. For his boys.

5

LONGSTREET

He rode out of Gettysburg just after dark. His headquarters were back on the Cashtown Road, and so he rode back over the battlefield of the day. His staff recognized his mood and left him discreetly alone. He was riding slumped forward, head down, hat over his eyes. One by one they left him, moving ahead, cheering up when they were out of his company. He passed a hospital wagon, saw mounded limbs glowing whitely in the dark, a pile of legs, another of arms. It looked like masses of fat white spiders. He stopped in the road and lighted a cigar, looking around him at the tents and the wagons, listening to the rumble and music of the army in the night. There were a few groans, dead sounds from dying earth, most of them soft and low. There was a fire far off, a large fire in a grove of trees, men outlined against a great glare; a band was playing something discordant, unrecognizable. A dog passed him, trotted through the light of an open tent flap, paused, looked, inspected the ground, padded silently into the dark. Fragments of cloth, trees, chewed bits of paper littered the road. Longstreet took it all in, began to move on. He passed a black mound which seemed strange in the dark: lumpy, misshapen. He rode over and saw: dead horses. He rode away from the field, toward higher ground.

Lee would attack in the morning. Clear enough. Time and place not yet set. But he will attack. Fixed and unturnable, a runaway horse. Longstreet felt a depression so profound it deadened him. Gazing back on that black hill above Gettysburg, that high lighted hill already speckled with fires among the gravestones, he smelled disaster like distant rain.

It was Longstreet's curse to see the thing clearly. He was a brilliant man who was slow in speech and slow to move and silent-faced as stone. He had not the power to convince. He sat on the horse, turning his mind away, willing it away as a gun barrel swivels, and then he thought of his children, powerless to stop that vision. It blossomed: a black picture. She stood in the doorway: *the boy is dead*. She didn't even say his name. She didn't even cry.

Longstreet took a long deep breath. In the winter the fever had come to Richmond. In a week they were dead. All within a week, all three. He saw the sweet faces: moment of enormous pain. The thing had pushed him out of his mind, insane, but no one knew it. They looked at the plain blunt stubborn face and saw nothing but dull Dutch eyes, the great darkness, the silence. He had not thought God would do a thing like that. He went to church and asked and there was no answer. He got down on his knees and pleaded but there was no answer. She kept standing in the door: *the boy is dead*. And he could not even help her, could say nothing, could not move, could not even take her into his arms. Nothing to give. One strength he did not have. Oh God: *my boy is dead*.

He had tears in his eyes. Turn away from that. He mastered it. What he had left was the army. The boys were here. He even had the father, in place of God: old Robert Lee. Rest with that, abide with that.

His aides were all gone, all but two. Goree hung back from him in the growing dark. He rode on alone, silently, Goree trailing like a hunting dog, and met one of his surgeons coming up from camp: J. S. D. Cullen, delighted, having heard of the great victory, and Longstreet succeeded in depressing him, and Cullen departed. Longstreet lectured himself: depression is contagious; keep it to yourself. He needed something to cheer him, turned to two men behind him, found there was only one, not an aide, the Englishman: Fremantle. Exactly what he needed. Longstreet drew up to wait.

The Englishman came pleasantly, slowly forward. He was the kind of breezy, cheery man who brings humor with his presence. He was wearing the same tall gray hat and the remarkable coat. He said cheerily, tapping the great hat, "Don't mean to intrude upon your thoughts, General."

"Not 't'all," Longstreet said.

"Really, sir, if you'd rather ride alone . . ."

"Good to see you," Longstreet said.

The Englishman rode up grinning broadly through widely spaced teeth. He had entered the country by way of Mexico, riding in a wagon drawn by a tobacco-chewing man who had turned out to be, in his spare time, the local judge. Fremantle had seen many interesting things: a casual hanging, raw floods, great fires. He was continually amazed at the combination of raw earth and rough people, white columned houses and traces of English manner. He had not gotten used to the crude habit of shaking hands which was common among these people, but he forced himself. He was enjoying himself hugely. He had not changed his clothes in some days and he looked delightfully disreputable, yet mannered and cool and light in the saddle. Longstreet grinned again.

"Did you get a chance to see anything?"

"Well as a matter of fact I *did*. I found rather a large tree and Lawley and I sat out in the open and there was quite a show. Lovely, oh lovely."

"You didn't happen to see a cavalry charge?" Stuart: not yet returned.

"Not a one," Fremantle gloomed. "Nor a hollow square. You know, sir, we really ought to discuss that at length on some occasion. Provided this war lasts long enough, which most people seem to think it won't. You fellows seem to do well enough without it, I must say. But still, one likes to feel a certain *security* in these matters, which the square gives, do you see? One likes to know, that is, where everyone is, at given moments. Ah, but then—" he took a deep breath, tapped his chest—"there's always tomorrow. I gather you expect a bit of an adventure tomorrow."

Longstreet nodded.

"Well, I shall try to find a position of advantage. I will appreciate your advice, although of course if I'm ever in the way at all, you must feel free, I mean, one must not hamper operations. Don't spare my feelings, sir. But if you'll tell me where to stand."

"I will."

Fremantle whacked a mosquito. "Another victory today. When I am clear about it all I shall write it down. Expect you chaps are getting rather used to victory, what? Damn!" He swatted another bug. "Must say, enormously impressive, this army. Yet the Federal fellas just keep on coming. Curious. I have a bit of difficulty, you know, understanding exactly *why*. Some time when there's time

. . . but the war is ending, of course. I can feel that myself. That is the message I shall transmit to my people. No doubt of it."

He eyed Longstreet. Longstreet said nothing.

"Your General Lee is a wonder."

"Yes," Longstreet said.

"A thing one rarely sees." Fremantle paused. "Remarkable," he said. He was about to say something else but changed his mind.

"He holds this army together," Longstreet said.

"Strordnry dignity."

"Strordnry."

"I mean, one does not expect it. No offense, sir? But your General Lee is an *English* general, sir. Strordnry. He has gained some reputation, sir, as of course you know, but there is a tendency in Europe to, ah, think of Americans as, ah, somewhat behind the times, sometimes what, ah, how do I say this? One is on tricky ground here, but, sir, of course you understand, there are these cultural differences, a new land and all that. Yet, what I mean to say is, one did not expect General Lee."

"To be a gentleman," Longstreet said.

Fremantle squinted. After a moment he nodded. Longstreet was not offended. Fremantle said wonderingly, "Sir, you cannot imagine the surprise. One hears all these stories of Indians and massacres and lean backwoodsmen with ten-foot rifles and rain dances and what not, and yet here, your officers . . ." He shook his head. "Strordnry. Why, do you know, your General Lee is even a member of the Church of England?"

"True."

"He has great forebears."

"Yes," Longstreet said.

"I have noticed, sir, that you are always in camp near him. I must say, sir, that I am touched."

"Well," Longstreet said.

"Ah." Fremantle sighed. "We have so many things in common, your country and mine. I earnestly hope we shall become allies. Yet I feel you do not need us. But I must say, I am increasingly indebted to you for your hospitality."

"Our pleasure."

"Ah. Um." Fremantle cocked his head again. "One thing I'm very glad to see. Your General Lee is a moralist, as are all true gentlemen, of course, but he respects minor vice, harmless vice, when he finds it in others. Now that's the mark of the true gentleman. That is what distinguishes the man so to me, aside from his military prowess, of course. The *true* gentleman has no vices, but he allows you your own. Ah." He patted a saddlebag. "By which I mean, sir, to get to the heart of the matter, that I have a flagon of brandy at your disposal, should the occasion arise."

"It undoubtedly will." Longstreet bowed. "Thank you."

"You may call on me, sir."

Longstreet smiled.

"A small weakness," Fremantle went on cheerily, "of which I am not proud, you understand. But one sees so little whisky in this army. Amazing."

"Lee's example. Jackson didn't drink either. Nor does Stuart."

Fremantle shook his head in wonder. "Oh, by the way, there's a story going around, do you know? They say that General Lee was asleep, and the army was marching by, and fifteen thousand men went by on tiptoe so as not to wake him. Is that true?"

"Might have been." Longstreet chuckled. "I know one that I heard myself. While ago we sat around a fire, talked on Darwin. Evolution. You read about it?"

"Ah?"

"Charles Darwin. Theory of Evolution."

"Can't say that I have. There are so many of these things rattling about."

"Theory that claims that men are descended from apes."

"Oh *that*. Oh yes. Well, I've heard—distastefully—of that."

"Well, we were talking on that. Finally agreed that Darwin was probably right. Then one fella said, with great dignity he said, 'Well, maybe *you* are come from an ape, and maybe *I* am come from an ape, but General Lee, *he* didn't come from no ape.'"

"Well, of course." Fremantle did not quite see the humor. Longstreet grinned into the dark.

"It is a Christian army," Longstreet said. "You did not know Jackson."

"No. It was my great misfortune to arrive after his death. They tell great things of him."

"He was colorful," Longstreet said. "He was Christian."

"His reputation exceeds that of Lee."

"Well, pay no attention to that. But he was a good soldier. He could move troops. He knew how to hate." Longstreet thought: a good Christian. He remembered suddenly the day Jackson had come upon some of his troops letting a valiant Yankee color sergeant withdraw after a great fight. The men refused to fire at him, that man had been brave, he deserved to live. Jackson said, *"I don't want them brave, I want them dead."*

"They tell many stories of the man. I regret not having known him."

"He loved to chew lemons," Longstreet said.

"Lemons?"

"Don't know where he got them. He loved them. I remember him that way, sitting on a fence, chewing a lemon, his finger in the air."

Fremantle stared.

"He had a finger shot away," Longstreet explained. "When he held it down the blood would get into it and hurt him, so he would hold it up in the air and ride or talk with his arm held up, not noticing it. It was a sight, until you got used to it. Dick Ewell thought he was crazy. Ewell is rather odd himself. He told me Jackson told him that he never ate pepper because it weakened his left leg."

Fremantle's mouth was open.

"I'm serious," Longstreet said amiably. "A little eccentricity is a help to a general. It helps with the newspapers. The women love it too. Southern women like their men religious and a little mad. That's why they fall in love with preachers."

Fremantle was not following. Longstreet said, "He knew how to fight, Jackson did. A. P. Hill is good too. He wears a red shirt when he's going into battle. It's an interesting army. You've met George Pickett?"

"Oh yes."

"Perfume and all." Longstreet chuckled. "It's a hell of an army." But thinking of Pickett, last in line, reminded him of Pickett's two brigade commanders: Garnett and Armistead. Old Armistead, torn by the war away from his beloved friend Win Hancock, who was undoubtedly waiting ahead on that black hill beyond Gettysburg. Armistead would be thinking of that tonight. And then there was Dick Garnett.

"Pickett's men are extraordinary men," Fremantle said. "The Virginians seem different, quite, from the Texans, or the soldiers from Mississippi. Is that true, do you think, sir?"

"Yes. Have you met Dick Garnett?"

"Ah, yes. Tall fella, rather dark. Wounded leg. Odd that . . ."

"Jackson tried to court-martial him. For cowardice in the face of the enemy. I've known Garnett for twenty years. No coward. But his honor is gone. You will hear bad things from people who know nothing. I want you to know the truth. Jackson was . . . a hard man."

Fremantle nodded silently.

"He also court-martialed A. P. Hill once. And Lee simply overlooked it. Well, come to think of it, I had some trouble with old Powell myself once; he wanted to fight me a duel. Matter of honor. I ignored him. It's an interesting army. Only Lee could hold it together. But the thing about Garnett troubles me. He thinks his honor is gone."

"A tragic thing," Fremantle said. There was tact there, a tone of caution.

"The papers, of course, all side with Jackson." Longstreet blew out a breath. "And Jackson is dead. So now Garnett will have to die bravely to erase the stain."

And he saw that Fremantle agreed. Only thing for a gentleman to do. Longstreet shook his head. A weary bitterness fogged his brain. He knew Garnett would die, no help for it now, unturnable, ridiculous, doomed with a festering, unseen wound.

Fremantle said, "You are not, ah, Virginia born, sir?"

"South Carolina," Longstreet said.

"Ah. That's in the far south isn't it, sir?"

"True," Longstreet said. He was weary of talk. "Honor," he said. "Honor without intelligence is a disaster. Honor could lose the war."

Fremantle was vaguely shocked.

"Sir?"

"Listen. Let me tell you something. I appreciate honor and bravery and courage. Before God . . . but the point of the war is not to show how brave you are and how you can die in a manly fashion, face to the enemy. God knows it's easy to die. Anybody can die."

In the darkness he could not see Fremantle's face. He talked to darkness.

"Let me explain this. Try to see this. When we were all young, they fought in a simple way. They faced each other out in the open, usually across a field. One side came running. The other got one shot in, from a close distance, because the rifle wasn't very good at distance, because it wasn't a rifle. Then after that one shot they hit together hand to hand, or sword to sword, and the cavalry would ride in from one angle or another. That's the truth, isn't it? In the old days they fought from a distance with bows and arrows and ran at each other, man to man, with swords. But now, listen, now it's quite a bit different, and quite a few people don't seem to know that yet. But we're learning. Look. Right now, take a man with a good rifle, a good man with a good rifle which has a good range and may even be a repeater. He can kill at, oh, conservatively, two, three hundred yards shooting into the crowd attacking him. Forget the cannon. Just put one man behind a tree. You can hardly see him from two hundred yards away, but he can see you. And shoot. And shoot again. How many men do you think it will take to get to that man behind a tree, in a ditch, defended by cannon, if you have to cross an open field to get him? How many men? Well, I've figured it. At least three. And he'll kill at least two. The way you do it is this: one man fires while one man is moving, and the other is loading and getting ready to move. That's how the three men attack. There's always one moving and one firing. That way you can do it. If you forget the cannon. But you'll lose one man most probably on the way across the field, at least one, probably two, against a cannon you'll lose all three, no matter what you do, and that's across the field. Now. If you are attacking uphill . . ."

He broke it off. No point in talking this way to a foreigner. Might have to fight him sometime. But the man would not see. Longstreet had spoken to his own officers. They found what he said vaguely shameful. Defense? When Lee dug trenches around Richmond they called him, derisively, the King of Spades. Longstreet took a deep breath and let it go, remembering again that damned black hill, fires like eyes.

Fremantle said, bewildered, "But, sir, there is the example of Solferino. And of course the Charge of the Light Brigade."

"Yes," Longstreet said. Like all Englishmen, and most Southerners, Fremantle would rather lose the war than his dignity. Dick Garnett would die and die smiling. "Had he his hurts before?" Aye, then he died like a man. Longstreet, who had invented a transverse trench which no one would use, filed the matter forcefully in the dark cavern of his swelling brain and rode into camp.

That night, at supper, someone remarked casually that since the army needed ammunition, wouldn't it be proper for the ammunition factories to stay open on Sunday? Most of the officers agreed that it had not yet come to *that*.

Longstreet stayed up talking, as long as there was company, as long as there was a fire. Because when the fire was gone and the dark had truly come there was no way he could avoid the dead faces of his children.

6

LEE

Lee rode north through the town and out the Heidlersburg Road. There was a joy in the night all around him. The men yelled and whooped as he passed by. Many stopped and just smiled and some took off their hats. They had won again. The joy on their faces, the look of incredible pride, the way so many of them looked at him going by as if waiting for some sign of his approval of a job well done, another fight so nobly fought, lights in all the starry young eyes, and beyond that the way some of them had tears in their eyes as he went by, tears for him, for the cause, for the dead of the day; the sight of it was something very nearly unbearable, and he set his face and rode through saying nothing, nodding, touching his hat. Then he was out the other side of town, and there were piles of stacked Union muskets, blankets and canteens and wagons, the abandoned implements of war.

Ewell had made his headquarters in a farmhouse. He was there, along with Early and Rodes. They were all standing at a white gate as Lee rode up at the beginning of the night, enough light still in the sky so that the black mass of the hill to the east, the untaken hill, could still be seen against the evening sky. Lee thought: why did you not attack? Why? But he said nothing.

Ewell had the look of a great-beaked, hopping bird. He was bald and scrawny; his voice piped and squeaked like cracking eggshells. He had lost a leg at Manassas and had just recently returned to the army, and he was standing awkwardly balancing himself against the unfamiliar leg and scratching his head and swaying nervously, clutching a fencepost. Early stood beside him, dark, formal, composed. Rodes off to the side bowed formally at Lee's approach.

"Good evening, sir, God bless you, did you see them run? Did you see them? We whipped them again, by God, yes, sir, we did, sir." Ewell chattered. Lee sensed a strange thin quality in his voice, a wavery exuberance. He escorted Lee through the house, hobbling awkwardly on the wooden leg, talking about the bullet that had hit him there that afternoon while he was mounted on his horse. They went out into an arbor and sat in the warm evening under the grapevines and the soft sky and Ewell sat on the ground and hiked up his pants to show Lee where the bullet had hit, a Minnie ball just below the jointed knee, a vast gash of splintered white wood. Ewell was giggling, grinning, cocking his head off to the side like a huge parrot, chortling.

Lee asked the condition of the corps, the number of wounded. Early spoke up. Ewell deferred. Early stood with his legs wide apart, his hands clasped behind his back, heavy in the jaw, his face bleak and grim, black beard dirty and untrimmed. He had been a West Pointer, had left the army to become a lawyer, a prosecutor. He was utterly sure of himself. Lee watched and listened. Early explained the situation coolly and logically. Behind him, Ewell nodded in punctuation, his head twitching, his fingers fluttering. Lee felt a strangeness in the air, a coolness. Ewell should speak for himself. Rodes sat silently leaning forward, his hands on his knees, looking at the ground. There was a pause.

Lee said, "I had hoped you would move on through the town and take that hill."

Ewell blinked, rubbed his nose, looked at Early, looked at Rodes, patted his thigh. Lee, watching, felt a sudden acute depression.

Ewell said, "I didn't think it was, ah, practical. We were waiting, ah, for many reasons. We had marched all day, and fought, and your orders were a caution against bringing on a general engagement." He jabbered, rambling, moving about in his chair. Early walked over and sat on the railing of the arbor. Ewell turned to him for confirmation.

Early said calmly, silently, bored, "There were reports of Federal troops in the north. We couldn't bring artillery to bear, and no word came from Hill, as you know. We decided it would be best to wait for Johnson." Yes, yes, Ewell nodded vigorously, thumping the wooden leg. "But he did not arrive until dark, just a while ago. He's out now, looking over the terrain."

Ewell went on nodding. Lee looked at Rodes, who said nothing. After a moment Early said, "You may remember, sir, that I passed over this ground a few days ago and am familiar with it. The hill is named Cemetery Hill. It has another hill beyond it, also occupied. It will be a very strong position."

Lee closed his eyes for a moment, was very tired. Think of all of it later. An aide brought a cup of hot boiled coffee, thick with sugar. Lee drank, revived, abruptly saw the face of Jackson in his mind, a flare of cold blue eyes. He looked up, blinked. Could almost see him. Jackson was here. Jackson was looking on.

Ewell was drinking coffee. Early had folded his arms. Rodes still gazed at the ground, plucking at one of his fingers. Lee said, "Can you attack on this flank, in the morning?"

Ewell sat up. Early did not move. Lee felt the depression, cold and slow and steady like a wind in his brain, shook his head to blow it away.

Early said, "That hill will be a very strong position. Once it is fortified. Which they are doing right now."

"Very strong." Ewell nodded violently.

"Have you looked over the ground, sir?" Early asked.

"From a distance."

Early leaned back into the dark. He spoke slowly, deliberately. "I do not think we should attack this point. This will be the strong point. Our troops have marched hard today and fought hard today. I suggest we hold here while the rest of the army makes an attack on the other flank."

"You think an attack here would succeed?"

"I think it would be very costly."

Ewell nodded. Lee turned.

"General Rodes?"

Rodes looked up, glanced away, shrugged.

"We'll attack, of course. But the men have had a good fight. And it will be a strong position." He looked up at Ewell, then quickly away. "I'm sorry we did not take it today."

"Well," Lee said. "Today is done."

"General Longstreet has not been engaged," Early said. "His Corps has not been fought for some time." He was referring to Chancellorsville, where Longstreet's men had been detached. "If he were to attack on the right he would draw the enemy from this position and we could then attempt the assault. Supported, of course, by General Hill."

Lee thought: Longstreet cannot stand the man. I wonder why? Something too cold here, something disagreeable in the silence of the eyes, the tilt of the head. Jubal. Strange name. Old Jubilee. Nothing happy about the man. And yet, unmistakable competence. Lee said, "Longstreet proposes that we move our army to the right around the enemy flank and interpose between Meade and Washington."

"And vacate this position?" Ewell popped his eyes, slapped the splintered wood again. "Leave this town, which we have just captured?"

Lee said, with some irritation, "The town is of no importance."

Ewell looked to Early. Early said slowly, "To move this entire Corps, in the face of a fortified enemy?" He smiled slightly, with a touch of the disdain for which he was rapidly becoming notorious.

"Hardly fitting," Ewell piped. "Hardly. Troops fought so hard for this town, do we move them out and march them off into the woods, in sight of the enemy? Morale will suffer, General. The boys are ready. Our boys are ready."

"Longstreet is on the defensive again." Early grinned. "I suppose that's to be expected. But really, sir, it seems to me, we are here and the enemy is there, and Hill and General Ewell have engaged and Longstreet has not. If Longstreet can be induced to attack on the right, we can give you this hill tomorrow by sundown."

Ewell was nodding again, pointing at Early, wagging a bony finger. They talked. Lee made no decision. Must not judge Ewell now. The man had been a good soldier for too long. First day in command of the Corps. Jackson's old Corps.

Hill is sick. Ewell indecisive. The hill untaken. Longstreet broods on defensive war. Lee said, "Would you gentlemen retreat?"

"Retreat? Retreat?" Ewell sat with his mouth open. Rodes looked up.

"Would you suggest that we fall back behind South Mountain?"

"Retreat?" Ewell was amazed. "But why?"

Lee said, "If we do not withdraw, and if we do not maneuver in the face of the enemy, then we must attack. There is no other alternative." He rose, not waiting for an answer. They accompanied him to the door. He saw a vase filled with flowers on a small wooden table. A picture of an old man frowned down out of an old round frame. Lee was thinking: very dangerous to withdraw. To pull this army with all its trains back through that pass. Without cavalry, it cannot be done. Stuart, I have waited long enough.

He thanked the men for their day's work, told them to get a good night's rest. Once again he saw Jackson's blue eyes, probing, reproachful. He thought: General, we miss you.

He rode off into the dark. Taylor was there with messages. Lee answered them, one to Imboden, one to Chilton, sent Taylor off to find the raider, Harry Gilmore, who was with Johnson. He rode off with Venable and then, moving in out of the night to greet him, saw old Isaac Trimble, astride a pale horse, fiery old Isaac. Lee smiled a greeting. General Trimble was almost sixty. Not much older than *you*, old man. But he looks ancient. Do I look that old? I was tired before, but I am not tired now. No pain now. God's blessing. What will I do about Ewell?

Trimble said, "Sir, I beg your pardon, but I will not serve the man." He was furious. He raised one huge hand like a vast claw and made a gesture as if pushing a disgusting thing away from him, into the black air. "I will not serve the man. I am a volunteer aide with the man, sir, as you know. I most respectfully request another assignment." He shook his head violently, almost displacing his hat. "The man is a disgrace. Have you heard it all, sir? What they have been telling you? Ask the aides, sir, or General Gordon, or Johnson."

He went on. He was a marvelous old man who had sworn to be a Major General or a corpse. Lee gathered that he was talking about Ewell. Lee calmed him, but he wanted to hear.

Trimble said, "We should have taken that hill. God in His wisdom knows we could have taken that hill. Beyond Cemetery Hill there is another hill and it was totally unoccupied. There was no one there at all, and it commanded the town. Gordon saw it, sir, he was with us, me and Gordon and Ewell, all standing there in the flaming dark like great fat idiots with that bloody damned hill empty, begging your pardon, General, but that bloody damned hill was as bare as his bloody damned great head and it commands the town. We all saw it, General, as God is my witness, ask anyone here. McKim was there, Smith was there, they were all there. I said, 'General Ewell, we have got to take that hill. General Jackson would not have stopped like this with the bluebellies on the run and plenty of light left and a hill like that empty as, oh God help us, I don't know what.' But nobody there at all. And the Federals running, no guns set up, nothing but one battery and one regiment in line."

He was running out of breath. Lee had stopped to listen. He sensed, among the anger, the bitter breath of truth. Trimble took off his hat and wiped it across his brow, and his white hair gleamed in the moonlight like wadded cotton. Lee said, "Go on."

"Yes, sir. Sir, I told him, General Ewell, I said to him, 'Sir, give me one division and I will take that hill.' And he said nothing at all. He stood there! He stared at me! I said, 'General Ewell, give me one *brigade,* and I will take that hill.' I was becoming disturbed, sir. And General Ewell put his arms behind him and blinked. So I said, 'General, give me one *regiment* and I will take that hill.' And he said nothing; he just shook his head, and I threw my sword down." Trimble gestured helplessly, actually close to tears. "Down on the ground in front of him." He raised both arms. "We could have done it, sir. A blind man should have seen it. Now they are working, up there, you can hear the axes. Now in the morning many a good boy will die."

He wiped his face. It was all out of him. The fire died. He slumped forward in the saddle.

"General, sir, I request another assignment."

Lee said softly, "Thank you, General. You will be of great service, thank you."

Now that Trimble was quieter Lee could question him. Dick Ewell had frozen; he had deferred to Early. Lee thought: I must look into this. He told Trimble to rest and he rode back to his headquarters in the dark. He was becoming increasingly tired, but there was much to do. Food. Get some fuel. The ancient body had no reserve. His chest was stuffed, a feeling of cool bleakness there, no strength in him. He thought of that and of Stuart off somewhere, possibly dead, and of Ewell's weakness and Hill's illness and the Union Army growing now in the night on that hill, blossoming darkly across the field like a fungus, a bristly fungus.

The headquarters was in a small stone house on Seminary Ridge. An elderly woman, the resident, was cooking for him. Lee chatted with her politely, his mind on other things, while aides came and went, Generals pushed in and out, reporters and artists and the Prussian and the Austrian passed in and out. There was a rocking chair for Lee; it received him like an enfolding arm. Taylor appeared with a squad of men, led by a man named Watters, a Marylander. Now late at night it was becoming difficult to recognize people, to remember their names. Lee prepared sealed orders to be given to each of Watters' men; they were to scatter out over the countryside and find Stuart and get him back to Gettysburg with all possible speed. When that was done Lee looked for Longstreet, but the stubborn face was not there. Lee closed his eyes. The uproar of jokes and joy went on around him. Must see Ewell *now*, without Early. He motioned to Marshall, sent for Ewell. The room gradually cleared. Lee signed orders. I do too much myself. He was thinking: retreat is not even an option; we must assault or maneuver. If we assault, Longstreet must bear the load.

Lee took a quick nap. He was awakened by the arrival of Ewell. He rose and went out into the night. The strange beaked figure waited with deference. Lee said, "How are you, sir?"

"I am fine, sir. The leg troubles me a bit."

Lee suggested a doctor. Ewell shook his head. "Drugs injure a man's thinking. The leg is minor. Sir?

"Johnson's men are in position now. He is very optimistic, much more than Early. I believe we ought to attack *there,* sir."

"Attack the hill?"

"Yes, sir. Culp's Hill or Cemetery Hill, or both, sir."

There was a new certainty in his voice. Lee was very glad to hear it. A small relief blossomed like a flower. Lee said only, "I have made no decision yet. But in your opinion, we should attack on your flank."

"Yes, sir."

Lee nodded. "I will consider it. I am glad to hear you are well."

"General," Ewell said. His face was not clear in the evening light, the lamplight from inside, the moon from the heavens, but there was a sadness in his voice, regret apparent in the motion of his head, the beak above the wild mustache bobbing. "I think I was too slow today, sir. I regret that very much. I was trying to be . . . careful. I may have been too careful."

Lee was moved. My good old soldier. He was embarrassed. He said quickly, "You won a victory, General." Ewell looked up. His eyes were strained. "It was not a large victory, it might have been larger, we might have pushed harder. But it was a victory. I am satisfied. The men fought well. This was your first day. It is not as easy as it sometimes appears."

"No, sir," Ewell said.

"Now get some rest." Lee sent him off. He went back into the house feeling much better. The old man had been a good soldier for too long; you cannot worry about Ewell. And then Lee thought: but sometimes I have seen it happen. A man loses part of himself, an arm, a leg, and though he has been a fine soldier he is never quite the same again; he has lost nothing else visible, but there is a certain softness in the man thereafter, a slowness, a caution. I did not expect it with Ewell. I do not understand it. Very little of a man is in a hand or a leg. A man is in his spirit and he has that in full no matter what part of his body dies, or all of it. But, Lee thought, you may not understand. It has not happened to you, so you don't understand. So don't judge. He was a good soldier. He is not Jackson. Jackson is gone—not entirely gone; Jackson was there today watching, and Ewell sees *his* eyes—but you cannot blame him for not being Jackson. You must make do with the tools God has given for the job. Richard Ewell, old Baldy . . . and his ridiculous horse.

Lee went back to the rocker. Midnight came, and he had not yet slept. Headquarters grew steadily more still. Lee thought again of Rooney Lee, wounded, and prayed for him. There was no time for a letter to his wife, that troubled woman. He closed his eyes and thought of Meade, out there, gathering the army. John Reynolds was dead. He prayed for the soul of Reynolds. And in the morning?

This is the great battle. Tomorrow or the next day. This will determine the war. Virginia is here, all the South is here. What will you do tomorrow?

No orders were out. Now he was alone. It was cooler. Taylor came and tucked a blanket around his knees and Lee did not argue. He was drifting off. Longstreet would be up in the morning. Pickett would be up by late afternoon. In the afternoon all the army will be here. And we will hit them. We will hit them with everything and drive them right off that hill and send them running back down the road to Washington. If Stuart's cavalry . . .

He woke briefly. Without cavalry in the rear no victory would be complete. Should we attack before Stuart comes? And if he comes with tired horses and weary men? If he comes at all . . .

Don't think on that. Lee closed his eyes. And let himself fall into the bright dark. For Thine be the Kingdom, and the Power . . .

7

BUFORD

He came back at last to the cemetery on the hill. All down the ridge they were digging in, all around the crest of the hill. He sat on the horse and watched the picks swinging in the moonlight, listened to the sound of shovels in the earth. The army was still coming in, marching by moonlight. It was almost two o'clock in the morning.

He rode slowly along the ridge, looking for headquarters. He had been hit once in the left arm and the bleeding had stopped but the genuine pain was just beginning. They had wrapped the arm and put his coat back on and he did not show the injury. He rode stiffly, dizzily, looking for someone to give him orders for what was left of his cavalry.

He found a small farmhouse, center of many lights, many horses tethered outside. The musk of cigar smoke was heavy in the warm air. He remembered an old Indian joke: follow cigar smoke; fat men *there*. Bright moonlight, a warm and cloudless night. They were posting cannon along the ridge by moonlight: pleasant looming shapes, rolling caissons. Buford thought: I need a drink. Whisky stiffens. He rode to the farmhouse and stopped in a crowd of horses and sat there. Rather not get down. Men were passing in and out, much conversation. A cloud of officers had clustered by the small lighted door, looking in. One glanced up, saw him, noted the star, turned, saluted quickly. Buford wiggled a finger; the man came forward: a major. Other men were turning. Buford rode the horse almost to the door.

Buford said, "Who's in command, and where do I find him?"

"Good evening, sir," the major said. A very high voice. A lisp? "The officer in command is General Howard, sir. He may be found—"

"Don't be a damn fool, Edgar," another man said. He saluted Buford. "Begging your pardon, sir, but the truth is that General Hancock is in command, and if you'll—"

Another major, skinny, grinning. The first major said angrily, "I must remind you, sir, that General Howard is the *senior* officer on the field."

"But General Hancock has orders from General Meade himself."

They argued, ignoring Buford. He looked down in wonder. Other officers voiced opinions. Oliver Howard was the commander of the Eleventh Corps. He had arrived this morning with Reynolds. He had fought on the right and been broken, just as he had been broken at Chancellorsville. He was a one-armed man for whom Buford had no admiration. The majors confronted like wispy chickens; it was very strange. Behind them Buford saw suddenly a familiar face: John Gibbon, of Hancock's corps. Infantry. A cold, silent man. His brothers fought for the other side. Buford nodded. Gibbon nodded. A major was giving a lecture on military precedence: Howard could not be relieved except by written order or by Meade in person. Gibbon came up and took the reins.

"Evenin', John."

Buford bowed.

"A hard day?"

"Long," Buford admitted.

"Hancock's inside, if you want to see him." Gibbon led the horse out of the crowd. The argument went on behind them. Buford watched it with awe. Never get used to it, the mind of headquarters, not if I live a thousand years.

Gibbon said, "That's been going on all night."

"I gather Meade's not here yet. Who's in command?"

"Take your choice." Gibbon grinned. But he was one of Hancock's fanatics. Good soldier.

"I have to refit my outfit," Buford said. "I need orders."

"Hancock got here late this afternoon, just as Howard's Corps was falling apart. They ran, them Dutchmen, just like they did at Chancellorsville. Hancock took command and reformed them on this hill, along with the First, and ever since then everybody's been coming to him for orders, and not Howard, and he's hopping mad. Kind of funny. He claims he's senior officer." Gibbon chuckled.

"But Hancock has a verbal order from Meade. It's all very funny. Thing is, when Hancock's on the field the men naturally turn that way. Old Howard's really steamed."

"I just want orders," Buford said. "I'm kind of weary." He was thinking: need the long quiet again, want to get away from here. He dismounted, held briefly to the horse.

Gibbon called a man to take the reins. He said, "I'll get your orders. Why don't you wait out here?"

Buford sat on a rail. The arm was alive with pain. He said, "Is the army here?"

"Just about. All but Sedgewick. We've got Sykes and Geary and Sickles, along with Hancock. And Howard. Sedgewick will be here tomorrow, but he has a long march."

"Good," Buford said. He nodded, closed his eyes. Can relax now. He felt the beginning of sleep, even among the pain, the quiet dark coming, the soft rolling dreamless rest.

Gibbon said, "They're all inside."

Buford stirred, began to head toward the door. Gibbon said casually, "Why don't you stay out here?"

Buford moved sleepily toward the door. Need one last order, then a good long sleep. The aides near the door were parting, but something in Gibbon's voice caught him. He stopped, turned. Gibbon was there.

"Howard has made a complaint against you, John. He says you should have supported him on the right."

Buford nodded dumbly, then blinked. He raised the pained arm. Gibbon said, "He lost half his strength. Most of them got taken prisoner. He's mad as a hornet, lookin' for somebody to blame it on. I think he's picked you."

Buford felt nothing for a moment, a sort of sodden silence all through his brain, then the anger began to rise like a metal wave, like a hot tide in the dark. Buford could say nothing. No words came. Gibbon said softly, "Stay out here, John. I'll tell Hancock you're here."

He moved past Buford into the room. Buford blinked and blinked again and then began moving, pushing his way into the light, the smoke of the room. It was jammed with officers, all the brass. The anger made Buford dizzy. He tried to push his way through and the pain went all the way up his arm and into his chest and shocked him stiff. He could see faces: Sickles, the bully boy, the bright politician, a fat cigar clamped in a fat mouth, the man who was famous for having shot his wife's lover. Geary and Sykes were sitting, brooding; that damned Howard was making a speech. And there was Hancock against a wall, writing a note, talking to aides, issuing orders. Buford's vision blurred. The room was very hot and there was too much smoke. He had to push his way back out of the room into the open air. He kept saying aloud, God damn him, God damn him. He sat on a rail. In a moment he looked up and there was Hancock.

"How are you, John?"

Handsome face, watching. Buford focused. Hancock looked down with bright dark eyes. Buford said, "I'm all right."

"Heard you were with John Reynolds when he died."

"I was."

"Tell me."

Buford told him. Hancock would write the letter. Good, very good. Hancock was older since last time Buford saw him. Calm and cocky, damned good-looking man. Buford felt suddenly better. Cool, clean air.

Hancock said, "I'm sending the body back to his folks in Lancaster. They might appreciate a note from you."

"I'll send it."

"How's your division?"

Buford told him. Hancock was surprised. He hadn't known Buford was that involved. Buford said, "We were involved."

"Well, get yourself refitted. May need you in the morning."

There was commotion behind him. A mass of aides were riding up. Somebody blew a discordant bugle. Hancock stood up, grinned. Buford noted: why, Hancock's wearing a clean white shirt. Isn't that amazing. Clean as a whistle. Hancock said, "Here's Meade."

They all came out to meet him, the angry man with the squeaky voice. They gathered around him as he dismounted. Buford was pushed to the side. He heard Meade greet Hancock.

"Damn dark. I can't see a damn thing."

Hancock said he was very glad to see the General. Meade said, with great disgust, "Well, I hope to God this is good ground, General. Is it good ground?"

"Very good ground, General."

"Well, by God it better be, because we're going to have to fight here sure enough in the morning."

Buford was pushed too far away. Meade went on into the house. Flocks of officers gathered at the windows. Buford had enough; he had his orders. He got back on his horse and rode slowly back toward the cemetery. He had not much strength left. He called for one of his aides, but the buck-toothed boy was dead, and the yellow-haired boy was dead, and the Sergeant was down and would never recover. Buford stopped in the cemetery. He could not find the white angel. But he looked out across the town and he could see a great ocean of Rebel campfires, flooding the town, with fire burning all over those ridges to the west, flooding fire right up to the base of the hill. Buford took off his hat, looked up to the stars. He said to John Reynolds, "Well, John, we held the ground." He wiped his eyes. He thought: *have to get some more lieutenants.* Then he rode off down the hill into the black beneath the trees.

N

ANDERSON

EARLY

RODES

JOHNSON

HETH

LEE

PENDER

SEMINARY

GETTYSBURG

EARLY

HOWARD

Oak Hill

CARLISLE ROAD

MUMMASBURG ROAD

UNFINISHED R.R.

CASHTOWN ROAD

Willoughby Run

HAGERSTOWN ROAD

YORK PIKE

HANOVER ROAD

Cemetery Hill

Culp's Hill

Seminary Ridge

DOUBLEDAY

CODORI

Cemetery Ridge

TANEYTOWN ROAD

BALTIMORE PIKE

Rock Creek

WILLIAMS

EMMITSBURG ROAD

Peach Orchard

Wheat Field

BUFORD

Devil's Den

Little Round Top

BIRNEY

Big Round Top

0   500   1000
Yards

SITUATION
AT CLOSE OF
First Day

THURSDAY,
JULY 2, 1863
THE SECOND DAY

He hath loosed the fateful lightning . . .

1

FREMANTLE

Awake in the dark, the stars still brightly shining, Fremantle, a slow riser, staggered into the dawn not quite knowing where he was. These people might conduct these things at a civilized hour. Three in the morning. Incredible. He washed in dirty water. Came vaguely awake. War!

The army awakened around him. He could sense the red battle forming today, coming like the sun. His senses shocked him awake. He expected cannon at any moment. He saw the first light of dawn a dusky rose in the east, the sun coming up from the direction of the enemy. He felt sleepily marvelous. He bid a cheery hello to Sorrel, Longstreet's aide.

"Major Sorrel, sir, good morning! I say, could you direct me to the battle?"

Sorrel, a neat and natty person, smiled and bowed. "Would you care for a bite to eat before the assault? We can serve Yankees done to order, before or after breakfast."

Fremantle could not suppress a yawn, smothered it politely with his hand. "I suppose there is time for a bun or two. How's General Longstreet this morning? My compliments, and I trust he slept well."

"Doubt if he slept at all. He's gone over to speak with General Lee."

"Does the man ever sleep? Amazing. He rarely even sits *down.*"

Sorrel smiled. A bird, annoyed at being awakened early, began chattering in the tree above him. Other officers began stepping out into the dark of the morning. There was Ross, the fat Austrian with the Scotch name. He was all aglow in the powder-blue uniform of the Austrian Hussars, complete with shining silver chamberpot for the head, waving a blue plume. As he came closer Fremantle observed with alarm that the man was spotlessly groomed; even his mustache was waxed, the ends slim and sharp like wiggly rapiers.

Ross boomed happily, patting himself fat-handedly across the stomach. *"C'est le sanglant appel-de Mars,* eh, old chap?" He popped the slender Fremantle on the arm, unsettling him.

Fremantle said with distaste, "Early in the morning for that, old friend. Could you wait until after tea?"

The others were gathering around the breakfast table. Scheibert, the beardless Prussian, moody, prim, was dressed all in white, white coat, floppy white hat, the inevitable glittering monocle. While most of the officers of the army could speak French, few could speak German, and Scheibert's pride was continually offended, but he went on stubbornly using German military terms in conversation, was not understood, would not explain, sat fatly, whitely to the side, a rare sight, oddly comical in that company. Lawley, the correspondent, seemed ill again and had not made up his mind whether or not to ride today. There were the three medical people—Maury, Cullen, Barksdale—and others of Longstreet's staff: Latrobe, Goree, and the charming little Jew, Major Moses. They sat down to a splendid breakfast, and although Fremantle continued to wake up slowly, coming alive as the day came alive, warmly, brightly, with no clouds anywhere, the wind beginning to pick up and rustle the trees, the light beginning to sift down through the cool leaves, the dark branches, still Fremantle remained vaguely asleep.

The morning at war. Marvelous. Good men around a table. What a joy to be with the winners! All these men had nothing but contempt for the Yankees, whom they had beaten so often. There was even an air of regret at the table, a sense of seize the day, as if these bright moments of good fellowship before battle were numbered, that the war would soon be over, and all this would end, and we would all go back to the duller pursuits of peace. Fremantle enjoyed himself enormously. Southerners! They were *Englishmen,* by George. Fremantle was at home.

He ate hot eggs, warm bread, reveled in steaming tea, although the water from which the tea was made left an aftertaste in the mouth, afterthoughts in the brain: from what nearby barn? The men all chatted, joked. Fremantle was sorry to see breakfast end. But the sun was fully up. Now once more he could expect the big thunder of cannon. Must not miss it today. Sorrel promised to keep him informed. They rode together toward the lines, hoping for a good view.

So Fremantle came to Gettysburg, saw the bodies unburied in the fields, beginning to become offensive in the heat of the morning, poor chaps. They turned off to the right and rode up through a grove of trees to higher ground, and through the trees Fremantle could already see the blue ridge to the east, soft in the morning haze, where the Yankees were camped. But he could see no troops, no movement. He felt his stomach tighten, his breath grow sharp. In the presence of the enemy! In range of the guns! He passed a battery of Southern artillery, mixed Napoleons and Parrots, served by wagons stamped USA.

Sorrel said, "We got most of our wagons from the enemy. Many of the guns. Their artillery is very good. But ours will get better."

The Austrian, Ross, had ridden up beside them. One of the gunners, a lean, barefoot man in dusty brown, stared at him unbelievingly as he passed, then bawled in a piercing voice that carried all along the line, "Hey, mister. You in blue. What you do, man, you look like you swallowed some mice."

Sorrel put his hand over his mouth. Ross stared back, uncomprehending.

Fremantle said cheerily, "The fellow is referring to the waxed mustache, old friend."

Ross grumbled, twitched the mustache, stroked the ends lovingly, glowered. They rode to Lee's headquarters, then beyond, up the ridge to where the Generals were meeting.

There was a gathering of officers, too many men. Sorrel suggested that if Fremantle wanted a good view, he should find a convenient tree. Fremantle wandered forward, with Lawley, through the cool green woods, to the same commanding position he had the day before, climbed the same wide oak. There below him, not fifty feet away, he recognized Longstreet, then Lee. The officers were in consultation.

Lee was standing with his back to the group, bareheaded, the white hair flicking in the breeze. He was gazing out toward the Union lines, which were clearly visible in the east. He put his field glasses to his eyes, looked, put them down, walked two or three paces south, turned, looked again, slowly walked back and forth. Longstreet was sitting on a camp stool, whittling slowly on a stick, making a point, sharpening the point, sharpening, sharpening. A. P. Hill, looking much healthier than the day before, was chatting with another officer, unidentified.

Sitting next to Longstreet, on a stump, also whittling, was a tall slim man with an extraordinary face, eyes with a cold glint in them, erect in posture even as he sat, cutting a stick. Fremantle asked, impressed, "Who is that?"

Lawley: "That's Hood. John Bell Hood. They call him 'Sam,' I think. He commands one of Longstreet's divisions. From Texas, I believe."

"Does his behavior in battle match his appearance?"

"He does his job," Lawley said laconically.

"An interesting army," Fremantle said. "Most interesting."

Lee had turned, was saying something to Longstreet. Longstreet shook his head. Hill came closer.

Lawley said, "The Yankees have dug in. But I don't see any trenches anywhere here. That means we'll attack."

The "we" was inevitable, but Fremantle noticed it. He felt a part, almost a member, of this marvelous group of outnumbered men. Englishmen. They called themselves Americans, but they were transplanted Englishmen. Look at the names: Lee, Hill, Longstreet, Jackson, Stuart. And Lee was Church of England. Most of them were. All gentlemen. No finer gentlemen in England than Lee. Well, of course, here and there, possibly one exception. Or two.

Nevertheless, they are *our* people. Proud to have them. And perhaps they will rejoin the Queen and it will be as it was, as it always should have been.

They had talked of that the evening before. Every one of the officers had insisted that the South would be happier under the Queen than under the Union. Of course, hard to say what they meant. But if England came to help now, would it not be possible? That this soil would once again be English soil?

He had borrowed glasses from Sorrel, was looking at the Union lines. He could see the cannon now, rolled out in front of the trees. He could see men moving among the caissons, men on horseback moving in the trees; here and there a pennant blew. He saw a flash of gold. Breastworks were going up, twisted sticks, small, very far away. There was an open valley below him, partly cultivated, then a long bare rise to the Union line. To the left was the high hill, Cemetery Hill, that Ewell had failed to take the day before, the hill that had worried Longstreet. To the center was a wooded ridge. To the right were two round hills, one rocky, the other wooded. The Union position was approximately three miles in length, or so it seemed from here. All this Fremantle saw with continually rising excitement.

He looked down, saw Longstreet rise, move off, shoulders bowed, wandering head down and lumbering, like a bearded stump, to stare out at the lines. Hood joined him. Once more Longstreet shook his head. Lee came back to a small table, stared at a map, looked up, back toward the Union lines, keeping his hand on the map. Fremantle had a good look at that extraordinary face. Lee looked weary, more pale than before. The sun was climbing; it was noticeably hotter. Fremantle felt a familiar rumble in his own stomach. Oh God, not the soldier's disease. Those damned cherries.

There seemed no point in remaining in the tree. Soldiers had observed him, hanging in the air like a plump gray fruit, were beginning to point and grin. Fremantle descended with dignity, joined the other foreigners. He heard, for the first time that day, music: a polka. He listened with surprise. He could not identify the sound but he knew the beat. It was followed by a march.

Ross said, "They play even during an attack. Not very good. But inspiring. Have you heard the Rebel yell?"

Fremantle nodded. "Godawful sound. I expect they learned it from Indians."

Ross opened wide his eyes. "Never thought of *that*," he said. His silver helmet shifted. Sweat was all over his brow.

"I say, old friend, you really aren't going to wear that thing all day, are you? In this charming climate?"

"Well," Ross said. He tweaked his mustache. "One must be properly dressed. Teach these fellas respect."

Fremantle nodded. Understandable. One tried to be neat. But that *helmet*. And Ross did tend to look a bit ridiculous. Like some sort of fat plumed duck. These chaps all looked so natural, so . . . *earthy*. Not the officers. But the troops. Hardly any uniform at all. Brown and yellow Americans. Odd. So near, yet so far.

He saw Moxley Sorrel, walking briskly off on a mission, "corralled him," as the Americans would put it.

Sorrel said, "We've sent out engineers to inspect the ground to our right. We'll be attacking later in the day. Don't know where yet, so you can relax, I should say, for two hours or so at least."

"Have you heard from General Stuart?"

"Not a word. General Lee has sent out scouts to find him." Sorrel chuckled. "Cheer up, you may have your charge."

"I hope to have a good position today."

"We'll do all we can. I suggest you stay close to Longstreet. There'll be action where he is."

Sorrel moved off. Through the trees Fremantle saw Longstreet mounting his horse. Fremantle led his own horse that way. Longstreet had Goree with him, the aide from Texas. The greeting was friendly, even warm. Fremantle thought, startled, he *likes* me, and flushed with unexpected pride. He asked if he could ride with the General; Longstreet nodded. They rode down to the right, along the spine of the ridge, in under the trees. Most of Longstreet's staff had joined them.

Longstreet said to Hood, "I'll do what I can. His mind seems set on it."

Hood shrugged. He seemed smaller now when you were close. He had extraordinary eyes. The eyebrows were shaggy and tilted and the eyes were dark as coal so that he seemed very sad. Fremantle had a sudden numbing thought: by evening this man could be dead. Fremantle stared at him, transfixed, trying to sense a premonition. He had never had a premonition, but he had heard of them happening, particularly on the battlefield. Men often knew when their time had come. He stared at Hood, but truthfully, except for the sadness in the eyes, which may have been only weariness, for Hood had marched all night, there was no extra sensation, nothing at all but a certain delicious air of impending combat which was with them all. Longstreet most of all, sitting round and immobile on the black horse, gazing eastward.

Hood said, "Well, if he's right, then the war is over by sundown."

Longstreet nodded.

"We'll see. But going in without Pickett is like going in with one boot off. I'll wait as long as I can."

Hood cocked his head toward the Union lines. "Do you have any idea of the force?"

Longstreet ticked off the corps so far identified: five, counting the two involved in the first day's action. He thought there would be more very soon, that perhaps even now the entire army was up. Lee did not think so. But yesterday he had not thought the Yankees would be there at all, and they were there in force, and now today the Yankees were on the high ground and with Stuart gone there was no way of knowing just how many corps lay in wait beyond the haze of that far ridge.

Fremantle rode along politely, silently, listening. He had developed a confidence that was almost absolute. He knew that Longstreet was tense and that there was a certain gloom in the set of his face, but Fremantle knew with the certainty of youth and faith that he could not possibly lose this day, not with these troops, not with Englishmen, the gentlemen against the rabble. He rode along with delight blossoming in him like a roseate flower, listening. Longstreet looked at him vacantly, saw him, then looked at him.

"Colonel," he said abruptly, "how are you?"

"By George, sir, I am fine, I must say."

"You slept well?"

Fremantle thought: everyone seems concerned that I sleep well.

"Oh, very well." He paused. "Not *long,* mind you, but well."

Longstreet smiled. There seemed to be something about Fremantle that amused him. Fremantle was oddly flattered; he did not know why.

"I would like someday to meet the Queen," Longstreet said.

"I'm sure that could be arranged. Sir, you would be considered most welcome in my country, a most distinguished visitor."

There was firing below, a sharp popping, a scattering of shots, a bunch, another bunch, then silence. Longstreet put on his glasses, looked down into the valley. "Pickets," he said.

Fremantle, who did not know what to expect, started, gulped, stared. But he was delighted. He saw puffs of white smoke start up down in the valley, like vents in the earth, blow slowly lazily to his left, to the north. He looked up at the ridge, but he could see only a few black cannon, a single flag. He said abruptly, "I say, sir, you say you won't be attacking for a bit?"

Longstreet shook his head.

"Then, ah, if I may be so bold, what's to prevent the Yankees from attacking *you?*"

Longstreet looked at Hood.

"I mean, ah, I don't see that you have bothered to entrench," Fremantle went on.

Longstreet grinned. Hood grinned.

"An interesting thought." Longstreet smiled. "I confess, it had not occurred to me."

"Me neither," Hood said.

"But I suppose it's *possible,*" Longstreet said.

"You really think so?"

"Well," Longstreet hedged. He grinned, reached up along the edge of his hat, scratched his head. "I guess not." More soberly, he turned to Fremantle. "It would be most unlike General Meade to attack. For one thing, he is General Meade. For another, he has just arrived on the field and it will take some time to understand the position, like perhaps a week. Also, he has not yet managed to gather the entire Army of the Potomac, all two hundred thousand men, and he will be reluctant to move without his full force. Then again, he will think of reasons." Longstreet shook his head, and Fremantle saw that he had again lost his humor. "No, Meade will not do us the favor, the great favor. We will have to *make* him attack. We will have to occupy dangerous grounds between him and Washington and let the politicians push him to the assault. Which they will most certainly do. Given time. We need time."

He paused, shook his head. They rode on in silence. Fremantle began to realize how remarkably still it was. Down in the valley the fields were open and still, the breeze had slowed, there was no movement of smoke. A few cows grazed in the shade, rested in dark pools of shade under the trees. Fremantle could feel the presence of that vast army; he knew it was there, thousands of men, thousands of horses, miles of cannon, miles of steel. And spread out beyond him and around him Lee's whole army in the dark shade, moving, settling, lining up for the assault, and yet from this point on the ridge under the tree he could look out across the whole valley and see nothing, hear nothing, feel nothing, not even a trembling of the earth, not even one small slow rumble of all those feet and wheels moving against the earth, moving in together like two waves meeting in a great ocean, like two avalanches coming down together down facing sides of a green mountain. The day had dawned clear, but now there were clouds beginning to patch the sky with hazy blots of cottony white, and not even any motion there, just the white silence against the blue. It was beginning to be very hot, hotter even than before, and Fremantle noticed perspiration on all the faces. He had not slept well, and suddenly the silence and the heat began to get to him. He was a man from a northern clime and England did not have this sort of weather, and when you have not slept . . .

He was most anxious to move on with Longstreet, but he saw Lawley and Ross pull off into an open field and sit down, and so he bade Longstreet goodbye and rode off to join his fellow Europeans. He let his horse roam with the others in a fenced field and found himself a grassy place under a charming tree and lay flat on his back, gazing up serenely into the blue, watching those curious flecks that you can see if you stare upward against the vacant blue, the defects of your own eye.

They chatted, telling stories of other wars. They discussed the strategy of Napoleon, the theories of Jomini, the women of Richmond. Fremantle was not that impressed by Napoleon. But he was impressed by the women of Richmond. He lay dreamily remembering certain ladies, a ball, a rose garden . . .

This land was huge. England had a sense of compactness, like a garden, a lovely garden, but this country was without borders. There was this refreshing sense of *space*, of blowing winds, too hot, too cold, too huge, raw in a way raw meat is raw—and yet there were the neat farms, the green country, so much like Home. The people so much like Home. Southern Home. Couldn't grow flowers, these people. No gardens. Great weakness. And yet. They are *Englishmen*. Should I tell Longstreet? Would it annoy him?

He thinks, after all, that he is an American.

Um. The great experiment. In democracy. The equality of rabble. In not much more than a generation they have come back to *class*. As the French have done. What a tragic thing, that Revolution. Bloody George was a bloody fool. But no matter. The experiment doesn't work. Give them fifty years, and all that equality rot is gone. Here they have the same love of the land and of tradition, of the right form, of breeding, in their horses, their women. Of course slavery is a bit embarrassing, but that, of course, will go. But the point is they do it all exactly as we do in Europe. And the North does not. *That's* what the war is really about. The North has those huge bloody cities and a thousand religions, and the only aristocracy is the aristocracy of wealth. The Northerner doesn't give a damn for tradition, or breeding, or the Old Country. He hates the Old Country. Odd. You very rarely hear a Southerner refer to "the Old Country." In that painted way a German does. Or an Italian. Well, of course, the South *is* the Old Country. They haven't left Europe. They've merely transplanted it. And *that's* what the war is about.

Fremantle opened an eye. It occurred to him that he might have come across something rather profound, something to take back to England. The more he thought about it, the more clear it seemed. In the South there was one religion, as in England, one way of life. They even allowed the occasional Jew—like Longstreet's Major Moses, or Judah Benjamin, back in Richmond—but by and large they were all the same nationality, same religion, same customs. A little rougher, perhaps, but . . . my word.

Fremantle sat up. Major Clarke was resting, back against a tree. Fremantle said, "I say, Major, Longstreet is an English name, I should imagine."

Clarke blinked.

"No, as a matter of fact, I don't think it is." He pondered. "Dutch, I think. Yes, come to think of it. Dutch all right. Comes from New Jersey, the old Dutch settlements up there."

"Oh." Fremantle's theory had taken a jolt. Well. But Longstreet was an exception. He was not a Virginian.

Fremantle again relaxed. He even began to feel hungry.

The morning moved toward noon.

2

CHAMBERLAIN

The Regiment sat in an open field studded with boulders like half-sunken balls. Small fires burned under a steam-gray sky. Chamberlain wandered, watching, listening. He did not talk; he moved silently among them, hands clasped behind his back, wandering, nodding, soaking in the sounds of voices, tabulating the light in men's eyes, moving like a forester through a treasured grove, noting the condition of the trees. All his life he had been a detached man, but he was not detached any more. He had grown up in the cold New England woods, the iron dark, grown in contained silence like a lone house on a mountain, and now he was no longer alone; he had joined not only the army but the race, not only the country but mankind. His mother had wanted him to join the church. Now he had his call. He wandered, sensing. Tired men. But ready. Please, God, do not withdraw them now. He saw illness in one face, told the man to report to sick call. One man complained. "Colonel, it keeps raining, these damn Enfields gonna clog on us. Whyn't we trade 'em for Springfields first chance we get?" Chamberlain agreed. He saw Bucklin, together with a cold-eyed group from the old Second Maine, nodded good morning, did not stop to talk. A young private asked him, "Sir, is it true that General McClellan is in command again?" Chamberlain had to say no. The private swore. Chamberlain finished the walk, went back alone to sit under a tree.

He had dreamed of her in the night, dreamed of his wife in a scarlet robe, turning witchlike to love him. Now when he closed his eyes she was suddenly there, hot candy presence. Away from her, you loved her more. The only need was her; she the only vacancy in the steamy morning. He remembered her letter, the misspelled words: "I lie here dreamyly." Even the misspelling is lovely.

A mass of men was coming down the road, unarmed, unspiked, no rifles visible: prisoners. They stopped near a long rock ledge which walled the road. Some of his own troops began drifting over that way, to stare, to chat. They were usually polite to prisoners. The accents fascinated them. Although some of the Regiment were sailing men, most of them had never been out of Maine. Chamberlain thought vaguely of the South. *She* had loved it. *She* had been at home. Heat and Spanish moss. Strange hot land of courtly manners and sudden violence, elegance and anger. A curious mixture: the white-columned houses high on the green hills, the shacks down in the dark valleys. Land of black and white, no grays. The South was a well-bred, well-mannered, highly educated man challenging you to a duel. *She* loved it. Dreamyly. She had liked being a professor's wife. She had been outraged when he went off to war.

Square-headed Kilrain: "Is the Colonel awake?"

Chamberlain nodded, looking up.

"I have found me a John Henry, sir."

"John who?"

"A John Henry, sir. A black man. A darky. He's over thataway."

Kilrain gestured. Chamberlain started to rise.

"I heard him a-groanin'," Kilran said, "just before dawn. Would the Colonel care to see him?"

"Lead on."

Kilrain walked down a grassy slope away from the road, across the soft field, marshy with heavy rain, up a rise of granite to a gathering of boulders along the edge of a grove of dark trees. Chamberlain saw two men standing on a rock ledge, men of the Regiment. Kilrain sprang lightly up the rock. The two men—one was the newcomer, Bucklin—touched their caps and wished him "morning" and grinned and pointed.

The black man lay in the shadow between two round rocks. He was very big and very black. His head was shaved and round and resting on mossy granite. He was breathing slowly and deeply, audibly; his eyes were blinking. He wore a faded red shirt, ragged, dusty, and dark pants ragged around his legs. There were no sleeves in the shirt, and his arms had muscles like black cannonballs. His right arm was cupped across his belly. Chamberlain saw a dark stain, a tear, realized that the man had been bleeding. Bucklin was bending over him with a tin cup of coffee in his hand. The black man took a drink. He opened his eyes and the whites of his eyes were red-stained and ugly.

Chamberlain pointed to the wound.

"How bad is that?"

"Oh, not bad," Kilrain said. "I think he's bled a lot, but you know, you can't really tell."

Bucklin chuckled. "That's a fact."

"Bullet wound," Kilrain said. "Just under the ribs."

Chamberlain knelt. The black man's face was empty, inscrutable. The red eyes looked up out of a vast darkness. Then the man blinked and Chamberlain realized that there was nothing inscrutable here; the man was exhausted. Chamberlain had rarely seen black men; he was fascinated.

"We'll get him something to eat, then we'll get him to a surgeon. Is the bullet still in?"

"Don't know. Don't think so. Haven't really looked." Kilrain paused. "He sure is black, and that's a fact."

"Did you get his name?"

"He said something I couldn't understand. Hell, Colonel, I can't even understand them Johnnies, and I've been a long time in this army." The black man drank more of the coffee, put out both hands and took the cup, drank, nodded, said something incomprehensible.

"Guess he was a servant on the march, took a chance to run away. Guess they shot at him."

Chamberlain looked at the bald head, the ragged dress. Impossible to tell the age. A young man, at least. No lines around the eyes. Thick-lipped, huge jaw. Look of animal strength. Chamberlain shook his head.

"He wouldn't be a house servant. Look at his hands. Field hands." Chamberlain tried to communicate. The man said something weakly, softly. Chamberlain, who could speak seven languages, recognized nothing. The man said a word that sounded like *Baatu, Baatu,* and closed his eyes.

"God," Kilrain said. "He can't even speak English."

Bucklin grunted. "Maybe he's just bad wounded."

Chamberlain shook his head. "No. I think you're right. I don't think he knows the language."

The man opened his eyes again, looked directly at Chamberlain, nodded his head, grimaced, said again, *Baatu, Baatu.* Chamberlain said, "Do you suppose that could be 'thank you'?"

The black man nodded strongly. "Tang oo, tang oo, baas."

"That's it." Chamberlain reached out, patted the man happily on the arm. "Don't worry, fella, you'll be all right." He gestured to Kilrain. "Here, let's get him up."

They carried the man down out of the rocks, lay him on open grass. A knot of soldiers gathered. The man pulled himself desperately up on one elbow, looked round in fear. Kilrain brought some hardtack and bacon and he ate with obvious hunger, but his teeth were bad; he had trouble chewing the hardtack. The soldiers squatted around him curiously. You saw very few black men in New England. Chamberlain knew one to speak to: a silent roundheaded man with a white wife, a farmer, living far out of town, without friends. You saw black men in the cities but they kept to themselves. Chamberlain's curiosity was natural and friendly, but there was a reserve in it, an unexpected caution. The man was really very black. Chamberlain felt an oddness, a crawly hesitation, not wanting to touch him. He shook his head, amazed at himself. He saw: palm of the hand almost white; blood dries normally, skin seems dusty. But he could not tell whether it was truly dust or only a natural sheen of light on hair above black skin. But he felt it again: a flutter of unmistakable revulsion. Fat lips, brute jaw, red-veined eyeballs. Chamberlain stood up. He had not expected this feeling. He had not even known this feeling was there. He remembered suddenly a conversation with a Southerner a long time ago, before the war, a Baptist minister. White complacent face, sense of bland enormous superiority: *my dear man, you have to live among them, you simply don't understand.*

Kilrain said, "And this is what it's all about."

A soldier said softly, "Poor bastard."

"Hey, Sarge. How much you figure he's worth, this one, on the hoof?"

"Funny. Very funny. But they'd give a thousand dollars for him, I bet. Nine hundred for sure."

"Really? Hell." It was Bucklin, grinning. "Whyn't we sell him back and buy outen this army."

Chamberlain said to Kilrain, "He can't have been long in this country."

"No. A recent import, you might say."

"I wonder how much he knows of what's happening."

Kilrain shrugged. A crowd was gathering. Chamberlain said, "Get a surgeon to look at that wound."

He backed off. He stared at the palm of his own hand. A matter of thin skin. A matter of color. The reaction is instinctive. Any alien thing. And yet Chamberlain was ashamed; he had not known it was there. He thought: If I feel this way, even I, an educated man . . . what was in God's mind?

He remembered the minister: and what if it is *you* who are wrong, after all?

Tom came bubbling up with a message from Vincent: the Corps would move soon, on further orders. Tom was chuckling.

"Lawrence, you want to hear a funny thing? We were talking to these three Reb prisoners, trying to be sociable, you know? But mainly trying to figure 'em out. They were farm-type fellers. We asked them why they were fighting this war, thinkin' on slavery and all, and one fella said they was fightin' for their 'rats.' Hee. That's what he said." Tom giggled, grinned. "We all thought they was crazy, but we hadn't heard a-right. They kept on insistin' they wasn't fightin' for no slaves, they were fighting for their 'rats.' It finally dawned on me that what the feller meant was their 'rights,' only, the way they talk, it came out 'rats.' Hee. Then after that I asked this fella what rights he had that we were offendin', and he said, well, he didn't know, but he must have some rights he didn't know nothin' about. Now, aint that something?"

"Button your shirt," Chamberlain said.

"Yassuh, boss. Hey, what we got here?" He moved to see the surrounded black. The surgeon had bent over the man and the red eyes had gone wild with new fear, rolling horselike, terrified. Chamberlain went away, went back to the coffeepot. He felt a slow deep flow of sympathy. To be alien and alone, among white lords and glittering machines, uprooted by brute force and threat of death from the familiar earth of what he did not even know was Africa, to be shipped in black stinking darkness across an ocean he had not dreamed existed, forced then to work on alien soil, strange beyond belief, by men with guns whose words he could not even comprehend. What could the black man know of what was happening? Chamberlain tried to imagine it. He had seen ignorance, but this was more than that. What could this man know of borders and states' rights and the Constitution and Dred Scott? What did he know of the war? And yet he was truly what it was all about. It simplified to that. Seen in the flesh, the cause of the war was brutally clear.

He thought of writing Fanny a quick letter. Dreamyly. He wanted to tell her about the black man. He wanted time to think. But the 83rd Pennsylvania was up and forming. Ellis Spear was coming along the line. It came to Chamberlain suddenly that they might move from here to battle. Under his command. He took a deep breath. Bloody lonely feeling.

He moved back to the cluster around the black man. The shirt was off and Nolan was attending him. The light was stronger; the sun was a blood red ball just over the hills. Chamberlain saw a glistening black chest, massive muscles. The black man was in pain.

Nolan said, "He'll be all right, Colonel. Bullet glanced off a rib. Cut the skin. Looks just like anybody else inside." Nolan clucked in surprise. "Never treated a Negro before. This one's a tough one. They all got muscles like this one, Colonel?"

"We'll have to leave him," Chamberlain said. "Let him have some rations, try to give him directions. Buster, can you talk to him?"

"A little. Found out who shot him. It was some woman in that town there, Gettysburg."

"A woman?"

"He came into town looking for directions and a woman came out on a porch and shot at him. He don't understand. I guess she didn't want to take a chance on being caught with him. But *shoot* him? Christ. He crawled out here figurin' on dyin'."

Chamberlain shook his head slowly.

Kilrain said, "He's only been in this country a few weeks. He says he'd like to go home. Since now he's free."

Bugles were blowing. The men were moving out into formation. Tom came up with the black mare.

"I don't know what I can do," Chamberlain said. "Give him some food. Bind him up. Make a good bandage. But I don't know what else."

"Which way is home, Colonel?"

"Let's go, Buster."

"Do I point him generally east?"

Chamberlain shrugged. He started to move off, and then he turned, and to the black face looking up, to the red eyes, he looked down and bowed slightly, touching his cap. "Goodbye, friend. Good luck. God bless you."

He rode off feeling foolish and angry, placed himself in front of the Regiment.

The Division was forming on level ground, down the road—great square blocks of blue. The colors were unfurled, the lines were dressed. A stillness came over the corps. They were expecting a review, possibly Meade himself. But no one came. Chamberlain sat on his horse, alone in the sun before the ranks of the Twentieth Maine. He heard Tozier behind him: "Dress it up, dress it up," a muffled complaint, whispers, the far sound of hoofs pawing the ground. His own horse stood quietly, neck down, nibbling Pennsylvania grass. Chamberlain let the mare feed. The day was very hot. He saw a buzzard floating along in the pale blue above, drifting and floating, and he thought of the smell of dead men and chicken hawks swooping down and the only eagle he'd ever seen, in captivity, back in Brewer, a vast wingspread, a murderous eve.

Colonel Vincent came down the line, trailing aides like blue clouds. Chamberlain saluted. Vincent looked very happy.

"We'll be moving up soon. No action this morning. I expect we'll be in reserve."

"Yes, sir."

"Reserve is the best duty. That means they'll use us where we're needed. 'Once more into the breach.'" He grinned brightly, showing teeth almost womanly white. "How does that go, Professor?"

Chamberlain smiled politely.

"You spell breach with an 'a,' am I right? Thought so. I'm a Harvard man myself." Vincent grinned, looked thoughtfully at the Regiment. "Glad you got those extra men. You may need 'em. How they getting along?"

"Fine."

Vincent nodded, reached out cheerily, patted Chamberlain on the arm. "You'll be all right, Colonel. Glad to have you with us. I'm having some beef driven up. If there's time, we'll have a good feed tonight in this brigade."

He was interrupted by bugles, and there it was: *Dan, Dan, Dan, Butterfield, Butterfield.* He swung his horse to listen, saw riders approaching, began to move that way. Over his shoulder he said, "Anything you need, Colonel," and he rode off.

The call came to advance. Chamberlain turned to face the Regiment. He ordered right shoulder arms; the rifles went up. He drew his sword, turned. Down the line the order came: advance. He gave the long order to Tozier, guide in the next regiment, the 118th Pennsylvania. He raised his sword. They began to move, the whole Corps in mass, at slow march forward through a flat farm, a peach orchard. He ordered route step. Looking far off down the line, he saw the men moving in a long blue wave, the heart-stopping sight of thousands of men walking silently forward, rifles shouldered and gleaming in the sun, colors bobbing, the officers in front on high-stepping horses. Chamberlain sucked in his breath: marvelous, marvelous. Behind him he could hear men joking, but he could not hear the jokes. Details of men, in front, were removing white rail fences. He rode past a house, slowed to let the men flow round it, saw a fat woman in a bonnet, a gray dress, standing on the porch, her hands in her apron. She extracted one hand, waved slowly, silently. Chamberlain bowed. Some of the men wished her good morning. A sergeant apologized for marching through her farm. The Regiment moved on across the open place and through a cornfield and some low bushes. Then there was high ground to the right. The front of the Corps swung to face south, rolled forward down a slope through more cornfields. The corn was high and the men tried not to trample it, but that was not possible. It was becoming a long walk, up and down in the heat, but Chamberlain was not tired. They came to a brook, cold water already very dirty from many men moving upstream. Chamberlain sent back word that no one was to fall out to fill a canteen; canteen bearers would be appointed. On the far side of the brook they came upon a broad road and the rear of the army. He saw a long line of dark wagons, a band of Provost guards, men gathered in groups around stacked rifles, small fires. To the right there was an artillery park, dozens of guns and caissons and horses. Beyond the road there was a rise of ground, and at that moment, looking upward toward a broad tree on a knoll just above, a tree with huge branches spread wide in the shape of a cup, full and green against a blue sky, Chamberlain heard the first gun, a cannon, a long soft boom of a gun firing a long way off.

A short while later the Corps was stopped. They were told to stop where they were and rest. The men sat in a flat field, an orchard to the left, trees and men everywhere, higher ground in front of them. They waited. Nothing happened. There was the sound of an occasional cannon. But even the crows nearby were silent. Some of the men began to lie back, to rest. Chamberlain rode briefly off to find out what would happen, but no one knew. When he returned he found himself a place under a tree. It was very hot. He had just closed his eyes when a courier arrived with a message from Meade to read to the troops. Chamberlain gathered them around him in the field, in the sunlight, and read the order.

Hour of decision, enemy on soil. When he came to the part about men who failed to do their duty being punished by instant death, it embarrassed him. The men looked up at him with empty faces. Chamberlain read the order and added nothing, went off by himself to sit down. Damn fool order. Mind of West Point at work.

No time to threaten a man. Not now. Men cannot be threatened into the kind of fight they will have to put up to win. They will have to be led. By *you*, Joshuway, by you. Well. Let's get on with it.

He looked out across the field. The men were sleeping, writing letters. Some of them had staked their rifles bayonet first into the ground and rigged tent cloth across to shade them from the sun. One man had built a small fire and was popping corn. No one was singing.

Kilrain came and sat with him, took off his cap, wiped a sweating red face.

"John Henry's still with us." He indicated the woods to the east. Chamberlain looked, did not see the dark head.

"We ought to offer him a rifle," Kilrain said.

There was a silence. Chamberlain said, "Don't know what to do for him. Don't think there's anything we can do."

"Don't guess he'll ever get home."

"Guess not."

"Suppose he'll wander to a city, Pittsburgh. Maybe New York. Fella can always get lost in a city."

A cannon thumped far off. A soldier came in from foraging, held a white chicken aloft, grinning.

Kilrain said, "God damn all gentlemen."

Chamberlain looked: square head, white hair, a battered face, scarred around the eyes like an old fighter. In battle he moved with a crouch, a fanged white ape, grinning. Chamberlain had come to depend on him. In battle men often seemed to melt away, reappearing afterward with tight mirthless grins. But Kilrain was always there, eyes that saw through smoke, eyes that could read the ground.

Chamberlain said suddenly, "Buster, tell me something. What do you think of Negroes?"

Kilrain brooded.

"There are some who are unpopular," he concluded.

Chamberlain waited.

"Well, if you mean the race, well, I don't really know." He hunched his shoulders. "I have reservations, I will admit. As many a man does. As you well know. This is not a thing to be ashamed of. But the thing is, you cannot judge a race. Any man who judges by the group is a peawit. You take men one at a time, and I've seen a few blacks that earned my respect. A few. Not many, but a few."

Chamberlain said, "To me there was never any difference."

"None at all?"

"None. Of course, I didn't know that many. But those I knew . . . well, you looked in the eye and there was a *man.* There was the divine spark, as my mother used to say. That was all there was to it . . . all there *is* to it."

"Um."

"We used to have visitors from the South before the war. It was always very polite. I never understood them, but we stayed off the question of slavery until near the end, out of courtesy. But toward the end there was no staying away from it, and there was one time I'll never forget. There was this minister, a Southern Baptist, and this professor from the University of Virginia. The professor was a famous man, but more than that, he was a good man, and he had a brain."

"Rare combination."

"True. Well, we sat drinking tea. Ladies were present. I'll never forget. He held the tea like this." Chamberlain extended a delicate finger. "I kept trying to be courteous, but this minister was so damned *wrong* and moral and arrogant all at the same time that he began to get under my skin. And finally he said, like this: 'Look here, my good man, you don't understand.' There was this tone of voice as if he was speaking to a stupid dull child and he was being patient, but running out of patience. Then he said, 'You don't understand. You have to live with the Negro to understand. Let me put it this way. Suppose I kept a fine stallion in one of my fields, and suddenly one of your Northern abolitionists came up and insisted I should free it. Well, sir, I would not be more astonished. I feel exactly that way about my blacks, and I resent your lack of knowledge, sir.' "

Kilrain grunted. Chamberlain said, "I remember him sitting there, sipping tea. I tried to point out that a man is not a horse, and he replied, very patiently, that *that* was the thing I did not understand, that a Negro was not a man. Then I left the room."

Kilrain smiled. Chamberlain said slowly, "I don't really understand it. Never have. The more I think on it the more it horrifies me. How can they look in the eyes of a man and make a slave of him and then quote the Bible? But then right after that, after I left the room, the other one came to see me, the professor. I could see he was concerned, and I respected him, and he apologized for having offended me in my own home."

"Oh yes." Kilrain nodded. "He would definitely do that."

"But then he pointed out that he could not apologize for his views, because they were honestly held. And I had to see he was right there. Then he talked to me for a while, and he was trying to get through to *me*, just as I had tried with the minister. The difference was that this was a brilliant man. He explained that the minister was a moral man, kind to his children, and that the minister believed every word he said, just as I did, and then he said, 'My young friend, what if it is you who are wrong?' I had one of those moments when you feel that if the rest of the world is right, then you yourself have gone mad. Because I was really thinking of killing him, wiping him off the earth, and it was then I realized for the first time that if it was necessary to kill them, then I would kill them, and something at the time said: you cannot be utterly right. And there is still something every now and then which says, 'Yes, but what if you are wrong?'" Chamberlain stopped. A shell burst dimly a long way off, a dull and distant thumping.

They sat for a long while in silence. Then Kilrain said, softly smiling, "Colonel, you're a lovely man." He shook his head. "I see at last a great difference between us, and yet, I admire ye, lad. You're an idealist, praise be."

Kilrain rubbed his nose, brooding. Then he said, "The truth is, Colonel, that there's no divine spark, bless you. There's many a man alive no more value than a dead dog. Believe me, when you've seen them hang each other . . . Equality? Christ in Heaven. What I'm fighting for is the right to prove I'm a better man than many. Where have you seen this divine spark in operation, Colonel? Where have you noted this magnificent equality? The Great White Joker in the Sky dooms us all to stupidity or poverty from birth. No two things on earth are equal or have an equal chance, not a leaf nor a tree. There's many a man worse than me, and some better, but I don't think race or country matters a damn. What matters is justice. 'Tis why I'm here. I'll be treated as I deserve, not as my father deserved. I'm Kilrain, and I God damn all gentlemen. I don't know who me father was and I don't give a damn. There's only one aristocracy, and that's right here—" he tapped his white skull with a thick finger—"and *you,* Colonel laddie, are a member of it and don't even know it. You are damned good at everything I've seen you do, a lovely soldier, an honest man, and you got a good heart on you too, which is rare in clever men. Strange thing, I'm not a clever man meself, but I know it when I run across it. The strange and marvelous thing about you, Colonel darlin', is that you believe in mankind, even preachers, whereas when you've got my great experience of the world you will have learned that good men are rare, much rarer than you think. Ah—" he raised his hands, smiling—"don't you worry about ministers. The more you kill, the more you do the world a service." He chuckled, rubbing his face. His nose was fat and soft, rippling under his fingers.

Chamberlain said, "What has been done to the black is a terrible thing."

"True. From any point of view. But your freed black will turn out no better than many the white that's fighting to free him. The point is that we have a country here where the past cannot keep a good man in chains, and that's the nature of the war. It's the aristocracy I'm after. All that lovely, plumed, stinking chivalry. The people who look at you like a piece of filth, a coachroach, ah." His face twitched to stark bitterness. "I tell you, Colonel, we got to win this war." He brooded. "What will happen, do you think, if we lose? Do you think the country will ever get back together again?"

"Doubt it. Wound it too deep. The differences . . . If they win there'll be two countries, like France and Germany in Europe, and the border will be armed. Then there'll be a third country in the West, and that one will be the balance of power."

Kilrain sat moodily munching on a blade of grass. More cannon thumped; the dull sound rolled among the hills. Kilrain said. "They used to have signs on tavern doors: Dogs and Irishmen keep out. You ever see them signs, Colonel?"

"They burned a Catholic church up your way not long ago. With some nuns in it."

"Yes."

There was a divine spark."

Chamberlain grinned, shook his head. Kilrain turned away. Chamberlain sat for a while silently and then took out a copy of *Harper's Weekly* he'd carried up with him and began to look through it. There was an article by a general from Argentina concerning the use of Negro troops. He said that they fought very well, with training.

Chamberlain's nose wrinkled. The world around him grew silent; there was something in the air. The odor of dead meat came down on the wind, drifting through the trees. Soft and sour, the smell of distant death. It passed like an invisible cloud. Kilrain said, "Make you a little wager, Colonel. We'll sit here all day and in the evening we'll march away again." He lay back. "So I might's well get some rest."

Chamberlain moved back against a tree. He was not tired. He closed his eyes, saw a sudden shocking memory of death, torn flaps of skin, the black rotted meat of muscle.

Kilrain said sleepily, "I bet nothing happens today."

But Chamberlain knew. He was certain. He looked toward the odor of death. Still early in the day. Long time until nightfall. They'll come. He could not relax. But what if it is *you* who are wrong? But I am not wrong. Thank God for that. If I were an officer for *them,* on the other side, what would I be feeling now?

The cannon had stilled. The old soldier was popping corn: pop pop poppity pop.

Chamberlain put down the paper, folded his arms. Waited.

3

LONGSTREET

They had taken a door from its hinges at the Thompson house and placed it across fence rails to serve as a map table. Lee stood above it with his arms folded behind him, staring down. Although the morning was warm and humid his coat was buttoned at the throat, his face pale. He put one hand down, drummed on the map, shook his head, then turned abruptly and walked off to the edge of the trees to look toward Cemetery Hill.

Longstreet sat gazing at the map, fixing it in his mind. Johnston and Clarke had scouted the Union position and it was drawn now on the map in blue ink. Longstreet looked down at the map and then up at the hazy blue ridge in the east, trying to orient himself.

There were two hills beyond Gettysburg: first Cemetery Hill and beyond that Culp's Hill. The Union Army had dug in along the crest of both hills, in a crescent. From the two hills ran a long ridge, like the shaft of a fishhook, Cemetery Ridge, sloping gradually down to the south to two more hills, one rocky and bare, the other high and thickly wooded. Meade had put troops along the ridge so that his position was shaped like the fishhook, but there were no troops yet on the rocky hills.

Longstreet sat alone, a forbidding figure. He was thinking: Lee has made up his mind; there's nothing you can do. Well. Then there will be a scrap. He took a deep breath. Ought to get something to eat.

"General?"

He looked down, saw the handsome face of Taylor, Lee's aide.

"General Lee wishes to speak to you, sir."

Lee was up on the rise by the Seminary, walking back and forth under the shade trees. Officers sat quietly by, joking softly, respectfully with each other, keeping an eye on the old man walking back and forth, back and forth, stopping to stare at the eastern hills, the eastern haze. Longstreet came up.

"General," Lee said.

Longstreet grunted. There was bright heat in Lee's eyes, like fever. Longstreet felt a shudder of alarm.

Lee said, "I like to go into battle with the agreement of my commanders, as far as possible, as you know. We are all members of this army, in a common cause."

Longstreet waited.

"I understand your position," Lee said. "I did not want this fight but I think it was forced upon us. As the war was." He added, "As the war was." He stopped and frowned, put up his fingers and rubbed the bridge of his nose. "Well," he said. He gestured toward the north, toward Ewell. "General Ewell has changed his mind about attacking to the left. He insists the enemy is too firmly entrenched and has been heavily reinforced in the night. I've been over there personally. I tend to agree with him. There are elements of at least three Union corps occupying those hills."

Longstreet waited. Lee had been over to the left, through Gettysburg, to inspect Ewell's position, but he had not been to the right to check on Longstreet. It was a measure of his trust, and Longstreet knew it.

"I spoke to Ewell of your suggestion that he move around to the right. Both he and Early were opposed."

"*Early.*" Longstreet grimaced, spat.

"Yes." Lee nodded. "Both Generals were of the opinion that an attack on the right would draw off Union forces and that they would then be able to take the hills. They insist that withdrawing from Gettysburg, giving it back to the enemy, would be bad for morale, is unnecessary, and might be dangerous."

Lee looked at him, the deep-set eyes still bright, still hot, still questing. Longstreet said nothing.

"You disagree," Lee said.

Longstreet shrugged. He had disagreed last night, had argued all morning, but now he was setting his mind to it. The attack would come.

THE
SECOND DAY
-Morning-
Estimated Union position

"We must attack," General Lee said forcefully. "We *must* attack. I would rather not have done it upon this ground, but every moment we delay the enemy uses to reinforce himself. We cannot support ourselves in this country. We cannot let him work around behind us and cut us off from home. We must hit him now. We pushed him yesterday; he will remember it. The men are ready. I see no alternative."

"Yes, sir," Longstreet said. He wants me to agree. But I cannot agree. Let's get on with it.

Lee waited for a moment, but Longstreet said nothing, and the silence lengthened until at last Lee said, "You will attack on the right with the First Corps."

Longstreet nodded. He took off his hat and wiped the sweat from his brow. He was beginning to relax inside, like an unclenching fist. Now that you knew for sure it was coming a man could rest a bit.

"I want you to attack *en echelon,* to take Cemetery Hill in reverse. Hill will support you with Pender and Anderson. Heth's Division will be in reserve. It had a hard day yesterday. Ewell's people will demonstrate, to keep them from reinforcing against you."

"All right," Longstreet said. "But I don't have Pickett. I have only Hood and McLaws."

Lee said, "You will have to go in without him."

Longstreet said stubbornly, "Law's Brigade is still coming up. I must have Law."

"How long will that take?"

"At least another hour."

"All right." Lee nodded. His head bobbed tightly; he was blinking.

"It will take time to position the men, the artillery."

"At your discretion, General."

"Sir." Longstreet bowed slightly.

"Let us go to the map." Lee turned back toward the table. "I am suspicious of written orders since that affair at Sharpsburg."

Back at the map table men waited for them expectantly. Someone told a joke; there was a ripple of laughter. Lee did not seem to notice.

McLaws and Hood were at a table, along with A. P. Hill. Hill had looked well in the morning, but he did not look well now. Lee bent down over the map. He said, "You will attack up at Emmitsburg Road, up Cemetary Ridge, passing in front of the Rocky Hill. Your objective will be to get in the rear of the Union Army."

McLaws bent over the map. He was a patient man, stubborn and slow, not brilliant, but a dependable soldier. He had a deep streak of sloppy sentimentality to him and he loved to sit around fires singing sad songs of home. He tended to be a bit pompous at times, but he was reliable.

Lee said to McLaws, "Well, General, do you think you can carry this line?"

McLaws shrugged, glanced briefly at Longstreet. He was well aware of Longstreet's theory of defensive tactics. He said pontifically, "Well, sir, I know of nothing to *prevent* my taking that line, but then, of course, I haven't seen it myself. I wouldn't mind taking out a line of skirmishers to reconnoiter the position."

"Unnecessary," Longstreet said. "Waste of time. We've had scouts out all morning. Let's get on with it, General. I don't want you to leave your Division."

McLaws looked to Lee. Lee nodded.

"Yes. Well, we will step off in echelon, from right to left. Ewell will wait until he hears your artillery. The left of your advance will be on the Emmitsburg Road. Your right will sweep under those rocky heights."

THE
SECOND DAY
-Morning-
Lee's plan for Longstreet's
attack on the Union
left flank

"We'll have enfilade fire coming down on us."

"Not for long," Lee said. "You'll be up over the ridge and take them in the rear. When you are heavily engaged, Ewell will take them in front."

Longstreet nodded. It might work. Heavy loss, but it might work.

Hood, who had been silent, said suddenly, softly, "General Lee?"

They turned to face him. Lee considered him a fine tactician, and more than that, Hood was a man you listened to. He said, in that soft voice, "General, I'd like to send one brigade around those rocky heights. I think I can get into their wagon trains back there."

Lee shook his head quickly, raised a hand as if warding him off.

"Let's concentrate, General, concentrate. I can't risk losing a brigade."

Hood said nothing, glanced at Longstreet. McLaws was not quite sure where to post his Division. They discussed that for a while, and then explained it to Hill. Longstreet turned suddenly to Sorrel, who was standing by.

"Major, I need something to eat."

"To eat, sir? Of course, sir. What would you like, sir?"

"Marching food," Longstreet said, "I don't give a damn what."

Sorrel moved off, Longstreet looked up and saw Harry Heth, a white bandage on his head, standing weakly by a tree, looking down vacantly to the map table, trying to comprehend.

"How are you, Harry?" Longstreet said.

Heth turned, squinted, blinked. "I'm fine," he said. "What's happening? Are you going to attack? Where's my Division?"

Lee said, "Your Division will not fight today, General. I want you to rest." There was that tone in his voice, that marvelous warmth, that made them all look not at Heth but at Lee, the graybeard, the dark-eyed, the old man, the fighter.

"Sir, I'm fine," Heth said. But he could not even stand without the hand on the tree.

Lee smiled. "Of course, sir. But I would rather you rested. We will soon be needing you." He turned back to the table. "Gentlemen?" he said.

They moved out. Alexander was off to place the artillery. McLaws moved out to join his Division. Hood walked for a moment at Longstreet's side.

"We marched all night," Hood said. "Took a two hour break, from two A.M. to four, then marched again to get here."

"I know," Longstreet said.

"Law's people will come even farther, with no rest. It's twenty-four miles to Guilford. He left at three A.M. When he gets here he'll be pretty tired." Hood squinted at the sun. "Not that it makes much difference, I guess. But one thing, General. Everybody here's had first crack at the water. I want to round some up for Law's boys when they arrive. They'll be thirsty, wells may be dry."

"See to it," Longstreet said. "Any way you can." He paused, watched the men around him moving into motion, men mounting on horses, cannon moving past and swinging into position, the artillery people beginning to dig trenches alongside the guns. He said, "Your idea of moving to the right was sound, but his mind was set. Well, we'll do what we can." He turned. At moments like this it was difficult to look a man in the eye. He put out his hand.

"Well, Sam, let's go to it. Take care of yourself."

Hood took the hand, held it for a moment. Sometimes you touched a man like this and it was the last time, and the next time you saw him he was cold and white and bloodless, and the warmth was gone forever.

Hood said, "And you, Pete." He walked away, thin, awkward, long bony strides. Longstreet thought: Best soldier in the army. If it can be done, *he* will do it. He and Pickett. My two. Oh God, there's not enough of them. We have to spend them like gold, in single pieces. Once they're gone, there will be no more.

Sorrel appeared with a tin plate, a steaming slab of meat.

"What's that?" Longstreet sniffed.

"Bit of steak, sir. Compliments of Major Moses."

Longstreet picked it up in his fingers, too hot, sucked the ends of his fingers: delicious.

"Major Moses thought you wanted fighting food, sir."

Longstreet ate with slow delight. Hot food for a hot day. Will be much hotter later on.

Longstreet moved toward his command. The corps was to be led into position by Lee's engineer, Captain Johnston, who had scouted the area this morning. Lee had gone off to see Ewell, to explain the attack to him. Longstreet told Johnston, "Time doesn't matter here. What matters is surprise. We *must* go on unobserved. We're hitting them on the flank. If they see us coming they'll have time to swing round their artillery and it'll be a damn slaughter. So you take your time, Captain, but I don't want us observed."

Johnston saluted, his face strained. "Sir," he said, "may I make a point?"

"Make away."

"General Lee has ordered me to conduct you to the field. But, sir, I scouted the Union position this morning, not the roads leading to it. I don't know much more about how to get there than you do."

Longstreet sighed. Stuart's fault. If there were cavalry here, the roads and routes would be known. Longstreet said, "All right, Captain. But anything you know is more than I know."

"But, sir, General Lee is giving me responsibility for an entire corps." Johnston sweated.

"I know, Captain. It's a weight, isn't it? Well. You lead on as best you can. If you get nervous, call. But I don't want us observed."

"Yes, sir, very good, sir." He rode off.

Longstreet took out a treasured cigar, lighted it, chomped it. Stuart. He ought to be court-martialed.

Would you do it? Court-martial Stuart?

Yes, I would.

Seriously? Or are you just talking?

Longstreet thought a moment. Lee wouldn't. Lee won't.

But I would.

The long march began at around noon, the sun high in a cloudless sea of burning haze. A messenger came in from Law: he had joined Hood's column back at Willoughby Run. A superb march. Longstreet sent his compliments, hoped Hood got him the water. On little things like that—a cup of water—battles were decided. Generalship? How much of a factor is it, really?

He rode in the dust of a blazing road, brooding in his saddle. The hot meat had fired him. He rode alone, and then there was cheering behind him, raw, hoarse cheering from dusty throats, and there was Lee—the old man with the slight smile, the eyes bright with new vigor, revived, the fight coming up to warm him like sunrise.

"General." Longstreet touched his cap.

"You don't mind if I accompany you?" Lee said in the gravely formal gentleman's way.

Longstreet bowed. "Glad to have you with us." There was a peculiar hilarity in Longstreet's breast, the mulish foolish hungry feeling you get just before an assault. There was a certain wild independence in the air, blowing like a hot wind inside his head. He felt an absurd impulse to josh old Lee, to pat him on the back and ruffle the white hair and tell immoral stories. He felt foolish, fond and hungry. Lee looked at him and abruptly smiled, almost a grin, a sudden light blazing in black round eyes.

"Heat reminds me of Mexico," Longstreet said. Visions of those days rolled and boiled: white smoke blowing through broken white buildings, wild-haired Pickett going over the wall, man's face with pools of dirt in the eyes, sky wheeling in black blotches, silver blotches, after the wound. *Lieutenant Longstreet: for distinguished service on the field of battle* . . .

"Yes, but there it was very dry." Lee squinted upward. "And I believe it was warmer. Yes, it was undoubtedly warmer."

"That was a good outfit. There were some very good men in that outfit."

"Yes," Lee said.

"Some of them are up ahead now, waiting for us."

And the past flared again in Longstreet's mind, and the world tilted, and for a moment they were all one army again, riding with old friends through the white dust toward Chapultepec. And then it was past. He blinked, grimaced, looked at Lee. The old man was gazing silently ahead into the rising dust.

"It troubles me sometimes," Longstreet said. His mind rang a warning, but he went on grimly, as you ride over rocks. "They're never quite the enemy, those boys in blue."

"I know," Lee said.

"I used to command those boys," Longstreet said. "Difficult thing to fight men you used to command."

Lee said nothing.

"Swore an oath too," Longstreet said. He shook his head violently. Strange thought to have, at the moment. "I must say, there are times when I'm troubled. But . . . couldn't fight against home. Not against your own family. And yet . . . we broke the vow."

Lee said, "Let's not think on this today."

"Yes," Longstreet said. There was a moment of dusty silence. He grumbled to himself: why did you start that? Why talk about that now? Damn fool.

Then Lee said, "There was a higher duty to Virginia. That was the first duty. There was never any doubt about that."

"Guess not," Longstreet said. But we broke the vow.

Lee said, "The issue is in God's hands. We will live with His decision, whichever way it goes."

Longstreet glanced at the dusty face, saw a shadow cross the eyes like a passing wing. Lee said, "I pray it will be over soon."

"Amen," Longstreet said.

They rode for a while in silence, a tiny island in the smoky stream of marching men. Then Lee said slowly, in a strange, soft, slow tone of voice, "Soldiering has one great trap."

Longstreet turned to see his face. Lee was riding slowly ahead, without expression. He spoke in that same slow voice.

"To be a good soldier you must love the army. But to be a good officer you must be willing to order the death of the thing you love. This is . . . a very hard thing to do. No other profession requires it. That is one reason why there are so very few good officers. Although there are many good men."

Lee rarely lectured. Longstreet sensed a message beyond it. He waited. Lee said, "We don't fear our own deaths, you and I." He smiled slightly, then glanced away. "We protect ourselves out of military necessity, not fear. You, sir, do not protect yourself enough and must give thought to it. I need you. But the point is, we are not afraid to die. We are prepared for our own deaths and for the deaths of comrades. We learn that at the Point. But I have seen this happen: We are not prepared for as many deaths as we have to face, inevitably as the war goes on. There comes a time . . ."

He paused. He had been gazing straight ahead, away from Longstreet. Now, black-eyed, he turned back, glanced once quickly into Longstreet's eyes, then looked away.

"We are never prepared for so many to die. So you understand? No one is. We expect some chosen few. We expect an occasional empty chair, a toast to dear departed comrades. Victory celebrations for most of us, a hallowed death for a few. But the war goes on. And the men die. The price gets ever higher. Some officers . . . can pay no longer. We are prepared to lose some of us." He paused again. "But never *all* of us. Surely not all of us. But . . . that is the trap. You can hold nothing back when you attack. You must commit yourself totally. And yet, if they all die, a man must ask himself, will it have been worth it?"

Longstreet felt a coldness down his spine. He had never heard Lee speak this way. He had not known Lee thought of this kind of thing. He said, "You think I feel too much for the men."

"Oh no," Lee shook his head quickly. "Not too much. I did not say 'too much.' But I . . . was just speaking."

Longstreet thought: Possibly? But his mind said: *No.* It is not that. That's the trap all right, but it's not my trap. Not yet. But he thinks I love the men too much. He thinks that's where all the talk of defense comes from. My God . . . But there's no time.

Lee said, "General, you know, I've not been well lately."

That was so unlike him that Longstreet turned to stare. But the face was calm, composed, watchful. Longstreet felt a rumble of unexpected affection. Lee said, "I hope my illness has not affected my judgment. I rely on you always to tell me the truth as you see it."

"Of course."

"No matter how much I disagree."

Longstreet shrugged.

"I want this to be the last battle," Lee said. He took a deep breath. He leaned forward slightly and lowered his voice, as if to confide something terribly important. "You know, General, under this beard I'm not a young man."

Longstreet chuckled, grumbled, rubbed his nose.

A courier came toiling down the dusty lane, pushing his horse through the crowded troops. The man rode to Lee. In this army Lee was always easy to find. The courier, whom Longstreet did not recognize, saluted, then for some unaccountable reason took off his hat, stood bareheaded in the sun, yellow hair plastered wetly all over his scalp.

"Message from General Hood, sir."

"Yes." Politely, Lee waited.

"The General says to tell you that the Yankees are moving troops up on the high Rocky Hill, the one to the right. And there's a signal team up there."*

Lee nodded, gave his compliments.

---

* The Confederates did not know that the local name for that hill was "Little Round Top." During the battle their most common name for it was simply "The Rocky Hill."

"That was to be expected. Tell General Hood that General Meade might have saved himself the trouble. We'll have that hill before night."

The courier put his hat back on and rode off. They rode on for a while in silence. Then Lee halted abruptly in the center of the road. He said, "I suppose I should be getting back. I'll only be in your way."

"Not at all," Longstreet said. But it was Lee's practice to back off, once the fight had begun, and let the commanders handle it. He could see that Lee was reluctant to go. Gradually it dawned on him that Lee was worried for *him*.

"You know," Lee said slowly, looking eastward again, toward the heights, "when I awoke this morning I half thought he'd be gone, General Meade, that he would not want to fight here. When I woke up I thought, yes, Meade will be gone, and Longstreet will be happy, and then I can please Old Pete, my war-horse."

"We'll make him sorry he stayed." Longstreet grinned.

"They fought well yesterday. Meredith's brigade put up a fine fight. They will fight well again today."

Longstreet smiled. "We'll see," he said.

Lee put out a hand. Longstreet took it. The grip no longer quite so firm, the hand no longer quite so large.

"God go with you," Lee said. It was like a blessing from a minister. Longstreet nodded. Lee rode off.

Now Longstreet was alone. And now he felt a cold depression. He did not know why. He chewed another cigar. The army ahead halted. He rode past waiting men, gradually began to become annoyed. He looked up and saw Captain Johnston riding back, his face flushed and worried.

"General," Johnston said, "I'm sorry, but if we go on down this road the enemy will view us."

Longstreet swore. He began to ride ahead, saw Joe Kershaw ahead, on horseback, waiting with his South Carolina Brigade. Longstreet said, "Come on, Joe, let's see what's up."

They rode together, Johnston following, across a road crossing from east to west. On the north corner there was a tavern, deserted, the door open into a black interior. Beyond the tavern was a rise—Herr Ridge, Johnston said, a continuation of the ridge leading out from town, facing Seminary Ridge about a mile away, not two miles from the Rocky Hill. Longstreet rode up from under a clump of trees into the open. In front of him was a broad green field at least half a mile wide, spreading eastward. To the south loomed the Rocky Hill, gray boulders clearly visible along the top, and beyond it the higher eminence of the Round Hill. Any march along here would be clearly visible to troops on that hill. Longstreet swore again.

"Damn!" he roared, then abruptly shut his mouth.

Johnston said worriedly, "General, I'm sorry."

Longstreet said, "But you're dead right. We'll have to find another road." He turned to Kershaw. "Joe, we're turning around. I'm taking over as guide. Send somebody for my staff."

Sorrel and Goree were coming up, then Osmun Latrobe. Longstreet outlined the change: both Divisions would have to stop where they were and turn around. Longstreet rode gloomily back along the line. God, how long a delay would there be? It was after one now. Lee's attack was *en echelon*. That took a long time. Well, we'll get this right in a hurry. He sent Sorrel to Lee with word of the change of direction. Then he scouted for a new path. He rode all the way back to the Cashtown Road, getting madder and madder as he rode. If Stuart had appeared at that moment Longstreet would have arrested him.

To save time, he ordered the brigades to double the line of march. But time was passing. There was a flurry over near the center. Longstreet sent Goree to find out what was happening and it turned out to be nothing much—skirmish of pickets in Anderson's front.

They marched, seventeen thousand men, their wagons, their artillery. Captain Johnston was shattered; it was all his fault. Longstreet propped him up. If it was anybody's fault, it was Stuart's. But it was maddening. He found a new route along Willoughby Run, followed it down through the dark woods. At least it was out of the sun. Most of these men had marched all the day before and all the night and they were fading visibly, lean men, hollow-eyed, falling out to stare whitely at nothing as you passed, and they were expected to march now again and fight at the end of it. He moved finally out through the woods across country in the general direction he knew had to be right and so came at last within sight of that gray tower, that damned rocky hill, but they were under cover of the trees along Seminary Ridge and so there ought to be at least some semblance of surprise. Sorrel rode back and forth with reports to Lee, who was becoming steadily more unnerved, and Sorrel had a very bad habit of being a bit too presumptuous on occasion, and finally Longstreet turned in his saddle and roared, "Sorrel, God damn it! Everybody has his pace. This is mine."

Sorrel retreated to a distance. Longstreet would not be hurried. He placed Hood to the right, then McLaws before him. Anderson's Division of Hill's Corps should be next in line. The soldiers were still moving into line when McLaws was back. He was mildly confused.

"General, I understood General Lee to say that the enemy would be up on the ridge back there and we would attack across the road and up the ridge."

Longstreet said, "That's correct."

McLaws hummed, scratched his face.

"Well?" Longstreet said ominously.

"Well, the enemy's right in front of me. He's dug in just across that road. He's all over that peach orchard."

Longstreet took out his glasses, rode that way, out into the open, looked. But this was a poor point, low ground; there was brush country ahead and he could not see clearly. He began to ride forward. He heard the popping of rifle fire to the north. Nothing much, not yet. But then there was the whine of a bullet in the air, here and past, gone away, death sliding through the air a few feet above him, disappearing behind him. Longstreet grunted. Sniper? From where? He scanned the brush. God knows. Can't worry now. He rode to a rail fence, stared down a slope, saw a battery a long way off, down in flat ground beyond the peach orchard. Blue troops speckled a long fence. He could see them moving rails.

Behind him, McLaws said, "Lot of them."

Longstreet looked up toward the ridge. But he could make out nothing at all. You don't suppose . . . they moved down here? Forward, off the ridge? How many? You don't suppose a whole Corps?

He looked around, spied Fairfax, sent him off with word to Lee.

McLaws said, "What now?"

"Same plan. You hit them. Hood goes first. You key on his last Brigade. That will be G. T. Anderson."

"Right."

Longstreet was running low on aides. He found Goree, sent him off to Hood, telling him to send vedettes ahead to scout the ground. There was not a cavalry-man near, not one horse. Longstreet swore. But he was feeling better. Any minute now it would all begin. All hell would break loose and then no more worrying and

**LONGSTREET'S
COUNTER-
MARCH**

fretting and fuming; he'd hit straight up that road with everything he had. Never been afraid of that. Never been afraid to lose it all if necessary. Longstreet knew himself. There was no fear there. The only fear was not of death, was not of the war, was of blind stupid human frailty, of blind proud foolishness that could lose it all. He was thinking very clearly now. Mind seemed to uncloud like washed glass. Everything cool and crystal. He glanced at his watch. Getting on toward four o'clock. Good God. Lee's echelon plan would never work. Send messenger to Lee. Let's all go in together. The hell with a plan.

But no messenger was available. A moment later one of Hood's boys found him, riding slowly forward, watching McLaws moving into position.

"Sir, message from General Hood. He says his scouts have moved to the right, says there's nothing there. Nothing between us and the Federal train. He suggests most urgently we move around the big hill there and take them from the rear."

Longstreet sighed. "Sonny boy," he said patiently, disgustedly, "you go back and tell Sam that I been telling General Lee that same damn thing for two days, move to the right, and there aint no point in bringing it up again. Tell him to attack as ordered."

The young scout saluted and was gone. Longstreet sat alone. And there was happy-eyed Fremantle, dirty and cheery on a ragged horse. He seemed never to change his clothes.

"General, are things about to commence?"

"They are indeed." Longstreet grinned. "I suggest you find a convenient tree."

"I will, oh, I will indeed." He turned, pulling the horse away, then turned back. "Oh, sir, I say, best of luck."

"Charming," Longstreet said.

Barksdale's Brigade, Mississippians, was passing him, moving into line. He watched them place all extra baggage, all blankets, all kitbags, and post one lone guard—a frail young man who looked genuinely ill, who sagged against the fence. Longstreet approached and saw that the cornsilk hair was not young, not young at all. The frail young man was a gaunt man with white hair. And he was ill. He opened red eyes, stared vaguely upward.

"Howdy, General," he said. He smiled feebly.

Longstreet said, "Can I get you anything?"

The old man shook his head. He gasped. "Aint nothin' serious. Damn green apples. Damn Yankee apples." He clutched his stomach. Longstreet grinned, moved on.

He saw Barksdale from a long way off. The famous politician had his hat off and was waving it wildly and his white hair was flowing and bobbing, conspicuous, distinguished. Longstreet was fond of this Brigade. Privately he thought it the best in McLaws' whole Division, but of course he couldn't say so. But everybody knew Mississippi was tough. What was it that old man said back in Chambersburg? "You men of Virginia are gentlemen. But those people from *Mississippi*." Longstreet grinned. Another fella had said the same thing about Hood's Texans. The joke about breastworks. Oh God, let's go.

The same officer, back from Hood. The face was wary, the voice was firm, "General Hood begs to report, sir, that the enemy has his left flank in the air. He requests your presence, sir, or that of General Lee. He begs to inform you that in his opinion it would be most unwise to attack up the Emmitsburg Road. The ground is very bad and heavily defended. Whereas if we move to the rear, sir, there is no defense all. The enemy has uncovered the Rocky Hill."

Longstreet said, "Tell General Hood . . ." Then he thought: they uncovered the Rocky Hill. McLaws has troops in front of him. Good God. They aren't back on the ridge at all; they've moved forward. He took out the map he had drawn of the position, tried to visualize it.

The Union Army was supposed to be up on the ridge. But it wasn't. It was down in the peach orchard.

He stared at the map again.

So Hood had found an opening to the right. Of course.

Longstreet stared again at his watch. Almost four. Lee was miles away. If I go to him now . . . He saw again the grave gray face, the dark reproachful eyes. Too late.

Well, Longstreet thought, Lee wants a frontal assault. I guess he'll have one. He turned to the messenger.

"Tell General Hood to attack as ordered."

McLaws and Barksdale came up together. Barksdale was breathing deeply, face pale, ready for the fight. He said, "When do we go in?"

"In a while, in a while."

There was a cannon to the right. The beginning? No. Hood was probing with his batteries. Longstreet extracted another cigar. The supply was low. Calmly he told Goree to go get some more. He looked up to see Harry Sellars. Hood's AG. Longstreet thought: Sellars is a good man, the best he has. Hood's trying to impress me. The cannon boomed. Sellars started talking. Longstreet said gently, "Harry, I'm sorry."

Sellars said, his voice touched with desperation, "General, will you *look* at the ground? We can't even mount artillery."

"All right." Longstreet decided to ride with him. Time was running out. Even now, if Lee attacked *en echelon,* some of the brigades could not attack before dark, unless everything went very smoothly, and it would not go smoothly, not today. Longstreet rode, listening to Sellars, thinking: when you study war it's all so clear. Everybody knows all the movements. General So and So should have done such and such. God knows we all try. We none of us lose battles on purpose. But now on this field what can we do that's undone?

He came on Hood, preparing to move out. There was something rare in his face; a light was shining from his eyes. Longstreet had heard men talk of Hood's face in a fight, but he had not seen it; the fight had not yet begun. But Hood's eyes, normally so soft and sad, were wide and black as round coals, shining with a black heat.

Hood said, "General, the ground is strewn with boulders. They are dug in all over the ground and there are guns in the rocks above. Every move I make is observed. If I attack as ordered I will lose half my Division, and they will still be looking down our throats from that hill. We *must* move to the right."

Longstreet said nothing. He looked down; through thick woods he could begin to see the boulders, great boulders tall as houses, piled one upon another like the wreckage of a vast explosion.

Hood said, "How can you mount cannon in that?"

Longstreet: "Sam . . ." He shook his head. He thought of it again. No. Too late. I cannot go against Lee. Not again. He said, "Sam, the Commanding General will not approve a move to the right. I argued it yesterday. I argued it all morning. Hell, I've been arguing against any attack at all. How can I call this one off? We have our orders. Go on in. We're waiting on you."

Hood stared at him with the black round eyes. Longstreet felt an overwhelming wave of sadness. They're all going in to die. But he could say nothing. Hood stared at him.

THE SECOND DAY
-4:00 P.M.-
Actual line attacked by
Longstreet after Sickles'
move forward

Hood: "Let me move to the right, up the Round Hill. If I could get a battery up there . . ."

Longstreet shook his head. "Not enough time. You'd have to cut trees; it would be dark before you were in action."

But he was staring upward at the top of the Rocky Hill. Everywhere you went, that damned hill looked down on you. The key to the position. Once they got a battery up there. Longstreet said, "You're going to have to take that hill."

He pointed.

Hood said, "They don't even need rifles to defend that. All they need to do is roll rocks down on you."

Longstreet said, "But you're going to have to take it."

"General, I do this under protest."

Longstreet nodded. Hood turned. His staff was waiting. He began issuing orders in a low voice. Longstreet backed away. Hood saluted and rode off. Longstreet rode back toward McLaws.

Goodbye, Sam. You're right. You're the best I've got. If I lose you, I don't know what I'll do. God bless you, Sam.

Longstreet was rattled. Never been this rattled in a fight. But the guns began and the sound livened him. We'll brood later. We'll count the dead and brood later. With any luck at all . . . but did you see those rocks?

He rode out into the open. That damned rocky hill stood off to his right, overlooking the field. That they should leave it uncovered was incredible. He saw motion: signal flags? Something was up there. Not a battery, not yet. The fire of Hood was spreading. The first brigade had hit. There was no wind now, the air all dead around him. Hood's smoke stayed where it was, then slowly, very slowly, like a huge ghost, the white cloud came drifting gracefully up the ridge, clinging to the trees, drifting and tearing. The second brigade was following. The fire grew. Longstreet moved to where McLaws and Barksdale were standing together. Wofford had come up.

They all stood together, waiting. The old man who was guarding the clothing of that one Mississippi regiment was asleep against the rail fence, his mouth open. Longstreet rode forward with Barksdale. The man was eager to go in. McLaws moved back and forth, checking the line.

There were woods in front of them, to the left a gray farmhouse. The men were scattered all through the trees, red pennants dipped down, rifles bristling like black sticks. Longstreet saw a shell burst in the woods ahead, another, another. The Yanks knew they were there, knew they were coming. God, did Meade have the whole Union Army here? Against my two divisions?

McLaws came up. Even McLaws was getting nervous.

"Well, sir? When do I go in?"

"Calmly," Longstreet said, "calmly." He stared through his glasses. He could see through the trees a Union battery firing from an orchard on the far side of the road. He said, "We'll all go in directly." Something in Longstreet was savage now; he enjoyed holding them back, the savage power. He could feel the fire building in McLaws, in Barksdale, as water builds behind a damn.

But it was the point of an echelon attack. You begin on one side. The enemy is pressed and begins to move troops there. At the right moment your attack opens in another place. The enemy does not know where to move troops now, or to move any at all. He delays. He is upset where he is, not quite so definite. With luck, you catch him on the move. He does not realize the attack is *en echelon* for a while; he thinks perhaps it is a diversion, and he will be hit on another flank. So he waits, and then gradually he is enveloped where he is, and if his line was thin to begin with, you have not allowed him to concentrate, and if he gambled and concentrated, then he is very weak somewhere, and somewhere you break through. So restraint was necessary now, and Longstreet got down off the horse and sat astride the fence for a while, chatting, the fire growing all around him, shells coming down in the woods ahead, beginning to fall in the field around him, and McLaws stood there blinking and Barksdale running fingers through his hair.

"Not yet, not yet," Longstreet said cheerily, but he got back on his horse and began riding slowly forward into the trees. In the dark of the trees he could smell splintered wood and see white upturned faces with wide white dirty flowers and he looked out to see a battery working steadily, firing into the woods. He heard the first moans but saw no dead. Almost time now. At his elbow, Barksdale was saying something, pleading. The Mississippi boys were staring not at Barksdale but at Longstreet. Longstreet looked down.

"Well," he said, "I guess it's time. If you're ready, sir, why don't you go take that battery, that battery right there?"

He pointed. Barksdale screamed, waved his hat. The men rose. Barksdale formed them in line, the shells zipping the leaves above them. They stepped out of the woods, Barksdale in front, on foot, forbidden to ride, and Longstreet saw them go off across the field and saw the enemy fire open up, a whole fence suddenly puff into white smoke, and the bullets whirred by and clipped among the leaves and thunked the trees, and Longstreet rode out into the open and took off his hat. Barksdale was going straight for the guns, running, screaming, far out in front, alone, as if in a race with all the world, hair streaming like a white torch. Longstreet rode behind him, his hat off, waving, screaming, Go! Go you Mississippi! Go!

4

CHAMBERLAIN

. . . heard the cannon begin. Sat up. Kilrain sat up. Tom Chamberlain went on sleeping, mouth open, saintly young, at peace.

Chamberlain said, "That's mostly in the west."

Kilrain cocked his head, listening. "I thought the Rebs were all up at Gettysburg." He looked at Chamberlain, eyes dark. "You don't suppose they're flanking us again."

The cannons were blossoming, filling the air with thunder, far enough away to soften and roll, not angry yet, but growing.

"At Chancellorsville they came in on the right. This time they could be on the left."

"Do you think they'll ever learn, our goddamn generals?"

Chamberlain shook his head. "Wait."

The men in the field were stirring. Some of the newer men were pulling the tent halves down, but the others, professionals, had rolled over and were staring in the direction of the firing. The corn popper remained asleep.

Chamberlain thought: Alert the men? Some of them were looking to him. One stood up, yawned, stretched, glanced unconcernedly in his direction. Not yet. Chamberlain put the novel away.

Kilrain said, "That's a whole division."

Chamberlain nodded.

"Good thing their artillery aint very good."

A rider had come over the crest of the hill, was loping down through the tall grass among the boulders. Chamberlain stood up. The courier saluted.

"Colonel Vincent's compliments, sir. You are instructed to form your regiment."

Chamberlain did not ask what was going on. He felt a coolness spreading all the way through him. He began buttoning his shirt as the courier rode off—no hurry, why hurry?—and began slipping on the belt and saber. When he was done with that he began smoothing his hair, yawned, grinned, turned to Tozier.

"Sergeant, have the Regiment fall in."

He looked down on Tom, sleeping Tom. Mom's favorite. He'll be all right. Did not want to wake him. Delayed a moment, buttoned his collar. Hot day for that. Shadows growing longer. Cool soon. He nudged Tom with his foot. Tom groaned, licked his lips, groaned again, opened his eyes.

"Hey, Lawrence." He blinked and sat up, heard the thunder. "What's happening?"

"Let's go," Chamberlain said.

"Right." He jumped to his feet. Chamberlain walked out into the sun. Some of the men were in line, forming by companies. The Regiment was bigger now; Chamberlain was glad of the new men. Ellis Spear had come sleepily up, disarranged, eyes wide. Chamberlain told him to bring everybody, cooks and prisoners, sick-call people. Chamberlain took a deep breath, smelled wet grass, hay, felt his heart beating, looked up into God's broad sky, shivered as a thrill passed through him. He looked down through the woods. The whole Brigade was forming.

And nothing happened. The guns thundered beyond the hill. They were in line, waiting. Chamberlain looked at his watch. Not quite four. The men were remarkably quiet, most of them still sleepy. Sergeant Ruel Thomas, an orderly, reported from sick call. Chamberlain nodded formally. Meade had ordered every soldier to action, even the Provost Guards. This was it, the last great effort. Don't think now: rest.

Here, at last, was Vincent, riding at a gallop down the long slope. He reined up, the horse rising-and kicking the air. All the faces watched him.

"Colonel, column of fours. Follow me."

Chamberlain gave the order, mounted, feeling weak. No strength in his arms. Vincent gave orders to aides: they galloped away. Vincent said, "They're attacking the left flank. Sickles has got us in one hell of a jam."

They began moving up the slope. The Twentieth Maine came after them, four abreast. Vincent was shaking his handsome head.

"Damn fool. Unbelievable. But I must say, remarkably beautiful thing to see."

They moved up between rocks. The artillery fire was growing, becoming massive. They found a narrow road leading upward: high ground ahead. Vincent spurred his horse, waved to Chamberlain to come on. They galloped across a wooden bridge, a dark creek, then up a narrow farm road. The firing was louder. A shell tore through the trees ahead, smashed a limb, blasted rock. Fragments spattered the air.

Chamberlain turned, saw Tom's white grinning face, saw him flick rock dust from his uniform, blinking it out of his eyes, grinning bleakly. Chamberlain grimaced, gestured. Tom said, "Whee."

Chamberlain said, "Listen, another one a bit closer and it will be a hard day for Mother. You get back to the rear and watch for stragglers. Keep your distance from me."

"Right, fine." Tom touched his cap, a thing he rarely did, and moved off thoughtfully. Chamberlain felt an easing in his chest, a small weight lifted. Vincent trotted coolly into the open, reined his horse. Chamberlain saw through a break in the trees, blue hills very far away, hazy ridges miles to the west, not ridges, mountains; he was on high ground. Vincent paused, looked back, saw the Regiment coming up the road, shook his head, violently.

"That damn fool Sickles, you know him?"

"Know of him."

Another shell passed close, fifty yards to the left, clipped a limb, ricocheted up through the leaves. Vincent glanced that way, then back, went on.

"The Bully Boy. You know the one. The politician from New York. Fella shot his wife's lover. The Barton Key affair. You've heard of it?"

Chamberlain nodded.

"Well, the damn fool was supposed to fall in on the left of Hancock, right *there*." Vincent pointed up the ridge to the right. "He should be right here, as a matter of fact, where we're standing. But he didn't like the ground." Vincent shook his head, amazed. "He didn't like the ground. So he just up and moved his whole Corps forward, hour or so ago. I saw them go. Amazing. Beautiful. Full marching line forward, as if they were going to pass in review. Moved right on out to the road down there. Leaving his hill uncovered. Isn't that amazing?" Vincent grimaced. "Politicians. Well, let's go."

The road turned upward, into dark woods. Shells were falling up there. Chamberlain heard the wicked hum of shrapnel in leaves.

Vincent said, "Don't mean to rush you people, but perhaps we better double-time."

The men began to move, running upward into the dark. Chamberlain followed Vincent up the rise. The artillery was firing at nothing; there was no one ahead at all. They passed massive boulders, the stumps of newly sawed trees, splinters of shattered ones. Chamberlain could begin to see out across the valley: mass of milky smoke below, yellow flashes. Vincent said, raising his voice to be heard, "Whole damn Rebel army hitting Sickles down there, coming up around his flank. Be here any minute. Got to hold this place. This way."

He pointed. They crossed the crown of the hill, had a brief glimpse all the way out across Pennsylvania, woods far away, a line of batteries massed and firing, men moving in the smoke and rocks below. Chamberlain thought: Bet you could see Gettysburg from here. Look at those rocks, marvelous position.

But they moved down the hill, down into dark woods. Shells were passing over them, exploding in the dark far away. Vincent led them down to the left, stopped in the middle of nowhere, rocks and small trees, said to Chamberlain, "All right, I place you here." Chamberlain looked, saw a dark slope before him, rock behind him, ridges of rock to both sides. Vincent said, "You'll hold here. The rest of the Brigade will form on your right. Looks like you're the flank, Colonel."

"Right," Chamberlain said. He looked left and right, taking it all in. A quiet place in the woods. Strange place to fight. Can't see very far. The Regiment was moving up. Chamberlain called in the company commanders, gave them the position. Right by file into line. Vincent walked down into the woods, came back up.

An aide found him with a message. He sent to the rest of the Brigade to form around the hill to the right, below the crown. Too much artillery on the crown. Rebs liked to shoot high. Chamberlain strode back and forth, watching the Regiment form along the ridge in the dark. The sun was behind the hill, on the other side of the mountain. Here it was dark, but he had no sense of temperature; he felt neither hot nor cold. He heard Vincent say, "Colonel?"

"Yes." Chamberlain was busy.

Vincent said, "You are the extreme left of the Union line. Do you understand that?"

"Yes," Chamberlain said.

"The line runs from here all the way back to Gettysburg. But it stops here. You know what that means."

"Of course."

"You cannot withdraw. Under any conditions. If you go, the line is flanked. If you go, they'll go right up the hilltop and take us in the rear. You must defend this place to the last."

"Yes," Chamberlain said absently.

Vincent was staring at him.

"I've got to go now."

"Right," Chamberlain said, wishing him gone.

"Now we'll see how professors fight," Vincent said.

"I'm a Harvard man myself."

Chamberlain nodded patiently, noting that the artillery fire had slackened. Could mean troops coming this way. Vincent's hand was out. Chamberlain took it, did not notice Vincent's departure. He turned, saw Ruel Thomas standing there with his horse. Chamberlain said, "Take that animal back and tie it some place, Sergeant, then come back."

"You mean leave it, sir?"

"I mean leave it."

Chamberlain turned back. The men were digging in, piling rocks to make a stone wall. The position was more than a hundred yards long, Chamberlain could see the end of it, saw the 83rd Pennsylvania forming on his right. On his left there was nothing, nothing at all. Chamberlain called Kilrain, told him to check the flank, to see that the joint between Regiments was secure. Chamberlain took a short walk. Hold to the last. To the last what? Exercise in rhetoric. Last man? Last shell? Last foot of ground? Last Reb?

The hill was shaped like a comma, large and round with a spur leading out and down:

The Twentieth Maine was positioned along the spur, the other regiments curved around to the right. At the end of the spur was a massive boulder. Chamberlain placed the colors there, backed off. To the left of his line there was nothing. Empty ground. Bare rocks. He peered off into the darkness. He was used to fighting with men on each side of him. He felt the emptiness to his left like a pressure, a coolness, the coming of winter. He did not like it.

He moved out in front of his line. Through the trees to his right he could see the dark bulk of a larger hill. If the Rebs get a battery there. What a mess. This could be messy indeed. He kept turning to look to the vacant left, the dark emptiness. No good at all. Morrill's B Company was moving up. Chamberlain signaled. Morrill came up. He was a stocky man with an angular mustache, like a messy inverted U. Sleepy-eyed, he saluted.

"Captain, I want you to take your company out there." Chamberlain pointed to the left. "Go out a ways, but stay within supporting distance. Build up a wall, dig

Peach Orchard

EMMITSBURG ROAD

Wheat Field

ANDERSON

3rd
ARK.

1st TEX.

Devil's Den

40th
N.Y.   155th PA.

146th N.Y.

4th   4th   91st PA.
ME.   TEX.   140th N.Y.

Little Round Top

44th   48th
ALA.   ALA.

5th TEX.   15th
5th TEX. 47th ALA. ALA.

McLAWS

HOOD

BENNING

Plum Run

TANEYTOWN ROAD

a 16th MICH.
b 44th N.Y.
c 83rd PA.
d 20th ME.

THE SECOND DAY
-5:00 P.M.-
Defense of Devil's Den and Little Round Top

0   500

Yards

Big Round Top

in. I want you there in case somebody tries to flank us. If I hear you fire I'll know the Rebs are trying to get round. Go out a good distance. I have no idea what's out there. Keep me informed."

Company B was fifty men. Alone out in the woods. Chamberlain was sorry. They'd all rather be with the Regiment. Messy detail. Well, he thought philosophically, so it goes. He moved on back up the hill, saw Morrill's men melt into the trees. Have I done all I can? Not yet, not yet.

Artillery was coming in again behind him. All down the line, in front of him, the men were digging, piling rocks. He thought of the stone wall at Fredericksburg. *Never, forever.* This could be a good place to fight. Spirits rose. Left flank of the whole line. Something to tell the grandchildren.

Nothing happening here. He hopped up the rocks, drawn toward the summit for a better look, saw an officer: Colonel Rice of the 44th New York, with the same idea.

Rice grinned happily. "What a view!"

He gestured. Chamberlain moved forward. Now he could see: masses of gray rock wreathed in smoke, gray men moving. If Sickles had a line down there it had already been flanked. He saw a Union battery firing to the south, saw sprays of men rush out of the woods, the smoke, and envelop it, dying, and then the smoke drifted over it. But now more masses were coming, in clots, broken lines, red battle flags plowing through the smoke, moving this way, drifting to the left, toward the base of the hill.

Rice said, glasses to his eyes, "My God, I can see all of it. Sickles is being overrun." He put the glasses down and smiled a foolish smile. "You know, there are an awful lot of people headin' this way."

Chamberlain saw gleams in the woods to the south. Bayonets? Must get back to the Regiment. Rice moved off, calling a thoughtful "good luck." Chamberlain

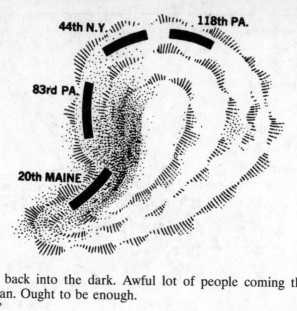

44th N.Y.   118th PA.

83rd PA.

20th MAINE

walked down back into the dark. Awful lot of people coming this way. Sixty rounds per man. Ought to be enough.

"Colonel?"

At his elbow: Glazier Estabrook. Incapable of standing up straight, he *listed*, like a sinking ship. He was chewing a huge plug of tobacco. Chamberlain grinned, happy to see him.

"Colonel, what about these here prisoners?"

Chamberlain looked: six dark forms squatting in the rocks. The hard cases from the Second Maine. He had completely forgotten them.

Glazier said slowly, around the wet plug, "Now I wouldn't complain normal, Colonel, only if there's goin' to be a fight I got to keep an eye on my cousin. You understand, Colonel."

What he meant was that he would under no circumstances tend these prisoners during the coming engagement, and he was saying it as politely as possible. Chamberlain nodded. He strode to the prisoners.

"Any of you fellas care to join us?"

"The Rebs really coming?" The man said it wistfully, cautiously, not quite convinced.

"They're really comin'."

One man, bearded, stretched and yawned. "Well, be kind of dull sittin' up here just a-watchin'."

He stood. The others watched. At that moment a solid shot passed through the trees above them, tore through the leaves, ripped away a branch, caromed out into the dark over the line. A shower of granite dust drifted down. The ball must have grazed a ledge above. Granite dust had salt in it. Or perhaps the salt was from your own lips.

Chamberlain said, "Any man that joins us now, there'll be no charges."

"Well," another one said. He was the youngest; his beard was only a fuzz. "No man will call me a coward," he said. He rose. Then a third, a man with fat on him. The other three sat mute. Two looked away from his eyes; the last looked back in hate. Chamberlain turned away. He did not understand a man who would pass by this chance. He did not want to be with him. He turned back.

"I'll waste no man to guard you. I'll expect to find you here when this is over."

He walked down the hill with the three men, forgetting the incomprehensible three who would not come. He gave the three volunteers to Ruel Thomas, to post along the line. There were no rifles available. Chamberlain said, "You men wait just a bit. Rifles will be available after a while."

And now the softer roar of musketry began opening up behind him; the popping wave of an infantry volley came down from above, from the other side of the hill. The Rebs were pressing the front, against Rice's New York boys, the rest of the brigade. Now there was sharper fire, closer to home; the 83rd was opening up. The battle moved this way, like a wall of rain moving through the trees. Chamberlain strode down along the line. Tom came up behind him, Kilrain above. Private Foss was on his knees, praying. Chamberlain asked that he put in a kind word. Amos Long was sweating.

" 'Tis a hell of a spot to be in, Colonel. I cannot see fifty yards."

Chamberlain laid a hand on his shoulder. "Amos, they'll be a lot closer than that."

Jim and Bill Merrill, two brothers, were standing next to a sapling. Chamberlain frowned.

"Boys, why aren't you dug in?"

Jim, the older, grinned widely, tightly, scared but proud.

"Sir, I can't shoot worth a damn lying down. Never could. Nor Bill either. Like to fight standin', with the Colonel's permission."

"Then I suggest you find a thicker tree."

He moved on. Private George Washington Buck, former sergeant, had a place to himself, wedged between two rocks. His face was cold and gray. Chamberlain asked him how it was going. Buck said, "Keep an eye on me, sir. I'm about to get them stripes back."

A weird sound, a wail, a ghost, high and thin. For a vague second he thought it was the sound of a man in awful pain, many men. Then he knew: the Rebel yell. Here they come.

He drifted back to the center. To Tom he said, "You stay by me. But get down, keep down." Kilrain was sitting calmly, chewing away. He was carrying a cavalry carbine. A great roar of musketry from behind the hill. Full battle now. They must be swarming Sickles under. Kilrain was right. Flank attack. Whole Reb army coming right this way. Wonder who? Longstreet? He it was behind the stone wall at Fredericksburg. Now we have our own stone wall. Chamberlain hopped down along the line, telling men to keep good cover, pile rocks higher, fire slowly and carefully, take their time. Have to keep your eye on some of them; they loaded and loaded and never fired, just went on loading, and some of them came out of a fight with seven or eight bullets rammed home in a barrel, unfired. He looked again to the left, saw the bleak silence, felt a crawling uneasiness. Into his mind came the delayed knowledge: You are the left of the Union. The Army of the Potomac ends here.

He stopped, sat down on a rock.

A flank attack.

Never to withdraw.

He took a deep breath, smelled more granite dust. Never to withdraw. Had never heard the order, nor thought. Never really thought it possible. He looked around at the dark trees, the boulders, the men hunched before him in blue mounds, waiting. Don't like to wait. Let's get on, get on. But his mind said cheerily, coldly: Be patient, friend, be patient. You are not leaving here. Possibly not forever, except, as they say, trailing clouds of glory, if that theory really is true after all and they do send some sort of chariot, possibly presently you will be on it.

My, how the mind does chatter at times like this. Stop thinking. Depart in a chariot of fire. I suppose it's possible. That He is waiting. Well. May well find out.

The 83rd engaged. Chamberlain moved to the right. He had been hoping to face a solid charge, unleash a full volley, but the Rebs seemed to be coming on like a lapping wave, rolling up the beach. He told the right to fire at will. He remained on the right while the firing began. A man down in E Company began it, but there was nothing there; he had fired at a falling branch, and Chamberlain heard a sergeant swearing, then a flurry of fire broke out to the right and spread down the line and the white smoke bloomed in his eyes. Bullets zipped in the leaves, cracked the rocks. Chamberlain moved down closer to the line. Far to the left he could see Tozier standing by the great boulder, with the colors.

Then he saw the Rebs.

Gray-green-yellow uniforms, rolling up in a mass. His heart seized him. Several companies. More and more. At least a hundred men. More. Coming up out of the green, out of the dark. They seemed to be rising out of the ground. Suddenly the terrible scream, the ripply crawly sound in your skull. A whole regiment. Dissolving in smoke and thunder. They came on. Chamberlain could see nothing but smoke, the blue mounds bobbing in front of him, clang of ramrods, grunts, a high gaunt wail. A bullet thunked into a tree near him. Chamberlain turned, saw white splintered wood. He ducked suddenly, then stood up, moved forward, crouched behind a boulder, looking.

A new wave of firing. A hole in the smoke. Chamberlain saw a man on his knees before him, facing the enemy, arms clutching his stomach. A man was yelling an obscene word. Chamberlain looked, could not see who it was. But the fire from his boys was steady and heavy and they were behind trees and under rocks and pouring it in, and Chamberlain saw gray-yellow forms go down, saw a man come bounding up a rock waving his arms wide like a crazy Indian and take a bullet that doubled him right over so that he fell forward over the rocks and out of sight, and then a whole flood to the right, ten or twelve in a pack, suddenly stopping to kneel and fire, one man in fringed clothes, like buckskin, stopping to prop his rifle against a tree, and then to go down, punched backward, coming all loose and to rubbery pieces and flipping back so one bare foot stood up above a bloody rock. A blast of fire at Chamberlain's ear. He turned: Kilrain reloading the carbine. Said something. Noise too great to hear. Screams and yells of joy and pain and rage. He saw bloodstains spatter against a tree. Turned. Fire slowing. They were moving back. Thought: we've stopped 'em. By God and by Mary, we've stopped 'em.

The firing went on, much slower. Smoke was drifting away. But the din from the right was unceasing, the noise from the other side of the hill was one long huge roar, like the ground opening. Kilrain looked that way.

"Half expect 'em to come in from behind."

Chamberlain said, "Did you hear Morrill's Company?"

"No, sir. Couldn't hear nothing in that mess."

"Tom?"

Tom shook his head. He had the look of a man who has just heard a very loud noise and has not yet regained his hearing. Chamberlain felt a sudden moment of wonderful delight. He put out a hand and touched his brother's cheek.

"You stay down, boy."

Tom nodded, wide-eyed. "Damn right," he said.

Chamberlain looked out into the smoke. Morrill might have run into them already, might already be wiped out. He saw: a red flag, down in the smoke and dark. Battle flag. A new burst of firing. He moved down the line, Kilrain following, crouched. Men were down. He saw the first dead: Willard Buxton of K. Neat hole in the forehead. Instantaneous. Merciful. First Sergeant Noyes was with him. Chamberlain touched the dead hand, moved on. He was thinking: with Morrill gone, I have perhaps three hundred men. Few more, few less. What do I do if they flank me?

The emptiness to the left was a vacuum, drawing him back that way. Men were drinking water. He warned them to save it. The new attack broke before he could get to the left.

The attack came all down the line, a full, wild, leaping charge. Three men came inside the low stone wall the boys had built. Two died; the other lay badly wounded, unable to speak. Chamberlain called for a surgeon to treat him. A few feet away he saw a man lying dead, half his face shot away. Vaguely familiar. He turned away, turned back. Half the right jawbone visible, above the bloody leer: face of one of the Second Maine prisoners who had volunteered just a few moments past—the fat one. Never had time to know his name. He turned to Kilrain. "That was one of the Maine prisoners. Don't let me forget."

Kilrain nodded. Odd look on his face. Chamberlain felt a cool wind. He put a hand out.

"Buster? You all right?"

Bleak gray look. Holding his side.

"Fine, Colonel. Hardly touched me."

He turned, showed his side. Tear just under the right shoulder, blood filling the armpit. Kilrain stuffed white cloth into the hole. "Be fine in a moment. But plays hell with me target practice. Would you care for the carbine?"

He sat down abruptly. Weak from loss of blood. But not a bad wound, surely not a bad wound.

"You stay there," Chamberlain said. Another attack was coming. New firing blossomed around them. Chamberlain knelt.

Kilrain grinned widely. "Hell, Colonel, I feel saintly."

"Tom'll get a surgeon."

"Just a bit of bandage is all I'll be needin'. And a few minutes off me feet. Me brogans are killin' me." Lapse into brogue.

Tom moved off into the smoke. Chamberlain lost him. He stood. Whine of bullets, whisking murder. Leaves were falling around him. Face in the smoke. Chamberlain stepped forward.

Jim Nichols, K Company: "Colonel, something goin' on in our front. Better come see."

Nichols a good man. Chamberlain hopped forward, slipped on a rock, nearly fell, hopped to another boulder, felt an explosion under his right foot, blow knocked his leg away, twirled, fell, caught by Nichols. Damned undignified. Hurt? Damn!

How are you, sir?

Looked at his foot. Hole in the boot? Blood? No. Numb. Oh my, begins to hurt now. But no hole, thank God. He stood up.

Nichols pointed. Chamberlain clambered up on a high boulder. Going to get killed, give 'em a good high target. Saw: they were coming in groups, from rock to rock, tree to tree, not charging wildly as before, firing as they came, going down, killing us. But there, back there: masses of men, flags, two flags, flanking, moving down the line. They're going to turn us. They're going to that hole in the left . . .

He was knocked clean off the rock. Blow in the side like lightning bolt. Must be what it feels like. Dirt and leaves in his mouth. Rolling over. This is ridiculous. Hands pulled him up. He looked down. His scabbard rippled like a spider's leg, stuck out at a ridiculous angle. Blood? No. But the hip, oh my. Damn, damn. He stood up. Becoming quite a target. What was that now? He steadied his mind. Remembered: they're flanking us.

He moved back behind the boulder from which he had just been knocked. His hands were skinned; he was licking blood out of his mouth. His mind, temporarily sidetracked, oiled itself and ticked and turned and woke up, functioning. To Nichols: "Find my brother. Send all company commanders. Hold your positions."

Extend the line? No.

He brooded. Stood up. Stared to the left, then mounted the rock again, aware of pain but concentrating. To the left the Regiment ended, a high boulder there. Chamberlain thought: What was the phrase in the manual? Muddled brain. Oh yes: refuse the line.

The commanders were arriving. Chamberlain, for the first time, raised his voice. "You men! MOVE!"

The other commanders came in a hurry. Chamberlain said, "We're about to be flanked. Now here's what we do. Keep up a good hot masking fire, you understand? Now let's just make sure the Rebs keep their heads down. And let's keep a tight hold on the Eighty-third, on old Pennsylvania over there. I want no breaks in the line. That's *you*, Captain Clark, understand? No breaks."

Clark nodded. Bullets chipped the tree above him.

"Now here's the move. Keeping up the fire, and keeping a tight hold on the Eighty-third, we *refuse* the line. Men will sidestep to the left, thinning out to twice the present distance. See that boulder? When we reach that point we'll refuse the line, form a new line at right angles. That boulder will be the salient. Let's place the colors there, right? Five. Now you go on back and move your men in sidestep and form a new line to the boulder, and then back from the boulder like a swinging door. I assume that, ah, F Company will take the point. Clear? Any questions?"

They moved. It was very well done. Chamberlain limped to the boulder, to stand at the colors with Tozier. He grinned at Tozier.

"How are you, Andrew?"

"Fine, sir. And you?"

"Worn." Chamberlain grinned. "A bit worn."

"I tell you this, Colonel. The boys are making a hell of a fight."

"They are indeed."

The fire increased. The Rebs moved up close and began aimed fire, trying to mask their own movement. In a few moments several men died near where Chamberlain was standing. One boy was hit in the head and the wound seemed so bloody it had to be fatal, but the boy sat up and shook his head and bound up the wound himself with a handkerchief and went back to firing. Chamberlain noted: most of our wounds are in the head or hands, bodies protected. Bless the stone wall. Pleasure to be behind it. Pity the men out there. Very good men. Here they come. Whose?

The next charge struck the angle at the boulder, at the colors, lapped around it, ran into the new line, was enfiladed, collapsed. Chamberlain saw Tom come up, whirling through smoke, saw a rip in his coat, thought: no good to have a brother here. Weakens a man. He sent to the 83rd to tell them of his move to the left, asking if perhaps they couldn't come a little this way and help him out. He sent Ruel Thomas back up the hill to find out how things were going there, to find Vincent to tell him that life was getting difficult and we need a little help.

He looked for Kilrain. The old Buster was sitting among some rocks, aiming the carbine, looking chipper. Hat was off. An old man, really. No business here. Kilrain said, "I'm not much good to you, Colonel."

There was a momentary calm. Chamberlain sat.

"Buster, how are you?"

Grin. Stained crooked teeth. All the pores remarkably clear, red bulbous nose. Eyes of an old man. How old? I've never asked.

"How's the ammunition?" Kilrain asked.

"I've sent back."

"They're in a mess on the other side." He frowned, grinned, wiped his mouth with the good hand, the right arm folded across his chest, a bloody rag tucked in his armpit. "Half expect Rebs comin' right over the top of the hill. Nothing much to do then. Be Jesus. Fight makes a thirst. And I've brought nothin' a-tall, would you believe that? Not even my emergency ration against snakebite and bad dreams. Not even a spoonful of Save the Baby."

Aimed fire now. He heard a man crying with pain. He looked down the hill. Darker down there. He saw a boy behind a thick tree, tears running down his face, ramming home a ball, crying, whimpering, aiming fire, jolted shoulders, ball of smoke, then turning back, crying aloud, sobbing, biting the paper cartridge, tears all over his face, wiping his nose with a wet sleeve, ramming home another ball.

Kilrain said, "I can stand now, I think."

Darker down the hill. Sunset soon. How long had this been going on? Longer pause then usual. But . . . the Rebel yell. A rush on the left. He stood up. Pain in the right foot, unmistakable squish of blood in the boot. Didn't know it was bleeding. See them come, bounding up the rocks, hitting the left flank. Kilrain moved by him on the right, knelt, fired. Chamberlain pulled out the pistol. No damn good except at very close range. You couldn't hit anything. He moved to the left flank. Much smoke. Smoke changing now, blowing this way, blinding. He was caught in it, a smothering shroud, hot, white, the bitter smell of burned powder. It broke. He saw a man swinging a black rifle, grunts and yells and weird thick sounds unlike anything he had ever heard before. A Reb came over a rock, bayonet fixed, black thin point forward and poised, face seemed blinded, head twitched. Chamberlain aimed the pistol, fired, hit the man dead center, down he went, folding; smoke swallowed him. Chamberlain moved forward. He expected them to be everywhere, flood of brown bodies, gray bodies. But the smoke cleared and the line was firm. Only a few Rebs had come up, a few come over the stones, all were down. He ran forward to a boulder, ducked, looked out: dead men, ten, fifteen, lumps of gray, blood spattering everywhere, dirty white skin, a clawlike hand, black sightless eyes. Burst of white smoke, again, again. Tom at his shoulder: "Lawrence?"

Chamberlain turned. All right? Boyish face. He smiled.

"They can't send us no help from the Eighty-third." Woodward said they have got their troubles, but they can extend the line a little and help us out."

"Good. Go tell Clarke to shift a bit, strengthen the center."

Kilrain, on hands and knees, squinting: "They keep coming in on the flank."

Chamberlain, grateful for the presence: "What do you think?"

"We've been shooting a lot of rounds."

Chamberlain looked toward the crest of the hill. No Thomas anywhere. Looked down again toward the dark. Motion. They're forming again. Must have made five or six tries already. To Kilrain: "Don't know what else to do."

Looked down the line. Every few feet, a man down. Men sitting facing numbly to the rear. He thought: let's pull back a ways. He gave the order to Spear. The Regiment bent back from the colors, from the boulder, swung back to a new line, tighter, almost a U. The next assault came against both flanks and the center all at once, worst of all. Chamberlain dizzy in the smoke began to lose track of events, saw only blurred images of smoke and death, Tozier with the flag, great black gaps in the line, the left flank giving again, falling back, tightening. Now there was only a few yards between the line on the right and the line on the left, and Chamberlain walked the narrow corridor between, Kilrain at his side, always at a crouch.

Ruel Thomas came back. "Sir? Colonel Vincent is dead."

Chamberlain swung to look him in the face. Thomas nodded jerkily.

"Yes, sir. Got hit a few moments after fight started. We've already been reinforced by Weed's Brigade, up front, but now Weed is dead, and they moved Hazlett's battery in up top and Hazlett's dead."

Chamberlain listened, nodded, took a moment to let it come to focus.

"Can't get no ammunition, sir. Everything's a mess up there. But they're holdin' pretty good. Rebs having trouble coming up the hill. Pretty steep."

"Got to have bullets," Chamberlain said.

Spear came up from the left. "Colonel, half the men are down. If they come again . . ." He shrugged, annoyed, baffled as if by a problem he could not quite solve, yet ought to, certainly, easily. "Don't know if we can stop 'em."

"Send out word," Chamberlain said. "Take ammunition from the wounded. Make every round count." Tom went off, along with Ruel Thomas. Reports began coming in. Spear was right. But the right flank was better, not so many casualties there. Chamberlain moved, shifting men. And heard the assault coming, up the rocks, clawing up through the bushes, through the shattered trees, the pocked stone, the ripped and bloody earth. It struck the left flank. Chamberlain shot another man, an officer. He fell inside the new rock wall, face a bloody rag. On the left two Maine men went down, side by side, at the same moment, and along that spot there was no one left, no one at all, and yet no Rebs coming, just one moment of emptiness in all the battle, as if in that spot the end had come and there were not enough men left now to fill the earth, that final death was beginning there and spreading like a stain. Chamberlain saw movements below, troops drawn toward the gap as toward a cool place in all the heat, and looking down, saw Tom's face and yelled, but not being heard, pointed and pushed, but his hand stopped in mid-air, not my own brother, but Tom understood, hopped across to the vacant place and plugged it with his body so that there was no longer a hole but one terribly mortal exposed boy, and smoke cut him off, so that Chamberlain could no longer see, moving forward himself, had to shoot another man, shot him twice, the first ball taking him in the shoulder, and the man was trying to fire a musket with one hand when Chamberlain got him again, taking careful aim this time. Fought off this assault, thinking all the while coldly, calmly, perhaps now we are approaching the end. They can't keep coming. We can't keep stopping them.

Firing faded. Darker now. Old Tom. Where?

Familiar form in familiar position, aiming downhill, firing again. All right. God be praised.

Chamberlain thought: not right, not right at all. If he was hit, I sent him there. What would I tell Mother? What do I feel myself? His duty to go. No, no. Chamberlain blinked. He was becoming tired. Think on all that later, the theology of it.

He limped along the line. Signs of exhaustion. Men down, everywhere. He thought: we cannot hold.

Looked up toward the crest. Fire still hot there, still hot everywhere. Down into the dark. They are damned good men, those Rebs. Rebs, I salute you. I don't think we can hold you.

He gathered with Spear and Kilrain back behind the line. He saw another long gap, sent Ruel Thomas to this one. Spear made a count.

"We've lost a third of the men, Colonel. Over a hundred down. The left is too thin."

"How's the ammunition?"

"I'm checking."

A new face, dirt-stained, bloody: Homan Melcher, Lieutenant, Company F, a gaunt boy with buck teeth.

"Colonel? Request permission to go pick up some of our wounded. We left a few boys out there."

"Wait," Chamberlain said.

Spear came back, shaking his head. "We're out." Alarm stained his face, a grayness in his cheeks.

"Some of the boys have nothing at all."

"Nothing," Chamberlain said.

Officers were coming from the right. Down to a round or two per man. And now there was a silence around him. No man spoke. They stood and looked at him, and then looked down into the dark and then looked back at Chamberlain. One man said, "Sir, I guess we ought to pull out."

Chamberlain said, "Can't do that."

Spear: "We won't hold 'em again. Colonel, you know we can't hold 'em again."

Chamberlain: "If we don't hold, they go right on by and over the hill and the whole flank caves in."

He looked from face to face. The enormity of it, the weight of the line, was a mass too great to express. But he could see it as clearly as in a broad wide vision, a Biblical dream: If the line broke here, then the hill was gone, all these boys from Pennsylvania, New York, hit from behind above. Once the hill went, the flank of the army went. Good God! He could see troops running; he could see the blue flood, the bloody tide.

Kilrain: "Colonel, they're coming."

Chamberlain marveled. But we're not so bad ourselves. One recourse: Can't go back. Can't stay where we are. Results: inevitable.

The idea formed.

"Let's fix bayonets," Chamberlain said.

For a moment no one moved.

"We'll have the advantage of moving downhill," he said.

Spear understood. His eyes saw; he nodded automatically. The men coming up the hill stopped to volley; weak fire came in return. Chamberlain said, "They've got to be tired, those Rebs. They've got to be close to the end. Fix bayonets. Wait. Ellis, you take the left wing. I want a right wheel forward of the whole Regiment."

Lieutenant Melcher said, perplexed, "Sir, excuse me but what's a 'right wheel forward'?"

Ellis Spear said, "He means 'charge,' Lieutenant, 'charge.'"

Chamberlain nodded. "Not quite. We charge swinging down to the right. We straighten out our line. Clarke hangs onto the Eighty-third, and we swing like a door, sweeping them down the hill. Understand? Everybody understand? Ellis, you take the wing, and when I yell you go to it, the whole Regiment goes forward, swinging to the right."

"Well," Ellis Spear said. He shook his head. "Well."

"Let's go." Chamberlain raised his saber, bawled at the top of his voice, "Fix bayonets!"

He was thinking: We don't have two hundred men left. Not two hundred. More than that coming at us. He saw Melcher bounding away toward his company, yelling, waving. Bayonets were coming out, clinking, clattering. He heard men beginning to shout, Marine men, strange shouts, hoarse, wordless, animal. He limped to the front, toward the great boulder where Tozier stood with the colors, Kilrain at his side. The Rebs were in plain view, moving, firing. Chamberlain saw clearly a tall man aiming a rifle at him. At *me.* Saw the smoke, the flash, but did not hear the bullet go by. Missed. Ha! He stepped out into the open, balanced on the gray rock. Tozier had lifted the colors into the clear. The Rebs were thirty yards off. Chamberlain raised his saber, let loose the shout that was the greatest sound he could make, boiling the yell up from his chest: *Fix bayonets! Charge! Fix bayonets! Charge! Fix bayonets! Charge!* He leaped down from the boulder, still screaming, his voice beginning to crack and give, and all around him his men were roaring animal screams, and he saw the whole Regiment rising and pouring over the wall and beginning to bound down through the dark bushes, over the dead and dying and wounded, hats coming off, hair flying, mouths making sounds, one man firing as he ran, the last bullet, last round. Chamberlain saw gray men below stop, freeze, crouch, then quickly turn. The move was so quick he could not believe it. Men were turning and running. Some were stopping to fire. There was the yellow flash and then they turned. Chamberlain saw a man drop a rifle and run. Another. A bullet plucked at Chamberlain's coat, a hard pluck so that he thought he had caught a thorn but looked down and saw the huge gash. But he was not hit. He saw an officer: handsome full-bearded man in gray, sword and revolver. Chamberlain ran toward him, stumbled, cursed the bad foot, looked up and aimed and fired and missed, then held aloft the saber. The officer turned, saw him coming, raised a pistol, and Chamberlain ran toward it downhill, unable to stop, stumbling downhill seeing the black hole of the pistol turning toward him, not anything but the small hole yards away, feet away, the officer's face a blur behind it and no thought, a moment of gray suspension rushing silently, soundlessly toward the black hole . . . and the gun did not fire; the hammer clicked down on an empty shell, and Chamberlain was at the man's throat with the saber and the man was handing him his sword, all in one motion, and Chamberlain stopped.

"The pistol too," he said.

The officer handed him the gun: a cavalry revolver, Colt.

"Your prisoner, sir." The face of the officer was very white, like old paper. Chamberlain nodded.

He looked up to see an open space. The Rebs had begun to fall back; now they were running. He had never seen them run; he stared, began limping forward to see. Great cries, incredible sounds, firing and yelling. The Regiment was driving a line, swinging to the right, into the dark valley. Men were surrendering. He saw masses of gray coats, a hundred or more, moving back up the slope to his front, in good order, the only ones not running, and thought: If they form again we're in trouble, desperate trouble, and he began moving that way, ignoring the officer he had just captured. At that moment a new wave of firing broke out on the other side of the gray mass. He saw a line of white smoke erupt, the gray troops waver and move back this way, stop, rifles begin to fall, men begin to run to the right, trying to get away. Another line of fire—Morrill. B Company. Chamberlain moved that way. A soldier grabbed his Reb officer, grinning, by the arm. Chamberlain passed a man sitting on a rock, holding his stomach. He had been bayoneted. Blood coming from his mouth. Stepped on a dead body, wedged between rocks. Came upon Ellis Spear, grinning crazily, foolishly, face stretched and glowing with a wondrous light.

"By God, Colonel, by God, by God," Spear said. He pointed. Men were running off down the valley. The Regiment was moving across the front of the 83rd Pennsylvania. He looked up the hill and saw them waving and cheering. Chamberlain said, aloud, "I'll be damned."

The Regiment had not stopped, was chasing the Rebs down the long valley between the hills. Rebs had stopped everywhere, surrendering. Chamberlain said to Spear, "Go on up and stop the boys. They've gone far enough."

"Yes, sir. But they're on their way to Richmond."

"Not today," Chamberlain said. "They've done enough today."

He stopped, took a deep breath, stood still, then turned to look for Tom. Saw Morrill, of Company B, wandering toward him through thick brush.

"Hey, Colonel, glad to see you. I was beginning to wonder."

Chamberlain stared. *"You* were beginning to wonder?"

"I tell you, Colonel, I keep thinking I better come back and help you, but you said stay out there and guard that flank, so I did, and I guess it come out all right, thank the Lord. Nobody came nowhere near me until just a few minutes ago. Then they come *backin'* my way, which I didn't expect. So we opened up, and they all turned around and quit, just like that. Damnedest thing you ever saw." He shook his head, amazed. "Easiest fight I was ever in."

Chamberlain sighed. "Captain," he said, "next time I tell you to go out a ways, please don't go quite so far."

"Well, Colonel, we looked around, and there was this here stone wall, and it was *comfortin'*, you know?"

Tom was here, well, untouched. Chamberlain opened up into a smile. Tom had a Reb officer in tow, a weary gentleman with a face of grime and sadness, of exhausted despair.

"Hey, Lawrence, want you to meet this fella from Alabama. Cap'n Hawkins, want you to meet my brother. This here's Colonel Chamberlain."

Chamberlain put out a hand. "Sir," he said. The Alabama man nodded slightly. His voice was so low Chamberlain could hardly hear it. "Do you have some water?"

"Certainly." Chamberlain offered his own canteen. Off to the right a huge mass of prisoners: two hundred, maybe more. Most of them sitting, exhausted, heads down. Only a few men of the Regiment here, mostly Morrill's Company. Ironic. Chamberlain thought: well, he's the only one with ammunition.

Firing was slacking beyond the hill. The charge of the 20th Maine had cleared the ground in front of the 83rd Pennsylvania; they were beginning to move down the hill, rounding up prisoners. As the Reb flank on this side fell apart and running men began to appear on the other side of the hill the attack there would break up. Yes, firing was less. He heard whoops and hollers, felt a grin break out as if stepping into lovely sunshine. We did it, by God.

The Alabama man was sitting down. Chamberlain let him alone. Kilrain. Looked. Where? He moved painfully back up the rocks toward the position from which they had charged. Hip stiffening badly. Old Kilrain. Unhurtable.

He saw Kilrain from a distance. He was sitting on a rock, head back against a tree, arm black with streaked blood. But all right, all right, head bobbing bareheaded like a lively mossy white rock. Ruel Thomas was with him, and Tozier, working on the arm. Chamberlain bounded and slipped on wet rocks, forgetting his hurts, his throat stuffed. He knelt. They had peeled back the shirt and the arm was whitely soft where they had cleaned it and there was a mess around the shoulder. Great round muscle: strong old man. Chamberlain grinned, giggled, wiped his face.

"Buster? How you doin'? You old mick."

Kilrain peered at him vaguely cheerily. His face had a linen softness.

"They couldn't seem hardly to miss," he said regretfully, apologizing. "Twice, would you believe. For the love of Mary. *Twicet.*"

He snorted, gloomed, looked up into Chamberlain's eyes and blinked.

"And how are *you,* Colonel darlin'? This fine day?"

Chamberlain nodded, grinning foolishly. There was a tight long silent moment. Chamberlain felt a thickness all through his chest. It was like coming back to your father, having done something fine, and your father knows it, and you can see the knowledge in his eyes, and you are both too proud to speak of it. But he knows. Kilrain looked away. He tried to move bloody fingers.

"In the armpit," he gloomed forlornly. "For the love of God. He died of his wounds. In the bloody bleedin' *armpit.* Ak."

To Tozier, Chamberlain said, "How is that?"

Tozier shrugged. "It's an arm."

"By God," Chamberlain said. "I think you'll live."

Kilrain blinked hazily. "Only an arm. Got to lose something, might's well be an arm. Can part with that easier than the other mechanics of nature, an thass the truth." He was blurring; he stretched his eyes. "Used to worry about that, you know? Only thing ever worried, really. Losing wrong part." His eyes closed; his voice was plaintive. "I could do with a nip right now."

"I'll see what I can do."

"You do pretty good." Kilrain blinked, peered, looking for him.

"Colonel?"

"Right here."

"The army was blessed . . ." But he ran out of breath, closed his eyes.

"You take it easy."

"Want you to know. Just in case. That I have never served . . ." He paused to breathe, put out the bloody hand, looked into Chamberlain's eyes. "Never served under a better man. Want you to know. Want to thank you, sir."

Chamberlain nodded. Kilrain closed his eyes. His face began to relax; his skin was very pale. Chamberlain held the great cold hand. Chamberlain said, "Let me go round up something medicinal."

"I'd be eternal grateful."

"You rest." Chamberlain was feeling alarm.

Tozier said, "I've sent off."

"Well I've seen them run," Kilrain said dreamily. "Glory be. Thanks to you, Colonel darlin'. Lived long enough to see the Rebs run. Come the Millennium. Did you see them run, Colonel darlin'?"

"I did."

"I got one fella. Raggedy fella. Beautiful offhand shot, if I say so mesel'."

"I've got to go, Buster."

"He was drawin' a bead on you, Colonel. I got him with one quick shot offhand. Oh lovely." Kilrain sighed. "Loveliest shot I ever made."

"You stay with him, Sergeant," Chamberlain said.

Thomas nodded.

"Be back in a while, Buster."

Kilrain opened his eyes, but he was drifting off toward sleep, and he nodded but did not see. Chamberlain backed away. There were some men around him from the old Second Maine and he talked to them automatically, not knowing what he was saying, thanking them for the fight, looking on strange young bloody faces. He moved back down the slope.

He went back along the low stone wall. The dead were mostly covered now with blankets and shelter halves, but some of them were still dying and there were groups of men clustered here and there. There were dead bodies and wounded bodies all down the wall and all down through the trees and blood was streaked on the trees and rocks and rich wet wood splinters were everywhere. He patted shoulders, noted faces. It was very quiet and dark down among the trees. Night was coming. He began to feel tired. He went on talking. A boy was dying. He had made a good fight and he wanted to be promoted before he died and Chamberlain promoted him. He spoke to a man who had been clubbed over the head with a musket and who could not seem to say what he wanted to say, and another man who was crying because both of the Merrill boys were dead, both brothers, and he would be the one who would have to tell their mother. Chamberlain reached the foot of the hill and came out into the last light.

Ellis Spear came up. There were tears in the corners of his eyes. He nodded jerkily, a habit of Maine men, a greeting.

"Well," he said. He did not know what to say. After a moment he pulled out an impressively ornamented silver flask, dented, lustrous.

"Colonel? Ah, I have a beverage here which I have been saving for an, ah, appropriate moment. I think this is—well, would the Colonel honor me by joining me in a, ah, swallow?"

Chamberlain thought: Kilrain. But he could not hurt Spear's feelings. And his mouth was gritty and dry. Spear handed it over solemnly, gravely, with the air of a man taking part in a ceremony. Chamberlain drank. Oh, good. Very, very good. He saw one small flicker of sadness pass over Spear's face, took the bottle from his lips.

"Sorry, Ellis. 'Swallow' is a flighty word. An indiscriminate word. But thank you. Very much. And now."

Spear bowed formally. "Colonel, it has been my pleasure."

Here through the rocks was a grinning Tom. Young Tom. Only a boy. Chamberlain felt a shattering rush of emotion, restrained it. Behind Tom were troops of the 83rd Pennsylvania: Captain Woodward, Colonel Rice of the 44th New York. Chamberlain thought: Rice must be the new commander of the whole brigade.

Tom said with vast delight, ticking them off, "Lawrence, we got prisoners from the Fifteenth Alabama, the Forty-seventh Alabama, the Fourth and Fifth Texas. Man, we fought four Reb regiments!"

Four regiments would be perhaps two thousand men. Chamberlain was impressed.

"We got five hundred prisoners," Tom insisted.

The figure seemed high. Chamberlain: "What are our casualties?"

Tom's face lost its light. "Well, I'll go check."

Colonel Rice came up. Much darker now. He put out a hand.

"Colonel Chamberlain, may I shake your hand?"

"Sir."

"Colonel, I watched that from above. Colonel, that was the damnedest thing I ever saw."

"Well," Chamberlain said. A private popped up, saluted, whispered in Chamberlain's ear: "Colonel, sir, I'm guardin' these here Rebs with a empty rifle."

Chamberlain grinned. "Not so loud. Colonel Rice, we sure could use some ammunition."

Rice was clucking like a chicken. "Amazing. They ran like sheep."

Woodward said, "It was getting a bit tight there, Colonel, I'll say."

Rice wandered about, stared at the prisoners, wandered back, hands behind him, peered at Chamberlain, shook his head.

"You're not Regular Army?"

"No, sir."

"Oh yes. You're the professor. Um. What did you teach?"

"Rhetoric, sir."

"Really?" Rice grimaced. "Amazing." After a moment: "Where'd you get the idea to charge?"

Chamberlain said, "We were out of ammunition."

Rice nodded. "So. You fixed bayonets."

Chamberlain nodded. It seemed logical enough. It was beginning to dawn on him that what he had done might be considered unusual. He said, "There didn't seem to be any alternative."

Rice shook his head, chuckled, grunted.

Chamberlain said, "I heard about Colonel Vincent."

"Yes. Damn shame. They think he won't make it."

"He's still alive?"

"Not by much."

"Well. But there's always hope."

Rice looked at him. "Of course," Rice said.

Chamberlain wandered among his men. Ought to put them in some kind of order. He was beginning to feel an elation in him, like a bubble blowing up in his chest. A few moments later, Rice was back.

"Colonel, I have to ask your help. You see the big hill there, the wooded hill? There's nobody there. I think. General Warren wants that hill occupied. Could you do that?"

"Well," Chamberlain said. "If we had some ammunition."

"I'll move a train up. That hill's been unoccupied all day. If the Rebs get a battery there . . . it's the extreme flank of the Union line. Highest ground. Warren sends you his compliments and says to tell you he would prefer to have your regiment there."

Chamberlain said, "Well of course, sir. But the boys are tired. May take a while. And I sure need that ammunition."

"Right. I'll tell the General you'll be up soon as possible."

Chamberlain squinted. A wall of trees, thick brush. He sighed.

Tom was back. "I count about one hundred and thirty men, Lawrence. Forty to fifty already dead, about ninety wounded. Lot of boys walking around with minor stuff, one hundred thirty for the hospital."

Chamberlain thought: one hundred thirty down. We had three hundred in line. Almost half the Regiment. Kilrain is gone.

He told Spear of the move. He was becoming very tired. But along with the weariness he felt spasms of pure joy. Spear formed the Company, Rice took over the prisoners. Rice came by to watch them go.

"Colonel," Chamberlain said. "One thing. What's the name of this place? This hill. Has it got a name?"

"Little Round Top," Rice said. "Name of the hill you defended. The one you're going to is Big Round Top."

Little Round Top. Battle of Little Round Top. Well. I guess we'll remember it.

"Move 'em out, Ellis."

He went back to say goodbye to Kilrain. The white head was visible from a long way off, sitting stumplike, motionless in the dark of the trees. He had leaned back and was staring at the sky, his eyes closed. He had welcomed Chamberlain to the

Regiment and there had never been a day without him. He would be going to the hospital now, and Chamberlain did not know what to say, did not know how to express it. Blue eyes opened in a weary face. Kilrain smiled.

"I'll be going, Buster," Chamberlain said.

Kilrain grumbled, looked sourly, accusingly at his bloody wound.

"Damn."

"Well, you take care. I'll send Tom back with word."

"Sure."

"We'll miss you. Probably get into all kinds of trouble without you."

"No." Kilrain said. "You'll do all right."

"Well, I have to go."

"Right. Goodbye, Colonel."

He put out a hand, formally. Chamberlain took it.

"It was a hell of a day, wasn't it, Buster?"

Kilrain grinned, his eyes glistened.

"I'll come down and see you tomorrow." Chamberlain backed off.

"Sure." Kilrain was blinking, trying to keep his eyes open. Chamberlain walked away, stopped, looked back, saw the eyes already closed, turned his back for the last time, moved off into the gathering dark.

He moved forward and began to climb the big hill in the dark. As he walked he forgot his pain; his heart began to beat quickly, and he felt an incredible joy. He looked at himself, wonderingly, at the beloved men around him, and he said to himself: Lawrence, old son, treasure this moment. Because you feel as good as a man can feel.

5

LONGSTREET

The hospital was an open field just back of the line. There were small white tents all over the field and bigger tents where the surgeons did the cutting. Hood was there, in a big tent, on a litter. Longstreet came in out of the dark, bowing under a canopy, saw the face like cold marble in yellow candlelight, eyes black and soft like old polished stones. Cullen and Maury were working together on the arm. Longstreet saw; not much left of the hand. Exposed bone. He thought of Jackson hit in the arm at Chancellorsville: died a slow death. *Let us cross over the river.* Hood's black eyes stared unseeing. Longstreet said softly, "Sam?"

Cullen looked up; Maury was tying a knot, went on working. Troops had gathered outside the canopy. A sergeant bawled: move on, move on. Hood stared at Longstreet, not seeing. There was dirt streaked in tear stains on his cheeks, but he was not crying now. His head twitched, cheek jerked. He said suddenly, in a light, strange, feathery voice, "Should have let me move to ri—" He breathed. "To the right."

Longstreet nodded. To Cullen, he said, "Can I talk to him?"

"Rather not. We've drugged him. Sir. Better let him sleep."

Hood raised the other arm, twitched fingers, let the hand fall. "Din see much. Boys went in an' hit the rocks. I got hit."

Longstreet, no good at talking, nodded.

"Should have moved right, Pete." Hood was staring at him, bright, drugged, eerie eyes. "How did it go, Pete?" "Fine, Sam,"

"We took those rocks?"

"Most of 'em."

"Took the rocks. Really did."

"Yes," Longstreet lied.

Hood's eyes blinked slowly, blearily. He put the good hand up to shade his eyes.

"Devil's Den. Good name for it."

"Yep."

"Worst ground I ever saw, you know that?" Hood laid the back of his hand across his eyes. His voice trembled. "Got to give my boys credit."

Longstreet said to Cullen, "Can you save the arm?"

"We're trying. But if we do, it won't be much use to him."

Hood said, "Casualties? Was casualties?"

"Don't know yet," Longstreet said. And then: "Not bad." Another lie.

Cullen said gloomily, plaintively, "He ought to go to sleep. Now don't fight it, General. Let it work. You just drift right on off."

Longstreet said softly, "You go to sleep now, Sam. Tell you all about it tomorrow."

"Shame not to see it." Hood took the hand away. His eyes were dreaming, closing like small doors over a dim light. "Should have gone to the right." He looked hazily at the hand. "You fellas try to save that now, you hear?"

"Yes, sir, General. Now why don't you . . . ?"

"Sure will miss it." Hood's eyes closed again; his face began smoothing toward sleep. Longstreet thought: he won't die. Not like Jackson. There was a blackness around Jackson's eyes. Longstreet reached down, touched Hood on the shoulder, then turned and went out into the moonlight.

Sorrel was there, with the silent staff. Longstreet mounted, rising up into the moonlight, looking out across the pale tents at the small fires, the black silence. He heard a boy crying, pitiful childish sobs, a deeper voice beyond soothing. Longstreet shook his head to clear the sound, closed his eyes, saw Barksdale go streaming to his death against a flaming fence in the brilliant afternoon, hair blazing out behind him like white fire. Longstreet rode up the ridge toward the darker ground under the trees. Barksdale lies under a sheet. They have not covered his face; there is a flag over him. Semmes is dead. How many others? Longstreet cleared the brain, blew away bloody images, the brilliant fence in the bright gleaming air of the afternoon, tried to catalogue the dead. Must have figures. But he was not thinking clearly. There was a rage in his brain, a bloody cloudy area like mud stirred in a pool. He was like a fighter who has been down once and is up again, hurt and in rage, looking to return the blow, looking for the opening. But it was a silent rage, a crafty rage; he was learning war. He rode purposefully, slowly off into the dark feeling the swelling inside his chest like an unexploded bomb and in the back of his mind a vision of that gray rocky hill* all spiked with guns, massed with blue troops at the top, and he knew as certainly as

* Little Round Top.

he had ever known anything as a soldier that the hill could not be taken, not any more, and a cold, metal, emotionless voice told him that coldly, calmly, speaking into his ear as if he had a companion with him utterly untouched by the rage, the war, a machine inside wholly unhurt, a metal mind that did not feel at all.

"Sir?"

Longstreet swiveled in the saddle: Sorrel. The man said warily, "Captain Goree is here, sir. Ah, you sent for him."

Longstreet looked, saw the skinny Texan, gestured. Sorrel backed off. Longstreet said, "T. J. Want you to get out to the right and scout the position. No more damn fool counter-marches in the morning. Take most of the night but get it clear, get it clear. I've got Hood's Division posted on our right flank. Or what's left of it. I've put Law in command. You need any help, you get it from Law, all right?"

The Texan, a silent man, nodded but did not move. Longstreet said, "What's the matter?"

"They're blaming us," Goree said. His voice was squeaky, like a dry wagon wheel. He radiated anger. Longstreet stared.

"What?"

"I been talking to Hood's officers. Do you know they blame us? They blame *you.* For today."

Longstreet could not see the bony face clearly, in the dark, but the voice was tight and very high, and Longstreet thought: he could be a dangerous man, out of control.

Goree said, "You may hear of it, General. I had to hit this fella. They all said the attack was your fault and if General Lee knowed he wouldn't have ordered it and I just couldn't just stand there and I couldn't say right out what I felt, so I had to hit this one fella. Pretty hard. Had to do it. Ain' goin' to apologize neither. No time. But. Thought you ought to know."

"Is he dead?"

"I don't think so."

"Well, that's good." Longstreet meditated. "Well, don't worry on it. Probably won't hear another thing if you didn't kill him. Probably forgotten in the morning. One thing: I want no duels. No silly damn duels."

"Yes, sir. Thing is, if anything bad happens now, they all blame it on you. I seen it comin'. They can't blame General Lee. Not no more. So they all take it out on you. You got to watch yourself, General."

"Well," Longstreet said. "Let it go."

"Yes, sir. But it aint easy. After I saw you take all morning trying to get General Lee to move to the right."

"Let it go. T. J. We'll talk on it after the fight."

Goree moved out. There goes a damn good man. Longstreet felt the warmth of unexpected gratitude. He swung the black horse toward Lee's headquarters back on the road to Cashtown. Time now to talk. Good long talk. Watch the anger. Careful. But it is true. The men shied from blaming Lee. The Old Man is becoming untouchable. Now more than anything else he needs the truth. But . . . well, it's not his fault, not the Old Man. Longstreet jerked the horse, almost ran into Sorrel. They came out into a patch of bright moonlight. Longstreet saw: the man was hurt.

"Major," Longstreet said harshly. "How are you?"

"Sir? Oh, I'm fine, sir. Juss minor problem."

"That's a godawful piece of horse you've got there."

"Yes, sir. Lost the other one, sir. They shot it out from under me. It lost both legs. I was with Dearing's Battery. Hot time, sir." Sorrel bobbed his head apologetically.

Longstreet pointed. "What's the trouble with the arm?"

Sorrel shrugged, embarrassed. "Nothing much, sir. Bit painful, can't move it. Shrapnel, sir. Hardly broke the skin. Ah, Osmun Latrobe got hit too."

"How bad?"

"Just got knocked off the horse, I believe. This fighting is very hard on the horses, sir. I was hoping we could get a new supply up here, but these Yankee horses are just farm stock—too big, too slow. Man would look ridiculous on a plow horse."

"Well," Longstreet grumbled vaguely. "Take care of yourself, Major. You aint the most likable man I ever met, but you sure are useful."

Sorrel bowed. "I appreciate your sentiments, sir. The General is a man of truth."

"Have you got the casualty figures yet?"

"No, sir. I regret to say. Just preliminary reports. Indications are that losses will exceed one third."

Longstreet jerked his head, acknowledging.

Sorrel said carefully, "Possibly more. The figures could go . . ."

"Don't play it down," Longstreet said.

"No, sir. I think that casualties were much worse in Hood's Division. Won't have an exact count for some time. But . . . it appears that the Yankees put up a fight. My guess is Hood's losses will approach fifty percent."

Longstreet took a deep breath, turned away. Eight thousand men? Down in two hours. His mind flicked on. Not enough left now for a major assault. No way in the world. Lee will see. Now: the facts.

"I need a hard count, Major. As quickly as possible."

"Yes, sir. But, well, it's not easy. The men tend to suppress the truth. I hear, for example, that Harry Heth's Division was badly hurt yesterday, but his officers did not report all the losses to General Lee because they did not want General Heth to get into trouble."

"I want the truth. However black. But hard facts. Soon as you can. I rely on you. Also, I want an account of artillery available, rounds remaining, type of rounds, et cetera. Got that? Get out a note to Alexander."

Up the road at a gallop: a handsome horseman, waving a plumed hat in the night. He reined up grandly, waved the hat in one long slow swop, bowed halfway down off the horse—a broad sweeping cavalier's gesture. Fairfax, another of Longstreet's aides.

"General Pickett's compliments, sir. He wishes to announce his presence upon the field."

Longstreet stared, grunted, gave an involuntary chuckle. "Oh grand," Longstreet said. "That's just grand." He turned to Sorrel. "Isn't that grand, Major? Now, let the battle commence." He grimaced, grunted. "Tell General Pickett I'm glad to have him here. At last."

Fairfax had a wide mouth: teeth gleamed in moonlight. "General Pickett is gravely concerned, sir. He wishes to inquire if there are any Yankees left. He says to tell you that he personally is bored and his men are very lonely."

Longstreet shook his head. Fairfax went on cheerily: "General Pickett reported earlier today to General Lee, while General Longstreet was engaged in the entertainment on the right flank, but General Lee said that General Pickett's men would not be necessary in the day's action. General Pickett instructs me to inform you that his is a sensitive nature and that his feelings are wounded and that he and his Division of pale Virginians awaits you in yon field, hoping you will come tuck them in for the night and console them."

"Well," Longstreet mused. "Fairfax, are you drunk?"

"No, sir. I am quoting General Pickett's exact words, sir. With fine accuracy, sir."

"Well." Longstreet smiled once slightly, shrugged. "You can tell General Pickett I'll be along directly."

Fairfax saluted, bowed, departed. Longstreet rode on into the dark. Pickett's Division: five thousand fresh men. Damn fine men. It was like being handed a bright new shiny gun. He felt stronger. Now talk to Lee. He spurred the horse and began to canter toward the lights on the Cashtown Road.

Headquarters could be seen from a long way off, like a small city at night. The glow of it rose above the trees and shone reflected in the haze of the sky. He could begin to hear singing. Different bands sang different songs: a melody of wind. He began to pass clusters of men laughing off in the dark. They did not recognize him. He smelled whisky, tobacco, roasting meat. He came out into the open just below the Seminary and he could see Headquarters field filled with smoke and light, hundreds of men, dozens of fires. He passed a circle of men watching a tall thin black boy dressed in a flowing red dress, dancing, kicking heels. There was a sutler's store, a white wagon, a man selling a strange elixir with the high blessed chant of a preacher. He began to see civilians: important people in very good clothes, some sleek carriages, many slaves. People come up from home to see how the army was doing, to deliver a package to a son, a brother. He rode out into the light and heads began to turn and fix on him and he felt the awkward flush come over his face as eyes looked at him and knew him and fingers began to point. He rode looking straight ahead, a crowd beginning to trail out after him like the tail of a comet. A reporter yelled a question. One of the foreigners, the one with the silver helmet like an ornate chamber pot, waved an intoxicated greeting. Longstreet rode on toward the little house across the road. Music and laughter and motion everywhere: a celebration. All the faces were happy. Teeth glittered through black beards. He saw pearl stickpins, silky, satiny clothing. And there against a fence: Jeb Stuart.

Longstreet pulled up.

The cavalier, a beautiful man, was lounging against a fence, a white rail fence, in a circle of light, a circle of admirers. Reporters were taking notes. Stuart was dressed in soft gray with butternut braid along the arms and around the collar and lace at his throat, and the feathered hat was swept back to hang happily, boyishly from the back of the head, and curls peeked out across the wide handsome forehead. Full-bearded, to hide a weak chin, but a lovely boy, carefree, mud-spattered, obviously tired, languid, cheery, confident. He looked up at Longstreet, waved a languid hello. He gave the impression of having been up for days, in the saddle for days, and not minding it. Longstreet jerked a nod, unsmiling. He thought: we have small use for you now. But you are Lee's problem. Longstreet slowed, not wanting to speak to Stuart. The crowd was beginning to press in around his horse, shouting congratulations. Longstreet looked from face to breathless face, amazed. Congratulations? For what? The crowd had moved in between him and Stuart. He pressed stubbornly forward toward Lee's cottage. It was impossible to answer questions: too much noise. He wished he had not come. Ride back later, when it's quiet. But too late to go now. One of Lee's people, Venable, had taken the reins of his horse. Someone was yelling in an eerie wail, "Way for General Longstreet, way for the General!" And there across the crowd he saw an open space by the door of the little house, and there in the light was Lee.

Quiet spread out from Lee. The old man stepped out into the light, came forward. Stuart swung to look. Longstreet saw men beginning to take off their hats in the old man's presence. Lee came up to Longstreet's horse, put out his hand, said something very soft. Longstreet took the hand. There was no strength in it. Lee was saying that he was glad to see him well, and there was that extraordinary flame in the dark eyes, concern of a loving father, that flicked all Longstreet's defenses aside and penetrated to the lonely man within like a bright hot spear, and Longstreet nodded, grumbled, and got down from the horse. Lee said accusingly that he had heard that Longstreet had been in the front line again and that he had promised not to do that, and Longstreet, flustered by too many people staring at him, too many strangers, said, well, he'd just come by for orders.

Lee said watchfully, smiling, "General Stuart is back."

The crowd opened for Jeb. He came forward with extended hand. Longstreet took it, mumbled, could not meet the younger eyes. Jeb was grinning a brilliant grin; hands were patting him on the back. Longstreet felt mulish. Damn fool. But he said nothing. Lee said that General Stuart ought to know how worried they had all been about him, and Stuart grinned like a proud child, but there was something wary in his eyes, looking at Lee, some small bit of question, and Longstreet wondered what the old man had said. Stuart said something about having seen a lot of Yankee countryside lately, and it was getting kind of dull, and slowly the noise began to grow up around them again. They moved toward the house, Lee taking Longstreet by the arm. They moved in a lane through hundreds of people, like Moses at the parting of the Sea. Somebody began a cheer, a formal cheer, a *university* cheer. A band struck up, oh Lord, "Bonny Blue Flag," again. Hands were touching Longstreet. He went up into the small house and into a small room, the roof closing in over him like the lid on a jar, but even here it was jammed with people, a tiny room no bigger than your kitchen, and all Lee's officers and aides, working, rushing in and out, and even here some people from Richmond. A place cleared for Lee and he sat down in a rocking chair and Longstreet saw him in the light and saw that he was tired. Lee rested a moment, closing his eyes. There was no place for Longstreet to sit except on the edge of the table, and so he sat there. Taylor pushed by, begging Longstreet's pardon, needing a signature on a letter to someone.

Lee raised a hand. "We'll rest for a moment."

Longstreet saw the old man sag, breathe deeply, his mouth open. Lines of pain around the eyes. He put the gray head down for a moment, then looked up quickly at Longstreet, shook his head slightly.

"A bit tired."

He never said anything like that. Lee never complained. Longstreet said, "Can I get you something?"

Lee shook his head. Aides were talking loudly about artillery, a message to Richmond. Longstreet thought: no rest here. Lee said, reading his mind, "I'll clear them out in a minute or two." He took another deep breath, almost a gasp, put a hand to his chest, shook his head with regret. His face was gray and still. He looked up with a vagueness in his eyes.

"It was very close this afternoon."

"Sir?"

"They almost broke. I could feel them breaking. I thought for a moment . . . I saw our flags go up the hill . . . I almost thought . . ."

Longstreet said, "It wasn't that close." But Lee's eyes were gazing by him at a vision of victory. Longstreet said nothing. He rubbed his mouth. Lee eyes strange: so dark and soft. Longstreet could say nothing. In the presence of the Commander the right words would not come.

Lee said, "The attacks were not coordinated. I don't know why. We shall see. But we almost did it, this day. I could see . . . an open road to Washington." He closed his eyes, rubbed them. Longstreet felt an extraordinary confusion. He had a moment without confidence, windblown and blasted, vacant as an exploded shell. There was a grandness in Lee that shadowed him, silenced him. You could not preach caution here, not to that face. And then the moment passed and a small rage bloomed, not at Lee but at Longstreet himself. He started to try to speak, but Lee said, "It was reported that General Barksdale was killed."

"Yes, sir."

"And General Semmes."

"Sir."

"And how is it with General Hood?"

"I think he'll live. I've just come from him."

"Praise God. We could not spare General Hood." He was gazing again into nowhere. After a moment he said, almost plaintively, "I've lost Dorsey Pender."

"Yes," Longstreet said. One by one: down the dark road. Don't think on that now.

Lee said, "He would have made a Corps commander, I think." The old man sat looking half asleep.

Longstreet said stiffly, "Sir, there are three Union corps dug in on the high ground in front of me."

Lee nodded. After a moment he said, "So very close. I believe one more push . . ."

A burst of shouting outside. The band had come closer. Longstreet said, "To-day I lost almost half my strength." And felt like a traitor for saying it, the truth, the granite truth, felt a smallness, a rage. Lee nodded but did not seem to hear. Longstreet pushed on.

"The way to the right is still open, sir."

Lee looked up slowly, focused, slowly smiled, put out a hand, touched Longstreet's arm.

"Let me think, General."

"We have enough artillery for one more good fight. One more."

"I know." Lee took a breath, sat up. "Let me think on it. But, General, I am very glad to see you well."

Taylor pushed in again. Longstreet reached out, gripped the young man in a metal clasp.

"General Lee needs his rest. I want you to keep some of these people away."

Taylor drew back in frosty reproach, as if Longstreet's hand smelled badly of fish. Longstreet felt the coming of a serious rage. But Lee smiled, reached out for the papers in Taylor's hand.

"A few more moments, General. Then I'll send them off. Now, what have we here?"

Longstreet backed off. The white head bent down over the papers. Longstreet stood there. All his life he had taken orders and he knew the necessity for command and the old man in front of him was the finest commander he had ever known. Longstreet looked around at the faces. The gentlemen were chatting, telling lively funny stories. Out in the smoky night a band was mounting another song. Too many people, too much noise. He backed out the door. Come back later. In the night, later, when the old man is alone, we will have to talk.

He moved out into the crowd, head down, mounted his horse. Someone pulled his arm. He glared: Marshall, red-faced, waving papers, cheeks hot with rage.

"General Longstreet! Sir. Will you talk to him?"

"Who? What about?"

"I've prepared court-martial papers for General Stuart. General Lee will not sign them."

Longstreet grimaced. Of course not. But not my problem. Marshall held the reins. He was standing close by and the men nearby were backed off in deference and had not heard him. Longstreet said, "When did he finally get back?"

"This evening." Marshall, with effort, was keeping his voice down. "He was joyriding. For the fun of it. He captured about a hundred enemy wagons. And left us blind in enemy country. Criminal, absolutely criminal. Several of us have agreed to ask for court-martial, but General Lee says he will not discuss it at this time."

Longstreet shrugged.

"General. If there is not some discipline in this army . . . there are good men *dead,* sir." Marshall struggled. Longstreet saw a man closing in. Fat man with a full beard. Familiar face: a Richmond reporter. Yes, a theorist on war. A man with a silvery vest and many opinions. He came, notebook in hand. Longstreet itched to move, but Marshall held.

"I'd like your opinion, sir. You are the second-ranking officer in this army. Do you believe that these court-martial papers should be signed?"

Longstreet paused. Men were closing in, yelling more congratulations. Longstreet nodded once, deliberately.

"I do," he said.

"Will you talk to General Lee?"

"I will." Longstreet gathered the reins. Men were close enough now to hear, were staring up at him. "But you know, Marshall, it won't do any good."

"We can try, sir."

"Right." Longstreet touched his cap. "We can at least do that."

He spurred toward the cool dark. They opened to let him pass. Hats were off; they were cheering. He rode head down toward the silent road. He was amazed at the air of victory. He thought: got so that whenever they fight they assume there's victory that night. Face of Goree. They can't blame General Lee, not no more. But there was no victory today. So very close, the old man said. And yet it was not a loss. And Longstreet knew that Lee would attack in the morning. He would never quit the field. Not with the Union Army holding the field. Three Union corps on the hills above. Lee will attack.

Longstreet stopped, in darkness, looked back toward the light. A voice was calling. Longstreet turned to ride on, and then the voice registered and he looked back: a grinning Fremantle, hat held high like the cloth on the arm of a scarecrow, bony, ridiculous. He looked like an illustration Longstreet had once seen of Ichabod Crane.

"Good evening, sir! My compliments, sir! Marvelous evening, what? Extraordinary! May I say, sir, that I observed your charge this afternoon, and I was inspired, sir, *inspired.* Strordnry, sir, a general officer at the front of the line. One's heart leaps. One's hat is off to you, sir." He executed a vast swirling bow, nearly falling from the horse, arose grinning, mouth a half moon of cheery teeth. Longstreet smiled.

"Will you take my hand, sir, in honor of your great victory?"

Longstreet took the limp palm, knowing the effort it cost the Englishman, who thought handshaking unnatural. "Victory?" Longstreet said.

"General Lee is the soldier of the age, the soldier of the age." Fremantle radiated approval like a tattered star, but he did it with such cool and delicate grace that there was nothing unnatural about it, nothing fawning or flattering. He babbled a charming hero-worship, one gentleman to another. Longstreet, who had never learned the art of compliment, admired it.

"May I ride along with you, sir?"

"Course."

"I do not wish to intrude upon your thoughts and schemes."

"No problem."

"I observed you with General Lee. I would imagine that there are weighty technical matters that occupy your mind."

Longstreet shrugged. Fremantle rode along beamily chatting. He remarked that he had watched General Lee during much of the engagement that day and that the General rarely sent messages. Longstreet explained that Lee usually gave the orders and then let his boys alone to do the job. Fremantle returned to awe. "The soldier of the age," he said again, and Longstreet thought: should have spoken to Lee. Must go back tonight. But . . . let the old man sleep. Never saw his face that weary. Soul of the army. *He's* in command. You are only the hand. Silence. Like a soldier.

He will attack.

Well. They love him. They do not blame him. They do impossible things for him. They may even take that hill.

". . . have no doubt," Fremantle was saying, "that General Lee shall become the world's foremost authority on military matters when this war is over, which would appear now to be only a matter of days, or at most a few weeks. I suspect all Europe will be turning to him for lessons."

Lessons?

"I have been thinking, I must confess, of setting some brief thoughts to paper," Fremantle announced gravely. "Some brief remarks of my own, appended to an account of this battle, and perhaps others this army has fought. Some notes as to the tactics."

Tactics?

"General Lee's various stratagems will be most instructive, most illuminating. I wonder, sir, if I might enlist your aid in this, ah, endeavor. As one most closely concerned? That is, to be brief, may I come to you when in need?"

"Sure," Longstreet said. Tactics? He chuckled. The tactics are simple: find the enemy, fight him. He shook his head, snorting. Fremantle spoke softly, in tones of awe.

"One would not think of General Lee, now that one has met him, now that one has looked him, so to speak, in the *eye,* as it were, one would not think him, you know, to be such a *devious* man."

"Devious?" Longstreet swung to stare at him, aghast.

"Oh my word," Fremantle went on devoutly, "but he's a tricky one. The Old Gray Fox, as they say. Charming phrase. American to the hilt."

"Devious?" Longstreet stopped dead in the road. "Devious." He laughed aloud. Fremantle stared an owlish stare.

"Why, Colonel, bless your soul, there aint a devious bone in Robert Lee's body, don't you know that?"

"My dear sir."

"By damn, man, if there is one human being in the world *less* devious than Robert Lee, I aint yet met him. By God and fire, Colonel, but you amuse me." And yet Longstreet was not amused. He leaned forward blackly across the pommel of the saddle. "Colonel, let me explain something. The secret of General Lee is that men love him and follow him with faith in him. That's one secret. The next secret is that General Lee makes a decision and he *moves,* with guts, and he's been up against a lot of sickly generals who don't know how to make decisions, although some of them have guts but whose men don't love them. That's why we win, mostly. Because we move with speed, and faith, and because we usually have the good ground. Tactics? God, man, we don't win because of tricks. What were the tactics at Malvern Hill? What were the tactics at Fredericksburg, where we got down behind a bloody stone wall and shot the bloody hell out of them as they came up, wave after wave, bravest thing you ever saw, because, listen, there are some damn good boys across the way, make no mistake on that. I've fought with those boys, and they know how to fight when they've got the ground, but tactics? Tactics?" He was stumbling for words, but it was pouring out of him in hot clumps out of the back of the brain, the words like falling coals, and Fremantle stared openmouthed.

"God in Heaven," Longstreet said, and repeated it, "there's no strategy to this bloody war. What it is is old Napoleon and a hell of a lot of chivalry. That's all it is. What were the tactics at Chancellorsville, where we divided the army, *divided* it, so help me God, in the face of the enemy, and got away with it because Joe Hooker froze cold in his stomach? What were the tactics yesterday? What were they today? And what will be the blessed tactics tomorrow? I'll tell you the tactics tomorrow. Devious? Christ in Heaven. Tomorrow we will attack an enemy that outnumbers us, an enemy that outguns us, an enemy dug in on the high ground, and let me tell you, if we win that one it will not be because of the tactics or because we are great strategists or because there is anything even remotely intelligent about the war at all. It will be a bloody miracle, a bloody miracle."

And then he saw what he was saying.

He cut it off. Fremantle's mouth was still open. Longstreet thought: very bad things to say. Disloyal. Fool. Bloody damned fool.

And then he began truly to understand what he had said.

It surfaced, like something long sunken rising up out of black water. It opened up there in the dark of his mind and he turned from Fremantle.

The Englishman said something. Longstreet nodded. The truth kept coming. Longstreet waited. He had known all this for a long time but he had never said it, except in fragments. He had banked it and gone on with the job, a soldier all his life. In his mind he could see Lee's beautiful face and suddenly it was not the same face. Longstreet felt stuffed and thick and very strange. He did not want to think about it. He spurred the horse. Hero reared. Longstreet thought: you always know the truth; wait long enough and the mind will tell you. He rode beneath a low tree; leaves brushed his hat. He stopped. A voice at his elbow: Fremantle.

"Yes," Longstreet said. Damn fool things to say. To a guest.

"If I have disturbed you, sir . . ."

"Not at all. Things on my mind. If you don't mind, Colonel . . ."

Fremantle apologized. Longstreet said good night. He sat alone on his horse in the dark. There was a fire in the field. A boy was playing a harmonica, frail and lovely sound. Longstreet thought of Barksdale as he had gone to die, streaming off to death, white hair trailing him like white fire. Hood's eyes were accusing. Should have moved to the right. He thought: tactics are old Napoleon and a lot of chivalry.

He shuddered. He remembered that day in church when he prayed from the soul and listened and knew in that moment that there was no one there, no one to listen.

Don't think on these things. Keep an orderly mind. This stuff is like heresy.

It was quieter now and very warm and wet, a softness in the air, a mountain peace. His mind went silent for a time and he rode down the long road between the fires in the fields and men passed him in the night unknowing, and soldiers chased each other across the road. A happy camp, behind the line. There was music and faith. And pride. We have always had pride.

He thought suddenly of Stonewall Jackson, old Thomas, old Blue Light. *He* could move men. Yes. But you remember, he ordered *pikes* for his men, *spears,* for the love of God. And the pikes sit by the thousands, rusting now in a Richmond warehouse because Jackson is dead and gone to glory. But he would have used them. Pikes. Against cannon in black rows. Against that hill in the morning.

They come from another age. The Age of Virginia.

Must talk to Lee in the morning.

He's tired. Never saw him that tired. And sick. But he'll listen.

They all come from another age.

General Lee, I have three Union corps in front of me. They have the high ground, and they are dug in, and I am down to half my strength.

He will smile and pat you on the arm and say: go do it.

And perhaps we will do it.

He was approaching his own camp. He could hear laughter ahead, and there were many bright fires. He slowed, let Hero crop grass. He felt a great sense of shame. A man should not think these things. But he could not control it. He rode into camp, back to work. He came in silently and sat back under a dark tree and Sorrel came to him with the figures. The figures were bad. Longstreet sat with his back against a tree and out in the open there was a party, sounds of joy: George Pickett was telling a story.

He was standing by a fire, wild-haired, gorgeous, stabbing with an invisible sword. He could tell a story. A circle of men was watching him; Longstreet could see the grins, flash of a dark bottle going round. Off in the dark there was a voice of a young man singing: clear Irish tenor. Longstreet felt a long way off, a long, long way. Pickett finished with one mighty stab, then put both hands on his knees and crouched and howled with laughter, enjoying himself enormously. Longstreet wanted a drink. No. Not now. Later. In a few days. Perhaps a long bottle and a long sleep. He looked across firelight and saw one face in the ring not smiling, not even listening, one still face staring unseeing into the yellow blaze: Dick Garnett. The man Jackson had court-martialed for cowardice. Longstreet saw Lo Armistead nudge him, concerned, whisper in his ear. Garnett smiled, shook his head, turned back to the fire. Armistead went on watching him, worried. Longstreet bowed his head.

Saw the face of Robert Lee. Incredible eyes. An honest man, a simple man. Out of date. They all ride to glory, all the plumed knights. Saw the eyes of Sam Hood, accusing eyes. He'll not go and die. Did not have the black look they get, the dying ones, around the eyes. But Barksdale is gone, and Semmes, and half of Hood's Division . . .

"Evening, Pete."

Longstreet squinted upward. Tall man holding a tall glass, youthful grin under steel-gray hair: Lo Armistead.

"How goes it, Pete?"

"Passing well, passing well."

"Come on and join us, why don't you? We liberated some Pennsylvania whisky; aint much left."

Longstreet shook his head.

"Mind if I sit a spell?" Armistead squatted, perched on the ground sitting on his heels, resting the glass on his thigh. "What do you hear from Sam Hood?"

"May lose an arm."

Armistead asked about the rest. Longstreet gave him the list. There was a moment of silence. Armistead took a drink, let the names register. After a moment he said, "Dick Garnett is sick. He can't hardly walk."

"I'll get somebody to look after him."

"Would you do that, Pete? He'll have to take it, coming from you."

"Sure."

"Thing is, if there's any action, he can't stand to be out of it. But if you ordered him."

Longstreet said nothing.

"Don't suppose you could do that," Armistead said wistfully.

Longstreet shook his head.

"I keep trying to tell him he don't have to prove a thing, not to us," Armistead brooded. "Well, what the hell." He sipped from the glass. "A pleasant brew. The Dutchmen make good whisky. Oh. Beg your pardon."

Longstreet looked out into the firelight. He recognized Fremantle, popeyed and grinning, rising awkwardly to his feet, tin cup raised for a toast. Longstreet could not hear. Armistead said, "I been talking to that Englishman. He isn't too bright, is he?"

Longstreet smiled. He thought: devious Lee.

Armistead said, "We put it to him, how come the limeys didn't come help us. In their own interest and all. Hell, perfectly obvious they ought to help. You know what he said? He said the problem was *slavery*. Now what do you think of that?"

Longstreet shook his head. That was another thing he did not think about. Armistead said disgustedly, "They think we're fighting to keep the slaves. He says that's what most of Europe thinks the war is all about. Now, what we supposed to do about that?"

Longstreet said nothing. The war was about slavery, all right. That was not why Longstreet fought but that was what the war was about, and there was no point in talking about it, never had been.

Armistead said, "Ole Fremantle said one thing that was interestin'. He said, whole time he's been in this country, he never heard the word 'slave.' He said we always call them 'servants.' Now you know, that's true. I never thought of it before, but it's true."

Longstreet remembered a speech: *In a land where all slaves are servants, all servants are slaves, and thus ends democracy.* A good line. But it didn't pay to think on it. Armistead was saying, "That Fremantle is kind of funny. He said that we Southerners were the most polite people he'd ever met, but then he noticed we all of us carry guns all the time, wherever we went, and he figured that maybe that was why. Hee." Armistead chuckled. "But we don't really need the limeys, do we, Pete, you think? Not so long as we have old Bobby Lee to lead the way."

Pickett's party was quieting. The faces were turning to the moon. It was a moment before Longstreet, slightly deaf, realized they had turned to the sound of the tenor singing. An Irish song. He listened.

> *. . . oh hast thou forgotten*
> *how soon we must sever?*
> *Oh has thou forgotten*
> *how soon we must part?*

It may be for years,
it may be forever . . .

"That boy can sing," Longstreet said. "That's 'Kathleen Mavourneen,' am I right?" He turned to Armistead.

The handsome face had gone all to softness. Longstreet thought he was crying, just for a moment, but there were no tears, only the look of pain. Armistead was gazing toward the sound of the voice and then his eyes shifted suddenly and he looked straight down. He knelt there unmoving while the whole camp grew slowly still and in the dark silence the voice sang the next verse, softer, with great feeling, with great beauty, very far off to Longstreet's dull ear, far off and strange, from another time, an older softer time, and Longstreet could see tears on faces around the fire, and men beginning to drop their eyes, and he dropped his own, feeling a sudden spasm of irrational love. Then the voice was done.

Armistead looked up. He looked at Longstreet and then quickly away. Out in the glade they were sitting motionless, and then Pickett got up suddenly and stalked, face wet with tears, rubbing his cheeks, grumbling, then he said stiffly, "Good cheer, boys, good cheer tonight." The faces looked up at him. Pickett moved to the rail fence and sat there and said, "Let me tell you the story of old Tangent, which is Dick Ewell's horse, which as God is my final judge is not only the slowest and orneriest piece of horseflesh in all this here army, but possibly also the slowest horse in this hemisphere, or even in the history of all slow horses."

The faces began to lighten. A bottle began to move. Pickett sat on the rail fence like old Baldy Ewell riding the horse. The laughter began again, and in the background they played something fast and light and the tenor did not sing. In a few moments Pickett was doing a hornpipe with Fremantle, and the momentary sadness had passed like a small mist. Longstreet wanted to move over there and sit down. But he did not belong there.

Armistead said, "You hear anything of Win Hancock?"

"Ran in to him today." Longstreet gestured. "He's over that way, mile or so."

"That a fact?" Armistead grinned. "Bet he was tough."

"He was."

"Ha," Armistead chuckled. "He's the best they've got, and that's a fact."

"Yep."

"Like to go on over and see him, soon's I can, if it's all right."

"Sure. Maybe tomorrow."

"Well, that'll be fine." Armistead looked up at the moon. "That song there, 'Kathleen Mavourneen'?" He shrugged. Longstreet looked at him. He was rubbing his face. Armistead said slowly, "Last time I saw old Win, we played that, 'round the piano." He glanced at Longstreet, grinned vaguely, glanced away. "We went over there for the last dinner together, night before we all broke up. Spring of sixty-one." He paused, looked into the past, nodded to himself.

"Mira Hancock had us over. One more evening together. You remember Mira. Beautiful woman. Sweet woman. They were a beautiful couple, you know that? Most beautiful couple I ever saw. He sure looks like a soldier, now, and that's a fact."

Longstreet waited. Something was coming.

"Garnett was there, that last night. And Sydney Johnston. Lot of fellas from the old outfit. We were leaving the next day, some goin' North, some comin' South. Splitting up. God! You remember."

Longstreet remembered: a bright cold day. A cold cold day. A soldier's farewell: goodbye, good luck, and see you in Hell. Armistead said, "We sat around the piano, toward the end of the evening. You know how it was. Mary was playing. We sang all the good songs. That was one of them, 'Kathleen Mavourneen,' and there was 'Mary of Argyle,' and . . . ah. *It may be for years, and it may be forever.* Never forget that."

He stopped, paused, looked down into the whisky glass, looked up at Longstreet. "You know how it was, Pete."

Longstreet nodded.

"Well, the man was a brother to me. You remember. Toward the end of the evening . . . it got rough. We all began, well, you know, there were a lot of tears." Armistead's voice wavered; he took a deep breath. "Well, I was crying, and I went up to Win and I took him by the shoulder and I said, 'Win, so help me, if I ever lift a hand against you, may God strike me dead.'"

Longstreet felt a cold shudder. He looked down at the ground. There was nothing to say. Armistead said, shaken, "I've not seen him since. I haven't been on the same field with him, thank God. It . . . troubles me to think on it."

Longstreet wanted to reach out and touch him. But he went on looking at the dark ground.

"Can't leave the fight, of course," Armistead said. "But I think about it. I meant it as a vow, you see. You understand, Pete?"

"Sure."

"I thought about sitting this one out. But . . . I don't think I can do that. I don't think that would be right either."

"Guess not."

Armistead sighed. He drank the last of the whisky in a swift single motion. He took off the soft black hat and held it in his hand and the gray hair glistened wetly, and the band of white skin at the forehead shone in the light. With the hat off he was older, much older, old courtly Lo. Had been a fiery young man. Lothario grown old.

"Thank you, Pete." Armistead's voice was steady. "Had to talk about that."

"Course."

"I sent Mira Hancock a package to be opened in the event of my death. I . . . you'll drop by and see her, after this is·done?"

Longstreet nodded. He said, "I was just thinking. Of the time you hit Early with the plate."

Armistead grinned. "Didn't hit him hard enough."

Longstreet smiled. Then was able to reach out and touch him. He just tapped him once lightly, one touch, on the shoulder, and pulled back his hand.

Out in the camp in the light of the fire Pickett was winding down. He was telling the story about the time during a cannonade when there was only one tree to hide behind and how the men kept forming behind the tree, a long thin line which grew like a pigtail, and swayed to one side or the other every time a ball came close, and as Pickett acted it out daintily, gracefully, it was very funny.

Armistead said, "Wonder if these cherry trees will grow at home. You think they'll grow at home?"

In a moment Armistead said, "Let's go join the party. Pete? Why not? Before they drink up all the whisky."

"No thanks. You go on."

"Pete, tomorrow could be a long day."

"Work to do." But Longstreet felt himself yielding, softening, bending like a young tree in the wind.

"Come on, Pete. One time. Do you good."

Longstreet looked out at all the bright apple faces. He saw again in his mind the steady face of Lee. He thought: I don't belong. But he wanted to join them. Not even to say anything. Just to sit there and listen to the jokes up close, sit inside the warm ring, because off here at this distance with the deafness you never heard what they said; you were out of it. But . . . if he joined there would be a stiffness. He did not want to spoil their night. And yet suddenly, terribly, he wanted it again, the way it used to be, arms linked together, all drunk and singing beautifully into the night, with visions of death from the afternoon, and dreams of death in the coming dawn, the night filled with a monstrous and temporary glittering joy, fat moments, thick seconds dropping like warm rain, jewel after jewel.

"Pete?"

Longstreet stood up. He let go the reins of command. He thought of the three Union corps, one of them Hancock, dug in on the hill, and he let them all go. He did not want to lead any more. He wanted to sit and drink and listen to stories. He said, "I guess one drink, if it's all right."

Armistead took him by the arm with a broad grin, and it was genuine; he took Longstreet by the arm and pulled him toward the circle.

"Hey, fellas," Armistead bawled, "look what I got. Make way for the Old Man."

They all stood to greet him. He sat down and took a drink and he did not think any more about the war.

6

Lee

He worked all that night. The noise went on around him until long after midnight. His staff was too small: must do something about that. But he could handle the work and there were many decisions that could be made only by the commanding officer, and the commanding officer should know as much as possible about the logistics of the situation, the condition of the army down to the last detail. He found that he could work right through the pain, that there came a second wind. If you sat quietly in a rocking chair you could work all night long. The trouble came when you tried to move. So he worked from the chair, not rising, and every now and then he rested his head in his hands and closed his eyes and blanked the brain, and so rested. The noise did not bother him. But he did not like people crowding too close. After a while he knew it was time to be alone. He told Taylor to ask the people outside to disperse. In a few moments it was very quiet. He rose up out of the chair and stepped out into the night. Time to make a plan now, time to make a decision.

The night air was soft and warm. Across the road there were still many fires in the field but no more bands, no more singing. Men sat in quiet groups, talking the long slow talk of night in camp at war; many had gone to sleep. There were stars in the sky and a gorgeous white moon. The moon shone on the white cupola of the seminary across the road—lovely view, good place to see the fight. He had tried to climb the ladder but it turned out not to be possible. Yet there was little pain now. Move slowly, slowly. He said to Taylor, "What day is it now?"

Taylor extracted a large round watch.

"Sir, it's long after midnight. It's already Friday."

"Friday, July third."

"Yes, sir, I believe that is correct."

"And tomorrow will be the Fourth of July."

"Sir?"

"Independence Day."

Taylor grunted, surprised. "I'd quite forgotten."

Curious coincidence, Lee thought. Perhaps an omen?

Taylor said, "The good Lord has a sense of humor."

"Wouldn't it be ironic—" Lee could not resist the thought—"if we should gain our independence from them, on their own Independence Day?" He shook his head, wondering. He believed in a Purpose as surely as he believed that the stars above him were really there. He thought himself too dull to read God's plan, thought he was not meant to know God's plan, a servant only. And yet sometimes there were glimpses. To Taylor he said, "I'll go sit with Traveler awhile and think. You will keep these people away."

"Yes, sir."

"I am sorry to keep you so late."

"My pleasure, sir."

"We should have a larger staff."

"Sir, I shall be offended."

"Well, I want to think for a while, alone."

"Sir."

Lee moved off into the dark pasture. Now in motion he was aware of stiffness, of weakness, of a suspended fear. He moved as if his body was filled with cold cement that was slowly hardening, and yet there was something inside bright and hot and fearful, as if something somewhere could break at any moment, as if a rock in his chest was teetering and could come crashing down. He found the dark horse in the night and stood caressing the warm skin, thick bristly mane, feeding sugar, talking.

Two alternatives. We move away to better ground, as Longstreet suggests. Or we stay. To the end.

He sat on a rail fence. *And so we broke the vow.* Longstreet's bitter phrase. It stuck in the mind like one of those spiny sticker burrs they had in the South, in Florida, small hooked seeds that lurk in the grass. Honest and stubborn man, Longstreet. We broke the vow. No point in thinking.

He remembered the night in Arlington when the news came: secession. He remembered a paneled wall and firelight. When we heard the news we went into mourning. But outside there was cheering in the streets, bonfires of joy. They had their war at last. But where was there ever any choice? The sight of fire against wood paneling, a bonfire seen far off at night through a window, soft and sparky glows always to remind him of that embedded night when he found that he had no choice. The war had come. He was a member of the army that would march against his home, his sons. He was not only to serve in it but actually to lead it, to make the plans and issue the orders to kill and burn and ruin. He could not do that. Each man would make his own decision, but Lee could not raise his hand against his own. And so what then? To stand by and watch, observer at the death? To do nothing? To wait until the war was over? And if so, from what vantage point and what distance? How far do you stand from the attack on your home, whatever the cause, so that you can bear it? It had nothing to do with causes; it was no longer a matter of vows.

When Virginia left the Union she bore his home away as surely as if she were a ship setting out to sea, and what was left behind on the shore was not his anymore. So it was no cause and no country he fought for, no ideal and no justice. He fought for his people, for the children and the kin, and not even the land, because not even the land was worth the war, but the people were, wrong as they were, insane even as many of them were, they were his own, he belonged with his own. And so he took up arms wilfully, knowingly, in perhaps the wrong cause against his own sacred oath and stood now upon alien ground he had once sworn to defend, sworn in honor, and he had arrived there really in the hands of God, without any choice at all; there had never been an alternative except to run away, and he could not do that. But Longstreet was right, of course: he had broken the vow. And he would pay. He knew that and accepted it. He had already paid. He closed his eyes. Dear God, let it end soon.

Now he must focus his mind on the war.

Alternatives? Any real choice here?

Move on, to higher ground in another place.

Or stay and fight.

Well, if we stay, we must fight. No waiting. We will never be stronger. They will be gaining men from all directions. Most of the men will be militia and not the match of our boys, but they will come in thousands, bringing fresh guns. Supplies will come to them in rivers, but nothing will come to us. Richmond has nothing to send. So if we stay, we fight soon. No more chance of surprise. No more need for speed or mobility. But no more delay. We cannot sit and wait. Bad effect on the troops.

And if we pull out?

He saw that in his mind's eye: his boys backing off, pulling out, looking up in wonder and rage at the Yankee troops still in possession of the high ground. If we fall back, we will have fought here for two days and we will leave knowing that we did not drive them off, and if it was no defeat, surely it was no victory. And we have never yet left the enemy in command of the field.

I never saw soldiers fight well after a retreat.

We have always been outgunned. Our strength is in our pride.

But they have good ground. And they have fought well. On home ground.

He saw a man coming toward him, easy gait, rolling and serene, instantly recognizable: Jeb Stuart. Lee stood up. This must be done. Stuart came up, saluted pleasantly, took off the plumed hat and bowed.

"You wish to see me, sir?"

"I asked to see you alone," Lee said quietly. "I wished to speak with you alone, away from other officers. That has not been possible until now. I am sorry to keep you up so late."

"Sir, I was not asleep," Stuart drawled, smiled, gave the sunny impression that sleep held no importance, none at all.

Lee thought: here's one with faith in himself. Must protect that. And yet, there's a lesson to be learned. He said, "Are you aware, General, that there are officers on my staff who have requested your court-martial?"

Stuart froze. His mouth hung open. He shook his head once quickly, then cocked it to one side.

Lee said, "I have not concurred. But it is the opinion of some excellent officers that you have let us all down."

"General Lee," Stuart was struggling. Lee thought: now there will be anger. "Sir," Stuart said tightly, "if you will tell me who these *gentlemen* . . ."

"There will be none of that." Lee's voice was cold and sharp. He spoke as you speak to a child, a small child, from a great height. "There is no time for that."

"I only ask that I be allowed—"

Lee cut him off. "There is no time," Lee said. He was not a man to speak this way to a brother officer, a fellow Virginian; he shocked Stuart to silence with the iciness of his voice. Stuart stood like a beggar, his hat in his hands.

"General Stuart," Lee said slowly, "you were the eyes of this army." He paused.

Stuart said softly, a pathetic voice, "General Lee, if you please . . ." But Lee went on.

"You were my eyes. Your mission was to screen this army from the enemy cavalry and to report any movement by the enemy's main body. That mission was not fulfilled."

Stuart stood motionless.

Lee said, "You left this army without word of your movements, or of the movements of the enemy, for several days. We were forced into battle without adequate knowledge of the enemy's position, or strength, without knowledge of the ground. It is only by God's grace that we have escaped disaster."

"General Lee." Stuart was in pain, and the old man felt pity, but this was necessary; it had to be done as a bad tooth has to be pulled, and there was no turning away. Yet even now he felt the pity rise, and he wanted to say, it's all right, boy, it's all right; this is only a lesson, just one painful quick moment of learning, over in a moment, hold on, it'll be all right. His voice began to soften. He could not help it.

"It is possible that you misunderstood my orders. It is possible I did not make myself clear. Yet this must be clear: you with your cavalry are the eyes of the army. Without your cavalry we are blind, and that has happened once but must never happen again."

There was a moment of silence. It was done. Lee wanted to reassure him, but he waited, giving it time to sink in, to take effect, like medicine. Stuart stood breathing audibly. After a moment he reached down and unbuckled his sword, theatrically, and handed it over with high drama in his face. Lee grimaced, annoyed, put his hands behind his back, half turned his face. Stuart was saying that since he no longer held the General's trust, but Lee interrupted with acid vigor.

"I have told you that there is no time for that. There is a fight tomorrow, and we need you. We need every man, God knows. You must take what I have told you and learn from it, as a man does. There has been a mistake. It will not happen again. I know your quality. You are a good soldier. You are as good a cavalry officer as I have known, and your service to this army has been invaluable. I have learned to rely on your information; all your reports are always accurate. But no report is useful if it does not reach us. And that is what I wanted you to know. Now." He lifted a hand. "Let us talk no more of this."

Stuart stood there, sword in hand. Lee felt a vast pity, yet at the same time he could feel the coming of a smile. Good thing it was dark. He said formally, "General, this matter is concluded. There will be no further discussion of it. Good night."

He turned away. Stuart stood holding the sword, but he had too much respect for Lee to speak. He began to move slowly away. Lee saw him stop before going back out into the night and put the sword back on. A good boy. If he is a man, he will learn. But now he will be reckless, to prove himself. Must beware of that. Longstreet would not approve. But court-martial would have destroyed him. And he is spirited, and that is a great part of his value. Keep him on rein, but on a loose rein. He has to be checked now and then. But he's a fine boy. And I am sorry to have to do that. Yet it was necessary.

He sat back on the fence. Another figure was coming. He sighed, wanting silence. But the man was Venable, back from Ewell's camp. Like all of Lee's aides he had too much to do and had slept little in the last two days and he was nearing exhaustion. He reported, speech blurred.

"Sir, I think I've, ah, pieced it together. I've been studying General Ewell's, ah, operation. Regret to say, very strange. There is much confusion in that camp."

"Is General Ewell in firm command?"

They had discussed it. Venable, who was fond of Dick Ewell, paused before answering. Then he said slowly, "Sir, I think General Ewell defers too much to General Early. He is . . . uncertain. I regret the necessity for speaking, sir. I would have preferred not . . ."

"I know." Lee bowed his head. So. The choice of Dick Ewell had been a mistake. But how was one to know? Honest Old Baldy. Had been a fine soldier. But cannot command a corps. Could I have known? Who else was there? Dorsey Pender . . . is wounded.

Venable said, "General Ewell could not get his corps in position for the attack this afternoon until some hours after Longstreet had already begun. General Rodes got his men bottled up in the streets of Gettysburg and never attacked at all."

"Not at *all?*"

"No sir. General Early attacked at dusk—"

"At dusk. But that was hours late."

"Yes, sir, Longstreet's attack was virtually over before Early got into action. But Early made no progress and called off the attack very soon. General Johnson managed to capture some trenches. Casualties were, ah, light."

Lee said nothing. He thought: Jackson would have *moved* . . . no time for that. He stared at the bold moon.

"You gave General Ewell my orders for the morning?"

"Yes, sir. He understands he is to be in position to attack at first light."

"He understands that."

"Yes, sir."

"He will have all night to prepare. That should be nearly ample time." There was in Lee's voice a rare touch of bitterness.

Venable paused warily, then said, "Are there further orders, sir?"

"Not just yet." Lee rested against the rail fence. Cannot depend on Ewell, nor on Hill. There is only Longstreet, Pickett is fresh. Longstreet has fresh men. Virginians. For whom we broke the vow. Lee shook his head. Well, one thing is sure, if we attack tomorrow, it will be with Longstreet. He meditated a moment, weariness flowing through him like a bleak slow wind. Think *now,* before you get too tired. He dismissed Venable and turned back to the night.

He sat down once more against the rail fence. The horse moved in over him; he had to move to keep from being stepped on. He sat on the far side of the fence and reviewed the facts and made the decision.

It did not take him very long. He was by nature a decisive man, and although this was one of the great decisions of his life and he knew it, he made it quickly and did not agonize over it. He did not think of the men who would die; he had learned long ago not to do that. The men came here ready to die for what they believed in, for their homes and their honor, and although it was often a terrible death it was always an honorable death, and no matter how bad the pain it was only temporary, and after death there was the reward.

The decision was clear. It had been there in the back of his mind all that night, as he worked, remembering every moment the sight of his blue Virginia flags going up that long slope to the top, almost to victory, so close he could feel the world over there beginning to give like a rotten brick wall. He could not retreat now. It might be the clever thing to do, but cleverness did not win victories; the bright combinations rarely worked. You won because the men thought they would win, attacked with courage, attacked with faith, and it was the faith more than anything else you had to protect; that was one thing that was in your hands, and so you could not ask them to leave the field to the enemy. And even if you could do that, cleverly, there was no certainty they would find better ground anywhere else, not even any certainty that they could extricate themselves without trouble, and so he had known all along that retreat was simply no longer an alternative, the way a man of honor knows that when he has faced an enemy and exchanged one round of blows and stands there bleeding, and sees the blood of the enemy, a man of honor can no longer turn away. So he would stay. And therefore, he would attack. The rest was clear as an engraving, so natural there seemed no alternative. There would be no surprise now; speed no longer mattered. So motion meant nothing. The enemy had been attacked on both wings; he had reinforced there and would be strongest there. So the weak point was the center.

The enemy had high ground on each wing, but in the center there was a long slope. So he would be softest there, and if you hit him there with everything you had, all the artillery firing to prepare the way in a *pont au feu,* if you sent Pickett's fresh Virginians straight up the center with Longstreet's hand the guiding force, the dominant force, you would drive a split in the center and cut Meade's army in two, break the rotten wall and send the broken pieces flying in all directions, so that if you sent Stuart's cavalry around to the rear he could complete the rout, in among the wagons to finish the wreckage, yes, Stuart raw with wounded pride and so anxious to redeem himself that he would let nothing stop him, and neither would Pickett, who had come in that day so desperately eager for battle.

Lee knelt and began to pray. His engineer's mind went on thinking while he prayed. He could find no flaw: we will go up the center and split them in two, on the defense no longer, attacking at last, Pickett and Hood and McLaws. By the end of the prayer he was certain: he felt a releasing thrill. This was the way, as God would have it. Face to face with the enemy, on grounds of his own choosing. End with honor.

The weight of it was gone. He felt a grave drowsiness. The horse nuzzled his ear; he smiled and rubbed the delicate nostrils. Then he began to drift off. He should go into bed now, but he was not comfortable lying down; he could not breathe. It was far better to sit in the night alone with the beautiful horse standing guard above him. It was not so bad to be an old man, drifting. Soon to see the Light. He wondered what it would be like to enter the Presence. They said there would be a fierce blinding light. How could they know, any of them? He wondered: Do you see all the old friends? At what age will they be? Will I see my father?

But it was all beyond him, and he accepted it. He had done his best: the Lord knew it. The heart thumped twice, a grave reminder. Lee nodded, as if at a summons, and prayed to the Lord for a little more time. After a while, he slept. He dreamed of little girls, dancing a cotillion. Then he dreamed of horses, herds of great horses, thundering by through black canyons of cloud. Beyond his tree, as he slept, the first blood light of dawn was rising up the sky.

SITUATION
AT CLOSE OF
SECOND DAY

FRIDAY,
JULY 3, 1863

Of His terrible swift sword . . .

1

CHAMBERLAIN

At dawn he climbed a tree and watched the day come. He was high on the summit of Round Top, higher than any man in either army. The sky was thick and gray, smelling of heat and rain; long mists drifted down between the ridges, lay in pools in the woods, rose toward the sun like white steam. He could see campfires burning in groups and clusters, like little cities sparkling in the mist, far, far off toward the blue hills to the east. He could look directly down on the gray crest of Little Round Top, saw the gunners there rising and stretching and heating coffee near black cannon. There were lights all down the Union line, a few horses moving, here and there a bugle, lights in the cemetery, a spattering of lights in Gettysburg. Here at the summit of Round Top the air was cool, there was no wind, the odor of death was very slight, just that one pale yellow scent, a memory in the silent air. The odor of coffee was stronger. Chamberlain sniffed and hoped, but he had none. All rations were gone. He lay back and watched the morning come.

The men lay below him in a line below the crest, receding down into the trees, the dark. In the night they had built a stone wall, had set out pickets, had taken prisoners. They had been joined at last by the 83rd Pennsylvania and the 44th New York, but they were still the extreme end of the Union line, the highest point on the field. Chamberlain kept pickets out all night, changing them every two hours, making them report every half hour. He did not sleep. As long as he kept moving the pain in the leg did not trouble him, but the foot kept bleeding and annoying him. No one had any rations. They had left Union Mills with three days' worth, but the troops had philosophically eaten most of that first chance they got. Chamberlain searched for coffee, which he badly needed. Just before sunup he began to get very, very tired, and so he climbed the tree and rested his legs. Dawn was always the worst time. Almost impossible to keep the eyes open. Close them and he thought of her, the red robe. This morning, oddly, he thought of her and of his two children. He could see them clearly, when he closed his eyes, playing at her feet like cubs, she looking up at him smiling calmly, waiting, pouting—but they would not even be up yet. Too early for them. They will sleep two more hours, at least. And here I sit on a hill in Pennsylvania. High on a hill, perched in a tree, watching the dawn come. A year ago I was in Maine, a teacher of languages. Amazing. The ways of God. Who would have thought? Well. It will be hard to go home again after this. Yesterday was . . . He closed his eyes. Saw the men behind the rocks, Tozier with the flag, the smoke, white faces, a scream for bayonets. Yesterday was . . . a dream.

He almost dozed. Came awake. Need someone to talk to. Sky all thick and gray. Rain? I hope so. But no, another scorcher. They don't know about this kind of weather back in Maine.

"Colonel?" At the foot of the tree: Tom. Chamberlain smiled.

"Hey, Colonel, I got you some coffee."

He held aloft a steaming cup. Chamberlain's stomach twinged in anticipation. Tom clambered up, reaching.

Chamberlain took the hot cup, held it lovingly. "Oh, that's fine. Where did you find that?"

"Well . . ." Tom grinned. "Gee, you sure can see a ways from up here." He squinted. "Golly, that's the whole damn Reb army."

"Don't swear," Chamberlain said automatically. He thought of yesterday. I used him to plug a hole. My brother. Did it automatically, as if he was expendable. Reached out and put him there, as you move a chess piece.

"We sent out a detail," Tom said cheerily, yawning, "and found some poor departed souls down there and they were carrying coffee for which they had no more use, so we took it."

Chamberlain grimaced. "Ghoul," he said. But he drank, and the coffee was sweet with brown sugar, and strength boiled into him.

"How you feel, Colonel, sir? You notice I don't say 'Lawrence.' "

"I feel fine."

"You know, I bet we're higher than anybody in the whole army. In *both* blame armies." Tom was pleased. "Now there's a thing to tell your children. My, what a view."

Chamberlain drank. After a moment he said, without thinking, "I miss old Buster."

"Kilrain? Yep. But he'll be all right."

The vacancy was there, a hole in the air, a special kind of loneliness. You wanted to have Buster to talk to when it was all over, to go over it, to learn, to understand, to see what you should have done.

Tom said, "You know, Lawrence? I close my eyes, I fall asleep."

"Better get down off the tree."

"You know what?"

"What?"

"I don't like bayonets." He squinted at Chamberlain, shrugged foolishly, blinked and yawned. "One thing about war I just don't like. Different, you know? Not like guns and cannon. Other men feel the same way. You know what I mean?"

Chamberlain nodded.

"I couldn't use mine," Tom said ashamedly. "Yesterday. Just couldn't. Ran down the hill, yelling, screamed my head off. Hit one man with the rifle barrel. Bent the rifle all to hell, pardon me. But couldn't stick nobody. Didn't see much of that, either. Am glad to say. Most men won't stick people. When I was going back and looking at the dead, weren't many killed by bayonet."

Chamberlain said, "Nothing to be ashamed of."

"Lawrence?"

Chamberlain turned. Tom was gazing at him, owl-eyed.

"You weren't afraid, much, yesterday."

"Too busy," Chamberlain said.

"No." Tom shook his head. "I shoot and run around and all the time I'm scared green. But you weren't scared at all. Not at all. But at Fredericksburg you were scared."

Chamberlain said, "I was too busy. Had things to do. Couldn't think about getting hurt." But he remembered: There was more to it than that. There was an exultation, a huge delight: *I was alive.*

"Well," Tom said stubbornly, "you did real good." It was the old family expression, used by one brother to another, down the years. Did I do good? You did real good. Chamberlain grinned.

"You know what?" Tom said. He grabbed a branch, swung himself into a better position. "I think we're going to win this war." He looked to Chamberlain for confirmation. Chamberlain nodded, but he was too tired to think about it, all those noble ideals, all true, all high and golden in the mind, but he was just too tired, and he had no need to talk about it. He would hang onto these rocks, all right, of that he was certain. But he didn't know about another charge. He looked down on the men, the line running down the hill. A little ammunition, a little food. We'll hang onto these rocks, all right. Now if I could just get a little sleep . . .

"Lawrence? The way them Rebs kept coming yesterday . . . You got to admire 'em."

"Um," Chamberlain said.

"You think they'll come again today?"

Chamberlain looked out across the open air, gazed at the miles of campfires. "Doesn't look like they're planning to depart."

"You think they'll come again?"

"They'll come again," he said. He stirred himself on the branch. They'll come again, for sure. Must get more ammunition up here. What in God's name is keeping Rice?

"We only got about two hundred men," Tom said thoughtfully. Not with worry but with calculation, a new realist, assessing the cold truth.

"But the position is very good," Chamberlain said.

"I guess so," Tom admitted. Rumble of cannon. At first he thought it was thunder, out of the dark sky to the north. But he saw the flashes sparkle on Cemetery Hill and knew it was too early for thunder, and as he looked northward he could see sunlight breaking through the overcast, to the north and west, and shells falling on the far side of the cemetery. He put his glasses to his eyes and looked, but all he could see was smoke and mist, an occasional yellow flash. Below him, on the hilltop, the heads of the men turned north. Chamberlain thought: diversion. To Tom he said, "You go down and alert the pickets. May be a diversion on that flank. They may be coming this way again. Send Ruel Thomas to me, tell him to send another call to Rice for ammunition."

Tom started down the tree. He scratched himself, swore feebly.

"Lawrence, we're going to need another runner, sir, old brother. I go up and down this hill much more my legs going to fall off."

Chamberlain said, "Yes. Tell Ellis Spear to pick a man, send him to me."

Tom moved down into the dark. Chamberlain waited in the tree. It was a very good position. The hill was flat across the top, about thirty yards of flat rock, an occasional tree, but the ascent on all sides was steep. The ground facing the enemy was rocky and steep and heavy with trees, and the ground behind him fell away abruptly, a sheer drop of at least a hundred feet, no worry about assault from that side. The men had built another rock wall, and now, with enough ammunition, he could hold there for a long time. The end of the line. Overlooking all the world. They'll come again. Let 'em come.

He half expected another assault. But there was no sound from below. The sky was brighter now, breaks in the overcast; light streamed down in blinding rays. He shaded sleep-filled eyes, gazed out across the Southern lines to the blue hills to the east. Lovely country. If I close my eyes, you know, I'll go to sleep. If they come again, could use some rest first.

He heard a man snoring loudly just below his tree. He saw a round face, bearded, mouth open, flat on his back on a rock ledge, hands folded on his chest. Chamberlain smiled in envy. He thought: guess I better get down from here, look around.

But now he had sat for a long time and his leg had stiffened, there was a brutal pain in his foot. He limped along the rock, trying to work out the stiffness. Thirty-four years old, laddie, not the man you used to be. He walked painfully past the sleeping man. A tall thin boy grinned happily upward, touched his cap. Chamberlain said, "Good morning."

"Colonel, sir."

"How you getting along?"

"Hungry, sir." The boy started to get up. Chamberlain held out a hand.

"Never mind that. Take it easy." He looked down on the round-faced sleeper, smiled.

"Jonas can sleep anywhere," the boy said proudly.

Chamberlain moved on down the line. The battle in the north was growing. No diversion. Well. He felt oddly disappointed. Then a trace of pride. They tried this flank yesterday and couldn't move us. Now they're trying the other flank. He wondered who his opposite number was, the colonel on the far right, the last man on the right of the Union line. What troops did he lead? What was he thinking now? Good luck to you, Colonel, Chamberlain said silently, saluting in his mind. But you don't have soldiers like these.

He limped among the men, passing each one like a warming fire. He shared with them all the memory of yesterday. He had been with them to that other world; they were in it now, the high clear world of the last man in line, and all the enemy coming. Tozier on the rock with the flag in his hand, Tom plugging the gap, bayonets lifted, that last wild charge. He looked down smiling as he passed, patting shoulders, concerned with small wounds. One boy lay behind a rock. He had been shot through the cheek yesterday but had not gone to the rear, had charged, had come all this way to the top of the hill. Now he was down with a fever, and the wound in the face was inflamed. Chamberlain ordered him to the field hospital. There were several signs of sickness, one possible case of typhoid. Nothing to do but detail the men down the hill. But none of them wanted to go, some deathly afraid of the hospital itself, some not wanting to be away from men they knew, men they could trust, the Regiment of Home.

Chamberlain began to grow restless for food. He thought: we're forgotten up here. Nobody knows what these men did yesterday. They saved the whole line, God knows, and now I can't even feed them. He was becoming angry. He clambered back up the hill and tore open the wound inside his boot, which began again to bleed. He sat down at the top of the hill, listening to the cannon fire and musketry raging in the north, momentarily grateful that it was over *there,* and took off the boot, bound the foot, wished he could get something to wash it down with, but what water there was was dirty and bloody. There was a creek down below: Plum Run. Choked with yesterday's dead. Good to be high up here; the smells of death don't seem to be rising. Wind still from the south, blowing it away. You know, the Regiment is weary.

That thought had taken a while to form, had formed slowly as he moved up and down the line. Just so far you can push a man.

He thought: a little food. A little rest. They'll be right again in a bit. Fewer than two hundred now. And there on the rock, sitting staring down at the long line of dark men shapeless under dark trees, he felt for the first time the sense of the coming end. They were dwindling away like sands in a glass. How long does it go on? Each one becoming more precious. What's left now is the best, each man a rock. But now there are so few. We began with a thousand and so whittled down, polishing, pruning, until what we had yesterday was superb, absolutely superb, and now only about two hundred, and, God, had it not been for those boys from the Second Maine . . . but the end is in sight. Another day like yesterday . . . and the Regiment will be gone. In the Union Army that was the way it was: they fought a unit until it bled to death. There were no replacements.

He shook his head, trying to shake away the thought. He could not imagine them gone. He would go with them. But if the war went on much longer . . . if there was one more fight like yesterday . . .

The sound of the battle in the north grew steadily in intensity. Chamberlain, alone, wished he knew anything at all about what was happening. He could not even talk to Ellis Spear, who was down in the woods with the other flank of the Regiment, where it joined the 83rd. He waited, alone, staying awake, listening. After a while there was a courier from Rice. He was a puffing lieutenant staggering up among the rocks.

"Colonel Chamberlain? Sir, that's some climb." The lieutenant paused to gasp for air, leaned upon a tree.

"My men need rations, Lieutenant," Chamberlain said. He stood up on his bloody foot, boot in hand.

"Sir, Colonel Rice instructs me to tell you that you are relieved, sir."

"Relieved?" Men were gathering around him. Sergeant Tozier had come up, that big-nosed man, towered over the lieutenant, gloomed down at him.

"Colonel Fisher's people are coming up, sir, and will take over here. Colonel Rice informs me that he wishes to compliment you on a job well done and give your people a rest, so he wants you to fall back, and I'm to show you the way."

"Fall back." Chamberlain turned, looked around the hilltop. He did not want to go. You could defend this place against an army. Well. He looked at his tree, from which he had watched the dawn.

He gave the words to Tozier. The Twentieth Maine would stay in position until Fisher's brigade came up, but in a few moments he heard them coming—extraordinary, he had not expected anything quick to happen in this army. The lieutenant sat against a tree while Chamberlain moved among the troops, getting them ready to move. Chamberlain came back for one last look around. For a moment, at least, we were the flank of the army. From this point you could see the whole battlefield. Now they were going down, to blend into the mass below. He looked around. He would remember the spot. He would be back here, some day, after the war.

The men were in line, all down the hill. Tom and Ellis Spear were waiting down below.

"You'll guide us, Lieutenant."

"Yes, sir."

The lieutenant moved off, downward into the dark. Chamberlain said, "I'll be wanting to go back to Little Round Top as soon as possible. The Regiment will bury its own dead."

"Yes, sir, but I'm to lead you to your new position first, sir, if you don't mind."

Chamberlain said, "Where are we going?"

"Oh, sir—" the lieutenant grinned—"a lovely spot. Safest place on the battlefield. Right smack dab in the center of the line. Very quiet there."

2

LONGSTREET

Goree was back in the gray dawn. The move to the south was still possible; the road to Washington was still open. But Union cavalry was closing in around Longstreet's flank. He sent orders to extend Hood's division. He sat in the gray light studying Goree's map, smelling rain, thinking that a little rain now would be marvelous, cool them, cool the battle fever, settle the dust. Wet mist flowed softly by; dew dripped from the leaves, pattered in the woods, but the morning was already warm. The heat would come again.

He drank coffee alone, dreaming. Scheibert, the Prussian, chatted with him about the Battle of Solferino. Longstreet could hear the laughter from Pickett's boys; some of them had been up all night. They were moving into line in the fields behind Seminary Ridge, out of sight of the Union guns. He was curt with Scheibert. The Prussian was not a fool; he bowed, departed. Longstreet studied the map. Rain would be a great blessing. Rain would screen our movements.

Lee came out of the mists. He was tall and gray on that marvelous horse, riding majestically forward in the gray light of morning outlined against the sky, the staff all around him and behind him, Lee alone in the center, larger than them all, erect, soldierly, gazing eastward toward the enemy line. He rode up, saluted grandly. Longstreet rose. Lee rested both hands on the pommel of his saddle. The mist thickened and blew between them; there was a ghostly quality in the look of him, of all his staff, ghost riders out of the past, sabers clanking, horses breathing thick and heavy in thick dank air.

Lee said, "General, good morning."

Longstreet offered him coffee. Lee declined. He said, "If you will mount up, General, I would like to ride over in that direction—" he gestured eastward— "some little way."

Longstreet called for his horse, mounted. He said, "I've had scouts out all night, General. I know the terrain now."

Lee said nothing. They rode toward the high ground, an opening in the trees. Longstreet looked out across a flat field of mist, fenceposts, a ridge of stone black against the soft-white flow mist, then across the road and up the long rise toward the Union defenses, high out of the mist, fires burning, black cannon in plain view.

Longstreet said again, "Sir, I've discovered a way south that seems promising. If we would move—"

"General, the enemy is *there*—" Lee lifted his arm, pointed up the ridge in a massive gesture—"and there's where I'm going to strike him."

He turned and looked back at Longstreet for one long moment, straight into his eyes, fixing Longstreet with the black stare, the eyes of the General, and then turned away. Longstreet drew his head in, like a turtle.

Lee said slowly, face to the east, "The situation is basically unchanged. But you have Pickett now, and he is fresh. I want you to move your corps forward and take those heights, in the center, and split the Union line."

Longstreet took a deep breath. Lee said, "I have sent word to Ewell. He is to attack when you do, keeping the enemy pinned on that flank. Yours will be the main effort. Hill will be the reserve. You will have all our artillery preceding you, fixed on that one point. A *pont au feu.*"

He was watching Longstreet's face, gazing at him without expression, the eyes set far back under white brows, dark, touched with the cool light of the morning. Longstreet said, "Sir." He shook his head, groping for words. Lee waited.

"Sir, there are some things I must say."

Lee nodded, again without expression, immobile. The staff had moved back; the two Generals were alone. Longstreet said, "Sir. My two divisions, Hood and McLaws, lost almost half their strength yesterday. Do you expect me to attack again that same high ground which they could not take yesterday at full strength? With so many officers lost? Including Sam Hood?"

Lee was expressionless. The eyes were black and still.

Longstreet said, "Sir, there are now three Union corps on those rocky hills, on our flank. If I move my people forward we'll have no flank at all; they'll simply swing around and crush us. There are thirty thousand men on those heights to our right. Cavalry is moving out on my flank now. If I move Hood and McLaws, the whole rear of this army is open."

Lee's head shifted slightly, imperceptibly; his eyes shifted. He had been set, now he turned, looked away, looked down at the ground, then east again.

After a moment he said, "You say there is cavalry moving on your right? In what force?"

"Two brigades, at least."

"You have that from Goree?"

"Yes, sir."

Lee nodded. "Goree is accurate," he said. He sat pondering.

"General," Longstreet said slowly, "it is my considered opinion that a frontal assault here would be a disaster."

Lee turned, frowned; the dark eyes flared for a moment. But he said nothing. Longstreet thought: I do not want to hurt this man. He said slowly, "They are well entrenched, they mean to fight. They have good artillery and plenty of it. Any attack will be uphill over open ground. General, this is a bad position. Have you ever seen a worse position? Here we are in a long line, spread all around them, a line five miles long. How can we coordinate an attack? They're massed all together, damn near in a circle. Anywhere we hit them they can bring reinforcements in a matter of minutes. And they can move up reinforcements behind those hills, out of sight of our cannon. But if *we* try to move in support it has to come from miles off, and their cannon can see every move. Hell, their cannon are looking down at us right now. General Lee, sir, this is not a good position."

Lee said, "They will break."

He said it very softly. Longstreet barely heard him. "Sir? Sir?"

"They will break," Lee repeated. "In any case, there is no alternative."

"Sir, I do not think so."

I am making him angry. Lee turned and looked at him, but there was a difference in the face now; the weariness was suddenly apparent. The old man had lost control for a moment and the pain was there; the exhaustion dulled the eyes.

THE THIRD DAY
-2:30 P.M.-
Lee's plan for
Pickett's charge

Longstreet felt a surge of emotion. He wanted to reach out and touch the old man, but that was impossible. You could not show affection here, no place for it here, too many men will die, must think clearly, but all the while he felt an icy despair, a cold dead place like dead skin. And then the guns began, cannon booming off to the left, where Ewell was. Longstreet swung in his saddle, saw A. P. Hill coming up, chatting with Pickett, and heads all turning at the sound of the guns. And now Lee's face was aflame. An anger Longstreet had never seen before contorted the old man's face. He pulled his horse savagely, almost snarled.

"What is Ewell up to? In God's name, can he follow no order at all?"

Lee galloped off to the left. Longstreet remained behind. Pickett came up, good cheer in his eye, babbling that his boys had been up for hours, and what was the plan? Longstreet said: nothing, and they recognized the mood and left him alone. Fits of weariness began to pass over Longstreet, as clouds pass over and dull the heat.

Colonel Marshall came back, from Lee. The word was that the Federals had opened an attack on Ewell, just as he was getting set. So. At least Ewell hadn't gone off half cocked. No. But what does Lee expect? How can we coordinate across all these miles? And now Meade is attacking. Good, very good. Meade begins to stir himself. Now that's excellent indeed. Given a bit of luck now, we can lure him down out of those damned bloody rocks. He's moving on my flank now. Good, very good. Let him come, let him come, and then when his arm is out far enough, when his nose is extended, I will chop it off with a chop they'll feel in London.

Lee was coming back. The sun was beginning to break through, the mist was rising. Lee rode slowly up, slouched a bit, no longer quite so trim. He smiled a haggard smile. Longstreet thought: He got mad at Ewell, now he's embarrassed.

Lee said, "No need for hurry now. General Ewell is engaged. General Meade has made a move. I must confess, I did not expect it." He pointed. "We'll ride forward."

They moved out toward the lines. Lee was thinking; Longstreet kept silent. The heat came slowly, steadily. They rode down to the Emmitsburg Road, in clear view of the Union lines. There were smells flowing up from the hospital. Out in the fields the dead lay everywhere in the litter of war. Here and there surgeons were moving, burial parties. Above them, on the Union lines, a cannon thumped, the ball passed overhead, exploded in an open field among the dead bodies. Two of Lee's aides rode up, insisted that the Union gunners could see them much too clearly. They dismounted. Lee walked forward across the road into the peach orchard, where Barksdale had streamed to his death the day before. Lee cautioned Longstreet to keep his distance so that if a shot came down it would not get both of them at once. They were nearing the lines now; men began rising out of the ground, ragged apparitions. The aides quieted cheering, which would draw Union fire. The men stood awe-stricken, hats in their hands, whispering kind words, words of hope, words of joy. Longstreet looked into lean young grinning faces, bloodstained clothes, saw bodies bloated in the fields, dead horses everywhere. Ewell's fight in the north was stiffer, but down here the sound was softened; the wind was in the south, blowing toward the battle, blowing up between the lines. They were walking now in Wofford's line. Wofford came out to greet General Lee.

Wofford's Brigade had pushed up the ridge almost to the top the day before. Lee listened to him tell of it, then Lee said, "General, you went up there yesterday. Surely you can do it again."

"No, General, I think not," Wofford said. He seemed embarrassed to say it.

Lee said, "Why not?"

"Because yesterday we were chasing a broken enemy. They've been heavily reinforced. They've had all night to entrench. And my boys . . . lost many friends yesterday."

Lee said nothing. Longstreet saw him clamp his jaw. He was walking slowly, hands clasped behind him. He said suddenly, "Well, but Pickett is here. And Stuart. Don't forget Stuart."

A sharpshooter's bullet shirred by overhead. Longstreet looked for it curiously. Shooting downhill, snipers always overshoot. They were moving into the front of the line, the bloody wheat field. Longstreet saw a battery being moved, guns being pulled back. He saw young Porter Alexander, his chief of artillery, in personal supervision. Good, he thought absently, very good, Alexander is seeing to it himself. The technical commander was Parson Pendleton, but Pendleton was a fool. There was high ground at the peach orchard. Alexander was posting some Napoleons there, waved as he rode by. Lee saw, approved wordlessly. He took his hat off, gazing upward at the long rise toward Cemetery Ridge. The sun gleamed on his white hair, the dark ridge along the brow line where the hat had pressed the hair down. Longstreet thought: he was not all that white-haired a year ago. He remembered yesterday: "I'll tell you a secret: I'm an old man."

I wish we could take the hill. Could flood right on over it and end the war, wipe them all away in one great motion. But we can't. No matter how much I wish . . . or trust in God . . .

Lee turned back. His face was again composed; he put the soft black hat back on his head. He called an aide: Venable, then Taylor. Longstreet waited to the side. Soldiers were drifting up to stand happily by, gazing with paternal affection at Lee, at Longstreet.

"Mornin' to ya, General. You look pert this mornin', sir."

"General, beggin' yer pardon, sir, I'd like to complain about the food, sir."

"We's back in the Union now, General."

They were ready. That superb morale. Lee touched his hat to the men. They moved away from the line. The sun broke through at last and poured heat on the roadway; the mist was gone. A rider came up from Hood's division, commanded now by General Law. Law reported Union cavalry moving in force across his flank, suggested strengthening his line with Robertson's Brigade. Longstreet agreed, Lee listening silently. Then they rode back toward the ridge where Pickett's men waited.

Ewell's fight was going on. They could see smoke blowing now across the top of the hill. Ewell reported that Johnson was being compelled to fall back from the trenches he had won the night before. Lee sat alone for a while, Longstreet a small way away. A slowly growing swarm of aides and other officers, reporters, foreigners, musicians, began gathering a respectful distance away. A band began playing "That Bonny Blue Flag," in Lee's honor. Skirmish firing broke out in the fields below Seminary Ridge; musketry popped in patches of white smoke as the lines felt and probed.

At last Lee turned, summoned Longstreet. Longstreet came up. Lee said, "General, we will attack the center."

He paused. Longstreet took a long breath, let it go.

"You will have Pickett's Division. But I think you are right about the flank. Leave Hood and McLaws where they are. I will give you Heth's Division. It was not engaged yesterday. And Pender's."

Longstreet nodded.

"You will have three divisions. Your objective will be that clump of trees . . . there."

He pointed. The center of the Union line, the center of the ridge. The clump of trees was clear, isolated. In the center of the clump was one large tree shaped like an umbrella. Unmistakable. Longstreet nodded, listened, tried not to think.

"Your attack will be preceded by massed artillery fire. *A feu d'enfer.* We will concentrate all our guns on that small area. When the artillery has had its effect, your charge will break the line. The rest of Hill's people will be waiting. Stuart has already gone round to the rear."

Lee turned. Now the excitement was in his eyes. He leaned forward, gazing at Longstreet, hoping to strike fire, but Longstreet said nothing, stood listening, head bowed.

Lee said, "Those three divisions . . . will give you fifteen thousand men."

Longstreet said, "Yes, sir." He stared at the ridge. He said suddenly, "Hancock is up there."

Lee nodded. "Yes, that's the Second Corps."

Longstreet said, "Hard on Armistead."

Lee said, "You can begin at any time. But plan it well, plan it well. We stake everything on this."

"Sir?" Longstreet thought: I can't. "Sir," Longstreet said, "you are giving me two of Hill's divisions, only one of mine. Most of the troops will be Hill's. Wouldn't it be better to give the attack to Hill?"

Lee shook his head. He said, "General, I want *you* to make this attack." Longstreet took another deep breath. Lee said, "General, I need you."

Longstreet said, "Sir, with your permission."

Lee waited. Longstreet spoke and did not want to look him in the face, but did, spoke looking at the weary face, the ancient eyes, the old man who was more than father of the army, symbol of war. "Sir, I have been a soldier all my life. I have served from the ranks on up. You know my service. I have to tell you now, sir, that I believe this attack will fail. I believe that no fifteen thousand men ever set for battle could take that hill, sir."

Lee raised a hand. Longstreet had seen the anger before, had never seen it turned toward him. It was as if Longstreet was betraying him. But Longstreet went on: "It is a distance of more than a mile. Over open ground. As soon as we leave the trees we will be under the fire of their artillery. From all over the field. At the top of the hill are Hancock's boys—"

Lee said, "That's enough."

He turned away. He called Taylor. For a long moment Longstreet thought: he is relieving me. But Lee was sending for someone. Longstreet thought: he should relieve me. He should give it to A. P. Hill. But he knew Hill could not take it, no one could take it; there was no one else Lee could rely on, nothing else to do. It was all set and fated like the coming of the bloody heat, the damned rising of the damned sun, and nothing to do, no way to prevent it, my weary old man, God help us, what are you doing?

Not thinking clearly anymore, Longstreet composed himself. Lee came back. Lee said calmly, "General, do you have any questions?"

Longstreet shook his head. Lee came to him, touched his arm.

"General, we all do our duty. We do what we have to do."

"Yes, sir," Longstreet said, not looking at him.

"Alexander is handling the artillery. He is very good. We will rely on him to break them up before Pickett gets there."

"Yes, sir."

"Heth is still too ill for action. I am giving his division to Johnston Pettigrew. Is that satisfactory to you?"

Longstreet nodded.

"Pender is out of action, too. Who would you suggest for the command there?"

Longstreet could not think. He said, "Anyone you choose."

"Well," Lee meditated. "How about Isaac Trimble? No one in the army has more fight in him that Trimble."

"Yes," Longstreet said.

"Good. Then that's agreed. Pettigrew, Pickett, and Trimble. The new commanders won't really matter, in an attack of this kind. The men will know where to go."

He went over the plan again. He wanted to be certain, this day, that it all went well, laying it all out like the tracks of a railroad. He was confident, excited, the blood was up. He thought the army could do anything. Longstreet felt the weariness, the heat of the day. The objective was clear. All fifteen thousand men would concentrate, finally, on a small stone wall perhaps a hundred yards wide. They might break through. It was possible.

Lee said, "The line there is not strong. Meade has strengthened both his flanks; he must be weak in the center. I estimate his strength in the center at not much more than five thousand men. The artillery barrage will upset them."

"Yes, sir."

"Is there anything you need? Take whatever time you need."

"I have always been slow," Longstreet said.

"There is no one I trust more."

"If the line can be broken . . ." Longstreet said.

"It can. It will." Lee paused, smiled.

"If it can be done, those boys will do it." Longstreet moved back formally, saluted.

Lee returned the salute, tall, erect, radiating faith and confidence. He said slowly, the voice of the father, "General Longstreet, God go with you."

Longstreet rode off to summon his staff.

What was needed now was control, absolute control. Lee was right about that: a man who could not control himself had no right to command an army. They must not know my doubts, *they must not.* So I will send them forward and say nothing, absolutely nothing, except what must be said. But he looked down at his hands. They were trembling. Control took a few moments. He was not sure he could do it. There had never been anything like this in his life before. But here was Pickett, wide-eyed, curious, long hair ringed and combed, mounted on a black horse, under a great tree.

Longstreet told him the orders. Pickett whooped with joy. Longstreet let him go off to form his troops. He looked at his watch: not yet noon. It would be some time yet. He sent for the other officers, for Porter Alexander. The fight on the far left was dying; Ewell was done. There would be no support there. He felt a moment of curious suspension, as when you have been awake for a long time you have certain moments of unreality, of numbness, of the beginning of sleep. It passed. He heard cannon fire to the left, closer. A. P. Hill was shooting at something. Alexander rode up: a young man; nondescript face but very capable. He was excited, hatless. He apologized for the loss of the hat.

"Sir, ah, we seem to have upset Colonel Walton. He has just reminded me that he is the senior artillery officer in this Corps."

Longstreet moved out to the edge of the trees. He indicated the limits of the attack, where the fire should converge. He explained it slowly, methodically, with great care. The Union cannon up on the Rocky Hill would cause trouble. Alexander should assign guns to keep them quiet. He should have more guns ready to move forward with the attack, keeping the flanks clear. It occurred to Longstreet that this was a grave responsibility. He interrupted himself, said suddenly, "How old are you, son?"

"Sir? Ah, twenty-six, sir."

Longstreet nodded, looked into the unlined face, the bright, dark, anxious eyes. Best gunner in the corps. We make do with what we have. He said, "Can you clean those guns off that hill, son?"

"Sir? Well, sir, I don't know about that, sir."

"Well," Longstreet said. He thought: I'm seeking reassurance. Let it go. He said, "I am relying on you, son."

"Yes, sir." Alexander bobbed his head several times, kicked the turf. "I'll sure keep 'em shootin', sir."

"Don't open fire until I give you the word, until everything's in position. Then fire with everything you have. Get yourself a good observation point so you can see the damage we're doing. We've got to drive some of those people off that hill. If we don't do that . . . I'll rely on your judgment."

A great weight to put upon him. But nothing else to do. Alexander saluted, moved off. Here came Sorrel, bringing with him, on horseback, Generals Pettigrew and Trimble. Longstreet greeted them, sent for Pickett. He got down from his horse and walked over to the open space on the ground where the staff had spread the camp stools, and asked for coffee. They sat in a circle, lesser officers at a distance, almost in files, by rank. Longstreet wore the expressionless face, drank the coffee, said nothing at all, looked at them.

Johnston Pettigrew: handsome, fine-featured. An intellectual. Very few intellectuals in this army. He had attended the University of North Carolina and they talked of his grades there with reverence and awe. Curious thing, Longstreet thought. He smiled slightly. Here's our intellectual, Pettigrew, going into battle side by side with old Pickett, last in his class. He chuckled. The men were watching him, sensing his mood. They seemed to see him grin. Longstreet looked at Pettigrew.

"They tell me you've written a book."

"Sir? Oh, yes, sir." Firm sound to the voice, clear calm eye. Lee thinks the world of him. He will do all right.

"What was it about?"

"Oh, it was only a minor work, sir."

"I'll have to read it."

"You will have a copy, sir, with my compliments." To Longstreet's surprise, Pettigrew rose, summoned an aide, dispatched the man for the book.

Longstreet grinned again. He said, "General, I doubt if I'll have time today."

"At your leisure, sir." Pettigrew bowed formally.

Longstreet looked at Isaac Trimble. He was breathing hard, face red and puffy, a bewildered look to him. He had a reputation as a fire-breather. He did not look like it. His beard was fully white, his hair puffed and frizzled. Well, Longstreet thought, we shall see.

Pickett came up, joined the circle. Introductions were unnecessary. Longstreet ordered coffee all around, but Trimble would not take any; his stomach was troubling him. Sorrel was the only other officer to hear the orders. Longstreet explained it all slowly, watching them. Pickett was excited, could not sit still, sat rubbing his thighs with both hands, nodding, patting himself on the knees. Pettigrew was calm and pale and still. Trimble breathed deeply, rubbed his nose. His face grew more and more crimson. Longstreet began to understand that the old man was deeply moved. When he was done with the orders Longstreet drew the alignment in the dirt:

They all understood. Then Longstreet rose and walked out to the edge of the trees, out into the open, for a look at the Union line. He pointed to the clump of trees. There were a few minor questions. Longstreet told them to keep that clump in sight as they moved back to their troops, to make sure that there was no confusion. The attack would guide on Pickett. More minor questions, then silence. They stood together, the four men, looking up at the Union line. The mist had burned away; there were a few clouds, a slight haze. Hill's guns had stopped; there was a general silence.

Longstreet said, "Gentlemen, the fate of your country rests on this attack."

All eyes were on his face. He put out his hand.

"Gentlemen, return to your troops."

Pettigrew took his hand. "Sir, I want to say, it is an honor to serve under your command."

He moved off. Trimble took the hand. He was crying. He said huskily, tears all down the red glistening cheeks, "I want to thank you, sir, for the opportunity you have given me, sir, to serve here. I have prayed, sir." He stopped, choked. Longstreet pressed his hand. Trimble said, "I will take that wall, sir."

Pickett stayed. Longstreet said, "George, can you take that hill?"

Pickett grinned. My curly boy. He rushed off, hair flying. Here was Alexander, galloping up through the trees, exasperated.

"Sir, General Hill's artillery is dueling the Union people for some damned barn, sir, excuse me, but it's a tragic waste of ammunition. We don't have a limitless supply."

Longstreet said, "Give General Hill my compliments and tell him I suggest he reserve his ammunition for the assault."

Alexander rode off.

And so it's in motion.

Seminary Ridge was thick with trees, but the fields on both sides were bare. Pickett's troops were beginning to form in the fields to the west, out of sight of the Union line. Longstreet rode to watch them, then back out through the trees to face east, looking up toward the Union line. His staff was with him: gaunt Goree asleep in his saddle, refusing to lie down. Longstreet saw a familiar figure standing some distance out in the field, alone, looking toward the Union line. He rode that way: Armistead. Looking up toward Hancock's wall. Longstreet stopped, nodded, let the man alone, rode away. Poor old Lo. Well. All over soon. One way or the other.

Lee was coming back down the line, aides preceding him, to keep the men from cheering. Alexander's guns were moving, realigning; horses were pulling caissons into position, stirring the dust. Lee was trim and calm, all business. He suggested they ride the lines again. Longstreet agreed silently. Pickett rode up, asked to accompany them. All the attack would guide on Pickett; it was necessary there be no mistake at all. The three men rode together along the front of the dark woods, in front of the cannon, the troops, the woods behind them a dark wall, and the long flat green rise in front of them, spreading upward and outward to the Emmitsburg Road, the rise beyond that, the visible breastworks, the stone wall near the crest, well named, Cemetery Ridge. Lee discussed the attack with Pickett; Longstreet was silent. There was a dip in the ground near the center; they rode down out of sight of the Union line. Lee was telling Pickett how to maneuver his troops sideways when he reached the road so that they would converge on that clump of trees toward the center. He had many suggestions as to how to use the ground. Longstreet dropped slightly behind them. They came out into the open again, in front of the point of woods from which Lee would watch the assault. Longstreet looked up the long rise.

He could begin to see it. When the troops came out of the woods the artillery would open up. Long-range artillery, percussion and solid shot, every gun on the hill. The guns to the right, on the Rocky Hill, would enfilade the line. The troops would be under fire with more than a mile to walk. And so they would go. A few hundred yards out, still in the open field, they would come within range of skirmish, aimed rifles. Losses would steadily increase. When they reached the road they would slow by the fence there, and the formation, if it still held, would begin to come apart. Then they would be within range of the rifles on the crest. When they crossed the road, they would begin to take canister fire and thousands of balls of shrapnel wiping huge holes in the lines. As they got closer, there would be double canister. If they reached the wall without breaking, there would not be many left. It was a mathematical equation. But maybe the artillery would break up the defense. There was that hope. But that was Hancock up there. And Hancock would not run. So it is mathematical after all. If they reach the road and get beyond it, they will suffer fifty percent casualties. I do not think they will even reach the wall.

Lee asked his advice on artillery support. Longstreet gave it quietly. They rode back down the line. A quietness was beginning to settle over the field. The sun was rising toward noon. They came back toward Longstreet's line. Lee said, "Well, we have left nothing undone. It is all in the hands of God."

Longstreet thought: it isn't God that is sending those men up that hill. But he said nothing. Lee rode away.

Pickett said earnestly, "Sir, how much time do we have?"

Terrible question. But he did not know what he was asking. Longstreet said, "Plenty of time. The guns will fire for at least an hour."

Pickett slapped his thighs.

"It's the waiting, sir, you know? Well, sir, I think I'll have the troops lie down. Then I'll write to Sallie. You'll see it's delivered, sir?"

Longstreet nodded.

Pickett rode off.

Nothing to do now but wait. The guns were in line, the caissons were stacking shot, the gunners digging their small trenches. One hundred and forty guns. And the Union boys will reply. It will be the greatest concentration of artillery ever fired.

Longstreet got down from his horse. He was very, very tired. He walked toward a cool grove of trees. Sorrel and Goree followed, but Longstreet waved them away. He sat with his back against a tree, put his head in his hands.

There is one thing you can do. You can resign now. You can refuse to lead it.

But I cannot even do that. Cannot leave the man alone. Cannot leave him with that attack in the hands of Hill. Cannot leave because I disagree, because, as he says, it's all in the hands of God. And maybe God really wants it this way. But they will mostly all die. We will lose it here. Even if they get to the hill, what will they have left, what will we have left, all ammunition gone, our best men gone? And the thing is, I cannot even refuse, I cannot even back away, I cannot leave him to fight it alone, they're my people, my boys. God help me, I can't even quit.

He closed his eyes. From a tree close by Colonel Fremantle saw him, thought he was resting before the great battle, could not help but wonder at the enormous calm of the man. What an incredible time to go to sleep!

3

CHAMBERLAIN

Past Little Round Top the ground dipped down into a saddle but the line ran straight, unbroken, along the saddle and up the ridge, rising toward the trees and the cemetery, that northern hill. The line was a marvelous thing to see: thousands of men and horses and the gleaming Napoleons, row on row, and miles of wagons and shells. Marching along the crest, they could see back to the Taneytown Road and the rows of tents, the hospitals, the endless black rows of more cannon, wagon trains. The sun was hot along the ridge, and men had stuck bayonets in the ground and rigged shelter halves, and here and there through scarred trees they could see down into the rocks below, bodies there in black clumps, soft among the gray boulders. Back in the woods of Little Round Top, up on the summit of the hill, they had been alone, but now they were in the midst of the army, the great army, a moving fragment of this unending line of men and guns lined along the spine of that ridge going out of sight to the north. Chamberlain gathered strength, limping along the ridge, tucking himself in under his soft black hat, out of the sun.

The lieutenant who was their guide was a dapper young man named Pitzer, who liked to gossip, to show that he was privy to great secrets. He had a runny nose and he sneezed repeatedly but seemed to be enjoying himself. He pointed out the place where the First Minnesota had made the charge that had the whole army talking. Three hundred men had charged, under Hancock's direction; only forty had come back. But they had broken a Reb assault, giving reserves time to get up. Chamberlain thought: their casualties much worse than mine. In a fight, it always seems that your fight is the hardest. Must remember that. What happened to them was much worse than what happened to us.

Pitzer said conversationally, "We very nearly retreated this morning."

"Retreated? *Why?*" Chamberlain was aghast.

"Meade wanted to pull the whole army out. Had a meeting of corps commanders last night. He really did." Pitzer sneezed emphatically. "Damn ragweed. Happens every sum—" He exploded again, plucked out a bright red handkerchief, wiped his nose, his wheezy eye, grinned. "Meade wrote an order for the whole army to withdraw, then held a meeting of corps commanders and asked for a vote. This army is great for meetings, Colonel. Old Sedgewick did the right thing. He fell asleep." Pitzer chuckled. "Old Uncle John, you can count on him. He voted, then he fell asleep."

"What was the vote?"

"Well, hell, *all* the corps commanders voted to stay. I mean the *only* one felt like pulling out was Meade. *General* Meade," he added thoughtfully, eyeing Chamberlain. Never knew how to take these civilian colonels. "It was unanimous. Meade had 'em write it out, so it's all on record. I was watching through a window, saw the whole thing, even old Sedgewick asleep. Now *there's* an officer. Him and Hancock." Pitzer shook his head admiringly, wheezing. "Hancock was something to behold. He says they'll come again one more time and we ought to be right here waiting."

"He says they'll come again? Hancock?"

"Yep."

"Where did he say they'd come?"

Pitzer grinned, pointed, wheezed. "Why, Colonel, right about here."

They were moving higher up the crest of the hill. They were coming out on a long space of open ground along the crest before a grove of trees, the Cemetery. Down across the field there was a small farmhouse surrounded by horses, flags, many soldiers. Chamberlain could see, even at this distance: the high brass. To the left was a clump of trees, a stone fence, two batteries of artillery, the long line of troops lying in the sun, in the shade of the trees, dug in, waiting.

Pitzer said, pointing, "That's Meade's headquarters, over there. Position of your regiment will be back there, down near the road. You'll be in reserve behind the crest. Don't have to dig in, but don't go way." Pitzer led them down the grass, pointed to a flat space just above the road, the masses of guns and wagons, in plain sight of the headquarters. "Here it is, Colonel. I'm to place you here. Colonel Rice will be by in a bit. Says you are to report to General Sykes later on." He saluted, sneezed, wandered off, in no great hurry, wiping his nose.

Chamberlain placed the regiment. They sat in the field, in the sun. There were questions about rations. Chamberlain thought: All those wagons down there, there ought to be something. He sent Ruel Thomas out to scrounge. Brother Tom went off to find the hospital, to see how the boys were, to see how Buster Kilrain was getting along. Chamberlain smelled coffee, the lovely smell of cooking chicken. He tried to follow his nose, was interrupted by another odor. He climbed a stone fence, knee high, saw a shallow depression filled with dead horses, dragged there to get them off the crest, legs and guts and glaring teeth, beginning to smell. Wind still luckily from the south. Chamberlain went back across the stone fence, looked up toward the crest. Couldn't see much from here. Could sure use some food. Felt incredibly lonesome, no one to talk to anymore. Sat by himself. The men around him were rigging shade, collapsing. Ellis Spear came up, sat down, said hello, fell asleep. The sun was too much. The men were moving with slow, drugged movements. Chamberlain thought: Any minute now I will go to sleep. Dreamyly. He smiled. Did not want to sleep. Food. Get some fuel. Mustn't sleep.

A rider. Man stopped before him. Chamberlain squinted upward. Message from General Sykes. Would like the pleasure of Colonel Chamberlain's company.

Chamberlain squinted. "Where is he?"

The rider indicated the crest, trees at the far end. Chamberlain said, "Haven't got a horse, but I guess I can make that."

He staggered to his feet. The rider, solicitous, hopped down, offered him the horse, led the animal by the bridle, making Chamberlain feel boyish and ridiculous. Chamberlain took the reins, woke Ellis Spear, told him to take over. Spear agreed blearily. The messenger led Chamberlain up the crest.

Past a clump of trees to his left the view opened. He could see a long way down across open fields to a road, a farmhouse, a long sweep of wheat rising up to green woods on the far ridge, at least a mile off. Lovely country. Heat shimmered on the road. Chamberlain thought: must be ninety. Hope my next war is in Maine. Where I will fight dreamyly. Owe her a letter. Soon. Kids be playing now. Sitting down to lunch. Eating—cold, cold milk, thick white bread, cheese and cream, ah.

He rode up into the shade of the trees. Sitting there ahead . . . was Hancock.

Chamberlain perked up, straightened his uniform. He had seen Hancock only a few times, but the man was memorable. Picture-book soldier: tall and calm, handsome, magnetic. Clean white shirt, even here, white cuffs, hat cocked forward slightly jauntily, shading his eyes. He was sitting on a camp stool, gazing westward intently. He moved; his arm came up. He was eating a piece of chicken.

He was surrounded by Generals. Some of them Chamberlain recognized: Gibbon, of Hancock's Corps, the cold man with the icy reputation. He had three brothers with the South. How many out there today, across that silent field? There was Pleasanton, of the cavalry, and Newton, new commander of the First Corps. Chamberlain saw a vast pot of stewed chicken, a pot of hot tea, a disappearing loaf of battered bread, some pickles. His mouth opened, watered, gulped. The Generals went on eating mercilessly. The messenger took Chamberlain on past the food to a dark spot near a white barn. General Sykes was sitting there, smoking a cigar, staring down at some papers, dictating an order. The messenger introduced him as he dismounted, then departed with the horse. Sykes stood up, extended a hand, looked him over as you look over a horse you are contemplating buying.

"Chamberlain. Yes. Heard about you. Want to hear more. Want you to write a report. Rice says you did a good job."

Chamberlain nodded and said thank you and went on smelling chicken. Sykes was a small, thin, grouchy man, had the reputation of a gentleman, though somewhat bad-tempered. Chamberlain thought: There are no good-tempered generals.

Sykes said, observing Chamberlain with the same look one gives a new rifle, "Rice says you're a schoolteacher."

"Well," Chamberlain said, "not quite."

"You aren't Regular Army."

"No, sir. I taught at Bowdoin."

"Bowdoin? *Oh*, you mean Bow-doyn. Yes. Heard of it. Amazing." He shook his head. "Tell me you ordered a bayonet charge, drove those people halfway to Richmond."

Chamberlain shifted his feet idiotically.

"Well, I'm going to look into it, Colonel, and let me tell you this, we need fightin' men in this army, any way we can get 'em, Regular Army or no, and one damn thing is sure, we can use some Brigade commanders. I'm going to look into it. Meantime, well done, well done. Now you go rest up. Nothing going to happen today."

He was finished, turned back to his work. Chamberlain asked about rations. Sykes told a lieutenant to see to it. Chamberlain saluted, backed off, out into the sun. No horse now, have to walk. Right foot on fire. Damn. He limped along the crest, not paying much attention to the view. He was a picturesque figure. He had not changed clothes nor washed nor shaved in a week. His blue pants were torn in several places and splotched with dried blood; his right boot was torn, his jacket was ripped at the shoulder, his sword was without a scabbard, was stuck into his belt. He hobbled along painfully, sleepily, detouring around the front of a Napoleon, didn't notice it until he opened his eyes and looked straight into the black maw, the hole of the barrel, and he blinked and came awake, momentarily, remembering Shakespeare's line: "the bubble reputation in the cannon's mouth." Doesn't look like a mouth. Looks like a damn dangerous hole. Stay away from that.

He was passing the group with Hancock and the chickens. He sighed wistfully, smelling fresh coffee, looked that way, was too proud to ask, saw a familiar figure: Meade himself. The crusty old stork, munching on a chicken leg. Chamberlain paused. Never saw much of Meade, didn't quite know what to think of him. But if he wants to retreat, he's a damn fool. Chamberlain had stopped; a number of the group of officers noticed him. Chamberlain looked down, saw blood coming out of his boot. This keeps up, I'm in trouble. Foot wounds always slow to heal. Wonder why?

An officer had detached himself from the group. Chamberlain had started to move on, but the officer came up, saluted. He was older than Chamberlain, but he was only a lieutenant. Sitting with all the generals. Chamberlain could feel the massed power; it was like being near great barrels of gunpowder. The lieutenant asked if he could be of service. Chamberlain said no thanks, wondering how to conquer pride and if a general would part with some chicken, and then felt ashamed, because his boys had none and would be guilty to eat something up here, but on the other hand, don't get something soon, and keep losing blood, might pass out, in all this damned heat, like you did the other time, and be no good to anybody.

The lieutenant introduced himself: Frank Haskell, aide to General Gibbon. He recognized Chamberlain's name. His eyes showed respect; now *that* was pleasant. Chamberlain explained that he'd been to see General Sykes and had no horse, and the foot was bothering him, and did the lieutenant think they might spare one scrawny leg, or even a neck? The lieutenant bowed, came back with *three* pieces of chicken, hot and greasy, wrapped in a dirty white cloth. Chamberlain took them with gratitude, staggered off down the hill. He ate one piece, preserved the other two. It was awful but marvelous. When he got back to the company he gave the two surviving pieces to Ellis Spear and told him to figure out a way to share them with somebody, that rations would be here soon, Sykes had promised.

He rested and took off his boot. Nothing to wrap it with. He tore off a bit of his shirt, was working away diligently, saw Tom coming.

Tom was losing the chipper edge. Chamberlain thought: Be all right in a bit. The young recover quickly. Must think on the theology of that: plugging a hole in the line with a brother. Except for that, it would all have been fine. An almost perfect fight, but the memory of that is a jar, is wrong. Some things a man cannot be asked to do. Killing of brothers. This whole war is concerned with the killing of brothers. Not my family. He thought of Gibbon. Praise be to God. Must send Tom somewhere else. In that moment, Chamberlain made up his mind: Tom would have to go. Tell him soon. Not now.

Tom sat. Lines in the face. Something wrong. Chamberlain saw: Kilrain?

"Lawrence, I been down to the hospital. Godawful mess. No shade, no room. They lying everywhere, out in the sun. They cuttin' off arms and legs right out in the open, front of everybody, like they did at Fredericksburg. God, they ought to know better, they ought not do that in public. Some of them people *die.* Man ought to have privacy at a time like that. You got to yell sometimes, you know? Lord . . ."

"Did you see Kilrain?"

Tom nodded. He sat with his back against the wall, the small stone wall this side of the dead horses, plucking grass. He sighed.

Chamberlain said, "How is he?"

"Well, Lawrence, he died."

"Oh," Chamberlain said. He blinked. The world came into focus. He could see leaves of the trees dark and sharp against the blue sky. He could smell the dead horses.

"He died this morning, 'fore I got there. Couple of the boys was with him. He said to tell you goodbye and that he was sorry."

Chamberlain nodded.

"It wasn't the wounds. They say his heart give out."

Chamberlain had stopped wrapping his bloody foot. Now he went on. But he could see the weary Irish face, the red-nose leprechaun. Just one small drink, one wee pint of the cruel . . .

Tom said, "I tell you, Lawrence, I sure was fond of that man."

"Yes," Chamberlain said.

Tom said nothing more. He sat plucking grass. Chamberlain wrapped the foot. The moment was very quiet. He sat looking down at his bloody leg, feeling the gentle wind, the heat from the south, seeing Kilrain dead on a litter, no more the steady presence. Sometimes he believed in a Heaven, mostly he believed in a Heaven; there ought to be a Heaven for young soldiers, especially young soldiers, but just as surely for the old soldier; there ought to be more than just that metallic end, and then silence, then the worms, and sometimes he believed, mostly he believed, but just this moment he did not believe at all, knew Kilrain was dead and gone forever, that the grin had died and would not reappear, never, there was nothing beyond the sound of the guns but the vast dark, the huge nothing, not even silence, just an end . . .

One sharp report, one single cannon. His head turned unconsciously to listen. A long flutter; the ball passed over, exploded on the far side of the road, along the edge of the hospitals there. He saw white smoke, splintered wood. He sat up.

Another gun. One single shot. And then the long roar as of the whole vast rumbling earth beginning to open. Chamberlain twitched around to see shells beginning to come over, falling first on the left, then almost instantly on the center, then to the right, then overhead, air bursts and ground bursts and solid shot. There was a blaze in the air obliterating his sight, hot breath of death noise. He was rolled over in the dirt, came out on his knees, facedown. Very, very close. He looked down, around, amazed. Tom was near, flat on the ground. All right, all right. He saw other troops behind boulders, molded into depressions in the earth. The world was blowing up. Had been under artillery fire before but never like this. Am I all right? Sat up to probe, found self intact. Looked out over the wall, saw no one moving anywhere. Moment ago there had been men moving all along the crest, men sitting and wandering and riding horses, artillery moving here and there, a wagon, a caisson. Now they were all gone, as men vanish from a busy street when rain comes. There was burst after burst in the dirty air, yellow lightning shattering the ground, splintering rock, ripping limbs off the great trees and sending them twisting swirling dancing along the ground, along the ridge. But no man anywhere, no man at all, as if the whole army had suddenly sunk into the earth. There was a horse moving riderless; another came out of the smoke. Blowing smoke was . . . another shell very close shook the ground, shook his vision. He hid behind the stone wall, stared very hard for a moment at a circle of greenish dried moss, the fine gray grain of the rock the most vivid thing he had ever seen, what marvelous eyesight one has now, and he thought: must tell the men to keep down, but of course that's stupid, they're down, any fool knows that. Peeked up along the rock, saw down to where shells were bursting along the road, saw cooks and bakers scrambling to escape, horses and wagons wobbling away down the road. A shell hit a caisson; it blew up in a great black tower of smoke, small black fragments whirling up into the air, fine dust sifting down everywhere, settling on the lips, into the eyes. More sound now. Chamberlain turned, saw the Union guns beginning to open up, to give it back, saw forms moving in the smoke, saw a whole line fire at once, wondered if an attack was coming, thought: how can you form to repel an attack? You can't even stand. But it went on and on, all the guns in all the world firing, and the dust drifted down and the smoke began to envelop him, and he lay finally facedown in the dust, the grass, thinking, well, I'll just wait a bit and look out again, and then gradually the world softened and the sound was a great lullaby, thunderous, madly, liquidly soothing, and he fell asleep.

Slept, but did not know how long. Woke to the sound of the continuing guns. No difference. Looked out across the rock, smoke everywhere. Union guns firing, men moving among the guns, hunched, a bloody horse running eerily by, three-legged, horrible sight, running toward the road. Another horse down with no head, like a broken toy. Man nearby, lying on his back, one hand groping upward, oddly reaching for the sky. Chamberlain closed his eyes, slept again. Opened them and lost all sense of time, had been sleeping since Noah in the sound of the guns, had slept through the mud and the ooze and thousands of days since Creation, the guns going on forever, like the endless rains of dawn. The earth was actually shuddering. It was as if you were a baby and your mother was shuddering with cold. More of the shells seemed to be passing overhead. He looked: there was a rider moving along in the smoke. Unbelievable. Familiar: Hancock. Chamberlain rose for a better look. It was Hancock all right. General Hancock had mounted his horse and was riding slowly along that ripped and thundering crest, chatting through puffs of smoke and showers of dirt to the men behind the wall, the men crouched in holes. There was an orderly behind him, carrying the flag of the Corps. The two horses moved slowly, unconcernedly along, an incredible sight, a dreamlike sight. They moved on up the line, ethereal, untouched. But the shells were definitely beginning to pass overhead. The Rebs were lengthening their aim, beginning to fire high, too long. Chamberlain saw a solid shot furrow the earth, an instant hole, almost a tunnel, black, spitting, and the shot rebounded a hundred feet into the air, spinning off across the road. Another caisson went; the hospital was pooled in smoke, as in the morning mist. Chamberlain rolled over onto his back and lay for awhile longer, hands clasped on his chest, gazing at the sky, trying to see the balls as they passed. He became aware for the first time of the incredible variety of sound. The great roar was composed of a thousand different rips and whispers, most incredible noise he had ever heard or imagined, like a great orchestra of death, all the sounds of myriad death: the *whicker whicker* of certain shells, the weird thin scream of others, the truly frightful sound made by one strange species that came every few moments, an indescribable keening, like old Death as a woman gone mad and a-hunting you, screaming, that would be the Whitworth, new English cannon the Rebs had. Then there were the sounds of the bursts, flat splats in the air, deeper bursts in ground, brutal smash and crack of shot into rock, shot splattering dirt and whining off, whispers of rock fragments and dirt fragments and small bits of metal and horse and man rippling the air, spraying the ground, humming the air, and the Union cannon braying away one after another, and an occasional scream, sometimes even joy, some of the cannoneers screaming with joy at hitting something as when they saw a caisson blow up across the way. They could see the explosion from here, above the smoke, but not much else, too much smoke; possibly that's why the Reb shells were going overhead. Reb artillery never very accurate. Thank the Lord. Elevation too high now. And *we* ought to conserve our long-range stuff. They'll be coming now in a few moments, once the guns stop. God knows how many of them will come this time. Right in the path, Joshuway, aren't you? Well, we ought to save our artillery then, damn it, and let them get out in the open. But they'll be coming again. Please God, let's stop 'em. I have this one small regiment . . .

He thought: must form the regiment, face the crest. Enough ammunition. Send Tom to the rear. Poor old Kilrain. We'll miss you. We're right in the path. Would not have missed this for anything, not anything in the world. Will rest now. Dreamyly.

He put his face down. The shells fell all down the line, all over the crest, down in the road and back in the woods and on the hospital and in the artillery park. Chamberlain went to sleep.

4

ARMISTEAD

. . . Saw it all begin, saw the guns go off one by one, each one a split second after the last, so that there was one long continuing blossoming explosion beginning on the right, erupting down through the grove and up the ridge to the left like one gigantic fuse sputtering up the ridge. Armistead looked at his watch: 1:07. He could see shells bursting on top of the ridge, on the Union lines, saw a caisson blow up in a fireball of yellow smoke, heard wild cheering amid the great sound of the cannon, but then the smoke came boiling up the ridge and he began to lose sight. Pickett was in front of him, out in the open, waving his hat and yelling wildly. Longstreet sat on a fence rail, motionless, crouched forward. There was too much smoke to see anything at all, just Longstreet's back, black, unmoving, and Pickett turning back through the smoke with joy in his face, and then the Union artillery opened up. The first shells came down in the trees beyond them. Longstreet turned slowly and looked. Then they began coming down in the field back there, where the Division was. Armistead turned and ran back through the trees across the ridge.

The Division lay in the open fields beyond the ridge. They had been there all morning, out in the open, through the growing heat. There was no protection: knee-high grass, low stone walls, off to the left a low field of rye. The shells began to come in on them and there was nothing to do but lie flat and hold the ground. Armistead walked out into the open, saw the men lying in long clumped rows, as if plowed up out of the earth, here and there an officer standing, a color sergeant, the flags erect in the earth and limp, no winds at all, and the shells bursting in sharp puffs everywhere, all down the line. Armistead walked among them. There was nothing he could do, no orders to give. He saw the first bloody dead, heard the first agony. Men were telling him angrily to get down, get down, but he went on wandering. Off in the distance he could see Garnett doing the same, on horseback. After a while it was not really so bad. The shells were not so thick. They came down, and here and there a shock and a scream, but the masses of men lay in rows in the grass, and in the distance a band was playing. Armistead walked slowly back toward the trees, hoping to find out what was going on. His chest was very tight. He looked at his watch: 1:35.

He wanted some moments to himself. The firing would stop and then they would line up for the assault. Between that time and this there ought to be a private moment. He came in under the trees and saw Longstreet writing a note, sending it with a galloping aide. There was Pickett, writing too, sitting on a camp stool as if composing a poem. Armistead smiled. He was closer to the guns now and the sound of the cannonade was enormous, like a beating of great wings, and all around him the air was fluttering and leaves were falling and the ground was shaking, and there was Pickett writing a poem, face furrowed with mighty thought, old George, never much of a thinker, and all that while in the back of Armistead's mind he could see Mary at the spinet: *it may be for years, it may be forever.* He could see the lips move, see tears on all the faces, but he could not hear that sound, the sound of the cannon was too great. He moved up closer to Pickett. Abruptly, not knowing beforehand that he would do it, he plucked the small ring from his little finger. Pickett looked up; his eyes glazed with concentration, focused, blinked.

"Here, George, send her this. My compliments." He handed Pickett the ring. Pickett took it, looked at it, a sentimental man; he reached out and took Armistead's hand and pumped it wordlessly, then flung an arm wildly out toward the guns, the noise, the hill to the east.

"Oh God, Lo, isn't it something? Isn't it marvelous? How does a man find words? Tell me something to say, Lo, you're good at that. Lord, I thought we'd missed it all. But do you know, this may be the last great fight of the war? Do you realize that? Isn't that marvelous?"

There was a long series of explosions; a tree limb burst. Armistead could hardly hear. But Pickett was profoundly moved. He was one of those, like Stuart, who looked on war as God's greatest game. At this moment Armistead seemed to be looking down a long way away, from a long, sleepy, hazy distance. George was grinning, clapping him on the arm. He said something about Sallie having the ring mounted. Armistead moved away.

He saw Longstreet sitting alone in the same place, on the same rail, drew comfort from the solid presence. Some officers had that gift. He did not. Hancock had it. Superb soldier. *It may be for years, it may be forever* . . . don't think on that. He looked at his watch: 1:47. Cannot go on much longer.

But he did not want to think about the attack right now. All the plans were laid, the thing was set, the others had planned it, Longstreet and Lee and Pickett, now he would carry it out, but for these few moments at least, the old soldier knows enough not to think about it. Shut the mind off and think on better days, remember things to be grateful for. Perhaps, like Pickett, you should write a letter. No. Would say the wrong things.

He went back toward his men, sat with his back against a tree, facing the open. He closed his eyes for a moment and he could see her again, Mary, *it may be for years, it may be forever,* and Hancock's face in tears, may God strike me dead. He opened his eyes, looked a question at Heaven, felt himself in the grip of these great forces, powerless, sliding down the long afternoon toward the end, as if it was all arranged somewhere, nothing he could have done to avoid it, not he or any Virginian. And he had said it and meant it: "If I lift a hand against you, friend, may God strike me dead." Well, it is all in His hands. Armistead took off his black hat and ran his hands through the gray hair, his forehead wet with perspiration, the hair wet and glistening in the light.

He was a grave and courtly man, a soldier all his life. He had a martial bearing and the kind of a face on which emotion rarely showed, a calm, almost regal quality. It had hindered him in the army because men thought he was not aggressive enough, but he was a good soldier, a dependable soldier, and all his life he had felt things more deeply than anyone knew—except *her,* so very briefly, before she died, as she was dying . . .

Don't think on that. But I loved her.

And loved much else. Always loved music. And good friends, and some moments together. Had much joy in the weather. So very rarely shared. I should have shared more. The way Pickett does, the way so many do. It's a liquid thing with them; it flows. But I . . . move on impulse. I gave him the ring. Premonition? Well, many will die. I'm a bit old for war. Will do my duty. I come from a line . . . no more of that. No need of that now. An Armistead does his duty, so do we all. But I wish, I wish it was not Hancock atop that hill. I wish this was Virginia again, my own green country, my own black soil. I wish . . . the war was over.

Quieter now. The fire was definitely slackening.

2:10.

He sat patiently, his back to a tree. The attack would be soon enough. When he thought of that his mind closed down like a blank gray wall, not letting him see. No point in thinking of that. He sat quietly, silently, suspended, breathing the good warm air, the smoke, the dust. Mustn't look ahead at all. One tends to look ahead with imagination. Must not look backward either. But it is so easy to see her, there at the spinet, and all of us gathered round, and all of us crying, my dear old friend . . . Hancock has no time for painting now. He was rather good at it. Always meant to ask him for one of his works. Never enough time. Wonder how it has touched him? Two years of war. Point of pride: My old friend is the best soldier they have. My old friend is up on the ridge.

Here was Garnett dressed beautifully, new gray uniform, slender, trim, riding that great black mare with the smoky nose. Armistead stood.

Garnett touched his cap. A certain sleepiness seemed to precede the battle, a quality of haze, of unreality, of dust in the air, dust in the haze. Garnett had the eyes of a man who has just awakened.

Garnett said, "How are you, Lo?"

Armistead said, "I'm fine, Dick."

"Well, that's good." Garnett nodded, smiling faintly. They stood under the trees, waiting, not knowing what to say. The fire seemed to be slackening.

Armistead said, "How's the leg?"

"Oh, all right, thank you. Bit hard to walk. Guess I'll have to ride."

"Pickett's orders, nobody rides."

Garnett smiled.

"Dick," Armistead said, "You're not going to ride."

Garnett turned, looked away.

"You can't do that," Armistead insisted, the cold alarm growing. "You'll stand out like . . . you'll be a perfect target."

"Well," Garnett said, grinning faintly, "well, I tell you, Lo. I can't walk."

And cannot stay behind. Honor at stake. He could not let the attack go without him; he had to prove once and for all his honor, because there was Jackson's charge, never answered, still in the air wherever Garnett moved, the word on men's lips, watching him as he went by, for Jackson was gone and Jackson was a great soldier . . . there was nothing Armistead could say. He could feel tears coming to his eyes but he could not even do that. Must not let Garnett see. There was always a chance. Perhaps the horse would be hit early. Armistead put out a hand, touched the horse, sorry to wish death on anyone, anything.

Garnett said, "Just heard a funny thing. Thought you'd appreciate it."

"Oh?" Armistead did not look him in the face. A shot took off the limb of a tree nearby, clipped it off cleanly, so that it fell all at once, making a sound like a whole tree falling. Garnett did not turn.

"We have some educated troops, you know, gentlemen privates. Well, I was riding along the line and I heard one of these fellas, ex-professor type, declaiming this poem, you know the one: 'Backward, turn backward, oh Time, in your flight, and make me a child again, just for this fight.' And then there's a pause, and a voice says, in a slow drawl, 'Yep. A *gal* child.' "

Garnett chuckled. "Harrison and I found us some Pennsylvania whisky, and experimented, and found that it goes well with Pennsylvania water. Wa'nt bad a-tall. Tried to save you some, but first thing you know . . ." He shrugged helplessly.

Their eyes never quite met, like two lights moving, never quite touching. There was an awkward silence. Garnett said, "Well, I better get back." He moved back immediately, not attempting to shake hands. "I'll see you in a little bit," he said, and galloped off along the ridge.

Armistead closed his eyes, prayed silently. God protect him. Let him have justice. Thy will be done.

Armistead opened his eyes. Had not prayed for himself. Not yet. It was all out of his hands, all of it; there was nothing he could do about anything anywhere in the whole world. Now he would move forward and lead the men up the ridge to whatever end awaited, whatever plan was foreordained, and he felt a certain mild detachment, a curious sense of dull calm, as on those long, long Sunday afternoons when you were a boy and had to stay dressed and neat and clean with nothing to do, absolutely nothing, waiting for the grownups to let you go, to give you the blessed release to run out in the open and play. So he did not even pray. Not yet. It was all in God's hands.

Pickett rode toward him, staff trailing behind. The fire was definitely slower now; the air of the woods was clearing. Pickett's face was bright red. He reined up, but was hopping around in the saddle, patting the horse, slapping his own thigh, gesturing wildly, pointing, grinning.

"Lewis, how's everything, any questions?"

Armistead shook his head.

"Good, good. As soon as the guns cease fire, we step off. Garnett and Kemper the first line, you're in the second. Route step, no halting, no stopping to fire, want to get up there as fast as you can. I'll keep toward the right flank, to cover that side. Do you need anything?"

"Nothing."

"Good, fine." Pickett nodded violently. "How are you feeling?"

"I'm fine."

"That's good. One other point. All officers are ordered to walk. No officer takes his horse. Utterly foolish." Pickett's horse, catching the General's excitement, reared and wheeled; Pickett soothed him. "So you go on foot, no exceptions."

"Yes," Armistead said. "But what about Garnett?"

"What about . . . oh." Pickett grimaced. "That leg."

"I don't think he can walk."

Pickett said slowly, *"Damn* it."

"George, order him not to make the charge."

"I can't do that."

"He's in no condition."

But Pickett shook his head. "You know I can't do that."

"A man on a horse, in front of that line. George, he'll be the only rider in a line a mile wide. They'll have every gun on that hill on him."

Pickett rubbed the back of his neck, slammed his thigh.

"He can't walk at all?"

"He might get fifty yards."

"Damn," Pickett said, caught himself guiltily. Not a good time to be swearing. "But you know how he feels. It's a matter of honor." Pickett threw up his hands abruptly, helplessly.

"Order him not to go, George."

Pickett shook his head reprovingly.

Armistead said, "All right. I understand. Yes. But I think . . . I'm getting a bit old for this business."

His voice was low and Pickett did not hear it, was not even listening. Armistead rode with him back into the woods along Seminary Ridge. The woods were dark and blessedly cool. He saw Longstreet sitting on a rail fence, gazing out into the glittering fields toward the enemy line. Pickett rode toward him and Longstreet turned slowly, swiveling his head, stared, said nothing. Pickett asked him about the guns. Longstreet did not seem to hear. His face was dark and still; he looked wordlessly at Pickett, then at Armistead, then turned back to the light. Pickett backed off. There was a savagery in Longstreet they all knew well. It showed rarely but it was always there and it was an impressive thing. Suddenly, in the dark grove, for no reason at all, Armistead looked at the dark face, the broad back, felt a bolt of almost stunning affection. It embarrassed him. But he thought: Before we go, I ought to say something.

Longstreet had moved suddenly, turning away from the rail. Armistead saw Pickett running up through the trees, a note in his hand, his face flushed. Longstreet stopped, turned to look at him, turned slowly, like an old man, looked at him with a strange face, a look tight and old that Armistead had never seen. Pickett was saying, "Alexander says if we're going at all, now's the time."

Longstreet stopped still in the dark of the woods. The huge glare behind him made it difficult to see. Armistead moved that way, feeling his heart roll over and thump once. Pickett said, pointing, "Alexander says we've silenced some Yankee artillery. They're withdrawing from the cemetery. What do you say, sir? Do we go in now?"

And Longstreet said nothing, staring at him, staring, and Armistead felt an eerie turning, like a sickness, watching Longstreet's face, and then he saw that Longstreet was crying. He moved closer. The General was crying. Something he never saw or ever expected to see, and the tears came to Armistead's eyes as he watched, saw Pickett beginning to lift his hands, holding out the note, asking again, and then Longstreet took a deep breath, his shoulders lifted, and then he nodded, dropping his head, taking his eyes away from Pickett's face, and in the same motion turned away, and Pickett let out a whoop and clenched a fist and shook it. Then he pulled a letter from his pocket and wrote something on it and handed it to Longstreet and Longstreet nodded again, and then Pickett was coming this way, face alight, look on his face of pure joy. And tears too, eyes flashing and watery, but with joy, with joy. He said something about being chosen for glory, for the glory of Virginia. He said, "Gentlemen, form your brigades."

Armistead moved out, called the brigade to its feet. He felt curiously heavy, slow, very tired, oddly sleepy. The heat was stuffy; one had trouble breathing.

The brigade dressed in a line. The fire had slackened all down the line; now for the first time there were long seconds of silence, long moments of stillness, and you could hear again the voices of the men, the movements of feet in grass and the clink of sabers, muskets, and that band was still piping, a polka this time, tinny and bumpy, joyous, out of tune. The men dressed right, line after line. Armistead moved silently back and forth. Down to the left he saw Garnett still on the horse. A mounted man in front of that line would not live five minutes. Every rifle on the crest would be aiming for him.

The orders came, bawled by a bull sergeant. The line began to move forward into the woods, forward toward the great yellow light of the open fields on the other side. They moved through the woods in good order, past the silent guns. Almost all the guns were quiet now. Armistead thought: Give the Yankees time to get set. Give Win Hancock time to get set. Move up reinforcements to the weak spots. Win, I'm sorry. Remember the old vow: May God strike me dead. And so the words came. I wish I could call them back. But Win understands. I have to come now. All in God's hands. Father, into your hands . . .

To the left of the line a rabbit broke from heavy brush, darted frantically out into the tall grass. A soldier said, close by, "That's right, ol' hare, you run, you run. If I'se an ol' hare, I'd run too."

A murmur, a laugh. They came out of the woods into the open ground.

The ground fell away from the woods into a shallow dip. They were out of sight of the Union line. To the left there was a finger of woods between them and Pettigrew's men. They would not see Pettigrew until they had moved out a way. The day was lovely and hot and still, not a bird anywhere. Armistead searched the sky. Marvelous day, but very hot. He blinked. Would love to swim now. Cool clear water, lake water, cool and dark at the bottom, out of the light.

The Division was forming. Garnett was in front, Kemper to the right; Armistead's line lay across the rear. It was a matchless sight, the Division drawn up as if for review. He looked down the line at the rows of guns, the soft blue flags of Virginia; he began to look at the faces, the tight faces, the eyes wide and dark and open, and he could hear more bands striking up far off to the right. No hurry now, a stillness everywhere, that same dusty, sleepy pause, the men not talking, no guns firing. Armistead moved forward through the ranks, saw Garnett on the horse, went over to say goodbye. Garnett no longer looked well; his coat was buttoned at the throat. Armistead said, "Dick, for God's sake and mine, get down off the horse."

Garnett said, "I'll see you at the top, Lo."

He put out his hand. Armistead took it.

Armistead said, "My old friend."

It was the first time in Armistead's life he had ever really known a man would die. Always before there was at least a chance, but here no chance at all, and now the man was his oldest friend.

Armistead said, "I ought to ride too."

Garnett said, "Against orders."

Armistead looked down the long line. "Have you ever seen anything so beautiful?"

Garnett smiled.

Armistead said, "They never looked better, on any parade ground."

"They never did."

Armistead heard once more that sweet female voice, unbearable beauty of the unbearable past: *it may be for years, it may be forever. Then why art thou silent. . . .* He still held Garnett's hand. He squeezed once more. Nothing more to say now. Careful now. He let the hand go.

He said, "Goodbye, Dick. God bless you."

Garnett nodded.

Armistead turned away, walked back to his brigade. Now for the first time, at just the wrong time, the acute depression hit him a blow to the brain. Out of the sleepiness the face of despair. He remembered Longstreet's tears. He thought: *a desperate thing.* But he formed the brigade. Out front, George Pickett had ridden out before the whole Division, was making a speech, but he was too far away and none of the men could hear. Then Pickett raised his sword. The order came down the line. Armistead, his voice never strong, bawled hoarsely, with all his force, "All right now, boys, for your wives, your sweethearts, for Virginia! At route step, forward, *ho!*"

He drew his sword, pointed it toward the ridge.

The brigade began to move.

He heard a chattering begin in the ranks. Someone seemed to be trying to tell a story. A man said, "Save your breath, boy." They moved in the tall grass, Garnett's whole line in front of them. The grass was trampled now, here and there a part in the line as men stepped aside to avoid a dead body, lost the day before. Armistead could still see nothing, nothing but the backs of the troops before him. He saw one man falter, looking to the right, gray-faced, to the sergeant who was watching him, had evidently been warned against him, now lifted a rifle and pointed it that way and the man got back into line.

The Northern artillery opened up, as if it had been asleep, or pulled back to lure them in. Massive wave of fire rolled over from the left. Pettigrew was getting it, then on the right batteries on the Rocky Hill were firing on Kemper. Garnett not yet really touched. Nothing much coming this way. But we didn't drive off any Yankee guns. Win's doing. He made them cease fire, knowing soon we'd be in the open. Guns to the left and right, nothing much in the center. Garnett's doing well.

He began to see. They were coming out into the open, up to where the ground dipped toward the Emmitsburg Road. Now to the left he could see the great mass of Pettigrew's Division, with Trimble coming up behind him, advancing in superb order, line after line, a stunning sight, red battle flags, row on row. Could not see Pettigrew, nor Trimble. The line must be a mile long. A mile of men, armed and coming, the earth shuddering with their movement, with the sound of the guns. A shell exploded in Garnett's line, another; gaps began to appear. Armistead heard the sergeants' hoarse "Close it up, close it up," and behind him he heard his own men coming and a voice saying calmly, cheerily, "Steady, boys, steady, there now, you can see the enemy, now you aint blind anymore, now you know exactly where's to go, aint that fine?" A voice said hollowly, "That's just fine."

But the artillery sound was blossoming. A whole new set of batteries opened up; he could see smoke rolling across the top of the hill, and no counterfire from behind, no Southern batteries. God, he thought, they're out of ammunition. But no, of course not; they just don't like firing over our heads. And even as he thought of that he saw a battery moving out of the woods to his left, being rushed up to support the line. And then the first shell struck near him, percussion, killing a mass of men to his right rear, his own men, and from then on the shells came down increasingly, as the first fat drops of an advancing storm, but it was not truly bad. Close it up, close it up. Gaps in front, the newly dead, piles of red meat. One man down holding his stomach, blood pouring out of him like a butchered pig, young face, only a boy, the man bending over him trying to help, a sergeant screaming, "Damn it, I said close it up."

Kemper's Brigade, ahead and to the right, was getting it. The batteries on the Rocky Hill were enfilading him, shooting right down his line, sometimes with solid shot, and you could see the damn black balls bouncing along like bowling balls, and here and there, in the air, tumbling over and over like a blood-spouting cartwheel, a piece of a man.

Armistead turned to look back. Solid line behind him, God bless them, coming on. Not so bad, now, is it? We'll do it, with God's help, Coming, they are, to a man. All good men here. He turned back to the front, Garnett's men were nearing the road. He could see old Dick, still there, on the great black horse. And then the first storm of musketry: the line of skirmishers. He winced. Could not see, but knew. Long line of men in blue, lined, waiting, their sights set, waiting, and now the first line of gray is near, clear, nearer, unmissable, an officer screams, if they're soldiers at all they cannot miss, and they're Hancock's men. Armistead saw a visible waver pass through the ranks in front of him. Close it up, close it up. The line seemed to have drifted slightly to the left. Heavy roll of musket fire now. The march slowing. He saw Garnett move down, thought for a moment, but no, he was moving down into that one swale, the protected area Pickett had spoken of. Armistead halted the men. Stood incredibly still in the open field with the artillery coming down like hail, great bloody hail. To the left, two hundred yards away, Pettigrew's men were slowing. Some of the men in front had stopped to fire. No point in that, too soon, too soon. Pickett's left oblique began. The whole line shifted left, moving to join with Pettigrew's flank, to close the gap. It was beautifully done, superbly done, under fire, in the face of the enemy. Armistead felt enormous pride, his chest filled and stuffed with a furious love. He peered left, could not see Trimble. But they were closing in, the great mass converging. Now he moved up and he could see the clump of trees, the one tree like an umbrella, Lee's objective, and then it was gone in smoke.

Garnett's boys had reached the road. They were slowing, taking down rails. Musket fire was beginning to reach them. The great noise increased, beating of wings in the air. More dead men: a long neat line of dead, like a shattered fence. And now the canister, *oh God,* he shuddered, millions of metal balls whirring through the air like startled quail, murderous quail, and now for the first time there was screaming, very bad sounds to hear. He began to move past wounded struggling to the rear, men falling out to help, heard the sergeants ordering the men back into line, saw gray faces as he passed, eyes sick with fear, but the line moved on. Dress it up, close it up. He looked back for a moment and walked backward up the long rise, looking backward at his line coming steadily, slowly, heads down as if into the wind, then he turned back to face the front.

To the right the line was breaking. He saw the line falter, the men beginning to clump together. Massed fire from there. In the smoke he could see a blue line. Kemper's boys were shifting this way, slowing. Armistead was closing in. He saw a horse coming down through the smoke: Kemper. Riding. Because Garnett rode. Still alive, even on the horse. But there was blood on his shoulder, blood on his face, his arm hung limp, he had no sword. He rode to Armistead, face streaked and gray, screaming something Armistead could not hear, then came up closer and turned, waving the bloody arm.

"Got to come up, come up, help me, in God's name. They're flanking me, they're coming down on the right and firing right into us, the line's breaking, we've got to have help."

Armistead yelled encouragement; Kemper tried to explain. They could not hear each other. A shell blew very close, on the far side of the horse, and Armistead, partially shielded, saw black fragments rush by, saw Kemper nearly fall. He grabbed Kemper's hand, screaming, "I'll double-time." Kemper said, "Come quick, come quick, for God's sake," and reined the horse up and turned back to the right. And beyond him Armistead saw a long blue line, Union boys out in the open, kneeling and firing from the right, and beyond that violent light of rows of cannon, and another flight of canister passed over. Kemper's men had stopped to fire, were drifting left. Too much smoke to see. Armistead turned, called his aides, took off the old black felt and put it on the tip of his sword and raised it high in the air. He called for double-time, double-time; the cry went down the line. The men began to run. He saw the line waver, ragged now, long legs beginning to eat up the ground, shorter legs falling behind, gaps appearing, men actually seeming to disappear, just to vanish out of the line, leaving a stunned vacancy, and the line slowly closing again, close it up, close it up, beginning to ripple and fold but still a line, still moving forward in the smoke and the beating noise.

They came to the road. It was sunken into the field, choked like the bed of a stream with mounded men. Armistead jumped down, saw a boy in front of him, kneeling, crying, a row of men crouched under the far bank, an officer yelling, pounding with the flat of his sword. There was a house to the right, smoke pouring from the roof, a great clog of men jammed behind the house, but men were moving across the road and up toward the ridge. There was a boy on his knees on the road edge, staring upward toward the ridge, unmoving. Armistead touched him on the shoulder, said, "Come on, boy, come on." The boy looked up with sick eyes, eyes soft and black like pieces of coal. Armistead said, "Come on, boy. What will you think of yourself tomorrow?"

The boy did not move. Armistead told an officer nearby; "Move these people out." He climbed up the roadbank, over the gray rails on the far side, between two dead bodies, one a sergeant, face vaguely familiar, eyes open, very blue. Armistead stood high, trying to see.

Kemper's men had come apart, drifting left. There was a mass ahead but it did not seem to be moving. Up there the wall was a terrible thing, flame and smoke. He had to squint to look at it, kept his head down, looked left, saw Pettigrew's men still moving, but the neat lines were gone, growing confusion, the flags dropping, no Rebel yell now, no more screams of victory, the men falling here and there like trees before an invisible axe, you could see them go one by one and in clumps, suddenly, in among the columns of smoke from the shell. Far to the left he saw: Pettigrew's men were running. He saw red flags streaming back to the rear. One of Pettigrew's brigades had broken on the far left. Armistead raised his sword, saw that the sword had gone through the hat and the hat was now down near his hand. He put the hat up again, the sword point on a new place, started screaming, follow me, follow me, and began the long last walk toward the ridge. No need for hurry now, too tired to run, expecting to be hit at any moment. Over on the right no horse. Kemper was down, impossible to live up there. Armistead moved on, expecting to die, but was not hit. He moved closer to the wall up there, past mounds of bodies, no line any more, just men moving forward at different speeds, stopping to fire, stopping to die, drifting back like leaves blown from the fire ahead. Armistead thought: we won't make it. He lifted the sword screaming, and moved on, closer, closer, but it was all coming apart; the whole world was dying. Armistead felt a blow in the thigh, stopped, looked down at blood on his right leg. But no pain. He could walk. He moved on. There was a horse coming down the ridge: great black horse with blood all over the chest, blood streaming through bubbly holes, blood on the saddle, dying eyes, smoke-gray at the muzzle: Garnett's horse.

Armistead held to watch the horse go by, tried to touch it. He looked for Garnett ahead; he might be afoot, might still be alive. But vision was mistier. Much, much smoke. Closer now. He could see separate heads; he could see men firing over the wall. The charge had come to a halt; the attack had stopped. The men ahead were kneeling to fire at the blue men on the far side of the wall, firing at the gunners of the terrible cannon. Canister came down in floods, wiping bloody holes. A few flags tilted forward, but there was no motion; the men had stalled, unable to go on, still thirty yards from the wall and no visible halt, unable to advance, unwilling to run, a deadly paralysis.

Armistead stopped, looked. Pettigrew's men were coming up on the left: not many, not enough. Here he had a few hundred. To the right Kemper's brigade had broken, but some of the men still fired. Armistead paused for one long second. It's impossible now, cannot be done; we have failed and it's all done, all those boys are dead, it's all done, and then he began to move forward automatically, instinctively, raising the black hat on the sword again, beginning to scream, "Virginians! With me! With me!" and he moved forward the last yards toward the wall, drawn by the pluck of that great force from within, for home, for country, and now the ground went by slowly, inexorably, like a great slow river, and the moment went by black and slow, close to the wall, closer, walking now on the backs of dead men, troops around beginning to move, yelling at last the wild Rebel yell, and the blue troops began to break from the fence. Armistead came up to the stone wall, and the blue boys were falling back. He felt a moment of incredible joy. A hot slap of air brushed his face, but he was not hit; to the right a great blast of canister and all the troops to his right were down, but then there was another rush, and Armistead leaped to the top of the wall, balanced high on the stones, seeing the blue troops running up the slope into the guns, and then he came down on the other side, had done it, had gotten inside the wall, and men moved in around him, screaming. And then he was hit, finally, in the side, doubling him. No pain at all, merely a nuisance. He moved toward a cannon the boys had just taken. Some blue troops had stopped near the trees above and were kneeling and firing; he saw the rifles aimed at him. Too weary now. He had made it all this way; this way was enough. He put an arm on the cannon to steady himself. But now there was a rush from the right. Blue troops were closing in. Armistead's vision blurred; the world turned soft and still. He saw again: a bloody tangle, men fighting hand to hand. An officer was riding toward him; there was a violent blow. He saw the sky, swirling round and round, thank God no pain. A sense of vast release, of great peace. I came all the way up, I came over the wall . . .

He sat against something. The fight went on. He looked down at his chest, saw the blood. Tried to breathe, experimentally, but now he could feel the end coming, now for the first time he sensed the sliding toward the dark, a weakening, a closing, all things ending now slowly and steadily and peacefully. He closed his eyes, opened them. A voice said, "I was riding toward you, sir, trying to knock you down. You didn't have a chance."

He looked up: a Union officer. I am not captured, I am dying. He tried to see: help me, help me. He was lifted slightly.

Everywhere the dead. All his boys. Blue soldiers stood around him. Down the hill he could see the gray boys moving back, a few flags fluttering. He closed his eyes on the sight, sank down in the dark, ready for death, knew it was coming, but it did not come. Not quite yet. Death comes at its own speed. He looked into the blue sky, at the shattered trees. *It may be for years, it may be forever* . . . The officer was speaking. Armistead said, "Is General Hancock . . . would like to see General Hancock."

A man said, "I'm sorry, sir. General Hancock has been hit."

"No," Armistead said. He closed his eyes. Not both of us. Not all of us. Sent to Mira Hancock, to be opened in the event of my death. But not both of us, please dear God . . .

He opened his eyes. Closer now. The long slow fall begins.

"Will you tell General Hancock . . . Can you hear me, son?"

"I can hear you, sir."

"Will you tell General Hancock, please, that General Armistead sends his regrets. Will you tell him . . . how very sorry I am . . ."

The energy failed. He felt himself flicker. But it was a long slow falling, very quiet, very peaceful, rather still, but always the motion, the darkness closing in, and so he fell out of the light and away, far away, and was gone.

5

LONGSTREET

Longstreet sat on a rail fence, hugging his chest with both arms. He suspended thinking; his mind was a bloody vacancy, like a room in which there has been a butchering. He tried once formally to pray, but there was no one there and no words came, and over and over he said to himself, Heavenly Father, Heavenly Father. He watched the battle dissolve to nightmare: the neat military lines beginning to come apart as they crossed the road and no order beyond that but black struggling clots and a few flags in the smoke, tilting like sails above a white sea, going down one by one. A shell burst near Longstreet and he felt the hot brutal breath, and then the sounds of battle were softer, the smoke began to blanket the field. But there was still a few flags moving toward the top of the hill. Longstreet put glasses to his eyes, saw ghost figures stumbling in white smoke, yellow blaze of cannon, black flakes of men spattering upward into a white sky, and then the smoke was too thick and he could not see anything and it was like going blind. A paralysis came over him. He sat staring off into the white sea where the guns still flashed and boomed softly, at a great distance, until he saw the first men beginning to come back out of the smoke. They came slowly up the long green slope, a ragged crowd of men. No one was running. They were moving with slow set stubborn unstoppable looks on their faces, eyes down, guns dragging the ground, and they were moving slowly but steadily, even though the Union guns had elevated and shells were still falling on them as they came back up the field. The smoke parted for a vision: the green field dirtied a vast mile with lumped bodies, white and red, and far across the field the whole army falling back in a speckled flood across the road to the safety of the woods, and there at the top of the hill one flag erect near the center of the Union line. Then that flag was down in the smoke, and Longstreet could no longer see, and the retreat began to flood by him.

The men parted as they passed him, not looking at him. He sat on an island in the stream of retreating men. He made no attempt to stop them. A man rode up on a black horse, a frantic man with blood on his face: Harry Bright, Pickett's staff. He was screaming. Longstreet stared at him. The man went on screaming. Longstreet made out: Pickett was asking for support. Longstreet shook his head, wordlessly, pointed down at the field. Bright did not yet understand. Longstreet said patiently, "Nine brigades went in. That's all we have." There was nothing to send now, no further help to give, and even if Lee on the other side would send support now it would be too late. Longstreet hugged his chest. He got down off the fence. A black horse rode up out of the smoke: familiar spot on a smoky forehead, blood bubbling from a foaming chest: Garnett's mount. Longstreet nodded. He told Bright to instruct Pickett to fall back. He sent word for a battery to move down the slope in front of him, to fire uphill and protect Pickett as he retreated.

The wind had changed. The smoke was blowing back across the field against his face. The guns were easing off. The men streamed by: nightmare army, faces gray and cold, sick. Longstreet felt a cold wind blowing in his brain. He stood up. He had sat long enough. He looked up to see Fremantle. A moment ago the man had been cheering wildly, not understanding what was happening. Now he was holding out a silver flask. Longstreet shook his head. It was all done. Along with all the horror of loss, and the weariness, and all the sick helpless rage, there was coming now a monstrous disgust. He was through. They had all died for nothing and he had sent them. He thought: a man is asked to bear too much. And he refused. He began slowly to walk forward. He was all done. He would find a gun somewhere and take a walk forward. He walked down the long slope in front of him toward that one battery that was still firing toward the blue line. He saw a rifle by a dead man, the man missing a leg and the leg nearby, bent and chewed at the knee, and the rifle clean and new and cold. He bent down to pick it up, and when he looked up he saw Lee.

The old man was riding the gray horse across the open ground in front of the trees. He had taken his hat off and the white hair and the unmistakable white head were visible from a long way off. He was walking the horse slowly along the ground among the first rows of dead where the cannon had begun to take them as they stepped out of the trees, and the retreating men were slowed at the sight of him. Longstreet stopped. The old man reined up and stood for a moment immobile, head turned eastward toward the enemy, the gray hat on the horn of the saddle. He sat there motionless as a statue and the men coming back began to turn toward him. He sat looking down, talking to them. Longstreet stood watching him. He knew that he would never forgive the old man, never. He stood paralyzed holding the rifle and tears were running down his cheeks. The old man saw him and began riding toward him. Longstreet could hear him: "It is all my fault, it is all my fault," and men were already arguing with him and shaking their heads in rage and shame, but Lee said, "We shall rest and try it again another day. Now you must show good order. Never let them see you run."

There were men all around him, some of them crying. A tall man in a gray beard was pleading with Lee to let them attack again. A bony boy in a ripped and bloody shirt had hold of the halter of his horse and was insisting that the General move to the rear. Lee said again, "It is all my fault," but they were shaking their heads. Lee saw Longstreet.

Longstreet waited, the rifle in his hand. Lee rode slowly forward. A crowd of men was gathering now, a hundred or more. The stream to the rear had slowed. Now it was quieter and the nearby cannon were no longer firing and Lee came forward out of the smoke and the nightmare. His face was hard and red, his eyes bright and hot; he had a stiff, set look to him and both hands held hard to the saddle horn and when he looked at Longstreet his eyes had nothing in them. The old man stopped the horse and pointed east. He said in a soft, feathery voice, "I think they are forming over there, General. I think they may attack."

Longstreet nodded. The old man's voice was very soft; Longstreet could hardly hear. Lee looked down on him from a long way away. Longstreet nodded again. There was motion in front of him and suddenly he saw George Pickett, blood-stained. His hat was gone; his hair streamed like a blasted flower. His face was pale; he moved his head like a man who has heard too loud a sound. He rode slowly forward. Lee turned to meet him. Longstreet was vaguely amazed that Pickett was still alive. He heard Pickett say something to Lee. George turned and pointed back down the hill. His face was oddly wrinkled.

Lee raised a hand. "General Pickett, I want you to reform your Division in the rear of this hill."

Pickett's eyes lighted as if a sudden pain had shot through him. He started to cry. Lee said again with absolute calm, "General, you must look to your Division."

Pickett said tearfully, voice of a bewildered angry boy, "General Lee, I have no Division." He pointed back down the hill, jabbing at the blowing smoke, the valley of wrecked men, turned and shuddered, waving, then saying, "Sir? What about my men?" as if even now there was still something Lee could do to fix it. "What about my men? Armistead is gone. Garnett is gone. Kemper is gone. All my colonels are gone. General, *every one*. Most of my men are gone. Good God, sir, what about my men?"

Longstreet turned away. Enough of this. He looked for his horse, beckoned. The groom came up. Longstreet could look down across the way and see blue skirmishers forming across his front. The land sloped to where the one battery was still firing uphill into the smoke. Longstreet nodded. I'm coming. He felt a tug at his leg, looked down: Sorrel. Let me go, Major. The staff was around him, someone had the reins of the horse. Longstreet felt the gathering of the last great rage. He looked down slowly and pulled at the reins slowly and said carefully, "Major, you better let this damned horse go."

And then he pointed.

"They're coming, do you see? I'm going to meet them. I want you to put fire down on them and form to hold right here. I'm going down to meet them."

He rode off down the hill. He moved very quickly and the horse spurred and it was magnificent to feel the clean air blow across your face, and he was aware suddenly of the cold tears blurring his eyes and tried to wipe them away, Old

Hero shying among all the dead bodies. He leaped a fence and became aware of a horse following and swung and saw the face of Goree, the frail Texan trailing him like the wind. Ahead of him the guns were firing into a line of blue soldiers and Longstreet spurred that way and Goree pulled alongside, screaming, "What are your orders, General? Where do you want me to go?"

A shell blew up in front of him. He swerved to the right. Goree was down and Longstreet reined up. The bony man was scrambling, trying to get to his feet. Rifle fire was beginning to pluck at the air around them. Longstreet saw some of the staff riding toward him, trying to catch up. He rode to Goree and looked down but he couldn't say anything more, no words would come, and he couldn't even stop the damn tears, and Goree's eyes looking up, filled with pain and sorrow and pity, was another thing he would remember as long as he lived, and he closed his eyes.

The staff was around him, looking at him with wild eyes. Someone again had the bridle of his horse. Bullets still plucked the air: song of the dark guitar. He wanted to sleep. Someone was yelling, "Got to pull back," and he shook his head violently, clearing it, and turned back to the guns, letting the mind begin to function. "Place the guns," he bawled, "bring down some guns." He began directing fire. He took another shell burst close by and again the great drone filled his ears and after that came a cottony murmury rush, like a waterfall, and he moved in a black dream, directing the fire, waiting for them to come, trying to see through the smoke where the shells were falling. But the firing began to stop. The storm was ending. He looked out through the smoke and saw no more blue troops; they had pulled back. He thought, to God: if there is any mercy in you at all you will finish it now.

But the blue troops pulled back, and there was no attack.

After a while Longstreet sat on a fence. He noticed the rifle still in his hand. He had never used it. Carefully, he placed it on the ground. He stared at it for a while. Then he began to feel nothing at all. He saw the dirt-streaked face of T. J. Goree, watching him.

"How are you?" Longstreet said.

"Tolerable."

Longstreet pointed uphill. "They aren't coming."

Goree shook his head.

"Too bad," Longstreet said.

"Yes, sir."

"Too bad," Longstreet said again.

"Yes, sir. We got plenty canister left. If they hit us now we could sure make it hot for them."

Longstreet nodded. After a moment Goree said, "General, I tell you plain. There are times when you worry me."

"Well," Longstreet said.

"It's no good trying to get yourself killed, General. The Lord will come for you in His own time."

Longstreet leaned back against a fencepost and stared up into the sky. For a moment he saw nothing but the clean and wondrous sky. He sat for a moment, coming back to himself. He thought of Lee as he had looked riding that hill, his hat off so that the retreating men could see him and recognize him. When they saw him they actually stopped running. From Death itself.

It was darker now. Late afternoon. If Meade was coming he would have to come soon. But there was no sign of it. A few guns were still firing a long way off; heartbroken men would not let it end. But the fire was dying; the guns ended like sparks. Suddenly it was still, enormously still, a long pause in the air, a waiting, a fall. And then there was a different silence. Men began to turn to look out across the smoldering field. The wind had died; there was no motion anywhere but the slow smoke drifting and far off one tiny flame of a burning tree. The men stood immobile across the field. The knowledge began to pass among them, passing without words, that it was over. The sun was already beginning to set beyond new black clouds which were rising in the west, and men came out into the open to watch the last sunlight flame across the fields. The sun died gold and red, and the final light across the smoke was red, and then the slow darkness came out of the trees and flowed up the field to the stone wall, moving along above the dead and the dying like the shadowing wing of an enormous bird, but still far off beyond the cemetery there was golden light in the trees on the hill, a golden glow over the rocks and the men in the last high places, and then it was done, and the field was gray.

Longstreet sat looking out across the ground to the green rise of the Union line and he saw a blue officer come riding along the crest surrounded by flags and a cloud of men, and he saw troops rising to greet him.

"They're cheering," Goree said bitterly, but Longstreet could not hear. He saw a man raise a captured battle flag, blue flag of Virginia, and he turned from the sight. He was done. Sorrel was by his side, asking for orders. Longstreet shook his head. He would go somewhere now and sleep. He thought: couldn't even quit. Even that is not to be allowed. He mounted the black horse and rode back toward the camp and the evening.

With the evening came a new stillness. There were no guns, no music. Men sat alone under ripped branchless trees. A great black wall of cloud was gathering in the west, and as the evening advanced and the sky grew darker they could begin to see the lightning although they could not yet hear the thunder. Longstreet functioned mechanically, placing his troops in a defensive line. Then he sat alone by the fire drinking coffee. Sorrel brought the first figures from Pickett's command.

Armistead and Garnett were dead; Kemper was dying. Of the thirteen colonels in Pickett's Division seven were dead and six were wounded. Longstreet did not look at the rest. He held up a hand and Sorrel went away.

But the facts stayed with him. The facts rose up like shattered fenceposts in the mist. The army would not recover from this day. He was a professional and he knew that as a good doctor knows it, bending down for perhaps the last time over a doomed beloved patient. Longstreet did not know what he would do now. He looked out at the burial parties and the lights beginning to come on across the field like clusters of carrion fireflies. All that was left now was more dying. It was final defeat. They had all died and it had accomplished nothing, the wall was unbroken, the blue line was sound. He shook his head suddenly, violently, and remembered the old man again, coming bareheaded along the hill, stemming the retreat.

After a while Lee came. Longstreet did not want to see him. But the old man came in a cluster of men, outlined under that dark and ominous sky, the lightning blazing beyond his head. Men were again holding the bridle of the horse, talking to him, pleading; there was something oddly biblical about it, and yet even here in the dusk of defeat there was something else in the air around him; the man brought strength with his presence: doomed and defeated, he brought nonetheless a certain majesty. And Longstreet, knowing that he would never quite forgive him, stood to meet him.

Lee dismounted. Longstreet looked once into his face and then dropped his eyes. The face was set and cold, stonelike. Men were speaking. Lee said, "I would like a few moments alone with General Longstreet." The men withdrew. Lee sat in a camp chair near the fire and Longstreet sat and they were alone together. Lee did not speak. Longstreet sat staring at the ground, into the firelight. Lightning flared; a cool wind was blowing. After a while Lee said, "We will withdraw tonight."

His voice was husky and raw, as if he had been shouting. Longstreet did not answer. Lee said, "We can withdraw under cover of the weather. If we can reach the river, there will be no more danger."

Longstreet sat waiting, his mind vacant and cold. Gradually he realized that the old man was expecting advice, an opinion. But he said nothing. Then he looked up. The old man had his hand over his eyes. He looked vaguely different. Longstreet felt a chill. The old man said slowly, "Peter, I'm going to need your help."

He kept his hand over his eyes, shading himself as if from bright sunlight. Longstreet saw him take a deep breath and let it go. Then he realized that Lee had called him by his nickname. Lee said, "I'm really very tired."

Longstreet said quickly, "What can I do?"

Lee shook his head. Longstreet had never seen the old man lose control. He had not lost it now, but sat there with his hand over his eyes and Longstreet felt shut away from his mind and in that same moment felt a shudder of enormous pity. He said, "General?"

Lee nodded. He dropped the hand and glanced up once quickly at Longstreet, eyes bright and black and burning. He shook his head again. He raised both palms, a gesture almost of surrender, palms facing Longstreet, tried to say something, shook his head for the last time. Longstreet said, "I will take care of it, General. We'll pull out tonight."

"I thought . . ." Lee said huskily.

Longstreet said, "Never mind."

"Well," Lee said. He took a long deep breath, faced the firelight. "Well, now we must withdraw."

"Yes."

They sat for a while in silence. Lee recovered. He crossed his legs and sat looking into the fire and the strength came back, the face smoothed calm again and grave, the eyes silent and dark. He said, "We must look to our own deportment. The spirit of the Army is still very good."

Longstreet nodded.

"We will do better another time."

Longstreet shook his head instinctively. He said, "I don't think so."

Lee looked up. The eyes were clearer now. The moment of weakness had come and passed. What was left was a permanent weariness. A voice in Longstreet said: let the old man alone. But there had been too much death; it was time for reality. He said slowly, "I don't think we can win it now."

After a moment Lee nodded, as if it were not really important. He said, "Perhaps."

"I don't think—" Longstreet raised his hands—"I don't know if I can go on leading them. To die. For nothing."

Lee nodded. He sat for a long while with his hands folded in his lap, staring at the fire, and the firelight on his face was soft and warm. Then he said slowly, "They do not die for us. Not for us. That at least is a blessing." He spoke staring at the fire. "Each man has his own reason to die. But if they go on, I will go on." He paused. "It is only another defeat." He looked up at Longstreet, lifted his palms out, folded them softly, slowly. "If the war goes on—and it will, it will—

what else can we do but go on? It is the same question forever, what else can we do? If they fight, we will fight with them. And does it matter after all who wins? Was that ever really the question? Will God ask that question, in the end?" He put his hands on his thighs, started painfully to rise.

He got to his feet, laboring. Longstreet reached forward instinctively to help him. Lee said, embarrassed, "Thank you," and then where Longstreet held his arm he reached up and covered Longstreet's hand. He looked into Longstreet's eyes. Then he said, "You were right. And I was wrong. And now you must help me see what must be done. Help us to *see.* I become . . . very tired."

"Yes," Longstreet said.

They stood a moment longer in the growing dark. The first wind of the coming storm had begun to break over the hills and the trees, cold and heavy and smelling of rain. Lee said, "I lectured you yesterday, on war."

Longstreet nodded. His mind was too full to think.

"I was trying to warn you. But . . . you have no Cause. You and I, we have no Cause. We have only the army. But if a soldier fights only for soldiers, he cannot ever win. It is only the soldiers who die."

Lee mounted the gray horse. Longstreet watched the old man clear his face and stiffen his back and place the hat carefully, formally on his head. Then he rode off into the dark. Longstreet stood watching him out of sight. Then he turned and went out into the field to say goodbye, and when that was done he gave the order to retreat.

6

CHAMBERLAIN

In the evening he left the Regiment and went off by himself alone while the night came over the field. He moved out across the blasted stone wall and down the long littered slope until he found a bare rock where he could sit and look out across the battlefield at dusk. It was like the gray floor of hell. Parties moved with yellow lights through blowing smoke under a low gray sky, moving from black lump to black lump while papers fluttered and blew and fragments of cloth and cartridge and canteen tumbled and floated across the gray and steaming ground. He remembered with awe the clean green fields of morning, the splendid yellow wheat. This was another world. His own mind was blasted and clean, windblown; he was still slightly in shock from the bombardment and he sat not thinking of anything but watching the last light of the enormous day, treasuring the last gray moment. He knew he had been present at one of the great moments in history. He had seen them come out of the trees and begin to march up the slope and when he closed his eyes he could still see them coming. It was a sight few men were privileged to see and many who had seen it best had not lived through it. He knew that he would carry it with him as long as he lived, and he could see himself as an old man trying to describe it to his grandchildren, the way the men had looked as they came out into the open and formed for the assault, the way they stood there shining and immobile, all the flags high and tilting and glittering in the sun, and then the way they all kicked to motion, suddenly, all beginning to move at once, too far away for the separate feet to be visible so that there seemed to be a silvery rippling all down the line, and that was the moment when he first felt the real fear of them coming: when he saw them begin to move.

Chamberlain closed his eyes and saw it again. It was the most beautiful thing he had ever seen. No book or music would have that beauty. He did not understand it: a mile of men flowing slowly, steadily, inevitably up the long green ground, dying all the while, coming to kill you, and the shell bursts appearing above them like instant white flowers, and the flags all tipping and fluttering, and dimly you could hear the music and the drums, and then you could hear the officers screaming, and yet even above your own fear came the sensation of unspeakable beauty. He shook his head, opened his eyes. Professors' minds. But he thought of Aristotle: pity and terror. So this is tragedy. Yes. He nodded. In the presence of real tragedy you feel neither pain nor joy nor hatred, only a sense of enormous space and time suspended, the great doors open to black eternity, the rising across the terrible field of that last enormous, unanswerable question.

It was dark around him. There was one small gray area of the sky still aglow in the west; the rest was blackness, and flashes of lightning. At that moment a fine rain began to fall and he heard it come toward him, seeking him in a light patter up the slope. He had dust all over him, a fine pulverized powder from the shelling, dust in his hair and eyes and dust gritty in his teeth, and now he lifted his face to the rain and licked his lips and could taste the dirt on his face and knew that he would remember that too, the last moment at Gettysburg, the taste of raw earth in the cold and blowing dark, the touch of cold rain, the blaze of lightning.

After a while brother Tom found him, sitting in the rain, and sat with him and shared the darkness and the rain. Chamberlain remembered using the boy to plug a hole in the line, stopping the hole with his own brother's body like a warm bloody cork, and Chamberlain looked at himself. It was so natural and clear, the right thing to do: fill the gap with the body of my brother. Therefore Tom would have to go, and Chamberlain told himself: Run the boy away from you, because if he stays with you he'll die. He stared at the boy in the darkness, felt an incredible love, reached out to touch him, stopped himself.

Tom was saying, "I guess you got to hand it to them, the way they came up that hill."

Chamberlain nodded. He was beginning to feel very strange, stuffed and strange.

"But we stood up to them. They couldn't break us," Tom said.

"No."

"Well, nobody ever said they wasn't good soldiers. Well, they're Americans anyway, even if they are Rebs."

"Yes," Chamberlain said.

"Thing I cannot understand. Thing I never will understand. How can they fight so hard, them Johnnies, and all for slavery?"

Chamberlain raised his head. He had forgotten the Cause. When the guns began firing he had forgotten it completely. It seemed very strange now to think of morality, or that minister long ago, or the poor runaway black. He looked out across the dark field, could see nothing but the yellow lights and outlines of black bodies stark in the lightning.

Tom said, "When you ask them prisoners, they never talk about slavery. But, Lawrence, how do you explain that? What else is the war about?"

Chamberlain shook his head.

"If it weren't for the slaves, there'd never have been no war, now would there?"

"No," Chamberlain said.

"Well then, I don't care how much political fast-talking you hear, that's what it's all about and that's what them fellers died for, and I tell you, Lawrence, I don't understand it at all."

"No," Chamberlain said. He was thinking of Kilrain: *no divine spark.* Animal meat: the Killer Animals.

Out in the field nearby they were laying out bodies, row after row, the feet all even and the toes pointing upward like rows of black leaves on the border of a garden. He saw again the bitter face of Kilrain, but Chamberlain did not hate the gentlemen, could not think of them as gentlemen. He felt instead an extraordinary admiration. It was as if they were his own men who had come up the hill and he had been with them as they came, and he had made it across the stone wall to victory, but they had died. He felt a violent pity. He said slowly, in memory of Kilrain, "Well, they're all equal now."

"In the sight of God, anyways."

"Yes," Chamberlain said. "In the sight of God."

Tom stood up. "Better get moving, Lawrence, there's a big rain coming."

Chamberlain rose, but he was not yet ready to go.

Tom said, "Do you think they'll attack again?"

Chamberlain nodded. They were not yet done. He felt an appalling thrill. They would fight again, and when they came he would be behind another stone wall waiting for them, and he would stay there until he died or until it ended, and he was looking forward to it with an incredible eagerness, as you wait for the great music to begin again after the silence. He shook his head, amazed at himself. He thought: have to come back to this place when the war is over. Maybe then I'll understand it.

The rain was much heavier now. He put on the stolen cavalry hat and blinked upward into the black sky. He thought: it was my privilege to be here today. He thanked God for the honor. Then he went back to his men.

The light rain went on falling on the hills above Gettysburg, but it was only the overture to the great storm to come. Out of the black night it came at last, cold and wild and flooded with lightning. The true rain came in a monster wind, and the storm broke in blackness over the hills and the bloody valley; the sky opened along the ridge, and the vast water thundered down, drowning the fires, flooding the red creeks, washing the rocks and the grass and the white bones of the dead, cleansing the earth and soaking it thick and rich with water and wet again with clean cold rainwater, driving the blood deep into the earth, to grow it again with the roots toward Heaven.

It rained all that night. The next day was Saturday, the Fourth of July.

"Thus ended the great American Civil War, which must upon the whole be considered the noblest and least avoidable of all the great mass conflicts of which till then there was record."

—Winston Churchill,
*A History of the English-
Speaking Peoples*

AFTERWORD

ROBERT EDWARD LEE

In August he asked to be relieved of command. Of the battle he says:

No blame can be attached to the army for its failure to accomplish what was projected by me. . . . I alone am to blame, in perhaps expecting too much of its prowess and valor . . . could I have foreseen that the attack on the last day would fail, I should certainly have tried some other course . . . but I do not know what better course I could have pursued.

His request is not accepted, although he cites his poor health, and he serves until the end of the war. He never again attempts a Napoleonic assault. When the war is over, he believes that the issue has been settled by combat, that God has passed judgment. He lays down arms, asks his men to do the same. His great prestige brings a peace which might not otherwise have been possible. He asks Congress for pardon; it is never given. Dies of heart disease in 1870, perhaps the most beloved General in the history of American war.

JAMES LONGSTREET

That winter he requests relief from command, on the ground that he no longer believes the South can win the war. Lee prevails upon him to stay. He is wounded severely in the Wilderness, 1864, but returns to be Lee's most dependable soldier, his right hand until the end at Appomattox.

After the war he makes two great mistakes. First, he becomes a Republican, attempts to join with old comrade Grant in rebuilding the South. For this he is branded a turncoat, within two years of the end of the war is being referred to by Southern newspapers as "the most hated man in the South."

Second, as time passes and it becomes slowly apparent that the war was lost at Gettysburg, Longstreet gives as his opinion what he believes to be true: that the battle was lost by Robert E. Lee. This occurs long after Lee's death, when Lee has become the symbol of all that is fine and noble in the Southern cause. The South does not forgive Longstreet the insult to Lee's name. At the great reunion, years later, of the Army of Northern Virginia, Longstreet is not even invited, but he comes anyway, stubborn to the end, walks down the aisle in his old gray uniform, stars of a general on his collar, and is received by an enormous ovation by the men, with tears and an embrace from Jefferson Davis.

His theories on defensive warfare are generations ahead of his time. The generals of Europe are still ordering massed assaults against fortified positions long years after his death, in 1904, at the age of eighty-three.

RICHARD EWELL

Serves with courage until the end, but as a corps commander he is fated never to achieve distinction. Of the Battle of Gettysburg he is later to remark: "It took a great many mistakes to lose that battle. And I myself made most of them."

AMBROSE POWELL HILL

Never to take his place in the Richmond society he so dearly loved, so richly deserved. Five days before Appomattox, at the Battle of Five Forks, he is killed by a sniper's bullet.

JOHN BELL HOOD

Loses not the arm but the use of it; it remains withered within his pinned sleeve for the rest of his days. Complains bitterly about the handling of the army at Gettysburg, is later given a command of his own: the Army of Tennessee. Defeated in Atlanta by Sherman, he spends much of the rest of his life justifying his actions in the field.

DORSEY PENDER

His wound grows steadily worse. An operation is performed within the month, at Staunton, but he begins to hemorrhage. The leg is amputated. He dies within the month. His wife attributes his death to the judgment of God.

ISAAC TRIMBLE

Wounded, is left to be captured by the enemy. Loses his leg, survives the war. Of the charge at Gettysburg he says: "If the men I had the honor to command that day could not take that position, all Hell couldn't take it."

JOHNSTON PETTIGREW

Survives the charge at Gettysburg with only a minor wound in the hand. Is shot to death ten days later in a delaying action guarding the retreat across the Potomac.

GEORGE PICKETT

His Division is virtually destroyed. No field officer is unhurt. Of the thirteen colonels in his command that day seven are dead, six are wounded. His casualties exceed 60 percent. The famous Charge of the Light Brigade, in comparison, suffered casualties of approximately 40 percent. Pickett survives to great glory, but he broods on the loss. When the war is over he happens one day on John Singleton Mosby, on the way to see Robert Lee, and together they visit the old man. The meeting is, in Mosby's words, "singularly cold." After it is over, Pickett comes outside and says bitterly: "That man destroyed my Division."

JUBAL EARLY

Serves until near the end of the war, when Lee finds it necessary to relieve him because of complaints against him by citizens he has offended. His conduct after the war is notable for two episodes: he becomes the Southern officer most involved in trying to prove that Longstreet was responsible for the loss at Gettysburg, and he becomes the central figure in the infamous Louisiana lottery, which cost thousands of Southerners thousands of dollars.

ARTHUR FREMANTLE

Returns to England after three months in the Confederacy and writes a book on his experience, which is published in the South three months before the end of the war. It is a very readable and entertaining book, which predicts a certain Southern victory.

HARRISON

He vanishes from Longstreet's records. Years after the war Moxley Sorrel attends a play, notices something vaguely familiar about one of the actors, recognizes Harrison. He goes backstage for a moment, they speak for a moment, but Sorrel is a gentleman and Harrison is a player, and there is no further connection. Nothing else of Harrison is known.

JOHN BUFORD

Never to receive recognition for his part in choosing the ground and holding it, and in so doing saving not only the battle but perhaps the war, he survives the summer but is weakened by wounds. In December of that year he goes down with pneumonia, and dies of it.

WINFIELD SCOTT HANCOCK

Survives the wound at Gettysburg. When the war ends it is found that his Second Corps captured more prisoners, more colors, and suffered more casualties than the entire rest of the Army of the Potomac. An enormously popular man all his life, in 1880 he runs for the Presidency on the Democratic ticket, against Garfield, but the country has had two terms of Grant and is weary of Generals in high office, and so he is defeated, retires from public life. The package Lew Armistead sent Almira Hancock was Armistead's personal Bible.

JOSHUA LAWRENCE CHAMBERLAIN

In August he is given a brigade. Shortly thereafter he is so badly wounded, shot through both hips, that he is not expected to live. But he returns to become one of the most remarkable soldiers in American history. Wounded six times. Cited for bravery in action four times. Promoted to Brigadier General by special order of Ulysses Grant for heroism at Petersburg. Breveted Major General for heroism at Five Forks. He is the officer chosen by Grant from all other Northern officers to have the honor of receiving the Southern surrender at Appomattox, where he startles the world by calling his troops to attention to salute the defeated South.

He is given first place in the last Grand Review in Washington. For his day at Little Round Top he is to receive the Congressional Medal of Honor.

In Maine he is elected Governor by the largest majority in the history of the state and returned to office three times, where he alienates political friends by refusing to agree to the impeachment of Andrew Johnson.

In 1876, elected President of Bowdoin College, where he attempts to modernize the school, introducing courses in science, de-emphasizing religion, and becomes involved in student demonstrations over the question of ROTC. Receives medal of honor from France for distinguished efforts in international education. When he retires from Bowdoin he has taught every subject in the curriculum except mathematics.

Dies of his wounds, June 1914, at the age of eighty-three.

ANDERSONVILLE

by
MacKinlay Kantor

MacKINLAY KANTOR was born in Webster City, Iowa, the son of Effie Mac-Kinley, a young woman of mixed Scottish, English, Irish and Pennsylvania Dutch blood, and John Martin Kantor, a Swedish-born Jew. His parents were soon divorced and Kantor spent his childhood and youth in his grandparents' home in Webster City. He began his writing career at the age of seventeen as an apprentice to his mother, who was the editor of the daily paper in Webster City. By the end of 1927, Kantor had been married to Irene Layne, (a young commercial artist) and gained and lost "the last regular job I ever held"—on the Cedar Rapids *Republican.*

The publication of *Long Remember* in 1934, Kantor's novel about the battle of Gettysburg, marked his first significant financial and critical success. It was followed by such well-known works as *Arouse and Beware,* another historical novel, *The Romance of Rosey Ridge* and *The Voice of Bugle Ann.* With the publication of *Andersonville* in 1955, MacKinlay Kantor became established as one of the most distinguished and widely-read American authors.

The study of prison life was something of a literary interest for Kantor during much of his writing career, beginning with the research for *Arouse and Beware,* gradually focusing on the horrendous history of Andersonville itself. But it was not until his experience on entering the Buchenwald concentration camp with the U.S. Army the day after it was liberated, that the interest became an obsession. Ten years later, *Andersonville* was published, and is today generally regarded as the great American novel of the Civil War.

MacKinlay Kantor died in 1977. He is survived by a daughter, Mrs. Layne Shroeder, and a son, Tim Kantor.

To Irene

"The future historian who shall undertake to write an unbiased story of the War between the States, will be compelled to weigh in the scales of justice all its parts and features; and if the revolting crimes . . . have indeed been committed, the perpetrators must be held accountable. Be they of the South or of the North, they cannot escape history."

—R. Randolph Stevenson,
formerly surgeon in the Army of
the Confederate States of America

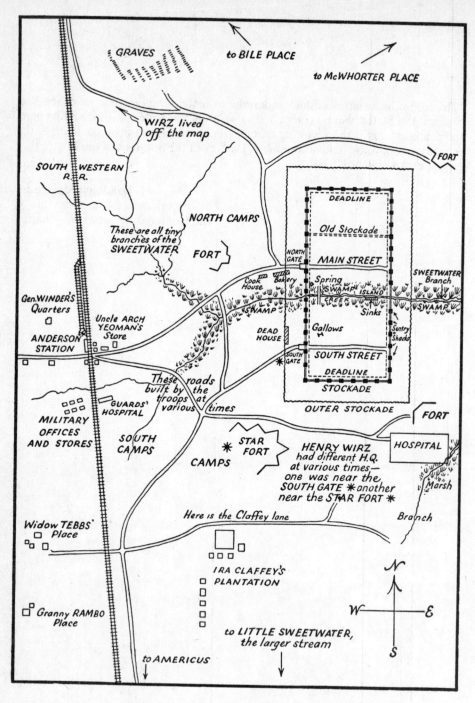

Chart showing approximate location
of various points and areas at Andersonville.

1

Sometimes there was a compulsion which drew Ira Claffey from his plantation and sent him to walk the forest. It came upon him at eight o'clock on this morning of October twenty-third; he responded, he yielded, he climbed over the snake fence at the boundary of his sweet potato field and went away among the pines.

Ira Claffey had employed no overseer since the first year of the war, and had risen early this morning to direct his hands in the potato patch. Nowadays there were only seven and one-half hands on the place, house and field, out of a total Negro population of twelve souls; the other four were an infant at the breast and three capering children of shirt-tail size.

Jem and Coffee he ordered to the digging, and made certain that they were thorough in turning up the harvest and yet gentle in lifting the potatoes. Nothing annoyed Ira Claffey like storing a good thirty-five bushels in a single mound and then losing half of them through speedy decay.

In such a manner, he thought, have some of our best elements and institutions perished. One bruise, one carelessness, and rot begins. Decay is a secret but hastening act in darkness; then one opens up the pine bark and pine straw—or shall we say, the Senate?—and observes a visible wastage and smell, a wet and horrid mouldering of the potatoes. Or shall we say, of the men?

In pursuit of his own husbandry on this day, Ira carried a budding knife in his belt. While musing in bed the night before, he had been touched with ambition: he would bud a George the Fourth peach upon a Duane's Purple plum.

Veronica was not yet asleep, but reading her Bible by candlelight beside him. He told her about it.

But, Ira, does not the Duane's Purple ripen too soon? Aren't those the trees just on the other side of the magnolias?

No, no, my dear. Those are Prince's Yellow Gage. The Duane's Purple matures in keeping with the George Fourths. I'd warrant you about the second week of July. Say about the tenth. I should love to see that skin. Such a fine red cheek on the George Fourths, and maybe dotted with that lilac bloom and yellow specks—

But she was not hearing him, she was weeping. He turned to watch her; he sighed, he put out one big hand and touched the thick gray-yellow braid which weighted on her white-frilled shoulder. It was either Moses or Sutherland whom she considered now. Dully he wondered which one.

She said, on receiving the communication of his thought, though he had said nothing— She spoke Suthy's name.

Oh, said Ira. I said nothing to make you think—

The Prince's Yellow Gage. He fancied them so. When they were still green he'd hide them in the little waist he wore. Many's the time I gave him a belting—

She sobbed a while longer, and he stared into the gloom beyond the bed curtains, and did his best to forget Suthy. Suthy was the eldest. Sixteenth Georgia.

It was away up at the North, at a place no one had ever heard of before, a place called Gettysburg.

In recent awareness of bereavement had lain the germ of retreat and restlessness, perhaps; but sometimes Ira spirited himself off into the woods when he was fleeing from no sadness or perplexity. He had gone like that since he could first remember. Oh, pines were taller forty-five years ago . . . when he was only three feet tall, the easy nodding grace of their foliage was reared out of all proportion, thirty times his stature. And forests were wilder, forty-five years ago, over in Liberty County, and he went armed with a wooden gun which old Jehu had carved and painted as a Christmas gift for him. It had a real lock, a real flint; it snapped and the sparks flew. Ira Claffey slew brigades of redcoats with this weapon; he went as commander of a force of small blacks; he was their general.

Hi, them's British, Mastah Iry.

Where?

Yonder in them 'simmons!

Take them on the flank.

Hi, what you say we do, Mastah?

He wasn't quite sure what he wanted them to do. Something about the flank. His Uncle Sutherland talked about a flank attack in some wild distant spot known as the Carolinas. . . . Of course this was later on, perhaps only forty years ago, when Ira Claffey was ten. . . .

Charge those redcoats! They advanced upon the persimmon brake in full cry and leaping; and once there came terror when a doe soared out of the thicket directly in their faces, and all the little darkies scattered like quail, and Ira came near to legging it after them.

In similar shades he had been Francis Marion, and surely his own boys had scuttled here in identical pursuits. It was a good place to be, treading alone on the clay-paved path curving its way to the closest branch of Sweetwater Creek. God walked ahead and behind and with him, near, powerful, silent . . . *words of my mouth, and the meditation of my heart, be acceptable in thy sight, O Lord, my strength, and my redeemer.*

He had budded the peach upon the plum as he wished to do, though he feared that it was a trifle too late in the season for success. He budded each of the two selected trees five times, and then went back to the potato field. Coffee and Jem were doing well enough, but they were plaguèd slow; Ira had been emphatic about the tenderness he required of them, and they handled the big sulphur-colored Brimstones as if they were eggs. Well, he thought, I shan't speed them on this. Better forty bushels well-dug and well-stored than eighty bushels bumped and scratched and ready to spoil as soon as they're covered.

Keep on with it until I return, and mind about no bruising. I shall look up some pine straw—where it's thickest and easy to scoop—and we'll fetch the cart after the nooning.

Yassah.

Frost had not yet killed the vines. Some planters always waited for a killing frost before they dug, but Ira was certain that the crop kept better if dug immediately before the frost struck.

He was newly come into his fifty-first year; the natal day had been observed on October sixth. Black Naomi chuckled mysteriously in the kitchen; there had been much talk about, Mistess, can I please speak with you a minute *alone?* He had to pretend that he was blind and deaf, and owned no suspicion that delicate and hard-to-come-by substances were being lavished in his honor. The fragrant Lady

Baltimore cake appeared in time, borne by Ira Claffey's daughter because she would not trust the wenches with this treasure.

There they sat, the three surviving Claffeys left at home, sipping their roast-grain coffee and speaking words in praise of the cake, and now Ira had lived for half a century . . . fifty years stuffed with woe and work and dreams and peril. He sought to dwell in recollection only on the benefits accruing. With Veronica and Lucy he tried to keep his imaginings away from far-off roads where horses and men were in tragic operation.

The best I've tasted since the Mexican War.

Poppy, you always say that. About everything.

Come, come, Lucy. Do I indeed?

You do, agreed his wife, and gave him her wan smile above the home-dipped candles.

Yes, sir, chimed in Lucy. It's always the best and the worst and the biggest and all such things, but always dated from that old war.

After this night, said Ira, I presume that I should date everything from my fiftieth birthday?

Poppy, love, you don't look even on the outskirts of fifty. Scarcely a shred of gray in your hair.

Well, my dear, I don't have much hair left to me.

That's no certain indication of encroaching age. Is it, Mother? Take Colonel Tollis. I declare, he can't be aged over thirty-one or two, and yet he's got less hair than—

Lucy. Do you consider it ladylike, to discuss baldness so—so intimately?

Well, I declare—

So it had gone; they uttered their little jests and remonstrances; they had their affection; the stringy candles sank and died in chipped gilt candelabra, and in the end Ira Claffey sat alone in his library and treated himself to port. He had tasted no port since the previous winter (there was so little of it left now) and he made a silent gesture and toasted each of his sons in turn as they stared from ambrotype frames beside him. His hand went down and rubbed along his right leg; it caressed his shabby fawn-colored pantaloons above the knotted hole which for years he had bandaged afresh each day. I'd be with you, fifty or no fifty, he tried to tell his sons, reaching to them across uncharted distances and dimensions. I'd be among the muskets if it hadn't been for Monterey. I wonder who that Mexican was! I wonder if he is living still—sorrowing as I am sorrowing, going through repeated and sometimes doleful mimicry. Still able to love, however? Not so frequently? But still able, and most eager at times.

The wine affected Ira Claffey because he drank so little of it in this time of strife and paucity. He thought of Veronica and the fever which came over him sometimes in darkness, the drawing up of her nightdress, the muffled hysteria of their encounter, the shame which she always admitted afterward because she had been taught that carnal enjoyment was lewd and Ira could never persuade her otherwise. He thought of the mistress he had had in Milledgeville when he was in the Legislature, he thought of pretty strumpets he'd known in the brief time when he was a soldier, he thought of the first brown girl he ever lay with at seventeen or thereabouts in age.

How do you countenance such goings-on? You, professedly a religious man—

I suppose each of us must be guilty of certain sins. We'd be less than human if we weren't blemished a bit. And I strive earnestly not to envy, not to grow little snips and slips and buds and seeds of jealousy. I deplore cruelty, and own no avarice—at least none I'm conscious of. But lust—

I'm steeped in that particular brand of iniquity. At least—when I was younger— And now, now, tonight, the night I'm fifty—

Silently he opened the library door and looked across the dark hall. Lucy and her mother were scraping lint at the big table in the crowded parlor; they had a servant helping them, but Lucy was yawning. He felt a fire as he saw that yawn. Soon, then— To bed, to bed! Incestuous sheets, sweet prince? Nay, my Veronica and I lie within the embrace of a mortal primness known as Holy Wedlock.

Thus we contrived eight children, and thus the four small graves within the red rusty fence—the longest no longer than my walking stick— Thus we had four children to grow to full stature—or close to it— Thus we came to another war.

I was a Stephens man from the first, but what possible difference can that make now, to Mr. Stephens or to me?

I was no Secessionist. Quite the contrary. But dress yourselves in gray, Suthy and Badger and Moses, and be off with your shooting-irons. Scrape the raw white fabric, Lucy. Put up the calves-foot jelly for the wounded, my Veronica. And cry and cry, and read your Bible, and pray again, and cry once more. . . .

Mist had condensed thickly after a chilly night, and Ira walked through it like a swimmer moving erect, walking rapidly though lamely, a man with broad round powerful shoulders, and carrying his head tipped forward as if to resist the weight of the flat-brimmed black hat pulled low on his forehead. His brow was channeled horizontally by four distinct wrinkles like deep narrow scars. His pale eyes shone from a covert of long dark lashes and coffee-colored eyebrows. His nose was insignificant, his wide full-lipped mouth the best feature in a round smooth face. Ira Claffey demonstrated the manner of a keen-eyed hunter who was forever on the watch for birds and expected that a covey would go crackling up and out, only a few steps ahead.

He would have been able to name the week—and possibly the day—of the year; he would have been able to name it by evidence before him if startled quickly awake from a century's repose. The long-leaved pines themselves, their banks of dark green plush in milky distance, with the outer tips of pine needles touched by autumnal tan, and yet this tan was invisible until you came close. Sunflowers, the little susie flowers still blooming spiritedly; sodden cornfields shrunken merciless, every ragged stalk of fodder soaked with mist; sandy, clayey bare spots in yard and gardens standing out silvery—intense spots, never casual, but seeming to have been cleared and stamped recently, and for a special purpose . . . eight o'clock in the morning, as told by his silver watch, with the sun burning low and solid in a cloudless sky but with farthermost groves still fogged; jack-oaks half green and looking withered and scrofulous; the scrub swamp gums well turned at this date, and some of them burning in artificial pinks; tulip trees half green; some of the buttonwoods verdant as in summer.

The air hung clammy, but still good because it was wild, unprovoked by many men or their machines or structures. Ira heard the squeal of a train whistle (the service was untidy and uncertain on this Southwestern line from Macon to Americus and Albany. Claffey could not have told you with accuracy just how many trains jounced puffing up and down the line each day; at least he knew that the service was sadly confused because of military necessity) and far above the hill and western pines there frothed some woodsmoke as the cars halted at Anderson Station. Nothing much there except a wretched store, several houses, and a pyramid of old sawdust from Yeoman's mill, no longer operating.

. . . Air good because it was wild, and because deer had run through it, and turkeys also. It was long since the Creeks trotted those easy slopes, but you could still smell them when fall came on. Cold weather was their time, the time of

Indian ghosts, and Ira loved to sense them; he loved the ghosts as well as any boy and better than some. More than the Indians, however: air was tanged with sweet-gum and persimmons and nut trees and dry goober vines and thistles. Ira Claffey worshipped vegetation; he understood the small or wide-spread miracles appurte-nant to chlorophyll, photosynthesis . . . oh, list to the botanizing, the rub or splitting of cotyledons! . . . Any plant was his love, some were near to being his spiritual mistresses (he remembered making love and crushing infinitesimal pur-plish flowers while they did it; he and a slave girl, when he was young, when he was very young; but he could never get a white woman to lie with him in grass and blossoms, though he had tried. Ladies wanted beds). More than these affections, too: Ira had an enormous respect for vegetation beyond loving it; yet he was disciplined and sensible, and recognized that weeds must be ripped out, and some trees also.

Here, in the last field at his left hand, once the cotton had flourished . . . dry toughness of the stalks, the long long picking-sacks, the dark hands going like beaks to bite and swallow the cotton. No cotton now, markets were gone. A few good melon vines had volunteered and come running over the ground, squarely over the bottom rail of the fence; and more gourd vines and some pumpkins had volunteered from another quarter, and doubtless cucumbers as well, though Ira Claffey hadn't checked. They interbred as all gourds will. Now their awful prog-eny rotted amid visible ruins of a cotton planter's hopes. They were not melons, not pumpkins; they were monsters; not even the hungriest hand would eat them. Children came and kicked them loose and rolled them around. The green worms had come, too, and the green worms worked their especial penetrating assassina-tion: once the air was admitted to these fruit, spoilage was hurried. The bastard product of vines lay exposed where leaves had fallen, like bulbous rotting bodies —skulls, perhaps—and they made an almost visible awfulness of odor. Ah, said Ira Claffey to himself, I didn't realize that this was such a horror. Well, there's no pride in having an old field turned into a sink, even though we have nothing to plant in it. Send Coffee down here post haste with a cart and let him get rid of these nuisances; he can dump them into the swamp —bury them, if necessary. . . . No, Coffee's instructed with the Brimstones, I shan't take him from potato digging, I'll take Jonas from the woodpile and send him instead.

He left the orbs and jellies of noxious cross-breeds behind him thankfully, and turned north on a path which led from northern limits of his own plantation . . . pines cool in their brittle dignity, and a stile to be mounted over. This was a serious obstacle because his right leg could not be made to bend past forty-five degrees at the knee without pain. Something about a quadriceps tendon fastening itself to a femur; Ira did not know; he was no surgeon. He wrinkled his small nose, thinking of surgeons and probes which looked something like knitting needles— uncompanionable needles, to say the least.

Halfway down the northern slope of this ridge was where the stile bothered him; now he lurched on a downward path through land belonging to the McWhorters, the Yeomans, the Biles. Wilderness barely fit for pasture, these eminences were; no one was ever quite certain just where the joining lines ran, and no survey had been made since the earliest times. The McWhorter heirs lived in Americus and did nothing about their woodland except to pay microscopic taxes; the Yeoman place no longer operated as a plantation, with both the young-middle-aged men gone to the army and their wives dwelling with cousins in Tattnall County. The Biles were old, sedentary, retiring—their house stood two miles away, and they lived off their garden-patch with two slovenly house servants to bear them company. Ira Claffey himself had given them meat as a neighborly gift in winter and trusted that some other folks had done the same.

Irvine Yeoman, aged forty-one, had died in the same battle which claimed Sutherland Claffey—that Gettysburg place. For the moment Ira had forgotten.

In speculation on death (even secret half-realized contemplation of the misery) and on the scrawny barrenness which fell over remote holdings like this when war ruled, Ira desired keenly all faith and sustenance which the forest might give. . . . No deer here nowadays; one had not been shot in these woods for years. Raccoons and bobcats and other vermin, the spotted skunks and weasels darting at night on urgent autumnal errands . . . but lean stringy dancing legs of the deer went piercing other thickets. It was a miraculous thing how a deer could be frightened loose and go rising and plunging through tough jagged windfalls from some old hurricane; then you'd go and examine the route where he'd run, and you wouldn't think that a rat could have gotten through there; but the deer had, and the remarkable mechanism of his small hooves and elastic sinews was even now carrying him at a fool's pace through tighter fences of tumbled roots and pine boughs at the other end of the wilderness.

The Sweetwater branch to be crossed, a fine fair small stream to visit, generous in its treatment of roots of gums and willows which marked its way. Ira went across on the trunk of a tree he'd had his hands fell for that very purpose: to make a bridge where strollers could pass dry-shod. This portion of the valley belonged definitely to the McWhorters; Ira requested and received permission for the tree to be cut. It was a willow, hurt badly by lightning, and no great sacrifice in any event. He thought of kneeling to drink from the clean black water, he knew that this branch of Sweetwater would taste cold and leaf-mouldy, it would be a balm to mouth and tongue and throat and would pour slowly and darkly as if rinsing at a gentle course through his whole big body, into every extremity. He had risen before sunrise and worked long and well, and he needed a drink.

But better to try the spring beyond. Only a short way above the marshy plashy boundaries of the creek there stood clay and brown boulders exposed. . . . Here, he explained once to Lucy when he took her that way— Here is where the fairies live.

What kind of fairies?

Good ones, my dear. They are wet, very tiny, very green—

As big as me, Poppy?

Heavens, no. Miniature fairies of the damp sort, scarcely as big as your finger.

Where do they sleep?

Ah, there's that moss. Where do you think?

Yes, Poppy, I think they use the moss. And for table linen, too. Would they let me drink their water?

Assuredly. That's the reason they keep it running. Here, child, I'll make a cup of my hand. Beneath this rock, so. Now you bend down—take care, don't wet your boots and skirts— That's the way.

She faced him with plump pink face dripping, and said, I saw one, whilst I was drinking.

Where was he?

In the moss.

Alone he squatted now amid kindly memories and held out his hand. The water looked like a sheer fluted icicle. Ira had seen icicles long before, when he went to Washington City in winter. Water drenched his heavy hand, and curled along his wrist and tried to make its way up his sleeve, and he laughed and drew back his hand and shook it. This was the smallest, loveliest spring of several which

he knew in these few square miles of domestic woodland. Especially the moss
. . . his daughter was too grown-up to dream about fairies; she was twenty; the
youth she loved had died of fever in the Yankee prison pen at Camp Douglas,
Chicago, the winter before . . . or maybe she did dream secretly about fairies
still. She owned a pretty mouth filled with all the young lady chatter and some of
the young lady slang. Veronica would say impatiently, I declare, sometimes I
believe that youngun has scarcely a wit in her noggin. But both the Claffeys were
glad to boast Lucy as their own. She was dainty and valiant, she was skillful and
kindly at nursing the sick be they white or black. Sick people followed her with
their eyes. She would have made a noble wife for big Rob Lamar. But he was
dead. So many were dead.

A chill came from darker gloom of pines and touched Ira's face and heart.

He shook his head, removed his hat, and—kneeling deeper and more painfully
in the niche of stones and moss—he turned up his face beneath the steady pouring of the spring. He opened his mouth and drank deeply, swallowing steadily
until he was satisfied.

Distantly sounded the slow talking of shod hooves on rock and hardpan clay.
Ira heard the approach as he was drying his face with a yellow bandana; he heard
voices also, and a light metallic drag and jingle. With curiosity he examined the
nearer paths to see who might be coming. Seldom did you meet hunters or
planters in this quiet place; this section of the county was but sparsely settled—all
the hunters gone to more dangerous hunting, some of the planters gone too.

A sorrel horse and a gray came in sight, moving cautiously down the steep trail
from the north—from the direction of the empty Yeoman plantation—and ridden
by two young men. They appeared to be in uniform, at least as to pants and boots
and hats, though one wore a jacket of checkered brown and drab denim. Behind
them stumbled a youth in Confederate gray, bearing a surveyor's rod over his
shoulder; and in the rear followed a tall ragged Negro who carried some sort of
wooden satchel-box in his right hand and held a tripod and a looped linked chain
in heavy coils upon his other shoulder. What's this, demanded Ira Claffey of
himself in astonishment. Surveyors? Have the McWhorters sold out?

I want a drink, spoke the man in the checkered coat. He seemed to be in
charge, for the little procession turned promptly along the declivity toward the
spring. Ira walked to meet them.

Good day, gentlemen.

Good day to you.

The two horsemen dismounted. Both were officers or so Ira took them to be.
Something about the undersized denim-jacketed fellow made Ira recoil instinctively if slightly as the man moved past him.

Look out you don't slip, Sid, said the other. The young private soldier and the
slave were standing back, waiting to drink in their proper turns.

The unprepossessing man called Sid finished his refreshment and stood wiping
his mouth on his sleeve. His jacket was smeared with clay, his boots greased
reddishly with it. He had been walking in a marsh first; there was black muck
higher on his legs.

You own this property? He was addressing Ira curtly.

No, sir. I believe we're standing on McWhorter land at the moment. My place
begins yonder. He pointed to the fence barely visible among trees, south across
the branch. He said, My name is Claffey. He offered his hand, but not eagerly.

Both officers shook hands with him. I'm Captain W. S. Winder—

In belated respect to Ira's elder years he added *Sir*.

—This is Captain Boyce Charwick. He's from the topographical engineers.

Ira gave his grave smile. Are you looking up a new battleground? This would be rather remote from the lines.

Prison, said Winder.

A prison? Here?

It's possible. I'm charged with locating a site. We're considering several locations. This is one of them.

Ira had a thought of murderers and lunatics in chains. What sort of prison would that be?

A stockade to keep damn Yankee prisoners in, replied Charwick.

A stockade to keep God damn Yankee prisoners in, Captain Winder amended. They both laughed.

Ah, I see. But it's so far from—

Winder grimaced in a manner to show impatience or impertinence, Claffey could not be sure which. The captains climbed back into their saddles and stood waiting for the other two to drink—first the white boy, then the Negro.

It's a long way removed from the theatre of war, is it not?

My father, General John H. Winder, is Superintendent of Military Prisons. I have been authorized to seek a site for a new stockade. You've got railroad transportation here—

His hand swept and stabbed the horizon, pointing out things which Ira Claffey had known for years. He talked impolitely as if the planter were a child retarded in mind.

Excellent drainage. Bountiful supply of water; not that the Yankees are over-prone to bathe, or so I've heard.

Laughter.

I'm considering this area seriously because of the provender situation. You folks hereabouts are not tributary to Virginia when it comes to food. Self-sustaining, I'd say. Bountiful crops—or at least the areas where they could be raised. How was your own corn this year?

Fair, sir, said Claffey guardedly. Merely fair. Locally we received inundation at the wrong season. But—How on earth could you build sufficient structures to house—?

See these pines? How many million board feet of pine's around here, anyway? I didn't say anything about structures. We can take those trees and square them off, and slap them together, and build a fence around ten or twenty acres—a fence so high that the meanest living Yankee couldn't get over the top if he had an aerial balloon.

Laughter. Sid, you're a caution, said Captain Charwick.

Claffey stared. I was told that you are a topographical engineer. Do you agree, sir, that this location is ideal for a prison site?

Charwick said, his smile gone, Well, I agree in general theory with Captain Winder's observations. Of course I'm present strictly in an advisory capacity. His decision will be tailored by demands other than those of topography. He may be aware of military exigencies of which I know nothing—

Oh, thought Claffey, talk, talk, talk. I know your sort. We had mealy-mouths like yours when we were baking in the sun at Matamoras.

Captain Winder took up his reins. I want you to see the lay of the land on this southern ridge, Boyce. I went over it yesterday—

They were turning, the boy and the Negro waited in the path.

Where would you get your labor, to build such a large stockade?

Winder's rodent mouth puffed out as he wiped his teeth with his tongue. Mr. Claffey, sir, and he emphasized that address—Mr. Claffey, we can obtain the authority to impress all the labor we need. Tom Twitt's niggers, Bill Bump's niggers, your niggers, anybody's niggers. Also the authority to take your acres for our purpose—as much as we need.

Ira said coolly, I trust you'll require none of my acres. If my surviving son returns from the army, he'll need the land.

I take it you've lost a son? Young Winder set his boots tightly into his stirrups. My sincerest regrets, sir.

Two, said Ira. The youngest at Crampton's Gap, the eldest at Gettysburg.

Ah. Sad. A mere boy, I presume—a private soldier?

He was a major.

Winder looked disconcerted momentarily. He felt a stinging rebuke against his bumptiousness and cavalier attitude; it was apparent, yet he could not locate it, or discern in just what words and intonation it was phrased. He gave a kind of half salute. Captain Charwick touched his hat-brim. The Negro and the boy were already far up the slope with their burdens. The officers rode quickly away up the difficult steep, both riding effortlessly as if they had spent years in their saddles, as undoubtedly they had.

The party went into the woods. Claffey did not see them again after he crossed near the stile; he saw only the marks of their going. He saw traces where rails had been taken out beside the stile in order for horses to pass, but the rails had been restored carefully to position again. Ira wondered whether, if these people had not chanced to meet him at the spring near the Sweetwater branch, they might have left rails lying after taking them down. Perhaps he was doing the officers an injustice in the thought.

But he did not like their attitude. They seemed to bring a meanness to war. There should be nobility about the business of risking life, even the business of taking it. Why did we all respect more the memory of the benevolent knight who died in battle—the profound and kingly knight—more than the memory of the truculent, self-seeking warrior? . . . The memory—or the legend? Which? . . . Both the godly knight and the cruel one wagered the same; they wagered hopefully that they would not need to lay their lives down; yet each took the same hazard in the wagering, and one might fight as stoutly as the other, and each would be just as dead as the other when the end came. It was a thought to baffle him. Ira squinted his eyes shut and shook his head like a horse shaking off flies; he always did that when he was perplexed, when he was alone and there was no one to see him. He had to guard against doing it before his family and his servants, for he felt that simple dignity was an honest and important thing. Yet somehow the shaking seemed to help.

He brooded his way back to the potato patches. It was now long after nine o'clock. He had wasted a good hour and a half in his wanderings and musings, and in conversing with the military party. He considered it wasted, because for the first time in—when?—the forest had not granted him the peace and food he sought. A prison, here where always there had been the green pleasure of growth, or water having its way with lichens—the blessing of gum, pine cones, sly animals feeding, rare birds meeting their kind? Let them build their prison someplace else, he'd have none of it. He knew the President, or had known him slightly seventeen years before. He should go to Richmond (but it would cost a sight of cash, and cash was not plentiful in these days) and utter a protest. He should take a firm stand, if this supercilious young captain sought to preëmpt any of the Claffey acres.

Oh, bother, bother. That Winder person said that they were merely considering the site. No doubt they'll select another area, Lord knows where.

He said farewell to the forest, and heard birds buzzing through it, and had some thought of taking a shotgun soon and fetching a few birds for the table. Claffey did not truly enjoy shooting birds (he was an excellent shot; so all his boys had been) and he pitied the blood and drooping which followed. But Veronica was like a child—she beamed and giggled like Lucy herself—whenever he proffered wildfowl. Black Naomi had a special blue earthenware dish in which she cooked them. She used wine and onions—

Coffee and Jem had made great strides with the potatoes. A good two-thirds of the Brimstones were dug, and by noontime the hands would doubtless be ready to start in on the Hayti yams, which they preferred for the table, and which it was easier to raise as fare for the slaves because the Hayti yams were more prolific and they stored well. Common yams were the most prolific of all, but had rather a pumpkinish flavor. Ira couldn't abide growing them.

Coffee. Did you dig these?

Coffee was a long-armed, long-faced fellow with Indian blood apparent. Nossuh, Mastah, I use the hoe. That Jem there—he got the old potato hook. I done told him to look sharp.

Well, Jem, suppose you try the hoe instead. Potato hook's a tricky implement. You've hurt a few in this hill. Look there. And there, in the next. . . .

Real sorry, Mastah. They just jump up out of the earth and get themselves tore, fore I know what they's about.

Hear me, Jem. Do you use the hoe from now on, and give the hook to Coffee. And slow with the hoe. You'll need to eat the ones you bruise, and they don't keep long so. That you know.

Jem, wide and black and rubbery as to body, stood grinning weakly in an attitude of shame.

Caution, Jem, use caution. Hear me, now?

Mastah, I surely take care.

Gracious, thought Ira, I neglected to look into the pine straw situation. But there'll be sufficient, over on Little Sweetwater. We fetched none from there last year. . . . He continued to give the slaves detailed instructions. He had decided that they shouldn't get into the yams today. There was sun, and the crop would have to undergo a good drying for several hours before the piles were started. There were the floors of piles to be built, the trenches to be dug around the floors; then a few days of sustained drying should continue under pine straw only, before the piles were finally earthed up and barked up.

Ira went on toward the big house (oh Lord, if only he had paint) and stopped a moment at the implement shed, which he unlocked with a key selected from the hefty wad at his belt. He cleaned his budding knife and hung it in its groove. Then, locking up, he walked on around through the narrow carriageway, aiming for the west end of the gallery where he wished to examine some cold frames he'd built. But he was surprised to find a gig under the big oak, with an old black horse tied and eating oak leaves. At first Ira thought that the advent of this horse and rig must have something to do with the surveyors he encountered; they had so few callers these days. Then he recognized the horse as belonging to the Reverend Mr. Cato Dillard of Americus.

He heard a voice— Poppy, she said, and it was Lucy, rising drunkenly from the top step where she'd been sitting. She is grown suddenly ill, thought Ira. An epidemic, perhaps? Some fever has struck? He limped toward her and held out his arms as the girl came swaying down the steps.

Oh, Poppy, and she nuzzled deep into his wide-flung coat. Poppy. It's Badge.

Lucy— The minister's horse—

They wrote to him. A colonel did—and—a surgeon. They wrote to him first. Reckoned it'd be easier on— On us.

Where's Mr. Dillard? Where's your mother, child? He shook her as if he hated her.

She's on her bed. They came— It was an hour ago. The letters only reached them last night. Mrs. Dillard is with Mother, and he's praying up there. He wished me to stay for prayers. I didn't wish to pray.

Still holding her in his arms, he waited and waited. Finally he could command his voice and make it do what he wanted. He could make it talk and sound like a human being, not like a beast's whine. Lucy, where did it happen?

Some place up in Tennessee. Chick-a-something. He was hurt on the twentieth of September, and we didn't know it, Poppy, we didn't know it all this time, we were in utter ignorance. Why didn't they tell us? You might have gone to him. So he died of his wounds, just as my dear Rob died in that Yankee pen of his sickness.

. . . Lucy, are you certain that you don't wish to pray? I think—it would—be —well—if we both went in to—prayers. Later Mr. Dillard can hold a service for the hands.

It will do no good, said Lucy, but she came quivering along with him. It never does any good. We should know that by now.

. . . *And there sat in a window a certain young man . . . and as Paul was long preaching, he sunk down with sleep, and fell down from the third loft, and was taken up dead.*

And Paul went down, and fell on him, and embracing him said, Trouble not yourselves: for his life is in him.

Ah, it was not, life not in him in the slightest, but only abysmal decay and bad sight and odor, like the cross-bred pumpkin-gourd-cucumbers in that unholy field yonder, nigh to the woods. He was the last: Moses, the youngest, first; then Suthy, the eldest; now Badger, the middle son. Get up from your mounds, you small fry behind that old rusty fence, and join in lamentation, for we've only Lucy to help us with the task of weeping.

The Yankees got Moses and Suthy. Yankees now destroy Badge. They got him, with their many cannon and many men, and their quick-shooting breech-loading rifles. Damn the Yankees. Damn them forever, damn them to a hundred hells with their cannon and their money and their blankets and their medicines. God— damn—the Yankees. God damn the Yankees. God *damn* the Yankees. Amen.

2

Having shared the grief of the Claffeys for some hours, the Reverend Mr. Cato Dillard at last handed his wife into the gig and prepared to drive away. Grief was nothing new to Cato Dillard, whether he suffered his own or witnessed it in that portion of humanity he considered to be within his charge; and he believed that all mankind he had observed since leaving the seminary came within his charge.

Excepting, possibly, Roman Catholics. Sometimes he wasn't even too certain about those. And, of recent years, Yankees. . . .

Veronica Claffey stared sightlessly at the canopy above her bed, and lay unable to read her Bible or to respond to any prayer offered. Lucy was in her own room, also, with the servant Ninny rubbing her ankles. Ira Claffey attended the brief service to which the slaves had been called. The black people's wail and chanting hung bitterly protracted in the sunlight of early afternoon; the whites wished that the slaves would not manufacture such sounds, but there was no way of hushing them.

The servant Pet came with a withe basket containing corn bread, fried chicken and a bottle of beer to refresh the Dillards on their drive to Americus. Cato Dillard embraced his friend and then drove away without looking back; it was better so.

He wished with recurrent regret that Ira Claffey was not averse to metaphysical discussion, but Ira was averse to it. Ira was one of three men among the parson's acquaintances who possessed sufficient scholarly background to indulge in such activity. Still Ira always changed the subject as soon as Cato Dillard was well-embarked and as soon as his tiny eyes burnt bright with intellectual zeal and as soon as his eager voice thrummed with a new range and timbre of enthusiasm. Ira's religion was of a gentle, affectionate, pantheistic variety, and he refused stubbornly to be tricked into any exercise of theology.

I fear the beer may be flat, Ira said in parting. It's from the only brewing which kept, and this year we can't spare the grain. What with military levies and all.

Flat or not, it'll be tasty. Goodbye, my dear friend.

Goodbye, Mrs. Dillard. I can say but Thank You. Goodbye, Brother.

And the dry shivering handclasp saying more.

God bless you, Brother Ira. I'll pray daily.

Whatever benefit that may bring! Bitterness of the deep and stunning hurt.

I'll pray, Brother Ira.

And light wheels going away, and the gloom on all hearts.

Halfway down the lane with its magnolias on one side and its small oaks on the other, Cato turned to his wife and began to quote, So we say farewell to our lamented dead, and know only that we shall reassemble on that great day when all shall foregather—some from the East, and some from the West, some from the South— And it may even be that a few shall come from the North.

Muckle wish have I that any should come from the North. Effie Dillard was a Scotswoman. The words of her Rothesay youth came easily from her wide thin lips when she was stirred. She was wearing a faded frilled pink cap and now she lifted her straw bonnet and drew it on over the cap, which act would have seemed astonishing to a stranger. Mrs. Dillard had suffered fever many years before—had nearly died of it, and all her hair was lost. She wore caps, waking and sleeping. No one except a trusted servant had ever seen her without a cap, since she recovered. Not even the Reverend Mr. Dillard.

She was a bony, bent woman with knobs on her shoulders and a face like a yellow witch. Everyone in the region knew that she had a heart bigger than the area of Sumter County itself, and many traded on her accordingly. Her skin was marred by smallpox which she had acquired when nursing a brood of Negroes from whom the rest of humanity fled.

Effie, don't talk hatred.

I feel it. If I feel it I should utter it.

Thus purging your soul? The minister smiled a tired sly smile.

Aye. She gave him the ghost of her own smile.

Mr. Cato Dillard was plump and squat, and loose flesh squeezed out around his short neck in rolls. His hazel eyes lost themselves in chasms of veined wrinkles; they peeked out like twin squirrels in hiding. He was brilliantly far-sighted, literally as well as figuratively, and donned his spectacles only when working on his sermons or when reading tracts aloud to some blind or illiterate sufferer unable to read the tracts himself. He was sixty-six years old and still moved with the bounce of youth. The Dillards had no living children, but five of their eight grandchildren were serving in the army, all alive as yet.

Mr. Cato Dillard had one vanity: the tufts of luxuriant tingling curly silver, growing down past his ears on either side of his firm fat face, and so fluffy that the lightest breeze set them rippling.

Cate, she called him in private, and sometimes in public when she forgot. Now she cried, Cate! in a manner of alarm.

Is something wrong, my dear?

You've turned off the road. You're not bound for Americus. There's the railroad ahead.

Only bound down this side track on an errand. Briefly.

Where are we bound?

He wriggled guiltily. If you must know, we're bound for the Widow Tebbs' place.

Cate, are you daft?

The Cloth can be worn anywhere and remain unsullied. It is my Christian duty. And I might add—yours also, Effie.

Let me out of this gig, man. I'll not go.

You've been before.

On a fool's errand!

Effie, don't be difficult. She's a poor miserable creature, with no great happiness behind her, and only iniquity and grief to make up her present, and flames reaching ahead. But she's human, and I knew her grandfather well, and as a ruling elder he represented our congregation in the presbytery.

Scarlet is as scarlet does. What charity can you give her? I mean what charity would she accept? Neither The Word nor the practice thereof. She does not know the meaning of repentance.

Perhaps, at one time, neither did Mary Magdalene.

Ah. Touch pitch, I say.

Now, how often do you suppose The Saviour touched pitch? And how severely was He tarred?

Cate, you're daft.

But Mrs. Dillard gave no further remonstrance—only a reedy sigh now and then, as the little vehicle bumped down the miserable side road.

Over the railway tracks they rocked, the horse snorting when wheels grated on the rails: Blackie recognized the railroad and tossed his head at the notion of encountering a locomotive which always set him to spreading his legs and lifting wild ears. The Widow Tebbs' place was just beyond—a small house with a sloping roof like the tilt of a water-soaked visored cap. There was a ruined stable, a pigpen, several miscellaneous sheds; and across a wide dirty yard stood a cubicle structure which had once served as a storage place for corn. That was when Dickwood Tebbs was alive. Nowadays it was fitted out with curtains, lamps, a reedy music box, and definitely a bed. In this building the Widow Tebbs did her entertaining. Her children referred to it as The Crib, as did Mrs. Tebbs' regular patrons. This collection of buildings was bounded by a fence of split palings, heavy with gourd vines, some sections leaning in and some sections leaning out. A few tattered specimens of poultry fled jabbering as the gig came closer.

To think you'd carry your own good wife to such a spot.

My dear, be benevolent and forgiving. Her eldest's just back from the battles, and he's wanting a foot. This is sad poverty, dire poverty.

When they halted before the sagging gate, they saw the flight of something other than poultry: a small brown object which sped under the house like a bunchy high-backed varmint. It was a child, a boy of three or four, dressed in a loose skirt and shirt of filthy material. He traveled on his hands and knees with a speed to baffle the eye. One moment he was crouched, gazing fearfully at the approach of the gig; the next he had streaked between the chunks of stone which supported the old cottage, and had gone into darkness like a rabbit or a pig.

The Reverend Mr. Cato Dillard smiled. That would be her youngest.

Never knowing who his father is or was!

Doubtless none of them knows, save the eldest.

A flat-chested youth of thirteen came out on the stoop and stared warily. Mr. Dillard said, Good afternoon, Floral.

The boy mumbled a reply. He had a head small for the skinny body and long neck on which it was perched. His head was covered with spiny golden hair, kept clipped raggedly close by his mother's shears. He wore a dirty undershirt, and patched pantaloons were held around his thin waist by a knotted cord.

Is your mother at home, Floral?

Yes, sir.

Then fetch her, please. And when you've done that, come down here to the buggy. I've something for you.

The boy ducked through the door, there were mumblings inside and then an exclamation of surprise, then Floral reappeared. He came down the two steps and across the littered yard, walking gingerly and seeking smooth places to set his bare left foot as he came.

What's ado here, Flory? Cato Dillard spoke with light jocularity which it was difficult for him to muster, faced with the want and degradation he witnessed, faced with the boy's wizened face and round blank gray eyes. Did you hurt your foot?

Yes, sir.

How did that occur?

Stepped on a damn old nail in a board.

Hush that profanity, child, said Effie Dillard sharply. Now you climb up here on the hub and show me your foot.

With agility, even if in some pain, Flory obeyed. Solemnly he presented the dirty sole of his foot to the woman's gaze. Effie took her specs from her pocket, examined the wound, and gave an exclamation of disgust. I'll be bound. That needs green ointment, and I must see to it.

Will it hurt?

Never you mind about that. It's got proud flesh in it.

Yes, ma'am.

From his jacket pocket Cato Dillard drew a comfit-case of battered silver; he had carried it since his youth. Solemnly he opened the lid and revealed a hoard of lozenges. These are wintergreen, he said. One for you, one for the little lad— What's his name, my boy? He went under the house.

That's Zoral.

Very well, one for Zoral. One for Laurel—

She ain't to home. She's over helping tend old Mrs. Bile. Both the niggers is sickly, and so's the old Mrs.

Save it for her. These are hard to come by.

Well I know. Flory sucked his lozenge with relish.

Where is Coral?

Coral wouldn't want no sugarplum. He just don't want nothing since he got himself wounded. Flory had a greedy eye on the lozenge offered for his elder brother.

He might fancy it. Where is he, bubby?

Took the shotgun and gone a-hunting.

What? On one foot?

I done whittled him out a crutch. Flory still eyed the lozenge. Had it all ready for him when the wagon set him down at the door. First thing he says was, I'll learn you to make gawk at my crippledness, and he took a swipe at me with the crutch. Coral's mean as sin.

The Widow Tebbs appeared on the stoop, noticeably unstayed but wearing a fringed shawl over an old blue poplin gown which had been obviously a hand-me-down and was too tight for her. Her ruddy hair was wound up in a mass of curl papers. Heavens, said Cato involuntarily, behold the Gorgon Medusa.

Don't you choose to light, Parson? And Ma'am? Her voice was high of key, nervous as a fledgling girl's voice . . . she had no great share of wits. Her soft chin was weak, sagging; her bright brown eyes kept up an incessant blinking. Her body bulged, but in keeping with its original construction. A walking fleshly altar to Eros, thought Cato. Nothing could be done with her or about her. Nothing, not from her maiden days which must have ended when she was ten.

Despite the fact that she had a son nearly seventeen years old, she was barely in her thirties. Marget Lumpkin she had been born, and her father once conducted a tannery in Americus. He drove his children from him by fiendish exercise of the most antique and ascetic religious profession. Marget, or Mag as she was more commonly called, was in trouble at fourteen, wife to a slovenly young farmer and mother of his child at fifteen. . . . She had a persistent pitiable fondness for color, whether in flowers or in ribbons; the rougher boys of the town in her young time knew for a literal truth that Mag would lay herself down for the mere gift of a brass button or a spool of crimson thread. Lumpkin was a respectable—even an honored—name throughout most of Georgia, but the poor girl had always loathed the sound of it, when meaner children teased her muddled little brain and called her Bumpkin. Hence she groped for some sort of beauty when she named her scrawny troop of children (three of them fathered by men other than her husband). She named them Coral, Laurel, Floral, Zoral. Dick Tebbs had been dead for ten years, but poor Mag was gone into whoredom long before he died; and he spent his last sullen sickly winters in cutting enough wood to keep The Crib warm while she did her entertaining.

Won't you light? The widow asked it a second time, as the Dillards sat in silence, pitying her. Effie Dillard's bark was savage at times, but she did not even know how to bite.

No, thank you, Sister Marget. We stopped by to offer a small gift; but it is a long homeward journey.

The Widow Tebbs brightened at the thought of a gift. Probably she thought of ribbons. She said, I do implore you not to call me Sister, Parson. Puts me in mind of Pa, and he was so cross all the while.

She came forward eagerly as she spoke, her soft red mouth spreading in a smile which enhanced her degenerate beauty.

Paint, said Mrs. Dillard, and lifted an accusing bony finger of her mitted hand. Whereabouts?

On your face, woman. On your very lips.

Oh, no, ma'am. This is red off of a candy stick. I keep it special.

Effie groaned. Cato Dillard bent his head to conceal his own amusement; he knew that he was transgressing mildly in finding any glee in the situation, yet he could not help himself. He reached beneath the seat and brought out a solid weighty bag of soiled cotton cloth. Tis meal, he told the widow. A member of the congregation brought us a generous gift from his mill this week, and I'm sharing it with you, Marget.

Perhaps she would rather have had a wornout bonnet or the feathers or flowers from it, but Mag was grateful. Why, Parson, I give you thanks. Times are so hard with—

She was about to say, With so many menfolks gone to the army, but innate and unsuspected delicacy restrained her. Instead she said after hesitation, With things the way they be.

What about the boy's foot?

It's gone complete. Marget blinked more rapidly than ever, and tears were spilling. Poor little Coral—it was only his third big battle. He got a ball right through the foot, and them surgeons hacked it off. He said they held him down a-doing it. Always cutting. All a surgeon knows how to do.

Effie declared that they might be losing a second foot in the family unless precautions were taken about Flory. She produced a bottle of green ointment of her own manufacture, one of several medicines without which she would seldom travel abroad. She made Flory fetch a cup, and measured a portion of the medicine. Enthusiastically she recited the recipe while Flory listened with horror. Good refined turpentine and lard, also honey and beeswax; these had been melted together with a bit of finely pulverized verdigris stirred in. Did the widow have any beeswax? She reckoned there was some around, somewhere. . . . Well, Effie was determined to enter the house and prepare the poultice herself—or rather a little tent, stiffened with warm beeswax and worked into the oozing wound—but the widow said that her fire was cold and it would take time to build it up. Effie extracted a promise and had to be content with that. Flory still clung to the gig wheel and sucked on the second lozenge which he had wheedled out of the minister by mere exercise of longing in his pinched face.

While they were thus engaged, the whistle of a train sounded, and Blackie's ears arose and Blackie's feet spread apart, and Cato had to climb down and take Blackie's head and speak soothingly. The others watched the train come lurching, smoking past. The engineer managed a couple of extra whistle-toots when directly in front of the cottage; he knew the widow well, and always saluted her. There were a few soldiers guarding the burden cars—foodstuffs for the army, probably —and they waved and shouted pleasantries which could not be understood. The widow waved urgently in reply.

Just as last cinders were flying and while Blackie still snuffled, a thin youth progressed slowly around the corner of The Crib. He stopped when he saw the gig, then came on, looking at the ground beneath and ahead of him. He swung his body from side to side, pivoting on the homemade crutch, putting his right foot forward, hopping the pole of the crutch into a new position . . . thus he traveled. His pantleg flopped in rags around the stump where his left leg had been severed at the ankle. Coral did not resemble his mother in appearance, and bore no resemblance to the other children. His black hair was shaggy, his thick black brows pulled together in a hairy scowl, his cheeks were darkened with young untrimmed beard. In his right hand he carried a shotgun with a mended stock, and Cato Dillard rejoiced to see that a quail—no, two—hung suspended from Coral's belt.

I see you did well, my boy. Dillard spoke with enthusiasm as soon as Coral was within hearing.

Got two.

I never did hear that old gun at all, said Floral in surprise.

Well, it's an accomplishment, declared the minister. And working without a dog.

Coral glowered as if he'd expected the minister to say, Without a foot. He stopped near the steps and said guardedly, Old Zack got himself kilt whilst I was gone to— Just went to sleep on the tracks and let the cars run over him. Least that's what they tell me.

Coral, cried his mother, come down out the gate and make some nice manners to the parson and the Mrs.

No, said the youth. He moved painfully up the steps.

You got no call to be so mean, sonny. And they fetched meal for us; and Flory's saving you a candy.

Don't want no candy. He was gone into the cottage.

I told you so, said Flory, and popped Coral's designated wintergreen into his own mouth. He's just poison mean.

You shut your trap, Flory. His mother struck at him but the boy dodged.

We must go. Dillard had climbed back into the gig. Marget, daughter, I merely want you to know that you are often in my prayers.

Thank you kindly, Parson, but I don't want to be in nobody's prayers. Had enough of prayers when I was little.

I speak now from the Larger Catechism: *We are by nature children of Wrath, bond slaves to Satan, and justly liable to all punishments in this world and that which is to come.* God bless you, Marget.

He began to turn Blackie away from the gate.

God bless you folks, too, and then Marget stopped in alarm at having been lured into saying it. She cried after them, I do thank you for the meal.

Save the poke, Effie Dillard yelled. Allow no one to make off with it. The dominie can pick it up one day.

Wait, the widow screamed. She sent Flory into the cottage to dump meal into a pan, and then he flew out again, waving the dusty sack in his hand. He hustled down the road at a limping gallop, and grinned shyly up at the pair when he handed them the bag. He breathed, Could I have just one more candy?

You're a little pig. Effie spoke severely. You should save some for your sister and your baby brother. Cate, do you give me that comfitbox. She counted out three more lozenges while her husband sighed. One for you, one for Sister, one for Brother. Mind, now.

Yes, ma'am.

And mind about that tent of green ointment, lest you be like poor Coral.

I'll mind. Ma can fix it, soon as we get a fire going.

They looked back at the house. Zoral was emerging from his den under the house but the widow seemed paying no attention to the child. She kept waving earnestly at the Dillards until they were gone across the railroad. She could not hear him, but the Reverend Mr. Cato Dillard concerned himself audibly with The Gospel According to Saint John.

Woman, where are those thine accusers? hath no man condemned thee?

Revelation comes later than you, said his wife. *Mystery, Babylon the Great. The Mother of Harlots and Abominations of the Earth.*

Oh, Effie. I prefer The Gospel. *She said, No man, Lord. . . . Neither do I condemn thee.*

Back at the Tebbs house, Floral worked reluctantly for a time, fetching wood and kindling of pine splinters which his mother demanded. Coral was hunched on a stool by the table, plucking the first bird. He had put the shotgun on its pegs, and hung the shot flask and powder flask where they belonged. Flory went to take them down, and his brother spewed out a stream of profanity and struck with his crutch. You leave them things alone, God damn you, you little squeak.

Now, you youngsters—

Tain't your shotgun any more'n it's mine!

Tis, by God!

I used it whilst you was in the army. I got some ground doves and—

Ground doves! No wonder I'm shy a foot! That's the unluckiest thing a mortal can do: kill a ground dove. Any nigger in the county could of tolt you that. You hadn't no call to use the shotgun. Tis mine; because I'm the eldest and a gun is handed down from a father to his eldest.

God damn lie.

You touch my gun again and I'll beat the poop out of you.

Ah, you and your old crutch—

Coral hurled the crutch. It might have injured Flory but it only grazed his hip. Nevertheless the younger boy burst into squalls and hurried blindly out of the door, calling spitefully, You damn cripple! Crip, crip, crip, crip, crip, crip, cripple —! He tripped over Zoral below the stoop, and the stunted baby set up a bellowing. Mag flew to the rescue, calling loudly on the world to witness what troubles possessed her.

Floral retreated into woods behind the privy and solaced himself with a wad of pine gum. It occurred to him that if he carried a heavy club, and crept up silently on a covey of quail without disturbance, he might be able to get a bird for himself by flinging the club, much as Coral was forever hurling his crutch. Flory had tried unsuccessfully before with rocks, never with a club. He hunted around for a suitable bludgeon, found one, and tottered off among the trees. He played that the stick in his hands was a gun. Not just a shotgun, but a regular military musket. Maybe even a modern rifle. Maybe even a modern Henry rifle, a repeater with copper cartridges; he had seen such weapons carried by soldiers on several occasions when soldiers called upon his mother. Such weapons were captured from Yankees.

He played that he was killing a Yankee. Hold still there, you Yankee scum. You heard me. Don't move or I'll blow your guts out handsome. Hold right still, don't try to get away, you Yankee bastard! Look sharp; I warned you.

Flory lifted the stick to his shoulder. His face was contorted and he squeezed his eyes shut as he fired. *Poom.*

3

At this same hour in Paris a rain came blackly. It was mid-afternoon in Georgia, evening in the region near the old Medical College where the good Dr. Cordier had lectured hoarsely above his cadavers more than twenty years before. The good Dr. Cordier was long since in his tomb, but at a favorite café two of his former students now sat with wine. There was a tablecloth of flowered green, the crusty bread lay broken upon it, the big shiny casserole still stood on its seared frame above a burning lamp.

Dr. Bucheton reached over and selected a mushroom which had eluded him in gravy; he speared it with surgical precision, ate it, put down his fork and nodded across at his companion.

You see how it is, Henry. I not only take some pride in myself as a gourmet; I'm also a glutton. He patted the belly which stood out under his tight white waistcoat.

The bearded Henry Wirz said, I am a dyspeptic. He was a round-shouldered thin-faced man, past forty, sallow of skin, and with blood vessels apparent in his pale eyeballs which suggested constant pain, sleeplessness, a constriction of various forces clamoring for release. His French was spoken shrilly, almost explosively, with a pronounced German accent. Many people took him to be a Jew, but he was not a Jew. It was as if he sought to relieve the somber acids moving through his digestive system and in his leaden blood, by gauding himself in tints commonly worn only by younger men. His jacket was saffron, his shirt of checkered cambric, his stock of Stuart tartan silk. His right arm rested in a black sateen sling, and the arm was giving him misery this night; he kept groping across the tablecloth with the fingers of his left hand, and caressing and kneading the slim bandaged bulk within the sateen.

You still have the sulphate of morphia? In your lodgings?

The devil—yes. I have plenty. But I can't take too much of that stuff. Henry Wirz had something else in his lodgings in the Rue d'Assas: he had it hanging in the big wardrobe: a uniform of Confederate gray.

Be sure to reduce the dosage by degrees.

You don't have to tell me that. But you don't understand how it is with us in the Confederacy, Pierre. These things are unprocurable. The blockade is tighter all the time.

Dr. Bucheton nodded sympathetically, and filled Henry's wine glass, then his own. I don't pay much attention to what goes on over there. My dear friend, you'll forgive me when I state a simple if unpleasant professional fact. Between my own patients and what goes on at the hospital and my lectures at the school— Well, my wife tells the children not to run shrieking to their nurse that a strange impostor has forced his way into the house, on those rare occasions when I do appear. As for my mistress—

He shrugged. I should not beat her if she began to dally with a younger and more light-hearted man. It would be only justice if she did. Thus I cast my speeding eyes over the printed page, and I see that your Mr. Mason and your Mr.

Slidell are still on this side of the Atlantic, and I wish them well, and I also would like to have you shipping to us cotton and rice and tobacco and other good things, but I don't want to go to war with the Americans about it. And I assume also that when the old friend of my student days appears, and lo and behold he is *Captain* Henry Wirz— I assume that he has possibly some business with Mr. Slidell in France? But I don't give it more thought than that. It's a physical and mental impossibility. Do you forgive me, Henry?

Wirz nodded. My arm is particularly troublesome tonight.

Come, I've just ordered cognac.

I have no head for cognac. You should remember.

Well, perhaps we should call it the poor man's sulphate of morphia or— Do you have cognac in the Confederate States, Henry?

Only what is left in a few people's cellars. Some we get from the Yankees. Damn this thing, Pierre. I think you injured the nerves when you removed the *sequestra*.

Hush, you very stupid fellow! The great Dr. Bucheton does not go about butchering nerves with his scalpel. Do you wish me to draw another diagram? Here, upon the tablecloth; give me your pencil—

Nonsense. I want no more of your diagrams. I want only for the pain to go away.

In time, Henry, in time. You must needs be patient. You've undergone a great deal of treatment—some of it very inept and messy, according to what I found when I got into that wrist of yours last Monday. This is merely Old Dame Nature's way of saying, My God, I've been stabbed, I've been raped, I've been slaughtered. Watch closely. The drainage has already decreased to a bare trickle. The efflores- cence has decreased as well. And the seropurulent matter which came out of there! Where did you say you got this wound? In the battle of Louisiana?

No, no, no, Louisiana is my *home*. Or was. The wound I received in the fighting near Richmond, our capital. That was a year ago last summer. They called the place Seven Pines. God damn the Yankee who did this to me.

The fortunes of war, Henry. You know, I did some soldiering myself in '48. Have I yet told you about—?

Fortune of war or no fortune of war, may the good God damn the Yankee who did this to me. I say, Give him to me. Let me meet him face to face. Who are you, Yankee? Was it your fingers on the lanyard which did the wickedness? Show them to me; I will show you my hand, or my arm which you did such cruelty to; now show me, Yankee, your own evil hand which performed the act. So what is that hand like, and where is the Yankee? Is it a young man's hand—lively, tanned, hairy, a strong right hand? Or maybe the Yankee was left-handed?

Henry Wirz was speaking with such passion that Madame bent down from her smoky perch under the archway and gave him a searching look. An idle old waiter had drawn near, in alarm at having to deal with a foreign inebriate; a party of students and girls from the half-world had given up all conversation of their own and were united in attention.

Henry, said Bucheton in disquiet.

I tell you, I should like to meet that hand, and the man to whom it is attached! Ah—

No doubt you should, no doubt you should. Here, waiter, we'll both have another cognac. Immediately, if you please!

In his sudden outpouring of frenzy, Wirz had thudded his bandaged forearm against the table, and the act brought forth a single exclamation of agony. He sat silently, his glance turned down, the sweat standing like fragile pebbled topaz bulbs upon his high bony forehead.

Bucheton began chattering in rapid sequence punctuated by low laughter intended to be soothing. He spoke a string of gossip and reminiscence concerning their mutual student past. Not for one moment did he think that Wirz was imagining or magnifying the misery dancing amid the nerves of his right arm. Pierre Bucheton had seen the slivered radius and ulna exposed, and his own small bright tongs had tightened on crumbs of corroded bone which he found serrated amid the tissues of Henry Wirz. He was a companion of this patient a solid generation previously, but had not fallen in with him again until the current year. Ah, yes—in 1849 Henry had indeed sent him a letter; that was when Henry passed through Paris en route for America, his dead wife left behind beneath her slab in Zurich, his living children left with their grandparents. The note had reached Bucheton belatedly since he was gone with the army. So he had not encountered Wirz again until this modern time of 1863. He had never thought that Wirz would be one to bear adversity with the dignity which passes for serenity. Old Cordier and others had signalled their awareness that Wirz was a talented youth—alert in the extreme, but too taut for his own well-being. His mind was an engraver's stone, ready to be saturated with the inks of acquired knowledge; but reasoning did not come to him with ease. There was no flavor of humor about him except the taste of humor which is found in most youths; maturity would dry it up—yes, and had.

Bucheton had been willing—even keen—to benefit Wirz with his skill and experience in surgery, and with no mention of a fee. Academically he regretted that Henry must suffer this persistent pain; but as a truth Bucheton had never suffered any great physical agony within his own experience; he had only seen others suffering. He knew that physical anguish was bad; he was sorry that it must occur. But he could dismiss it, since the ache did not lie within his own experience or within his own flesh.

A last draught of cognac?

No.

They went outside into a dark city fresh washed, but it was raining no longer. Bucheton's coachman hurried up to the next wide turning to bring the doctor's chaise. You'll squeeze in beside me, friend Henry, and I'll set you down at your lodgings.

I will walk through the night air. It is chilly, and a stroll may help to clear my poor head and make me forget this.

There are purse-snatchers about. We've been warned.

Even in this quiet area? Well, I have very little money.

They made their goodbyes, Wirz gave his thanks for the dinner, Bucheton cautioned him about the reduction of the sulphate of morphia dosage by measured degrees, he set a day and an hour when Wirz should appear for his next examination. He dared not insult the Herr Doktor Wirz by instructing him about dressings, though he longed to. But Wirz said that the young son of his *concierge* was a tractable youth, and had been taught to hold the basin and bind the ends of linen—so—and now and then got a franc for his trouble.

Bucheton embraced the captain perfunctorily, and then drove off in his chaise. Wirz strolled, rigidly round-shouldered, beyond the Boulevard St. Germain; he held his gold-headed walking stick gripped tightly in his left hand, and it was a heavy stick, and would offer punishment to any slovenly mendicant or possible footpad who approached him. Yes, be he pickpocket or ruffian, Wirz could lift the stick and bring it down hardily.

Be he a Yankee— The pale knuckles grew paler.

Through the cool glistening, Wirz walked homeward slowly. Later he crossed through a corner of the Luxembourg gardens, and two becaped policemen strode toward him, bearing their batons, and one was carrying a lantern. The lantern was lifted, Captain Wirz spoke a salutation, the policemen gave him their respects and marched away. His arm shriveled, grew cold, grew hot, grew fatter; it was at times made of iron; it was at times an elongated toad which squirmed; always it was an irritant, sometimes a beast.

—Very well. So if you'd undergone an amputation—

—But my hand. *Ach.* It is my hand which I need to retain— Condemn Bucheton and his smugness! If I'd but owned three hands I could have used two of them to operate on myself—

—But you have been your own surgeon at times. The first pink scraps, when they came near the surface; the older more recent bits, turned black as coal, and honey-combed— You worked in sweat, the bottle of whiskey beside you, the scalpel cleanly wiped, the tufts of lint soaking up the liquid— You worked methodically and well, and even on that night when you were home, and your wife was ill with the female curse, and Cora had the croup and was gagging with it— You worked as your own surgeon, with a Negro bug-eyed beside you—

—But still the leaping pain, the nerves like frogs in their jumping, the frogs bounding and saying, Let us out or we'll burst your skin.

—*Ja.* Frogs.

With discipline he sought to break his recollection away from the concern it held with his wound. Libby—he saw the desk, he put muster rolls into the narrow pigeon-holes when they had been checked, he heard the slam of guards' musket butts on the stones when they halted outside the door—not his door, the other door . . . sat outside the office of Mr. Seddon's deputy, he sat there during three whole forenoons and two and one-half afternoons, he sat motionless or nearly motionless, with his beard neatly brushed and his small gray cap held upon his knee like a bright-beaked bird he had trapped. Then he had his appointment. *Inspecting Officer of Prisons.* That sounded very well indeed.

Special Minister Plenipotentiary in Europe. That sounded even better. Of course he wasn't the only one, and also he was on leave of absence officially.

And why had they not made him a colonel? They had promised that he should be a colonel. Here he was now, doing a man-sized task with only boy-sized rank to wear. A captain!—no wonder he was treated like an errand boy. Actually he had never laid eyes on Mr. Slidell (though he pretended to Bucheton and others that he had). A secretary came into an anteroom on both occasions—once to accept the dispatches which Wirz had brought; the other time to give him an envelope of instructions.

His German was profound and scholarly, because he was native to Zurich and educated also in Berlin. His French was fairly secure, accent or no accent, because he had learned the language when very young; but he was twenty-seven years old before he began to speak more than a few words of English, and was handicapped further (as a loyal Confederate he disliked to admit this) because he had spent most of his thirteen or fourteen American years with the soft long drawl of R-slighting of Southerners in his ears.

So perhaps that was the reason his promotion had been passed over repeatedly? They thought that a man who talked like a Tam Tutchman wasn't worthy of higher grade? What about that Prussian giant—what was his name?—who worked for General Stuart? Wirz had heard him laughing, bellowing delightedly, twisting up his whiskers; he stood close to him once; and Von Borcke was unmistakably of field grade, with his English nothing like so extensive as Henry's.

You had to know influential people, you had to know them well. You had to know—

Ach, mein lieber Gott im Himmel! The arm.

He was walking, measured hurtful step by measured hurtful step, on a stone-bordered path in the Luxembourg gardens, where he had strolled so often when he was a youth; and one day he had even helped two little boys with their sailing of boats, and a great breeze blew the fountain spray loose from its jeweled column and spattered them thoroughly, and they all shrieked with laughter and so did young Henry Wirz, and kindly he took off his shoes and stockings and rolled up his dove-colored pantaloons, and he waded in to retrieve the two white sailboats which the wind had tossed upon their beam-ends—

He was walking, grasping that slung arm which bred its torture, he was walking in midnight amid the damp Luxembourg gardens; and it did not seem real— walking in New Orleans would seem more real nowadays, if only he could walk there; and in the Luxembourg gardens all of the Parisians turned out in full force each Sunday, except for the thousands who went gabbling to the *Bois,* and all of them had their dogs along with them. French dogs were a race apart: not like American dogs, not like Southern American dogs, with their long ears and jaunty scratching and their loose addiction to raccoons or brawling, or their fondness for copulation in the open dusty roads. French dogs marched in harness, they took tight little steps, they seemed to sniff in French, they carried the pinned-up ears of one breed, the ruffles of another, the hard-curled tails of still another heritage; they were indubitably French—they gestured with their strange tails as they met and conversed—

The dogs. The Yankees were dogs. Oh, God. My arm—

Wirz walked there, and saw and felt no more than the barest impress of a fading past, hung like bleached wall paper against the facade of the October night. What was more real was blackness of a late May storm—*ja,* the night between May thirtieth and May thirty-first, it was—and Blanchard's Brigade was moving up through steady pouring rain, and the arm did not hurt at all because there had been no metal entering to mutilate it. Come the next day, and the next . . . all plank highways built up out of the marsh, and trees thick and dripping, and the uncertain scattered fire of skirmishers cutting through the forest where another brigade of Huger's Division was already making contact with the enemy—

Then came the smash of pain like a fist striking simultaneously his arm, his eyes, his nose, the soft thin hollow of his belly.

Go to the rear. And look out for those batteries moving up, and go stumbling off the corduroy while the great wheels draped with mud come skating past, and hold your arm and watch the blood run down between your fingers and— *Go to the rear.*

And never a moment, from that moment, divorced from the feel of the wickedness. Never a tingling second to escape it, never a long hour of waking to know that the throbbing was subdued. Only in sleep, only in blank blackness, with the bitter small brew of morphia to bring a void before you, and force you over the edge and into it.

Henry Wirz moved across wet and ancient stones. With his left hand he opened the iron gate; he went up to the steps and rang the bell for the *concierge.* A night-walker came past the fence, he heard the light conversation of her heels resounding under barren chestnut trees. She called with low fervor, Oh, *Monsieur,* one moment, please— He coughed and turned his thin face away. The *concierge* came muttering inside with a candle, chains were unfastened, the door swung.

One might then have gone far beyond Henry Wirz, through darkened bricks of the tall old house which once had been occupied by a marshal who died in Egypt, and over the soot and tiles beyond— One could have gone out in thought through the wastes of the *Bois de Meudon* where a suicide and a huddled hare and a softly wailing servant girl (newly and rudely taught a rite supposed to deal with affection) lay nearly in the same thicket— One could have swept on an instant past the spires of Versailles and over secret countryside where the River Eure rose in its initial brimming; and might have passed near Alencon in a twinkling, and given a blessing to old women who spent years with their lace and dangling shuttles; and sped across thrashing coasts of southernmost Brittany where the racket of night-time winches was forgotten at Lorient and last lanterns were put out by the fog—

Away, away, going in thought or imagination above the long black swells, west and a little south, west and steadily bearing a little to the port dots of the compass, ignoring the marble which emerged from waves and was then sponged into spray by a fresh slapping of salt and was reconstructed into more jet and snowy marble far in the depth, and pushed up and out again to frighten the fishermen in their small plunging boats and to be seen by birds flying at night, except that none was flying—

And on past a Swedish vessel and a blockade runner which bore no lights because Yankees were looking for her, even in these eternal wildernesses of marble and salt which couldn't be measured easily or plumbed; and on, in the single flaming of a thought, ignoring lonely islands of the Atlantic and into the growing color which suggested a twilight and became finally a sunset and then a remnant of late October afternoon in which coastal cities stood out boldly, and where guards walked above the batteries of some forts which had been attacked and some which would never be hit by any shells—

Above estuaries and over camps the fast wild thought might have gone fleeting, born in a brain which truly had no power to bear it; for this moment became a part of the future where a man can never dwell, and where gods are merely invented, and where the new unseen sun gives off its roaring, and new unseen stars are intact.

The Fifth Maine Battery was bivouacked behind a knotty board fence. When Portland Hyde and his friend Caldwell walked the nearby lane at night they could see cooking fires showing pale red in reflection above the fence, and raw living red through the cracks. Now they moved in dusk, less than two months away from the winter solstice; dusk or not, they did not care, for they carried a duck with a fresh-wrung neck. Got him safe under your coat, Porty? You just bet I have. Don't want no sentry putting down the law to me about foraging. Yes, and then taking our duck for his own self. How do you say we boil him? Twould be easier. Maybe so; but I just couldn't stomach boiled duck. No, sir, I'd as lief toast him bit by bit on a ramrod. I wish we had some peas; a pot of peas would go well along with him. Well, why don't you wish you was to home, and having Betty fetching in beans and biscuits? O laughter. . . .

Companies E and K of the Eleventh Vermont guarded a great pile of earth-works and logworks outside Washington City. Here John Appleby was freshly come on picket duty. He had retreated like a smart soldier below a broken-off sycamore tree where he was cooped safely from any wind or weather, and had a good sight at the road in either direction whenever he felt in his bones that an officer or a provost detail might be approaching. Mainly he thought about his friend Adam Garrett, and how well things must be going with him. Adam was recovered from his Gettysburg wound, which he had received while serving with Stannard's Brigade. Now that the Sixteenth Vermont was mustered out, Adam had re-enlisted in the Eleventh and was still at West Dummerston enjoying veteran's furlough.

Where was Adam? Maybe gone to take supper with the Smalls? John groaned to himself, thinking of the Smalls and their big low kitchen; well, yes, he'd liked Hallie Small too, but Adam always shone up to the girls more successfully. Mrs. Small was noted for her fruit pies all over the town of Dummerston, all the way from East Dummerston across the forest through Dummerston Center and down to West Dummerston on the river. (Fact of the matter was, Adam Garrett was gone to a church supper on this evening. Next Tuesday he'd ride with his father to Brattleboro and take the cars, and head for Northern Virginia to join his new regiment and his old friend John Appleby. Time was when Adam never thought he'd get over talking about that piece of rib which was shot out of his side—he was so proud of it, and rejoiced in the realization that he wasn't actually killed, just hurt a mite. But lately he'd grown weary of telling the same story to the same rural garden-variety of ears. Nobody understood truly what he was talking about. He sat beneath a bower of bunting, and ladies bustled behind him with their big flat blackened pans of chicken pie, and he tried to see Hallie beyond the bunting, and prayed that she wasn't still mad because of that tiff they'd had when he caught Hepsy Clark and kissed her when they played Ruth and Jacob at the Jennings place— He said to old Deacon Root and young tongue-tied Mr. Willis and of course the minister, beaming gravely beyond— He said, Well, you see our regiment was on the left of those trees. There was a stone wall just ahead of us, but the stones was knocked loose and scattered. The Rebs give us one volley before they moved forward past the barn. I forgot to tell you there was a barn and farmhouse towards the Rebel lines from us—I mean, in between. He kept peering past the bearded listeners, trying to see Hallie. He caught a flurry of her plaid gown—)

Old Tom Gusset, Saddler, Ninth Ohio Cavalry, said to the sutler, That's a pretty price. Thirty cents currency for that one little tin? Look, old man, them preserves are strawberry and they got a little brandy in them, or so tis said. Would you guarantee that? Not me; I ain't guaranteeing nothing. How do I know it's true what it says on the label of the tin? Well, by cracky, if you don't know, who does? How much is that there tin marked quince and nut? That's dearer, partner. Thirty-five cents I got to get for that.

In a bleak ravine west of Chattanooga, a private of the Twenty-sixth Wisconsin said, Haltoogoesthere? Friends with the countersign. Advance singly and be recognized. Billy stood with his rifle directed on dim shapes moving among the trees, and he resented the added weight of the bayonet. What in the devil—? Oh, yes; the countersign was *Tippecanoe*. Advance singly, mister. You come one at a time. Advance with the countersign. . . . *Tippecanoe*. Hey, there, Billy—you sounded scared—I didn't recognize your voice. Gol damn it, I ain't scared, I'm just sick. Sick of what? Sick of beef dried on the hoof. Well, we may fare better, now that they've got rid of old Rosy Rosecrans. Think Pap Thomas will do better by us? I surely do—rumor has it that the first thing old Pap is going to do is open up a cracker line.

In a Richmond bedroom two great sagging wide-fleshed faces met and stared; one was cased in glass backed by crinkled quicksilver, and the quicksilver had flaked away from the mirror's back to make the imprisoned face more pocked, more scabbed, more seamed than it was in fact. Brigadier-General John Winder put up his pulpy fingers and inspected tenderly the bleeding notch which a razor had made in a ridge of loose skin beside his mouth (his mouth was a thin old scar, wide and long-healed and stitched together by mythical sutures; it was a fierce blue mouth). Amos, you black son of a bitch, what were you trying to do—murder me? A frightened slave in a frayed white jacket hovered behind Winder. Please, General, sir, I don't know what did happen. That old razor seem like it was nice and sharp when I strop it, but it just didn't glide tonight, sir, it just didn't glide. . . . Winder snarled in reply, saying no words, but he was a master of the snarl, his snarls spoke volumes of invective on complicated ugly subjects. Now he must appear at the President's table with a freshcut face. . . . You son of a bitch, go fetch a lump of alum! Don't stand there like a gawk, God damn it—*fetch!*

Aboard the United States sloop *Sea Sprite,* bumping on patrol beyond Mobile, a shaggy Irishman named Patrick was squatted in the head, doing his business at the same hour he always liked to perform it. On the same deck, at another place, another seaman was soliciting the youth whom Patrick adored.

I'll give you five dollars, Val, the man muttered—no, I'll make it six. Just think —six beautiful gold dollars.

I don't think you got six dollars.

Yes, I got them, right in this here sock. Hear them jingle? Val, if you'll wait till it's my watch below and—

I don't dast. He'd be mad; he'd maybe beat me black and blue.

Val, he won't know nothing about it, because he'll be on watch. I'll never tell, Val boy—you can trust old Sprit.

The boy backed slowly away, his ferret eyes gleaming with cupidity, his ferret head shaking. No, I don't dast.

Say ten, by God. I'll raise to ten; hain't got no more.

Well, for ten—

In the lines near Knoxville a boy from the Thirteenth Kentucky slid his rifle across a rock, elevated the sight slightly, and fired at a dark shape which had been drifting in front of him through the thickening mountain dusk. *Yipe,* and then swifter howls going away. I'll be blamed. Just one of those damn dogs again. Hey, Charley, what did you pop? Blame dog. Hey, listen, Charley, you got any crackers left? Got three. Give me one? If I crawl over? Thanks kindly.

Near the Rappahannock the woods were witches' woods where the One Hundred and Forty-eighth Pennsylvania crouched along a side road. Ennis, I noticed something. Well, what? It's the quartermaster; notice anything odd about it? No. Well, I did. Tonight's the first night he set up his tent right *in camp—not out with the wagon train.* Now, way it looks to me, we're stuck here for good. Might as well start work on a shebang tomorrow; I give my oath, I'd bet every shinplaster I got that we'll go into winter quarters right here. First time we've settled down since Bristoe Station. What do you say—about the shebang? There's whole loads of wood around, and if we get started before the rest pitch into it, we'll get first pick. By gum, Jake, I think you're maybe right. Get Balder and Timmelpennick and Douglas and Puffy; let's get after that wood *tonight.* Shake on it, Ennis, I'm with you.

A youth from a New York tenement who bore the name of Torrosian, a youth from the Catskills whose name was Plover, a youth named Mutterson whose mother was reputed to be the best cook in their Pennsylvania valley: Brewster's Brigade divided itself across a creek west of Warrenton, Virginia; pork was sizzling. Eric Torrosian tripped over a root and sent the coffee can spattering into the fire. Amid curses of some men and laughter of others he was sentenced to make up the wasted coffee grounds out of his own store. He had no more coffee in his knapsack, he had to walk a quarter of a mile to the sutler's cart, he went in resentment even though he recognized the justice of it.

At the headquarters of Major-General George H. Thomas in a corner of

Tennessee, a tired bearded man leaned between his crutches and peered into a circle of lamplight where papers were spread. A man named Baldy Smith was explaining intently how he had prepared lumber for bridges. Did you establish a sawmill, General Smith? Yes, sir—cobbled one together—utilized an old engine we *borrowed* in the neighborhood. Building the pontoons right now for Bridge Number Three. In addition we're well progressed on a steamer for plying between here and Bridgeport—as soon as we achieve possession of the river. The man on the crutches said, Boat building? Have you a shipyard, General? Smith said, Oh, it's not much, but I think it should turn the trick. It's a scow made from planks we sawed in our mill—all well housed in—and the stern wheel is to be propelled by another steam engine we *borrowed* from a local factory. The man on crutches meditated; there was a tired smile under his brown beard. Seems to me you always were a good provider, even when we were Kay-dets at the Point. Don't think I've seen you since graduation, twenty years ago. Pleased to find you doing such outstanding work. . . . Smith looked at him earnestly. Thank you, sir. It's good to see you again, but I'm sorry to find you on crutches. Is that from the accident you suffered out West? . . . General Grant nodded. It was in August, when I went to New Orleans to talk to Banks. My horse fell. It's been pretty troublesome for over two months. By the by, I haven't notified General Halleck of my arrival here. Will one of your people please to take a message over to the telegrapher for me? . . .

Other crutches rapped across the rough planks of a prison hospital in central Virginia. An ugly beak-nosed man tossed on his pallet and mouthed, Why'n't you quit making all that racket? I was trying to sleep. . . . Oh, shut up, Chicka-mauga! Some fine day maybe that old hacked-off festered limb of yours will get well, and then you'll have some crutches of your own, and you can see how you like it. . . . Not far away, in a mire named Belle Isle, a New York City rough called Collins clamped his fingers around the throat of a sick Ohioan until there was no breath left in the man; then Collins went through the man's pockets and found the watch he sought, the watch wrapped in a dirty handkerchief with *Enoch from Louella* cross-stitched upon it.

Woods' Brigade of Osterhaus's Division of the Fifteenth Corps trailed along a road in northeastern Mississippi, marching still, they would march until after dark, and how long was it since the day they left Memphis? Willie Mann gave only automatic attention to demands of the march, the watching where to plant his feet, the watching to avoid ruts or rocks. He dreamed, as the last pink warmness of sun touched the heavy knapsack bulking on his shoulders, he dreamed of a girl named Katty. Right now, back home in Missouri, she might be putting a big pan of apples into the oven to bake for dessert that evening. Willie had eaten apples baked by Katty, and they were marvelous things: the scraped flakes of cinnamon bark toasted to black, the sugar changed to apple-nectar-syrup, the thick Alderney cream swirling slowly down through the hollow where the apple had been cored. . . . Beside Willie Mann a big-framed comrade was singing in a monotone as he strode. Titus Cherry couldn't carry a tune on a shovel, but he beguiled himself with song whenever they traveled as hard as they'd traveled this autumn day. The other boys didn't relish the sounds he made, but none of them was big enough to silence him . . . *what signifies the life of man if twere not for the lasses, oh? Green grow the rashes, oh, green grow the rashes, oh.* The tuneless rumble of Titus Cherry hung like a weight on the hearing of the rest, it seemed to retard them while they tramped. . . . On an adjacent road the Fifth Iowa Infantry trailed up a low slope where the Seventeenth Corps was pushing, and Eben Dolliver saw a bird he couldn't quite recognize: was it a jay? It didn't look like the jaybirds back home in Hamilton County—seemed to have more gray on it—it was over there in that scraggly oak—he wished he could leave the column, to see it at close range—maybe bluejays in northern Mississippi had more gray than Iowa birds would have at this season. Of course! he thought drolly. Confederate birds, Secesh jaybirds, they're bound to be gray. The man ahead of him snarled over his shoulder, Ebe, quit goosing me with your rifle butt. A butt in the butt, said someone else. A weak chuckle drifted up.

Pines, mountains, stones upon stones, the flat pocked farms below, the burned houses and disordered towns, the girl waving her kerchief, the crone spitting as the enemy passed, the armies squatting or moving, the oceans along margins where hunted craft and hunters went lurching as the wind of night rose. And scattered, dotted singly or by couples or by dozens from Texas to the White Mountains and down to the lead-speckled clefts of Tennessee once more, there labored a pulse and breathing of fifty thousand men whose fate bayed behind them—never seen, never heard, but driving them with the dedicated relentlessness of time itself, driving them toward a common destination.

The next morning before it was light, Ira Claffey walked in the woods with his grief.

4

Often in early December the north wind beats thinly, steadily across the hillocks of Georgia; it comes like a sickle cutting unseen but felt, and the edge is rawly mean; and before dawn a woman should shiver from her nest (if an indulgent woman who could not presume to awaken her husband first to the task) and let her sleepy grasp go hunting charred billets piled in the corner. . . . The log sinks loosely, deeper and deeper among pink flakes after she has put it there, and for a minute or two there are no flames, only a sizzling. Then the resin has melted out, it pops and fries with a smell like cooking, there are spurts and explosions of crystallized juices as they burn to evaporation in a twinkling: the first solid flame is accomplished. Up it goes, crawls onto a splinter, hangs, droops, falls off, rises wider and more solidly. Its cousin flame joins it from the rear and over the top; the wide hot ruffle is a fringe and a high one, in seconds. The warmth comes out . . . it is good that the warmth comes, for that unseen sickle swings across every upland where the stalks have dried.

In this December darkness, Coffee's wife lifted and fired the small log.

She ran back, long-legged and monstrous in her rough short shirt; she rolled back the old comforters and plunged beneath them, and bundled them behind her muscular back and wadded them beneath her thin buttock. Her knees drew into the warm space behind Coffee's knees, her right arm slid around his hairy chest, her chin pressed close between his shoulders, and her own breath burnt in its regular strength beneath the covers, helping to warm them both.

Ung, said Coffee.

It's time, old man.

He was twenty-five years old, Pet was nineteen. Coffee could count to forty and a little past, which was often a convenience in his work, and he had learned proudly. Old Leander taught him. Pet could not count past the sum of her fingers, though sometimes she tried to add the sum of her toes; but this bothered her because she had lost one toe from the bite of a rat when she was small, and she could not quite understand why she never seemed to have as many toes as she had fingers. The bite of the rat came in that unhappy antiquity when she and her mother belonged to Mr. Ganwood. It was a filthy plantation where they were owned, and there was never enough wood or coverings or potatoes, seldom any meat except what the slaves stole or hunted down; there was a whipping-morning for accumulated misdeeds every week—just before holiday, so that the slaves whipped might have a chance to recover before they went into the fields again . . . never any Christmas fit to speak of. Old Mr. Ganwood died a smelly death in bed—slaves said that the Devil came and got him, and certain slaves even declared awesomely that they had seen the Devil coming: he wore a tall black hat, and had two hands with him to fetch out the box in which old Mr. Ganwood was finally nailed. Mr. Ganwood's hands were then parceled out at public auction, and Pet and her mother Naomi became the property of Mr. Ira Claffey. From then on (during the next fourteen years, except for privations which occurred because of war) there was every sort of decent generous allowance which you could name. The Claffeys always made a wonderful Christmas for all their people, and they called them people, and the people were pleased. And these very quilts beneath which Pet now snuggled with her wedded husband, had once covered white folks and made them warm; they were a trifle frayed now, the green squares fading to yellow, the yellow squares fading to white . . . this top quilt was warm, and had a softness.

Time, old man.

Ung.

Time.

How you know, old woman?

I just knows.

Coffee stirred, grunted, settled warm but lifelessly again. They lay like a frieze taken down from the wall and placed flat upon the solid roped bed. There were three of them, in this order: Pet, Coffee, Sukey. Pet was married to Coffee when she was fifteen, and she had lost three other children before they grew very large inside her. Each time she had to stay abed for many days, and both the old and the young mistress came to help attend her, and oversee just what Naomi did for her daughter; and the young mistress made her drink of a tea she herself had prepared. This was all very painful and disheartening, and in weakness Pet was certain that she cried enough tears to fill the largest bucket in the kitchen. But now Sukey was an accomplished fact, and the child grinned all day long, and crawled everywhere; she pulled herself up beside chairs, and grinned at the old master and snatched at the finger which he presented with its gold Masonic ring. Soon she would be walking.

How that child, you Coffee?

She all wet. He giggled sleepily. She wet but she sleeping. She got me wet too.

Time, old man.

He yawned enormously. Still got time, and his big strong hand came hunting amusement. He began to struggle around to face her.

No, no, no! You be decent, man.

Still got time!

No, old man. No time now. Them chickens started in.

I don't hear them.

You listen, you hear them. Don't you come funning with me now. You come home tonight, I let you make fun then.

Oh, yes, old woman. I come home all tuckered out.

Sukey awakened and began to yell. Give her to me, you Coffee. Coffee gathered up the dripping child and helped her to crawl across his strong body until she whimpered happily at her mother's fat breast. Pet was built like a bean-pole, but she carried plenty of milk. The milk was rich, and Naomi said, Hi, just see that fat in it. Once Sukey was born she had never been sick a day in her little life.

Get out of there. You hear me?

The chickens were increasingly vocal; Coffee dared not ignore their summons any longer. He could hear the roosters in their high wailing whooping, all the way across the world. He guessed he could hear them away over at the Tebbs place, and in the scrawny village of Anderson itself. *Urr-a-urr-a-oo.*

Bell ain't spoke yet.

It'll speak, but don't you wait. You fly round, get your clothes, put on one more log, make yourself some count.

The bell spoke: pound, pound, pound. It hung in its gallows on the corner of Old Leander's cabin two cabins away from the home of Pet and Coffee, and it was one of Old Leander's proud tasks to ring the bell according to direction. He would beat it ferociously, then go hobbling back to bed. He had worked for a lifetime, he had toiled well and hard, he could sleep as late as he pleased. Nowadays however he spoke of Heaven with increasing frequency; he prayed hourly. He said that he had seen the three young masters in a dream, and they were dressed in raiment. The rest of the hands were impressed. They cried a little whenever Leander spoke of the young masters, and they too talked about raiment.

Alternately groaning and snorting, Coffee emerged from bed and put on the loose shirt and jeans which he had wadded under the foot of the bed. Wind cut through the few cabin-cracks and made even his strong frame shiver.

Where our shawl, woman?

On that peg with my frocksies.

He found the shawl, tied it around his shoulders, and padded away toward the door.

Don't you go making dirt by the door, you hear me? Old Mastah say everybody go down to the privy, else we get a plague.

Coffee mumbled that he had no intention of making dirt. However, the privy was a long way down the hind path, and cold made him squirm. It was dark, no one could see; all he wanted to make was water, and he went between the two small Walker's Yellow apple trees and made it. Around him rose the sounds of earliest morning, though still the night clung black; you could make out the blot of horizon in the east, you could separate the lighter darkness of sky from the darker darkness of earth, that was all. Jonas and Buncombe, his eldest child, were busy at the stables; Coffee could hear them talking to the horse and the mules. That little Buncombe was stepping around smartly these days; before long he would graduate on the rolls and be listed as half a hand. . . . Coffee put his fingers into both of the buckets on a split bench before the cabin door. Empty or practically so. He carried the pails to the nearest well, beyond the line of cabins on a rounding small hill above stockpens and stables. He put down the sweep, brought up water, filled the pails and carried them home. At the well he'd splashed water all over his face, and had rubbed his eyes and ears with his big wet thumbs. He was thoroughly awake at last.

Pet was up and gowned. She had put a second log into the fireplace and flames were merry; the room was cosier. Sukey sat squealing on the bed. Pet was digging around in the wide heaps of light loose ashes, hunting for yams she'd put there the night before. Coffee had reproved her a dozen times: he claimed that she was always getting the yams too close to the center, too near the logs, too near the actual burning. Well, she had done it again, but with only one yam. She lifted out the four—one charred nearly to a husk, one half raw, two excellently baked, and these two happened to be the biggest. She put them down on the table, and Coffee grabbed, and burnt his hand, and swore.

Don't you go a-cursing, old man.

Woman, I like to roast my fingers off!

Coffee, I don't favor no cursing. Dear Lord never favor cursing. Won't never rear this child mongst cursing.

Oh, hush you prattle, woman. He slapped at her playfully, and she assaulted him with the scorched forked stick she'd used for the yams.

Coffee said, pushing the muffled words out of his mouth while it was filled with potato— He said, I got to tote lunch for noontime.

You want me send a child down with your dinner? Coffee, we low on rations.

We eat too much. You burn too much our rations way! Old woman, know what we do today? We start working for the army.

Who all?

I told you once, I told you twice: me and Jem and Jonas. We all queesishunned.

What that mean?

Big soldier man, he come riding up and old Mastah go out to the gate, and they talk right next me. Bet you old Mastah he mad through and through. Soldier man say, I can't help that, Mr. Claffey, sir. What it say here on this paper: how many hands you got for me? Can't take no women; got to have men cut down trees and dig the ground. So we all get queesishunned, what he say.

What that mean, though?

Just what he say. He say slack work now, won't make no hard times, but old Mastah mad just same.

What you do? Whereabouts?

He say cut down trees, dig ground. Reckon over on Mr. Bile land or mostly on McWhorter land; maybe some on our land.

Well, I got cold pone you fetch along.

Ain't we got no meat?

Well, I let you fetch one piece of pork with your pone. Tomorrow Sunday, tomorrow blessed day, holiday, old man. You take your club, go get us some rabbit.

Dad fetch, we do-go through our rations! Bless the dear Lord you get plenty snick-snack up in the big house.

No snick-snack like we used to get. White folks eat mighty plain nowadays; old Mistress watch the platters, and she count and watch careful, and she warn Naomi no waste, and she carry her keys right on the belt of her gown, and she lock up all the time.

Get me my dinner-snack. Don't you hear Jem a-calling?

She wrapped a generous slab of pone and a smaller chunk of greasy pork in clean corn-shucks, and Coffee put the bundle inside his shirt. He tried to kiss Pet, she fought him off, the child shrieked, and Coffee went fleeing. It was much lighter outside and before he got to the tool shed he could see Jem and Jonas standing ready for work ahead of him.

There was a slight ripple of excitement through their uneventful lives at this thought of going to work for the army. Perhaps Coffee was more steeped in melancholy than the other two, and thus he had sought to keep up his own spirits by chatting with Pet while they breakfasted. Behind his long ruddy-tinted face and within his close-cropped skull Coffee had a brain which contained machinery both for imagination and recollection. He remembered, he remembered. In the old days, and during a December week like this, they would have had eighteen or twenty field hands picking cotton, maybe four hands employed constantly at the gin, to say nothing of the people bringing in corn, the people minding pigs, the people hauling boards, the people weaving and making rope or mule-collars, the people inevitably sick. These in addition to house-servants flying round at the big house, or busy in dairy and wash house and store-houses and kitchen. The Claffey place was something to behold, before the war.

After the unresolved campaigns of 1862, the drawn battles and tightening of the blockade, Ira Claffey had witnessed the *Mene, Mene, Tekel, Upharsin* in no uncertain characters. He sold his people right and left, and at great loss, for he would not separate families and would not sell to strangers unless he went personally to see where his sold-off people would be dwelling and under what conditions. In this late season of 1863 another year of protracted butchery and short commons had proved Ira's wisdom. The place could feed the Claffeys and the hands still remaining to them; that was about all it could do, after the military took their tithe.

Coffee might understand but dimly what his master had been about, and why; nevertheless he recalled autumns abounding in prosperity, autumns unperforated by worms of war and death.

He listened idly to the mumbling of Jem and Jonas while they waited for the master to appear.

One of the mules was sick with colic, and Jonas was reciting the remedy he desired to employ and the cure which would follow. It was something Old Leander had taught him when Jonas was young. Take a big plug of tobacco and cut off a slice maybe as thick as your little finger was long. Put the tobacco in cold water —about the size of that crockful, over there on the bench; then throw in four or five shovels of hot oak ashes, and let the mixture set awhile before you give it to the mule. Ask master or overseer to use his watch; ask him to tell you when fifteen minutes had passed. Then the solution was ready to use, and better not use more of it than a chunk bottle full at one time. It still had to be warm when you used it to drench the mule. Chances were that the mule would be well at once; but never let him near water for a good ten hours. If it were noon when you drenched him, you shouldn't let him drink till close to midnight. And never let him eat corn right afterward, nor do any more work that day.

Then old mule get well.

You drench that Devil mule like that?

I got tobacco waiting in the water. I got oak ash in my fire. When Mastah come I tell him about Devil; but I can't go work for old army and drench Devil mule same time. Can't be no two places same time.

A rear door of the big house was heard to open, and Ira Claffey appeared, followed by a setter who was partially paralyzed by the ills of old age, and dragged his rear quarters, sniffing himself into a succession of sneezes.

The Negroes watched with ready amusement. He think he young again, that Deuce. Think he go after partridge.

Claffey left the dog inside the house fence and prepared to latch the gate. Deuce vented a long shuddering whine, and held up his front paw. This was a ritual of his, to gain attention, and never failed whether he approached black or white.

Poor Deuce, said Claffey, turning. Have you a thorn in your foot?

Whine, said Deuce, still holding out the paw.

What have you here? An old sand-spur?

Whine.

Claffey returned to the gate, reached through between the palings and pretended to extract a thorn from one of the crumbling split toe-pads. There, got it, he said. Deuce dropped his foot to the ground as if relieved of enormous trouble, and went capering about. The slaves laughed aloud, watching. Morning, Mastah.

Morning, Jem, Jonas, Coffee. I trust you said your prayers.

Jem and Jonas bobbed their heads vigorously, and after a guilty second Coffee nodded also, but in a lie. Ira Claffey looked at his watch, and Jonas stepped forward to tell him about Devil.

Very well, Jonas. I know about that drench. Leander used it for many years.

Yassah.

Have you oak ashes in your fireplace? Good—I'll drench Devil myself, and pen him away from food and water.

The slaves felt a great pride that they were owned by a master who did not stand helplessly, or labor among his fruit trees to no avail, or who did not spend the bulk of his time at whist or in lounging with liquor and no purpose. The dumb affection and faith they gave to Ira stemmed (much of it) from an awareness that he could do many of the same tasks they performed, and often do them better. In such an absolute monarchy, and in the shadow of such a monarch, there was the flourishing of a strange democratic pride; you had to see it and feel it and live it to know it, but it was there, and always exerting.

Claffey did the things an overseer would have done. He performed these tasks with reluctance because he did not approve the work laid out for his hands, demanded of them by their Government. He unlocked the door of the implement house and parceled out three axes and three spades which the slaves put across their shoulders. The tools had been well smithed to begin with; axe-helves and the handles of spades were of timber cured for the purpose. Ira gave to Jonas a whetstone and warned him not to lose it. Each tool had a *C* branded on it; Ira instructed the hands to guard the plantation property jealously. No telling what sort of raggle-taggle herds might have been assembled by the army folks who were impressing labor.

Ira Claffey took his people to the front gate. Daylight came clearly but no troops or workers appeared. He sent Coffee to the kitchen with instructions to fetch from Naomi a small pail of the burnt-grain brew which had to serve in these times, together with a cup and saucer for the master. He poured out his own cup and gave the rest to the people. They drank the hot stuff eagerly, smacking their lips in turn above the tin pail's rim.

Before they had finished, a disturbance moved along the lane from beyond the magnolias. There appeared a wagon drawn by two mules, the box heaped with miscellaneous axes, picks, mattocks, shovels. A bearded sergeant rode on the board beside the Negro driver, and a band of some two dozen blacks trailed behind, gabbling noisily. The rearmost file was closed by a fat youth of fifteen or thereabouts who burst fairly out of his shabby gray clothing, and who wore accoutrements and carried a musket slung from his shoulder.

The wagon halted in front of the gate. The sergeant took out a notebook and consulted it. . . . Mr. Claffey, sir?

Yes, Sergeant. I have three hands ready for you.

Says here you're supposed to have four.

So your impressing officer thought, but the fourth of my black people—full-grown males—is Old Leander, and he's in his dotage. I'll never send him.

Well, sir, right here it says, Mr. I. Claffey, four hands.

If there's any question about it, the officer may complain to me in person. Might send the provost.

Let him.

Very well, sir.

Jem, Coffee and Jonas had been waiting with docility, grinning at friends from neighborhood plantations they saw before them, conversing in low tones. The sergeant swung round and called, You three nigs fall in with the others.

They stood, deeply puzzled.

Fall *in,* God damn it!

Don't curse my people, Sergeant. Ira Claffey spoke sharply. They're not accustomed to it. The sergeant means, Jonas, that you shall march along with the others.

Yes, Mastah.

They went, and Ira stood watching the procession as it traveled to the head of the lane and then turned north on a wood road past abandoned cotton fields. He closed his eyes, his head blurred quickly in its traditional shaking, he took a deep breath. Not enjoying the December breeze which continued to wield its knife, he strode off to drench his Devil mule.

The three Claffey Negroes went in docility with their fellows, and presently the sound of axe-strokes came spanking from a valley ahead. Halfway down the slope a man who seemed to be a soldier signalled to the sergeant, and the wagon turned off to the left. This man wore a fine overcoat of bright blue; it had a cape across the shoulders, and instantly all the blacks coveted those gleaming brass buttons.

That Yankee coat for sure.

How you know, boy?

Count of blue. All them Yankee wear blue, blue, blue. Young Mastah Badger tolt me.

But that gentleman ain't no Yankee gentleman. Old Mistuh Bile—he got blue coat too, and he no Yankee.

That gentleman captivate he coat in the war, yes, boy.

They found in the throng people from nearby plantations and smaller farms, people drawn from big places miles away, enormous holdings which they had heard of in legendary fashion. There were hands belonging to the Groovers, the Nickersons, the Rackleys, the Vinings. A larger share of the impressed laborers were engaged in carving out a narrow trench some five feet deep, cleaving down the slope and passing disordered rails where old fences had been ruined. The stile was pulled apart. Gangs dotted up the other slope, felling pines ahead of the diggers; and one troop worked at nothing but rolling fallen trunks aside, or heave-hoing with chains and oxen to tear the roots and stumps loose. It was a fable of the circus which the Claffey hands had never seen but hoped to witness before they became as old as Old Leander. Something was going on in every direction, and they found an added pepper of excitement in observing the white youths who brought a show of force and urgency by strolling about with their guns. Coffee felt his blood warming and his pulse bounding.

What folks do here, you Jem?

White captain say they make jail.

Hi. Jail all over these here woods?

Jail for Yankees.

Hi. Reckon they got ten hundred dozen thousand Yankees cotched already.

Yes, boy. They got ten hundred dozen villain nillain hundred Yankees cotched.
You nigs get over here and line up for axes.

Mastah Captain, sir, we got our own axes. Old Mastah say we keep them by us.
They marked with the word, Mastah Captain. Old Mastah say—

Ah, the hell with your Old Mastah! Step lively, over here by the driver—

The driver was an impassive middle-aged creature named Scooper. He belonged to Mrs. Barney Yeoman and was a power at the sawmill when it was in
operation. Also Scooper had local fame as the owner of a vicious fighting-cock
which had torn the feathers and throats and bellies of all rivals in the region. The
Claffey people had lost heavily to Scooper in the past . . . dimes and quarters
too. They offered him no resentment; only respectful admiration. They assembled
under his command, and Scooper put them in a squad of three; he knew that they
were accustomed to toiling in unison and would do better so. With regret Coffee
heard the order for them to deposit their shovels in the wagon bed to be drawn by
other hands, but Scooper muttered that he would try to keep an eye on the
implements.

These two pines here. Cut them down. Fell them over on this side.

The slaves cleared away the thin undergrowth, took their positions, and as
chief axeman Jonas set pace and cadence. One, two, three; one, two, three; hink,
hank, hunk; hink, henk, honk . . . blades tilted with power, evenly, deeply into
fresh jeweled wood; the chips whirled out. . . . Hold up, you; I take a look; now
stand back, I cut me a butt kerf. Hink, hink, hink, hink. That good, boy? It good,
boy. Old tree lie right over here where Scooper say. Now we go again . . . hink,
henk, hunk . . . already it seemed that the needled summit was quavering steadily, gracefully in knowledge of its own death. Behind the slaves another tree came
roaring down, making the brown cones and dry needles fly amid dust, and all the
people yelped and jumped and let their laughter rise.

Air did not grow much warmer but the workers did. Long since they had
dispensed with wraps and hung them on the remains of the fence separating Bile
and McWhorter land. Dumbly they were grateful that this clearing of forest did
not take place necessarily in August . . . you could work up a mighty sweat,
putting that old axe into the pine. But their muscles scarcely recognized the
demand put upon them. There was always a demand upon their muscles, an order
calling for bending, stooping, lifting, toting, kneeling, bearing, squatting, digging,
heaping, covering, flailing. Jonas was thirty-eight or so, Jem perhaps the same age
(nobody knew) and Coffee in his youngest prime. They were the sole male active
survivors of a troop which once had thronged the cotton rows, cornfields, pig-
pens, goober patches, wood brakes. Nowadays they performed any and every task,
dreaming no further ahead than the cold potatoes of noon, hot potatoes of night,
the boiled turnips, the tasty chew of pork, the picked game bones, the dog yelling
that here were squirrels . . . dreaming certainly no further ahead than the next
turkey gobble or Christmas gift or yielding of a giggling shiny body in a bed or
down a fence-row.

Coffee and Jem stood aside, responding to Jonas's direction, and they watched
his last quick heaving of the blade. Piny tendons grew taut, pulled, snapped . . .
patch of shade tilted quickly off into space above their heads as Jonas leaped
away. Then the hillside jumped beneath their feet, the mincing slam was in their
ears.

Scooper, you want we cut him up?

No, cut-up gang do that. You take next one, like I bid you.

. . . Hink, hunk, honk. The heavy slicing once again, the designing of the kerf
. . . cadence thrumming out to suggest a song.

Put old Yankee in?

Put old Yankee in the jail. How long?

Long, long, long! In the jail—

This here jail. Put old Yankee long, long, long. Put him in the jail.

Oh, how many do you say?

Six-teen-hun-dred-vill-ain-mill-ain-Yankee-in-the-jail.

The smash again, cones bounding like grenades, the cold good woods axed apart, and far away the buzzing of a stubborn and belated covey as they whizzed out of the forest; and did not know it, but they would never fly there again, they would never nest or hide or peek or feed or run, now that trees were coming down and stumps being wrenched and the long roots rending clay.

At noon the Claffey hands sprawled in solid sunlight, protected from wind by the bulk of a broken tree, warm as toast and with a few flies bothering them. Preparations for the stockade were more extensive than people of the countryside had dreamed. Parties of impressed laborers kept arriving all forenoon—also soldiers, with wagons containing ragged tent flies beneath which some of the workers would be housed temporarily. Labor was being brought from points as far as a day's journey distant; the Claffey people said, I wouldn't do it, reckon I'd run off, not sleep in these here woods but put for home and my own good bed. They saw a young captain master riding around on a sorrel horse; rumor said that also there were a major master and an old colonel master somewhere about, but none of the Claffey contingent saw them. Axe parties were kept toiling while the diggers had their nooning, in order to have progressed well ahead of the shovels. A certain grim if slatternly efficiency was now apparent in the whole enterprise.

When the first yells rose about nooning, the welcome fever spread visibly from gang to gang. The Claffeys saw the gang south of them putting their axes at rest and hunting their lunches; in turn they struck their own blades into logs and sought their jackets, or the corn-shuck parcels hung up somewhere; in turn the next gang to the north and east saw what they were doing, and followed suit. Someone had stolen Jem's corn pone, and Jem had nothing left but a jar of cooked rutabagas scorned by the thief. Generously Coffee and Jonas shared their own lunches with their fellow and partook of his rutabagas, changing about in employment of the old iron spoon. They were accustomed, at the Claffey place, to much more variety in the way of vegetables than most slaves ate; the plantation health was that much better in consequence. Old master had a green thumb—two green thumbs—and just wait till those peaches and plums grew ripe again, and berries too. Watch for that lettuce and those onions and those okras when spring-time came; yes, and collard greens or mustard, with pork.

You Jem, reckon they put Linkum in this jail?

They never cotch Linkum!

Take a powerful lot of soldiers cotch Linkum.

They is powerful lot of soldiers right here now in these woods.

They soldiers, they got guns, but they young. Take old soldier, lot of big majors like young Mastah Suthy, catch Linkum. Old Linkum he smart as old coon.

Old Linkum, he wear big blue coat like that Yankee coat soldier gentleman captivate from the Yankees.

Yes, boy, all buttons gold.

Never cotch Linkum, insisted Jem stubbornly.

You black little old turd, you not know Linkum.

Jem rose and glowered. Who you call black little old turd?

Scooper came round the crest of the fallen pine, snapping his fingers for them to get back on the job. They rose—not with too much alacrity; they knew Scooper well, and would have been astonished had he driven them as hard as he might drive a gang of strangers. Scooper was full of talk about what would be done with the pine trees, and the people listened with curiosity. Trunks would be trimmed to fit tightly each against the next, with branches and boles chopped clean; they would be set upright in the trench, with earth scraped back and beaten down to hold them solidly. They would be immovable, twenty feet tall, with a quarter of their length held in the ground; thus the fence they made would be a good fifteen feet in height, tall as the front gallery on a goodsized house. Jonas was the only one who understood readily the measurements and dimensions described by Scooper, but the slaves listened to his tale with interest. Jem had forgotten utterly his cross words exchanged with Coffee; they chuckled and nudged each other and said, No Yankee get across that big fence.

But old Linkum, said Jem. He get across.

Maybe he do that, agreed Scooper. He run up them post like bobcat.

The humorous thought of Lincoln running up the posts like a bobcat struck them with full force. They went back to finish felling the next tree in bright merriment. A corporal scolded them later and then they were comparatively silent, working with strong docility, doing what they were ordered to do and doing it well. Until near sunset the axe-strokes were snapping.

5

The next day, perhaps two hours after his hands were on the job, Ira Claffey appeared in a small two-wheeled cart, driving behind a brown mule and with little Buncombe, Jonas's son, beside him. Bun was only six years old but already Jonas had taught him to drive this mule, which was as tractable and dependable as a mule could be. After making inquiries Ira made his way down the slope and found the sergeant who was in charge of implement supply.

I wish to pick up my shovels, sir. My hands did not fetch them home last night.

Carelessly the sergeant declared his ignorance of the shovels, and was not choice about his language when he did it. Instantly Ira Claffey knocked him flat, and while the younger man lay amid the pine trash rubbing his jaw, Ira spoke calmly, describing his situation. There had been no requisition addressed to him about tools; merely he had been instructed verbally that he must equip his slaves for whatever work was demanded of them. Since his people were put in the chopping gang, he had requested that the unused portion of his property be returned. Such articles commanded a premium throughout the Confederacy, which fact Ira knew very well. He was unwilling for some Home Guardsman to profit from the sale or trade of those shovels.

There was every impress of honesty in Ira's statements; nor did the dull sergeant wish to encounter that fist again. Ira Claffey was distinguished in that community and the sergeant knew it. He had a loaded revolver in a holster on the wagon seat, but who would dare to use a weapon against a former member of the State Legislature, and the father of three dead sons, two of them officers? Grumpily he ordered the diggers to file by and present their spades for Claffey's inspection. One, marked plainly with the *C* brand, turned up within a couple of minutes; a second was found farther north, across the branch, but only after much searching. The third and last eluded them until a slave whispered that there was a spade with a broken handle in the wagon-box. It seemed that someone had tried to pry a big rock with the spade. Claffey put the shovels into his two-wheeled cart and took out a game bag, ammunition pouches, and a fine silver-chased English fowling piece which had belonged to his elder brother, Felton Claffey, and had been left to him in Felton's will.

Mastah, breathed the child shyly, you going take old Deuce?

No, Buncombe. Deuce is too badly paralyzed. His hind end hurts him because he is old; he grows very tired.

Mastah, what you do for you dog?

I heard dogs up in the old pasture when I left the place; that's the reason I went back for gun and ammunition. I think that pair from the Yeoman place— what are their names? Twink and Wink?— They're out hunting by their lonesome. I've shot over them before.

Mastah, said Bun with great conviction, reckon we folks ought to have a new dog.

Well, Bun, if you find any good young dogs, free of charge, please inform me.

Sir?

Let me know if you find any dogs—free.

Yes, Mastah, and the child grinned on his way, delighted beyond description at this first intrusting to himself of the two-wheeled cart for a solitary errand. He drove the mule, whose name was Tiger, very slowly all the way home. He listened with rapture to each thud and crackling of the animal's slow pace, and yet with agony because each step meant that they were a trifle nearer home. He thrilled to the twitching of the reins, patched from scrap material as they were. Bun sang, tunefully but singing no recognizable words, all the way home.

Ira Claffey heard the Yeoman dogs giving voice on distant uplands after he had left the area where forest was in the process of being spoilt. These pointers he sought were damaged through neglect—they came from a line with good noses, and had undergone a certain amount of proper schooling—but now a resident overseer and his family were the only whites left on the Yeoman place, and the overseer did not shoot. The pointers galloped in complete abandon; like mongrels they scented and chased squirrels and varmints, they dug for little beasts in burrows. Ira went through a pine grove where the hubbub from the construction gangs (they were actually *de*struction gangs, and he frowned at the thought) barely reached his ears. He saw a black-and-white tail waving above the scrub; he whistled, and both dogs rushed to him like rowdies. Wink would accept no discipline and finally Claffey had to drive him off; the dog returned to his excavation of a rabbit's tunnel. Twink, on the other hand, reverted handsomely to better behavior when he became aware that Ira Claffey bore a shotgun. He could not be depended upon, but at least he might give some hint of birds waiting unseen ahead.

They hunted across one of the old cotton fields where now weeds were romping, and raised only four ground doves, which Claffey would not shoot because he had been reared in the superstition surrounding them. . . . What other grief, he thought, could possibly befall? Well, I presume that if I were now to lose Lucy or —God forbid it—Veronica—

There was a trick of his imagination which recurred persistently; it had recurred, ever since the last ghastly news was brought by the Dillards. Ira kept seeing his sons around the place, he kept hearing their voices. Sometimes at home he would be in his tool shed, and it seemed that a corner of his vision caught the impression of young Moses going out the door. He was positive that sometimes, lying dry and wakeful in the middle of the night, he heard the faint ring of china from Sutherland's room as the young man got up and used his chamber pot. Ira did not believe in ghosts as such. But he thought that perhaps the actual impress of the boys' living had left a variety of sights, sounds and scents which had never been expended and were not dead, even though the boys were dead. He thought that all trees and shrubbery and walls and fences on the plantation might have absorbed the day-by-day activities of his sons, and still gave them forth, but faintly —as a roasted brick retained its heat long after it had been pinned up in flannel, and so afforded comfort to the cold feet of an invalid who needed warmth. And Ira needed this reassurance that his sons had once been part of a waking, busy scheme called Life; ah, he needed it.

He did not consciously imagine these figments of reappearance, but welcomed them when they befell. He could not share the knowledge with others; he had tried. He said to Veronica, Strangest thing, my dear. I was in the seed house looking up seed for top onions—you know, the tree onion: that's *Allium Cepa,* variety *viviparum*—because I thought it high time to start the onion beds. And distinctly I heard the house door open and close, and it seemed that Badger started down the path. I thought I heard him stumble across the little stones which border it—you know, walking heedlessly, rather floundering like the hobbledehoy that he is— That he was—

Veronica was racked with a fit of dry sobbing on the instant, and walked slowly out of the room with her hands pressed against her cheeks. It would never do to mention such things to her again. So he would never do it, not if he saw clearly all three boys ranged before the fireplace, toasting their parents with good humor, drinking strong drink from the small silver cups they'd had when they were babies.

In a prank which Veronica might have deemed cruel but which Ira thought beneficent, he saw the boys hunting beside him. He missed a fair shot at the first two quail which rose, because he was watching Badger and how the youngster carried his gun. Badger wore an old jacket of yellow tow which his mother had thought so disreputable that repeatedly she begged him to give it to a servant, but it was Badge's favorite. He wore also a powder-horn with a shiny brass plug or stopper, a powder-horn carried long ago by his grand-uncle Sutherland Claffey when Unk warred against the redcoats. The plug was a gem in sunlight and cast out little glistening daggers to stab the eyes.

Sometimes Badger was there, hunting, and sometimes the land was untenanted except for the pointer and the shadow which walked beneath Ira's own bulk. Sometimes he saw the other boys also, but today they were mistier than Badge, and Ira could not have recited what they wore nor what they said when birds went up and escaped their firing, or whether they got any birds at all. He saw them. . . .

He himself missed some more birds, finally got his eye back, and observed the feathers struck and buffed by fine shot, he watched the birds tumbling and felt sorry for them. He put nine quail into the game bag before he was tired. He could have shot many more if he'd had a proper dog; but the half-ruined Twink had done his best, and Ira praised him and gave him a biscuit from his pocket. He regretted the little speckled bodies still warm, dumped in a weight against his hip; he felt a gloom when he thought of blood on a beak, blood in a bright eye soon to be no longer bright. But death was walking the land with such enormous crushing strides that who was he to mourn this microscopic butchery? The birds would be a fair tribute to Ira's womenfolks; the women would know that he had thought of them with love, that he had tried to please.

As he returned slowly to his home at an hour approaching midday, the chorus of axes, shouts, songs, whistles, bellows and thuds came steadily louder, the nearer Ira approached to the Sweetwater branch and astounded hills hemming it. What ugliness—to know that there would soon be a prison adjacent to one's dooryard! He supposed that prisons were necessary, but the thought of this stockade pained him before it was even made. He counseled himself that he should be glad there was a prison—and in such a healthy area as this—for a prison meant that the young fellows who'd be placed in it were living still; they were not extinct as the Claffey boys were extinct, but they were breathing and able to walk around, even restrained by the fence of massacred pine trees. If there were no places of military detention it would mean that every individual who yielded to superior force was slaughtered when he yielded. That would be a massacre in truth.

But isn't all war a massacre?

Scarcely—not in the sense that we employ when we speak of Indians and massacres. It's not a complete wiping out. It is a knightly contest.

In what knightly fashion did your comrades the volunteers behave in Mexico?

That was a brutal and unprovoked war, although at the time I was comparatively young and did not understand. This is the War for Southern Independence. The Yankees call it a Rebellion. Indeed it is one: a Rebellion against a power whose authority is denied.

But you did not favor Secession.

Neither did Aleck Stephens. *Revolutions are much easier started than controlled, and the men that begin them seldom end them. . . . Human passions are like the winds—when aroused they sweep everything before them in their fury. The wise and the good who attempt to control them will themselves most likely become the victims.*

Georgia—

Sutherland died for Georgia. Badger died for Georgia. Moses died for Georgia. Rob Lamar died for Georgia—

The devil they did. They died for— They died—

That's it. The Alpha and the Omega. They died.

Yet in private philosophy unvoiced, unrecognized, chained in a dark place remotely in his belief, Ira knew that he was undervaluing his sons and perhaps undervaluing his own dreams. The legend must still be alive—the grave and powerful and courteous legend—it must be exalted somewhere, if so many young spirits had embraced it. And elder spirits as well. The legend must be shining, as the slain were shining in whatever realm they occupied. Ira wished doggedly that he could see the shining. But it seemed that he went home in the dark (midnight at high noon) and sounds from the region toward the northeast stunned him as he walked.

6

In February the one black gown remaining to Lucy was worn shabby, pulled loose at many of its seams. She tried discussing this problem with her mother, but Veronica was treading farther and farther away from both husband and daughter. Often it was hard to win a response from her on any topic in the world. If you spoke of the boys, her face turned more haggard than ever and tears flowed. In speaking of black gowns Lucy had in fact spoken of the boys. Still addled with her own grief, the girl felt torture afresh as she saw her mother withdraw to her own room. Veronica slept alone, Ira Claffey had moved into Badger's old room. This began when he suffered a catarrhal attack during the Christmas season and wished to avoid infecting his wife. He had enjoyed no physical relationship with Veronica since the last black draught was given them to drink. It seemed expedient for them to continue dwelling apart.

Poppy, I must seek your advice.

What is it, my dear?

About my wardrobe. I tried discussing it with Mother but— You see, Poppy, my last black has gone by the board; and of course we daren't spend money on goods even could we find the proper goods at Mr. Campbell's.

But, Lucy, do you wish to remain in black?

For the time being I'd prefer it. At least until it's been a year since—I've the pale green silk—you know, the old one, my first silk when I was seventeen—and I'm positive it would take a strong black dye mighty well. I hadn't thought to dye a wool, though, for goodness knows how I'll feel about my wardrobe in the autumn; I might choose to remain in black, and then again I might not. Can't scarcely tell.

Her small tender laugh, the laugh he loved, but coming seldom nowadays.

Well, child, you can't wear silk daily.

Oh, about the house I don't mind—I've plenty of fixings for home use, unless we have callers. But when callers appear, or going to church, or just going to Americus— Now, I've the blue figured poplin I could dye; I've two cottons for summer wear which I'm sure would take it well—the blue sprigged on white, and the pink patterned walking gown we had made when I was at the Female Institute. You may remember it: all the girls were required to have them alike, and I surely never did like being all alike.

Ah. And now the uniform turns to black. For Georgians.

Father and daughter stood regarding each other mutely, and Lucy had paled at this observation which escaped him whether he wished it or no. She shrugged wearily, and he bent to kiss her on her high smooth forehead. I suppose there must be a great deal of black in other States. And at the North also, Poppy, she said in her soft voice.

Yes, yes. I've thought of that. He added hastily, Lucy child, I'd recommend the pink walking gown for the dye-vat, since it has an unhappy connotation of seminary days. I remember how miserable you were, forever begging to return home.

And at last you let me, like a dear sweet Poppy, and over Mother's protestations. I regret it deeply, but I never could keep up that old French, and I promised faithfully.

You're a dear good child, and you don't need French. All you need is to go on being Lucy.

Thank you, sir. And I'll take your advice about that little walking gown.

But who can do the trick for you? Ninny, Pet or Extra? Or does Naomi—?

Oh, you've forgotten what a remarkable dye-woman I did become in my very early youth. Before old Ruth died I learned heaps from her. I used to watch her by the hour—just plain fascinated by all the colors and the way things dripped. I wrote down some of her receipts on the blank leaves of Grandmamma's cook book. I've explored carefully: we've all the necessaries for black. I'll take Extra to do the dipping and fire-making; she's mighty slow, but she doesn't talk a body's arm off like the other wenches. I just never can compel Ninny to remain quiet.

Three pounds of sumac, lime water, half a pound of copperas, two and one-half pounds of logwood . . . Lucy assembled her materials. She ordered Extra to prepare kettles and tubs under shade of the wash shed and to build up fires there. She needed blue vitriol also, for the silk, and bichromate of potash for both dresses; she knit her brows above the scales as she weighed the portions with care.

Lucy's hair was not so fair as her mother's, it was nearer the color of honey in the comb, and of fine texture. Rob Lamar used to insist that it was not a natural growth, that no hair could be so fine, that Lucy had ordered it from a shop maybe in Paris, France, and then had it sewn to her scalp. She could cry no longer, no tears were left to her to expend on Rob and her brothers. Now Rob had been dead for some fourteen months; his wide-jawed face and merry straight gaze and pomaded hair were beginning to be confused, to fade in recollection. When she thought of him, which was at least hourly, he seemed always to be mounted and riding rapidly away from her—she could see his back, she could not see his face, he did not turn around to wave in the saddle, he kept riding.

She wore her delicate hair drawn straight up from her brows, and coiled high, knotted with narrow black velvet ribbons. She had not curled her hair for over a year, and wondered whether she should ever curl it again. Her brows were slightly darker than her hair, and they arched in high bent bows, and were luxuriant, as were her dark lashes. She was the only one in the family with brown eyes which were so dark as to be almost black; Grandmamma Sutherland's eyes, everyone said; eyes like Lucy's shone duskily, challengingly from the primitive portrait in the lower hall. Lucy's slim body was made for activity; she rode excellently, could fire a pistol without squeezing her eyes shut, had owned a better skill than her brothers when they played with bows and arrows. She learned to swim in the Gulf of Mexico when the family visited the Gulf coast when she was small, and she lamented that there was no place for her to swim at home, and lamented further because her mother refused her permission to bathe in the Flint River, partly because of water-snakes but mostly because ladies of the region did not bathe commonly in the Flint River.

While Lucy was still very young the exploits of Florence Nightingale were discussed in newspapers and magazines. Lucy burned to emulate the English-woman, and was discovered to have set up hospital in a bake house which had been damaged by fire and was not being used at the time. She had five unwilling small blacks for patients and was dosing them with her father's best brandy and Trask's Magnetic Ointment which she had prepared out of lard, raisins and fine cut tobacco. Her brothers dubbed her Florence Nightmare and applied the name until she stormed into tears; then they were contrite. A brother and a sister died as infants before Lucy was born, but she witnessed the arrival and eventual departure of two more little sisters during her childhood, and was stricken with the notion that if she had been grown-up and a capable nurse, the children might have lived. When her mother was ill Lucy tended her eagerly, banishing the wenches, banishing even old Ruth who was the wife of Leander and a skilled nurse in her own right.

There was no instruction in the art Lucy loved most, at the Americus Female Institute. An attempt was made to teach the young ladies French, religious history, geography, Use of the Globes, *Belles Lettres,* velvet and landscape painting. Lucy learned more of value at the plantation than she ever absorbed from this bewildering hodge-podge. From her father she drank of Keats, Wordsworth, Lord Byron and earlier poets such as Herrick, and could recite from their works at length. The Claffeys had a family game they played, quoting verse and the Bible, and Lucy excelled in this, and other members of the family delighted in hearing her recitations. She hated to sew, she loved to take off her shoes and stockings and run barefooted on the grass. Her father greeted her often in the morning with, *Hail to thee, blithe spirit! Bird thou never wert,* and her mother did also until blows of later bereavement were more than her mother could bear, and it was impossible for her to venture a pleasantry.

It grieved Lucy that she found no balm in prayer; privately she felt like a heretic about it. She spoke her prayers dutifully on retirement, and she had a small morning prayer which she almost always murmured on rising. But she had believed, simply and sincerely, that if she prayed intently enough she would keep her brothers—and later, Rob—protected from bullets. This had proved not to be true, and thus the act of prayer seemed of little consequence any longer. But Lucy did still believe in God as a personal Father, resembling considerably her own father but with whiskers similar to the Reverend Mr. Cato Dillard's. She saw him presiding in a gilt courthouse which rested on cumulus clouds—very high, and always in the west, and frequently lit fiery by sunsets—and the courthouse was populated chiefly by Claffeys, Arwoods, Sutherlands and their kin; and Rob Lamar's horse was tied outside at evening.

Innocently she maintained a deep-seated feeling (it was a feeling, it stemmed solely from emotion, it was not a conscious or deliberate reasoning) that there was a promise wider, warmer, kindlier, prettier than might be contained in the creed or practice of any established religion. At least of established Presbyterianism. She had been taught to regard Roman Catholics as misguided antiquarians, and she knew little of Oriental beliefs: she supposed that they were all barbarous if ornate. But this warm good life which suggested itself as a vague mixture of conduct and dream— It was both balm and provocation each time it affected Lucy. It was not solely the simple worship of Nature enjoyed by Ira Claffey and in no way conflicting with his faith. It was more personal and more feminine, an illusion of the world's sheer beauty mingled with sensuous and sensual delight.

She had supported dreams about Rob, beginning with the first touch and kiss he awarded her; but with Rob's long death (it took him months to die in her imagination) other men supplanted him, and most of these she had never met, and perhaps they did not exist. Babies were mingled in her hidden fancies, along with the act of love. Lucy did not know exactly how the act of love was performed —she had only wicked whispered girlish gossip to go by—but in lonely nights she lay charmed by the contemplation of her own body, excited nearly into fever. Somewhere there might still be a man's body constructed for the express purpose of gratifying her own . . . when she cooled she was crushed by the enormity of her sin, and prayed with moving lips and half-voiced sounds, seeking impossible perfection, swearing to the Saviour that she would never countenance such emotions again.

But the dreams persisted as she grew older and more lonely; in one breath she said that they were a product of Satan, inserted in her drowsy brain in order to disease her immortal soul; in the next breath she yielded lustfully, and went springing down long flowery avenues of the future—she scented blossoms never designated by any botanists, ate fruits beyond the ken of her father or any green-thumbed horticulturist, she counted the stars and knew each of their colored shafts as a light wielded by a friend. She tussled with chuckling dimpled boy and girl babies, lying naked among them on rich mattresses of violets (forever violets; her favorites; she wore them in their season) and waiting the muscular man who would step toward her, smiling and courteous but not to be restrained, out of tapestried shadows.

Inadvertently once she had come upon Moses and Badge and a group of their cronies, when they were all fifteen or thereabouts, splashing nude in Little Sweet-water. So she knew how young boys looked; she supposed that full-grown men must appear the same, but larger.

If she had possessed that intimate trusted friend whom girls in stories seemed often to have but whom she'd never valued, she would never have dared to tell the friend. And of course Lucy could not tell her father; although she had an inkling that he might understand better than most, and might not condemn her for her passion.

She drudged assuredly, bitterly, suffering the vanishment of her brothers, suffering a quasi-widowhood. Recurrently she tried to pray for particular guidance, but prayer as an unguent for burns seemed to have failed.

7

Long since the mustering officer who assembled laborers for the stockade had yielded to entreaties of many small planters. He had released every slave (excepting trained carpenters) drawn from a plantation where there were less than five male hands; he had released half of all the rest. This left a crew of not more than forty hands still hewing fallen pines and planting them in the five-foot trench. Ira Claffey had never begged the return of Jem, Coffee and Jonas, but he welcomed them; now his hands were plowing and planting diligently, happy also at having hot rations prepared by their wives, no longer reduced to cold fare at noon. The ridges sustained a comparative silence; the chopping, the whoops of ox-drivers echoed only sporadically. A portion of the fence near the southwest corner remained to be set in place; the rest of the structure towered in a raw parallelogram enclosing seventeen or eighteen acres. A narrow strip at the south was Claffey land, the balance was requisitioned from the neighbors. Posts, so recently the trunks of living pines, had been coarsely stripped and squared to be planted tightly side by side. A dense odor of fresh gum occupied the air; it was sweet to smell; and blue smoke drifted by day from smouldering fires where stumps and roots were charring, and at night there was a devilish glow. Underbrush—there had been little of it to begin with—was scorched off. Less than twenty trees still lived within the area, most of these of little account as to size.

Ira's feet were drawn to the region on two or three occasions, but each time he walked away sick at heart. Beloved narrow deep valley where the branch of Sweetwater made its light music— This had been a place precious to him. He would have deplored the ruination on aesthetic grounds if it had been worked five counties away; but here, gashed on personal timberland, it ached like a sprain. Tight, tight, solid, solid, yellow, tanned, bleeding, the stockade stood, a savage excrescence fifteen feet in height. It marched its short side across the south (except for the gap still remaining), its long side stamped down the declivity through the creek and across it, and stamped up the hill to the north, and across the north once more, and back down the long east side. Better trained hands among the Negroes worked at putting up numerous sentry-boxes along the exterior; they worked under close supervision of uniformed soldiers, they were building ladders. More troops tenanted the neighborhood than ever before, and more came daily; they had cut a road beside the creek, a road leading up to the railway station. Disks of stumps stood up-ended every which way along the route, heavy with clay; ruddy roots curled like snakes and fingers.

Lucy said to Ira at their supper, You're somber, Poppy. She hoped to make a jest of it. More somber than at any time since the Mexican War.

He closed his eyes and shook his head, as she had known he would do. In her place at the table Veronica Claffey ate in rapt cold silence and refused to lift her gaze. Oh, said Ira, it's merely that I walked over there again and observed the destruction they've made and are making.

Lucy shuddered. I shan't go.

. . . But she did go at last for curiosity's sake, lifting skirts to climb above the tangle and the cruel rough places, her father putting out his hand to steady her as he limped beside. The blacks stared and lazed at their tasks, to see a woman there; soldiers stared also, admiring Lucy and thinking of girls at home, or perhaps many of them looked at her with desire as young men might.

She screamed softly when they approached the creek. Poppy! It's gone. Oh, oh, how dreadful! They killed it.

What, Lucy?

The spring. Our spring—where you used to fetch me for a drink when I was tiny— She turned away blindly. No, let us go back. I can't bear more, I just naturally can't.

Nearing the gateway where carpenters worked, she looked up at her father with angry eyes. Her eyes were wet above their blaze. Ira offered his handkerchief.

Poppy, where did it go? The spring—

Crushed down, Lucy. Tamped and dragged and beaten and stifled.

But what became of the water?

I imagine, with all that weight of earth forced over it when they dug the ditch and dragged the trees— It had to make a new way for itself. Likely the water seeps through behind rocks, far under all that weight of material, and finds its way down to the branch. Travels underground, you see.

What a pity. It was the fairy place, truly. Reckon you don't recall how I used to see them in the moss?

He made his grimace. Reckon I do, daughter.

It held a lovely flavor, that water. Didn't it?

Yes.

They walked homeward, they passed the place where black workmen scooped at strange angles of earth, where white soldiers in sweaty undershirts were toiling as well.

What are they making?

A fort, my dear. To guard the prison.

Oh, they've a cannon back there in the pines. They'll put it in the fort?

Doubtless. And more than that.

When they walked in their own lane, when noises of dragging and pounding and shoveling fell farther behind them, Lucy still wore her white face. Poppy, I've thought of something. Perhaps the Yankee who killed Suthy— The one who killed Mosey-Wosey— The one who killed Badge— And who captured my Rob. Perhaps they'll all be taken prisoner, perhaps they'll all be brought to the prison here.

Perhaps, Lucy, they're gone already. As the boys are gone. Perhaps they were slain in the same battles.

But it would be mighty strange if all of them—

In war, said Ira Claffey, seldom do you know whom you've slain. You fire, all fire, both sides fire their volleys, and singly. People are hit. You do not know. Artillery is anonymous also. It's better so.

There's nothing better about war, Poppy. Nothing *best*.

He turned and stood still and looked back, but thank God nothing of the evil could be seen from where they waited. However a smell came to Claffey's nostrils, and he glanced quickly at his daughter to see whether she too had sensed it. She gave no indication, but moved on, stroking the back of her hand with a magnolia leaf she had gathered, and she did not know why she had picked it up: an idle thing to do. The smell was one familiar to Ira Claffey but he could not recognize its source. It might have been that one of the plantation cats—there were several —had found its fate in being worried by a stray dog, and now lay beneath the bushes. A rank tangle hugged the fence, and bloated flesh might have been concealed there . . . or an unfortunate recollection of the bastard melons which had oozed their evil until the Negroes, at Ira's behest, got rid of them? Or a varmint of the woods? He did not know, but he detected stench for a time, and then lost it as he went to join Lucy, and to join her in dwelling on happier things if there were any way for them to do so.

8

Old Ruth had declared long ago that it was impossible to achieve a permanent black on cotton with less labor, but still it was incredible labor. Lucy estimated that the goods might weigh five pounds; hence she'd assembled three pounds of sumac, wood and bark together. This sumac had been boiled half an hour, then the goods had steeped overnight. Extra removed the cotton after breakfast and hung it on a rope to drip for an hour. Lucy added eight ounces of copperas to the sumac liquor, and ordered Extra to dip the goods for another hour.

We put it back in the lime water, Miss Lucy?

Yes, Extra, for fifteen minutes again. Did you make a new dye of logwood as I bade you?

On this other fire. It been a-boiling already.

How long?

I don't know, Miss Lucy. It just been a-boiling.

It should boil for an hour at least. Then the goods must be dipped for another three hours before I add potash.

They worked in the wash house, which was a shed with a roof but only two sides or parts of sides, and a great wide chimney arching above to accept the smoke. When gusts of spring breeze assailed the area, smoke was rejected by the chimney and came down to smart the eyes of girl and servant. Fires sizzled and spat beneath cranes in a row. Simultaneously Lucy was dyeing her silk, and that necessitated still another vat containing blue vitriol compound; the same logwood mixtures could be used for both, but would need to be diluted for the silk.

Extra was plump and slow-moving and had hips like a stall-fed animal. Her slab of wide-nostriled nose turned squarely up in the middle of her broad purplish face, and dripped with sweat; Lucy saw the sweat on Extra's nose, and it made her feel hotter than ever.

Extra, like Ninny, was a daughter of Old Leander—one of the eight daughters whom he had fathered and whom the dead Ruth had mothered—but the other six had all been sold along with their husbands and children, if any. Extra was married to Jonas, and they had two of the plantation's current four children: little bright Buncombe and four-year-old Gracious. Also Orphan Dick, a four-year-old boy, was tended by Extra. His parents had perished of galloping consumption during the first year of the war; but Orphan Dick was giggling and spirited and strangely the mark of consumption did not seem to be upon him; it might reveal itself later, Ira Claffey feared.

Lucy would be twenty-one during this year of 1864, Extra would be twenty-three. As children they had played contentedly together; there were few white girls of Lucy's generation among the neighbors. Pet was closer to Lucy's age, but they were not so harmonious in disposition. Extra and Lucy had little shops in shade under the magnolia rustle—shops well stocked with pine cones, acorns, bits of broken glass which they said were jewels, and nosegays of seasonable flowers. Lucy was the proprietor, and Extra came to buy, paying in currency of pebbles. Sometimes they could persuade adults or older children to patronize their store; then both became shopkeepers. When they tired of such play, and in hotter days, they had a playhouse amid lower limbs of an oak. The playhouse had been built for Sutherland originally in 1844, but by this time he considered himself too grown-up to enjoy it. Lucy inherited the playhouse, and sometimes she and Extra would permit Moses, two years younger, to attend them there; mostly they did not welcome him because he was a boy, he was too obstreperous, he liked to pound and dance on the warped old planks. When they were alone Lucy might set Extra to braiding flowery adornments. She would say, Now, Extra, I shall read to you from my new book of verses which Cousin Sally Sue sent for my Christmas book.

Yas, Miss Lucy.

Mind, you're to pay close heed. Should you like to commit some verses to memory?

Do I got to, Miss Lucy?

No. But I daren't teach you to read—it's against the law, you see—but I'd be very glad to help you commit a verse or two.

I don't want to, I guess, Miss Lucy, please.

Very well. I shall read to you. Mind.

> *. . . The Child is father of the Man;*
> *And I could wish my days to be*
> *Bound each to each by natural piety.*

Is that not beautiful, Extra?

Yas'm.

I'll read it again:

> *My heart leaps up when I behold*
> *A rainbow in the sky—*

We out of daisies, Miss Lucy. Better I go fetch more?

Go pick enough to finish the collar, and I shall wear it to tea.

She would sit dreaming over her book, the tree would speak to her, her own voice would drift low to a murmur and then to silence . . . she dreamed across the book and saw Extra—a dumpy, dutiful, black-legged figure in faded yellow calico—tramping through weeds for more daisies to complete her fabrication.

Now, in adult state, slave and young mistress worked at preparing the black gowns for the young mistress. Extra toiled as seriously as she had when weaving flowers. Even her plump arms showed a dye not put there by the God who had designated her as a black. Lucy wore a pair of ancient kid gloves to protect herself, but be she ever so careful it was certain that her hands would absorb some of the color; there would be blotches; she would have to wear mitts or gloves if company came, until the color wore off.

Company came now. It was between ten and eleven in the morning, hot for middle February. The wash house reeked; this task should have been done in an earlier week tinged with frost. More chilly weather would arrive, but it was very bad luck that today the sun was willfully unblemished by clouds. Cauldrons steamed. Lucy saw the beads drip from Extra's wide nose, and felt more perspiration growing amid roots of her own hair. She had bound her hair in a brown net, and had her skirts caught up, pinned in two places so that she would not trip as she moved in the combined chores of overseer and fellow-dyer.

Company appeared behind her: there was the clearing of a man's throat, an ahem and growl with which some stranger sought to announce his presence. There was no place for Lucy to flee. She felt supreme high-pitched feminine wrath that a man should creep close without warning. She faced him, her face looked boiled and baked, and she knew it; it was dreadful.

I'm sorry, Ma'am, to intrude upon you.

He wore a single spur, he must have been riding, probably he had tied his horse out in front. Naomi was in the kitchen, Ninny was doubtless above stairs, making beds belatedly . . . Ninny was slightly deaf, or pretended to be so habitually when the bell rang. (The Claffeys used to argue as to whether Ninny's deafness was actual or feigned; certainly it was periodic.) Pet, had Lucy but known it, was gone to the root cellar when the stranger rang, and Ira Claffey was gone to the fields. No one could have heard the bell except Veronica, and she was dedicated to a new and dreadful task: she searched wardrobes, presses, cupboards, shelves throughout the house, she hunted for any and all personal relics of the three fallen sons, and was putting them away—fabrics, china, wood and steel—in low chests in the room of Moses, the baby. Then, when they were filled and there was nothing more to put into them, the chests would be locked and shoved under Moses's bed. That was Veronica's plan; her husband and her daughter guessed at it, but said nothing. Ira looked for the boys' silver cups, and found them under infant flannels in one of the carved chests. He removed the cups and put them behind Scott on his own library shelf. Maybe in time Veronica might be cured of this burial passion, and again the cups could take their proud pathetic place in view.

I did try to ring, Ma'am, but there seemed to be nobody about.

I'm sorry no one heard the bell, sir. You see—we're dyeing—

He would think that she meant *dying!* He bowed. He spoke with the genial scratchy voice of an adolescent, though he appeared to be older than Suthy had been—perhaps he was near to thirty. Permit me to introduce myself, Ma'am. My name is Harrell Elkins. Have I the honor of addressing Miss Lucy Claffey?

She stood with hot face and soaked gloves, she edged behind a bench so that her hiked-up skirts mightn't be observed too readily. Mr. Elkins, sir, I'm Lucy. But, you see, we're engaged in dyeing and—If you would be so kind as to rest in the house, I'll have my servant escort you— I'll send to the field for Father—

He was in shabby gray uniform, there were dark blemishes where insignia had been removed. His old hat had faded nearly to green on the crown, and he held the brim in front of his middle with big pale hands on which a pink of very fresh sunburn was showing. He was a rangy man, with rounded shoulders detracting from his natural height; and his head was small for a man of six feet or thereabouts, and his ears stuck out, roundly, quizzically. He wore silver-rimmed spectacles; these glassy wafers attempted to conceal but could not conceal the dance of dark-blue-black eyes behind them. In no degree was Mr. Elkins handsome. In every degree he was a man peculiar to himself.

Miss Lucy, permit me. Do you recall that your brother Sutherland ever mentioned a Captain Elkins?

The steam from logwood and sumac and copperas blinded Lucy. Elkins thought that she was fainting. He stepped forward with strange animal grace and put his hand beneath the girl's elbow to steady her. He brought out a clean bandana and unfolded it. I'm sorry.

Thank you. It's only— Oh, that was mighty sudden. She tried to laugh, she made a sound, it wasn't laughter, it was a small cry. Of course. Captain Elkins! He called you Harry, didn't he?

Yes, Miss Lucy, people do.

You were not with him at—at Gettysburg?

Elkins shook his head. You see, I was with them both in the early days of the Sixteenth. I knew your youngest brother but slightly, since he was a private soldier and in another company; but I was near him when he died at Crampton's Gap. It was the same engagement in which Colonel Lamar lost his life.

She nodded limply. I—I was affianced to a distant cousin of Lieutenant-Colonel Jefferson Lamar.

Ah, yes. That would have been Rob?

Yes, Captain.

His eyes leaped with a spurt of life behind the lenses. Just Surgeon Elkins now, Miss Lucy. I hadn't yet finished my medical studies when the war came, and I was determined on deeds of derring do. So I served as a soldier.

And you performed the deeds.

He chuckled. Mighty few, I fear.

Not according to the accounts we received from my brother, sir.

Miss Lucy, you're more than kind and I fear your brother was more than generous to his friends. But I stopped a few pieces of scrap-iron last spring, and thus was made unfit for further service in the field. That was some two months before Sutherland—died. Naught for me to do but resume my medical studies again; thus I've become a surgeon—very much of a neophyte.

Then you'll not be returning to the field?

I'd hoped for that, but our Government had other plans. For the moment I've been detailed to this region on what might appear to be a peculiar mission. I did welcome the assignment to this duty, for I've long wanted to call upon the Claffeys, if you'll pardon my saying so. . . .

At sunset, when Ira Claffey himself escorted his guest above stairs, he led the way down a short main hall, turned sharp right into the narrower passage which ran from east to west, and stopped at the second door on the right. With his hand upon the round white doorknob, Ira said, This was Sutherland's, and ushered Harrell Elkins inside. Elkins' saddle bags, with the waterproof roll containing his personal belongings, had already been fetched up by Ninny and stood upon a chair. There was nothing of Sutherland's in the room. Veronica had banished every young man's trinket and treasure to entombment.

His things are no longer here. Ira spoke in a manner of apology. His mother's put them all away. She has— Possibly you observed it, Harry. She has grown remote.

Elkins went to the front window and looked out at rows of trees fronting the lane. Then he moved to the smaller west window and glanced at plum-colored clouds and strips of glint between them. He turned. Thank you, Mr. Claffey, for calling me Harry. I was fond of your son. I fear I'm mighty shy, as a social individual, and have not made as many friends as some. Suth used to call me Cousin Harry.

We shall be glad to continue the designation, Coz.

I appreciate your welcome more than I can say.

Please to join me in the library at your convenience, Cousin Harry, and we'll taste a glass of wine.

Ira went down to the little library and found Lucy there before him. She was wearing her wornout black dress, but Ira squinted to observe that some one had been very busy with needle and thread, drawing the spread seams together so that the gown would serve. She wore also a pair of ancient black lace gloves: the dye had left its stain.

It would seem, said Ira, that you've taken especial pains with your hair.

She stared at him indignantly, as occurred seldom. Father!

I apologize, my dear. This is no occasion for levity. Nevertheless I'm glad he's come. Ira bent to unlock a cupboard, and drew out the glass decanters which he had not touched since the New Year.

Poppy, may I join you gentlemen?

What might your mother say?

Nothing. She merely bowed when I introduced Mr. Elkins to her. She bowed and said, Pray sit down, sir. Then she was out of the room in another minute, gone to Moses's room.

We'll be honored to have you. Now that I think of it, I wasn't awarded my morning kiss today.

You may have it belatedly. Lucy offered her face. When her father kissed her, she clutched his arms spasmodically, and whined.

Now, now.

Poppy, I think he knew my Rob! When he spoke of Crampton's Gap, he mentioned also Lieutenant-Colonel Lamar and how he died. I said that he was kin to the man I was to marry, and he said, That would be Rob. So he must have known him.

Ira thought about it for a moment. Likely that was at the University. Cousin Harry tells me that he served as assistant to the medical chemist there whilst pursuing his early medical studies.

You call him Cousin Harry? cried Lucy with disbelief.

He requested it. Daughter, remember that he and Suthy were struck by the same shell-burst at Chancellorsville. Though Suthy's was a minor wound.

Harrell Elkins appeared in the doorway, in obvious embarrassment because they were talking about him.

A small wood fire burned on the hearth; coolness possessed the later hours of the day. There had been no matches in that household for many months except homemade ones, and often the homemade matches would not strike. Lucy took a sliver of pine from an old glass vase standing handy, and brought fire from the hearth to wan leaning candles on the table. The light glared on Elkins' spectacles and made him appear as a monster with great orange eyes.

My daughter hoped that she might be allowed to join us, Coz.

I'm pleased. Harry Elkins' rough high voice was unsteady; but he spoke as if he meant what he said. You had a feeling that he might never speak other than a sincere belief, profound or trivial. He said, I trust that Mrs. Claffey is not indisposed, and then stood in shock at having said the wrong thing.

I believe she'll join us at dinner. Lucy, in honor of Cousin Harry's arrival, will you indulge along with us?

Thank you, yes, Poppy.

Ira reached behind the calfbound row of Sir Walter Scott and brought out three small silver cups. Lucy exclaimed; she was positive that her mother must have buried the cups in one of those dreadful chests, and Lucy was surprised but delighted to see that her father had recovered them.

These were the boys'. Lucy, do you take Moses's cup. I'll drink from Badger's. You, sir, Cousin Harry, may observe that the cup which I've handed to you bears the name of Sutherland.

Elkins peered closely at the little silver thing, the child's cup nearly concealed in his broad smooth steady hand. He saw the name, or did not see it: firelight and candlelight were tricky, and not much light of sunset remained to reflect into the room. A streak of water appeared on his slightly hollow cheek. Lucy turned her glance away, but she was glad that he had cried.

Ira Claffey poured dark sherry for all three, though Lucy's was but a token. I give you, he said, and then could not say the names. They drank, and when Cousin Harry Elkins put down his cup he said shrilly, scratchily but in reverence, God bless them all. Wherever they may be.

Lucy repeated it to herself when she was in her bed at ten. Wherever they may be, and she was pleased with Cousin Harry for saying those words and for thinking the thought. He was awkward, strained, almost self-consciously rustic as to habit; yet there was a benefit in being near him. In this single day of acquaintance she considered him as a kind of evangelical relative.

Between mellow yellowed sheets and under a woven blanket some two rods distant from the girl, Harrell Elkins stretched watching toward the ceiling, the ceiling which he could not even see without spectacles. He considered the six pairs of spectacles which he had toted to the army; and he had broken four pairs the first year, and how they cost, and where might one secure good magnifying spectacles now? This was the last pair of the six—here, on the stand beside Suth's bed—and it was remarkable that they had survived the burst at Chancellorsville; they needed only a bow repaired. A watchmaker did that while Harry was in the hospital—or rather, hospitals, since he had been in three.

He lay now savoring the sweetness of Ira Claffey and Lucy. He lay pitying the mother, and wishing that something might be done for her. Short of a general resurrection of the war's dead, he did not know of any act or treatment which might effect a change. He feared that Veronica Claffey must march without deviation toward the solemn retreat which awaited her: a retreat wherein people sat unspeaking in their rigid chairs, and did not listen to what others said, and took their meals alone, and when they smiled—rarely—it was as if to say, I know a secret but I shan't tell. It was terrible when they smiled. Harrell Elkins had seen them.

He felt drawn to Lucy and her father not alone because they were Suth Claffey's flesh and blood, but because they embraced him with a tenderness. All his life Harry had dreamt of warm companionship; he had not found it at college: only in the army, where the general scale of values resolved in his favor. Through young years he had walked in the discomfort of weakness, he had suffered varieties of scorn because he had a strange voice, because he was bookish, because he wore spectacles in a civilization where most young folks never wore them, because he could not see well enough to catch a swift ball or shoot a quail.

He could barely remember his mother. There was a faint recollection of a fleshy, frilled lap and the scent of cologne (it might have been a Sunday when she held him. He knew that she read from a book of Bible stories, and must have simplified them as she read). Also in memory he heard her saying to the cook, Do you let Master Harrell make thimble cookies if he wishes. Then no other memory except black nodding plumes, and his own shrieks because he did not understand death, he did not understand, he feared for his mother; who were all these people, and why did they hold their voices low and musty? His father was bitten by a rattlesnake while hunting, when Harrell Elkins was seven, and died two days later. Harry was reared, until ready for the academy, in the home of a second cousin whose ward he became. The cousin was a physician and surgeon, a cruel man, but brilliant and scientifically experimental by turns. Doctor Epps disliked Harry, whose funds he squandered to the possible enrichment of brokers in cotton and foodstuffs in distant Savannah. He devised strange punishments when the boy was driven to rebellion, when he did wicked things out of resentment at loneliness and immurement.

Once Harry dragged a load of loose cones and pine needles against the ell of the house, and tried to set the place on fire. Nothing burned except a wooden sill, since the structure was of brick. Servants caught the boy red-handed and gave him over to Doctor Epps. The doctor said that he must go to jail and be fettered, and live on bread and water. The jail was a barren windowless entry off the doctor's private sitting room; slats were nailed across the door, and Harry was incarcerated there, fettered with knotted hemp, and with a chamber pot and the traditional pallet of straw for furnishings. Bread and water were given him by the doctor, morning and evening. When Doctor Epps was at home, and not calling on patients or performing operations, he had his meals brought to him on a tray within sight and sound and smell of the child beyond the lattice. Doctor Epps was fond of boiled foods, and they smelt particularly pungent: Harry Elkins recalled the rich odors of ham and cabbage, pork and turnips, beef and onions. His cousin kept him in jail for five days, and then word got abroad through gossip among the slaves. The rector came to call, with fire in his old eyes, and Harry was released, counseled, prayed over, fed.

These were things which he might not tell the Claffeys now. He might tell them in time, if friendship grew as he petitioned that it would; he had told Suth a few of the incidents. It would have offended Harrell Elkins to know it, it would have wounded him immeasurably had he known that Sutherland Claffey's initial interest in him and attention to him were engendered first by a sense of the ridiculous and then by pity. Suth had written to his family: I dislike being a tale bearer, but then you must remember that young Moses and I are new at this task of soldiering, and shall wish to parade the story in completeness before your eyes. It is probable that I shall write to you more frequently than Moses, the idle scut. Of course his company is removed from mine by three companies, and we are separated by the rigid distinctions of rank and cast (sic!) but little birds tell tales now and then. I hear that he and another prankster of his ilk *borrowed* two of their officers' mounts, and went for a fine gallop yesterday. Tricks like that will land the youngster in durance vile, you may be certain; but I doubt they will get him shot by a firing squad! In my own company we have the most absurd *coterie* of individuals. Not that there are not splendid chaps as well, and those who will stand out gallantly when we face the enemy. Not in all the myths of the ancients have such *phantasmagoria* been assembled! In all my days at Oglethorpe I never saw the beat, in classroom or on campus. One *lieutenant* in particular— Ah, what a figure for legendry! It is said that he achieved his appointment because his late father was a classmate of the Hon. Gen. Howell Cobb at the U. some thirty years ago. The Yankees should see him: they would take off and flee, not a doubt of it. He is somewhere near my own age, but half bald already; he wears the ears of an ape; his voice squeaks like a warped windlass; and surmounting all this *manly beauty* he employs a great pair of specs—to make it easier for him to spy the foe, no doubt. His name is Elkins, and already to myself I call him Elky—you recall?—after the colt in the Rollo tale. Only yesterday I ordered him to engage his platoon in drill according to the time-honored Poinsett tactics. He had no sword to give him a manner of command; it seems that, lean of purse, he is still bargaining for sidearms. Upon my word, he appeared on the drill-ground with a grass *sickle* in his hand. The men were close to splitting. Elkins was immensely serious about the whole thing. . . .

'Another letter, later. Your box arrived on a Saturday in fine order. Only the peaches were broken, and leaking rum along the way, no doubt to the satisfaction of sundry *baggage-handlers*. Nevertheless I salvaged them with content, and rinsed off the glass and mildew. Tell our loyal Naomi that her tin of *Federal Cake* made many mouths water and many hearts beat high. The sugar itself would have been a treat, since recently that commodity was lacking in our messes—why, I know not. Tell Naomi that henceforth, however, it must be dubbed *Confederate Cake*. Come evening, a few of the elect assembled in my narrow quarters to taste and to enjoy: those gentlemen around me with *chicken-guts* on their sleeves. Lucy will shrink, but that is merely soldier slang for the braid we officers wear. The redoubtable Lt. Elkins was in attendance. I must say, he is a saint as to good humor, never complaining, and always ready to crack a joke in his peculiar voice. It has come to my attention that the men respect him, and find comfort and perhaps inspiration in his dry sallies. . . .

Another letter. Elkins is a remarkably fine horseman, at least for the demands of a martial life. He is not spectacular in the saddle, he does not cut a fine figure, because of his odd posture; but he can take a horse anywhere. After our arduous *traverses* of the past week, several officers were complaining of saddle boils, chafing and the like. Including The Undersigned. Rob Lamar should be with us— there is a *Centaur* for you! But I must add that the *un-Centaur-like* Harry Elkins had no complaint of *mayhem at the hands of a horse,* and was fresh as the proverbial daisy. . . .

Another. It was our baptism of such concentrated fire. They were fairly focal upon us. With all that smoke and banging and—I regret to state—the sight of blood round about, many in the company might have felt like taking *French leave.* It seems in battle that sometimes there is a concentrated if brief period of silence —a vacation between the cannonading and musketry. In such a *holiday of silence* there spoke the easily recognizable accents of one Harry Elkins. He was re-marking with a degree of pain that he wished the Yanks would cease throwing stones at us. In fact, dear parents and Lucy, what he said was not *stones* but another equally commonplace commodity in a stableyard where animals have been segregated for some time. You should have heard the men roar with laugh-ter. It made matters indubitably easier for all concerned. . . .

. . . I have had to lecture Harry severely about exposing himself to enemy fire. He looked contrite, but finally faltered out with a statement that he was sure he was constantly more *scairt* than anyone else in the Confederate States Army, and that if he didn't consciously ignore the bullets snapping about him he might be guilty of some unfathomable act of cowardice. Furthermore, his opinion was that since a rank of infantrymen are compelled to stand up and attempt an advance in the face of withering fire, it behooves their officers to be nonchalant, even to the point of suicide, in disclaiming any attitude which might suggest that they were not invulnerable to *minié* balls. I wonder if there is wisdom here?? Certainly food for thought. . . .

. . . He is so kind hearted. I feel that he is like a brother, now that Moses is no more, and Badge far away. Sunday night we had a fine talk by the fire. Harry told me of his ambitions as a physician and surgeon. Strangely he was instigated in these ambitions by the example of a relative who possessed experience and tech-nical skill, but no Christian heart and soul. Harry declares that as a youth he swore that, since this relative was a *bad* doctor, he should grow up to be a *good* doctor. There is a strange and valuable salt flavoring his conversation; I enjoy it heartily. When this war is over we shall all be the patients, when necessary, of *Doctor Harry Elkins.* He says that he will give me physic without charge! . . .

. . . My own wound is a bagatelle: a mere splinter near the left elbow, which made me bleed *pints* and causes some pain, but will not disqualify me for full duty after a fortnight or so. But the thought of Harry occupies more attention. We are eager for word of him, and nothing is heard. His hemorrhage was severe: he was struck in the neck, at the base of his head, in the shoulder and chest. He kept insisting that no one should carry him to the rear; he was quite comfortable; no one must leave the firing line on his account. The last time I spoke to him he murmured something about, Give those Yanks a belting for me. They broke my specs. . . .

Harrell Elkins heard his own voice saying those words, now, as he sought sleep in Sutherland Claffey's old room. They had held that deep love which is disassoci-ated from sex because of the nature of the lovers: they are men made for women, never men made for men. Abhorrent as decay itself was the notion that ever either of them could have loved physically one of his own fashioning, in intimacy. Elkins hoped wistfully that after long search he might find a woman who would (according to the Scriptural phrase he learned early) cleave unto him. The affec-tion between himself and Suth was an attraction of opposites, solidified by peril into a union which only those who'd functioned together in equal peril might ever know.

Suth had known many women, although he was too much the well-taught young gentleman to discuss them. He was handsome, devoted to any phase of the patriotic career to which he had dedicated himself, pleased by his own accom-plishments, a bit too vain for popular taste until the close song of bullets blew the swelling from his head. Fear of the death which was to come made him admirable at last, and so he remained to the end. In passing Sutherland Claffey was bewailed by his superior officers, envied in retrospect by subordinates, mourned by his men. He became the complete effigic pattern of a Crusader on a tombstone. So Harry Elkins thought of him now, resting in that sacred bed.

From the first moment of contact, from Lucy's primary flutter in the wash house in front of dyeing-kettles, and from Ira's handclasp and gentle knowing manner, and from the worshipful agony they shared as they sipped from silver cups— From these and subsequent sharings through the evening hours, Harry Elkins knew the Claffeys, father and daughter, as new dignities and beauties to be respected. In no degree could he have considered Lucy as a love for himself. He dared not look at her romantically (not yet) even if he had admitted for an instant that he longed to. She belonged in sanctified association with a dead lover, with her brothers' memory, and with a father who was so obviously a man above most men, and with a mother who suffered as a casualty of the conflict.

He thought, It was so good of them to take me in. He thought, It was more than good of them to accept me as I scarce dared wish I might be accepted. I am very fortunate. His twenty-five-year-old body (not yet twenty-six, despite the scrubby hair and barren scalp and the facial lines) relaxed in a baby's contentment. His arms slid up across the pillow, his big fists were bent loosely, his fingers curved in rest. He slept, but feeling in the last coverts of awareness that some benevolence would be offered him.

In the middle of the night, Lucy Claffey walked and rolled once more in that pagan dream wherein violets grew, laughing children tumbled, the man come bare and heartily to claim her, to bear her down among flowers while distant flutes were playing and the fallow deer of legend were running past. The man was Harrell Elkins. She roused herself from this sinful illusion with strength and in decided horror. Never again, dear Lord, never, never, she prayed. Oh, that I could be so carnal. Desperately she flung out her hand and found the Shorter Catechism of her childhood, a thin brown tiny volume on the round table by her bed. *What is forbidden in the seventh commandment? The seventh commandment forbiddeth all unchaste thoughts, words, and actions.* She held it as a talisman until she slept again deeply and her limp fingers fell away from the book. She was inordinately silent at the breakfast table, and her father wondered about it to no avail. He had been up early, showing Cousin Harry about the place.

Lucy avoided being left in the room alone with Harrell Elkins; that did not take much managing, since he was so shy of her. Soon after they had breakfasted he asked for his horse, and little Buncombe led the animal proudly to the front. Cousin Harry thanked them for their hospitality, and rode toward the new stockade. It seemed that Ira Claffey had invited him to be their guest while he proceeded on duty in the region, and Harry accepted willingly. Lucy told herself that she did not approve of the invitation, but Suthy would have wished it, so she must say nothing. Never again, she swore, would she dream such a dream.

9

Eben Dolliver shouted at the guard in thickening darkness. What in thunder did you lam me for? Like to busted my head—

The guard called across the heads and shoulders of other prisoners jammed fast. I'll bust it sure enough if you don't shush.

I wasn't talking—

Somebody back in that corner of the car was talking. You heard me order you to cease.

You like to busted my head, repeated Eben in fury.

Again the guard drove his musket butt toward the obscure corner of the box car, but men squatted and ducked and the butt thudded against the wooden side. Keep quiet, Ebe, a boy whispered. He's mad. You'll but make him crosser.

The guard withdrew his weapon and again took up a station beside the closed door, speaking with fervor to a fellow guard about what he would do if the prisoners didn't shut up. The prisoners were talking about exchange, the all important subject, but the young guard believed that they shouldn't talk about exchange or anything else. He had been commanded to maintain order in the box car, and to his nervous taste maintaining order was synonymous with maintaining absolute silence. He was a frightened, fat, stupid youth, trembling at being shut into this small space with dozens of savage Yankees. No telling when they might spring at you, seize your musket, perhaps twist your arms and legs out of their sockets.

Certain of the prisoners were considering that very course. Sounds resolved into a disordered fluttering mutter, submerged by coughing, nose-blowing, a continual crunch of timbers as the car jerked into its couplings and again tried to pull loose from them, a chorus of clanking metal underneath. Woodsmoke from the antique engine drifted along the train's top and found its way through every aperture. People were half gagged by smoke, including the guards.

Pushed into a forward corner by weight of the mass on every downgrade, Eben Dolliver and his friends made queer plans and then abandoned them. How many's in here? I was third in, I watched the door and counted: we got forty-seven. With the guards? No, there's either four or five guards extra; I couldn't make out exactly. That makes fifty-one or fifty-two in all.

What I thought was we could pass the word around and have a signal. Somebody yell a signal. Then all at once we could climb on the guards and get their guns. Got enough to do it, weak as we are. Both doors locked on the outside. Couldn't get them open. We could wait, Charley. They're bound to open them in time. Then we'd have four or five muskets, and maybe even some knives or bayonets—Have they got bayonets on? One has. I seen him when he crawled in. Maybe we could bust out.

Eben Dolliver whispered, And get mowed down. They always got troops standing by with rifles ready-aimed, the second they sling the doors open. Wouldn't have a prayer.

Guess you're right. Well, it's better than Belle Isle. Hain't you droll? Least we could breathe on the Island. Can't breathe in here. After while maybe they'll stop, and march us out in the woods like they done the other nights.

The engine struggled slowly on a long upgrade. The load of smelly people fell gradually away from the front end of the car, displaced by the pull of gravity, and a mingling of pleas and curses and bitter chuckling rose from the herd now squeezed toward the rear. Members of the Moon Hotel mess dug their fingers into cracks and around interior braces of the forward end. Thus they clung in comparative ease for a time. Two of them found room enough to sit down.

Get stepped on down there, Kirke.

Don't care if I do. Good to stretch my limbs out. Gad.

They called themselves the Moon Hotel mess after a hotel conducted in Iowa by the father of one of the members. Nine in all had messed together on the Island: three were Iowans, one was from Indiana, one from eastern Kentucky, the rest from Michigan. Andrew Kirke had enlivened earlier days of starvation with detailed descriptions of the table set by his father. That was when they were in a primary stage of hunger, fascinated unduly by any consideration of food. As they dried and thinned (one died) on the limited diet of the Belle Isle winter, they found themselves losing interest in such fragrant illusions. No longer did they prompt Andrew to describe black pepper scattered on the surface of prairie chicken gravy. His favorite tale had concerned a political dinner during 1860, when plank tables were erected under cottonwoods in front of the Moon Hotel, and guests came all the way from Fort Dodge to join in the rally and to partake of Mr. Kirke's fare. Fried prairie chicken, two roast pigs, venison, platters of grilled pike; boiled potatoes, greens, hominy, green corn . . . Andrew had been fond of going into precious detail concerning the gravy. He said it had a brown film over the top as it cooled, being well thickened with flour, but when you put the spoon down through it the steam came drifting out, and the skin of the gravy was broken, and hotter softer gravy was paler underneath. Also Andy had a great deal to say about crab-apple pickles, and sauerkraut made by the local German saloon-keeper. Andrew was very fond of crab-apple pickles and plum butter; he said that he dreamed often of these luxuries. By February the dreams had fallen away, they no longer provoked in taunting routine, they no longer comforted in sleep as a promise of what might be if ever the men got themselves exchanged. (They did not refer to exchange in the cynical sense, but in the hopeful one.) Rarely did the fancies of food recur; then they came sharp and baking and quick, and left the dreamer staggering.

The Moon Hotel mess promulgated certain rules; any person not conforming would be banished. Everybody had to take exercise, they had to walk about, it would help to keep their bodies and brains alert. They must boil every spoonful of water they drank. A man must keep himself as free from vermin as circumstances would permit. A lane lined by high boards ran from the Belle Isle pen down to waters of the James; at night this lane was closed by a high gate, but the gate was reopened each morning. Guards were on duty at the river's edge: no chance for a prisoner to swim away, even if he felt stout and bold enough to try it. But he could wash, and every member of the Moon Hotel mess must wash daily. Above all no despondent conversation was permitted. Members should talk, laugh, jest openly about their situation. They had a debating society, although three or four of them did most of the talking. Andrew Kirke could sing Irish ballads, Ebe Dolliver sang like a minstrel, most of the others sang passably hymns or popular doggerel learned at school and singing school. They sang almost nightly, even on the evening after the morning when Sam Michols, Twentieth Michigan, was carried out dead. That night they sang, Rock of Ages, and, Glory, Glory Hallelujah. They considered it a direct result of their discipline that Sam was the only one they lost on the Island, and he had been feverish to begin with.

Eben Dolliver referred to himself as middle-aged, meaning that he was the precise middle individual, in age, of the original nine. Four were older than he, four younger. Eben became twenty years old the month before he was captured in the Chattanooga campaign. He had marched four hundred miles with the Fifth Iowa, all the way from Memphis to Chattanooga, to take part in that fight, and it was hard lines to be captured in your first battle after such a wearing march. The Fifth Iowa had marched upwards of two thousand miles in two years; half the men of the regiment were already casualties; now they were serving under their third colonel. At Chattanooga they took to boats, and most of them had to find boats in the dark. They went floundering two-by-two on the edge of the Tennessee River, slipping in greasy wet places, barking their shins on stones they couldn't see, when a calm voice spoke through the November night. The speaker was so close that Eben Dolliver could almost have reached out and touched him.

Be prompt as you can, boys. There's room for thirty in a boat.

. . . Who was that, talking there on the bank?

Didn't you know? Austin tolt me he was here, overseeing us.

No. It wasn't Captain Byers—

Not Captain Byers's voice. Guess again.

The colonel?

Naw, naw, naw. Uncle Billy!

Get along, now! You mean Uncle Billy himself?

Sure enough.

It made you feel better inside, turning with slowness on the broad black cool water, expecting to have Rebel pickets start poking holes through you every foot of the way— It made you feel better to know that General Bill Sherman was right there alongside, taking at the moment the same risk you were taking.

Less than two days later, when the adjacent Army of the Cumberland ordered itself to take the top of Missionary Ridge after the commanders had only ordered it to take the bottom, Eben Dolliver was jumping over logs and rifle pits along with the rest of the Fifth Iowa. A lot of people started to scream warning ahead on the right—and there they were, seeming like more Secesh than Eben had ever seen at one time and in one place. They looked a lot meaner too. They were boiling and Rebel-yelling out of a tunnel which drilled the side of the mountain, and boiling up out of the railroad cut beside the tunnel. A few minutes later there was nothing to do but drop your gun and stick your hands up and waggle them desperately to attract attention so's you wouldn't get a hole through you. Looked like part of Company H was taken, and part of Company G, and some from A and B also. Only two or three fellows from C. Sixty-odd men gobbled by the Rebs in less time than a heifer'd take to switch her tail. And here they had thought they were winning a battle. Just went ahead too fast and too far. The Confederate artillery was already limbering up and streaking for the rear when they reached the artillery positions. Rebs marched them twenty-five miles that night to avoid their being freed by the Union advance. They were just about as dismal a gang of Hawkeyes as ever chewed biscuit.

They were marched and shipped by way of Bristol, Virginia, denuded of most of their possessions by guards before they reached Bristol. Ebe Dolliver had no blanket with him at the moment of his capture, but he was wearing an overcoat, which he peeled off as bidden to do. A couple of days later he got even. The prisoners were being hustled through icy mountains, and Ebe Dolliver spied a guard who didn't appear to be overly intelligent and who was wrapped in a crazy quilt. The quilt, a dirty one, was adorned with every color of the rainbow, but the material itself was tightly stitched, well stuffed, wearable. Hey, Johnny, what'd you say to selling your quilt for greenbacks? You can get another one from home. Yank, you all know we ain't lowed to have greenbacks. Look, nice and green, and Dolliver displayed his roll. How many dollars you reckon you got there, Yank? Thirty-five.

The quilt slid over to Eben's shoulder, and a lean hand extended for the money; the Iowan pressed the wad into the hand and moved away. Also the guard moved away, for he saw an officer approaching; he thrust the money into his pocket without looking at it. Two hours later the guards were changed, and Eben Dolliver never saw again the man he had victimized. The currency which had appeared so temptingly green was in reality wildcat currency, printed by Western stage companies and irresponsible and probably defunct banks. Masses of that scrip floated through the army, and became the joke and toy of soldiers; but Eben and his fellow Fifth Iowans talked the matter over and decided that the old guard wouldn't have known the difference even if he had looked at the bills. They doubted that he could read. Soon after they were captured, a Rebel said, All you Yanks that can write your names line up over here, and the entire group moved over. The Rebel officer was indignant because he thought they were making fun of him. To Eben's knowledge there had been one man in his company who couldn't read or write, and he was not captured. These ignorant Secesh just didn't realize what it was like to be raised in the North, especially in Iowa.

Wind cut across the mountains, and Ebe Dolliver was more than glad that he had acquired a quilt. Wintry wind blew them to Richmond and Belle Isle; they landed on the Island at the end of the first week of December. First thing they saw was a troop of armed guards dressed in blue, and some goose of a prisoner danced with loud cheers, smitten by the notion that Richmond had fallen to the Yankees and they were now among friends. Those blue-clad guards soon showed him how wrong he was, as they shoved him back into the file and threatened to fire. Next thing they saw was a line of twenty-two bodies—Dolliver counted—being carried out of camp feet first. It had been colder than usual during the night.

On the afternoon of February fourteenth the eight surviving members of the Moon Hotel mess were counted out of Belle Isle with exactly five hundred and ninety-two other prisoners. Wishful gossip in camp suggested that they were about to be exchanged, perhaps aboard a warship at some coastal port, but most of the wiser guessed the truth. They would be sent South, possibly to Savannah or Charleston. They hoped to go South because there they would find sunlight and maybe oranges and flowers; rivers would not be nearly frozen over as the James had been. The Moon Hotel mess had no business being numbered in this first contingent. Not a man of them was in the designated Hundreds. They flanked out, adroitly as imaginative and resourceful young men might do. Others—incompetents—sought to accompany them and were hustled and dragged away. You had to be sly about a thing like that. The foppish discipline of the Moon Hotel mess, once derided by people in adjacent tents, was showing its profit.

In this railroad train now, according to testimony of more talkative guards, they were being shipped to a prison called Camp Sumter. Yep, that's at Charleston, said some, recalling the first month of the Rebellion. Hope we get some decent shelter from rain. Hope the Rebs didn't blow down all them walls when they first fired on the Nationals there. Wiser folks knew that Camp Sumter and Fort Sumter must be two entirely different places. One night, while encamped beside the track, Dolliver and his friend Kirke had some conversation with a genial Rebel officer in command of the guards. This captain wore his left sleeve folded and pinned at the forearm; he said that he had encountered a chunk of red-hot shot at Sharpsburg. He said that he needed buttons for a new jacket which his wife was remodeling from the uniform of a friend who'd died. Dolliver traded four gilt metal buttons for four whittled from bone, which the Rebel was then wearing; he thought that he could get the bone ones sewn on sooner or later. In appreciation the Confederate disappeared for the better part of an hour and then came back and whispered, Sonny, here's some rations for you. He offered a little wooden pail containing thick stew—one of the most delicious substances Dolliver and Kirke had ever tasted in this life. It included potatoes, sweet potatoes, onions and a delicate meat which they thought might be squirrel or possum —it had a gamey flavor. Loyally they awakened the other six, and they ate the stew, turn and turn about, a spoonful at a time, until there wasn't a drop of grease left in the bucket. The captain had given them information also: he said that the Camp Sumter for which they were bound was in Georgia, not South Carolina, and was brand new—no prisoners had ever been kept there before. This was wonderful, for there would be no lice. Georgia in February would be Heaven compared to Virginia. The officer never came back for his bucket, so they took it along with them.

. . . Eben Dolliver's head ached where the gun butt had jabbed it. The skin of his scalp was broken, a trickle of blood stiffened his hair. Wonder the blow didn't crack his dome wide open! Throb or no throb, he made light of his injury: that was the manner of the Moon Hotel mess—to make light of unpleasant things, after a primary howl of distress. Also it was the manner of the Dolliver family, a jovial set of millers (for five generations). Certain distant cousins were lawyers and politicians, prominent in the new State of Iowa from its inception. Eben's branch of the family was comparatively humble, but open-handed and proud. His father had been responsible for organizing the first Campbellite church in the county when Eben was a little shaver. Jotham Dolliver was a long-armed long-legged man with a red beard which turned silver when he was still in his forties. His booming untrained voice lifted continually above the mill's whine . . . Joth Dolliver loved to chant of celestial hurricanes, far golden rivers, forested shores, mansions in the sky . . . his joy was in the rich illusion of Paradise as pictured by David and the Prophets, dripping with flame and jasper in The Book of the Revelation, solidified in song by Isaac Watts and later poets. He practiced his benevolent preachments through every waking moment, and communed pleasantly with his Creator when asleep. Never shrewd or tight-fisted in the grasping fashion ascribed to millers, Joth kept his numerous family on short commons because of his native improvidence, his native generosity. When a poor man came to mill, Joth was willing to grind his grain for nothing. The family loved him as they would have loved a prankish elder brother or a rollicking sheep dog, instead of as a father. In straitened wartime hours when Eben Dolliver thought tearfully of Home and its beauties, he recalled how his father towered at the front of the one-room church, admired by the preacher (the greater share of whose keep came from Joth) and leading in hymns; and how the shrunken yellow-haired little mother, with seamed face and big-knuckled warped hands and faded gray-and-pink shawl, would look up at him with quicksilver in her glance as if to say, My Joth, my dear Joth, how splendid you are, truly.

Dolliver's Mill stood on the west bank of the Boone River. Thickly forested hills, seeming like young mountains to the gaze of prairie dwellers, arose on the east side; but smaller hills on the west bank of the river already stood denuded of

timber, and white men had lived in that country only a few years when Joth
Dolliver moved up from Poweshiek County.

Again and again the dam was torn out by crunching barges of ice at the end of
winter. Black walnut posts had to be re-established at great expense and with
grueling labor. Once, when Eben was thirteen, the entire end of the mill was
knifed away by towering shifting masses of ice: it dropped into the ravenous river,
and was swept off, and left machinery and piles of flour sacks exposed to view.
The Dolliver family lined on the bank, watching the tragedy, weeping loudly—
weeping, every one of them, from the eighteen-months-old baby up to mighty
Joth. It was strange, but other men didn't cry, simply and naturally in the way of
children, as Joth cried.

When very young it had seemed to Eben that his father was a normal man; and
other fathers and neighboring men were not at all normal because one never saw
them cry. Once Jotham rented a breaking plow, to open a breadth of raw prairie
on a ridge across the road from his house (no sense in letting that fine land go to
waste! Many days there was no grinding to be done at the mill, no one came with
grists; Joth would be a farmer as well as a miller, and prosper at it) and little Eben
ran after the big plow, trying to help. The plowshare ripped through a bumblebee's nest, and the next moment Jotham Dolliver was on the ground, rolling and
bellowing. No, no—stay away, little Ebe, he was gasping between sobs. Oh, oh,
oh, how it hurts, oh God, oh Lord forgive me for taking Thy name in vain, ow, ow,
it hurts. Didn't know bumblebee stings could hurt like—Ow, ow! The unstung
oxen stood and regarded him mildly. Eben jigged and wrung his hands; then he
scooted to the house, bawling for his mother. She came to comfort her wailing
husband, to plaster his swellings with cool mud.

Was Joth honestly a baby? Not so's you'd notice it.

The Campbellites joined with parent and somewhat snobbish Methodists—and
with their fellow immersionists the Baptists—in organizing a camp meeting that
same year. They chose the season after corn was too high for plowing and before
small grain needed to be cut. In this brief period there might be only haying to
interfere with an intense, informal period of devotion. Since Dolliver's Mill was
more or less a gathering point for neighbors, and since the river offered charm for
the young—they could wade in mud, catch crawdaddies, hunt for mussel shells
while their elders listened to preaching—a platform was built in the walnut grove
across from the mill. The idea appealed, socially as well as religiously, and people
rode or drove or even walked from miles around. The grove held from a hundred
to three hundred devotees at any given moment during the four-day session.
Naturally all the ministers in southern Hamilton County took turns at preaching,
together with various laymen (Joth Dolliver was one, to the pride of his family)
who got up and exhorted.

This rural festivity, with sagging baskets of good things and with pretty girls
bound to turn up, excited the interest of certain hulking youths who had a dangerous reputation throughout the community. Folks called them the Monger gang or
the Monger tribe. There were two Monger brothers and a Monger cousin, with
several cronies trailing along. Most other young fellows from respectable homes
gave them a wide berth; they were said to go armed, the tricks they played were
cruel and ugly, often they staggered drunkenly in public. Well, they came along to
camp meeting on the second day and stood haw-hawing on the outskirts. Slowly
their deviltry crept into the session and before long was close to disrupting it.
They lounged, grinning contemptuously under the wide-brimmed black hats they
all affected, and when hymns were tuned up the Monger gang made meeowings
and calf-blattings under cover of the music. Old Reverend Grosscup went tiptoe-

ing toward them and was heard to say, If you boys can't act civilized in true Christian fashion, we ask that you withdraw. They pretended not to have heard his quavering voice, but kept winking at one another; they planned fresh mischief. Eben Dolliver could watch his father's face getting redder and redder, and he shivered to think what might happen . . . perhaps his father would order the riffraff away, and one of them would pull out a pistol and. . . .

One of the Mongers had a bottle of turpentine; a yellow dog trotted near. People at the back of the congregation could see what actually happened, the rest could only hear the outcry. Those young men caught the yellow dog and smeared turpentine on its rear. The creature rushed howling in circles, alternately bounding into the air and dragging its burning bottom across the grass in a frenzied attempt to allay the hurt. Joth Dolliver arose and called in a rough voice, Excuse me, Parson, and then forced his way back through the crowd.

The Mongers saw him coming. They stood in a tight group, waiting. The nearest fellow brought up a sly knee as Joth came close, but Joth stepped back quickly and caught the young man's leg with his two hands. He had tossed grain sacks about for thirty years. He turned this youth upside down in the air and dropped him on his head; folks nearest thought that the fellow's neck must be broken. Next thing Joth snatched the two biggest—Arney Monger and Benton Hakes—He caught them by their shirt collars, one by the back of his collar, one by the front. He flung them together, head against head, with all his strength, and both dropped to the ground. Arney Monger was rendered unconscious . . . you could hear the crack of those two skulls coming together, clear across the grove.

Bent Hakes got up on his haunches and reached for his clasp-knife, but before he could get it out of his pocket Joth Dolliver kicked him in the jaw. Bent shrieked to high heaven. His jaw was broken, and he gasped and struggled on the trodden-down grass, spitting out blood and teeth.

Sorry I was compelled to ruin you, Bent, but if it takes ruination to teach you Christian decency I'll work the ruin. Used to be the meanest rough-and-tumble man in Dubuque before I saw the New Light. I'll take you together or singly.

The Mongers were in full flight by this time, hustling toward the underbrush— all except the three on the ground. People gathered around them, and Doctor Dawson went to his wagon for his satchel. People feared that the Monger gang might try to shoot Joth Dolliver from ambush, after that, but so far as was known they never attempted revenge—perhaps for fear of the lynching which might follow. One youth went to California that same year and was said to have been killed by the Comanches on his way back to Iowa. Well did Eben Dolliver know the fate of two others: Benton Hakes and Elston Monger. They died at Shiloh along with numerous others of the Thirteenth Iowa Infantry.

Watching his father deal out justice as he dealt it, Eben yearned for the day when he also would be grown and imposing in stature, and generally looked up to. But he grew only to average height by the time he was twenty. They had no accurate method of measuring in the prison pen, but he stood barefoot and back-to-back against Olin Claver from Michigan, and Olin had his growth long since— he was twenty-seven, and said that he stood five-feet-nine-and-a-quarter. They were of identical height. Eben had grown but an inch since he enlisted over two years before. He was pleased that from birth he had exhibited the reddish coloration of Joth Dolliver—reddish skin, reddish hair with a curly shine to it. Also he had his father's clear eager gray gaze, and usually through his childhood and teens Ebe's gaze wore the expression of a hungry youngster who has just been told that he may eat with the grown-up folks—he need not wait for second table. Joyfully he appreciated the commonplace and felt pity for those who could not. His laughter rang easily until he was weakened by captivity; still he laughed more readily than most.

His father's glee was found in song, his mother's in flowers. However demanding the cares of the family, Elizabeth Dolliver always snatched an hour to go gathering the first pasque flowers which blew like lavender bolls of cotton on breezy summits. She would cry in rapture, and sit by the furry little things with unheeded bees coming near—She actually talked to flowers, and her children smiled to see and hear her do it. There were six living children in 1861; three others had died. All had Biblical names: the living were Eben, Neri, Ruth, Jacob, Naomi, Jesse. All could sing. People used to stop their teams in the road to listen to the Dollivers. The first banker in the county seat cried in scornful envy, Guess I'd better go out and get myself a pile of debts and work my fingers to the bone, and not have a dime to show for it at the end of every year. Then maybe I could sing like those Dollivers. . . . Those Singing Dollivers, everyone said. When Ruth and Naomi were just knee-high to a bunny and a mouse, respectively, they were in demand to warble at patriotic or political functions. Three Cheers for the Red, White and Blue (Blue-blue-blue)—That was one of their mainstays in the way of secular songs, along with Robin Adair and Flow Gently, Sweet Afton. The boys had a quartet—Jesse joined it when he was only four—and they did noble things with The Minstrel Boy, and Hail To the Chief, and Open Thy Lattice, Love. But their father liked best to hear Land Of the Leal, and of course he always joined in and drowned them out.

Song was born in Eben's heart, song thrilled in his ears from his first moment of awareness; possibly that was why he was drawn to the birds. As his mother worshipped bloodroots which came up leaf-wrapped and pearly through poplar glades each spring, so her eldest saw a charm in the first robin to appear—a charm and a lure which he could not describe. In May, going out at daybreak to begin his chores, the caroling from nearby heights of trees would turn Eben into a statue. His father said, Come along there, Pillar of Salt. Come along, Lot's Wife. Those are tuneful robins, but they won't put any mush on the table.

Old Reverend Grosscup had a book called Our Feathered Friends, With Copious Illustrations, and Eben borrowed the book so frequently and kept it so long that finally Reverend Grosscup declared with some heat, Well, I see nothing to do but to present the book to you, Eben. Then you won't always be pestering me for the lend of it. He wrote Eben's name on the smudged fly-leaf with a flourish and gave him a little smack with his frail hand after the boy was holding the volume to his heart.

Ebe went into the fish business when he was nine or so. An old Indian, a Pottawatomie called John-John, used to come up the river on solitary excursions with his gun and traps, and he would beg for tea or sugar at Mrs. Dolliver's cabin door. John-John watched young Eben trying to catch fish without success; he grunted and made signs, begging twine from Joth Dolliver. They had to keep plenty of twine at the mill, to tie and repair sacks. Well, that John-John sat down and wove a beautiful fish net. In only one day he put it together. Then he borrowed an axe, and shaped a wooden block, and into that wooden block he inserted four limber poles of willow. This block John-John mounted on a post something like a well-sweep, and the net was suspended to the four light springy poles. Above the mill flume the Indian placed this apparatus, and showed Eben how to lower the sweep until bending boughs of willow had spread the net across the bottom of the flume. There John-John insisted on leaving it stretched, though Eben was highly excited when he saw a large pickerel come nosing through the shadows. John-John knew how fish loved to swim away from sunlight, away from heated shallows, and lie twitching contentedly in cool shade of the flume. More fish came, more; Eben was fit to be tied. At last John-John let him throw his weight on the exalted sweep, and release the willows from their bending, and bring the net aloft, closing as it came. Little fish flopped out through the wide mesh but big fellows were trapped securely. Eben would always remember with a bounce of his heart: there were three pickerel and two enormous pike in that first net-load. John-John said, Uh, good, and made signs to the boy that the fish trap was his for keeps.

In time the net grew rotten, the willows corroded because of their constant drowning at the flume's floor. But Eben could make other nets, he could cut more willow limbs. No one of his subsequent traps was as efficient as the one John-John had made, but they caught many fish. In certain seasons the mill ground day and night. Often there'd be a whole line of wagons whose owners waited their turn with grists. When the farmers were ready to head for home, they'd find Eben standing by. Wish some nice fresh fish to take home, Mr. Clark? Shouldn't you like to give your folks a treat of fine fresh bass, Mr. Hurst, sir? I got five beauties —just pulled them up—some are still kicking. The prices had to be low, for no one on the prairie owned much cash in those years. But five cents here, ten cents there, twenty-three cents one day, twenty-nine another: it added up. Eben kept his money in a cracked ginger jar. When he thought he had enough, he approached Mr. Corey, the watchmaker in Webster City, on one of those rare occasions when he accompanied Joth Dolliver behind a borrowed nag across more than a dozen miles of grass. Sir, have you by any chance't got a telescope for sale? No, bubby, but I got a catalogue with some pictures. It turned out that Eben didn't have enough money as yet; but Mr. Corey said that he would order the telescope, and keep it for Eben until he was ready to pay. Ebe bought it that fall in time to watch the birds moving south. That was why he had yearned for a telescope: it could bring a bird into his lap, he could count the feathers in a jay's tail, he could watch a distracted dainty warbler feeding the slob of a cowbird fledgling which she believed to be her own because he had been hatched in her small nest.

Eben Dolliver's fingers were cased only in flesh. It took years for them to wear the golden finish off the telescope's cheap brass, but they did wear it through. By the time he was sixteen you could see where his fingers clamped most often. The lenses were well ground nevertheless, and through them he won an intimacy with wrens which he would never have had without this device. His ambition outran all common sense. He read that nowadays, in cities, photographers had a splendid new method in their work, and could secure accurate likenesses on their wet plates of any object which remained still. If the object moved, of course the image was blurred. But take a brooding hen lark or a bobwhite. Sometimes she'd never flicked a feather or rolled her eye for as long as Eben observed her. Might it not be possible to take a picture of a brooding bird? But where might he find a modern machine for such photography, and how might he ever get together enough money to purchase it, and who might teach him to employ it? It would be more accurate than any artist's conception in Our Feathered Friends, With Copious Illustrations.

Other people might have spoken severely about Eben's addiction, except that he was known to be a stalwart worker. Joth Dolliver liked to say that he had two right hands. This one, attached by the arm to his shoulder— And that one. Over there. He meant Eben. Men chuckled when he said it, and Eben turned from tanned pink to beet red. It seemed a piddling sport, to most neighbors, when they discussed how Ebe put up a little shelf among plum trees next to the new-sided house, in winter, and begged scraps of gristle from his mother to place thereon for nuthatches and chickadees to eat. Also he learned that sunflower seeds were relished by birds, so each fall he worked among dry heads of rusty sunflowers, harvesting against the snowy season.

Strangers came to the mill—new people, usually, who had just taken up land in the vicinity—and they heard that Eben was by way of being an ornithologist. That's interesting, boy. Have you got a lot of them stuffed? Eben stared, horrified at the idea. He thought that he might be able to shoot a human being if Fate required it of him, but was positive that he could kill no bird. Some boys from the village of Homer came past the mill with a pocket rifle; they were shooting at kingfishers along the river; they said that the feathers would make a beautiful dressing for ladies' bonnets. Eben dove off the loading platform and attempted to impound the instrument of death, and got a trouncing for his pains; there were three of the boys, two of them huskier than he. But in the process he awarded two bloody noses to the victorious party, and they did not stalk kingfishers within his domain again. Honestly he thought that the birds were his, even on land not belonging to his father, even in thick timber which was the property of Bells and Bryans. He watched a yellow-breasted chat and thought, No one could make gold like that. No human, no mint in the world.

He was seventeen when cannon roared on a South Carolina shoreline and a call went up for volunteers. Eben and his father attended a rally at Homer where the Democrats broke down the Republican flagpole and Republicans dislodged the Democratic pole. The two poles were spliced together and raised on high in a new location, and the Colors went crinkling to the top. White-haired Beriah Seton, who had served in the War of 1812, stood up on a wagon seat and fired a pepper-box revolver at the sky. Men joined hands—a few women joined hands too, and a great many small boys. They circled slowly around the spliced poles, singing, Hail, Columbia, Happy Land.

Joth Dolliver was silent as they walked the five miles toward home under stars that evening. For Joth to be silent was to say that he was sick in bed.

What ails you, Pap?

Ebe, I was just trying to cipher out some way to go.

I'm going.

No you ain't.

Yes I am. You forget I'm practically man-grown. Seventeen.

Ebe, you'd have to have my permission, and I won't give it. Your Ma would be broken-hearted if I let you traipse to the army. I'm bigger'n more able than you, if I am past the age; and I'm a better scrapper. I can still lay you on your back. Do you reckon you could conduct the mill by your lonesome?

No I don't. Furthermore, there's that hundred and sixty-five dollars to be paid to Mr. Bell for the machinery you bought off him, and how'd I ever manage to pay that, come July first?

I know, Ebe . . . it beats me. But somehow I'm going. You ain't.

We'll see about that.

No we won't.

They stopped on the old Mesquakie trail through springtime thickets, and looked at each other in darkness. They laughed, and shook their heads in much the same manner, and then went on. Presently Eben struck up, Father And I Went Down To Camp. Joth joined with him. Elizabeth Dolliver and the younger children heard those voices among bare trees and spreading through the glades where hepaticas grew (hepaticas couldn't be seen in the dark, but they were there, ready to reveal silk on their stems when daylight came), long before Jotham and

Eben struck their feet against the bridge's timbers. They fell silent, pausing there and listening to the rush of water across the dam. They stopped at the mill to see that everything was right; then they went home, and each lay awake for a time, planning.

Eben was the first to go. In mid-summer his father's sister fell sick in Marshall County, and wrote that she was having a hard time; could Dear Brother spare some cash? Her hands were crippled and she couldn't sew, and actually there was little in the house to eat. She had written to her married daughter in Kansas, but perhaps the letter had gone astray, for no word came. Jotham Dolliver dared not leave his mill; he was dressing both corn and wheat burrs against the next season, and had other repairs to make. Accordingly Ebe was dispatched with twelve dollars in currency—all that could be scraped up—and an old watch and snuff-box in his pocket which should be sold in Marshalltown and the money given to Aunt Esther. Stages cost too much; he walked part of the way, and was picked up by two movers in turn, so it didn't take him long to reach Marshalltown. There he sold watch and snuff-box for even more than the minimum which his parents had agreed that he should accept, and with delight he walked to a nearby village and presented the money to his aunt, trusting that it would see her through her disability until she was able to resume dressmaking once more. He spent the night on Aunt Esther's sofa, and at dawn was up and away, spyglass in hand, reveling in the activity of orioles and grosbeaks. Back in Marshalltown, he enlisted promptly in the Fifth Iowa Infantry, which was then being raised, giving his age as eighteen. This was a thing which explicitly he had promised his father that he would not do.

. . . Never have I uttered an untruth to you before, dear father, nor gone back on my word. But now I take up my pen for confeshin. I am bound to be a soldier and already am one in name. We were mustered in, here at Burlington, yesterday. I regret deeply that I was false to the vow you extrackted from me but trust you will forgive and forget. You are capuble of supporting the family whilst I am not. Hence it is My Stint not yours. Our Nation is in dire peril and if a nat's brain and a nat's fist may be of service, why, Uncle Samuel, here is your nat. Give my dearest love to Ma and remember me fondly to the girls and to Neri, Jake and Jess. Warn Neri not to attempt *crowbaticks* on the water gate as is his wont. I have my telescope along, and shall see many strange wildfowl in the Sunny South, so I hear. May the Heavenly Father keep and fend for thee. Y'r Affec'n't Son.

It was less than two years later, during the hundred-day siege of Vicksburg, when Eben received a letter from his father telling of the elder Dolliver's being commissioned as a lieutenant in Company G, Seventh Iowa Cavalry. A neighbor named Ennis, a man with some milling experience, was to look after operations at Dolliver's Mill; he agreed to pay Elizabeth Dolliver fifty per cent of the net profit. Jotham went out to Nebraska Territory, and one day, ten miles from Fort Cotton-wood, he was shot down by a party of Cheyennes who tore off his silver scalp and built a hot fire between his legs so that he might not be able to procreate in the Next World. Had they known that he took pleasure in song, they would also have cut out his tongue, since he was the enemy of the Indians and they did not wish him to have pleasure.

. . . Miseries such as these roved through Ebe Dolliver's brain as he lay wrapped in his tattered quilt, in an open Georgia forest along the Southwestern Railroad. He did not know the details of his father's death; he knew only that he had been killed by Indians. The letter reached him shortly before the long march from Memphis to Chattanooga. Also there came news that Mr. Ennis was doing well with the mill, which relieved Ebe of certain worries concerning his mother, the girls, and Jake and Jesse. Neri had already run away to war, and was believed to be somewhere in Arkansas.

Ebe thought of his father, he thought of Indians, he thought of old John-John, he wondered whether John-John had ever killed and scalped a white man. Maybe he had, in some remote period when Pottawatomies warred against encroaching settlers . . . head hurt. Blame that guard! There he was huddled against that tree over yonder past the nearest log fire. Like to crack him over his fat head with his own musket. Bet he'd never forget it.

Eben thought of the stew they'd been given, two nights before, and wished he had some now.

Suddenly he was sitting up, pushing himself up, holding himself up by his dirty hands spread against the ground. He had been lifted by a cry. There it was again . . . question and answer in the damp February sky, the sky holding no stars, no light. Only it held a mystic summons, a silver horning which might have been blown by the breath of ghosts or fairies. *Hear it?* he wanted to call to the guards and to the snoring, moaning, grunting herd of prisoners around him like swine in a wallow. Geese, ducks, elusive runaways, I know not. But they are birds of some sort, and they are going north, free and keen and shrilling about it as they have shrilled through the millennia. Oh, to be vaulting in empty blackness, to be flying with silent force as no others but the birds have gone. To unfasten from the throat that challenging whoop which is not a song, thin and far, and yet haunts as no other melody pealed. To understand the question asked, the answer awarded. . . .

Eben listened until the last hollering had left the limit of his hearing. Then he fell back and slept in peace, dreaming little but dreaming mainly of the mill and of a heron which kissed the willows as it soared.

10

What would it have been like in the old days at this same season? Ira Claffey tried to think. Not only the face and texture of the world had been altered, but also fundamental values underlying had been revised. It was difficult for him to envision the overseer's report which might have been handed him, say, in the late 1850's, if he had been absent, say, in Atlanta or Milledgeville. The corn land would have been ready for planting, but possibly sufficient manure would not have been hauled to cover it; some hands would haul manure for another fortnight. They would have been ridging up the land for cotton—perhaps fifty acres or more might be ridged up already. They would soon commence fencing. They would have finished rolling logs, perhaps? Usually the Claffeys were ready to plant as soon as anyone else in Sumter County, usually sooner. If the season weren't behindhand. . . . Ducks would soon commence laying.

What of the harness? Would it survive the rigors of planting, or shouldn't it be wise to set Putty and Shem to going over all the old harness? What of the twisted-cotton rope for plow-lines, the mule-collars constructed of sewn corn-husks? Would it be necessary to buy two or three new plows—cast plows, the Number

Fifty size? Perhaps one of those rare but violent February deluges would have occurred, washing out the low place in the main road, taking out the oldest bridge on the road to Americus, forming gullies in the cornfield, washing out part of the slope where the slave quarters were built (the old quarters, far down the south ridge toward the main Sweetwater, and all standing empty except for birds and varmints, now in this February of 1864).

. . . Wind south, cloudy. One and one-half hands sick: Putty, Lake. Ten hands hauling manure. Eight hands still ridging cotton. Three hands in kitchen garden. Two hands still rolling logs. Ten and one-half hands repairing road after storm. Three hands mauling rails. Japeth building, Ruth spinning, Naomi and Pet cooking for hands; Leander and Jonas with stock; Triton minding the hogs. The fare would have been plain but ample for all, and there would be treats on holidays, on Sundays, and when Badge and Suthy came from Oglethorpe. The week before Christmas Ira Claffey always went to Americus to buy Christmas for the black people; always he needed at least two people to help him, and they went with a four-mule team when the roads were bad, for the wagon swayed heavily on its return trip.

His people worked hard and ate well and were housed snugly, but he did not pamper them to the point of abuse. If Nestor or Dudley misbehaved they would be punished, and knew it; but if they misbehaved frequently they knew that they would be sold; and so they were sold.

Ira Claffey was shocked speechless at the thought of a general abolition of slavery. He imagined hordes of illiterates trooping the highways with no roofs to lie beneath at night, with no one to buy food for them, with no money and without sufficient knowledge to buy sustenance for themselves. Worse than that, he saw them exploited as tools of unscrupulous white men who might fetter them in an industrial slavery in cities, where sun and comfort of wild places would be denied them.

When he was young he had walked through an area in New York (it was somewhere near the place called Five Points, and he had been cautioned to carry a pistol if he ventured there alone even in daylight) where besotted people white and black sprawled actually in the swill of the roadway, and wild eyes rolled in kinky heads thrust, slathering, cursing inarticulately, from windows. What terrors lay inside those crazy dwellings he could only guess. Twice he felt that he was being followed, but when he turned, stood, and put his hand in his pistol pocket the followers found business elsewhere. He did not have to defend himself, but he could find no defense for the wretchedness. In a box of offal and rotten vegetables which he stepped away to avoid, he saw—scarcely could he believe it. Stench or no stench, he forced himself to halt and look. It was the body of a child, a black child, apparently the result of an extremely premature birth. Such hideous exposure might never occur on any plantation he'd ever visited or heard of. He fled the slums and found refuge at his Broadway hotel, but it was long before he could bathe away this most evil recollection.

In the worst of his current imaginings, Ira had visions of Ninny, Naomi, little Bun, Coffee and the rest, being herded into mines or sweatshops and compelled to live in those tenements before which he'd shuddered. He did not see them or their descendants made respectable, dwelling in homes comparable to those of the whites, schooled, taught to work in trades or even in professions, making a satisfactory economic way as individuals and as a mass. He did not see how that transformation could be achieved in a thousand years, let alone a hundred. And the thought of black men given uniforms and arms and trained to make targets of the whites against whom they were marched— Ira ordered himself to slay this thought, never to entertain it, never to consider that the reality was even now in existence.

He worked among his cabbages, he sought for kinder musings as he held his trowel. Consider Cousin Harry. How good it was to have him about, how good to hear a young man's enthusiasm and prayer for the future. Harrell Elkins had humor and high hopes left to him; they had not drained away through his wounds or been expunged by peril and bereavement.

. . . These were Early York cabbages. Ira was choice of the delicate seedlings, he would not permit Jem, Jonas or Coffee to remove them from the glass frames where they'd stood over the winter. This task he must perform himself. Each time he touched one of the pale immature plants with its sheen, its blush of frost and dust, he thought of the mature plant which it might come to be in time: an oval head slightly heart-shaped, a short stem, all very firm and with a flavor to remember. If the cutworms didn't devour it first.

. . . Salt should have been sown in the prospective cabbage patch last autumn, but salt was hard to come by, like so many other things; it would have taken perhaps ten bushels or even more. But there was another way of guarding against cutworms; Old Leander taught it to Ira some twenty years before. Ira had had two of the hands at work on a dry day, throwing the ground into ridges and trenches: he'd cut some sticks to the exact length for them to measure with. The ridges were sixteen inches apart, the trenches seven inches deep. In the bottom of these furrows tender flaky young cabbages should be transplanted now—it was a moist day, a perfect day for the job. He would set the plants a foot apart. As soon as they were well rooted he would have the soil stirred gently about them; but the trenches should never be filled until all danger of worms was past.

. . . A benefit to have Cousin Harry at the plantation; his presence aided in exercise of Ira's own intelligence and Lucy's . . . Veronica was becoming a pale spectre who stalked, only a spectre. The horticulture which claimed Ira throughout his days could not occupy his thoughts at mealtime, his attention during evenings.

Except for the old wound, life had been good to Ira's body; he had treated his body sanely, had not drunk or eaten to excess, had been scrupulous about not over-indulging at the greasy banquets which many others of his persuasion fancied. He cherished still the sensual appetite of a much younger person, but there was left in the small circle of existence no object to serve as partner in his sporadic but tempting lusts. There had been two experiences wherein he sought to seduce Veronica into rapture; the first time, she repelled him by saying, I cannot, I cannot. Never in her life had she demonstrated refusal, even after her change occurred. (Ira thought that her change came about earlier than in most cases, and with fewer of the unpleasant symptoms, and was more abrupt.) But there must have been some dread protraction; not all the substance of her cold mania could be charged sensibly to the recurrent losses.

Still, a nail of anguish had been driven through her coil of white-blonde hair and into her skull, each time a child died. The four small children died; each time, that nail hammered in. Then the pause, then in rapid succession the great spikes marked Crampton's Gap, Gettysburg, Chickamauga. In delusion her husband turned his sad eye upon her and saw the seven nails bristled out like quills. No wonder that her expression was glazed, her tongue lying silent! Oh, my Veronica, such joy we manufactured between us, divine joy, brutal joy, every variety. It was a charm, and now it is gone, now it is gone.

The second time, he tried to persuade her with tender courting, but she lay like marble under his touch.

I cannot.

Don't say that again.

Because it is grief.

For God's sake, woman! It's not a grief, and never was.

Isn't that the way we begat our children?

Yes, but—

Our children are a grief. All but Lucy. Doubtless something will befall her too. You'll see.

Don't say it, Veronica. For God's sake don't speak the thought! We must think of Lucy as having a good life, a long life.

If I let— If I let you do It now, it would be as if— As if we were doing It again to get Suthy. To get poor little Arwood. To get Badge. Poor little Peggy. Moses. Lucy. Poor little—

Cease naming those names! You heard me! His coarse whisper was intense and frightening as a roar. Veronica sobbed, but she went on and spoke the other poor little names: Sally, Courtenay.

I'll leave you now. You want peace, and you want to be left alone. By God I'll leave you alone. You want to wallow amid the graves; go lie in them. You want to remain in love with the dead, you forget the living, you forget your own living.

I loved my children, Ira. Now all are dead except Lucy. Do you not pity me? Does the Creator not pity me? Perhaps—neither of you! The boys are gone, claimed by the earth. The boys—

Ira flew to his own room, he would not attempt this thing again. Let the juice dry in his body, let the green go from it as it went from cactus growing in unkempt untillable portions of the landscape. When cactus slabs died they turned disgustingly red, like rotten fruit. In extinction they were dry, papery, thin, discarded, bleached snakeskin. So let him, Ira Claffey, bleach.

But body and spirit refused to accept this dictum without a struggle, so at times he rolled sleeplessly, or put on his clothes at some unseemly hour and went pacing out of doors. The hoary Deuce rose from his deep drugged sleep of infirmity and, blinder each week than the week before, came nosing to Ira in the dark, cursed by imaginary sand-spurs. Ira knew that he should shoot Deuce, or perhaps put him to sleep with chloroform; still, there was no chloroform to be had, and as for the rifle—

Death, withdraw, cease reminding me that you are.

On one of these disconsolate strolls, at perhaps three o'clock of a cold morning, Ira went wrapped in the cape which had belonged to his father; his father had died in 1842, but the cape was still warm and wearable. Like some sad romantic being stepped from the tumult of Shakespeare he went cape-wrapped along the lane and came at length to the railroad, and the spot where ruts led to the house of the Widow Tebbs.

Poor Mag . . . even thought of her could come fairly to Ira in his extremity.

Fair, fair, she was more than fair; why, consider her: she was a glutton for It. What would she be like under the husks of her clothing, once those limp husks were removed? Why, she would be a pet, an adoring partner in the gayest crime of all: adultery.

She would be his fleshy little plaything—the welter of ruddy hair, the weak mouth wide with pleasure, the soft arms around him, thighs squeezing his own thighs.

Ira dropped his cape to the ground; too hot, too hot. Ah, could he ever permit himself to go up that doleful road, even sneaking in darkness? He picked up the cape once more, shook it, folded it across his arm, the while he was torn between seeking forgiveness and prayer and considering the spasm of excited debauchery which Mag might afford. Touch of his father's cape suggested the press where it had hung long among scent of camphor contained heavily by other garments there. There was his own military jacket with its epaulets turned dull by time, there were gowns of another day in which little Lucy had loved to swathe herself and then mince about with a fan. There was— He started, to think of it. A red silk wrapper which had belonged to an aunt. Veronica never chose to wear it, she did not approve of herself in red. What might not the gift of this wrapper to the Widow Tebbs provide for him? A devilish boy in Americus had made a rhyme about, Old Mag Lumpkin, I think she's nice, I gave her a ribband, she did It twice; that dull rhyme was recited in Ira's hearing years before, and he rejected it as unworthy of being blamed even on a child. He had not thought of it consciously since, but here it was, he thought of it.

If secretly he took the silk wrapper from the press no one would be the wiser. He could hide it somewhere—as he hid the cups from Veronica's grim collecting. And, when whips of ardor drove him at last to the Widow Tebbs' door, he'd have a present for her . . . am I weaker than old Deuce? Why dwell on this, why countenance the savage lurid yielding? I'm not twenty. I'm fifty. I'm old. I should be old. . . . I must be demented. What would Lucy think of me if she learned of the depravity of my plan? She would grow pale with the knowledge. What would Harrell Elkins think? He respects me sincerely; would I still command respect? Cato Dillard would mourn for me. My sons— If they saw, if they could see, if they do see and know—

At this moment of private torment, wavering still in the dull darkness of that road, Ira saw prickles of light ahead and across the tracks. Somebody opened a door, somebody came out. Later, as the muffled approach of feet grew louder, he realized that at least two somebodies were coming. He withdrew past the edge of the road and seated himself; he could not be observed against a mat of vines overhanging the fence and small trees there. Two shapes, men's shapes, formed in the road. Ira smelled tobacco.

She give you good treatment? Sounded like it.

I hope to shout. What did you pay?

She wanted a dollar, wanted a greenback sure enough. I says, Honey, I got nary a greenback, so she up and settled for five dollars Confed.

Identical what I give her. She sure did take the blaze out of my breeches.

Oh, she ripped and she tore—

They went on, singing not too loudly. Military personnel from the stockade camp. So this is the depth to which your passion has sunk you. You'd share with them, stand in line as men stood in line outside those squalid huts at Matamoras, you'd mingle yourself with hogs.

Are they more swinish than I? Where does the man end and the brute begin? Whom do I hear saying, Brute? Is it my own voice?

He returned to his house, petted Deuce, allowed the wheezing setter to climb the stair. This was a rare award and brought forth a wild waving of the rusty tail. Ira lifted Deuce to the high bed, Badger's old bed. At the foot of the bed Deuce curled gratefully, glorying in close contact with his master. With care Ira kept his feet to the left side, that he might not disturb the dog on top of the covers. Deuce went to rest in the early morning hours. When Ira awakened belatedly after seven o'clock, roused by sounds from below, the old dog was still curled as he had been hours before. Perhaps the heartworms had reached his gentle heart at last; he was fourteen. Ira had bought the pup especially for Suthy when the boy was ten, but forever Deuce regarded Ira as his one-and-only. Ira Claffey dressed quietly, in respect to the friend who lay upon his bed. Strangely he found a sweetness and warmth in this death, in the manner of its coming. Had he cried, Death, withdraw? It did not seem possible now, when one considered the gift and its healing permanent perfection. He carried the friend down to the library and placed him on the couch, covered with the old cloak; then he went to tell the others. Harrell Elkins said, Poor creature. He must have perished of pure happiness at being allowed to sleep with you. Lucy went to the library and cried softly, lifting the cloak to stroke Deuce's white hair, thinking of her brothers as she did it. Poppy, maybe he can hunt with them now. In the Hereafter. He'll be so happy to have someone shoot over him again, to be able to go for birds. I declare, I love to think of it.

Of course you do, you dear sweet girl, girl with the tender heart, blithe spirit.

Veronica said, So he's gone too. I ask you to save his collar for me. I wish to put it with the other things.

Jem dug a grave in the pet cemetery not far from the family cemetery where a number of dogs, a parrot, a pony, and three especially favored cats were already ensconced. Ira and Lucy bore Deuce to his place, after they had breakfasted, and after Elkins was gone to the stockade; they were attended also by the three black children. Bun whispered to the others, Seed Old Mastah cry. Big tear on he face.

Harrell Elkins could not stand smiling tenderly through specs at the funeral scene. He thought that he should be on duty in the stockade region. He wriggled guiltily inside himself at realization that he was extending that duty beyond its demand. The task to which he had been ordered was vague but loaded with responsibility to the future.

Elkins was selected because he had two years of experience in the field as well as a medical degree. His orders read that he should examine carefully the new prison site, and set forth recommendations as to hospital facilities for an expected ratio of sick among a maximum of ten thousand prisoners. This entailed a study of climatic conditions, water, transportation, shelter. The diet of the prisoners was an unknown quantity; Harry assumed that they would receive the ordinary field ration of the Confederate soldier.

He applied himself seriously to the work, but by his third night in the Anderson community he recognized that there was little excuse for staying longer. At Milledgeville he had secured what crop and weather reports were available; from other sources he had scraped together figures on British campaigns in the Crimea and on illness incident to given numbers of troops in the Italian wars. He possessed also a lengthy report on hospitalization and the diet of prisoners at Dartmoor prison in England.

Superimposing this technical information on the structure of a firsthand study of a not-yet-completed-and-unoccupied stockade, he hoped to present a coherent report with attendant recommendations. *Surgeon H. Elkins will proceed to Camp Sumter, at the village of Anderson, in Sumter County—* No time limit was mentioned in his orders; paper work at most headquarters was performed sketchily these days. Harrell knew that he was naughty in drawing out his stay; this was the eighth morning he had risen at the Claffeys'.

11

Veronica locked herself in her own room, to examine minutely a collection of beetles which Badger had gotten together when he was twelve or thereabouts. The beetles had been discovered atop a huge wardrobe in the boy's old room; wenches never dusted that surface—it was beyond their reach—and apparently the collection had been forgotten by Badger when he went away to college and later to the army. Beetles of various sizes and shapes were impaled on pins and the pins were thrust into a thin planed board. There were no differences in their coloration now: time and heat and tinier insects had had their way with the creatures. They were shells of shapes, more brittle than straw. Dead as he is dead, said Veronica to herself, playing over that dirge. Creatures smaller than they have long since made dust of their insides. So must similar creatures have made ruin of Badger's body e'er now.

At times she journeyed through her past—a limited past, on the whole, circumscribed by her own limitations as an individual. For years her body and her affection had been able to accompany Ira's, but never her mind. Intrinsically she was a selfish creature, not sufficiently elastic to examine herself; but taught the habit of kindliness toward others in her rearing and by example. In wartime the suffering of the South as a whole she deplored; never had it wounded her truly. She was not aware that in loving her offspring with such abandon she was loving herself. Her children, living, were important to her mainly because they were hers. Her children, dead, were a woe greater than the accumulated woes of all tribes, nations, peoples, places, centuries.

She thought, But I cannot leave them on this board. The pins will come loose. But if I should remove them—each beetle, singly, pin and all—I should be destroying the collection *per se,* as Badge put it together. So must it be wrapped for storage with everything else, but how, how, how? Cloth will not protect the delicate dry bugs. Jem is fair to middling as a carpenter; might I not have him build a little box? I shall try to make him understand. . . .

She saw seven children, assorted as to sex and age, set on pins in a row and labeled much as Badger had labeled these creatures—not Order, Family, Subfamily, Genus— But labeled with the names and pet names her children had worn. There was an empty pin, waiting for Lucy. I have a collection also, she told herself.

But the assemblage must be put away, it must be kept, retained in private, guarded. It will be— What is the term? I recall Doctor Kennebrew lecturing to us when I was at Miss Benham's. A study collection. Not displayed to the common view.

Secret, smelling of camphor, the more fragile things smelling of lavender amid camphor.

What is a scarab? A kind of beetle, to be sure. There is some association with mummies—

Instantly there rose before her the picture of seven mummies large and small, spaced in their colored coffins. There was a vacant mummy-case awaiting Lucy.

Doctor Kennebrew did not lecture about mummies. His bent was for zoology and botany. Someone else— It could have been Miss Benham herself who gave the lectures.

The pages of the *Southern Recorder* rustled at an 1830 breakfast table. It was always quiet at the Arwoods'. The servants were made to wear felt slippers as they moved about. In some slovenly households servants walked with their feet bare, but never at the Arwoods'. Bare feet made a slap-slap on the painted boards, slippers made a gliding sound.

Mr. Arwood. So Veronica's mother addressed her husband.

My dear.

Possibly have you discovered some notices concerning schools? As to the subject of our discussion on Sunday evening—

Ah, yes. One moment, my dear. Here it is. The issue of January second. Miss Benham, late Principal in several distinguished Female Institutions at the North, will reopen her Select School for Young Ladies in Milledgeville. . . .

Veronica was close to fourteen years in age. It was high time.

She remembered the winter school dress, the very next winter when she was close to fifteen. Miss Benham required her students to appear in what she termed Livery. The gown was of brown Circassian material, with a belt and tippet of the same. With these brown dresses the girls wore aprons of either black silk or of Holland cloth (Veronica's was of silk) and black leather shoes. They walked out as a troop of young Quakeresses.

Orthography. She remembered: the very name terrified her. So did Civic Knowledge and Statecraft. Some parents grumbled, that Miss Benham should instruct young ladies in such subjects. One would think, said old Judge Beatenbough at a dinner, that young ladies might be bound for the Senate.

Perhaps, said a lady timidly, Miss Benham is ahead of her time.

Ahead, Mrs. Rutland? Behind, by gracious! Portia's been gone some centuries, has she not? Or, more likely, she never existed!

. . . Miss Veronica.

Yes, Miss Benham. And a curtsy.

Please to recite the statistics on Milledgeville.

Milledgeville, Baldwin County, is the capital of the State of Georgia. According to the most recent census there are in Milledgeville a total of one thousand five hundred and ninety-nine souls.

That is correct. How many white and black, Miss Veronica?

There are whites to the number of eight hundred and thirty-one, blacks to the number of seven hundred and sixty-eight. There are attorneys to the number of twenty, there are—uh—eight physicians—

Six.

Six physicians, twenty-one merchants, nine innkeepers, two joiners, six bootmakers, uh—six tailors—

Eight.

Eight tailors, four silversmiths—

(Veronica had no intention of going to the Senate, nor the desire to go. She thought of herself as marrying eventually a man quite unlike her father; yet she knew that it was wrong in her to wish to marry a man quite unlike her father. *Honor Thy Father.*)

Sixteen shopkeepers, five blacksmiths—

That will do, my dear. Well done, on the whole.

Eight children, seven dead. Not well done, my dear, on the whole. But in the individual parts—

Like her daughter, Veronica had recurrent dreams, similar in general and sometimes identical in detail. They were not erotic dreams. Thought that she had ever indulged in the act of copulation was increasingly repugnant to her, and thought of the variations of this art which she and Ira had practiced (and which they did for entertainment, for sinful pleasure, not in the doleful dedicated solemnity of Begetting) was worse than repugnant. It outraged not only a code of personal conduct but all religion, all philosophy, all virtue.

Her dream recurred not only when she slumbered, but with increasing persistency when she was erect and seeming to be awake: saying, Ninny, you neglected the vessel in the room where Mr. Dillard slept on Tuesday night. It is smelling. Attend to that at once, do you hear? Saying, Naomi, we shall have beaten biscuits to our luncheon. Saying, So Deuce is dead. So he's gone too. I ask you to save his collar—

Her dream swept her into a flat bare neighborhood and along a straight road lined with high stiff cedars or yews, very like the cypresses she'd seen in Europe when the Arwoods went abroad, a year or two before Veronica met Ira Claffey. She walked and walked, holding her shawl about her against an increasing chill, and soon she met a stranger who said not a word, but pointed to the left with his stick. Obediently she turned to the left and passed through a gateway; sometimes she turned to look back at the stranger, sometimes not, but whenever she did look back he would be gone. Down a slight slope, turning to the right again . . . grass over which she wandered was cropped close, as if sheep had been keeping it down —or deer, in an English park . . . presently she reached a place made of white stone. It was not marble, it had not the sheen of marble; could it have been granite, was there white granite?

Come in.

But the iron door of the structure stood open already, she did not need to turn the knob.

Come in. It was a throaty voice, it might have been a man speaking, or more likely a contralto with a very deep voice, far in lower registers.

She glanced at the western sky. It was orange, the cedar-yew-cypresses inked black against the color.

Veronica went inside, after passing down three or four steps to reach the door. This building was half above ground, half buried. It seemed to continue indefinitely, reaching back into the hill which now appeared swelling above—

She went inside, and there the sarcophagi were spaced; but there were more than seven, many more than seven, they stretched on and on, on both sides of the room. And the voice echoed, echoed, echoed—the voice which had said, Come in —distantly through space of the room until it lost itself in a single *sostenuto* organ tone—

She went inside. Somebody, a stranger dressed in white (never a child of hers), sat up suddenly in one of the open coffins.

She came from her dream.

12

On the evening of Wednesday, February twenty-fourth, they sat in the library, playing a game. The three: Lucy, Ira, Cousin Harry.

They were continuing a gentle rite established a few days after Harrell Elkins arrived. In conversation Ira quoted from The Bard; he said: *For sweetest things turn sourest by their deeds; lilies that fester smell far worse than weeds.* Instantly his daughter responded with, *We shall grow old apace, and die before we know our liberty.*

She said, Shakespeare for you, Poppy.

Herrick for you.

They giggled, and Elkins was puzzled. I'm sorry, sir. . . . Lucy explained the pastime of rhymes and quotations which had been their custom before the war, in family recreation.

I'm afraid I don't understand. That grating voice was become strangely a joy to her hearing. Mr. Claffey said *weeds.* Shouldn't you have begun with the letter *S?*

Oh, no, no. It's simple as simple can be. The next player begins with the *first letter* of the *last word.* And you should be able to identify the previous quotation, or it'll be a Black Mark.

I fear I would have many Black Marks.

Oh, come, sir. Come, Poppy. It'll be just like old times. Do let's try—

At first it was difficult, with the boys gathered close. Furthermore it turned out that Cousin Harry was either martial or morbid in his selections, and very often both. He apologized. He said that when he was a boy he had visions of himself as a soldier, but had never believed that he would be one in fact. Strutting through the hours, harassed by self-abnegation but determined to play alternately the part of Hector or Patroclus, he had read brave chants before a glass, he had put on a casque made of newspaper, had dragged his grandfather's sword.

. . . Very well. What was your last, Miss Lucy? Shyly he clung to this formality.

She addressed him in comparative intimacy for the first time, and her father grinned within to hear her. —*Before we know our liberty,* Cousin Harry.

Liberty, liberty. Ah. . . . *Lightly they'll talk of the spirit that's gone, and o'er his cold ashes upbraid him.*

There was silence. I give up, said Lucy. So do I, said Ira.

It's a quotation from Charles Wolfe. The Burial of Sir John Moore. It might be that I wasn't playing correctly?

No, no, Cousin Harry. You were quite correct. Poppy, it's your turn next, so you must accept the Black Mark.

Very well. The boys were still lounging close, but their shades were good-tempered and warming. *He is gone on the mountain, he is lost to the forest, like a summer-dried fountain when our need was the sorest.*

Oh, Poppy!

It's a Black Mark for you, Miss Lucy, cried Harrell Elkins gleefully. That's Sir Walter.

Raleigh or Scott?

Scott, you benighted wretch, said Ira. Thus they played willingly. Ira did not again stray into the cemeteries mourned over by Cousin Harry, but gave himself up almost completely to Shakespeare and the Psalms. Lucy roved among her favorites: Herrick, Wordsworth, Keats. Elkins would have been sonorous, but his tone was incapable of the designation, with *Ah! no;—the voices of the dead sound like a distant torrent's fall,* with, *My love is dead, gone to his death-bed, all under the willow tree,* with, *When the goodman mends his armor, and trims his helmet's plume.* Lucy looked at his earnest face, the round chunks of glass holding back the candlelight, the round ears standing out, and thought, He recites of heroes and is loath to admit that he is one. So were the boys, so was—Rob. But they are no longer in the flesh; and here we sit, playing at being the children they were.

Hours passed in concert were not all decked with such simplicity. They held conversation, often quite bitter, about the conduct of the war. Knowing that he could find trust in his faith and sympathy for his opinions, Elkins was outspokenly bitter against President Davis. Ira welcomed this expression of opinion as a man does when his own views are reflected, and presented perhaps with more authority than that with which he can present them.

If Fate had given us Stephens—

With that I'm not wholly in accord, Coz. I'm a respecter of Mr. Stephens, not a worshipper.

Nor am I, sir. But our President is scorned by many in the army. When General Toombs—

Oh, Poppy knows Mr. Toombs very well indeed, cried Lucy in interruption. And Mr. Stephens also—he's known him practically since boyhood.

Ira said in deprecation. Not since boyhood. It happened that in his youth he acted as tutor in a family with whom we were acquainted.

And Poppy pulled that brute of a Judge Cone off of poor sickly Mr. Stephens when he sought to cut Mr. Stephens' heart out, at the Atlanta Hotel. Didn't you, Poppy?

Did you indeed, sir? Suth never told me.

Oh, said Ira, I happened to be standing near when the attack occurred. Several of us jumped to the rescue.

They were young, they were insistent, Ira had to relate each detail again. Lucy had heard the story more than once, she had heard it a dozen times; but always it gave her excitement and the kind of delicious horror contained in threatening fairy tales (since everything came out well in the end).

Harrell Elkins said meditatively, Hearing such an experience recounted by an eyewitness— It offers us obscure folk a kinship with the great.

No one might ever presume to term as obscure a gentleman who has commanded a company of the Sixteenth Georgia, Cousin Harry.

But, Lucy, I— Miss Lucy, it—

Thus he floundered, rustic and bashful, and Ira Claffey let him flounder, he spoke no word of rescue. He thought, Let him learn. He's a man. Let him admit it. In time I trust she'll teach him. Indeed he was a man, and Ira could not believe that in any face-to-face encounter Elkins would come off second best. He recalled how, on the third or fourth evening of his stay, Cousin Harry came from deep thought to ask, Sir, have you chanced to meet up with a Captain Winder? It's under his supervision that the stockade has been built.

Ira thought of the surveying party in long ago October. Captain Sid Winder. I'm afraid I don't care for him. If recollection serves, I met his father also, during the Mexican War. He was an extremely courageous man, unfortunately as ill-mannered as they come.

I met him today, said Harry. Captain Winder.

Ah?

Slowly the story came out. Elkins was interrupted by Lucy's coming into the room, and postponed the telling until her departure, since it was necessary for him to use profanity in quoting accurately.

. . . He said, Captain, will no barracks be constructed before the arrival of the first prisoners?

. . . Winder said, That's none of your damn business, Surgeon.

. . . Will you permit me to quote you verbatim in my report?

. . . We didn't build any barracks, I have no intention of building any barracks.

. . . Will any shelter of any sort whatsoever be erected?

. . . Not by me.

. . . Then why, for God's sake, did you cut down all the trees? At least trees within the area might have afforded a certain degree of shelter to the inmates, protecting them from the sun.

. . . Why protect them from the sun?

. . . Because direct exposure to the sun's rays, in this climate, and especially during the summer months, may cause a high degree of mortality.

. . . I hope it does, Surgeon, I hope it does. What the hell's the use of coddling a pen full of Yankees? I've got a pen here that ought to kill more God damn Yankees than you ever saw killed at the front.

Harrell Elkins arose from his chair and moved restlessly across the room. He stood looking out of the window, though it was dark, though panes shone back at him, though nothing could be seen.

What was your reply?

Oh, I asked him how many Yankees he had seen killed at the front.

And, Coz?

He said that he had a good notion to call me out. That he would call me out, if I weren't bespectacled.

And then?

Oh, I said that I wished that he would call me out, since as the challenged party the choice of weapons would rest with me. Informed him that I would select cavalry sabres at two paces.

What said he to that?

Oh, he kind of barked. He rode off.

For a moment Elkins and Claffey gazed blankly at each other; then their shouts arose. It was long since such lawless laughter had sounded within that room. Should it come to such a pretty pass, said Ira between gasps, I would be most proud to officiate in your behalf. In the kitchen servants heard the laughter and came creeping through the hall to listen closer, to wonder at the laughter, to grin and giggle in distant fellowship without knowing why. In Moses Claffey's old room Veronica heard the laughter. She arose, the candlelight making a nervous vulture of her shape upon the wall, and she crushed a pair of baby boots in her cold hands and said, not aloud, How *dare* they? In her own room Lucy heard the laughter and she sat with uplifted hair brush, smiling at herself in the mirror. She remembered how, when she was younger and before war overwhelmed them, it had seemed natural as life to have Ninny brushing her hair each night. But now Ninny, Extra, Pet and Naomi must do all the work of the house, which meant all cooking, baking, washing, sewing, mending, dyeing, weaving, spinning, soap-making, candle-making . . . the list stretched on. In these activities Lucy was mistress, driver and participant, much of the time. At night she slept as soundly as any of the black people, with as good reason to sleep. She brushed her own hair, one hundred strokes each night, even when she was really too tired to do it.

In a wine glass of water on her dressing table two violets posed for her. The violets were of different shape and color; one was much paler than the other, and curled its petals, and was bluer. The other violet, more purple, was of the crow-foot species.

Where on earth did you find them, Cousin Harry?

Twas inside the stockade, actually.

Seems like it's so early for them. Yet—no—Extra and I used often to find them there, sometimes even in January. I do thank you.

I just happened to glance down—saw one first, then later the other one. I recalled that you said violets were your favorite flower.

Surely they are.

I presume these are the last violets which will grow in Andersonville. When prisoners are put inside, the place will be trampled flat.

But it's Anderson, Cousin Harry, not Andersonville. The station was named for Mr. John Anderson, of Savannah.

So I've heard. And the official designation of the new post is Camp Sumter. But you know how troops are, Miss Lucy: forever applying a special name to something or other. They call the depot village Anderson, but they term the stockade Andersonville, to distinguish it. . . . His rough voice sawed on, and Lucy turned the fragile violet stems between her thumb and finger, and considered how she and Rob Lamar had gone violet-picking three years ago. She could pick twice as fast as could Rob—he was always hearing birds about, always calling to his dog. But between the two of them they'd gathered so many violets that her one hand could not enclose the stems.

No longer did they speak of Rob Lamar, she and Cousin Harry. Elkins had known him barely, at college; he remembered going to a picnic party where Rob also was a guest. Just that one picnic, said Harry. I wasn't exactly what you might call a social butterfly. And medical books and lectures do require a power of concentration.

But apparently there had been time for him to apply that power of concentration to literature as well as to medicine. Cousin Harry could grasp and identify more quotations than either Lucy or Ira when they played their game. Thus far he was in the lead, with only nineteen Black Marks against his name on the torn sheet of gilt-lined notepaper they used as their scoring tab. Ira had twenty-six Black Marks, Lucy thirty-eight.

By the evening of Wednesday, February twenty-fourth, Harrell Elkins had left high-piled clods and blood-drenched claymores behind him. *She cannot fade, though thou hast not thy bliss, for ever wilt thou love, and she be fair!* This he spoke with enthusiasm. Ira Claffey found impish satisfaction in witnessing this slow fondness, grown obviously out of proximity and sentimental tragedy. Cousin Harry had announced that he must leave for Macon on the next day; his work was finished, his reports and recommendations needed amplification and resort to other advices at headquarters. Lucy received the news coolly; Ira observed her. She ate little at supper. When Pet took away her plate she mumbled in alarm, Miss Lucy, is you poorly?

I fear thy kisses, gentle maiden;
Thou needest not fear mine;

My spirit is too deeply laden
Ever to burden thine.

On this evening of Wednesday, February twenty-fourth (it was after nine o'clock), Elkins sprang up in the middle of Ira's deliberately wicked quotation of Shelley, crying, Beg pardon—looks like a fire! They joined him at the window: the entire valley to the north was colored brilliantly. The Biles' house was much farther beyond, the Yeoman house farther to the west, the McWhorters' farther to the east. Could the damp forest itself be burning, could the few sprawling houses of Anderson be alight?

In glow the three left the house and hurried west along the lane. Ira led sharply to the right on a footpath worked out by slaves going to and from the village. Years before, he had had his people build a crude bridge with a handrail across the little branch of Sweetwater and squashy ground surrounding it at this point. Looking ahead through the trees as they hastened, they could see that the newly carved-out road was become a sluice of ruddy light. It looked as if bonfires had been kindled for a gay homecoming (except that no one was coming home) or some such festivity (except that there was little to be gay about). Stumps, roots, branches, tops and needles: the debris of slain pines was heaped regularly to illuminate the road. These brush piles howled and crackled on high.

The snapping blazes revealed a train halted beside the Anderson depot; the train had been loaded with goblins, and several hundred goblins had trooped already from their box cars. Pine knots burned at intervals along the front and wispish lantern lights went scouting between ragged ranks, coming together again by twos and threes as if lightning bugs assembled for conference.

Next car, called a distant voice of authority. Count them as they come out, align them in ranks of fifty, two ranks deep, form them by Hundreds. Hold on! March those first eight men over here to complete this Hundred.

Many guards convened along the borders of the muddy road, and they were being ordered into position like posts of a loose fence stretching from fire to fire: one fire, three guards between like a short post and tall posts, next fire larger and farther away, five guards in between, next fire and three guards, more fires, more guards, the color of flames reflected as on splinters of broken looking glass by pine gum dry and icy on the stumps. Some of the guards had bayonets fixed to their weapons, others had not; there was a tingling gleam to the bayonets. Some of the guards wore blue and the blazes turned them to purple.

You men in this formation are First Squad, First Hundred. Repeat after me: First Squad, First Hundred. The ragged mumble following. You men in this formation are Second Squad, First Hundred. Repeat after me: Second Squad, First Hundred. Mumble, mumble in the manner of an extended groan. A thin mad voice soared, Hey, Johnny, how are the rations here?

Silence in the ranks! You men in this formation are Third Squad, First Hundred.

Something popped and burst in one of the fires, perhaps it was a bottle. Two guards approached the flames cautiously, they found nothing, they moved to their posts. You men in this formation are Second Squad, Second Hundred. Past trees and stumps the twin rows of blaze were spaced, curving slightly south, curving sharply north again all the way to the stockade.

Ira turned quickly at the sound of a familiar voice. In a cluster his black people were grouped—all of them seemed gathered, even Old Leander and the children. Yes, all: Pet held the sleeping Sukey wrapped in her arms. A reek of orange touched their polished dark faces.

Mastah, please, Mastah. We come. . . .

Feared something was afire, said Jonas.

Mastah, is them Yankees over by them cars?

Ira cleared his throat. Yes, Coffee, I believe they are.

Look just like folks.

Mighty poor white trash, said the skinny voice of one of the wenches. There was a shiver of laughter.

A hand slid into the grip of Ira's hand, it was Lucy's hand, it trembled. Beyond her Harrell Elkins said, It's well that I was delayed until now. I can look them over tomorrow before I leave, and gain some notion of their general physical condition. It might affect my recommendations.

Yes, Ira heard himself saying, it might. But these prisoners are not newly captured?

I was informed that they were to come from Richmond.

Then there will be a difference in the physical condition of these, and in the condition of those who are brought here shortly after their capture?

Bound to be, sir. It was an inclement winter at Richmond, with severe mortality among the Northern prisoners. . . . Reminded speedily of the dead Rob Lamar, and how Rob must be pinned in Lucy's thought at this moment, Elkins felt chagrined.

Would these guards be the same troops who've been assigned here lately?

Twenty-sixth Alabama and Fifty-fifth Georgia. Or rather—remnants of those regiments. But I'm told that they'll soon be sent to the front, and some of the new Georgia Reserve regiments will be stationed here in their stead.

Orders shouted alongside the depot . . . goblins began to move. They straggled in a column of twos, guards hovering. Squarely through the avenue of flames they advanced, fifty couples, more guards, another fifty stumbling couples, more guards, the next shambling Hundred in their grotesque wedding march, the next. They were dressed in every variety of rags afforded by their own uniforms at the time of capture, every variety of garment flung out from Sanitary Commission barrels at Belle Isle, every variety bartered for, stolen, traded for, ripped from the dead. Pancake caps, slouched hats, citizens' hats, no hats at all, hair of the hatless looked like wads of leaves in oaks where crows had nested. Blue jacket, undershirt, a man wrapped in a shawl, another Indian shape with a blanket folded around him, more blue jackets and flannel shirts. (The Claffeys did not see him, he did not see them, he did not know them, they would never know him; but a youth named Eben Dolliver walked in his crazy quilt.) Some carried cloth-wrapped bundles, a few wore knapsacks on their backs, there were haversacks and rolls of bedding slung across the shoulders in Confederate style, one man carried a carpetbag, there were skillets and buckets hanging. The more mature were grizzled wildly in their beards . . . dirty crusted faces of sixteen-year-olds were pinched and squeezed. Oh thank Heaven, cried Ira Claffey in his heart, that Moses was never captured. He might have looked like one of these, like one of these; he might have been marched to one of those evil places of which I've heard, Yankee prison pens, Rock Island or Johnson's Island or Point Lookout.

. . . But if he had been captured, instead of shot in Maryland, he might be alive still.

. . . Are these alive? Walking, it is true—parading now before our gaze—but are they The Quick? Might not this be a procession of The Dead?

Few sounds did they make, they coughed, there were hawkings of those with maladies of the throat; one man kept bending out to blow his nose between his fingers. God damn it, he cried impatiently but recognizably, now I've tooted myself into a nosebleed again.

Hush up, Yank. You heard the order. No talking!

In all there were six Hundreds, although the final Hundred did not move with its full complement. There came a burst of steam, froth of sparks from the railroad engine; it jerked forward with the line of empty box cars, heading for Albany and foodstuffs which must be loaded. Driving wheels shivered and spun with racking clatter; no voice of guard or prisoner could be heard against the engine's riot.

Distantly on the fiery boulevard Yankees seemed fumbling in indecision. There were delays outside the stockade gate, where names were being checked, rolls written out. Flames wavered, expunged them for a moment, brought the last batch into final glare and showed them for what they were: insects disturbed in a sandy channel, progressing sluggishly as their own larvae.

With the train's departure, Ira could hear his Negroes returning in an orderly drove across the branch. They were discussing the Yankees, and had been sadly disappointed in the Yankees' appearance.

Harrell Elkins said, Did I tell you there's still a broad gap on one side of the stockade? We've artillery mounted there.

Oh, Lucy cried, some may escape. They're such a desperate lot.

Never fear. A squad of guards remains on duty through every hour of the twenty-four, and will until the gap is closed.

The torchlight procession has passed, said Ira. He led the way back toward the plantation. He kept thinking, Why, they came too early! I had not expected prisoners so soon. Lucy and Cousin Harry followed slowly on the path, Cousin Harry helping Lucy in the dark. There was not such strong light now; fires were burning down. But a deepening glow could be seen from Claffey windows even after the three people had said Goodnight and had gone to their rooms.

13

At nineteen years of age Edward Blamey was a corporal in the First Rhode Island Cavalry, and had been a captive since he was dismounted near Chancellorsville when his horse broke its leg. Edward was somewhat the worse for wear after an autumn and winter at Belle Isle, but his practiced eye still rolled keenly. Blamey had remarkable eyesight, inherited from generations of fishermen who put out daily past Point Judith, although he did not incline toward the sea.

The first morning after he'd arrived at Camp Sumter, he mounted a wedge of pine-root and clay which lay like the bulb of a giant's onion tossed aside. This was at a point of vantage on the northern summit, a few rods from the north fence, and Edward Blamey had a clear view of the whole interior. Most of the men were at work, rigging shelters out of the forest's wreckage left by axemen, but some were sitting in apathy, too tired or ill or depressed to join in this general pioneering. Groups gathered opposite the breach in the wall, staring at a brass cannon which glared back with its blank black muzzle.

Blamey's ancestors, who awarded him such vision, had been accustomed to gauging the activities of birds on distant waters and thus discovering shoals of fish they sought. In the cavalry, men used to amuse themselves by saying, Ed, I hain't got my spy-glasses handy. What are those critters doing on that road down yonder? Are they Federals or Johnnies? Or maybe a herd of muley cows? Ed Blamey could examine the tiny moving figures, and report that they constituted a foraging party of four men, driving in some rather sorry beeves. This he could do with his naked gray eyes narrowed to telescopic power. His comrades used to lay wagers as to whether he was right or wrong, but usually he was right. In this way he formed a perpetual diversion for himself—measuring distances, estimating numbers, evaluating faraway activities of troops or wagon trains. Most men would have needed field-glasses to do this; and Blamey's developed skill helped to win him two wide stripes.

As a cavalryman he had been compact as to stature, a spruce figure in spite of violently bowed legs that folks made jokes about. The spruceness was long since departed: Blamey appeared as a dried bean or nut, rattling in the husk of his short jacket and patched sodden pants. The big patch on the seat had come loose and flapped and sagged, every step that Ed Blamey took. No one of the people with whom he messed had needle or thread to repair the damage, and it annoyed Edward's dignity to have his grimy buttocks exposed to the world. Here his search could be pursued more widely and, he hoped, successfully. That was his main reason for climbing upon the hillock of stump: he wished to estimate the number of prisoners assembled in this new stockade, and pick out a likely group where men seemed better dressed and better supplied than the average; such a group might include a man with a housewife in his possession. That was Ed's chief compulsion; but also he knew that he would have done it if he'd needed no patch at all—merely for the challenge, merely from habit.

He stood breakfasting on part of the cornmeal mush he had saved from yesterday's ration. It had weighed nearly two pounds—a sizeable chunk of cold mush, and he hadn't eaten it all, because his mess still had some boiled sweet potatoes they'd purchased on the railroad. Ed Blamey assorted days in his mind. This was Saturday the twenty-seventh. Well, folks said that the first shipment had arrived on the twenty-fourth—five hundred and ninety-one strong. Those represented the six hundred who had been told off and marched out of Belle Isle on St. Valentine's day . . . there were rumors that they were to be sent to the North for exchange, and many men not included in this detachment tried to flank out with them, and were struck or—if unduly persistent—punished in other ways. Men yelled after the departing gang, Hey, give The Girl I Left Behind Me a pretty valentine for me! . . . Five hundred and ninety-one, they had reached this place: nine either died of disease en route, or were shot by guards in trying to escape from the cars. Two more detachments of three hundred each came on the twenty-sixth, one of these being Edward Blamey's crowd. The Rebs didn't seem able to handle more than a few hundred at one swoop. There was such a jumble of box cars coming south and troop trains going north, that the two groups had arrived within a few hours of each other. Officers commanding the guards hurried wildly about at the station, cursing. They said that rations had not been made available for such numbers. Some of the new men would have to go hungry, and they did go hungry, but they were accustomed to going hungry.

There must be nearly twelve hundred prisoners now penned inside this place. It was nothing like so crowded as Belle Isle, and Edward felt relief about that. His glance roved the fence. Somewhere above fifteen acres was the area contained. Later he would pace the length of the walls and then he'd know exactly. Of course that creek took up space, and obviously men and teams had trampled the adjacent sides into a mire when they were building the prison. A certain amount of uninhabitable space must thus be deducted from the whole. Blamey watched the creek, and stiffened with disgust: some people were squatted down, there, doing their business. Fine business indeed—didn't they realize that that was the only source of drinking water in the entire place? Well, he couldn't whip the lot of them (his spirit was dry, selfish and quiet; but he was impelled by the small man's demand for assertion) or he'd have gone down there and tried it. Doubtless guards or prison officials would put a stop to that dirty habit soon.

He thought of the James River, boiling coldly past the side of the Belle Isle camp, rushing foamy brown among its rocks. This creek wasn't much. Suppose it ran dry?

Edward Blamey thought to select the family engaged in building the most efficient-looking and best-equipped shelter of the lot. Over there, black figures tussling and heaving: it was beyond the creek valley on the south hilltop, and they were actually setting tall poles in the ground, and roofing them with what shone like India rubber blankets, fairly new ones. Men as well supplied as those men must have needles, thread, all such things. Ed Blamey chewed the last of his solidified mush and spat out a stray piece of unground cob. He slid down through the red twist of roots to the ground.

He called himself Number One, in slang he had picked up after joining the cavalry (which he and many of his companions still called *calvary* as they had when they were children) and one reason why he was in fair shape now was that he looked after Number One with care. At Belle Isle he had jeered and thrown clods like the rest when a few turncoats yielded to the inducements of Rebel emissaries, and marched out of the camp to accept food, clothing and liberty as Confederate States' soldiers. Ed's grim small conscience would not have permitted such deviation on his own part; at least his nervousness regarding The Wrath To Come would not have permitted it. But within limitation of a prisoner's existence Edward Blamey was adept at finding the dryest corner of any shebang, the freshest chunk of pork, the least weevily meal, the warmest spot by a winter fireside. His common expression, when anyone else touched an article belonging to him, was, That's mine. Take care. That's mine. He was not admired as generous or entertaining; still he kept himself as clean as possible, he would share his scrap of blanket if someone else offered a share in a waterproof in return; he would do his share in any task, but only his share. Here's Number One's chunk of kindling, he'd say, and put it down for the fire; but it would have taken much persuasion for him to go out and seek kindling for one of the invalids. He was not loved, he was accepted.

(Edward's father was treasurer of the Baptist Church at home in Rhode Island, and neighbors thought or pretended to think that the elder Blamey found certain unmentionable perquisites in his office. This was untrue. Mr. Blamey's accounts could always be balanced to the penny, and he was fond of asserting that they could be.)

On the south hill of the prison pen, Edward encountered the busy batch of men he had observed from afar. Critically he paused to watch their activity. A fine cabin was being constructed by their united efforts. Slighter, weaker folks came lugging armloads of dry pine boughs for stuffing chinks, more powerful men were disrupting roots and stumps, dragging them into the outline of a primitive castle.

Dolan, you rat, said a deep vibrating voice. Blamey jumped to hear it.

Hey? What did you say, Willie?

Dolan, you rat, that main pole's not resting proper. Put it deeper, man—deeper. Make it stout.

Seated on a pile of blankets and overcoats, a mighty figure held his huge arms folded across his chest. His head was oversized, covered on top by scraggly ginger-colored hair, covered on the jowls and cheeks by a scrubby ginger-colored beard. His eyes rolled large and white. His arms were forest logs. My, my, said Ed Blamey in his thought, so he's here too. Mosby the Raider! At Belle Isle he and Mosby had been numbered in the same Hundred. The man's name actually was William Collins, and he had earned the appellation of Mosby the Raider through exertion of a piracy which might have caused the Confederate Mosby to shudder, and surely would have filled him with loathing. Willie Collins's philosophy was plain, abrupt: a weak man has no business in this place nor in any place where physical force may rule. An invalid should die and be an invalid no longer. A strong man should be strong to begin with, and should remain powerful. He cannot do that unless he feed and shelter himself. I shall feed and shelter myself at whatever expense of anguish by another. Is there a luxury, a dainty, a pair of handmade boots, a Shetland shawl to be had? These I shall have. Only a power greater than I can exert shall prevent me from having them.

Edward Blamey had first observed William Collins in the ice of December, in that week when many Belle Islanders limped on frozen feet, making the same sound which Edward remembered his three-year-old sister as making after she fell from a bag-swing and broke her arm: a steady high keening like a fiddle string consistently tortured by rosin and horse-hair. You heard it everywhere, it lived in the air, and on the earth where less heartened victims crouched, rocking their shoulders and striking at their feet, trying to thaw them. Through this sound came the blast of Willie Collins's rich voice saying, Take them off, God damn it, you heard me. He had found a fellow prisoner with feet the size of his own, and was forcing the prisoner to give up his shoes. It seemed that Collins's own shoes had disappeared during the night. The prisoner had huge feet but no other hugeness about him; he was a rack of bones, his right arm hung idle from an old wound. Collins twisted the prisoner's ear between thumb and finger, forcing the man to the ground. There he stood over him, threatening with the flat of his hand until the fellow untied his shoe-cords with his one good hand and kicked off the shoes. Edward and others stared glumly, but only one man tried to interfere. He was a sturdy Kentuckian whom they called Dark And Bloody. Dark And Bloody plunged suddenly toward the Irishman, caught hold of his arm and swung him around. Before he could deliver the blow he'd aimed, Willie's foot came up like a rock from a gunpowder blast and caught the Kentuckian squarely in the crotch. One man fainted at the sound of that scream. After Willie Collins had paraded away in his stolen shoes, people picked up the kicking figure from the ground and carried it, twisting and blubbering, to the hospital. Folks said that Dark And Bloody's testicles were mashed to a pulp and that the whole bottom part of his belly was turning blue. Dark And Bloody, indeed. Few people even thought of resisting Willie Collins after that. As would be bound to occur, he gathered round him a mob of gentry of his own persuasion: some were incompetents, mere chinless starvelings, but they were feists who might hamstring a bull while a bolder dog had him by the throat. Since dashing exploits of the partisan John Mosby were common lore in that year, Collins was called Mosby. The name stuck.

Loot was taken from all and sundry, either through open assault in daylight or by sneak thievery at night. Loot could be traded, sold to the guards in exchange for any comfort obtainable. Cash exchange, the exchange of barter: it mattered not what machinery was employed so long as stewpots bubbled and raw corn whiskey was delivered in jugs. The more venal among the guards tolerated William Collins and his gang because they were a source of knives, watches, scissors, needles, buttons and clothing no longer commonly to be procured in the South. Other guards looked upon Collins with disgust, and swore to shoot him at the first opportunity. At Belle Isle Willie never went near the boundary ditch in consequence. When a new prisoner had been selected as a victim for search and seizure, and he chanced to be a prisoner located near the ditch, Willie would send subordinates to do the job.

In one whistling icy evening, a henchman named Tomcat O'Connor was engaged in stripping the flannel shirt from a fifteen-year-old newcomer whom he had hammered into submission. The attack took place close to the north ditch and came under observation of an old guard whom folks called Father Time—a patriarchal mountaineer who never swore at the inmates when ordering them about, but who misquoted liberally from the Prophets instead. There was still light enough to see, although lamps were winking on in Richmond and Manchester. Father Time halted in his leisurely sentry's pace, took his unlit pipe out of his mouth, lifted his musket and took painstaking aim. The report of his gun jarred nearer groups, and sent people crawling away from their small fires. But Father Time wasn't shooting at random, as depraved guards sometimes did: he was shooting at Tomcat O'Connor and he was shooting to kill, and he did kill. Tomcat leaped high off the ground when the ball broke through his chest; his arms shot out to their fullest spread and he gave a loud gulp as he fell. The next sound was a roar of laughter from Willie Collins as he stood safely beside a crowded tent, half screened by his associates. Did you see that Tomcat? he hallooed, pealing again with glee. Did you see him? Faith, I thought he was trying to jump over the moon! Then, in a lower tone, Barney, do you get over there like a brisk kiddie and go through him, and fetch his clothes—soon twill be dark, and the guard can't see to shoot you well.

So Edward Blamey had chanced to be counted into Belle Isle in the same Hundred with this monster. Here at Camp Sumter or Andersonville or whatever they called the place, here, caged in a fresh stockade, Ed Blamey was dully grateful that he was no longer in dangerous proximity to an unprincipled force. . . . But he maintained a loathing respect for the giant just the same. Mosby certainly did look out for Number One in more than a fair way. You had to give him credit.

Willie sat in well-fed massiveness, boss and lord, the imperfect picture of a prisoner, the perfect figure of the New York City gangster which it was said that he had been all his life. Ed Blamey knew nothing of New York except that it was a noisy and bewildering place to travel through, and when he traveled through New York he had been cheated by a motherly old Scotswoman who offered the boys chocolate fudges to taste. Aren't these fine fudges, dearie? and I'm letting them go cheap: a shilling a box, and that's not much for fine sweeties, is it, now? Everybody tasted the crumbs she gave out, and she sold all the boxes she was carrying—twelve—as fast as the quarter-dollars could be handed to her. Then she disappeared in the crowd, saying she would be back soon with more sweeties. Edward Blamey was one of those who bought; but when the boys opened their treats they found that the boxes contained only bits of brick and shavings and no fudges at all. New York also was said to be the home of the Plug Uglies. Blamey rather supposed that Willie Collins had been a Plug Ugly.

For now Willie owned a plug hat, and it rested on his knee, that knee thewed as thickly as some men's trunks. He wore a long blouse of blue, a plaid waistcoat, and a woolen tippet was tied around his squat neck. A gold watch chain hung across his front, and he carried a pair of officer's gauntlets stuck into his belt, and in his pockets he had two slung-shots which he might wield simultaneously when the need arose: these weapons he called his Neddies.

Also he was said to own dirks, and rumor armed him with a pistol. He took from his pocket a green silk handkerchief and, unwinding it, produced a thick sandwich of biscuit and meat which he chewed up in three or four bites. Oh, thought Ed Blamey, that was beef. How I'd like to have—

In front of Willie's kingly gaze the gang labored. This was still the winter season and night winds could stab you. The residence in construction was half a cave and half a fort: when the stout stump was torn out by chains and oxen it had left a hole, and this hole was utilized shrewdly in the construction design. Walls formed of wood and earth, the cavity enlarged and deepened, the sheets of rubber, the portions of canvas shingled aloft. If he dwelt here until summer Willie would have a tent constructed, for air and coolness; now he wished to be snug. Three of the men fabricated a mud chimney, as he had ordered them to do. Several of the company were apes close to Mosby the Raider in size and threat; but he had taken the measure of each as their resentfulness or ambition dictated, and at last they served consistently—if with occasional rebellion—the cause of Willie's enrichment and their own.

His ponderous head turned, his glance identified the gawking Blamey, his finger crooked. Ha.

Blamey did not stir; he supposed that Willie must be summoning a man beyond him. He looked back, there was no one else close.

Ha. You in the cavalry jacket. It's you I'm beckoning to.

Blamey approached with reluctance.

Come near me, Rubber Legs. God, a man could put a beer barrel betwixt them. Are you not from Belle Isle? It's in my own Hundred you were.

Ed Blamey nodded and made a sound.

What want you here?

This patch on my pants. I thought—maybe one of your men would own a needle and thread.

Ah, your ass is ragged, and that's the truth. Ho there, Lipsky. He summoned an undersized black-bearded man with a devilish face and one blind eye.

Lipsky can see to sew, for he was a tailor in his time. Lipsky, fetch you your tools and stitch this gentleman where he needs to be stitched. He wagged his rough boulder of a head while Lipsky sulked off to delve into a ragged bundle.

Once he tried to come at me with a knife, and I rubbed my thumb in his eye. That should teach him, hey?

Yes, chattered Edward Blamey, it ought to.

Speaking of eyes, I must needs speak with you.

Lipsky, the former tailor, unclean even among those droves of unclean and building a private stench wherever he moved, came up and prepared to thread a needle. So I can't sew pantaloons when a customer is wearing them, he moaned.

Be taking them off, Rubber Legs.

Blamey had little wish to remove his trousers but he obeyed. He stood in a shred of under-drawers while Lipsky arranged himself on a hummock and bent to the job.

Rubber Legs, they say you've the ogles of a hawk. Weren't you the one, now, who was forever spying out what went on near Libby? Sure, the fire in November! Every man of us saw the flames and people on roof-tops a-watching, but it was you who could spy how many there were, and could tell of the women you saw amongst them. Ah, it's good to be blessed with a brace of ogles such as yours. It should teach Lipsky a trick or two, should it not? Lipsky, you dirty sheeney, it's only one eye you've got for your sewing now, and why did you ever attempt to open up Willie Collins? So he rambled on while the tailor stitched, while Ed Blamey stood shaking, while other ruffians appraised Blamey's masculinity and were rude in their evaluation of it. Mosby the Raider pulled a second sandwich from his pocket and sat munching. He did not offer to share, but Blamey would never have offered to share had that been his own sandwich. Mosby talked on with his large mouth full, and crumbs of biscuit flew out each time he opened his lips on certain words.

And a multitude of his words were incomprehensible to the bowlegged young Rhode Islander—the argot of organized brawling throngs in whose ranks Willie Collins had slugged since he was a child. Sure, and there was another fire after the New Year, near to Libby, and you were telling all that went on. . . . It's little more than a fortnight since the Union cavalry, bless their barking irons, tried to capture Richmond and got themselves anointed for it; and the Rebs were pitching about on their forts and fetching up new cannon, and it was every motion you could see when they looked like mice to the rest of us. Ah, what a fine pair of gagers you're a-wearing in your head. May God damn you, Lipsky, bestir yourself with the gentleman's pants! Now, which of you kiddies has made off with Willie's flask of bingo? Nickey help me, I'll tear the wattles off your skulls if you've drunk it! He kept grubbing around among overcoats on which he lolled, and finally he gave a grunt of satisfaction and his hand brought up a brown glass bottle filled with some sort of liquor. Collins smirked at Edward Blamey and drew out the stopper with his teeth. The guards call it pine-top. It cost me a bean, and it would burn the gob out of most men; but to Willie it's like the milk from his dear mother's tits.

He spoke as if he could remember his dear mother, but he could not. He was brought from Ireland when a boy, by a father who died of what Willie called barrel fever in a Fourth Ward slum, in 1845.

Lipsky finished sewing the patch. It looked like it would last as long as the rest of the garment. This was the best tailoring which had ever been the fortune of Ed Blamey. He mumbled thanks to Lipsky, but the wretched fellow gave only a glare of his one good eye and put away needle and thread. Ah, you dead-ogled sheeney, roared Collins as the tailor passed him. He threw out his great platter of a hand in an attempted slap, but Lipsky dodged away. Willie Collins laughed, slid the brown bottle into his pocket, and again crooked his finger at Edward. Come, Rubber Legs. I've business with you. What's your name?

Ed finished knotting the cord which held up his pants. He forced himself to step closer to the giant, fearing that the slap thrown at Lipsky might now be directed at him.

What's your name?

Blamey.

Is it Delaney you say? I've a friend—

No, sir. Blamey.

Don't go to sirring me, or I'll tear the velvet out of your head. Collins is the name, you addle cove—Willie Collins!

Yes—Willie.

When did you come from Belle?

Got here a yesterday.

What's your Hundred?

Second Squad, Eighth Hundred.

And where do you dwell? Where do you come from? You look like a joskin from the hayseeds to me! Delaney, harken to Willie Collins. I've use for a pair of gagers like your own.

In that moment Edward Blamey thought wildly that Collins must be planning to gouge the eyes out of his head; he would have stumbled in flight, but Collins's hand had clamped on his jacket. Collins dragged him closer and explained his plan. This stockade enclosed a large area, far larger than Belle Isle. It was difficult to tell what was going on at one end of the pen when you stood at the other. Blamey should serve as a scout, an observer. He could tell when new prisoners were coming in at the gate, and which of those new prisoners possessed blankets or bundles, and where they went to domicile themselves. From far distances Blamey might be able to see whether men pulled watches from their pockets to look at the time; he might know which prisoner held a jackknife in his hand, and which only a bit of stick. Cannily he might discover whether there were four men or fourteen gathered in a remote well-furnished shebang—whether the crowd was weak enough to be attacked, or strong enough to put up a dangerous defense. Ah, Willie would rather own eyes like Delaney's than the finest field-glass in the land!

It's on the best you'll be faring, along with these snafflers of mine. No more chicken shit, but fine sawney and stews, with a swig of pine-top to help it along. I've the best cooks in the land; you'll be my nose, man, my very nose! We're a jolly crew, a jolly crew, and so is Willie a jolly rabbit. You should hear the ditties I can sing. Ask any man from the Eighty-eighth Pennsylvania that I was captured along with. I've jumped a dozen bounties; and Willie Collins's pockets are lined forever, man, they're lined with beans. Ask any from the Seventy-second New York or the Hundred and Twenty-fifth New York or the Fourteenth Connecticut or the Hundred and Nineteenth Pennsylvania, for I've been in all of them; and they know my ditties. Should another man seek to take the brass from your pockets, you'll cry O Yes, O Yes, and my kiddies will be about you in a twinkling. And isn't that better than living on hog-fodder, and gadding the hoof? Sure, with me a fellow has everything he's needing except a ladybird.

Edward Blamey backed to the limit of his jacket's length and said No. It took courage for him to say this, but he did so through no conscious heroism. The peculiar mixture of promises, boasting and prophecy—the mingling of unfamiliar thieves' jargon with familiar slang of the army—left him puzzled and unnerved. His quick rejection of the offer was his father's rejection, Rhode Island's rejection, his elder brother's rejection, the rejection of the Baptist Church. The Wrath To Come was a flame kindled for robbers, adulterers, murderers, atheists; in time it would scorch Willie Collins and all like him. Ed Blamey did not wish to sizzle. The next instant he was jerked whirling, he was smacked by the bottom of Collins's shoe, he went through the air and landed on his face. Blamey got up and ran for his life. Blood began to ooze from a dozen small lacerations on his cheeks and forehead where tough roots had abraided him. Behind, he heard Mosby bellowing, I'll teach you to say No to Willie Collins! Edward Blamey fled to the north slope which now he knew he should never have left, and he promised himself that he would not go to the South Side again.

When he came puffing up to the site of the previous night's encampment, he found acquaintances at work constructing a shebang. He had no special friends among them, but they asked about his injuries. Fell down, he said. Was up on a stump and a root busted under me. Later he warned that the Belle Isle raiders were present in force, and that it would be well for all their crowd to be armed with clubs in case of an attack. Soon blood stopped running from Blamey's abrasions; they were not deep but painful. He went to the western edge of the stockade where the creek came in below the high fence. A young guard peered down to watch him as Edward Blamey bathed his face, but the guard did not offer to shoot nor did he order Ed away. Apparently there was no observance of a deadline here in this new place; and he mentioned it to his companions when he returned to do his share (no more than his share) in preparing shelter. No deadline? Just you wait, said a grim New Hampshireman, they'll have one.

Edward contributed his lone two-thirds of a louse-ridden blanket to the roofing of the shebang, he fetched boughs and poles for half an hour. Then he went searching for a cudgel with which to fend off possible raiders; he wanted a club heavy enough to drub a big man's head and make him feel it. Any greenish pine he found would be too awkward for convenience, and he roamed farther afield. Luck attended him when he discovered a dressed length of hardwood amid the litter on the ground. There was a rusty bolt or rivet hole discernible at the broken end; this seemed to be the handle of a spade or shovel which had been snapped when workmen were there. Blamey observed that the letter *C* had been scorched into this handle as if to mark it for identification. It was the tool he sought for a weapon of defense, and he started back to the new shebang in an emboldened mood.

During his search he had chanced upon a lone blue figure curled in a hollow and partly sheltered by roots. The first time he passed he did not bother to make further examination; that looked like a good place to sleep, and Edward Blamey supposed that the man was sleeping there—it was out of the wind. But as he circled the hole on his homeward trip he heard a wail and chattering. The figure moved, and there was the sound of weak retching. Edward paused and looked down. He could see foam on the man's mouth. Hi there, he said, out of some sense of Christian duty. He remembered his father reading about the Levite who passed by on the other side. The man did not move.

Hi, mister.

The curled-up man opened his eyes, they were glass, they saw nothing, the eyes fell shut again.

Want something?

A weak voice said, Catherine.

What say?

The fellow wore a short cavalry jacket very like Edward's own, but newer and cleaner; he could not have been long imprisoned, but was about to be Exchanged. That was what they'd called it on the Island—and probably in every other prison camp, North or South. When someone died the others were apt to term him as Exchanged. When someone was shot by a guard they called him Paroled.

Hi, mister. What's your name?

The eyes failed to open, but the fellow shook quickly in spasm, and more fluid issued from his mouth. Swarner, he said.

What name did you say? Warner?

Swarner. J—H—Swarner.

Where from?

Second New York Ccccavalry. He managed to stutter the last word loose, but it was an almighty effort for him to do it.

You sick?

No.

Yes, you be. It was contrary to Edward's habit, but again he considered his father's favorite Chapter about the Good Samaritan (the moral of this text was cited often but practiced seldom by Mr. Blamey). Also his encounter with Willie Collins had stirred Edward into a recognition of Virtue as opposed to Wickedness. He supposed that he must be virtuous in the sight of God, if it would cost him nothing. He got down into the hole and bent over the huddled Swarner. Want some water, mister? I could fetch some.

No.

I hain't got any rations. You want rations?

No. Ccccatherine.

His attempted ministering thus unsuccessful, Edward climbed back out of the depression and walked to his shebang. Found a sick feller up yonder, he said casually to the others, but they gave little attention. They had seen many sick, many dying, many dead. In the middle of the afternoon they drew rations, and the food seemed munificent: nearly a quart of uncooked cornmeal, half a pound of beef, and a spoonful of salt per man. Mess Two still had five sweet potatoes left as well, and under the leadership of the New Hampshire sergeant—a mason by trade—a furnace of mud and sticks had been constructed. Ed Blamey and his family fed well, and they babbled about the improvement over conditions at Belle Isle. However, Ed still imagined that New York cavalryman bent like an abandoned cruller in his hole. Before dusk he turned his steps in that direction again, drawn as much by curiosity as by saintly intent. He came back from the east faster than he went.

Fellers, that man's dead as mackerel.

What man? Man you saw?

Said his name was Swarner.

Well, what do we do about it? Ain't he got no friends?

There don't seem to be nobody about.

The New Hampshireman, whose name was Colony, went back with Ed Blamey; so did the brothers Wingate, when they heard that the dead man was from York State. They were from Troy. The four men stood around and looked at the curved stiffening morsel in the fairly new and fairly clean jacket.

Got a good coat on him, said the youngest Wingate. I could use a coat like that.

Take it, said Colony. He'll never need it more.

Si Wingate slid down into the hole and, with some struggling, removed the jacket from the corpse. He climbed out, shook the garment violently, and turned out each pocket in turn. There was nothing in any of them except a half-gnawed turnip and, in the breast pocket, a letter worn to dirty tissue, a letter without an envelope. It was written in pencil and the penciling was blurred from much handling. Tup Wingate held the paper up to the fading light and spelled out a few words.

Seems to be from his sister, for she calls him Beloved Brother. Her name is Catherine. Hain't no address that I can see.

Take care with that coat, said Sergeant Colony darkly. Maybe he's dead of a plague.

No, looky there. He ain't broke out in any way.

He's too nigh to us for comfort, and if we leave him laying here he'll stink. Get a hold on him and we'll fetch him over to that nearest gate.

They went, carrying Swarner gingerly by his cold hands and rag-wrapped feet. As they approached the gate the adjacent guards called down a question from their sentry shacks.

He ain't from our mess. Don't know where he's from. We just come acrost him in a hole.

Well, Yank, put him next the gate. Somebody'll tote him out, the next time the gate's open.

They did as instructed and turned away through windy gloom. Then Edward Blamey owned an idea. He had a pencil in his pocket. Give me that there letter of his, Wingate, and the York State man handed it over. Blamey held the letter spread against a flat chip, and across the fading text he printed in big black capitals: *J. H. Swarner, 2 N Y Cavalry.* He returned to the gate and stuffed the paper beneath the ragged trouser-band of the corpse where someone would be apt to see it. It was odd, but again it seemed that he could hear that weak stutter of, Ccccatherine.

The others were waiting silently, and they all walked back to their new shebang together. Scratches and cuts on Blamey's face were stiff and puffing; his entire face felt as if it were on fire. He wished that he were older and hairier, he wished that he had more beard than this dirty mouse-colored down which he still wore at nineteen. A beard would have protected his skin somewhat when Collins kicked him to the ground.

I wonder if he's the first to die in here? said Tup Wingate.

Colony said, Won't be the last, I'll warrant you that.

Next fellow dies, I trust he has some socks, said Si Wingate. I got great need of socks. This here jacket is a good fit.

Colony spoke again lugubriously. Won't be the last.

Oh, come now, Sarge. We victualed well today. This puts Belle Isle in the shade.

Ed Blamey walked in silence, feeling the hurt of his torn face, but feeling also immeasurably noble as compared to an ogre like Willie Collins. Once back in Rhode Island he would be bound to tell his father that he had assumed the role of Good Samaritan, or at least had tried to.

Won't be the last, repeated that dreary clipped voice.

14

Captain Oxford Puckett was in bed with the Widow Tebbs that evening when Floral answered their hallooing and stood outside the door of The Crib and responded with, Huh?

The widow said, Flory, Captain Ox has got a bottle of sorghum liquor in his saddle bag. Please to go fetch it.

Ox Puckett called out genially, I'll give you five cents.

Secesh, thought Floral resentfully. Can't buy much with that. Can't buy scarcely nothing. Nevertheless he ran off on the errand—running because he was a nervous child and liked to move rapidly, and could move rapidly now that his sore foot was healed. Also he knew that it filled his elder brother Coral with furious envy to see him loping. The feud between them was blind, unreasoning, intense, a feud almost to the death.

Oxford Puckett had known Mag Lumpkin from her infancy; he could remember her mother when she was large with child and the child was Mag. As a butcher's boy he had delivered meat to the Lumpkins. His father was the butcher, a savage hulk who kept a strip of tanned hide cut neatly into the shape of a paddle for the express purpose of beating his sons for trivial offenses. As fast as they grew tall enough the sons ran away from home; Oxford was the third to flee. He ran away to the army, and later served heroically in the campaign of invasion against Mexico City; he was given a sergeant's stripes in the field. After that the army was his life periodically, although he turned an unsuccessful hand at farming, butchering and harness-making between enlistments. He drank a great deal, but no one ever saw him when he could be described as drunk. He was a jovial round-shouldered little man, capable of extreme lewdness. Ox Puckett boasted calmly that he had practiced every sin in the decalogue of sexual crime at one time or another (he could not have employed such phraseology, however, in describing his wickedness, since he was poorly educated and had a limited vocabulary). Now in young middle age his silky beard and silkier hair were almost snow-white; his pale blue eyes shone like bits of bottle glass from a lined face the color of an old saddle. The beard concealed a chuckling sensual mouth and made him appear like some patriarch of religious pursuits. He had served wherever the Fifty-fifth Georgia served. His wiry abused body was marked with wounds received in two wars and also in brawls.

The captain and the woman lay resting. Mag giggled as she explored his scars with her loose hands.

Ow, lady.

Hurt you, honey? I'm sorry.

Got that from some damn Yankee at Cumberland Gap, and it was right slow to heal.

Ox, what's this here blue one down here next to your cock?

That's old. Got that at Chapultepec. Like to shot my manhood clean away.

Few's got more manhood than you, Ox Puckett. Well I know.

Reckon you ought to know if anybody does. How many men you reckon you've lain with, Mag, sweet?

Oh, I couldn't never calculate. You know I hain't got no head for figures and such. Maybe a hundred different ones in the course of a year . . . that was before the war. I guess so, honey. I've had a sight of folks a-loving me in my time.

Well, I'm a-going to love you again, right now.

Wait till Flory gets back with your liquor. I'd like a taste myself, if you'd be so kind; hain't swallowed a drop all week.

It's not much slouch of a drink. My, my, how I'd relish a canteen full of *mescal!* That'll put the Old Scratch in any man's breeches.

What did you call it, honey lamb?

Mescal. What folks drink down Mexico way. They make it out of cactus, so they say.

We got right smart of cactus here on my place.

Reckon it's a special kind they use. But this here other stuff— The boys over to the stockade call it pine-top. Sutler who sells it claims he puts a fresh rattlesnake head in every barrel, and it does taste like it, sure enough.

Flory returned with the bottle he'd found in Captain Ox's saddle bag, and tapped at the door.

Oh, hell. You'll have to go let him in, Mag.

Door hain't bolted. Fetch the bottle in, Flory.

There was no especial novelty in Flory's seeing his mother in bed with a man. He had seen her so ever since he could remember. As a very small child he had hidden in an empty barrel in The Crib, in order to peep out at operations carried on there. His mother saw the barrel head lifting and lowering; she caught him, and gave him a thrashing with the belt belonging to her customer of the moment. But in later pursuit of her vocation Mag became less sensitive to the scrutiny of watching eyes. Her daughter she would not permit to enter The Crib; some peculiar warped sense of delicacy kept her from allowing another female to observe her there; but both Coral and Floral had fetched and carried everything from peaches to firewood, more times than they could count. Sometimes the callers gave them gratuities, sometimes not.

Captain Puckett said, That's a good boy, bubby. Reach me my pants from yonder chair. When Flory brought the garment, the captain rolled over in bed and got out his purse. He extracted a good hard round Federal half-dime.

Godsakes, thank you, mister, said Flory.

You got some real live greenbacks in there, cried Mag.

No lie about that. Took exactly eleven dollars and sixty-three cents off of a Yankee this very day; and one of them green dollars is for you, Mag. What say you to that, hey?

Well, to tell the truth, Ox, I was suspecting you'd maybe give me a Yankee dollar. Or at least ten dollars Confed. It's so hard to get along nowadays; and since Coral come back from the fighting that makes another mouth to feed.

What I mean, lady, it's an *extra* dollar, all for you. Kind of a wedding present, on account of I'm happy to see you again.

You mean you'll give me two greenbacks?

Sure as hell don't mean nothing else.

Ox, you surely are a lamb. They don't come no better-natured than you.

Right now I feel like a red-hot lamb filled with hellfire. Christ, this pine-top hain't so bad! *Vamoose,* you small fry.

Flory said, Captain, sir?

Vamoose. It's foreign talk—it means to get to hell out of here. Same as *puk-a-chee.* But that's Sioux Injun talk.

Flory ran out into a dusk which grew colder by the minute. He hesitated wildly, swinging this way and that. At the house he had a piece of blanket which he wore tied across his shoulders for a coat— With this sudden chill in the air he'd like to have his blanket— But Laurel was at the house, and she'd ask him where he was bound, and she'd want to know where he got the money to spend at the village store, and she'd beg candy from him— Well, he might give her part of a stick— Coral he would never give a bite to, but of course Coral didn't like candy; all Coral wanted to do was snarl and curse, and clean that old shotgun, and tote it around in the fields as he staggered with his crutch—

His mind made up, Floral headed for the Anderson depot, coatless. There was one store in the place, consisting of a miserable collection of junk hawked to the public by a dirty old man named Uncle Arch Yeoman, no relation to the Yeomans who owned the sawmill. In other seasons Uncle Arch would have shut up shop long before this hour, but with the coming of two regiments or parts of two regiments on duty at the stockade he kept his door open until late at night. Uncle Arch was a reformed drunkard, a fanatical railer against The Curse of Drink, and he refused to peddle that commodity much desired by soldiers; but he kept candy, a few spices, grain coffee, vinegar, and a scanty supply of medicines. The troops visited his store frequently when off duty, so Floral Tebbs would not have to wait until tomorrow for his treat.

Floral had the candy associated with his mother in his mind. He could not read or write and could barely count; therefore the spelling meant nothing to him, and there was no difference in the sound. Horehound candy—he liked it better than peppermint or cinnamon sticks, or the wintergreen lozenges fed him by the Reverend Cato Dillard. Horehound candy . . . people said that his mother was a whore, he had heard the word applied to her often; he had heard coarsest conversation on the subject. The squared brown sticks, with a splintery dust of sugar on the outside . . . he thought of his mother whenever he rolled dissolving fragments in his mouth or, more frequently, when he hung about the store with not a penny in his clothes and could only glare worshipfully at the fly-specked jar where this delight was sealed.

He trotted down the railway track. At one point a portion of the distant stockade's interior was visible by day, and Floral halted in dimness to peer across the ravine . . . fires, little freckled winkings and glowings: that was all he could see now. He ran on. Lanterns hung high in Uncle Arch Yeoman's store, and soldiers lounged within the door or against the counters. Most of the soldiers seemed almighty old and tall to Flory, but some few of them were near to his own age . . . they always swaggered disdainfully when they knew that he was regarding them. In these few weeks since hordes of troops had camped down in the woods Flory had learned to avoid them except in some public place, such as the store, where the presence of grown men granted him a certain security from persecution.

He wormed his way through the gossiping crowd and confronted Uncle Arch across the counter where tobacco and candy were kept.

Well, what you want, Flory?

Five cents worth.

Horehound, same as usual? Five cents won't get you much. Maybe a teeny little hunk.

Floral opened his grubby hand and displayed the five-cent piece. Yankee money.

. . . Them Reserve regiments, a voice was saying behind him.

Flory, that's hard money for a fact. Uncle Arch began to rig a small poke of soiled newspaper, and he fumbled on the shelf for the sacred jar.

. . . Robbing the cradle and the grave, too.

. . . If'n Joe Brown comes around to rob *my* cradle back home. . . .

Uncle Arch's palsied hand dragged a few sticks of candy from the jar, and he began to crumple the poke.

More! demanded Floral. You give me that much for three cents tother time.

Times is hard hereabouts, Flory; prices have risen up. Well, reckon I can let you have one more little stick.

. . . Do tell. A man of seventy-seven? Pretty regiment that one will be.

. . . Georgia Reserves! Ought to call them *Pre*serves. Laughter.

Here you be, Flory. How's that wicked old whorehound, your Ma? Whorehounding about, same as ever, I reckon?

She's fine, said Floral, and began to burrow out of the store.

. . . And boys as young as thirteen, tis told.

. . . Sure enough. I knowed one that wasn't but twelve, and they took him.

. . . Drummer boy.

. . . No, sir, private soldier.

Floral Tebbs halted, bare feet frozen against the planks. For a few minutes he forgot even the treasure of brown sticks gripped in the newspaper bag. He had turned, he squatted down, he was listening, he wished he had a dozen ears. At last, when talk strayed to another topic, he slunk out into darkness. Now the sky was black, deadened by clouds; it was difficult to see the way until he reached the railroad. Then he ran on the rails, for they were scrubbed by wheels, they could be seen on even such a night. Floral ran lightly. Usually in this sport he was counting the number of paces he could take on a rail before losing his balance and needing to step to the ties; this night he did not count. The conversation of Uncle Arch's store roared back at him from raw fields, from pines and vines and roadway; he heard it all again; he battened on it. Not until he was halfway home did he open the paper and wedge candy into his mouth until he could scarcely move his jaws.

At the Tebbs house little Zoral, the baby, had whined himself to sleep in the bedroom; Zoral had been howling about something or other when Flory first left the place in response to the summons from The Crib. Coral crouched by the fireplace, popping corn in a skillet; it was his favorite evening occupation, but seldom would he share his corn with the rest, never with Floral. The sister, Laurel, was trying to stitch up a rent in her petticoat by light of a feeble rag lamp. She was a listless child of fifteen with a pinched sharp-featured face and eyes like a mink's. She ate clay continually in secret, though her mother tried to break her of the habit by frequent lashings of tongue and willow whip. Laurel's coarse carroty hair, untidy as it was, became a singular beauty in the dull glow of the primitive lamp.

What you got there, Flory? What you eating at?

Horehound.

Whereabouts you get it?

Uncle Arch's.

Whereabouts you get any money?

Captain Ox done give it to me for being valuable to him.

Coral said, Get some wood.

I ain't no nigger of your'n.

God damn it, tonight's your turn! I fetched it last night. Wish to God you had to tote wood on one leg like I got to.

Yes, said Laurel, tis your turn, Flory. Go get some wood like a good boy.

Well. . . . Generously he offered an entire stick of the brown candy to his sister, and she crushed it with her little teeth in rapture.

Reckon, said Flory, speaking casually from the doorway— Reckon I'll be going for a soldier.

Reckon you'll shit, said his brother.

Coral, you forget I'm a lady! came Laurel's thin moan. Ma won't tolerate no such talk from you. She'll give you a whipping if'n I tell her, crutch or no crutch. What makes you think they'd take you for a soldier, Flory?

Hope to shout they would. I heard them soldiers a-telling of it. Down to Uncle Arch's just now. Said they had them new regiments name of Georgia Reserves, and they'll take any number of boys my size. So I reckon I'll go.

Well, you get that wood first, dad blast you, cried Coral.

Intoxicated by notions of military accomplishment, Flory obeyed. He would not have responded to a just and deserved summons at any other time, but he was entranced by the thought that soon he might be marching and fighting in gray. No longer a child, no longer creeping in the guise of an outcast from even a portion of his own family. . . . Soldiers owned money. They must own it, else how could so many of them visit Flory's mother? She did not give her female valuables away: she sold them. (Had Floral but known it, he was contrived from a gift. His father had tried to sell Dr. Krieder's Ague Pills to Mrs. Dickwood Tebbs; his father had failed in the attempt simply because Mrs. Tebbs had no cash with which to buy pills, and said that she would rely on soot coffee, as most people did, for the ague. But she liked the blond limber-tongued young ignoramus who came soliciting her. He offered also a panacea for looseness of the bowels which he called Mother Felch's Blackberry Balm. . . . Blackberry?—repeated the woman. We got a sight of blackberries in our lane. Come nighttime I like to have myself a little stroll, and nibble at them blackberries. . . . Reckon you'll be strolling amongst them blackberries tonight? . . . Could be, mister. . . . She strolled, he was waiting, they rolled in illicit rapture. The salesman went drifting away with satchel and pack, with glib speech and limited jokes; he left the ripe seed which was Floral within her body.)

Flory had heard soldiers speak of chicken-guts. In time he'd have chicken-guts upon his sleeves.

Old pistols? No. A navy revolver, captivated off of the Yanks.

A horse. He'd never ridden a horse, but— He'd ridden a lame mule when they owned one. A horse—

We jumped them Yankees nigh side of the stream. They was shooting our asses off. I got turkey bumps all over my blame body.

Right oblique—hah!

Pre-sent—hah?

Rear, open order—hah!

Would they actually pay him eleven dollars a month? Even Secesh?

Flory brought in the wood, he brought in three armloads of wood. I declare to God, said his brother.

Floral Tebbs felt his way in darkness to the remains of the stable—half of the roof still hung there, but badly supported—and found that Captain Oxford Puckett's mule still chewed at old corn-shucks. Quietly Flory crept to the doorstep of The Crib. He hunched, entertaining fancies. At the house he'd gathered his section of blanket, he'd twisted the rag around him, it gave him as much warmth as he needed. The entrance to The Crib was on the south side and out of the wind. From within came muffled exclamations, the grunting of weight on bed-ropes, a faint light through cracks, and suddenly the caroling of the old music box. The instrument played well despite the grim treatment it had suffered. It had been kicked and dropped, ignored, wound up hour after hour, not oiled for years, oiled too lavishly and with the wrong sort of oil. The spiny cylinder turned slowly, and some of the spines were worn or broken away, but tunes had an elfin tinkle about them despite gaps and cluckings.

Inside the building, Captain Ox Puckett spoke loudly as if come to a sudden decision. Ma'am, you got all the smart out of my marbles. Reckon I'll head for that blame camp.

We drunk all the pine-top, honey?

Sure enough.

Oh, I do hope you come back to see me again.

Surely will, when the spirit starts a-working. Here's them two greenbacks, and I wish they was more, but also I got to live. Hain't many Yanks come in with cash in hand; the bulk is from Danville or Belle Isle, up Virginia way, and they got cleaned long ago.

Ox, bless you, I do love that extra greenback.

Fitten you should have it.

Floral listened to Captain Puckett getting into his clothes and stamping in his boots. Prompted by a vague shame, Floral arose and walked to a respectable distance. He stood, palpitating with illusions, until the door of The Crib opened and Puckett was revealed with the shine of candlelight on white beard and hair. He was creasing his old slouched hat, smoothing out the brim preparatory to wearing the hat.

Captain, sir, said Flory.

Ox Puckett squinted into the gloom. Sakes, Flory, is that you?

I want you should tell me something.

Come here to the door, you Flory.

The Widow Tebbs appeared behind the man, pulling a ragged beribboned wrapper around her. Flory, child, you ought to be abed.

It hain't late. Captain, I was scheming to go for a soldier.

Puckett laughed shrilly. God, you got the milk still wet on your mouth, bubby.

But I was down to Uncle Arch's and I heard them soldiers a-talking. They call it the Georgia Reserves; and tis said they'll take folks my size.

Ox Puckett said judiciously, Well, I know of four regiments of Reserves they're planning to muster, and maybe there's many more. But that hain't no life for a soldier: the lame and halt and blind. Course, you're just a mere child.

The widow cried, He hain't but twelve.

That's a no count lie, yelled Flory. You know well enough I'm growed to thirteen, nigh onto fourteen.

Looky here, Ox, said Mag fervently. What befell my eldest? Skun away to the army when he weren't more than fifteen, and now he's got to hop on a crutch for the rest of his days.

The bearded captain turned, leaned toward her, whispered something. Floral could not hear what he said.

Do tell? Just guard duty?

The captain whispered again.

And they do get paid?

Oh, like all armies. When and if.

But they get their provender?

Field rations. Keep soul and body in the same piece.

Floral stood ragged and wispy, barely within the vague spot of light which fell from the open door. With that cape of blanket hooded over his close-cropped head and around his weak shoulders it was hard to tell whether he was boy or girl. He was all of five feet tall. My, said his mother, Government must be hard up for soldiers if they'd take Flory.

Captain Ox Puckett fastened his belt buckle. You give forth a mouthful, lady. Where's the flower of the South? It got scythed down. We won't never have the Nation we had before. But if ever we're to whip them Yanks, the boys and old folks got to help. Take my regiment or take them Alabama troops alongside us, measly as they be: we got experience in the field. We could be used in the field. Even a younger size of Flory could stand up on that parapet over yonder and keep an eye on them prisoners so's they wouldn't bust loose.

Well, I never.

You hear that, Ma? cried Flory in delight.

Yah, yah, yah, I heard. Now you cut for bed.

Captain Ox, please, sir. Do you know any generals?

Puckett put his heels together. Bubby, you can't serve in two wars and not know some generals. More'n once I've stood as close to General Lee as I'm standing to you. And once I fit along of One-eyed Jeff when you couldn't tell beans from musket balls count of the powder smoke.

One-eyed Jeff?

President Jefferson Davis, if you like. Twas in Mexico.

Captain Ox, please, reckon you might fix it up for me to get in the army?

Just in them Georgia Reserves, Flory.

But ain't they going to be a army?

Oh, kind of. Hell, I weren't much bigger'n you when first I went hunting for a yard of skirmish line.

Well, I never, said the Widow Tebbs. Flory, you cut for bed like I bid you.

Flory cut. Half the night he shivered restlessly beside the snoring half-brother who hated him, and whom he hated. His thin brain rattled with shots, bugle calls, orders, cannon rumblings, stirrup squeakings, the clangor of bayonets. By God, he thought in a last succumbing to weariness, I might even get to shoot a Yankee. . . . *Poom.*

15

In one of his several military capacities (in this case in the role of provost-marshal at Richmond) John Winder had spent most of the morning in preparation for the calling of a court martial and of inquiry. Also he had assailed verbally, with bellowing heard through four flimsy partitions, heard with fright by the five men and two women who waited his whim in the barren reception hall— He had assailed a Goochland County planter whose crime was not that of proven disloyalty but of anti-Secession sentiment uttered in his own neighborhood some three years before. The fact that the planter had since lost a son and a son-in-law at Cedar Mountain, and had had another Confederate soldier son crippled in a skirmish just before Second Manassas, did not serve as extenuation for his previous sin—not in General Winder's opinion.

Denied recourse to any code of chivalry, the unhappy Virginian was compelled to stand like a criminal before the desk of a Marylander and hear himself likened to spies, hirelings, Abolitionists, nigger-lovers, Lovejoys, Butlers and Thaddeus Stevenses, each epithet hurled with its dressing of profanity. The egg-smell of sulphur was in the air of that office and of adjacent corridors. The planter stumbled out, hurt and maddened, fortunate at not being ordered into prison for the evil he had committed: requesting a pass through the lines for a sister who was married to a Pennsylvanian and had long sought to leave the Confederacy and join her sickly elderly husband at the North.

Old J.H.W. is raring, whispered a one-legged corporal to a palsied sergeant.

Lordy, yes. You got those letters of appointment and assembly duly copied?

Right here, but I don't want to put my head through that door.

Better wait till he's calmed, Joey.

If ever!

John Winder was in no hurry for the letters of appointment and assembly. He had formed a habit through his sixty-four years of life; he preferred to sit brooding silently on whatever foul nest he'd constructed with the beak and claws of his hatred. He would warm those tough little orbs of wrath, let them hatch logical fledglings when again his rage needed reinforcement. He sat nearly motionless, glowering at the present, resentful of the future, distasteful of the past. His untidy gray hair dripped in strings below fat crooked ears, there were ink stains and stains of age upon his fat crooked fingers, the scars of consistent bitterness came down between his bulging eyes. The scar where Amos the slave had wounded him with a razor last October— It was whitely apparent on the pulp around his compressed mouth.

He had witnessed his own red blood turning to black in the year of 1814, when he was fourteen. The blood had been black ever since; he knew it, waking or sleeping; he felt it moving like pitch through the veins tangled throughout his big body. When his skin was pierced and blood ran, John Winder was invariably surprised to observe its crimson, for truly it was acrid black, he must be color blind—the world must be color blind not to know—his blood had been black since that day on the oyster bar in Somerset County not far from Rewston where John Winder was born.

What my father said, said Gay Chastain.

That old Winder was a coward? asked Freddy Darlington.

Father said he should be shot because he let the British take Washington.

Freddy was nigh to sixteen in age and nigh to eighteen in size, Gay Chastain was even heavier and more dangerous if not so old; what might Johnny Winder do about this? Not one thing. What could he do? Nothing. The slur was there, the tale of his father's inefficiency (at the best) or demoralization (considered possible in less charitable opinion) or downright cowardice and resulting deeds which named him as a traitor. It should not happen to you at fourteen, to have your father named as a traitor because he was held responsible for losing the fight at Bladensburg. It should not happen to you, it should not happen to a dog, not to the meanest slave in the parish, not to the most sluggish oyster crab, not to the wounded oyster eaten by the crab.

Johnny Winder stood rooted to the muddy bar, hammer in one hand, bucket in the other. It had all begun as a lark. He was glad that these elder youths had invited him to come oystering with them, for a lark like this might help him to forget the whispered odium newly attached to his father's name. They had fetched crab-cakes and biscuits, they had filched Tipsy Squire pudding from a suspicious brown tyrant who presided over the Chastain kitchen and larder, they had ridden far in their cart, had prided themselves on the size of the oysters they would break loose in a secret cove.

But in this moment wine was gone from the strong cool wind, ragged waves of tidewater bit like rats at John Winder's wet boots. He stood behind the shoreline thicket and heard his playmates turning themselves into torturers because they repeated some common gossip, and thought that John was fifty rods to the windward instead of prowling that same shaggy bar.

Attack them with his oyster knife, with his hammer? No, they owned similar weapons, they were bigger than he, they were two. Run home, fetch his double-barreled pistol, lie behind the oak at Five Corners, shoot them down as they drove past on the homeward trip (and probably wondering what had become of John even as the round bullets flew through their young bodies)? One could not shoot down the entire county, not shoot down the Nation, all the States. (Or could one? Later he pondered. Ardently John Henry Winder welcomed the advance of Secession forty-six years later, even before his commission as a major in the Regular establishment had been signed.)

Nothing could be as black, nothing had ever been blacker . . . mud in empty shells, old housings of dead oysters, the mud was squeezed into ink, almost it dyed the wet skin when it touched the skin. He looked down through the smart of tears and saw cold jet dripping from his fingertips . . . jet, jet, his blood had turned, oh watch it dripping.

Somewhere between that awful island and the wilderness of low mainland John Winder dropped his oyster bucket with its carefully selected freight, and so the bucket must have been buried beneath Chesapeake tides later. But still he gripped his hammer; he found the small boat which belonged to Fred Darlington and which they'd used for many an expedition, and he burst the boat's ribs, mauling away in blind fury; it seemed that he owned the bull strength of the most powerful blacksmith. He found Nap the pony tethered at a fence corner where they'd left him, and Nap belonged to Johnny Winder although the cart didn't. He unharnessed Nap, he rode him home bareback, he left the others to guess, to grieve over the ruined boat, to walk all the way to the nearest plantation and borrow a nag to draw their deserted vehicle.

They sought John Winder later for questioning, they demanded that he give an account of himself, that he pay for the boat, that he apologize. Eventually he drew out his penknife. The Chastain youth gave him a thrashing and threw the knife into the inlet nearby. John Winder went home to load his pistol—his father found him, loading the pistol. He was reprimanded, threatened with the lash, exhorted to manly conduct, informed that an eventual court of inquiry would most certainly exonerate his father when those orders issued to his father by General Armstrong came to light. This prophecy was correct. General William Henry Winder was acquitted in the spring of 1815; he was reassigned to his command, but resigned promptly.

When John was a cadet at the Point three or four years later, he thought of that silly double-barreled pistol, and how he'd intended to take the lives of young Darlington and young Chastain because of their slurs; he thought of it when his father expressed to him a copy of the *Trials of the Mail Robbers, Hare, Alexander and Hare,* published in Baltimore with his father's pleas in behalf of the accused presented verbatim. *What is the* use *of dangerous weapons which can occasion* jeopardy *of life? . . . The use of dangerous weapons, to produce* fear of life *may be very different from the* use *of dangerous weapons, to put life in* jeopardy. . . . But certainly he, Johnny Winder, had intended to slay his quondam friends and thus get himself hanged triumphantly; he had not intended merely to frighten them. Ah, he would have accomplished his purpose if not restrained, for already his blood was black (he thought of the paint of oyster muck running down his hands) and it was a secret, naturally; but still it was odd that all might not see and understand.

Florida, Contreras, Churubusco, Mexico City. Consistently he exposed himself through those old campaigns. Twice came the brevets—once as major, once as lieutenant-colonel. No medals were offered, the brevet was sole recognition for a man who'd nerved himself to suicide when he was fourteen and had never recovered from the nerving. The National government became a composite demon. It was like the demons who beset an uncomfortable childhood . . . composed of moonlight, sycamore shade, mists, the shade of other trees, the distant thin light of stray stars which vied with the moon. Amid tangles of garden or driveway John Winder had glimpsed demons when he was small; they attended him, labeled Federal Government or National Interest, through a military career which covered forty-odd years (if a man subtracted the four years he'd spent as a resigned lieutenant, and added the years when he was a cadet).

Federal Government. Ogre. Tarred his father, pilloried him before the public gaze, drove the son into a studied heroism amid powder smoke when he would have been happier in flight, turned the son's blood to black.

John Winder had desired that children should be trained to scorn the National government as he scorned it, to loathe the Yankees as he loathed them, to crush all supporters of that Faith as one would snap the shell of a cockroach with his boot sole and feel the shell pop, feel gush and squirting, find happiness in the smear made so.

. . . His aide tiptoed into the office, making himself appear as insignificant as possible. This was not difficult since the aide was an insignificant man to begin with. Winder found a bully's satisfaction in towering beside insignificance.

Where is the list of officers eligible for the court martial and of inquiry?

The aide came hastening to lift a paperweight in the shape of a pink cat with two paws broken off. Once General Winder, in ordinary temper, had thrown that paperweight through a windowpane. Clerks scrambled into the street to recover it; the paws had been glued back but they would not stick for long.

Here is the list, sir.

What of the letters of appointment and assembly?

All copied, sir. I'll have them fetched—

Never mind now. I want the classification of charges!

I'll fetch it, sir.

Well, God damn it, hurry up! He had brooded on eggs of anger, they were ready to hatch, he could feel them cracking under the weight of his broad stagnant bottom.

Court would convene, a heart or two might be broken (that would be fair, if many hearts were mashed), the details relating to proceedings and sentences would be written up, the long confinement would commence. Let newspapers say what they would of him. He cared nothing for newspapers.

When, a furious editorial writer had demanded lately, will Richmond ever be rid of Old Winder?

Let them scream, spread their type, let them print, foam, froth, weep, clench their fists, gnash futile teeth.

He sat at the table of the President, he sat there frequently. John Winder might not be the most popular officer to enter the bar at the Spotswood Hotel, he might not be regarded too affectionately by fellow Episcopalians, meeowings might sound behind him in the street if there were a safe crowd about; but he wondered often if there was another brigadier who had the ear and unalterable patronage of Mr. Seddon and Mr. Davis as he held them. He knew that there was none. His curiosity on the subject was perfunctory, a judicious exploration of other political intrigue observed by him, resulting always in the fatuous knowledge that his position would not be changed until he desired it to be changed.

Brigadier-general, commander of the Department of Henrico, inspector-general of camps in the Richmond area, Supervisor of Prisons, provost-marshal-general of Richmond . . . in time, perhaps, Commissary-General of all prisoners held by the Confederacy? It would be a wise move on the part of the President to initiate this appointment, it would be a wise move for Mr. Seddon to expedite it. John Henry Winder would see to it that those same Yankees did not plague the Confederate nation further.

. . . In the 1820's weather was cold, the valley of the Hudson was a polar ice-cap, the Hudson was frozen tight. Students of the United States Military Academy blew out white steam as they ran to their classrooms, they ran through heavy snow, there was a great deal of snow and it was impossible to clear it away.

Cadet Davis could be remembered mainly as a hobbledehoy with glinting eyes and abnormally large hands which always twitched (contrary to regulation) when the youth delivered a recitation in the presence of his tactical instructor.

His tactical instructor was a lieutenant named J. H. Winder.

Gentlemen, the Grecian army, at the period when the military art was in greatest perfection among the Greeks, was composed of infantry and cavalry. The former was made up of three different orders of soldiers. I shall request one of you to describe to us the three orders of Grecian infantry. Mr. Davis.

Huge hands gripping tightly, gripping nothing. Sir. Heavily armed were the *Oplitai.* They wore very complete defensive armor, and bore the *sarissa.* Macedonian pike—a formidable weapon about twenty-four feet in length. Light infantry were the *Psiloi;* no defensive armor; customarily they carried javelin, bow and sling. Intermediate between these two grades—

Not grades, Mr. Davis. Orders.

—Between these two orders— Thank you, sir. Between these two orders of infantry were the *Peltastae.* They wore a lighter defensive armor than the *Oplitai;* also bore a shorter pike.

Thank you, Mr. Davis.

. . . Thank you indeed, Mr. Davis. You will be Secretary of War when I am still a Regular captain, and you will not remember my skillful tactical instruction at the time, nor seek me out for well-deserved promotion, but— But that will be the fault of the Federal demon whom we both serve. When once we are no longer serving that demon— Thank you again, Mr. Davis.

The aide placed the classification of charges upon Winder's desk.

Who's outside?

The usual, sir.

Nothing usual about any of them. Except they're always a God damn nuisance. That man Betterson come back?

No, sir. Not yet, sir.

Tis just as well. Who's there?

Those two ladies again—Mrs. Polling and Mrs. Leftwich.

Yes, yes—son and husband in the calaboose. Son of a bitch ought to hang— feeding an escaped Yankee prisoner—

Doctor Kendrick—

He'll get no pass from me! Tell him to go way.

Yes, sir.

Tell him I'll place him under arrest next time he comes bothering!

Yes, sir. A Mr. Lee from over in Manchester—

Any kin to the general?

I don't think so, sir. He wants—

What mean you, Captain? *You don't think so!* Do you *know?*

No, sir. I didn't ask him, sir. I mean to say—

Anyway I'm too dratted busy. Tell him to go way.

A Mr. Buckland and a Mr. Prentice—they seem to be together, sir. Mr. Prentice has but one arm—I think he's a veteran, sir.

Did you ask him? Do you *know?* Why don't you present a few *facts,* God damn it?

And a Captain Wirz—

Who? Ah. With a beard?

Yes, sir. He's here in response to an order—

So he is. Send him in.

Henry Wirz had been sitting as he sat before in other offices, cap upon his knee, pained eyes darting inquisitively and disapprovingly over fellow petitioners in the anteroom. Once again he was in uniform; he had worn that uniform since he crept aboard the blockade runner in a French port, he had worn it for fear of capture by the Federals, he had no wish to be executed as a spy. The swollen right forearm was wound in its dirty black cloth, the thin face was set in the ice of longing. Wirz dreamed of freedom from hurt, he dreamed of rank and emoluments, he wished that his name were known, he prayed that one day his name would be known throughout the Confederate States. Captain Peschau came to bend down, put his pomaded head near Wirz's and to announce in a stage whisper which all might hear (and thus know that they were kept waiting, because Wirz had arrived later than the others), General'll see you now, Captain.

Danke— Thank you.

When Wirz stood alone before the wide cracked marble-topped table which served as one of Winder's desks, the general grunted and motioned toward a chair. He sat staring moodily at Wirz for at least twenty slow seconds after the captain had seated himself. Winder was applying deliberate discomfort, putting Wirz in his place, castigating him silently for wrongs which Henry Wirz could not identify or even recollect; yet he felt that he must have committed them, and hoped that he would not be stripped of his tiny rank.

Uh—Wirz.

Ja, mein General.

Worked for me before. . . .

Ja, sir. It was at Libby. Also in that Tuscaloosa.

Uh—long leave of absence—

Sir, in Europe I was. It is my arm. The wound I got from Seven Pines. But also I take dispatches and they name me Special Minister Plenipotentiary.

Uh—how's the arm?

The great pain I have. Sometimes it is so bad—

I'm no surgeon, said Winder harshly. Don't fret me with your ailments. It matters only that you're fit for duty or you're not. Are you fit?

Henry stiffened briskly and nodded his head many times. *Ja,* General Winder, I am fit.

Stop bobbing about.

Ja, sir!

After a time John Winder had softened his tone until it was near to a caress. Captain Wirz, do you bear any love for the Yankees?

Ach! Love?   •

I put a question to you. That same soft voice.

Is it I must now love the enemy? *Nein.* I hate them much!

Why, Captain?

Because— Why, because it is coercion! They invade the Sister States, they come with sword and fire, our rights they would trample—

And—your arm, Captain?

Ja, I tell you what they do to me! *Mein* General, I also was one surgeon before the war, and I tell you that my radius and ulna—

You wouldn't feel like—coddling Yankees?

What means this coddling, General?

Oh, treating them soft as silk. (His voice was softer than silk.) Babying them. Being—kind to them, Captain.

Kind? We must be stern. We must show them who is boss!

The thin mouth in the huge face began to curl lazily at its lined corners. John Henry Winder was cooing. Since you went abroad, Captain, we have constructed a new prison. My own son Sid was empowered to select the site and get the place in readiness; and it seems that he has performed his duties capably. It's in Sumter County, Georgia, near a little village called Anderson—

16

Dear *Cousin* Lucy, wrote Harrell Elkins, making a great gesture of his use of *Cousin* and underscoring the word in red ink as a pleasantry which he considered reckless. It is a weary hour, ten after ten by Grandfather Elkins' gold watch which is my sole fortune, if one excepts those acres at present untilled! I am weary to the point of desolation, yet find a comfort in projecting myself into the Claffey home and partaking of the company of those whom I cannot help but regard with fondness. May I be permitted to do so?

Why, you forward creature, thought Lucy in response to the mood. And then, stirred with secret guilt in remembering that Harrell Elkins now appeared consistently in her sensual dream, she could not drive him away although consciously she tried. She lowered the letter in her hand, closed her eyes, and reconstructed Rob Lamar. Far gone, far gone. She lifted the letter and absorbed Cousin Harry's polite inquiries as to her health, her father's health, his expressed hope that the condition of her mother had improved.

. . . You ask me to tell you of my work, yet it might be considered a repulsive task to any individual not of the medical persuasion. Lately I have traveled to one of our hospitals where hospital gangrene caused severe mortality. I assisted Dr. Joseph Jones in performing a series of *post mortems* and learned much. At his behest I wrote a preliminary report for the eyes of our Surgeon General; doubtless this will be promptly filed away; but how could one act upon it if he had the inclination to do so? Suppose I write—and I quote with pride: While the clots were absent in cases in which there were no inflammatory symptoms, their presence in other cases sustains the conclusion that hospital gangrene is a species of inflammation in which the fibrous element and coagulation of the blood are increased, even in those who are suffering from such condition of the blood, and from such diseases as are naturally accompanied with a decrease in the fibrous constituent. Suppose I write this (and I did). Is there any immediate and direct decrease in human suffering, is the ugliness alleviated? Are our men—more of them—returned in good fettle to their arduous hazard in the field? Not that it can be noticed! What may a scientist do but recommend? The practicalist, the Chief of Staff, the quartermaster, the commissariat: these and only these may expedite a reform. One fair shipload of drugs from the Continent of Europe would serve more purpose than a thousand such reports; and (gloomily) would serve more purpose than a thousand such men as write the reports. . . . On re-reading the foregoing I diagnose myself as suffering from a severe case of *cholera morbid,* if the pun may be excused.

. . . We fellows, when serving at the front, were accustomed to cracking raucous jokes in imitation of the orator who, secure in the certainty that age or physical disability or political expediency kept him from courting bullets, puffed forth his bombast: Would that I were only younger (or less corpulent or less generally bombproof)! How gladly would I shoulder a musket beside you brave lads, with what lightness of heart would I march at your side & & & et cetera.

Well, be it said, dear *Cousin*, that now I find myself in that peculiar position which two years agone I would have scorned to High Heaven. Has your father need of a good overseer? Assuredly I could keep the black people contented and industrious; my very jocularities should turn the trick! May I apply to you for Good Character??

. . . Must have underestimated the Yankees in more ways than one. Now we approach the entering of the *Fourth Year* of conflict. At first it appears that we underestimated their *fighting* qualities. (I did, for one, and to my pain.) Next, their *staying* qualities. Over all, their *productive* capacity. Were we ever whipped, it should be a sad thing were we whipped by this ironclad blockade and (array me at strict Attention before the muzzles of a firing squad) by the blunderings of our Executive and his Fellow Cooks Spoiling the Broth. The administration of the Confederacy's military affairs approaches poltroonery! We had our opportunity, we had it on a round dozen occasions. No one might be allowed to act upon it. Now, after toiling for nearly three years, what is the sum? The lines in Virginia lie within a comfortable stroll of where they lay in 1861 (but there are little birds speaking of a vigorous onslaught soon to be entered upon by the Yanks, following the inevitable change in command). The ligatures of the blockade are shutting off our life's blood. The Federals control the Mississippi and its affluents. Thus the Department of the Trans-Mississippi must be written off, except for its nuisance value. Who owns New Orleans? The Federals. Who have swept not too triumphantly to the very doorstep of Georgia (yet indeed they have swept)? The National army. Who have invaded boldly upon Florida soil, even though sent packing at Olustee? The National army. *Cousin*, my lamentation is longer than Jeremiah's, and could get me a prison cell at best were it made public. Observe how I trust to your discretion?

. . . So there is naught to do but to proceed with one's task as faithfully as one may. There is naught to do but close one's eyes to the infernal maneuverings of arm-chair busy-bodies who, to indulge slangily, rule the roost. I have applied repeatedly for a post of more activity; but there seems to be an especial pigeon-hole wherein my applications are stuffed, with passage pigeons flying nobly away with them from tother end. Daily (or rather nightly, when I am alone and seeking slumber) I recreate a panorama of Claffey acres, Claffey verandah, Claffey repasts, Claffey beauty & courage. See what selfish fruit your combined hospitality bore! Are there more violets in adjacent woodlands, *Cousin?* Or have you time for the seeking? I judge there must be none any longer within the confines of the prison pen itself, since it must be in an increasingly trampled condition.

Now it is past midnight, and the spirit weakens along with the flare of this inadequate lamp. Pray think of me kindly. I think of thee & thine with respect and admiration and with whatever degree of tenderness might be allowed. Y'r servant, *Cousin*. Harrell Elkins, Surgeon, P.A., C.S.

Lucy Claffey wrote to him, Would that I could offer better news of my mother, but I cannot. She has taken to having her meals above stairs; and, even worse, insists that her tray be brought not into her own room but into the room once occupied by the youngest, Moses, where also she keeps all objects pertaining to the memory of my brothers. In vain might I insist that her course is unhealthy and bound to destroy sanity. Such contention is useless: she has a will of iron, but a cold and unseeing will. Frequently she ventures forth in the evening, walking alone in her cloak if the air be chilly. Poppy attempted to accompany her at first; she would have none of it; then he ordered one of the wenches to accompany her, which Ninny does but ineffectually.

Enough of gloomy topics, Cousin Harry. What shall I tell you of those Claffey acres which you prize? I just fear I'm a poor interpreter of horticultural activities and always was. (Would that I might be allowed to be a nurse. Then should I meet you eventually in the tented field, no doubt?) Father is deeply concerned with asparagus at the present, and thus we have asparagus for dinner—as a topic of conversation, not as yet garnished with sour sauce. It seems that we are shy of salt, and not likely to obtain salt in quantity for some time to come, with the railroad so busy feeding both Lee's and Gen. Johnston's armies. The asparagus beds should have had a top-dressing of salt, two pounds to the square yard; hence Father is fretful about it. Mighty little do I understand, as well, about the production of beans which are now being planted or have been planted; but it appears that we have had such an awful lot of rain during March that the seed is liable to spoil without germinating! Land sakes. I do listen, and try to understand, for Poppy has no one else in whom to confide or to whom to complain! There is something about the pole beans which should have been planted simultaneously with the main crop of bush beans; but this he must explain when again he takes pen in hand &c.

Jem cut his foot severely, poor old black thing, on some instrument of endeavor—is it called a dibble?—and goes hobbling about. I really can't say that I wished for Jem to be hurt, for he is a good hand if he has no more wits than a duck; but it *did* give me a fair opportunity to indulge in what the boys used to call my Florence Nightmare tactics. Thus I have bathed his foot and tended him devotedly, and am rewarded by observing a good healthy uniting of his tissues in the laceration of that broad ebony foot. Once again, Surgeon, have you employment for me in the field?

. . . As an infrequent guest we welcome one Lieut. Col. Alexander Persons, now in command at this post.

(This statement was received with disquietude by Surgeon Elkins.)

. . . It seems that the command is divided, in theory, into three separate and distinct departments. I append this information for the interest of yourself as a military man. One officer in command of the *troops,* another in command of the *prison,* a third in command of the *post.* Colonel Persons is post commander; I think there is no prison officer on duty as yet, though he informs me that there are upwards of seven thousand Yankees in the pen at this writing, and a lot more to come. Land. What if they should get loose? Colonel Persons says it is needless to worry. He does not come often, since he is so hard put to, as he declares, make bricks without straw.

. . . The Rev. Mr. Cato Dillard, whom I called Uncle Dayto when I was small (and he insists that I apply the appellation still) was here with his wife for a night. Sakes. I do not mean that she is his wife *temporarily*—that could scarcely be, for they have scads of grandchildren—two lately dead in the army at the North, poor things. I mean that we were fortunate to have them as guests for one night, and Col. Persons came along to help eat the *pig.* Dearie me, the pig's name was Sec Stanton, and he was one of my favorites. Poppy said that he shouldn't be killed, now that the merc. rose to eighty-seven degrees the other day; but we were fresh out of meat, and Man must be served. (Also Woman. Naomi did a just heavenly fresh ham.) Do you enjoy theological—or is it metaphysical?—discussions, Coz? I just don't understand them, but beg leave to report, since my father will not *participate.* He says there is too much theology in the world, and not enough food to go round, and not enough honeysuckle, and too many tears. Well.

. . . While we award much learning and piety to men, we search the Scriptures, and bring every man's theory to this inspired test. That is Uncle Dayto speaking. Col. Persons: Every man's theory must differ. Rev. Cato Dillard: We accept or reject his theory, just as it may be in accord with, or differ from, God's revealed will. Mr. Ira Claffey: There's a nearly full moon; shall we adjourn to the gallery outside? Col. Alex Persons: I must return to the post. So many matters to claim my attention—Uncle Dayto Dillard: You have said that you did not believe in the doctrine of election because you did not understand it. But do you understand the mystery of Godliness—God manifest in the flesh? You agree that you believe that, and yet you accept it on the divine veracity. Col. Persons: Four hundred and fifty more Yankees due tonight, or so I was informed. I can't trust to the telegraph, sir. Mr. Ira Claffey: As I was saying awhile back, if you don't wash in the slips of the Hayti yam when you take them up in dry weather, it is of great advantage to grout them. Rev. Mr. Dillard: Can you not believe the doctrine of election simply because it is taught in the Bible, even though you do not understand it? Mrs. Effie Dillard: Cate, don't be an old blether. (She is Scotch.) Col. P.: What is *grout?* Mr. Claffey: That means to dip the yam slips into water thickened with rich earth—a thin mud, a muddy soup, I suppose you'd term it. It refreshes the slips, and gives them a thin coating of earth as a protection against the atmosphere. Rev. Dayto Dillard: If it be a doctrine of the Bible—and you cannot deny, according to your lights, that it is clearly taught—then you are *bound to believe it,* or make God a liar! Mrs. Effie Dillard: God's no liar, mon! Set a watch upon your lips. Uncle Dayto: Ah, we must have reverence enough for the perfections of His character to believe all that He has revealed, whether it comes in antagonism with our own previous opinions or not! Col. P.: Did they say four hundred and fifty Yanks, or was it five hundred? I must take leave, Mr. Claffey, and— Mr. Ira Claffey: Such a pleasant night. I'll walk a piece with you, Colonel. The Rev. Mr. Cato Dillard: Ah, tis a pity, Colonel, that I did not first meet you when you were a boy.

You will see, Cousin Harry, life at the Claffeys' is not sedentary these days.

(Damn Colonel Persons, remarked Surgeon Elkins honestly.)

. . . Trains come plunging with a regularity they did not exhibit in the piping times of Peace. Should I be at work on the west side of the house, I salute them through the window or through springtime foliage, and trust (when they bear to the North) that they are well loaded with viands for the armies. I know that I should reverence each sharp-pointed cow-catcher, each set of tall wheels, each funnel-shaped stack like an enormous weight above the cab & boiler and— What call you those round things? I shall go and ask Poppy. He says steam-dome. But they *do* make noise and ugliness, and soot blows far across the fields and (of this I am nearly positive) finds lodgment in the stray tresses of one Miss L. Claffey, and must needs be washed out.

. . . There is little more to relate, except the vagary of Nature herself, which as we know is a pattern and a repetition; yet each act of Nature seems new. I rise to the colored sunrise before six, and make my sad hymn of approval to the Creator as I dress myself. The field of onion tops is richly green; and above and beyond lie flat broken platters of mist hanging at various levels over the terrain— thin, solid, motionless. Somewhere (could it have been at the Female Institute, where I studied *useful and ornamental branches, including the French language)* I have witnessed such a beauty. Was it some strange print brought from the Orient? I know not. Friend *Coz,* I must up and be busy; the world's work is to be done, and I must do my share. These last lines are penned whilst I lie abed in the morning, but I am no lady of leisure. Breakfast odors soar aloft. Uncle Dayto is stopping by again this week; he and my father are soon to view the interior of the prison pen, as invited by Col. P. to do so. I presume they will stand upon one of the sentinels' platforms. Seven thousand ferocious Yankees? I should not call that a pleasant sight, nor should I desire to join the gentlemen in their junket had I been included in the invitation. Still it is no pastime for a lady, so they say. Will military exigencies prevail upon you to visit this region once again? I pray that they will. I have gathered no violets of late. With all wishes for your health & happiness, I remain, Y'r fond *Cousin,* Lucy C.

This letter lay in Cato Dillard's pocket, to be put into the mail by him later, when he stood crowded atop the stockade with Ira Claffey and Lieutenant-Colonel Persons. The Reverend Mr. Dillard and the post commander had many acquaintances in common in the Fort Valley region; Dillard had lived in that area where Macon, Houston and Crawford Counties pressed together. In whimsy the minister was constantly inquiring about the fishing in Mossy Creek, Bay Creek, Indian Creek—all the creeks adjacent to Fort Valley which he was sure that Persons should know now as well as he, Cato Dillard, had known them years before.

Ira stared at the prison and was in no mood to consider quiet streams and shiners flickering. He witnessed an ugliness which his worst imagination had balked at contriving. The last occasion when he'd gazed at the area was before those first scrawny columns moved in by firelight. Now he did not know how to term the nastiness. A rabbit warren, a den of rats tangling, chunky snakes upturned by a bottom-land plow? The free-piled stumps and brushy tangles were evaporated. A community of huts spread loosely over the slopes like warts, like protruding wounds with corners on them. Rags, brown pine boughs, blankets, sodden overcoats and oilskins: the earth festered with tunneling, cellaring, burrowing; materials were draped on sticks; and all space between was pimpled with moving humanity. Or name it inhumanity—

Shebangs, said Persons. That's the term the Yanks apply to their shelters.

How many men living in each one?

Any number you wish to name. Some live alone, many by twos or fours. The larger huts hold more.

Why are the men's faces so black? I thought in the first glimpse that you were holding all niggers.

Fat pine, said Persons. The smoke of their fires has darkened them.

How many thousand prisoners did you say?

Upwards of seven thousand, at the moment.

It appeared to Ira Claffey that there were not enough huts to furnish shelter for all.

You're correct in that assumption, sir. Many of the prisoners had no coats or blankets in the hour of their capture, or were robbed before entering the stockade, or afterward. They've had nothing to build with; thus they didn't build.

They sleep out, in complete exposure to the elements?

As you can see, no shelter was provided when the stockade was raised.

Ah, yes. I remember when Captain Winder was approached on that topic, and I recall his reply.

At this mention of Sid Winder the glance of Persons and the glance of Claffey met and held. The soldier recognized even more painfully than the citizen that there was a malignant connotation in the name of Winder as applied to individuals associated with this place. Both men had encountered the ruling genius—the father and cousin—and had formed their opinions of his character independently of whatever noisome reputation he possessed in the Confederate capital. Both knew the son. As for Cousin Dick (commonly believed to be General Winder's nephew because of disparity in age) only Persons was unfortunate enough to hold contact with him. Richard B. Winder was like his cousin a staff officer of the general's, and now wore the title of quartermaster of this expanding pest-hole. Lieutenant-Colonel Persons had been forced to stand by helplessly while Dick Winder superintended, in bored surly fashion, the construction of a bakery. The sheds stood on a slope above the creek immediately west of the stockade; Persons pointed out that its drainage would flow into the creek before the stream entered the pen; Captain R. B. Winder ignored the field officer as pointedly as the cousin of a commanding general might if he were particularly inept and selfish.

The quartermaster remarked to a subordinate within Persons' hearing, I have no orders to report to any quartermaster at all, no orders to report to any officer commanding troops in another capacity. I report directly to Richmond. I receive my instructions from Richmond.

In this application of nepotism even the headquarters of the Georgia Reserves at Macon were by-passed. Alexander Persons detested nepotism as any fair-minded man was compelled to detest it; and forced to nibble its rotten fruit in the discharge of his duties he grew particularly incensed. . . . Sidney Winder's levies of workmen, ignorant and unsupervised, had left lower reaches of the Sweetwater branch choked with felled trees and a mat of brush. The creek pushed sluggishly out from the east stockade, its normal insufficient velocity reduced to a trickle by this careless damming. When and if the bake house were ever completed, equipped and operating, what could be the result of its natural drainage and debris except to pollute to the saturation point a marsh already teeming with fecal matter and the hungrily copulating flies of spring?

I report directly to Richmond. I receive my instructions from Richmond. The weak voice bland and smug.

Sometimes Alex Persons came close to wishing that a bullet had found him at Cumberland Gap. Sometimes he wanted to scream to the dirty mendicants caged by the up-ended logs, I too am a prisoner. You think you know the entire story of restriction, do you? Each of us wears manacles, mine are not apparent, they are heavy, they chafe more than my ankles and my wrists, do you wear irons in your dreams as I am compelled to?

With the platform fairly sagging under their combined weight, the Reverend Mr. Cato Dillard stood as aloof from his friends as the meager plane would permit. But Cato was drained of all trivial talk about the Fort Valley community. Belatedly he saw the enormity of the thing below the fence; he was trying to justify it by poking for texts and muttering them softly. *Egypt is like a very fair heifer, but destruction cometh; it cometh out of the north.*

Did Cato think deeply and sadly about his two grandsons killed not long before? Ira Claffey could not know, but Ira felt for a moment that savage selfish brutality—the hideous latent desire of the bereaved to see other men drink the same juice.

Thus saith the Lord. Behold, a people cometh from the north country . . . they are cruel, and have no mercy . . . I will cause you to dwell in this place.

But why the devil without shelter, Brother Dillard? Ira put the question so sharply that it came as a rebuke as well as a profane echo to the Biblical murmurings.

Cato Dillard twisted his silky side-whiskers between nervous fingers. *Judge me, O God, and plead my cause against an ungodly nation.*

Persons cleared his throat. His handsome face had grown darkly intent as always when he stood aloft and examined the stockade and its people. About the question of shelter, Mr. Claffey. I've been hard after it since I came here, to no avail. Repeatedly the superintendent of the railroad has promised me a train;

each time I thought I'd get eight or ten cars of lumber; thus far none has come through. I still have hopes.

Ira said, There are sawmills in this vicinity.

Certainly. I took that matter up with Macon.

Without result?

Persons said deliberately, It would not be becoming in me, as an officer, to discuss my superior officers, and with citizens. As a former soldier you must know that.

Colonel, you have my sympathy and my respect. But this pen is turning very rapidly into one vast latrine.

Into worse than that, sir.

What could be worse? The Reverend Mr. Dillard wished to know.

This place called Andersonville.

Persons continued, but still in the manner of changing a subject. The stockade . . . he pointed out where the last breach had been closed. Yes, those were new guns being put into position on the high southwest fort nearest the Claffey place. Captured from the Yankees in Florida, Persons declared with satisfaction. And fetched here to use in turn against the Yankees when and if an emergency arises. . . . The two box gates on the west; they worked efficiently; observe the rectangular stockade enclosing an area outside the actual stockade fence in each case; the outer gate could be opened, wagons driven inside, the outer gate closed, the inner gate opened. Thus the prisoners never had a possible access to the outer world at any given moment, thus they could never carry the gate in a rush by sheer mass of numbers. . . . Yes, the North Gate was used mainly for ingress, the South Gate for egress. Yes, those were more or less streets extending through the stockade's interior from each gate; it was essential that there be some cleared space for the distribution of rations, for the assembling of prisoners in formation. Therefore no prisoners were permitted to construct their shebangs within the area contained by those more or less streets . . . it was odd: the Yanks referred to the street opposite the South Gate as South Street, but the street opposite the North Gate was called by some Broadway and by others Main Street. Very odd indeed; you would think that they'd say North Street, but they didn't. Very odd lot, these Yankees . . . yes, many foreigners. Many roughs from the New York streets. Had the gentlemen witnessed any fist-fights since they stood atop the stockade? Well, watch . . . bound to see a fight sooner or later.

I've no wish to witness their wicked brawling, said Mr. Dillard in high disgust.

Persons touched his lips with a clean but frayed handkerchief. There was no way in which he might make these civilians appreciate the problems besetting him, so he would not try. Persons was accustomed to the stern indelible procedures essential to service in the field; he believed the things which were told to him—at first.

. . . A telegram came ticking: three hundred prisoners were due to arrive the next afternoon, and thus Persons arranged for their reception, and notified the quartermaster. . . . The train would not appear. It would not appear on the stated afternoon, nor during the next morning, nor the next afternoon. Rain would fall to soak the meal on carts where rations waited with no covering because no covering was available. Then, perhaps at eleven o'clock of the second night, and with more rain sweeping and with cold wind deadening the heaps of burning knots, not one train but three would arrive in the space of half an hour. Eleven hundred prisoners instead of three hundred (one engine had snapped a driving-rod above Macon, another train had been shunted to the Southwestern from the Savannah line; no one was expecting it, no telegram had been received).

Lieutenant-Colonel Alexander Persons grew pearly of face, his stomach hurt him, he wanted to belch but there seemed to be an obstruction. The pain went higher in his chest. His meticulous legal mind began to jerk from this subject to that; he thought he heard the snap of a leather whip lash, a thin whip lash like the tongue of a blue racer, curling and popping inside his skull.

Lieutenant, how soon can you procure rations for this new contingent?

Well, sir, reckon I got rations for six-seven hundred over to the tent, but I ain't got no transportation. Got two mules down sick, and a wheel just come off that old wagon. If Captain Winder—

Get your men out of bed, prepare five hundred more rations, I'll see that you have transportation. Mr. Ussery, fetch those two wagons that were hauling logs for the artillery revetments this afternoon.

Sir, I haven't got any drivers.

By God, Mr. Ussery, *find* some drivers! Drive a wagon down here yourself if necessary, then go and fetch the other.

. . . Colonel Persons, did you hear them whistles? Another train's halted down the track behind that one there; the sentry done tolt me.

Department of Georgia, Department of Georgia, and who was commanding the Georgia Reserves? Brigadier-General Howell Cobb. Or was Cobb now become a major-general? The Nation knew him better as a politician. Inspector General of Prisons, and who was that? Brigadier-General John H. Winder. Secretary of War, and who was he? Mr. James A. Seddon. Have you rations for these prisoners, Colonel? No. Why not? No one informed me that they were coming. How many wagons have you at the post? Four—no, I think five. Have you tools? No. Lumber? No. Is it night? Yes. Is it raining? Indeed, yes. Is there adequate drainage inside the stockade? Hold on a minute, old fellow, drainage for whom, drainage for what? Have the prisoners any shelter? No, no, no! But I didn't build the prison, I didn't lay it out, I didn't plan it, I didn't construct it, Sid Winder did that. *Directly after my command was captured at Cumberland Gap, I went to Richmond and reported directly to the Secretary of War for duty. He gave me instructions to report to General Winder. General Winder instructed me to report to Andersonville.*

Colonel Persons, I've had these men in formation for an hour. Do you want me to keep them standing here in the rain?

Well, what's the difference, Captain? There's no shelter for them inside the stockade.

But all our boys are soaked, sir, a-guarding them. I just thought if we turned them inside, our sentries wouldn't have to stand out here and—

What matters it, Captain Hamrick? You're soaked through. I'm soaked through, everybody's soaked through; and two more train loads to come. No, three: another just arrived—and from the south.

From the *south,* sir? Whereabouts?

Here's the escort officer's communication. Hold that lantern closer. Whom have we here? Ah, there seem to be above seven hundred . . . portions of the Seventh Connecticut, Forty-eighth New York, Forty-seventh New York, Seventh New Hampshire, One Hundred and Fifteenth New York . . . Sherman's Regular battery . . . Sherman, indeed! . . . here it says: Olustee, Florida. So that's where they were taken. But it says also: *colored* troops—from the Eighth United States and the Fifty-fourth New York. Damnation, Captain, we have no facilities for the retention of *colored* troops. *Colored* troops! What do they mean? What can we *do* with them?

Way I see it, Colonel Persons, sir, there's no such thing as a colored soldier. Now, if I had my way, I'd form my command into a series of firing squads and—

Ah, hush up, Captain Hamrick. We can put them to work. Appears to be some two hundred of them. Yes, yes—we shall put them to work outside, we have need of many hands. They could drive— But we have no teams for them to drive. They could fabricate— But we have no implements. They could build— But no lumber. Was that another train whistle?

Inside the stockade the newly arrived prisoners could not see where to go. They sat down in mud. They sat shivering. It was dark, they could not see. They huddled close together; but even so, the more energetic of the raiders found them in midnight and rain. A lament went up as a man was hit and his overcoat was taken from him, and a worse lament arose as another man felt gripping arms upon him in the streaming darkness, and struggled to resist: and so the rest of his captured company found him motionless in muck when gray light fell upon the place where he had resisted.

Fresh fish: that was the universal appellation for the newly arrived as it had been in some of the other pens. Look at them! Here's where you get your fresh fish! *Fresh* fish, *fresh* fish: *hooooot,* whistle, whistle; they come so cheap; who wants *fresh* fish? A dime a dozen, lady, a dime a dozen: herring, cod, mackerel and sticklebacks. Who'll buy, who'll buy, who'll buy *freshhhhh fishhhhh?* . . . The Olustee hundreds comprised the first large batch of unskinned victims who might be possessed of more than their usual complement of jewelry, buttons, blankets, shoes, tobacco and other useables or tradeables. Their scales had been scraped by Home Guards along the way but they had not been gutted. There would come more, there would come more.

Despite the withdrawal evinced by Lieutenant-Colonel Persons while he spoke of surface activities and refused to state the length to which he was plagued, Ira Claffey gave ear to the true complaint of the commander. Ira had not served as a soldier for many years, but he brought a quiet understanding to the soldier who stood beside him. Ira was not limited as many men, Ira could sense things beyond his experience. He knew that the entire Confederacy labored now in confusion and dismemberment. It was more than unlikely that the subordinate upon whom fell the responsibility of administering the affairs of a new prison in this remote spot should be given the equipment and personnel to serve his purpose; it was impossible. Engines would not run because irreplaceable parts fell away or because makeshift engineers were incompetent (the competent engineers were occupied with artillery at some crucial point). Fuel and food went astray, tires came off of wagons. Where is the quinine? There is no quinine. These muskets must be altered; we have no locks to fit; where are the locks? Stored in a warehouse? Who has the key, who has the manifest, the bill of lading? Someone knew, someone had these things, someone could tell; but he could not tell—he was dead at South Mountain, he was dead on the Chickahominy, he was dead at Fort Donelson.

. . . A new superintendent for the stockade, Persons was saying.

When?

This week. He comes directly under General Winder's office. I am to command the post only.

But is not the stockade a part of the post?

In geography only, not in the echelon of command. I wish, said Alexander Persons, scraping the inner surface of his heart as with a silver spoon, that I was back in the field with my regiment.

The new commander: who is he?

Some captain named Henry Wirz. He's a German or something of the sort, added Persons with obvious distaste. Mr. Claffey, sir, I'd just as soon not have his job. A goodly number of these prisoners were sick when they came in; many more sickened here; they're not getting the proper rations; I'd give them proper rations willingly, but I'm not the quartermaster and I haven't *got* proper rations for them. I don't consider even that my own men are properly fed! The meal is coarse and mouldy, the bacon's tainted—*when* we get bacon, and we don't get nearly enough. You ought to go up on that hill over yonder, past those pines.

Persons' hand shook as he pointed toward the north, east of the Bile property. His hand shook suddenly as if it had been employed as the instrument for spewing these words, as if he had torn loose the plaint, the volley of resentment and futility, by act of hand rather than by act of speech.

What would we find in the pines up there?

Graves, sir. We've carted off over two hundred already. . . . Turn the other way. Look at that dirty stream of water.

Once, said Ira, the stream was clean. I was accustomed to drink from it.

You wouldn't want to drink from it now. But the Yanks have to, unless they can dig wells deep enough to supply them.

Once there was a spring. Down here, almost directly below us. It was spoilt when they built the stockade.

I don't know anything about that, Mr. Claffey, sir. I didn't build the stockade. He added, as in a sudden dream, I have to keep telling myself that I didn't build it, that Captain Sid Winder did. There is another stream over south of your place —maybe a mile—?

Ira said, Little Sweetwater.

Is that the name? I thought this oozing marsh was Sweetwater. Though the prisoners call it Stockade Creek.

This was a branch.

Just the same, sir, that other creek is four or five times the size of this. It flows now perhaps twelve or fifteen feet wide and more than five feet deep in spots. I'm no engineer; preparing a legal brief is more in my line; but I'd estimate that the velocity of that other stream is possibly a mile an hour. Well, sir! Couldn't the stockade have been placed to include that stream instead of this one? I mentioned as much to Sid Winder. All other things were about equal: drainage, timberland, amount of clearing to be done—

What was Winder's response?

Rather vague. He declared that he had absolute authority in the selection of the site. I have understood from other sources that a site near Albany—a place infinitely superior to this—was under consideration also. But he selected this place. Damn it all, sir!

Persons wiped his forehead. I'm talking entirely too much. But, to sum it up, we've got prisoners with diarrhoea, prisoners showing signs of scurvy, prisoners dropsical, prisoners gangrenous. What we need here is a first-rate hospital; thus far I haven't been able to lay hold on any tents, much less lumber. . . . Do you wish to go below, gentlemen? I reckon you've seen enough.

Ira said, I saw no fights. The men were merely milling about. Idly, stupidly. . . .

That's all they have to do—mill about. You were fortunate in not observing any of those roughs pursuing their chosen vocation of robbery and mayhem. It goes on all the time.

Can't you stop it, Colonel? Ira was regretful that he had stated the question the moment it passed his lips, for Persons froze upon the ladder and looked down at him with scorn, while the sentry stood at a distance, waiting to resume his post.

How, sir? Appeal to their better instincts? Send armed guards among them? The kind of material I'm commanding here and now: old men and little boys, or dullards incapable of serving at the front? Send them inside with weapons and ammunition? It's bad enough to have to put people like that On Parapet.

Ira said, I'm sorry, Colonel. Then, when Persons stood beside him (the officer was breathing heavily, not because of the exertion of descent) Ira put his hand on his arm. He said, Obviously it's no fault of yours, and there's nothing you can do about it.

Yes, said Alexander Persons, I might be able to do something about it. If I had the wisdom of Solomon, the patience of Job, the courage of the Lion of Judah. How is that for Scriptural summation, Parson Dillard?

Cato told them, It was prophesied in the Book of Joel. *I will remove far off from you the northern army, and will drive him into a land barren and desolate.*

Brother Dillard preaches a very stern war, said Ira. But if he owned a tub of fresh collard greens and pork at this moment, he'd be inside distributing it to the hungry.

Dillard's face shone. A very fine notion, Brother Ira! Why shouldn't we do that at the first opportunity?

First off, said Persons, you should have to consult with Captain Wirz, the new commander of the stockade. And I assure you that he appears to be a gentleman of very short temper. He added in a low voice, He's ill. Suffering from an old wound.

The commander took leave of his guests and went rapidly away toward his headquarters tent where he knew that twenty problems, assorted but equally ugly, would be sitting like patients in a doctor's parlor; they would be aching, they would be waiting. In thought he saw the thin frantic face of Henry Wirz, and he recoiled from the thought: he had not liked that face in his first glimpse of it. This occurred during one of those hours of duplicated entanglement now traditional with the struggling Department of Georgia. Wirz appeared, bearing an order requiring him to assume command of the stockade. Simultaneously appeared a Major Griswold from some other direction, producing an order almost identical with Wirz's. Discreetly Lieutenant-Colonel Persons retired from the complication; he said merely, Gentlemen, you'll have to get your own orders straightened out. The matter's in abeyance, so far as I'm concerned. Wirz disappeared for ten or fifteen days, Griswold fussed about . . . at last came a telegraphed order which took the major away to some other station. Wirz reappeared, triumphant but more habitually irritable than ever. Alex Persons doubted not that the bearded little fussbudget had been all the way to Richmond to invoke the power of Winder's office. Strange business, he thought despondently. Who'd want a task like that? Thank the Eternal it's no chore of mine any longer. . . . Secretly he felt a stirring of pity for the caged scarecrows who had followed him, supplicating, each time he went inside. All he could do for them was to mention the bright probability of exchange, and Persons knew that he lied each time he used the word. So did most of the men; he knew that they spoke disgracefully of him the moment his back was turned. Remotely he forgave them. They reminded him— many of them—of his own Fifty-fifth Georgia boys he'd commanded earlier, and who were captured in the mountains, and must now be penned somewhere at the North. . . . Lieutenant-Colonel Alexander W. Persons discovered that he had a severe headache. The afternoon sun was too bright, it hurt his eyes. He went to his tent and found the row of lame halt problems waiting, just as he had known that they would wait, waiting in their home-cobbled bandages, smelling of their home-applied arnica. Gad.

Ira Claffey saw Cato Dillard set forth upon his way to Americus, provided with a lunch of boiled eggs and fresh lettuce sandwiches, but with no Mrs. Dillard beside him today. Once again she was nursing the sick somewhere. There seemed to be more sick than ever before. Many wounded soldiers were come home, unhappy families had been forced from their homes by Sherman's advance and now were compelled to hunt shelter with relatives in these out-of-the-way counties. Suppose that Georgia should turn into one vast poorhouse or hospital or similar charitable refuge, thought Ira (as the area termed Camp Sumter was turning into the latrine he had described)? He held a sudden impressive vision of beds, beds, beds, cots, cots, pallets, pallets laid out in rows, as he would arrange patches of vegetables, stretching from Bibb to Chattahoochee and south: Macon, Sumter, Dooly, Lee, Worth, Colquitt, name the counties, minister to burdens in the beds.

He went into the plantation's seed house and tried to concentrate the energy of his thought upon carrots. Carrot planting had been delayed by this and that. If he wanted a late crop the seeds should be put in before the middle of April; in his opinion they came up badly if you waited for warmer weather. He thought the carrot a remarkable plant, both from the point of food value and medicinally as well. He remembered carrot poultices which his grandmother had applied in those departed frontier days when Indian wars ruled the regions barely west of them, when he was young and saw imaginary Creeks lurking in each tangle of gum shoots, and heard with apprehension the tales of wagoners dragged from their seats and scalped in timberland roads. Carrots revived the thought of his youth; carrots would be a manner of refuge.

In neat rows in small paper bags, his seeds awaited him, ticketed first by year, then subdivided alphabetically. Let me cull out these few packets of '61 carrots; how did they ever come to be left? They should have been thrown away long ago; the seed will seldom germinate properly if more than two years old. Have we a sufficiency of the '63's? More than a sufficiency. Then throw out the '62's, all of them, along with the '61's; they would be uncertain, they would be a hazard. Thus into the refuse basket go the '61's (who died then?) and the '62's (Moses) and we shall plant the 1863's (Suthy, Badge) and they, the carrots, shall arise from the ground in this holy year of 1864—but not upon the Third Day—and who shall be The Departed in this holy year? Many Secessionists, no doubt; also many Northerners. Many Yanks in the nearby stockade. Colonel Persons said over two hundred were gone to their graves already. Granny, should you have used a carrot poultice for the nursing of these? Suppose you wished to give them butter (ah, who has butter except as a treat?): then you should use the carrots for butter coloring as you did in wild early days. Bend forward seriously in your cap and gray-fringed shawl and say to the servant (with her kinky hair tied with pink yarn to scare witches), as you did in the free remote wild early days: One will be enough, Rhody. We'll have perhaps eight pounds of butter in this lot and more than a single carrot might spoil the flavor. Grate it fine, grate it into *cold* water, Rhody; mind, I said grated *fine.* And Grandfather declared that one bushel of corn and one of carrots were worth more than two bushels of corn as feed for hogs. . . . But let the hogs run untrammeled for the most part, let them feed on mast, feed on acorns, let them rub snouts into the ground and trench it and roll the turf, hunting for other food they like. . . .

Always Ira Claffey prepared his carrot seed wisely according to rule: he had saved only the principal umbels; each head was cut as it turned brown, the seeds had been dried carefully in shade, rubbed out, and then dried further in the paper. . . . A carrot poultice. Had one been prepared for Lucy's young man when he lay giving up the ghost in Illinois? But indeed what disease, what hurt, required the use of this particular remedy? Ira could not remember. It was peculiar (as his hands tried to tremble, working with the seed bags, and he labored to keep those hands from trembling) to think that he could name the remedy but not the ailment. Starvation? Dirt? Incarceration? Was incarceration a recognized disease? Could a doctor turn away from a corpse and inscribe upon the needed record: this man died of a severe case of incarceration?

He thought that the prisoners within the stockade were not too crowded—not as yet—but they would become crowded past the point of mere discomfort if trains kept fetching them. But at the moment: seven thousand squatters on, say, fifteen acres of habitable ground. Not too deplorable. . . .

They occupied his attention as a combined wretched curiosity because they or their kindred had killed his sons. In this way they made their intimacy with Ira. His wife progressed into straitened madness, his daughter felt her young hopeful strength still asserting itself and so she might open ears and eyes to the possibility of love. For himself Ira could contemplate no longer a personal physical attachment which might affect his emotion and thus in turn color the activities of heart, intellect and dream which others typified as soul or spirit (indistinguishable to him: always they had been). Sometimes he thought that he was dried from the waist up, frozen from the waist down, saturated with morphia from ear to ear. Yet a strange awareness of humanity as a whole had come upon him and he dared not deny it; it had not lived in him before save as an abstraction. He'd found that in standing on that splintery post above the fence, with a piece of rotten canvas hanging from the sloped shake roof to give the guard partial protection from sun or driving rain— He'd found that he was identified closely with Lieutenant-Colonel Persons, closely with the youthful guard who came down to give them room, even more closely with the prisoners beyond. They began to appear as his problem and his pain solely because they were human, not because he knew them; he did not know them.

Again and again through weeks to come he would reappear on that sentinel's box, passed first by Persons and later in negligent fashion by subordinate officers of the guards because they knew Ira's face and learned that he lived next door, and sometimes drifted over to the plantation to receive a gift of fresh things from the garden. Lucy gave fried eggs to one lieutenant, milk to another, gingerbread to any of the younger enlisted men who visited briefly, shyly, but ready to talk eagerly of their mothers, sweethearts, hound dogs, if given half a chance. Illusions of his own dead children faded away from Ira Claffey. No longer did he see the boys hunting beside him nor did he hear them walking on path or stairway; and that was because his mind was still level, still sound; he had not gone astray with Veronica, his balance would not permit him to accompany her. For this he gave thanks in prayer even while he prayed for his truant wife. The convocation of young slain Claffeys was replaced by disordered anonymous Yankees . . . the one he saw crawling, laced doubled in the corset of scurvy, the one he saw crawling to the marsh with his unsoldered half canteen in hand . . . the Yankee he witnessed thumbing his nose arrogantly at Ira up on the parapet . . . the boy picking lice from his pubic hair, the freshly-arrived boy displaying a scrap of newspaper to others who crowded close, the boy who whanged away on a jewsharp, the two bearded men wrestling and slugging about something-or-other, the narrow-shouldered graybeard sliding his ragged trousers below his knees as he prepared for evacuation at the swamp's edge.

Sometimes in the middle of night, when pacing on desperate solitary rounds in his nightshirt, Ira fancied that he heard the warblers which had loved that tilted pine forest when it was a forest, the nocturnal animals which had lapped at the stream when it was a stream. But mostly he went prying among the present occupants. Had the graybeard died as yet? Who won the fight, and did one prisoner now own the other's pocket comb? What had those boys read about in the newspaper? A Rebel retreat, a brazen Northern lie? The musket shot rapped out, prisoners yelled in distance and midnight, fires of the outside camp shone hard through trees, a wagon rattled, an engine whistled, frogs hallooed in a steady stream of bird-like music along the low places of farther woodland (they had gone from regions closer at hand, the waters had become too dirty for them). Who fired the musket, and at whom, and did he hit him; and why did that dog bark? Did Ike or Johnny or Silas cry in his sleep, did Ike or Johnny or Silas find sleep?

More and more the power of Andersonville poured over Ira Claffey like a glistening dark tide; it was there, reaching around him, it was sticky (he thought of molasses leaking from a barrel but the tide was not sweet). . . . . Once more to the stockade the next day, wondering, staring, absorbing increased terror of the thing. The mean strength in number of the prisoners rose to ten thousand during April, the graves were said to be over nine hundred.

One time the very cones were clean, unsaturated, untrodden. One time peaceful trunks stood warm and ruddy with sunset on them, purplish when you looked toward the sunset and watched their shadowy eastern sides. There was pure silence, the ground doves' cooing instead of the cooing which lorn invalids made. Wood of the stockade might have absorbed those wonders, wood of the stockade could never radiate them now. Wood of the stockade stood cut, hammered, malformed, mute in its resentment of the use to which it had been put. Once, said the night hovering above the increasing stench. Once.

17

When Henry Wirz arrived in March he rented a house owned and occupied in part by a man named Boss. It was a double house with scabby window frames, and on the side which was to be the Wirz habitat several of the outer shutters were missing. Mr. Boss offered but weak hope that these could be replaced by the time Elizabeth Wirz and the children arrived: where might he get shutters, where might he find a carpenter to make them, what of the hardware? In the rear yawned an abandoned cistern into which a gray cat had slipped to drowning a few days earlier, and now the cat's body floated like a striped bladder breaking the surface of dark seepage, and nobody'd even tried to get it out. This old cistern had been replaced by a more efficient one hollowed beneath the kitchen floor. There was no need for a disgusting spectacle, no excuse for it; Wirz's physician's soul revolted at the idea. The cavity might make a fit trap for an enemy but the gray cat had been nobody's enemy. Also Wirz feared that little Coralie might fall in as the cat had done. He requested assistance from Lieutenant-Colonel Persons and received it lamely (he felt that it was lamely, since he was sourly certain that Persons did not like him at first sight; God knew why). Shortly thereafter Wirz came riding in a wagon driven by a Negro and containing, besides Henry Wirz, another Negro and some tools and scrap lumber. He presided glowering and barking over the two blacks while they toted stones, shoveled earth, and finally turned the trap into a cylindrical morass less frightening. The cat's body was out of sight and out of smell. Scrap lumber served to construct a curb and platform ragged but efficient. Cora could not fall in. Susie and Cornelia were big enough not to endanger themselves heedlessly.

There. This was done. Had anyone ever said that he was not a good father, not a good stepfather? Who had said it? How dared they say it? They would not say it again. For Henry was a man who thought of his family even before he considered the interior of the double house or his own comfort, or which room would be shared by himself and his wife. Henry had wedded himself to the widowed Mrs. Wolfe in a Kentucky village near Louisville ten years previously. She possessed two children already whom Henry accepted as vague compensation for the boy and the girl he had left with their grandparents in Switzerland. With dedication during those moments when he was not burning with the zeal to earn money and thus become rich, or to serve ardently the Confederacy and thus become a storied hero, he had worked at making Elizabeth Wolfe into a good Zurich *Hausfrau*. Sometimes an acid of indignation burned his stomach and told him that such labors were in vain.

The Major Griswold incident gave Captain Henry Wirz fresh self-confidence to the point of exuberance. His arm was no better, sometimes he thought it worse; Bucheton's surgery in Paris had been useless, worse than useless because it caused additional hurt and inconvenience. Wirz should strike Bucheton from his list of friends (*ach*, where was that list and how long might it be?) and never consult with him personally or professionally again! It was as if the enormous quantities of sulphate of morphia absorbed by Wirz's body had built up a wall through which the drug's beneficence might no longer penetrate; except that it leaked surprisingly through unperceived crannies at times. But exercise of such power as was decreed to him, knowledge that he owned prestige above and beyond his rank— They were neither food nor medicine but they were dazzlement. Aloof he could stand blinking at these brightnesses and feel no pain for a time. Griswold had been of field grade; but Wirz, the lowly captain, had managed to have Griswold sent packing and to another post. Wirz was bitter because allowed to wear no major's insignia, but delighted at his own immediate accomplishment. He would accomplish more. The demonstration should begin at once. As for General Winder, one must remember that Winder meted out promotions grudgingly. His own cousin, his own son—these were but captains, and after three years of war too. This was said to be the case because the elder Winder had been so long in securing his own promotion through lower echelons. It had taken him forty years to attain his majority in the Regular establishment. Well, let him permit Henry Wirz to administer this new stockade; let Henry Wirz be executive, reorganizer, jailer, shrewd schemer. He would do more for the Government in this capacity than the most vaunted leaders might do at the front. Then General John Winder should see who was worthy of field grade. *Ja.*

During that first night in the new house which soon would shelter his family, Wirz dwelt without furniture because the furniture had not yet been moved in. In austere extension of courtesy Persons had offered a tent to the newcomer for his convenience, but Henry Wirz wished to be withdrawn from the coughing and foot-pounding and challenging and rattling of camp life; he was no campaigner in the enviable sense; always he preferred to be withdrawn. He brought his blankets to the bare house, took silent supper with the Boss family, insisted on paying them— He could not understand why they pretended reluctance when he offered to pay them; food cost money; they were not in the restaurant business, but food cost money, you could not deny that.

Wirz sat cross-legged beside a candle on a box and worked out his plans in a manifold order book with a lead pencil. The book said *U.S.* and must have been captured, or perhaps preëmpted from some depot long before at the outset of the war. There was justice in the notion that now it was employed as a tool in the manipulation of Yankee prisoners.

. . . Thousands. Lieutenant-Colonel Persons had explained that the prisoners were divided into detachments of Thousands and subdivided into Hundreds, as was the case in other prisons. Ha, Thousands were too large, too unwieldy! Prisoners should never be unwieldy, they should be maneuvered as easily as one pushed dominoes. Ninety men were enough for a squad, a hundred men were too many. How many squads to be in a detachment? Henry Wirz pushed his scraggly dark brows together and peered through waving candlelight at the diagrams he had drawn, the numerals he had put down with neatness. Three squads per detachment—that was enough. Two hundred and seventy prisoners in the largest unit. It might make for more bookkeeping but he, Wirz, would find somebody to keep the books. . . . The population of Camp Sumter must become more fluid, more malleable. He himself would make them more fluid and malleable.

If any voice were raised, if one person beneath his authority sought to resist reforms— *Ach!* Almost it would be a pleasure.

He worked with his left hand; he had learned to write with it, his right hand hurt him sorely. . . . Three squads per detachment, ninety men per squad. Should he term them squads? *Nein.* That gave him an idea, and the bilingual connotation caused Henry nearly to smile. They should be Nineties.

Prisoner, who are you? Sir, I am James Büttner, Third Detachment, Second Ninety— What mess? . . . Thirty men to a mess; that should be convenient for the quartermaster's purposes, convenient for Wirz's own, convenient for the men themselves (he did not wish to afford them any convenience truly). But the double series of threes would simplify things. Three Messes to a Ninety, three Nineties to a Detachment. Three Detachments to a— To a what? A regiment, a brigade? Leave it there. Let the area swarm with detachments, not with strictly military designations. It would be well for the prisoners to realize that they were no longer troops, they were prisoners. He would never refer to them as men, he would refer to them always as prisoners.

Prisoner, Attention! Speak up, Prisoner, tell me your name. Sir, I am James Büttner (*ja,* you traitor, James Büttner, with a German-sounding name!), Third Detachment, Second Ninety, First Mess. Perhaps it should be the other way around? Instruct him to say in order, First Mess, Second Ninety, Third Detachment? Best to wait and see. He would tolerate no nonsense from prisoners. This they must get into their thick Yankee skulls at the very start. Suppose a prisoner did not speak correctly, did not reply in the prescribed manner? Then he should go supperless. Suppose that the prisoner continued to prove insolent, even so? . . . There were punishments. Chains could be forged. Wirz would cause stocks and whipping posts to be constructed; there should be arrangements for the bucking and gagging of mutineers; order should come from confusion. Confusion bred waste, expense, incompetence among the administrators. Everything here at Camp Sumter should be orderly. Promotions did not come about as a result of disorder. Henry Wirz blew out his candle and sought such sleep as his arm would permit him to find. It was not a good sleep.

Early he was awakened by children's talking and running about in the Boss premises. He arose, pleased that for the moment he did not have to dress his forearm amid uncomfortable surroundings. The bone infection healed and opened alternately; he had lost track of the number of times when flesh grew in scarred covering over the minced tissues, the number of times when inflammation redeveloped, swelled, heated, throbbed, puffed, to be relieved only by its own bursting forth through the taut thin surface or by the slash of an instrument which he or some other person wielded. Midway through the act of donning his clothes, Henry Wirz remained motionless for a full five seconds while a delightfully bitter thought overwhelmed him. Suppose that the Yankee artillerist who had hurt him was even now a prisoner within the stockade! What justice in that! . . . But how would he know, how could ever the prisoner confess his crime, how could ever the prisoner know that he had been guilty of that most heinous offense: the Maiming of Doctor Henry Wirz? Impossible. But still the creature might be there, one of those scrofulous pinched-faced gypsies he had observed when he peeked from a sentry station. As yet Henry had not entered the stockade proper, he had only observed. Today he would go inside; he would walk with keen deliberation, estimating necessary changes which must be brought about under his jurisdiction. It was good that he needed not to go with his forearm swathed; it had healed when last he was in Richmond, perhaps it would remain with dermis and epidermis intact for a time, torturing him slowly but not draining, not making yellow stains and smelling like bran.

Elizabeth had worked a new shirt for her husband. The day was fair (he glanced through the six-paned window with one broken pane) and thus he should not be forced to wear a jacket. He was an individual, he was no professional soldier (although he knew that he could offer wisdom, courage and efficiency beyond the ability of many professional soldiers) and as he sought to relieve the drabness of his being by use of bright colors when in citizen's attire, so he tried to vary the meanness, the uniformity of dun badly-dyed Confederate clothing. A few officers looked askance at him from time to time, but no one had ever lectured him for his lack of conformity. This was an army where few conformed or could conform. Uniform habiliments were scarce. In the field, men fought in red or tawny undershirts in summer, many of them were apt to be in Yankee overcoats when winter came. Officer X had a green velvet collar on his dress jacket because no gray velvet had been available when that jacket was stitched, Officer Y had a turned-down collar, Officer Z had a stiff standing collar. Officer Q wore the British vest he had worn when fighting for the Queen, and Officer P rode to inspect the pickets in a flat straw hat. Henry Wirz's reluctance to garb himself according to regulation was neither unique nor ununderstandable. If Elizabeth presented him with a beautiful calico shirt (*ach,* where had that woman gotten calico? She was clever at times) it was his own business; and he would wear the shirt because he liked new clothing and could not often come by it.

Actually it was not a shirt but a waist, a waist such as was worn by young boys, and it gave him a fleeting sense of extreme youth and energy to put it on. White pearl buttons adorned the bottom hem of the waist—Elizabeth had sewn them at the proper intervals—probably she had used an old wornout pair of his uniform pants to measure with. He pressed the staring pearl wafers through button holes and stretched his thin chest and tried to square his round shoulders. *Ja.* Very nice. She should receive from him a letter of thanks as soon as he had time to write it; but perhaps his duties would keep him from writing until Elizabeth and the children arrived.

He pulled on his boots with some trouble, reaching across with his left arm to drag at his right boot, not daring to stretch the tender right arm. He tied a black scarf about his neck and reached for his revolver belt. The new weapon was a pride. He had bought it while abroad after concentrated search amid the shops of Parisian gunsmiths. This revolver was in fine condition, though it was secondhand, and a special holster had been sewn to contain it. The cylinder itself was built of barrels, ten small barrels; and from the larger bore in the center of the cylinder a musket ball could be projected whenever one chose to pull the trigger which operated it. Do not fool with me, Yankees. No monkey business from you! . . . The acrid but pleasing scent of barley coffee came to his nostrils. Ha, this was a good day, his first day of duty at Camp Sumter. He wished that he might enjoy an egg, but Mr. Boss said that rats or mink or some such vermin had taken off the chickens. Doubtless he would be served corn pone and fried hog-meat, the common fare of these backwoods ignoramuses. Henry Wirz felt in his pocket for the silver dime which he must offer in payment, and went clumping to his breakfast.

. . . Yes, a very fair day; birds were straining with song as he rode toward the stockade half an hour later. This was a borrowed horse, a bad one because he was close to being fractious, and difficult to manage with but one arm and a half. Henry must procure another mount. He must speak to Captain Dick Winder at once, and convey the unpleasantly perfunctory greeting which General Winder had sent to Cousin Dick, and inquire after a sedate gray-white mare he had seen in the pine-pole paddock behind a kind of outhouse indicated as Winder's office, the previous day. The quartermaster was absent—a lounging sentry said with little respect, Well, Captain, sir, he's away someplace like he usually is. The sentry had spat tobacco juice dangerously close to Wirz's boot-toe. Discipline was needed sorely in these parts. He would instill it. Wirz pushed back his shoulders as he rode.

He called at Dick Winder's shack, could not find him, left word that he had called, and rode to the North Gate where he dismounted and tied his sore-flanked horse firmly to an adjacent railing from which all bark was already chewed. Henry Wirz would show this ragged hireling horde of Yankees that he was not afraid of them; he would go inside on foot, man to man (no, no—man to prisoner) and look them fiercely in their eyes. Wirz's own nervous pink-lidded eyes shone with fresh fire when he glanced at his shabby patent-leather boots. His boots would be dirtied by prisoners' filth but he would get a Negro to clean them for him. Yes, and he should have an orderly; he must have clerks; he concluded shrewdly that such might be found readily among the mass of Yankees. Errand boys, clerks, personal servants; he would make them walk chalk—no funny business from any of them; but if they volunteered to come Outside in response to his summons they would receive in turn many morsels of food not obtainable in the pen. Would he be justified in offering prisoners double rations if they came to serve him? Assuredly. No one could complain about that.

At the outer gate of the boxed-off rectangle the sentry did not recognize him as the new superintendent and refused to let him pass. Wirz shrieked, flew into the German which temper always made him spew, shaped the German into broken English once more—English interlarded generously with the oaths and obscenities which at least he could speak clearly. The sentry was unmoved: a stupid elderly fellow with lack-lustre eyes, split lip, stringy beard. Wirz brandished his orders under the fellow's nose; the fellow could not read, and Henry Wirz would make him sweat for this. He would write out a complaint to the lieutenant-colonel commanding! He—

Once on duty at this stockade you come, you dumb sentry you, God damn you are my boss! I mean—son of a bitch—*I* am boss! It is under my orders you come!

(*Ach,* why could he not speak the English better? It baffled him. Elizabeth had tried to teach, even the little girls had tried to teach. He knew that he was yelling like an idiot, and the recognition of this fact made him but more enraged and yelling the louder. Lack of facility at English had held up his promotion, lack of English—)

By God, I make you smell hell *oder* you let me in!

A coughing and apologetic Captain Hamrick was drawn to the scene by Wirz's fuming; he identified the new superintendent of the prison, the sentry accepted a furious tongue-lashing from Wirz which seemed to draw no blood—perhaps the creature was deaf as well as illiterate. Wirz passed through the enclosure, halting to survey it critically although there was really nothing to see except log walls, a broken wagon wheel leaning against the logs, and a bedraggled slave stretched at full length in the sun which by this time was high enough to find the interior of the box: the black was either sick or asleep or both. Well! In time there should be built a complete second stockade rather than this mere border around each gate. What was to prevent devilish Yankees from digging tunnels underneath a single stockade? Then might they come squeezing through like fastbred rodents, emerging into freedom, ready to pillage the countryside—burn houses and stores, corrupt the crops, ravish the women, seize guns, shoot, shoot—ready to constitute a threat behind the Confederate lines more appalling than that faced at the front. Certainly. A second stockade should be constructed as soon as Wirz could wheedle such security from the Winders.

He paused at the interior gate, quickly putting himself to rights for the prisoners' eyes. His revolver hanging at his left side, ready for his left hand . . . yes, fully capped, ready to spit. He made his heavy gold watch chain hang true, and felt the forepiece of his cap, and drew the cap jauntily to one side.

Going inside, sir? A pimply child at the inner gate put the nasal question.

I am Captain Henry Wirz, commanding now this prison!

Just a second till I lift the bar, Captain, sir. The boy exerted skinny arms under the wooden bar. Wirz helped him with his hand, together they worried the bar aloft and the wicket door scraped open. Wirz stepped over the sill, wrinkling his sharp nose as an odor swept to possess him. It smelled like an alley in one of those Parisian slums where he had walked gingerly, not pitying the poor, but scorning them for their filth, thinking that they should know better.

Wry-necked Smith was calling the roll. That was his regular task. He was a Rebel sergeant on whom devolved many duties not too complex but savoring of any ceremony which exemplified discipline. He was a middle-aged man with a squeezed face, sandy mustache and goatee, and a perpetual frown of concentration. In Taliaferro County he had sought public office assiduously and was bound to be disappointed always on election day, but the next election found him undiscouraged. Smith was barely literate. He pronounced many names so remarkably that it was difficult for their owners to recognize them. Years before, on the way to a gin, driving a cart with his own bale of cotton atop, Smith had managed to upset the vehicle and was pinned beneath the load. His recovery amazed the Taliaferro County medical profession; but after that time his head was riveted around to the right; he could not turn it. When he wished to look in another direction he had to turn his whole body. At this late date the wastage of war had raked even this misshapen relic into the army, and soldiers of his company said that Wry-necked Smith was frozen permanently at Eyes Right: an officer had called the order, Smith had obeyed, and then the officer had forgotten to give the order of Front. Northern prisoners, as soldiers also, had come naturally to the same conclusion.

Wirz had never seen this sergeant before, and now regarded him with disfavor. His darting examination told him immediately that the prisoners were playing roots with the non-commissioned officer. It was an old trick; Wirz had seen them attempting it during his brief service in an Alabama prison and even at Richmond. They tried the trick but did not perform it successfully when Henry Wirz held the roll! It consisted, mainly, of making eighty-seven men, perhaps, seem to count as a hundred. Smith edged warily in front of the formation, moving a few steps at a time, moving to the right where his congealed gaze led him. Yankees responded to their names at one end of the rank, then ducked behind the bodies of their fellows and reappeared in line farther along, squeezing in, answering to the name of Johnson or Langley later as boldly as they had responded to Adams or Atherton earlier. One hundred rations were more to be desired by eighty-seven men than eighty-seven rations. And the game of roots could be played in divers other ways also: it was an aggravation to authorities, a positive swindle to the unalert.

By God, Sergeant!

Wry-necked Smith stepped promptly around to look at Henry Wirz.

These God damn Yankees, you watch them better!

Smith shifted his tobacco quid. Who're you?

Sergeant, it is now I command this stockade. Better you better watch all these damn Yankees. You watch them close! They come around behind, beating you every times!

A few prisoners hooted in the ranks, the rest watched apathetically, the rest were too tired to do more than that. For the most part only the young lean whipper-snappers in their teens had this dance and energy left to them. Ragged slouching ranks were of a sameness; there was such variety to torn attire or lack of it, such infinite variety in people's shapes and sizes that they seemed starved down into common face and form. Who had answered to the name of Lewis when previously he had answered to Gilmore? Wirz might not know; their uniformly tarred faces baffled him whether they wore hair or whether they didn't, whether they were scurvy-ridden and bent between sticks or whether they stood erect, whether they were well-fed raiders or waifs preyed upon by the raiders. Not knowing, feeling his way to absolute authority with caution, Henry Wirz let his patent-leather boots take him away.

He moved along Main Street toward the center of the stockade, holding his left hand upon the flap of his holster. His right forearm began to knock like the pulse of an aching tooth. Proximity to these devils had done that, *ja, ja*. The arm responded; the arm said, So these are the people who tore me, these are the inventors of my misery? *Throb, throb*—let me out, I am cased here in agony. Let me *out! Throb*, let me *out, throb, throb!* said the reeking suffering spirit fastened inside the arm, *let me see the Yankees*.

Wirz traveled almost blindly, moisture on his forehead, cold moisture on his stringy neck. He looked down: one boot-toe was befouled by excrement, fresh soft yellow human excrement; it had to be human, there were no dogs in the place. He said aloud, God damn shit, Yankees are shit— He kept walking.

A string of monsters great and small began to attach to him. They followed calculatingly, trying to evaluate this slight grizzled man, many recognizing immediately the power which he would hold over them, and wondering in the same breath how they might profit from it or avoid its impact. Since Wirz announced himself to Wry-necked Smith the word had gone coursing through mildewed formations and on and on . . . a limp word was spoken, a head was turned . . . group to group among the shebangs. Him? Yup, him. There he goes. What? Who? New commander. Where? Over there. Hey, leave us have a look . . . shoed feet, shoeless feet pattering in muck behind the solitary visitor in gray uniform trousers, the armed man in the calico waist. What is he, an errant boy for Persons? Hey, bubby, does your Ma know where you're at? Bet you a red cent he's got some sugarplums in that there pocket of his. Who? That's him . . . word was ahead of Henry Wirz now, people of the stockade were following in a drove, the news had spread faster than Wirz walked.

A dozen voices were blatting, their owners concealed behind huts or taking refuge back of their mates.

Hi, mister, where in tunket did you get that great big awful pistol?

Will it shoot?

Beardy, don't shoot me!

Who's that specimen, anyways?

Wirz stood his ground, face twisted partly by pain and partly by desperate assertion. You hear to me, Yankees, you dumb damn prisoners! I am Captain Wirz. Now this stockade I command! You watch, you know what is good for you!

They seemed to have their faces corked like actors, they were hooligans from some weird treacherous minstrel troupe. Yah, sneered evil boys hiding behind other evil boys. Older ones or the more sickly (and all the sickly ones looked older than they were; so they were sick, they were fundamentally as vicious as the rest, but too weak to manifest their viciousness!) clung closer to Wirz. Some had actually the effrontery to touch the sleeve of his waist, and he drew back offended.

Captain. Please, Cap'n Wirz. . . .

You know anything about exchange?

Heard anything about exchange?

We're bound to get exchanged soon, aren't we, Captain?

They can't keep us here forever, can they?

We'll get exchanged, won't we, huh, Captain, please?

Ja, said Henry, who knew nothing whatsoever about the exchange or its stoppage—because he had been in Europe when that occurred—and who might not divine the resumption of exchange, because he owned no crystal ball nor knew how to use one. *Ja.* You all get exchanged pretty quick I guess.

He thought that he was being kind no matter how cruel he was in fact. These prisoners who clustered close were behaving like good children for the most part, and good children should be given peppermint sticks, horehound, barley sugar. This was barley sugar which he offered cheerfully, though it would turn to wormwood later. Bad children should be punished. That also would he do.

Several times during his march through this populated mire and during his businesslike return, he halted to examine the stockade from the prisoners' vantage. His glance bounded about like a mouse fallen into a slop-jar. Ha: one stockade only. So they *could* dig tunnels. Ha: Yankees swarmed tightly against the fence, some of them had even attached their jungly huts to the tall logs, seeking shelter from wind or sun. The most innocent shebang might mask fiendish preparations: elaborate ladders to be raised in the dead of night, a concerted rushing of the gate when ration carts entered or when a fresh draft of prisoners arrived or when— A deadline! There must be a deadline. And tomorrow—at once on paper, tomorrow in the fact—the personnel within the pen should be squadded over. The Thousands and Hundreds should disappear forever, supplanted by Detachments and Nineties.

With sycophants trailing Wirz returned to the North Gate. One fellow begged to go out to cut wood, another had written a letter which he wished mailed, another insisted that he was an officer—by rights a captain like Henry Wirz—and should no longer be confined here. Henry accepted the letter (which he neglected to mail for the petitioner, and which got mixed in with some old newspapers later on, and so was thrown out, and the prisoner's wife never heard from him again; never did she know that he died in Andersonville on June twenty-third, 1864, and was taken to the deadhouse without his name tied to his rags; so he became one of the Unknowns; but his wife and sons always thought that he had died gloriously if anonymously in the battle of Olustee). Henry said that there would be no wood-cutting at this time—later on, perhaps, and under heavy guard; he told the pre-tending officer to be off, to try no funny monkey business with him. He went to his new office, a rough plank shanty on the slope opposite the roadway below the large southwest fort. There, with considerable labor and recourse to the dictio-nary taken from his saddle bag, Wirz inscribed an advertisement to be tacked on the inside of the North Gate. He desired two prisoners, bilingual as to German and English preferably, with experience in the routine of military offices. Such men must give their paroles and could dwell outside the stockade. They would receive double rations; other emoluments were hinted at but not specifically promised. . . . Promptly there were five applicants for this seeming sinecure, and Wirz had them fetched outside later on. He interviewed them with increasing disappointment and finally made himself select his two. Neither of them did he consider to be of even average intelligence. (One was named Charles, the other Viggo—he was truly a Dane but he spoke German with a Schleswig accent. Charles was sickly, fated to die of a phagedenic ulcer within a few weeks. Viggo stole things to sell to the guards; Wirz caught him stealing soft soap, and had him turned back into the stockade.) They were but the forerunners of a host who would serve Wirz in his office or at and around his quarters, and some would serve efficiently. How many there would be Wirz himself could not guess, any more than he could have guessed how many prisoners would be confined there eventually.

That same day a guarded herd of Negroes found themselves sinking posts inside the stockade. Wirz's instructions to the youth in command were to drive small posts into the ground firmly so that some three or four feet of their length remained exposed; upon these posts would be nailed scantling strips to mark the deadline. Twenty feet inside the stockade, said Wirz, but the lieutenant was no surveyor and had not a good eye for measurements. At some points the deadline was established not more than sixteen feet from the fence, at others perhaps twenty-two. A howl arose from scores of unfortunates thus dispossessed. They had labored like insects to achieve their shelter; now treasured stakes were pulled out, pine lattice tossed aside; the men were told to take their blankets and coats and move. Furthermore the habitable area within the pen stood reduced by per-haps three acres. Indignation meetings were held, fists were waved, a few stones were thrown at guards.

Just let that Dutch son of a bitch show his face in here!

Deadline, hell. A Wisconsin man stepped angrily past the new posts and jeered up at the parapet, spreading his arms as he hallooed. Promptly several of the nearer guards began to aim their guns at him, and friends dragged the foolhardy man to safety. There was some doubt about whether Wirz meant business, whether the guards would really shoot. This doubt was dispelled quickly the next morning. Ironically the first victim was a German; the prisoners called him Sigel in derogatory reference to his crescent badge of the ill-fated Eleventh Corps. Exposure and illness had sent Sigel into the nodding ranks of the lunatics. Men called him the Old Clothes Man because he went jerking about in a kind of St. Vitus' dance, searching for stray rags or socks in the mud. Sigel observed a checkered scrap of cloth dropped probably by one of the blacks who had driven posts into place. Scantlings had been nailed already at this point, but a scantling meant nothing to the deranged wanderer, and he went pawing under the little barricade, white crescent corps badge and all. He was killed almost instantly by a handful of buckshot smashing through his chest. Prisoners screamed their hatred of the young guard who had fired, they drove him from his perch with mud and billets before he could reload. Another guard took his place. Later Wirz himself crept aloft to survey the situation . . . missiles flew again, obscenities smoked, the hatred was given freely and accepted just as willingly. The construction detail ran out of scantling before they had marked the entire deadline, and there would be dangerous gaps for a long time to come; wiser people tied cords at night, with tufts of rag to wave in warning, but always these cords were being stolen by other people.

The squadding over which began on the day of the death of Crazy Sigel was attended by a protracted insurrection. Henry Wirz was a fanatical believer in the Oriental philosophy of Go Thyself. If he depended on some other person's count, how could he establish the correctness of it? Imagine Wry-necked Smith charged with this task! Wirz was certain that half the private soldiers available to his purposes could not count to twenty without a mistake; he detected signs of unruliness among sergeants and the handful of commissioned officers subordinate to his command. Lieutenant-Colonel Persons himself had introduced the familiar system of Thousands and Hundreds. Through a smoked-up tent fly Wirz heard Alexander Persons denounce the projected Detachments and Nineties as purest fertilizer. *Ach,* was ever a prison superintendent so put upon, was ever a prison superintendent less coöperated with? So must he parade the prisoners and count them himself.

It took him hours to achieve the count, manifold order book in hand. By the time he had completed checking the Seventh Thousand, prisoners of the first detachments were out of formation and wandering all over the place. Bad children—they should be punished (what did he do to Cora when she was naughty? Send her to bed without her supper! So should he do with these!)—he was the man for the job, God damn.

Today for your badness no rations will come!

The howl which answered this announcement made Claffey slaves rise in alarm from their planting of a distant field, it brought men running out of Uncle Arch Yeoman's store.

This incident was unfortunate, but if it served to teach the prisoners to stay in line when they were ordered to, it should have served its purpose. One could not line up Thousands and tell them off into fresh Detachments unless orders were obeyed. In a melancholy drizzle next morning bayonets were fixed, the gate was swung, guards marched in with Wirz trotting in their midst as if he also were a prisoner.

Maybe you Yankees stay until dismissed, this day? he asked witheringly. . . . Once more he proceeded with his labored count, once more the sickly tired resentful beggarmen said, Oh, cowshit, and skulked from the ranks. Here was Henry Wirz, counting the new Detachment Twenty-three; and beyond him those vagabonds in the as-yet-uncounted Detachment Twenty-six were strolling down to the marsh because they claimed they had to do their business. Never could two hundred and seventy men need to do their business at once! Did they take him for a fool? They would learn the temper of the officer with whom they trifled!

Famished throngs swayed opposite the North Gate all that afternoon, watching with such hope that even sentries stared down to pity them. But no patched harness jingled, no wheels squeaked, no rabbit mules flicked their ears, no cornmeal was transported to its parceling out. Now forty-eight hours had passed since a bite of food had been issued. Only the acknowledged raiders had anything saved up for a rainy day, and even these joined in the din and grumble. Fierce youths who still had the litheness of willow and the verve of cats about them— They gathered in trembling groups, talk flew wildly.

Come along, old top, I'm with you: better off dead than starved!

If we get enough poles to batter with, we can bust out that little wicket door.

Certain—some of us are going to get shot, but the bulk will get through.

Harvey, I'll be right alongside you!

Let's every fellow grab a club and—

The gravel of these verbal torpedoes spread stinging; yet there was no leader, no supreme chemist to mix the desperation and hunger and rage, no one to shake the mixture and let it spurt. Far into hours of darkness the boys huddled and snarled; yet it was only a pathetic snarling, only a huddle.

Once more in early morning the Rebel fife squeaked its message of Roll Call. Once more came bayonets and the skinny bearded man, now so universally loathed, scooting in the shadow of their security. This day the prisoners' swollen feet seemed fastened to the ground with a mucilage of despair. They did not go ranging afield after they were first counted, they remained in ranks. Scores of them collapsed or sat down through sheer weakness; but they stayed, they did not drift, they were in the counted Thousands when the superintendent came back to make his final conversion into Detachments.

He rewarded them with their day's ration, but only that day's ration. (This he debated in his mind, after he was once back in the shed: might he not give them the meal for the two other days? *Nein:* too much all at once, it would make them sick, the incidence of mortality might rise abruptly. One day's rations: enough. They had earned this by good behavior. But their bad behavior of the two previous days had earned them exactly nothing save empty bellies. Like naughty children they must be brought to time, *ja.*) The toy mules came straining, the mess sergeants drew their meal, it was divided.

. . . He was but doing his duty, they must be aware of that. Since the squadding over was now complete, Henry Wirz had no thought that he needed longer a retinue of guards. The next morning he ventured into the stockade alone. Within minutes he came dodging out again, his unfired revolver shaking in his left hand, his calico waist dripping with mud and offal, his neck dirtied, his arms dirtied, his shoulder bruised where a rock had struck.

Gott, they were devils! But if he had emptied his weapon into the bodies of some, then the others would surely have torn him to pieces, no matter how many dropped to the guards' volley. He thought of a snake pit, thought of a lions' den. Prisoners seethed through his aching head all that day; he could not eat dinner, no longer did he have appetite; he wished he could drink but liquor made him sick; *ja,* even food made him sick, even the idea of food, for he was a dyspeptic. Prisoners jabbered and seethed in his dreams that night, he cried out hoarsely, he awakened the neighbors. Henry Wirz wished for his wife, for his family. He felt alone and misunderstood.

18

Two older but not so hefty boys showed Willie Collins how to make a bully out of a dead rat and handfuls of shot. This was in 1843 when Willie was nine years old. A common play for boys in the Fourth Ward (and in regions equally depraved in other portions of the United States) was to attach a dead rat to a stout cord and whirl the rat over your head, or round and round beside you as you ran and shrieked. Live rats abounded, a dead rat was to be avoided only because of its putridity . . . you whirled the plummet, smaller children got out of the way, girl children ran screaming. You could have battles with other boys, biffing them with your rat until its tail broke off; then you had to tie the cord around the neck, and it did not swing so well; eventually the rat would be mashed apart, flogged out of all usefulness; then you had to get another dead rat, but there were plenty of those to be had.

The boys who taught a better trick to Willie were Danny Crogan and Gabriel Seek; one was white, the other colored but with red hair. Danny was dead at fourteen, his head splintered in a street fight. At sixteen red-headed Gabe was shot by a coachman who said that Gabe had raped his young daughter, and maybe Gabe had; but previously he bragged to friends that the girl gave herself to him, and she sneaked out to him a dinner bucket filled with delicious fried smelts almost every day.

Get you your rat, said Danny. Slit him open and take out the guts. . . . Get a fresh rat what ain't swoll up yet, said Gabe. Nail him to a board, scrape the skin so's it won't have much smell, so twill be good and soft. . . . Go you down to that tannery, end of Cherry Street; steal you a handful of the tan stuff and rub it on. . . . First thing you know, you got you a well-tanned rat. . . . It's then you sew him up. . . . First you got to put in them shot, said Gabriel Seek. . . . Och, sure: and it's tight you must stitch it, with the hide doubled, or the shot will leak. . . . Buckshot—that best. . . . Och, yes, said Danny Crogan. Go you down to Cowley the gunsmith, and he's got buckshot in the third keg from the door; and wait you till he's back at his bench with some crusher who's brought a pistol to him, and it's then you can snatch your buckshot and get away before he fibs you. . . . Stuff that rat full and sew him tight, said Gabe Seek, rolling his eyes.

Willie Collins listened, Willie Collins learned. Within a few days he had his rat ready, tanned at least well enough to suit him. But use stout cordage, he had been told. Rawhide is best; and tie it to the neck, for the tail would snap, it's that heavy.

Willie went out into the gloaming—it was autumn, and trees drifted their dry spicy leaves when you got where there were trees. Willie had been instructed to look for a hockey. There were many hockeys staggering in narrow passages close to the Gotham Court tenement where he dwelt; but these drunken men were half naked, and none of them might have so much as a hogg, a single ten-cent piece, in his rags. Willie traveled farther afield, swinging the heavy rat-pouch from time to time, to pretend that he was an innocent lad, playing innocently with a dead rat and that was the truth. He idled his way toward the East River. Nearby there survived a short row of prim mansions, their iron gates locked against incursions, holding red brick shoulders stiff against the loose hordes now spilling across Franklin Square where once George Washington had dwelt, where once John Hancock had walked.

A man moved toward Willie through the wan purple light. Most certainly he was a hockey; he was an elderly man, but he tottered as if he had swallowed an entire decanter of brandy before weaving on his homeward path. How was Willie Collins to know that Mr. Hans Van Auken, a long retired watchmaker, had suffered a stroke of paralysis the previous winter and could now walk only with difficulty? And would it have made any difference at all whether he was a hockey, fuddled with drink, or only an ancient with twitching limbs? Mr. Hans Van Auken leaned on his silver-headed cane, he wore a brushed beaver hat, his pantaloons were strapped neatly beneath his slippers. Had he seen danger approaching, he would have blown upon the shrill-noted whistle he carried on a ribbon around his neck, to alert policemen or servants or private watchmen, to send a thief scotting. But he saw no danger; he saw only a lad wheeling a dead rat round his head— Oh, poor lad from a poor home, and that was all he had to play with. Mr. Van Auken thought to give the lad a penny, and began to fumble in the lower left pocket of his waistcoat. A minute later he was dead. He died, he drained away unconsciously there on the cobbled sidewalk without a cry, without a whine, with the front of his fragile egg-shell skull crushed in, with several of his pockets turned out, and the treasured ebony walking stick gone from his dying grasp.

Two streets away Willie Collins thought suddenly about the walking stick. Were he seen carrying it, someone might know— He penetrated an alley, felt about until he found a narrow cranny between two jammed-up buildings. He put the silver head of the cane into this cranny and snapped it off. With the lump in his pocket, and still swinging his rat, he ran home to Gotham Court to see how well he had profited. He had profited to the extent of one gold watch, a few silver coins and coppers—and one gold eagle in the lot; and a beaded doeskin purse of Indian manufacture which Mr. Van Auken had carried as a precious souvenir sent by his son who traded with the Winnebagoes. This purse was found to contain twenty-eight American dollars, an English sovereign, and a promissory note for two hundred dollars drawn to Mr. Van Auken's favor and signed by a man named Cameron. (Since Willie could not read, this information escaped him and he put the note into the chamber pot.) Purse and money he put into his pocket along with the cane-head, and he was gloating over the watch by candlelight when rudely interrupted by Big Biddy.

Big Biddy was a gangling mulatto woman, deeply in love with Willie Collins's father when she was drunk—which was most of the time—and resenting him (because he was an Irishman, and white) when she was sober. Which was now.

A yack. Where you get that yack, Willie?

And wouldn't you like to know?

Give me that yack.

In a pig's ass I will.

She fell upon him, they fought, at nine years he might have been taken for twelve or older. Big Biddy had her hands full. (He had concealed his rat in a favorite hideaway, which was beneath a loose board under the pallet whereon Willie's father and Big Biddy slept commonly together or singly; otherwise Willie might have used the rat on her. They might look for purloined goods under the mound of rags which was Willie's, they had not wits enough to look under their own. . . . When their noisy ardor was spent, and when they were roaring with sleep, it was an easy matter to work the loose board out from beneath their couch.) At length, amid mutual buffetings and squawkings, Big Biddy was able to draw a fresh-filled gin bottle from the pocket of her red cloak, and she gave Willie such a bang on the head—but never breaking the bottle—that he went squealing down the stairs. The watch had fallen upon the bricks they used for a brazier in cold weather; when opened it proved to have the crystal broken and it would not run. But it was a gold-cased watch with the initials H.I.V.A. engraved elaborately. When Aloysius Collins came gasping in (you could hear his breathing as he approached, the grating wheeze of it, you could hear it from the bottom of the stairway) Big Biddy displayed her loot.

You black bludget, you. Where did you hoist it?

Kiddie had it, Al. She had drunk half the gin and was warming to him.

He's but a babe.

God damn, man, he had it.

Likely twas in the street he found it, muttered the gigantic decrepit Aloysius.

Yah, she sneered, disapproving of Willie because he had hurt her breast during the struggle. I bet you, man, he hoist it from some shop.

He's but a babe, ladybird, but a babe.

The next morning the elder Collins sold Mr. Van Auken's watch to a popshop proprietor for five dollars: he should have received much more, but he was stupid and quivering, and it seemed that wild animals were roosting above his bed when he awakened; he stood in need of liquor. During the day policemen came searching the stores of all the Uncles in the area, for the murder of Hans Van Auken had caused a great hue and cry . . . one of the dead man's sons was a rich merchant, another was a city official. They discovered the watch, Collins was pointed out as the man who'd sold it to the pawnshop proprietor, police came thundering into Gotham Court. But twenty men, including the proprietor of the Diving Bell (and the proprietor was well acquainted with the dead man's politician son) swore that Aloysius Collins had slept on a bench in the corner of the Diving Bell from five p.m. until long after the body of Hans Van Auken was discovered. Thus Collins's insistence that he had found the watch, broken in the street on his way home, could not be refuted. His wailing word was accepted as gospel in the end.

Al Collins could never have done it, anyway, declared the proprietor of the Diving Bell. He's a mighty man, but drink has took the pepper from him.

No one even thought of nine-year-old Willie. They said, Be off with you, when he came slinking around, when the police had his father in tow. They said, Away with you, you spalpeen. This is a sorry business.

Later, when the freed Aloysius was sufficiently sane, he beat half the life out of his son with a chair-leg.

Willie endured, although he screamed loud enough to awaken all of Gotham Court. He did not awaken all of Gotham Court; they were accustomed to screams. Willie had the money tucked safely away, and the head of the silver walking stick was hidden against a future emergency (he used it eventually to make a slung-shot which he lost in a fight) and he would savor sugarplums, oysters, fried cod, hot corn and any other dainty he chose—forever and a day, it seemed then. He was thunderstruck and delighted to learn that he had killed a man. He walked with puffed chest, he snarled at smaller children, he stood around with other colts in front of public houses on Water Street, watching men and prostitutes moving in and out, watching with glee the fights which always developed. Sometimes there would be several fights in the course of an hour, sometimes men were left for dead, sometimes they were dead.

It's myself who's kilt a man already, he told Gabriel Seek and Danny Crogan when he felt expansive.

You're not elderly enough to have hair in your crotch!

But I did. With my leaded rat, as you showed me.

And who did you give the nope to, kiddie?

Twas an old hockey.

Who you think you fool, Willie? . . . Ah, you're not elderly enough to—

And where are you after thinking I got all the brass I got?

Hoisting purses off of owls! cried Danny in great pride at his own humor. Willie grappled with him and they rolled in the street, gouging and biting, until some passing sailors thoughtfully kicked them apart and into flight.

At sixteen Willie Collins, grown already to some thirteen stone, drifted into river piracy with the Daybreak Boys, operating under the banner of Nick Saul and Billie Howlett. He was not yet nineteen, in 1853, when he stood in the Tombs yard and with interest watched Saul and Howlett drop from their scaffold. He did not wonder how it would feel to be hanged, he did not wonder about anything. A smarter slyer youth might plan the forays; he, Willie Collins, would carry them out. At least that portion of the work which fell to him commonly—the strong arm, the club on the skull, the kick in the groin, the arm around the neck until breathing stopped.

Wait till it's two o'clock, Willie.

Yes. Two.

Then get to Tanner's wharf; it should take you ten minutes. The watchman keeps a fire in an iron drum, to keep him warm. I think he'll be setting by the fire; if he's making his rounds he'll come back to it. Get him by the neck—take care he gives no yell, take care he has no chance to yell—and kick the fire into the river, drum and all. Then there'll be no glim.

That I'll do.

Mind, there must be no yelling.

He'll never yell, cove, that he'll not do.

. . . That he did not do.

It was said that a fellow named Slobbery Jim would take over command of the Daybreak Boys after Billie and Nick were hanged at the Tombs. But Willie Collins was not a favorite of Slobbery Jim. To begin with, the new captain was afraid of Willie, and still regarded him as even more stupid than he really was.

Willie drifted up into the Eighteenth Ward where he heard that pickings were easier, and so they proved to be. The system there was exceedingly simple, much more to Willie's liking and understanding than the devious split-second-timing incursions of the Daybreak Boys among docks and shipping. A man who called himself Paddy Delaney (he was built much as Willie was built, although he was not as large as Willie; and yet he was older, and more experienced) was Willie Collins's immediate superior. Take the corner of Twenty-ninth and Madison: that was all Willie had to do. Take the northeast corner—that was as good as any; and Saxey would have the northwest corner, and Cuban Cookie the southwest, and Skibbereen Mahone the southeast. If a well-dressed man approached in darkness— Well, take him and go through him. If there were two men together, as often happened, one of the other kiddies could step over from yonder corner.

They, and the roughs who worked with them, were known as the Honeymoon Gang—a satirical tribute to their cruelty. If a pedestrian strolling through the fog appeared to be well clad, and then, on close and violent examination, proved no fit subject for profitable keel-hauling, the Honeymooners would batter him to ribbons merely for the sport of the thing. Willie took to this stand-up-and-slam-a-man-down simplicity with gusto. The second week of his operations he was lucky enough to observe a lone gentleman in an opera cloak leaving a nearby cat-house from in front of which his untipped hackman had long since driven away in dudgeon. Willie put his hand over the stranger's bearded lips, carried him into a blind areaway and throttled him into insensibility. The man turned out to be a wealthy coffee merchant from Latin America; Willie could not know that; he knew only that he acquired over six hundred dollars in banknotes, to say nothing of jewelry. The newspapers cried that Juan Santa Maria Lopez, Esq., a visiting exporter, had been half-killed and was now under the care of surgeons at his lodgings, and had lost a fortune in jewelry to the roughs who attacked him. Juan Santa Maria Lopez affirmed that there were at least five men in the band who fell upon him.

I don't know who the other man was. Paddy Delaney sat with a cocked pistol in his hand. But let us be after seeing the sparks and the fawneys, you dirty buzzers, or I'll pop the bladder of one of you.

Saxey, Skibbereen and Cuban Cookie were loud in their protestations of ignorance of the affair, but it was not easy for Willie to lie with aplomb. Soon all four of them were arrayed against him, and that was too many, for Delaney and Skibbereen both approached him in size. He handed over a silk handkerchief containing the baubles, and gave up three dollars in currency which he swore by heaven and earth was all the money the foreigner had had upon him. In delight over emeralds Delaney did not press him further; but awarded Willie only a tenth share in the later proceeds as punishment. Willie never told about the six hundred dollars; in his mutton-headed musings he thought that he had out-smarted Patrick Delaney. He did not know that Delaney divvied up only a fraction of the money received for the jewelry. . . . The Honeymoon Gang waxed rich, then poorer as more police crowded that neighborhood in response to the agony of citizens. Some months later they were driven down into the Bowery by the intrepid Captain Walling and his Strong Arm Squad. It was merry while it lasted.

His giant's stature began to tell on Willie Collins, to make him a marked man. If a shorn and bleeding sheep complained to the authorities that he had been pounded by a robber of enormous height and girth, the police (or such of them as could be persuaded by bribery) went seeking Willie. Thus he was charged with crimes he did not commit . . . he had committed many . . . he did not know how many men he had killed before he entered wartime captivity, he supposed a dozen or so. Several times he was imprisoned; once he escaped, once he bought his way to freedom, the other times he served the brief terms to which he was sentenced. He thought of leaving New York but New York was home, he did not know where else to go. The body which had once been his bonanza was now a positive handicap. At rare intervals fortune sent a rich weakling into his grasp, and then he made sure that no evidence would be given against him. . . . Willie flaunted new duds in Barney Bright's Joy Mill where, according to the gilded sign outside, the mill ground out Joy, Joy, Nothing But Joy—and a little mayhem and venereal disease along with the Joy.

He lived—bellowing, pompous, frightening, thick-headed. He leaned on the rail of an excursion craft off Bedloe's Island and poked his shoulders and his whiskey bottle through the bunting in order to watch Albert Hicks, the high seas murderer, as Hicks fell through an open air gallows trap and struggled in strangulation. And if they ever come to hang me, howled Willie Collins, they'll have to hang me twice! A well-fleshed woman cooed beside him and wiggled her hip against him; she wore red gloves and red stockings; faith, and she wore little bells on her garters, the bells tinkled when she moved. Willie lived . . . he lived even-

tually with the Bowery Boys, he had fought alongside them when they raided the
Dead Rabbits at the election polls back in 1856, but it did no good: Fernando
Wood was reëlected anyway. But it was a fine fight. And again he had contended
against the Dead Rabbits in the historic Bayard Street riot of the following summer; and could you guess the man he met there, slugging in the ranks of the Dead
Rabbits with a paving stone in one hand and a shoemaker's awl in the other?
Patrick Delaney it was, the erstwhile Honeymooner. They grappled in long anticipated rivalry . . . sure, and Willie was confident that Delaney died beneath the
stamping of his brass-heeled boots. Willie lived!

For a fact Paddy Delaney did not die. The next time the monsters met, it was
on Rebel soil with Rebel guards rimmed beyond them. It might have been that
the two roughs were rocked in the same cradle in a Dublin slum, if anyone ever
bothered to rock babies in Dublin slums: they embraced like grizzly bears, they
wept and swore their loyalty, they drank what smuggled liquor was available and
brayed for more. Ah, and I thought I had kilt you surely that day at the Bowery
and Bayard. . . . Willie darling, it's me that was certain I was kilt; and months it
took me to regain my strength, with half my ribs stove in.

Willie came to the sad pass of Confederate prison life through a series of
misadventures. He emerged from another type of prison in New York after the
war had begun. A turmoil of alternate patriotic demonstration and felonious
interference was ruling the town. It was hard for Willie to turn a dollar or even a
dime. Though they had a wary respect for Collins's proficiency the ruling gangsters held him to be bad luck and would have none of his services. He eked out an
existence in Mulberry Bend, preying on the same sort of stumbling drunks and
drugged seamen he had preyed on when he was a boy. In his late twenties Willie
looked to be at least forty. The skin of his face and neck bore the coarse-seamed
texture of middle age, there were stray shreds of glint in his ginger-colored beard,
his hair-line receded. Soon he heard that he was being sought by the police again
—something about a Norwegian cook who had been squeezed to death in a cellar,
and the Norwegian ship's master had friends among the new Metropolitan Police.
There was nothing for Willie to do but enlist, which he did quickly, and then
deserted just as quickly, bounty money sewn in his drawers. In this way he went
from regiment to regiment. It had never occurred to him that he might be sent
into combat, but that was what happened after he joined the Eighty-eighth Pennsylvania, before he'd found opportunity to take his usual French Leave.

He had done well enough at Belle Isle but here at Andersonville he was doing
even better. There were vastly more prisoners to provide the luxuries of existence
both directly and indirectly. Day after day fresh drafts were pushed into the
stockade: there were riches to be had, a plethora. For indeed there were no police
to bother! Once more Willie was marked, towering above the rest, but his mark-
ing was as great a benefit to him here as it had been a handicap in the city streets.
By April he needed not to stir hand or foot if he did not choose to move; he grew
fat; but it would take a long while for his grotesque thews to become so wadded in
corpulence that they would not serve him. He kept his own band well under
control—not too many of them, but whittled down to comfortable size. There
were a round dozen sluggers, also the cooks and housekeepers—two of these
latter were homosexuals whose affection some of his men enjoyed, but Willie
himself did not crave such peculiar ecstasies, his laughter burst at the very idea.
There was Lipsky the tailor, and a few other scrofulous hangers-on who served for
one purpose or another. Collins's Raiders were not the largest band in the stockade but they were feared above all others.

Collins's Raiders, Delaney's Raiders, Sarsfield's Raiders, Curtis's Raiders. The name of Terence Sullivan was an imprecation; the names of Heenan and Pete Bradley and Dick Allen conjured obscenities; you shuddered as well when you thought of the Staleybridge Chicken or the Harlem Infant, for these creatures had been pugilists and brought their nasty experience like weapons into the stockade.

The population swelled steadily through March, train whistles bleated at the station, the columns of rag-pickers toiled through the ravine to the North Gate; they had picked enough rags in Virginia, now they could pick them in Georgia. Stray infantry skirmish here, stray cavalry encounter there—the gaping blue-clad flat-hatted seamen from an unhappy sloop, the battery men gathered in by the Rebs when they were still limbering up to flee: all appeared. All had a certain small wealth in their pockets or on their backs or in the very clothes which dressed them. The raiders took what they wished, and were seldom disappointed. Their victims lost anything from their buttons to their lives.

A hopeless teeming disorder was apparent in this polluted rectangle from the very first. In tag-end days of February the initial thefts were committed under cover of darkness or behind tumbled wafers of clay and pine-roots: you knew that something bad was happening, it had happened at Belle Isle and Danville, it had happened to some degree in all the Virginia prisons, you didn't see it happening often, it happened out of sight, it was treacherous and to be feared.

What was the need of waiting for night? At first Willie Collins and those like him had a notion that guards might shoot. They recalled the death of Tomcat O'Connor, they saw no reason to die jumping as he had died. But one morning John Sarsfield himself, with his minions, was standing near the North Gate when a small detachment of Westerners (they included pickets gobbled up by a swift Confederate movement in northwest Georgia) found themselves staring at Andersonville for the first time. These people had not been robbed of their blankets. As did many folks from the West, they wore blanket rolls in Confederate fashion, they carried no knapsacks. The blanket rolls seemed bulky to Sarsfield's practiced gaze. He shouldered forward and wrenched the roll away from the nearest prisoner. The man hallooed, Sarsfield knocked him flat, the balance of the fresh fish leaped toward Sarsfield, Sarsfield's Raiders swatted, stabbed, kicked. This fight was over in less than a minute. Six of the Westerners lay on the ground and the rest had fallen back into the watching throng—several others shy of their blanket rolls, as was the first man. All of the new-come prisoners were bleeding, two were unconscious. Sarsfield's Raiders were the richer by eleven blanket rolls filled with combs, socks, extra shoes, Bibles (these could be bartered), gilt melanotypes, housewives, knives, eating utensils and name-it-if-you-like. The guards on the parapet stations had not fired a shot; they watched idly or in downright amusement; they said, Look at them Yanks a-fighting like a lot of dogs, just look.

Willie Collins and Pat Delaney lifted a leaf from Sarsfield's book. Sarsfield was intelligent; it was said that he had read law, had served three years in the army, had been wounded, his wound had healed, he had been promoted First Sergeant and later commissioned; his commission had arrived but he had not been mustered when he was captured. Hence he'd landed here with the enlisted men. Folks said that a bright fellow like Sarsfield had known all along that the guards would not fire. Or perhaps he had made a private agreement with the guards; and now guards might profit from each robbery occurring before their eyes and under the muzzles of their unfired muskets. No longer could the vice be relegated to darkness. It was here in daylight, stalking; it was an animal grown tall as the Methodist Church steeple back home, it was Force and Force only, it could and would maul you to a wet bloody rag if you lifted your fist in protest, or sometimes even if you lifted your voice.

A twenty-year-old named John L. Ransom, Ninth Michigan Cavalry, wrote in his diary: Colonel Persons commands the prison, and rides in and talks with the men. Is quite sociable, and says we are all to be exchanged in a few weeks. He was informed that such talk would not go down any longer. We have been fooled enough, and pay no attention to what they tell us.

John Ransom wrote in a sodden notebook that said *Pickell & Co., Commission Merchants. Chicago. Ills.,* on the cover in faded gilt letters. Get almost enough to eat, such as it is, but don't get it regularly; sometimes in the morning, and sometimes in the afternoon. Six hundred more prisoners came last night. . . . We have no shelter of any kind whatever. Eighteen or twenty die per day. Cold and damp nights. The dews wet things through completely, and by morning all nearly chilled. Wood getting scarce. On the outside it is a regular wilderness of pines . . . can just see the cars go by, which is the only sign of civilization in sight. Rebels all the while at work making the prison stronger. Very poor meal, and not so much today as formerly. . . . Prevailing conversation is food and exchange. A good deal of fighting going on among us. . . . Prison gradually filling up with forlorn looking creatures.

Johnny Ransom had a broken stub of pencil, and he chewed the pencil and made it smaller and found difficulty in writing with it; but he was determined to write a diary. Well, well, my birthday came six days ago, and how old do you think I am? Let me see. Appearances would seem to indicate that I am thirty or thereabouts, but as I was born on the twentieth day of March, 1843, I must now be just twenty-one years of age, this being the year 1864. Of age and six days over. I thought that when a man became of age, he generally became free and his own master as well. If this ain't a burlesque on that old time-honored custom, then carry me out—but not feet foremost. . . . The pine which we use in cooking is pitch pine, and a black smoke arises from it; consequently we are black as negroes. Prison gradually filling from day to day, and situation rather more unhealthy. . . . It is a sad sight to see men die so fast. New prisoners die the quickest. . . . It's a sickly dirty place. Seems as if the sun was not over a mile high, and has a particular grudge against us.

There was a dull man named Dawson who rose each day during that first month of the prison's existence and made his comment about the weather. If the sun came clear, ready to accumulate and radiate the fierce stout heat of a Georgia sun in spring, the dullard would declare, Well, Old Sol the Haymaker is going to get in his work on us again today. And if—as came about more often in March—the skies were cased with zinc and ready to leak or burst, Dawson called the skies and the day Old Boo. Well, Old Boo gets us again today. The terse keen wisdom of the ages can be recollected and quoted by a few; it is the dunces who conceive or incubate the old saws, the slang, the common parlance. Dawson stood daily and turned his bleared gaze upward, and spoke his piece. In no time at all most of the men capable of observing an anecdote were talking about Old Boo. Dawson fell sick, he died, he smelled badly, he was lugged away, no one cared much about him, he was not missed. Months later new prisoners would enter and soon would hear about Old Boo, and they would laugh about Old Boo and in time would shrink in their terror of Old Boo; and then like Dawson they would go down to death, blaming Old Boo; or if they were more fortunately tougher they might survive, and thus live to procreate, to have their children procreate, to sit one day in a rocking chair out on the shady grass under maple trees and tell their grandchildren about Old Boo; and then the grandchildren would go to bed, and cry out in the middle of the night with bad dreams, and when Mother came soothing they would say, He was going to get me, he was going to grab me. Who was going to grab you, dearie? Old Boo! Now, there is no such thing as Old Boo; I never heard of Old Boo; that's just silly. Say Now I Lay Me again, and go to sleep, and don't dream about Old Boo any more because there isn't any such thing.

Johnny Ransom took the wet stub out of his sore mouth and wrote painstakingly: Seems as if our government is at fault in not providing some way to get us out of here. The hot weather months must kill us all outright. Feel myself at times sick and feverish with no strength seemingly. . . . Raiders getting more bold as the situation grows worse. Often rob a man now of all he has, in public, making no attempt at concealment. In sticking up for the weaker party our mess gets into trouble nearly every day.

So indeed did the boys of John Ransom's mess; so did many others. But their resistance (heroic in starved slight youths who battled against a vast anonymous cruelty) was ineffectual. There was no concert in action, no assembling of a force sufficient to cope with well-fed enemies most of whom had practiced the arts of subjugation from infancy. Charity, Christianity, eagerness, righteousness: these were lame swords with which to be armed no matter what the Scriptures had to say on the subject. History had taught a million lessons, history would teach a million more; few might profit from the teaching. Angry and continually apprehensive, the prisoners said, If we all get together . . . take a hundred men, every man jack of them carrying a club; why, we ought to be able to— No one mustered the hundred, no one prepared the cudgels. Say, fellers, we'll make agreement with you folks in that Ohio tent; we'll swap protection with you. If any raiders tackle you, we'll join in; and you got to swear you'll side with us if we get jumped. How about them new folks yonder in the next shebang? Hellfire, twon't do no good to even ask them. Seventh New Hampshire, the whole boiling, and you know what that means: bounty jumpers who enlisted for the heavy pay. Not a true New Hampshireman in the lot, and I vow they'd turn tail in the first pinch.

The frantic disorder pertaining to housing—such as it was—and rations—such as were furnished— Disorder, crowding, the speedy rise of disease and resultant mortality: these ills worked for the raiders' benefit. One noon news came skimming through the mobs: smallpox—didn't you hear? It's rife. No, I didn't see the sick ones; but a boy from the next mess seen them: all blotched up and feverish, and itching like the Old Harry. Tis said the Rebs are going to vaccinate us. Well, by mighty, they'll have to cinch and hog-tie me before they'll get their rotten horse-piss into *my* arm! I seen a nigger man up in Virginia, and he lost his arm because of that damnable vaccination, and like to lost his life as well.

One day, urged by the bayonets of a seedy regiment marched inside for the purpose, the seven thousand men assembled in the stockade were walked to one side of the creek and made to return by slow files while the few contract surgeons scraped vaccine into their arms as they passed. Once beyond the surgeons, there was a growing rush to the marsh and boggy creek despite the fumes which now smoked above each turgid pool. People feared the vaccine more than they feared this noxious ooze—many of them did. They scrubbed madly at their abraded flesh, washing with mud and slime, trusting that they were expelling tainted medicament. There followed numerous cases of swelling and local putrefaction, with amputation and sometimes death as the logical result. Men who had bathed their vaccinations developed enormous sores, men who had not bathed their vaccinations developed enormous sores. There were as many theories about the sores as there were sores; some believed that the vaccine had been adulterated deliberately with blood taken from syphilitic invalids. The surgeons exhausted their store before half the men had been treated; the threat of later vaccination was another of the clouds lying above the stockade.

It was a community demoralized in its inception, demoralized through rapid growth, exploded into wreckage as each cap was detonated by a falling hammer: the cap of starvation . . . *bang!* and more lives flame out . . . the cap of illness, the cap of chill at night . . . *bang! Bang* . . . the dread of a beating, the water poisoned by human filth . . . Godsakes, Piper, I dipped out a half-canteen of that stuff and lifted it up to drink and— Godsakes, there was a turd floating right under my nose! . . . The hammer of the rifle falling, the fresh cap exploded spitefully . . . *bang* . . . the trigger pulled by an unseen finger, by a finger far away, by a finger inert, by a finger fumbling.

In such a teetering confusion there were crops to be gathered by savage simple people who knew but enough to strike a blow and had the power to strike it. Willie Collins was happier in Andersonville than he had ever been before. Other toughs emerged from their brutal obscurity—a man in sailor's dress named Rickson, another alleged sailor named Munn. They had been worms in the outer world; there they stood in secret dread of manacles, a flogging, in dread of discipline itself. Here there was no discipline except such as the Goliaths chose to inflict upon their subordinates. Among themselves they brawled for fun, and to reassure themselves constantly as to their status as chieftains. The handsome Munn scowled his ponderous way among shebangs; weaker prisoners hurriedly freed a pathway for him. The heavy-fisted Sarsfield commanded more power than he would have commanded as the officer he never became in fact. Charley Curtis reminded some prisoners of the orangutans pictured in books of travel . . . low-browed, massive, his voice was a grunt, he had a trick of tearing the ear off any victim who offered resistance.

Sentries clucked at their stations. By God, Holley, I'm damned if them Yanks don't just beat the devil.

Sure enough. Like a pack of wolves.

Holley, I hain't never seen a pack of wolves; but if'n they're as mean-tempered and all gone filthy as these Yankees I sure as hell don't want to!

. . . Ah, Delaney, and it's over to my own headquarters you must come immediately; and wait till you see what I've got to treat you with. Pine-top, man? Never! It's a bottle of the finest brandy I've tasted since first I joined up. Devil knows where the guard at Station Thirty got it. A fine pocketknife I gave him for it, with four blades and a bone handle. It's from a fresh Marylander I took it— Ah, you would have split a gut! Nickey snatch the lot of us if he didn't make to jab me with it when I asked him for the knife politely. Sure, and there he lies yonder; hark you to the noise he's making still; his jaw went to pieces like a teacup when I tapped him.

Hymns receded from the hearing of a bowlegged Rhode Islander named Edward Blamey; he could not hear his father reading aloud: *Therefore I say unto you, Take no thought for your life, what ye shall eat, or what ye shall drink; nor yet for your body, what ye shall put on. Is not the life more than meat, and the body than raiment? Behold the fowls of the air—*

So regularly that it became a commonplace, a frightened-looking young officer in a shabby dun-colored jacket appeared within the stockade on muleback; he rode from point to point, rattling off his memorized screed whenever he thought there was an audience sufficient, and receiving invariably the same vociferous response.

. . . Your Government has cruelly abandoned you, as you can now see, for it makes no attempt to release you and refuses all our offers of a fair exchange of prisoners, North and South. Since your capture you must have become increasingly aware that the Southern Confederacy will soon succeed in achieving its complete and undisputed independence. The Southern Confederacy now offers you an opportunity to enter its service. You will be taken out of this uncomfortable spot, you will receive bounteous rations and adequate apparel; you will be given an attractive bounty, and, at the conclusion of hostilities, you will receive a land warrant establishing your right to—

Aw, go fuck a duck.

Got any of those bounteous rations along with you now?

Why, your adequate apparel hain't much better'n my own.

Where's my farm going to be, with that land warrant and all? I don't want no farm in Texas. Got a nice farm in hell?

Who the devil told you I wanted to be galvanized?

Now and then a lone man—sometimes two or three at a time (comrades who had talked it over and decided that they would dishonor themselves before they would die; but they were few)—slipped to the gate in dark. They asked to speak to an officer, they mumbled the words, the guards had no respect for them and they knew it, they felt a fierce hot breath of living Unionists down their spines, they felt a fierce cold breath of Unionists who were dead.

Some men wondered why, above all, the professional bounty jumpers and roughs did not take advantage of an opportunity to crawl out of this obnoxious slough. But the more discerning might understand easily; within these precincts there was prosperity for the rapacious. Unless driven frantic by the need for women, few of them cared to enlist as Confederates; they saw the Rebel sentries ill-housed, ill-fed, ill-equipped; where was the profit? As galvanized Rebels they would be suspect for a long time, and might not enjoy the freedom awarded to ordinary enlistees. They would have no eminence, they would be regarded suspiciously, accepted by their mates with a grudge. As ordinary Outsiders who had given their parole, even though they did not take the oath as Secessionists, they might not leave the region of the stockade under penalty of being shot. Women? . . . Sometimes you overheard officers joking about an obliging widow who lived nearby. Where were women, what were women when one considered food and drink and other comfort to be secured through bestiality and—later—barter? The more articulate thugs muttered about frying pans and fires; the less articulate thugs said nothing, but proceeded with their program of theft and murder in sullen dedication.

Edward Blamey recognized that Number One was doing poorly by himself. His grandmother used to make the best beach plum preserves anyone had ever tasted; Ed Blamey dreamed nightly about beach plum preserves; he saw himself ladling out the winy richness into a saucer, he felt himself spooning up the preserves and swallowing with-love . . . his grandmother fried a chicken the day he went to visit her. With his three-tined black-handled fork and with his sharp black-handled knife he worked steaming white meat free from the little bones, and ate chicken with beach plum treasure spread thereon; there were sage and onion dressing, boiled potatoes, chicken gravy . . . he said, Grandmother, guess I'm feeding like a hog, but I do want to ask you for another saucerful. He heard his grandmother chuckle, complimented to the point of endearment; and then he awoke and knew that he dwelt in steadily increasing filth, that he owned a small amount of rough corn-meal-cob-meal in which black bugs were crawling; that was all he owned, he had no salt; he had a raw place on his right shin which pained and worried him; the shebang leaked badly, and water came around you with awful freshness, awful chill until the faint heat of even one's own weak body warmed it, but the bodily heat could not warm it enough. The gums of Ed Blamey's mouth were touchy, his teeth loosened in their sockets. . . . *Eat, or what ye shall drink; nor yet for your body.* . . . The Wrath To Come was less effectual, it moved shapeless beyond this horizon of up-ended logs, it moved far past the sentries, the sentries were more of a plague than The Wrath To Come. Suppose he was jostled in a crowd, as some prisoners had been jostled when clawing for rations, and so was jostled against the deadline until some half-brained guard thought that he was trying to escape, and shot him through the head? His father wouldn't want him to die . . . Edward, you got to look out for Number One; if you don't, who will? His elder brother wouldn't wish him to die of bleeding toothless gums with which fabrications of coarse cornmeal could not be chewed. There was a rumor that some day, somehow, bread would be baked Outside and issued to the prisoners instead of meal. But Ed would not be able to chew corn bread if his teeth were gone.

The Baptist Church would never demand that he die. Oh, certainly—die in battle, die in a charge, have a bullet rip his rags, have a hot bulb of grapeshot take the top from his skull. But not to decay by inches and parts of inches . . . folks at home, all of Rhode Island; nobody demanding that he die as men now died near him; no idols or human patterns of the past exacting an assurance that he must spoil here while some people were stout and gay and able, living in plenty.

No one had said a word about this smelly eventuality when he joined the cavalry. At least, he couldn't remember that they had. *With the garlands of victory around her, when so proudly she bore her brave crew . . . the shrine of each pa-triot's devotion, a world offers homage to thee.* Good enough for singing on the Fourth of July when everybody crowded on the green, and Judge J. T. Day stood up on the bandstand and talked about hosannahs of filial devotion arising even unto the blue Empyrean; and the Daughters of the King Sunday School class had decided to serve a public dinner for the appalling sum of twenty cents per person in order to raise money for the new Baptistry (the old Baptistry leaked down into the cellar), and that meant more chicken and dressing and other sorts of pre-serves besides beach plum, and apple butter and coconut cakes; and Edward Blamey and some of his friends had stuffed a toy cannon with powder and wad-ded newspapers, and they touched it off right in the middle of Judge J. T. Day's speech, and then they ran like whiteheads when they saw the constable coming . . . ran long and lightly and youthfully with their pockets filled with torpedoes and Chinese crackers and squibs . . . *three cheers for the Red, White and Blue!*

No. Scarcely. You didn't feel like cheering for the Red, White and Blue when your teeth were coming out, or threatening to come out, and when your shebang leaked dolefully (By Mighty, said the scarecrow Sergeant Colony, we got more rain than roof) and when Si Wingate whined with fever for three days and nights and was then carried to join a row of fat-eyed motionless people near the gate, and when Tup Wingate squatted in agony with his ragged pants pulled down and bloody stool dripping from his haunches.

Got to look after Number One. Well—

Weavers, malleable iron workers, machinists, railroad men, printers, tanners, shoemakers—oh, above all shoemakers in this nearly shoeless domain!—Rebel emissaries appeared, guarded, every day or two. Any millers, saw or grist? Oh, shoemakers. . . . Who'd like to work in Macon? All you got to do, Yank, is sign this here little old piece of paper; make your mark if you can't sign. Yes, sir, Yank, I got a golden opportunity for you: any man who knows the cobbler's trade! Nice boarding place, good bed to sleep in, that old lady sets a fine table, and wages on top of it. You boys *are* tight run here, sure enough. But I reckon you can see which way the cat's jumping now. Just chew on it, Yank; don't need to make up your mind today; I'll be back a Friday, and I'll tell that old lady to put on a mess of pork and turnips against your coming. . . .

Aw, dry up.

That old lady got any *young* ladies with her, mister?

Any *young* ladies in that good bed you was talking about?

I hate turnips! Tell her to cook some nice green peas instead.

Can't read nor cipher, so *you* make my mark for me—great *big* mark.

Hey. Go stick a weasel up your ass. Right beside the cobbler's bench, Mister Monkey!

The bulk of the men knew that in cutting shoe-leather or in reaming bolts or in tanning hides or in mixing mortar or in baking bricks for anyone in this bleak hated region, they would be fighting for the Bonnie Blue Flag (where was it? They had never seen the enemy with a Bonnie Blue Flag; they had seen him with the diagonal cross and stars on his red battle flag) as surely as if they rode with Forrest or marched in Hood's columns. The bulk of the men resisted these commercial missionaries as they resisted the gangling lieutenant with his claptrap chatter about Adequate Apparel and Conclusion of Hostilities.

The bulk of the men, again. . . . There was the silent haggard louse-ridden harness-maker from Indiana; people in his mess referred to him as Fort Wayne; he disappeared one day, and folks said that they had seen him near the South Gate; and other folks said later that they had heard Fort Wayne was gone to Albany to fashion the tug-straps which were his specialty. His mess argued about it.

A parole is just a parole, after all. What difference whether you're paroled to work Outside, taking care of mules, or whether you're paroled to work in Albany?

Plenty difference!

Bet your life. One way you're just here at the stockade, same as if you were on the Inside. Other way, you're helping the Reb artillery to shoot your own God damn brother.

Well, Fort Wayne had three kids to home.

Do tell. I got *four.*

A Pittsburgh printer vanished, so did a stationary engineman from Schenectady: one was said to be working in Macon, the other in Savannah. . . . No one knew. The men were gone; not many of them went; perhaps seven or eight went in March out of the whole stockade. More than seven thousand others stayed and drank the water or didn't drink it, and popped the lice like popcorn from their frayed jacket seams when they held the jackets over blazing pine scraps. The pine scraps were fewer now, you couldn't just pick them up, you had to bargain for them. A lean Scandinavian corporal called Nellie Bly because his name was Nels —he cut his wrist deliberately with a piece of tin and died quietly at sunrise, saying nothing. Adoniram Kempley insisted on taking off what remained of his clothes and sitting naked on the edge of the marsh, day and night; he said that he was waiting for somebody, he would not utter the name of the person he was waiting for; he perished within the week. An artilleryman they called Indian Giver was throttled in broad daylight by one of Curtis's Raiders because he refused to part with his pocket comb. Paul Hexley tore his heel on a crumpled cooking pan, and soon he had no heel, nor any foot to have a heel on; soon he had no life. An undersized sixteen-year-old musician called Wabash huddled around, unable to play the fife with which he had entertained his fellows earlier. His gums looked like spongy rotten plums, they thrust oozing far out of his mouth, his lips spread back to let the gums protrude, it looked as if he were holding a bit or a gag in his mouth, a bit or a gag heavy and purplish and artificial.

That's scurvy, said Edward Blamey, and I got a touch of it. He lay alternately perspiring and shivering until the eastern sky grew murky instead of Stygian above obtruding sentry stations. Then he took silent terrified leave of companions who did not even sniff, who thought that he might have gone to the sinks. He crossed Stockade Creek and crouched down within a pole's length of the unearthly root-and-oilcloth-and-log-and-blanket structure known as Collins's Castle on the South Side. Later he was challenged by hangers-on; he stood with docility while they ripped out his pockets and found nothing except an uneven set of small flat grayish stones which he used to play checkers with, with Sergeant Colony. The roughs threw the stones away, biffed Edward Blamey until his ear rang and seemed deafened; they swaggered off toward the gate. After nine o'clock in the morning Willie Collins emerged from his castle, a furry half-naked trunk, the walking trunk of a ginger-colored tree, yelling for someone named Donner: where the hell was that meat he was after frying? Edward Blamey went to the ruffian's side at once. He could not feel his feet touching the ground in their broken-soled shoes. But still The Wrath To Come was a long way off, he could not hear its roaring.

Member me, Willie?

Agh. . . . The giant rolled his red-rimmed eyes, yawned, snorted. What want ye with Willie Collins?

I got a sharp pair of eyes. You called them ogles . . . made me a kind of proposition. Member?

That I do. Inside with you, Rubber Legs. He took Edward Blamey into the wide cave above ground, the cave half in the ground, and it was warm inside, whatever uncertain springtime chill and wetness ruled elsewhere, and it smelled of fried food and vomit and dirty males and liquor, and oh Heavenly Father it smelled of food, and oh Heavenly Father there was a fire beaming on the baked mud hearth, and oh Heavenly Father don't send The Wrath To Come.

Look you. There's a shebang yonder, name of Parker House. Artillerymen, so tis said.

Nigh the North Gate, Willie? I think I know it.

That you must. Striped blankets on the roof? Twould be the one. Watch you well this day, and run to me the first minute there's not more than two—mark you, kiddie, I said *two*—of the Sams inside. We've tried them before; they're hell on wheels; but they've greenbacks buried there. Mark well, or I'll tear the velvet from your head! Not more than *two*.

Willie . . . what's velvet?

Your red tongue, you addle cove! I'll rip it out of your throat with these fingers if there's more than two men in that shebang when we hit the place.

He gave Edward Blamey some fried potatoes and onions, gave him half a cup of pine-top on which the Rhode Islander choked, but which coursed like fury through him. Ed Blamey wandered idly afield, selected a vantage point, watched with care. The Boston men might never dream that he was observing them. He counted carefully: there were six about the place. Two went away, another left later . . . he couldn't be certain . . . by noon there were but two about? Suddenly he saw three men standing in front, talking; then one picked his way toward the North Gate; the other two went back inside the Parker House. Blamey shot himself into the presence of Willie Collins like a misshapen bowlegged projectile. Five minutes later the yells had gone aloft. Raiders! had been cried to no effect, for the other partners in the Parker House could not reach the scene in time. A thatch was torn aside, a tin can of currency was gathered up, blankets were pulled from the roof. One of the two defenders lay gulping spasmodically, holding his

abdomen where kicks had smashed his bowels; the other defender lay unconscious, his head cracked, bystanders had heard the bone crack when he was
clubbed.

Edward Blamey drank deeply of pine-top that night, trying to forget the thing
that had happened, the thing which he had brought about. Och, what a pair of
ogles! cried Willie Collins. And there was a hundred and twenty-nine dollars in
that wad! Cookie, break open another box of biscuit for our friend Delaney, and
where's that cheese, and what came of that tin of mushroom pickles? Sure and I
feel a song coming on.

> *In Athol there lived a man named Jerry Lanagan—*

Is it a song you can sing me, Delaney? A good melody to tickle the heart—
No, said Edward Blamey, I can't. Can't sing a note.

19

One bright morning at the end of April late sleepers awoke to find both South
Street and Main Street tenanted by recumbent bodies on which fresh sun shone
brightly blue, from which fresh sun tore spasms of gilt where buttons spangled or
where patent-leather chevrons reflected. Hundreds of new prisoners had been
herded in through both gates during the night, and they bedded in those streets
because they had nowhere else to sleep and feared to go wallowing in the dark.

Well, by God, these are the freshest fish that ever got hooked.

Fresh fish, hell! Looks like the Rebs gobbled up a brigade of major-generals.

Looky. Silk chevrons on some.

Patent-leather. . . .

Looky that gang. Got feathers in their hats, I swear.

Hey, there, Yank! If you be a Yank. What you from?

A man roused slowly as if he had drunk himself to sleep on liquor, as if his
head puffed and rang, as if he saw rats gnawing close. He gazed at the blackened
hairy skeletons a-crowding. Huh?

I said, What you from?

Hundred and Third Pennsylvania.

Where you get grabbed?

Huh?

Whereabouts were you captured?

Oh. Plymouth, North Carolina.

Plymouth? You must be Pilgrim Fathers for certain. Hey, Pee-leg, come take a
look at these Pilgrim Fathers!

The term Plymouth Pilgrims would cling to them throughout their captivity; it
would be a short captivity for many. They awakened in the pit squarely beneath a
privy used by devils, the shock numbed and dumbed them, the devils' evacuations
poured over them, they were mired, they were suffocated, they drowned, they
died.

For most their war had been a light and easy war until the seventeenth of April. These regiments dwelt at quiet if important forts along the coast all the way from Fortress Monroe to Beaufort, and good food came in on supply ships, and the quarters of such garrisons were dry and clean. On a Sunday you might attend services at Grace Church. . . . Off duty, a man could lie along old pilings and whip a line around his wrist, and toss the plummet and baited hook out into shifting water, and prepare for a stripèd fish to flap and lunge and delight him. . . . The Eighty-fifth New York, the One Hundred and First Pennsylvania, the One Hundred and Third Pennsylvania: every man waited contentedly for boats to bear the regiments northward. It would be a lark, sailing for home on a veteran's furlough. Instead came a powerful ram called the *Albemarle,* and three brigades of troops attacking by land. Cannon thudded from the forts, the *Albemarle* ripped past unscathed and sent the *Southfield* rolling into the sea and pounded the *Miami* into flight. Federal troops on land held out for two more days, then they surrendered to what seemed like a million polite North Carolinians who did not even search their knapsacks.

Looky, Charley, at them bureaus.

I swan. Member when I was a new recruit, I packed one of them big bureaus off to the front. How it like to gauled the shoulders off of me. Hey, Yank, what you got in your bureau? Got any spare crackers to swap?

I'll warrant you he's got everything but the kitchen stove.

He'll have that under that big feathered hat of his.

You actually tried to fight a battle in rigging like that? No wonder you got grabbed.

The newcomers explained haltingly that since they stood in momentary expectancy of sailing north from Plymouth, they were wearing their best new uniforms at the time the Confederate onslaught began; after that they had no chance to change, they never even thought of changing their clothes. They fought from the seventeenth until the twentieth of April and then were captured in finery. Along with the veterans' brigade were the Sixteenth Connecticut Infantry, the Twenty-fourth New York Independent Battery, a company of the Twelfth New York Cavalry, and two batteries of Massachusetts heavy artillery. Two-thirds of these captives arrived on this day; the rest reached Andersonville on May third. Not a man of them had ever envisioned a place like Andersonville in his ugliest imaginings. The immensity of smell, the shrunken limbs, the pot bellies of the dropsical, the oozing mouths of the scurvy-ridden—Blackened masses of faces which pressed close with hungry eyes staring—The bundles of lousy hair bristling out, wads of lousy beards a-stringing—

There they sat with freighted knapsacks, the heavy oblongs with good rolled blankets atop, and stuffed with every civilized comfort known to the easy regime of garrison troops—troops who'd never marched a thousand miles or (many of them) even a hundred miles—There they sat, with sun glittering on their niceness. They could not arise from the ground.

How in tarnation did they ever get in here with all that truck? It's a sight for sore eyes.

You know the answer to that one. Guarded by Regular troops instead of these chicken-shit Home Guards!

Hey, Corp. You with the fancy mustache. Swap you two good blanket poles for that canteen? You got to have blanket poles or else you got no shebang to dwell in. Come along, old top, I'll show you what I mean—

They moved in stricken daze, their eyes saw things, the brains behind them would not believe. Raiders began swooping down, the moment individuals were separated from the mass which might have given protection—and did, for wiser ones, for a time.

Wiser and more resilient than many of his fellows loomed a broad-shouldered young man of twenty-three with a well-trimmed mane of black hair and ears wide and outstanding. His mouth was full-lipped, his brown eyes brooding and thick-lidded, and he had the Semitic nose fancied by cruel cartoonists and seldom seen in fact. His name was Nathan Dreyfoos. He was well at home in the world although never had he thought to find himself domiciled in a roost such as this. Born in Boston, he had spent most of his life abroad, traveling from country to country with his father and mother, taught by English tutors the while. His father was a purchasing agent for merchants in eastern American cities, buying every-thing from tweeds to olive oil, and back again to watches and Parisian perfumery and Bavarian china and Flemish glass. Nathan was tri-lingual as to English, French and Spanish, speaking also subordinate dialects of the latter language. He spoke a good deal of Yiddish and some German, Italian and Swedish. He owned no ambition in life except to worship the better elements of the past and (in some vague manner as yet undecided) to acquaint people with lessons and glories of the past, to the eventual comfort and enrichment of humanity.

Abroad when the war began, Nathan Dreyfoos felt no upsurge of nationalism. His parents were barely removed by one generation from their separate Euro-pean backgrounds, and thus had returned easily to Continental attitude and thought. The young man heard about the burst of civil warfare with disquietude and regret, because wars inflicted miseries, and he was benevolent of heart and did not wish to have miseries inflicted. He liked Boston, New York, Philadelphia; he grew momentarily and remotely saddened at thinking of Bostonians, New Yorkers, Philadelphians being slain in battle. He liked Charleston and New Or-leans; was it not a horrid thing that people from South Carolina and Louisiana must now die or be mutilated? He would have felt a personal concern of infinitely greater depth if he had learned that in Madrid they were raising an army to invade France, or that the Dutch were assembling a navy to sail against England.

When again he walked an American street he strolled in citizen's clothing tailored by Desborough. One evening he stood sipping wine in the public room of the Astor House when two young officers of the Eighty-fifth New York moved close to him and, having absorbed more drink than their heads could carry, felt it incumbent upon them to discuss in clear ringing tones the worthlessness of well-dressed stay-at-homes who permitted braver men to go out and do their fighting for them.

Present company excepted, said Lieutenant Corley elaborately.

Oh, yes, indeed, said Lieutenant Stevenson. As a matter of fact, my dear Tom, I've heard that our Hebrew brethren are disinclined to violence of any kind. A fellow couldn't hold them responsible. . . .

I beg your pardon, said Nathan Dreyfoos, but they pretended not to hear him, although most men in the place were turning to watch. Nathan paid for his wine, and stepped into the street. He had not long to wait in the reflected glare of gas. Soon the lieutenants appeared, flushed and talkative, bound for another bar-room. Politely Nathan invited them to step back inside and apologize to the company there—not so much for the insults directed at him personally as for the remarks about Hebrews. Corley, the broadest and longest, said that he would see Nathan in hell first. Very well, said Nathan Dreyfoos, let us go. By way of this alley.

In the alley he flattened Corley with his first blow, and Stevenson rushed upon him. Stevenson struck the cobblestones while Corley was rising and thus it went for a time, amid yells of servants and guests pouring from the Astor House. The two officers were alternately smashed and toppled, while Nathan received no damage except to his attire. Mr. Halliburton, his favorite tutor, was a Cantabrian athlete with not-too-thwarted ambitions as a pugilist. Once Mr. Halliburton cracked Nathan's jawbone; then the guilty pair had to connive to keep this dark secret from the senior Dreyfooses. Nathan was a seasoned expert at boxing as well as a seasoned expert at fencing, and felt regret at what he was doing now. Yet, in some disquieting manner, this performance seemed called for. A policeman put a cautious hand on the young man's shoulder while he was bending over the bleeding and amazed Lieutenant Corley, and told him that he was under arrest for brawling in public. Nonsense, said Nathan, and gave the policeman a five-dollar bill. With his arm around Corley and with Stevenson stumbling sore-faced against his right side, Nathan led the way to his own quarters upstairs, and of course they were handsome quarters. A doctor came with plasters, a mumbling Negro carried off the officers' clothing to be repaired; more wine appeared, together with cold beef and chicken. The gentleman talked long. Corley and Stevenson spent the balance of the night in Nathan's big bed and Nathan slept on the sofa. In this way the Eighty-fifth New York gained a somewhat poetic linguist who insisted on enlisting as a private soldier because he feared the responsibility of command.

. . . But, damn it, my dear boy! Your father must know heaps of men with influence, and you just heard what Tom said about *his* father and the senator. There's bound to be a vacancy soon and—

Now, listen, old chap. I'm acquainted with Colonel Fardella *personally,* not just as a subordinate company officer. When once he hears that you can speak Italian—

In France, said Nathan, my best friend was my father's coachman.

But a fellow of culture and—

In Spain, Nathan told them, Olmedo the gardener was my best friend. I knew poor people, I knew a charcoal burner in the hills, I knew bandits. I am very much at ease with such people.

Oh, damn it, Dreyfoos! We've got no charcoal burners, and not too many gardeners or coachmen, I'll wager that. Our men are mostly young chaps, boys from good Christian homes—Beg pardon—

Blessed are ye, when men shall revile you, and persecute you. . . . Nathan smiled at Lieutenant Stevenson and put a hand on his throbbing arm. In Málaga I was accustomed to playing my violin for the monks. And I know the Beatitudes of your Faith. And I do come from a good home. I could be harmonious with the men in your command.

He served under First Lieutenant Corley and Second Lieutenant Stevenson and was promoted by rapid degrees to the rank of sergeant, with the approval of those surrounding him. In the attack on Plymouth both Corley and Stevenson were killed—the former by a shell from the *Albemarle,* the latter by a stray musket ball half an hour before the Unionists surrendered. During the days which followed his capture, Nathan walked with a heavy heart. He was disconsolate at losing his friends, yet he thought they had died for a sound purpose. That long ago night, in the Astor House, the ebullient youths grew articulate in stress of emotion following their thrashing. They had persuaded Nathan that since he turned out to be historically minded, he must look at the present conflict in the historical sense. The Nation had been founded in bitter conflict, and had achieved to world importance through further conflict and through its own crowding growth to the West. Broken in half, the impact of America on the world and on the future would be lessened; the United States and the Confederate States would resolve into puny second-rate powers. It was so throughout history . . . look at the federations which made strength; look at Grecian history, Roman, western European.

The Union *must* survive! cried the blond young Corley, with his bruised mouth full of chicken.

And, as a born American, it is your strict duty to aid in that survival!

But I love the South of this country as well as the North.

Do you suppose that General George H. Thomas, for example, does not love Virginia? He was born in Virginia, Virginia is his mother State! Why is General Thomas fighting for the Union? Because he recognizes the necessity of resistance against armed rebellion! The Nation is bigger than any one State or group of States, Friend Nathan. *It is historically demanded that this Nation survive as a single entity.* If you go to the army, as you are *obliged* to go to the army, you will be fighting—not as a renegade American returned to these shores, not as a native Bostonian, not for the State of Massachusetts. You will be fighting for the greatest, noblest commonwealth which ever gave a benefit to mankind: the single, Federal commonwealth of sister States, the United States of America!

Cracky, Tom, cried Salem Stevenson. I can't wait for this war to be over, so's you can hang out your shingle and strike for the Albany assembly!

Corley was duly modest. Well, I used to twist a mean verb, as they say, when I was on the debating panel at the Academy.

Stevenson mounted stiffly to a gilt-tasseled chair and, champagne glass in hand, demanded to know of Nathan whether he had ever seen Daniel Webster in the flesh. He, Stevenson, had.

When my eyes shall be turned to behold for the last time the sun in heaven, may I not see him shining on the broken and dishonored fragments of a once-glorious Nation . . . on a land rent with civil feuds and drenched, it may be, in fraternal blood—

Toby the floor-waiter knocked softly at the door. If the gentlemen could kindly be a mite more quiet. Lady in Number Twelve she feeling poorly. And it's nigh to four o'clock.

They talked more softly, but still they talked earnestly. Nathan was forced to admit that his grandparents on both sides had been immigrants because they sought the opportunity and safety which America afforded. He was forced to admit that his father had advanced in a fashion impossible in most other countries . . . was this not, then, a debt which he owed to the Federal Union and which he must pay by offering his own body and spirit? Stirred to intimacy, Nathan now told how his grandfather Margolis's father and mother had been beaten to death and hurled into the flames of their own house, while the baby which was Grandfather Margolis lay covered by straw nearby and thus escaped extermination in that *pogrom.* His new friends (the heedless Jew-baiters of a few hours before) paled at the description and clucked in sympathy.

These memories returned with blinding force during the heartbreak of defeat and surrender, during the pain of being transported as a chattel of war. Because he was accustomed to travel and acutely sensitive to each impression, Nathan did not dwell, however, in a stricken doze. Automatically his mind said, This is new. This I have not seen before. This I will remember. . . . The enemy's reserve pickets marching us forth. They say this village is Jamesville. The last was Foster's Mills. . . . Why this desolation, why the white and fire-marked chimneys of houses no longer standing? The damage must have been done by our Union troops when they raided to Whitehall. . . . Our guards say they are from the Thirty-fifth North Carolina. A very decent set of fellows; and civil war becomes increasingly dreadful when I realize that it was they or their brothers-in-arms who killed my friends the two lieutenants, without whose instigation I would not have come to fight in the first place. . . . Suppose my father and I had sailed to New Orleans (and we might have done so, but for the blockade) instead of to New York? Then I might have met some Southerners and been insulted by them, and might have whipped them in the same way; and then, over wine and meat, might have been persuaded that their Cause was the Cause truly just, and so might have found myself wearing their uniform. . . . No, no, impossible! Because a civil war proves in its very waging that it is the nastiest business afoot; and it is to prevent for all time the recurrence of such strife that we thinking Union troops are willing to endure. Corley and Stevenson are now wiped off the slate, along with so many thousands of others. Perhaps the damp sponge of Fate is waiting to rub out my own name. If so, I am willing to let it be rubbed, because I came earnestly into this situation. I am confident that the North will prevail; I am assured that, eventually, the forces of dissolution will crumble; I know in my heart and soul that one day both sections of this Country will again be forged together, never more to be split.

The great lamentation of the future will be concerned only with the fact that, by and large, the most energetic and high-minded youths of all these States involved were the ones who perished; and most of them were too young to leave their seed behind them. It will be a long weakness for the united Nation of the future. The soul which might have written the compelling opera went winging at Manassas Junction. The hand which might have sculptured a shape fairer than *Moses* was shot off on the Chickahominy. The brain which could have managed the richest agronomy of all time was drilled by a conoidal bullet at Stone's River. The hearts which might have beat with the rhythm of philanthropist and priest and educator . . . O wicked Gettysburg, O doleful Vicksburg, O thrice lewd Fredericksburg!

> *Lang wull his lady look*
> *Frae the castle doon,*
> *E'er she see the Earl o' Murray*
> *Come soonding through the toon.*

. . . Good old Halliburton, and the ballads he sang before the fireplace; and Mother chording on that ancient gilt spinet in the corner, and candle flames bowing in obeisance to the legendry, and the warm sea touched with stars at the foot of our lawn. Will ever I see them again? Will ever I know the future?

O sad maimed Future! Where is your prime inventor? The ocean covered him with barnacles when the *Monitor* went down. Where is the saint whose scalpel or microscope was intended to still the scream of cancer? We Federals spattered his skull at Missionary Ridge. O long discordant Future drowned in tears, as now my soul is drowning! Where is the President whose power and nobility might have led a healed Nation to world-enfolding glory? The fever took him at Rock Island, in Arkansas, in Libby Prison, at Fort Delaware. He wore blue, he wore butternut. He drew a lanyard, he tore the paper of a cartridge with his teeth, he galloped behind John Morgan, he rode to meet the lead on that last charge of Farnsworth's in a Pennsylvania glen. Minister and explorer, balloonist and poet, botanist and judge, geologist and astronomer and man with songs to sing . . . they are clavicles under leaves at Perryville, ribs and phalanges in the soil of Iuka, they are a bone at Seven Pines, a bone at Antietam, bones in battles yet to be sweated, they are in the soil instead of walking, the moss has them.

So Nathan Dreyfoos had mourned, seeking adjustment to new situation and recent tragedy . . . a town called Williamston, the prisoners resting in a pine grove, guards lounging about and some of them flirting with girls who came tripping fearfully in the crowd scampering to see the Yankees. The village postmaster, fat and old and pink-faced, came trotting up with his leather pouch like an amiable Saint Nick; he promised to mail letters for any of the prisoners who wished to write to the folks at home. Yes, sir, boys, them letters'll be sent through your lines at the first opportunity. Don't thank me, boys—glad to do it—my own Andy got took by your fellows up in Maryland and he's still a prisoner of war; but once't in a while we get a letter from him. Nathan Dreyfoos blinked away the tears which came suddenly, and smiled down at Saint Nick. I hope he's keeping well, sir. Oh, yes, Sergeant, tolerable, tolerable.

Nathan wrote hastily on half a sheet of paper, he gave the rest of his paper away to boys who had none. Dear Father and Mother, I trust this will reach you with the assurance that I am unwounded and in fine fettle. But there is sad news: Plymouth has fallen to the enemy and those of us who were not killed were taken prisoner. My friends Stevenson and Corley are among the dead. I do not know where we will be imprisoned; some say at Charleston or Savannah. If all our warders are as gentlemanly as our present guards and as the kind person who has promised to mail this, then shall we be well treated indeed. Please advise Halliburton of my situation; I think he is still at the Embassy in Paris—People in gray began ordering the prisoners into column; there was not time to write more; he scribbled, Y'r Devoted Son Nathan, and Saint Nick took the letters away in his pouch, and girls' shrill voices began to sing in the grove, *Hurrah, Hurrah, for Southern Rights, Hurrah,* and the marching prisoners answered with a roaring *We'll hang Jeff Davis to a sour apple tree,* until they were silenced by the guards. Tramp, march, stride, the long shadows on the dust, the long dusty blue column in rising dust, the dogs coming out to yap, the Negroes staring and laughing.

They had some sickness that night; the Rebels put up a tent for the sick; the prisoners slept in a void something like bliss. At least nobody is a-prosecuting us, said one serious countryman from up the Hudson; and most of the others knew that he meant to say persecuting, and that was a joke, and they made much of the joke. They were filled with crackers and raw pork, and knew that they had nothing to fear from captors who would put up a tent to shield sufferers from the night.

They lost their charitable North Carolinians at Hamilton the next day. A new band of Confederates succeeded them, but still there was no brutality; still appeared the nightly ration of black-eyed peas, meal and bacon. . . . The twenty-fourth was a Sunday, and before the prisoners were formed in column for the march to Tarboro a throng of them got together for prayers and Bible reading. They sang, Sweet Hour of Prayer, and Nathan hummed along with the rest for he did not know the words. . . . Should I chant *Kol Nidre* for them? I fear that I do not know that, either. Ah, my poor violin, neglected in its case in New York. Or is it in New York? Father said that he would keep it safe. I wonder where it is.

The train at Tarboro, and striking the main road at Rocky Mount, and rattling on into the South to meet a warmer spring. . . . Now the men were weary of singing; there was a good deal of arguing and one fight in Nathan's box car, a disturbance which he quelled with haste. Their guards were from the Twenty-eighth Georgia and a very stern officer of the guard—a captain named Johnson—ordered the doors closed at dusk. Then there was mashing and pressing and squeezing and jerking through the long noisy night. A drummer boy wept that he was being smothered.

And I bet you wish you were home with your mother, Tyke.

Yes, God damn it, I do!

Well, so do I. So does every last man of us. So quit bawling, Tyke. It won't help none.

All right, Corporal Reeves. Sniffle, snuffle. I'll quih-hit—

Pikeville, Goldsborough, Wilmington with its lean blockade runners lying silver gray by the docks. There was some firing out at sea, the prisoners crowded hopefully against their ferryboat's rail and soon were rewarded by observing the return of a steamer which had tried to run the blockade. Yeh, yeh, yeh, the men yelled. Try again, Johnny—better luck next time!—but the crew of the steamer could not hear them, and a few sailors waved affably, and shouted jocular insults across the water, or appeared to be shouting them. . . . The new train had platform cars. Various men whispered about jumping off and striking for the woods, but the armed Georgians beside them looked as if they could shoot so no one made the attempt. Younger prisoners waved and hooted at the people, black and white, in every village which the train went smoking through. Cinders came back to sting their eyes, and sometimes glowing flakes were lashed out of the air to sting and burn; but still it was better than being crushed in box cars. . . . In Charleston the ropy beards of Spanish moss swayed dreamily, the flowers were magenta and pink and gold; in Charleston an old Negro came up to the cars with a bucket of hot fried shrimps to sell and his bucket was emptied in a twinkling.

Look at those women. Picking peas in their garden.

Man alive! Wait'll I write Pa about that. Up home I don't think he'll have the peas scarcely planted.

They changed trains again at Savannah and only thirty-five men were put into each box car. There was room to stretch out. It was good to lie down, even though the cars did seem to run on square wheels, even though grit came flying in all night and the sound of hammers deafened a fellow's ears. The next day they stopped in a wilderness where there was a shack marked Station Number Thirteen, and here the prisoners were marched to an adjacent stream and permitted to wash.

. . . I'll be beat, Lewis. You know, my brother Lafe was in a prison pen in Virginia, up until he got exchanged, and he said they never had a chance to wash. So they got lice all over themselves. This is pie. If this keeps up we won't be doing badly at all.

. . . And, Sim, look at the rations they're issuing, up ahead. Looks like soft tack and fresh pork. And beans. By gum, so tis!

. . . Well, if this be a sample, bring on your hippypotymus. Georgia for me!

That night they were marched into the Andersonville stockade; and so they woke up staring, and they could not believe, they could not believe.

Nathan Dreyfoos said, It was too good to last.

But, Sarge, they can't mean to *keep* us here.

Look at the other prisoners, Allen.

But they must have made a mistake. Maybe they sent us to the wrong place. Maybe this is a *punishment* camp. Eh, Sarge? Oh, for God's sake, Sarge, please do ask the guards if there hain't been a mistake! A man can't *live* in a place like this.

A great many of them don't, said one of the blackened hairy creatures who stood watching and listening.

What say?

A great many of them don't.

The boy who had been pleading with Nathan Dreyfoos buried his head in his arms and began to blubber.

Nathan sat quietly in the bright stinking sunshine for a while, trying to decide what to say to Private Allen. At last he put his arm around the boy's shaking shoulders and said, Don't do that if you can help it, Allen. Weeping is the easiest but the worst thing that any of us can do here.

Yyyyeh.

You still have your strength. We have arrived at this ugly place in splendid condition. Instead of indulging in tears, we must keep our spirits up and our wits alive. There may be some way out.

Yyyyeh, Sarge.

Perhaps you can escape. Perhaps many of us can.

The man who had said, A great many of them don't, moved off slowly through the crowd. He thought of Nathan, He talks like an officer, but is only a sergeant like me. He oughtn't to delude himself about escape. . . . Oh, well, I used to try to escape, myself. Eventually I learned that it was wiser to devote myself to the science of living here, living as well as possible and as long as possible. . . . I wonder what that big Jew has got in his big knapsack? Maybe we can make a swap.

The man's name was Seneca MacBean, and he came from Galena, Illinois. He was long a prisoner, shrewd in experience with mankind before he became a prisoner, shrewder now a thousand fold. MacBean had served with the Eighth Illinois Cavalry until that storied afternoon of July first, 1863, when dismounted troopers of Gamble's Brigade went stringing east from a certain bullet-pocked seminary building, still firing their carbines if they had any rounds left to fire. In the town beyond they ran down this street and that, hunting for a way to safety, darting across backyards, trampling the rhubarb and onion tops and moss roses. Eventually the way behind them was barred by panting gangs of strangers in sweat-drenched gray shirts and undershirts, and the way ahead was thronged with other sweaty people who advanced on them meaningly with muskets at the ready.

Drop that carbine, Yank.

One man tried to get away by climbing a brick wall, and several guns banged, and the man fell into a tangle of tomato vines. This is *futility*, said Seneca MacBean, imagining that he was setting the word in Italic antique boldface; it was an odd trick, emphasizing words in that manner, but he was a printer by trade; he had been a printer's devil at ten. He called to those of his men who were near, ordering them not to resist. Forms all locked up, he said. We've gone to press, gentlemen. The cavalrymen did not know exactly what he meant by this, but the example of Sergeant MacBean was unmistakable: he had dropped his carbine, and was holding up a yellow bandana in lieu of a white flag. . . . At Belle Isle he tried to escape by swimming the James River but was picked up by Home Guards on the Richmond side and returned to the Island. Here at Andersonville he had tried to escape by tunneling, along with a great many others; some dogs scouted him out, less than an hour after he left the tunnel. Seneca MacBean was resting, exhausted, on a cypress knee in the nearby swamp. My tongue, he told his friends later, was hanging longer than the dogs'. He spent a week in the stocks, which he endured stoically, and was then marched back into the pen.

Wirz remembered him well, because of his height (his rangy body towered four inches over six feet) and the circumstances. So, Henry Wirz would say each time he encountered the bony Illinoisan, Maybe you want you should go back in the stocks, *nein?*

No thanks, Captain.

Then no more tunnels you make, you bad sergeant, you!

Nope. I won't.

MacBean sustained himself at Andersonville by conducting a laundry. He had two wooden buckets which he cared for lovingly in order to keep them from springing leaks. He had no soap, but ashes and sand served. He'd made himself a scrubbing board, buying the end of a wide planed plank of hardwood, and this piece of plank he had grooved diligently. It did not work as well as his grandmother's well-remembered scrubbing board, back home at the shady end of Bench Street, but it worked.

Often he thought of his grandmother; he could see her scrubbing under a morning-glory arbor as she had scrubbed when he was small—when his grandfather lost his job, when Gran MacBean took in washings, when Seneca MacBean drew those same washings—pressed beautifully by Gran's hot irons—back to the tall homes of the Campbells or Gratiots or Kittoes on his squeaky-wheeled wagon, or sometimes in winter on his sled.

Senny, did your Gran say how much it was, this time?

Yes'm. She said she guessed a shilling.

Wait till I get my purse. . . . Here it is, in fractional currency. Count it carefully. Or can you count, yet?

Yes'm. I can count to a hundred.

What are you sniffing at, Senny? Those muffins Ellen is baking for tea?

Yes'm.

You shall have one. Ellen, fetch a strawberry muffin for the MacBean child. Fetch two. . . . And little Mrs. Gratiot smiled down at him, and he thought that she was beautiful.

It had been a good childhood, marred only by trivial matters like poverty, like being an orphan, like having a grandfather who often lay on his bed for days at a time . . . mumble, mumble, mumble, sometimes in English, sometimes in the Gaelic which John MacBean couldn't recollect when he was sober. Then, at the age of fifty-nine, John MacBean signed The Pledge. I've never gone back on my word, he told the plain-faced woman who loved him devotedly. No more do I intend to go back on this word I've given now. He did not go back on his word; he never took another drink, and repeatedly counseled Seneca never to take The First Drink.

It was drink that took that fine handsome father of yours, laddie, and, in a way, it was drink that took the fair young mother who bore you, for she had not the will or strength to survive. Never take The First Drink.

Seneca did not, until he was seventeen. Then, while working across the big river in Dubuque, he fell in with a riotous crowd of Irishmen, and attended a picnic where the whiskey called forty-rod was flowing. He took The First Drink, the second, the third and more. He became furiously drunk, scrapped with the Irish, thrashed several of them, was himself thrashed by the survivors. He throbbed to wakefulness in the middle of the night, pounded, aching, black-eyed, scratched. He lay abandoned in that same horrid grove, lying in his own vomit.

He washed in the first stream he came to, and tottered back to his lodging house where he wrote out a pledge for himself and signed it with a quivering hand. In the morning he looked at that pledge and could scarcely make out his own signature, so he signed it again. Like his grandfather and the other storied MacBeans whom he had never seen but of whom he had heard much, Sen MacBean did not go back on his word. He owned immeasurable strength. Sometimes he felt that he needed all of it, to keep going in Andersonville.

Seneca was proud of his sign and pleased often by his own humor. In early March, when there was still an abundance of forest trash all over the place, he had amused himself by hunting for curly splinters, chips and other morsels of pine wood or roots which had dried into the shape of letters. At first he tried merely to assemble an alphabet; then he got the idea of a sign to advertise his laundry. He had assisted another man periodically in washing the prisoners' clothes at Belle Isle; but now the other man was dead, so Sen went into business for himself. He pulled little nails out of a pair of wornout boots which he acquired, and tacked the rustic letters on a branch suspended above his hut. Since Illinoisans were often called Suckers, he had a name ready-made for this concern. *Sucker Laundry & Cleaning Co.* read the sign, *S. MacBean, Prop.* Only the *k,* two *a*'s, the *b* and one *p* (and the & sign) had needed to be cobbled together a bit. The rest of the letters were natural, just as he had found them, and Seneca MacBean was fond of pointing this out. In time he met a few fellow printers, and they had discussions as to the type style of the various letters—Gothic, Tudor black, German text, and so on.

He prospered if anyone could be said to prosper in the stockade. The more intelligent and resourceful prisoners recognized that cleanliness would aid in their survival; scrubbing would allay the activities of vermin; it was as simple as that. But few owned the facilities for even an attempt at washing their clothes, and many did not own the strength to try. Seneca MacBean accepted any currency, for he could barter away things which he did not need. Except corn bread (later)—he would not accept that. He would take wood, clothing, buckles, vegetables, bones, pieces of string, buttons, fragments of reading matter—any and every object—in payment for his services. His arms and shoulders were powerful, even after the Belle Isle winter. He ate sparingly, he ate not to allay his hunger for that was impossible; but he ate only those materials which he thought would be good for him; if he thought that something might make him sick he would not feed on it, no matter how hungry he was. He drank only water from wells dug on the higher ground of the North Side; this he received as laundering pay from the proprietors of the wells. He weighed in the neighborhood of a hundred and eighty pounds at the time of his capture, went down to perhaps a hundred and fifty on Belle Isle; now at Andersonville he managed to hold this weight very well, it even seemed that he had put on a few pounds, or was he dreaming?

Collins's Raiders had begun operations the moment they entered the stockade; Sarsfield's Raiders and Curtis's Raiders and the rest were not far behind with thefts and incursions. If there was any man whom Willie Collins feared that man was Seneca MacBean. Collins never attacked Seneca, and discouraged those of his herd who suggested it. The man named Tomcat O'Connor, who was shot by Father Time on Belle Isle—He was a former member of the Daybreak Boys in New York City, who found as much delight as actual profit in overhauling a weaker man. A few days after he reached the Island, O'Connor attempted to remove from Seneca MacBean's finger the old seal ring which had belonged to John MacBean's father's father, in Glasgow. Perhaps Tomcat outweighed Seneca by twenty-five or thirty pounds. A starved assemblage actually left the ration wagon to watch the beating which MacBean awarded to Tomcat O'Connor.

People screamed, Kill him, kill him! You should have killed him. You could have killed him—

Yes, I think so, said Seneca, and licked his raw knuckles. Along with the raiders he recognized that this was a violent world, and violence was a necessary adjunct to reaching a desired end. The difference was that the gangsters and he had different conceptions of what might constitute a desired end. They were selfish and avaricious; Sen was not. He enjoyed serenity, but (like so many Scots before him) he was willing to engage in conflict to attain serenity. *We shall have Peace if we must fight for it* was a philosophy jested about through the generations, but to Seneca MacBean this seemed not incongruous.

The morning when the Plymouth Pilgrims arrived he was halfway back to his shebang when consideration prompted him to halt and then to retrace his steps. He found the big Jew at the same place where he had seen him first, except that now he was standing with knapsack and blanket roll at his feet, gazing curiously toward the South Side. A hullabaloo ascended over there; it sounded and looked like a riot. Morning, said Sen MacBean, and told the stranger his name and regiment, and held out his hand.

Nathan Dreyfoos responded in kind, but when he released MacBean's hand he looked down at it and smiled. I cannot understand why your hands are comparatively so clean and—

And the rest of me dirty? That's the result of my laundry business. Scrubbing for hours, every day. But it does crack my hands and make them sore. Tell me, Sergeant, have you been squadded yet?

Last night before they turned us into—this place. I'm Thirty-ninth Detachment, Second Ninety, Third Mess.

But you've got no quarters as yet?

No. They said— The Rebel sergeant's words were, Pick out a place.

It's getting increasingly difficult to pick a good one. How'd you like to come over to my shebang, and see how we live here?

A fresh series of yells and shrieks issued from the South Side, and Nathan Dreyfoos jerked his head. What's going on, over there?

Raiders. Probably attacking some of you new men.

Raiders? Nathan would learn in another hour that three boys of his regiment had strayed incautiously near the headquarters of Charley Curtis. When attacked these boys screamed for help and several more of the Eighty-fifth New York went to their assistance. The battle ended—if such battles could be said to ever end— with three of the Pilgrims kicked and clubbed into insensibility . . . one had a fractured skull, and died four days later. The rest had their jackets and shirts literally torn from their backs, and of course all of them lost their knapsacks.

They are gangsters, robbers, said MacBean. The majority of them come from the slums of New York. Come along. I'll show you my shebang.

Thank you. I'd best stay with my men, here. Do you mean that the Confederates do nothing to ameliorate this situation? They allow hoodlums to go unpunished?

Friend, said Seneca, you've got a lot to learn about this place. You fetch the people of your squad together, and bid them sit on their knapsacks. Get at least six or eight together, and bid them keep together. What have you got in the way of arms?

Nathan looked his astonishment. But all our weapons were taken from us when we surrendered.

All, mister? What's in these bureaus? Knives, forks—You got any scissors amongst you? Any Barlow knives? Even a spoon; you can break off the bowl, sharpen the end on a stone: it makes one of the meanest weapons alive because you carry it concealed in your hand. . . .

Nathan went with Seneca MacBean to the northwest central portion of the area, not far above Main Street where they had met. MacBean lectured him all the way there. He said frankly that he had been struck by Nathan's size and physical makeup, and by the manner in which he addressed Private Allen.

You have qualities of leadership, Dreyfoos.

Thank you, but I fail to see what good—In a place like this—

Too few retained those qualities. Some had them before they came in, and lost them immediately or gradually. I want to see you retain your strength; hence my special interest in you, and overtures on your behalf. This business of these raiders: they're all over the place, growing worse and worse by the day. First off, it was sneak thievery at night. Then jostling and hustling by daylight. It's getting so bad that a couple of them will walk up to a man and knock him flat, right in plain sight, and take what he's got. Only way a man can survive is to keep big enough and mean enough for them not to tackle. But the bulk of the prisoners aren't big enough to begin with . . . some of those pests are regular giants, and they muster anywhere from a dozen to four dozen helpers and hangers-on apiece.

Nathan meditated on this. Then the only way to overpower them would be by concerted action.

I guess you'll get along, said MacBean. He exhibited the new shebang into which he had been compelled to move when the hospital was set up in the northeast corner. Oh, he said, we had a fancy domicile to begin with. Snug as a bug. Then they got the notion of a hospital on that very site, and we were condemned out of there.

Could you not move your house?

No, twas pine. All too dry to stand moving; the tufts fell to pieces. Of course this wood which you see now—ridgepole, front poles and so on—all came from there.

Where will we newcomers get wood for our poles?

Buy it. You can buy anything here. From the guards, from other prisoners, from that skinflint sutler. If you have no money you will pay in kind, so to speak; it's barter, but still it's buying and selling.

Do you have any poles to spare, Sergeant?

MacBean lowered his voice. Got four beauties hid underneath that trash there. They belonged to my comrade, fellow name of Lawrence, also from the Eighth Cavalry. He died this month and I was his sole heir.

How many have died this month?

Close to seven hundred by actual count.

Out of how many prisoners?

We might have numbered ten thousand before you folks arrived.

Nathan said something in another language.

What say?

Never mind, Sergeant. It is difficult to—Ah. I should like very much to buy your poles so that we may rig our blankets and overcoats. I'll offer you—He thought for a moment. You mentioned scissors. I have a beautiful pair. I won them in a game of bluff, he added with a grin.

Mister, said Seneca slowly, I'll take you on that. No—hold on—on second thought, you keep ownership of the scissors, and give me something else. Here's a proposition: how'd you like to be a barber? Shears, even little ladies' needlework shears like they have sometimes in a housewife—They're awful hard to come by, in here. A haircut is equally hard to come by. Suppose you set up shop as a barber right here alongside my laundry. That will give you various benefits: you can win a small income—food, bits of this and that to bargain with. It'll all help. Mind what I said about a man retaining his qualities of leadership! *And* his power to take care of himself!

But the rations which they give you aren't—?

You'll see. Wait till this afternoon. Nothing but that damnable cornmeal, I'll be bound. Our mess hasn't tasted meat in nine days—I've counted. A little salt once; extra peas on two occasions. But they were pretty wormy. I warn you, Dreyfoos, you'll go downhill unless you take extra special precautions.

I thank you for the advice. I'll be a barber although I've never been one. Will it be difficult to learn the trade?

Don't think so. Never tried it—but then I never was in the laundry business before—except as a delivery boy, back home. I suppose it's just a case of clip, clip and more clip. If a man gets clipped close enough it helps with the bugs. Beards, same way. I haven't got trimmed for some time—too busy washing. So I'll be your first customer. And mind to warn your men away from that deadline. Don't even step close to it. The Twenty-sixth Alabama guards aren't too bad, but those damn Georgians would rather shoot than eat.

20

Sometimes General Howell Cobb, one-time cabinet officer and now serving as commander of the Department of Georgia and of the reserve troops, wondered why circumstance had ever compelled him to assume a charge which demanded so much and paid so little. Emolument was nothing. One could not set a cash value on service to one's Country but there should be a clean spiritual benefit accruing. Howell Cobb received no pence of this sort to put in the purse of his soul. He was a big man with a mane (sometimes in dreams he saw himself stepping about in a toga; and sometimes—worse—he was uncomfortably aware that he resembled a rustic auctioneer with a loud voice whom he had known as a boy). His most important immediate duty as he saw it was the raising, arming, equipping and training of Georgia Reserves. This was not even making bricks without straw, it was making bricks without clay. He had seen the first railroad trains go through Macon, bearing off-scourings of Belle Isle and other Virginia garbage heaps. He thought that even this starved and ragged human material would have served better in construction than the scrappings allotted to him. He stood with thick pompous face set, he stood with lowered hatbrim, and reviewed in solemn gaze and more solemn spirit the worthless ranks which formed his regiments. Blank-eyed little boys with oozing noses; shambling uncouth illiterates better cast as village idiots in this dreadful drama; hollow-cheeked doddering bearded relics who stood with trousers wet, their prostate glands turned to jelly by age. His worry was such that it could admit but little space for consideration of Yankees penned by a pine wall he had never seen—Yankees stalking in a Winder-contrived cage, Yankees Winder-fed, Yankees guarded by a Winder-appointed minion.

Nevertheless someone in Richmond was hearing groans and ghoststories, and orders could not be ignored when they arrived over the signature of the adjutant-general. Howell Cobb brushed his locks, had his servant pack a satchel, and traveled the sixty miles to Camp Sumter accompanied by his chief surgeon and whatever other staff officers might be spared from headquarters. Wednesday, May fourth, was a fine fair day. In this dressing of warm spring sunlight the stockade did not appear so ugly as General Cobb's active imaginings had painted it. Henry Wirz, panicked into flutter by the influx of braid and crusted stars, pranced nervously on the left of the mighty slowtreading statesman as the little party toured the prison with guards lounging ahead and behind.

A general break was the first bugaboo which must be laid, and Cobb devoted his attention to this chore. Wirz prayed for battery after battery of artillery to be placed here and there; but General Cobb assumed wisely that the four pieces of cannon now in position could rake the pen handsomely if need arose. He inquired into the state of ordnance, the quantity of grape available for quick reloading; he thought the supplies ample, and said as much in a report which he began to indite within a few hours after his return to Macon.

Headquarters Georgia Reserves, Macon, Georgia, May 5, 1864 General: Under your orders to inform myself of the condition of the prison at Andersonville, with a view of furnishing from the reserve corps the necessary guard for its protection and safety . . . ha. His service in the field had not been lengthy, but he felt at least that exposure to enemy fire had made a veteran of him promptly, completely. O curling scraps of down on cheeks of jaundiced hobbledehoys; O sodden pants of the aged; O nitwit cropper able better to handle a hoe than a musket, and bound to chop out the corn, in your foolishness, and leave the chickweed! *There are now in the prison about twelve thousand prisoners, in an area of less than eighteen acres, with a stockade around it about fifteen feet high. I presume the character of the prison is well understood at Richmond, and therefore give no description of it.* Might one be able to box or bottle a smell? Even a small phial of smell? How shrewd it might be to ship off a well-packed box, the squat glass medical tube wrapped in cotton to prevent breakage, the label traced in an indecipherable script used by surgeons in jotting down their requirements: Contents, 10 cubic centimeters Smell, Andersonville, Camp Sumter, Sumter Co., Ga., May 4, 1864. By the Eternal, sir, it would cause a sensation in those pothersome offices with their rows of meddling clerks, their snidish field grade officers who built a supercilious wall between High Command and Reality! The unpacking, the group around the desk, the peeking and wondering, the stopper withdrawn, the stench bursting out of its concentration, the panic to follow. . . .

Howell Cobb's massive face did not bulge in a smile, but he felt an awful smile shaping inside him. He went on writing.

I took the liberty of making several suggestions for rendering the prison more secure; and if the tools could be had, I would recommend that the entire prison grounds should be surrounded by fortifications, which could be put up by the troops, whose health would be promoted by the employment. Health—a pretty word, a worthless one under the circumstances. What was health among troops? Health was a singing of the blood, a bellowing of energy to be released in horseplay, high jinks, conflict, the mass surge and peril and murder of a campaign. Health was a chicken roasted on a ramrod, a bayonet jammed between the ribs of a hireling, a fist-fight on an embrasure, a thumbing of the nose. Health was sacrifice, dash, shooting coolly or in frenzy, health was a Rebel yell which went aloft until it seemed that unknown stars must seize and hold it . . . contain it to be given back to future heroic generations when future heroic generations might need to hear the sound, to tell babies in their cradles to listen for that long hoot and be inspired by it when once again the drums came beating. Health was the lusty war fought by vigorous youths with braided muscles on their bones, with God's own good hot butter husbanded in their testicles. Where were the healthy? Name the spots in no necessary order of geography or chronology: Fair Oaks, Corinth, Vicksburg, Sharpsburg, Gettysburg, how many other *burgs?*—Gaines's Mill, Mechanicsville, Manassas, Pittsburg Landing. Take your spade, historian, and go to digging. You might unearth Leonidas, Varus, King Harald; or at least anonymous Jakes and Johnnies who were cast proudly in their mold. Assuredly you could not dig up these spindle-shanked Antiques and Horribles who comprised the command of Howell Cobb.

He sighed, he wished for a long just peace, and himself rising in the Senate to a Point of Order. He wrote.

The most important change is the one suggested in the accompanying report of my chief surgeon, Dr. Eldridge, that is, the erection of hospital buildings outside the prison. Upon that point there cannot be two opinions among intelligent men. It ought to be done at once, and such is the opinion of every sensible man who has examined the prison.

Here was himself, who had practiced the usage of words with dignity and color throughout his adult life, who thought that language was tonic and decoration— Prison, prison, prison; prisoners, prisoners, prisoners. Had he not a synonym in his cartouche of verbiage? What did you call a prisoner except a prisoner? What did you call a prison except a prison? Might you term Andersonville anything other than Andersonville? Call it mire, muck, sink, morass, dump, dung, cesspool, chamber pot, hog-wallow, cow-pie? Somewhere there must be proper synonyms . . . they did not come readily.

Wirz had said, General, I tell you I am a physician! Those sick should not be so many among the well ones.

I presume, Captain Wirz, that you have done what you could.

Always I do. *Himmel,* at night I keep thinking, What should I do?

I observe that you have made some attempt to provide shelter for the sick in that northeast area—

Tent flies we got, and some—what you call it?—canvas. But to make the hospital, must I have many men move from their huts. *Ach,* they make my head hurt when they yell from it! And so many more men without shelter it has now become; so, so many more sick we have. General, better I was a colonel, this should not be!

It is not a matter of your rank, Captain. It is simply a case of our possessing neither tools nor materials, nor sufficient personnel.

And such a bunch of guards, they are bad and foolish. Much trouble have I got from them, as also from these damn Yankees.

The prison is already too much crowded, and no additional prisoners should be sent there until it can be enlarged. The effect of increasing the number within the present area must be a terrific increase of sickness and death during the summer months. Prison, prisoner, increasing, increase . . . what had befallen his vaunted claim to the majesty of words spoken or set down in ink?

Poor Alexander Persons. A good just capable dependable man in peacetime— and, thus far, in wartime, though he seemed overcritical of superiors. It gave Howell Cobb a wrench to see Persons placed in such a position. (It gave Howell Cobb an even more severe wrench to observe the position in which he himself had been placed.) Wirz was a blundering snapping sputtering little wretch; but at least he stood devoted with a whole soul to the task of superintending prisoners; he was busy at the job; you could see that he was busy at it, he was not playing checkers in a tent nor swimming in sorghum whiskey. Where could you find another Persons, another Wirz? Oh, you might replace the other, you could never replace the one. But Henry Wirz was a direct appointee of Winder; and in essence Howell Cobb would be impugning Winder's ability if he so much as suggested a criticism of Wirz.

I understand that an order has been given for enlarging the prison. If it was possible to make another prison it would be much better, for I doubt very much whether the water will be sufficient for the accommodation of the increased number of prisoners. Prison, prison; much better, I doubt very much; should it be If It Were Possible or If It Was Possible? Suddenly Cobb had grown weary of words.

He recalled smell and faces. Sharply, sharply. Might one not box up a face and send it to that same Richmond office to be looked at, to be regarded with horror?

The general management of the prison under Colonel Persons is good, and he manifests a laudable desire to discharge his duties in the most efficient manner. There, that takes care of Alex Persons. *The duties of the inside command are admirably performed by Captain Wirz—*

Howell Cobb's tired sense went wool-gathering for a time . . . he recognized at last that his sense was vote-gathering, in retrospect or in dreamy ambition . . . vote-gathering must be really wool-gathering when a man had military responsibility ravaging him.

—Whose place it would be difficult to fill. There, that takes care of the little German-Swiss captain. *I take the liberty of enclosing a copy of Dr. Eldridge's report.* Oh, he should have said Surgeon Eldridge instead of Dr. Eldridge, but what in damnation was the difference! *I am, General, very respectfully yours, & c., Howell Cobb, Major-General Commanding.*

He penned his own endorsement, and told his adjutant to have the thing sent along with the enclosure of Eldridge's report. He wondered what other endorsements these papers would bear eventually. *Received A. & I. G.O., May 21, 1864. A. & I. G.O. Received May 26, 1864.* The best, the speediest of military mails were slower than lame blind mules these days. He thought of Richmond, and labored in the thought under that increased lethargy and blank doubt which overwhelmed any good mind when it considered Richmond and the pale clerks and ambitious limited majors skittering about like white rats denned in a cracker box. To whom might General Cooper pass along this report if indeed he chose to pass it along? To what generals, to what gentlemen in rumpled linen suits, to what musing bespectacled bigwigs in shabby frock coats—bigwigs more interested in the portraits for which they might be sitting than in the flow of life represented by neat stacks of mail arranged in square little islands on their desks, in front of yawning pigeon holes? Howell Cobb had seen such gentlemen and such islands of mail, and knew the amazing depth of a pigeon hole. A pigeon hole was not a well; a well was of lesser depth, and so was a vertical mine-shaft with its steam windlasses lowering. A pigeon hole went straight down to China, and papers fluttered out at the other end, and the Chinese picked them up and squeaked and clacked at the strange symbols, and burned them later in censers before their idols with due ceremony. Already Secretary Seddon's endorsement had become traditional. There were carping children who told tales out of school. *Noted.* That meant that he had read the contents, or at least had cast his weak gaze across the lines. *File* or *filed.* That meant that the report should be filed or had been filed, personally. *J.A.S.* That meant James A. Seddon, Secretary of War. It was more efficient to employ initials than a signature, it took less time and required less effort.

Well, Eldridge's accompanying report would make good reading for someone, sometime, somewhere, if anyone should bother to read it, if it should not be awarded the mere cursory scratch of those three initials. *I found the prisoners, in my opinion, too much crowded for the promotion or even continuance of their present health, particularly during the approaching summer months. . . . At present their shelters consist of such as they can make of the boughs of trees, poles, & c., covered with dirt. The few tents they have are occupied as a hospital . . . very many of them suffering from chronic diarrhoea combined with the scorbutic disposition, with extreme emaciation as the consequence.*

Extreme emaciation. Howell Cobb looked down at his own fist, clenched like a solid creased pillow upon his desk. Might not many of those skeletal creatures have once worn the flesh which now dressed his bones? Might they not, like he, have worn even too much flesh? Likely.

The hospital being within the enclosure, it has been found impracticable to administer such diet and give them such attention as they require, as unless constantly watched, such diet as is prepared for them is stolen and eaten by the other prisoners.

Thieves, said Howell Cobb in response to his surgeon's elucidation. Roughs. Hooligans. Why, Captain Wirz had told him—

Enemies of my Country. Brutes to be restrained. Monsters to suffer durance, fiends to be boarded in their cell. Pray to Almighty God that the necessity for grapeshot should not arise, but once it does arise let the lanyard be quick, the cap in instantaneous flash, let the powder be dry as toast, let the mass of balls go flying.

He sighed, he put thought of his and Eldridge's reports as far away from him as his thick mental arm could reach. Let him now go back to the dread task of building bricks without—Without anything.

By long lamplight, until very late at night that same week, Henry Wirz worked at preparing his own report. This was directed not to General Cooper, the adjutant-general, but to Major Thomas Turner in Richmond. Wirz had been instructed by Winder's office that Turner was next superior in the echelon of that command. A direct appeal to General Winder would have suited Wirz much better, but he feared that any attempt on his part to skip echelons would defeat its own purpose promptly.

By this time he had acquired a more tolerable military family, being rid of both the ailing Charles and the light-fingered Viggo. He hoped with all his heart that the report would be free from grammatical errors, and the necessity for this he enjoined constantly upon his clerks. The clerks went to bed at eleven o'clock that night, but Henry Wirz stayed awake until nearly twelve; and continually he peeked at the final copy.

. . . The number of prisoners on the 1st day
      of April was   7,160
  I received up to today, from various sources   5,787
  I received today, recaptured   7
                         Total   12,954
  The number of dead from the 1st of April to
      8th of May is   728
  The number of escaped from the 1st of April
      to the 8th of May is   13   741
  Leaving on hand   12,213

. . . I am here in a very unpleasant position, growing out of the rank which I now hold, and suggest the propriety of being promoted. Having the full control of the prison, and consequently of the daily prison guard, the orders which I have to give are very often not obeyed with the promptness the occasion requires, and I am of opinion that it emanates from the reluctance of obeying an officer who holds the same rank as they do. My duties are manifold, and require all my time in daytime, and very often part of the night. . . .

H. Wirz,
Captain Commanding Prison.

His small harried heart would have shivered with anticipation could it have known how favorable would be the endorsements to come. Wirz was open to just damnation on almost any charge conceivable but the sorest prisoner within the stockade could never call him lazy. He owned a virtue commonly respected: its name was diligence.

Strangely enough another man named Turner was now active in the life of Henry Wirz. Argument raked persistently between them as to whether a stipulated price amounted to thirty dollars or to thirty-five. The stipulated price was the standard amount on the head of a runaway Yankee. Wesley Turner was a master of hounds; previously he had worn gray, but now he operated in civilian capacity as a professional Yankee hunter. The dogs were most of them ordinary foxhounds or coon dogs with good noses; also the hunter mustered three vicious snapping creatures of mixed breed: perhaps they were a cross between the mastiff and the bull terrier—no one could tell for a certainty. These were known as catch-dogs; they were worthless at a scent, but would race along with the hounds. They served splendidly for scaring, treeing and sometimes tearing escapees (runaway Yankees were not called Escapees but Escapes, in prison slang).

Armed with pistol and horn, Turner rode his mule on a circuit outside the stockade early each morning; dogs sniffed and snorted ahead and behind. Often they trailed a guard or a Negro instead of a Yankee, and brought up yelling among tents of the Georgia regiment, among the Alabamans. Their master tried to beat sense into their heads with a long pole; soldiers stood jeering to watch him. Many of these youths had heard guns fired in anger, some had been wounded, a few had even been captured early in the war, to be exchanged later (fortunate prisoners, in a day when the process of exchange existed still). They had little respect for the man on muleback and no respect at all for Wirz; all who served at the stockade stations were disgruntled at coming under Henry's command during their tour of duty. As soldiers they recognized the obligation of any man to escape if he could manage it. The more depraved of the lot were trigger-happy, and boasted of Yankees they had shot at the deadline; however they saw nothing outlandish in the effort of a Northerner to tunnel out, flank out, or even to leap on the back of a guard while scratching through the forest with a wood-detail. In all justice they knew that they would have tried the same trick were the situation reversed. Dogs were an ignominy, a bullet was more to the point. The very baying of trail-dogs suggested that a black man had fled rather than a white.

My Daddy used to keep a catch-dog. Big brindled bastard.

Whereabouts was this, Nucky?

Wayne County. If a nigger walked off, man who owned the nigger might have hounds, but mostly they never owned no catch-dogs. Use to hire Buster from my Daddy, and Daddy'd have to go along to handle Buster, and times he'd take me along with him. Old Bus he trailed a damn nigger in the brush along Goose Creek —What I mean to say, them hounds did the trailing, but Bus was right in there with them, and when he come up to that nigger he just gave that nigger sut! Like to tore all the hide off one of his legs. God, you ought to heard that nigger holler.

Leastways he was a nigger.

Nigger ain't got no damn right to put for freedom!

But these here greasy mechanics ain't no niggers.

God damn, boy, some of them is!

But not the white ones. What I mean, a soldier is a soldier, I mean a white soldier. How'd you feel to have a catch-dog coming for you, like you was black? Nucky, I'd sure enough taste piss in my mouth fore I'd like to be niggerfied in such fashion.

That fucking Dutch captain! He's white-livered for sure.

Liver so white that chalk'd make a black mark on it.

God damn, sure enough.

Nevertheless Wesley Turner's pack of hounds was feared with reason by every prisoner who possessed the boldness and energy to attempt flight. If roll call disclosed that new Escapes were loose, or if a tunnel was discovered, or if the guards noted any peculiar activity among Outsiders—In any situations such as these Wirz shrieked for Wes Turner; the horn tooted, hound voices soared, catch-dogs growled and galloped. Through springtime only thirteen men managed to avoid being overhauled, as noted in the superintendent's report; and four of these were among the seven picked up by patrols in farther regions and fetched back to Andersonville. (The other three unfortunates had fled from a railroad train near Savannah and were brought to Andersonville because it was the prison nearest their point of recapture. Out of the frying pan into the fire, they said when once they stood inside the gate. None of them would survive the summer.)

Wes Turner was richer by nearly one thousand dollars Secesh before the first week of May. He increased his pack in consequence, and traded for a Colt's revolver to replace his old smooth-bore pistol.

Look a here, Captain. I never got no pay for them last two.

Ja, ja, ja, you was paid!

I never was paid, and I lost old Trip out of it. One of them damn Yankees had a knife, and he cut old Trip bad when Trip come up to him. I had to shoot him, by God.

The Yankee you should shoot instead!

Well, I did beat the poop out of him. But you never paid me for him, nor for the one I took over behind Widow Tebbs's place.

Ja, I show you on the book. You are bad, you Wes Turner, come always to bleed me for money. You think maybe the army is made from money, *nein?* Maybe I am made from money? Benny, it is you show this bad Turner in the book. . . . Here you see it, *mit* your own eyes!

Look a here, Captain Wirz, you know I can't read.

Benny can read, and now you he will show. Benny, you God damn Yankee, you show him!

First May, 1864. Paid to W. Turner sixty dollars, two prisoners recaptured.

So what you say to that, hah?

Well, it should a been seventy dollars. First off you promised me thirty-five dollars apiece, and then when I come to claim my rightful money you said thirty dollars—

Get from my office out, you Wes! Son of a bitch—

Don't you dare call me no son of a bitch, you little Dutch bastard!

Ja, I call you son of a bitch. Never do you call me one bastard!

Ahh—

Ahhhh, also! Now get out once!

Thus they contended with the meaningless futile insult of the weak and surly and suspicious.

A brilliant idea for the discouraging of tunnels had occurred to Wirz. He planned to put it into effect as soon as enough spades could be secured. His notion of a second, outer stockade must remain in abeyance for the time being, since the labor would be monumental; but he thought that a deep ditch might be dug without too much trouble. Prisoners (Negroes taken at Olustee) could do the excavating, since all his offers of double rations and other blandishments were refused scornfully by the bulk of the whites. But Negroes were an element apart. Neither he nor his superiors countenanced the assumption that they were bona fide military prisoners. He thought of them as wicked slaves who not only planned that nightmare, a slave insurrection, but who had actually participated in such an attempt. Most of the black captives from the Florida campaign had been pre-empted for outside duty as wagon-drivers, grave-diggers and the like. These creatures he would set to digging as soon as he could put spades in their hands. Whenever an engine squawked at the Anderson Station he set a youth flying to see whether the long-desired shovels might have arrived along with a new batch of prisoners. Sid Winder told him scornfully that he had experienced little difficulty in requisitioning necessary tools when the stockade was built, but there was a sudden paucity of spades when Wirz sent a detail abroad to seek such necessaries from nearby plantations and smaller farms. His status was understood throughout the neighborhood. People told the would-be requisitioners that Wirz was merely in command of the pen and had no authority to levy on the countryside for anything; only military engineers had such authority. Since this was uncomfortably the truth, Henry Wirz was forced to content himself with the hope of coöperation from headquarters at Macon; General Cobb had promised to do what he could. . . . A ditch, a very deep ditch. Guards should patrol it day and night. How deep would Yankees have to dig in order to avoid projecting their tunnels into that ditch? Very deep; and this they could not do, they were not all coal-miners.

Wirz worked zealously, feverishly at devising punishments for the insubordinate, and once the strap of punishment was prepared he wielded it with gusto. He arranged a row of foot stocks and another of spread-eagle stocks wherein men were locked to stand with their arms extended. (This latter colony caused him private discomfort, since when fastened therein a Yankee bore an unpleasant resemblance to Christ on the Cross. Henry considered himself a good Catholic, although he was not a good Catholic; in secret he felt that he had been guilty of profaning a symbolic sacredness; yet like an Oriental he would lose face if his orders were rescinded and the spread-eagle stocks taken down.) He conferred lengthily with smiths at the camp, and the result was a complicated series of chains and balls among which sinners could be manacled in a double rank and soon were. Trying to escape was a crime, so was complaining about the rations, so was the act of insulting a Confederate soldier or even remonstrating with him. The application of these tortures depended upon the superintendent's mood. Thus prisoners were puzzled and terrified by his capriciousness since Henry was a slave to moods. Sometimes a Yankee amused him in the manner of his attempt to break loose or in the manner of his recapture; then Wirz might greet him tolerantly, almost affectionately, and turn him back Inside with barely a slap on the wrist. Sometimes (mornings after his right arm had kept him awake were especially evil) a prisoner might offend him merely by way of address, solely by the earnestness of supplication. Then chains were fastened on, then the divided stock-arms were locked firmly.

I teach you to tell me bacon is bad.

Captain, for God's sake—

Son of a bitch Yankee, I teach you. Here you stay two days.

You dirty Dutch shit-heel, if I had a gun—

Now you stay one week!

True, he regarded his own punitive measures as painful and ugly, but pain and ugliness must be the lot of all vile humanity who walked in such filth, who planned to escape in order to burn munitions and ravish tender Southern girls, who had been so cruel in their warfare as to inflict a hurt which went throbbing through the years. . . . Devils who hurled mud at him . . . he would show them.

. . . The other Turner, the Richmond Turner, endorsed Wirz's report of May eighth with flattering alacrity. He wrote: *Captain Henry Wirz, commanding prison, reports in reference to the general condition of the prison, and suggests the propriety of increased rank being given him. . . . Respectfully forwarded, recommended. Thos. P. Turner, Major Commanding.*

General Winder in turn added his cramped agreement: *Approved and respectfully forwarded. Captain Wirz has proved himself to be a very diligent and efficient officer, whose superior in commanding prisoners and incident duties I know not.*

But the insignia of field grade shimmered only in a worthless future. There was no new metallic sheen on Wirz's jacket. Winder did not promote him, he only wrote the words Approved and Forwarded, he wrote words of praise. A simpering clerk in a remote office pinned the report to a sheaf of others and placed the pile under a paperweight to curl. Promotion would be awarded this hysterical tyrant only when he had no prison left to command; it would come as the accolade of a hopeless and disheveled Confederacy.

Under his consciousness Henry Wirz thought of the prisoners as animals, although he was not sure what sort of animals. They varied their coats and colors and shapes from time to time; some days they had hoofs, some days claws, some days they were strip*è*d, some days shaggy as bison. Monkeys they appeared to be when they were picking lice, fabled more ferocious apes when they fought in torment, herds of two-legged domestic beasts (but unfriendly, apt to burst through rails and perhaps trample children) when they were marshalled about in a squadding. Finally one night while in bed Henry had a recollective illusion. It was part memory, part dream and nightmare.

He was very young, perhaps eight years old, and had journeyed with his parents from Zurich to Bern to visit his grandmother. He had heard about Bern and the bears there, kept traditionally in their pit. It was the thing to do, to take children to see the bears; all children of Bern were taken so, and thus the little visiting Henry was escorted to this zoo in his turn.

He had not expected that the bears would be so large, and there was a growing feud between the two great males; perhaps the mating season approached. They growled horribly, slapped at each other, one bit the other on the shoulder and a scream arose. Keepers came with long poles and separated the combatants; one was driven into his den and made to remain behind a grating. At this roaring fearful confusion the throng of children gazed wide-eyed, and some little girls hid their faces in their aprons. Henry had no apron, but he could never have hidden his face had he possessed an apron, for his glaring dark eyes were nailed against the bear pit; he could not look in any other direction, frightened as he was. A few other children were led away, Henry could not be dragged.

At last when comparative peace reigned among the fierce brown animals, he saw that people were tossing carrots over the ledge. Two bears, trained to expectancy by long association, sat down with fuzzy legs spread and opened their mouths to catch the morsels. One, a mother bear, had a trick of making cumbersome gestures with her paw, indicating her mouth, indicating that she wished more carrots.

There was a vendor with a pushcart nearby, and Henry begged a few sous. He went to the cart, bought a bunch of carrots, and returned to the feeding. One by one he tossed the small tapering vegetables (they were clean, they were crisp, almost he wished to eat them himself but it was better to feed the bears; the carrots were of a delicate pinkish orange, they were beautiful). Not once did the bear miss, though Henry Wirz's aim was far from accurate . . . the bear weaved on her haunches, she leaned far out, she swayed from side to side. As the bright morsel flew, seeming to go past her, her jaws would snap and No More Carrot.

This trivial recollection, half dreamed in the night, resolved the identity of the Andersonville prisoners for Wirz into a common dark hairy form. They were bears, they seemed very stupid but they could bite and rend, worse perhaps than African lions.

A few days later he was in his splinter-new office, checking a roll of arrivals which Ben Dilley, one of his Yankee clerks, had put before him. He was eating a lunch at the same time. He had bacon sandwiches and a thin bundle of well-scrubbed carrots, also a canteen of weak elderberry wine. Wirz had eaten his two sandwiches and had drunk most of the wine, and was snapping carrots between his prominent front teeth. The clerk jumped each time that Wirz bit—it sounded like a cap snapping—and then would come the fast grinding sound as Henry Wirz chewed, opening his mouth under his beard.

Suddenly the report of a sentinel's gun popped through the air, and there was yelling in the pen. Wirz sent Benny to see what had happened, to find out about the shooting.

Ben came back. Prisoner, sir, he said.

Is he dead?

No, sir, he's kind of kicking around. Guess it went through his thigh.

I go see, said Henry Wirz.

He went to the nearest sentry station, climbed, and looked down. The wounded man was lying well inside the deadline at the edge of the marsh, and seemed wallowing in pain but making very little noise.

You shoot him? Wirz demanded of the wan-faced guard.

Huh-uh. Twas Tom Luckey over yonder, and the boy pointed.

The superintendent called across thirty yards to the next station where the sentry had just finished reloading. For why you shoot?

He was scooping up water clean inside the line, Captain.

Then it is good you shoot. . . . Wirz spoke to the staring prisoners below, whose permanent anger was always so obviously intensified by such occurrences (they came more frequently all the time). Some from you son of a bitch Yankees get that Yankee who was wounded. From out the deadline take him; I let you move him.

The victim's friends sprang into the fatal area promptly and lifted the youth from slime in which he writhed. They carried him across the narrow footbridge and up the hill toward the South Gate, planning apparently to have him ready for examination should any of the stockade surgeons appear. Wirz turned from watching the departure and studied the mass of wild dark faces upturned below, and felt their hatred sweep through him, and he fired back his own silent hate. They were bears . . . here he stood with carrots again, he had come up with the things in his hand, he had not realized that he was carrying them.

Before he knew what he was doing, Wirz had shifted the five remaining small carrots to his weak right hand, and his left hand went over to feel for a single vegetable and to toss it out and far.

There was a scramble, more faces turned up; there sounded profanity, scattered insults, a scatter of laughter. Again Wirz threw a carrot. Bern, he said in his soul. It was long ago, I was so little. *Ja*, they are bears.

Fresh carrots were seen seldom in that place except by raiders who might purchase them from guards. (It was against the rules, of course; but much trading went on every night, much buying and selling, and often even in the daytime. Wirz would have been powerless to stop the practice even had he cared to.) Hands groped, waved, snatched at space, the bears were grabbing and fighting, bears were growling as in that ancient pit in Switzerland. One at a time Henry Wirz threw the rest of the carrots and saw them vanish into turmoil. Wirz turned away and descended the ladder carefully; he had no wish to fall, to fall and hurt his arm. Bears, he kept saying to himself.

21

Chickamauga possessed almost no beard at all; he said that it was because of a disease he had suffered when young. It was at Chickamauga that he was wounded (the same battle in which Badger Claffey received fatal wounds); it was at Chickamauga that he was captured; in the hospital he had talked incessantly about these experiences, so the name clung to him. But also he was called by a variety of other names. Poll Parrot, Pretty Polly and Fortune Teller were some of the designations applied to him—this last because he carried a deck of ragged dirty cards in his pocket, and would tell your fortune for one dollar Confed. If he liked you he would give you a very good fortune indeed; he would say that he saw you alive, well, returned safely to Michigan or Massachusetts, sitting down to dumplings and chicken-pie, the admired of a beautiful young woman, and rich too. But if you had offended him in some way (and many people did offend Chickamauga daily, and well did he merit offense) he would see all sorts of dreadful things in your future. His protruding eyes, green as peas, would glow devilishly as he related his advice. Keep away from water, and did anyone in your family ever die of dropsy, or was anybody in your family ever burned to death—I don't know for sure, but it says right here in these cards that someone in your family got burned to death or maybe will get burned to death . . . these things he saw for you. His head was bald, and people had a joke and said that his head was perhaps the only place where Chickamauga was balled. Some people said that Chickamauga's true name was Hubbard, some said Hulburt; some said he was from the Ninety-sixth Illinois, some said the Thirty-eighth. If you asked him he would try to tell you, but he had the sort of deformed lip which made it impossible for him to enunciate with complete clarity. The sobriquet of Poll Parrot was apt also; you had only to look at his nose. Chickamauga talked to anyone, everyone, jabbering on in every waking moment; and when he slept his mouth fell open, and his snoring was the grunt of a hog. It seemed often that he did not sleep at all, but went crutching nervously throughout the stockade even by night, and thus was as well known to folks on the North Side as on the island in the marsh. He wore a pair of Rebel pants, and the right trouser leg, empty throughout the greater part of its length, was turned up and pinned by several large thorns. The smell of his breath might have been an emetic. It was difficult to believe that he had come to exist through the natural process of conception and birth and growth; it was as if he were a changeling from a Grimm tale, delivered by a troop of elves, and wicked elves at that. It was impossible to believe that anyone had ever loved him, and yet somewhere sometime someone must have kissed his horrid face and held him tenderly.

Chickamauga had learned early in life that benefits might accrue to him if he curried favor in high places, so he came to know Henry Wirz very soon after his draft of prisoners was sent down from Richmond. Wirz, thinking about it distastefully, came to the conclusion that he must have seen Chickamauga the very first time that he, Wirz, came into the stockade. Always that wheedling hare-lipped murmur, high in the mouth and throat of the cripple . . . we don't get enough to eat, and Captain, if I tell you when someone is going to escape, and prove it too, will you let me have a piece of meat?—not jackass, but real honest to God meat; and, Captain, I heard some fellows talking, and I think they're digging of a tunnel, and I think I know where it is, and if I find out just where that tunnel is, will you let me go Outside and pick berries? Look, I won't try to Take Leave, I couldn't try to Take Leave, I've only got one leg, and I couldn't very well run away with these here crutches.

Wirz disliked Chickamauga as he disliked most people except his wife and little Cora; also the weird Poll Parrot face was a Yankee face. But Henry recognized the necessity for having spies and informers within the stockade, and since Chickamauga's half-mad babblings were looked upon as the outpourings of an idiot child by the prisoners, it was possible that they might speak unguardedly in his presence. Wirz did give the one-legged man small favors from time to time. Maybe the prisoners thought that it was out of pity, but few of the prisoners believed that Henry Wirz had any pity in his heart. Henry Wirz did have. He had pity for himself.

Chickamauga prayed constantly to be taken Outside, but the Outsiders must be able-bodied in order to perform work demanded of them; and once he was put on Wirz's list of informers he might as well have ceased praying to go out, except that he was granted two brief sumach berry excursions with the wood gang. From these sorties he returned more voluble than ever, carrying extra berries in half of a broken wooden bucket. The first time he set up shop on Broadway and sold his berries (one at a time, for the most part, but some customers had sufficient means to buy a dozen) at a sublime price. Sumach berries, dried on the bush or not, were a recognized antiscorbutic and thus valued highly by the prisoners, who ascribed all sorts of tonic values to the bitter fruit.

After the second trip Chickamauga made the mistake of going into business on South Street and that was near the haunts of the raiders. A foot came out slyly and hooked itself around one of Poll Parrot's crutches, the crutch was jerked from under the bald man's weight, he went sprawling. Of course when he arose the berries were halfway to the sinks; people pointed out the thieves, but what might this plundered salesman do against raiders? Naturally he sought each day to find favor with them just as he did with Wirz; he followed the chiefs, wheedling and lying and offering information about fresh fish who were reputed to own enormous bankrolls or gold watches. He went capering after Collins or Sarsfield or Delaney, after any and all of them, until the epithet of Brown Nose was added to the weight of those other names he bore already. But the raiders who stole the berries were young boys, mere hangers-on, ambitious ruffians who strove to emulate their lords. Willie Collins laughed when Chickamauga came complaining. He said that the berries were all eaten, and why hadn't Chickamauga brought some to him, to Willie Collins? This the cripple planned to do, next time he went Out, but he didn't go Out again.

When the Plymouth Pilgrims appeared the raiders came into luxuriant funds; they enjoyed banquets of pork, rice, milk, green vegetables, they even had coffee and army crackers at times. Bundles of canteens filled with pine-top were smuggled in dusk to the conical tent which now rose alongside the headquarters near South Street. They sang, bellowing through night hours, singing off-key and sometimes ending up with a free-for-all, a battle royal among the chiefs. They owned strength enough to fight, for their board was better set than it had been when they were campaigning; the food was excellently cooked (why not? They had kettles, iron skillets, plenty of wood) for they'd found trained cooks among the horde of New Yorkers who clung in satellite formation around them; and one skilled cook had been impressed bodily, captured and kidnapped and retained in slavery, mourned as dead by his Philadelphia comrades on the North Side.

Liquor bubbled, voices grated into the night.

> *In Athol there lived a man named Jerry Lanagan;*
> *He battered away till he hadn't a pound.*
> *His father he died, and he made him a man again;*
> *Left him a farm of ten acres of ground.*

Estimates of the wealth brought in by the Plymouth Pilgrims ran as high as one hundred thousand dollars in greenbacks; probably the actual amount was but a fraction of that sum. Nevertheless in hands of the raiders the Pilgrims were bunnies gripped by hounds. The raiders soon had most of the money . . . thus they had eatables, they had potables, they had prime and power.

> *It's of a fierce highwayman my story I will tell:*
> *His name was Willie Brennan and in Ireland he did dwell,*
> *He rob-bed from the rich and he gave unto the poor,*
> *And all the folk did call him Willie Brennan On The Moor.*

Somebody was persistently singing John Brennan instead of Willie.

Who the hell is singing John? Tis Willie—

Hell it is. It's John.

God damn you, tis myself will show you! Willie!

Thwack and tussle, and burbled shouts and hootings, and people nearby crawling away because they feared that guards might fire.

Willie Collins's voice roaring out, Hold up, you shitty spalpeens! I'll clout the skulls of both of you.

Clout them he did, and then there was only a snarl and moaning.

I'll teach you, you bastards. When you sing it you'll never sing John. Nor Willie Brennan. Willie Collins! Me! Do you hear? Me—Willie Collins! For isn't that the thing I do—a-robbing from the rich and a-giving to the poor?

Dread laughter in darkness.

Sing it, devil suck it, as I bid you.

> *It's of a fierce highwayman my story I will tell:*
> *His name was Willie Collins and in Ireland he did dwell—*

In New York he did dwell—

In Andersonville he did dwell—

In the stockade he did dwell.

Laughter, with Willie's booming the highest.

Chickamauga was fascinated by these monsters as pimps and mendicants forever are fascinated by might and especially by the might of the cruel; but they would have little of him. They did not fancy his bad breath, his snoring, his split-lip chatter. Even Lipsky the tailor knocked him out of his path, threw his crutches aside and delighted in observing him as he crawled to get them. Furthermore the leaders feared that in his approach to idiocy he might apprise intended victims that raiders were at hand, and so they'd meet with no success in stripping the victims. They drove Chickamauga from their neighborhood more frequently than they welcomed him. They welcomed him only when a credulous superstition was ascendant in the drunken state, and they wished their fortunes to be told.

Chickamauga cringed at what he hoped was a safe distance, trusting to be summoned.

Poll, you devil. Pretty Polly, come you here.

He would jerk along eagerly.

Polly, do you tell my fortune. Have you your broads?

Yes, yes, yes, got my cards. What will you give me?

I'll give you the toe of my boot if you don't hasten—

Yes, yes, but you want a good fortune. A real good fortune? Give me a bowl of them beans and bacon—Give me a big bowl and I'll tell you a great big fine fortune—Give me—

Ah, hush your jawing. Here, Cookie, fetch the bastard a bowl of that kitchen physic. Hurry up, God damn you.

They stood, begrudging the Fortune Teller even this moment of good faring, while he spooned the stew with a trembling hand.

And, please, Willie—Please, Willie—Just one little drink of sorghum whiskey —Just one swallow—

I've no bingo for the likes of you.

But I'll give you the best fortune I ever gave—

Give him a slop of bingo, Willie, to hush his guff.

Ah . . . that bottle there. Damn you, Cookie, never pour too much. Don't be wasting of it on the likes of him. . . . Now, then, hustle with that fortune before I snitchel your ugly conk.

The thick soiled cards spread on a barrel head, the mumbling and scowling as Chickamauga bent above, and moved the cards in a pattern, and rejected some, and shook out others. He was nearsighted, and had secured a gift of spectacles while in the hospital, but the spectacles were long since broken.

Hurry up, you addle cove.

I see you going out of here.

Exchange?

I can't tell. Maybe exchange.

And how soon would that be? Speak up, you vampire.

I think it's July, cried the Fortune Teller in triumph. Yes, yes, it's July. You go out of here—

And to where am I going? To another stockade? I'll fib the living—

No, no, please, Willie—Not another stockade! I see you going—I see you wearing citizen's clothes! Beautiful, beautiful citizen's clothes. You are sitting in a great big gilded dining room—it's a lobster palace. You got a pretty lady with you. You got—you got *champagne!* And beefsteak! And strawberries! You got—

Ah, enough of your—

You mustn't hurt a fortune teller, Willie, wailed Chickamauga in fear but in severity. That's very bad luck. Don't you dare hit me again—

Well, it's not me that will club you. Willie Collins laughed richly; he liked the idea of himself with a pretty lady in a lobster palace. Now, tell me, Poll—What's the hair that lady's got upon her head?

Golden.

Golden? Why—

Yes, sir—lovely golden hair, and she's got a red hat with a pink feather on it—

With what? You vampire, speak up like a man! Don't you come at Willie Collins a-spitting and a-clacking like a bludget.

Pink feathers! What I said. Pretty pink feathers on her red hat—and curly yellow hair—

Doubtless a whore from a goosing slum on Water Street.

This was said by someone behind Collins, and Willie whirled, waving his club. His friends scattered, laughing uproariously, but bound to keep away from that angry club. Unable to select a particular target at the moment, Willie turned back and kicked the barrel and sent the cards fluttering. Chickamauga sought to elude him, but fell over his own crutch, and Willie Collins gave him stripes to turn his bottom black-and-blue. You ugly pigeon, you've sought to plague me. Don't you know that I like them with brown hair? I hate all women with yellow hair, indeed I do, for one of them gave me the Venus curse when I was a lad. Get out of this and don't you never be coming back! *Whack.*

No, no! Willie—

Get—*whack*—out— *Whack.*

No—oh God—

Chickamauga was now in pain, and would be for days, but he was hurt by these blows no worse than already he had been hurt by repeated woundings of life itself which offered no caress to him, only blows, blows, blows; and he did not know how to earn a caress from anyone. He crawled to his crutches and went weeping away, helped along by a few charitable persons who had been watching the scene, and who perhaps risked the wrath of Willie by ministering to the wretch. Chickamauga did not again seek the company of the raiders; his playing cards were lost; Collins had trampled them into the mud.

About the time of the arrival of the elegantly garbed prisoners from North Carolina, the quantity of rations began to decline; the quality had been non-existent for a long while. Men estimated as to whether they were getting one-quarter or one-third as much food as they needed to keep them going. To augment his slim pickings, Chickamauga could now be seen peeking and prying with double energy; he was bent on gathering some small detail concerning an escape plan which he might sell to Wirz or to the Officer of the Day. Even his insipid reason assured him that he must have accurate identifiable evidence; no mere rumor would suffice. On the morning of May second, when the first load of pone came rocking into the stockade behind its sorry mules, there was a concerted rush by a band—not of raiders, but of ordinary prisoners who had aligned themselves for the purpose. The cart was swept clean in an instant, and all over the vicinity men could be seen, darting or creeping off with two, three, four flat loaves clutched to their bodies . . . in some cases other prisoners hustled after them, bent on robbing the robbers. The cart-driver scratched his woolly head, the guard picked up the musket which had been knocked from his grasp. With two sergeants comprising this detail they drove back out to make their report. Guards on the parapet stood threatening, but mercifully no one was fired upon except one foolish man who went clambering past the deadline near the sink, seeking a scrap of stolen pone which had tumbled there. He was shot dead, shot through the head.

Wirz shrieked when the news came. An edict was pronounced at once, delivered to prisoners at both gates, and spread rapidly by word and shouting until the population was apprised wholly: no further rations would be delivered that day in punishment for the offense. Wirz was so righteously indignant that for once he forgot all about the necessity for personal guards. Revolver on his belt and holster unfastened, he came through the South Gate wicket . . . he had been awake all night with his arm, and stepdaughter Susie (his family was now arrived) had an illness and whinnied with it. Henry Wirz sent about among surgeons as soon as he reached his office that morning, seeking for sulphate of morphia, but the surgeons had none to give him.

He stood, teeth bared under his beard, cursing the ring of scarecrows who threatened and jeered.

By God, I find who stole that bread. Who stole bread? You, fellow there—tall —Did you steal bread?

A slow shake of the head.

By God damn, I find out.

Behind the nearer rank facing him, other voices ranted. Oh, shut up, you dirty Dutchman. Kill the son of a bitch. Take his pistol away from him!

He was getting nowhere with this crowd, so he turned with precision on toe and heel and started in the opposite direction, advancing toward a portion of the encircling throng who resembled the ones he'd just faced with a quality identical in appearance: they had the same thin blackened frames, the same clumps of matted hair and beard, the same rags, the same shedding of humanity.

A stone sang past his head. Wirz turned and drew his revolver. Two wads of mud struck him from the rear, one on the rump, one near his collar. Again he whirled.

I teach you to throw mud at me!

Teach us, teach us, you Dutch son of a bitch! Go ahead, old boy, teach us! What?—with that fucking pistol of yours? Yah, yah, yah, yah, yah—

His voice pressed thin and shrill from a shaking throat. I wish I find out—

Buck and gag the bastard! Let's buck and gag him!

—Wish I find out who says to me such insulting words, I kill the damn Yankee, soon as I eat my supper!

Hear, hear! Aw, listen, Hartley, the poor little critter never had his supper. Hard lines, old fellow, hard lines—

Mud flew toward Henry Wirz. He shut pained eyes and tried to squeeze the trigger of his revolver as he aimed it; he could not squeeze the trigger, the hammer hadn't been pulled to cock, he tried to cock the hammer, his twitching thumb knocked off a percussion cap. What would befall if he stood unarmed before these fiends?—oh death, oh beating and pain and death and lynching— suppose they got hold of his arm—his *right* arm—

He turned and ran violently toward the wicket gate, trying to jam the revolver into its holster as he ran, ducking his head to avoid stones. Voice from the parapet: Hey, open up that little door down there for the captain. And then the wicket swinging, and his own boots bumping the ledge as he clambered through, and mud striking the gate, and the prisoners howling as if they had done a brave thing. What was brave about that? Why should they exult? They were thousands against one, and he was a wounded man, and he had been aching all hours of the night—

He rubbed sweat from his forehead. I want a squad, he ordered. I want I should have two squads with muskets loaded and fixture of bayonets. Then I go back inside, I find those thieves who stole bread from the wagon.

Chickamauga was neither a witness to this event nor a participant in it. Chickamauga was skulking far over on the North Side close to the western border of the stockade. He had reason to think that several tunnels were being constructed, and Henry Wirz was driven wild by the threat of tunnels, and hoisted into glee when he could find a tunnel and break it in. Wirz would pay well for the news, granted it were correct, or at least he should pay well if he had justice about him. Sometimes Chickamauga doubted lugubriously and correctly that there was any justice in anything. But he held some small clues and itched to find more.

That night the Fortune Teller went to the sinks to relieve himself—not through any sense of sanitation or natural tidiness, but because he had learned that he would be pummeled if he grew careless near the habitations of other men. Diarrhoeic prisoners might be forgiven their lapses by the charitable—not Chickamauga. Sometimes he cried, to himself or to others—it did not matter—because he thought that no one ever forgave him for anything.

So he was at the sinks. In twilight he might have been mistaken for a stump, though by this time there was no visible portion of a stump left in the area. All stumps had been splintered apart by the population's knives, forks, bits of tin, sharp stones, or even their own fingernails. The digging up of subterranean roots was in progress, to continue through the summer. But since Chickamauga squatted motionless on his one good leg, half supporting a portion of his weight by means of his leg-stump and a trusty crutch, there was nothing about him to cause alarm.

The man who came and stood nearest him did not indicate by word or gesture that he saw the mutilated figure amid shadows and spongy mats of excrement. If Chickamauga was not a stump then he was a rock, a harmless ghost, a blot before night-seeking eyes, an ink-blot spotted on a copybook of the past, a grease-stain on the muster roll of the future.

The man stood quietly, he did not squat, he might have been taking a leak. But at nighttime no one bothered to go far in order to leak; all the earth was becoming rapidly saturated with those poisons which sick men exude, and it wasn't worth a fight (except in the more fastidious messes, and most of these people would live longer because of their care) to challenge a man when he leaked close to you. There was no sound of urine spraying. What could the man be a-doing? Chickamauga watched, he could not see.

For perhaps three unyielding minutes the man stood there, and as he faded off another figure came to take his place. The watching cripple could not be satisfied as to just what went on—his nearsightedness provoked him—but it seemed that the men made some slight contact . . . maybe it was a word they exchanged. Then the second man took the place of the first, or stood a few feet to the left of where the first man had stood. As in the initial case there was no stream of water. Only a dry trickle or so it seemed. Chickamauga had the ears of an owl; he could hear much, especially at night.

He hoisted up his ragged Confederate pants and crutched to a more comfortable post of observation after the second man departed. He waited, he waited and listened and observed as adroitly as he could, he crouched on watch for another hour or two. The life of the pen continued to make itself felt and heard with that groaning, hacking, contending crystallization which lost all variety because it had too much variety, and so came into a sameness like a single musical note played with monotony and forever . . . half-hourly reports of the guards, the boy who came creeping to the sinks soaked in tears and kept sobbing repeatedly for Aunt Ida and saying again, Aunt Ida, if I could only see you, if I could only see you and old Fan and the pups, Aunt Ida . . . *hulp, look out! Raiders!* (This very distantly.) Station Number Three, eight-thirty o'clock and all's well. Aw, go fuck a duck . . . the mumble, mumble of how many thousand voices, dressed underneath with individual gagging, individual bursts of wind, noise of the fight which may have meant death to some boy weaker than the monsters who bore him down . . . Station Number Four, nine o'clock and alllllls welllll. Station Number Four, nine o'clock and Jeff Davis just buggered himself. And the very earth which was earth no longer, but instead a wet blanket of fecal matter laid across the rounded ribs of the sad punctured world—this apology for earth made its own conversation around Chickamauga; the unseen pools bubbled and stank, the bubbles came out of them as if forced by slow bellows underneath, and worms were working in that slime, or phantom snakes or toads. The bubbles popped, swallowed themselves, the smell came thickening.

But there was living going on, quite near the sentry Poll Parrot whose name may have been Herbert or Hurlburt or Hulburd or Hubbard, and what matter what it was? Or what mattered now whether it was the Thirty-eighth Illinois or the Ninety-sixth Illinois that he came from? Sometimes he thought that he had forgotten all; sometimes he was confident that he remembered clearly, even back unto the day when he was drafted and left the steam and boiling water and floating bits of food in that restaurant kitchen where he washed dishes on Madison Street in Chicago. He had washed dishes in Michigan and in Toronto and Milwaukee too.

There was living going on, a brief dwelling and visiting marked by men who came and went repeatedly. By judging their shapes against the night he thought that identical figures stood near him again and again. They didn't leak, there wasn't any water about the business they did, they only let go with a dry trickle.

At last, puzzled but still suspicious, Chickamauga went up the slope to his lonely shebang made of pine bark and portions of an overcoat. As often occurred, someone else had preëmpted his sleeping space. This interloper was an invalid on his last legs, or rather on his last raw wounds and swellings. He offered no resistance when Chickamauga spanked him cruelly with a crutch and drove him away to weep and die without shelter above. (The man was dead, with his head turned on one side and syrup congealed from his mouth, when Chickamauga saw him the next morning. . . . By gum, you won't come stealing my bed no more.)

The cripple pondered concerning those figures moving in darkness near the sinks, he pondered as well as his lame brain would let him, but he could not understand. He thought with self-recognized slyness that he would go and investigate further at dawn, as soon as it was light enough to see, but before daily activity of the camp had destroyed whatever revealing evidence might exist. Then he settled himself beneath mouldy rags and dreamed of food.

Since he was a boy he had toiled in proximity to food and in proximity to big coal and wood ranges; he had heard and seen and smelt cookery, he had scraped away pungent food left on many plates and platters, he had saved the best of these leftovers for himself, and so he'd dined almost daily on the best. Sometimes the stuff was of a nature which might not bear reheating, but still it was of the very best. He had eaten veal chops with mushroom ketchup, he had eaten *Hasenpfeffer* along with rich dumplings speckled with caraway . . . oh, a fat lobster claw, dripping with butter and drenched in lemon juice . . . peach cobbler . . . just at this moment he thought of *Königsberger Klops* and that dish also he had rejoiced in, in the last German restaurant where he worked. He could not pronounce the name recognizably. His fellow kitchen employees teased him through the hours, trying to get him to say *Königsberger Klops*, but they were always teasing him. They said that he said *Whaneywhagger whop*. He thought of food.

Sometimes there was a falsehood about the dawn. Some of the dawns were honest, murky as old dishwater, draining gradually lighter to reveal the jagged parapet, guards on high, the insane panorama of those masses of huts and sagging shelters, the scrawny wretches who stalked. Other mornings were honest in the fog they brought, for fog made the place the nightmare landscape which it was— fog accentuated nearer angles and ugliness, it turned the inhabitants into those visible apes they'd become in spirit. Chickamauga snored through his beaked nose and dreamed that he was being held down while people sawed his leg, as actually they had held him, with whiskey dashed into his mouth; he dreamed of this particular past and awoke yelling. Winking and shivering in cold he eyed the sky. This was surely the most dishonest dawn ever climbing up. It had a gentle yellow pinkness, and mockingbirds and redbirds were piping with spirit beyond the fence. In such an approaching sunrise one should be forever a child, and have a rosy street to scurry down on the way to work, with no one else abroad except an occasional stomping laborer or a night watchman turning his steps toward the warm breakfast awaiting. Chickamauga had known such sunrises, years before he became cut apart and confined.

He got up hurriedly, shivering in his trunk and three stiff extremities as he tried to stretch himself for the task of exploration. He clawed round in his pockets and found some bits of corn-and-pea bread and gobbled them. On his way down the slope he discovered the dead man whom he had beaten; so he searched the dead man's clothing and found more pone: two ragged rocks of it which the dead man had been unable to eat because his teeth had fallen out from scurvy, or most of them had. Chickamauga found a stub of red pencil less than an inch long, barely big enough to write with, and a fold of dirty paper covered with scribbling. Chickamauga could read quite well, but he was uninterested, so he tossed the paper aside . . . probably a last love note or a last Will & Testament, and who cared about that?

Something firm and flat, sewed within the lining of the corpse's gummy blue jacket (it was a cavalry jacket, short, with some of the seed-shaped buttons still attached down the front, and—Chickamauga bent closer, squinting through colored dimness—yes, there were a few stray threads still clinging to the shoulders, enough pattern of thread knobs to mark the shape of a bent rectangle on each shoulder. So the man had been an officer, one of those strangely dedicated beings who chose to accompany their men rather than go to an officers' prison; and so he must have torn off his shoulder straps before his rank was noted, and he must have given his name as Silas Fassett, Private, Co. G, Eighth Michigan Cavalry; and so he must have come here with his men, and he must have watched them all die off or else he would not have been alone and untended, worming about for a place to lie in and a place to die in, and finding both while his bones still throbbed from the punishment of Chickamauga's blows).

Chickamauga brushed aside the assembled lice and tore open the rotten jacket lining. He brought the flat object out, he snorted with excitement as he ripped shreds of decayed dun-colored silk which wrapped it. It was an ambrotype, a double ambrotype in a frame folding face to face. Cheeks and ribbons of the females therein had been tinted pink and yellow. From the left-hand frame smiled a young girl with bunched-up black curls, and in the right-hand frame that same young girl, a bit more grown up and certainly more than a bit more serious, held a fat stout-legged baby on her plaid lap, and both of them stared directly into your eyes and deep beyond them. They would have stared directly into Chickamauga's soul if he'd possessed more than a shred of one. He dug the woman and baby out of their frames, wondering earnestly if the frames could be gold, but probably they were only of brass and gilt. Nevertheless he'd rub the thing up; and when he set up shop to market it, he would do so on Main Street in order to escape the raiders' attention if possible. He threw the ambrotypes away and went off toward the sinks, pausing occasionally to polish the frame upon his rags. . . . He threw the ambrotypes away, and the one of the mother and child would be unheeded, trodden deeply into muck before an hour had passed, never being recovered, going to demolishment in time. But the picture of the mother before she was a mother—this would be picked up by a lonely youth, Opie Brandel, Co. E, Nineteenth Maine Infantry, and Opie would love and cherish her until he died in June; he would pretend that she was his girl, when in reality he had no girl because he was shy and hoarse-voiced and toadlike; he would call her Ellen because once he had loved from distance a Sunday School teacher named Miss Ellen; he would take her out, when he lay alone at night and when he felt strong enough, and he would turn her small face close to his own hairy one, and he would whisper, Ellen; and sometimes moonlight would find her there with him, and they would be quite alone, and there would be love between them.

Chickamauga ventured near the sinks. His crutch-marks had long since disappeared in slime, but he moved here and there until he was confident that he had found the exact spot where he squatted the evening before, and thus could select the place where mysterious men had appeared to do a mysterious errand. Here it was and . . . ah . . . other places nearby. He balanced his weight on his leg and poked about with one crutch. . . . It would all sink down and disappear during the day, but these traces were unmistakable. Clay and sand, that's what it was— clay and sand, and occasional shreds of brown wet roots too slender for use as firewood . . . a few pebbles. Earth, dirt, soil. Those men had fetched quantities of sandy soil in their pockets or in bags, and had stood sifting it into the bog so as to escape detection.

Who was digging that tunnel, and where was the mouth of it? Under a folded blanket and secreted planks or a lattice of brush, most likely—under the ragged roof of somebody's shebang. Well, there were so many huts. Yes, and so many tunnels or attempted tunnels. His split mouth grinned, thinking of how the men would swear if they knew that he, Poll Parrot, knew their secret already or at least a portion of it. He knew that they were digging the tunnel, and they thought that neither he nor anybody else except the loyal workers themselves knew that they were digging a tunnel. And in time Wirz would know about it, too; and Wirz would give him at least jackass meat, or maybe even currency, or salt which he could trade, or a chance to go Outside for sumach berries. Shrewdly Chickamauga sifted a little of the brown-yellow-sand-clay into his pocket for a specimen, and then he went away: there was nothing more to be done here just now.

That day, after his Ninety had received their rations (each prisoner was given a quarter loaf of corn bread, weighing possibly six ounces, and a piece of smelly pork weighing a little less) and after he had eaten his, and had eaten the portions taken from the dead cavalryman's pocket—after dining so, he crouched on Main Street and held up his ambrotype frame for sale. Soon a man came by who had been a jeweler when he was a citizen; when Chickamauga begged him to, the jeweler examined the frame and hefted it lightly in his thin hand, and scratched with a bent fingernail. It was, he said, merely gilded brass, just as the vendor feared. Well, the brass could be broken apart to serve for little tools or implements if no one needed it to frame pictures in.

Here's where you get a nice daguerreotype frame, cried Chickamauga. Step this way, gentlemen, and see a fine frame, beautifully gilded, fit to put pictures of your loved ones in. He would have tried to pass it off as solid gold but knew that he could find no takers; also he might attract Collins, John Sarsfield or their ilk. Best to admit that the thing was merely gilded brass. Step up and see, step up and see. . . . Other voices contended against his; men selling rice, men offering tobacco, men with buttons to sell, and boiled potatoes; a man with a ragged *Harper's Weekly* to let, another with a New Testament for sale. Right this way, a beautiful gilded frame to put your loved ones in.

A tall well-built youth with every look of fresh fish about him stopped to examine the merchandise. Chickamauga was excited. This man might be laden with currency.

What did you say this was?

Ambrotype frame! Beautiful! You got a picture to put in it—?

I can't understand you, so quit trying to make me understand. The youth opened the frame, closed it again. How much?

Five dollars currency. Five dollars greenbacks.

The boy laughed, threw the frame at him, turned to go.

Wait, wait! Chickamauga was desperate. This was the first person who'd shown any interest. How much will you pay?

Fifty cents Yank.

Fifty cents Yank? For this fine gilt—?

The customer started away through the crowd, but Chickamauga hastened after him. Wait, wait, mister. Give me seventy-five. Seventy-five. He kept repeating it until he was sure that he was understood.

Look here, Old Clatterpuss. I'm a watchmaker by trade, and I can do some tinkering whilst I'm in this prison pen. Got a few of my tools and—I could use that brass, but I'd have to cut it up—

In the end they compromised on seven dollars Confed, and now it was Chickamauga himself who went shopping. He bought nine small onions with one of the dollars, and a pinch of salt for fifty cents Confed extra, and later he traded two of the onions for a bit of raw meat and bone which the vendor insisted was veal but which was probably dog. He went back to his shebang and cooked a stew in the battered stewpan he'd stolen two weeks earlier, using pine splinters he'd brought from the outside on his last berry trip. Once he bothered to look down the hill to see whether the dead cavalryman was still there; he was, but neighbors were complaining; soon some of the more able-bodied neighbors would carry him away. Chickamauga finished his stew with relish.

He spent on the whole a peaceful and satisfying day. He watched two fights from a safe distance, he saw a wounded man bleeding after he'd been stabbed, he stood in a circle of other rubbernecks and observed a priest from Outside administering Last Rites to a consumptive old man; for a time he followed the priest on his rounds. Wirz appeared in the sentry-box at Station Number Nineteen, accompanied by another Confederate officer with a gray beard, and was roundly screamed at by the inmates. A prisoner was shot and killed near the deadline of the east stockade; the guard insisted that he'd tried to cross the deadline; other prisoners said the victim hadn't tried to cross—that he had been jostled. The guard was ordered out of the sentry-box afterward; there was a rumor that he was a patriarch eighty years of age, and how had his eyesight been good enough to enable him to shoot so accurately? Chickamauga attended also a prayer service conducted by an exhorter of the Methodist faith. He attempted to join in hymns because he enjoyed singing, but no one would ever let him sing—he made such a harsh noise—and this time was no exception. The prisoners manhandled him, hustled him, pushed him away, while the exhorter called warnings and quoted Christ in a loud voice. Vaguely Chickamauga felt a kinship with Christ, for He too had been pounded and scorned.

On the whole however it was a good sunny day, beginning with his discovery of the ambrotype frame in the dead man's jacket, and on through his examination of guilty sand deposited near the sinks, and on through all the rest. The events proceeded as on many other days, but sun shone for hours, a pleasant relief from the chill soaked skies which had clung recently.

That night he posted himself on a route where he might detect the sanddistributors passing, but rain swept down to drive him to cover. The next day Chickamauga shook with the ague for hours and lay miserably in his shebang; he took down the remnants of overcoat to wind around him. He still had currency, and bribed a neighbor to fetch rations. The man brought corn bread and a cup of coffee made from roasted okra seeds; Chickamauga paid more currency to have the coffee heated up. Gradually he regained sufficient strength and initiative to resume his detective operations.

On the night of Tuesday, May tenth, he followed the sand-carriers to the door of their shebang. It took him several hours to accomplish this feat, but Chicka-mauga felt that luck was with him, and relayed himself, as it were, from man to man through the sleeping, waking, growling, snoring, praying, gasping populace. The shebang was a large one, solidly made—there was even one whole rubber blanket incorporated in the roof. It was tenanted by a mess of Westerners, most of them Iowans. This information Chickamauga pumped from not-too-close neigh-bors the following morning, by means which seemed to him shrewd.

That morning Chickamauga was at the South Gate long before even the order-lies had arrived to examine prisoners who pleaded for hospitalization. He did not wish to meet the orderlies; he sought Captain Henry Wirz himself. When Chicka-mauga could get a sentry to heed him, he was stunned by the news that Wirz was sick abed. He moped about . . . should he approach the Officer of the Day or should he not? Wirz might pay better. He wanted to be certain that Wirz knew the source of the information which would be whispered, so that he might appreciate Chickamauga in the future; Chickamauga had no currency, but maybe the Officer of the Day was also flat of purse; certainly some food should be forthcoming; Chickamauga had fasted the day before; he suffered diarrhoea following his ague, and feared to eat corn bread because it irritated his intestines; how could he wait for Wirz and the next day? Perhaps someone else would stumble upon this tunnel project in the meantime and retail the information to guards, and Chickamauga's hopes would be dashed because he had delayed. It was this latter consideration which kept him hanging there, and finally sent him bounding toward the officer, the moment that familiar soiled red sash came in view.

Please, Lieutenant—Please—

What's ado? The Officer of the Day happened to be a plump oyster-eyed man named Gholson, resentful at serving as a lieutenant in middle age when people with half his years were sometimes captains, majors, even colonels.

Outside, whispered Chickamauga, bending close with wretched breath.

The lieutenant drew back in disgust. What the hell do you want to go Outside for?

I got some information. He had to repeat it two or three times before the officer made out what he meant. I don't want to talk in front of all these prisoners. Please—Outside—

The lieutenant turned pompously, called up to the parapet to have the wicket opened; and, squeezing his gray shape through, he beckoned for Chickamauga to follow. At that moment a shower of rain came down; it had been threatening since daylight, and the Officer of the Day directed the cripple to follow him under doubtful shelter of the nearest sentry-platform. Here they stood screened from all eyes, with outer gates of the protective cubicle closed firmly beyond them.

What do you know? The officer turned down the brim of his old yellow hat.

Chickamauga had no hat or cap. Water pearled on his bald head and pinched beardless face, it dripped from his bent nose. Please, will you pay cash? Cash?

Gholson put his hand in his pocket, then took it out again. He said, lying obviously, Left my purse in my quarters. I hain't got no cash to pay you. Speak up.

Please, sir, just a little something to eat. Maybe you could get hold of some meat?

Meat. Everybody dreamed about meat.

You stay here. As a gesture the lieutenant unsnapped the flap of his holster, and then walked over to the outer gate and knocked loudly, calling for someone named Sipes. The wicket opened, a face appeared, and Chickamauga stood chilled and dripping but watching eagerly.

Sipes, send up to the kitchens for a dish of them nigger-peas. And a spoon. Make it lively—I hain't got all day.

Big dish, Lieutenant?

A can full will do.

In the background Chickamauga jiggled on his crutch, eyes swelling out as he thought of hot peas.

There was a degree of shelter beside the outer gate, for rain was driving from the west. The fat Gholson lounged there while leisurely he cut a chew from his tobacco plug, put the plug and pocketknife away, and began to roll the fresh chew about in his mouth. He called through moist brown lips, You better have that information, crip. I'm wasting a sight of time.

Presently the wicket reopened and a small mess tin and a spoon were handed through to Gholson. The lieutenant signalled to Chickamauga, and the man came hopping across. Actually the nigger-peas were still warm, even in cold rain, and there were a few fragments of bacon in them. The lieutenant handed the treasure to the informer, saying, Just like the Planters' Hotel in Charleston. You even got a spoon. What do you know? You can talk while you're eating.

Chickamauga tried to talk while he was eating, but the officer soon stopped him. You cow-mouth bastard, I can't make you out. Eat them peas, and then talk, and talk sense or you'll go in the stocks.

Nothing had ever seemed so wonderful since the last dream of *Königsberger Klops.* Well, and he spooned up the last tasty drop of sauce, I know where there's a tunnel.

He told all, he gave a clear description of the Westerners' shebang.

Reckon I know that one. They got them a rubber blanket on the roof?

Yes, yes! Rubber blanket—

Chickamauga tried, again without success, to beg currency; then he asked for more peas or for an Outside pass with the next wood squad, but was refused. He began to cry. The lieutenant gave him a fair-sized piece of tobacco cut from his plug. Chickamauga did not chew or smoke, but this would be excellent for barter. He was ushered back into the stockade and went in, feeling that in some way he had been cheated. But Wirz might still let him go for berries when Wirz heard the tidings; anyway, another tunnel would be dug sooner or later. The memory of those heavenly peas lingered in his mind and on his tongue.

About forty-five minutes later a file of twelve guards followed Lieutenant Gholson into the pen. Ten of the men carried guns with bayonets fixed, and the lieutenant had his revolver out and cocked, carried dangerously in his hand. One of the men lugged a shovel and one a pick-axe. Gholson had no inclination toward the circuitous; he led his little army to the guilty shebang as directly as the crazy unsystematic arrangement of huts would allow.

The Westerners were lined up. Five had been caught at home, but two others escaped because they happened to be away. The five said that they were the only dwellers in that place; this they would still affirm, even in torture of stocks and balls-and-chains. They did not admit that people from adjacent shebangs had also helped in the digging (this was true of course). Away the prisoners were marched, to be put into a chain-gang. Wirz regarded a prisoner's attempt to escape not as a duty, a military obligation to his own cause, but as a fiendish effort to visit murder and rapine upon an innocent countryside. The shovel man and pick-axe man remained behind with Gholson still in command, breaking the ground around the tunnel's entrance, and filling in the hole. A hundred silent neighbors stood and glowered. Others went about their ordinary affairs in an elaborately casual manner, fearing to be associated in any demonstration of sympathy or resentment. The tunnel itself was well-made and well-executed . . . it was rumored that the leader in the enterprise had engineering experience. The tunnel began with a vertical shaft, shored up in its more crumbly portions, and other people could only guess at its depth before the horizontal passageway began. As was usual, the opening had been concealed by a blanket near which a couple of men were forever lounging during daytimes.

Chickamauga kept away from the immediate neighborhood while the arrest and destruction took place. He ambled along Main Street, seeking the best possible rate of exchange for his tobacco, and he said, What do you know about that? when people discussed the tunnel and pointed to the little squad of prisoners being marched Outside for punishment.

Chickamauga made finally a handsome bargain in which he paid his tobacco as rent for a deck of cards; he would be allowed to keep the cards for twenty-four hours, but was instructed not to lose so much as a single card under penalty of having his parrot's nose mashed flat. With these tools so necessary to the fortune teller's trade, he went about through the afternoon with satisfaction and profit. He devised fortunes for a few cents here, half a spoonful of salt there. He encountered a prosperous newcomer who delighted in hearing that positively he would be exchanged within either three days, three weeks or three months (could it have been three years? the man worried later) and he paid Chickamauga with a wooden plate filled with freshly fried potatoes of which the newcomer had a supply. After delighting in these viands and others, Chickamauga turned in and slept until sunset when the sky was clearing.

He returned to Main Street, trusting to earn a supper by means of his art, and was calling for clients along the muddy strand when a hand fell upon his shoulder. He turned and looked into the narrowed eyes of a seventeen-year-old stripling whose muscles had not yet fallen into threads. Two other men, older but equally grim, were with the prisoner.

We're from the Fifth Iowa, he said sternly to Chickamauga. You're the one who give our friends away.

No, I ain't!

Hell you ain't. You were all around there early today, asking questions about who lived in that tent—

No, I wasn't! You let me lone—

Hell you wasn't. Didn't you say he was, Ebe?

Yes. One of the other men had moved around behind the cripple to bar his escape. I saw him and heard him.

The tall youth struck Chickamauga on the mouth and knocked him against Eben Dolliver; he would have fallen if Eben had not been there, and he lost his crutches. He tottered forward on his left leg as Dolliver shoved him away. The youth punched Chickamauga twice more—in the belly, and he doubled forward; then on the side of the jaw. The victim tried to scream but could make only guttural growlings and gaspings, for his breath had been nearly knocked out of him. He stretched his length in the greasy mud, he tried to roll away from punishment. The youth wore shoes, or apologies for them; and with these shoes he kicked Chickamauga in the ribs four or five times.

Stop killing that poor cripple, cried a shocked voice.

Try and stop me. He got our friends on the chain-gang!

The youth awarded several more kicks, and so did the man beside him. Ebe Dolliver did not kick, but he approved the treatment, shocking as it might have seemed to him when first he was captured. They went away and left Chickamauga, who began to sob stupidly as soon as he had enough wind.

Some kind men were nearby, and they stood appalled at witnessing what seemed to them such unprovoked viciousness, yet they were not strong enough to interfere. They helped Chickamauga to stand up, they wiped blood from his mouth; one prisoner who professed to a knowledge of anatomy felt along the unhappy creature's ribs and assured him that they were not broken—only bruised. These benefactors even offered him a jacket at the edge of their shebang where he rested for a time. But it was growing dark, and there was not room for him there. People were settling down, tightly packed in spoon fashion, to spend another May night and to pray for August. (In July they would pray for November, in February they would pray for June.) Chickamauga could hobble, though stiffly. He traveled to his own shebang.

A stranger was there, and he was more powerful than Chickamauga, crutches and all.

This here's my shebang.

Do tell. It's mine now.

I'll larrup you with this crutch—

I don't know half what you're saying, but I've moved in here and I'm going to stay.

Chickamauga begged and cajoled, he asked for people in nearby shelters to aid him in expelling the intruder, but deaf ears were turned to him: he had won no regard from any by his previous conduct. Justly or not, this claim-jumper was going to stay. It was very chilly for a spring night. Chickamauga suggested that it would be warmer for two of them than for one; so the man agreed to share his stolen couch with the true owner. They lay together, shuddering . . . the other man had been drinking, and where had he got liquor? After an hour or two he became nauseated, and staggered off in search of water. He did not return, probably because he was unfamiliar with the lay of the land and could not find his way. Chickamauga took down the wisp of overcoat and wrapped it around himself. He could not sleep for a long time, his ribs hurt him terribly. Sniveling and mourning, he fell asleep and dreamed about his father. He was a little boy again, his father was drunk and chasing him with a strap. Chickamauga awakened in tears, but slept later and dreamed no more.

Morning came with sun, but it was misery for the lame man to haul himself up on his left foot. Knives were thrust into his side, a hammer had mauled his jaw and left it out of shape. But he hungered. He took stock of his stores . . . only salt, and not more than a few cents' worth. However, no one of the playing cards had been lost when he was beaten the previous evening, and thus he might hope to earn a breakfast at even this early hour. Fearing the Fifth Iowa boys more than he now feared the New Yorkers, he picked his way past the sinks over to South Street and solicited for an hour or two without success. His voice worn shabby by repetition of his slogan, Chickamauga was squatted alongside a temporarily deserted shebang when two men passed; they were not strangers, they were men he knew.

News traveled like birds in that community, and a rumor flapped its wings. The men were talking close at hand as they dawdled painfully along . . . one was bent forward with scurvy. They did not see Chickamauga beside them, though he could have reached out and touched them with his crutch.

Hear about the cripple?

Heard he give away about a tunnel on the North Side—

So he did; he told Wirz. Well, one of them Iowa boys was shot last night on the Outside, trying to Take Leave from the chain-gang. You know that fellow they call Big Mizzoo: he just tolt me; and he had it that them Iowa boys are hunting all over hell and high water for old Poll Parrot, and I reckon they'll make him sweat. The men moved on, their voices weaker in the camp's noise.

Wirz, Wirz. Wirz was the only hope now. Drooling, perspiring between his shiverings, Chickamauga set out for the South Gate as fast as he could travel. He had only twenty rods to go. As he approached the deadline and dead-row he saw a wagon drive in belatedly for a load of bodies, and Henry Wirz rode behind the wagon on his gray horse. With an armed guard near, the wagon guard, Wirz did not feel menaced and alone.

Wirz recognized an essential nastiness in this mutilated gabbler and dreaded encountering him, despite the various traitorous services Chickamauga had performed. Gentle and tired with age, the white-gray mare shied away from the figure which came humping. Wirz, an awkward but determined horseman, brought the beast under control with strong use of the bit.

Get away, you—You frighten my horse!

Captain, please, please, Captain, I want to go Outside.

It is nonsense. Why you go Outside?

This was a dilemma. Had the lieutenant told the captain of Chickamauga's recent service to them? If Chickamauga mentioned it now, it would come as an assertion of guilt to all ears listening nearby.

Because—there's bad men here. They beat me last night. Captain, they beat me! I didn't do nothing bad. They—

Such stories I do not wish to hear. Go away, you damn Yankee!

The boys—the men—they made up lies about me! They—they hit me and knocked me down and kicked me—God's sake, Captain Wirz, they'll kill me unless you take me Outside!

Now you get away from my horse.

Chickamauga tottered forward, hand straining for a grasp on the stirrup. Wirz kicked out with his boot, he drove him off. You damn fool son of a bitch, you get away from my horse or my pistol I take and shoot you dead!

Men were close, herded close to the deadline, and many as always had petitions for their keeper. Aw, get out of that, Poll Parrot, somebody yelled. The Flying Dutchman don't want you.

Outside! Captain, please—they'll kill me—

Wirz took the mare past him, and Chickamauga toppled fairly against the scantling which ran on deadline poles. Tears were spurting afresh . . . oh, not again, he wailed within his soul. Not to be hit and kicked again, kicked until I die of it.

. . . The deadline! He said either My God or Mother—those closest could not tell which words he uttered, or whether it was only a discordant mumble of M-sounds. Chickamauga adjusted his crutches, bent down deliberately and placed his hand on the scantling. In a tumbling tilting maneuver he got his crutches over the scantling, and used them as vaulting poles to hop his left leg across. He stood poised on forbidden ground.

You damn fool son of a bitch, get out from that deadline! the superintendent screamed.

Chickamauga faced him. No, I won't, he said more distinctly than he said most things. Not unless you take me Outside.

Wirz swore in German and drew his revolver. Come out, or I kill you dead.

Then kill me, God damn it.

Light was spreading behind Chickamauga's tight-shut eyes, light was battering with a sound against his brain. That's what you want to do, a voice rang at him, and not a voice from any human. It said, Stay. It said, They'll never dare shoot you. They'll let you go Outside.

He spoke again, with something close to clarity, I won't come out unless you promise—

Wirz took aim, then lowered the weapon. He turned his thin bearded face upward and began to berate the sentry. My job is to keep these damn Yankees, never to shoot them, you lazy, you! Your job it is to do that. That Yankee is inside the deadline. Shoot him!

The sentry was a sixteen-year-old from the Twenty-sixth Alabama named Ben Drawhorn. Had he been one of the Fifty-fifth Georgia, Chickamauga would have been dead in a twinkling; but the Alabamans were schooled to hold their fire better than the Georgians. Ben held his old Queen Anne musket, it was loaded with buckshot, the muzzle went from side to side and up and down in an extravagant circle.

I can't shoot that man, Captain—

I fix you, you bad sentinel, you! Now (to the prisoners closest to Chickamauga) you get that damn cripple out from that deadline! You I will not shoot! Wirz put away his revolver.

Promptly fellow prisoners dragged Chickamauga back to safer territory despite his struggles and strident protestation. Wirz was at the gate, he was beating and hallooing to have the portal swung, and slowly the hinges began to squeal. Wirz rode out with intent to discipline the reluctant boy on the parapet, the private who had disobeyed an order from a captain.

Look at that bastard.

A solitary voice said it, and then there came a dozen concerted yells mingled with laughter. Chickamauga had crept back inside the deadline, once hands released him, and while all attention was directed to the exit of Henry Wirz.

Again the white-faced boy lifted his Queen's-arm. It was one of the ancient pieces altered for percussion. His act, as well as the hullabaloo within the stockade, told Wirz what had happened.

He screamed beyond the wall. If that damn bitch cripple is again in the deadline—Shoot him! Shoot, damn you, like I command you shoot!

Chickamauga was a good three yards within the line. No man could reach him to draw him out without exposing himself to that musket.

People understood him to say with stubbornness, I want to go Outside. There's some bad folks—

Young Ben Drawhorn stood with open mouth and bowed shoulders, but he was aiming the musket. He pulled the trigger. The cap did not explode.

God damn you! They heard Wirz's boots clumping on the ladder outside. I come up there and show you—

The explosion of the powder charge interrupted his cry. Ben Drawhorn had recocked his musket and this time the cap did not misfire. The buckshot tore Chickamauga's lower jaw into a loose red spray and went deep inside him, to rest in his breast somewhere. He fell, jaw-less, blood spurting wide. Up on the sentry's platform Ben Drawhorn dropped the musket and staggered back with both hands forced against his face, covering his eyes, but if he exclaimed no one heard him. Wirz soon appeared beside him on the box; he scarcely glanced down at the fallen Chickamauga, but instead began a violent accusation of the silently sobbing boy.

Someone called up, Can we carry him out? and Wirz told them to go ahead. They picked up Chickamauga and bore him off a little way, and then put him down to die. Though he could not speak without that lower jaw, his tongue was still active, and waved violently as he tried to talk. People wondered later what he would have liked to have said. On the whole there was little regret at his passing, but men laughed about that stoutly wagging red tongue in its crimson nest. It haunted some of the more sensitive in their sleep and for long.

22

It had been early in May that Ebe Dolliver, the Iowa bird-lover, first munched a ration of cooked bread. This came about a day or two after certain men were detailed to go Outside as bakers. The prisoners looked for a grand improvement in their rations as a result, but did not find it. As the novelty of a loaf instead of loose meal wore off, they realized that cobs were being ground along with the corn, and that the resulting cake was nearly as hard as hickory and scratched a man's bowels to the quick as material passed through. People complained in communication to folks Outside, and the reply came back that the Outside men's job was not to grind the corn, only to mix paste and bake the pones. In grinding quantities sufficient (or insufficient) to feed twelve thousand prisoners many cobs found their way among the kernels through accident, more through carelessness on the part of stupid blacks and shiftless whites, and still more through deliberate criminal neglect. From being a wealth and a much-sought-after currency, which the bread was at first, it changed to garbage. People went around with the stuff in their pockets, offering to trade; there were few takers among the old prisoners, but some among new ones until they became prison-wise.

You began to find slabs of uneaten corn pone among personal effects of the dead. Soon you began to see chunks of the stuff lying outside doors of shebangs— unwanted, cast aside. Wood was a treasure compared to bread, for you could cook other things over wood if you could secure other things to cook. The character of the morass along Stockade Creek changed in color; it was no longer composed solely of feces and organic slime; there was now a brownish yellowish crust, a flotsam of corn bread in every stage of spongy decay. Great metallic flies, frightening in burnished brassy armor, whirled above with a humming louder than bees. Some few prisoners might have had bowels of iron: they ate the stuff stoically, it did not rake their insides, the blood did not appear.

In revulsion from this stony ration, Eben Dolliver considered meat. Adjusted to the protraction of his starving, he did not beguile himself with discussion of Moon Hotel dinners and the like—with thoughts of his mother's marble cake, fresh baked hermits, apple salad. Meat appeared as a medicine in his ideal, meat might have been bottled or put into pills, it might have rested in huge ornamented jars, well stoppered, on the shelves of some apothecary. Ebe tried to count the varieties of meat he had known, and sometimes in the middle of the night he thought of a new variety to add to his list. He tried to make up a hundred sorts of flesh which he had eaten in his young life, and was well on his way toward that goal. At first he said only pork, beef, lamb and the like, but soon recognized how different they were. Bacon was quite another thing from sausage, ham hocks were not to be confused with pork chops. Yet all came from the same beast. Eben argued with himself in detached philosophy on the subject, and at last yielded to his own importuning. Every variety of pork should be counted, and so with other products of other beasts. A catfish was not like a bass, nor was a wild goose like a tame chicken.

(Strangely he had never objected to killing chickens, and had killed many at his mother's behest. He did not think of poultry as being birds: they were filthy and cannibalistic in their habits, they did not sing a dainty song, they did not enliven the hazel brush with miraculous flashes of blue and rose. They were wedded to the dirty ground where they fed, and he loathed their squawking; he was willing to kill them, for they were not a free wild glory which lifted him.)

The Moon Hotel mess clustered still in brotherhood, they tried to keep to their rules. Their effort at bathing was become a sorry thing. Hull of Michigan and Mendenhall of Pennsylvania were gone into scurvy: the linings of their mouths puffed and spotted, cords hurting in their legs. Still they made an attempt to speak cheerfully, to join in weak choruses. Everyone had heard the stories and anecdotes of the rest over and over again; yet now and then a man thought of something new to tell.

Mendenhall thought suddenly of a neighbor of his, a fat bachelor who did not have all his reason and was the butt of jokes. The man's name was Johnny Jober; tales of Johnny, told in Mendenhall's best Pennsylvania German style, enlivened the mess for days. The boys would say, Let's hear it again, Mendy. Tell about Chonny Yober and how he put the shingles on his roof upside down. I like to split over that one. So Mendenhall would gather strength and tell again . . . the neighbor sat in his wagon and called to Johnny on the roof and said, Hey, ain't it you put on them shingles ass backward? And how Johnny sat and gazed at the whole of that shed roof he'd shingled, starting at the ridgepole instead of along the eaves, and how he burst into tears and how he said—

People lay in shade of the shebang, tittering at these fine new stories of Chonny Yober, the stronger men breaking out with guffaws at the proper time. Other prisoners arose and came near, staring mutely, as if wondering what all the laughter was about, and yet not really caring. They drifted away slowly to be replaced by other mute watchers. The shuttle of this vagabond audience wove itself back and forth, flies hummed and bit, the blistering yellow stench of May sun was high. A wave of heat stole up to distort the looming fence and sentry stations, to turn them watery.

Often Ebe Dolliver drifted loose in thought from broken accents of Mendenhall's recounting; he went off alone in his mind to dream of meat. Once, at play in the woods, he and little Neri had killed a groundhog; they had butchered the creature and cooked it over a small fire, trying to live like wild men or outlaws in hiding. Had he counted the groundhog among his meats? He thought he had; maybe not. That would make eighty-three varieties of flesh, if he hadn't counted groundhog previously. Eighty-two, eighty-three. . . . Had he counted the last buffalo killed in their section when he was a little tad? Roll Brewer gave a chunk of the meat to Joth Dolliver as he came past the mill. Ebe remembered how they gathered round when the roast was removed from the baking pan—rare lean meat looked like gigantic rare beef but more orange in color; the fat was yellower than beef fat. . . .

Forever, in time, he wandered to the birds. When wearied of enumerating medicinal meats, Eben found ease in following a ground-robin. He had heard that towhee was also a name for this bird, perhaps a name given by the aborigines. Black-white-and-bay, the industrious little folk scratched their way among old leaves in a silent place. Eben had lain motionless and watched their coming . . . sometimes walking like hens upon the ground, but prettier and more delicate than hens . . . no sound but the watery trill of a fly-catcher hidden in some ravine, no other sound except light wind making poplars tremble their coins of leaves in pride, and the *ink, cheerink* made by ground-robins themselves as they gossiped.

Again he saw his first indigo bunting. . . . He sat on a special hill said to have been once a place of massacre; larks rose and descended and rose with spirit again, giving out their long fluting . . . more of them, more out in the grass, they played pipes across the boundary where an ear could still hear them; and then the ear lost strength to pick up their piping, but somehow a sleepy brain knew that they were practicing by multitudes in remoter pastures . . . their sound was a wonder, a promise of brave simple measures to be rippled Up Yonder . . . *or if on joyful wing, cleaving the sky . . . sun, moon and stars forgot, upward I fly.*

He examined a catbird's ragged nest, he saw the lettuce tint of eggs contained therein. (They looked like candied eggs in a grocery store jar.) He'd bound a handkerchief across his mouth, not to taint the catbird's eggs so the mother would refuse to return; it told that one must do that in Our Feathered Friends, With Copious Illustrations. . . . Male redwings, polished like shoe leather with soot from the pot rubbed into it, redwings so black that they were silver in the morning as they swayed on reeds around a prairie slough. Their Quaker wives, wearing The Garb, more modest than sparrows. . . .

When Eben arrived at Andersonville there was still activity among the tousle of mutilated pine. He'd explored past stumps that first day, observing how the gum oozed from every cut. It had turned white, crystallized, flaky; he chewed some, but he wasn't accustomed to it—too much taste of turpentine, so he spat it out. Small birds, some he knew, some he'd never seen before—They took wing, streaked away through air before Eben as he walked. Come back, stay with us, he said in his heart, with the enchantment of eerie high-going larger birds still fresh in memory—the unidentified northbound tribes he'd heard two nights previously. But the birds would not stay, prisoners frightened them, they went to live in less disturbed areas beyond the rectangular fence.

Through the remainder of springtime Eben heard their mating tunes, their early salute, one light instrument's sound imposed on the trickle of a hundred others, many of them different. But now in May it was hot summer, a Georgia summer. Birds sang less, they sang little. If he'd had his precious telescope he might have spotted them and fetched them nigh to him again: there were many places on the North Side where you could see the outside fort at the southwest corner, and woods beyond that. On the South Side, near the South Gate, you could look across the fence where it dived toward the creek; you could see past the pine-roofed deadhouse, see smoke spilling up from the bake house, see guards and Outsiders trailing about their work, mule teams moving. Sometimes, oh sometimes, there shafted a blade of gold, an agate of whirring slate and white, the red speck which was a redbird. That was all Eben could see of gods and goddesses. His telescope had been stolen out of his knapsack in front of Vicksburg; never had he found the thief.

Eben Dolliver knew that his body had changed, but he did not feel an alteration of his spirit; only it seemed easier nowadays for his spirit to separate from the body and go hiking into underbrush which his corporeal shape was restrained from entering. Bell's Woods, Bryan's Woods, the single towering hill far north of Dolliver's Mill which settlers called Mount Washington: Ebe could visit those places in turn or simultaneously as impulse directed. In those places he discovered painted buntings he had never glimpsed, the groove-billed ani of which he'd only read, mockingbirds he'd seen during his first Andersonville week on the one happy day when they were sent Outside under guard with axes in their hands. . . . Flights of passenger pigeons came to impress the Iowa groves with uncountable numbers when they roosted; but peculiarly they wore no longer the dove and peach colors of orthodox pigeons—they were as tropical immigrants, with blazing crests and the plumes of peacocks.

Eben sat with skeletal hands around his knobby knees, sat in shade furnished partially by the crazy quilt he'd cheated away from the Rebel, a quilt no longer crazy but patterned with dun in varying degrees. Exposed skin of his lank frame was pigmented with the pitch from burning oily wood, hardened in, baked in: it could not have been scrubbed away by soap of whatever strength; Eben would have needed to be flayed in order to be cleaned. His mop of pink hair hung stiff with dirt and twisted in a curl at the nape of his neck. His meager beard was a lichen spread over the weathered grime of his face. This was the afternoon of May twenty-fourth, a Tuesday.

Within a few minutes the more active prisoners went wild. They leaped into the air, they found stones to throw, and threw them, and the stones came down and struck other prisoners to their grief. They began capering with lengths of board or dry pine torn from walls of their shebangs; with these improvised cudgels they battered at space above their heads. Now and then there was uplifted a howl of triumph, and several men converged, scrambling on the ground, snatching at something; and then one man would rise, the obvious victor, waving something in his hand.

Birds had come. They were swallows, a multitude, planing low in any direction, giving out irascible cries. They came like bats past the guards loafing on the stockade's rim and made the guards jump as wind of their passing brushed the guards' faces. One swallow came alone, a dozen swept in a different direction to intercept his flight . . . now they spread and teetered in point-winged circles, so numerous in a given space that they must have broken themselves to bits and hatched a dozen new birds from each whirring fragment. High, aloft, squeaking, their pale swift breasts turned dark as their wings against the low motionless sun; then down to fairly comb the earth, and crowds gesticulating there and trying to kill them, and killing some. The birds' wings clapped like limber scissors, their split tails were sharp as if drawn by pen and ink, the plumage of breasts and bellies was pearl when they came close, low. It was one of those convocations to which swallows are addicted under seasonable conditions; but no man might know why they had herded into this ugly place, and the swallows did not know.

The stockade became a trap holding them in its grip. To the swallows it appeared that the sky was not sky—a favorable avenue, an uninterrupted lake wherein they might soar to any independence they desired. The sky was the lid of the trap, it seemed pressing down on them, they resisted its pressure with new squealings, and swarmed up to burst through it and were forced back to earth again by some compulsion impervious as the screening of a cage. With speed of insects they cut here and there, up, down, across, behind. Never did swallows halt to roost atop the huts; they rubbed the angles of huts, disturbed the hot motionless air, you felt it blowing this way and that as if fans were wielded. By how many scores, how many hundreds, how many thousands, did they appear? Were they as numerous as the tramps who grabbed at them? They seemed more numerous.

Killing birds, said Eben Dolliver aloud. They're trying to kill birds. He heard a boy's voice speak from distance. Give me that there pocket rifle. You got no business shooting kingfishers. Another boy saying, Just try and take it from me. Joth Dolliver saying mildly from the mill door, Now, Ebe, don't you try to pick a fight.

Killing birds.

Again they were bats, their wings were pointed like the wings of bats, perhaps in fact they were bats deployed from some awful cavern of history, and dressed in disguise of feathers to tempt these people into wickedness. It sounded as an Indian fight must have sounded; men voiced their stuttering chorus of yaps and yelps, the swallows burbled their own cries. Two huts away from him, Eben saw a tall man bounding up and down, a jacket spread between his hands. He was trying to batter the birds with his jacket, trying to swaddle them with the cloth; even as Eben looked the man swaddled one. He wadded the garment around the bird, made a ball of it, he killed the swallow by crushing the jacket-wad beneath his feet. Then he sank down on his knees, and when he arose half a minute later with a grin on his hairy face there was bright blood on his chin. Raw? said Kirke behind Eben. Not for me, mister. If I got one I'd pluck it and toast it on a fire.

Why, declared Eben, once more aloud, they're meat.

Meat might be concentrated in pills and potions, it was tonic. The doctor said, Now you go straight home and take a dose of meat. Swallow down a big dose of blood, hot blood. It's the anodyne you stand in need of. . . . Had ever he thought that birds wore flesh beneath their down? Never before had they done so, now they must be wearing it. For all those thousands of years since they left off being snakes (this he believed; early in 1861 he had read a borrowed copy of Darwin, mostly in secret since his father did not approve) they had dressed their bones with thistledown instead of tissue, and doubtless the bones were leaf green, fragile as new maple leaves.

Myrtle warbler shy and peeking, goldfinch bold upon the milkweed plant, the fleeting dust of rust which blew when fox sparrows shot themselves across a road in spring . . . what was that soul bubbling its wet poetry from solitude of the dry brush pile? Call it angel, call it brown thrasher, call it heartbreak, call it God's blessing. Call it meat.

Call it a swallow.

Eben Dolliver pulled out the heavy stick which anchored his comforter to the shebang's roof in daytime, and could be drawn loose when the quilt was needed for a blanket. Hey, Ebe, take it easy; trying to tear down the whole roof? He emerged into open bird-haunted space, and a flight of the frantic things went up and away from him, and raced like moths toward the marsh, and new stragglers came flipping above. He waved his club this way and that, he beat it in a circle. Many other prisoners had been making desperate attempts at capture since the swallows first swarmed, and had not managed to strike a single specimen, but they did not own the luck of Eben. At the fifth or sixth ferocious smash of his stick there was a light thud, and something bounced on the ground like a crumple of blue-black-pale-gray paper blown by a wind. Other pirating hands tried to snatch it, but Eben plunged at full length, he fell on the bird and crushed it with chest and arms. He wrung its neck as he arose. Vaguely he heard surviving swallows condemning him with tiny words as he pushed his jaws, as he sucked, as he spat out feathers.

23

An unbearable announcement was made in the Claffey household some time around the end of May or the first of June. When Lucy thought of it drearily, afterward, she could remember the season, not the date. It was just before the Big Rains began. There had been heavy rainfall in March, the weather improved generally during April, May was mostly hot with some unseasonably cold nights . . . ah, yes, the unbearable announcement was made perhaps during the first few days of June. Lucy counted rains that month as the unsheltered prisoners beyond the surviving fringe of pines counted them. It rained during twenty-four of the thirty June days that year. It rained on twenty successive days.

Her mother—Before the Big Rains—

The thing began with the misdeed of a white cat designated as Columbus. Lucy had named the creature thus because of his exploring propensities in kittenhood. He was always crawling about somewhere and getting stuck, and then sending out piercing yowls for assistance. He climbed high into trees, and ladders had to be brought; he entombed himself for two days within an unused chimney; once he crept into the west wall of the library and strips of siding had to be removed in order to rescue Columbus. The blacks could not pronounce the kitten's name— mostly they spoke of him as Cumbus, and the Claffeys fell into the habit. Having now attained great size and some age, Cumbus had left off dangerous explorations. He'd turned half wild, he prowled savagely in the woods, whipped or assaulted other cats frequently, and only approached the kitchen to steal. He was a powerful animal, built like a wrestler, pink scars showing all over his white head, green-eyed and selfish.

Ira Claffey brought a hat filled with mushrooms from the woods, and Lucy clapped her hands. These were a favorite of theirs; Ira had identified them as *Russulas,* unmistakable with broad caps of lavender-rose, short stems, gills delicate as the flesh of a nicely cooked fish. They had a tender nutty flavor when prepared with care, they were tastier far than the common agarics which Ira used to grow on trays in a dark shed, before the war, when he had time to spare for such nonsense.

Poppy, I declare they're remarkable. Regular honey lambs. Where did you find them?

Among oaks above Little Sweetwater. Shall we have a pie?

I'll take them out to Naomi myself, and I'll most certainly count them so's there'll be no foolishness; I'll warn Naomi that all—yes, sir, Poppy, fifteen of them —had better be in that little pie! We'll be just as selfish as selfish can be, and eat that whole pie our own selves.

Ira said with anticipation, Twill be the best thing I've eaten since the Mexican War.

Course it will. With scads of gravy under the crust, and just a mite of onion.

I've fresh chervil and marjoram! Chervil in the third row of the kitchen garden, and marjoram in a pot on the shelf yonder.

Well, Poppy, not too much, or you'll sacrifice the woodsy taste. I'll snip just a teentsie bit with my shears and give it to Naomi in a poke. What a pity—

She stopped speaking on the instant, hurt by thought of the silent woman who remained mainly above stairs. A pity, she repeated, that Mother nor the boys never liked mushrooms.

No, they did not. She does not. Father and daughter held a brief merciful silence between them. Automatically they both began to look toward the ceiling and then away quickly again, neither wishing the other to realize how they had responded.

The mushroom pie came pungent and brown-crusted from the big oven in proper season for dinner, but at that moment Coffee and Jem turned up a den of small snakes in the south pasture lot, and the resulting squalls sent Ira to the scene to make sure that no one had been bitten and that the snakes were destroyed. During this interval the treasured pie waited on a kitchen table, half covered with a padded tea-cosy to keep it warm, sending its odor far. Lucy heard a combined clatter, thud and shrieking from the kitchen; she groaned and wondered What Now? She was going to investigate, but Extra came lumbering into the house to offer a report, her rolling eyes wet with tears of joy, black face shining . . . gulping for breath between yells as she tried to talk and could not manage it.

What *is* it, Extra?

Miss—Luce—yah—

What *is* it?

That—Cumbus cat—

Lucy was standing at the foot of the front stairway. Extra writhed and gesticulated before her.

Extra, do wait until you can talk.

Yah! That Cumbus cat—

It came out that Cumbus had been drawn to the kitchen by gravy scents. Unnoticed by servants he had leaped upon the table with thievish intent, and in his approach to the pie he had somehow upset a leaning platter. The platter smashed against a pitcher, other pots and pans had gone tumbling; the terrified cat jumped for the window but instead had landed in a tub of warm water—The chronology of this misadventure was confused by the narrator's gasps and cries of delight. From the recounting emerged a picture of a bandit righteously punished by immersion, soaring off between cabins as if Old Satan were after him.

Old Satan, Miss Lucy! That old cat, that what he think—

Well, Extra, thank you for telling me, and I'm very glad our pie was saved—

Ira had reëntered the house by this time and stood quizzically regarding his daughter and the black woman. A sound from above drew their combined attention to the head of the staircase. Veronica stood thin and stiff in her shabby mourning-dress, and the icy indignation of her expression was a glare.

Please—daughter—Ira—Extra. Above all— *Ex*tra! She spoke the slave woman's name with guttural rage.

Lucy could not move. Ira took a step or two on the stairs. He said rapidly, My dear, what—?

You're making too much *noise.* You'll wake the *children.* We must have quiet in this house. They're *asleep.*

The mushroom pie went mainly uneaten that day; Lucy gave the remains, which were really the bulk of the pie, to the blacks. She thought, I am weary of staring dumbly. How long must we stare, how long must we be dumb, why can we not expunge this cloud which swelters and strangles us, takes away all air, takes away even the desire to breathe air? She was so young that she felt blind fury at injustice, she wanted to reorganize the scheme of birth and life and death (she thought not of reorganizing the scheme of procreation, but had she suffered a wound while loving she would have wished to alter this process too, because of wrath).

Soon it was learned that the children dwelt in Moses's old room; Ira had feared that was where they would be domiciled. It was not clear whether all the other Claffey children were there or only the boys who'd died in the war. Perhaps little Arwood, Peggy, Sally and Courtenay slumbered in the same chests with Suthy's knitted boots, Badger's brown plaid cambric dress, Moses's unblemished New Testament & Psalms which he was awarded for committing to memory one hundred and one verses of the Scriptures, most of which he promptly forgot. Did the children sleep rosy and in health, did they choke with the diphtheria which had claimed two, did they complain with whimpers that the surviving family and slaves walked too heavily, spoke too loudly? They might not complain about laughter, there would be little laughter for them to complain about. At first Ira was afraid to go into that room. He muttered to his daughter, By God, my child, I can't go. At last Lucy, braver in this hour than he, visited the ghastly chamber while her mother walked abroad with the mystified Ninny trudging dutifully behind. To Lucy's relief she found no little beds made up. These she had feared she would find, she had entertained visions of her mother arranging a row of spectral pallets. It was good to observe—No, there could be nothing good about it; but it was helpful to know that the dead young warriors occupied couches which were simple illusion, not actual linen and feathers and ticking.

Sometimes Veronica spoke of The Boys, more often it was The Children. *Shh.* This to a Pet or a Ninny who banged about while scrubbing the floor. You must work more quietly; I do not wish them waked. *Shh.*

Out across the yard in the kitchen Naomi blubbered about it.

Miss Lucy. Is Mistess gone *crazy?*

Hush, Naomi.

But she know the boys dead at the North. She know it! She know they not little babies in that room up there!

Now, Naomi. The middle-aged slave sobbed, hot and perspiring and smelly, against the white girl's slenderness; Lucy stroked the broad damp back with her hands; it seemed that she was reaching out through distance to touch Naomi. Now, Naomi, it's only that—My mother is ill, we hope she will be better soon. She is ill.

Suddenly the enormity of the cruel cycle weighted Lucy, it crushed and tore her inside and out. She said, louder and louder, She's not crazy, you fool thing! Ill —do you hear me? Ill! Her straining hands came up and crumpled Naomi's gown at the shoulders, and her pinch must have caught patches of the Negress's skin in its compression, for Naomi struggled and cried, hurt in body as well as in her bewildered soul. Upstairs in the house Veronica stiffened at hearing Jonas bawl at his mule in the lane outside. She went to the window, looked down to where Jonas must be working, but she could not see him for the trees. She put a cool finger against her lips. *Shh.*

24

The relationship between himself and Seneca MacBean worked to the immediate benefit of Nathan Dreyfoos and those close to him, but also it was a grain of reassurance for the rawboned printer from Galena. A strength like the strength Nathan had to offer (and would retain in considerable degree if he followed the direction of a more seasoned man) was another stud in the bludgeon which Seneca MacBean planned to fashion for wielding at some future date. Nathan had manual dexterity—Sen was not surprised when he heard that Dreyfoos could play the fiddle—and as a barber he was a success promptly, although at first he worked too slowly to make much profit. . . . Food, MacBean urged him, that was the thing. Try to get food first of all. Rice, barley, root vegetables, bones, salt: a stew was the thing. He knew; he lived mainly on stews, and he was keeping his grip. If a man couldn't pay in food, try for some article which you might barter for food. Nathan Dreyfoos was a willing pupil in the grim curriculum of stockade erudition, and he emerged with other talents peculiar to himself.

For example, Sen smiled when he noticed the hook-nosed sergeant's activity during periods when there were no customers for haircuts. He would look up from his scrubbing and wringing, to see Nathan toying with one of the tent poles he had bought. The pole was of hickory—light, smooth, tough, springy. Seriously with his penknife Dreyfoos was working one end of the pole into a short sharp point. Well, Seneca thought, he'll learn in time. Learn that it doesn't pay a man to twiddle himself by mere whittling—not in here. Too many other things to do: assemble firewood, swap, build a fire, cook, keep the vermin down. He was bitterly amused further when he saw Nathan toasting the sharpened end of the pole over a fire. What's he doing—pretending he's got a sausage on a stick at a pic-nic?

Not long afterward two of the worst characters in camp sauntered near—a pair of sailors named Bill Rickson and Al Munn. Close behind drifted a group of six or eight, the inevitable pack of hyenas.

Hi, Sergeant. Come here. We'd like to talk swap.

Don't move, said Seneca in a low voice. They carry brass knucks.

But Dreyfoos was advancing on the sailors, the slim tent pole similar to a cane in his hand.

Like to swap them scissors off of you. Now, I got a gold watch that—

A club came out of a pant-leg, another out of a sleeve. Blows were aimed and delivered on empty space. Munn bellowed and clapped his hand to his side where his sailor's blouse was ripped and his flesh torn. Rickson bored forward silently, wheeling his club; then he stopped, then he began to give ground. That pointed pole was everywhere, threatening his belly, jabbing at his throat, whipping right, left, up, down, in, out. It raked his hairy arm, the club flew. Munn circled, crouching, arms swinging wide, to take Nathan in the rear, but Seneca MacBean was there by that time, doubling his fists.

Oh, come out of it, Billy. Munn moved away, not looking back, examining his skinned side as he went.

The valiant cohorts had already disappeared, and people were crawling out of the shade of their shebangs to observe. Two or three rocks flew. One very nearly struck Nathan instead of striking the man for whom it was intended. The silent Rickson, now without a club, joined Munn in retreat. He stopped to rip a post from a shebang which he passed, tried its strength in his arms, the post snapped like a candy stick.

Hell, Billy, come along with you.

They went away; folks gazed wide-eyed. Usually an encounter with raiders ended in a manner different from this.

Nathan Dreyfoos stood watching the sailors as they pushed their way down the slope. Will they come back?

Not in daylight. It'd pay to be on the lookout at night; they might try to cut your throat for revenge. Sen MacBean slapped Nathan heartily on the buttock. To think I thought you were frittering your time in idle whittling. *Always whittle from yourself and then you'll never cut yourself.* What you call that thing—a spear?

Only a pointed stick.

How you handled it.

Well, you see, Seneca, I began the study of fencing when I was eleven.

Ever fight in the prize ring?

Never. But I have experience in boxing.

Dreyfoos, it'll take time but— Let's get back to work. I've got a pair of dirty pants half washed, and the owner has naught to hide his nakedness until I dry them. Now I think you'll get more customers to your barbering. Why? Because they'll feel safe from the raiders, merely being near you. By gum. MacBean brayed with one of his nasal peals of laughter. You handled that weapon (he called it weepon) like I'd handle a line gauge.

Nathan Dreyfoos messed apart from Sen MacBean and slept apart from him as well. He felt his obligation to the boys of the Eighty-fifth, though some of them were intractable, many would not be buoyed up . . . they had a fierce mistaken notion that their discipline ended with their imprisonment, and they only snarled at Nathan and others who attempted to set them to rights. But most daytime hours were passed at the combination laundry and barber shop. It grew to be a center of community interest, a meeting place and gossip mart. Nathan wore his knapsack to work each day, and carried off to his own shebang such articles as he had acquired for pay during the day. His ration of corn pone he broke up and put into the eternal stews. Every two or three days he had to spend some hours on shopping tours, bargaining his way along Main Street or to the sutler's shack, trading off rawhide shoe-laces or shirt buttons or tobacco for vegetables, sometimes even for meat. At times he went calmly to South Street, which was definitely raider territory, but always he carried his homemade spear. He was attacked once more in daylight; after that the raiders looked the other way. The thought of night did not worry Nathan Dreyfoos severely. Ten of them slept in a wide shebang made of their coats and blankets, and it was a rule that at least five must remain at home at all times, day or night, armed with knives, spoon daggers and clubs. Sarsfield's Raiders made an attack there one afternoon; the five housekeepers fought savagely until others of their regiment could lend a hand. Sarsfield got only one poncho for his pains, and it was announced that one of his men had been stabbed in the belly by Private Allen, the boy who had burst into tears the morning he landed in the stockade (it was rumored that the man died later as a result, but perhaps that was but a rumor).

Way I look at it, said Seneca MacBean. Oh, there's heroisms and heroisms, but more than heroism is going to be necessary to clean up this mess. It's like you've said and like I've thought: concerted action.

Often I do not understand you, Sen. Your speech . . . you speak much of the time with the—forgive me—rural dialect of so many Americans. You employ army slang and colloquial words. The average boy in my company would not use words like *concerted*. Or *overture*.

Seneca studied this. Well, my father was a schoolmaster but he died before I was born. My formal education was poorly come by. But I'm a printer, and my grandfather was a printer before me. Printers get to know language. We're faced with words, editorialwise and otherwise, which we mightn't face were we mechanics. . . . No, Brother Nathan, to proceed as I was going: concerted action is the only answer. Discipline, organization. I've friends who feel the same way, and one of them is a better organizer than I could be. That's Key, from the Sixteenth Cavalry—fellow who was just in here awhile ago, fetching this old blue shirt. He's also a Sucker, from Bloomington. Big courageous-looking man, isn't he? I warrant you he'll *be* courageous too, if the time ever comes. And take that fellow who looks like a red Indian—comes from the Sixty-seventh Illinois Infantry—you cut his hair a-yesterday—

They call him Limber Jim.

Limber Jim—that's he. And Ned Carrigan from Chicago. And Johnny McElroy—he's little but he's determined. They'll all fight, and fight well, but it means organization and thought and planning. It means a campaign to be mapped out, and troops to be selected and raised and mustered.

Nathan Dreyfoos gave his slow wide smile. It seems that you people are relying chiefly on your fellow Illinoisans. Can this be partisanship?

No, exploded MacBean sharply. And then . . . after a pause . . . well, could be. Now, take you. You're Eighty-fifth New York, but mighty un-New Yorkish. I suppose your life abroad has given you a kind of universalness.

Universality.

Thankee. Where's my sand bucket? Ah . . . trouble is, we *ought* to rely on Westerners. I'm one, I understand them, they understand me. Most of your New Yorkers—saving the raiders—and Pennsylvanians— They stick by themselves. Even the New Jersey boys tend to cleave together, and dog bite the man on the outside. Did you ever see anything like the way Massachusetts folks hang tight? And so with most of New England. Now, Michiganders are something like them —but I'd say humanized. Westernized New Englanders? Is that what you'd call them? They talk much the same way. Say *I be* instead of *I am.* But they're more awake, more Western.

Nathan Dreyfoos felt a lack and ignorance. This is my country. I was born in it; Corley and Stevenson taught me that I must attempt to live for it and die for it. Yet I know so little about it. He said, It must be like the difference between Catalonians and Madrilenos and Andalucians.

I don't know any of them, but it's doubtless the same. Take the people from Ohio, Indiana, Illinois, Iowa, Kansas—some of the Minnesotans—there aren't too many—and some of the Missourians too. Cut off the same bolt of goods. Sometimes you'd think that if one studied McGuffey they all studied McGuffey. If one studied Ray's Arithmetic they all studied Ray's Arithmetic. They think—

MacBean hunted for the word. They respond alike, he said.

—If we need police, and we do need police—

—I'm not condemning Easterners solely because they're from the East. A lot of Easterners could help, and a lot of them probably will help us out, if we get started—

—I've talked with Limber Jim, and Key, and you. Haven't talked to the others, but Key's been sizing everybody up. In due time—

—There's dire need of police right now. But Jerusalem wasn't built in a day. Rome.

Thankee, Brother Nathan. Rome.

The friendship grew like a seedling in a frame under glass under strong sun; it might have been manured by the manure of Andersonville, which was everywhere. The metaphor occurred to both men, separately and singly (it was inescapable) but neither would have defamed the friendship by citing it.

It was an attraction and trust of opposites, a mutual reliance on men identical in faith and sanity. The straitened horizon of Galena and Chicago and the few other towns where Seneca MacBean's fingers had streaked from upper case to lower case—It stretched to include the picturesque cities where he had never walked and probably never would walk. The young man who'd had no roots to let down into the soil of his birth found himself anchored increasingly, attached by invisible tentacles to loam of the Middle West which he had never trodden or dug or scented.

MacBean had had no confidant in his life, except his grandmother, his grandfather, and one young woman whom he'd adored in Chicago a year or two before the war. (She was frail, her heart hurt her. Her mother worked on occasion, part time, folding printed sheets in the shop where Seneca slugged the galleys. Generously and thoughtfully the elder woman invited the lonely young man to Sunday tea in rooms which she and her daughter Phoebe occupied. After that he was there each evening, and in time contributed to their support. There came a cold sleety morning when a little boy pounded on Sen MacBean's door at his lodging house and presented a note which read *Dear Friend Seneca. Can you come to me at once. Phoebe has died in her sleep.*)

Sen became garrulous at times, talked of his ambitions in civil life, said that he'd like nothing better than to be the editor of a small town newspaper. . . . Bet you I'd raise the fur along their spines. Always something which needs correction in any town: sidewalks, sewage, corrupt officials, or maybe a new railroad or canal. A newspaper editor never need look far for a stone on which to grind his axe. . . .

How did he come to join the cavalry?

That was an oddment. It began when he was a little boy, dragging those willow baskets of washings along the even east-and-west streets of Galena or—much worse—up and down the nearly vertical north-and-south streets of Galena. There was an older boy named Clovis Tibbetts and he had a black pony with a red saddle. The sight of this pony drove Seneca into fits of jealousy, quiet spasms of envy. In solitary imaginings he owned not a pony but a horse; the horse was as high as a house, and not merely black but black and white; the red saddle was crusted with gems on the saddle-bow. (I guess, said Seneca, that the stirrups were solid gold.) But this was mere wishful illusion: no creature except a rat ever dwelt in the MacBean stable during Sen's boyhood, no nervous fairy hoofs twinkled along the driveway. (I didn't want to *be* Clovis Tibbetts, he said. I just wanted a pony—or a horse—as good as his or better'n his.) Acutely he recalled one hot afternoon when he was lonely, he had nothing to do, he had no work to do, no one to play with; his grandfather snored in a stupor; his grandmother was ironing clothes. Gran, he said, I wish—

What do you wish, lad?

Wish (he whispered it) I had a pony.

What would you do with a pony, laddie?

I'd ride it.

She said brightly that she would prepare a pony for him. He must remain inside the house, he must not peep out until she gave the word. He waited, his throat dry, his breath coming fast; he hid himself in a closet so that he might not be tempted to disobey her command. When at last she chirruped from the lawn outside he came dashing. . . . What magic was here? She had said that she would fix a pony for him. Did she know a neighbor from whom a pony might be borrowed? Had she—? It was a pain and jabbing but— Had she *borrowed Clovis Tibbetts' pony?*

The woman had done her best. She had rolled a cask from the woodshed—a decrepit wooden barrel which had been salvaged from somewhere and was to serve as kindling. On this cask she had folded a makeshift saddle made from a shawl, and she had attached reins of faded ribbon. Now, lad, she said, bestride your pony, and ride far far away. Ride to the ends of the earth. . . . Sen nodded, he thanked Gran in a murmur, he waited until she was gone back to her work, and then reluctantly he climbed astride the barrel. It did not look like a horse, it did not smell as a horse smelled, it was a miserable makeshift, it did not feel between his legs as a horse must feel.

And damn, he said. Soon I looked up—might have heard a noise out in front, along Bench Street—and there he was. Riding past. Clovis Tibbetts on his pony. Red saddle and all. Right then was when I joined the cavalry.

Ah, yes. I understand. I have never been poor—I might be a wiser man had I been poor. But I understand.

Never rode a horse until I was grown, except— Oh, once in a while, bareback to water, on somebody's farm. But I had the notion.

I know. Anyone who's had dreams would know.

Then I was working away off, hell to yonder, when they fired on Fort Sumter. The paper I worked for was edited by a man who hated Abolitionists, and he declared that only Abolitionists were rattling the sword. Maybe I had absorbed some of his teachings—you know, putting his notions into type. He had a fine style with words, somewhat like Thomas Carlyle. And equally opinionated! So it took me a while to make up my mind.

. . . Funny what this prison life does to a body, Brother Nathan. I never told anyone about that heretofore, except one lady. But this awful place makes a man talk at times. And dream.

Nathan said, A man escapes in his dreams. I go far, even though I have not been here long.

Well, I can guess what you mean. Paris, Rome, England—all those lands where you've been. But take care you don't go too far. Man can't live sole alone on dreams.

I shan't go too far.

Not far enough to lose those qualities of leadership. They'll be needed. You'll be needed.

No, I shall not go too far.

Seneca MacBean said that he had a hero who demonstrated qualities of leadership. . . . Perhaps from the time his young fingers first plucked type Sen MacBean had been possessed of a desire to tell his own story in his own way. Between the ens and ems of his occupation had risen the legendary skill of the campfire yarn-spinner, the cracker-barrel raconteur. He loved a good story for the story's own sake, and told stories well; but when his own emotion or experience was involved he could rise to a simple dramatic height. He chewed the words with wide jaws, there was slyness in his eyes as he talked, he seemed meditating between sentences; yet the pauses were urgent in their very silence. Any listener would wait with eager ears and soul, his attention would not wander until the nasal Western voice carried along the narrative and made it march and shine in the telling.

So Sen had a hero. At home they called the man Cap, because one time he had been a captain in the army. He was not at all the embattled swordsman of antiquity, like the Gillies MacBean described by Seneca's grandfather. John MacBean said that forever any youth should be proud to wear the name of MacBean; the youth had only to think of Gillies. Gillies MacBean stood alone in some old Highland war, to guard a breach through which the enemy must advance. He fought until he became a martial saint; at last he was killed; the dead lay piled. Gillies MacBean was the subject of a lament which the wrinkled Scottish printer could recall only in part: *And each day the eyes of thy young son before, shall the plaid be unfolded, unsheathed the claymore.*

So be proud to be a MacBean, ye ken.

Yes, Grandfather.

Say, Aye!

Aye!—and then his grandfather would chuckle.

But the man called Cap, said Seneca, was styled differently. He remembered seeing him, the day Cap first came to town, progressing slowly off the boat which tied downtown at the wharf on Fever Creek; the wife came first, in charge of her little family, and Cap followed, carrying two kitchen chairs in his hands. He had failed in business since leaving the army (he drank himself out of his commission) and was being more or less pensioned by his father. His two brothers ran a business, and Cap was destined to help them, and people hoped he'd make a go of it. But the brothers were sharper than tacks. Cap was not.

Take a farmer: he'd come into the store to trade for some harness, and Cap would help him to select the harness, while the brothers watched suspiciously.

Farmer'd say, How much is this here harness?

Cap'd say, Let's see. Here's the tag. Twenty-five dollars.

Farmer'd steam and blow up. This here set? Twenty-five dollars? Why, by mighty, it hain't *worth* twenty-five dollars!

And Cap'd examine the harness all over, critically. Then he'd shake his head and say, Guess you're right. Doesn't look like twenty-five dollars worth to me, either.

And then those brothers would be fit to be tied.

Time the war busted out, Cap was eager to join up again, and they had a local militia company called the Jo Daviess Guards. But the folks in town held their own notions about who should be officering that company, and Cap wasn't included in their speculations. They held an election, but Cap wasn't elected; somebody else would command. Well . . . he couldn't carry liquor, and once he'd been compelled to resign from the army, and a man who had no brains for harness-selling probably wouldn't have any brains for commanding a company. With his tongue unhinged by a glass or two, Cap told a few of his friends that he'd written to Washington, written to the War Department. He said that he had been educated at the National expense and now thought he ought to repay his debt to the Nation; in his own opinion he was fit to command as much as a regiment. But no reply came. Some clerk had scorned the letter and filed it away.

Well, Seneca MacBean was back in town, called by his grandfather's last illness, the day that the Jo Daviess Guards marched to the train. They looked pretty fine, for green troops; they had a power of sparkle to them, and the young officers looked imposing. Then a few folks started to laugh. What did they see? Here came old Cap, walking or marching or whatever you want to call it, along the street. He was keeping pace with the Jo Daviess Guards, bound and determined to follow them at least as far as Springfield where troops were rendezvousing. There he trod along in his shabby citizen's clothes and faded hat, carrying a limp carpetbag in his hand. Quite a sight. No wonder the folks laughed and nudged one another.

My hero, said Seneca MacBean. What you might call Qualities of Leadership, in upper case.

Where is Cap now?

Some weeks ago I heard that he'd been given command of all the armies of the United States. Man by the name of Grant.

25

The first few days of Floral Tebbs's military experience had been marked by widespread festivity: the planning thereof, the excited contemplation thereof, the celebration itself. The Twenty-sixth Alabama was about to leave for the front and a majority of veterans in those ranks looked forward to departure with hysterical relief. They did not care how many Yankees shot at them in far hills where soon they would reëncounter the enemy. Battle would be a delight in comparison to the stench and monotony of this duty at Andersonville. Georgia Reserves would relieve them here, Georgia Reserves would go On Picket and On Parapet instead of the Alabamans. Good enough for them.

Flory Tebbs wished that he also might be bound for fields of glory, but still the primary appurtenances of soldier life were thrilling. Contemplation of the altered musket issued to him sent him into a blissful daze. He loved to touch the cracked walnut of the old stock, even though he forgot and left his piece leaning outside to rust against a tent-rope the first night, and was cursed by his sergeant. The sergeant was a pimply mentally retarded youth named Sinkfield whose chief accomplishment before this war seemed to have been in the killing of little pigs at an Atlanta slaughter-house. Sergeant Sinkfield was fond of reciting the death throes of little pigs and could imitate their squeals to dread perfection. After enduring a shove, slap and verbal blasting from this bestripèd hulk, Flory took to polishing his musket with sandpaper which he and two new cronies stole from an ordnance chest left untended at the big star fort. The musket barrel accumulated no more rust, it was abraded until it hurt the eyes in sunlight, it gleamed beneath the stars.

When not trooping through one of their disordered drills or digging fresh trenches for latrines, the raw Reserves were set to clearing a space on level ground among the pines near the road to Anderson Station. This area was dragged, pounded, wet down, stamped again, swept clean. It was to serve as a dance floor. Everyone prayed that no rain would fall on the thirteenth of the month. No rain came. Throughout the countryside folks made a holiday, and black people thronged to watch. The string band played for hours; The Girl I Left Behind Me seemed the only rendition on which fiddles, banjos and the two guitars could get together properly, but there was better music offered in solo by various musicians. Dust crawled in a cloud from the clay floor. Over to the east beyond the uneven palisade and sentry shacks Yanks stood in droves, watching the merry-making across that low place where the stockade dipped over the creek. They stood upon high ground on one side, the celebrants were upon distant high ground on the other side, they could see. It seemed funny to have Yanks watching you while you danced.

Floral Tebbs did not dance; he did not know how to dance any more than he knew how to read, and he did not like to have girls near him. The detail of unlucky guards who had drawn Parapet lounged on their platforms, peering toward this unprecedented frolic, paying more attention to the gaiety than to the Yanks they were set to watch. Thus no one was shot at the deadline during those hours, and sly bold prisoners took advantage of the opportunity to steal wood and comparatively uncontaminated water from the danger side of the scantlings.

Laurel Tebbs, her little witch's face afire with excitement, was whirled from hand to hand, from group to group. The gross Sergeant Sinkfield attended her persistently, hugging her thin body against his oversized body whenever he found a chance. Laurel wore an old purple gown of her mother's, gathered in wads at the waist to take up the slack of extra goods; she had done this alteration herself, and it was not wholly successful; but the color was bright, her petticoats were mended, she had scrubbed and pressed them, they showed when she swung and skipped, men found them enticing no matter how bare and brown and bony the scarred limbs which twisted beneath the folds. Laurel had upset a pot of boiling water over her feet and ankles when she was tiny. Plentiful scars still showed, mottled, pink, creamy amid the tan.

Flory regarded his sister with disgust, and stalked away to the pit where bodies of two foraged half-wild hogs were basted slowly above barbecue coals. Just look at my younger, cried the Widow Tebbs to Captain Ox Puckett as they bounced to the end of the line. Going along over there. He does make quite a soldier.

Flory? He won't never make no soldier.

But he is one. In that little Yankee jacket too big for him—

Honey, these here Reserves is slime. Just pure slime.

Ox Puckett, how dast you? Flory hain't no slime!

Oh, no, not him specially. What I mean: no fit drill, no fit discipline. The non-coms is quarter-witted and slothful, and anybody knows that non-coms are the backbone of the military. Leave us pray to God there don't come no general rising of the Yanks! These here Reserves would cut for it—I don't care how snipsish is the jacket Flory's a-wearing! . . . Come along, let's get into this new set. But let me kick off these boots first and go sock-footed.

Coral Tebbs attended the pic-nic, after declaring with oaths that he would die sooner than go. He spent some time glowering at dancers from a distance; later he accepted a gourd half filled with pine-top and was drawn into conversation by two of the Alabamans who happened to have been in the battle at South Mountain back in '62. The conversation became animated, rowdy; the pic-nic was ignored by Coral and nearly ignored by the others; little points of fire burned in Coral's black gaze. He drank more pine-top and later became sick at his stomach, and threw up behind a tree. The Alabamans had seemed suddenly like comrades, and he had had no comrade in a long time. Now the Alabama boys (comrades: what were their names? Loopy and Cox) would be going to the front, and he could not go to the front. He could not go anywhere much. He fumbled his head-aching way toward home long before the pic-nic was done. Uncle Arch Yeoman saw him reeling; he came out of his store and smelled liquor, and upbraided Coral, and offered him a Temperance tract.

God damn you, said Coral, I don't want no Temperance track. Go wipe your ass with it! He pressed the paper into a ball and threw it at Uncle Arch, and went on toward the Tebbs place, whimpering to himself, blowing his nose with his fingers as he traveled.

His brother Flory had found also boon companions in a manner which suggested that they might be more or less permanently welded in partnership, since they were members of Flory's new mess and slept beside him. Both were from Chatham County and had known each other before they came to serve. One was a tall starveling who'd spent early years at a Poor Farm, the other a runaway apprentice who declared that his father was executed early in the war for murdering his lieutenant. This latter youth, Irby Flincher, became Flory's favored compatriot because they were nearly of the same size although Irby was three years older than Flory. Times when they stood unclad Flory took pains to conceal his nakedness from the others because he had no hair and the other elder boys had hair. In anguish Floral inspected himself and petitioned the Almighty to grant him hair, and by June was rewarded in observing a few limp sprouts of blondish texture above his rudimentary organs. . . . Irby Flincher had a trick of giggling privately with the other member of this triumvirate whose name was Mackey Nall. They talked of corn-holing, browning and other mysteries unknown to Floral Tebbs.

Floral was beaten up several times during the early weeks of soldiering. He was whipped by Sergeant Sinkfield, by Corporal Woodall, by a loutish private from up in Bibb. Once he attempted to run away to the Tebbs place and scream his trials to the widow; but fleeter people fetched him back. Sinkfield talked of bucking and gagging, but Flory was sentenced finally to march back and forth on picket duty with a Yankee knapsack on his back—a knapsack filled with bricks. It appeared that he was turned to be a whipping boy, being one of the smallest and perhaps the youngest in his command.

One night he and Irby Flincher got into a discussion about which should sleep under a new leak sprung in their rotten tent, and Irby attempted to enforce his demands. Flory had come to the end of his rope. He shrilled, I don't give the shit off'n a tomcat if your Daddy *was* a killer, and very nearly gouged out one of Irby's large brown eyes in the resulting struggle. Irby shrieked for help, Mackey came to help him, Floral Tebbs bit the lobe from Mackey Nall's right ear. After that he was termed a devil-festered little runt, and respected accordingly. Within a few days he and Irby and Mackey were friends again, and swaggered together off duty.

Irby said, You know them bricks.

What bricks, Sojer?

Like old Stinkfield-Sinkfield compelled you to tote for punishment. Member where they come from? From nigh that bake house.

God damn, I don't hanker to carry no more bricks.

But I got a good idea come to mind. Let's get down back of them stumps where no one can't see nor hear us, and I'll tell you what.

Together the three squatted in hiding and Irby explained his plan. They were bothered by mud in their tent; water rose out of the trench beyond the canvas whenever new rains came pelting. Well, sir. There were plenty bricks over next to that bake house where apparently old Dick Winder planned to build a new oven. Well, sir. There wasn't any guard set over them bricks. . . . Irby Flincher's eyes were huge and pale-rimmed and luminous—they looked like the eyes of Holy folk in Bible pictures—they shone with wistful brilliance when he talked feverishly.

Sojers, we can crawl over there one at a time in the dark. No guards about, specially if it's raining pitchforks and nigger-babies. Make a tolerable platform, raise our beds out of the mud.

But twould be hard sleeping.

Ain't hard sleeping better than wet sleeping, Sojer?

Spose the quartermaster cotches us?

Oh, he couldn't cotch the pox! Where do you reckon he got them boards from —build himself a fine new office and quarters? Some of that same lumber Colonel Persons got to make barracks for the Yanks in the stockade!

Hell, it hain't fitten them Yanks should have barracks and us have none.

Reckon we'll have barracks fore long. So I heard tell. But meanwhile—

They made private creeping sorties, the bricks were transferred laboriously. Their other tentmate (an asthmatic Millerite with brown fangs who warned the three little ruffians to prepare for an eventual reappearance of Christ on earth) threatened to disclose their thievery unless they toted some bricks for him too. They whispered about a possible accident which might ensue; they had heard of such executions awarded to soldiers who made themselves obnoxious . . . a loaded gun might go off suddenly, unexpectedly. But none of them had yet whetted his savagery to the edge of cold-blooded murder: they liked to talk about it, that was all. They fetched bricks for old Ducky Duckworth, they had a dry and well-paved tent. There was never any official inspection of the tents . . . it was expected that barracks would be constructed soon, and so in time they were constructed. Meanwhile no one appeared to have missed the stolen bricks, and the three robbers prided themselves.

Together or singly they stole other things. The post adjutant owned a slab shack to which only he had the key, and rumor claimed that the shack was stuffed with good things to be sold at fancy prices to prison sutlers. Floral Tebbs watched sharply whenever he passed this structure on a slight incline above the road. He observed that it was set on posts, but that a very small person—one of his size or Irby's—might snake his way between the squat pilings and perhaps gain entry from beneath. Boards had been nailed tightly to the sleepers, ambition was thwarted to begin with. Later Flory discovered by candlelight, and with Mackey and Irby lying along the ground outside to shield the candle's flare— He discovered that one of the sleepers was worm-eaten. You could practically push the nails out with your fingers, or at least with a claw-hammer if one might be filched. In time this too was accomplished, and, under cover of the trampling and barking of a thousand new prisoners arriving in one night, the nails were dispensed with. Irby and Flory got into the adjutant's shack and passed things out to Mackey Nall beneath the floor. They made several raids before an investigation disclosed the nature and manner of this burglary, though not the perpetrators thereof; then the floor was rebuilt and a guard was stationed at the building twenty-four hours a day. Nevertheless the scrawny freebooters had made off with red pepper, honey, salt, saleratus, half a bushel of onions worth sixty dollars Secesh per bushel, an entire box of tobacco worth twenty-two fifty; and to crown their achievement they had drained away several quarts of precious sorghum from a vast barrel which was believed to be worth the startling sum of three hundred and twenty-five dollars— not Secesh, but in greenbacks.

But what's that there saleratus good for? (They had secreted their spoils in loose underbrush beyond the guards' sinks.)

Sell it to the Yanks, old Poop Brain.

What they want with it?

Oh, they use it for bread and truck. Maybe biscuits. Medicine.

What you get for it?

Buttons with hens on them, if not cold cash.

The brass buttons on Flory's jacket had been removed before the garment was handed to him, his own buttons were mere disks of wood. He longed for eagle-shine, he longed for the gleam of minted stars. Dog my cats, Sojer. How many buttons ought I to make a Yank give me?

Say a jacket-full for a teeny little sack. Don't you fret—they'll get the buttons if you got the other stuff.

That night they swung to a new shifting of the guards. Flory found himself On Parapet at sundown. He'd called his squealing eight o'clock and all's well . . . his half-after-eight, his nine o'clock and all's well . . . he heard taunts flung up because of his childhood and the baby squawk of his voice. He itched to kill a Yankee as he had itched long; yet he was afraid to fire his musket because old Ducky warned him that the kick would knock him off the platform and break his neck for him. Flory had never fired the musket; they had no gunnery range, no targets; he wondered if truly the kick was worse than the kick of Coral's shotgun. He had no idea how to begin negotiating with prisoners, but presently he became aware that something odd was going on at the next station. Several prisoners huddled near the deadline in the dark. A good-sized moon was rising in the east. Soon it would be light enough to see what was happening. But when the moon preened itself in unattainable yellow splendor the Yanks were vanished.

Flory looked down across the newly excavated ditch on the outside. No ser-geants in sight, no details moving about. The coast was clear. He called to the guard at Station Number Thirty-eight (a mere acquaintance, a nearsighted older man who ignored Flory usually); he called, trying to make his treble seem gruff and casual. What'd you get over there, Johnson?

Pair of shears, bub. I swear, won't the old lady be proud.

What kind of shears?

Sewing shears sure enough.

What you have to give for them, Johnson?

Bub, quit calling my name out loud. . . . I give some salt.

Sakes. Where you get that old salt?

Well, where you think, you little fart? I ain't telling nobody. Now you shut up—quit your yelling at me fore we get in trouble.

This warning caused Flory to fall silent. Soon he lost himself in a child's musings, the eternal Wish I Had of the scrawny and ill-favored. He dreamed of horehound candy (he would buy a quantity when he was paid) and favorite foods which he had tasted infrequently and thus considered rare, and he dreamed of foods he had heard about but had never seen or smelled, and of other delicacies of which he had never even heard . . . what were they? Off in delectable space somewhere beyond the buzz, the murmur, the squawling, the reek of this prison . . . great hot platters of tempting meats and colored fruits.

He wished he owned a pistol such as was owned by this officer and that. A gun was all right; he had been taught how to load his musket, how to cap it, how to draw the charge. But there was something especially man-grown about the idea of a holster rubbing beside your leg as you moved. Flory liked the flap of a revolver holster, he liked the way it curved and fastened down, he liked the feel and solidity and promise of guarding leather, the way it became polished by rubbing and by sweat (he had never worn a holster, he could but imagine). He had lost much of his curiosity about Yanks, knowing them with intimacy now when they congregated below him. But Flory had been told that there was money to be made out of them, profit to be gained; he desired money and profit. He did not know how to begin a transaction, he was afraid that the Yanks would laugh at him. Floral Tebbs hated to be laughed at, and yet he was laughed at frequently.

His imaginings were limited by primitive inexperience. He was an infant and an illiterate, but some illiterates had absorbed the stimulation of profound emotion and thus were above the beasts. Flory was not. He was a beast, although a weak and confused little animal and thus proportionately dangerous. He did not know exactly what occupied the thought and attention of the branded scoundrels whom he had been set to watch. If he considered that they had secret pulsations and agonies such as lacerated him, it was only to ascribe to them a concerted wickedness: they would like to get out, and rove horned and prankish through the unprotected landscape. He must give none of them an opportunity to do this.

(Within ten rods of Flory's sentry-box an ex-miner and an ex-baggage-handler and an ex-mule-driver and an ex-book-agent-who-longed-to-be-a-writer-of-novels huddled together in their rags busy with lice. They were wrapped by the tape of common knowledge, common tragedy. They had been comrades in the Forty-fifth Ohio, and already had watched numerous of their friends die, and these men also would die. The other three listened while the book-agent told of scuppernong grapes. He had traveled through gulfside wildernesses a few years before the war, and that was how he'd come to know scuppernongs. Three shriveled fuzzy skull-faces pressed near him and low moonlight touched them when they turned, and the blanched brains behind the faces played, each in its own fashion, with imagined joy of fruit juices, fruit crystals, the power contained in thin skins and rich pulp of a peculiar sort they had never tasted and now never would taste. The book-agent said that the grapes crawled on truant vines in wild places where you'd never think to find them. You drove along the forest road in a buggy or a wagon, and the driver stopped suddenly, and you said or he said, Here they be. You reached out and pressed the bulbous things into your mouth. They were salt and sugar and sustenance, deep purple purity and grace, tang and promise. You rolled an invisible morsel of their taste around on your tongue, and it struck the roof of your mouth and it occupied your soul and you could think of nothing else. Here it was: spice and fragrance and power. It was like the moment when you were with a hearty woman and she yielded with her drive and delicacy, and you yielded unto her your whip-snapping and private bitter concentrated flogging, and here it was and this was it, the summation of bountiful flavor. Your body lived and died and was revivified as you absorbed.)

Floral did not know how he might have appeared to the prisoners, or how his fellows might have appeared. It was impossible that it might occur to him to wonder how the prisoners thought of him and other Reserves. He did not realize that after the moon ascended farther, wafer-thin above the stockade, guard shacks along the eastern parapet became small haunted houses with death dwelling in them. The shaggy figures of guards stood motionless or rarely moving, but always with menace in their silhouetting; so he himself, not yet fourteen, was a menace. The guards said to the Yankees in essence between their throat-hawkings and tobacco-spittings, Try to get past us. Only try. We have bullets and powder, the musket barrels to contain velocity and expend it against you. We're up here On Parapet; you ain't; you're down below. We got our eyes on you. Just try it, Fourth Pennsylvania and Fourth Vermont and Fourth Kentucky and Fourth Iowa. Try it, Thirteenth U.S. Infantry and Cole's Cavalry and Michiganders and folks from Wisconsin in the Iron Brigade. Try to get past us.

Night and day, in sunlight and smell, or in moonlight or in darkness and increased and concentrated smell . . . we got our muzzles ready and the percussion caps ready on tubes at tother end, and the squeeze of powder and balls jammed in between. We loaf up here, excused by too old age or too young age from feeling any feeling but a blind unreasoning unreckoning undiscerning hatred. We loaf on our planks, we are bored, we cry the reports of the hours and half hours. Somebody starts off on the stroke of twelve or of seven or of two or of whatever hour of the night, and middling thereafter, and the calls drone from lair to lair along the fence. Post Sixteen, ten o'clock and all's well, or we yell for fun, Post Thirty-three, ten o'clock and here's your mule. Maybe some other members of our far-flung regiment are laughing their livers out along the rim, or maybe they aren't paying any attention at all, and wouldn't have sense enough to pay heed if they had the waking ears to pay heed. Just try to get past this stockade, just try to get past the deadline in shadows, Tenth Connecticut and Pennsylvania Lancers and Twenty-second Indiana and Pennsylvania Bucktails and folks from out West, from Crocker's Brigade and such. Just try it; all we ask, or sometimes we won't even wait to ask; just try. We got the muskets loaded and we ain't asleep by any chance. We got the fire ready, Chicago Board of Trade Battery and Second Maryland and Minnesota Indians and any God damn niggers that claim they're soldiers like white men, even Yankees, and haven't been sent to a labor detail in the burying trenches yet. Just try it. In stench of wormy black, in clarity of the thing in the sky, we linger amid haunted houses on the fence, and we dare you. You will die if you take the dare.

Hi, Reb.

Flory jumped from his vague blank retreat and looked down. He had thought it was a post, it wasn't a post, it was too wide for a post, and that post he'd thought it was (the toughened remains of a small pine from which prisoners ripped the last splinters) had disappeared under erosion of fingernails and homemade knives sometime previously.

Reb. Hi, Guard!

With shuddering hands Floral Tebbs slid his musket barrel across the fence.

Take care, don't shoot me, you damn fool.

Yank—get—away—from that—deadline. Flory spoke the words thinly with a mouth near to blubbering.

Hah. Thought you was the guard we call Little Tattnall. He's usually on this post.

Flory's jellied finger went inside the trigger guard. The Yankee stood close to death, he didn't know how close he stood. Flory's stagewhisper came down to him. Little Tattnall's took sick. They give me this post.

You might do. Be a sport, kiddie. Raise that gun barrel a trifle. . . .

He was safe, after all—he was up on the fence—no Yankee could jump fifteen feet into the air, although sometimes Flory imagined that a Yankee could. Flory tilted the musket toward the moon.

Thanks, kiddie. What I need is soda.

Who're you?

Kid, I'm Donner. You ought to know—Willie Collins's cookie?

Flory had heard of Willie Collins since the first time he went On Parapet. Collins had been pointed out to him, he had seen the giant, had watched him slugging and bossing.

You understand? Soda. You Rebs call it saleratus.

Flory shuffled loosely on his perch. I got some.

This was a miracle, the Yank asking him for saleratus; and all the time that twisted paper had been lying squeezed in his jeans' pocket.

Guess you didn't follow me. Little Reb, what's your name?

Flory.

Well, Flory, Willie wants some York biscuits. I got everything else—sufficient flour and butter and sugar, got the milk souring. But we need soda. Saleratus.

I—got some.

Devil suck it, here's luck! You know what I mean, now? Sal—
Saleratus.

How much you got?

Nigh onto a pocket full.

I'll be sucked. What you want for it? Greenback?

Flory spewed the low words in a stream. No I want buttons with hens on them.
Give you two dollars in good currency.

No. Buttons with hens on them.

You fool little Reb, I'll give you a bean, a gold piece.

Want buttons with hens—

The man named Donner swore softly and went stalking off until he was mingled in the noisy pattern of moonlight and tilted shebang roofs, until he could not
be seen moving, could not be separated from the wide-spread garbage dump with
its fire-flickers and bird sounds. A few minutes later the cry of *Raiders!* was raised
near the creekside. There was a feeling that a few people ran toward the spot and
many more went tottering away. More minutes elapsed, Donner returned. The
light swept increasingly brighter, increasingly shadows flattened as the moon
sailed. Flory could see that the cook held a loose dark patch in his hand.

I got here a jacket with them buttons on it.

Dddon't need no jacket, Yank. Just buttons—

Brown your God damn nose, I hain't got nothing to cut buttons off with!
Should I pull them off twould likely bust them little gilt loops. Kiddie, you got a
string?

Flory had no twine, he had not thought to bring a length of it.

I'll hurl it up. You catch. Donner wadded the garment and tossed it high. It
fluttered and fell short within the deadline. Casually the big Donner stepped
across the deadline and picked up the jacket. Johnson, the guard at the next
station toward the north, and the guard at the next station toward the south—
Both were watching, neither bothered to lift his gun. They were more accustomed
to such transactions than was Floral Tebbs, but Flory would grow accustomed.
Donner weighted the jacket with a wad of mud, wrapped it with care, threw it
high. It came hard and hurtfully against Flory's face with a button bruising his
eyelid when it struck. His calico hat was knocked from his head, but he held the
jacket, he had it in his arms, he had buttons with proud eagles threatening amid
circles of stars, those were the glory he sought.

Well, kiddie, I'm waiting. Toss the soda.

Flory tossed it and Donner caught the poke easily in one hand. He said nothing
more but strolled into the tangle of huts and population; and Willie Collins would
have his York biscuits the next morning, with butter and jam and rashers of fresh
bacon.

In the huge conical tent draped beside Collins's winter castle, Donner leered
through the firelight at Edward Blamey. Rubber Legs, you did a fair deed.

What?

Member that freshie you sighted this afternoon with the artillery jacket on
him? I was hard put to find some buttons just now, to buy soda for these biscuits.
Damn if I didn't mind that artillery jacket then and there.

Edward Blamey remembered. He was moved into that overcoat shebang, this
side of the sinks, wa'n't he?

Hah, he's still there. Little squirt—he weren't more'n sixteen and skinny too—
he tried to give me trouble.

Cookie looked critically at his big right fist and saw that there was blood drying.
He wiped the blood on his trousers. He quoted gaily to Ed Blamey before he

turned to his wooden trough, to begin raising the biscuit dough— He quoted, If you don't believe I'm a butcher, just smell of me boots.

Ed Blamey reached for his bottle of pine-top.

On the sentry platform Floral Tebbs stroked buttons of the stolen jacket, and considered how they would shine even more delightfully in the sun if tomorrow became one of the rare fair days of this month, if indeed the sun shone. He would rub buttons, they would be alive with golden fire, people who had no such buttons would look their envy.

Fifty rods away a gaunt Jewish sergeant of the Eighty-fifth New York (but still powerful, holding control of himself, not straying too far no matter how many similar moons he had worshipped above other lands) sat with big hands clasped across his ragged knees, worshipping this moon. Suddenly Nathan Dreyfoos realized that he had been craving the moon and the silent simplicity and clear freedom which it represented more than he had craved any delight or fulfillment during the twenty-three years through which he'd lived. He had forgotten that brothers-in-arms and brothers who had once borne arms alongside him had suffered and hungered and desired in the same manner. He had been selfish, insensitive to their need. He thought of the dead Corley, the dead Stevenson—he had neglected their memory utterly. He was blanketed with shame. In weakness he prayed to moonlight and to the Almighty God or Monster who made that moonlight, he prayed: Oh, give these other survivors the same release and independence, afford them the same ability to go kiting beyond the stockade, grant it more quickly and more firmly than you grant it to me!

He begged this; but it was as if some caterpillar of voracious falsity crawled active beneath the stalk of his benevolence—a larva who fed on the stem, and awarded rottenness before it could be recognized by his soul (but recognized only by the small portion which begged). Please me first, give me escape in the first moment you can manage it, I care not for the rest, find me a way out, leave me free, Devil take the others.

26

Sometimes it seemed to Henry Wirz that his brain was made of rubber, it was a rubber sack filled with stones, it stretched to paleness as more stones were necessarily introduced and as the weight grew. Stones were labeled Hospital, Crowding, Incompetence of Guards, Poison Swamp, labeled with many other unpleasant names and reminders. In contrast screaming temper Wirz bounded from desk to stockade to headquarters, back again to the office of the quartermaster, thence to the quarters of the surly Dick Winder, back on horseback to the stockade to mete out a new punishment or to make a new observation. If it were possible for him to loathe the prisoners more each hour of his life he loathed them so. But his trained physician's attitude could not countenance the filth of these creatures without wishing to exorcise it merely on the grounds that it was filth. A row of sinks— these he'd built (they were totally inadequate, and this he knew; but they were placed on the lowest ground within the pen for purposes of drainage; and half the sick were too sick to use them, to muster strength to creep or stagger to the sinks; and he ran out of lumber). A bridge across the creek—this he'd managed to have constructed (but it was too narrow, it sagged: again the shortage of lumber and tools). A shoring of the creekside, a fumbling attempt to deepen the stream and thus increase its flow . . . this hopeless effort was achieved amid shrieks. Almost before his eyes Henry saw planks of the shoring melt away, split for tent poles, hacked into bits for firewood. His shivering hands were tied, the entreaties he sent to higher echelons were lost or filed. Who cared? Not the Winders.

By God, I get that damn hospital out of there once.

Odds seemed at times insurmountable but he toiled with frenzy, he hated the sight of those few tent flies packed in the northeast corner, hated the sight and clamor and stink of invalids motionless or gesticulating. In heat of late May he would have rested with pride if rest were ever a state to be attained by Henry Wirz (but it was not). He saw the tent flies sprouting in a new location, and outside the pen at last. He'd procured more tents, lumber to build bunks (not enough lumber, not enough bunks) and had even built a portion of a separate fence around the establishment. It was not a good hospital. At least it was outside the main stockade. Outside, *ja* . . . he kept telling himself that it was better, better. Rotten tent flies, a considerable number of small A tents, a limited number of wall tents scraped from some camp farther at the North and dumped off a flat car one rainy day along with the sodden supply of A tents. . . . This collection of awning rose on a few acres of land east of the star fort, east also of the surgeons' offices. The ground was higher than the areas immediately adjacent, and sloped toward the southeast, but marshes sent up their aroma on two sides. A small stream, one of the many branches amid those valleys, ran through a corner of the hospital enclosure. Quickly this became a thing of reek and evil.

This was the place where Ira Claffey's black people had dumped their loads of bastard melons months before. A more noisome cargo of decay was now dumped here on the twenty-third and twenty-fourth of May. After that many people were carried out daily on carts, and more came to take their places, puffing, drooling, hullooing; they were lugged in blankets or on makeshift stretchers, they were carried in the arms of stronger men.

Still it was better. It was outside the stockade. Outside! Much better, *ja*.

Four patients were jammed into each of the A tents, eight patients in the wall tents; under common flies lay as many as could be crowded together—six or eight men—sometimes more, under the larger flies. Bunks had been made by driving forks of saplings into the soil and placing scraps of planking—or, more frequently, pine poles—across them. But— Not enough bunks. The sick lay on the ground, some had pine straw, some had no pine straw. If Henry Wirz had been able to devote a greater share of his time to this task he would have seen to it that all had pine straw to lie in. He was a very busy man. He had to be many places at once.

Captain Winder, I tell you now, it is again I make request for you to— Requisition for spades and axes! It is I must have a larger prison, God damn!

Oh, that's all very well, to speak of implements; and I got them last year and I presume I can get them again; but these damn planters won't coöperate. All of them want to keep their niggers at home. They raise hell all the way from Macon to Milledgeville every time I try to get hold of a few niggers.

By God, mine own niggers I got. Prisoners I got, nigger prisoners. In the carload I got them!

Well, wouldn't that be forced labor? Contrary to the Rules of War? Next time I have communication with my father I'll—

I tell you, you Sid Winder, those picks and spades and axes, those I got to have. God damn, I blow them Rules of War up somebody's ass, I tell you!

Sid Winder had been manicuring his nails with his penknife. After Wirz left he saw a great bluebottle fly upon the barrelhead beside him, and tried to impale the fly with his knife blade, and missed. He thought, Little bastard of a Swiss squirt. I don't understand how the old man tolerates him. But we surely are killing off a lot of damn Yankees here. Everybody's got to do his share. Sid Winder thought of Harrell Elkins, thought of him with undying hatred and with a fear which he could never quite put down . . . cavalry sabers at two paces.

Wirz hacked fiercely at the problem, and eventually he secured his coveted tools. Once more the chant of black voices moaned among trees, this time due north of the existing stockade. Once more resin dripped, chips spun, shaggy tops came crashing.

Oh, he gone up there. Never come back again.

Where you say he gone?

Ooohhh. . . .

Work went forward with speed surpassing far the laggardly construction of the original stockade. Only some ten acres were to be enclosed, the ground was mainly flat, there was no creek to be crossed, no gates to be made. Simply it was an extension of the rectangle by about six hundred feet. Main Street and South Street would still serve as arteries for traffic and commerce. It was told lugubriously Inside that the raiders would undoubtedly preëmpt the fresh space for themselves—it would not be saturated with slime, it would be higher, more healthful, farther away from effluvium of the marsh. In fact the raiders had no intention of moving. Why should they move? They had their castles, their pavilion, they had all the room they wanted; as for effluvium, most of them had been born in it. Faster, faster sounded the click of axes, drone of the diggers, sharp cries of overseers beyond the north wall. Henry Wirz was no lounging Sid Winder. He drove unceasingly.

Where you say he gone?

Ooohhh, ooohhhh, way up there above.

He gone up there, up in the sky. Never come back no more.

Ooohhh. . . .

A strange calm, comparative silence came in the middle of June: heavy work was done. Now was essential only the final touch on ladders and sentry stations. On the evening of June eighteenth there came the sound of digging and prying. The more energetic prisoners gathered outside the deadline to gape up at shacks on the north rim. There were no longer any guards on those platforms. A portion of the fence began to sway, first one log toppled, then three or four others were pried and they fell thunderously. That's enough, a voice called outside. Big enough hole for them to get through.

Provident prisoners had taken up already their dirty bundles of personal belongings, their cooking tins; they rolled the fabric of shebangs and were treasuring the poles. Men seeped gingerly across the abandoned deadline at first, but soon a minor riot ensued as more and more sought to force their way through the aperture, to make claims on new holdings in the clean area. There were more than twenty-two thousand people in the place on this day, and if these twenty-two thousand were distributed evenly throughout the old acres and the new there would be an end to unbearable swarming. But—Hold on. What of the future? How many more trains would come wrenching to the Anderson depot? It was rumored that all prisoners held by the eastern States of the Confederacy might be concentrated in this one place. For how long would pressure be relaxed? Oh, dear Lord above, it would tighten, it would tighten.

By the hour of darkness the bulk of migration was concluded. In human and animal fashion grass had appeared greener on the other side (it was greener, it would not be for many hours; by the next day there would be no grass) and more folks stampeded into the north enclosure than could be accommodated. Many late arrivals limped back to their old haunts in disgust, and in turn found their original quarters occupied by men who had moved up from marshy regions; there were fights throughout the wet moonlit hours. Henry Wirz rode home pleased with himself. They had said that it was impossible to move the hospital outside; the hospital was now outside. They had said that it was impossible to enlarge the stockade; the stockade had been enlarged. His immediate project was for the removal of the old fence. Seven hundred and eighty feet of palisading, each log twenty feet in length . . . dried out; and the buried ends would not have been long enough in the earth to decay. What might not he build with this treasure? A separate punishment stockade—he had thought of that, he had planned for that with what amounted to affection. And bridges and trestles. On the morrow he would cry for wagons, wagons. Should he not obtain wagons from some source or other the logs could easily be snaked out at the ends of chains, hauled by mules. If worst came to worst he might harness gangs of Negroes together and have them pull the logs.

Chastised into performance by tightening of narcotic energy, he was back at the stockade soon after sunrise on the morning of June nineteenth. He climbed fussing to a new sentry station north of the corner of the old stockade. At first he became sick at his stomach and tottered dizzily; then he began to rave, literally, until frothy spittle flew from his beard. The fence was gone. The old fence was gone. The solid palisade was vanished as if giants had leaned down from the sky and plucked the pines like toothpicks. It was not merely that the old line of stockading had been dug up or knocked down: *there were simply no logs in sight.*

Who, who, who? That damn Sid Winder? That damn Dick Winder? That damn colonel commanding the post? No one had authority to do this thing. The lumber was his, his—it belonged to Henry Wirz, he had plans for using it— He stood gasping for breath at last, German curses still lingering in echo— He would find curses in English when—When he had more strength— He would go to General Winder in person— His property had been stolen. A seven-hundred-and-eighty-foot line of logs twenty feet tall. Someone had taken his logs.

Prisoners, sir, the old guard was saying weakly behind him.

Vas? What you say, guard?

I said, Captain, twas the prisoners as done it.

Them damn logs? *Mein* logs? Them damn Yankees? Son of a bitch—

Yes sir, Captain. We heard them a-doing it. All night long. But nobody'd give us any orders to fire. And they wasn't inside the deadline—not much, anyways—

Yankees. They had taken his fence, with their bare hands they had taken it, picked it apart with striving fingernails, scraped it to nothingness with puny primitive tools. Firewood, flooring, roofing: it bloomed about the fuming area. As Henry's vision cleared, he could look down and recognize split pine posts here and there, the rows of newly splintered material.

They do that, he croaked again, not daring to believe.

Yes, Captain, they did so, sure as white blossoms make little apples.

He crept down the ladder, his head was aching. Twenty-two thousand three hundred sixty-two Yankees. Was that the last report he had drawn up? No, no, he could not recollect. Twenty-two thousand Yankees, each had eight fingers and two thumbs . . . *ach, ja,* some had been amputated; but there were more than twenty-two thousand prisoners, and so— Call it two hundred and twenty thousand fingers. He closed his eyes and he could see the mass of those clawing twitching curling fierce fingers like a nest of worms as big as a house— As big as— As big as the Louvre? Not that big.

He was so beaten by his loss that he could perform little work that day. He was very nearly gentle with the people who worked in his office. He gave his errand boy part of his lunch brought from home. Wirz muttered that he had no appetite. He rode home early and in a near stupor. He went to bed at dusk and lay staring up at the low ceiling, and said *Nein, nein* when Elizabeth offered chicken broth. Two hundred and twenty thousand fingers pulling his logs apart.

Papa, said little Coralie when she came barefoot and in her nightdress, Please, Papa, can I get in bed with you?

Ja, Liebchen, he said after a moment or two, when the knowledge of her request reached through befuddlement. He held up the covering with his left hand, and the child giggled and hunched with pleasure, snuggling close to his side.

Shall you sing me the song, *Mein Vater?*

He liked to have her call him Father in German, he had taught her to do so. In his cracked nasal voice, but softly, softly, he began to sing a little song which a kind old lady had sung to him first in 1826 when he was but four. He wished that it were 1826 now, he wished that he were but four. Cora lay still as a mouse, her gentle appreciative breathing reached his ears.

27

Laurel Tebbs came in shyness to the Claffey plantation, seeking the loan of a thimble. I did have one, she said in her high-pitched voice. Her voice was a whine suggesting some kind of animal inheritance, an inheritance from an animal whipped too frequently for its own good, and fearing more blows. Did have one, silver one what belonged to Granny or so twas said; but Zoral he kept a-playing with it, dropping it down a crack; and then I'd have to give him a lick and make him crawl under the house after it; and one day he couldn't find it no way, nor could I, though I went under the house my own self; and I surely hated to do that, count of the dead chickens and rats he's always a-dragging under there. Reckon maybe he dropped it down—She lowered her tone, faced with the delicacy of Lucy's presence. Down the privy.

Lucy said, I'm sorry it was lost.

Coral he was kind enough to make me a thimble out'n a big acorn; but that split in two today; and I was part way through sewing myself a gown, and I hain't got no other gown fit to put on, cepting this one, and the purple one used to belong to Ma. That's for dress-up.

Lucy said, Come into the house, child, and let me look about. She addressed Laurel thus naturally, not realizing that the girl was fifteen, thinking of her still as the shrunken bag-of-bones she'd always been, peering from behind fences and weed-brakes at the doings of the Claffeys and their people.

Laurel's father was a frightened Americus widower who had the devil's own time trying to support his five children on meager returns from his occupation as cooper. Mr. Marion Padgett was hopelessly pale, his kinky hair was orange, his sad small face was spattered with orange freckles and so were his hands and wiry arms. When he made a statement of a fact it sounded like a question, for every sentence ended with a rising inflection which said, Excuse me, was it all right for me to say this, to say anything at all? His children sounded the same way, even when speaking to one another. Marion Padgett hovered over them ceaselessly, putting clothes to soak at ungodly hours of the morning, running from his workbench to take a boiler from the fire, putting down his hammer to take up a soup ladle. He was fortunate in that the children never needed discipline or punishment, they were all too wan and apologetic to fight even among themselves. The Padgetts trotted to the Methodist church each Sunday like a covey of starved redheaded warblers, but mainly silent warblers who did not know how to warble. One day in 1848 a bearded stranger with a tall beaver hat marched into the cooperage which stood in the same yard as the Padgett cottage. It appeared that Marion's sister had died in Charleston, and her husband had preceded her to the grave by only five days. There were no children, no other relatives, no heirs but Francis Marion Padgett. The property consisted of a house and furniture and some jewelry of value, together with a large lot on Meeting Street and five well-trained Negroes, and forty-two hundred dollars in cash. Marion Padgett spat the nails out of his mouth and wandered in a daze. His children wept to see him go, and he was deaf to the stranger who hastened for a time at his side saying, But, sir, where are you going—? Damn it, sir! Mr. Padgett, I request that you pay some heed to what I am saying— Come back to your house, sir! Your children are in tears! Eventually the lawyer had to return to the cooperage alone, and he parceled the children out to neighbors, and sat in a nearby inn awaiting Marion's return, in dudgeon. He had to wait three days.

Reports drifted back of a Marion Padgett who wandered from one seller of brandy to another seller of brandy. Mistrusting any orthodox depository, he carried always what few funds he had about him in a chamois-skin bag tied to the belt which held up his pantaloons. Through rigorous saving and self-denial and child-denial he had accumulated thirty-seven dollars against a mortgage payment of forty dollars, plus the quarter's interest which must be paid soon. Reports drifted of a Marion Padgett who hired a horse and chaise and was seen driving madly over rough roads in the adjacent wilderness. In time he arrived at the Tebbs place. Thus he fathered Laurel. (There was always some doubt about this in the Widow Tebbs's mind, since it chanced that she had entertained two other red-headed gentlemen in that same week. Well, she said, my little girl does look a sight like that Marion, and I knowed him when I was scarce more'n a infant myself; but I reckon she looks a sight like one of the others, too. And I weren't yet a widow then, and— But it's been quite a time since; and all them doses of gunpowder never did do no good at all. She had a vague thought of puppies and kittens. The child cried, and Mag picked her up and cuddled her. She thought briefly of Marion Padgett, now said to be living in distant luxury. She thought once more of Marion, then he strayed from her simple mind, he returned seldom.)

This was an especially hot day, and Lucy was conscious of the strong odor of Laurel Tebbs as the round-shouldered little creature moved beside her. She said sharply, Miss, have you bathed yourself of late? as she might have said it to one of her own servants, and then felt that she had been heedless and cruel, and was ashamed.

Nome, spoke the languid voice. It's so hard to bring up water from our well, and Coral he's always off to the forest, and Flory's gone to the army, and Zoral's but a babe. Ma she's always a-entertaining or a-sleeping. I just can't scarcely pull that big sweep, hain't got the power.

Then you shall go over to Little Sweetwater, said Lucy brightly. For I have some rose oil which I pressed, and I shall give you a bit of that, and it's no earthly good, of course, if you're not freshly scrubbed. And I shall give you a square of Windsor for your own.

Miss Lucy, whined Laurel, I'd be plumb scairt to go naked in the creek. Too many sojers about.

Then go far up the creek, the big creek, where there's no one.

That I'll do, if'n you say I got to. Please, what's Windsor?

Tis a toilet soap I've made myself, and scented with caraway, and it's just the best! Except for variegated toilet soap, and I used to make that too, with Extra shaving the bar-soap fine; but we've no longer any Chinese blue and only a teentsie bit of Chinese vermilion.

This conversation occurred in the hall and on the stairs, and Laurel now stood with her hostess in Lucy's chamber. Oh, just lots of pretties, she said without envy. She was accustomed to seeing silver and portraits, certain elements of grandeur although decayed grandeur, when she helped at the Biles'. But she had never entered a dainty young lady's room before.

Lucy searched though work-basket, work-table, drawers, appraising her stock of thimbles. She thought that she owned four but could find only three. One of these had belonged to Great-aunt Mary Flo; Lucy remembered this woman as a waspish invalid in a scarlet silk dressing gown; she cherished no particularly pleasant memories of Great-aunt Mary Flo. And the thimble was too narrow for her own finger now that she was grown.

This you may have.

For to keep?

Certainly, for your own. Mind and don't let Baby Brother get his paws on it.

Reckon I can hide it from him. The girl smiled in wan delight. Didn't figure to come a-begging. Twas just for the lend; but I do thank you, Miss Lucy.

Now for rose oil and the Windsor! Lucy found the oil on her washstand shelf and poured a trifle into an empty pill-flask which had been saved with care. Here's the toilet soap in my cupboard. And—

Critically she inspected the stringy hair of the child beside her; actually she expected to see vermin, but did not find any; she spread the hair with her fingers with disgust but also in explorative curiosity. She was very curious about fellow human beings—wondering privately how they ate, cared for their bodies, washed or did not wash, felt, thought, lived, died. Certain influences in her rearing cried that this was unwomanly, and Lucy had pride as a woman, she did not wish to be unwomanly although often she knew that she was unladylike in the generally accepted sense, and felt impish about it.

Such a lovely color to your hair, Laurel. It's like a wild orange, and I remember how Uncle Felton fetched a sack of them.

Hain't never ate no orange. Ma says they're good to suck but mighty puckerish.

But pretty hair should be tended—I suppose it's like the oranges themselves—they must need sun and rain, and your hair needs soap and water.

Well, I did wash it with soap but it like to burnt the hide off my head. And it got all stiff as weeds.

You had no fit shampoo, I fancy. Lucy scribbled a note at her desk and rang for one of the blacks; after some time there was a response. Ninny looked injured at finding Laurel Tebbs in the young mistress's bed chamber; she stood in a silently sneering attitude, firm in conviction that the young mistress was demeaning herself.

Do you go, Ninny, to my father. He is in the seed house or store shed, and do you give him this note.

In this way Laurel was endowed further with a vial of Lucy's own shampoo contrived of aqua ammonia, salts of tartar, and alcohol flavored with bergamot. Lucy instructed the girl how to mix the potion with rainwater, and how to rub it through her hair into her scalp until the lather had gone down, then how to lave it out in the clearness of the creek or in more rainwater. Laurel promised faithfully. By this time she was enamored to the point of idolatry. Lucy whirled before her eyes in a froth of the room's pretties.

Is them your brothers what got kilt, Miss Lucy?

Not this one, child. Tis a miniature of my father when once he was a soldier too. But this daguerreotype, here, and the two ambrotypes yonder. Those were my brothers.

Surely is a pity. . . . My brother Coral, surgeons cut the foot off'n him.

I have seen him since, poor lad, with his crutch.

You got—? Laurel whispered it, and could not look at the young woman as she whispered. Got yourself a fellow?

Lucy did not speak for a moment. . . . I fear not. There is a friend, a gentleman who writes letters sometimes. But— She busied herself in emptying a basket of woven bull-grass, and this too would be a gift for Laurel; the girl could carry home her bottles, soap and thimble. Child, have you a—fellow?

Kind of. He sure did pull me round when we danced, when them Alabama sojers was a-leaving. And he held me tight against himself, she managed to breathe in confidence. A few minutes later she was running down the lane with the speed of a field-mouse, her scarred legs flashing under tags of calico. The spring of extreme youth was in her frame, appreciation for the gifts was foaming, the certainty that she must follow Lucy Claffey's injunctions (and the sooner the better) was a delight intense enough to be named as a pain. Laurel bubbled to herself shrill bits of worship which she felt might be profanity, yet not the obscenity which she heard spoken often by Coral and Floral. Mercy God, she cried with pulpy pale lips, Mercy God, damn, hell, Jesus, damn hell, Mercy God. She stopped once shortly near the railroad, for a train approached, and she scarcely saw or heard the engine until she was beside the track. Boys rode on some of the platform cars or sat in box car doorways. They shouted, whistled, pretended to shoot Laurel with their guns, but she gave no heed. She had taken the tiny phial containing rose oil from the basket, and had withdrawn the glass stopper and was drinking in the odor with long rewarding sniffs. When the train had gone Laurel fled homeward, her sunbonnet spreading wide soiled wings above her shoulders where it had fallen.

Old Mrs. Bile taught Laurel to sew when the girl was eleven, and thus her thin fingers could fly about the business of it. Coral had caught a string of catfish that morning, and the widow fried balls of cornmeal to go with them. There were turnip greens and pork as well, but Laurel declined all invitations to join her family at table. The rest ate eagerly, greasily, washing down their feast with quantities of okra coffee. Zoral gagged on a fish-bone and choked himself into purple regurgitation before his mother could extract the bone. Through this excitement Laurel did not lift her head from her work, she did not leave her bench and basket. Her gown was finished before two o'clock, fashioned from pieces of calico sent by Effie Dillard. Waist and skirt did not match—the one was of a green pattern, the other of gray—but to Laurel they were measureless beauty and pride.

What you a-doing there, Sissy? inquired Captain Ox Puckett when he came stamping in. By Ned, ain't you a regular little Betsy Ross, like they claim stitched a flag for General Jackson or somebody! Soon Ox and the Widow Tebbs had retired to The Crib, Coral was asleep on his bed, and Zoral was a train growling back and forth in front of a chicken-coop depot. Laurel crammed her new gown into the bull-grass basket and carried off soap, shampoo and rose oil which Lucy had given her. She took also two torn towels, reasonably clean, and some scraps of underclothing. Not even to Lucy could she have expressed her desire to be fresh and scented and neatly put together, in body and hair and dress alike. Passion was in her, her eyes snapped with it as she darted across the field behind the old Rambo homestead next door and sought upper reaches of Little Sweetwater.

In a shallow calm pool among willows she whitened the water; frogs leaped away, crayfish scuttled to safety. No one came to spy upon Laurel's nakedness, although she blushed in this fearful solitude, made small squeals when she found a leech upon her leg, felt malarial fever through her limbs at every crow-call. Once she was scrubbed and dried the rose oil made aromatic madness on her skin and in her hair. Why had she not fetched her mother's looking glass? Oh, to gaze upon herself, to see whether her bright hair was the damp loose cloud of ecstasy which she believed it to be when her hands went through it and let it fall and then strayed aloft wonderingly again . . . an idea came to her, in the end. With skirt held high she waded to a dark untroubled place beneath a cypress, and stood motionless, not breathing until the water was cleared, unrippled; then the girl bent forward, squatting, and saw her own thin wild face wavering up at her, and saw the hair . . . oh, Mercy Jesus, God, hell. . . . Oh, Miss Lucy, lady, I do thank you for them soaps and the potion.

That evening Captain Ox was long since departed; but another mule was tethered, and a lamp burned in The Crib and was then put out at the caller's request. Zoral slept in a wet place of his own making. Coral had gone crutching off to Uncle Arch's, empowered to buy navy plug, meal, and a stick of red candy for his mother's use. The late lopsided moon had not yet risen, nor would rise for hours; but starlight yielded golden brownness to enrich each tuft of nearby trees. Laurel Tebbs sat on the step, leaning her shoulder against a post. My, she had the unspoken thought, it surely does stink bad. That there prison pen yonder. Them Yankees must be powerful dirty, dirtier than ever I been in my born days. She thought of Little Sweetwater, and how savage and lonely must be the region where she had bathed; perhaps dangerous wild beasts were prowling beside the very pool wherein she had splashed—formless ferocious wild beasts—she trembled before the notion of their stealth and blackness. She thought of the shampoo, the cake of Windsor worn to a flake; she thought of the rose oil, and scrambled up to bring her bottle out of hiding. She had concealed the bottle within an old clock (the clock did not run, it stood dusty on a high shelf, it was a good place to hide her thimble or any other treasure which might be coveted by Zoral). There was still a spoonful or two of oil in the flask, and the girl resumed her place on the step and held the bottle to her nostril, and believed that the stockade's vapor could not reach past this immediate fragrance. Presently a dark shape detached itself from hollowness of the roadway, seemed to halt indecisively, then drifted forward. It was a man who tripped over the crude two-wheeled cart which Mag had prevailed upon Coral to build for the baby; the man swore heatedly and then came closer. Laurel stood up. Ma ain't in the house, she said automatically. She's over'n The Crib, she's got a caller.

The man laughed. Honey, I never did come to see your old lady. Come to see you.

She roasted quickly in the heat of her own flesh. Now, you look a here, Sergeant! I'm but a girl. It's my Ma who does the entertaining.

Sinkfield came up to the step and stood with hands on his wide stuffed hips. Sakes, honey child, I wouldn't want no truck with your old lady. I like young ladies, like you. Member how we danced at the pic-nic?

Hain't no pic-nic going on tonight.

Look what I brung you, and he brought forth a crumple of paper. Brown sugar. What they call maple sugar, manufactured away at the North. Ain't that nobby?

Laurel tossed her head, and brushed her wiry hair with her hands, then smoothed it against her scalp once more. Oh, she said, I don't much care for sugar no way.

Took it off a Yank that I went through at the depot. Thinks I, Well, now I wonder who'd like this? Thinks I, Bet I know who'd like it. That pretty little Laurel Tebbs, that's who. So reckon I'll just mog along that way, once't I get off duty and get myself a pass. His big hand reached out to touch her knee, Laurel slapped the hand. Sinkfield laughed, he took his hand away. Aw, come along now, honey. Just please to take one bite.

Well, she said, I will try it.

Sinkfield lounged against the post, he seemed to tower tall above Laurel, although he was not truly tall, he was only heavy and loutish. She pressed the stopper of her rose oil bottle into place, put the bottle in her lap, and explored the wad of newspaper which the sergeant had pressed upon her. She liked the odor which came up, she examined the flat lump and few granules which had broken loose. She tasted cautiously.

Now, ain't that fine, Laurel?

Oh, it don't taste like much.

Ah, you know it does.

No, it don't neither, she snapped.

Aw, does so.

Well, she said, twill do for Zoral.

Who's that?

My baby brother. Baby half-brother, mean to say. We're all halves.

That Flory just a half-brother also?

Uh-huh.

Little snot.

I'll have Ma take a stick to you, you go saying bad words front of me!

Why, snot hain't a bad word, it's just what comes out of your nose. And I do have a task, keeping Flory in line. But he's really scairt of me, so I fetch him up sharp. Never had to thrash him but a couple of times.

Officers and sergeants and such— They ain't *sposed* to hit the boys under them. I heard Captain Ox say so.

Sinkfield grasped the girl's hand and tried to draw her to her feet, but she exclaimed and held back, and with her left hand hugged the paper of sugar and the bottle into her skirts.

Laurel, honey, less you and me take a little walk—

Her heart was thudding like a hard fist knocking at a door, nok, nok, nok, nok, nok. No, I don't want to. Look out there, you'll spill my ssssugar, and her voice also was a slippery entity and seemed to writhe out of management. She twisted her hand loose from the sweaty grasp.

Well, less put it away somewheres.

Well, I—

Just a little bitty walk, honey?

Well . . . you got any sulphur matches, Sergeant? Please to strike a light for me, so's I can see where to put my sugar. She retreated into the house and Sinkfield groped after her. He lighted the match, Laurel brought a candle (in times of comparative plenty they used lamps and candles in this house, they did not have to use greaselights). She put the rose oil into the clock, the sugar into a dusty pitcher. She stood, short rapid breathing hurting her chest, heart breaking itself apart inside her. She stood with slightly lowered head, gazing at Sinkfield through the flickers of tawny light, conscious of an indefinite limitless power which she now held. She thought that she should like to use that power to hurt Sergeant Sinkfield, she wished that his face was not so broken into pink and yellow rash; but if she hurt him severely he might not come back again, he might never dance with her again, he might never pull her tightly against his overgrown body again.

You want—? Her voice shook with the excitement ruling the room and the lout and herself. Want a drink of wwwater?

He grinned. I don't need no water, honey. He came around the corner of the table, and Laurel retreated before him.

Want a peach? We got some.

Why ain't you just like a little peach your own self! That pretty peachy hair and— He had her hand again, he had both hands; she laughed shrilly, without reason. She shook her head and felt the loose clean hair whipping. Again it must be like a loose cloud, a lovely scented cloud; she wished she could see herself in a mirror.

Laurel, listen—

Whwhwhat?

Less take that little old walk.

Reckon Ma might give me a whipping.

Pshaw, she won't know nothing about it. Just a little bitty walk.

Well, if'n I do go—

Ah, strength was in her, strength of mules and horses and cruel spring winds a-twisting, power of red blood flowing in rivers, power of engines and staring stars. You know I ain't but fifteen. We got to stay in earshot of the house, now you mind that.

Sure we will, honey.

And— And you got to promise you won't hit Flory no more.

Why, sure I won't if you ask it. Little snot like him—

Ser*geant!* And you got to swear you'll stop a-saying that word. If'n I go. For a walk. Just a— A little way. Real close to home.

Sure enough, honey, I'll do anything you say. He drew her out into the broken wilderness of tan light and umber shade.

Within one hour she had returned to the house, and alone, alternately running a few steps, driving her bruised pelvic region into the motion of flight; but it would pain her severely, and cause her to move more slowly, and then she would walk as one entranced. One sleeve was torn nearly loose from the new-stitched gown and fluttered as a light wind came to toss it. Certain sundered tissues scraped rawly each step that Laurel took, hot moisture oozed, her ragged drawers were stained with it. Had she said she'd go for a walk? Yes, she had said— She had said, We got to stay nigh the house, but he had drawn her on and on, across the railroad and beyond a fence into a bushy corner of the Claffey acres (which site he had selected previously with an eye to solitude and convenience; the grass was long there, no houses stood near). The unidentified power which had coursed in Laurel's frame and spirit was frozen solid, it was no longer a power, it was ice and wail and terror. She heard a mushy voice battering her ears as later the big dry rod had slain her maidenhood. I'm just the funniest feller. She heard her own treble drawling, How so? . . . Count of the jokes I make, and tricks. I just keep them boys at the camps a-laughing all the while. You mind what my name is: I told you at the pic-nic: tis Jester. Jester Johnson Sinkfield. And what Jester means is a feller doing stunts and jokes. You got a funny-bone, Laurel? Less see— And the clumsy hand digging her side, her own protestation resounding. . . . You ever see a little pig hung up by his hind legs a-squealing? Funniest thing you ever did see! Twas my task at the slaughter-house up Atlanta way; I took care of the little ones, and didn't they just rip. Way you do is first tie their legs, like this. No, no, honey, I hain't a-going to tie your legs together; here, give me your hands; no, give me both hands; we'll play like you was a baby pig, just the prettiest little baby pig, and like your hands was his hind legs; here, I'll use this big handkerchief; and I'll tie them tight, see? Like this; ah, that's good. Ho, ho! Well, look at little Laurel, and I got your hands tied tight. Yes, by God, so I have. And you ain't a-going to squeal, are you? Cause you don't know how—and cause I'm going to take this other nice clean handkerchief *and stick it in your mouth,* by God, I'm going to stuff it in, ah, that's better, ain't it better, honey, because you can't squeal no way, and now I got you, Laurel, *get this damn dress out of the way,* and by God, hot damn, holy Jesus H. Christ, I'm a-going to stuff something else in somewhere, ah, aha, aha, *aha*— And her own cry gagged to a mumble, a mumble and shudder turned back by the fabric in her mouth and rolled angrily in reverse to poison the very soul which had sent it forth.

28

Ought to call them the Black Brigade or the Dark Avengers or something similar, said Seneca MacBean. He was going over the list of secret Regulators in his mind. He knew a man who'd dug for gold in California (well, he knew several such men, but none of them had ever found much gold) and that man spoke of this new contingent, organized so slowly, quietly, solidly, as Vigilantes. That sounded foreign to MacBean's ears, so he always used the term Regulators. He would have called them The Blacks or The Darks—he had heard of the Scots Greys—because so many were black-locked. It wasn't just the pitch which stained their faces; they were dark to begin with. Take Bill Rowe, Michigander from the Ninth Cavalry. Very swarthy as to hue. Take the fellow everybody called Limber Jim, from the Sixty-seventh Illinois. Looked like an Indian, and maybe he did have Indian blood. Well, there were even some full-blooded Indians on this team! Take Nathan Dreyfoos, take himself: both black as to hair. And take the ruling genius of the lot: he was a printer like Sen MacBean, but from Bloomington instead of from Galena; his name was Leroy Key and he was a sergeant in the Sixteenth Cavalry. Fully as dangerous to toy with as MacBean, Key had a talent for organization and planning which matched Sen's, and an outright executive capacity far exceeding the Galenan's.

Lord smiled on us when he sent Key here, said Seneca.

Key has the manner of a colonel.

And he'll *be* better than a colonel, mark my words!

I have a new recruit, Sen. I spoke to him again this morning, and he'll be at the meeting tonight. Certainly he will be accepted and sworn.

Name?

His name is Hill, a sergeant from the Hundredth Ohio Volunteers. Extremely broad shoulders and the mildest manner in the world. But—

Sen MacBean slapped the board with the tattered drawers he was washing. Don't need to tell me. I wonder I never thought of Hill before! Just goes to show how stupid I can grow. Why, when we hit Belle Isle there was a bully name of Jack Oliver, Nineteenth Indiana. Had everything pretty much his own way until one day he got to picking on an old man in A.R.'s mess. I mean Hill—that's his initials —A.R.

MacBean paused for a time as if he were considering what style of type to use to set A.R. Hill's name and initials.

A.R. says to this bully, Mister, I don't think that's a nice way to talk to an old man. Talking slowly, the way he does, kind of spelling out the words like a chorister would line a hymn. Up jumps Oliver with, Maybe you want to take it up? Well, mister, says Hill, I don't go around hunting trouble, but I generally take care of all that's sent me. . . . Oh, you should have seen it, Nate. A.R. went around that fellow like a cooper round a barrel. Oliver's front teeth were out, his ribs busted, his face looked like it had been run through a job press. He was what you might call better mannered after that.

Nathan nodded but he was still seeking recruits. Is Oliver now in Andersonville? Is he one of the Raiders? If not, possibly we could enlist him.

Nope. Scurvy. He's a sorry picture now. I saw him tother day going along Main Street. His cords had pulled in on him and he had to travel on all fours. Pitiful sight.

Six new recruits were accepted into the band at the assembly that night. Sergeant Key'd worked cleverly at organizing a screen of singers and religious exhorters. These pickets were trustworthy men who approved heartily the plan for concerted action against the raiders, but who would be prevented by age or infirmity or small stature from taking active part in any pitched battle. A sergeant named Waddell, whose home was in Kenton, Ohio, had founded a prayer meeting late in May, and from the devout boys and elders who had been regular attendants Key could levy with no fear of betrayal. As dusk came down the communicants assembled according to prearranged plan beyond Main Street but not too close to the north fence. There were a number of ordained ministers among the prisoners, and some one of these discoursed fervently, turn and turn about. There was a bearded lay preacher named Frank Ives who served his stint. . . . Brothers, I will take as my text this evening Romans Fourteen, Twelve. *So then every one of us shall give account of himself to God.*

Hymns arose simultaneously from other circles nearby.

> *My heavenly home is bright and fair,*
> *No pain nor woe can enter there;*
> *Its glittering towers the sun outshine—*
> *That heavenly mansion shall be mine.*

All hail the power of Jesus' name!
Let angels prostrate fall;
Bring forth the royal diadem—

Tho' ev'ry prospect pleases
And only man is vile—

Come, Thou Fount of every blessing—

Behind this mask of humanity and psalmody the canny destruction was in planning. The band of Regulators crouched in tight concentric circles; a few sentries walked their beats on the outskirts while Key stood tall before serious eyes watching him. It was impossible to keep raiders or their spies from knowing that something unusual and foreboding was in progress, but at least it was hoped that specific information—the personnel, equipment and tactics to be employed —might be kept from the enemy.

Key's sober nasal Illinois voice droned calmly under cover of sacred choruses.

I'm going home to die no more,
To die no more, to die no more,
I'm going home to die no more.

Bring forth the royal diadem,
And crown Him Lord of all.

Tune my heart to sing Thy grace—

Armament was the chief problem; that, and coöperation from Rebel authorities. A fear was voiced that when warfare commenced actually on a decisive scale, Wirz would make good his threat to sweep the stockade with canister. His jumping nerves might cry that here rose Insurrection, here came Riot, now the Yankees were trying to storm the gates as he had feared.

We must figure out some plan for apprising our jailers in advance.

Key, that ain't no good. Too many spies among the Paroles outside, and they'd get word to Curtis or Collins or Sarsfield or somebody in the twinkling of an eye.

That's correct, Goody. There would necessarily be the briefest of intervals between the apprisal of our intentions, and the actual attack.

But spose the Rebs refused us permission?

I don't think they would, Ned. Mike Hoare, you got anything to say on the subject?

Hoare was a slim powerful man from Jackson, Michigan, who had been captured during Dahlgren's abortive raid against Richmond. He spoke, feelingly and to the point, on the subject of armament. In battle they would be going against a horde possessed of knives, slung-shots, brass knuckles, probably some pistols. God was usually on the side with the heaviest artillery. Well. . . .

O that with yonder sacred throng
We at His feet may fall!

It took more nighttime meetings, and shrewd manipulation and bargainings by day, to equip even squad leaders with anything like decent arms. The men were determined that no more of them should commingle with that yonder sacred throng than became absolutely necessary, but that as many raiders as resisted should commingle. The Sucker Laundry and its adjacent barber shop served as a market-place where owners of weapons or incipient weapons might be questioned judiciously and persuaded to part with these essentials when bribed by community resources. MacBean and Dreyfoos gave liberally of their world's goods to this cause, and MacBean was effective as a missionary enlisting financial support. In this manner nearly two dozen makeshift knives and eight real knives were secured, together with two lead-filled billies and many improvised slung-shots; leaders worked at improvising more. But clubs would prove most effective when the army took the field, and it was lack of these implements which perplexed Key and his lieutenants. Long ago the few trees left standing in the area had been torn apart, the very roots had been excavated piecemeal and burned, every remainder of the old north boundary had vanished as if eaten by ants. Few tent poles could be found which were tough enough to serve.

Face the music, said Sen MacBean. Pine just doesn't make a good solid club. Maybe a green branch, properly cut and peeled; the rest's too brittle and splintery.

Nathan said, I should have made more pointed lances or rapiers last spring when still they could be had.

Certainly, you ought. But no use crying over spilt milk. Maybe we can take enough clubs away from the toughs before they bowl us over?

No firearms came to light during a first cautious census by the Regulators. On the hot morning of July second it became known that a shriveled little Italian of the Forty-eighth New York had died in his shebang during the night. Nathan Dreyfoos was called to the scene to act as interpreter during a debate which ensued between neighbors and fellow Forty-eighth New Yorkers. The neighbors sought to have the corpse removed immediately, the comrades wished to wait until a priest named Father Peter Whelan appeared on his rounds; he came inside nearly every day. Nathan spoke only a little Italian, but by resorting to French and Spanish he managed to persuade the survivors to convey the body to the deadline and await Father Whelan there.

The Forty-eighth New York was known commonly as the Dead Ducks or Lost Ducks (their official designation was *Les Enfants Perdus*) and it was said that every nation in Europe was represented in their ranks, and wags insisted that no two of them could speak the same language. Nathan looked down at the dirty corpse still dressed in its short-tailed jacket and kilt-like nether garment, he looked down at this morsel come so far from some olive-grown hill to give itself to Georgia soil, he pitied the morsel. In helping other lank paupers to lift their dead he felt a lump against the sunken chest and found, to his delight and astonishment, that the little man had been possessed of a small revolver of German manufacture. Apparently *L'Enfant* had never felt called upon to use or even brandish the weapon since he entered the stockade; his companions expressed obvious wonder at this discovery. Despite their shrieks, Nathan appropriated the revolver in true raider fashion and carried it away with him, as well as nine rounds of ammunition and a box of caps.

I felt that the greater good would be served, Seneca.

Course you're right. Isn't that what they call the End justifying the Means?

We could use it. Some one of us. Perhaps Key?

Key it should be. I happen to know that he shoots passing well with a pistol. You know how the bulk of us cavalrymen are, with a hand-gun: passing bad. But I was told that Key won a pig one time in a pistol match when he was with the Sixteenth. And those other Dead Ducks don't deserve such a prize. Only interesting thing I ever knew that bunch of riffraff to do was to capture and cook and eat a snake they found in the bog, last spring. Brother Nathan, did you ever eat cooked snake? No? Not even in Europe?

I have eaten eels.

Mister, to think I've got you for a comrade!

Nathan traded a haircut for some rancid grease and with this substance he scrubbed off rust which had formed, and took the stiffness out of the weapon's mechanism. Soon he had action restored to a serviceable state, and presented the revolver to Leroy Key whose firm face broke into a grin when he saw it.

Before nine o'clock that night three figures rose out of gloom beside Key's hillside shebang. The Illinois sergeant heard his name spoken.

Need to see you, Sarge. Talk with you.

The Illinoisan's first thought was, They've heard about the revolver. They mean to take it away from me.

He knew that these evening callers were not Regulators; a Regulator would have given the password on approaching the chief's tent at night; this countersign was changed daily, and on this day the countersign was *Sangamon,* and no one had said *Sangamon.*

Sergeant Key stepped out into the putrid disorder, into poultry sounds and far-worse-than-poultry smells which saturated the dusk and seemed always worse when you left the kindness of your own lodging. . . . Even rags stretched between you and the sky seemed to afford a comfort, a guardianship.

He could not have remained inside; they would have sought him out, he would have been stabbed or bludgeoned as he lay.

To the gaze of these three emissaries who squinted their challenge he seemed to stand weaponless.

He said later that he thought one of them was Mosby the Raider's man Dolan; he was almost certain that it was Dolan; he could not identify the other two.

Will you listen, Key? We people on the South Side have been hearing things.

What did you hear?

Talk of police and such.

You did?

They had been sent to kill him. Their bosses were most of them not brainy men, but they knew enough to squelch an uprising (it amounted to an uprising against authority, since from the beginning the raiders had been the supreme power operating in Andersonville) by cutting off its head. Who had talked, who had carried information? No use figuring that out, you couldn't figure it out. Too many cooks stirring this particular kettle of broth.

Is it true? They asked it naively.

Yep, said the Bloomington printer.

A tiny fire was burning some twenty yards away; it was strong enough to make a glint on the knife which showed in the hand of the nearest man. The others moved in closer, Key heard the rasp as a club or billy was drawn from under a belt. He flung up his right hand holding the fortuitous revolver, and clicked back the hammer as he lifted it. He would have fired on the instant, but felt that he must wait almost until the men were upon him. He dreaded missing one of the dusky shapes and shooting some innocent person in a hut beyond. The metallic sharp *kack* was as good as a bullet except that it did not kill. The raiders' committee fell back before the sound so rapidly that it seemed they must have anticipated Key's gesture. They ran off like cattle blundering; one of them crashed into and through a shebang, there were grunts, wails, sounds of ripping, the sound of entanglement, the sound of a big man wrenching himself loose from fabric and then thudding away after other creatures who galloped in ruthless retreat.

On the fence a nervous guard fired at the sky, you could tell from the direction of the painted flash that his musket was pointed upward as he fired. Key stood listening and deciding what to do.

He thought that he had given sufficient discouragement to these individuals, but more might creep up on him later. He hated the event more than he hated peril to himself: it was forcing the Regulators' hand. They were by no means ready for an engagement. But from now on none of them would be safe from murder under cover of darkness, nor would they be safe in daylight unless they clung together. Key released the hammer of his gun, put the revolver inside his belted jacket, and went in search of Nathan Dreyfoos. He owed his life to the present of the revolver on that day.

He called softly outside Dreyfoos's hut, and the lame voice of Private Allen said, No, he's not here.

Where's he at, son?

Gone over to MacBean's place.

In the region of the Sucker Laundry & Cleaning Co. several dark shapes were motionless as stumps while Sergeant Key approached, then detached themselves from the ground to greet him as they recognized his figure. There were MacBean, Dreyfoos, a long-armed man from the One Hundred and Eleventh Illinois known as Egypt, and Ned Carrigan from Chicago. Carrigan was a jolly youngster of enormous frame who had fought in the ring and admitted reluctantly that he had killed another pugilist with one blow during a prize fight held in a hay barn near St. Louis. Had he emerged from another environment Carrigan might have been one of the raiders; as it was he stood ready to march in phalanx with fellow Westerners.

What you doing, boys?

Talking things over.

Where's Brother Nathan? That was what Seneca MacBean called Dreyfoos continually, and Key had adopted the address.

I am here, Sergeant Key.

Key felt through darkness, found Nathan's hand, shook it with spirit. That pistol saved me, Brother Nathan.

The others pushed closer around him as he told of the experience, and there was a general cluck-clucking. Glad you're sound, Key. But that surely is a poser.

A restlessness rose within the stockade on this night, and through regions close around. It affected the mass of the living. The raiders (such as were sufficiently sensitive to recognize the thing, to feel) ascribed this uncertain tingling to the fact that a definite organization was being formed to controvert them. Key and MacBean and Limber Jim and Nathan Dreyfoos and the rest— They ascribed their nervousness to the indisputable evidence that now their enemies had knowledge of the Westerners' plan, and the hand of the Regulators might be forced to bring about calamity. The flame-spit of a sentry's gun, fired from the parapet when hoodlums ran away from Leroy Key and his revolver, had never initiated this quivering but had underlined it, punctuated it, emphasized it, shown that it was there. Camp Sumter with its thousands and the pen controlled by Camp Sumter were become a loose black jelly on the saucer of Georgia.

A boy named Dolliver felt the tremor and he thought of blackbirds. They dwelt in wavering tribes amid prairie sloughs, they clung festooned on reeds and made amiable metallic sounds; but something occurred suddenly to disturb them, and you might not descry the signal given, you might not identify the messenger. He flew in without your seeing him . . . or he could have been a hungry animal approaching soft-footed, wet-footed, intending to feed on blackbirds. He could have been a snake winding there, intending to feed on blackbirds' eggs. Whatever the peril, the redwings flocked up above grasses, glint of jewelry came off their shininess, the small throats rang with what they were saying and fearing.

A man who hailed from farther on the plains, and like the Indians had crept in a coyote's skin in order to approach buffalo herds closely, thought of buffalo as Eben Dolliver relied on birds for comparison. Where were this man's comrades of the Eighth Kansas, where were Williams and Gensarde and Freeman? Dead they were, dead during the month past. Where was Weidman? He was here, he was close, and he would not die until October. But the erstwhile buffalo hunter did not linger for long, dwelling on the tragedy of his friends, thinking of how they had rotted or were rotting, and how he himself was putrefying while still he could walk and talk. He sensed the drift of the night, sensed its peculiar qualm. In comparison he thought of a herd, and could smell fairly the bitter dusty buffalo, the oily perfume shed by kinky manes. He could feel the plain shaking like a drumhead merely because so many creatures stood and moved upon it. They were feeding quietly . . . then a surge reached them and alarm was conveyed to thick brains within the mountainous skulls. Heads lifted, eyes rolled, hoofs touched the ground, refused the ground, there was a telegraph wire stretched under dry earth, a message was tapped there. Was it arrow or bullet or wolf which would come? There was a fright not yet become a true fright (call it rumor spoken silently from cow to cow, call it legend never dignified as fact). A message reeked in the unseen telegraph wire. Which bull might read it, who could read the code? Was this disaster, or merely mosquitoes, or sharp seeds of the spear grass itching their moulting hides? Might one become reassured in time and thus stand ready to munch, chew a cud, lift a tail, let the dung go splashing? The Kansan believed vaguely that such a herd was around him. He was one member of it. In his dream he wore horns bent upon his head.

And also this was the ominous swaying and bawling of cattle who felt a storm on the way. It was sleepy clucking of poultry on lime-smeared perches (perhaps a weasel slunk like a rapid worm, skimming, twisting amid the stones on which the poultry shed was built. The weasel was trying to find a way in).

A wounded veteran of the Seven Days—one of the few such veterans now serving with the Reserves—sniffed suspiciously on the platform of Station Number Thirty-nine. He rolled his quid into his cheek, spat across the jagged chopped pine, called to a fellow guard in darkness thirty yards away.

What you say, Pokey?

Didn't say nothing. Thought you said something.

Didn't say nothing myself until now. But hain't something funny going on?

Somebody down there by the deadline?

Can't see nothing. Too blame dark. But it feels like they was up to something. Feels that way.

Station Number One, eleven o'clock and allllls wellll. Station Number Two, eleven o'clock and alllls wellll. Station Number Three . . . repeated yell, voice to voice, boy to man, man to boy, boy to boy, boy to man, man to very old man, going along the rim in yapped solo and chorus, overlapping, muttered, squealed, neglected by two guards who were asleep, finished within a minute or two, seldom derided and interrupted by prisoners in this unsubstantial night.

Men who knew cities felt the tremor of a crowd which might turn into a mob and go to breaking windows and upsetting freight cars to loot them. They thought of a mob not yet a mob, yet ready to spring into a mob if the stone were hurled or the oath were cried.

There was a Turk who had worked in a zoological garden; he understood wild animals; he knew that there were nights when lions walked unceasingly, when mothers carried their cubs into farthest corners and lay licking them, when big fierce faces rubbed against the bars. He knew that there were nights when a rumbling growl came without a reason which could be guessed, yet the growl sounded and was coughed and grunted from cage to cage. No lightning trickled above the horizon, no storm approached across the peasantry beyond the town; but electricity occupied the air. Animals smelled stronger on such a night, and this was such a night, Andersonville smelled stronger now.

MacBean said, Going to turn in, Brother Nathan?

Somehow I am not sleepy.

Lieutenant Davis, Wirz's deputy, swung sock-footed legs off his hot bed and groped around for his boots. The officer who shared Davis's quarters mumbled, Going to check the Posts?

Reckon I'll take a look around.

Not time for regular check, is it?

No, but I just can't sleep no way.

And there was a man who had spent much of his youth in fishing for mullet. He recalled the glassiness of pools amid mangrove islands, and how on a still day there might be no mullet; then suddenly the treasure would be leaping, drove after drove plunging up out of the water, throwing themselves with curve and flip, thousands of pounds of mullet racing under shallowness which had been quiescent and now so quickly was torn. In this man's thought the prison was a bay and prisoners were fish. What might occur to set them into antics beneath the salty surface, ripping out with their burnished heads, arching in long thrusts of purplish silver, high and wet, jumping by hundreds, the sun sharp upon them? Something in secret avenues of shell and sands, something moving fiercely; a summons and threat among mullet; there was something. . . .

> Now, the mayor he knew Brennan. And, I think, says he,
> Your name is Willie Brennan, ha? You must come along with me—

Devil suck you, Sarsfield! Tis Willie Collins, never Brennan.

Way I heard twas Brennan.

Och, nay, never! It's myself who trained my kiddies to sing it different. Give heed:

> Your name is Willie Collins, ha? You must come along with me—

> Oh, Collins on the moor, Collins on the moor!

Fuck Willie Collins! Laughter, laughter. . . .

Now what rat has thieved my bottle of bingo? Hand it over, or I'll tear the wattles—

They were gathered in and around the tall conical tent of Mosby the Raider (seldom called Mosby at this late day, called Willie Collins by most). The roll was a roll of the damned and damnable, the rich, the blind uncaring cruel, the selfish, the powerful, the exalted of this place. The sailors Munn and Rickson, Patrick Delaney of the Dead Rabbits, Curtis with brick-red brow and brick-thick bone above the brow, John Sarsfield the renegade hero from the One Hundred and

Forty-fourth New York: these were the leaders. If a roll of colossi had been called they would have answered Here; Willie Collins would have roared his response along with theirs. Turbulence possessed them, they drew together, drank pine-top, sent underlings with loot to the deadline to bargain for more. They said, These greenbacks are enough, and be after telling that snot of a guard I'll never pay more for a gallon; and he's to let it down in buckets with no leak to them.

> In Athol there lived a man named Jerry Lanagan;
> He battered away till he hadn't a pound—

Their cohorts sat or lay, attendants encircling the captains. The cooks cooked late, a smell of fried meat came up to vie with the wide mat of ordinary stench (and other prisoners watched this convention of monsters from a distance they hoped was safe; on scenting the meat and watching the orange reek of flames they thought of Hell. The meat of sinners was burning). Edward Blamey had learned to drink unmeasured quantities of sorghum whiskey. He was become the first drunkard in uncounted generations of stiff New Englanders, Old Englanders, Norman French. His eyeballs were laced with pink veins like silken thread tangled on oystery whiteness, but his fantastic vision still served . . . excepting in night-time, then it did not need to serve. One of the homosexuals crawled close to importune him. This fellow had been hounding Edward Blamey for some time. Edward kicked out with a strong sound stolen boot, the homosexual screamed like a frightened spinster and told Edward that he was perfectly horrid. Where was The Wrath To Come? Out yonder—oh, out yonder—stalking through the spread of tremulous hours. The Wrath To Come was kept at bay, Willie Collins could keep it at bay forever. Edward Blamey grunted, belched, rolled over on his blanket, rested his untidy head on a bent elbow, slept immediately. But he had a nightmare wherein the leaky baptistry of his Rhode Island boyhood was filled with pine-top, and Willie Collins said, Delaney, you rubber-legged louse, it's you must drink it up. Edward Blamey set to work laboriously to remove planks which formed a lid above the immersion tank; first he had to shove back the old oak pulpit, and that was a job; next he had to roll the faded greenish carpet, with its worn place where the preacher always stood; next he had to lift the planks one at a time. And when he had raised the last plank, and peered down into a dim splashing interior, there sat his own father, totally naked, bathing himself in raw burning whiskey. Mr. Blamey rolled his cold narrow gaze toward the frightened son crouched above him and said, *But if thine eye be evil*—

Edward awoke yelling. No one paid attention to him. The leaders were drunker than ever, they were boasting what they'd do if any self-appointed police came against them.

By God! That joskin Key. I'll tear his pecker off.

And the other—?

MacBean? Also a printer.

Take him at the back, Johnny boy. I'll take him in the front, same time.

Ah, but give me a chance at that Jew-boy, the Plymouth Pilgrim, him with the pointed stick!

Hell, you had your chance, and he beat you out!

Why, you son of a bitch, I'll— So he beat me, did he? Why—

Pass that canteen my way—

Coarse laughter, the bellow bursting out, uncaged cats sitting large and two-legged, the hoot and lashing of them.

Now, Brennan is an outlaw, all on some mountain high.
With infantry and cavalry to take him they did try.
But he laughed at them and he scorned at them—

Ha, and what are you saying there? *Collins,* you bastards. *Collins! Collins* is an outlaw, all on some mountain high—
Oh, it's Collins on the moor—
Bold gay and undaunted—
He batter'd away till he hadn't a pound—
Take your God damn hand off my—
Edward Blamey slept again, he slept a better sleep for a time; then he saw his father, but it was not the face of his father after all; it was the body of his father, but the face was the face of a fellow Rhode Islander whom Edward had observed in June, digging a hole and secreting something therein. Acting on this observation, raiders circled promptly to dig up the hole again and take what it contained. It contained a tiny miniature painting of the boy's mother (his branch of this Rhode Island family was well-to-do) in a gold frame set with pearls. The boy strove to defend his property with his life, and so he did until his life was taken from him along with the miniature in its frame. Edward Blamey saw his face, somehow it was the same face, both before and after what occurred; and how could that be when a two-hundred-pound man had stood upon that face and stamped it with cavalry boots?

Oh, it's Collins on the moor, Collins on the moor!
Bold, gay and undaunted stood young Collins—

Other men did not think of buffalo or blackbirds or mullet or city crowds in this midnight, because they had no knowledge of these creatures; but there was a quiet boy from a quiet shore who thought of seabirds he had seen when he walked the coast at evening. Gulls roosted far out on an island little more than a shoal, for the sea was calmer than usual and there was dry space for them to roost upon. They settled in white and dark and golden throngs as the last sun caught them (the boy thought of angel throngs). He looked away from the sea and island and sitting gulls, and progressed homeward along the shore path . . . it was like a moorland of his ancestors' past, with wraiths to be avoided if one traveled when the fog came in. The boy walked on, carrying his heavy wooden tool-kit slung by a wide strap over his shoulder, for at seventeen he was close to being an expert at his craft, and had been repairing a dory that afternoon. Again he looked to the east, and there they were, there they were, rising. Some matter had caused dissent or alarm among the gulls, they boiled up like masses of dark leaves flung in October. Sun was down and hidden, no longer were the seabirds colored or angelic with natural cream or ivory. They flaked in a storm-cloud of black fragments, whirled in a peevish choir, their penetrating squall came across the crush of waves on rocks. Oh, what had caused this uneasiness and hurled them into the wind again? Something, something.
The devout man named Frank Ives said, Sleep's impossible. Are you awake, Brother Ellicott?
Yes, Brother Ives. So're Berwick and Harper.
Dunlop, over there? Are you awake, Brother Dunlop?
Brother Dunlop squeezed the swollen fingers of his left hand with the unswollen (yet soon to be swollen, soon to be decayed) fingers of his right hand. I'm here. Shall we pray?

I had been thinking that we might read in response. Been thinking of Second Corinthians, also First Thessalonians.

We got sufficient light, Brother Ives?

Private Harper said eagerly, I've a lot of pine splinters left, wrapped in my jacket.

Pass them over. Ah, there's still a coal or two.

I'll blow, said Ellicott. Soon there was flame showing, soon there was enough light to read by and would be for some time if splinters were fed into the blaze with care. The men of this shebang pushed in a wad around the bright tiny wavering flare, and Frank Ives turned to Page Sixty-three of his ragged Hymnal, whereon one of his favorite Readings was printed. Move your head a little, Brother. No—this side—put it under Alex's arm. Now we can all see.

I know Corinthians and Thessalonians practically by heart, all four books of them, said young Percival Berwick. Don't need to see. Read away, Brother.

For all things are for your sakes, that the grace, being multiplied through the many, may cause the thanksgiving to abound unto the glory of God.

Chant of response, tuned in that lower octave used by congregations, the same sound as in a Mass, the same faith as in a Mass, the faith to make gangrene of secondary importance, faith to make a soul exult and feel that it was hung on an accompanying Cross, and would soon be with Someone in Paradise. *Wherefore we faint not; but though our outward man is decaying, yet our inward man is renewed day by day.*

The starving Frank Ives read serenely, *For our light affliction, which is for the moment, worketh for us more and more exceedingly an eternal weight of glory.*

Low concerted murmur of the response, the S-sounds laving as it were read in the village churches most of these people had known before they came to endure Andersonville. *While we look not at the things which are seen, but at the things which are not seen: for the things which are seen are temporal; but the things which are not seen are eternal.*

Their neighbors—some of them—had cat-called before, then had grown tired of jeering when they learned that they could not affect the radiant purpose of these consistently practicing Christians. Neighbors tolerated songs and services, or else paid no attention; some neighbors died, some moved away; one was now a convert and living in this shebang. He was Dunlop, the man with the gangrened hand. He would speak Salvation as long as breath was left to him, with the ardor which only newly made zealots may know.

Outside the fence a patterned scrap of brown light moved reluctantly along the hard-trodden path communicating from sentry station to sentry station. In some instances Lieutenant Davis went to the trouble of swinging his heavy body up the ladder-rungs and standing beside the guard for a while, staring down at the interior, rubbing his chin whiskers as he gazed. Then down the ladder again, and on to the next station, carrying his tinkling lantern, walking with the flap of his holster unbuttoned and often letting his hand slide around the revolver butt to find reassurance. Close, so close to the angry beasts, close to storied crocodiles. They were lying in their mud only a couple of rods away. They could do anything. Think how they had melted away that old north fence on the night of June eighteenth. If they could nibble a pine wall—timbers twenty feet tall, including the portion dug out of the ground, and extending seven hundred and eighty feet from east wall to west wall— If they could chew that to vanishment in a single night, what might they not now effect if they chose? Look sharp, there, his heavy voice drawled to the perched sentries in those instances where he felt too weary to climb. Hear me, now. You watch sharp, you hear?

Yes, sir.

You see anything queer, anything different?

Well, sir, they seem to be doing an awful lot of circulating.

What you mean, there, circulating?

Kind of keep moving about.

And at Post Number Forty he would hoist himself up the ladder again. He was a coarse lustful young man more or less popular with the troops he commanded, and hated not too cordially by the prisoners. When he became brutal he was brutal only through lack of feeling and not in a calculated fashion. He was the sort of man who might have found delight in the act of rape, if lured to commit it through a girl's petting; and then he would have felt sorry afterward, and would have begged abject pardon . . . he would have brought the girl later some ugly but (to him) expensive gift. His small pale eyes protruded abnormally, his mouth was loose, he should have worn a full beard instead of chin whiskers to conceal his weakness from the world. He was not above taking bribes; on the other hand he declared loudly that it was a shame and a sin to see how these God damn Yankees were compelled to live. Man couldn't keep no self-respect whilst living like a hog, no sir. Secretly he was very much afraid of the Yankees, especially afraid of the lean silent ones. Thus he swaggered, talked loudly whenever he entered the stockade, glared when Yanks came up to him with their petitions, pushed his eyes even farther out of his head and stood scowling while he listened, but he did listen. Often he granted the prisoners' requests. Yes, he would ask Captain Wirz to release Willis Lowell, citizen teamster, from the stocks—Lowell had been there three days, that was sufficient punishment for his offense. Yes, he would permit three men from the Eleventh Kentucky Cavalry to go outside and pick berries— they had a touch of scurvy, but still only a touch, berries might save their lives. No, emphatically, he would not demand that Lucas Rensem, Fifteenth Missouri, be put into the hospital—that was solely up to the stockade surgeons, he could not go around interfering with stockade surgeons in their performance of their duties (besides, it would have been too much trouble for Lieutenant Davis).

He insisted that he had a bad heart, he could not perform any heavy work, any task too arduous. He took refuge in his disability the moment trouble loomed. Lieutenant Davis hated and feared trouble of any kind. He declared repeatedly that he was an easy-going man and he liked people to be easy-going. When Wirz screamed at him (as he screamed at anyone and everyone except his small daughter when he was in the mood to scream—which was every hour, and with increasing frequency)— When Wirz screamed at him, Lieutenant Davis's fat face sagged in offended alarm, and he put a fat hand on the breast of his tight-fitting gray jacket and cried in an injured tone, Captain Wirz, sir, now you quit abusing me; I'll enter complaint to the colonel; mind, now, I got a bad heart—

Ach, you and your bad heart! Also a bad brain you got!

Captain, mind, now— I ain't a-fooling. Surgeon said I got a greatly enlarged heart, and can't suffer such abuse no way. I warn you, I'll just fall out!

It is I wish you *would* fall out!

Just keep on like that if you want a corpse on your hands! Gluey tears seeped in Davis's eyes.

What a fat lazy corpse I would have once.

He was lazy in truth, but also he held a certain addiction to duty (again, if the duty were obvious and apparent to all, and if any lapse on his part would be apparent to all). The threatening magic of these hours had drawn him from his cot, sent him patrolling, hauled him up to several of the platforms.

He went aloft for the last time at the southwest corner, breathing heavily from his mile-long journey and the climbings and descents. Davis eyed the high-blazing raider fires with resentment, and listened to the Brennan On the Moor, Collins On the Moor song and imprecations accompanying. Now you just bet they're a-whooping it up.

Sure are, Lieutenant.

If twas solely them burglars from New York— He said this much aloud, and then realized that he should not reveal his perturbation to the round-shouldered child who leaned on his musket beside him. Davis descended, contemplating responsibility on every rung of the ladder, fearing as always that the ladder might break, feeling inexpressible relief when again he stood on the ground, and yet feeling a persecuted sadness that any momentous decision must be his. If he called Wirz from bed, and Wirz decided that nothing was wrong with the stockade's population, Wirz would make him sweat for it. But if some conflict did develop during the remainder of the night, if the dreaded outbreak did occur, if twenty-five thousand brutes and cripples pushed against one of those gates, hammering even only with their heads and their fists— If they built a stairway of the dead, if they piled up only a thousand dead men and then twenty-four thousand living men mounted on their bodies to flow over the stockade in a filthy tide, as all had feared that they were capable of doing—

Davis heard the One o'clock and all's well begin to wail along the parapet as his feet took the path toward headquarters. That cry decided him. There were several hours of darkness remaining; he could not shudder through those hours single-handed. Now he wished for Henry Wirz longingly. Even if Wirz cursed him, brandished his fists under Davis's little knob of a nose, told him that he would see to it that Davis got no leave for six months at least— It would be near to a comfort.

The superintendent's office was closed and dark and locked. Davis's lantern revealed the sentry stretched on a bench at the right-hand side of the door with several hound puppies intertwined on his chest.

Wake up there, you. By God, you ought to be court-martialed and shot, and that sure is the truth. I got a great mind to—

Lieutenant, sir, I ain't asleep. No, sir. Just laying here playing with the pups— Puppies flew, the sentinel got up stiffly, white-haired and shaking, and reached for his gun. You got to remember that I'm an old man, nigh on to seventy, and I do get tuckered a-standing up.

Where's Red Cap? He round here somewheres?

Sleeping inside the shack, Mister Lieutenant.

Say, Sir, you old goat.

Yes, sir. Sir!

Davis slapped on the closed door with his flabby palm and bawled, Whah-ye! Red Cap! This yell of his was the lieutenant's traditional signal for order, for attention; it was a summoning and a prelude. The more sprightly among the prisoners used to imitate Davis's cry very much to his wrath, but the fomentation of a Davis rage was not to be feared like a Wirz rage. Some believed that in bawling, Whah-ye! the man was in fact calling, Where are ye? Others said that it was a corruption of the time-honored Oyez uttered by a bailiff. In any case it attracted immediate compliance, and now Red Cap arose from his pallet and answered at the door. He slid the big bolt and peered out, his tousled hair spun gold in the lantern flickers. He had been a drummer boy with Company I, Tenth West Virginia Infantry and was fourteen years old at the time of his capture. Wirz took him Outside as personal orderly and messenger; there was something faunal and winning about the boy. It may have been that Henry Wirz thought to save him from those deviates who slunk among the raiders or followed their sailor protectors like mincing bitches. The youth's name was Ransom Powell, but prisoners and Rebels alike called him Little Red Cap, and they pictured the home he came from as a kind and lovely place, with a mother who wore pink aprons, baked pans of spicy gingerbread, and taught Little Red Cap his prayers. His face shone eternally for he was well fed, he starved not, and in his favored position he could do much for less fortunate comrades. Little Red Cap smuggled everything from hopeful tidings to pork ribs and onions whenever an errand took him back into the stockade.

Want you to go seek the captain, boy.

Yes, sir. Want I should ride? Course the captain took the Old Gray Mare home with him.

I reckon you do have to ride, you little Yankee limb! Can't walk all that way, and I want Captain Wirz bad, and I want you to hustle! You take my own Mouse mule.

Quickly the boy filled and lighted another lantern and put on his tiny shoes . . . small shoes indeed on his small feet, they might have been cobbled by elves, they were solid patches. In rare good humor Wirz had promised the boy boots, but thus far no boots could be found small enough to fit him. Ransom Powell clapped upon his head the crimson peaked cap with its tarnished gilt lace which had given him his name. Davis watched the freckled light go bobbing down to the pen where Mouse was kept; soon the lantern was blown out, and Davis could hear the shrill eager voice of Red Cap ordering Mouse into speed on the narrow road, and could hear him switching the mule's flank, and it sounded as if Mouse were bucking in resistance. Dimly it seemed to Davis that even a domestic animal might feel the tautness of this hour. Davis sat heavily on the step and felt the pressure of apprehension wrapping him like an overcoat unwelcome in July.

He growled at the sentry. Old Man, you get up there and walk your beat like you're sposed to. Don't you know nothing? Joe Brown ought to feed you to the hogs!

. . . Later he grew too nervous to sit idly, and went slouching off to the South Gate, and listened to the guttural hum and wailing of that terrifying herd beyond the up-ended logs; and then he thought that he was too tired to stand listening longer, and he thought that his heart was swelling large and painful within his ribs. Some day twill bust, he thought drearily. Just like a bottle busting in a fire. . . .

Davis considered that Wirz was long overdue when at last Wirz arrived; indeed the captain was long overdue, for he had been operating on his forearm when Little Red Cap arrived at the Boss house. He had been picking out scraps of honeycombed bone with a steel knitting needle. Henry Wirz cursed Little Red Cap vehemently (this was not unprecedented but it was unusual. Like many another of the most savage of his type, Wirz had a genuine fondness for children. He remembered his own childhood with nostalgia, thought that he had been happy then, cried sometimes when he thought of Paul and Louisa Emily left perforce with their grandparents in Switzerland. *Ja*, so tall they had grown by this time; and it was nearly a year since he had seen them. Nowadays he was impatient with his stepdaughters because they were of awkward and seemingly unmanageable age; they had been sweet tiny creatures when first he knew them, but now their skirts were long, the girls were flighty, unpredictable, openly disobedient at times. Coralie was still wistful and birdlike, she was only nine-and-a-half, not quite nine-and-a-half).

So God damn you, you bad Little Red Cap, you!

Captain, please sir, I couldn't help it. Lieutenant Davis ordered me to come fetch you—

Nothing you know why I should be fetched? God damn, did you *ask? Nein!* So all the way to that damn stockade I must worry, worry, worry. Now, you bad Red Cap, this strip of linen you hold here. . . . Nah—*here* you hold it, I hold it *here.* Now you wind it once. *Ja*—son of a bitch—I tell you—not *once* only around the arm. Wind, wind, *wind!* Sweat gleamed on Henry's thin forehead, fell from his sharp nose, made wet places on the thickening bandage. The pressure on the tangled tissues became a steady ache; yet it was a benefit; frogs in the arm kept piping as always, Let me out, let me *out,* and the bandage would keep those frogs in check.

Seneca MacBean said one day to Nathan Dreyfoos, after a particularly lively encounter with the superintendent, You know, Brother Nathan, Wirz is the most even-tempered man I ever saw in my life. He's always foaming mad.

So he was foaming mad as he rode through threatening woods toward the pen, and little Ranny Powell wisely and cheerfully fell farther back into darkness, pretending that Mouse would go no faster. So Wirz was foaming mad when he encountered the unhappy Davis in thick hot smell (Andersonville seemed to smell worse in the night than in the daytime, and how could that be?). True to the lieutenant's lugubrious prophecy, Henry swore that he would grant no leave to any subordinate so derelict in his duties. . . .

For why you call me from *mein* house? All the nights I got to work too, all the daytimes too? You say nobody is shot, nobody is making escaping, *oder* they not set fire to the fence, *ja?* So what are you good for, you damn Davis?

Captain, now you quit. You know I got a weak heart and—

Ja, a fat ass you got also, lazybones!

All right, by God! Just you go up on some of them sentry stations. I bet you never heard them act like this afore, not so's you could notice it. . . .

The captain went blaspheming to the southwest corner of the prison and climbed to the same platform where Davis had stood before him. He came down so quickly that the aggrieved exhausted young officer was frightened anew. Why you not call me more quicker? *Gott,* I think those bears they try to force the gate!

Captain, they ain't tried, yet. But they make so much noise and—Kind of act so funny, all over the place, and—

Now you get the Officer of the Day, you have him get two guards on every station. Not *one,* God damn son of a bitch, get *two* on every station! How you say— Double these no good guards! Now I go over to the fort, I get that battery commander from his bed out!

The battery commander on the star fort was not in his blankets or on them; he was sitting unsteadily on the earth fort above the rude fascines, smoking his pipe. He was nearly as glad to see Wirz as Davis had been. He declared that he had not slept all night. The guns were already shotted up.

And fuses in those touch-holes you got?

No, the fuses had not been inserted. He was always fearful of an accident. . . .

Better accidents we have than Yankees break out maybe!

Well, he couldn't insert fuses without an order. . . . And, listen to me, you damn Switzer, you don't rank over me, and don't go giving me no orders.

One order you get from the colonel, and that damn quick! Wirz went fuming away, and decided also that he would ask that an order be issued to have every piece of artillery manned completely until daylight, and that the gunners not only have the fuses inserted in the touch-holes but that they be standing literally with lanyards in their hands. Thus at a second's signal the stockade could be raked.

Momentarily Henry Wirz closed his strained sore eyes as he rode. Not with those eyes but with the lenses of memory he saw once more that tussle in the pit at Bern, and stood frosted in terror at sight of it. Oh, the bears. . . .

But there was no plan for a sundering of the barrier, no intention for a mass swarming. The weird impatience could not be chained to a fact unless there existed some cloud of precognition, which spilled to affect nearly every man of the region and shiver him into alarm. Far beyond fancied cities and blackbirds' swales and upland prairies where the buffalo pawed and Arapahoes were tented— Thousands of miles away, that restive spirit might have risen like a wind with no one to say its origin. It seemed to come from the top of the world and perhaps from airless space beyond the top of the world—the restiveness of time itself which will not be quiet or comforted, but travels unceasingly. And where, a few more wise and humble men thought, does time begin? And what shall be the ending, and shall there be one?

29

Implacably the sun came up steamed and polished. Ready to fry you, said the sun. Yes, yes, this day you shall fry; forty or fifty of you shall be carried off on the sizzled tray of the day when the day is through; the last grease shall be cooked from those forty or fifty; declare them to be cracklings; put them into the loaf of the soil, and I shall bake the whole loaf anew on the next day.

Old Sol's going to get us again, prisoners said. Hell, I'd ruther have Old Boo get me. Hell you would; you cried your ass off in the rain, all of June.

Among pine barrens north of the Anderson depot a locomotive halted, steam was down, there was no wood left on the fuel tender. Cars bumped to a halt and three Negroes descended with their axes from the tender. A rail fence little more than a relic yielded to their blows, but there were only a few panels of fencing left there; then they had to attack a scorched fallen tree. In less than an hour's time the tender was loaded once more, steam was up, the line of decrepit box cars dragged toward Anderson, axles rattling and trusses loose and clanking.

Three hundred and fifty-two strained embittered Unionists were counted from the cars. A majority were native to the mountains of western Virginia, and thus were objects of particular scorn to guards who refused to admit the existence of the new State of West Virginia (those who had heard of it. Little Red Cap was accepted and favored because of his youth and charm and handsome vitality. At the worst the Secessionists put him down as a misguided child, they did not think of him as a traitor to his State).

Duly enrolled as prisoners, the West Virginians began to file in through the North Gate. Edward Blamey blinked away his alcoholic tears, spotted the vanguard, evalued their rolls and haversacks, reported to his master. Collins's Raiders were thus the first into the fray, but other bands were not far behind. They descended upon the newcomers with ferocity unmatched. It was as if they were driven by an impulse which had not ruled the raiders when they slugged merely through cupidity, merely through the craving to exert their strength. The night of unrest had tempered them with beastliness. Haversacks flew from hand to hand and were distributed through the air, jackets were ripped, buttons flew, sleeves were pulled out. In earlier months there had been a pretense of innocence, a masquerading as humans on the part of the raiders. That was when incursions were limited to nighttime; and later the bulk of them might lounge or stroll or play chuck-a-luck, elaborately aloof from strife when six hooligans descended on, say, two Westerners who happened to own a poncho. But in this sharp hot morning the evil element rose in an unrestrained body, they were a single baboon. There were a few stray calls of *Raiders!* from more knowledgeable prisoners who fled the area; then a hush lay over the two or three thousand people who stood near at hand, backing off, pressed together in ragged watching ranks, an audience who had paid their admission in the coin of long starvation, the coin of sickness and penury.

Raider forces whirled around the West Virginians like the outer wheel of a corn-sheller cranked by Furies; and each newcomer was a cob to be expelled from the inner mass, to be hurled out, minute by minute, with all his kernels wrenched off. A hand was grasped, an arm was jerked, a bloody bewildered youth staggered free; he collapsed to feel the pounding throbbing draining swelling of his smashed nose, to wonder at scratches seared along his naked ribs, to wonder why he lived barefoot and in his under-drawers, to wonder why and how he lived at all. A quarter of an hour earlier he had been a man, an entity defeated and captured, but still a man with a name and with masculine pride.

He had been Miller Sprouse, Sixth West Virginia Cavalry, age eighteen, a brown-eyed brown-haired brown-faced person with small hard freckled fists and owning better-than-ordinary skill with a carbine. Here he was, captured, but guards on the train had been—most of them—wounded veterans missing a hand or an eye or an ear here and there; and thus they had been stern but decent. Miller Sprouse owned a good uniform, shabby but clean, and he had a rubber raincoat rolled around his blanket, he had a canteen, a spoon, fork, pocketknife, soap, a comb; he had a well-equipped housewife, a diary in which he scribbled painfully a few misspelled lines each day (this was an especial promise made to a girl named Tildy Freeborn; and when he came home they would be married and would raise corn, melons and younguns on a small farm on Beasley Run; and his father had said that Miller could pay him for the farm, so much per year, depending on how crops did. He was to help his father and Tildy's father mine coal during cold weather). Miller Sprouse had sixteen dollars and fifty-seven cents in currency; the Rebel guards had taken nothing except his cap and the old silver watch which wound with a key, and the key had been lost. He had his health, his identity, he had high hopes of escape; folks said that Andersonville was just a place with a fence around it, and surely that would be more promising than imprisonment in a tobacco warehouse or an abandoned factory in a city; you ought to be able to dig a hole and crawl out, or something.

Then suddenly a gate closed. They were crowded into a cubicle; they said, Hell, this is a little bitty prison, and people laughed about it. Then another gate opened ahead, and they passed into unavoidable unbreathable smell like all the untended privies in all the United States put together; it smelled also like dead skunks or polecats before birds got at them and cleaned them up; it smelled also like Grandpa Abbott smelled when he was dying of that there throat-cancer. A roar and a howl, and thousands and thousands of hairy shaggy black-faced devils swaying all around the place, and then lifted another roar with a different sound. Suddenly he thought that Paul Handland and Scott McConkey were fighting, just ahead of him; but no, they were fighting with two or three strangers, great big fellows. Something hit young Miller Sprouse on the side of the head, and he saw stars, and through the stars he saw a wide scarred face like a monkey's face (he had seen a monkey once in a circus)—that was how the face looked, except much larger. A hand twisted across his shoulder and jerked on Miller's blanket roll; he said, By Gol, and he punched and twisted and gulped. Something struck him in the belly, it felt like a cannon-ball driven against him. He was on the ground, gasping for breath, unable to find any breath in the mass of struggling bodies. Hands fought over him, his jacket was twisted, they like to pulled his arms out of the sockets as they pulled that jacket off; his shoes were gone, his trousers hauled from his kicking legs; he was propelled, shunted, flung; he landed painfully on dirty ground again; he was peeled, shucked, shelled; why was he here, where was he, what had happened, what was his name, he was half naked, marred, bruised. Still he couldn't get his breath, it seemed that his ribs were cracked, he could scarcely lift his left arm, one eye was closing, why, what, when, how, what had happened, why?

Seneca MacBean said, It's the beat.

Nathan Dreyfoos took his brooding gaze from the scene and looked a question.

I say it's the beatingest!

Leroy Key nodded. Worst yet. What you think, Brother Nathan?

Nathan thought, This is the repetition of history before our eyes. There comes no answer from philosophy, religion, morality. There is but one answer to a manifestation of brute strength; that is a manifestation of greater brute strength.

Aloud he said, Have we the strength?

That's as may be. Think so, Seneca?

Beyond him the silent Limber Jim scowled his half-breed scowl.

Key swallowed. Shall we put it to a vote? If we try now, and get whipped— That'd be the end.

Mister. The halting voice of the mighty Ohioan, A. R. Hill. There ain't no need to vote. Them roughs have really put it to us.

Get clubs, somebody said.

Anyhow we'll make a try for it. Come on, Brother Nathan.

Key, MacBean and Dreyfoos moved toward the North Gate. The struggle was done, it had been completed with incredible speed. The last of the raiders trailed triumphantly toward the South Side, waving trophies. Feists and hyenas loped ahead, bound to explore the haversacks they'd taken; Willie Collins and Pat Delaney strolled almost benignly in the rear. Willie was counting greenbacks, Delaney drinking from a bottle. A howling began on the South Side in the vicinity of the raiders' pavilion; there ensued a private tussle, men came crowding and pushing and punching, to see. A collection of obscene cards had been found in a pocket of one of the stolen jackets. They were of the sort vended by unscrupulous sutlers—made in Germany, it was said, and colored gaily. They depicted mass orgies in which men and women copulated on sofas, beds, tables, even on the floor. The ungodly had leered at them before, but all old cards were long since defaced or lost or handled into ruin; these were bright, they were new and trim; the boy who'd owned them crouched moaning at the end of Main Street, spitting out blood and splintered teeth. His fellows sat weeping or cursing, stripped to the hide.

Little groups of kindly intentioned prisoners assembled to do what they could, to offer sips of water, bits of corn pone. This was the most flagrant assault which had ever occurred, and affecting by far the greatest number, and was pursued with swiftness beyond imagination. The bulk of the helpless Yankees appeared stunned by it.

They were stunned further a moment later at the latest pronouncement of the prison superintendent. Almost simultaneously news was posted at both North and South Gates. A general wail ensued: Wirz said that no rations would be issued that day. He hinted that he might not issue any more rations until the prisoners had seen to it that no such disgraceful episodes would be repeated.

Puts it up to us with a vengeance, said Seneca.

Actually, Nathan told him, we would seem to have Wirz on our side.

Key started toward the deadline but MacBean pulled him back. Key, you got folks to go home to. I have none. Deadline's an infernal jumpy business, with all these trundle-bed soldiers so nervous on the trigger. He pushed fairly up to the scantling and was greeted by a gun muzzle from Station Number Eight. We need to speak to Captain Wirz, he called to the calico hat behind the gun.

He ain't here, Yyyank. Get off'n that deadline!

I'll get, but you get Wirz.

I'll ask the sergeant when he comes round. Get back, you. Hear me?

I hear you, but you get Captain Wirz.

They waited in staring sun for more than twenty minutes, but after a time Nathan believed that he heard the guard talking with someone on the path outside. They hoped for the best, they knew that spies were watching them, they prayed only that raiders, emboldened by their morning's feat, might not charge in mass attack upon Regulators or suspected Regulators before the ranks were filled. Presently the wicket in the North Gate squealed open and the plump face of Lieutenant Davis appeared.

Whah-ye!

We don't want you, Lieutenant. We want your boss. The three moved toward the wicket.

What you want to see him about? He's busy.

Tis important.

A matter of life and death, said Nathan Dreyfoos.

All of that, said Key.

Davis's puffy little eyes looked their alarm. I'll let the three of you into the enclosure here; but you better be sure it's important or the captain will make you smoke.

Course, said MacBean, settling his long shape in shade of the palisade— Course we're correct. Whole prison's a matter of life and death.

Death, mainly.

If we prevail, said Nathan, it will become a matter of life for some who otherwise would have died.

Blame you for a philosopher, Brother Nathan.

A very childish one.

They relaxed in the gift of shade. There was no real shade within the prison except in the best-constructed shebangs. Here, in this cubicle surrounding the North Gate, a fifteen-foot height of logs built a barrier against the scorch and would until the sun reached its zenith; in that same hour the western end of the cubicle would begin to furnish shade. Davis had gone, but he left one armed guard beside the outer gate. Suddenly this guard jumped aside almost guiltily as the outer wicket was jerked open. Henry Wirz tripped across the sill. He wore his calico waist with no collar—there was a naked collar-button showing below his Adam's apple—and the waist was wet with perspiration, and he bore his arm in its black sling. The three prisoners got up quickly and moved to meet the smaller man. He stood with thin hot face lifted toward them, beard stringy and damp, angry eyes jumping.

Captain Wirz, sir, said Leroy Key.

To me you come to beg rations? *Nein.* I have said it, it will be so: no rations you get today!

We're not here to beg for rations.

You I know not. Him—pointing to Nathan—I know not. You—to MacBean—I know. Speak it out once, you bad sergeant. *Was gibt's?* You want you should go in the stocks again?

Not so's you could notice it. What we want is clubs.

For why you should get clubs, God damn?

To handle those raiders.

Wirz swore in German, then in English. To the surprise of the others Nathan Dreyfoos began to speak laboriously in German. Almost no words of German had passed his lips in several years; still, there was the similarity to Yiddish, and he was getting on tolerably when Wirz interrupted him with a sharp gesture.

Parlez-vous français?

Oui, Monsieur le Capitaine.

The conversation was continued and concluded in French, at which Nathan was more proficient than Wirz. Still the linguistic barrier fenced them apart from the rest of mankind at this moment; Henry Wirz felt inferior when compelled to speak in English, as he was compelled to speak it through most of his waking hours. His inferiority begat an underlying resentment to sustain the heap of his other resentments. This was sensed by Nathan Dreyfoos, it was the reason he had attempted German.

Leroy Key, capable commander though he was, might not have obtained the promise of armament. Wirz would have been dyed in suspicion because of the Bloomington printer's essential American qualities, his essential Yankeeness. Seneca MacBean would not have persuaded Wirz to furnish clubs: already MacBean had tried to escape, he might be planning some new trick when he appeared with an artless request for Rebel cooperation.

But Dreyfoos was recognizable to the superintendent as a European whatever his nativity. Wirz held the ancient Teutonic-Swiss distrust of Jews; and as they talked he became hurtfully aware of the tall young man's culture; Nathan's fund of culture exceeded Wirz's obviously. Nevertheless this employment of French brought back student days, young days, better days. It suggested old Doctor Cordier and Bucheton and Jacques and Annette and Mimi and Louis Modave (young things, gone, some dead, Bucheton scorned but still representative of youth and freedom) and other boys and girls of the past who danced together and drank together and worked together and made love as in a careless mural depicting some opera. In the long ago, when Henry Wirz spoke chiefly in French, his arm had not pained him, it had not been pierced by hot iron and made into a draining hurt. Fate had not then compelled him to superintend the mess of muck and vagabonds which now he was called to boss. Each flowing nasal phrase, spoken and heard, was redolent of a past superior to this baking hour with sunshine flaring and hordes of human vultures to be detested for their dirtiness as Henry detested slum-dwellers because of their poverty.

Nathan spoke briefly but impressively of the Regulators. He pointed out that they were mainly non-commissioned officers, men accustomed to discharging responsibility. If given the help of Confederates they might conceivably bring about an orderly regime within the stockade which had not abided before. Prisoners existing in a city ruled by surly barbarians were assuredly less tractable than prisoners existing without the dread of robbery, kicks, strangulation: was that not plain to see? If the raiders were put down a better authority might prevail, and certain worries of Andersonville's supervisors would be lessened or even vanished. This made sense to Wirz, no matter what fright he had endured throughout the previous night. Promptly Nathan won the promise of clubs.

He won more than that. There had been fear that clubs might be torn from the hands of those who wielded them, as happened so often in brawls. Therefore Nathan asked that each club be provided with a loop of hemp or rawhide, as in a policeman's billy club. Henry Wirz nodded and believed that he could furnish these thongs.

Time was of the essence. Wirz said that he would order a company of Reserves to the Yeomans' sawmill at once. The sawmill, though not now in operation, had spawned a large trash heap. Quantities of seasoned hardwood of odd sizes and lengths could be found there.

And additional rope, Nathan insisted. With which to tie our prisoners.

This I give you.

When it comes to that, said MacBean, where we going to put the bastards on trial?

Key requested, Might we use one of these gate cubicles for a place of detention, maybe a court room?

Was—?

Nathan explained in French. Again Wirz agreed on grounds of practicality. But he said that they must not take too long about the trial of their prisoners; they must be quick, efficient.

Got to be quick and efficient about the whole blame business.

They thanked Wirz for his coöperation and trusted secretly that no vagary would cause him to change his mind. They returned to the stockade to assemble squads of Regulators.

Had it not been for a broken grindstone, Ira Claffey might not have been forewarned of the encounter which was to take place, he would not have witnessed it.

It was share and share alike in these times of stringency: the grindstone at the Yeoman place had been broken beyond repair several months earlier, and in this week the big shining Scooper had appeared with a cart, to borrow the Claffey grindstone and sharpen Mrs. Barney Yeoman's hoes, knives, axes, other implements. Now he came driving to return the stone, and Jonas and Jem lifted it from the cart. In shadows of the implement shed Ira heard the deep-voiced conversation of the slaves, punctuated as always by their falsetto laughter. Scooper was guiding his mule down the lane when Ira walked out to see that the grindstone was undamaged and had been returned to its proper situation under the low roof built to shelter it.

Big doings, Mastah!

What say, Jonas?

With them Yankees. They going fight!

It came out that a party of soldiers had visited the Yeoman sawmill to seek for hardwood fragments in trash heaps, fragments which, according to information furnished by Scooper, were to be made into bludgeons. Scooper had sworn that this was true: he had seen it with his own eyes. No telling what those Yankees might do next. The soldiers were cutting the cudgels to size, and fastening a loop to each club.

He say all them Yankees set to kill each other today, Mastah.

Save us folks the trouble, said Jem with patriotic virtue.

Ira told the black men, I think Scooper must be mistaken. Do you get on with your rebuilding of that fence. He returned to his work in the shed, cataloguing seeds which had been dried from the choicest of the earlier vegetable crops. But Ira could not rid himself of the bizarre notion which the hands' conversation had evoked. At last he put his pencil down, locked the shed, and started deliberately toward the stockade. Tension of the night now lay over the sunburnt region as an implacable silence. Ira quickened his pace. When he had passed the star fort and looked back to see cannoneers at their posts he forced himself to go even faster. Sentry shacks loomed: two of the Georgia Reserves instead of one stood on every platform, and Ira identified officers ganged at those stations nearest the gates. At the post by the south corner the fat figure of Lieutenant Davis, wearing his familiar ragged straw hat, went toiling up the ladder. At the next post were two guards. Ira mounted to the platform and looked into the shrunken face of Floral Tebbs. A bearded Reserve with frightened eyes stood behind the boy.

What's ado, Flory?

Them prisoners, Mr. Claffey, sir. Just you look.

Beyond the marsh, where the slope piled steeply toward the north, the hillside had become a mosaic. This was a mosaic composed of Yankee faces by the thousands. The prisoners congregated, raw shoulder to raw shoulder, thin belly crowded above thin buttocks; if they were toys, and had been placed so by many busy children, they could not have been packed more securely. Above each mat of tangled hair was a portion of another countenance. Some way speedily, without plan or reckoning, those mobs had managed to sort themselves for observation. There was no hill, no bare mud to be seen, no shebangs—nothing but this studding of fierce small faces. Here was their amphitheatre: they had found it, were employing it.

Denizens of the southern area had drawn back, squeezing perilously near the deadline in a crescent; it was a crescent which lapped from both ends into the battle array of the raiders. Ira had heard of raiders, as who had not, yet he was unable to single the beasts out, designate them as such. He saw only that the core of the throng—massing near the conical tent close to South Street—was composed of men in prime, men of stature, some wearing better garments than Ira wore. He wondered who might dare to come against them. Then, picking their way up the slope from creek and bridge and marsh, he saw a column of men deploying with military precision into a wider rank, becoming a sickle blade as they reached the top of the hill. He thrilled to observe that many of these prisoners were of a stature comparable to the hoodlums at the summit.

There had been a tactical error on the part of the raiders, in their not pushing ahead to resist volunteers approaching from the north. The cat-walk and its approaches were narrow; they could have been held indefinitely. Forces attempting to move by flanks through the adjacent mire would have been bogged down in the most literal fashion. But the raiders' supreme self-confidence was born justifiably of a thousand successes speckled with a scant dust of failures. Their assault on the West Virginians that morning had strengthened belief in their own invulnerability.

Key instructed his lieutenants, Proceed with all caution, approach in silence. Then, at the first stroke of encounter, drive with every ounce you've got.

The raiders were expending precious breath on obscenities and threats. Man for man, no matter how ample their diet of recent months, they were inferior in condition to the Westerners now breathing in their faces— Westerners who came without a word to say. (No orders were cried. Their plan had been dinned into every man's brain.) The raiders were soaked in pine-top, they'd caroused through-out the night into this day.

The front rank of the attacking force feinted toward the right, then veered obliquely to the center where the most gigantic of their enemies were grouped, and their supporting flanks veered accordingly.

Brother Nathan, said Seneca, I'll think of Clovis Tibbets on that pony. I'll make like I was pulling him off of it.

(So was Michael Hoare now gathering strength to expend against a neighbor-hood bully who had pounded a beloved younger playmate, while little Mike Hoare sat up in bed, tremulous with scarlet fever, and watched through a window. The bully moved away from town before Mike was grown to a size which might have permitted revenge. The fact that he had not revenged himself was bitterness for years. . . . So was Bill Rowe about to smite an officer who had hounded him when first he joined the cavalry. . . . Dad Sanders told himself that here stood the rich Methodist who had extracted the life's savings of a gentle relative who sickened and died under the strain. . . . Key himself was lifting a club against a boss who had wounded him particularly. . . . Consciously, or deeply un-perceived and yet present, the same notion instilled a flaming fury in the souls of other men, Egypt and Sergeant Goody and Ned Johnson alike. Tom Larkin said that here stood the neighbor who poisoned his dog; A. R. Hill was about to encounter the schoolmaster who had beaten Hill's tongue-tied chum with a strap. . . . Nathan Dreyfoos saw a squat Spaniard with the face of a Moor, he had watched this man stoning a puppy to death in a slum by the sea when he, Nathan, was too small to do more than scream; so grown with skill and power he could find the Malagüenan again. Ned Carrigan was hitting against death; death itself had been a monster ever since the day he killed unwittingly a grinning rockfaced pugilist with whom he had been drinking jolly beers two nights before. . . . Limber Jim, the sinewy man from the Sixty-seventh Illinois who looked like a Sioux, did not have to tax his imagination; this was well, since he had almost no imagination. He grunted within himself. He picked out the huge gingery shape of Willie Collins. Limber Jim knew that Willie Collins or one of his gang had killed his, Limber Jim's, brother.)

They wore the visors of desperation but they were not blinded by the visors. Their desperation rose from the knowledge that this was The Moment, they had primed for it, The Moment would not come again. If they failed in the first onslaught they would fail in the second. If they failed for an instant they would fail for all time. Their line would be broken, individuals would be wrenched from it—as witness, again, the West Virginians of that morning—and individually they would be tackled until they were stamped to ribbons on the ground or gargled their bloody way back down the hill. They thought of weaker comrades who were here now, they thought of the weak and disconsolate to be tossed into this place next month. The same mayhem which had ruled before would terrorize through-out a heartless future. There was only one thing to do; they said it again in their hearts: win quickly, win decisively, crush the head of every constrictor before its coils twisted in the fatal pulling.

Help one another to win, feel no obligation of pity or quarter. If a comrade staggered an enemy with his blow, and the raider came weaving toward you, and you had the split second to do it, you were to stagger him again. Forget decency and Christianity, because decency and Christianity themselves had absolved you of any necessity to observe them. The bite would be here, the kick in the crotch, the pressing out of the eyeball, the tearing of the nostrils, the champ of your teeth to rip the muscle from an arm before the enemy's fangs went into your own. Win this first battle, in truth it would be the last.

The issue was decided more speedily than any Regulator could have dreamed. Vaguely some sensed that the climax of their endeavor had not yet come: it would come only when the most formidable of the raiders were put to death. By the massing and delivering of disciplined strength they achieved a victory which might have been achieved long before, had they put themselves to the test.

They dealt first with the core and spine of the gangs; the extremities and supports fell magically from the huge leaders with each blow put down. To gallery gods like Ira Claffey and the Reserves, watching from the platforms, there was only a roaring tangle, with lines swaying for two or three minutes; then a breakage, a sloughing off of defenders.

In microcosm the assault had its history in the experience of Willie Collins. He stood grumbling and scornful, bleared hot gaze trying to single out the largest and most contemptible of the joskins, as he called them. It was a term of opprobrium: joskin meant a rube, an oaf, a bumpkin untried and without danger in him. So these joskins had approached, and even while Willie Collins was aiming his fists at the pressing serious individuals who dared to challenge, a club sang against the base of his skull, it made loose explosions of silver within his head. A youth from Wisconsin—one of the smaller agile Regulators, who had been ordered merely to prevent spectators from joining the raiders if he could— This seventeen-year-old countryman (a German, a young dairyman, a joskin if you please) had filtered his way behind Willie. He struck with the whole force of his young arms and body. Collins turned with a howl. Even as he turned a heel drove into the soft place above his left hip-bone and dented his bowels. Collins swung back, slamming out the hairy freckled rocks which were his fists. He mashed down two men, one was a man of his own gang, Willie was confused. A longer club hurtled from somewhere into his right eyesocket and half the world turned to blood. Even while he struck down two more men, others were diving beneath his fists. Another kick in his groin . . . the welter of his own people seemed turned against him, impeding him, they got in the way, they got in the way. His left eye observed the blank face of Limber Jim. Shrieking he tried to reach that face; but there was a small body diving between his legs, a larger body contending for the possession of his right leg. The next instant the horizon of close-riding figures descended with a jerk. Willie's head went back; he was down, more feet danced upon his face, more feet beat his belly with staccato blows. He entertained a ruling perplexity of Why, How now, This is not the way it should be, What am I doing on the ground? He is dancing on me. . . . The bastards fear me. Faith, I'm greater than they. Hammer stroke. A wooden stick forced past his spread lips and breaking off some of his teeth and wounding his tongue, he could taste the bitter sap in that piston of wood. Something was wrapping his left wrist. He tried to utter the rallying cry, O Yes, O Yes, as he had yelled it in New York; but the sole of a boot trod his left eye and closed it, another boot crushed into his stomach. His left arm was jerked out and to the left and twisted. A dozen hands were on his legs, prying—and now the right wrist—What was that, a rope? Wrench, wrench, wrench; the noose brought the two thick wrists together and wrapped them, no matter how he strained. Willie could only say, Agh, agh.

Sarsfield also was down. Patrick Delaney had flattened a row in front of him before his shin was cracked by a kick, and so he staggered; then whiteness burst inside his skull, he heard nothing more, he went into deepness. Many raiders began to break and run.

Flying in appalled retreat was the bowlegged figure of Edward Blamey. The favorite weapon which he had fetched with him when he came to subsist with Willie Collins, in the spring: he had it still, he'd tried to use it to advantage. But an Ohio quarryman rose in front of him, and Edward Blamey could not resist a man of such size. He turned and ran. He fell into a shadow well; the next thing he knew, people were dragging him out and tying him. One of them damn sailors, he heard someone crowing. It was an error understandable. Edward Blamey had long since thrown away his cavalry rags and was garbed in stolen navy blouse and bell-bottomed trousers. Now, what of The Wrath To Come?

Hangers-on went skulking toward the marsh; but people who might have sheltered them before out of terror of their masters were now shrieking, Here's one, that little bastard, went down that way. Throngs of lightweight Regulators spread in successful pursuit.

It was an object lesson for all time; yet man might never learn that a wickedness must be singled out and struck if it is to be done away with. Man would keep on equivocating, searching himself for a sore. He would declare to internal rottenness here and there, would declare that there was no concentration of sin among the enemy merely because he had discovered a wrong within his own structure. The lesson was reiterated during those intense minutes; yet it would be ignored and forgotten. The pulsing organs of raider vitality were separated from their body abruptly. People saw that the body could not survive. In bruised awe they offered thanks to their Spook of battles. Forty or fifty chief offenders were tied and dragged toward the gate. A hundred more could be hunted down and singled for trial during the afternoon and day to follow.

Twas easy, someone gasped later to Seneca MacBean.

MacBean sponged at a flap of skin torn from his stubbly cheek, and grinned crookedly. No, mister, twasn't easy. But if the world ever saw concerted action it witnessed it right here today.

30

The Claffeys sat upon the gallery in rocking chairs moved out into the dusk when hot rain stopped and the sky dried slightly and pale stars appeared. There was a boon in that the wind blew from the southwest for a time. Wind came lightly but with persistence, and kept the prison's smell away as if the wind were a strong bold hand held steadily at arm's length, palm outward, restraining the stockade and that murmur more apparent at night than in the day.

Lucy held a mended blue fan which had been a prize won for accomplishment in ball room deportment when she attended the Institute, and her father was armed with a Macon newspaper with which he might fan himself; but it was unnecessary to employ these fans more than languidly until the wind changed.

It changed, it shifted to the east, then bore farther from the north. Smell walked the trees in a cloud and swept across the open veranda among short squared primitive posts which supported the upper gallery. Now the fans switched steadily.

Poppy, shouldn't I have the wenches make a smudge?

It all depends. Whether you wish to be smoke-dried or whether you wish to breathe—this.

Reckon I'd rather have smoke in my eyes, said Lucy with a nervous giggle. She lifted a copper camel-bell which Uncle Felton had brought from Egypt before she could remember, and rang it. She waited, rang again, waited, rang, rang, rang.

From loneliness at the far end of the gallery Veronica called a warning in her weak dried voice. I just got them to sleep, she complained.

Mother, I'm merely summoning the wenches.

But you'll wake the children.

Ninny came shuffling. Lucy sighed, it would profit nothing to upbraid Ninny for tardiness, Ninny would pretend that her feelings were hurt because the young mistress did not recognize her deafness and excuse her because of it.

Do you make a smudge, Ninny.

Yas'm. In that old kettle?

Did Jonas cut fresh evergreens today as I bid him?

Yas'm.

Wet the boughs thoroughly, dip them in water before you pile them on the coals. And do you put the kettle over there, Ninny, this side the jonquil bed, for the smoke to reach us.

Presently two dark figures lurked in the gloom, the glow of fresh coals went aloft, Ninny and Pet were lined against the glow. Each was a sorceress, you could imagine that they assembled ingredients for a potion.

Round about the cauldron go, said Ira. *Gall of goat and slips of yew sliver'd in the moon's eclipse, nose of Turk and Tartar's lips.* He left off quoting Macbeth abruptly as he realized that the next was *finger of birth-strangled babe,* and neither he nor Lucy cared to mention babes, birth-strangled or otherwise. Wet greenery was pressed into the kettle, spice of cedar swept the Claffeys. They waved the thickest smoke away but still it was wreathing close, protecting them, building a wall to keep out Andersonville. The black women went away.

Poppy, I heard Mrs. Yeoman's Scooper talking with our hands.

And?

He was telling them that the smell reaches all the way to Aunt Ella May Piggott's place when wind is right.

When the wind is wrong, Lucy.

Her laugh a phantom. Ah, certainly. When the wind is wrong.

Ira measured distances in his mind. At least two miles.

All of that. Well.

Smell fought to get through the aromatic cedar. Sometimes it wormed past the clouded drift, sometimes it accompanied the smoke, riding on top of it, crawling beneath slyly. The smell was crafty, it found a way . . . wall of smoke was rifted, leaky. Smell said, Do not forget *me.* Do not forget *us. I* will not—*we* will not—permit you to forget.

Poppy, is it— Is it the Dead?

Partially, I suppose. Although they're so far in the other direction. But mostly the marsh and its filth, and the Yankees themselves.

How many have died by now?

Thousands, tis said.

I overheard you speaking with Uncle Dayto, Poppy.

Ah, I regret that.

About—the hogs— In the cemetery—

Such things are bound to happen. I mean—when burials are so shallowly and carelessly made. In any event, more earth is used now. They're—deeper. Lucy, shall we speak of other matters?

Mean little drafts, guerrilla breezes, they hovered close to the ground, went aloft suddenly, took smoke high, reduced it to no value. Ira went down and moved the hot kettle with a stick, shifting it into a position he thought more favorable. Soon the wind worked capriciously once more, Andersonville was upon the gallery, the gallery was within the stockade.

Lucy strangled. We must go into the house, Poppy. Oh, this is the worst yet! And close all windows tightly.

Daughter, it's too blamed hot!

Yes, yes— Poppy! I've just recollected: I've still some Balm of a Thousand Flowers. I'll go fetch.

Her limp-skirted figure fluttered away against the gleam of one low lamp inside and Ira heard her speeding on the stairs. He got up heavily and pushed through the heat and smoke and night and smell, making his way to Veronica, hoping that a share of smoke traveled to her thickly enough to do some good. She too was in a rocking chair, but she sat bolt upright, she did not rock, the claws of her hands were bent tight under the old silk shawl. She ate very little nowadays. She must have raised her eyes to look at Ira although she did not move her head. She whispered, At least that youngun is not clattering her bell.

Of course not, my dear.

See that you walk with care. This old gallery pounds so.

Certainly. I came to see if the cedar smoke reaches you.

Veronica drew a long breath with intense and lingering satisfaction. I like it, Ira.

He said brightly, So do I. Evergreen smoke is one of the pleasantest things. Somehow it causes one to think of holidays and good times, does it not?

She said, Noooo, said it softly and drawn out like the plaint of some animal. Not the evergreen smoke, Ira. The other. The Yellow Smell.

He was cast, cast in his shabby rough but dignified clothing, he was metal poured and cooled. His body was a portion of the statue that he made inside his garb. The spirit which dwelt in that body was molded also (might it ever again walk abroad, witness beauty and thrill to suffocation to it, be proud, be generous, might it know the fierce satisfaction of suffering?) and the spirit was the skeletal structure which a great and awful Molder had strung together to hold his illusion together; so by some accident in a foundry the original skeleton was part of the finished bronze.

Not solely a statue . . . he was a group. He was Laocoön with serpents wrapping him.

Yellow smell, my dear? Smell has no color. He said it because silence knocked at his ears—this nearer silence, separated by leagues from the crooning of the stockade.

I like it. It's Them.

She said again, They smell because it hurts Them. So. I want Them to be hurt. A chuckle crawled beneath the stilted calm of her tone.

Why? Oh, why? And he was not certain whether he spoke the scream of query aloud or whether it rose only within him, and was unvoiced; yet she found question or answer to his communication as often she had found them when sane.

They killed Moses.

My dear. It's a war. People are—

They killed Sutherland.

Veronica, you hear me? People are killed in wars. They take risks. It—it finds them—

Killed my Badger—

Hush up, you— You idiot! You idiot woman! Didn't you yourself just insist that the children were safe, safe asleep upstairs, I shouldn't walk heavily on this gallery? You know they're there— They're asleep upstairs! You said so—

O smell. Well he knew it, he had known it longer than anyone else. He found it when the first cross-bred vines tangled under a fence and dragged their rotting fruit shaped like skulls, and he sent a slave to rid the region of their presence. He'd smelled it—unidentified, unticketed but still noticed—in the long ago when he and his daughter journeyed to their plantation from the incompletely fenced area and he wondered: was it a dog, was it a worried cat, what was the nuisance which lay gassy?

Course they're asleep.

She agreed to this austerely and did not seem to be aware that he had named her an idiot; or, if she were aware of it, did not resent it.

Ira knew for the first time that there were two notions and knowledges claiming Veronica's belief simultaneously. There was no rhyme or reason to this. Veronica was a youngish mother still, of childbearing age, haughtily maternal. She owned a troop of boy-and-girl children possibly all of the same size. This unseen litter she tended with selfish devotion. They were dead but they were alive, she saw that they were fed but offered no bottles or breasts or mugs or spoonfuls; they wailed when they were sick and Veronica soothed them, changed their napkins, did the nursing stint herself, would not let old Ruth do it if old Ruth were about.

And, in identical moments and treading in a quite different avenue of fancy, she was the bereaved lioness whose cubs had been slaughtered . . . yet crueler far than a lioness, not only willing to perform more slaughter in revenge but willing—nay, eager—to brood on an awfulness and call it a Love.

She tittered about it. She said again, I like it. It's Them. Surely it must hurt Them when They smell like that.

Some of this she spoke aloud . . . the rest seethed inside her and only bubbled out in laughter.

Lucy was close, Lucy stood beside her father and her skirts were brushing him. He stumbled away and bruised his shoulder hard upon the nearest column; this alone kept him from falling off the gallery onto plants and rocks beneath— because he could not see, the night loomed black as a student's slate, he could not see through it. Lucy held a bowl in which she'd mixed her Balm of a Thousand Flowers cologne with water. In this bowl three of her small pocket handkerchiefs were saturated and should be wrung out: one for her mother, one for herself, one for Ira. They had done this a few other times when the stink overwhelmed them. Lucy thought that her cologne was all gone, used up, and then she remembered another older bottle in her cupboard with a small quantity of cologne remaining in it. They might make masks through which to breathe and thus be able to remain on the porch in comparative coolness. The night was so stifling. In the house it would be worse.

This was the first occasion when Veronica rejected the aid, the boon, the ministration.

Mother, Lucy insisted again, but the woman waved her off.

Tis a pleasing scent. Tis—attar—

Surely it is pleasing. But let me spread the cloth over your face. See—it's all wet—and cool—

With dread strength her mother pushed the hand away. My dear young lady! Don't be insistent. Don't be impudent—

Mother—

Gifts should never be forced by the giver! Mind, now. I worked it once in cross-stitch. Twas something like that. Twas a motto—

But, Mother, if you insist on breathing that noxious scent you'll be ill. Cousin Harry warned by letter that the very air must be laden with miasma. And—and the effluvia of so many who are sick—

Dying, said Veronica. Dead. Better dead.

Her thin iron hand and arm swept up and out, hurling the bowl from Lucy's clutch. It was a heavy vessel, not fragile, it did not break immediately. There came a loud splash on the gallery's floor, then no sound but the bowl's rolling as it made small thunder across the hollow boards (Ira thought of skulls again, he thought of a skull rolling) and then for a portion of time, the part of a second, there was silence as the bowl went through space; then it struck the ornamental ridge of stones bordering a flower bed. The smash said, This is termination. Something definite has happened. Something is over and done with.

Balm of a Thousand Flowers rose up to vie with the stockade's smell and the faint odor of charred cedar lingering, to be defeated first by the other, and soon they were both defeated by the one. Andersonville towered and struck, almost you could see it in the night, it slapped as the hand of Veronica had slapped the bowl gone to atoms.

Lucy found her father and sank her head against his arm. Veronica Claffey sat motionless, no longer giving forth her laugh. That was one kindness in a life grown dank otherwise.

Lucy whispered, Question Forty-two.

Ah, in the Shorter Catechism? You learned it all so well. You were a good child, you've always been a good child.

The sum of the ten commandments is, To love the Lord our God with all our heart, with all our soul, with all our strength, and with all our mind; and our neighbor as ourselves. Poppy, I did. I tried to. With emphasis upon the neighbor part—

My dear, in loving thy neighbor you are also loving God. That's apparent within the Scriptures. And outside them.

I tell you, I tried!

Good child.

Don't call me blithe spirit, Poppy. I'll never be again.

Yes, yes, you'll—

Never! Poppy, I want to— I want to *damn God.*

Oh, poor Lucy. Poor—

What did you do, to deserve this? What did I do? What did *she* do?

Nothing at all, my dear. It's—but a misery—

Is not all life, as it's come to us? Oh, dear God, let me damn God! Let me damn Him and damn Him and damn Him—

Now the weeping came with a puppy's cry, and Ira stood holding the girl as she sagged. Behind them Veronica told Lucy to use caution. Never waken little Arwood, she said. Troubled with colic as he is.

31

Sometimes Our Dear Lord (or was it Our Lady?) let Father Peter Whelan dream, and did not cause him to repeat endlessly in ritual the offices he managed through waking hours. Sometimes Our Dear Lord made him a boy again, running through dim beech woods in County Meath. Our Dear Lord allowed him to go for an evening stroll, as when he was in the seminary, and he heard cosy laughter of Terry Shanahan ahead of him and the solemn grunt of red-faced John Gilligan waddling black-cassocked close behind, the solemn voice of John Gilligan declaring that primroses were worldly objects and so not to be admired, since admiration might lead to worship, and thus would be committed a transgression of the soul if not of the flesh. Sometimes. Only sometimes.

Father Peter Whelan was a very old man, aging a year each day he served in Andersonville. He had come to Andersonville from Savannah on the sixteenth of June, bearing in his hand and in his intelligence the same Roman Ritual which Benedict the Fourteenth authorized nearly one hundred and forty years before. When he slept he was an effigy, except that no effigy wore so many facial lines, compressed into the texture of woven fabric, perhaps coarse linen, perhaps fine lace. When Father Whelan slept he seemed to be dead. There was the smallest possible respiration of his thin chest, his gray hands were folded across his body, he lay motionless upon his back, the wide thin firm lips did not twitch.

Only bright watery blue of his eyes made Father Whelan live when he opened his eyes; still, the prisoners never saw him asleep, they did not know that he went into death when he slept. When they saw him it was to observe him prowling without rest, papery under weight of an old umbrella with broken bows, an umbrella faded, mildewed, hit by the steady sun; but the umbrella became a symbol of strength which amounted to audacity in one so frail, so old.

Haley Ladden was dying, Haley knew that he was dying, his breath was a long hard rattle. Priest— Father. His imaginings twitched off to Dubuque and he named Father Whelan as Father Jackson whom he had known when he was a little boy.

No, no, me son. I'm Father Whelan.

Not—same priest—here—awhile back?

In May, me son? Twas Father Hamilton from Macon. I'm Father Whelan. Sip of this water now, me boy.

A surgeon would have said that Haley Ladden was close to total blindness from extravasation of blood as well as from fluid in the posterior parts of his eyes. A surgeon would have said, His ulcers have assumed a phagedenic appearance and extend over a large extent of surface, and present irritable, jagged, and everted edges, and are destroying the dead tissues down to the bone. Except that no surgeon had observed Haley Ladden because he had no friends to carry him to the gate for examination; and when Haley had been able to totter in that direction supported by his own limbs and canes he had not been able to get within fifty yards of the gate.

How old are you, me boy?

Don't know. Nnnnnnn. Sseventeen. . . .

And where was your home?

Dubuque . . . Ioway. . . .

And are you a Catholic, me boy?

Yehhhhh. . . .

Oremus. Domine Deus, qui per Apostolum tuum Jacobum locutus es: Infirmatur quis in vobis? Inducat presbyteros Ecclesiae, et orent super eum, ungentes eum oleo in nomine Domini—

Ernst Kamphoefner was dying, Ernst did not know that he was dying; instead he would be paroled, and his captain and the village grocer and a girl named Anna had just called on him to tell him so; they said, Pack your plunder, boy; home we go maybe tomorrow, and forget all about what happened to the Seventy-fourth Pennsylvania nearly a year ago—

Here, me son. Let me wipe your poor mouth; and taste the cup of cool water I bring you.

Ja. . . .

And what is your name, me poor lad? And where do you come from?

Anna, she was by me. The parole I got now. *Ja,* I go home. Ernst Kamphoefner writhed and thought that he was standing, thought that he was walking off between Anna and Captain Dromke; but he was only lifting his head a trifle; more of the evil liquid poured from his mouth; and a surgeon would have said— What would a surgeon have said?

Ah, I know that you're a good Catholic, me brave boy, for you've got the Holy Cross around your neck. Taste another sip of the water I've brought you.

Ja. . . .

Tattered umbrella building its shade upon them, the bone handle of it thrust into oozing ground. *Et oratio fidei salvabit infirmum, et alleviabit eum Dominus: et si in peccatis sit, remittentur ei: cura, quaesumus. Redemptor noster—*

A surgeon would have said, In cases of ulceration of the mucous membrane of the intestinal canal, the fibrous element of the blood is increased. Bill Skelly would have said, Ah, I fear to die, Father, for I've sinned— How I've sinned— But Bill Skelly could not speak; only his great swollen eyes could roll wildly, watching the seamed austere but gentle face pushing close above. *Gratia Sancti Spiritus languores istius infirmi, ejusque sana vulnera, et dimitte peccata, atque dolores cunctos mentis et corporis ab eo expelle—*

Eyes, ears, nostrils, mouth, hands, feet. The smell of oil upon the cotton, little wads going into the bashed tin cup, the dab of corn bread rubbed upon Father Whelan's thumb; fire reaching for these remnants once Father Whelan was finished with them. Oh, were other deeper more dangerous fires reaching for Tim and Jackie and Barney and Olin and Fritz and Owen and the rest? He must hasten, he must tread far and pray long, he must not let the flames sear the young pale souls which had been caged within rotting ribs and horny skin, but which would soon be freed. They must go shrived if they were to be freed.

Violet stole hanging on the tall frame, that frame wasted by age and by the giving out of unmeasured pity . . . sun coming through a split in the umbrella's top to blaze upon the violet stole and try to fade it. *Et ne nos inducas in tentationem.*

Hoarse mumble of response made by Father Whelan himself, because the dying boy could not speak the words. *Sed libera nos a malo.*

Salvum fac servum tuum.

Mumble running down into a whisper. *Deus meus, sperantem in te.*

Some might have thought that the bishop should never have sent so elderly a man to labor amid agonies, but to Peter Whelan this was the accolade supreme: ardently he had dreamed of martyrdom, this was martyrdom, it was a reward scarce to be expected while he remained upon Earth. He went about his tingling earnest creepings nerved by bitterness of the task. He felt a pride; pride was sin, he recognized this sin in himself, he was abject, he prayed with humility again. *Refresh the soul which Thou hast created, that being bettered by Thy chastisements, he may feel himself saved by Thy healing.*

Are you a Catholic, me son?

Mais oui.

Ah. And what might be your name?

Please. André Fromentin.

Ah, I've never the French to help you—the vernacular—and I pray daily that the good bishop may see fit to send Father Clavereul from Savannah, for he's French and could warm your soul with his speech, me boy.

Please— *Monsieur le Curé.* We get exchange, *non?*

Now, me boy, concern yourself with affairs of the spirit, concern yourself with God.

But, you hear—? Those officers, of *la Confédération.* We get exchange, very quick now, *non?*

Me son, those are temporal affairs, I have no knowledge of them. Truly it's enough, and it's essential, that you heed only the word of God, the love and law of the Mother Church.

But, *Monsieur le—*

There were so many of them, too many of them. More and more Father Whelan found it necessary to employ the short form for Extreme Unction, the short form for the Apostolic Blessing. A demented man rambled in confession and recited all manner of lewdness, another demented youth begged to partake of Communion (it turned out that he was a Campbellite, not a Roman Catholic; that was the form of Communion he sought). Father Whelan turned his wet blue gaze toward the depot when, once out of the stockade, he set out on a tiring homeward march. Perhaps others would be sent to aid— Not him, he wanted no aid, he asked for none. But to aid those dear lads yonder, whose souls were crying for blessings, who might sputter and yell in pits and lakes of The Damned if the Rites were not available. *Ego, facultate mihi ab Apostolica Sede tributa, indulgentiam plenariam et remissionem omnium peccatorum tibi concedo, et benedico te.* Oh, let the poor child be strengthened to resist all temptations of the Devil and to die happily in the Lord! Eyes, ears, nostrils, mouth, hands, feet? Nay, no time for that —the gagging sounds in the throat, the eyeballs are glue— Quick swipe of oil on the forehead only, a hasty jumble, Latin falling over Latin with recklessness to beat the fiends, to exorcise them permanently. *Per istam sanctam Unctionem, indulgeat tibi Dominus quidquid deliquisti. Amen.* And now the boy is dead, but— kiss the Holy Cross— He died in the Lord, he died happily in the Lord!

Perform only the essentials, the skeleton rite established by Christ. Give the Sacrament without additional prayers ordained by the Church. It is a sadness but— Give it, give it— Quickly—

If Father Clavereul should be sent to help the prisoners Peter Whelan would kneel in thanks. There had been some talk of sending also Father John Kirby from Augusta. And— Ah, the Jesuit from over Mobile way, Father Hosannah— He spoke three or four languages, perhaps more. Perhaps in time Bishop Verot himself might appear; he had hinted as much; and with him might come the vicar-general, Father Dufan. These were a hope, they could be sought in prayer. They might never be secured but they could be prayed after.

O Lord, hear my prayer.

And let my cry come unto thee.

During those weeks when Father Whelan was on the point of taking up his burden and did take it up, Andersonville suffered the loss of another benignant influence and was afflicted with a baleful one. Lieutenant-Colonel Persons was relieved of his command: the creased spongy face of John Winder pushed above the Georgia horizon. It was an added cruelty that General Winder should arrive to assume personal control at the very moment when Alexander Persons had finally achieved some success in his long hunt for lumber. Rolling stock was at a premium but Persons possessed the grave stubborn spirit which does not recognize defeat. He knew but to apply and receive a rejection, make a new application, find it rejected or ignored, apply again. The first train which he won was composed of nine carloads of lumber, the second—weeks later—of six, the third held eight cars. Lumber was being unloaded from Persons' sixth train on the afternoon when General Winder and his little party descended upon the graveled platform of Anderson Station. Persons had gathered fifty-one carloads of lumber in all. Long yellow planks lay stacked in an orderly little city and sent up their fresh clean odor to vie with the stockade's efflux. Then disaster stamped down from a newly-arrived train, the meaty face came pressing.

As I remember it, Colonel Persons, you were the first officer to suggest that the hospital be taken out of the local stockade.

No, sir, that's scarcely correct. Captain Wirz came to me, urging the removal.

What was your reply?

I told him, sir, that I had no authority to effect the transfer.

And then you addressed a communication to me in Richmond?

Yes, sir, that is correct. I asked for permission to take the hospital outside.

Can you recall the reply?

As I recall it, General, the permission was denied.

I presume you have copies of the correspondence in your files, Colonel Persons?

Sir, I retain all copies as instructed.

If you chose to refresh your memory you would find that permission was most definitely denied. I don't forget things like this, God damn it!

The general choked with rage and walked up and down the platform for a time, muttering to himself; you could see his jowls twitching spasmodically, his face growing dark, then lightening gradually as a new thought came to him. He halted, turned, and crooked a finger at Persons, who moved forward in obedience to the silent summons but was consumed with a fury to match Winder's.

You acted on your own recognizance, didn't you? Did anyone try to persuade you to ignore the fact that I'd declined to give you permission for the removal? Did Wirz persuade you?

It would be incorrect, General, to say that he did. We were both of the same mind about it. When permission was refused or declined or however the general wishes to state it, Captain Wirz remonstrated with me.

What did you tell Captain Wirz?

I told him to proceed with the hospital's removal.

Upon whose authority, then?

I told Captain Wirz that I would take full responsibility.

Bare-faced disobedience! And, by God, you're positively smug about it!

Persons thought, still in a rage by no means blind— He thought, as a hundred other military men had thought, as a thousand civilians had thought while Winder served as provost-marshal— He thought, If you were my own age, sir! If you didn't have those dratted stars wreathed upon your collar! How I'd like to knot my fist and push it into your doughy phiz! How I'd like to stand up to you with a pistol!

He said, speaking with a pained deliberation which would have revealed to his intimates that he was very near to physical assault, age or no age, rank or no rank— It occurred to me, sir, that if the general were here in person, on the ground and possessed of firsthand evidence as to the necessities, the general would very likely revise his opinion. Since I held this belief, I gave Captain Wirz instructions accordingly. I repeat, sir, that I assume full responsibility.

Winder growled meaningly, The general is now here, he's on the ground, by Jesus Christ. I'm going to get you out of here so fast your head'll spin!

Persons said nothing, he dared not speak.

The entire system is being reorganized, d'you hear? I shall be in sole command of all prisons east of the Mississippi. That's General Cooper's plan, and it meets with Mr. Seddon's approval and with President Davis's approval, by God!

Persons' throat and mouth and lips were chalk. I have seen no orders from the I.G. to that effect, sir.

So you haven't. But it's in the offing, and I'm giving it to you directly from the horse's mouth, Colonel. Do you think for one moment that you field grade officers, supposedly occupied with your duties in the field, know everything that goes on in Richmond? In a pig's ass you do!

Respectfully, General Winder, I am bound to call your attention to the Article of War which states that superiors of every grade are forbidden to injure those under them by tyrannical or capricious conduct, or by abusive language. . . . I shall instruct an officer to extend to you and your party the courtesies of my post. Until I am relieved, sir. Persons saluted, ground his heel into the platform, walked away. He was on the point of throwing up, he hoped that he could control his palpitating stomach until he was out of sight.

Winder bellowed after him, Very well, Colonel, the hospital's outside and it shall remain outside; we've no people to spare for the task of mopping up milk that other men have spilt! I'm here, I'm on the ground, but I tell you that I'll never set foot inside that damned stockade, I'll not sully my boots with Yankee scum!

His military family stood clustered fawningly behind him; Captain Peschau cluck-clucked his tongue, shook his head, and spoke in deprecation of Lieutenant-Colonel Persons to the others.

. . . Find himself commanding Fort Shit on Ass-hole Creek.

. . . Find himself a captain, you mean!

. . . Shouldn't be a bit surprised. Just look at old J.H.W. He's in a slather.

. . . Well, walk softly, Major.

. . . Soft as silk, Jack my boy.

Alex Persons had gone so far as to prepare plans for the barracks which he hoped to erect within the enclosure, working until all hours at night with one Lieutenant Wright of the Fifty-fifth who owned some engineering experience. Sid Winder would have been the logical officer for this task, but Persons knew better than to broach his plan to any of the Winders. With Wright he had labored to secure the maximum amount of effective shelter at a minimum expenditure of planks. So a master drawing had been made, and copies traced through impression paper. Reports were being drawn on the quantity of tools and labor available, some of the lumber had actually been carried as far as the North Gate. Persons strode, defeated and ill, past aromatic stacks of sawed pine. His hope, his accumulated treasure . . . now it would be stolen. He knew what would happen to the lumber after he was sent packing (and it did happen thus). Forty or fifty structures growing over the trampled hillsides, but not within Andersonville. No shelter for the prisoners, but offices and quarters for General Winder, Cousin Dick Winder —dear Cousin Dick!—and Sid Winder. A hospital for the guards, perhaps—they had nothing but tents, but better tents than the Yankees had. Perhaps more barracks for the officers of the Georgia Reserves. Sutlers' shacks— Reserves would floor their tents with precious boards, they would shade their canvas with more precious boards— Agh.

Lieutenant-Colonel Persons stumbled behind a tree and was sick in fact. Cold sweat stood out, his temples were pounding him to death. He halted at a nearby well with its leaky tub, washed his face, then went on to headquarters.

He didn't like Wirz, he didn't see how anyone could ever like Wirz; but he had grown to admire the sickly man's zeal. Every frenzied blundering attempt of Wirz at providing better facilities had met with Persons' approbation. Persons had loaned his best men to aid Wirz in the hospital's removal, in the shoring of the ugly stream. Lieutenant Wright himself had volunteered to supervise the stockade's extension. Paroled prisoners and black labor had done the trick, and would have done this trick of barracks-building if allowed to proceed. Alex Persons understood the whole truth at last. Henry Wirz was a frothing little ferret, a martinet of a repulsive sort, but at least his brain was oozing with ideas and some of the ideas were good ones. He was not impelled by humanitarian motives but by a desire for efficiency; had he been provided with the means he might have superintended a cleanly prison if a cruel one. Obviously he wished revenge, but at the same time he was given seriously to stewardship (his own version of stewardship).

General Winder wished to kill as many of the prisoners as he could. It was as simple as that.

Now he would kill them in increasing droves. Persons had seen those reports assembled with so much cursing and fussing. Wirz was always brandishing reports under his nose. He could not recall the exact figures, of course, but he did remember round numbers. The mean strength in March was about seventy-five hundred, the deaths about three hundred. Mean strength in April ten thousand, deaths six hundred. Mean strength in May fifteen thousand, deaths seven hundred. Morbidly he had asked Lieutenant Wright to count marked graves in the cemetery (there were believed to be many unmarked, because of the carelessness surrounding burial) and Wright had reported fifteen hundred and eighty-two marked graves. Alex Persons presumed that the mean strength of prisoners might rise as high as twenty-two or twenty-three thousand when figures for all of June were summed up; that would mean an additional twelve or thirteen hundred dead. What would be the value of prisoners' barracks in summer? Alex Persons was a Georgian; he knew very well what the value of shade would be. Once he had put a thermometer out in the June sun and the temperature was marked at one hundred and twenty-nine degrees Fahrenheit. In winter he had witnessed as much as twenty-two degrees of frost. The hospital would never have been removed from the stockade unless he, Persons, had exceeded his authority—had, in fact, deliberately disobeyed an opinion if not an order. And now he would be whipped away from this command, the barracks would never be built. Winder would toast Yankees throughout the summer as surely as if he held them impaled on a ramrod above a camp blaze. And, next winter— If it were an especially cold winter— And often in Georgia an especially cold winter followed an especially hot summer, as this was growing to be—

Lieutenant-Colonel Persons thought that his removal from this command would save his life, but it would rob him of an opportunity to save whatever dignity was left to the Confederate States Government insofar as Andersonville was concerned.

He performed courtesy chores for the general and his party, and then left the post in charge of Major Flournoy. His own head was on the chopping block, he had put it there himself, the blade would come down today, tomorrow, next day, it didn't matter.

He rode to the Claffey plantation, he hadn't the strength to walk there. He found Ira among peach trees, and Ira offered him a green peach.

That's all I'd need, Mr. Claffey, sir! Already I've been nauseated today. I mean that truly.

Ira looked at Persons' face, and picked up his implements promptly. We shall go into the house, Colonel. Why not lie awhile on the sofa in my library?

I fear I'd take permanent possession of it.

They did go into the house. Persons sat with a glass of blackberry wine.

One of my daughter's many triumphs, Colonel. And most settling to the stomach.

Persons sat hunched on the sofa. Soon he was pouring out the Winder story. I speak to you, sir, because I must speak to someone. You're a citizen, and I'd probably be churched if it came out that I was blabbing. But— Oh, devil take us. I'm going to be churched anyway!

He sipped the wine and said presently in a calmer tone, You have patience and tolerance, Mr. Claffey. And you have been a soldier.

I did know Mr. Davis, said Ira. It was during the Mexican War.

Twould mean nothing. That senile wretch has the President's ear, or so everybody says.

Will this change in command result in immediate deterioration of the local situation? Ira laughed dryly. You see, I'm trying to speak in military parlance.

Persons told him, biting off his words: It will mean this, sir. No individual of whatever rank will have the right to interfere with General John H. Winder in any shape, form or fashion. This order will give him absolute dominion and control over every Yankee prisoner east of the Mississippi—and of course that's where most of them are. The extended engagements now being fought above Atlanta and below Richmond— You can understand that, Mr. Claffey. The bulk of all Yanks captured by us during the progress of these campaigns, which campaigns I pray will be terminated by the success of our arms—

Amen, sir!

The bulk of the captured Yanks will land *here*. That old monster has planned it so, else he'd not be sending all these trainloads. I've exceeded my authority—he calls it bare-faced mutiny—and I shall be flogged or broken for it. So farewell, Mr. Claffey, and bless you for your hospitality.

He stood up, and Ira took his arm and walked with Persons to his horse.

Persons went but Winder stayed. And in his dedication Father Peter Whelan stayed. Peter Whelan dwelt sparely in an unpainted shack nearly a mile from Andersonville. His stove was a charred hollow stump at the door with a half-burned-out grating spread over the top and blackened stones to hold his little kettle in place. There was an open frieze of sky and pines showing around the edges of the roof where shakes had peeled; when rains came there fell steady leakage all along the ridgepole. There was no door, only a gaping doorway and a half of a cedar log for a step. Father Whelan's army blanket was spread over a compressed mound of pine straw and oak leaves. Rats came to visit him at night but they did not offer to bite; he'd hoped that the persuasion of Saint Francis of Assisi might rule these small creatures away from their natural savagery, and it did rule. Father Whelan wore a coat of faded blue linen, and this jacket was busy with lice throughout its seams. He tried to keep the lice in check, burning them off over a flame as he had seen the Yankees do, but it was only a gesture. There were too many hovels into which he must crawl, too many shivering skeletons beside whom he must crouch or even lie to hear their mutterings. Lice lived in every beard, every squirming tuft of hair. Father Hamilton had warned him about vermin after the Macon priest made his explorative visits during May. Indeed, said Father Hamilton, it's such a filthy place. The men huddled together, crawling with filth. Ah, hear me—I went in there wearing my white coat, and I'd not been there but one quarter of an hour at the most, when a guard kindly drew my attention to the condition of my coat. It was fairly alive. I had to take my coat off and leave it with the guard, and perform my religious duties in my shirt sleeves, the place was that filthy.

Och, the poor boys!

But you're an old man, Father Whelan. Do you think you can bear with it?

If Bishop Verot should send me— Ah, no. If Our Lord should send me—

I fear you'll but sicken and die.

Jesus, Mary and Joseph, may I sleep and rest in peace in your holy company.

Henry Wirz showed not the slightest objection to providing Peter Whelan with a pass to visit stockade or hospital as he chose; perhaps he might have objected had Whelan been a minister of the Protestant faith. (Thus far only one Protestant had evinced a desire to enter Andersonville to preach; and he was a die-hard Secessionist who preached Secession intermingled with Christianity, and came near to being thrown out bodily by the prisoners.) Henry Wirz placed the leaky shack at the priest's disposal and saw that rations were issued to him by the guards' commissary. Other than that Wirz did not seek the venerable Father's company; he felt that Whelan was disgusted if not appalled by boorish profanity, and since Captain Wirz might not conduct his superintendency of the prison without employing boorish and worse than boorish profanity—

The old priest. You got him a place to sleep, *ja?*

Yes sir, Captain. Sergeant Prather fixed him up tolerable in that old shanty over past the sawmill.

Every day inside among the Yankees he goes?

Yes sir, Captain. I just seen that old bumbershoot of his a-flapping along the road. Generally he gets inside by nine o'clock, don't come out till nigh onto dark.

The Church had a power greater than the power of all armies of all countries and all centuries put together; partly because its equipment and tendons and the valves of its bejeweled heart were disciplined, but mostly because it was the Church. (When Henry Wirz thought of the Church, which was seldom, he thought of a certain dark portal in Bern where columns of midgets and saints and beasts with gargoyle faces marched unendingly toward some sort of doom; medieval craftsmen had made them march that way, and so they frightened a little boy worse than the Bern bears.) Naked Christians stood with bellies exposed to tigers' claws in Rome, they quailed at a subterranean roar which came up from dens in Italica (then they saw a light shining). A prelate was squeezed into an iron basket, and to and fro he swung above the coals; and so many thousands of fires had cooked other flesh through the ages (yea, there were fires in Smithfield as well). The poisoned wine, the small hidden dagger, the ring with the needle's prick, the solemn walling-away . . . road of rocks bruised by sandaled feet or multitudes of feet which wore no sandals . . . heavy fall the pikes of Cromwell's men, down comes the axe. . . .

Father Whelan lay like that same effigy again in hot darkness, rude-shirted and bitten by bugs; he lay in temporary death; there was no one to see him unless saints peered through split shakes of the shed's roof. Sometimes he ran as a youth in beech woods again— There was a path which went to old Brigid Shacklin's house, and she would roll a hot potato from the ashes to thank him for the fish he'd fetched her—

The Church was greater than sun, moon and stars; because God had made these, but the Church was God's extension in time.

Quid petis ab Ecclesia Dei? Fidem. What to ask, indeed, of the Church of God? Faith, nothing but faith. *Was begehrst du von der Kirche Gottes? Den Glauben.* (As learned by Henry Wirz, as learned by the boy named Ernst Kamphoefner who now lay Exchanged in a ditch to the north— Why, his illusion had been correct; there was Exchange, he was now at the North with a vengeance.) *Que demandez-vous à l'Eglise de Dieu?* Respond, André Fromentin, and say *La foi.* Ah, if Father Hosannah came from Spring Hill College—the Jesuit school— He could speak many languages, not merely the Latin and the English and the Gaelic like Father Peter Whelan. He could Baptize any converted soldier of the polyglot Forty-eighth New York, and in the vernacular; he could Baptize a Bohemian. *Co žádáš od Církve Boží? Víru.* He could Baptize a Pole. *Czego zadasz od Kościoła Bozego? Wiary.* The Church was taller than MacCillicuddy's Reeks, taller than the Rocky Mountains were said to be; because God made the mountains, and God founded the Church, and the Church was God's action extended from eternity into time. . . .

Pilgrims went barefoot to Lourdes, pilgrims crawled on stairways, they crawled up hard brown rocky hills to pray to the Virgin of Guadalupe, the *Virgen de la Cabeza.* Lame pilgrims crawled the gray-green rocky cone of Puig above Pollensa and planned to leave their crutches at the top. The servant girl wept in the Confessional. The beggar stole silver from the poor box and thus he became a thief instead of a beggar; but he could be forgiven, he could do a penance, not necessarily was he deeded to the flames. The sickly child in Seville—sickly, but with a face like a rock-rose—shivered and danced when *pasos* went swaying past, when drums rolled hard, when gypsies wailed from the balconies. *¿Qué pides de la Iglesia de Dios? La fe.* The Church was more majestic than blue sky or dun sky or black sky, for God had made the sky of whatever color. *Che cosa chiedi dalla Chiesa di Dio? La Fede.* The old Italian was trodden to death by a crowd pressing forward to see the Pope.

Through endless dusty muddy decades nuns went walking to beg, nuns lifted the heavy stinking sick, nuns put gruel into sagging mouths of the idiots they tended, nuns unwound the swelling abraiding bandage and put on the newer sweeter kinder bandage, nuns sponged the soiled buttocks, nuns changed the bed. The monsignor stole the orphans' money, the cardinal employed the assassin, the priest seduced the sniveling young lunatic put into his care. The Church was greater than any force or inhuman beauty dreamed or named by man or men because the Church was above these wickednesses. The knife of perfidy could not disembowel the Church, worms of jealousy could not gnaw its structure, the powder of hypocrisy could not explode to shatter its columns. *What doth faith bring thee to? Life everlasting.*

In the morning Father Peter Whelan arose again. He prayed. He washed himself at a wooden bucket, and shaved in cold water, and cooked a bowl of mush and another of peas; then he was fed sufficiently until night. He rid himself of as many lice as he could. He walked the long hard hot distance to Andersonville, walking in broken shoes which he himself had tried to sew together, walking under the ruin of his umbrella. *Salvum fac servum tuum.* Sun hurled itself against him, against the prisoners; the thick stench came to meet and claim. He would not come dragging out through that gate until dusk; another day would have passed, he would be a year older. Still he would serve.

32

Johnny Ransom, the twenty-one-year-old from the Ninth Michigan Cavalry, scrawled his scrawl. The farther advanced the summer, the death rate increases, until they die off by scores. I walk around to see friends of a few days ago and am told, Dead. Men stand it nobly and are apparently ordinarily well, when all at once they go. Like a horse, that will stand up until he drops dead. . . . Was ever before in this world anything so terrible happening? Many entirely naked. . . . Sores afflict us now, and The Lord only knows what next. Scurvy and scurvy sores, dropsy, not the least thing to eat that can be called fit for any one, much less a sick man, water that to drink is poison, no shelter. . . .

He knew whereof he wrote when it came to scurvy. Johnny Ransom was barely able to walk; he had been unable to participate in the raider fight however much he applauded the Regulators.

He wrote: A new prisoner fainted away on his entrance to Andersonville and is now crazy, a raving maniac. That is how our condition affected him. My pants are the worse for wear from repeated washings, my shirt sleeveless and feet stockingless; have a red cap without any front piece; shoes by some hocus-pocus are not mates, one considerable larger than the other. Wonder what they would think if I should suddenly appear on the streets in Jackson in this garb. Would be a circus; side show and all. The Glorious Fourth of July. How shall we celebrate? Know of no way except to pound on the bake tin, which I shall do.

In fact it was the Glorious Fourth of July, and raiders knelt in subjugation. Solemnly the bent scurvy-racked Johnny Ransom beat upon his bake tin.

He wrote: The men taken outside yesterday are under rebel guard and will be punished. The men are thoroughly aroused, and now that the matter has been taken in hand, it will be followed up to the letter. Other arrests are being made today, and occasionally a big fight. Little Terry, whom they could not find yesterday, was today taken. Fought like a little tiger, but had to go. Limber Jim is a brick, and should be made a Major General if he ever reaches our lines. . . . The writer hereof does no fighting, being on the sick list. The excitement of looking on is almost too much for me. Can hardly arrest the big graybacks crawling around.

John Ransom was loved and tended by a mighty Indian from Minnesota named Baptiste, called Bateese by all. You get well soon, said Bateese. He brought to Johnny the potato parings which his industry had purchased. Like Seneca MacBean the Indian conducted a laundry of sorts, and said that he had no time to fight, must wash. But he would grunt his approval when he saw the worst of the raiders suspended by ropes.

The young diarist traced his words with slow devotion: Have taken to rubbing my limbs . . . badly swollen. One of my teeth came out a few days ago, and all are loose. Mouth very sore. Bateese says, We get away yet. Works around and is always busy. If any news, he merely listens and doesn't say a word. Even he is in poor health, but never mentions it. An acquaintance of his says he owns a good farm in Minnesota. Asked him if he was married—says: Oh, yes. Any children? Oh, yes. . . . Is very different from Indians in general. Some of them here are despisable cowards—worse than the negro. Probably one hundred negroes are here. Not so tough as the whites.

Stub pencil fell from weakened fingers, the hurting head came forward and lay on Johnny Ransom's arm; Johnny dreamed of the Pepys whom he had read avidly and strove to emulate. He dreamed that he would survive agonies to come, and in some fine fair future hour would journey through that gate. His diary, his precious stained scrubby notebooks saying *Ledger* and *Day Book* and *Cash Receipts* and *Pickell & Co.*— These would accompany him.

He stood in the office of a publisher, the publisher was portly and sagacious. What cash down payment would it be necessary for us to put forth, Mr. Ransom, in order to secure the highly estimable privilege of printing your remarkable diary? By Heaven, young man, what a ghastly experience you have passed through —and yet, memorable, memorable indeed. And to think that you are one of the few survivors! Yet the vast American public should no longer be denied the cultural advantage which will redound and we are prepared to lay a goodly sum on the line, Mr. Ransom, a goodly sum.

The publisher toyed with his thick gold watch chain, the fraternal emblem dangling there was diamond-encrusted. So if you would venture to suggest an appropriate sum, to serve as binder for our agreement—?

Frankly, sir, I'd thought in terms of one thousand dollars.

One thousand dollars? Perfectly preposterous, young man, pre*post*errrruss!

But, sir, I—

It would amount to an insult to my professional integrity, Mr. Ransom! A thousand dollars? Humph, I'll pay you a hundred.

But, sir, one hundred dollars—

I didn't mean one hundred dollars! I meant one hundred *thousand* dollars! Beamingly the publisher opened his desk, scratched around here and there, and then began to toss small bags filled with gold coins, to toss them at John Ransom. John dodged and ducked, the plummets fell faster, one struck him in the eye and he yelled with the grief of it. A horse-fly had bitten him on the right eyelid. He sat awake and scorching in the dry bath of the shebang. Bateese came near to feel the back of Johnny's neck, to feel fever there, to say, I bring water.

July 5, wrote the young man a day later. Court is in session outside and raiders being tried by our own men. Wirtz—

(Never could he spell this name correctly.)

—Has done one good thing, but it's a question whether he is entitled to any credit, as he had to be threatened with a break before he would assist us. Rations again today. I am quite bad off with my diseases, but still there are so many thousands so much worse off that I do not complain much, or try not to however.

Boiling hot, camp reeking with filth . . . men dying off. . . . Have more me-mentoes than I can carry, from those who have died, to be given to their friends at home. At least a dozen have given me letters, pictures &c., to take North. Hope I shan't have to turn them over to some one else. . . . Rebel visitors . . . look at us from a distance. It is said the stench keeps all away who have no business here and can keep away.

(All except Ira Claffey, who appeared on a sentry platform daily. Guards begged tobacco from him, he tried to remember to carry a plug at all times; though often he would forget, he used tobacco so rarely himself. He looked down and saw Newgate, Bedlam, and camps where he had heard that Spanish torturers herded the rebellious in colonies of New Spain. He watched the pen where Andy Jackson had suffered and sickened when he was a boy, when the spunky Andrew refused to clean a British officer's boots. He observed the misery of Seminoles, saw Osceola dying in filth and stony pride. Here was an inclusion of every indignity and deprivation which a captor might visit upon those he'd shackled. Shackles? So identified: Ira saw the chain gangs dragging as he walked back to his plantation. He marvelled how Henry Wirz could sleep at night, he did not know that often Henry Wirz never slept.)

At the end of the week, first decisions of the court trying the raiders were written out on a sheet torn from the manifold order book (captured: a Federal manifold order book) which had been donated by Wirz for judicial purposes. This paper was posted upon the South Gate. Many crowded there to read it; the news spread far within minutes, and was the signal for congratulatory hullabaloo.

Willie Collins, Patrick Delaney, John Sarsfield, Charles Curtis and the sailors Munn and Rickson had been sentenced to be hanged by the neck until dead. Seventeen other men were sentenced to floggings, buckings and to the stocks or chain gang for various terms.

The court's deliberations were still proceeding when Henry Wirz sent for Leroy Key and Seneca MacBean. The two were conveyed to his office under guard.

The Gate pen I got to have back!

Captain, you told us we could have it to keep our prisoners in, to use for the trial—

Ja, how many days you have it now?

Key still objected, MacBean said nothing. Seneca had deplored the leisurely garrulous aspect of the trial; he thought that it was a mistake to lean over backward in selecting a court of thirteen sergeants, all of whom were recent arrivals at Andersonville. He supposed that this was a weakness inherent in American institutions; he called it creaky justice. It had worked to the Nation's detriment many times before, and no doubt would until the end of time. Those new-come sergeants had no true conception of what occurred within the stockade during raider-ridden months. They had but academic secondhand knowledge of the fear which had gripped, hands which had gripped, the rupturings and burstings and fracturings so commonplace. MacBean would have been perfectly willing to place any and all of the captured roughs before the muzzles of a firing squad. He would have been willing, if not eager, to stand with that squad. But the dubious chimera of fair play fogged the scene. Cogitations and ramblings of witnesses and counsels alike had long since passed the point of practicality.

You God damn Yankees got lead in your ass, Wirz was screaming. All day you take to tell one man you hang him, one more day you take to tell one more man! Maybe a year you take for the rest, hah? *Gott,* I must use my gate. Those damn prisoners I put back Inside!

Wirz granted but an hour's grace, and said that he would turn the remaining prisoners back into the stockade, using bayonets if necessary. The Illinoisans were dismissed with a few more execrations, but MacBean lingered, even when a guard jerked at his sleeve.

You go when I tell you, you bad sergeant! *Oder* you also I put in the stocks!

Captain, one thing: we've got to have some wood. Planks, timbers, plenty of ropes—

For why should I give you those things, God damn?

Can't hang the guilty folks on thin air. We can't make a gallows out of our shebang poles.

All you damn Yankees thirst for blood!

MacBean stood grinning with saturnine calm, and let Wirz brandish his fist until the arm tired and the fist fell. He saw fierce darting pain in the captain's face, and was annoyed to find himself pitying Wirz. Resolutely he put the pity down.

Going to be a good fellow, Captain, and give us a nice sound gallows? We got hundreds of qualified carpenters who'd be willing to work without pay—

He won the promise of adequate materials for the execution, to be delivered— on loan, not as a gift—within the stockade on Monday morning. Wirz had shrieked that the hanging should occur the very next day. MacBean pointed out that the next day was Sunday, and thousands of prisoners might object to a sextuple execution on the Sabbath. It wouldn't matter to him, he said.

But you might get a riot, Captain.

At that dread word the superintendent winced and agreed that Monday would be best. MacBean went back to the cubicle, provoking guards to rage by his sauntering, and found that the six condemned hooligans had been placed in stocks to await their death. Key adjourned court permanently. The seventeen men already sentenced were herded off to punishment; but more than a hundred others still sat with bound hands (the feet of the more recalcitrant were also bound).

Can't turn them back inside, MacBean told Key, without taking off those ties. They'd be torn to death instanter.

The innocent along with the guilty?

Hells bells, they're all guilty.

Word of the intended repatriation of untried, unconvicted raiders had seeped into the pen; prisoners were roaring. Many, who had been reluctant to assist the Regulators until tide of battle turned in their favor, were now vociferous in declaring their hatred of the accused. They brandished cudgels, declared that they would pound the accused to a pulp the moment they appeared.

A hasty trip through the wicket convinced Key that the danger was real and not fancied. He sent another appeal to Wirz but it fell upon deaf ears. Several squads of guards with fixed bayonets entered the enclosure through its outer gate, and Key shrugged hopelessly.

I don't like it, Seneca.

Don't like it too well myself, but what's a feller to do? Let's you and I haste back inside for keeps.

There was not time to marshal the Regulators. They were scattered over the entire stockade, and had it been possible to marshal them, nothing could have resulted except the burden of perpetual guarding and tending. Swarms of the furious came milling as Key and MacBean stepped through the narrow portal.

Make them run the gantlet, said MacBean in inspiration.

This notion was accepted with roaring enthusiasm. To the end of his life Seneca would believe sincerely that he had saved many lives in this way, although what was the purpose in saving lives such as these? It was apparent that when those hated men were shoved individually through the door they would be mobbed as fast as they appeared. . . . A gantlet was something else: it appealed to a sporting instinct however savage. It suggested in its very form an Indian tradition that if a man managed to flee under a lengthy rain of blows, and survived them, he would achieve to some asylum.

Before the first unhappy New Yorker was shoved through the wicket, a vengeful population had formed a lane for the man's reception. Hundreds of others rushed to extend the course of punishment. The first New Yorker through the gate was an undersized long-armed man called Monk Galloway, ticketed appropriately because of the length of his dangling arms, the flatness of his bald dome, the jut of jaw and scrolling of face. He had trailed with the Roach Guards through a number of street brawls. He knew Willie Collins by sight, if Willie did not know him, before either of them ever heard of Andersonville. Monk was afraid of Willie, and thus had joined the gang captained by Curtis. He was not large, but a dangerous fighter: a man who delighted in cries and blanchings of his victims; then his eyes shone hot, his breath puffed short, spasmodic. Had he come to trial, Monk Galloway might not have been hanged but would have been condemned to a chain gang.

A guard's weapon prodded him, he stepped across the bottom plank. Immediately someone kicked him in the thigh; a club was swung at his head, the blow missed. Holding arms lifted and bent for protection he was propelled down the line by a succession of swats and punches. He fell beneath howls and punishment, leaped up and closed in a tussle with the nearest men. A club snapped against his right ear, already corrugated with scars of old feuds; when he was torn out of this grip and hammered on to the next, he bled at ears and at the nose, his eyes protruded with gleaming fear of death. Any individual of the herd assailing him, he felt that he could have handled alone—in many cases two or three of them together. But neither were they now fellow prisoners nor a flock of bleating creatures to be snapped at by wolves of his species. They were turned into gesticulating Indians, cannibals. They could have been weaker than cats; still the blows would have fallen, there were too many of them.

A new chorus of shouts rang at the gate, another and larger man was hustled. His name was Myles Crickland, his home had been a lumber camp in Michigan. He'd never stolen so much as a dime, and never whipped a smaller man for gain, until he came to Andersonville. But while being shipped he had fallen in with John Sarsfield. Crickland had not wished to starve any more than Edward Blamey wished to starve: he lent size and ferocity to the Sarsfield cause. The same prisoner who'd aimed the initial cudgel stroke at Galloway now whirled his club at the target of the Michigander's head; this time the blow did not miss. The dazed lumberman faltered in a blind circle, his weight carried him completely through one pouncing screaming line before he fell. He could have been pounded to death then and there, but another raider was forced into the arena, attention was distracted. Crickland fell to his knees, fell further. His length stretched across the ground, his shoulders shook as he blubbered. Three contorted youths stood above him, alternately kicking with bare feet and jabbing with poles wrenched from some nearby shebang. . . .

The third man was one Ross from Boston; the fourth a stupid longshoreman, middle-aged, who'd supported the banner of Patrick Delaney. A voice yelled, I think he killed one of our boys, and Ross ran away from that voice. He pushed his bulk down the lane with lurching strides until he was tripped and fell to be stomped upon. Old Cleary made rough agonized progress behind him; most of Cleary's clothes were torn off before he'd gone as far as Ross. . . .

So they came: Murphy, Rae, Billings, Apgar, a dozen more, to receive hackings and thwackings, to be swatted, bloodied . . . beasts of prey turned miraculously into dogs, to accept that cruelty visited upon homeless animals, to know—for the first time, perhaps—what it was to sustain the attack of wretches who gave quarter only when distracted by a new victim.

The eleventh man through the gate was Edward Blamey. Seemingly his legs were more bowed than ever, since he wore a sailor's clothing. In an instant boys were yelling, Look out! Look out, he's got a knife! Certainly Edward Blamey had a knife. In looking after Number One he'd kept gold pieces sewn in the collar of his blouse, and with a gold piece had bought a butcher knife from the venal Mackey Nall, unperceived by Regulators who also guarded. How Ed Blamey had concealed that knife: whether in blouse or sleeve, how he had hidden it when his hands were tied, no one might ever know. The blade flashed in Edward Blamey's freed hand, files of prisoners scattered before him. He went tearing away down the slope; but all The Wrath to Come which had been preached and which he had dreaded, cried at his heels.

Blamey had never been a fast runner. Desperation gave him speed. He fled squarely through one shebang, tried to rush through another and was staggered by the collision. He went to the left . . . no, that way lay the deadline; he held a swift vision of guards lifting their guns above him. He raced back to the east. A small group stood in his path, he yelled, knifed at them, did not strike anyone. The men jumped apart, then joined the pack baying on Ed Blamey's trail.

A lone man watched his rapid approach. His name was Lynn, a solemn farmer from Indiana who had been in the stockade only since the first of the month; he had not been set upon by raiders on his arrival; his uniform was fairly new and fairly clean. Lynn had bull strength left to him. He'd been busy this day, had helped to carry two dead bodies to the habitat of the dead, and was rewarded with the common premium of being allowed to go Outside with a wood detail. His own wood was secured in the shape of a long rail of pine; once the rail had been part of a Claffey fence. Lynn returned through the North Gate. He lugged his pine pole all the way to the shebang he shared with friends on the southern slope, and had been wondering what to do with his prize . . . whether to seek help in cutting it up, whether to sell all or only part of this wooden treasure. He must consult with friends, and they were not at home. He stood as if once more armed and with the Union forces, holding his rifle at Present Arms; actually he held the tall rail straight into the air.

Edward Blamey might not have seen this man; again, he might have seen him and decided flashingly to run the risk. His rubber-legged stride carried him directly in front of Farmer Lynn, and when Ed was two leaps distant the rail began to speed in lowering. It came down rapidly. It had been vertical, it went through its portion of an arc. The sound rapped clear as it struck squarely atop Edward Blamey's bare head. The knife flew. Blamey never thought again, there was no waking mind surviving to reason or repent. The Wrath overtook him. He did not know that Number One was dying, did not know when Number One died.

33

Lord, have mercy on us.
Christ, have mercy on us.
Lord, have mercy on us.

Death On A Pale Horse: people described Henry Wirz so, because of course he rode the old gray-white mare and wore his one suit of white duck.

More and more was Wirz departing from prescribed military usage in his habit and attire. One might have thought that John Winder would upbraid him for these lapses and bring about a reformation. The fact was that the old general paid little attention; but rarely did awareness of slip-shod deportment penetrate the toughening hide which wrapped that senile brain. The guards were slovens, their officers slovens. Sid Winder wore a plaid shirt and a straw hat; Cousin Dick was neater than he, but still he wore red knit galluses. The general himself had streaks of egg and fat upon his tunic, he belched heavily after eating, he ate prodigiously, you could hear him belch if you were standing in the yard outside his quarters. On a single occasion was it observed that his tantrum rose from recognizing that the Swiss captain was not up-to-snuff. An edict had come from Richmond forbidding anyone to issue an order for transportation except on the orders of chiefs of bureaus, or commanders of Armies and Departments. Wirz complained that this dictate locked up the post decisively and hampered him in discharging his duties. He appeared before John Winder with a request that the general obtain an order which would make him, Wirz, an exception and would allow him to issue transportation at least in Winder's name if not merely above his own signature. No one else was in the room with the two, but Captain Peschau sat at an improvised desk on the outside stoop, and two sentries lounged near. They heard a familiar bellow, a wail which stemmed apparently from physical anguish. They heard John Winder roaring, God damn it, can't you grant me the courtesy of appearing *in uniform?* Henry Wirz emerged trotting, with his face ashy; lips trembled under his beard as he muttered, as he ran. It was believed that old J.H.W. had emphasized criticism by grasping the captain's arm, his wounded arm. On this day Wirz wore the bright-piped calico waist, pearl buttons and all; but he had worn it many times before in the general's presence without engendering annoyance. Peschau decided uncomfortably that General Winder had eaten too much pork again. Peschau wondered how soon he himself would stand to endure a verbal thrashing. He watched Henry Wirz retreating on horseback after his usual struggle to hoist that round-shouldered tormented body into the saddle. Peschau thought that he should not wish Wirz's job—not for a fortune in greenbacks, a fortune in gold; not for all the flimsy banknotes which ever poured from Confederate presses.

Death on a white horse, Death on a pale horse, Death warmed over, Death cooled off. So the prisoners typified Henry during this forenoon of July eleventh, when he headed a procession into the stockade.

Holy Mary, pray for them.
All ye holy Angels and Archangels, pray for them.

Holy Abel, pray for them.
All ye choirs of the just, pray for them.

Several thousand new prisoners had arrived since the first of the month, and it was rumored that the raider element might thus be heavily reinforced; there were the usual complement of ex-Bowery Boys, ex-Atlantic Guards, ex-Dead Rabbits in all drafts of Northerners who'd served with the Army of the Potomac and had been captured during the campaign against Richmond. Leroy Key was taking no chances with gangs: when it grew light enough to see, in the Monday dawn, he mustered Regulators and sent each detail to its task.

Early came the scream of ungreased wheels. A wagon rocked slowly through the South Gate rather than the North which was the more common portal of ingress. With an eye to drama and emphasis, the southern hill had been selected for a gallows site. The wagon contained beams, posts, planks, together with a keg of tools and a huge coil of precious rope. Volunteer carpenters set to work promptly inside a hollow square of Regulators whose clubs were ready to discourage any attempt at interference. Willie Collins's castle and the conical tent, which had served as unofficial headquarters for the raider chiefs, were but a few rods distant (beneath the latter shelter one could see disordered heaps of dirt where prisoners had dug, looking for buried treasure—some said that they had dug successfully, some said that they found skeletons of anonymous murdered men— as soon as the ringleaders were bound and hauled away on July third). The frame was of simple construction but would serve to hang six giants, or so its designers believed. They'd drawn a rude sketch the day before, and MacBean relayed the plan to Wirz so that proper materials might be secured. Two posts were set into the ground and a heavy beam secured across their tops. Within this structure, at about the height of a man's head, two wide planks met in the middle—their outer ends resting on cleats nailed against the side posts, their inner ends supported by braces pierced with holes in which ropes were tied.

Get the idee, Archibald?

Not quite.

See, they'll put them fellers on top of the planks, make them stand there. See them ropes coming down from the top brace? Each of them ropes will be noosed around a feller's neck. That's what them sailors are doing now—making nooses. Then, when they get the condemned all noosed up and ready to go, and when the boss gives the word, some folks will jerk on them other ropes down beneath—

And the braces will be ripped out, and the two planks fall, and them sons of bitches will join the Heavenly Choir!

What choir did you say?

Oh, they'll be in hell alongside Judas Priest and Captain Kidd and my own fatherinlaw!

Holy Abraham, pray for them.
St. John the Baptist, pray for them.
St. Joseph, pray for them.
All ye holy Patriarchs and Prophets, pray for them.

Sun rose hotter, people said that this would be the hottest day yet suffered. The great glaring mass of sun seemed concentrated as in a locomotive's headlamp, burning against the fresh gallows on the South Hill. The mosaic on the northern slope began to shape and tighten long before carpenters completed their task; boys selected vantage points and sat to watch, but soon they were forced to stand as other vagrants came crowding, there was not space in which to sit. They stood wearily, stared, jostled. For pity sakes quit sticking me with your elbow. Who, me? I ain't sticking you—blame arm's too weak to stick anybody, Charley.

Yes, and know what your legs look like? So I do: two darning needles with pumpkin seeds stuck on the bottom of them. O laughter, it is food and tonic; the brave have it, the brave drink of it and give it back to those in need. . . . A singing-school teacher from Danbury lay motionless in a shebang beyond Main Street or Broadway or whatever you wished to call the distant sluice; his heart pushed lazily inside his ribs, shuddered, bubbled for a moment, went on beating reluctantly again; the songster from Danbury did not know that anyone was about to be hanged, he did not have an illusion to stimulate or hurt him, he knew nothing, felt nothing. A Delaware oysterman lay motionless near the east dead-line, he lay in no shebang but exposed fully to the sun, he had no shebang, not a friend to carry him to thin shelter, soon he would need no shebang, his back was a water blister, his bony arms were blisters; under raw ribs the heart twitched gamely, fluttered—why, in that very moment it stopped, it ceased while we stood observant! A thousand men lay or huddled in a thousand far-flung places and did not care about a hanging; did not care who was hanged or why; but more than twenty thousand others plastered slope and ridge with their staring, their press.

Carpenters built a rough stair at the south end of the gallows; there were several cleats nailed across runners; they built their ladder stoutly, the con-demned were heavy men.

St. Peter, pray for them.
St. Paul, pray for them.
St. Andrew, pray for them.
St. John, pray for them.
All ye holy Apostles and Evangelists, pray for them.

Where ground tilted upward beyond the southwest corner of the stockade, where guns of the star fort threatened the stockade's interior, citizens and slaves of the county stood waiting. Women white and brown held their children up, they told their children to watch. Long before sunrise carts had been a-rumble on the road from Americus, mules stalked piny ways from the high region to the west, old men trudged out of damp lonely settlements along the Flint River. To begin with, a cordon of Reserves had lined with their bayonets, ordered to keep the populace in check, to hold them back from space directly in front of the cannon. There was room, it was pointed out, for all to see.

Just stand over there past the end of them rifle pits. You can see tolerable well.

Few people will assemble to watch a man living, most will congregate to watch him die.

The region immediately under the muzzles was higher, the view broader there, you could grasp a wider panorama of the interior. Bit by bit, moment after moment, the throng of ragged farmers, blacks and children came edging. Reserves were not trained to this task, their officers had ascended to sentry stations; they began to disperse and mingle with the very crowd they'd been set to restrain.

On the hill to the immediate north, across the Sweetwater branch, there was an area below the guards' camps where more than a glimpse of the fascinating interior might be obtained across the stockade's dip through the ravine. Here also humanity clustered—hangers-on of the Reserves, homeless servants who'd wan-dered from raided plantations in Alabama and northwest Georgia, who'd starved their way along the railroad line and here were impressed to serve as wood-choppers or grave-diggers. They massed, wondering, giggling.

They going put Yankees on that thing.

Yes, boy, sometime you hang a man—he fall down—old rope just pull he head square off—smick, smack—clean off he body.

Yi!

Ma, what's they a-doing yonder?

Them Yankees are going to *kill* each other.

Why, Ma?

Cause Yankees is bad.

How they going to kill each other, Ma?

Now you just shut your trap, and watch.

All ye holy Disciples of our Lord, pray for them.

All ye holy Innocents, pray for them.

St. Stephen, pray for them.

St. Lawrence, pray for them.

All ye holy Martyrs, pray for them.

Six assistant hangmen had been selected by lot from the ranks of Regulators and stood close together, watched with round eyes by prisoners nearest them; they were ready for their task with meal sacks and cords, the two youngest sought to minimize the strain of the hour by clowning. They tussled, wrestling, they did not fall to the ground, it was a sham battle, each was trying to force his meal sack over the other boy's head. Key said testily, Come along, come along, you'll get plenty of action in a few minutes; and they permitted the rebuke to turn them more sedate, as if deliberately they had sought rebuke.

An audible murmur drifted from outside the stockade, it spread in a quiet but distinguishable wave, born in throats and on the lips of the hundreds who grouped in two galleries on God's side of the fence, not on the Devil's; and it fell across the jagged parapet and rolled slowly through and over observant thousands within the pen.

Must be coming. Must be fetching them now.

Can't fetch them too soon to suit me.

That God damn bruiser of a Curtis like to killed me when he took my watch.

Well, he did kill one of our Twenty-second Connecticut boys.

You see him do it?

Don't you wherrit yourself: he done it.

The South Gate squawked open and crunched against posts set to receive its weight, the parade came in. Death On A Pale Horse rode ahead, and close behind the mare walked Father Peter Whelan wearing his soiled violet stole. The six condemned giants swaggered together, moving between double files of Rebel guards; Willie Collins's laugh echoed booming, he was laughing at something Delaney had said. There were no wan Floral Tebbses and Irby Flinchers bearing arms alongside the raiders; ranks of the Reserves had been combed to select a handful of veterans available for this chore. The guards had been ordered to shoot at the first sign of a break. These shaggy gray- and blue-clad men walked ready to fire, their hands lay across the locks of their guns.

Sure, you bandogs, and it's men like us you think you can fright with your twaddle of hanging?

Let's jump the bastards, Paddy!

Wait till we're rid of these guards.

St. Sylvester, pray for them.

St. Gregory, pray for them.

St. Augustine, pray for them.

All ye holy Bishops and Confessors, pray for them.

Swarms of black-faced Yankees split and fell away from the cautious advance of Wirz's mare, they did not wish to be stepped upon. Wirz traveled toward the gallows as directly as terrain and assortment of huts would allow; he bent past the mare's neck, watching for wells or dangerous pits, he had no desire to be thrown. Father Whelan followed Wirz on foot. He had washed his old jacket and it was still wet from the washing, so he came in his patched shirt. A smelly breeze lifted from somewhere to sway the ragged hems of his stole; prisoners looked with interest at the pretty color, the pretty violet. Nowhere else within the stockade was there violet. There were so few bright colors to be seen except often the color of blood. Father Whelan carried his umbrella beneath his arm, he did not have it spread, fractured bones of the umbrella thrust out and dangled. The Ritual was clasped in the priest's withered hand, his Crucifix was detected by glaring sun.

Wirz turned, motioned, jabbered an almost unintelligible order. Three or four Reserves moved forward hastily to open a wider path with their bayonets, and around the gallows area the hollow square of Regulators broke in obedience to Leroy Key's command. Make way, hurry up, so's we'll get them inside. The procession came to a halt. Wirz nudged his mare to one side, the square tightened once more in additional security. Seneca MacBean was horrified to see that the raiders walked unbound; this was a most stupid oversight on the part of Confederate authorities. He muttered softly about it, and with Dreyfoos, Corrigan and Limber Jim he stepped closer. Ready with your clubs, boys, minute those guards go out.

Prisoners!

Wirz's voice cut the fetid air, and as usual a few people on the outskirts began to mock his accent.

To you now I return these men, good as I got them. You say you try them yourself, you find them guilty. Nothing do I have to do with this—it is you, you prisoners.

The porcelain face of Henry Wirz was more drawn and gleaming than ever; he kept pausing in his speech, hunting for proper words. Those closest could see his pointed pink tongue coming out to moisten his lips under the ravelled beard.

Now to you I commit these men. Of everything with them I am washing my hands! Do to them what you wish, for it is you—you prisoners—who find them guilty.

He hesitated for another second, scowling, perspiring.

May *Gott* have mercy on them *und* you prisoners.

His wiry nervous voice went high. Guards, About—*Face!*

Lines swung into position with the click and thud of shoes and weapons.

Forward—*March!*

They went toward the gate. The square of Regulators squeezed closer, smaller, no longer a square, it was become a twisted circle under force of compression from the outside.

St. Benedict, pray for them.

St. Francis, pray for them.

St. Camillus, pray for them.

St. John of God, pray for them.

All ye holy Monks and Hermits, pray for them.

The manner of Wirz as much as the speech he uttered had its quick effect upon the six condemned. They looked at one another, they looked into hard faces of the Westerners who approached them cautiously but grimly. Had this been a threat, a kind of malignant jest? They'd sneered at the sentence when it was pronounced, boasted mutually of what they would do to the first person who put a hand on them, what they would do to the last person. They'd marched for long in the chain-mail of their established wickedness, bragged of their established wickedness; most of them had known little besides wickedness; they ate of it, drank of it, embraced and made love to a quaking rotting harlot called Wickedness. For what reason did there exist weaker mortals except to serve as foils, targets, scullions, spies?

Were they come to an End? They had never come to an End before. Their seizure and the comedy of court and trial were but a trivial interlude. Organ grinders had brought a Jocko or two to Andersonville in order to entertain them. Soon the monkey tricks would be finished, and somehow— In some way— By swindle, bribery— Through blow or cutting or strangulation the roughs would win back to the peerage they'd enjoyed, grown fat in, continued bloody-handed in.

Sarsfield gazed in disbelief at the gallows. His soldier's eye took in the crude but solid construction, his criminal's eye saw the nooses and rolled away from them and then came back to congeal.

He brayed, You don't really mean to hang us up there?

That seems to be about the size of it.

They might roar now, at least all except Rickson were howling; yet they'd had their fun before. They had taken joy in tormenting Father Whelan. From the moment word reached him that the six were condemned to death, the priest burned with ardor. Never was such challenge offered him before! To Peter Whelan, the Devil was an entity as real as himself, real as Wirz or the last boy he'd shrived. The Devil had maintained strict possession of these six souls, obviously, through their lifetime. What a triumph for the Church could Whelan loose those tight slimy tentacles, cause them to unwrap, extract the bruised suffering souls and wash them to purity! Examination disclosed that all except the close-mouthed Rickson had, in dim forgotten childhood, partaken of some semblance of Catholicism, or admitted to a Catholic inheritance however remote. Sincerely the priest hoped to bring them to admission of guilt. This admission might be achieved properly only if the men recited transgressions in detail and came eventually to repent. Because of their mutual imprisonment in the stocks, the privacy of a Confessional might not be observed; but Peter Whelan would do his best. . . . None of the six could believe that they were to die, and this ceremony became a sport.

Collins, man, you must go to confession. Our Lord is beseeching you to go.

Faith, I'll be going.

I want you to make a good confession.

Sure, and Willie rolled puffy blood-traced eyes at Delaney and Munn in stocks beyond him.

When did you make your last worthy confession, Collins?

Twas in my mother's belly.

The others guffawed.

Sins you shall confess in a good confession are the sins you have committed since your last worthy confession; but I'm praying, me son, that you will make a general confession.

What the hell might a general confession be?

Tis every sin of your entire past life you must confess, or at least the sins you may remember most clearly.

And why must I be doing this?

You are about to die, me son. They tell me that you've been found guilty— Oh, how I hate the word! Of *murder.* And you shall be executed, you shall be put to death for *murder.* I am but a humble servant of the Church; still I'm striving to engender contrition in your poor soul. I'm striving to loosen the grip of the Devil; he's had his claws upon you for so long, that he has.

What should I be after telling you, priest?

Call me Father, me son.

What should I be after telling you, Father? and Willie Collins winked so enormously that you could very nearly hear the snap of his eyelid.

Recite your past sins, and try to feel as much real sorrow as you're capable of feeling.

Well— There was a priest in New York—

And was he the one who heard your last confession?

Shit, never! He was the one I killed!

May God have mercy on your soul—

Sure, I cracked his throat with this very hand! And after he lay dreaming, I tied him to the top of his altar. And then— I set fire to the church! What a pretty blaze it made!

Delaney twisted his head in the adjoining stocks. Willie, lad. Was that before or after you were raping of the nun?

St. Mary Magdalen, pray for them.

St. Lucy, pray for them.

All ye holy Virgins and Widows, pray for them.

All ye holy Saints of God, make intercession for them.

Confronted actually with a machine erected for the express purpose of wrenching their lives away, they felt that they had been tricked. Their unanimous reaction was a rage the more blinding because of its complete futility. How now, how now? They stood without a tie of restraint upon them—now they should lift their hands, they must grasp and tear—let feet and elbows go flailing into the rank of blank-visaged men pressing close.

But— But—

The joskin called Key stood beyond their reach, he stood— Nickey snatch the lot of us! He stood with a revolver in his hand! And that black Indian of a Limber Jim stood with a bowie knife exposed. A bullet could reach or a steel blade slice before a man might crack more than a head or two; and here formed a hundred or two hundred of the damnable police with hate freezing their faces.

Howl no longer, thought Willie Collins, as his whole awareness and minor intelligence went draining into his boots. Howl no more.

He gave a shivering gulp. Thick tears began to ooze. His voice was shaking, humble. He called through the almost visible spume of threats and curses, Be quiet, you bastards!

Strangely they became quiet. Their terrified calm went spreading like a cloud's shadow through the population around them, and raced over the stockade as a moving representation of that same cloud, a brown silent formless wraith darkening the hill it passed across. The pen was more quiet than it had been, day or night, from the moment the first prisoners passed through the gate in that distant torch-lit February. At one end of the world sounded a locomotive's whistle, at the other end of the world crows made their wah-wah-wah; slopes of staring people were unspeaking and uncalling in between. At last Willie Collins and the rest might seek the very help they had derided.

Be still, lads. Willie added, with that pitiful dignity achieved by the brutal when they have fallen, Let the priest speak for us.

Ah, prisoners, cried Peter Whelan. Soldiers, if you like. Hear me now, please to give ear to me words. Can you not find forgiveness in your hearts? Have you no pity and no mercy? Remember our dear Lord who died upon the Cross to save us all from shame and sin! What would our Lord say, think you now, if He were standing among us at this moment, with His dear face aglow with inner mercy, with the light of compassion shining from His dear eyes? Would He ask for blood? Nay, nay— He would be beseeching you to spare the lives of these, your fellow men—

No, said one flat voice in the nearer crowd.

Be merciful, spare them, O Lord!

Be merciful, deliver them, O Lord!

Be merciful, deliver them, O Lord!

From Thy Anger, deliver them, O Lord!

From the danger of death, deliver them, O Lord!

The dry shivering voice continued its plea. What will it profit you if you demand now the death of these six miserable men? Sure, they're sinners. But aren't we all, does not each of us here on earth have his faults, are we not mortal as these poor condemned men are mortal? Oh, lads, prisoners, men of the North— Will this gallows bring back from the grave the boys who've been done to death? Never. Can this gallows expunge, lads, the miseries which have been done, the pain that's been inflicted? Never, never. A gallows cannot make, it can only mar. Search your hearts, now, lads— And find pity for these miserable sinners— And find mercy again in your hearts, for surely you shall find God when you find mercy— Spare them, lads!

No, that same single voice came biting.

Ferocious hating brothers of the lone boy (whoever might he be? And perhaps his mother or sweetheart or Sunday School teacher had said many times, Luke is the tender one. Just see how gently he handles Tab's kittens. He's such a gentle lad, wouldn't harm a flea) put their cry up against his, and supported him a thousand fold and supported him ten thousand fold. Peter Whelan's supplication went drowning. No. No. *No.* The short grunting yells thudded as if a master chorister stood with ferule uplifted, beating rhythm. No. No. No. No. *No!*

Hang them, rose the high-pitched hoot of a mountain boy who'd been stripped at the North Gate eight days before. Hang them, by Mighty! Haaaang them.

Hang them, said posts of the fence. Haaaang them, said every sentinel's platform. The gallows cried, Haaaang them; each beam and timber implored a choking. You could see that lacy face of old Peter Whelan turned in agony. (He was more miserable than he would be at any moment until he dragged himself out of the gate for the last time, in October.) His lips were moving, his jaws went up and down, but no man standing at his elbow could have heard him now.

From an ill end, deliver them, O Lord!

From the pains of hell, deliver them, O Lord!

From all evil, deliver them, O Lord!

From the power of the devil, deliver them, O Lord!

No, no, no, no, *no!* Never deliver them, let them strangle and stretch. Let the long jarring fall snap their necks, let nooses crunch, let the men's breath fail, let them die hard. Never deliver them, O Lord. Hang them, hang them, haaaang them!

Henry Wirz had reached his office some minutes before, but the wide slamming chant brought him out immediately, he stood bewildered on the step. What were those prisoners up to? Bears, what message do you growl?

Was gibt's?

Said the clerk who stood behind him, speaking in German— Captain, it is the prisoners, all calling together. They demand that the big men be hanged.

Why don't they get on with it, then?

Charles Curtis stood at the right of the file against whom the implacable demand of Hang them, Hang them, was cried. His gorilla shape was shortest in stature of any of the condemned. When honest (but dull and brutal to those about him) he had wielded a tamping-bar on the railroad in Providence. There was trouble because he struck a fellow workman with that same tamping-bar; his fist would have been nearly as lethal. Curtis decamped to Boston, found employment on the docks, found opportunities for profitable banditry. Again the police chased him, this time to Brooklyn, where he and a partner went buccaneering in a stolen boat through several lucrative seasons. In time they quarreled over the use and abuse of an anguished housemaid, a Scandinavian immigrant whom they'd kidnapped and lugged to a deserted wharf. Curtis's partner was found floating a day or two later, minus a portion of his skull; Charles Curtis sought seclusion in a battery of the Fifth Rhode Island Artillery. He was believed to have killed at least a dozen men with his own hands while in Andersonville, and to have been responsible for the murder of many others in his role as gang leader. But still he did not wish to hang, and now roared that he would not hang. Other Fifth Rhode Island artillerymen would sink to their doom in the mire of this place: Doyle would die in August, Calvin would die in September, Fay in August, Garvey in August, Sisson in August, Eaton in October; even at this moment one William Wallace lay in final stupor; and all were comrades, some from Charles Curtis's own battery. Not one of them but would have prayed to see him swinging. Still he did not wish to hang. I'd ruther die this way, his thick harsh voice came bursting. With arms folded across his face he dove into the line of Regulators.

His weight and force and suddenness flung their bodies away on either side of him, and two men went flat and his feet came down upon them as he plunged. Some idiot shrieked that Curtis held a weapon. He's got a knife, got a gun, look out, he's got— A mass of crowding prisoners outside the ranks of policemen scattered in terror. Curtis made rapid progress down the slope, he did not need to fling people away, they flung themselves in fear. A string of Regulators sped yelling a few rods behind. Get him! That's Curtis! Stop him, you down there! and the emphasis of their hollering cancelled the chorused litany which was still being called on the northern slope.

To the taut mind of Henry Wirz this commotion suggested but one thing: a prison break. It had been so long a dread that now, in coming (he thought it coming, he thought it in progress) it was nearly welcome. Gus, he screamed, tell the battery commander— When Gus the clerk lingered useless, dumb and rooted to planks whereon they stood, Wirz himself leaped from the stoop with a jar which racked him and went flurrying up the hill toward the star fort. He extracted his revolver from its holster as he ran, nearly dropped the weapon, he tried to cock it as he ran. Fire! soared his anguished cry, slender and shrill as the voice of a child at play, a child playing Indian. Fire! Son of a bitch! Why do you not fy-urrrr? . . . All soaked and gasping he stumbled past an embrasure, fighting through a tangle of country people and slaves who pushed first one way, then another; they did not know where to run, they felt that they must run somewhere.

The battery's commander glared in disgust. Gol damn, Captain Wirz, can't you see nothing? Those prisoners are running away from the fence, not towards it—

They try to break loose—

Naw, naw, naw. The artilleryman reached for Wirz's arm, clutched the right arm which was of course the wrong arm. Wirz howled. The artilleryman managed to turn the hysterical superintendent around, he tried to soothe him. Anyway, how the hell would I dare pull a lanyard with all these niggers and youngers and old folks too, square in front of my guns? Them Reserves ain't worth shit.

Henry Wirz bullied the Georgia Reserves back to their task. They came with shamed faces from sentry platforms, came out of the crowd itself. Responding to their brandishing of bayonets and threat of muskets, citizens and blacks allowed themselves to be folded away from the cannon. Guns could fire now were it necessary, but no necessity lived. People within the pen were become more static; they thronged to watch the capture of Charles Curtis, who'd halted mired to his middle in the slough of feces and maggots.

Regulators halted their pursuit at the margin of the swamp when they saw how speedily the Rhode Islander's excursion into freedom was halted. Well, here he is. A voice sang it from somewhere in the rear, as such voices always sing. Who in hell's going to go into all them worms and turds after him?

Without a word Nathan Dreyfoos waded to the task. He thought, In some fashion I can cleanse myself later. Someone must fetch the beast or he'll never come. At least I am strong enough to resist him in turn if he resists.

For some time Nathan had been reduced to the wearing of sandals carved and stitched by himself; but with the overthrowing of the raiders he was well-shod from Patrick Delaney's private hoard of boots. In amusement he felt now that it grieved him more to insert these new (to him) beloved shoes in the sickening bog than it did to know that ooze was working steadily higher on his torn pants and pasting putridity against his skin—skin perhaps not too clean, but at least pure, purer than the slow-foaming lake of drainage human and inhuman. A line came to his fancy: *Not all the perfumes of Arabia*— He felt young pardonable pride in knowing that others behind him were admiring the fortitude he displayed.

Curtis stood gasping in an attitude of defense, arms half bent, fists but half clenched. No, Nathan told him in a low voice, you will not die here. You shall hang; you have been sentenced; you shall hang.

Nathan pushed his long left arm forward, but holding the hickory club ready in his right hand, until he felt and saw his fingers grow around the open collar of Charles Curtis's flannel shirt. Bulbous green eyes stared into his own eyes with no hatred which Nathan Dreyfoos might detect; first he saw a fear and then a yielding, a blankness. He thought to himself, I have hypnotized him, or else he has hypnotized himself through his very flight—and how foolish it was! and where could he have fled to?—

Come, Nathan commanded in a stronger voice.

Curtis moved with him humbly, almost as if pleased to return. But his heavy breathing was a frog's grunt; his breath came quicker and quicker, he shook visibly with each labored respiration.

Want— Want a drink—

You shall have water.

Not— Not this—

There is water waiting you. At the gallows.

A certain amount of whistling exultation rose protractedly out of the thousands who observed; there were a few hands which spatted in applause; for the most part the inhabitants watched in silence. His hands holding Curtis's wrists behind his back (Nathan heard his tutor's suave voice out of the past: I say, old chap, shall we wrestle today?) the captor brought the condemned man up to more solid earth. First their brown shining dripping thighs were visible, then knees and lower limbs; maggots dropped along with the breakage of muck reluctant to be severed. Once Nathan slid and tripped, but the rock of Curtis's body kept him from falling.

The Rhode Islander continued with painful gasping. Give me—Drink—

Yes, you'll get water—

There was a tangle of Regulators on the margin; Nathan delivered his prize into this clump. Then he staggered toward even firmer ground; he did not realize it, but he was breathing almost with the force and noise of the man he'd caught. His mouth hung open, sweat drenched down from his bony face, dripped from the high point of his beaked nose; but his eyes were luminous with triumph. People gave him plenty of room because of the pudding which clung to his clothes. Curtis was dragged up the south side of the ravine, but Dreyfoos made his way along an avenue which opened before him to the west. He saw the creek gurgling under and around the posts, heard it gurgling. When he'd come fairly against the dead-line he looked up at the sentry station with smiling appeal.

Let me—go inside—if you please. In the stream—

Yank, get away—!

Please! I wish— Only to—stand in the creek? The water's comparatively—clear—within the deadline. My legs—are plastered with—

The little sentinel gabbled a threat, but someone pushed him out of the way, and the plump chin-whiskered face of Lieutenant Davis looked down in excitement amounting to anguish. Nobody's to fire at this Yank, he said distinctly. Pass it to them other stations, hear me? The word went along the fence, called to each guard within range. Don't fire, don't fire at that big Yank. All right, tall feller, said Davis to Nathan. I've done got you covered with my own pistol, so's you can get inside that deadline and clean yourself off. *If* you can! Gratefully Nathan obeyed. The swarm of nearer prisoners watched with envy. Numerous men had been shot at that point, trying to scoop cleaner water from beyond the deadline. Nathan splashed and scrubbed with his hands.

On the hill Seneca MacBean told Limber Jim, Well, that ought to help a little. But if we all club together, we can buy better water from some of the wells. Kind of think we owe it to Brother Nathan. He'd present an awful problem to the Sucker Laundry and Cleaning Company right now.

What about Curtis? asked someone.

Lived dirty, can die dirty, said Limber Jim.

Limber Jim felt satisfaction in the knowledge that only one raider had sought to follow the runaway Curtis. That was Patrick Delaney: he'd taken a tentative step or two and then Limber Jim was in front of him with uplifted knife. Delaney backed away and allowed himself to be tied as the others were now tied, as the wretched smelling Curtis would be tied whenever he got up from the step where he had collapsed.

He sat for five or ten minutes, he sat on the bottom rung of the rough stair on which the six must ascend to execution. His legs had crumpled inside their dreadful coating. Give me drink, he kept saying, over and over. The charitable bucket turned toward him with each request. He drank with sputtering gulps, pushed the pail from him, gasped, belched, water ran from his beard and from the corners of his mouth. His eyes were fat as clams. It was as if he saw nothing but the bucket, wanted nothing but water.

Through Thy nativity, deliver them, O Lord!

Through Thy cross and passion, deliver them, O Lord!

Now indeed would Willie Collins kiss the object so foreign to his thick lips. He was not to die taunting; for the first time he knew that he was about to die, and in a fashion in which he'd never believed that he would die. Along with Curtis and the rest he drowned himself in water. Gossiping wonder rose from nearest crowds, those who could see the thirst of this grotesque clan and hear their petition and swallowing. Already one—twas Rickson, people whispered—had filled his belly until it was bursting . . . he threw up, threw up water and whatever else was inside him. Regulators jumped out of the way. Yet a minute or two afterward Rickson was beckoning to the boys with pails. Several of them kept trotting back and forth to supply this inordinate demand.

Sergeant Key, please— Them Clevelanders said to tell you they want to know who's going to pay for all this water.

Too bad, said Key. But their well is nearest.

Tell them Clevelanders, came the drawl of Seneca MacBean, that the Good Lord will reward them in His own good time. And no funny business, or I'll be over there directly and drop them down their own well.

A suggestion was made: Give them Mosby's watch. Reckon he'd ruther have water than his watch.

MacBean went to speak to the giant. Father Whelan was busy with Delaney beside him, and Seneca was compelled to push next to the priest; he apologized at disturbing him. Peter Whelan did not even hear him. His lined face was blue with effort, his wide firm mouth had become a blur, the soul within him must be blurring as it labored—embracing the doomed with one spiritual arm, jogging the Devil away with the other. Sen MacBean came back with a gold watch chain hanging over his finger.

Says he gave the watch to a guard outside, hoping to have his bonds cut loose, but I assume the guard didn't dast. Anyway here's the chain to it.

Mister. The slow-spoken question of A. R. Hill. Is that chain made of little oak leaves kind of hanging together?

Yep.

Than I guess twould be Martin's chain. Willie Collins took it off of him whilst we were at Belle Isle.

Know the heirs?

That I do.

Give them avaricious well-owners maybe a link apiece? Twould more than pay for the water; and you take the rest to the heirs, should you ever survive to get back to Ohio.

That I will. Hill put the chain in his pocket.

Through Thy death and burial, deliver them, O Lord!

Through Thy glorious resurrection, deliver them, O Lord!

Through Thy admirable ascension, deliver them, O Lord!

On the platform of distant Station Number Thirty-three, Ira Claffey spoke to the Reverend Mr. Dillard.

(Cato Dillard had come early from Americus with some idea of visiting the six hoodlums and praying over them. Ira explained to his friend that he'd heard the men were all Catholics and thus would not desire Presbyterian attention. Cato breakfasted lengthily at the Claffey house, could not make up his mind whether any good purpose would be served if he witnessed the hanging; he said that he had never seen anyone die except in bed. He believed that the gravity and horror of the thing might be reflected valuably in future sermons wherein he should describe certain penalties awaiting the unregenerate. Ira Claffey himself had intended all along to watch the execution were it possible. Lucy shivered away from him, and did not understand, and spoke indignantly of Morbid Curiosity. Ira had seen a man hanged long before, in Mexico—a man put to death for a criminal assault upon a child. He had approved that sentence and was glad to witness the dealing out of punishment—as now, he believed, he would be glad to observe the final agony of these rogues. Had it fallen to him to be a hangman in such a case, he would not have cringed, he would have done the work. He thought that a man might not know how to be gentle toward recipients who needed gentleness, did he not know how to be savage with the proper targets for savagery. He thought his a just and honorable code. Secretly he believed it should be followed internationally, but doubted that it ever would be. Thus, after toilsome examination of their separate philosophies in the matter, the two gentlemen arrived in the vicinity to find the roughs already marched inside; and it was cried that one of them had broken away in flight but was recaptured. Every station near the scene was weighted with spectators past the point of safety. Officers and men hung upon the ladders. Ira and the minister were compelled to walk the stockade's path to the far east wall. Accompanying Ducky Duckworth on Station Thirty-three roosted a corporal who came often to the Claffeys' for garden truck. This youth took the guard's musket and sent the frightened sputtering ancient down the ladder, to his immense relief. The two citizens climbed up and gazed at gallows and thick knots of humanity corded there, they saw the infinity of paupers who looked on.)

I have Sutherland's field-glasses by me, Brother Dillard.

Ah, I saw. Captain Poe fetched them to you, after—?

After Gettysburg. Watch closely—they're like twin spy-glasses—each tube must be adjusted of itself, to suit the eye.

Cato Dillard stood with white whiskers pushed by the mild breeze, and had much difficulty in adjusting the glasses to suit his vision. Ah . . . *The wicked are like the troubled sea, when it cannot rest, whose waters cast up mire and dirt.* And the priest proceeds with his pagan rites!

You know, Brother, doubtless he feels sincerely that our rites are the pagan ones.

Them there Catholics, said Corporal Yount. They bow down to wood and stone. Yes, sir, they worship idols. My own brother he went into a Catholic church one time, at the North, and he seen the idols with his own eyes.

Caught in the circle of vision, never knowing or caring whether men put a stare on him or not, Peter Whelan toiled with eyes, ears, lips, hands and the opening and pressing out of his own honest soul. In this fierce moment recollection cried for blessings on a group of serious men in the Rome of long ago, who had made it possible for him to award these poor creatures an apostolic blessing. In his youth —When first he entered the Church— No, it could not have been done then. As a young man Peter Whelan had been taught the clear theology of the time: the sacrament of Extreme Unction could not be given to those who stood in danger of death from a purely external cause. So it stood even today. But in Father Whelan's young time there was no clear theology about the last blessing. Bishop Miter announced his belief that the apostolic blessing could be given only when Extreme Unction could also be given, Cardinal Cassock said Nay—he felt that the blessing might be awarded to even those in danger of death from external cause. So the argument abounded, it had abounded for a long time. Peter Whelan's memory went back to a chilly night in front of a welcome fire—why, it was in 1841; he was still in Ireland; he sat before Father Monell's peat—and the eager voices spoke on every side.

. . . Very definitely. Twas announced by the Sacred Congregation of Propaganda.

. . . And what was the question submitted?

. . . Truth is, it concerned a condemned criminal.

. . . You mean to tell me, Father, that the Sacred Congregation declares the last blessing can be given on the same day that a man dies?

. . . Sure and I do. How grateful all the condemned, of the present day and the future as well, should be for this leniency! Blessings be upon the Sacred Congregation of Propaganda! Sacrament of Extreme Unction or no Sacrament of Extreme Unction—

Oh, Father—

Yes, man.

Twas a hockey. I broke his head with a rat. I was but a child—

What are you saying, Collins?

A drunken man. He was that elderly! I killed him, Father, killed him dead—

And do you truly and fervently repent of that crime?

Father, I do, I do—

And all your multitude of other sins?

Och! But it was never true about me slaying the priest. Nor about the nun, Father—

I'm endeavoring to awaken in the poor soul of you as much real sorrow for your past sins as you are capable of feeling.

I repent, Father! Truly, truly, truly I do.

Through the grace of the Holy Ghost, the Comforter, deliver them, O Lord!

In the day of judgment, deliver them, O Lord!

And which are you again, you poor miserable creature?

Name's Munn.

Yes, indeed, I get you mixed, lads. And Munn, me boy—for it's not more than two and twenty you can be— Ah, Munn. Name your sins and be contrite. Feel the sorrow of them!

There—there was a boy. Cabin boy.

And when was this?

When first I served aboard the *Kitty Cat.* But—we were in dry-dock—

Did you commit murder, Munn?

Twasn't that. My watch below and— He was there. Weren't no others about. He—he was little. Kind of a pretty little boy. Not more'n twelve or thereabouts. So I tied him up and pulled down his pants—He did yell and cry! I put it up— Up his—

Time is fleeting, you poor miserable Munn. Do you truly repent of your abominable sins, me boy?

Oh, Father— I do, I do repent!

We sinners, beseech Thee, hear us.

That Thou spare them, we beseech Thee, hear us.

Lord, have mercy on us. Christ, have mercy on us. Lord, have mercy on us.

Leroy Key had been glancing at his watch again and again. Now he stood with watch in hand, and nodded, and made a clicking sound toward the hangmen who were grouped close behind the condemned and seemed so slight in comparison. Those designated as actual executioners were two named Harris and Payne; at Key's signal they moved toward ropes which lay coiled neatly on opposite sides of the scaffold. A grimy youth with caked pinkish hair (he came from Hamilton County, Iowa—his name was Dolliver) put a cautious hand at Willie Collins's back and poked him several times, and finally pushed Willie into motion. Willie blubbered whole-heartedly, his vision was so watered with tears that his blundering feet had difficulty in negotiating the ladder's steps. Eben Dolliver helped him to climb. First step, said the young man, pushing the hulk along. . . . Next step . . . now the third. . . . Next one. Take care, he said, it's wider. . . . Now up you go, onto the planks. Dolliver prodded Collins along the braced boards to the farthermost noose. Willie went with the docility of an agèd blind dog. Eben Dolliver took him by his rigid elbow and made him turn to face the east, as others were being made to turn, close beside one another, bound arms pressed close, their thighs pressed close. There they were lined in another minute or two: Collins, the reeking Curtis, Munn, Delaney, John Sarsfield, William Rickson; and Rickson was the only one who made no sound. Father Whelan had offered the Crucifix even to this Unbeliever, but Rickson turned away with an annoyed jerk of his head. Whelan sought to follow the parade of the dozen men up the ladder, but Sen MacBean restrained him. Sighing audibly, the old priest moved to the east of the scaffold and opened his precious little book. He began with *Adjutorium in nomine Domini. Qui fecit caelum et terram,* but soon realized that little time remained; he must seek a shorter form. He began again: *Ego, facultate mihi ab Apostolica Sede tributa—*

Three minutes to talk, said Key. If any of you want to talk. You'll go at eleven o'clock.

All were talking except the iron-jawed Rickson. John Sarsfield's voice rose above the rest; he was telling of his being wounded in the field, of his life being blameless before he came to Andersonville. Munn said, Four months ago, when I came here, I'd never stole a dollar in my life. I—I got a mother and two sisters in New York— And this made Willie Collins think of a wife and child who had been merely incidental in his life and whom he had deserted calmly. Boys, he wailed, don't hang me! Spare my life, boys, for I've a wife and child at home—

Indulgentiam plenariam et remissionem omnium peccatorum tibi concedo.

Aw, said Paddy Delaney, shut your jaw, Willie Collins. You'll never be getting the governor's stiff. If I had to live on the rations the rest of you live on— Faith, I'd rather hang! Only if a man were to steal would he get enough to eat in this damn place.

Peter Whelan looked up at him in admonishment. Me son, did you not truly repent of your crimes? Concern yourself with God.

Father, I've got this watch in my pocket—pants pocket, I can't reach it with my hands tied— But I see Pete Donnelly a-standing below; and Pete, tis in my pocket on the right side; so you shall have the watch after I'm gone—

Two minutes, said Key, looking closely at his own watch. Payne and Harris had uncoiled the ropes attached to the two stout braces beneath the planks, and stood in soldierly fashion with the ropes' ends in their hands.

Pete Donnelly, there's this ring upon my finger; has a fine jewel in it, and be after giving it to Pete Bradley, him that was once a jaw cove at the City College—

Father Whelan interrupted his reading with increased sternness. Me son! Let go these matters of Here On Earth, temporal matters. Turn your attention to the things of Heaven!

But, Father, I've got to dispose of my property.

In nomine Patris, et Filii, et Spiritus Sancti. Amen.

Crows in faraway woods said, Wah-wah-wah. Sun came boiling and baking, people on the sentry platforms and ladders were motionless, the crowds on the two outside slopes were near to being motionless, the thousands of clustered prisoners were more near to being motionless than they had ever been before, the mosaic of faces beyond the marsh seemed to glisten and fry in the sun.

The thin hands of Eben Dolliver widened the noose, preparing it for Willie Collins; he had to reach far and up to spread the noose for Willie Collins. Slowly he worked the heavy rope over Collins's puffing trembling face and began to tighten it around the immense neck. Other hands toiled with other nooses. Voices of the five talkative condemned were a busy convocation of guinea-fowl. At the outbreak of the Rebellion I enlisted and served three years with the army thinking that my mother and sisters will hear of this makes me wish I'd neh-heh-hever been born oh lads be after finding mercy for me as the priest told you and Pete I've a few beans in my watch pocket, and distribute them to the kiddies. . . .

Amid babbling of the rest came the thick dull mutter of Charles Curtis: I don't give a fuck. Get ahead with the job. Don't take all day about it.

Per sacrosancta humanae reparationis mysteria remittat tibi omnipotens Deus omnes praesentis et futurae vitae poenas—

One minute, said Leroy Key, never lifting his head from the watch held close to his gaze. It had been his father's watch, presented to Key as a talisman when he went off to war; and Key's father had been opposed firmly to capital punishment. Leroy Key wondered what his father would think if he knew of the necessary use to which this watch was now put.

A meal sack went over the head of Rickson, a sack masked the face of John Sarsfield, muffling his voice. But continually that voice hurried with its explanation, boast, extenuation. Bad company it was, bad company—first off, the only thing I stole was rations. Sacks were drawn to cover the heads of the other four, and as with Sarsfield their murmurings went down proportionately in volume. Don't lay it on so thick, boys were yelling impatiently in nearby ranks of watchers. You're a God damn villain, Munn, and you know it! That bastard Sarsfield killed a fellow used to live in our shebang! Willie Mosby, you dirty— Yeh, he took Paster's blanket when he was laying sick to death. Get ready to hang, you noisy sons of bitches!

. . . *Paradisi portas aperiat, et ad gaudia sempiterna perducat. Amen.*

Time's up, said Key.

The vast chant had begun behind him, in front of him, sun burned hard, the hillside larded with its thousands was shaking, heat waves rippled, the pound of ten thousand voices and more became a steady beat of drums. *Hang* them. *Hang* them. *Hang* them. Four functionaries jumped from the scaffold more or less nimbly, two of them went down the ladder with caution. Sergeant Key looked questioningly at the executioners. They had the ropes ready . . . Payne nodded in reply. Key looked to see that the assistants were well away from the gallows, and they were. He held his hand high, pulled it down sharply. Payne and Harris dug their heels into the ground simultaneously and flung themselves back, toward the east and the west; the braces flew at them, planks came banging down. Men standing closest could hear the combined thud and snap as six huge face-swaddled bodies dropped, those in the center speeding down a fraction of a second before those at the ends . . . there was a suggestion of a V in the shape of the descending mass. Willie Collins's great feet struck the ground with a double thud: his rope was shorn in two.

The other five raiders gyrated slowly, some of them were struggling. Certain of the watchers thought of fowls hung outside a poulterer's. In an instant Munn and Delaney were without motion except for the dangling, the gradual heave and twitching of weights and ropes subjected to sudden shock. The necks of Curtis and Rickson and Sarsfield had not snapped. They died of strangulation, waggling their corded legs, gesticulating with their corded hands and arms in a strange leisure. Sarsfield died more ruggedly than the others. His knees came striving up; almost they touched his chin; he jerked his legs down once more.

Lookit that vein in his neck, said a low voice.

Thought twas going to bust.

He's still kicking.

Guess they didn't get that thing tight enough around his throat to begin with.

Most attention was centered on the tumbled shape of Willie Collins. Leroy Key and several others swore the slow powerful oaths of men who do not curse frequently or fluently. Eben Dolliver stood appalled, overcome by the belief that this accident had occurred through some neglect of his own. In no way might he be blamed. The Confederates had searched high and low to find sufficient rope;

some of it was old, long exposed to the weather in some other more prosaic use; and the section employed to build Collins's noose was rotten in its hempen core.

Take off the sack, said Key. Already it was stained with blood, and Willie's lips were pushing against the wet bright red surface. A shiny fly came with burnished buzzing intent, prisoners batted away other diving flies as they lifted the huge man's head, drew off the sack, and worked the noose loose. Willie's face was the color of cigar ashes. Blood came steadily from his nose and mouth, some people thought that it was issuing from his big ears also; boys would say later that Willie was bleeding from the eyes. Give us that bucket, called Seneca MacBean. A pail of water was brought forward, and MacBean dashed its contents over the waxy face. Blood ran away in pink rivulets, but fresher darker blood reappeared insistently. Father Whelan recited a private prayer for Willie, and held the Crucifix close. *Kyrie, eleison. Christe, eleison. Kyrie, eleison. Pater noster*— His old anguished voice slid to a whisper. *Et ne nos inducas in tentationem*—

They drew Willie into a sitting position. Men supported his shoulders and bleeding head while other hands worked furiously at preparing a fresh noose. His eyes were protruding from their sockets until it seemed they would burst forth and roll like crab apples on the ground. He said, Agh, agh. And then, Agh, where ammmm I? and drew the low words out lengthily. Ammm I innnn theee otherrr worrrld?

Soon see where you are, bastard, Limber Jim told him.

Och, boys, I've never hurted you—

Kilt my brother, said Limber Jim softly.

Willie twisted his sore neck, his head lolled back. As through waves of heat he must have seen the gallows turned to milk, and milky men standing aloft, making milky frenzy of the milky rope. For the sake and love of God! Do not be putting me up there again. God has spared my life, has he not, now? Father— Priest— Tell them, tell them! God meant that you should be merciful to me, indeed He did—

Rope's ready.

Hope you got it strong enough this time.

Hell, twould hold a dozen of him. Twould hang Wirz himself, and the laughter rippled as people thought of the meager round-shouldered despised captain.

Sed libera nos a malo. Salvum fac servum tuum—

Fffather, tell them— *Father*—!

Be putting your mind with God, me boy. Peter Whelan knew sadly that he could gain nothing by pleading again with these grim avengers. Repeat, son. Repeat the words: *O my God, who putteth his trust in thee*—

Och— My—God—who putteth—his—trust—in— Father! *Father!*

O Lord, hear my prayer—

Och, Lord—hear my—prayer—

Hands spread around Willie Collins as they had spread on July third when he was kicked and beaten. Hands and arms held him, he was being carried, lugged like a great sack of booty. He heard the priest intoning, seemingly far below him: *And let my cry come unto Thee.* Willie struggled dutifully to repeat the words as bidden, yet he could say nothing more. A hasty vision occurred as cloth was pulled over his face again, as cloth covered the sun and diffused its royal glare. Something about a boat decked in bunting, and a woman's hip rubbing his own hip, and a man—that name? Was it Hicks?—dropping from his perch on Bedloe's Island. Said the bellow of Willie Collins through the years, And if they ever come to hang me, they'll have to hang me twice! In anguish he wished to speak to the audience before him and explain a variety of things. He wished to tell of his father, of Big Biddy, of turmoil in the long-forgotten Gotham Court. Something tightened against his windpipe. He was free in space. A cricket's voice said *tik* in his ear.

34

Lucy wrote. Dear Coz: Yours of July the 4th rec'd. and contents noted duly, with especial attention devoted to the illustration which was executed with a flourish remarkable in one professedly so weary. We did enjoy the row of Yankees sitting on the great Chinese cracker, with Mr. Lincoln's tall hat in prominence! What an excellent fashion in which to dispose of those grand nuisances at the North! You did not identify the rather furtive figure shown setting a torch to the fuse. Who in the entire Christian domain wears spectacles as large as those? Twould be someone very proud of his spectacles, or else ashamed of them. Tut. You would not know, because you do not wear spectacles. Or do you? I can't scarcely recollect.

Hereabouts the Yankees have no Chinese crackers, nor crackers of any kind, poor things. Dare I consider them as Poor Things? But charity should still be Christian virtue in an embittered age such as the one in which we dwell. Therefore, Miss L. Claffey, be virtuous and call them Poor Things! Poppy goes perpetually to watch. Wild horses could not drag me, though I hear that many ladies have been. Twas told that recently a bevy of simpering *beauties* from Americus or some nearby community ascended in daintiness to the guards' little stations, assisted gallantly up the ladders by eager officers; and from their lofty situation they amused themselves by sprightly comments made to the prisoners; asking them how many niggers they owned at the North, Shouldn't they like to have currant cakes baked for them?—*et cetera*. Had I been one of the unfortunates thus goaded, I should have hurled mud balls at Their Sweetnesses. Father became surly when he heard of the event. But still he himself insists on going to the pen each day, though not to taunt the captives. He says the mere thought of the place keeps him disturbed of nights. I conclude tis the unpleasant odor which causes me to lie restless.

But even amid such squalor there can arise amusement at times. For instance, immediately following the execution (which I recited to you in some detail. Second-handedly, of course: I fear that my letter must have gone astray, and trust that eventually it shall turn up) the bodies of those executed were cut down, and preparations made to convey them to the graveyard. While this was being done, the *gallows itself* just naturally melted away! Wood is very hard to come by over there; the sight of those fine posts and boards was more than the wood-starved populace could bear. My father watched, he said it was a sight: Tom going off with a length of rope, Dick and Harry scuttling with a rafter betwixt them. There were no guards inside the enclosure at the time, so the light-fingered *gentry* made off safely with their plunder. Tis understood that the prison's superintendent became apoplectic at the news.

I have met him barely: a glum bearded gentleman of *foreign* extraction. Some time since, Poppy thought that it would be an attention for me to call upon the

Captain's wife, so newly come amongst us. They dwell at the Boss place (one side, since it is a double house), and there I rode upon our tallest mule, ensconced upon my dearly-belovèd-but-seldom-used-nowadays saddle. With Jem stepping beside in the role of groom! I invited Mrs. Wirz to take tea at some future time, but she has never availed herself of the invitation. The two elder children—I understand that they are the progeny of a previous union on the part of the lady—are named Susie and Cornelia, and are quite young ladies. The only child of Captain Wirz and Mrs. Wirz is little Coralie. Is that not a pretty name? She is nine or thereabouts: a gay and bubbling creature with extremely fair skin. Proudly she displayed her treasures, much impressed especially by a necklace her father fetched her from abroad. The elder half-sisters speak of and to her tenderly as Baby Sister. The child was having her hair combed and curled when first I saw her. Twas sweet to see that fair head between her mammy's knees. The child said, with that definite air with which some infants impart nonsense, My Daddy is a Catholic, my Mother is a Methodist, but *I* shall be a Baptist when I am a grownup lady! I felt that I should attempt to persuade her into our Presbyterian fold; but had no such dramatics as *immersion* to offer. Later we talked of horses and riding. Her big eyes gleamed as I described the fashion in which my brothers used to cavort, the fences they used to jump.

I observe that I have said little of the mother. She is short, small-boned, a bit inclined to plumpness. Her voice is affable; poor thing, they have so little space in the small half of that double house, and it must be a trial. One of the elder girls possesses also a beautiful voice. I heard her singing in the garden. Mrs. W. set out her best to serve me what passes for *Java* nowadays (but her wench could not make miracles out of crusts or okra, as can Naomi): an Austrian china coffee set complete with pitchers, very lovely, purple flowers on white. As I said, she has never returned my call, but I do not think it rude. She has much to claim her time. The husband appeared before I left. He is grave, almost to the point of glowering, he seemed; but, poor man, he suffers from an old wound, and his arm was slung, and Poppy says tis often carried thus. He is commended to the tender mercies of the Old Scratch by guards and Yankees alike. Still, I should not be surprised but that he does the best he can, and with so little in the way of supplies or food available. I should not say food: tis sickening to watch the munificence of our garden go to waste beneath the sun. Even after our black people have eaten their fill. Poppy plants so much and tends with such care that we are surfeited with green things. One day I loaded the wenches with baskets of turnips and lettuces, and set out to play Lady Bountiful—even to Yankees. We were turned back by the guards, who said that we must have a pass. I knew not how to obtain one. I reported the matter to my father that evening, and thought that he would be highly indignant; but he only smiled his patient smile and said something about dipping the Nile with a sieve.

They do make *beer*, those Yankees. Now I shall offer you the formula, in the event that you may wish to tipple likewise. They mix cornmeal in water, and beg or buy some sorghum from the youths who guard them. This concoction is set out in the boiling sun to brew or ferment. Perish the thought! I should not wish to be a brewer, nor even to taste. On the other hand, Poppy declares that the mixture is good for them. Might it possibly delay the effects of scurvy from which so many are said to be suffering? What say you to this, out of your lore of medical wisdom? Please, Surgeon, do not prescribe such a dose for your ailing *Cousin!*

Enough of such jesting. Now to a sadder report: my mother's health concerns us greatly. We are powerless to cope with the situation. More and more through recent weeks has she ignored the plate put before her. I have tried broths, jellies,

egg-nogs and the like, have racked my brain to no avail. She appears to be
starving; it is self-induced. Were she to take a fever, the end would be near. But in
her demented state she is deaf to any plea or argument put against her. Weep for
me, Cousin Harry. I am so very tired of weeping for myself. . . .

Elkins wrote: Dear Cousin Lucy, Your letter of recent date has crystallized an
intention in my mind. I have requested an assignment to duty at Camp Sumter. I
cannot guarantee that I shall get it. Vaguely have I told myself, in viewing repeatedly those reports relating to shocking inadequacies at the stockade, that I would
be serving our Nation far better in that situation than I might in Macon or
Savannah. Sometimes there is naught upon my desk in the way of a paper. On
other occasions you might dig far beneath the heaps ere you unearthed a veritable
caricature of a surgeon who finds fewer and fewer *hairs* to scratch upon his head
each day. As you know, I earnestly desired further duty in the field, and this was
not to be. Were I at Camp Sumter, I might feel that I fought somewhere along a
line of battle, even though my task entailed saving a few lives among the very
human beings whom once I strove to destroy. Humanity seems crying aloud, and
who is there to listen? Certainly not those dullards up Richmond way! Report and
file, report and file: *that is all ye know on earth, and all ye need to know.* Our poor
and admired Keats! Would he not have had a quicker wastage had he dwelt in
that City Upon Your Doorstep, Coz?

But now I am impelled to add another motive, and that is to be of service to
you and yours, who have been so generous, more than generous, in the friendship
afforded me. I am not worthy of the name *soldier* in so putting my own desires
above whatever orders have been issued or may be issued. But let us observe, my
dear Lucy—

She read the line again and again. The first time he has addressed me so. . . .

—I am but one of mankind, proportionately selfish. I witness selfishness demonstrated in variety each day that I live; even did I see it so when engaged in the
field. Now I am not a *soldier;* I am a surgeon accompanying the military, and
subservient to military command. My intelligence is puny at best, I confess. But at
night, in or out of my slumbers, I hear a voice saying, Go to Camp Sumter. An
angel ordering me about? Could that be? I know not. Angel or fiend. But I have
applied as I described to you *ante,* and shall be in inner turmoil from now on.
There is this to be said, also: they are so woefully understaffed, and it is so
difficult to procure even the most indolent of the contract surgeons for duty at
Anderson, that someone might observe, Huzza! Have we here an imbecile who
actually desires to go there? By Heaven, he shall go!

Lucy wrote: Your most recent dispatch has Poppy and me agog. Frankly I
dread to inform you that not even your tender offices would aid my poor mother
now. She is sinking, all skin and bone she is, and with such a stare. We try to force
her physically to take nourishment. Grief, what a time. And the weather hotter
and hotter. May I say primly that twould be a comfort and a pleasure to Poppy
and myself to know that your kind person was at hand, not merely the kindness of
your thoughts? Poppy is so concerned with the desperate condition of those
prisoners. It occupies him night and day. Fairly does he walk the floor. I read to
him the portion of your letter describing your intent. He struck his hands together
and spoke something in this wise: I have seen the hospital, and am aware that no
individual might cope with the situation. There are too many lacks, too many
needs. But surely it would be better for those suffering youths, and better thus in
the sight of God, if at least one man of strong purpose were to be on duty at the
hospital.

Oh dear, I have made a botch of trying to convey the tenor of his thought. But at least, Coz, he hopes that you will be ordered here. And so, I confess with all maidenly decorum, do I. Now must I scamper off. Pet has the toothache, and I am to pull it. Your old room—Suthy's room—is awaiting you. Surely twill not be necessary for you to sleep yonder in that squalid place? No, unnecessary—I know that much—I see various of the surgeons lounging past in the lane, and hear their talk. They dwell elsewhere. Many I fear are very much *elsewhere* much of the time. . . .

Elkins did not appear until late in the month, and when he did arrive he was accompanied by a soldierly person named Chandler. They had become acquainted briefly at the Macon headquarters. When at last Harrell Elkins boarded the car which would jolt him sixty miles to the south, he found Colonel Chandler sitting with luggage beside him.

Elkins possessed and exuded the power and sweetness of the simple man who has suffered. Colonel Chandler might have been withdrawn, almost austere, confronted with a person more pretentious. Elkins's shape, appearance, voice, attitude made him a butt for the ignorant or unheeding; but identified him as trustworthy promptly to the experienced and discerning.

The two men bumped along through the hours, side by side on the scratched wooden bench with three militiamen and a wounded home-going corporal chattering distantly at the forward end of the car. Colonel Chandler was a graduate of the United States Military Academy. Like so many devoted to his cause he had felt that the Confederacy (like its army) was the repository of the best brains and abilities extant. He had never attempted to evaluate the economic factors, in fact was not too keenly aware of their existence, until repeated thudding defeats of 1863 made him aware. Now he saw his new proud Country prostrate before Northern assaults, armored only by its armies. The Confederacy was weaponed no longer with hope, only with determination. To most men Chandler would have voiced his opinion never; to a few he would have spoken directly if satirically. To Elkins, through the seven tiring laggardly hours, he opened his heart. The men were stronger friends when they got down from the ugly car at the Anderson station than many people would have been after an extended sea voyage. Harrell Elkins begged the colonel to accompany him to the Claffeys'—he knew that he would have been welcome. The colonel said No, he must get about his business. The assistant adjutant and inspector-general, Colonel R. H. Chilton, had ordered him to make a thorough examination of conditions at the prison, and to prepare a report as soon as was expedient.

Which report, came the grating voice of Elkins, who was no longer tempted by the illusion of justice, will be filed in the nearest chamber pot?

I fear as much. Nevertheless, what does one do?

Proceed according to the orders at hand!

Harry took up his residence at the Claffey place once more. Chandler went to live beyond the Sweetwater branch, where he was shrugged at by Henry Wirz (behind his back) and scorned by the Winders.

Harry had built his return to this region into an accomplishment: a savoring of all that was reassuring or noble. In common with those who dream too pleasurably in advance of an event, he suffered a letting down. His later warmness with Lucy had been constructed on paper; now, confronted with each other, the two young people remained aloof. But Ira offered affection and hospitality . . . Elkins felt himself received properly. Nevertheless there was a weakness, a lack of fulfillment here. The plague of Veronica's insanity pervaded the household as did the odor of Andersonville. Harry sat by the woman's bedside, was horrified but not too surprised at her shrinkage. He recognized fever, he felt the age-old perplexity of the physician who observes shadows of death merging, and feels that there is necessity in the approaching death; yet has sworn to hold it off as long as he may. In the end Elkins could recommend nothing but the hope that gruel and milk and soft eggs might be forced between the wooden jaws. He hoped the sufferer might be deluded into coöperation with those who would help her. Then he went to the prison hospital; he turned ghastly when he saw the prison hospital. He stayed for an afternoon and the following night; he slept heavily the next day, and was returned to the hospital before sunset.

35

They tortured Veronica through the night, cooking her on the griddle of her bed. Veronica wished to be free of the griddle and of Them. Who They were she did not know, but They were many; some were white, some colored, They had hands and voices, They did annoying things like sponging the shred which was her body, putting spoons to her lips. She would set her jaws, spill the contents of the spoons, laugh because she had tricked Them again.

Ninny, rouse yourself.

The servant grunted, sighed, rolled her head against the padded chair-back.

Ninny. I'm speaking to you! Rouse softly.

Eyes opened at last, the kinky head shook. Yas, Miss Lucy.

Lucy whispered intently, I'm falling asleep myself, watching so. It is after one by the clock, so I must snatch an hour's sleep or I'll be fit for nothing. Hear me now: the master is with Jem, doctoring the Blackberry cow again, trying to save her. Should he come into the house he is not to watch by my mother's bed, but also must rest. Hear?

Yas'm.

You can't tell time, mused Lucy unhappily. (She had tried to teach Ninny to tell time, she had taught Extra when they were small; Ninny could not be taught.) Do you come over here to the clock, Ninny. Now, watch with care. This large hand moves faster than the small one. It will go slowly around—like this—and will pass the small hand; then when it reaches *here*, you are to come to my room and awaken me. Understand?

Yas'm, whispered the black woman, bored and frightened by the soft ticking wooden clock.

Veronica heard low conversation, heard it unheeded. I won't, she told herself stubbornly. Definitely I shall not. They cannot compel me. She lay with eyes closed, dry lips hanging apart and revealing a protrusion of her small beautiful teeth.

Later there was no sound in the room but that conversational clock and the easy snoring of the slave who again had fallen asleep a few minutes after Lucy left. Through coarse cloth fastened across open windows in lieu of mosquito netting came the vile odor and an audible medley of birds or children. . . . Her children? No. Safe. Asleep and must not be routed out. They're gone to war. In the ground. The taller are dead. Nay, it is the smaller ones who are dead. Indeed, yes, Mrs. Ladshaw, Sutherland is still at Oglethorpe but this is his final year, commencement will occur in July. Moses has gone boating on the Flint with the McWhorters. Arwood lies sickly again, we fear for him.

She was ruled not only by craft of the demented but also by slyness of the cooked and dying. A deep resounding voice said, Come in, so she must respond to it as always. She'd heard the voice often in recent hours but, when she attempted to leave the pan in which she lay parching, certain creatures restrained her.

Miss Veronica, you must pretend to be tractable, pretend that you are submissive. With quiet leer and calm you must accept the heat over which They are baking you, even though you stick to the pan.

You are crying before a cupboard, you have shuddered down into a pile. This gown belonged to Baby Peggy, you have your face buried in it. . . . Move spectrally, or They'll put you back into the skillet and build blazes higher.

Remotely birds and children made incessant mild tumult, closer at hand the Yellow Smell walked. It surrounded the bed as if curtains were drawn to hold it in; but curtains were not drawn. Veronica had her eyes opened at last (hard scheming burning eyes) and could see that it was true: curtains were caught up. She could look past the foot of the bed and see that solemn clock on its table, and the frizzled head of a servant lolling. Snoring again, said Veronica. Abominable sound. She should be broken of the habit, but how?

Please to recite the statistics concerning Macon, Miss Veronica.

Macon, Bibb County, has a population of two thousand, six hundred and thirty-five souls, according to the census of 1830. Of these there are whites to the number of one thousand, four hundred and fifty-two; blacks to the number of one thousand, one hundred and eighty-three.

Correct, Miss Veronica. Well done.

Had she said Well Done On the Whole, had Miss Benham said something about beetles? No, she spoke of sarcophagi.

There was a vacant mummy-case awaiting Lucy.

Come in . . . deep voice echoing through the hill. The stranger pointed with his cane. Best to tread in the direction indicated.

She slid from bed, making no noise as she went but the light whisper of skin-and-bone gliding over a sheet and out from under another sheet, stealthy murmur of sheets folded to allow her to pass from their prisoning. Her white hair clung heated on her shoulders, fire in her shoulders must set it to crackling. At least the bed, the griddle, claimed its suffering prey no longer. She was free but frying. She found annoyance in this realization—snarled about it, drawing back lips until the full pearliness of her teeth shone. Even this sound did not rouse Ninny. Veronica swept from the room, holding up the long crushed muslin of her gown daintily. She paced over shadowy air of the hall, walked on a cushion of air. . . . Ah, who'd left that candle at the head of the stair? It might cause a conflagration: she'd extinguish the candle. *Puff.*

There was a pool . . . spring . . . pool where slippery green frogs were captured by the boys. Always a cool pool. Could she find that pool she would have herself in it, splash her face, wash off the scorching, expunge patterned streaks which the grid must have branded upon her.

Stay, twas a pan.

But wash off the burning.

Quietly, quietly down the stair, hands pressing the rail, bare foot after bare foot seeking the next lower step; how many feet did she possess? As many as a caterpillar owned, and each pair of delicate adhesive feet cushioned on a single segment. But, Badger, child—you are to fetch no more live worms into the house!

I know, I know—twill make a butterfly in time—but do you go to your father, and he can grant you space for your treasures in one of the sheds—all for your own. Shall you call it the Claffey Museum? Ah, indeed, a Museum of World-Wide Wonders? A splendid designation; and I shall be delighted to view it when you have your specimens in place.

Empty pin, waiting for Lucy.

Quietly, quietly—turning of the knob after the bolt is drawn—quietly, quietly. They shall not hear me and pursue, I shan't let Them pursue. It is incredible, but They might harm the children as They've sought to harm me.

Come in.

There was a star above stolid black heat, more stars yonder . . . tilt your head wisely and observe the combined low lamp of stars. They'll guide you to pool and coolness. Softly, easily, walking on empty cotton of the air, feeling nothing, nothing underfoot.

O heat, dry up my brains! tears seven times salt, burn out the sense and virtue of mine eye! So said Ophelia, so said Ira Claffey in the game they played. Your turn is next and you must identify it, so name the hour and minute of Shakespeare: easy to do so, since Ira has used that quotation frequently in the past. Now, then: *eye,* and your own line must begin with an E. Inculcate lessons for the children, since they sit rapt and listening. *Even a child is known by his doings, whether his work be pure, and whether it be right.* There, younguns—tis Proverbs, Twenty, Eleven—but I'll not tell you. The burden is yours, the guess and reckoning and bickering are yours also. A raw cold wet evening outside, and Christmas approaches—what a time that will be for all!—and the eldest boys home from school, and Moses shall enter when he is sixteen. Now they are rioting, the two eldest demanding more of the peach cider. Lucy, daughter, do not guzzle it; of course tis not fermented—but a trifle at the most: Ira has reassured me—but drink demurely, my daughter, drink demurely. Mere sips, the token of jollity, the barest token.

O heat, dry up my brains! There is too much heat, too persisting and head-twirling heat, so find the dark pool with dispatch . . . leaf mould making a cup above the soil, tiny scrolls of plants which swim and grow in their swimming, and Ira declared them to be algae. Unglimpsed, naturally, in this darkness and faint lamp of stars. But find the pool for its clamminess. The heat shall fade.

Halt, rang the changing voice of a young boy. Halt! Who goes there? His voice was a chicken-cry when he spoke so abruptly, he had the throat of a rooster.

What is a picket? I heard Them talking of pickets when They had me trapped in the pan. Once indeed there was mention of a war. . . . I have called, Mrs. Ladshaw, to pay my respects to you and to your husband, to offer what sympathy we may. We heard that your noble son gave a splendid account of himself before —before—

Someone else!

Yankees killed Moses. Yankees killed Suthy. Yankees killed my—my— Sally and Courtenay. They were but infants; the Yankees took them to the army and so they too—

Halt!

Sudden scratch of orange in the night, the singing and rush of some narrow pointed force close at hand.

Veronica continued walking the thick piled mass of dark air, her feet were unhurt by the pillow they trod. How strange that one foot should feel as if it were cut by a scrap of thrown-away metal or a splinter of wood, when her feet were swimming her forward to the pool and touching nothing, nothing.

Godsakes, Allie. What was that?

Me. Shot at something.

I heard you give a challenge. Who—?

Just seen something white. It kept a-moving and truly scairt the piss out of me. Think you hit anything?

Didn't hear no yell. Must have missed.

Better reload, cause the Captain of the Guard will—

I'm reloading right now. They any white mules around here?

I seen a gray one tother day. Might have been that, but I don't see how you could have missed a mule.

Sure as hell I did miss. Else I kilt him dead.

Heat, dry up my brains. For the sake of pity do not keep pounding them. Do not continue your scourging, Heat. Above all do not continue your ringing of bells and pushing of coals within me; and do not continue your dryness, dryness, dryness, my hands are dry.

Explosion of that gunpowder, contained within a musket barrel and booming free on the slope east of the Claffey house, brought Lucy upright in bed. Oh, blame, she thought, probably another guard has shot another prisoner. I'm positive it was a shot which disturbed me, seems I can sense its echoing, echoing. Is it too late, have I overslept, did Ninny fail to obey orders? Or perhaps Poppy has come into the house at last and sits nodding by that bed yonder— Poor thing, he should be asleep. Poor Poppy, he must sleep— In light gown and wrapper she trotted along the hall, and a moment later was cuffing Ninny savagely.

You black *wretch.* You— Where *is* she, where *is* she?

Ninny blubbered, Mistess, I done know! She—she gone from her bed—

Run, get my father. Hear me? *Run!* Lucy swung the palm of her hand, her hand grazed Ninny's hair and ear, the servant howled and went rushing. Through night below the rear windows Lucy could hear Ninny groaning her rapid way past cabins toward the cow shed, her cries of Mastah, *Mass*stah growing more prolonged and growing in volume. Lucy ran from room to room, she lighted a candle here, a candle there, lighted a lamp. She dropped down to look into threatening space below each bed in turn. Even Harrell Elkins's bed; it had not been made since he slept in it; she saw the creases his male body had put upon the sheet. . . . There were no closets in the house. Houses like the Claffeys' were never built with closets; but Lucy banged open doors of every wardrobe which might have contained the shape of her mother, that desiccated form gone to eighty pounds or less. She held a frantic notion that her mother might have sought to immure herself in one of those chests dedicated to the dead children; she beat fists against the chests; they were locked. Veronica was not above stairs. As Lucy sped down into the lower hall she heard Ira Claffey open the rear door with a crash. She floundered to meet him.

She's gone, Poppy!

Not in one of the other bedrooms?

No, no, I've searched all. That shiftless wench was dozing, and Mother left her bed— Poppy, Poppy! I should never have lain *down!*

Together they hunted hastily through lower rooms, then in disorder realized that which they should have noticed all along: the front door stood open to the night. Ira fetched a lantern from the rear stoop. She may have gone over to The Pines, child. He said that, not wishing to mention the family burying-ground. Often they spoke of their cemetery as The Pines.

I'll go see, said Ira.

Let Ninny rouse the hands!

But she's suffering hysterics because you struck her, child— I reckon you've never struck her before. Jem is fussing with her. Do you clothe yourself at once.

Ira hunted with no result among the graves; he'd thought that surely he would find Veronica there. He went to the blacks' cemetery, even to the pets'. Rouse up, old Deuce, and aid me in seeking your mistress, and he thought for a moment that Deuce came wagging. When he returned to the house Lucy had put on shoes and stockings, and a shawl over her wrapper. Already she had called Jonas and Coffee. Jem came lumbering a moment later. Ira told them off to the search. He warned the slaves about stopping in their tracks if challenged by pickets, and explained what they must say.

Lucy, you shall go with me. I can't let you explore by yourself, not with these vagabond troops about. Though we should surely cover more ground if you— We'll go toward the stockade.

Can't you fetch Coz from the hospital, Poppy?

How could he aid, other than to seek as we are seeking? If we do not find your mother promptly I'll appeal to the Officer of the Day.

One slave poked west toward the railroad, another (Jonas, the most trustworthy) moved among trees which screened the rifle pits and fort. They were told to cry, Mistress, Mistress, as they wandered. Also the black women were recruited; Orphan Dick wept along with Ninny, he did not know why. The women were ordered to investigate orchard and shrubbery, areas close to cabins and sheds. They went crying Mistess, *Missstess*. It was a strange fluting and rumble of calling voices spread farther and farther apart, muting in lonely black distance, small lights poking wan fluttering holes in the curtain of blackness, curtain of heat and decay.

Veronica Claffey discovered her pool. It had altered . . . oho, no frogs? Badger then shall have none to place in spirits, in glass jars within his Museum of World-Wide Wonders. Elsewhere he must collect his frogs. Veronica waded toward the pool, the earth grew spongier, looser, her bare torn feet began to slip through feather beds of air whereon she strolled, her feet began to splash. It was difficult to draw her feet free from ooze and plashing, they sucked deeply, something drew her feet down and mired them. This, she decided, is whence it cometh. The Yellow Smell. For it is here, and They must be here because it comes from Them. They make it.

They were a far different They from Those who'd baked her on the bed, on the griddle iron. They were Yankees.

Grid, pan, skillet?

A spider?

Come in.

Will you walk into my parlor, said the spider to the fly. This she began to sing in a crusty sharp tone. *Tis the prettiest little parlor that ever you did spy.*

But although wetness smelled, although Veronica struggled amid reek, she struggled in comparative coolness. The marsh was soft . . . a pool lay beneath, the pool would comfort her could she but reach it. *O heat,* a remembered voice was quoting. Assuredly heat would dry up her brains did she not lave and lave and lave. A slow gurgle sounded; why, the pool was moving. The collection of moisture would be treated serenely with moss and water bugs as she'd dreamed it; and Veronica Arwood was too wise a girl to be afraid of water bugs. Just skitter you hand, Mis Ronny, said Mammy Pen. Just skitter, skitter with you hand, child. Then all them bug they go a-fleeing.

Deep in the bog she squatted and began to skitter, and thought that bugs skated off from her disturbance.

. . . Halt!

I've halted, we're halted.

Who goes there?

Mr. Claffey from the plantation. We're hunting for Mrs. Claffey—she's stricken with fever—ill—wandering somewhere.

Is it Mr. Claffey sure enough?

Here, I'm holding the light on my face.

Why, Mr. Claffey, we hain't seen nobody.

Hold on there, Jeff, Allie done shot at something, while back.

Good God, did you—?

Yes, sir, I fired at something sure enough, but don't reckon I hit nothing.

What was it, what did you see?

Just something white kept a-moving even when I'd challenged.

Where? Which way?

Right down that way, sir. On that path winds around there, going over south side the hospital.

In time Ira found the woman. His lantern picked out her fragile figure now not so white, crouched in muck and painted with muck, the wide-spread slime of the hospital's drainage. He waded in, lifted the muttering creature, carried her out. So dry hot on that spider, she said distinctly. Shall need to drink more. The stuff dripped from her chin, plastered her night-dress, her babbling mouth was anointed with it. Ira strode lamely, carrying Veronica to her bed. Lucy scampered gasping ahead, she began to call to the black women before she entered the dooryard.

Come in.

Veronica went down those several steps as she had gone in fancy so many times. Smaller tombs within this larger edifice were open, and someone dressed in white lay within each marble shell. Or was it marble, was it granite? Off into nethermost reaches the bell-stroke of that voice resounded, and above outer roofs a sky must be painted mystically, yews or cedars must be black against retreating sunset.

Someone dressed in white sat up suddenly in one of the coffins.

A swathed arm stretched, grave-wrapped finger pointed, indicating the destination toward which Veronica must venture. In this instance she did not come from her dream. She thought of some great truth which she should announce, she should call it back to people behind her. Then she heard children running and laughing ahead, and began to laugh, herself, and to run toward the children.

36

John Winder stood with Henry Wirz on a sentry platform. John Winder did not see the bears witnessed by Henry Wirz; he saw scum, a marsh under the scum, pollywogs in the marsh. They were too thick, the marsh could not support their life, it was fated that many would die. Perhaps the survivors, if sufficiently cannabalistic, could sustain themselves directly by feasting on dead pollywogs. Or indirectly, as by swallowing fruits to be reared in a forest of growth which the dead creatures had manured.

I have not yet seen your most recent return, Captain.

General, that Gus Gleich he is sick. *Ach,* so much trouble I have with my office! And that Gus Moesner, he is good for the work, but with the English he is not so good. Slow he goes, *ja.* Tomorrow I present the return of prisoners to date.

Approximately . . . Captain?

Sir, it is maybe twenty-nine thousand now.

Because Winder was older in his mind than in his years, and sometimes worse than senile in his addiction to a crusty past, he sent Cadet Davis to the board again. Winder, aged perhaps twenty-seven, sat behind his small desk on a raised platform, and the cadets of this section sat before him, lining the sides of the long form—six on the left, five on the right, now that Mr. Davis had vacated his chair. Mr. Davis stood beside the easel which held the board, and gripped a pointer in one of his knotted bony young hands—the hand nearest the board, as prescribed.

Elementary tactical combinations of the Greeks were very simple, but they were methodical. An army corps was composed of—

The pointer found the long printed word at the top.

A *Tetraphalangarchia.*

Sprightly young Mr. Wayland at the lower end of the form wished to make a joke about this, you could see mischief peppered in his eyes, you could see his naughty soul fairly writhing for release within his rigid body; but he had a dangerous weight of demerits already, and the tactical instructor's hard eye was upon him.

This consisted of sixteen thousand, three hundred and forty-five *oplitai.*

The pointer moved.

An *Epitagma,* numbering eight thousand, one hundred and ninety-two *psiloi;* also an *Epitagma* of cavalry numbering four thousand and ninety-six men.

Might you explain to the section, Mr. Davis, the composition of the grand phalanx.

Yes, sir. Thank you, sir.

The tip of the pointer went walking. *Tetraphalangarchia,* four. *Phalanxes,* sixteen. *Chiliarchiae,* sixty-four. *Syntagmata,* two hundred and fifty-six.

. . . But in Andersonville these scraps of mouthing, hobbling, gurgling debris were neither Greeks nor Romans. Said old John Winder, They are Yankees, they are Nationalists; they must be treated so.

He cried at Henry Wirz, and so unexpectedly that Wirz's nerves gave a leap— He cried, I haven't yet set foot in this damnable place, nor do I intend to!

Ja, General. It is not good you do so. You they would attack!

Ah, I'm not afraid of the sons of bitches! Are *you* afraid?

No, no!

Ah, you fear them.

Sir, they are very bad. Like bears in Bern.

Where in hell's that?

Sir— I mean— General Winder, so many we have now; not more should be sent by me here.

God damn it, *you* don't send them.

I mean— *To* me at this stockade. They should not send more.

Winder made his stiff heavy way down the ladder, the ladder sagged and groaned under his weight. Flory Tebbs, displaced from the platform by the coming of these officers, stood bug-eyed and expected the ladder to smash and the general to fall with it. But to Flory's disappointment the ladder did not break.

Winder returned slowly up the hill to his office, breathing heavily as he went (he felt somehow that the prisoners had made him short of breath and he blamed them accordingly). Late that afternoon, when Wirz's delayed regular return was placed before him, he meditated upon it and then addressed himself with testiness to the adjutant and inspector-general, General Cooper.

Your indorsement on the letter of S. B. Davis, relating to the strength of the guard at this post, contains a very severe censure—

Winder sat for a time with the penholder shaking in front of his thin mouth. He wanted to chew the penholder, for thought, but he might press that infected tooth again. In old age he was trying to break himself of biting penholders.

—Which I am sure would not have been made if you had a clear comprehension of this post, of its wants and its difficulties. Reflect for a moment; twenty-nine thousand two hundred and one prisoners of war, many of them desperate characters—

Just how desperate, Cooper might never know. If Cooper could have stood upon that platform, if Cooper could have seen the lanceless *Oplitai—* God damn it! If Cooper could have seen squirming pollywogs in the marsh—

—A post a mile long by half a mile wide, the stockade for prisoners within one hundred and sixty yards of a mile in circumference, numerous avenues leading to the post to be guarded, public property to be cared for, guards for working parties—

He did bite the penholder at last. The jolt from that savage tooth-nerve went like a knife through his upper jaw and splintered the top of his head. He wrote on, as soon as his vision cleared. The ink was hot, the ink bitter, the ink black, black as John Winder's own blood had been for nearly fifty years.

You speak in your indorsement of placing the prisoners properly. I do not exactly comprehend what is intended by it. I know of but one way to place them, and that is to put them into the stockade.

He thought, And remember me to the President, devil burn you.

Again he retreated to the Hudson, he retreated into a classroom of 1827, a classroom of early 1828. . . . Did Mr. Davis have his pointer in hand? Had he advanced to the blackboard? Yes. Did the *Tetrarchiae* still number one thousand and twenty-four, the *Lochoi* or files, four thousand and ninety-six *Enomitiae* of four men each? Did Mr. Davis remember? John Winder remembered.

Perhaps ten days later, at two o'clock in the morning, Elizabeth Wirz roused up to see a dull brown bird on the ceiling above her and on wall and windows. This bird was the shadow of her husband Henry as he bent above and beside a stub of candle, extending his arm in a nest of rags and lint.

Husband, are you picking again? Her high-pitched voice was soft with sleep.

Gott, it is that I must pick. Almost it kills me, Ilse! He called her that often, it being an affectionate diminutive of Elizabeth with which he was familiar; also a favorite neighbor of his Zurich childhood had been named Ilse; the name had a connotation of warmth.

Elizabeth put on the nightcap which had come off while she slept, and in her wrapper went to help her husband. He had some surgical instruments in a pan, and had been trying without success to relieve the congestion of his old wound by establishing drainage. He cursed, not directly at his wife, but he cursed civilization around her, behind her, ahead of her. He complained that his left hand trembled with the pain engendered by his right arm: so he was making a botch. Furrowed hide of his forearm was a stubble field of angry corrugations—there were marks of old openings and old healings, there were long fresh ridges of cherry red drilled unevenly amid silvery scar tissue. Kinky black hair grew in disorderly patches, it did not grow upon scar tissue.

Will never I be rid of this?

You said you did not wish it amputated, said the little woman sadly.

Nein, rather would I be dead. He indicated an area which he wished to have sliced with his scalpel, and afterward he wished the incision deepened by use of a sharp probe. Elizabeth had performed this surgery for him several times before but once she fell in a faint while doing it. This was the first time Henry Wirz had made such a request of her since the day when she fainted.

You are giddy? he asked anxiously.

No, husband. I'll try the scalpel, as you bid. She tittered, trying to comfort him: My, I'm such a baby, Henry. And you, poor thing, suffering eternally—

He gasped, Ilse, do not scrape. It is sharp. Now you cut. Cut deep! The incision was made, the jiggling probe poked in. The woman felt a roaring in her ears. She shook her head and gritted her teeth, continuing with the task. There issued forth a secretion, but not in the quantity that Henry wished, and no flakes of separated bone came with it. Wirz thought that adjacent to the mutilated radius and ulna there was a reservoir of fluid which might later come pouring through the avenue made for it, and so pulsation and hotness would diminish, and so he might sleep again.

Bandage was constructed, linen was wound once more, the candle extinguished. The man and the woman got back upon the bed. Soon Elizabeth was breathing regularly in sleep. Henry's mind went jerking.

He was concerned with a chain gang. Twelve men had been shackled in this particular gang, ironed by the smith at Wirz's command. It was a creditable job: Captain John Heath, a commissary officer, superintended the blacksmith at the task and saw that all was well. The men thus confined were dangerous. All had tried to escape, two of them had attacked guards, one had tried to escape twice. Now he would not escape again or even try to! Each man had a chain and a shackle around each ankle, the chain leading forward to the man ahead of him; with legs so shackled, the prisoners could step but eight or ten inches at a time, and mechanically all were forced to keep in step. Each owned a small iron ball which he had to lift and carry in his hand when he moved, and there was a much larger ball chained to every group of four. By combined pulling of the gang the larger balls could be dragged.

At the present a problem intruded. One of the prisoners came down with diarrhoea in its most violent form, and Henry Wirz did not know what to do about this. The final plea brought to him when he left the prison at the end of the previous day had been a complaint of the well prisoners fastened to the sick one. At first they'd tried going along with him to the sink, whenever he had to Go Out; but he had to Go Out all the time. The Yankees fastened to him declared that it was ruthless to compel them—the well, the comparatively unsick—to share the groanings and splashings of a diarrhoeic prisoner. They did not wish to spend all their time at the sink. Nor did they wish to be sprayed with juices of the sick man when his explosions overcame him suddenly, unavoidably.

What was Captain Wirz to do about this? Also they were always complaining that the chain gang and stocks were inhuman. Henry responded cuttingly, jeeringly, asking them if they had ever heard of civil prisons and punishments awarded therein.

If you be good once—model prisoners—in those stocks you should not be, in this chain gang!

That made sense to Henry Wirz, why did it not make sense to the prisoners? Because they were bears. Because most of them had not the wits of bears. Could they not understand why they were being punished?

Him with the diarrhoea: he was something to think about. As a physician,

Henry deplored the sight or knowledge of men compelled to associate with the ordure of the sick. That was the reason he'd sought to move heaven and earth, that was the reason he'd managed to have the hospital taken outside the stockade months before. But as prison superintendent he must maintain discipline. Once committed to an act he should not falter, for any change would be interpreted promptly as a demonstration of weakness. The prisoners must not believe him weak. Suppose he yielded to their importuning and allowed the diarrhoeic Yankee to be separated from the others? They would feel that they had won a victory. They were not victors, they were prisoners. How should he decide? His arm hurt him so.

A hot wind came from the northwest, suggesting a shower to follow, and blowing before it the smell of Andersonville which had penetrated across dark low hills even as far as the Boss house. Pine branches were soughing, cardboard leaves of magnolia racketed. So, upon the high hurtful fence laced around a valley of sleep which he fought to enter— Perched on this indeterminate palisade, Henry Wirz had the notion that he was hearing waves, hearing a sea creasing under the bow of a blockade runner. Again an officer said to him, I'm sorry, Captain, we think the Yanks are chasing us, we've got to get up more speed, we've got to lighten ship. That's the reason those sailors are dumping out the cabin furniture. That chest of yours, Captain—

It was a handsome chest, carved—purchased in an old shop near the Seine, said to be of Italian origin. He was fetching it as a present to Elizabeth. It had not cost much, but his wife would think it beautiful.

Your chest's got to go, Captain. That's the order: every heavy object overboard that can be spared.

He did not protest for long, he saw the sense of the thing. They must lighten ship, so he must contribute his mite. He had no wish to be overhauled by a Federal cruiser. Only after the handsome old black cube (black as ebony, perhaps it was ebony) had gone tumbling into spray, heaved across the bulwark by two brawny sailors— Only after some small objects had scattered in the wind did Henry Wirz strike his right hand across his left and leap and sicken with the pain of it, and call himself a *Verfluchter Hund.* His chess set! The beautiful figures, the knights with ornate manes— How could he have done such a thing? Oh, old yellow ivory. He had left the chess set packed in the heavy carved chest. He could have taken pieces out and stowed them in his clothing one by one. He had loved chess when he was young; often he'd promised that he would teach Elizabeth to play; so when he saw this ivory set offered (the Jew who sold it declared upon his faith that it was stolen; thus he would let it go cheap, and to a foreigner, because he feared the police) Henry had envisioned contented hours when he sat beside his wife and taught her—first, the principle of the thing—later perhaps she might understand some fine points as well. Such relaxation it would be for him after a demanding day. Now the Atlantic had it.

Wind faltered, no rain came, magnolia leaves thrashed less noisily. Still Henry Wirz was not asleep: he ranged along that boundary which it seemed he could not pass.

A doll for Cora: that had been saved. It was in his big leather pouch (he was not requested to throw the leather pouch overboard). Also there were gloves for his stepdaughters, bottles of perfumery to be appreciated by Elizabeth, lockets for the older girls. Small things, old things, mostly second-hand, shopped for, bargained for with zeal. Henry Wirz had so little money, and the plantation he'd owned in Louisiana was gobbled by invading Federal troops during the Vicksburg campaign. He had managed to buy also a coral necklace for his small daughter: a coral necklace naturally, since her name was Coralie.

He passed into the haunted fen of sleep. He fastened the coral necklace around Cora's miniature neck. But, *Gott,* he found that he was fastening instead a metallic collar; from it would depend an iron ball, Cora would have a struggle to lift the ponderous orb whenever she moved.

He told himself, Now will I employ the sulphate of morphia. He had only one dose left, he did not know how soon he should be able to obtain more. The situation as to drugs and medicines was growing worse and worse.

Elizabeth awakened and found his shadow brooding. She hoisted herself on her elbow with a moan of sympathy and alarm. Oh, poor husband! Henry, can you not sleep at all?

Now maybe I get some sleep, he said heavily. He stumbled back to the bed, forgetting to put out the candle; so his round-shouldered parched body shone like a shadowgraph against candlelight, a desiccated body draped in false folds of the voluminous nightshirt.

Elizabeth, tomorrow to Augusta I go. I get things put together, I leave that damn Davis in charge. Maybe I am gone a week, maybe more.

But, Henry, why up to Augusta?

It is for the sake of *mein* arm, Ilse. I hear this week there is that Surgeon Greenaway in Augusta, and better he is with bones, better nor that damn Bucheton. I talk with one colonel, and he show me where he was wounded, and a bad wound from the scars; it is that Surgeon Greenaway fix him, and now he is well. In the arm, like me, but with him it is the left arm. He show me: his fist he clinch—clanch—how you say? *Himmel,* he punch a bag of meal with his fist, he punch hard, this I could not do! So now I ask leave. I go—tomorrow, next day—I report sick—

Husband, you didn't put out the candle.

Now I have my morphia I put him out. So.

No longer did the big bird flap his wings or crouch or move, there was only darkness, and wind growing.

37

The report which Colonel Chandler inscribed was conceived and projected with earnest intelligence and in contempt of human weakness, human blundering. Hatred he must put aside, hatred would render his pen insecure and detract from cogency. But he sat so astounded that he could not even write the dateline without error. *Andersonville, July 5, 1864.* It was August, and he wrote July; he did not realize his mistake, not even when he'd finished the report and sealed it. July had been a weary crowded month; in various tasks which he was ordered to perform, Chandler had written *July* a dozen times daily, thus he wrote the word of the wrong month now. *Having, in obedience to instructions of the 25th ultimo, carefully inspected the prison for Federal prisoners of war and post at this place, I respectfully submit the following report.* He went on to describe the dimensions of the pen, the deadline. He erred in his calculation as to the number of square feet available to each prisoner, and then discussed the stockade's creek. *Excepting the edges of this stream, the soil is sandy and easily drained, but from 30 to 50 yards on each side of it the ground is a muddy marsh, totally unfit for occupation, and having been constantly used as a sink since the prison was first established, it is now in a shocking condition and cannot fail to breed pestilence.*

He despised what he'd found here—disorganization, frailty, deliberate intent —because it reflected upon the Confederacy which he had embraced and which he had served with heart and body. He saw the Confederate lake which might have been pure (fed as it was by noble patriotic springs), muddied. He sat with ink upon his fingers, keen gaze turned against sheets of paper before him. He was aware of an awful truth while his pen scratched dutifully: the bravery of a Nation's men may resist the attack of outsiders, but what defense can be managed against creeping diseases within? Guard your legs with leggings (snakes cannot bite through them), glove your hands, helmet your head, wrap your belly and vitals to keep out cold . . . or even put armor outside to withstand blades and bullets. But an unseen worm will find its way down your gullet and make nuisance inside you until you sicken and fail; what will you drink for purge or tonic?

As Alexander Persons had put his own good head upon the block, so Chandler was laying himself open to censure with every curl of script, every indited comma. There were too many people of grade superior to his who would not countenance implied criticism. Yet Colonel Chilton had instructed him to make this inspection; by the eternal God he would set down exactly what he had seen.

He mentioned the efforts of Henry Wirz, his attempts to construct sluice and sinks, he told why this had not been done successfully. *No shelter whatever, nor material for constructing any has been provided by the prison authorities, and the ground being entirely bare of trees, none is within reach of the prisoners, nor has it been possible, from the overcrowded state of the enclosure, to arrange the camp with any system. Each man has been permitted to protect himself as best he can, stretching his blanket, or whatever he may have, above him on such sticks as he can procure, thatches of pine or whatever his ingenuity may suggest and his cleverness supply. Of other shelter there is and has been none.*

He discussed Nineties and Detachments. *But one Confederate States officer, Captain Wirz, is assigned to the supervision and control of the whole.* He spoke of the turmoil which had prevailed, and mentioned the sentencing and hanging of raiders as it had been described to him. He told of the absence of medical attendants within the stockade, and the parade which went creeping to the South Gate each morning, and the squeeze ensuing. *The hospital accommodations are so limited that though the beds (so-called) have all or nearly all two occupants each, large numbers who would otherwise be received are necessarily sent back to the stockade. Many—twenty yesterday—are carted out daily, who have died from unknown causes, and whom the medical officers have never seen.*

The face of John Winder seemed staring fixedly at Colonel Chandler across the field desk, the colonel's hand began to quiver. Desperately he sought to master vibration, to control his pen as he recounted the final horror observed that day. It was strange to entertain the apparition of Winder now, since the old general could not have been directly responsible for this particular wickedness—only indirectly responsible, only indirectly. *The dead are hauled out daily by the wagonload and buried without coffins, their hands in many instances being first mutilated with an axe in the removal of any finger rings they may have.*

Control was vanished. Chandler let the pen slide, and arose and went to the tent's door and lifted the rotten canvas and felt it tear bedraggledly under its own soiled weight as he held the folds. He peered out through stench and heard the faint voices of guards crying from the stockade's rim. Low in the west a bent flake of moon was receding and would soon be gone.

The colonel mastered his nervousness after a while and returned to discuss the condition of the hospital, the sick, the utter confusion of the medical staff. Most of this latter knowledge had been gained necessarily from second-hand sources; he was wary of it. But he put down a statistical summary: *the rate of death has been steadily increased from 37 4–10 per mil. during the month of March last to 62 7–10 per mil. in July.*

He wrote for nearly another hour, summing his recommendations and suggesting prisons in two additional localities which had been mentioned to him by General Winder before his exchange with Winder became acid. *In conclusion I beg leave to recommend that no more prisoners be sent to this already overcrowded prison. . . . Since my inspection was made, over 1,300 prisoners have been added to the number specified in the reports herewith.*

He felt his mind straying, it could not sustain him. He wanted to tell all, he had not told all. He began to worry about the uncertainty of his sources, especially with regard to hospital and surgeons. He must walk in the night and speak with someone—perhaps even have a glass of comfort, perform some selfish act in order to soothe the grating of his nerves. He thought of his assistant who had followed him to Andersonville, Major Hall; the mere fact that Hall was a direct subordinate ruled him out. There was another man whom he felt he could trust, this man he should seek.

Colonel Chandler did not wish to leave his report and the attendant papers lying about. He did not yet wish to lock his field desk, he might have a use for it later tonight. He folded the sheets carefully and put them into the pocket of his threadbare linen shirt. He took hat and sidearms and walked toward the Claffey place. Three times he was challenged, three times he identified himself and went past pickets. He was in no way confident that Harrell Elkins would be at the Claffey house or that he would be awake. But Elkins had gone on duty at four o'clock that morning, had slaved for twelve hours, had enjoyed whatever broken naps his frayed weariness permitted. Now he sat upon the gallery with Lucy.

Elkins said something about their not being gods, but they would offer the guest nectar in any event.

I should be glad to taste nectar. Colonel Chandler saw a white pitcher in the gloom. Elkins had gone promptly to fetch another tumbler; Chandler did not know what they meant by nectar, he was too strained to speculate.

Lucy explained, Tis from the Toccoa apples. A relative brought us slips from Habersham County long ago; but Poppy declares they don't flourish here as in those hills yonder.

I should think not. Colonel Chandler thought of ravines where the Chattahoochee rose.

But my father has a green thumb, so they do bear. The apples are just past ripe, and I direct Naomi to stew them with honey when honey can be had. We press out all the juice and express a kind of sauce, sir, and we've always called it nectar. I hope you'll think it's just the best. Tis mixed with cold spring water, so please to drink deeply and healthily. She added, when Harry came with the glass, I had some difficulty with Surgeon Elkins. She gave a little laugh which suggested a depth of other emotion.

Has the surgeon been ungallant, Ma'am? Has he been annoying you?

Truly he has. He refused to drink apple nectar at first; said he didn't thirst for it.

Frankly, Miss Lucy, he has no good taste.

The girl's voice shook. He would not drink it because the Yankee prisoners had none.

Elkins shifted his heavy feet and uttered a bleat of remonstrance.

Colonel Chandler lifted the glass in his hand and held it to vague light which came from inside the front room. My own victuals have choked me since I came here. Nevertheless I forced myself to eat them, and— To Elkins— Nevertheless you should force yourself to drink nectar.

Lucy thought that the visitor must have appeared for a purpose. If you gentlemen will excuse me, please. They arose, Lucy went rustling away.

So it stuck in your craw? Chandler felt an angry tendency to coarseness. The men seated themselves again.

You know how women are, Harry told him—Elkins, the man who knew so little about how women were. Perhaps I might mind the hospital less if it didn't accompany me perforce when I'd left it. Can I be of service, sir?

I have intruded upon you and the young lady.

Scarcely the place or season for romantic chit-chat, Colonel. The surroundings are not conducive to romance.

Mr. Claffey has retired?

He is abed and with either Shakespeare or the Apostle Paul. He asserts that he finds a refuge of almost equal character in the historic plays or in the admonitions to the people of Corinth. Mr. Claffey goes so far as to say that this is damaging to his religious stability.

Since we are alone, Surgeon, may we have a candle?

The candle was brought and stood leaning under its flame, attacked by tiger moths. By this light Chandler examined his papers. If you will be so kind as to confirm certain details I'll be in your debt. Let me see— I took my ratio of deaths directly from the report of the chief surgeon, Dr. White. We'll not bother with that.

To be frank, said Harry, I assisted Surgeon White in the report's preparation.

I'd guessed as much. Is it correct that such original hospital arrangements as were suggested were intended only for the accommodation of the supposed ratio of sick to a total population of ten thousand men?

That is correct.

Do you know how many prisoners were on hand, in camp and hospital, on the first of July?

Elkins's voice scratched. I was not present at that time, as you know, but I recall seeing a return recently. Something over twenty-six thousand on hand on the first of July.

And how many new prisoners were received during the month?

Something over seven thousand.

Making a total above thirty-three thousand, then. How many died during July?

Above seventeen hundred.

Would you guess as to how many are sick within the stockade, untended?

Impossible to state.

Now then, of the medical officers: how many hold commissions?

But ten hold commissions, sir. Most of the others are detailed from the militia. As for myself, I sought this duty because I was driven by the need.

Elkins stood up nervously and struck his hands together. I might admit also to more personal and selfish reasons for wishing Andersonville duty, but let that pass. Since I am ticketed as unfit for service in the field, I felt justified in trying to manipulate myself into a sphere where my conscience would assure me that I was needed. As a former officer I should be reluctant to state that many of our surgeons have accepted positions here to avoid service in the ranks. But, by God, sir, I do say it!

I know the type, said Chandler. They'll relinquish their contracts as soon as the present emergency exists no more and the militia is disbanded. Pray sit down, Elkins. You've been working long and hard—too long and too hard, I fear.

Harrell sank back into his chair. He said dryly, But little injury would result when those contracts are relinquished. The men who hold them are generally very inefficient. Many of them only visit the post once a day, at Sick Call. They bestow but little attention on those under their care.

What is your opinion as to the management and police of the general hospital grounds?

As good as the limited means will allow.

What are the facilities?

There is a necessity for at least three times the number of tents and amount of bedding on hand at this time.

What of medicines?

The supply is wholly inadequate. Frequently there is no supply of medicines. Great delays are experienced in the filling of requisitions.

Chandler folded his papers, put them away, pinched out the candle in order to discourage insects. Both he and Elkins had become oblivious to the hurt of mosquitoes. Hordes droned day and night, sometimes in visible clouds, again they were blown away by a wind. The two men sat in silence for so long that Harrell Elkins fell asleep and was roused by his own head snapping forward. He came awake to see the colonel's dark shape poised on the edge of the gallery, his back to Elkins. The young surgeon had a vague sleepy thought about some seeker for self-destruction teetering on the edge of an abyss.

Chandler was speaking of the past, something about his youthful days at West Point, and Elkins tried to send his attention hounding on the heels of Chandler's conversation, so that the visitor would not be aware of this lapse into slumber.

Walked the same paths in his time that I did in mine, said Colonel Chandler. And so, of course, did Grant and Sherman and most of the leading Yankees. They're enemies now, but I do not hold them to be arch-fiends. This old wretch seems to fit the description. I could not speak in this fashion to a subordinate or a superior; but you, sir, are a doctor—however young—and doctors must be father confessors to all.

Elkins managed to say, A portion of the responsibility which we must assume with the Hippocratic Oath.

Gad, sir, that man is completely indifferent to the welfare of the prisoners! He's undisposed to do anything to alleviate their sufferings. When I remonstrated with him I received only foul language in reply; when I spoke of the great mortality existing among the prisoners, and pointed out to him that the sickly season was coming on, and that sickness must necessarily increase unless something was done for the prisoners' relief—the swamp, for instance, drained; proper food furnished them, and in better quantity; and other sanitary suggestions which I made to him— He replied that he thought it was better to let half of them die than to take care of the men.

Elkins said, I have encountered the son, never encountered the father.

Major Hall had spoken to him previously. I'd suggested that he present some recommendations to the general whilst I was otherwise engaged. The major returned to me white of face; when he reported the fury and the obscenity employed, I could not well believe him, though I do trust Major Hall. I thought it incredible, thought that he must be mistaken! No, says Hall, he not only used those words once, but twice. Well, my friend, as I have just stated, subsequently General Winder made use of the same expressions to me.

Chandler took up the belt and sword and pistol which he had put aside when he sat down. I trust that you will forgive me, Surgeon. I'm better for the gift of Miss Claffey's nectar, and for your patience. My work here is concluded—if there can be any conclusion to such an effort—and I shall be proceeding to the head-quarters of the Army of Tennessee.

Their hands squeezed, the colonel wished Elkins success in his labors and cautioned him about wearing himself to the bone. He sent respects and sympathy to the Claffeys, then walked away across the black lane. Harrell Elkins was fast asleep in his chair before Chandler had reached the first picket.

It was almost lewd, thought the colonel, that he should now be entertaining memories of long-ago days at the Academy. Yet he presumed that it was because an illusion of idealistic service had been projected to youths there. At present, in observing the ideal trampled so cruelly and the service debased, he turned for comfort to thought of surroundings where this dream, now mutilated, had been born. Had John Winder been human when younger? Had he stolen bread-and-butter and hidden it in his leather bell cap, as Chandler had done when he was a cadet? Had he joined in a bread-and-butter feast after Taps in the old South Barracks? Had he gone illicitly to Benny Havens' and plunged his hot face into a mug of beer bought on credit?

> *When you and I and Benny, and all the others, too,*
> *Are called before the Final Board, our course in life to view.*
> *May we never 'fess on any point; but straight be told to go,*
> *And join the army of the blest, at Benny Havens', oh!*

In his tent Chandler relighted his lantern and stepped upon the path he had longed and yet feared to tread. He wrote a supplemental report to Colonel Chilton. In a small way he thought he would have been harming his own conception of the military ideal to which he was sworn if he did not do so. It was as if the flag had been befouled by Winder. He, Chandler, might not be able to scrub the colored folds clean again; but he wanted to own his soul, even if he were shorn of rank in the process.

My duty requires me respectfully to recommend a change in the officer in command of the post, Brigadier-General J. H. Winder, and the substitution in his place of some one who unites both energy and good judgment with some feeling of humanity and consideration for the welfare and comfort (so far as is consistent with their safekeeping) of the vast number of unfortunates placed under his control; some one who at least will not advocate deliberately and in cold blood the propriety of leaving them in their present condition until their number has been sufficiently reduced by death to make the present arrangement suffice for their accommodation; who will not consider it a matter of self-laudation and boasting that he has never been inside of the stockade, a place of horrors of which it is difficult to describe, and which is a disgrace to civilization. . . .

38

The young old friends from West Dummerston, Vermont—Adam Garrett and John Appleby—had taken up tenancy together on a portion of the crowded terrain commonly designated as the Island. Their green past was fled. Nowadays the fact that they had a halfway decent shebang (even though the Island lay surrounded by putrid bogs, and thus its inhabitants were named the Leper Colony) was more important than a remembrance that once, side by side, they'd walked to the covered bridge across the West River, and extended their fishing poles, also side by side. It was more important to Adam Garrett that he had been able to barter for a handful of dried beans, than that he had been wounded at Gettysburg when he served previously with the Sixteenth. It was more important to John Appleby that he brought home a fair mess of roots to repay laborious hours of digging, than that he had served under the admired Colonel James M. Warner, an actual graduate of the United States Military Academy . . . few of the Volunteer Regiments could claim such a commander! Camp Bradley at Brattleboro, with Hallie Small and Hephzibah Clark fetching loaded baskets on visitors' day: that was forgotten. So were forgotten old Austrian muskets put into the excited hands of awkward country boys. John forgot the filth of Cliffburne barracks since now he dwelt in an ocean of filth which would have made Cliffburne spotless in comparison.

The youths remembered only that they were both captured at the abortive Weldon Road battle southwest of Petersburg, in the early evening of June twenty-third.

Their principal friends on the Island, since so many of the Eleventh Vermont boys lay dead, were two artillerymen from Battery E of the Fifth Maine. One was sick, one was in comparatively good health. The Maine boys lived in a dugout adjoining. Sometimes in early days of captivity the four New Englanders argued vociferously as they cited the advantages of their respective States. Sometimes they came close to blows; then in the end, being good Christian village boys with a bounce of humor, they shook hands and said that it was a pity there weren't some New Hampshiremen in between to act as a buffer.

Through blinding heat, with mosquitoes keening thicker each night, they neglected rivalries and ignored the remembrance of Maine and Vermont. Might there be parents and clear-eyed tawny-haired girls who mourned them as Departed, or who had heard the truth of their capture and prayed for prison doors to be swung? Appleby had raked hay on his father's three mowings terraced above the gentle valley of the West River, Garrett had unpacked boots and weighed out sugar and sacked salt in his father's store. Portland Hyde had ridden logs in a river: he was a lumberman and proud of it; and the man Caldwell boasted earlier of how many cows he'd milked night and morning since he was knee-high to a cow. At last it mattered not what they had been, where they came from, what orderly dreams they'd once held. Congregationalism mattered not, nor did the fact that Hyde's mother had been a Quaker and his father was not a Quaker, but still his mother insisted on talking Plain in their home. . . . Andersonville reduced them to a single pattern: they were stamped out of that pattern by the enormous heavy die of confinement, like a row of four toy tin wretches holding hands.

Late one day the lumberman Hyde died of dropsy as the sun was draining down behind the fence. Adam Garrett and John Appleby tossed a penny to see which should go with Caldwell, carrying Hyde down to the dead row. Appleby lost —or won, depending upon how you looked at it: Caldwell had agreed to give Hyde's shirt to the man who helped him. It was not so much the weight of the body as the awkward task of handling a tall object like Portland Hyde, who weighed perhaps ninety pounds at death (exclusive of the fluid in him) but was still six feet and three inches in length. His flannel shirt was not good for much— tatters, mainly—but it had three large buttons on it. John Appleby planned to wash the shirt in a broth of ashes and get rid of most of the lice for a time at least.

Caldwell came over and said, He's gone. He ain't got a breath in him, and they all crept back to take a look at Hyde. The lumberman lay flat on his back with brown eyes protruding, and late flies settling stubbornly around the eyes, and moving in and out of the open mouth.

If there was some way to prick him and get rid of all that there dropsy water, he'd be simpler to carry. This was Appleby's idea.

I could use my penknife, Adam Garrett suggested.

Not on Porty, Caldwell cried, bristling. He may be gone to meet his Maker, but no one's to put a blade in him.

Hellfire. I was jesting.

I calculate we should hold a service. Porty was a good church man.

Garrett told John, Fetch your Scriptures.

John's Scriptures consisted only of Matthew with part of Mark and the last two pages of Malachi. He had them rolled around a bit of stick and tied with yarn, and covered with a piece of stained linen. Handling the flimsy leaves with care, he thumbed until he found the verses he sought.

. . . *He is not here: for he is risen, as he said. Come, see the place where the Lord lay.*

And go quickly, and tell his disciples that he is risen from the dead; and, behold, he goeth before you into Galilee; there shall you see him: lo, I have told you.

A few people came from surrounding shelters and watched apathetically; they stood with rough hair fuzzy against the pink sunset. A neighboring New Yorker called out, If I see him I hope he's not still sick. God, how he stunk. Hope you take him out of here tonight, Hay Rube.

I'll Hay Rube you, next time you get within reach of my club! Caldwell threw a stone which had braced the main pole of his shelter; he missed the New Yorker, but the little crowd dodged and scattered, and went back home.

Leave us repeat the Lord's Prayer.

Garrett felt that this service was miserable and inadequate, whatever the intention. They mumbled through the Lord's Prayer, and tied the dead man's big toes together with a bit of hemp. Then the Vermonters tossed their penny.

Caldwell stood musingly as he flicked lice out of his beard. Guess I'll pack up and move. Moving day for me. Or moving night.

Where to?

Member there was four fellows from our battery living over on the North Side? They come down to see us last month. Well, I hear that two are still alive. You know how it goes: man doesn't like to live alone.

He worked Hyde's body aside until he could remove the bark from their storehouse. They had some rice, a packet of dirty stationery imprinted with eagles and goddesses, a wad of soft soap in a rag, two pencils, a suspender strap, a few other odds and ends.

Caldwell wrote on a torn envelope, *Portland Hyde Battery E Fifth Maine Artillery* and with another strand of hemp string they tied this paper around Hyde's ear.

I'll bind these oddments up in the blanket, and Caldwell did so, folding the ragged edges tightly together so that nothing might be lost. With a last length of tent cord he tied the pack over his shoulder, and turned to shake hands with Adam. Drop in if you get up our way. It's in the furthest northwest corner, right past the last big well. They got two gray army blankets on top, and old pine boughs around the edges. It's about the biggest shebang in the neighborhood.

You'll still have to draw rations with your old Ninety, Adam warned him.

But I can dwell happier up there with my Maine friends. Maybe I can flank into their Ninety one way or another.

And get put in the stocks?

It'd be worth a try. Come along, Jim Along Johnny.

They lifted Hyde, Hyde made a belching noise; Caldwell had him by the feet, Johnny by the hands. We won't take off his shirt and drawers till we get him to the gate. They carried the corpse into the gloom.

Garrett cried while they were picking their way down the slope of the Island, Hi, Caldwell. Tent poles—

You can have them, Adam. More than I can fetch now. I don't want to come all the way back. His words floated faintly up the incline where tiny fires were glowing, with apes crouched above the colored flames, blowing in turn to keep the fire climbing through damp bits of splintered roots. For another minute or two Garrett could watch the two vertical shapes with that horizontal thing swaying between them; he lost them against deeper blackness of the marsh.

Adam wrenched up the four tent posts which had supported the blanket roof above that abandoned hole. He brought also the stones piled for extra bracing. Air smelled better already, with Hyde carried away. The New Yorker had been right . . . it was just the way he said it.

John came home half an hour later, picking his way stubbornly among shelters, and being roundly cursed when he stepped too close to any person or fire. You could follow his course up the low slope of the Island merely by listening to the oaths following as he moved.

He did some cursing on his own account after he reached home. That plaguèd God damn bitchy dropsy! Hope to high hell and hellfire I never get it! Scurvy's bad enough, but— Adam, I vow, I stopped down there in the creek and washed my hand a dozen times. Even them maggots smelt clean by comparison.

What was it? Dropsy— You mean Portland Hyde?

Damn, twas his hand. I mean the skin. We'd got his drawers and shirt off of him, and then we took hold to give him a heave across that little fence. I vow! The skin come loose from his hand like it was rotten cloth or something. Just peeled loose like a big glove. There he was in the row, and there I stood, a-holding onto the skin of his hand where it come loose on me. I like to puked my gizzard out.

Garrett muttered.

What say?

I said, Glad that I lost that penny toss. You can have the blame shirt and welcome.

I got it right here. Them three buttons will come handy, though one is split. What say? Want to turn in? Want some rations first?

They decided to eat half the piece of pone they were saving, and reserve the other half for morning. They still had one onion, but it was keeping well; they had agreed to save the onion for soup, in order to flavor the next meat ration when and if it was forthcoming. Mosquitoes hummed thickly while the men ate. They lay down, spooned closely; each covered his head with an old leg-of-drawers.

Garrett slept well, or at least better than usual; he dreamed of ferns. He tried to think of Hallie before he drifted into slumber; but rapidly she was joining the remote company of people in his past whom he could never reassemble, by voice or figment of face, no matter how earnestly he attempted to conjure them. He dreamed about a ravine of ferns below Black Mountain; it was summer, and there was agreeable coolness, and he walked through the bank of ferns. A woodpecker went down in long slicing flight from one tree and soared quickly up against another dead trunk, and clutched, hammering. Garrett didn't know what kind of woodpecker it was. But he saw the ferns clearly, and someone said something about blackberries in plenty.

Bam. Pam. Two shots woke them up . . . among mosquitoes . . . after midnight. The shots sounded like muskets but of different bore. There was a faint yell, whether the cry of the victim or a hoot of derision they did not know. A few voices called out the persistent litany of, Give the Rebel son of a bitch a furlough, then there was such silence as ruled—the wasting, crowded silence of mumbles and wails and snarls and hog-callings which went on forever, latticed like a visible structure beneath the stars.

With sunrise the vast population began to own a dimension of activity as well as sound, with men kindling fires anew, men beginning to bargain for food, men beginning to fight and tussle, men squatting at the sinks, men foraging for water in the marsh, men unable or unwilling to reach the sinks and squatting along the swamp's borders instead. Johnny was first out of the shelter, but he returned promptly and pushed his head back under the sagging overcoat with an expression of incredulity akin to amusement on his blackened face.

I swear, Adam. Damndest neighbors we got.

Adam Garrett joined him on hands and knees, and together they stared amazed at the transformation adjoining. When they went to sleep the night before, the dwelling-place which Hyde had relinquished through death and which Caldwell had given up as a matter of choice— The depression was a depression only, with no shred or twig to mark it. Now new poles had been put up, and a canvas cover which was close to being clean and white flaunted in the early breeze. The cover hung nearly to the ground on their side, but when currents of air twitched it, figures could be seen snuggled together in the scooped-out pit.

Did you hear anybody move in? No more did I.

Freshest fish in the ocean, I'll be bound. See how clean that cloth is, Johnny?

I'm going over. Appleby went away while Adam was still stretching and rubbing his eyes.

John came back soon, babbling with gossip. It's sailors, he announced in the gasping muted mumble with which they commonly maintained privacy when privacy was desired. . . . Two of them. Great big hairy fellow, big and fresh and strong, got meat all over his bones. Big old fellow, could be maybe of the age of thirty-five or forty. The other one is puny—just a boy fourteen or so. They're newly took by the Rebs—only last week, or so I make it out. But the old chap is some kind of foreigner; I can scarcely catch a word he utters.

Garrett's brother-in-law had served in the marines, and he remembered talk of weird doings aboard ships. John. That sounds like a seaman and his chicken.

Chicken? What in tunket is a chicken?

A little boy. Cabin boy, most likely. He belongs to the big man, and that chap takes care of him and loves him. He pulled Appleby's head closer to his, and lowered his voice to a bare whisper, and told more.

I never heard the beat of it! Appleby cried out in horror. Never heard the— Mister, you've heard of corn-holing, hain't you?

Oh, yes. But just imagine. On a National gunboat or warship! You'd think the officers—

I didn't say *all* the sailors. I just said some of them.

They soon heard it related that not one but three or four sailors had been accompanied by their chickens when the latest draft of fresh fish arrived. The Vermonters were busy with Hyde's obsequies, and did not notice excitement at the North Gate which had attended incoming squads. For the seamen had, for the most part, retained their sea-bags. This came about because they were guarded by a detachment of infantry newly removed from some position of coastal defense, now journeying north to aid in the resistance above Atlanta.

John cried indignantly, Just their damn good fortune! If they'd drawn a company of these volunteer Home Guards! I vow, it takes militia to comb you over.

The huge sailor domiciled in the Caldwell-Hyde hole told them about it later, when they could understand his speech more ably. He said that he had a razor, he carried it folded in his sleeve, and he could flip it out, opened and threatening, in a manner to strike terror. After the incoming prisoners got off the cars at Anderson, and were standing in uneven ranks waiting to be counted again and marched to the stockade, two Reserves did in fact descend on him and demand his sea-bag, and the boy's. The razor whistled close, the Reserves fell back, cocking their muskets. A voice snapped at them, an officer's voice, and the Reserves were ordered away before they had a chance to fire. A few of the forty-odd navy men in the detachment lost their possessions, but most kept them intact. It was lucky for them that they arrived after the breaking of the raiders instead of before. People guessed that they wouldn't have gotten halfway across the stockade with those bulging canvas bags.

The mighty sailor had slit his own bag to make this fresh canopy, since he owned no blanket or overcoat. He and the boy had short-cut pea jackets however; these they used for bedding. The big man was Irish, speaking an almost unintelligible collection of syllables which he tumbled round and round, deep in his thick throat. When he gave his name, to Garrett's ears it seemed to be Paydrog. Hence they called him Pay, and the other neighbors did too. He was a shambling, round-shouldered giant with a rim of cinnamon-colored brush shaped carefully down the boundaries of his cheeks and across his chin. Soon he gave up shaving, and used the razor for other purposes; then the razor was stolen from Pay one afternoon. He bellowed for a solid hour but it did no good: the razor did not reappear. Likely one of the New Yorkers got it.

They called the little boy Chickie at first, but Pay showed resentment; it seemed that the term was for use only by the adoring partner, or in the third person. The boy was named Valentine, and he had been born near the wharves of the Delaware River at Camden, New Jersey, and had gone to sea when he was twelve or thereabouts. Val sported a spoiled, simpering little face, a mouth which could smirk out of all proportion to its puffy pink fatness, and polished eyes reminding Adam of nothing so much as the eyes of a trapped garter-snake. Val could curse—and did, hourly—in a manner to put any of the raiders to shame. But Pay he addressed in cooing accents to drive the neighbors mad. Val seemed trying to imitate a mourning-dove.

Or a honey-bee, said Appleby in hate.

They do live high. Whilst you were digging roots this afternoon, and whilst I was on guard, they cooked up a stew—I mean, Pay cooked it. It had salt, too; he'd been down and made a barter opposite Stockade Creek. Had salt, onions, potatoes, some of that there Rebel vegetable—what you call it, all squashy—?

Okra.

That's the one. And two beef bones— reckon they're mule, though—and a big piece of tripe.

Tripe! Come along, I don't like being played for a fool.

Well, they had it. I set out there, and so did the New Yorkers, and that old saddler from Ohio. We set around on our marrowbones and watched them, and we could smell pretty good, too. They finished everything in that big pot, or pretty near, and Pay says to the lad, Did he want more? No, no, says Val, and made that silly face he's always making.

What did they do with what was left?

Pay give it a heave. You heard me. He flung it out.

Well, why didn't you—? *You* can go dig roots tomorrow.

I calculate to.

Then Garrett felt that he had had enough sport with his friend, and lovingly he produced the two bones he'd salvaged. There was gristle along the sides, the marrow would be intact for they had not been cut open, and there was actually a wad of lean meat and glutinous fat around the end of one bone. The New Yorkers made a dive, he said, but this little Vermont apple-knocker got there first.

The two flat hats, bobbing about next door, became a familiar spectacle, just as other familiar spectacles had existed before in the same locality during the tenancy of the Maine artillerymen, just as further familiar spectacles would in time supersede this one if the same eyes were there to witness. The flat hats bore in printed letters the words *Sea Sprite* but one day the bristly Irishman was not wearing his hat. He had sold it to a guard for brown sugar, a little envelope of brown sugar. Val had a sweet tooth.

The big sailor's store of money ran out quickly. Then, article by article, Pay hawked away his fortune. He bartered extra pairs of blue pantaloons for meat, his extra pairs of socks . . . he sold his sailor blouses, he sold tough linen thread, big hanks of waxed cord, many of his needles. He'd had something to do with the sails aboard that sloop on which he and the chicken were captured. In time he even sold the gold-beaded Rosary that hung around his own neck. Val was the possessor of a fine wardrobe—little white sailor suits trimmed in blue, little blue sailor suits trimmed in white. These costumes had been hand-sewn for him, lovingly, by his protector. Not a stitch of the chicken's possessions would Pay offer for barter—not until dire necessity on Val's part forced him to it. Then he disposed of them to some of the elder guards who bought the clothing for their children; he sold them for rice, turnips, a half-rotten melon, rancid bacon, anything he could get. Of course he was cheated roundly.

He had lost weight from the start, rapidly and visibly, as biggest men always did. It was as if a bony structure melted away beneath the stout countenance and let the exhausted cheeks and other features fall loosely, as if they were a mask grown limp and hung upon a curtain rod. Folds of flesh around his neck drooped like cloth, then tightened up in a turkey's wattles. The beard, no longer shaped, straggled out in tusks and horns. The ruddy skin became black as a miner's . . . Pay spent hours with his head pushed down in pine smoke, blowing at reluctant flames of his cooking smudge.

Also he washed Val's clothes stubbornly, hunting for less pestilential pools of the morass, prospecting here and there, and finally going to work with ashes and muddy water—wringing, rinsing, twisting, pummeling sodden cloth with a stick and with his fists—striving to keep Val the mincing blue-and-white dainty thing he'd been before. The neighbors, most of them, were beyond the point of catcalls and ribaldry about this; they only stared in a manner of bored impudence and disbelief. Pay himself was far beyond the practice of sodomy or any other mis-shapen act, but he proceeded in a pattern long established: he owned an affection, it had come to rule him, he was selfless, savagely devoted.

The silver-haired Ohio saddler, whose name was Tom Gusset, did a brisk trade in the repair of leather goods. He had managed to keep some of his knives, awls and the like, when he came in. Each day he set up shop, now near the North Gate, now near the South, and cried his skills aloud. He would cobble a strap or a shoe or a leather cartouche flap—he could do such things soundly and speedily with the aptness which lived still in his fingers—but he worked only for currency or for some victual he fancied. One day there was excitement when a batch of freshies came in from some fort in the Carolinas, and one of them had smuggled a packet of candy: gaudy, viscous sticks striped with red and white. Promptly the candy was distributed to the four winds; the newcomer needed a blanket, a cooking can, things more imperative than candy. Gusset acquired one stick; it was stared at and coveted by all. The saddler limited himself to a half-inch at a time. After two days there was still a sizeable stub remaining.

However, he found that the heat of his body was melting the sweetness as he carried it about in his clothing. Privately he dug a storage den, and buried the precious colored fragment. He'd put it in a chunk of hollow cane which he owned, and plugged up the ends. The chicken must have seen where the treasure was put away, though no one knew it at the time.

The next afternoon Garrett was root-digging and Appleby housekeeping, when an explosion occurred in the Ohio quarters. Previously a fight had begun, across the swamp on the slope of the North Side, and most of the stay-at-homes were down there watching the fight. Three angry skeletons were engaged in a battle royal over ownership of an old boot; literally they sought to club or gouge one another to the death. Then came the outburst closer at hand, and Johnny looked out to see Val in full flight, with the old saddler loping after him.

He told Adam, You should of seen it. Didn't know that old rooster could move so spry. He had a big belt in his hand, and he was wheeling it like all possessed. The youngster legged it like the Old Harry was after him. He'd dropped the candy prompt when Gusset spied him in the act of thieving, but Gusset was bound to teach him manners. I calculate the chicken would of got away scot-free, but he was tripped by Pay's own shelter-rope. That strap buckle sung out like it was a bullet, and it bit a piece out of his bottom. Should of heard him yip.

Garrett scratched the filth of his beard. Don't like that. Was it a big piece the buckle took out?

Well, he had blood on his bottom. He went dancing away, still yelling like possessed, and hanging on to his ass with both hands. But I could see blood on his little white cookie. Right side.

Take any kind of scratch or cut. Even a blister. Remember Greenberry? That was the way he went, from just a blister on the palm of his hand. Remember how that arm busted open, all the way up to the elbow?

Don't talk about it.

Reckon Pay will take it out on Old Ohio's hide.

Reckon he wanted to, but he couldn't find him. Gusset knew what was in the wind, and he moved off the Island before Pay come home. Likely he's joined some other Ohioans he knows, one place or another.

Appleby came closer to whisper, Pay's got Val under the shelter, bathing his
hind end. Heard him say he'd kiss it and make it well.

It would take Jesus of Nazareth to make that well.

Johnny was shocked. That's sacrilege.

I know, but ain't it true?

Remorselessly the spoilage began; Adam Garrett's prophecy came true and
more than true. The wound was puffed and swollen at first, then increasingly
discolored (this was what the Irishman told his neighbors later, after he had come,
leaking tears, begging them to help). Val fretted day and night, he had to lie on his
left side, then on his stomach . . . Pay bathed the wound, the bathing hurt, Val
cursed him with shrill hysterical fluency.

Johnny, that's a bad luck shebang, most certain.

Where?

The old Maine hole. First them other miseries, now the chicken.

Gad. I wish he'd stop his whining.

You'd whine the same way, with one side of your bottom swolled up and
turning blue.

He oughtn't to have tried to steal. Thou Shalt Not Steal.

Everybody steals around here.

I wouldn't.

Reckon we both might come to it in time.

There he goes, squealing again. Just like a porker at a butchering.

The Vermont neighbors advised hospital, so did the New Yorkers, but Pay
stood dumb and tearful and merely shook his awful head. They'd never be letting
me care for him in the hospital, now would they?

Not likely that they would.

Sure, I'll care for him myself. Ah, Chickie, Chickie, it's the fine good broth I'm
making for you now, do you hear, do you hear me, little Chickie?

In these days he began to sell Val's clothing from the sea-bag which had been
sacrosanct before. He would bribe a neighbor to sit by the shelter door and keep
an eye on things while he went to market. No longer did he fall in for rations, he
refused to take that much time away from the nursing of Val. He sold the once-
delicate uniforms which he had constructed, the two silk handkerchiefs, at last the
small bright shoes. He'd sold his own shoes long before; he was barefoot; he cut
one toe half off by stepping on a sharp broken cooking pan of tin. This injury did
not try to close itself up as the boy's did; it stood open, draining constantly, but
soon stuffed with worms. Pay was in pain along with his chicken, but never did he
complain of his own hurt.

Little cans of stew bubbled constantly, the slices of fair raw vegetable were
presented, they were pressed upon Val; he'd have none of them. He suffered a
night of delirium and hootings. John had looked at the buttock that day when the
Irishman tried to dress it, and the entire adjacent area of the thin small body was
polluted, discolored, sending out a stench. It was as if the boy wore a great black
pillow stitched against his frame from his knee to the middle of his back, and it
was splitting wide.

No, no, no hospital, mates—they'd never be letting me tend him. . . .

Another steaming, frying, boiling, stewing afternoon, when the whole marsh
crawled and lifted and sank in its maggoty tides. People went down beneath the
heat, they went flat in permanent submission. As the Vermonters sat weak in
sweat beneath the shelter, Garrett pointed out to John that four different dead-
parties were wending toward the dead row at one and the same time. . . . Watch

them, he said. Four, all at once't. Over there—just beyond that blue overcoat shebang.

I see them.

And there's two chaps— I'm certain they're carrying a dead one—yes, they are —right by that well where all them folks are haggling. And over there, above the sink-path. And just down here. . . . They dropped him. Fellow with a piece of blanket tied around him like a skirt. Now they're picking him up again. Four all at once't.

I see another. There, towards the North Gate. That'd make five.

Another evening of Val's clear-voiced agonies, but in the protracted hotness of the night his crying was muted; at last he sounded more like a crippled kitten than a pig about to be butchered. By morning he was giving no utterance at all. Pay fought to jam food into the blackened horny little mouth, but Val could not swallow; soup welled up and rose like water in a spring, and ran away down the emaciated face. Pay took the boy up in his arms and sat rocking back and forth, muttering in Gaelic. It must have been Gaelic, no one could understand what he said.

About three in the afternoon they heard a thin roar from the Irishman, and folks came to peer. Pay had the body wrapped in his arms, and he kept patting and slapping the shoulders crazily; but even his frenzy could put no heat in a shape which was cooling implacably, or limpness in a body which stiffened in that bent attitude into which it had been pressed.

Well, now he'll have to carry him down to the row.

Says he won't.

He'll have to.

Says he wants to bury him here where he can lie on his grave.

There's a hundred men hereabouts who'll say they're not going to dwell above a corpse. Anyway, they'd stop rations for the whole camp. You know that.

Might as well have corpses around as what we got. Couldn't smell much worse, now could they?

I vow, no.

The New Yorkers were moved to a kind of pity; they persuaded Pay to take the little body down to the line. Come, they said, we'll help.

Ah, none except myself shall carry him.

Tie his toes together. Here, I'll do it. . . . Very well, come along with you, Irish. It's hotter than hell today. He'll be swolled up before nightfall. You got to get rid of him.

Something told Garrett, Best go and watch. The final certain summation of tragedy would now occur; he felt it in his scorched and weary bones. Bring your Scriptures, Johnny.

But them fellers are Catholics. Holy Romans, next to being heathens.

Adam asked Pay if he wanted to hear some Scriptures read, or a prayer. . . . A Protestant prayer? Never.

They had difficulty in learning the dead boy's name; but from Pay's mutterings they decided that Valentine Connell must be correct, and they wrote it on a scrap of paper, along with *U.S. Navy* and buttoned the scrap on the chicken's blouse.

Get along, Irish, the New Yorkers were insisting.

Sun burned hard against Pay all the way down to the marsh. Adam and Appleby followed at a slight distance. Pay carried the half-curled body just as he'd held it in his arms all day—bare legs caught up over his right upper-arms, left forearm supporting the blue-bloused back. The hairy claws of hands which had slapped and stroked were motionless.

He carried him, without once adjusting the burden or moving his hands or arms, all the way to the dead row; there he put Valentine down. He placed him on his right flank where the wound was out of sight. Then slowly Pay stripped off his own ragged verminous blouse and spread it above the shrunken yellow face. He stood back, gasping audibly; there were no tears to come.

Put him down without a screech, muttered Appleby. Never thought he would.

Watch, said Adam. I got a feeling.

The fence was a swimming mountain of tan, tall and close through oily heat waves. Standing near the scantlings of the deadline which ruled behind the dead row itself, it seemed that you could hear the very pop of resin as it cooked from upright logs.

A young guard stood directly above them, leaning under the low sloping square of his roof. He held his musket poised idly across his chest. He stiffened and seemed to grow taller in an instant.

Watch this, said Adam again.

Hellfire, no. I'm getting out of the way.

The throng of prisoners who stood nearest the dead row began to step back, pushing backward with hasty steps, jostling and using their elbows. The crowd split, widened. Pay had put both his hands on the rail.

Yank. Take care, called the guard.

The Irishman bent down and slid one shoulder under the scantling. There came a warning whistle from the guard at the next station toward the right, the last station next to the gate. Up above, the nearest guard had his musket butt at his shoulder, but his hands were trembling and the gun barrel moved in a loose circle.

Get out of that, Yank.

The scattering of prisoners became a stampede. Even scurvy-ridden ones who sat closest, waiting for a first blessed shadow of the stockade to cool them when the sun went low enough— Even these cripples were hobbling and rolling and lurching away like stiff ungainly gnomes.

The guard directly above could not bring himself to pull the trigger. Pay stood erect inside the deadline and walked two steps toward the stockade. Guards at the right and left stations fired almost simultaneously.

Thirty days, thirty days, the prisoners were howling. Give the Rebel sons of bitches a furlough. Pay lurched when the balls went through him; he turned slowly and started back toward the deadline. Then he toppled forward, and the force of even his desiccated body snapped the scantling when he fell.

39

There were times when the sound of thirty thousand people assailed the senses more terribly than might have been imagined by one who was not there to hear them. Since the overthrow of the raiders the stockade was well-policed by Regulators, operating under command of the slow-spoken A. R. Hill of the One Hundredth Ohio Volunteer Infantry. Few civilian communities of comparable size could have boasted an equal passiveness and freedom from violent crime. But there were bound to ensue rivalry, fuss, abrasion. Men contended in a mere bickering or in a tussle to the death. Waldo took umbrage because Ned snored against the back of his head when they were pushed together at night, Amos claimed that Hez had stolen the bacon rind which Amos had bought on South Street the day before. A young agnostic, reared in an intensely Protestant environment (but who now shunned any established religion, and was darkly contemptuous of Catholics)— He called Herrity or Hanrahan a mackerel snapper or a Pope's child. Thus the private war which might be fought merely with words, more likely with fists and feet, not too rarely with slung-shots or hickory staves. Herman said that he had heard that a friend had told him (a friend who had it on good authority) that the whole Twenty-fourth Michigan Infantry was made up of bounty men; and Guy from the Twenty-fourth Michigan rose up to affirm that not a man in his regiment had received so much as a dollar in State or County money, and anyone who said he had was a lying son of a bitch.

Oh. Does that mean that I'm a son of a bitch?

You heard me.

Thus the ear torn off, the bitten nose, the kicked belly, the friends of both taking up the conflict, fists and feet and clubs mixed, the cries of, Keep your damn fighting over in your own territory. Don't come busting up our shebang or we'll beat the poop out of you.

Aw, shut up. Aw, hush your jaw. Aw, hush your gab. Aw, pound salt up your butt. Aw, bugger your brother. The talk of struggle . . . niceties worn off, the demons in every individual appearing unskinned (if he had such evil dwelling within him, and most men did have). The noise the men made.

The argument which resounded pointlessly, the sick red rheumy eye a-glowering. Any man who reads a word Charles Darwin has written is destined for Hell. Who said that? I did. Think you're a preacher or such-like? Think you're God? I didn't claim I was God; but it says clearly in the Scriptures that— Who are you, to interpret the Scriptures to me? Now, listen, Columbus Ohio, don't get gay. Take your hand off my arm. The devil I will. The devil you won't. *Whack. Thwack. Crack.* Come along, fellers, you'll spoil the mess! Hey, come aid me, he's too big for me to handle . . . looky here, Columbus Ohio, pick on somebody your own size. Well, you're my size and— The noise of strife: the men made it. Forever they constructed a contention if one did not exist naturally.

Thirty thousand men, so many making noises. The hullooing of the crazy, the whimpering of the bruised, the chop of knife or broken hatchet against a precious length of stovewood, the yell of the man offering five onions for sale, the quivering laughter of two friends who met suddenly at the North Gate (and each had supposed the other dead, and before winter both would be dead), the guard calling across to another guard, the bumping of wagon wheels at the South Gate, the wail like a cheer, the cheer identical with the voice of agony, the very small sound such as a canteen dropped, a stick snapped in two, wind broken from a body. The sound of Andersonville.

Nathan Dreyfoos told himself, Thirty thousand men might form a city of very fair size. But in a city of very fair size they would be spread far, some would be in homes, some in offices, others would be walking the streets, others would be down at the docks, others asleep in the park. Here the area is estimated at some twenty-nine acres, but that does not take into consideration that there is a deadline space twenty feet wide, or thereabouts, lining all four walls. How many acres should be subtracted to account for the deadline space? Two acres? The stockade is now said to measure, by engineers who have paced it, approximately sixteen hundred and twenty feet in length, and approximately seven hundred and eighty feet in width. Within the available rectangle, how many acres should be subtracted for the marsh? I am no engineer. Three acres less? Four acres? And the two streets must be kept unobstructed, so that wagons may drive in.

Let us say that our rectangle contains at least twenty acres of habitable space in which we may dwell—perhaps a trifle more. That would be a population of fifteen hundred men per acre. How many square feet in an acre? I know that there are six hundred and forty acres in one square mile, but how many square feet in—? I am no mathematician.

I am more fortunate than many people here, because I have patience, imagination, and recollections to stay me. My body may suffer, it has fallen away, it may fall into nothingness and I shall go into nothingness along with it. But my mental health is superb, my spirit was never better. It is strong, quiet. I muster my humor with a shrug when need be. I have known many quiet places, and now I may go to them, released to ride where I list in my cart or on my *mulo,* seeing warm gray mountains saluting the milky blue sky, seeing poppies, hearing a woman cry to her child, *Mah-ree-ah!* in the village below my feet.

Nathan Dreyfoos possessed a reservoir of pictures, perhaps he had more beauty stowed away than almost any other prisoner in the place. At will he could go to Suffolk or to Rome. There was the Swedish naval base; Karlskrona was the name; he could go there whenever he chose. Did Karlskrona have as large a population as Andersonville? He was positive that it had not. . . . He could go to Málaga. Málaga had many more people in it than did Andersonville.

But he did not want more people, so now he would leave. He would get into his *burrito* cart, the fine strong cart he'd had when he was eight or nine. But then his father insisted that José accompany him, unless he were to drive within restricted limits of the beach behind the big house . . . no, no! Better was the time when they'd come back to Spain again—Nathan recollected: he was fifteen at the time. That was when his father permitted him to go alone into the mountains. Nathan had begged endlessly that he be allowed to go, and alone; finally Solomon Dreyfoos weakened.

My son, there are bandits.

Father, I'm not afraid. Six feet one—

Yes, yes, yes, six feet one, and skinny as this pen in my hand!

Now, Father, did you ever know, personally, a man who was attacked by bandits on the road where I will go?

So which is the road on which you will go? You would go to Granada?

I thought I had rather go to Ronda; I've been to Granada by coach. I should like to go west to Marbella or Estepona. According to the maps, there are fine roads leading across the mountains to Ronda, by way of Ojen or Gaucín—

Fine roads? They're nothing of the kind. I was there, years ago, when you were small. Don Juan Huelín and I— A miserable road, very long, very winding, very steep, going no place at all, huge stones rattling down the cliffs, going no place whatsoever, our carriage nearly upset— Ah, I think it *did* upset! A wheel came off and—

Father. Did you meet any bandits?

I'm telling you, my son, there were bandits all about!

Did you meet any?

Go away, go away, don't twit me, I'm a busy man. Go get yourself hit over the head by bandits. No ransom will they get from me! Nathan, don't tell your mother that you contemplate anything so dangerous. Such a worry it should be for her.

But I've already told Mother. She thinks it's splendid.

Well, well, well, Mr. Halliburton says that you have done so fine in your studies. I promised you should have a treat if he gave a good report on your work for the recent months. Now it's late in July: a holiday you shall have. Oh, my poor son, going to the mountains with bandits—!

Nathan flew up the wide winding marble staircase from the ground floor of the house, where his father's office was located; he sprang up that staircase three steps at a time, and found his mother working at needlepoint in the high cool sitting room. She tortured her eyes to build the thing, but she was not happy unless she put in four or five hours of work daily. . . . She was creative: she wrote simple little rhymes about children and pets and gardens, and many of these had been published in newspapers and magazines. The money which she received in small amounts for her efforts was kept in a purse of blue brocade, especially to give to beggars or to nuns who came soliciting alms.

Nathan's mother had been Rose Margolis. She was brought together with Solomon Dreyfoos by a marriage broker in Boston when she was twenty-four and Solomon was forty-three. The match was made in Boston but little Nathan considered that it might have been made in Heaven. Never did he hear his parents exchange a word of doubt, rivalry or recrimination. They must have been solid in devotion from the day of their wedding. Rose was big-boned, homely, and had grown very fat by the time she was in her middle thirties; Sol Dreyfoos appeared to become more spare and stooped, if more energetic, each year of his life. He was nervous but dependable—a haggard black-eyed man with a little string of whiskers which looked false.

Nathan was an only child, but he wished that he had brothers and sisters by the dozen; it would have been such fun when they traveled, which was aggressively, constantly. Solomon's business took him to England and France, back across the Atlantic to Boston, Philadelphia, New York again; perhaps back across the Atlantic to France again; by boat to Spain; thence by boat to Genoa or Naples; back to Boston in the autumn once more. We, said Solomon, are the Wandering Jews. He said it often, he said it to Nathan when Nate was three, and Sol was holding him up at the rail of a fast mail ship, listening to fog horns announcing that Liverpool was near and the fast mail would become slow mail if the fog didn't lift.

. . . Went springing up those stairs, his brooding eyes alight, his wide loose-lipped mouth at a grin. His mother pushed down her specs and beamed at him, her plump hands came away from the frame whereon she was effecting seriously a collection of marble columns, bedizened ponies, incredibly lean and pink greyhounds, and a peasant population provided with baskets of fruit and vegetables. Sometimes she worked for a week on one figure, sometimes for a fortnight on another; when she was in a mood to work on flowers she could not work on knights and ladies. Therefore the assemblage of figures seemed suffering from ulceration at various colorful points, some looked like lepers, some were skeletal; but Rose could see far beyond this incompleteness, she could see the thing of beauty which would emerge.

What are you going to do with it, Rose? And what shall you do with it in the end, Madame? Is this destined for a museum, Señora? Oh, no, and her smooth contented laugh rippled, the sound which to Nathan was the most comforting music in the world (when he needed to be comforted, which was seldom: the world was so kind to him, so violent and mean to many other boys he saw). Oh, no. I just thought maybe it would make A Nice Present To Give Someone. She always said that, whether she worked at lace or embroidery: A Nice Present To Give Someone. Rose loved to give things away—personal things, toiled over. At this rate it would be a long while before her latest needlepoint became A Nice

Present; she had begun it in Holland early in 1854, and here it was July, 1856. Of course she worked on other things from time to time, and she had written a sonata in between, to say nothing of seven poems entitled respectively, Humility, The Happy Lambs, I Tread the Path, To My Kitten, Trust, On A Sleeping Baby, The Bobbins. Five of these had been accepted by editors and published, and now reposed in the album for which Rose had worked covers decorated with silver wire stitching, and which bore the imposing title, The Works Of Mrs. R. M. Dreyfoos.

Sol Dreyfoos thought the album a magnificent thing, and was eternally fetching it out to show to callers. Each poem or musical achievement of his wife's filled him with admiration. Always he said that he did not think he understood it completely (an old purchasing agent like himself—nothing but figures in his head —nothing but francs and dollar-signs and pounds sterling!) but that it was very beautiful. Secretly he was alarmed to see how little his wife's creations brought when they were sold; Sol wondered how composers and poets got along; he had heard that they didn't, that many of them starved.

. . . Mother, Mother!

Hm. You are smiling so hard I know you have great news.

Mother, he's going to permit me—

Now, I am glad! That is his business, Nathan; it is a father's business, not the business of a mother, to decide such things. But for your sake I am so glad he decided that you are to go. Nathan, come and look. I have finished my bananas.

Yes—they're wonderful. They're like gold—

Bananas, real bananas, are like gold—

Mother, I've been considering. I think I'll buy Tomás from the gardener.

Buy Tomás? I thought you planned to borrow a mule if—

But, you see, then I should feel that Tomás was *mine*. He's a splendid donkey, young enough not to tire, but splendidly disciplined. Nor does he bite or kick. Olmedo loads him with rock, halfway up to the old Gibralfaro, and brings him down with it—two great panniers, heavy as can be. Back and forth, all the day through, up and down. And still Tomás is ready for more. I've ridden him at sunset after he'd toiled like a slave, and he was fairly ready to canter—

Hm. That will take your savings.

But it would be such a lark, *ma chère maman,* to know that he was mine. I should feel like an emperor—like one of your people stepped from that needle-point frame. Hills, valleys, vistas, *las montañas, las colinas*—all mine, all mine, spread before my gaze as if I were king of the entire landscape—

Ah, young ambition! Nate, you should not wish to be a king.

Of course not. I don't wish to be one truly. But—you know the feeling I mean—

Ja, ja, ja, the feeling of possession. It brings security, and that is what we seek. But what would you do with Tomás after you're coming back from your jaunt in the mountains? Where would you stable him? We have no room in our stable.

Tomás isn't very large and he's *very* good tempered. I should think that Carlos might make room for him somewhere.

But Carlos says that horses do not like to be stabled with *mulos*. And who would feed and water poor Tomás? You should have to pay one of the servants; and you know how your father bids you not to be extravagant because you are a rich man's son.

Well, *es verdad*. I suppose you're right, Mother, as usual. Very well. I'll *rent* Tomás from the gardener!

That is my wise son. When shall you depart on your adventure?

Oh, not until Monday. Hang it all—I promised the monks I'd bring my fiddle and play for those old blind people on Sunday. They said it would be a joy to them.

Nathan, you play very well. I wish your dear grandfather had lived longer so that you might have heard him play—

I did hear him, when I was a little tad. Twice, in Boston.

But then you were too young to appreciate. I had hoped so that you would take up the violin in the way he did. But that means work, work, work, practice, practice, practice, the livelong day.

Ha. Precious chance I've had for that, living here and there as we do—

But, Nathan, you don't truly *like* to practice.

I know it, hang it all. But I don't play too badly as it is. And at least Mr. Halliburton says I've done well with my studies. He must have praised me to Father, or I'd never be permitted to go.

Nathan, he did praise you to your father; I heard him do so. And I think that Mr. Halliburton is the very best tutor we have found for you, ever. Should you like to invite him to go back to America in the fall, with us, after we leave England?

Oh, *Madre!* He's a hundred times pleasanter than that old Revere, and a thousand times more intelligent than Cuff was. That would be simply ripping!

Very well, I myself shall speak to your father about it. We will see. It will be expensive—the passage—but— Nathan, one thing. When you ride to the mountains, you must forget who you are. You must be dressed very simply—almost like—

I know—like a peasant—in rough clothes!

You speak almost perfect Andaluz, or so I hear the servants say. So I am not worried about— And you are tall and strong, you can run foot-races, you are a fine fencer. So I shall not worry about— But, my son, there *are* bandits in those mountains. Many.

But I'll travel like a poor chap, I'll put up only at the cheaper inns.

Well, God go with thee.

She looked at him after he had kissed her and was gone prancing away to dicker with the gardener— She looked at him as he left the room, and before she adjusted her specs again— She looked at him lovingly and thought, Life has been and is being too easy for my son. But what can one do? Should I want him to starve as I starved when I was a little girl, when my own father could not get work in the cafés? Should I want him to tramp the roads with a peddler's pack on his back, as dear Solomon did when he was of the same age? But Nathan does not seem cut out for a merchant. He does not seem cut out for anything except to be a dear sweet son! And he is kind of heart. Thank God!

Nathan's impulse was to buy beautiful accoutrements for Tomás; indeed this was nominated in his agreement with Olmedo. Reluctantly he decided that new harness must wait until his return: the crimson-and-purple halter, the embroidered bands of heavy stitched fabric to bind Tomás's chunky body, to pass below his efficient fly-batting tail—These might attract envy and cupidity along the road, they would most certainly attract attention. Accordingly the boy set forth with a newly curried Tomás but with the old patched stained furniture. One basket carried the few necessaries which Nathan allowed himself in the way of clothing and toilet articles, another held bread, cheese and wine against emergencies. He was armed with a damascene clasp-knife from Toledo and a rusty double-barreled pistol bought in Sheffield when he was twelve; his father warned him to keep this armament out of sight. He had also his long-saved hoard of money concealed in an old innocent-looking loaf of bread, together with a bottle of saleratus to be used in case of snakebite, and a volume of Lord Byron. The entire household gathered in the courtyard to wish Nathan godspeed and to criticize his appearance . . . his legs were so long that they nearly touched the ground. Solomon Dreyfoos said that if Tomás grew weary Nathan must pick the donkey up and carry him. Olmedo the gardener embraced first Tomás, then Nathan, then Tomás again; this would be the first time Olmedo and Tomás had ever been separated since Tomás was a colt and was first acquired. Olmedo's dark tinny cheek quivered at thought of it, and the tears ran and split amid his wrinkles. He always called Nathan *Hombre!*—which pleased Nathan exceedingly. The *camereras* waved their aprons, and mule and rider picked their way through the gate out into busy Málaga with its towering carts and moving black boulders of oxen. In this way Nathan rode into one of the most rewarding experiences of his young life, and he had been trained and had been shown the way to find a reward in almost any experience.

    . . . Soldier, is the sun staring meanly? Does it burn your eyeballs and crack your lips? Retreat into the cave.

    The steps had been formed as early as the Fourth Century A.D., or so an earnest and archeologically-inclined old priest believed . . . Nathan Dreyfoos and the priest crawled there together, Nathan going first across the slanted fissured crumbling stair, the priest following with cassock belted up, his bony legs arching down, his sandals seeking a safe hold on the surface. Down through fig boughs and blackberry vines, down through shadows where fat grass-green lizards held up their gargoyle heads in alarm and then scooted away. Down to the altars thirty meters below. Roofs of both chapels had fallen in—an earthquake was believed to have shaken the huge squared blocks apart, some hundreds of years since—and thin silky moss waved like miniature fields of wheat on the rich slimed slabs. No other people, no spectators, no ghosts . . . the priest knelt before the damp seeping altar with its defaced fresco depicting San Jorge above; he prayed briefly. Nathan Dreyfoos stood with straw hat in his hand, watching, listening to the flutter of birds in fig branches far overhead, the increasing flutter of speedy little bats in stalagmited caverns beyond San Jorge's ruined altar. Sun was low behind the mountains, soon it would be evening, Nathan's watch said that it was almost seven o'clock . . . but coolness coming from these fissures was never implacable, never born of decay. Something lived deep in the blackness, and that thing which lived was not a Fright, it was gentle and dignified, golden as a candle flame.

My son, you do not pray.

Often I pray, but I do not kneel here. I am a Jew.

But many Catholics in Spain are Jews, or were Jews. Why, what of the Jewish bishop of Burgos? What of the great artist Gil de Siloé—?

I know.

Some of our best Catholics are—

I know.

In your house, do your father and mother keep the Jewish holidays, the dietary laws of the Jews?

My father says that we are all children of the world at large, thank God—not children of a given Church or creed. He does not keep the prescribed laws, but he respects those who do. He respects all men who adhere to that in which they believe.

Then there was nothing in your training to prevent your kneeling with me here and now, young man!

Nathan said after some thought, My body remained standing but my soul knelt.

They crept back up the steps, stung by blackberry barbs.

I appreciate your guiding me to the cave, *Señor Cure,* said Nathan. Will you accept this small offering for the poor of your parish?

The mountains tawny as lions, their hide like the hide of elephants, their shape like a herd of oxen asleep, and blue light coming up behind them as if a great cool lamp were sending it . . . Tomás brayed in greeting at seeing his friend reappear. This time he brayed exactly fifteen times; Nathan counted—*aww, eeeh, aww*— fifteen times, and the most that Tomás had ever brayed was seventeen.

Can I reach the next village before dark?

No, no, no, my son, you'll be an hour short; and it is death to wander in the blackness of these mountains when you do not know the path. I have a bed to spare, but it is now given over to a Carthusian who broke his leg while crossing the hills, and some shepherds found him and brought him to me. Juan Solivellas takes travelers into his house. Go past the church ramp, then turn right at the first street beyond. His house is on the seventh step below; go with care on that old Moorish ramp: the cobble stones are in bad condition, the sewer is broken in. A red gate leads to his courtyard; and you'll see the stable beyond the well, and the house itself is on the left. You may smell the olive oil before you get there, the women may be cooking *churos.*

. . . In Andersonville there were no *churos,* no paste squeezed in long tubular sections, swirling in steaming oil, stirred round and round into concentric patterns with a hot smooth stick, giggled at by naughty boys who made the obvious jokes about their appearance . . . lifted from olives' fat at last, to drain and dry. O joy and warmth and crispness—joy of fat and brownness, joy of taste, taste, taste as your teeth went through and your tongue played and your soul sprang out to thank the beaming cooks.

The life of Nathan Dreyfoos had been rich as olive oil, rich as golden circlets manufactured therein. It grieved him that other men might not possess the variation of a past to comfort them. He felt that (except in cases of the very young) it was the people of enforced limitation who went down quickest. Had Evatt known nothing except a brindled cow, a milking stool, a street with elms? These were not to be had in Andersonville. They were not to be had in the army either; but it was one thing to live as a human, to march and contend as a human with other proud humans beside you; and it was another thing to be a black starved worm among black starved worms. Had Percival known nothing except a lexicon and a row of students? Had Hank known nothing except receding water and the clams he dug upon the flats? . . . Ah, the prisoners bent, they faded, they crawled—ah, they ceased their crawling, began to caterwaul; soon came the cessation of their cry. Even in the oven of this August, Nathan felt himself invulnerable. He could not be drained, cooked, panicked. Always there bloomed stanch memory of various beauties. Far away, but beauties still. The fence was fifteen feet high, the imagined mountains taller.

40

Eric Torrosian said, My mind's made up.

His friend Malachi Plover said, I wouldn't try it.

But I've made up my mind. I'm going to try it.

Hell of a way to flank out. I couldn't never do it. I'd get a gripe in my insides and just whoop them up.

Eric Torrosian had worked with his father up and down the city of New York, carrying bundles of rugs and trying to sell them from house to house. His mother, who was a German, insisted that he should attend school instead; and she and her Armenian husband engaged in conflicts over the matter and supported a grinding persistent feud between them. Sometimes the mother triumphed: Eric was sent to sit behind a desk at Mr. Gottfried Ringel's day school where the rooms were always too cold in winter and too hot in summer, and where the washroom smelled like poison. For such instruction as was awarded her son, Mrs. Torrosian had to pay two dollars per month. The father beat the air with his hands and wailed that the price was exorbitant. But Anna wanted her son to be a lawyer and this was the first step.

Eric didn't get to take more than the first step. His father managed to remove him from school periodically on various pretexts, and finally had sufficient excuse for a permanent cessation of Eric's school days. Henry Torrosian slipped on a flight of icy steps and rolled all the way to the bottom, not well cushioned by his pack of rugs. After that he was unable to carry bundles, and Eric had to go along as pack-horse, else there would have been nothing for them to eat. Eric pleaded with his father to get a pushcart, but the old man demanded, How would I get a pushcart up and down stairs?

You could leave the cart, and carry up one rug at a time to customers.

And have my stock stolen? You are a devil.

No, Father. You could get a little boy. You could give him a dime to watch the cart and keep thieves away.

You are a lazy devil. So I've got that many dimes? Come along with you, and mind you don't crush that packet of new laces.

This went on until Eric was sixteen, nearly seventeen, and one day he was walking alone on Broadway, on his way to pick up an express package, and he was attracted by a sign stating the large bounty offered to men who would enlist in the newest regiment being raised. He went into the tobacco store which served as recruiting headquarters, with two desks and a flag and a brilliantly-uniformed captain and an almost-as-brilliantly-uniformed sergeant and a not-too-brilliantly-uniformed pair of privates, accompanied by several neighborhood idlers who were not enlistees: they said that they were merely chewing the fat. One was a bearded old doctor whose hands shivered with palsy; but he guided Eric Torrosian into the back room among tobacco kegs and told him to take off his shirt. He pounded Eric's thin chest and cupped his hairy ear against Eric's ribs, listening. Also he whispered that Eric must unbutton his pants; he would see if he had any visible symptoms of syphilis. The entire examination took about three minutes, though they told him that a surgeon would look him over later. The old doctor, or so he claimed to be, begged the boy for a chew of tobacco, and, when he had none to give, the man said that a few cents in currency would be just as welcome; then the doctor could buy his own chew. Eric gave him a three-cent-piece and the doctor thanked him effusively. He propelled the boy into the front room, punching him alternately in the back and in the buttocks as he moved close behind him. He said, Captain O'Connor, I give you my word—a fine specimen of young manhood. A fine, fine specimen. This was the first time anyone had ever called Eric a fine specimen of manhood or even of boyhood, and he was proportionately pleased. He gave his age as eighteen and signed the roll. He was eager for the bounty, but they told him that the money could not be paid until he reported for duty at an uptown armory; that is, the State and Special bounties might be paid then. The National bounty would not be forthcoming until a certain amount of red tape had been untied.

Eric was sent home to get his personal belongings, and was warned to report at the armory not later than seven o'clock that night. Also he was given a ticket good for dinner and supper and breakfast at an eating-house near the armory, and the sergeant presented him with a paper nosegay of red-white-and-blue flowers to put in his button hole. Those soldiers laughed after he was outside, or as he was going out; he heard what they said; they knew well that Eric was not eighteen; in fact, one of them didn't think that Eric was even sixteen. He guessed his age as fifteen, which infuriated the boy, and made him consider going back inside and giving that soldier a piece of his mind. But he didn't go.

Instead he picked up the express package and took it home, where his father was mending the fringe on a mottled rug which had been chewed by rats somewhere in transit. Henry Torrosian was sitting cross-leggèd on the big wide work table shoved against the window to gain light. This alone prevented him from stabbing Eric with his needle when Eric gave the news. Anna burst into dreadful lamentation and cried and prayed in German, and when she could be understood she demanded that Henry go immediately to the recruiters and inform them that Eric was only sixteen, and couldn't go to the army.

You do that and I'll run away.

Where would you run to?

I'd walk, I'd catch rides on freight wagons. I'd get a job as a prentice in Philadelphia or Boston or somewheres. You'd never find me.

He spoke the truth, for he had planned to run away if they scotched his military plans.

Ai. Now by my own son I am deserted. My back is lame, boy. How can I carry carpetings up and down stairways?

Get a cart, get a boy, like I said. Then he played his trump card. He said that he would share his bounties with them. Was it one hundred dollars from the Government, fifty dollars from the State of New York, fifty dollars Special Bounty? Eric was not certain as to the amount but he would give his parents half the accrual.

Soon his father had put on his black beaver hat—he'd worn that same hat ever since Eric could remember, and long before Eric could remember; he mended it himself— Henry put on his black beaver hat and went to bargain for a used pushcart. Anna hung through the window, calling to neighbor women in the four-story building opposite, telling them that her bold son had enlisted and would soon go to fight Rebels; when the war was over he would return—as an officer, most likely—and then he would become a lawyer.

Eventually Eric and thirty-three other recruits were transferred, from the regiment in which they had originally enlisted, to the ranks of the One Hundred and Twentieth New York. Eric was a serious-minded youth with syrupy eyes, a mound of coarse black hair, hollow cheeks and thick, wide lips. No one picked on him because of his youth; firstly, there were many other fifteen- or sixteen- or seventeen-year-olds in the One Hundred and Twentieth New York; secondly, he had grown up in a neighborhood where one must maul or be mauled in a fight, and he had learned aptly several delicate tricks of mayhem. He served with no complaint and liked the life better than life at home, although a cannonade always frightened him, it made him turn sheet-white and shaking; still he trotted along with his musket as the others trotted, grunting and mumbling when he caught enough breath to do so. One day in May it was unbearably hot, and the Virginia woods were afire, and folks said that wounded men were being burned to death in the woods up ahead: if you listened closely you could hear them screaming. Eric listened but he couldn't hear the shrieks—too many cannon in the distance. What he did observe, however, was a broken tiny farmhouse barely visible through trees on the right, and he made out the remains of a wooden well-curb out in back. Even a ruined well might hold water, and he and Malachi Plover and a big youth named Kennedy discussed the problem in low tones. This task called for one man to climb down into the well, one to pass canteens back and forth, one to remain on guard. On a farm of that kind, a mere wasted shell of a farm, most likely there would be no rope remaining on the windlass or else the windlass wouldn't work. Every canteen in their company was dry as a bone; the regiment had sprawled in those woods for a long time. Eric Torrosian talked to his sergeant. The sergeant said that he didn't dare give him any Hitch Up And Go Ahead; their orders were to remain where they were, until ordered to move forward or back; but the sergeant guessed that the One Hundred and Twentieth would be lying right there on their lame asses the rest of that day. He handed over his own canteen to Eric and so did others. The sergeant turned his back and pretended not to witness their departure.

There were a few bullets whining through the forest from time to time and whacking into trees, and a few men in the regiment had been hit by this overflow of fire, so the boys kept low. Malachi and Eric left their muskets and other equipment behind; they were bedecked with canteens until they could barely crawl, and they wondered how they'd ever make the return when those canteens were filled—*if* they were filled. Kennedy crawled behind; they warned him to keep his musket off cock, they didn't want to be shot. In the shelter of the stripped old cottage and out-houses they scurried to the well, and Eric saw water shining at the bottom. Kennedy found an old wagon tongue lying in the grass, and they employed it as a kind of ladder . . . Eric crawled down, and Malachi passed him the canteens two at a time, dangling from extended straps taken from other canteens. It was cool and wonderful at the bottom of this mossy, slimy shaft; there were frogs and maybe lizards slipping about; the water was muddy as soon as he'd stirred it up, but it was water.

Suddenly in woods nearby a crashing wave of gunfire broke out in a string of sound like Chinese crackers at a celebration, and son of a bitch if you couldn't hear the Rebs a-hollering. Let's get, cried Malachi, and his face loomed patched with shadow, an inhuman face as he bent over the well-curbing. A piece of the rotten wood broke beneath his weight, and damp dust and splinters and punk came down all over Eric Torrosian's upturned face, and fairly blinded him. He wouldn't bother with those last two canteens— Yes, surely he would; maybe one was *his;* so he wound the straps around his neck and went pawing and wrenching up the wagon tongue, trying to shinny up rapidly, tearing his clothes as he went.

His left eye pained him, and it had dust in it and it stung and watered. When he got to the top and tumbled out on the ground the other canteens were lying there, just the way Plover had dumped them when he took flight. Malachi Plover was halfway to the fence, but he was looking back as he ran, and he beckoned wildly at Eric when the boy appeared. Kennedy was a couple of rods ahead of Plover, and Eric saw him turn, halt, lift his gun and fire, and he heard the ball tear the air past him. There was a loud *bum, bum, bum* of answering fire from the other side of the little farm. By this time Eric had dropped to the ground and so had Plover. They both saw Kennedy: he threw his arms out widely—his musket flew one way, something else from his right hand flew in the other direction, and he seemed to jump high and fall backward as if the wind had been knocked out of him by a boxer's blow. Back among trees the flags of the One Hundred and Twentieth were being hastened to safety, and the entire regiment was seeking safety too; the boys couldn't see hide nor hair of anybody, except for those bobbing wads of Colors. (When the regimental Colors were presented, they were presented by a rather pretty spinster sister of one of the field officers who said charmingly, These Colors are warranted not to run! Hah. Eric thought of her now—straw bonnet and black lace mitts and all.)

He stood up and held up his hands, for Rebels were all around him. A tall fellow with seasoned sunburnt face pointed to the doorway with a revolver in his hand and said, Yank, go over and set down on that stoop. Go on, youngster, move —move e'er I put a chunk of lead through you! So Eric went to the step of the ruined house and sat down. Presently an armed soldier brought Malachi Plover to sit beside him, and Malachi said that Kennedy was dead, stone dead. He had been pierced by at least five bullets. Malachi gave the news stupidly, and Eric received the news just as stupidly. They sat and looked at grassy ground before them, and now and then stole glances at the Rebels who guarded them. It seemed odd to see gray and tan and brownish dust-colored figures standing erect so close at hand. The only ones they'd seen previously, close at hand, had been lying mute.

In this manner Eric Torrosian was captured, and no enemy so much as touched an article of his belongings that first night. But the second day following, when the guardianship of seventy-two prisoners was taken over by irregular troops behind the lines, he was stripped of watch, pocketknife, new shoes and all such sundries. He saw what was happening to the column and managed to put slabs of currency inside both cheeks, for recently he had been paid. Hence the villains got only his small change. He talked oddly, with those folds of money bulking between his teeth and the wet flesh of his mouth's inner lining, but since the Rebels didn't know how he talked at other times they discerned nothing suspicious in his responses. His cheeks appeared smooth instead of hollow, and the Rebels didn't know that he was naturally hollow-cheeked. He saved twenty-nine dollars in greenbacks which would be about three hundred dollars Confed. It gagged him when finally he removed the money, and he vomited copiously, but at least he had the money; and it helped to keep him and Malachi alive after they reached Andersonville, and it fed them en route. Malachi's money was stolen.

They arrived at Andersonville in a pouring rain, and waded through mud all the way from the cars to the stockade.

They landed in a shebang with three fellows also from the Second Brigade of the Fourth Division of the Second Corps, who had been captured in the Virginia woods too. The other fellows said it was true about the wounded being burned to death in the forest fire; one man had been wounded himself, and, temporarily weakened from loss of blood, he had to lie there and listen to the squeals and *yaaah* and Mother, have mercy, shoot me for *Goddddssake.* Finally he summoned enough strength to drag himself out of the fire's course and into some smoking rubble where a blaze had swept already. The man's name was Toby Mutterson and Toby bragged that he had been a hero and had pulled out another man as well, but he didn't know what happened to the other man finally. Toby's clothing was pretty well scorched as he lay amid those soft embers, and he exhibited the holes and raw brown fibers to prove his tale. He said that his blood-soaked condition might have saved his life; and the bleeding had stopped, praise be, and didn't start up again. He was wounded in the fleshy part of his thigh, but the bone wasn't broken.

Toby did not thrive at Andersonville because worms got into his wound promptly, and the authorities wouldn't let him into the hospital because he made the mistake of walking down to the gate surgeons to apply for admittance, instead of being carried. He jerked and whined in his sleep, and then his wound would hurt him so badly that he'd get up and limp around outside the shebang and blunder against neighboring shebangs or step upon sleeping men, and would be cursed and pummeled. Someone told him that ground oak ashes would expel the maggots from his wound, and he begged Eric to buy oak ashes for him. Finally Eric found an old man among the guards who said that he could burn some oak and fetch the ashes for ten dollars Confed. When the twelve o'clock round of calls issued from the stockade's rim that night, Eric must be lying in wait in blackness, just next to the deadline in front of the old guard's booth. The guard would toss down a cord with a stone attached to the end, and Eric should fasten his currency to the cord; the guard would pull it up, and then he would toss out the cord a second time with the packet of ground-up ashes attached. . . . Faithfully Eric followed instructions; he crouched amid shadows and heard the yells go out, and the answering growls of prisoners. A guard would start in and call, Station Number Three, twelve o'clock and all's well, and immediately the prisoners would start yapping. Twelve o'clock and, Mister, here's your mule, and other things less polite. Station Number Five, twelve o'clock and all's well, and the whoop to confound all guards and all enemies, Station Number Five, twelve o'clock and go diddle your grandma.

The stone fell down, Eric found the cord by fumbling and raking with both hands; here was the rock, and a long end of string for tying; he knotted the folded one-dollar U.S. greenback into place and jerked the cord hard to signify that the money was ready. It went scraping and tapping up the wall, and after a few minutes there was another thud, and Eric Torrosian clawed round until he found the string and the precious solid little envelope tied to it. He took the packet and ran back to the shebang as fast as he could go, which wasn't very fast. Oh, thanks, thanks, thanks, you're a real sport, Eric; give me that stuff, so's I can start getting rid of them old cutworms; Eric, I swear that when we get out of here and get North, you come to Pennsylvania and my mother will take good care of you; cook you the best pork ribs you ever tasted, and shoo-fly pies and truck; and you can lie abed on a featherbed all morning if you want to. Come on, let's open the paper up. . . . They were out of pine splinters, they had no light, so Toby Mutterson had to anoint his wound in the dark. Pretty soon he began to howl like all possessed. Oh, God, it's killing me, help me get that stuff out of there, and he went plunging around, rolling and gargling in the dark, and asking for somebody to pour water in his wound. But you say you don't want swamp water, and that's all we got. It'll just give you more worms. Ow, ow, ahhhh, I don't care what God damn water you use; the hell with clean wells and well rights, the God damn hell with clean water; wash it, wash it out, it's killlling me. And people from other shebangs hallooing, For Christ sake, quit that noise, you crazy poop. . . . So they used swamp water, and washed out Mutterson's lively wound; Eric guessed that he and Malachi sponged the wound a dozen times with a scrap of rag. Toby would howl every time they touched the suppurating hole, but after numerous swabbings he subsided into a quieter whimpering. At dawn they woke up and looked; here were the remains of the packet. No oak ashes. Salt. That was it: just plain coarse salt.

Eric went to the old guard's station late that day when the old man came back on duty, and he stood below and assailed him. The old man said, Sonny, I couldn't find no oak like I said I could. I lowed salt would do tolerable well. Eric kept crying epithets which had sunk early into his memory, but the bearded guard stood looking earnestly beyond Eric and pretending that he was deaf. Just about dusk Eric came back, and this time he had a stone. It was a fine stone, round and brownish and hard, and it was half as big as a goodsized apple. He watched his chance, and when the guard (a skinny patriarch he stood against the pale yellow western sky) was looking the other way, Eric flung the stone. He had taken careful aim, and as a small boy he had thrown stones in numerous street fights and hurled them accurately, but he missed the guard's head by a few inches. The old man must have been astonished when he heard that whirring past his ear. He caught up his piece and fired into the stockade; in the dimness below there was a great scurrying and terror, but apparently no one was hit. The next day Eric saw a little throng around a shack of rags and pine bark, and people were pointing. He went over for a look, but naturally did not confess that it was he who threw the stone to provoke the guard. From the looks of that pine bark the musket had been loaded with buck-and-ball: maybe one of the old Sixty-nines from Harper's Ferry. They took three buckshot and one heavy ball as a standard load. The charge passed just beneath the roof-tree, out the other side, and into earth beyond. Six men spooned together in that shack, and not one of them hit. Eric felt better. But Toby Mutterson was carried to the hospital the next Sunday, and they heard within the week that he was dead. Almost nobody ever came back from the hospital.

Eric went down to the old guard's station and waited for him to appear. He wanted to have the satisfaction of telling him that he had killed Toby with that salt, although Eric's conscience assured him that Toby would have died anyway sooner or later. Pretty soon the guard was changed, but it wasn't the graybeard who came; it was a gaunt child. His gun was bigger than he was by far and maybe weighed more. Hey there, guard, where's the old man used to be at this station? The boy was frightened—it seemed to be his first time on duty—for he jumped in surprise when Eric addressed him. Go way, Yank. We can't speak to prisoners. Oh, don't be a dunce; be a good fellow; all the guards talk to prisoners. Come on, where's the old man? The boy looked around cautiously and then leaned his small shaggy head across the rim. He's dead, Yank. Just died today. . . . What do you mean, dead? How did he die? . . . Just had a fit and died; just fell in a fit after eating. . . . That seemed queer. It seemed almost that Toby had come back like an avenging angel and taken the old man away with him.

Well, Eric Torrosian had made up his mind, and he wasn't going to die like either of them; neither with worms and bad blood like Toby, nor in a sudden fit like the old man. He refused to shrink into slow wastage as he saw so many others doing. He was going to flank out of there, and it seemed that there was one way in which it might be done. He would flank out with the dead.

He hated and feared the dead, as most people always have, and sometimes when he looked at the long horrid row of them he questioned himself concerning his reason for this detestation. In actuality their ugliness was no worse than that of the living, except perhaps in those cases where the eyes had congealed open.

Somehow those eyes made Eric think of grapes he used to see in fruit-stalls off the Bowery—grapes that were a little squashed—shed of their skins but still bulbous.

The living around him were ugly and he himself was ugly. A man died, and Malachi Plover helped to carry him to the dead row, so Plover and another fellow took what was left in the dead man's pockets. Among other things the dead man had a mirror: a round flat wafer, tin on one side and looking glass on the other. It had been broken, perhaps long before, but two stiff shreds of the silvered glass remained stuck in the frame, and they were big enough for you to see yourself in, with the slash of the break cutting across your face and making a scar which didn't exist. Eric Torrosian regarded himself with fright when he looked in that mirror; he looked like dead people. Being swarthy as to coloration and cursed with a stiff black beard, he thought that by this time (more than three months a prisoner) he looked like his own father. But Henry Torrosian's beard was combed gently, and his hair was clipped by his wife's scissors; when he could afford it he brushed cologne into his beard and linen to make himself more agreeable to lady customers. Eric had no cologne and no shears. His beard was grown into a mass and swarmed with lice; his hair, always lengthy, was black disordered sedge. Thin by the determination of his own nature (and—he disliked recognizing the thought but the knowledge was there: he was thinned by excessive masturbation during his early teens. He had heard that masturbation would drive him insane, and he had bad dreams in which he saw himself insane and roaring) he had fallen away as a filthy ghost since he entered this stockade. Maybe he weighed ten stone when he came in; he doubted that he weighed seven stone now.

He could pass as a dead man if he could remain quiet, and could endure without a sound the persecutions to which he would be subjected in handling.

Therefore, the second evening after he said, My mind's made up, he was sewn into a blanket by Malachi. It was a mere shred of blanket, a pattern of holes held together by shoddy scraps, a spiderweb, a leaf chewed by bugs. Once in a while you saw a dead man bundled in such wrapping, although more frequently they were carried down in their pants or drawers, and very often nude. It appeared that no one would bother to rip the worthless remnant from Eric's body. Eric reached out and shook hands all round with his comrades, and then Malachi Plover stitched the upper part of the rags in two or three more places. No trouble about breathing; the holes took care of that. Malachi and a Pennsylvanian (a companion of the dead Mutterson whom they called Dutchy) lugged Eric to the dead row and whispered Goodbye before they put him down. The wagon wouldn't come in until dawn, it was feared, and Eric would have to lie in the mute flat rank all night. Sometimes the wagon did appear in the evening, and the dead were lifted on, twenty-five or thereabouts to the load. Eric had instructed the boys to put him down somewhere near the farther end of a section of twenty-five—say number twenty-three or twenty-four. That way he would be almost certain to be placed on top of the load. But more bodies had been deposited since they spied out the situation, and Eric was actually number twenty-five, but he did not know it. His friends feared for his life. Maybe the blacks who took him away would carry only twenty-three or twenty-four as the first cargo, and Eric would find himself at the bottom of the next load under hundreds and hundreds of pounds of bodies. Well, there was no help for it—he had demanded that they aid him in this attempt, so Goodbye, old fellow, and I'm glad I ain't laying there instead of you. They went away.

Slowly Eric Torrosian relaxed the few thin muscles remaining to him, which he had drawn taut to simulate the stiffness of a corpse. He dared not actually move his limbs while there was any daylight left, else a passerby might pay heed or a guard peer down and detect him. He lay in overpowering stench, for the man next to him had died of gangrene. This smell affected him, and at last he coughed involuntarily, and then gagged from trying to quell the coughing fit; thus he vomited. Not a soul heard him. Too many similar sounds in the area beyond that strip of scantling which ruled the dead from the living.

Another corpse was dumped at his right side. . . . Shadows deepened beyond Eric's blanket holes, the general brownness of twilight came down; this did not take long to occur, for it was late when the others fetched him. But it seemed as long again as all the days which had passed since he was captured. He thought of bursting from his rough shroud and crawling out of there—giving up the whole miserable effort—and then he heard a howl of gate-hinges and felt the damp earth shake beneath an approach of heavy wheels. The dead wagon, it was the dead wagon.

Negroes' voices talked to a guard, bodies were hoisted.

Hey, wait there. This one he got pretty good pants.

You nigs step lively. Take them pants off outside, not here! I want my supper.

They grumbled between themselves, but went on with the loading.

Said the guard, You got a full load. They were in the act of lifting the thing next to Eric. It was dark. Eric began to tighten his arms and legs and neck muscles and back muscles, he began to stiffen his toes and fingers.

Ain't but two more to go, Mastah Guard.

Oh. Step lively. . . .

Big paws grasped Eric's upturned naked feet and dragged him forward. More big paws went scraping under his shoulders and sank hurtfully into his armpits; yea, he was rigid, he was rigid, they were tormenting him, he bit his tongue, it seemed that he must squeak, cry out, confound them into thinking he had come alive, get rid of their clasping, he'd never thought that they'd try to tear a corpse apart. *Hoy.* They swung him back and forth. *Hoy,* they said together on the second swing; and *hoy!* they cried in unison at the termination of the third swing, and he went sailing. Let go my stiffness, he thought in terror as he rose through the air, and then his head struck the head of a corpse atop the load; it struck a fraction of a second before his feet came down on the pile. Eric was knocked senseless. Just one quick burst of light, a sound to go with it. Nothing after that.

When he recovered consciousness he was in the deadhouse and his face was bloody, and he didn't know where he was, but he was in the deadhouse. Could a man bleed after death, if his nose had been smashed? Eric had bled; he thought for a time that he was dead; maybe he was dead; he was cold, he had never been so cold before, the cold was through and all around him, it emanated from the cold dead, the earth was cold underneath, the air was cold above, Eric was cold, the dead were cold, all the world cold, all the world dead.

If ever he walked in the world of men again, he would tell that world how the dead smelled. They smelled like a dog run over by a beer wagon, and it crawled into a narrow space between two houses just off Houston Street, and there it lay whimpering unheard and unsought and unwanted for a day or two, rotting even before the rot of unliving flesh began. Eric went into that place after a ball he had tried to catch but had missed, and so he smelled the dog four days after it died, and he had to pick up the grimy ball lying beside the grimy dog. These Andersonville dead smelled like that. They were the reek of privies and corruption found in oozing drainpipes, they were the garbage box, the neglected fallen greasy flakes in gutters of fish markets, they were the greasy water put into an old bottle and stoppered and left in the sun (the boys whom Eric knew used to make bombshells like that, to throw at each other in warfare of their gangs; they called the bottles stink-bombs). The dead were old vomit, old bandages, old pus. They had no decency about them, they thought they were sainted and needed not to yield to manners required of men who were not dead. The dead breathed decay from lungs no longer breathing, and their lung cavities were putrid but they were cold. They had no fire or flame or query or statement about them; they lay grinning in beards and hayrick hair, their tongues were thrust out sometimes, their mouths were split open and tongueless sometimes, the fluid ran from their mouths sometimes, the fluid ran from other orifices of their bodies sometimes, the breath of their death went into soil on which they lay, and colored the cold air on either side of them, and it ascended in a noxious weighty metallic cloud above them, and the cloud was cold, and the people who made it were doughy and cold, and they were dead.

Baleful in their silent mockery of him, it was as if the very silence which they created laughed along with their smaller individual silences. No more to do a thing any child or man-grown object had ever desired or earned—never to make the sound or speak the word or hear the sound; never, never to dream. In weak and stricken dread of this motionless herd, Eric Torrosian reconstructed their lives in the same fashion in which his own life had been poured: he shaped their existences so. Never to taste furry red wine from a stone bottle, never to eat an egg (ah, he had been fond of hens' eggs) and never to eat the pickled herons' eggs which he had tasted once. . . .

The long Springfield with its proud eagle on the lock: never to clean it again, never to bite off the cartridge paper, never to abrade fingers with the crisp fine sandpaper bent as a polishing cloth. Nor to march, nor to suck boiling brown coffee from a blackened tin cup. Nor to fight in a street fight, and roll across stones, and drive your elbow against another's belly, and hear him yip in his hot squirming as you fought. All these things the corpses had renounced, and Eric loathed them for it, because in silent conclave they were censuring him for even remembering such events, and for wishing to relive them. . . . Never to walk a street and see white-tanned-stoutly-patched sails rising at the end of the street between brick buildings, and to hasten, hasten for fear of missing closer sight of the ship as it pushed the Hudson waters aside. Never to make torn wisps of wastepaper into a ball for a kitten to play with, never to watch the kitten propelled upward by invisible springs in its feet, to see it somersault delightedly with the paper wad caught between mossy-striped paws. Never to rub a dog's warm ribs until you found the Magic Place, and then, when you had found the Magic Place and while you were scratching it rapidly, you'd see the dog's foot beat mechanically in air as if he too were scratching the Place, and so you laughed and called it Magic. These matters were not agreeable to the dead. They scorned these matters, and gave out, in one solid and crippling stench, the verdict of their disapproval.

They refused also, these dead, to ever more carry great bales of rugs upon their shoulders, to ever more gaze past the bright curtains of eating-house windows and envy the well-to-do who sat before their porter and oysters, their beer and bread and pigeon breasts and lemonade and cod.

To heave rocks at sparrows shooting past, to be afraid of a priest because he might lecture or thump you, to hear a woman's voice teaching softly beside the warm stove, and with waxy smell of candles in your nose— To hear the woman's voice buried in the long ago, separated from this moment by trivial and crabbèd years, but coming out stronger as the scent of candles continued—

To hear her teaching, *Zu Betlehem geboren*—

Your voice. *Zu Betlehem geboren—*
Ist uns ein Kindelein—
Your voice. *Ist uns ein Kindelein.*

The dead would have none of it, never, never. They would abolish all treasure great and small, they would abolish pleasure, and assuredly they would abolish the rite of pain. They had voted to do so.

To read a tale and feel your fancy drift, to walk with Little John, to draw a stronger bow than Friar Tuck himself, to be bored with Rollo and his cousin James, to wheel the thick blade of Marmion . . . they said No, they said, We will not do it, they said, We decline and refuse. Sternly. Forever. And they said also, We renounce the right to creep into rich houses, rug-laden and awed, and sit small and dusky and self-effacing on a bench in the hall while the old man is explaining about rugs to a rich dame in her parlor, and to marvel at polished mirrors and embossed walls with purple ladies playing tag under green trees.

Nor would the dead approve of rioting over a dumping ground, and bringing up forgotten wealth from beneath the layers of soaked straw and barrel-staves. Clock weights they would not discover, nor the pestle minus its mortar, nor the brass false teeth so colorfully green in corrosion, nor the torn corset nor the horse-collar with a rat's nest inside and baby rats peeping. . . . Nor would the dead countenance a solid click of billiard balls, smells of cigar smoke, the rich ferocious male laughter, the small voice saying, Paper, sir? Paper? . . . Click of billiard balls, the odor of peanuts being chewed, broadcloth buttocks bulging up beside green tables, the deep hearty frightening male laughter.

Gone always, gone completely, never to be tolerated. The dreams lonely but enfolding . . . waking at night with nothing but your youth and the creamy lust of youth to keep you company . . . ah, vision . . . ladies appearing again, with the satin rustle in which they always tread, the imagined French scents in which they've dipped themselves, the delicate foot protruding coyly cased in its shiny slipper . . . and what is this? You are privileged: she has accepted you, this golden creature here, here, *here,* she has flung over all standard of deportment, she has gone wicked, she is a pure woman but also a strumpet; invitingly she draws up her gown to reveal the delicacy underneath, she is begging you to roll and tussle and lose yourself for eternity in the lacy lake of her female state . . . power of her prettiness rules you in hidden imagined rapture until once more you are weak and exhausted, and you lie spent, and no doubt will be a maniac soon, barred, groveling in a cage.

The illusions of Eric Torrosian flared for minutes only, but they were numerous, they ruled him hard. Leaden, chill and stiff as sticks, the dead knew secrets but the secrets were secrets concerning a business of rot and dripping.

From them now he would run away. Eric climbed to his feet. The deadhouse . . . he was beyond the stockade, he was in the deadhouse made of pine boughs, he'd heard of the place, now he would go retching out. He had no blanket to cover him any longer; even those skimpy tatters had been taken from him by Negroes while he lay insensible, and in their ignorance they thought he was dead.

He went staggering into the night and walked directly in front of a terrified guard. The man lifted his piece, fired, shot Eric Torrosian through the chest. At that close range the musket's charge tore a great chunk out of the boy's heart and it dangled behind his broken rib as he fell.

Eric did not witness pine flames which burned above his glazing eyes, nor hear the speculations voiced. A record of the event was noted down, and Eric Torrosian was carried back into the deadhouse, where he was welcomed by chuckling unvoiced, unheard, but still the chuckling was there; and the ground was cold, cold, cold, and now everyone in the place was dead, and soon Eric also was as cold as the others, an accepted member of their fraternity.

41

Willie Mann was determined not to drink water; drink water he would not, unless personally God awarded it to him as from rainclouds, as from dew condensing. People said, Rain is in the air, sometimes; and those were the times when Willie Mann heard them, and tried to pretend that he didn't hear the people because they might take advantage of his idea, which was somehow to suck rain out of the air before it broke loose in form of orthodox globules to be wasted, spraying or hammering against soil which could never absorb or appreciate rain, against men who were only chilled or killed by its coming.

Willie Mann, Twenty-ninth Missouri Volunteers, came into the stockade shortly before the six raiders were hanged. Thus he witnessed a big man breaking free from a mass, a core of blackened faces and striving thin arms half naked and half ragged; he saw that man plunging at a loose long pace all the way down the slope and into the marsh next to the Island. Willie saw what that marsh was made of; in his innocence he had not dreamed of its construction when first he arrived; he thought that the bad smell came sole alone from those bodies which supported those faces which stared and yelled and called him and his fellows fresh fish. He thought with tears spreading inside to drown him—he thought that these eviscerated cannibals or whatever they were— He thought that they were jeering and taunting; whereas mainly they were giving him a rowdy grim welcome filled with curiosity and a certain envy because he had not been compelled to suffer as they had suffered. But now he would suffer.

The stench had been their stench, in Willie's first diagnosis, but a bulk of it was the stench of Stockade Creek and ooze surrounding. He gazed, he couldn't believe it, after Curtis ran away and plunged until he was mired waist-deep, and Nathan Dreyfoos waded in after him. Also, when Willie Mann heard that the tallest of the condemned was named Willie Collins it brought a dread kinship with the captured ringleader. He tried to tell himself that there must be hundreds of Willies walled in here, and so he should not be absurd about it; but that night he dreamed fiercely of the monster . . . gallows stood on the southern hill's shoulder, and when planks were knocked loose and when (never tell Katty or Ma what happened then!)— When at last all six stretched shapes hung gyrating leisurely from their ropes, there seemed a dark completeness, a finality to the course of his initiation. Willie Mann was now a full-fledged prisoner with a parched tongue. One of the executed men had, in his unknowing way, helped to parch that tongue by once trying to walk on substance unsuited to man's support. He was not Jesus, not even an exaggerated cartoon of a wicked overgrown Jesus born in a sinkhole instead of in a manger; so he had tried to walk upon the stuff, and had gone down. Willie Mann wandered once more to stare at the place.

He witnessed prisoners floundering or creeping—senior prisoners of vast stockade experience but apparently with no sensitivity. He saw them with their cups and chunks of broken canteen material. They sought water and found it. It was putrid thick ink, and they called it water. It was the oil of corruption, the wine from dying human bowels, the lively acid of iniquity, and they dared to call it water. It was a soup rising from wet invisible wells drilled by the Devil himself, and stewed out of festering meatbones and rotting bits of cloth, corncobs, abandoned corn bread, the fresh tanned floating strings of firm healthy excrement which came borne on narrow tide from habitations of guards outside the jagged fence, the watery yellow slime drained from dysenteric hordes inside the jagged fence. A million million million worms worked in its borders, a black frosting of insects clung above and busy. These debased fellows of Willie Mann's were willing to voice the evilest lie of all, and say Water.

Maybe they had never known true water, but Willie had. To begin with, the well of his family on the edge of the tiny Missouri village where he was born— This well was famous in the neighborhood. It served four families including the Manns, and Willie's father said that the more the well was used the better he liked it. Doctor Zachary Mann was a slender solemn fellow with a sparse beard and mild brown inquiring eyes. His dappled mare Annette and his pale duster and his chaise with tall mended wheels: all were familiar to the entire northern end of the county and in southerly regions of the county above. When Doctor went to some farmhouse and found three or four children staring with fever (maybe one might be dead before he arrived) Doctor Zach Mann lingered eventually at the farm well. He noted the site where it was dug, he brought up water and held it to the light in a glass, he sniffed, sometimes he tasted wryly and spat the water out again and rinsed his mouth with some liquid carried in his own satchel. People said that Doctor Zach was foolish on the subject of water; but no one of the eight Mann children died in infancy. In this case it seemed that the shoemaker's children had shoes.

Willie's elder brother Sam had been killed at Wilson's Creek or else in a skirmish immediately preceding the battle—no one knew which, or could find out for certain—so Willie begged to go to the war in a manner of vengeance. Not until you're eighteen, said Doctor. You got your mother to see after, if Annette should be scairt by the cars and run away with me.

Of course fat Annette had never run away in the thirteen years of her life, and probably never would run away; but the doctor was a determined father, and he extracted his promise. Willie did not know how to deceive because he had never been taught nor had he suffered the example.

The week before his eighteenth birthday—that was the same week they heard the news about Vicksburg—recruiters came to the county seat, and Willie begged to go to the courthouse and sign the roll.

You're not eighteen. You promised—

But I'll be eighteen a Sunday.

Wait till then.

Want me to leg it all the way to Saint Louis and maybe join up with a batch of foreigners?

Doctor debated in his mind, and at last arose from the tattered sofa (Linda Moberly's baby had been slow, and it took all night, and they nearly lost both the baby and Linda, but everything seemed all right now). He told Willie to hitch up Annette and not say anything to Ma. Silently they drove the five miles to the courthouse, Doctor dozing beside his one surviving son. When they pulled up along the shiny hitch-rail with its little strings of horse-hair caught in the polish of horses' rubbing, Doctor opened his eyes alertly as if he hadn't been asleep actually any of the time.

Well, sonny, go in and sign.

Willie came back, pale-faced and beaming—he came down from the courthouse three steps at a time, and nearly landed on top of old Mr. Cull Calice, who remembered Indian attacks on that very spot, and had actually shaken hands with Daniel Boone though he always spoke of him as Colonel Boone.

Did you sign, sonny?

Yup. But it's all right, Pa—I mean about me being eighteen. I hain't got to report until a Monday, and I'll be eighteen by then.

They drove home slowly; on the way Doctor stopped to dress the stump of Mr. Rector's finger at the cottage by the sawmill; and he stopped also to peek in at the exhausted Linda Moberly and her baby girl. When he came out he said, Sonny, I don't want you ever to take up doctoring.

Don't reckon I will. Rather be a soldier or work on a railroad. But why?

Might vaunt yourself pridefully, and get puffed up.

How so, Pa?

Hard to explain. Way a doctor gets to feel sometimes. Not maybe like God, but like the dear Lord's little finger.

Up over the next green hills the weary Annette took them along, making hungry sounds inside her round empty belly, making louder sounds from her rear. They passed the abandoned Gentry house . . . Mr. Dolph Gentry had Rebel tendencies, and had left the county long before. They passed their next-door neighbors, the Garshows; and also Paul and Silas Garshow were wearing gray, and were said to be off fighting in General Sterling Price's army somewhere. It was funny and awful how the neighborhood was split up, and so were a lot of other neighborhoods in Missouri.

Anyway, I got old Garshow to move his well.

What say, Pa?

There—you can see it gainst the west.

He pointed with his whip. That's the new well: fine high curb, and observe where she stands. Under that cottonwood, high and convenient. But down the slope's where they had the old well; just lazy because twas a low spot, and they figured twas easier to reach water so. Tweren't more than six foot deep, I swear. And just go up amongst them cedars sometime—when you come home from the fighting, I mean—and count them graves. Seven Garshows and five of the inlaws, the Teddlers.

All from a rotten well, Pa? Could that be?

Could be.

First off that night, after they had broken the news to Ma and the five girls (Addie was newly married and moved away) Willie went along the edge of the oatfield behind the barn, he went in thin plum-purple light of a hot evening in Missouri (although he had never seen evenings in any place other than Missouri at that time). He went to call upon Miss Katrine Fiedenbruster.

The Fiedenbrusters had moved to the region only four or five years previously; they had come from Germany by way of St. Louis where Jake Fiedenbruster had been a thrifty shoemaker, but now he wanted to be a farmer and was one. The kids at school made fun of the little Fiedenbrusters because at first they spoke only a few words of English and those badly . . . it was during the winter term. Willie was not yet fourteen at the time, and very slight; but he was muscular from hard work, and also he liked to wrestle with his big brother Sam. Well, he was coming home through soggy snow, and he heard shrieks ahead. He looked and saw all the little Fiedenbrusters running and crying and yelling in German. It turned out that big Ame Moberly had ambushed them, and Ame wasn't merely playing Indian: this was a real devilish ambush he had arranged. In advance he'd prepared ammunition consisting of snowballs soaked and then frozen; the missiles were stony and dangerous. He'd hidden behind the low crab-apple trees at the corner, and when the contingent of foreigners came by in their blue knitted woolen winter caps and scarfs, he up and opened fire. It was a mean business—snowballing girls, especially with frozen balls—but Ame did have a mean streak in him. (No more, though: he was killed in the attack on Fort Donelson.)

All of a sudden it came over Willie: what would his father have done?—truly he worshipped his father. Well, he figured that Doctor would have lit into Amos Moberly, so that was what Willie did now. Ame was whooping and dancing and running after the wailing Germans, and then stopping to heave another accurate snowball, and then he'd yell, Why don't you talk *decent?* and then another ball and another shriek. Then Willie hit him like a cat off a limb; they were in the snow. Standing up, using fists solely, Ame might have thrashed Willie to a jelly, but on the ground the slighter boy held an advantage, after all those tussles with tall Sam. It was a bitter fight, however—gouge and punch and twist and choke. At least Ame was bent on choking in defense. But Willie brought his boot up against Ame's belly, good and solid; after that there was no fight left in the bigger boy—nor any wind, either.

The Fiedenbrusters stood like a gallery, watching, fearing, appreciating the virtues of their savior. Finally when Ame got his breath back, he went off homeward across the old stubble field, refusing to look back because he was ashamed of being beaten, and even more ashamed at his own crying. He wouldn't speak to Willie for weeks and weeks; but at last they became moderately friendly at a church supper in the spring; and certainly Amos never plagued the Fiedenbrusters again.

The day after the fight, Willie found a pink-streaked winter apple in his lunch bucket, and his mother hadn't put it there: he'd watched her preparing his and his sisters' lunches, while he leaped with impatience for fear Teacher would catch them with the tardy bell. Next day, some spicy heart-shaped cookies of a kind he'd never seen or tasted before. He saw Katrine Fiedenbruster watching him, and then her face turned red when she saw that he saw her watching him; she turned away quickly. But next day, more soft gingery cookies. It would have been easy for her to slip things into his lunch bucket undetected. All the buckets and baskets stood in a row on the long bench in the cloak room. . . . Willie realized suddenly how very pretty Katrine Fiedenbruster really was. Her skin was creamy white, her little cheeks were round as cookies but soft as fresh-stirred candy, her neck reminded him of ice cream. Suddenly he thought that he would like to eat Katrine Fiedenbruster—actually eat her up, and how good she would taste—and then he was overcome with embarrassment at having entertained such a thought . . . and he thought of other things that he would like to do to and with her; his face flamed behind his McGuffey . . . he made a botch of lessons on that day. But he made a great to-do about shoveling slush off the path for old Mr. Spriggs, after school, and his sisters went home without him, prepared to tell Ma how Willie had declared in geography class that Prussia was the capital of Russia. The Fiedenbruster tribe went home without Katrine, because she was the eldest girl and now partook of a special fifteen-minute lesson in English which Mr. Spriggs awarded because for some reason he declared that she was a noble little Dutchwoman, and pinched her cheeks and made them even pinker.

Willie scraped and scraped. When finally Teacher came out with his cane and

surveyed the results, he said, William, you may not anticipate a brilliant career as
a scholar—not after today's blots and witlessness—but I vow you could make a
living with a shovel.

Teacher locked up the schoolhouse and thumped Willie's head with his stiff old
finger, and turned west along the road toward where he boarded with the Patter-
sons. But Willie and the noble little Dutchwoman had to go east.

She walked fast, Willie walked faster, soon he was up with her and walking at
speed fairly beside her, but she kept her hot face turned away.

Katrine. . . .

She seemed fearing to reply, and why should she hide her face in the folds of
knitted blue?

Katrine. Let me carry your books.

Nein.

Why not, eh?

Cause—

Let me carry your stuff.

Nein. Mineself I—carry—

Katrine, listen here. He snatched her free hand, and stopped her, and held her
as a prisoner; she faced him with damp reddened soft face and blue eyes like
silver.

You put them cookies in my bucket—

Nein, she breathed, but of course she breathed a lie.

Yes you did. What kind of cookies are they?

Boy and girl, they stood alone in the slushy road, and nobody was about—no
Teacher, no brothers or sisters or schoolmates, no rigs or teams—nothing there
but February wind and a crow calling, and a pervading cold consciousness of
spring to come.

Lebkuchen, she whispered.

What? Them cookies? Is that what they're called?

Ja.

She did not resist when he took her books and little willow basket. They made
an awkward if not heavy burden along with his own things. In utter silence the
children walked the way to a lane which bordered the Mann farm on the west, for
the Fiedenbrusters lived down that lane on the old Carrington place. Katrine
thanked him in the thinnest of whispers, and dared not meet his glance when she
did it.

Willie stopped, halfway to his home, and stood looking across the field at that
gray-shawled, blue-topped little figure a-hastening, and then she turned to look at
him, and thus again each saw the other looking.

She was his girl, in this modern grown-up time; he was her fellow. They had
belonged to each other, in pure and solemn devotion, from the very first.

Five times he had managed to kiss her. But only in kissing games, when other
folks were looking on and laughing. And only on the cheek, because she'd try to
hide away from him— She would seem to fight him. But not too hard—

This night the plum light was intense around him and around the white house
of the Fiedenbrusters, and the strong glow went up as if from prairie fires beyond
a row of cottonwoods, and a chorus of whip-poor-wills challenged steadily from
black hollows of Beverly's Timber. Oh God, please God, to be alone with her, to
be alone in Beverly's Timber or any place else in this spooky nighttime wonderland, but to be alone—

They roosted on a small porch and on the steps, the Fiedenbrusters. Papa and
Mamma sat in the two rocking chairs received as premiums. Katrine and

Wempkie, her next youngest sister, had sold bluing and vanilla throughout the neighborhood in their spare time; the rockers were their own accomplishment, and they were proportionately proud, but tonight they sat on stools. The girls had put down their mending, because now it was too dark to see properly, and they had taken up their knitting because they could knit ably, by touch, in the half-dark. All the girls could—even Marta and little Lena.

Jacob and Fritz were gone to the army. Henry and Lou were giggling out behind the plum trees—smoking grapevine, they were, and they became terrified and heavy with guilt when Willie Mann came upon them. Peter and Buck chased fireflies around the yard in this rare dusky moment of playtime, and the toddler, Link, was staggering after them.

Good evening.

To you good evening, Willie Mann.

The party on the stoop and steps loomed before him in dark solidity; they were a unit, a strong sedate family unit. How could he ever pry Katty loose from them?

He burst out with his tidings. I signed the roll today. Pa drove me to the courthouse. I'll be eighteen Sunday.

Katty upset the work basket on her lap. Scissors and thimbles and a darning ball and things tumbled all over the stoop planks, and some things rolled down into the lily bed below. Willie had no matches; Willie did not smoke. Mrs. Fiedenbruster sent one of the girls into the house, and she came back with a small block of sulphur matches. Willie took the matches from her, and scouted amid tapering lily leaves until Katty's lost property was restored. He straightened to find big Jake, the father, standing beside him, a mighty post of hewn manhood in dead brown darkness when the last match sputtered out.

Jake Fiedenbruster shook Willie's hand. This is good. Now you are a man, like my Jake and Frederick are men, like your brother was a man. When do you go?

I reckon we go next week. They aimed to raise a company, but the recruiting captain said they'd never get that many in these parts—too many folks already gone to war. Ben Carrington's signed, and Hudson Moberly and both the Pittridge boys.

Ja, das ist gut. It is bad, but it is good. Were it not for *die Kinder* I too should go.

The girls sat motionless on their stools and on the steps, and Katrine seemed to exude a deeper silence than the others, and Mrs. Fiedenbruster rocked heavily in the chair too small for her fat body, and the chair protested with squeaks. Down at the gate the boys still cavorted after lightning-bugs, making few sounds in order to keep from frightening the bugs.

It was late—far too dark to lure Katty from her family circle by this time. They would say that it was dark, her family would not permit her to walk down the road with him; that much was certain. But he would not have to leave for several days and—

After he was in the army, especially after he became a prisoner, he liked to think of that night. Mostly he thought about an afternoon before he went away, and what had happened then. But he chose also to consider the firefly evening (*chose* was scarcely it: memories pushed over him and fed him and choked him with their color and scent and shadow, whenever he was not occupied by the immediate urgencies of war).

No longer did the town band blat forth its resounding Hail Columbia or Benny Havens, Oh! Two trumpeters were dead of smallpox in Kentucky, the piccolo would roll its sweet trills no longer when operated by the breath of big Tad Wheeling because big Tad Wheeling's breath was taken from him by grapeshot. Most of the drummers were scattered and drumming still, but drumming at remote guardmounts in remote places. No band—but throngs of people on the cindered platform, waiting for the cars to come; sisters to weep, mothers to weep and squeeze you desperately, fathers struggling to seem calm and unweeping, little brothers torn between wide-eyed fear for your lives and the ecstasy of envy. Everyone stood with bowed heads, after the engine pulsed to its hot and blowing stop, while Reverend Collins spoke his prayer. Baskets of lunch, the sacks and satchels, the umbrella Hud Moberly's mother made him take along (how they would play with that, on the cars, and brandish it out of the window at other towns until the sergeant shouted them down).

Katty. Jewels and weapons in her bright wet blue eyes, the knowledge of what had already passed between them, the knowledge of her fragrance and softness and tenderness striking him like intoxication. Mother—ah, yes, one loved a mother—Willie loved his mother. Father—ah, Doctor was a father to be respected, to give the charm of calm manliness, to receive it back as his natural due. Sisters? Willie put his arms around the lot of them, or tried to, and patted them as a choice sprigged calico bouquet. But—Katty—

Finally, people had the decency to let him stand apart from them, to stand with Katty alone, looking directly into her face. She was not a tall girl, but she was nearly as tall as Willie.

Look what I bring to you, and she gave him a package. It seemed to be a bottle, sewn up in clean muslin and insulated against breakage with wads of paper inside the cloth.

Katty. . . .

You do not ask me, but it is lemonade.

Katty, I. . . .

Loaf sugar, one pound. In a trance she recited the formula. Citric acid, one-half ounce: this I buy from Mr. Partridge in his store. Also lemon essence. In a mortar I mix it, and it is all very dry. You should be sure to keep the bottle tight all the while.

Katty, you'll write to me and let me know if. . . .

Then, when it is your lemonade you want, I have here this tablespoon for you to measure. Not heaping, not flat, but round—so. That will make it proper. *Ach,* the amount of water I did not tell you: one half-pint. But maybe you like it not so strong; then more water you should use. Be sure to use pure and cold water.

Yes, yes, pure and cold— Katty—

The whistle blasted, steam blew on high, wet spatters came down. The boys went fleeting up the steps into the car, the sergeant was already aboard, Allen Pittridge was waving Willie's bundle at him and screaming, Come on, Will, I got your plunder—

He kissed her, and all her folks were staring; long he mashed his face on hers, his lips grown fast around hers, and all his folks were staring too, and all the other folks were staring, the world was staring. Then he was in the moving car, and smoke went alongside to mask the people stumbling and waving and trying to sing, smoke lifted to disclose old Mr. Cull Calise waving his flask at the train and quacking an invocation: Give 'em hell, boys. Scalp 'em, scalp 'em!

Glory, glory, hallelujah. Glory, glory, hallelujah. Glory, Glory—

So the knowledge that he must absorb nothing but purest liquid was a lesson set first by Doctor, learned fervently by Willie Mann, and endorsed by Katty in the final adjuration she gave him. Pure cold water from pure cold wells and springs. In this way Willie learned to go without water; he went without water when he had to—and often when he didn't, because he was over-zealous and his comrades thought him possessed of a mania. Privately he recognized that indeed he was possessed of a mania, but believed that it would sustain him. At first he was inclined to grow costive. This tendency he disciplined sternly by muscular exercise of his own abdominal area, by rubbings and proddings and twistings and bendings. Eventually he was convinced that his body needed only the moisture brought to it in mouthfuls of ordinary foods, though he drank boiled coffee along with other boys, and reveled in sweet milk whenever it might be bought or begged.

He survived the rigorous and disappointing earliest months of soldier life; he survived two transfers, the first frightening skirmish, the first utterly terrifying pitched battle; he survived four later battles, and various bang-bangs of desultory musket fire from rocks and woodlands (he refused to dignify these as skirmishes, because not an enemy was in sight). People caught scarlet fever in the winter of 1863–4; Willie Mann did not catch it. People caught mumps—fifteen boys in his company had the mumps at one time, and the mumps went down on four of the boys, and one boy died—of mumps and respiratory complications and gosh-knows-what. Willie Mann had had the mumps when he was nine; he did not catch the disease now. People died of pneumonia, intermittent fever, remittent fever, camp fever. Willie Mann suffered no fever whatsoever. He had grown half an inch since he enlisted. He was five-feet-seven and weighed one hundred and thirty-eight pounds. His round tan-colored eyes were solid and all-seeing. His tan-colored hair grew wavy and thick, and twisted in a tuft like a queue at the nape of his neck. He was more wiry than ever, and still liked to wrestle; and one of the bigger corporals was a wrestler too, and taught Willie many new holds. Willie Mann read a Chapter nearly every day, as he had promised his mother that he would do; he failed to perform this rite only in times of fighting, or in times of marching when actually he fell asleep between strides and pitched to the ground or tumbled against the man ahead of him. Willie owned deep-driven lines on either side of his little-boy's mouth, and nets of spidery lines around the outer corners of his eyesockets. He kept his body as clean as he could, and he dreamed of Katty Fiedenbruster. He carried his little Bible in his left breast pocket, confident that it would stop any bullet which sought his heart, and he had a letter from Katty folded in that Bible which letter would most certainly amplify the defense of the Bible, and he dreamed of Katty always while sleeping and whenever he could while waking.

Her lemonade was, while it lasted, a chalky treasure to be jeered at by his fellows, and promptly to be begged by them. He would remember always: hot, hot, and hollyhocks drooping on their roadside spikes, and dust twirling ahead sometimes diagonally across the road from southwest to northeast, the way cyclones blew. Sun made shivers out of remote windbreaks of cottonwood and sawed-off willows, and when the green regiment lay gasping at rest on swales along the floury roadside they could hear roosters wailing about the heat on distant small farms. Roosters talked with their mid-afternoon midsummer crowing, wan and hot and limp: it was not the inspiriting cry they uttered at dawn. Squad by squad, Willie's company was allowed to approach the nearest well. The widow who lived on that place had given her permission when the lieutenant asked her, and the boys were cautioned not to step on nasturtium beds, and to treat the old gate kindly. Forcibly imprisoned within the house, a shaggy shepherd dog uttered his barks in regular pounding cadence, without let or variety. *Owgh. Owgh. Owgh. Owgh,* until you thought you'd go crazy with barking and hotness and dust and solid sun.

Then was the time for Willie Mann to produce that bottle which Katty had given him, and the spoon to go with it. He measured cannily: the rounded spoonful, as she had directed. What in tarnation, Will? What you got there? Medicine?

A physic? He shook his head and tried to look wise, and succeeded only in looking smug. The others sensed his smugness; they made uncouth remarks about the stuff he was stirring into his can of water and—soon—the stuff he was drinking. Oh, but that was a good deep clear cool well; his father would have approved.

But Tite Cherry and Rom Hillburner were his especial chums, and they had respect for Willie and knew that he wasn't a dunce; neither was he an invalid in need of salts and powders. They hung back and begged quietly for a taste. After plain water, Katty Fiedenbruster's gift seemed a nectar. The word got around. Consistently thereafter Willie was importuned each time the squad descended on a well . . . he set his jaw, and shrugged: to think he'd ever toyed with the notion that the powdered lemonade might last through an entire campaign! But a man couldn't be niggardly with his campmates—especially not when he and Tite and Rom and Rom's brother Reem all messed closely together. Remus Hillburner was a natural born forager; if he couldn't beg a basket luncheon from bonneted ladies in some village he could manage to subtract a tender pullet from one of those same ladies' hencoops. Once he came back into camp with a corned leg of beef, and where had he stolen that? Reem stood in fine favor with the lieutenant, and even the cross-grained sergeant regarded him with a tenderly appraising eye. Pity that he had to die of fever that winter.

Tite Cherry and the Hillburner brothers and a few others had their share of the deliciousness proffered by Katty; probably more than their share, for Willie was generous to a fault. The day he emptied the bottle, and smashed it against a brick wall in sacred ceremony so that nothing else would ever be contained therein— That day he thought to himself, Hard lines from now on. Oh, I'll drink; but maybe Katty's lemonade powder took away a lot of the sickness I might have found in those wells along the roads, and now I got to show caution. So he did, though often his dry innards coiled like snakes at the sight of his fellows plunging their faces into dark streams which edged through dirty towns—rioting around some broken-down open well or cistern with a privy on one side of it and a hog-pen on the other, and manure piles rotting close.

In arid moments like those he thought of Doctor, and somehow he managed to live and to train himself into Going Without. The discipline Willie wielded over himself was not so bad, in all likelihood, as the discipline which Doctor had had to muster. In rare intimacies Willie had learned the whole story, bit by bit: the bestial father, the blows and tortures and eventual flight, the busy lordly doctor whose garden-digger and stable-boy the senior Mann became, the medical books borrowed secretly—*thieved* would be more like it—and read by light of a tin lantern until the weary body fell off the bench and the weary brain hummed with a demons' litany of discutients, femurs, carminatives, and tartareous adhesions. The Latin learned so slowly, the trip to a strange city on borrowed money, the waiting-on-table, the long lectures listened to by tired ears, the shoveling-of-coal, the first cadaver to excite the spirit—

Doubtless his father was more of an ideal and symbol to Willie Mann than the National Flag; definitely more of an ideal and symbol than a vague thought of the President and the Congress and the engraved unfinished dome of the National Capitol. So what would Doctor say if he knew about Willie and Katrine? What would Doctor say—what would Doctor *do*—if—?

Hard lines, waiting to hear. Oh, hard lines.

The letter came finally, and gave to Willie a release and a freedom and vigor he did not well deserve, and knew that he did not well deserve.

It was not the only letter she wrote to him, but it was the only one which reached him until the spring of 1864.

It was after the Evening of Fireflies, and word had come that the soldier boys should prepare to depart on Wednesday. Sunday the skies wept at the thought of their going. The Fiedenbrusters attended one church, the Manns another, so there was not even a glimpse of Katty to be caught in the wet of noon. In the afternoon Willie put an old piece of blanket over his head in lieu of mackintosh, and walked to the Fiedenbruster place where things were dismal in the extreme. The two youngest boys were sick abed with whooping-cough and you could hear them whooping like animals or Indians or something as you sat in the sitting room. Wempkie and Marta insisted on keeping their elders company, and Katrine was indignant about this, and spoke shortly to her sisters and her face became colored as always when she was angry. She sat and looked out of the little window and Willie thought she was mad at him. He suggested Authors—the Fiedenbruster girls owned a set of the cards, each card decorated with imposing pictures of Dickens and Wordsworth and Shakespeare and folks like that; if Marta asked Wempkie for Love's Labour's Lost, Number Two, and Wempkie didn't have it, then when it came your turn you could say, Marta, do you happen to have Midsummer Night's Dream, Number Two? Sometimes Authors was a jolly business; but Mrs. Fiedenbruster wouldn't let them play on this day because it was Sunday. She said, No, *mein Kinder,* hickory nuts you can crack.

Katty said pettishly, *Ach,* Mamma, it won't do no good. All last year's nuts, and dried up. Not fit to eat.

It was dull indeed; the drizzle kept up outside. Jake Fiedenbruster slumbered noisily on the sofa in the kitchen-dining room with a red handkerchief over his bearded face; and the other children read Sunday School books around the kitchen table . . . those were all they were allowed to read. Willie went home early, and was cross with his sisters; and back at the other house Katty covered herself with a comforter on her bed and Wempkie's, and cried. He couldn't know that, of course, but she told him later.

Monday dawned as prettily painted as Sunday had been the tone of zinc. Willie went out to do his chores (only two more mornings would he do them) and he was so charged with life and strength that he roared martial songs at the top of his voice while he loped about with forks and pails. *We leave our plows and workshops,* sang Willie Mann or more properly chanted Willie Mann with sublime disregard of pitch because he could never carry a tune on a shovel, *our wives and children dear, with hearts too full for utterance, and but a silent tear.*

His mother heard him, and thought of how the dead Samuel had once sung, with more melody, and she lay crying as she looked at bright light making gilt out of the slanted walls across from her.

His father heard him, and snorted, half in his sleep and half awake. Not quite a silent tear, observed Doctor in a mumble.

But Willie's mother thought of the dead Sam, and of Willie's departure day-after-tomorrow, and she cried steadily if silently. Doctor was lying on his back with yellow hairs of his beard intertwined with darker curlier hairs of his chest where his nightshirt hung open, and he realized that his wife was crying and why she was crying. He struggled round in bed until he could put both arms around Minnie; so she cried, so he tended and soothed her by saying nothing but by holding her close.

We dare not look behind us, roared the youth at the stable, *but steadfastly before. We are coming, Father Abraham, three hundred thousand more.* Morning glories were candies of pink and blue where they crawled on the trellis against the privy wall, warming wider and wider although the sun was not yet high; nasturtiums were orange and gold butter spread on the green bread of the lawn beside the well-curb; the tiger cat named Victoria sat on the wooden walk with legs cocked wide, and scrubbed herself with a harsh pink tongue. *We are coming, we are coming, our Union to restore*— Florence had built up the kitchen fire, and smoke smelled sweet; it promised toast and eggs and fried salt pork to come, to say nothing of the best red cherry preserves ever made.

Willie thought of the holiday to be his as soon as morning chores were done, because soon he was going to the war. He thought of Beverly's Timber, and the crawling of Beverly's Creek, and the wide brown hole where first he had learned to swim, and where catfish hung dreaming outside the porticos of limestone where in earlier summer they made their nests and guarded their eggs. He thought of hazel thickets he had known in frosty fall; and now in July the grass would turn its tall length flat and lie in springy windrows like little glades of Nature's featherbeds stretching from bunch of brush to bunch of brush.

. . . Would you like to go there with me?

. . . *Ja.*

So that was the way he dreamed it. Within the hour after breakfast he stood at the Fiedenbruster kitchen door with his old stained straw hat in his hand . . . aw, Katty. Please ask your Ma. We could have a splendid pic-nic party: just you and me. You won't have to fix anything—I'd fetch all the sandwiches and truck, and we got half a hen left from Sunday dinner in the cooler. And a jar of Ma's grapejuice. I'll bait your hook and everything; you won't have to touch a worm.

My mother might not let me go. Alone in the woods—with a young man. *Nein,* she might not—

Dog my cats, I'll ask her myself! He shooed Katty aside with enthusiasm, and found Mrs. Fiedenbruster in the buttery, lifting a damp cloth filled with white curds. There he asked her. The old clock spoke persistently on its shelf above the sink—the clock brought from Bavaria with such care, and it had monkeys and vines and rose petals painted on the front. The rooms were strangely silent, except for that clock, for all the rest of the Fiedenbrusters worked in field or garden save for the ailing little boys, and they dozed.

The mother pushed her specs down on her round nose and peered intently over them. I do not know. Katty is so young a girl— But you are a good boy, Willie. And you go to war. Maybe you get killed, *nein?* She took up a corner of her wide blue apron to touch the honest wetness in her eyes.

Mutter, that you should not say!

But it could be. *Ja,* Katrine, you may go for pic-nic by Willie Mann. Across the road you must go, and through the long cornfield. I do not wish the neighbors should see you go—two, alone. And Willie, you take good care of *mein Katchen?*

Course I will.

No female Fiedenbruster dared permit a boy to prepare the luncheon to be carried to Beverly's Timber or anywhere else, so Katty was a long while about cutting and wrapping the food, and would have been an even longer while about fixing her curls and getting into her fresh checked gingham. But her mother hastened her up. Mrs. Fiedenbruster deemed it wise that the other children should be unaware of this rustic festivity. They might be allowed to think that Katty had been permitted to spend the day at the Mann house, with Willie and his sisters; ja, that was what they could think. Jacob she might tell, Jacob she might not tell: she would decide later . . . come, come, little daughter, away with thee before the girls come from the garden in; and at the gate thy Willie is already with fishing poles. . . .

Corn waited to conceal them, corn was a wilderness with its sharp-edged bent swords of leaves, and the new silk a beauty at the tip of every heartening ear.

Solemnly the girl and the boy moved down the long damp corn-row; it was a task; if Katty moved first the leaves chafed at her hands and face; if Willie went ahead the long leaves whipped back and spatted Katty; but they made their way, the corn smelled youthfully rich and filled with strong green juice; they made their way.

He took down two rails of Mr. Beverly's fence, so that he might aid Katty across with a minimum of skirt-hoisting, and then with care he replaced the rails —set them solidly back into their notches.

It is beautiful, Willie. Here I have never been.

Not in Beverly's Timber? Don't you folks ever come over here to fish or—?

By the creek at the bridge I have been. That is all. But with you I will not be afraid.

Well, what in— What could you be feart of?

She looked up shyly, then the brown lashes came down. Maybe bears.

Naw! Haven't been no bears in these parts for years and years.

Maybe a—wolf? Maybe wildcats? (There was still a touch of v in her w's; it sounded nearly like *volf* and *vildcats,* and Willie loved her for it . . . he loved her for many things.)

He remembered the two lines going loose into Beverly's Creek, and the way those lines broke at angles beneath the surface. The stream was brown and pale but you could see to a certain depth in the holes, and you could make out wide-headed shadows of catfish as they came to investigate the twin baits, and rejected them, but clung near, watching still, waving their limp feelers in derision. He remembered the unhappy turtle which did indeed bite hard on Katty's bait, and so she squealed and fetched it up: she was so excited that she kept talking in German (that was the language the Fiedenbrusters used at home, naturally enough); and part of her hair came down while she was cavorting and exclaiming and waving her pole about. The turtle marched grimly over grass, trying to go back to his deep home; and now Katty was deploring all fishing and fishermen.

Ach, and he has that cruel hook. In his poor mouth! *Ach,* Willie, it is so cruel. I cannot bear to see.

Naw, naw. It won't hurt him a speck. Here, I'll cut him loose.

Ach, the knife! It must hurt him so— She buried her face in her hands.

. . . All done, Kat. See, he's loose. Just look at them legs wiggle when I hold him up.

But he has the bleeding, Willie!

Just a trifle. His mouth is as hard as a rock—it'll well up in no time at all. Want to put him back in the creek, yourself? No? I'll put him in. In you go, Turt. Farewell, Turt.

He remembered great iridescent butterflies which whisked above a damp spot far in Beverly's Timber—the small black-and-orange-and-white butterflies which sat tasting the shallow pool, and shot up when you came too close . . . they wheeled and sped faster than flies . . . and a strange tiny bird of purplish blue beyond, the shyest of the shy, and making soft his song before they alarmed him with their coming.

Willie. Worshipping whisper, the quiet curls and peachy skin and smell of her so close . . . his breath clogged in his chest. Willie, so beautiful a bird. What name?

Dog my cats, Katty, I don't know. Never saw it before. Twasn't a bluebird.

Nein. He was even much more beautiful. Maybe a fairy bird?

They laughed about it, they wandered on, a groundhog raced heavily to his burrow, the girl yelled about it, and clutched Willie tightly and said that she had known there would be bears.

He remembered the sunny place, the deep ravine where a basswood had been undermined and had fallen across the thinning stream; thus it left a hole in the dark green roof, and sun beat through to stamp this one circle of hot gold amid the shadows. He remembered the willow basket placed between them, the red-bordered cloth which Katrine produced and spread: the pickles with cloves clinging to them, the ivory of hard-boiled eggs, the slices of dark cured ham and corned beef, bread-and-butter sandwiches, the jug of milk.

(Within the stockade men dreamt of food until the very dreams slew them as surely as bullets. It was this luncheon which Willie Mann dreamed of.)

The luncheon, the solitude, the laughter of the creek, the peewee songs, solid piling clouds hiding the sun at last.

It started with gingerbread. She offered gingerbread and then took it back roguishly and said, *Nein,* already you have eaten too much.

But—I—want—that—gingerbread!

Nein. She was on her feet, flying away from him . . . oh girl, oh goddess, oh the temptation in retreat and running, oh always in illusion the dear figure rushing away; and the hardihood of the male to pursue, the hardihood to effect the capture, to press the twisting arms tightly, to stumble, to sprawl together, to continue the embrace.

They had never kissed like this, their mouths had never touched before; they were alone, oh God the solitude, oh Katty, oh God the taste and smell of you, oh the hot ferocious breath of you, and breathing together with a gasping. . . .

She would cry softly, *Nein,* but when he sought to manage some denial and sought to drag his face from hers— Their mouths grew together again. And soon there was all the dainty majesty of her bosom revealed and touched and explored and slathered and warm with his kissing—

Nein. Ach, Gott— Not *mein* gown, Willie— It is wrong we do this! *Ach,* Willie— *Küss' mich, küss' mich, küss' mich—*

Long he heard the tender gasp and whisper of her maidenly protestation, long he surmounted all objection which propriety had taught the two of them. Virgin boy and virgin girl, their tears and exclamation of desire and fright and conscience and terror and sheer abandoned delight were commingled throughout their uniting. Somewhere beyond the ferocity which ruled them, there stood a vast disapproving congregation composed of parents, brothers, sisters, Reverend Collins, Reverend Mueller, Sunday School teachers, aunts, Jesus, neighbors, teachers, Disciples, Apostles, the county sheriff, God the Father.

In a later hour Willie was impelled to blubber when he stood alone in the forest where she had sent him. He heard the splashing of water; there at the brookside she must be striving to repair the damage to herself and to her costume; and when he returned it was to see her hastily hiding a small damp bundle in the willow basket.

She sat in grass, he sat near her; she was calmer than he as she did up her hair, working knowingly by touch for she had no looking glass.

Wretchedly he importuned her, and she looked at him calmly. You think I am a bad girl?

Naw! Katty, I made you do It.

So we have done It. It is as if always I knew that we would.

Katty, do you think—?

What do I think, *mein* Willie?

Do you think—? Mightn't—? Maybe now you'll have—a baby?

Ja. That could be.

Hi. He sat higher and stared at her. Let's get married. I'll marry you, Katty. We could get wed tomorrow.

Nein. Mein Vater und meine Mutter— They would say I am too young. I am only sixteen until October. If I say I should be wed to you, then they know that we have done It. My mother she was wed to my father at eighteen was the age. Always she has said her daughters must wait until also they are eighteen.

But if you— If—a baby—

Then so, a baby I will have. When back you come from the army, then we can be wed.

He urged, he pleaded and begged and cajoled . . . she repeated that she was too young. Again they lay in each other's arms, but there was a sainted serious-ness in their touching; and again they stared at close mysterious range, and seemed worlds apart, and never the youth and the girl who entered Beverly's Timber light-heartedly with their fishing poles and basket of lunch.

I guess somebody ought to horsewhip me. Or maybe shoot me. I promised your mother—

Quietly she placed her firm little finger on his lips. Talk no more, Willie. You are full of the talk. Some day we shall be older.

There was a noticeable sadness in the depth of her eyes and the depth of her tone; yet she was serene, she had courage, she had an amiable wisdom, and here she was fifteen months younger than Willie Mann. A burden seemed placed now upon her fine slender shoulders, and he marveled confusedly at the way she managed it: the weight she carried seemed not labeled as Guilt but as Wom-anhood. In vague wonderment the boy ascribed her strength to the discipline in which she had been reared and also to the heritage awarded to Katrine by genera-tions of good-hearted peasants with limited but sturdy minds. . . . Katty was his forever; and she seemed much older than he; strangely she seemed like his mother.

Nevertheless he fretted constantly, once he was away from her and coping with the first dread impersonal complications of soldier life. He lost weight, gave sharp retorts to his companions when they joked at him, was sullen if tractable beneath the scrutiny of his sergeant. Aloof on his sweat-soaked blanket at night, he envi-sioned all manner of complaints, disasters, social disgraces. Katty had a baby and the baby was born dead. Katty died in childbirth. Katty had a baby, and the baby was an idiot, waving foolish arms and legs and grunting like a pig. The neighbors drew in their skirts when Katty passed. Katty's father tied her in the woodshed as soon as he learned that she was pregnant, and beat her daily with a thick willow switch; and he walked up and down the road with his cowhide whip coiled in his huge hand, watching for Willie to return from the army so that Jake Fieden-bruster could savor the glee of thrashing Willie to a pulp. Sometimes these imaginings took the form of distinct colorful dreams and nightmares. Titus Cherry said, What in time ails you, Willie? You were groaning and growling in your sleep like my little brother when he et too many gooseberry tarts.

My dear friend, she addressed him timidly at long last, and that was the letter he carried folded in his Bible. (The Rebels did not take his Bible from him when he was captured; and sometimes he thought it was better for him than food; but the mere thought of locusts and honey made his mouth water.) My dear friend, I take my pen in hand to write that I hope you are well. Often I think of you and wish to see you. One letter from you I rec'd. but it is not wise that you should speak so freely of such matters, setting the words down in pencil and paper; for suppose my mother or my father should have chanced to read it?? Quickly I put it in the stove! But I write to inform you that no more such worries should be entertained in your thoughts. I have waited long in order to make certain; two months have elapsed and now I am certain that there is no fear. Willie, I am young and know very little of such matters! But I am sure now and you may be sure and free in your heart. By that I do not mean that you should be free enough to seek for another friend! For you are mine, Willie, and I am thine. And I am trying to remember the verses which Teacher set for us upon the big slate, but it is something about a vine entwining, and maybe about a stump. Oh, my Willie, the tears are flowing freely as I think of thee, and some have fallen upon this letter paper. Is it not handsome, with the Flag and spirit of Our Fair United Country standing side by side, and all in beautiful colors?? It is dear, costing five cents for each pretty sheet and envelope, but I paid for it with some of my berry money. May the Heavenly Father bless and keep thee safely, my dear friend Willie. Now I have covered all the little paper. The mother is calling to me to pare a pumpkin for the pies. Always I am thine, heart's dearest. Katrine Christine Ernestine Fiedenbruster.

There were other letters later, but none rang with the joy of this. As he wore it to a thin tinted rag, rereading and rereading, Willie thought that he heard the brown polished music box playing—a small music box which the Germans had brought from the Old Country along with their clock and the ugly silhouettes of two grandmothers and two grandfathers.

Now Willie could hop like a young frog in springtime. He was the life of the squad, sometimes the most bounding, least trammeled spirit in the column. No task was too arduous, no march too wearying, no shellfire too filled with threat. Remus Hillburner perished of his fever, Romulus Hillburner was shot through the knee and sent home to walk stiff-legged through the balance of his years, Titus Cherry was creased on the head by a bouncing piece of solid shot: they left him for dead, with blood pooling in his eyesockets, and then when they went back to fetch his body Tite wasn't there at all; and he came walking into camp that night with his scalp stiffening and painful where some old Rebel granny had kindly sewed it up with linen thread. Within the month Titus was well again, sound as a nut, and his mass of long black hair covered the huge scar. . . . Willie Mann suffered neither wound nor sickness, and was promoted to fourth corporal. The delighted Katty jigged and squeaked when she received the news, and that very day she wrote a letter to Willie with the word *Corporal* underscored with red crayon in the address, but the letter never reached Willie.

It was that same June day that three boys in torn brown shirts descended upon Willie from a cleft in Georgia rocks, and called him a Yankee son of a bitch, and told him to stick his bayoneted musket in the ground or they would blow his guts out of his ass. Willie's musket was empty, and his companions were scampering in retreat for the moment. He had no wish for his guts to be blown through any aperture whatsoever, so the bayonet sank quickly into earth. The boys (two of them appeared even younger than he) took all his accoutrements, along with his pocketknife and old silver watch, and the twenty-one cents in currency he had in his pocket. They snatched his knapsack and pawed through it, but they took nothing except the little blue housewife his sisters had sewn hastily for him before his departure. And later one of the boys came around with a shamed face and said, Yank, I reckon that was stealing, and stealing is a sin in the sight of the Almighty, and he gave the housewife back to Willie. Willie rather expected to have his watch returned also, and asked for it boldly; but another Rebel who now possessed it suffered no squirmings of conscience.

Along with other strays Willie was guarded rudely in various tanyards, school-houses, sawmill enclosures, cotton gin enclosures, and periodically on the cars. He arrived at Andersonville along with three hundred and fourteen fellow prisoners, only one of whom he had known by face but not by name when he was a recruit. This person, whose name was Dundridge, was no fit companion for anyone, be he man-at-arms or prisoner. One day Willie's ration disappeared while he rushed to answer a call of nature; he was almost sure that Dundridge took it and gobbled it, but he had no evidence. . . . Willie owned a capacious tin cup, fine to drink out of, fine to boil coffee in, or even stew or mush. Well, the cup disappeared also; and a day or so later Dundridge made a great to-do about a cup he had bought from a guard. Somehow secretly Dundridge had scoured off all the black, and he had twisted the handle to make it look different, but Willie snatched the cup and looked inside on the bottom. There it was: the crude symbol composed of W and M which Willie had scratched with his bayonet point long ago. Dundridge denied, protested and finally threatened; which vociferations Willie halted by means of the old-fashioned hip throw, and he banged Dundridge's head against the ground until a guard bruised his bottom with a musket butt and said, If you're such a smart scrapper, little Yank, why didn't you scrap harder and not get cotched? Dundridge and Willie remained distinctly aloof. In the hospital at Andersonville, Dundridge died, and his death was recorded as being due to marasmus—a wasting of flesh without fever or obvious disease. When Willie Mann heard of his demise he did not feel regretful in the least: he regretted only that so many others had to die. With an angry mustering of fanatic quality he was determined that he himself should not die.

If he had known more about the business of being a prisoner (he would learn) he would have recognized that he was of the type to last long. He was a knobby tanned streak of lean, such as you might extract from a bacon slice. He had youth, no extra weight, elasticity, a good humor, he did not require much food for sustenance, he had taught himself to drink very little water and now he would drink even less.

He held lengthy private conversations with his father, conversations in which he supplied the dialogue for both; yet if Doctor had been dropped into the stockade from a gas balloon his questions and comments would have been no more characteristic.

Sonny, tell me about that Dundridge.

Well, I know a fellow works Outside every now and again, and he was fetching pine boughs to the hospital. He heard it from another fellow from our Ninety—I mean from our mess. Said he died of marasmus.

Hain't no such disease in my book. Oh, I know the term; but it's employed to cover a multitude of sins. Did he have fever?

Not a grain, when he was sick here.

Flesh seem to fall away?

Reckon that's how you'd describe it. Didn't slough off—wasn't nary a sore on him. Teeth didn't come out, neither. Take that Canadian—the one they call Frenchy in that A-tent shebang over there. You can pull his teeth out betwixt your two fingers if you're game to try. I've seen him win money on it.

Dropsical?

Not so you'd notice. Entirely unpuffed-up.

Scurvy?

No trace. I kept three raw potatoes for days, and Dundridge saw they were there, but he never touched one. And he was a born thief.

Any signs of catarrhal affection, pleuritis, oedema, anasarca, ascites, hydrothorax or anaemia?

He just died.

I say twas water. What well did he use, this fellow Dundridge?

Pa. Come take a walk with me alongside that marsh. . . .

Willie was born to hardihood, for all his small size; Titus Cherry was not, for all his impressive bulk. Cherry wore a cap which would drop down on most other people's ears. He had a mane of hair black as a crow's back at midnight in the dark of the moon, and thick rounded eyebrows of the same material. His pale green eyes were slightly crossed, one of them was always looking off somewhere over the mountains. Once he rowed with Sergeant Buford about fatigue duty which Tite felt he hadn't deserved; one word led to another, and finally Tite said slowly, Well, I'll say no more. Dasn't make any proper argument with you—the kind I'm honing to make—long as you got them stripes on your sleeve. Buford was a gingery man who stood nearly as tall as Cherry and had served six years with Regulars in the Indian country. Also it was rumored that he was experienced in the prize ring. He said to Tite Cherry, If it's stripes that's bothering you, bub, they're easy taken off. So the two of them walked down behind the quartermaster's wagons and a grove which shielded them; they went with half the company following and making bets. Sergeant Buford took off his jacket, stripes and all, and began to roll up the sleeves on his tough freckled arms. Tite Cherry just stood observing the sergeant and kind of smiling at him while his left eye searched upper regions of the trees. Then, without removing his own jacket, he stolled over to the tailboard of one of the wagons. There stood a barrel of flour, all filled up, top nailed on solid. Usually it took four men to load or unload one of those barrels—two in the wagon, two on the ground. Tite dropped the tailboard on its chains and—standing beside it, with everyone watching with their jaws hanging open—he put his right arm halfway around that barrel and began to pull . . . pulled the barrel right over to the edge and past. Holding the barrel tight against his body and staggering only a little, he eased that barrel to the ground with scarcely a jar.

Everybody made a sound. The sergeant touched his lips with his tongue. Bub, can you put her back?

Reckon I can. But I'd have to use both arms.

Don't rupture your belly, bub.

Shan't.

. . . And all eyes still on him as he bent his knees and brought his body low, keeping his huge feet close together. He put both arms around that barrel and suddenly pushed himself erect and brought the barrel up against his chest. He slammed it back in the wagon and the whole wagon shook, loaded as it was. Tite turned around to face the crowd; he was laughing. Flour dust was on his black hair and his dark face, and tears or sweat ran down through the dust and left tracks.

Sergeant, I could break you in two.

By cracky, said Buford. (He was a model churchman; never swore.) I'm beat if you couldn't. Ain't but one thing to do. He offered his hard freckled hand, and it disappeared in Tite's dark hairy grasp, and they stood chuckling. Other folks went up to slap the flour barrel and to see if any two of them could move it, but they couldn't.

Willie Mann had been less than ten days in Andersonville when one morning he stood by the North Gate watching some fresh fish come in. Rebel sergeants were leading newly-instituted Nineties into various areas, designating these areas as places for them to settle themselves; which was all very well, except that by this time practically every square inch of habitable ground was already taken up by pioneer squatters, so there were bound to be fights. Suddenly a mighty black-and-blue shape loomed out at Willie, and he went scrambling past the populace to throw his arms around Titus Cherry.

Tite stared long, down into Willie's face. He said, You're mighty poor. Just skin and bone.

I never had much more than skin and bones, Tite. When'd they get you?

Twas a Friday. I was out a-foraging with Linton and MacCarrick. They tried to cut for it, and both got shot. I gave myself up. He said these things in a tired awed voice, not the genial rumble of the Tite Cherry whom Willie had known as a fellow campaigner. Both eyes seemed peering distantly into the sky; it was as if Titus had had one crossed eye before, now he had both of them crossed. This place, he said, this place. What is it?

Hell, Tite. They call it Camp Sumter. Andersonville. You had any rations today?

Not since yesterday. They gave us cowpeas when we were on the cars, and a little bit of mule.

Come along to our shebang. I got some corn bread saved.

So he had, but when he offered it to Tite the big chap squeezed his eyes shut and made a gesture of refusal.

Oh, come on. It hain't too bad. Just coarse and dry—no salt.

It's all dirty and got cobs ground in it. I'll go without.

Someone might have struck him a heavy blow with a fence-rail, the moment Tite entered at the gate. That was the way he acted—dazed and disbelieving. He appeared to be telling himself, This is not true, this will fade away. He answered the questions Willie put to him about the Twenty-ninth Missouri, and whether they had thought Willie dead, and whether Titus knew whether Willie had been reported as killed— He answered questions dutifully, sleepily, as if there were some secret Other Person whom he had to consult before he could come up with the answers. In between times he would turn his majestic head from side to side, taking in the stockade and its people and its stench and its noises—rejecting the whole business and probably assuring himself that he would wake up soon.

Going Without was one thing for a little shaver like Willie, and quite another thing for Titus. . . . There wasn't room for him in the ·shebang where Willie dwelt, though Willie tried to have his friend included, no matter which Ninety he was in. At nightfall Tite went down the hill to bunk with the fresh fish with whom he'd arrived, and to contribute his blouse as partial covering for a new shebang. He did everything demanded of him with docility, yet his thoughts seemed far away. Willie had not been long enough in the stockade to have observed intimately such cases; yet there were many. The hatchet of horror lay waiting for certain men the moment they stepped through the North Gate; it came up invisibly and struck them between the eyes, its blade went deep, the hatchet fractured their skulls and the will and the purpose and the reason lurking inside; everything was splintered, they could not put the pieces together again; so they died, so Titus Cherry died.

He would not eat. Willie ranted at him, cursed him, knelt and prayed beside him. He talked of Duty, parents, Tite's little brother who would long to see him return— He spoke deliriously of good times they would have, back in Missouri together— He should go to Canton and join Tite and Tite's people; Tite should come to visit him— They'd spread long tables out-of-doors under the wild grape arbor, they'd invite all the Fiedenbrusters and Moberlys, doughnuts and roast beef and baked apples and roasting ears would be theirs.

But in the meantime you got to feed on something, Tite. Can't exist solely on air. Bad as these rations be, you got to relish them.

Know what I saw, Will, know what I saw?

Oh, don't tell me that again!

It was down below there towards the sinks. Two men a-squatting with that running-off-of-the-bowels. And this other man—he was crippled—

Tite, you got to think of other matters! You got to keep your mind healthy. I tell you, it goes on all the time— I've seen it, everybody's seen it, tain't anything new!

He crawled right along behind them. Soon as one would get through with his business, he'd move along and then get the feeling and go to squatting again. This cripple would dig in his business. He was getting chunks of stuff—corn bread and it looked like potatoes—that the other man had et. Went right through him, never even changed color. And Willie, Willie, he was—

Oh, God alive! All right—say it, it ain't anything new— He was eating the stuff. Because he was hungry! Tite, you got to eat. I tell you, you got to. Not *that*. You don't—

Picking it out of all that loose business. I saw him. Little pieces of bread and— He was crawling along, eating it—

Or sometimes it was dead bodies which bothered him more, as his fever and lassitude grew intense; but usually it was a scene such as he had witnessed near the sinks. Flesh hung on him like loose clothing, his sagging hollow cheeks were pink and later yellow beneath the grime. He slept, sat, walked, later tottered alone. The sinks fascinated him, and the marsh beside the sinks, and he sat for long periods staring, with wide gummy lips moving soundlessly under his raw black beard.

Willie had little left to sell, but now he sold the housewife with its needles, pins, coils of thread, scissors, brass thimble, buttons. He bought meat, vegetables and rice, cooking them for Titus in his big tin cup, to have each offering declined as the first corn bread had been declined. . . . The meat was dog or cat, the rice had worms, the vegetables were poisoned by the Rebs. (This was later, when Tite's mind as well as his vision began to sweep to far and absurd places.) One cupful of stew he managed to upset and waste when he swept out a gaunt hand to gesture refusal. . . . Willie was a philosopher. He had been fond of Titus, he had loved him as much as any other comrade, as much as he had loved Rom Hillburner; he squeezed out tears for Titus, but he wolfed the other food as fast as Tite turned it away.

When Titus Cherry could stand no longer but lay jerking on his sodden blanket and recognizing no one, Willie prevailed upon two men from his shebang to help him carry Tite to the surgeons at the gate. First morning there was a dreadful press, and they couldn't even lug Tite through to be noted; the cries of That's All, No More, No More, Wait Until Tomorrow— These cries arose only fifteen minutes or so after they had fetched him. The other men growled about it; through his starvation Tite held only a fraction of the weight he'd owned when campaigning, but still the burden was nothing to be ignored by sickly men. Next morning Willie scratched amid his few effects and came up with a broken pocket comb and two iron staples which had fallen from the ration cart one day and which Willie had picked up quickly. The staples might be used as implements of some sort; he had hoped to keep the comb, because he could rid himself of many vermin with that; but nothing counted at this time but getting Titus to the hospital (though few people recovered strength in the hospital. The vast majority of them died as soon as they were lugged there. Still the thought of Hospital was a poultice to apply against whatever brotherly affection remained to Willie Mann). He offered these articles to the same men who'd helped him carry Tite on the previous day; one refused, one accepted the staples, and Willie enlisted a man from Tite's own mess through payment of the comb. They started very early, and thus got Tite through the gate and into a stall. There one orderly prescribed Dose Number Three, which was for scorbutus and all wrong; then a surgeon came by and shook his head, and tagged Titus Cherry for Hospital. He died there on a plank two or three days later, unconscious but mumbling until near the end.

I won't die, said Willie. God damn. I won't. Pa, I won't die. Katty (now the sheerest of visions, vague and papery), I won't die. Won't drink the water neither.

He chewed dryly, he chewed with his sore jaws, he chewed the bitter woody bread, chewed beans and the worms which dwelt in them. Part of the shebang where he lived was formed from a square of oilcloth which Willie had retained in his knapsack on capture. The first young Confederates did not preëmpt it, and— later, obeying some fortunate instinct—Willie put the oilcloth inside his shirt. So he brought it into the stockade, and it was impermeable at first, though the oiled part began to flake off under the burning sun. But August developed with recurrent fierce rains, many of them occurring at night; old-timers said it had been like that in June when it rained twenty days straight—some said it rained twenty-four days in June. Since early spring the earth of Georgia had held no thirst.

The loose soil was soaked, swollen past saturation. Occasionally it rejected a fresh onrush, and in one afternoon of early August its rejection was violent. Hour after hour a downpour thrummed on woodland, stockade; it pounded the dripping huddled masses of mankind within pine-stalked limits. Trickles ran down north slope and south, they widened into cascades; the stolid marsh became a lake pocked with infinite stabbings, the slow-crawling creek became a torrent. Yellow tide frothed and clung against those posts which were driven near the commonly-oozing streamlet. The tall logs had been high and dry before, now they were laved. Laving became a battering, each pole weakened in its socket. Deeply those trunks had been imbedded, but water weighted through the coarse ground; its constant pushing stroke could not be resisted.

First a single log of the eastern palisade swayed (benefit accomplished for a space: a portion of the accumulated sewage would be swept out of the stockade down the flat valley. But soon it would be replaced by new seepage) and the massive length of wood leaned hard against another beside it. The combined heaviness of the two was enough to urge a third post from its socket. So it went: in minutes a dozen thick jack-straws had tumbled and splashed. There was a gap in the stockade.

On high ground immediately west of this aperture, men rose from drenched hovels in disbelief. No wall, they cried in the rain, not believing it. Look at that hole! Promptly they came swarming from this same high ground, which was called the Island because ordinarily a pond of fetid ooze twisted to the north of it, and an equal morass curved to the south. Look at that hole! Stockade's gone!

They leaped swearing and screeching, some swam in the force of the cascade, others were running on the banks. Hundreds of prisoners on the twin slopes also had observed this catastrophe which might prove to be a release to all the thwarted and unkempt, so they came jumping.

Not a shot was fired by any guard. Some people thought later that the drilling rain had dampened their enemies' powder charges and caps, as it had cooled the prisoners' will to burst free. A wise battle-toughened sergeant cried an order, and frightened Reserves came tumbling from their shacks. The word was passed along, and quickly, around the south boundary. It reached the earthen fort and the camp to the southwest beyond and the camp to the northwest opposite the North Gate. Squads, companies, guards not On Parapet came to mill at the breach, urged by those few officers alert to the danger involved, urged by the babbling Lieutenant Davis.

Henry Wirz was not on duty. He was gone to Augusta, reported sick, the surgeon pecked at his arm. But among frantic subordinates left to discharge the duties he had laid out there were enough to form a nucleus of strength. They marshalled quaking boys, coughing graybeards, they held them along the boundaries of the raw river and formed them there with guns level, bayonets fixed.

Skies kept melting and falling, the hose of mettlesome gods was directed down. On one side of the gap scarecrow Yankees congregated, on the other side herded scarecrow hobbledehoys and patriarchs—but with the impact of weapons. No boy tried to gallop past them or sought to pierce the tide and swim to freedom beneath its crest. Reinforcements trotted through the dark rain until prisoners gazed across the breach into a solidity of muzzles and steel. Philosophers said wearily, It couldn't be. Twas too lucky to happen. They turned back to whatever shelter they had left, whatever other shelter they could find or imagine. In time the storm ceased its pounding. Within a night and a day laborers had made the stockade as solid as it was before, and no flash flood of equal proportions came again.

In such thudding storms Willie Mann claimed the right to adjust his portion of tent-patching to his needs. In darkness he would lie with the broken oilcloth funneled toward his mouth, and rainwater would drip or pour, depending on the amount and velocity of rain—It would be directed into Willie's open mouth. Thus he drank. These periodic dilutions were accomplished amid snarls and resentments of his tentmates . . . if you weren't such a plaguèd young fool, and bound to sop up rainwater, we could all be laying fairly snug. . . . After discussion and prevailing acrimony during saner hours, it was agreed that Eph Bainbridge's overcoat should be extended to help cover the gap left by Willie's oilcloth, and that Willie should betake himself into other regions—clear away from the shebang, over against the deadline, and that he should lie unsheltered—when again he chose to absorb the gift of the rain. He did not tell his mates how bad the rain tasted. It was tainted with the prison's effluvia as it came down; effluvia seemed to lie like a mattress above the thirty-odd thousand men and their reek. By the time the rain had dashed down to proximity with the crowded trampled earth it was noxious with retchings and throat-clearings and smells of disordered digestions, with the taint of corpses which had been more dead than alive when they were alive.

How many gallons less had he drunk in this year of 1864 than he had drunk in the year of 1863? There was no way of estimating. He saw a spreading fountain somewhere off in the past or the future, such a fountain as was pictured in the Versailles of their one European travel book at home; and that fountain, with foamy push and laving, represented the canteens and cups and reservoirs which Willie had not poured down his hard-surfaced throat. He thought that his throat was made of old harness, he thought that his throat was sunburnt and peeling as his bony face was peeling and burnt. Desperately he worked at manipulating the scrawny portion of his trunk which hung flat beneath the hoops of his ribs; it wouldn't do to grow costive, there were no physics to be had, and he was one inmate for whom diarrhoea held little threat—he'd only had a touch of it twice, both times mildly. When he witnessed his own feces he thought that a rabbit must have been halting there instead of Willie Mann.

. . . Thunder tussled in the southwest and a deluge burst upon the soaked stockade shortly before midnight. Clouds had gloomed and pressed low as if challenging the slivers atop the fence to rip them open; so in time they were ripped. Willie lay half submerged in a pool, close to the deadline on the steep north slope. Oilcloth covered the upper portion of his body, and stiffly he held his thin elbows immobile and pressed his palms up to tilt the long-punished fabric. The ill-favored ill-flavored storm distributed its substance into his mouth, flowing over cracks in his lips, filling cracks inside his mouth which felt like the cracks in a plaster wall.

Lightning had been gashing since the storm broke, but suddenly a thrust came close enough to singe the hair in any man's nostrils. Willie's ears popped; he thought that he had been struck and torn and melted by the blaze (vaguely he recalled a farmer back home who'd had the watch melted in his pocket and the nails melted in his boots when he was struck). For a while Willie could see nothing but the rough ball of fire which had seemed to bounce on earth beside him, he could smell nothing but scorched brimstone and sulphur and storied chemicals. Prisoners hallooed in the nearer shebangs, and wanted to know who had been hit. Maybe no one had been hit, but you would have thought that a dozen people had been tossed and carved by the lightning's lash, the crash of bursting cannon.

Willie felt cold all along his side. He was drenched, he had been drenched before, but this was a strange and different coldness. Had lightning tapped the blood from his body, was his blood chill instead of warm? He flung out his right hand. There was a bubbling, a running in the mud.

Willie Mann rose up on shaking knees. The next glare told him the truth . . . a stream, a small stream of clear water was coming his way, flowing desperately toward and around him. Another flare: he could see it rising in lather and bubbles from muck within the deadline space, carrying chunks of clay, swirls of mud, carrying scraps of bark and even pebbles on its crest. It wasn't the rain . . . this was colder than rain, by God it was clearer than rain. He could see it in repeated explosions of the crazy sky. It was a little brook, a spring, it was coming out of the ground.

He fell forward, burying his face in the flow, draining mouthful after mouthful, trying to condemn his stony throat to a banquet of swallowing. This was something to drown in, he would drown in it. Then he rose, supporting himself on trembling hands as he screamed with all his strength, Water! Fresh water! It's a spring! He did not distribute these tidings with any notion of sharing a treat with the rank and file of fellow men; it was only that he had to voice the discovery, bellow it above cracking thunder in order to reassure himself that it was true.

Within a matter of seconds there were fifty men tumbled around him, guzzling like spooks shed by the bursting night; and more scores came shoving on top of them.

Previous moisture had been nothing but the muck of obscenity; now there was Grace. How did it taste? It was Doctor's water and Katty's advised water: pure and cool and clear. It tasted as a forest pool where none but clean russet-coated beasts assembled to drink, and where unspoiled Indians bowed to drink and pray. It was the spring found by Daniel Boone when Boone came tramping in youth, prime, or frosty age. It tasted of simple and pretty things: violets, and taffy, and winter making pine-tree patterns on a thin sharp window pane. It was Beverly's Creek with crawdads scuttling, and the blue-purple-sky-colored bird being delicate in woodsy air overhead, the miniature bird the virgin boy and virgin girl had seen and heard, the bird without a name. It was the well at Grandpappy's house, where butter and cheese hung in a damp sack, and sometimes fresh little wild strawberries were put down there to keep them cool. O water, O bittersweet the cleanliness; it carried its own spice, not the meager drip of disconsolate rainfall; but you could taste the clarity of this stuff for all the rain which smashed upon it. The stream grew wider, it came in free panic seeping under the sagging timber of the deadline, it flowed and talked of Church and Christ Himself, it rippled of Home. Lightning reeked persistently, lightning was like fragrant lilacs in the bubbling reflection. Water, water, fresh water here, a hundred dollars a drink! Yells lost the restriction of words, all yells united in a single persistent whooping blast; and cripples tried to share as well, but many of them were knocked down or aside as the rush went on. Guards crouched under the slanting roofs of their sentry stations, they did not like to step out in the rain; some men feared that guards might shoot into the scrambling mass, and already weaker individuals were being shoved fairly across the deadline, and the deadline broke, but still the guards held their fire. *He clave the rocks in the wilderness, and gave them drink.* . . . Clear and cool and pure, as the saintly Doctor and the saintly Katty had ordered.

. . . Tasted of ferns, and wake-robins which opened early and pale when blackbirds were teetering on new green reeds and making their *chink* sounds . . . O springtime when bees came swarming, and sap had climbed clear up into the bundles of new maple seeds. Dear water—it might have been released by thunder's pulsation or the spear-thrust of lightning itself, and already a dozen prisoners announced staunchly that they had witnessed the very bolt which drilled the ground. It might have been released by the heaviness of saturation of soaked sandy soil . . . all those torrents of June, these new freshets of ugly August uniting to disturb the hard-tamped anchorage of a hillside where every tree had been felled, where a ditch had been spaded out, where roughly squared pine trunks had been socketed, where an ancient sweet spring had been hidden and trodden into muteness.

It was the deep round narrow haunted cistern at home, where you busied yourself with rope and bucket on washday, filling the family tubs before you took yourself off to school; yes, that wine from the cistern was rainwater, but not the rainwater of Andersonville funneled from rotten blankets, from draped overcoats with the taste of forgotten blood and forgotten piss in them . . . ah, so long tanked among dark buried limestone and cistern lining that the water awarded itself the flavor of a native spring, nor did it smell like rainwater longer.

Knowing nothing of this magic breaking forth, Ira Claffey stirred on his bed beyond the stockade and the southwest hill. He emerged from a dream about one of his dead sons, and was aware of lightning's brilliance and protracted thunder. He might have heard (he did not hear, at this time) a child speaking from memory. Lucy it was.

. . . Where do they sleep?

. . . Ah, there's that moss. Where do you think?

. . . And for table linen too. Would they let me drink their water?

. . . Assuredly. That's the reason they keep it running. Here, child, I'll make a cup of my hand . . . miniature fairies of the damp sort, scarcely as big as your finger.

. . . I saw one, whilst I was drinking.

It was not frozen, it was not ice, it was running loose in a summer night in Georgia, yet it had the perfume of icicles. You were a little boy again, and there came an exceptionally heavy snow to swaddle the roofs, and then a quick thaw, and then a freeze again. They hung in tapering clubs at the corner of the house where the slope of the rear portion met the slope of the front. Icicles were a menace, and Doctor said to knock them down with a pole; so you knocked them down, and it was sport. But the tiniest stilettos of all, the baby daggers on the summer kitchen eave—these you did not set to falling and crashing. These you broke off and carried in your red mitten until the hairs of yarn grew crimson against the icicles, and you sucked the icicles as you walked; they tasted crisp and of winter.

It was a fresh apple, this water, a harvest apple eaten before it was quite ripe, but still a softer apple than the one Katty had hidden in your lunch bucket. It was feast and comfort for a good elderly dog named Ben. Here, old fellow, you're panting at a great rate—and you're so warm in that heavy coat of yours— Here's the pan. And lap, lap, lap eternally after you had set the pan of clear water before him; lap, lap, lap, lap with a long tongue as pink as boiled meat; and the gratitude he offered when he came to sink his muzzle upon your knee. . . .

O wild grapes with their tan, O inner bark of slippery elm, O tang and tendril of sorrel growing crisp: these tastes were there. High on a shaded hillside in Beverly's Timber the winding gully cut its course, and there stood an elm in serenity—not a slippery elm, but one of another kind—with a great bared root outthrust, and the root had grown bark upon it like the trunk of the tree. Scored deeply across this mighty root, a little stream came down. Sometimes it dried to nothingness in late summer when no rains fell, but usually it was there, in winter it might be frozen, usually it was there, a baby waterfall across the root, a fall three inches wide and perhaps a foot long in the falling. It had built the dark depression by its own persistence over the bulk of that elm root, and when you were small you could lie at length beside the resulting pool and put your face beneath the hollowed root and let the waterfall wash your face and drown your mouth. Even slim Willie had grown too tall, by the time he was thirteen, to fit into the gully and force his face under the vertical pouring, but he remembered the wet clear drowning. So he remembered it this night.

As Willie Mann remembered, a thousand other men remembered beneficent drinks they had had; but not all of them were capable of entertaining the poetry Willie entertained; very few were capable of entertaining it. Something said in their souls, Water has come, it's here, it has burst from the hill, look out for that deadline, and when they'd scrambled and fought to absorb their share and more than their share, there might have been the briefest flash of recollection: a horse-trough in which a youth bathed his hot head, the welcome bitterness of cool beer in a riverside saloon, a natural flowing well where sulphur and other ingredients formed corded flowers and patterns beneath the foam, a lonely cave where stalactites dripped.

But it was Willie's water, he called it his own, he was the first prisoner to detect and taste it. For a time he lay recumbent beneath the scuffle, alternately sucking through the short tube he made of his lips, or plowing his entire face into the current. Then, as the rush and crush and fight developed to a point of actual danger—as men wailed and swore and caught weaker men by the arms or legs and dragged them away, bound to usurp their places— Willie had been kicked enough. He staggered off to a safe distance with water splashing inside him as if he carried a tin pail within his tight-drawn skin. He lay down and belched; a small portion of the water arose with belching and trickled from the corners of his mouth . . . but he had Gone Without, he had Gone Without for a very long time, and now he had drunk his rich reward and soon would drink again.

The riot continued. Lightning snapped at gradually decreasing intervals, but the flashes were quaking longer as the storm moved on. Wide-spread electricity revealed every filament of the scene with clear exactness: there was the stockade towering with the nearest sentry shack cut sharp on an impressive green-lilac sky —you could even see the shakes of the sentry-shack roof which had curled like leaves in a summer sun—you could see the guard and count his whiskers and see him spit. Then blackness ruled, hurting the eyes; groans and yells and admiration of the miracle continued; then another extensive glaring quivering, and closer at hand you witnessed the tufted heads, the bald heads, the tangle of ragged shapes bending, squirming, elbowing, beating about, making a herding as beasts should never herd—bound to drink, bound to drink the good water for which Providence exacted not one red cent; and no one else could put a price upon it, for it issued from beyond the deadline.

Wirz was gone, Wirz was sick abed. But the next day Lieutenant Davis looked down from the parapet and ordered a sluice to be built, conducting the flow past the deadline into camp. Make it long enough, he ordered. I don't want that gang busting them posts and scantlings down. Davis knew that if there was too much shooting by the guards at this particular point there would be some sort of investigation; Davis hated investigations chiefly because of the paper work entailed. It was no skin off his behind: there were plenty of springs outside the stockade to supply the Confederates amply, and so no need to conduct the new little stream in a westerly direction, through the fence itself. Davis would never have spent the effort or the attention necessary to drill a deep well for the prisoners; but since the storm had dug one the prisoners could have the use of it. Furthermore, there would now be less incentive for people to sink deep wells; thus opportunities for tunneling would be decreased.

A. R. Hill and his police brought about a form of discipline that day; the discipline continued tolerably. At any hour you could look that way and see two extensive lines of prisoners shambling along, moving by degrees toward the sluice and filling their cups, their cans, their broken canteens, their leaky kettles. Some who owned no such equipment merely stood in line, waiting for the treat of drinking from their dirty hands; and then they returned to the end of the line and gradually progressed springwards again for another drink; it was something to do.

Providence Spring, they called it universally. Many were the sermons recited by worshipping lay parsons who spoke their pieces throughout the stockade whenever and wherever a congregation might be assembled. They ascribed the phenomenon to direct interference by Celestial engineers, and more than one man swore that he had seen angels at the spot. Only the most hard-bitten heretics stood on the outskirts, heckling and desiring to know why God hadn't acted sooner, before their comrades died from drinking the maggoty reek of the marsh. By and large the flow was accepted as evidence that the One Above had not forgotten the stockade and the people in it, no matter how many generals and exchange commissioners had chosen apparently to forget.

Willie Mann read his soiled Bible with new energy, and was very near to becoming one of those same lay preachers. But he did not sermonize, he only read aloud from the Book to any friends who would listen. He thrilled at each reference to springs or brooks or just plain water which he might find, and he found them in the Psalms, but of course the seventeenth chapter of Exodus was his favorite text at the time, along with Numbers, Twenty. Sometimes Revelations. A mean scarecrow sauntered past and halted to jibe at him. Willie glowered in a rush of returning strength. It seemed that his bones jangled together when he moved, that his young muscles had shriveled from ropes to threads; but he rushed upon the profane scoffing heathen and hurled him flat in the mud. His congregation cheered him derisively. Willie went on reading aloud.

They shall hunger no more, neither thirst any more; neither shall the sun light on them, nor any heat.

For the Lamb which is in the midst of the throne shall feed them, and shall lead them unto living fountains of waters; and God shall wipe away all tears from their eyes.

More sharply, more eagerly distinct than in weeks, Katty moved through the Biblical incidents which came to his attention in reading. She wore Hebraic robes and trod the wilderness. Willie regarded Providence Spring as a portent . . . had he suffered doubts before, had he doubted when he watched Titus Cherry die? Now he knew. He would return to Missouri, he would walk once more in the timber, he would wed Katty, they would have flocks of children. They would have a deep well, clear and pure; and on August days the children would petition him for cool drinks, and so as soon as they were big enough he would train them to operate the well-sweep or maybe the windlass—he didn't know just what sort of machinery he would have. But he heard the water trickling . . . it was there for him to drink, for all men to drink.

Guards talked about it outside, and so Ira Claffey came to hear of the spring. He listened with wonder, he heard his sons chatting and drinking there, he heard the voice of small Lucy, heard his own voice. . . . Here, child, I'll make a cup of my hand. Beneath this rock, so. Now you bend down—take care, don't wet your boots and skirts— That's the way.

42

Cato Dillard searched his conscience and found himself remiss. In the first years of the war he had made a kind of game out of discovering Biblical support for the Secessionist cause. When Prophets discussed people of the North he knew of course that they referred to historic or fabled Hebraic wars. The Prophets were not cognizant of Abolitionists, or of greasy mechanics from urban New York and Pennsylvania who must now be considered as supporting the Republicans and Abolitionists, no matter how much they might differ in private theory. Cato Dillard was far too intelligent to believe so.

But still it was a game and titillating; it taxed his powers of research and application. Always he shone before a challenge.

Effie Dillard labeled the Southern cause as Right, and the Northern cause as Wrong. She prayed nightly that Lincoln would be packed out of his White House, and that Washington City, New York City, Philadelphia and Chicago might know the triumphant tread of gray columns. She let it go at that, she was too busy in the application of her flouncing ardent Christianity to waste hours in poking after a reassuring Text.

Both the old people suffered anguish as their grandsons were destroyed (five were gone by this August of 1864—and all in the past eight months: two dead of disease, two of wounds, one killed in a Hood's cavalry skirmish) and then they found comfort in the stout draught of Faith. They believed that a general family pic-nic of Dillards and their descendants would ensue during that sunny afternoon following Resurrection Morn.

In early months Cato had thought of conflict within Andersonville just as he'd typified it in speech: brawling. His witnessing of the raiders' execution, and subsequent examination of the motives involved, shattered this opinion. The men had died attended by an officer of the Catholic church; they were Catholics; surely the priest would have refused his services in the mere conclusion of a brawl. Ira assured the Reverend Mr. Dillard that those hanged had been sentenced by a Yankee court, defended by Yankee lawyers, prosecuted by Yankee lawyers or men serving as such. So Redeemed Yankees had sentenced Unredeemed Yankees to the worst penalty on earth . . . naturally there were worse penalties in the Hereafter . . . it was disquieting to think that, by law of averages, there must be many elect Presbyterians milling within the stockade . . . religionists conducted services, Cato himself had heard their songs arise.

He besought the Scriptures again to relieve his confusion.

Now, thou son of man, wilt thou judge, wilt thou judge the bloody city? . . . Cato read Ezekiel, on through all the talk of whoredoms and abominations which never ceased to offend him; because he was pure, had remained pure through his life, taught purity to his children, trusted in turn that they had passed this limpid inheritance on to the next generation. *And Aholah played the harlot . . . and she doted on her lovers, on the Assyrians her neighbors . . . which were clothed with blue, captains and rulers, all of them desirable young men, horsemen riding upon horses.* Yankee cavalry, beyond a doubt.

Mr. Dillard sighed, thudded his Bible shut, opened it again on the Gospels instead of the Prophets. Always he had imagined St. Mark as owning a voice firm but gentle, and especially gentle as he recounted the exploits and recited the words of the Gentlest Man. Cato Dillard's own father had possessed such a voice, such a spirit.

> *. . . So is the kingdom of God, as if a man should cast seed*
> *into the ground;*
> * And should sleep, and rise night and day, and the seed*
> *should spring and grow up, he knoweth not how.*

Cato Dillard lifted his gaze from the fine-lettered page, and snuffed his candle, and sat pillowed up in darkness beside his slumbering wife. He looked across sharp patches of moonlight on the old carpet, and through the window into moonlight washing warmly his own garden.

> *For the earth bringeth forth fruit of herself; first the blade,*
> *then the ear, after that the full corn in the ear.*

This is a desert place, came the words of that later Chapter, *and now the time is far passed.* Andersonville? It could be, could be. *They have nothing to eat.* And what had the Master said to that? *He answered and said unto them, Give ye them to eat.*

Effie, said Cato in the dawn, what of our green corn?

Yon patch is past roasting, dry in the husk. We've a bit left in rows past the woodshed.

Where might we get green corn in any quantity, roasting ears still soft and green?

Effie ceased her tinkling into the slop-jar, slid the cover into place (the knitted cap over the pottery cover prevented any clanking, there was only the dull *koom* of the jar's closing) and adjusted her skirts carefully before she stepped from behind a little screen of woven bull-grass which modesty dictated should be placed in its three unsteady sections to shield the commode.

From Brother Ira Claffey, man! He plants long, he plants late as well as early; his maize will no be dried to crispness yet—not all, to be sure. But what want you with green corn?

Roasting ears, said Cato. He slid his spotted old legs out of bed and removed his nightcap.

For whom?

Yankee prisoners.

Cate, you're daft.

He replied with that geniality coming easily to those who feel that they have arrived at righteous decision, Were I daft as often you've described me to be, woman, I'd have populated a dozen crazy-houses e'er now.

But what want yon Yankees with green corn?

They'd wish to eat it, don't you believe?

But— Cate— Would it be fair to our own grandchildren? Our brave boys in the field—?

Have you never become acquainted with the Sixth Chapter of the Gospel According To St. Mark?

Away with you. Those were—Disciples—

Five thousand Disciples? he asked archly.

Twas a congregation of The Just.

He mused pleasantly as he pulled on his stockings. Not only corn in roasting. But also root vegetables: we've turnips in plenty, carrots, beets—

Yon cabbages are rising into seed and waste, cried Effie in spite of herself.

Enthusiastically Cato wrote to Ira Claffey, telling him of his plan and inviting Ira's assistance and generosity. The minister had not been informed of Lucy's little march with wenches and baskets, and her inability to reach the stockade. He thought, as many well-intentioned people have often thought, that he had conceived of a particularly glossy charity—a bounteous impulse instigated by God, no doubt, but still a personal mercy. He wrote: *If a brother or sister be naked, and destitute of daily food*— The General Epistle of James eludes me for the moment, Brother Ira. Puss is asleep upon my Bible, and I shall not disturb her, since she may be dropping kits before nightfall. Last time she had them in the drawer containing my *drawers* and stockings! But what think you of the proposal? Neighbor Stancil has promised the lend of his big wagon, with a four-mule team; and he a Methodist! The Dennards, Lindsays and Nunns all express themselves as willing to give; and I should think a few bushels might also be got from the Lockridges and others, perhaps more than a mere few bushels; they might donate plenteously. Have you green corn enough and to spare? What of your cabbages and the general collard situation? I have set Buff to pulling turnips that they may be scrubbed. A further suggestion comes from Mrs. McCrary: her own dear child languished last year on an isle at the North, without sufficient coverings for his poor body; and she has sat with me, and we have explored God's opinion, or have attempted. Since the lad is now among The Blest (but they did have shelter; he died in a barracks, twas said) the lady has possessed an overpowering intent to find favor Aloft by exhibiting true Christian mercy to his enemies. She is assembling his entire stock of shirts, jackets, pantaloons and the like, to be offered to destitute Northrons. As we have observed, there is prevailing raggedness at Anderson, in some cases amounting to nakedness and resulting indecency. Poor as we have become in this struggle for Independence, and to repel invading hordes, I should think a goodly supply of serviceable clothing might be gotten together if each gave his mite. I myself am contributing boots—which pinch me, I admit, but might not pinch some shoe-less Yankee. *But the wisdom that is from above is first pure, then peaceable, gentle, and easy to be intreated, full of mercy and good fruits, without partiality, and without hypocrisy.* Mrs. Dillard goes flying about, attempting to collect medicines; and such a small stock can be assembled; and she dare not rob her own closet too grievously, since her attention is demanded by many ailing persons now and again. But boots, potions, turnips, green corn, undershirts or melons: all seem of value, all I should believe would be received thankfully by the lads there, misguided into cruelty though they have been. Now, dear Brother, what of the military who are in command? Will they see fit to admit of our charity? I grow alarmed at considering what has come to me of the superintendent and the general commanding: both obstreperously and insistently profane, tis said. I have not heard that either is addicted to The Bottle, but that they take a particular delight in cursing; and also this is reported of the troops under them. However, I should think that if we were to seek *not permission in advance,* but were to appear bag and baggage and basket, they would be bound to accept our small offering for the unfortunates *perforce.* Since many of the items are spoilable. Ah, also: Mr. Marshall has promised a pig. Though I had to fling Testament at him for an hour to get it! The pig must be butchered promptly before our departure. One cannot speculate as to the weather; but I should hazard an opinion that, all things being equal, and you receiving no advices to the contrary, our little caravan might arrive by Friday midday. If not on Friday, look to see us on Saturday. Mrs. Dillard is bound to come on for the distribution, and shall be accompanied by a few other ladies, I make little doubt. Do not feel that you must *feed* them, Brother, or the rest of us; but we shall pay our respects, and hope to gather up your own donation. Word has reached us of the miraculous spring bursting forth there. Could it be the same spring where you were wont to wander, and where we have sat many times; and where I told you of the Highland Presbyterians at Darien; and where in turn you told me of the so-called Dorchester Puritans, your own kinfolk in Liberty County, of more than a century since? *Behold, I will stand before thee there upon the rock in Horeb; and thou shalt smite the rock, and there shall come water out of it, that the people may drink.* Puss is still upon the Bible, but I need no reference. As a mere child I was enamored of Exodus, and all the dramatic events therein, and the building of the tabernacle, and what was a cubit? Theology should be awarded early to a youth, that he remember; but often I was naughty and put aside my Catechism, and loved to watch the Hebrews at their fights. Ah, me. My pen has been trailing about; but should that not be the privilege of an old man's pen? I wish it were yam time. Then we might assemble a quantity. Perhaps we can perform further philanthropy in the autumn. I have neglected to tell you that Neighbor Pace (Baptist) is giving carrots; and little Neddy Hinchley has just made an errand to inform me that his mother will contribute what fruit is left to her in all this hotness. Sakes, as your Lucy would say, what a scorcher is today! Heaven be praised that our dear Sister Veronica is no longer called upon to endure Earthly miseries; but sleeps, knowing no misfortune, and in fully justified hope, I am convinced, of a Glorious Resurrection. I pray for you daily, Brother, and please to include me in your prayers. Until the oncoming of our charitable migration, then. In Brotherly Faith & Hope, Yrs, C. Dillard.

Post Script. Will wonders never cease? I must have been inspired, truly, in getting my plot a-going. This missive was folded, I was seeking for wax to seal it, when appeared Mrs. Banister from across the way. You know her: an Episcopalian. She'd come for a Seidlitz powder, if Mrs. Dillard possessed any. (She did not.) Am informed by Mrs. Banister that General J. Winder is a *Communicant.* Their church here in Americus is new in organization; and the rector observed that he had seen General Winder, when in Richmond, partaking of the Holy Eucharist. They have been busy recently selecting their vestrymen and church wardens; and *Gen. Winder was named to be a warden.* Now certainly we have nothing to fear. A church warden could never refuse us permission. The tales borne to me of his profane utterances must have been made up out of whole cloth. Or were in error, since both names begin with a W; and only the Switzer must have been the sinner. C.P.D.

This letter was carried to Anderson on the cars next morning, and lay for three days in an old salt box at Uncle Arch Yeoman's, where mail intended for citizens of the community was left until neighbors or slaves distributed it. Jonas brought the letter in to Ira while the Claffeys were at breakfast with Harrell Elkins. The project was discussed with animation. Cousin Harry, so often gone into taciturnity these days and so often oblivious of them both, sat with spectacles shining . . . Lucy had the sly thought that the glass lenses were burnished by inner blaze stoked by brain and heart. Oh, and how he does need a joy, she thought. Would that I might afford it for him! He sees hospital, thinks hospital, will recognize nothing but hospital and wrongs contained there.

Cousin Harry talked constantly, with spirit; he'd interrupted Ira's reading several times with approving comments, with further suggestions. Now that the letter was put next to Ira's plate, Elkins discoursed on vinegar.

They appear to have forgotten it. Few other adjuncts to the diet could be more efficacious in treatment of scurvy. If you could get word to those Americus folks, they might fetch some barrels of it.

Our own supply is limited, said Lucy.

Elkins stared at her, watery eyes flicking rapidly in magnification. Surely you're mistaken, Cousin Lucy. You have that great cask on the roofed gallery beside your kitchen—

But it diminishes so rapidly.

However could we use much vinegar? asked her father. Solely for salads, and a trifle for spicing. Daughter, have you been making pickles in quantity?

Not I, not in this heat. And most of your gherkins were burnt by the sun, Poppy. But still there's less and less vinegar each day.

Have some of the black people developed a thirst?

I've detected no such addiction, said Lucy. She was replying directly to her father, but looking directly at Harrell, who sat with smooth face reddened and who made a great business of picking a muffin to pieces.

Lucy lifted her voice slightly, meaningly. It is as if some person came by day or night with a flask, opened the bung, and drew off vinegar.

For a moment the implied accusation and the expression of guilt held Ira perplexed, and he regarded the younger pair with amazement. Then, as the surgeon put his big hand to his forehead and concealed his face, Ira began to chuckle. Merriment spread among the three; Lucy collapsed in giggles; Elkins's shoulders were shaking, though it seemed that he might have been moved by sobs as well as by mirth; in fact he was close to sobbing.

Have you the tell-tale bottle about you? asked the girl.

Still refusing to face her, Elkins put his other hand down into his pocket and brought the flask forth. His voice shook as he confessed. A very small bottle, you see. A mere brandy flask.

Ring for more coffee, my dear, said Ira. Then, to Harry: Did you think we'd refuse you, Cousin?

Elkins removed his spectacles, wiped his eyes (He is almost comely, thought Lucy, without those great glaring things. I wish that I could see him more often thus) and managed to compose himself for confession. It was only— The first time the thought occurred to me— You see, none of you were about. I observed Naomi at the keg, filling a cruet, so of course I knew that it contained vinegar— I didn't wish to trouble anyone.

Have your depredations been confined solely to vinegar? asked Ira.

Elkins stared owlishly. Why do you ask that, sir?

Now that I'm put in mind of it, Jem complained that something had been at the cauliflowers.

But you have an over-supply of garden truck.

Not of cauliflowers. We're far from the seacoast, and enough salt's not to be had for preparing the beds. Just how have you been conveying cauliflowers to the hospital, Cousin Harry?

I put them in my pockets. And in corners of my medical kit.

What—whole cauliflowers?

You do appear right bulgy at times, said Lucy.

Not whole cauliflowers. I separate the small flowers, the segments—You see, sir, and Cousin Lucy— I've had no wish to run afoul of guards or of the Chief Surgeon. My small benevolence—the result of petty thievery—might not meet with his approbation.

Naomi had appeared with a steaming pot of grain coffee, to fill their cups, and had been interested and amazed. Miss Lucy, that Mastah Harry, he always asking me for bones.

Just leftovers, said Elkins weakly.

And he make me save potato parings.

Ira shook his head. But we've so many other things. Much has gone to waste, all through the summer.

I—I had no wish to bother you. And I feared to tote a basket. Twould have aroused suspicion, perhaps resentment.

He sipped the last of his coffee with rapid swallowing, he said that he must be up and away. He pushed back his chair, arose and spoke a thanks for the meal, bowed, and went into the hallway where his kit lay upon a chair. He cried a last goodbye through the open door and turned toward the outside gallery. He was halfway down the steps when the light tap of shoes sounded behind him, and he turned quickly. Lucy walked upon the gallery, she was coming toward him. The young man stood motionless, it was almost as if he knew what to expect; he saw her intent, and stood graven; he wished solemnly, he wished in his entire being to share with her; yet he felt wearily that the wrongs of the world and of this particular day and this particular portion of the world were overwhelming them; he dared yield to nothing but the demand of a task he had set for himself.

Lucy spoke two words— Dear Harry, she said. She bent forward and flung her arms around his neck and kissed him long on the mouth.

Do you mean love? he asked, when their faces were apart.

Twas for your great heart, Harry. I understand so well why Sutherland loved you.

But do you mean love? For a critter like me?

I don't know what I mean, she said softly. I but wished to—award you— Perhaps a kiss from me is nothing—

Elkins pushed her from him rudely. No, no, he mumbled (and it was odd, but she thought of a squirrel; he reminded her of a squirrel, a great baldish squirrel a-muttering). He said, I can't bear it. We can't— Not in this! There's so much filth and screaming. You should hear the gangrenous! No, no, you should not, I couldn't bear for you to hear them—

But I do, Coz.

You do? Where? Here?

All the way up here, she said with stoicism. I hear them screaming. My ears are keen.

May God damn the people who brought on this war. Elkins spoke in a whisper. He went away down the lane toward the first rifle pits, satchel swinging back and forth in accompaniment to his lunging pace. Lucy stood watching, and then tears washed him from her vision.

At the breakfast table Ira sat with a shred of bacon suspended on his fork, sat motionless and musing, unaware of the tenderness and hurt of this contact on the gallery. He was scarcely aware that Lucy had left the room. He considered his old friend the Reverend Mr. Dillard, and how native sweetness had transcended dry dictates put forth in the Directory for Worship. Very clearly did Ira recall an adjuration to the sick—was it in Chapter Twelve? Thirty-five years earlier Ira Claffey had hoped to become a minister, he had studied with diligence; but eventually saw himself standing before a frosty barrier over which he had no wish to scramble. What would a Presbyterian minister say to the wretched of Andersonville if he felt himself bound by the Directory? *He shall instruct the sick out of the Scriptures, that diseases arise not out of the ground, nor do they come by chance; but that they are directed and sent by a wise and holy God, either for correction of sin, for the trial of grace, for improvement in religion, or for other important ends. . . .* What wise and holy God had constucted the stockade? Was his name Winder? What sin had been performed by the Northerners? The sin of being Northern? Moses Claffey was born in 1845. . . . Let us select a Moses from Indiana or Vermont. He did not die at Crampton's Gap; at the age of eighteen or nineteen he finds himself in Andersonville, he lies in the hospital and is tended by Cousin Harry; or perhaps he is less fortunate, he is tended by a contract surgeon. Did not the disease of the Northern Moses rise from a putrid kennel in which he was compelled to crouch? Did it not come from the chance which fetched him into captivity in the first place? Oh, wise and holy God, I bless thee for correcting the sin of this Yankee youngun! I beseech thee to award him an additional and increasing trial of grace. Pray to improve his religion; he whimpers and gapes because you have removed his teeth, puffed his gums, fattened his tongue, put the poison in his belly and his blood. . . . And final admonition to you, you cringing Federal Moses: See that you do not despise God's chastening hand, see that you do not faint under God's rebukes! . . .

Lucy had gone to cool her face. Now she returned to the room, she came in slowly. Ira did not even look at her; he was lost in disgust at the prim and calloused, lost in admiration of a man who could rise above what fusty pettiness he'd been taught.

Your elderly Uncle Cato Dillard, said Ira. He's a man.

Yes, Poppy.

Daughter, I swear it: with each review of certain pages—in recollection, naturally—I approach agnosticism.

Yes, Poppy.

And he had thought to find her shocked. His eyes came up under wiry brows now turning whitish, and he saw that some fresh wrong had been visited upon the one great Love remaining to him.

But— Heed me. The thought of Mr. Dillard can expunge a variety of sins, it can draw a rusty nail from a wound—

Yes, Poppy.

Because he is *good,* so good that he is beyond precepts set forth by creaking meddlesome little minds.

Yes. . . .

My dear, about the vinegar. Did you catch Harry *in flagrante delicto?*

Her wan voice . . . Twas in the dawn. I looked from my room and saw him. Lucy's laughter rattled mechanically. There he was, crouched down, making a most serious business of filling his flask.

Then immediately we should go into the business of manufacturing it! Possibly Coz can fathom a method for smuggling it by the quart; he's a gentleman of resource. Have we another full barrel at hand?

In the pantry shed.

Then instruct Naomi to tap the fresh barrel, and we shall use the other for mothering. Have the wenches roll two casks beneath the roof—sugar casks would do nicely—and use a proportion of one gallon of sorghum to, say, eleven gallons of clear rainwater. Portion the current vinegar, remaining in what we should now call Coz's keg, into the other barrels, to supply the mother. Within the month, if the stuff keeps working and doesn't die, we should have fresh vinegar in quantity.

Ira considered, and then added a question. Have we any gauze or other coarse woven material, fly-proof, among the household supplies?

Not an inch. All used up, long since.

Then take it from the windows of an empty room.

Nnnone there, and he looked up in anguish to see her crying. Lucy made a strong successful effort to control her voice. I took down the last, months ago. I even took the material from the windows of Mother's room after—she— To make repairs. The only chambers with anything resembling a mosquito-bar are your room, mine and—Cousin Harry's.

Ira thought in annoyance that if the young people were married the gauze might be taken from one room or the other. He felt a rising impatience with Harrell Elkins. Then take it from my room. We must have it washed and dried with care, to cover the open barrels, to keep out flies. As our good Dr. Chase says, vinegar is an industrious fellow but he does need air in sufficiency.

I shall take it from my own windows, said Lucy stubbornly.

Damn it, you shan't, cried Ira in full testiness. He was appalled, he had not been driven to such expression of wrath with Lucy since she was fourteen, and sulked because he would not buy her a phaeton. He got up, stamped to his room, pulled down the cloth from both windows. By this time he was enraged with himself because he had become enraged. Below stairs he heard Lucy ordering the black women about, and soon came the rumpus of barrels being brought to the kitchen gallery. Ira descended grumpily, gave over the gauze to Extra for washing, and mumbled an apology to an ashen daughter who ignored him; he could not blame her for ignoring him. Ira was especially patient with the hands that day, fearing that his unsettled condition might cause him to display an additional sharpness to creatures wholly in his power. He still remembered, after forty years, his fright and disgust at witnessing a neighbor abuse an old horse solely because he, the neighbor, had achieved low score in a shooting-match.

Ira turned deliberately from contemplation of the stockade and its problems, and from any thought of Lucy and her grief (he did not fathom the exact nature of her grief, but was positive that it concerned Harry). He tried to soothe his spirit by renewed admiration of the generous Mr. Dillard, and this in turn led to his reflecting on Americus and its people. Ira had known the town well in years when business took him there, when his plantation was itself a business and not a region of weeds surrounding an orchard, a cornfield and a few garden-patches from which a living might be eked out for a handful of whites and blacks. When Cato wrote of Nunns, Dennards, McCrarys and the like, he was fanning a memory.

Eventually that day Ira Claffey worked in a daze. . . . Veronica was young and sane, a lovely morsel to tempt him with her eyes and slimness of her waist and conversation of her skirts . . . the children bounded noisily; they had to be hushed, but their eyes were gay and their cheeks ruddy; the surviving children . . . again Suthy broke his arm in falling from a chinaberry tree when he was four; again Badger shot his turkey through the head at one hundred yards at least —oh, lucky shot, and how he swelled about it . . . again Ira had a slave whipped —which one? was it that expensive sullen blacksmith called Caliph?—for beating his wife . . . again he persuaded Veronica to indulge in brandy—the only time; he could never persuade her to touch brandy again—and he seduced her accordingly, and what a seduction: he remembered her frenzy and bleatings; but the next day she was pickled in remorse perhaps because she had been pickled in brandy, more likely because of what she'd done in bed; twas often so; no wonder that the first thing she put aside, as she went into lunacy, was lust . . . again, in somber and quieter illusion, he chipped the stones for his babies' graves, so little time elapsing between the making of those small slabs. . . .

Thus he returned in thought to Americus. At least a portion of its inhabitants were not uncomprehending, unaware of that grotesque pen yonder and the pathetic bounty being assembled for its occupants . . . Dennards, McCrarys, Lindsays: there were many on the hill. The hill was shaded by oaks and cedars, and the monument of young Mr. Hudson, with its fine urn atop, was easily the handsomest. *In Memory of Leander M. Hudson. Born Feb. 22nd 1823. Died Nov. 21st 1851. A native Georgian and a resident of the town of Oglethorpe. He breathed his last among strangers where he now lies. Habitually active and energetic, he sprang to the duties of life, but looked beyond them to the rewards of Heaven.* Well, well, so should we all; and a year ago I would have sworn that I was serene in considering the rewards of Heaven; but what is this shaft sticking out from my breastplate? has an arrow come through? and what is the name upon it? Damnable stockade— you've taken my belief from me—

Oh, not yet, not yet; but the struggle is on—

Jem.

Yas, Mastah.

That end's not braced properly; those small stones will roll in the first freshet. Coffee, come to help. Do the two of you work that stump beneath the cross-piece to support it whilst you remove the stones. . . . Now then, see that boulder over there? Go dig it out, and roll it here to hold the cross-piece. Twill last out a hundred storms.

To the junior members of an orphaned family, he was a noble, generous and devoted brother, and to the suffering poor a prompt, liberal and benevolent benefactor.

Take lesson from the existence of young Mr. Hudson, and let us at once be prompt, liberal and benevolent. Indeed we are so. This bridge has been unsteady since the great rain of a week or two ago, and only carts could cross it safely. That wagon of Mr. Stancil's would have gone through it like a hog through a cucumber frame. And tomorrow is Friday, and if the fair weather holds, the wagon will come creaking this way with its freight of kindliness; and we must haste, haste to assemble the baskets of our own contribution. Turn out, all hands, to feed the guests; there are grown to be some thirty-two thousand of them. How many might Mr. Stancil's wagon feed?

Ira stood, overseeing the Negroes as they toiled in the gush and mud of Little

Sweetwater; he stood muddied, and nursing one finger which had been squeezed between logs of the bridge; he stood stricken out of all reverie by recognition of the futility of this enterprise. Let the loaves remain in the baskets, tell the little boy to run away home with his fishes. Cato Dillard, you wear no beard, you were not born in Bethlehem, there is no Aura about you. . . . But, stay. Tis a gesture, but not idle. If a single Yankee Moses is kept from starvation, the deed is worth the doing.

Returned to the plantation, he gave the hands a brief recess and urged them to put on dry things. Still wishing to avoid Lucy, he went to the burying ground and sat for a while beside the freshest grave. Several weeks had passed . . . he did not like to think of what was happening to the body packed in that homemade coffin; yet more dreadful was the recalling of what had happened to the mind and body when they were extant. The war killed her, Ira thought, as surely as if a Union sharpshooter squeezed his trigger.

And she was far out of his life before she died; so that was tragedy piled upon tragedy. He wondered if ever he would marry again, he wondered even if he would lie with a woman, ever again. He thought of Mrs. Lou Ella Mickley, often he thought of her. When Ira was much younger he had served two terms in the Legislature, but refused to run for a third term. He refused also to be a candidate for Congress; he'd found that honestly he loathed the trading, back-biting and double-dealing upon which many politicians thrived. It was during his freshman season at Milledgeville that he met Mrs. Mickley at a dinner. She had been widowed at twenty-one, and was a woman of means—chubby, brown-eyed, curly of hair—who kept no maiden aunt or other relative dwelling in chaperonage, and was completely oblivious to gossip which shafted around her until even the gossipers wearied of it, and selected other targets. Soon she and Ira became lovers. His relations with Veronica were unfavorable during much of that period, for he found himself aggravated by Veronica's selfishness and indrawn, Arwoodish ways. Not yet had he adjusted himself to the fact that she lacked certain virtues which in blindness and early passion he had awarded her. Never was there the delighted madness in his coming together with Lou Ella Mickley which ruled him when he was with his wife; yet they had their raptures, he profited from her serenity, they built pleasant childish humors between them, he thought her sage and valuable in most opinion about State and National affairs. The inevitable quarrel occurred when Ira announced that he would not run for a third term. She asked him why; he said honestly and artlessly that he did not wish to spend so much time away from his family. Family, family, family—you think nothing of *me,* care nothing for me—who am *I? I'm* a Nobody—I have cast aside all thought of womanly reputation because of *you*— She became the complete picture of the Other Woman Who Loves the Married Man, through all ages, nationalities, codes. . . . It seemed that the bruising of her reputation was less than fatal to Lou Ella Mickley. Within two years she married a vigorous bachelor senator, a rice-grower from the tidewater region; his name was Febresen, and he went off in 1862 to command a brigade. Promptly he was shot dead at Second Manassas. Ira had seen the lovely Widow Febresen just once since then; it was in the spring of 1863, when last he was in Milledgeville. He stopped at a crossing to let a carriage pass; he was looking, not at the lady who drove, but at the rubbery little groom in patched livery, sitting pompously up behind; and then the carriage slowed, he heard his name spoken. Ira, was all she said. Her hair was almost white—prematurely so, for she could not be much past forty. The bright brown eyes shone at him, then filled with tears. Ira had removed his hat, he was bowing, he moved toward the vehicle; then she had spoken to her horse and was driving rapidly away. She left an impression of daintiness and vivacity, as always. She left a memory, but it was not enough for him, probably not enough for her. He tried to envision Lou Ella as living here with him at the plantation, war or no war. He could not see her so.

. . . What if the malignant miracle should occur, and Sherman should take Atlanta? Any disaster might follow; blue columns might sweep even to Milledgeville. Possibly I'd best persuade Lucy to invite the widowed Mrs. Febresen to come to us, here and now. . . .

Wretched fellow! Sitting by your wife's grave, her frail unhappy mortality gone so recently into seclusion— Gad, man, what ails you?

Tis that monstrosity past the lane and fort and pits and barricades. It unsettles us all, unsteadies the world.

Now he resolved to make some sort of explanation to Lucy for his churlishness of the morning, perhaps to comfort her by finding the specific source of complaint, by offering a balm—he did not know what unguent it would be. Ira set the men to searching corn-rows for those ears which were still in the milk. He hunted through the house for Lucy, and found her at last below the front gallery. Little Gracious, the five-year-old daughter of Jonas and Extra, was propped against a pillar. The child's brown foot extended over the porch's edge; there was a basin in which the foot had been washed. Lucy stood in the lily bed, holding Gracious's tiny ankle in one hand while probing with a needle. The child made not a sound though her cheeks were varnished with tears.

She has picked up a sliver, said Lucy.

Shall I aid you?

I've most of it out, now. Gracious is being a soldier, and naturally soldiers do not shriek or squirm. And she is to receive a pink ribbon for her hair.

The last of the splinter was drawn out, the wound anointed with salve; Gracious had her pink ribbon, and went hopping off to parade it before her mother. Dear Lucy, said Ira gently. The girl looked up at him, then turned away blinded. Ira slumped on the step, and opened his arms. Lucy fell against him and sobbed for a time, she made inarticulate sounds in weeping, as if she were trying to tell a lonely story and could not.

You'll get no pink ribbon from me, Florence Nightmare.

Gggive it to little Gggracious, she gasped in the hysteria of laughter accompanying her wail.

No, to the Widow Tebbs!

. . . She could laugh more authentically at last, and sat away from her father. He offered his handkerchief, she mopped her flushed face with it, he suggested that she blow her nose, she blew her nose loudly. Her fine-spun hair was straggling. Ira brought a square mirror from the hall, that she might see to bind her hair properly again. They sat together on the gallery stair with the Andersonville smell intense, the Andersonville hum rising like the buzz of a rookery.

Twas here, Poppy.

Here?

On these steps, after he'd breakfasted. Just as he was leaving. I followed him here, I kissed him, I was the aggressor.

And—he—?

She said that her life was become a forlorn trial. She had not expected it to be such a trial, once her mother was relieved from the confusion which ruled her and ruled them all.

Is it right to wish people dead, Lucy asked. Is it ever right? For I wished her dead, I did, I did.

Good God, girl, so did I.

And I'd thought there would be some— Some peace in existence, some comfort for us, even in this ghastly war and with this ghastly pen— But no, no; twas worse than ever. He returned here, he shouldn't have returned. He says nothing at all. He comes home with that hospital stench hanging about him, he sleeps so long and with such exhaustion. He's thinner by far. His jacket fell open this morning; I saw the holes in his old belt, where the tongue of the buckle went through. There was the deep crease in the—the shabby leather, where he used to wear his buckle. I could see it, that little old crease. And now he wears it two holes farther along. And he wasn't plump to begin with, Poppy, truly I've never seen him plump. And such little bits of food he eats. Grief! And his abstraction is so intense—it's as if he were off in Macon or some such place. But I know where he dwells in his fancy, and always. It's over there. Oh, Poppy! No longer do we play our game—not even when Harry is supposed to be taking his ease. Ease? Grief, he knows not the word! One night we sat here on the gallery, and you were abed; you said you wished to read, but I know your notion was to leave us alone, and I— I did appreciate it, darling Poppy. But he would say nothing, do nothing! I gave a quote or two, to tempt him on. And silence, always silence. I fetched a pitcher of our nectar, and offered it, and he— He said, The folks in the hospital have no nectar. I bristled up and said I knew that well enough—I said they came to fight us, to invade, and this was the fate they found— And that—that Southern boys died at the North, as well— He drank the nectar then, but not as if he liked it. And then Colonel Chandler came, so I trotted off. But in the hall I heard them speaking. And Harry said a few words about, twas scarcely the proper time for romantic chit-chat; that was what he said, I'll never forget it. Romantic chit-chat! And I was only trying to be kind to him, to—to aid him—trying to make him rest his bones and—and his soul. I teased him about the vinegar, Poppy. Was that wrong of me? And then I fled after him, and kissed him; I'd never done such a thing before—not even to poor Rob—though law knows that *he* was forever after me, pursuing, trying to snatch a kiss—

Do you love Cousin Harry as much as you loved Rob, my dear?

Much—much—what is much? How much love is there in the world, how much can a girl give? How would I know? How would any girl know, any woman? Cause I'm a woman, now, Poppy—I was scarcely a woman then. At least—before Rob died. And—and all the boys. But we've had this dreadful thing come upon us, and then— Mother— Sakes, I know I'm speaking mighty disjointedly, scarcely making any sense at all, perhaps making no sense! But this is a different kind of love I feel now, because I'm older, and we've been through *plain hell*—oh, I know I shouldn't mention the Bad Place—just like a man might—Scarcely ladylike! If the folks at the Institute could hear me now!

Ira asked softly, How did Coz behave when you kissed him?

Just stood here like a stick, just like a plain old stick! Then he says, Do you mean love? My goodness, what did he think I meant? Oh, I told him he had such a great heart and—and I could understand why Suthy was fond of him. And then he says something about himself being an old critter, or something. And I said I reckoned my kisses didn't amount to much. And then he gave me a shove, Poppy —he just shunted me away from him. He just as much as told me there could be no love in his life, no love for me, not with that awful stockade and hospital around!

Poppy, she said much more quietly a little later. I don't believe he's right. Do you? Shouldn't love be bigger than—? And embrace more than just—? I mean, whether there were a stockade and a hospital or not? Or even a war. Seems like there've always been wars going on, one place or another. And boys dying in them. But people still managed to love one another.

A time to mourn and a time to dance. . . .

I wonder, Poppy.

You see, Lucy, men don't love as women love, my dear child; and the sooner you get that into your pretty little head, the better. But you never will, because you're a woman. And women go on forever, trying to see— It's like that looking glass in your lap. Women look into the glass and expect to find their own love mirrored; sometimes they delude themselves into thinking that they do see it; but actually they never do, never do. Men aren't capable of giving Woman Love— they can give but Man Love. And tis never enough, Lucy, never enough. Especially in the sensitive.

She muttered, Heavens knows I'm sensitive enough. I'm just a little old sensitive plant.

Forever, Ira told her, people speak of woman's intuition. But men have intuition also; perhaps they may call it by another name. They say that they observe, evaluate, study the evidence, arrive at conclusions—and half the time tis only intuition! And I'm equally as sensitive as you.

He spoke deliberately. Coz was enchanted by you from the very first moment of his arrival.

I can't believe that, Poppy.

Then continue being maidenly!

He kissed her hair and went away. It was better to go now. He had planted a seed, she announced that she rejected it; that meant nothing, the seed was there, it would grow.

The rest of the day Ira continued with preparations. He was proud of his vegetables, he saw that baskets were filled liberally. He found a boy's satisfaction in contemplating how Cato Dillard's eyes would bulge when he saw this store: pungent roots all scrubbed, carrots glowing orange, turnips with purple scalps, rippled wrapping of cabbages, the grainy opulence of fat squashes.

. . . How many people would these feed?

. . . Oh, quite a number.

. . . But, stay, what have we here? What populations stand milling, awaiting invitation to sit down at our table?

Ira took down his atlas and learned that they were planning to invite to feast the entire population of Columbus, Ohio; or the entire population of Kansas City, Missouri; or of Utica, New York; or of Wilmington, Delaware; or (this was closer to home, it jolted him) Savannah, Georgia.

Granted that permission would not be denied, he wondered how the good things might be divided and distributed. Many times Ira had watched the issuing of rations within the pen; he did not know how they were issued at the hospital; he must ask Cousin Harry about that.

He had stood, garbed with pity that stiffened into a coat of horror, and watched wagons entering the stockade, wheels screaming, drawn by miniature mules (they were mules with sores; and those were the same wagons in which he'd seen The Dead carted away).

. . . Wagons had their guards. The guards stood watching at the headquarters of each Detachment as that Detachment's portion was dumped upon the ground: mostly the long hard cards of corn bread, sometimes a portion of old bacon . . . and Ira had seen that bake house: he knew how the mixture was tempered with flies before the slabs were baked. Recently there had been stock peas on occasion, stewed to a mush. Watching through his binoculars, Ira could observe that some masses of the peas appeared half cooked, other masses were burned to blackness. Of course there would be no salt. . . .

So they entered: four-mule teams, a Negro riding on the nigh wheel mule of each team, the complement of four or five guards joining each wagon as it entered.

. . . Third Detachment sergeants?

The sergeants of the three Nineties stepped forward. Here we be.

Third Detachment rations.

Dry goods boxes dumped, the sound of shovels scraping. Food was ladled upon the ground. The wagon rattled on to headquarters of the Fourth Detachment, and left the three squad sergeants dividing seriously.

. . . Three Nineties in each Detachment, three Messes in each Ninety.

A prisoner stood with his back to the apportioned piles. Behind him a shaggy man put out a finger to indicate each pile in turn.

Who gets this?

Second Mess.

Who gets this?

First Mess.

Who gets this?

. . . Already the Third Mess sergeant was claiming the remaining pile.

So it would go in the Messes. One piece of bread about half the size of a brick, for each man—his ration for a day—and sometimes a piece of meat as large as two of his fingers, sometimes a wad of mush or stewed cowpeas such as he could hold in one hand.

Who gets this?

Number Nine.

Who gets this?

Number Fourteen.

Who gets this?

Number Five.

Ah, lucky Thompson! That was the biggest pile. . . .

Hell, he can't eat it, Bruce. Jaws won't work. . . .

Ira arose earlier than usual on Friday. It was a fair day, so he directed that the vegetables be fetched from the shed where they had been locked up to guard against thievery. There was a rough platform of planks in the side yard; Ira decreed that the baskets should be piled there, with room for Mr. Stancil's wagon to back and turn.

The gaunt Harry Elkins came down to observe the arrangement with interest. Harry went to fill his vinegar bottle, he went off to the hospital with pockets stuffed with parsnips and onions. Ira watched him depart. Come what may, he thought, there are a few vegetables which will in fact go down the gullets of the sick.

Ira lived in the high humor of a kindly man doing a kindly deed, and well aware of it. He admitted as much to Lucy when they breakfasted.

Poppy, I've been thinking. What about the chests upstairs?

(No one had touched them since Veronica's death.)

Would it pain you to open them, Daughter?

Everything hurts, she said. But I was so distraught yesterday that the notion didn't occur to me. . . . There's so many things of the boys'. Do you agree with me that it would be Christian in us to offer them?

Ira thought of jackets in which his boys had strolled and hunted, he thought of precious boots left behind them when they went a-soldiering. He considered

Moses's cambric shirts, fluffy rolls of well-darned home-knit stockings. Let us give some, Lucy—not all. In our little neighborhood we're now the sole family who can manage a charity. So many people are impoverished; also we know not what our own needs will be in the future.

He smiled. I may be reduced to wearing Badger's jeans. Although I fear I'd split them apart! And what of Cousin Harry? His old military clothing is worn thin.

Then will you help me to select, Poppy?

After I've parceled work to the hands.

There were delays. A farrowing sow accounted for much of the delay; then it was discovered that Old Leander was sick abed and must be tended. . . . A fence was down: rails stolen by Georgia Reserves or by paroled Yankee prisoners detailed on a wood squad.

It was close to high noon before the clothing chests were closed and shoved to their places again. A sad dreadful illusion of Veronica Claffey was locked inside each chest. Shoes and clothing had scarcely been prepared for distribution, along with the freight of vegetables, when the Americus procession ambled down the lane from the west. It consisted of three vehicles: the Dillards ahead in their gig, followed by a carriage containing three ladies of Americus; also young Dr. Pace, with empty sleeve pinned against his coat. He had been struck by a piece of solid shot in 1862. The Stancil wagon brought up the rear. A cluster of Negro boys were riding and driving and making great festivity out of the whole matter . . . some were singing as they came.

(What would it have been like in the old days? Ira wondered . . . August date, mention of a fair morning in the journal, mention of wind east or northeast. Who would have been confined, expecting her baby? How many hands would have been at the gin? . . . No, no, too early, no one would have been at the gin, they would not have started picking cotton yet; not nearly. But how many would have been pulling fodder, how many hauling leaves for manure, how many would have been out with their ploughs? Oh, let dark voices chant a soft chant . . . let simple recollections invoke the day I gave them a treat, and all unexpected . . . the time we killed a small beef and gave the black folks dinner, all because Badger'd won a race! And also I gave them a little bacon, and some syrup to go with it.)

Cries and compliments arose from the Americus contingent when they saw the outlay of the Claffeys. Cato Dillard beamed, his tufts of white whisker were frothy. *So they did eat,* he declared, *and were filled: and they took up of the broken meat that was left seven baskets.*

I doubt, Ira told him, that there will be any broken meat or loaves or digestibles to be taken up on this occasion.

He asked in a whisper, while slaves were stowing this additional treasure aboard the Stancil wagon, Have you received any news to indicate that your sanguine hope is justified?

The minister's chunky face was a wrinkling smile. We need no further word, Brother Ira! General Winder is a communicant of the church, as I advised you.

We might run into a stumbling block in the shape of subordinates.

Surely he will be able to override them!

Perhaps the general is not here? He goes away at times on other duties, or so I am told.

Twould be no fatal delay! Most of these things will keep, except for the hog; and that we could take to the hospital.

In some fashion Ira felt his own anticipation diminishing in proportion to the

Reverend Mr. Dillard's enthusiasm. Ira thought now that he should have taken the bull by the horns, he should have made judicious inquiries in advance. Well, no help for it: they were committed, they must be off to deliver. Lucy would not accompany them. She should remain at home to oversee a dinner for all.

Ira climbed aboard the wagon and stood in the rear, green corn ears sliding around his legs. The little parade jolted west on the lane once more, but with the wagon ahead. Ira pointed out to the driver: this road intersecting at the right . . . turn back on it, past the next intersection . . . swing left. He thought it wise to aim first for Wirz's headquarters, although gossip had it that the superintendent was absent. Also that road was closest to the stockade's entrance. There might be no need for journeying across the railroad to the Winder house.

Wagon advanced, gig and carriage followed on behind. As they approached the south camps, pickets stepped into the road to halt them. Ira Claffey got down to confer. Senior among these pickets was an elderly sergeant who came often to the Claffey place for garden truck.

Ira sought to bribe him with cabbages.

Mr. Claffey, sir, *you* could pass—no trouble bout that. But I can't let all these other folks through. And this here wagon . . . I got to send for the Officer of the Day. Maybe he'll admit you all past these posts.

The Officer of the Day never arrived. Instead came a chaise driven by a frightened gray-clad youth, and with General Winder's sagging face pressed out of it.

What the God damn hell's happening here?

Again Ira swung down from the big wagon. Sir, he said, there are some ladies in our party. . . .

I don't give a good God damn how many ladies there are! Tell them to go way! What are you people up to?

General Winder, we have here a load of green things, together with some clothing, to be distributed to needy prisoners. This is a contribution from the people of Americus.

Where do you think you're proceeding, and by whose authority?

Cato Dillard came from his gig, the wounded Dr. Pace followed with dignity. General, said Dillard, I have learned that you are warden of the newly-established Episcopal church in Americus.

I'm no such thing!

They named you to be one, sir.

What's that got to do with a wagon load of corn?

Not only corn: we are laden with fresh vegetables—a great variety of them. People have denuded their closets, sir, to furnish some clothing for the sick and ragged.

Winder climbed out of the chaise, grunting with the effort. He stood with folded arms, scowling first at the trio before him, then at slaves who watched white-eyed on their wagon perches. He stepped to the edge of the narrow road, and glared at the women in vehicles behind. He turned back.

You mean to tell me that you people are fetching these things to the prisoners? Not to the Confederate guards?

Cato told him, I have observed that the prisoners are in dire need.

Turn around, cried John Winder explosively. Go way! Drive back! Get out of here!

Dillard's voice was shaking; Ira knew that the quaver did not come from fear. General Winder, this is a gift, offered free out of hand. Please to let us pass.

I'll see you in hell first. You're a damn Yankee sympathizer, and so are all the rest of you!

The quiet sickly Dr. Pace had crept forward until there were but inches between his face and the old general's. Do you know where I left my arm, sir? In the Valley of Virginia.

I don't give a hoot in hell where you left your arm! I wish that all damn Yankee sympathizers—and every God damn Yankee prisoner too—were all in hell together!

Ira Claffey closed his eyes for a moment. He was biting his lips, finally he could speak. I do not believe, sir, that it is any evidence of Union sympathies to exhibit humanity. Nor do the rest of these people. Nor the ladies behind. . . . All of us have been bereaved by the war. Some still have young relatives at the front.

Winder howled, I know you, Mr. Claffey! You live right over there. You're always poking round—up on the sentry shacks. I've seen you with my own eyes. Well, by God, you'll poke no longer! I'll see to that.

He went waddling back to his chaise and stood muttering under his breath. Then he turned once again. You talk humanity, you citizens. There's no humanity about it. When you bring this stuff up here, it's intended as a slur upon the Confederate States' Government. And, by God—also an undercover attack on *me!*

Winder got into the chaise, then thrust his face out for a last cry. I'd as lief the damn Yankees would die here as anywhere else! By God, upon the whole, I don't know that it's not better for them. Now you folks vamoose!

Dr. Pace had turned back toward the carriage, his face chalked by this encounter. Cato Dillard was making strange breathless sounds, Ira did not know whether he was weeping or praying.

Ira gritted his teeth in final effort. He approached Winder's vehicle. One final request. The provisions are here, they're in the wagon; we shall promise to make no further attempt to convey things to the prisoners. But since these provisions have already come thus far, will you allow them to be taken inside the stockade, and distributed?

The pulpy face pushed toward him again. Not the first damn morsel shall go in! I only wish that I could issue an order to confiscate these goods. I haven't authority to do that; but I have got the power to prevent any damn Yankee prisoner from having them. By God, they shan't get them!

He yelled to pickets while the chaise was being turned: You heard me! You're not to let these folks move an inch further toward the stockade. . . .

Mr. Dillard and Ira went to rejoin the others. Some of the women were crying, Mrs. McCrary had her head on Mrs. Lindsay's shoulder. For him to say that I was a Yankee sympathizer! she sobbed. Mrs. Effie Dillard sat with fury of the Covenanters frozen in her pocked face. Her rage was so great that she could not yet begin to spout; presently she would spout.

Someone touched Ira's sleeve hesitantly. It was the old sergeant of the guards.

Mr. Claffey, sir. Wistfully. Since you can't take them things in to the Yanks, would you mind terrible if us folks got a little of the truck? Rations are mighty poor in these parts. Always have been.

. . . Clothing they took back with them, the vegetables and meat they gave to the guards.

43

Old Tom Gusset, Saddler, Ninth Ohio Cavalry, lingered far past the time which might have been allotted regularly to men of fifty-eight in Andersonville. His enforced retreat to a den filled with fellow Ohioans, when he fled from the wrath of the Irishman called Pay, wrought no change for the better. These were people from the Forty-fifth Volunteer Infantry, they were dying fast. Tom took the place made vacant by the demise of the ex-mule-driver, but the ex-miner and the ex-baggage-handler were in final disgusting stages of scurvy. The gums of the latter were sloughing away, he spat out wads of rotten membranes, it was feared that he swallowed other wads when he grew too weak to expel them. Only the ex-book-agent-who-longed-to-be-a-writer-of-novels was in fair shape, perhaps because he was slight and elastic to begin with. Once again this was an object lesson in the waning of the mighty athlete, the survival of the stringy and undersized.

Soon Tom Gusset let his implements lie idle, he lost ambition, he had no taste for the puny rations which his industry might have purchased. He did not wish to repair boots or straps, he said that he was too busy or too tired when customers approached. The ex-book-agent, one Woolstock, counseled and warned. Wool-stock had imagination, together with a great affection for the human race and an ardent interest therein. He knew that apathy was as destructive as any of the identifiable diseases which erased the population like a sponge in the Devil's own hand. Indeed he had manufactured this metaphor and made use of it, but Tom Gusset was not impressed.

Use your tools, old fellow! Don't just sit.

Wooly, I feel too sickly.

You'll really be sickly, too, if you don't perk up.

Don't feel like perking.

Think of your folks at home, Tom. Think of the glorious day of return, think of banners flying in the wind, and ladies strewing garlands, and—

Hell, young fellow. I'm old and I'm plain tired.

Tom had been vigorous previously, had done a young man's job in a young man's army, had held his own with people less than half his age. Now he sat and stared. Strangely he seemed suffering from no scurvy; diarrhoea did not wreck him; if he endured gripings he did not complain about them. He shook with no coughing, his eyes did not blaze, malarial fever did not shiver his frame. But suddenly he was become a vessel so empty that it seemed that vessel could never have contained the sauce of abounding life. Since he would not work he acquired no extra necessaries such as rice, salt, beans or bones. If he had owned any more candy he would not have had the energy to bottle it safely in a length of hollow cane. Certainly he would not have had the strength to chase a fleet young thief among the shebangs, punishing him (and thus killing him eventually; killing the shaggy Pay as well) with a belt buckle.

Woolstock quit uttering invocations because Gusset would not heed them, and soon did not even hear. Gusset ate less and less of the gnarly brick of corn bread which came his way each day. At last he ate none at all, he did not rise from the ground. The treasured implements of his saddler's career were stolen, and he did not care. The miner died, the baggage-handler died. Woolstock himself nursed a scratch on his arm and feared gangrene, and quickly saw and felt and smelled gangrene developing, and knew in last brilliant agonizing that now he too was doomed.

New prisoners, horrified and frantic at what they found here, shoved into the shebang and occupied mud where the Ohioans had suffered. Oh, they were new, not yet emasculated, they pitied Tom Gusset, thought it ghastly that a man nearing sixty should be in that place, thought it ghastly that anyone should be there, thought it a diabolical conspiracy on the part of the Confederacy, and on the part of the Union as well, that there should be such a place. They gave Tom Gusset his ration, they scraped away other mouldering rations which he had abandoned, they began to bet on how long he could live without food.

In fact he lived a surprisingly long time . . . day by day he shrank. It was discovered that he was dwelling in Ohio. He was living with his first wife, Lennie, who had died in early middle age after bearing Tom nine children. His second wife, Ada, was a vicious little shrew hated by her entire neighborhood. Tom had left his harness shop and joined the cavalry in order to get away from Ada. Not even in final insanity could he wish to rejoin Ada, but Lennie became a warm, good-scented vision. Of course he saw her always beaming at the end of the supper table, or rising to whisk more muffins from the oven. Little faces turned admiringly toward Tom all along the board. Olinthus boasted of the groundhog he had dug up, Eva and Leora giggled about a hair-pulling which had ensued at their Sunday School pic-nic, Willis begged to go and spend the night at a favorite cousin's. Tom Gusset, proud of his family, proud of his pink-cheeked wife and also proud of himself, spooned up the meat and gravy which his toil had provided.

Tommy boy, he'd say to his eldest, you better take some more pigeon pie.

God, said newcomers in the shebang, there the old bastard goes again. This time it's pigeon pie.

Now, Eva, don't say you don't like bean porridge. You know your Ma makes the best! It's from Granny LeMay's own receipt.

Artie, help yourself to another chunk of squash and please to pass the plate.

Think I'll take a little more of that hot slaw, Hiram. But help yourself first. Right in front of you.

The prisoners screamed, God damn you, old man, dry up!

He sat in mud, his thinning fingers no longer skilled and active, but frittering about with splinters, garbage, or even with rolls of mud which they took up and wadded. The splinters were Scotch scones, the garbage became tasty buttered onions with plenty of salt and pepper on them, the mud was cream pie.

Lowell boy, do have another fish ball. And Maudie's plate is nearly empty. Pass her some more of that boiled tongue and some of them parsnips.

Help yourself to another nice baked potato, Hiram.

The prisoners tried to stop their ears. I swear, they cried, if he don't cease that craziness I'll go crazy too. I swear, they cried, I got a notion to lam him over the head with this pole. Finish the old relic off! . . . Oh, leave him be, Mansfield. He's old, he hain't got long. . . .

He had far too long insofar as these new prisoners were concerned. Ain't this nice tenderloin, Linthus? Do take that last piece for yourself; now, hush, the rest of you—Linthus is titled to it, he split all them kindlings for his Ma while Hiram and Artie snuck away to play ball. Lowell, don't take that cold rusk; Ma is bringing some hot ones right now—better for you hot. Leora, you and Maudie got to toss a penny to see which one wipes the dishes. Here, I got two pennies right here in my pants; I'll give each of you a bright new cent, and you can match. Don't know how to match? Well, Pa'll show you. Watch careful.

I tell you, Lennie, you've baked some mighty good nut loaves in your time, but I never saw the beat of this one. Tommy boy, you spread that butter thick on your nut bread, for Granny always said there wasn't nothing like butter to put flesh on young bones. Eva, pass your saucer and I'll ladle you some more of these fine stewed cherries.

Nathan Dreyfoos strayed deliberately into remembered satisfactions with his good mind; old Tom Gusset strayed on whatever scraps of wounded fancy could still support him. The house rose before and around him, the small light green house overflowing with Gussets, the house which had supplanted the log house of Tom's father (the house of squared logs had been moved back to serve as wood-shed, dairy, cob house, general domestic repository. The children gave shows there; the minister thought it wrong for them to engage in theatricals; Tom Gusset shook his finger at the Reverend Mr. Sifert and said that his children could give all the blame shows they wanted to).

Gol damn, cried out one new prisoner in the shebang, think I ain't lonesome for my own wife and folks? Think I don't wish I was back in Frenchtown with Amy and Lily and Byron? Why the devil have I got to listen to this, night and day?

Oh, hang onto yourself, Melvin. He ain't got long.

Day after day Artie was offered his asparagus, Leora her buttered onions, Tommy boy his ham. Tom Gusset had been declared killed in battle through some misinformation by an alleged eye-witness. The evil-tongued Ada sold his harness shop and settled down to live comfortably in the old green house—peeking from behind curtains at the two young girls across the way, poisoning dogs, throwing boiling water at cats (which managed fortunately to elude her), shrieking at children to stay out of her yard. Naturally none of her stepchildren or stepgrandchildren ever came to see her. Thus the news that Olinthus was killed near Atlanta and that Hiram was captured and sent to a pen in Tyler, Texas— These griefs brought her no grief. . . . The silver hair and beard of her husband crawled with lice, the prisoners declared that he had a gallon of lice on him if he had a gill, he seemed thinner than paper, you could actually see his bones through transparent begrimed hide. His raw voice cackled without let, his eyes saw fairest and dearest forms, his shrunken nostrils smelled them out of the past.

He tried to get up a while ago and just couldn't.

That's what I been waiting for! He tried to resist us before, but I don't think he can resist us now.

Hospital! Good idee.

Next morning old Tom Gusset was carried to the South Gate; they carried him there before dawn so that the press would not be too great, so that they would not hear the No More Today, No More Today blasting hope that they would be rid of this nuisance once and for all.

Their luck took them to Contract Surgeon Number Six, one of the most hu-mane and resolute of the eleven contract surgeons working at the gate. When the Yankees brought up Tom Gusset in their turn, this surgeon, a bearded little wren named Crumbley whose home was in Albany, had already sent to the hospital the three patients whom he was empowered to assign there on this day. For some mysterious reason there had been but thirty-four hospital deaths since the previ-ous day; hence ten of the contract surgeons might each designate three prisoners —and the eleventh, four—to fill the vacancies. Dr. Crumbley begged the atten-tion of another surgeon whose allotted vacancies were not used up, and as a result

Tom was carried into a wall tent and placed with seven other patients. Four of these were in the two beds, or rather shelves with which the place was furnished; the rest lay upon the ground in trodden pine straw saturated with qualities unmentionable. From this low couch Tom's dramatization of recreated joys reached any ears willing to listen.

This was a rich and beautiful way in which to die. For he had no recognition of pain, stench, wail or ordure. He dwelt in an established past which was as good to his demented soul as was the cold compress to the feverish, the oven-baked flannel to the chilled. He dwelt in that content without chronology, he needed none. His conscious brain was ruptured, his cracked voice talked ahead. Tell you what I'll do, Mr. Lloyd—your boy Fred has owed me for them collars nearly two years now. Now, if you'll pay both bills—yours and his—today, I'll let you have that buggy whip at cost—just what it cost me. Thank you very much, Mr. Lloyd— you have been a good customer for years, but I just can't carry a heavy load of old Accounts Due. Yes, you bet— Thank you, Mr. Lloyd. Good day to you.

A ghoul crept in at night to rob the dead and the sick too; he stepped upon Tom Gusset's hand and broke the weakened bones, but Tom did not mind the crushing, not for long. He gave one bleat, and then muttered about it for a time, and then was beaming in his village again. Eva, you are a mighty good little currant picker! Ma told me about it, and it was a good thing you got them before the birds did, and I'm going to give you a dime all for your very own. May basket night? I thought I smelt taffy when I came in. How many baskets are you going to hang, Maudie? Eight? Ain't that more'n last year? And last year you got ten hung to *you.* Looks like you're a very popular young miss with your feller scholars!

A boy young enough to be Tom Gusset's grandchild lay beside him. He was mainly unconscious (this was good, since his lower bowel was in shreds, and some of these shreds protruded from his body), but at times he emitted little owlish cries. Queerly enough Tom was aware of these sounds, and ascribed them to a June dusk when his children marched purposefully along the street and he and Lennie sat on the bench he had built under the ivy. Screech owl, they call that one, dearie. Funny they call it screech. It's just as soft as the cooing of a squab. I do like to set and listen to it. I suppose he's calling to his mate. Listen to them kids—that's Willie's voice—guess he's captain of his side. Listen to them signals. *Danger,* he's calling. *Danger!* Bet that means the other side is getting further and further away. It's an old trick—we kids used to do it when we was little. Cept we called it Old Wolf, the best I can recall, instead of Run-Sheep-Run. There they go pelting off. Listen at them! *Run, Sheep, Run!* Old Wolf's going to get you!

We were lucky, Lennie. Think how our own kids all got through the diphtheria all right, and the Billingses lost two.

You know what I'd like, right here on this scrapple. Some of that sweet pepper hash. Well, I must be getting blind—didn't see it on the table, and here it was right in front of me all the time. Try some, Lowell, do. It just spices up this good scrapple to perfection. Yes, yes, that's Granny LeMay's old receipt also. . . .

First complaint I ever had, Mr. Conrad, that my workmanship was unsound! Sure, I can see it's broke, tore squarely in two. But it wouldn't tear like that unless you'd put undue strain on it. Ain't any journeyman harness-maker in the world could make a tug that bad out of such good leather. And I ain't no journeyman— I'm a master, as any other person in this community will bear witness. Fact is, Mr. Conrad, I think these two busted ends parted company *during* the runaway, and not before. Couldn't have been a busted whiffle-tree on that there ancient vehicle of yours that caused it, now could it? . . . Lennie, he looked like he could have gone through the floor. Don't know when anything has struck me so funny. He just slid out of the shop—you know, kind of mumbled something—and then skedaddled. I just set there and laughed till I shook.

Tom Gusset's vocal machinery was pulled apart by undue strain, as his good sound harness had been pulled. On the next day you would have had to bend close to his ghost's face to hear him speak (except that no one would have wished to bend close to such crawling ugliness, and there was no one to bend close). Lennie, dearie, don't turn your face away. Ain't nothing to be ashamed about. Everybody does it—married folks—and now we're married. Wasn't it funny, way they tied all them old shoes and pots and things on behind the rig? My, what a racket that made until we'd outdistanced them all, and I could get down and pull that blame stuff off of there. Lennie, dearie, let me kiss you again. You know what? That's a real pretty nightdress you got on. All that stuff around the top— what you call it? Yoke? Sounds like twas meant for oxen, now doesn't it? Cept you ain't no ox. You're just the sweetest prettiest little thing that ever. . . .

Artie, said the wispy raw voice, do have some more beans. Best you ever tasted, I'll be bound.

Tom spoke in this way until there was no mechanism left for speech, no germ to sustain the flower of life. Eventually mules took him away, he lay at the bottom of the load. Twas funny, said one of the black men who'd shoveled earth over him by indifferent spadefuls. They all smell pretty bad. Seem for a moment that this old one didn't smell so bad. Seem like I smell a nice place, with good things cooking.

How you talk, Jeff. Ain't no good things cooking round here.

44

Lucy cuddled upon an old cushion beside the gallery pillar. She gazed, not at Elkins and her father above and beyond her, but into dusk which seemed to flow and falter with a visible tide of sound and smell.

She asked, Have you spoken to any of your superiors about this matter?

I have made verbal suggestions to the Chief Surgeon.

From his own portion of dusk, Ira spoke. What did you tell him, Coz?

Asked him why the army didn't send us all away!

Harry Elkins thudded his tired boots upon the porch. I said that it was useless for surgeons to exert effort, when the patients were starved down to begin with. If the prisoners were receiving the vegetables which they should have—and if the prisoners had more room—at least half of them could be saved. They need the right kind of diet, more than they need medicines.

Did you tell him about General Winder—?

Indeed I told him! I said that it would be possible to have a large supply of green things brought from this plantation alone. I know that I was not presuming on your generosity, Cousin Claffey: I said that things were spoiling in your garden, I said that you would send him vegetables without charge. They were going to waste, doing nobody any good. . . . If he would connive with me to have them admitted to the hospital, lives might be saved. He observed that he would like to have the garden stuff; then turned off and spoke no more about it.

He feared the wrath of Winder, Coz.

He did—and does.

Elkins got up, pulled from his chair by the extremity which overpowered him increasingly. I wrote a report, with recommendations. Entirely unsolicited. Should you like to hear it?

I'll ring and have a light fetched, said Ira.

Sakes, I can fetch a light while we're still striving to enlist the attention of Ninny or Pet! Lucy brought a shielded candle from a nearer room. By this small light Harrell Elkins knelt with papers spread upon his knee. His spectacles were silvered, his face looked like hardened leftover dough.

Lucy thought, It rules him. What chance will he ever have to own a softness? The thing is too big, too stern and vengeful. Harry must succumb beneath it, thus must I succumb. . . .

Elkins's voice was grinding out the words: And to ascertain and report the causes of disease and mortality among the prisoners, and the means necessary to prevent the same, I respectfully submit the following. Causes of disease and mortality. One: The large number of prisoners crowded together. Two: Entire absence of vegetables as diet, so necessary in the prevention of scurvy. Three: The want of barracks to shelter prisoners from sun and rain. Four: Inadequate supply of wood and pure water. Five: Badly cooked food. Six: Filthy condition of prisoners and prison generally. Seven: Morbific emanations from the branch or ravine passing through the prison, the condition of which cannot be better explained than by naming it a morass of human excrement. . . .

There must be a fair place. . . . Again Lucy's youth served her in struggling against resignation. She would not accept this ordeal as a mode of life—never, never. It was not for this that women carried babies in their bodies and endured the torment of expelling them. It was not for this that an orb was set in the sky, and pin-holes and studding of stars gave suggestion of great glories, layer on layer, in regions outside the system of planets. Not for this did a purple bud rise gently out of compression against its stalk, and spread to make the rippled foil of a violet. Not for this did water set stones to grinding, nor did owls call, nor did warm rain spread and soak the ground. Not for this did tiny creatures work within the soil. . . .

Elkins read on. Preventative measures are suggested as follows. One: The removal immediately from the prison of not less than fifteen thousand prisoners. Two: The detailing On Parole of a number of Yankees sufficient to cultivate the necessary supply of vegetables; until this can be carried into practical operation I suggest the appointment of agents along the railroad line, to purchase and forward a supply of vegetables. Three: Immediate erection of barracks within the stockade, for shelter. Four: Let squads of prisoners proceed with axes, under adequate guard, to secure sufficient wood for their purposes, in thick forests nearby; and let proper wells be dug to supply the deficiency of water. A single bubbling spring, pure though it may be, cannot serve properly thirty-three thousand men. Five: Divide prisoners into squads, place each squad under a sergeant, furnish the necessary quantity of soap—which can be manufactured by prisoners themselves, working, again, under guard—and hold these sergeants responsible for the personal cleanliness of each squad. Six: Supply the prisoners with clothing at the expense of the Confederate States' Government; and if our Government be unable to do so, candidly admit our inability, and call upon the Federal Government to send clothing. Seven: There should be a daily inspection of bake houses and baking procedures. Eight: Cover over with sand the entire morass within the pen, not less than six inches deep. Board the stream or watercourse, and confine the men—also the Georgia Reserves outside the stockade—to the use of their sinks. Make the penalty for disobedience inescapable and severe.

. . . Why, my dear Harry, cried Lucy's crippled appealing fancy, you are up betimes.

My dear, did you not know when I left our bed?

I was sleeping so soundly that I scarcely heard you go. Then later I moved my limb, and the place where you had lain was still warm. But you were gone from it.

And were you alarmed, love?

No, I felt that you must have gone to call on old Mr. Bile.

So I did. Ah, the fruition of a lengthy peaceful life! It is a rest which cometh after the three-quarter century mark. I tell you, dear, there is a saintliness about the old. I would best describe it as the imminence of heaven.

Harry *darling.* Surely you must have encountered some of the old who were unsaintly in the extreme! I knew one such woman: twas a great-aunt: a regular little witch she was.

Ha-ha. And so have I encountered such, dear Lucy. But what of the Reverend Mr. Cato Dillard? Is he not nigh to sainthood?

Oh yes, Harry, Uncle Dayto is, of course; and some of the young are sainted too; but just *listen* to our own younguns.

What are they screaming about?

Rapture, beloved Harry, pure rapture! Their mammy has them at breakfast out amongst the plum trees. She has set up the little blue table which Jonas made for them, and she's lugged chairs. Ira and Suthy are having a fight, pelting each other with handfuls of plum blossoms; the girls are shrieking in protest. But come along with you, dear, you've been a mighty while without your breakfast.

To be frank, I could eat a horse.

No necessity for that. And certainly not one of *our* horses. . . . Naomi, you may bring the biscuits. Have you kept the sausages hot? And remember that the Doctor prefers his eggs basted over the top; but lightly, Naomi, very lightly, and peppered to a turn. . . . And—oh, Harry—I have a gift for you. Tis all your own; no one must touch it but you. The children have their own, but this is my dear Harry's jar. *Gooseberry jam,* my love, and what fun I had a-making it for you. . . .

Sheets of paper crinkled on Elkins's knee. A moth struck the candle flame, whirled, scorched. The candle sputtered lightly, flame resumed its small steady towering.

The dry voice kept growling. One: For the hospital I recommend that the tents be floored with planks; if planks cannot be had, with puncheons; and if this be impossible, then with pine straw, to be changed frequently. Two: There is an inadequate supply of stool boxes. It is recommended that the number be increased, and that the orderlies be required to remove them as soon as used; and before returning them, see that they are well washed and limed. Three: Diet for the sick is repulsive. They must be supplied with the necessary quantity of meat broth, with vegetables. Four: Surgeons should be required to visit hospital patients not less than twice a day.

Finally, I cannot too strongly recommend the necessity for the appointment of an efficient medical officer to the exclusive duty of inspecting daily the hospital and cooking facilities, requiring of him daily reports of their condition to headquarters.

I have the honor to remain, Sir, very respectfully. . . .

His words trailed away. Elkins rose, slapped the papers against his thigh, then smoothed them carefully.

Lucy drifted back from her private fairyland. Once again the prison smell was in her nostrils . . . and this was the present, it was 1864, they were upon the gallery, these things had happened, were happening, would happen.

Ira inquired, Coz, to whom did you make this report? To Chief Surgeon White?

I felt that it would be futile. Nor did I address Acting Assistant Surgeon Watkins. What power has he?

I thought that possibly you might have addressed Colonel Thurlow?

Merely does he command the Post, replacing your friend Lieutenant-Colonel Persons. What could he do? And as you know, Surgeon-General Moore is at Richmond, and has received many other reports heretofore.

Ira said dryly, I take it that there would be no point in addressing Brigadier-General John H. Winder.

No point whatsoever.

Then whom—?

This is not a copy, said Harrell Elkins, speaking not only to Ira and Lucy Claffey, but to swaddling stench and noise of the night—to the stockade's denizens, to corpses in earth on the hill—speaking to all people within the Southern Confederacy, to all within the Northern States.

This is not a copy. It is the original report. I would not waste time, sir, in sending a hopeless plea to Mr. Seddon, or even to President Davis.

One after the other, he held sheets to the candle flame; let the blaze broaden, let paper burn down to his fingers, let the flakes fall. Almighty God, please to note and file, said Harry.

Lucy caught her breath, her face went down into her hands. She wept quietly until Ira was gone. Then there came a wonder. She found herself in Elkins's arms; this was no dream; she found herself in his arms; but only for a moment. Firmly he said that he must go on duty.

45

Judah Hansom was one of many men who tried to escape from the prison through a tunnel. He was twenty-six years old, and had a thinnish face with small sad green eyes. His mouse-brown hair was mostly gone—premature baldness was said to have run in his mother's family—and his slanting forehead carried branded transverse lines which might have grooved the brow of a much older man. But Judah's shoulders were broad out of proportion to his medium height, and his great arms might have come swinging from a jungle. When a citizen he had been in fact a farmer, but first and foremost he liked to think of himself as a woodman—rather, a woodman before whom no trees should be spared unless especially desirable for shade, fruit or nuts.

Judah Hansom did not tell his comrades how much he dreaded lonely darkness below the earth's foul crust. A silent person by habit, he had never grown sufficiently articulate to voice other than commonplace utterances. The few people who had known him, and the further few who had been sufficiently interested to assay his nature for themselves, typified him as phlegmatic and unfeeling. He needed space around him in order to settle into security. When Judah worked through the first strength of his youth he gained more than pride as he saw the forest dissolve, yard by yard and stick by stick, under the clamor of his axe, under the assault of axes of his fellow workmen. He felt a private comfort, an exalted assurance, because he was achieving space; he was building it. Sometimes wide long vistas opened after trees lay toppled and the tops were stripped; he could stand sweaty, even when there was snow about, and soak his muscles and spirit in the blue boon of limitless distances surrounding him. He could look over the nearest ridge and see other feathered rolls of hills go inching toward the Adirondacks and always fading in shade, growing looser as to texture and detail, until they brought up unyielding against the mountain wall.

Knowing little except the ritual of helve and blade and forest silences, Judah found his God easily. He was devout after the manner of unimaginative men who have known little of human complication and the resulting perplexity. Moreover he had lived in civilian affairs as a practiced coward in that he avoided constantly, deliberately any situation which might bring him ill, any force against which he might not cope readily and with the assurance of victory. A town . . . he hated towns because there the trains champed and blew sparks from their cumbrous funneled stacks, there the teams tried to run him down, there strangers jostled and talked loudly of people and matters beyond his experience. He stood away from towns. Women and girls . . . they appalled him with their rustling and cackling, with constant reminder in every tone and gesture and mood that they were of a different pattern physically and yet were somehow glad and impudent about it. In that remote farmhouse called home there was only Aunt Annie, and she wore freckled blue calico caps, with a slatted bonnet literally bigger than a half-bushel measure when she worked in the garden; she had a scant black mustache turning gray, and clumped in heavy plain-toed slippers when she walked about the kitchen; she did not seem like other women, she could be endured because she never giggled and was fully as dour as Judah Hansom's father, her brother . . . it was just that she refused to wring a chicken's neck, and couldn't abide snakes, and you must never mention privies in her presence.

At a church or neighborhood sociable Judah squirmed in a corner on the most uncomfortable chair he could find, if the party were a small one; or he stood in a doorway and stared suspiciously from behind draped flags or corn-shucks if the party were large, a real merry-making. He mumbled Thankee when the hostess or her daughters offered a plate of pie and a mug of coffee. He went home early.

From the time he was sixteen or seventeen he feared that all women might wish to marry him because of the land—it totaled over six hundred acres—which his father owned. His father was niggardly, and bound to have Judah earn his salt, as Elijah Hansom expressed it. Judah developed craft with the axe very early, and had left school and was hiring out as a woodcutter at the age of fourteen. He did not mind hard work, he had never minded it; he preferred it to any sort of ease he knew (he had known very little ease of the body) because the Hansoms believed that there was a virtue in pain and discomfort. In another time, another civilization, the Hansoms might have squatted on pillars in order to bring about their own saintliness or to emphasize it to the rest of mankind.

But they did not court death, despite their eagerness to torture themselves. They wanted to live long and toil determinedly and reap what they were fond of hearing the preacher describe as a Bounteous Harvest. Whenever the preacher mentioned a Bounteous Harvest the elder Hansom reacted in thought to his six hundred and twenty-four acres, his livestock, the mortgages he held and which yielded him, under pressure applied, a steady and substantial interest. He thought of the three hundred and ninety-three double eagles and the small sack of silver coins locked in an iron box under the chicken house floor (the chickens would fuss and squawk if anyone came in there at night and started to dig) and which box only Elijah Hansom himself knew was buried. He had not yet informed his son Judah about the box, which had been brought from New Hampshire in a wagon before Judah was born. He planned to tell Judah in time. He thought of the lesser amount of cash placed to his credit in the Bindale Commercial Savings Bank, for convenience sake, and of the still lesser amount kept on the highest pantry shelf in a broken coffee-mill, and which of course Judah and Aunt Annie knew was there, although they never mentioned it. These comprised his Bounteous Harvest; it was to accumulations such as these that Reverend Burgess referred. Son Judah considered Bounteous Harvests in identical terms, although his own harvest was comparatively skimpy as yet.

They did not court death; death interfered with Bounteous Harvests unless death appeared as boon and release to an invalid. Take Elijah Hansom's wife Clementine: she died when Judah was two, and had not left her bed since Judah was born. It was a great relief to Elijah Hansom when Clementine was Gathered To Her Reward (Reverend Burgess preached a sonorous funeral sermon) because he had to hire a woman to look after her for thirteen months, until Annie could be prevailed upon to come and live with them. Disgusted neighbors who had bold tongues and who did not owe Mr. Hansom any money said that poor Clementine was brought to premature labor and consequent disaster through overwork and short commons. Mrs. Calkins went over there only two days before the skinny infant was delivered into Granny Ballentine's hands— She went to buy a set of eggs. Lo and behold, there was Clementine Hansom putting up currant jam, and the kitchen hotter than Tophet, and right behind her on the table were fifteen quarts of beans she had already put up—Mrs. Calkins counted. She said, Sakes a mercy, Clemmy, let them currants spoil. Oh, no, says Clementine, and she looked like a wrung-out dishrag, poor little body. If I let anything spoil, Lijah would make me rue the day. It's not the canning that I mind, really, because I can set down part of the time. But I hate picking berries so. Twas awful hot out there in the sun around them bushes, out of the shade. . . . Well, you saw what happened.

The Hansoms did not court death, but usually death seemed to find them without much trouble and without much warning. Judah's great-grandfather was killed instantly at the battle of Bennington. His grandfather, also named Judah Hansom, slipped on the ice while crossing a river in his old age, and lay peacefully unconscious until the end. Elijah, the one who fathered young Judah in York State, perished in 1860 through wrath at hearing of the nomination of Abraham Lincoln. Elijah said that the Democrats were bound to be defeated, come November, and all the ragtag and bobtail of Creation would ride into office on that quarter-witted monkey's shoulders or through his appointments. They would frisk in public offices like rats in a cheese-keg, they would squander public funds, their relatives would feed from the public trough; there might be a war, and certainly banks would close—not that Elijah had ever trusted banks. Nor had he yet brought himself to inform his son Jude about the hoard beneath the dirt floor of the chicken shed, which was basted generously in extreme secrecy every six months or so. By this time the iron box contained more than nine thousand dollars.

Elijah Hansom said that rats in public office would hold what he called High Carnival as soon as that lantern-jawed baboon was inaugurated. He was so mad that he would have beaten a wife if he'd had one, or Son Judah if Judah hadn't been too big for him to tackle. Well, he couldn't whip his sister Annie, so he decided to go out and cut down a tree. There was a maple at the corner of the woodshed, diseased and ugly; habitually it cluttered the yard with fallen branches, and one big live branch was scraping at the kitchen roof and threatening to dislodge shingles. The maple appeared as Lije Hansom's enemy, so he touched up his axe, and Annie heard him say that he was going to level that blame tree if it was the last thing he ever did. It was the last thing he ever did. Later it was decided that the grass was wet on that slope, and the man must have slipped in striding away from the trunk when it tipped. Aunt Annie heard the tree go down, but she heard no further remarks from her brother, and two hours later she went out to feed the hens. She saw the fallen maple, and saw something black-checked and reddish alongside the trunk. The black-checked material turned out to be Lijah's shirt, and the red turned out to be—

It took nine neighbors to turn the trunk off of Lijah Hansom, and Judah didn't know a thing about the whole business (he had driven to the lumber market in Bindale with a load of seasoned posts; the load weighed so much that he had to use oxen) until he was halfway home, late that afternoon. Then he met that squint-eyed little muskrat of a Benny Ballentine, and the Ballentines didn't like the Hansoms any more because Elijah had brought foreclosure proceedings against their nephew. No reason for them to act mean about it: Mr. Hansom asked only that which was his in the best judgment of God and man. Well, little Benny Ballentine looked Judah squarely in the eye and said, Howdy do, orphant. Judah thought, Tosh, that's a funny thing for him to say. Calculate he's trying to get gay with me, and maybe seeks a hiding. Except that Judah was mild of manner, and never brawled with the neighbor men; he hadn't been in a fight since he was eleven, and then he lost; but now he was too powerful for any of them to wish to tackle him. . . . When he passed the Petrie place, Sally Petrie ran out waving her apron, and she told him.

(The iron box reposed beneath chicken-droppings, while Judah Hansom dwelt in Andersonville. It would remain there indefinitely. No one ever found it. The chicken shed would burn down, much later, and bushes would grow on the site.)

Well, Judah was twenty-two when his father died, and twenty-four when he went into the army, and nobody expected him to go. Everybody thought that he would hire a substitute if the draft wheel turned against him. Strangely, it was that same squinting Benny Ballentine who really set the knapsack on Judah's back and the bayonet hanging at his belt. Benny went away with the first troops raised at Bindale . . . spunky little rat for sure. His father said admiringly in Wilkins's store, By mighty, my Benny hain't afraid of God, man, nor the Devil. When this was repeated back to Benny he grinned and squeezed his eyelids even tighter, and he said in his high-pitched voice that he was truly afraid of God and the Devil, but he hadn't yet met any man that he was afraid of. He doubted that the Rebels were any worse than Hulk Allen at the livery barn; and once Hulk Allen had knocked Benny flat with one slap of his big hand . . . when Benny got up he was holding a bottle with a broken neck, and he took off half of Hulk Allen's right cheek before the livery barn folks could tear him loose from the big fellow. So Benny went to war, and got himself shot through the chest at Big Bethel, Virginia, and he came home coughing. He kept coughing all the time. His mother said that although the wound had healed on the outside, front and back, it didn't seem to have cured itself in Benny's vitals. He had to keep a pan by his bed at night, to cough into, and sometimes he raised blood. It was silent at night under the high black-trunked maples on that cool road beyond the single business block of Bindale, and if you walked home late, like from prayer meeting on a Wednesday, you could hear only two sounds: the sound of your own feet on the hollow wooden sidewalk, and the sound of Benny Ballentine, hacking away on his bed past the white picket fence and the white lilacs and within the walls of the little white house.

Well, Judah stopped at the smith's to pick up two wagon wheels for which Mr. Whiteman had forged new tires. Jude, said hairy old Mr. Whiteman, whose son and son-in-law had both been killed in the ranks of the Forty-second New York at Ball's Bluff— Jude, I heard tell you was going for a soldier.

Mr. Whiteman was always saying that, every time Judah came around, and it was a provoking thing to say, because Judah had no intention of becoming a soldier. Judah preferred not to patronize Mr. Whiteman as a result; but he would have had to drive all the way to Herkimer otherwise, for Mr. Whiteman was the only blacksmith in Bindale since Uncle Delhi Lawrence died.

Even before Judah could open his mouth and ask, Where did you hear that?— Before Judah Hansom could say a word, up spoke Benny. He was sitting close to the forge because he had chills much of the time, and he wore his blue overcoat even when other folks had their sleeves rolled up against the springtime sun.

Not him, chirped Benny Ballentine. Might get shot.

Usually they were a talkative group, there at the smith's—the lame and old and idle. But now they didn't utter anything, and just went on chewing their tobacco and playing with nails. Judah felt his face go red as the forge. He didn't dare to look at Benny. From the remembered influence of his father, Judah had absorbed the notion that the war was somehow brought on by a group of capricious political bosses whose dupe Lincoln was. No sane person ought to support the war in any way because it might eventually ruin the country; banks would close, prices paid for lumber would go down, people wouldn't be able to pay their interest.

Might get shot.

He could hear that echoing tartly as he drove to the farm, he could hear it from afar in the protestation of sheep which his two hired men, and temporary assistants in the shape of three young boys, were dipping. The ewes seemed quacking in the nasal tone of Benny Ballentine. There had promised to be a great deal of money in sheep, for markets needed more and more wool, now that no cotton was forthcoming. Judah acquired a promising flock, pastured on hills cleared by his own axe. This day the smell of the dip nauseated him, and he regretted ever having bought the flock. Baaaa. Might get shot. Baaaa.

All night long he heard the sheep and he heard Benny, and as soon as he finished choring in the morning he sat down on the wash bench and made a list of things which he must do that day. His eggs grew cold upon his plate, his cakes steamed no longer, Aunt Annie called in vain. Judah saw his hired men disposed for the day, and then he hitched up and drove to Herkimer. The bank had been open only forty-five minutes when he got there. Jude did some business at the bank, and then he went to Mr. Endicott's office and made his will. He left five hundred dollars to the Congregational church, five hundred dollars to the one surviving cousin in New Hampshire (this cousin he had never seen, but he did it from a sense of family duty) and he provided for Aunt Annie through whatever years might remain to her. He supposed vaguely that you might term the rest of his property to be a backlog. Lawyer Endicott kept taking off his specs and putting them on again, and then losing them amid the papers on his desk. Obviously he thought that Jude Hansom was crazy, and maybe Jude was. Baaaa. Might get shot.

Judah drove directly—not home, but to the village of Bindale. It was an hour past dinner time when he walked into Mr. Whiteman's smithy. Benny Ballentine been here? No, Ben don't usually appear before mid-afternoon.

Judah didn't go to the Ballentine house because he wanted to tell Benny right there at the blacksmith's, right in front of that same crowd, right in the middle of the hot smells and tobacco juice and horse smells and scorched parings of the hooves, and fumes and heat. He had some business to do at the local bank and with a couple of folks whose property was mortgaged to him, so he went and did it. He hadn't eaten a bite all that day, and began to feel weak although he wasn't truly hungry. He went into Wilkins's and bought some crackers and cheese and salted codfish, and sat in his buggy beside the free-flowing town trough while he ate. It was shady there under the elms, and it was a good place to eat a luncheon however belated. He could drink from the wet-moss-draped old pipe, drinking from the stream before it fell into the stone trough below. Providently Judah always carried a nose-bag under the buggy seat, and he had brought along oats for Molly . . . she tossed the nose-bag contentedly while Judah munched as if it were a duty, and it was one.

About three-thirty Judah Hansom had done everything which he must do, so he went back to Whiteman's. He dropped Molly's block on the ground and snapped the catch against her bridle; this was merely a gesture, since Molly was docile and wouldn't have stirred unless too badly fly-bitten. Judah walked inside the smithy and found Mr. Whiteman busy shoeing Reverend Hathaway Burgess's old horse. The Reverend himself was there, chewing stick cinnamon instead of tobacco, and there were the regulars: Captain Mattice, Grandpa Corning, Lame Peter Jones (he was the only Negro in the community, and insisted that his father had once belonged to a British general) and a couple of little boys. And Benny Ballentine. Benny was sitting on a flat-bed wheelbarrow; of course he wore his army coat clinging around him. Everybody stared when Judah came in and walked to confront Benny. Mr. Whiteman dropped the horse's hoof to the cindery ground with a thud. The forge sent out its cherry-colored glow, and surprisingly the scorched odors were appetizing.

Judah turned around to Reverend Burgess and said, I left five hundred to the Congregationalists, and then he turned back to Benny.

I provided for my relatives. You'll get the backlog.

What?

I just call it the backlog. It's the bulk—what Mr. Endicott calls the residue. Pa's place—my place—the farm and all. It goes to you, in case; and I calculated you might wish to know.

Benny's mouth was open, and he had a sudden coughing fit. No one else could speak a word; they were gagged with amazement. Reverend Burgess went and got a dipper of water from the bucket and put his arm around Benny Ballentine's shoulders, and offered the dipper. Benny sipped some of the water and got control of his fit.

He asked of Judah, What in conscience are you talking about?

I made my will today. Might get shot.

He went out of the smithy, unsnapped the catch from Molly's bridle, picked up the block and tossed it into the buggy, got in and drove home. He arranged with the eldest hired man to bring his wife from Bindale and to live at the farm with Aunt Annie and to farm the place on a moderate share; but all disbursements and receipts were to be handled by Mr. Endicott at his office. . . . Aunt Annie said nothing, in her usual fashion. She cooked an especially fine supper for Judah; she went out to the garden and pulled a big dish of radishes, because Jude was fond of them, as also he was fond of chicken pie, and she had that, with plenty of mashed potatoes; she gave him also cold roast lamb, flint pickles, and opened her last jar of quince preserves. They ate in silence, they and the two hired men; but this was not the dull ordinary silence of people who are too tired physically to talk, and honestly have little in common to give them mutual pleasure or annoyance, and who do not even bother to speculate about where some neighbor was bound when he drove past that day. It was a silence laden with emotion and a sense of change, desperation, hazard, alteration, and some fear.

Judah ate well, however, and when he got upstairs to his room he was so stuffed that he couldn't even read his Bible. He lay back across his bed, and the world whirled high and far and speedily; he thought he heard a tree coming down, he thought he heard his father speak gruffly. He awakened hours later to find the lamp chimney burned black, and a horrid odor of coal-oil filling the chamber. He tiptoed down the stair, washed at the bench, and went upstairs with another lamp newly filled. He packed his satchel, being in much doubt as to what he should take. He thought of taking his favorite axe, but decided against it; they would have plenty of axes in the army, but perhaps he might be given no opportunity to use one. He packed his Testament. Judah felt slightly annoyed at finding how few things he owned or even wished to take with him; he even put in one of the Rollo books he had been given when he was a little boy. His Bounteous Harvest at the moment seemed to have run mainly to land, sheep, mortgages and cold cash. He was taking but fifty dollars with him—Mr. Endicott could send more, when and if he needed more, but Judah understood that everything was furnished in the army —you didn't have to pay for your food—maybe you had to pay for your uniform, or did you? It was a puzzle. He packed an extra pair of pants, and four more handkerchiefs.

Aunt Annie heard Judah moving about in his chamber, so she rose earlier than usual; the hired men, in accord, began their chores in the murk of dawn. One would need to drive Judah to Herkimer, and thus some hours would be lost from the work-day; it was best to be early birds. Aunt Annie cooked her usual platters of ham and eggs, and stood in dark gingham by the stove, cooking flapjacks as long as there was need for more.

Jas Wilkins said, Want me to hitch up Molly?

Judah nodded. I'll be ready in a trice.

Aunt Annie came and sat at the other end of the table, glad to be removed from the wood-range and its heat. They were alone in the long kitchen when Judah arose. She looked up at him, teacup in hand, and her small black eyes held a light.

You know, Jude, I'm nigh onto seventy. I was elder than your Pa.

Judah stood behind his chair.

Know who was president when I was born? George Washington.

Since Benny Ballentine had so strongly altered Judah's life, or maybe even taken it away from him, Judah was conscious of new emotions. He didn't like these feelings. An almighty thickness swelled in his chest and throat, his heart beat hard.

Never said nothing about it before, but if I'd been young and not a female, I'd have gone to fight e'er now.

Uh. Why?

Count of the Union. I mind Lijah used to fume about politicians, but the Union's bigger than any of them. Bigger than any one man, anywhere. It's got to be fit for.

Maybe so.

What was it altered your intentions, boy?

Uh . . . a fellow said something. Made out that I was scared of getting shot. Ain't you?

I calculate nobody ever wants to get shot. Except maybe a crazy man.

But you're going. I mind my own Pa, your grandpa, talking about Grandpa Elza Hansom. That was his father. He got kilt at Bennington when they was fighting the redcoats. Had his face to the foe when he fell. You got plenty stockings in your satchel? I mind Pa always held that a soldier needs fresh stockings more frequent than most folks.

These were more words than she had spoken to Judah or to anyone else in the past month.

Before Judah got into the buggy and took up the reins beside Jas Wilkins, Aunt Annie came out on the low porch. She shook hands with Judah, and gave him a parcel wrapped in store paper. Here's a luncheon to do you on the way. I put in a bottle of tea. It'll be cold, but it'll help to wash it down.

Thankee. Clumsily, hastily, the first time he had ever done it in his life, quite without intention or expectation, Judah kissed her hairy wrinkled face. He scraped the off wheel against the gate when they drove out, because he was embarrassed and annoyed with himself for yielding to such display.

He traveled from Herkimer to Albany; there he saw soldiers in the station, and asked them where he should go to enlist, and was directed properly. Five days later he was delighted to find that he should wear the crossed axes of a pioneer; he knew nothing of soldier life—except what Aunt Annie had told him about frequent changes of socks—but axes and other tools he understood very well indeed. Judah was helping to construct a log bridge in northwestern Georgia, more than two years after he enlisted, when a power of hoofbeats drummed on the pioneers' hearing, and they were captured before they could fire more than half a dozen rounds.

He spent blank appalling days after his arrival at Andersonville. As with so many of the incoming prisoners, Judah had no appetite and believed that God had forsaken him. Then his native tenacity and resource began a slow but growing assertion. He examined the lay of the land adjacent to the shebang which he shared with four other pioneers of his regiment, and decided after due deliberation that a tunnel was feasible. What Judah sought was freedom for freedom's own sake. He was actuated by no particularly noble patriotic motive; Aunt Annie had died of a stroke, the previous January; he had no person to return to—no person with whom he was deeply concerned, unless it might be Benny Ballentine. If Benny had coughed his life away by this time, no one had taken the trouble to inform Judah. Judah was driven by no strong intention of revenge; not necessarily did he despise Rebels and wish to kill them, although in fact he had killed two— one by mashing his head with a piece of railroad iron. He yearned for peace, quiet, woodland space. This must have been a nice piece of woods, right here, before this dratted stockade was built. . . . Also Jude deplored the stench, the pushing bickering mass. Except for the constant presence of smells of sweat and smells of manure (and sheep-dip) his had been a cleanly life before he entered the army, and cleaner than most lives after he was in the army. He wanted to smell again the juices of trees after he had cut them. He held the clear odor of sap and crushed leaves mingled with his ideas of Paradise. People said that the streets Up Yonder were golden, the walls of alabaster, but Judah was convinced that there were a lot of woods and hills as well, else no one should wish to go there.

He and the other York State people pooled their resources and prepared to dig. They had some half-canteens and cups, but there were no shovels anywhere about. Judah decided that serviceable little spades might be whittled out of hard wood, and he roamed ceaselessly, hunting for the right sort of wood to purchase. He possessed thirty-six dollars in greenbacks which he had concealed inside the split covers of his pocket Testament shortly after being captured. A Reb took the Testament, leafed through it, gave it back to Jude and never observed where the covers had been sliced and stuck together again. Also some of his companions had a little money. With luck they discovered a Marylander who owned a hoe, or the remains of one: the handle was only about eight inches long, the rusty blade was split in two places; still it was a tool. The Marylander was ridden with scurvy, and perishing for vegetables. They offered six dollars Federal, he held out for ten; finally they bought the hoe for seven dollars, and acquired two thin dried shakes which seemed made of some sort of hard wood—Judah had never seen that kind of wood before. Now they needed to buy or rent or borrow a knife for whittling the shakes into spades, and they owned no knife. Rumor had it that one of the men in that shebang over next to the deadline—the one with a piece of oilcloth forming part of the roof— One of those men was said to own a good knife. Judah went over there, and all the occupants were gone bartering or root-digging except for the lone housekeeper who sat reading a stained and ragged Bible. He was a stringy little chap, not much bigger than Benny Ballentine at home. No, he didn't own a knife, but it was true that one of his household did; the man would be coming back before long, so the little fellow bade Judah to sit down and wait. He reckoned that a bargain might be struck.

Want to hear a Chapter?

Don't mind. What are you on?

I just finished Nehemiah.

Hard going.

It is for certain, with all the children of Benjamin, and Levites and things. I read it through when I was just a little shaver, but now I swore to take her all the way through again. You a Baptist, by any chance?

Congregationalist.

And Jesus answering said unto him, Suffer it to be so now: for thus it becometh us to fulfil all righteousness.

Don't need to go preaching immersion, little chap. Not to me!

Well, I'll start on Esther.

Good enough. I only got the New Testament by me.

The youth began reading in a shrill wiry voice, and Judah Hansom sat in stinking shade, listening, with all the vast growl of the stockade muted somehow by heat, muted more in this mid-afternoon than at most other hours. The little chap's name was Willie Mann, and he was a Missourian. Willie liked the part about the beds of gold and silver and the colored pavement, and especially he seemed to like the part about the wine served in vessels of gold, for he read that verse twice in a row.

Ever drink any wine, Mister?

Judah said, Had an aunt used to make it out of cherries. But she said it wasn't an intoxicant. Tasted pretty good.

Ma made grapejuice, but it wouldn't keep none too well. I know some German folks that make beer at home. . . .

Willie returned again to Esther, and then once more he and Judah fell to talking. Willie told about Providence Spring and how it had started up, right on top of him, when God seemed to smite the hill. Judah had heard about this miracle, and under the watchful eyes of police he had stood in line twice daily for water since his arrival.

He said, I know where there's a dry well.

Where at?

Right in the corner of our shebang.

How deep is she?

Calculate it might go to twelve foot or so. Hain't no water in the bottom.

You know, said Willie Mann, a sight of tunnels have been dug from some of those wells.

They sat in considerate silence for a while, both thinking hard. Wirz had made good his threat to build a second stockade in order to discourage tunneling, and now in August the second stockade was a fact. Outsiders reported that it stood at a distance of perhaps one hundred and twenty feet, rimming completely the interior pen. Folks who had seen the fence said that it was not as high as the stockade proper, but still an effective deterrent to escape. Many believed, considering the Federal advance upon Atlanta, that this new work was as much a structure for defense as well as for restraint.

That there well, said Judah Hansom. Not too far from the deadline.

I know. But a hundred and twenty feet farther to go than earlier. Few boys have done much tunneling since July. Little profit in it.

So I hear. Do you know anybody who ever made it to the Outside?

Oh, I knew one fellow went out with that bunch of Buckeyes—guess twas a fortnight ago—but the dogs got him. But some have made it, folks do say. Course the Rebs found most of the tunnels and busted them in.

Judah said, Think your tentmate would part with his knife?

Not likely, but he'd rent it for a dollar, or so he has done before.

Mind speaking to him about it? How big is the knife?

A Barlow, about so big. Got two good blades on it still, and he keeps it well whet.

In this way their friendship began. Within a week Willie Mann was committed solidly to the task of excavation, and he kept at it with a passion exceeded only by the burrowing of Judah Hansom. Judah ached for trees and blue space, Willie had Katrine pictured in rosy soft flesh before him when he dug in loneliest depths. Most of the others worked with comparative apathy, and did not send out so much dirt, and could not stay underground as long as these two. Judah and Willie were more able-bodied than others of the group, although Willie was plagued by encroaching illness. He had loose teeth, one came out, his limbs hurt him, his mouth was sore perpetually. He kept the faithful large tin cup as a thing sacred to himself, to drink from, to feed from; he would not lend it or share from it because he feared in conscience that he might infect others.

The twelve-foot well had been dug by earlier inmates solely as a well and not as a preparation for escape. It went straight down and ended in a floor of caked clay. It had gone dry on the opening of Providence Spring, but Willie could remember when the fetid seepage of it sold for five or ten cents per cup. He had never consumed any of the water because there were too many sick in that hut above, but now they were all dead (or carried to the hospital, and thus probably dead). He remembered these things within the hour after Judah Hansom first came calling, for the knife. You knew things in this stockade, you recognized men or incidents of the moment; then, under the blanketing of days and nights and listlessness and dissolution, they were gone, scarcely a portion of memory, never a portion of recognized history. The past drifted from you because it was nearly identical with the present, and would be a stencil from which the future might be printed.

Seven men worked at the tunnel, the rest of the shebang dwellers crouched uncaring up above. There were Judah, four of his fellow York State men, Willie and a tentmate of his. They used the handcarved spades, the hoe, canteen halves, and a utensil made from twisted stovepipe. Each had special tools which he preferred, but there was room for only one man at a time to toil at the face of the tunnel. On the bottom of the perpendicular shaft which had formed the old well, the tunnel began. It ran at right angles to the stockade with a slight downward trend. People hoped that it would clear safely the region of Providence Spring, for now rocks could be seen when you peered down into the clear pushing water. Levering stones of any size would be beyond the prisoners' power. It was concluded that at a distance of sixty feet from the tunnel's commencement the passage would have extended to the line of inner stockade posts; eventually it would rise gradually like a long straight hollow blacksnake extending toward freedom.

The symbolism of the snake occurred to Judah as he shoved his shoulders through the orifice, and thrust his long arms in alternate attack against packed earth. He had devised a system of working with the two whittled-out wooden spades. They were rather like bent paddles with sharpened edges. He would dig-dig, dig-dig . . . a downward and backward shaving of the soil, until a harvest of loose dirt lay before his face . . . he could rest his chin on it, and particles got into his mouth and nose if he didn't take care. Then with the hoe which he had dragged along with him, he would work the loose earth under his body until he could surmount the pile of it and shave deeper into solidity ahead.

He thought of that blacksnake . . . tunnel inching forward. He thought of his father, of Aunt Annie, and more often of Benny Ballentine. . . . Might get shot. Well, he hadn't gotten shot, and now probably wouldn't get shot unless he were careless about the deadline. Baaaa. He did not prefer dying here, either, as he watched ungainly hosts weaken and starve and slough their manhood away. If he were bitten by catch-dogs outside and finally bled to death, it would be preferable to puffing with dropsy. Judah's body was transforming itself into a loose pulp inside his caked hide, and he wondered how many pounds of weight he was losing each day.

It had been agreed that no man should be compelled to lie cutting away at the penetration of the tunnel for more than one hour at a time. None of the party owned a watch, but a sun-dial of sorts had been rigged up with pebbles and splinters, although someone was always stumbling over it and spoiling it. This served moderately well as a reminder to the men above, but only on sunny days. Other days they had to guess at the time. When they were digging at night, it was simple; then guards signaled from their stations on the half hour. Night or day, it made no difference to the creature who mined below. All was empty earthiness, the raw earthiness of the grave. The world was composed of nothing but soil, and you could not see it—it had no color, there was no light, there was not even true blackness after you had once immersed yourself in the ground, because somehow it seemed that you needed the suggestion of associated light in order to recognize blackness. This color, this formlessness, this silence declaiming—you could recognize nothing except the feel of your implements, the sound of breathing and labor, the pumping of your heart, the drifting march of people and distorted events which came as a nightmare troop. You dug.

. . . Muskrat. That was the creature Judah'd always considered Benny Ballentine to be, but nowadays he couldn't be too sure. More like a squirrel.

The right-hand wooden shovel had a notch in its crude handle, and that notch hurt Judah's hand halfway up his first finger, and it rubbed it, and maybe made a blister; he must change paddles and hold that paddle in his left hand.

Mr. Endicott owned a letter press with a big iron wheel to work it, and once when Judah was little he went to Mr. Endicott's office with Pa, and he kept wanting to play with that letter press, so finally they said, Very well, bubby, go ahead. He liked to smashed his little hand in it; oh, how he did bellow; but Pa said it would teach him a trick or two. Maybe so. He never more wanted to play with letter presses.

And earth coming back around his chin, and he could lift his matted bearded chin and kind of nudge the soil back under his Adam's apple against his ragged breast; then he would have to grunt, and put down his spades, and lift himself on one arm, and get the hoe and work the loose earth farther back from the face.

O silence. The pressure of lurking solid tons above, every pound a threat. O pressure and squeeze and no clarity of vision. Sand in eyes, burning, and the moisture oozing from eyelids. Bad air draining from the crude noisy world upstairs, and impregnating soil it touched as it passed with its taint, and flowing gradually through the hard-won cleft until it oozed across Judah Hansom's sour body, drifted through the itching hair, the itching hair of his peeling scalp, the itching fungus of his beard, and found its way into those caked nostrils with which he still drew the breath of life (it smelled like the breath of decay).

He served more than his stint; so did Willie Mann. Each held his private reason for making perpetual sacrifice as he went worming a rod or nearly a rod beneath the populous sty on the surface. A man they called Old Bush—and a fellow pioneer of Judah he was—Old Bush said he couldn't breathe for long down there; he didn't know how the others breathed, he thought that they must be half mole or ground-puppy. He said he nearly smothered the last time he crept below. Now, fellers, you know I hain't no shirker; Old Bush has always tried to play fair and square, hain't he? . . . sat with pained legs bent beneath him, gluey tears coming down from his harsh pink-lidded eyes . . . tried to do my share. I want to get Outside just as bad as the next feller, but I can't stomach that chore thout no air.

Judah served Old Bush's shift, Willie Mann served Lew Ammons's turn when Lew lay crippled with cords taut as fishlines in his legs . . . a big fish pulling at those cords, and what was the big fish's name? Ah.

Judah recognized that he must have committed some unpardonable sin, and was now engaged in a fruitless attempt at expiation. He searched his past for the sin. He could not find it. Had he ever made unto himself a graven image? Well, if you could call a pumpkin head . . . he carved one of those when he was nine or so, and held it up to the window to frighten Aunt Annie, but she paid little heed. Had he taken the name of the Lord his God in vain? Only when a chip flew into his eye, or when—

Remember the Sabbath day . . . six days shalt thou labour . . . dutifully, willingly, piously he had bowed to these injunctions. He had honored a father in whom there was almost nothing to love. Why this restraint and tightening of lands and seas and antiquities? All Creation past and all Creation of the moment built into a box of clay, sand, pebbles, moistures, for the unique purpose of caging a Judah Hansom who had never liked to stand within a closet with the door shut, who felt manacled when he entered a room as small as the kitchen pantry, who had wept at crawling into the oat-chest in the barn when ordered there on an errand. Had he borne false witness, had he stolen? Nay, nay . . . oh, tarts and cream when he was small; he had stolen the prize Red Antwerp raspberries after being instructed not to touch them. Aunt Annie whipped him with a lilac switch. Had he committed adultery? Oh, Heavenly Father, he had not so much as kissed a girl when the rest were playing Spin-the-Platter; he'd just pretended to kiss Lydia Ruggles—he sort of pushed his face down past her cheek against her neck, and his face was a fiery furnace, and once again he was the first to leave the merrymaking.

Had he coveted? Well, once he saw a giant in Seth Howe's Circus, and the giant had such mighty legs and arms that Judah wished the giant's legs and arms were his own. Perhaps that was coveting.

He had worked hard and long. He had been frugal, he had prayed, he had eaten bread earned by the sweat of his brow; frequently he had fed tramps when his father wasn't around; in the army he had stayed awake many nights to nurse the sick, to help nurse the wounded, because he thought that God expected him to do these things, and he had done his full share of marching and hewing on the days following, no matter how sleepy he felt. He had slapped his own face to keep himself awake, he had given himself a bloody nose with a careless slap, and thus recognized himself as a martyr.

How long must this tunnel be, how long could a hollow blacksnake grow to be? Judah put back his hand and felt for the knotted length of rags and string which they used for their reckoning. It was like the dirty tail of a kite: there was one big knot tied every three feet, so that it could be felt in the lonely dungeon where no light ever fell. His hand found the nearest knot and pulled the strand tight against the peg to which it was anchored at the tunnel's beginning. . . . He'd scratched out another foot and a half, at least, since he came in.

Dark, dark, dark. The dread, the stifling, the granules in the mouth, the ache of ill-nourished arms which seemed mouldering away even as they were employed. Judah Hansom lay pressed in a vise of the ground. The Adirondacks tumbled all the way down from York State to heap themselves on Rebel ground in Georgia, to effect extinction, the worst extinction if one of the quickest, the extinction of the squeeze, the extinction of the stamp and mashing.

A light snapped ice-white, glaring behind his eyes even as his tired paw hunted for the hoe.

That was it: the truth.

Now it was revealed.

He saw, he saw—he had reasoned it out.

Deadfalls. Traps made of logs. He'd made them often in the woods in winter, balancing heavy logs, trimming triggers and notches deftly so they'd never slip. How many creatures had he crushed beneath those logs? Pine martens, weasels galore, even a lynx . . . he'd sold the furs, he'd made money out of them; never should he have slain those animals, not in that way. Not with deadfalls. For this must be the wickedness because of which he was now commanded to be a lonely beetle.

The stockade of Andersonville was a deadfall log, balanced prettily above him, ready to drop.

Willie Mann crawled to relieve him, Willie closed his hand on Judah's scabby ankle, and the perspiration was flowing anew.

Hey, Jude. Muffled voice booming stuffily.

Like I was under a deadfall.

What say?

Maybe a backlog. Like I told Benny . . . twould all be his, and now Aunt Annie's gone too.

Hey, what you talking about?

Oh.

I got a drink for you. I got the canteen and bucket and bootlegs. Here you be. I'll pass some up to you, and start filling back here. My, you done a sight. Lots of dirt.

Willie, I thought twas Eri's turn down here.

He's got running-off-of-the-bowels again. I'd rather do his chore myself than have him stinking everything up like he did the other day.

What time is it?

Six and after, hot as blazes still. Guard just shot a fellow in front of the Twenty-third station, clear over at the northeast corner. Everybody's yelling about it. Wirz came up to the station.

Oh. Who'd he shoot?

They say it was a Michigander, I don't know who. Here, I got water in your own cup. Harris fetched the bucket from the spring, and we all had a good swig. Sorry, but I reckon I spilt half of it a-crawling in.

Thankee.

Now I'll get out to the well with these bootlegs, and you can back out after me. We'll pass them up. Eri is holding the cord, if he hain't gone to the sink. Some-body's got the cord.

Air was shut off for awhile. I thought I was going to stifle. What happened?

Oh, couple of strangers came by, hunting for a man named Kennedy they thought was in your regiment. We were all sitting in front of the well, but we eased the overcoat across it just to be safe. They stayed about five minutes, but none of your comrades knew the man they wanted to find. Know him, Jude?

No. Could be he got captured after we did. It seemed longer'n five minutes.

Judah was shivering as he hitched himself out into the shaft and began to beat damply suspicious fresh dirt from his rags. They always did that before climbing to the top again. Thus far they believed that they had escaped the detection of informers. They were sly about their disposal of the dirt they hoisted up.

Judah was shivering, but it was the idea of the trap, the deadfall, the log pitching down, the tumbling Adirondacks, the power of a million tons of Georgia land coming down on him like a boulder squashing a grasshopper— It was this terror that ruled him. Willie Mann crawled to his job at the blacksnake's head, and Judah Hansom went up to join tribes who had at least light if they did not have freedom.

As had occurred throughout all the long hot months, heat bred a fury. It was in a pattern so repetitious as to be unworthy of note. First, the sunset swaddled with dun metallic clouds, lightning twitching sickly behind them. Then a distant sound of lonely caravans, caravans traveling with heavy loaded wagons, and their trip was pursued down a pike of corduroy construction, hollow, hollow underneath . . . great wheels a-rumble, the ravine and slopes of the stockade unsteadied by rumbling. Then the beckoning of wind above the fence, the beckoning changing to power and malignancy, scooping lower in whirls and whorls, papers and ashes caught in the wind's scope while thirty thousand rough male termagants began yelling with tonic of the wind which brought decent air to them for a moment (during most sunlit days no breeze moved between the walls, the stolid smell went aloft unbroken). They looked to props and fastenings of their huts, they hung onto scraps of overcoat, jacket, blanket, pine boughs; they hung onto their scraps of roofing material; but every now and then a chunk of clay-daubed chimney was blown free, or a loose leaf of Bible or a ragged leg-of-drawers went kiting on high, and showed black as a bat against the evening glare. Then, usually, rain hit them. Sometimes rain barely touched, and then lifted to assault another region; but more often it lingered to whip the people here. Guards turned up their ragged collars and hunched beneath sharp-sloped roofs of the sentry stations, but those high shacks offered little protection: soon the guards were as drenched as the men they watched.

To Judah, Willie, Old Bush, Eri, Lew and the rest, as they grubbed sporadically in turn—or to Judah and Willie as the responsibility of labor at their little mine's face came more and more to the two of them—freshet or tempest or cyclonic garbage flapping above could make no difference.

We grope for the wall like the blind, and we grope as if we had no eyes: we stumble at noon day as in the night; we are in desolate places as dead men.

That was Isaiah, and the Missourian and the York Stater had mourned like doves and roared like bears, each in his time; they knew Isaiah; the verse recurred to them separately in their struggles.

But Job persisted more strenuously with Judah, for Judah's bleak past life had been tinctured with the illusion of Job. He had thought it a compliment to any man to say, He has the patience of Job, and secretly had hoped that such compliment might in time be paid to himself.

Let that day be darkness; let not God regard it from above, neither let the light shine upon it.

Willie Mann had a grimness behind him, but there was music ahead. Judah had a grimness behind him and a grimness to go to. But still he thought of hills leading off to lakes and summits above West Canada Creek, he thought of the sound of a grindstone, he heard loons on one of those lakes, he felt his axe-blade sink cleanly into damp dressed wood, he saw the polished designs traced by God on a new chip as it lay prettily like a great coin.

Pelting through night the rain protracted, making gum of ground which had been gum before, recently, and would be gum consecutively again. Earth loosened, it was soaked sponge which amid the hours lost its spongy quality and dissolved into a paste as loose as cow manure. Dawn came gray, cooler than the dawn of yesterday; clouds were still soaked and soaking; at five-thirty o'clock, as time was told by the few watches still remaining to those hordes, no true light was discernible . . . clouds roosting above the eastern fence . . . barest hint of morning, perhaps imagined. At the bottom of the perpendicular shaft, knotted rags tightened once more in measurement, a new knot was counted.

Willie Mann came up with triumph in his shrunken face. He rubbed the colored spittle from his lips with a caked little hand, and his eyes were like pale brown buttons. Cracky, Jude. We ought to be under the stockade by now! Well past the deadline, at least.

How far do you make her?

Sixty-six feet, by cracky. Allowing for the curve in the slope, that'd bring her nigh the stockade or past.

Judah and Willie had saved their rations of bacon to eat for strength in the new day. Now they sat at the edge of the shebang, munching without more words for a while. The other York State men were spooned behind them (the rain had been unseasonably cold after the seasonable scorcher on the previous day, and men sought one another's warmth). Over in Willie's own shebang his comrades were still tented silently, none stirring. Close at hand Old Bush drove oxen in his sleep, as he did now with increasing fanaticism. Ho, he chirped, Bright . . . gee . . . he spoke to Bright more often than he did to the other ox of the team; apparently Bright had given him more trouble at home . . . gee, Bright!

Old Bush don't sound able to go down, Jude.

Wouldn't keep digging for more'n ten minutes if he did go. Tain't his turn, anyway. Whose chore is it?

Willie pointed. Lew Ammons's. But I reckon he's over in our shebang all twisted up. He's got the scurvy badly. I trust I don't get it that badly.

They chewed the last pulp of raw pork; it was called bacon, it was nothing like bacon except that now and then you found brownish gristles of lean amid the curdled fat. You hunted it over for worms, and pulled out those worms you could see; then you shut your eyes and popped the pork into your mouth, and chewed and chewed to get it down, and it hurt to chew if your mouth was getting the way Willie's mouth was getting.

Judah rose up on his haunches. I'll go down.

No, no. You did one spell at six, another around ten.

That was only part of an hour whilst you went to the sink.

Then you did a full hour in the middle of the night. Two or three o'clock.

Finished up at three.

Jude, you're doing a lion's share and more than a lion's share. There isn't any call for you to dig the whole tunnel.

Judah set his wide thin jaw. I feel rested like.

I'll go down myself.

What in tunket! You just finished your chore.

What about Eri?

Not till he gets over that looseness, if he ever does.

You can go for half an hour, said Willie with finality. Just let me take a breathing spell, and I'll be down to spell you.

William, we got to keep digging while we got our strength. If we tarry too long, we won't never get out.

I know. And I'm bound to get out.

So'm I.

That's why we're killing ourselves, Jude. But his fierce small face was grinning. We'll make it, comrade. Just think of that: sixty-six feet!

Judah Hansom made his way into the tunnel and set to work. He moved the last disturbed earth left by Willie; he filled two bootlegs with it, and then he fell to with his twin spades, shaving at the tunnel's face. He felt again, as perpetually, the dread of small space, close walls and roof, the pressure coming about him.

Let darkness and the shadow of death stain it; let a cloud dwell upon it; let the blackness of the day terrify it.

In the York State shebang, not in his own hut, Willie Mann stretched his brief narrow length and rested his cheek against his bony arm. Katty, are you there, are you somewhere? *Ja.* He liked to imagine that he heard her replying to him thus in a whisper; but he had forgotten what her whisper sounded like; he knew that she would often say *Ja* or *Nein,* but he couldn't remember how she sounded when she said it.

Considerable disturbance began growing, over around the deadline and stockade to the west, and now the dawn was strong enough for one to see the pen in all directions, to see filmy figures moving in a thin slow shuttling mass among planes and angles of the shelters. It seemed to Willie that he had heard, remotely, some sort of thud and squeaking—the squeal of wood on wood as if one heavy timber trembled in sliding across another.

Considerable disturbance. Of course the prisoners always made a noise, but this was a noise of wonder and speculation; a good many men seemed peering and pointing. Willie braced himself on his elbows to watch. Suddenly he got up and ran toward his own shebang as fast as his sore joints would let him.

Lo, let that night be solitary, let no joyful voice come therein.

There came the Adirondacks, rolling upon Judah Hansom. The deadfall log was made of mountains, and he was the pine marten beneath. He recalled lovely golden tones of a fresh-killed frozen marten's thick fur when he lifted the log which had crushed it.

Let the stars of the twilight thereof be dark; let it look for light, but have none; neither let it see the dawning of the day.

Judah in confusion observed a clear portrait, in memory, of Benny Ballentine. The portrait was clearer than a miniature painting, clearer than any type of photograph now prepared by modern methods: ambrotype, daguerreotype, wet-plate photograph, any modern thing he'd ever seen. Might get shot. But I didn't, Benny, didn't, never did get shot. What? Judah Hansom tried to speak to himself. What is this? What happened? In spite of the fears he'd hoarded, he was surprised to desperation . . . he heard his axe clanging as he stroked it, he heard a raven in fine fair winter woods ahead.

For now should I have lain still and been quiet. I should have slept: then had I been at rest.

Shoving dangerously near to the deadline, Willie Mann and lame Lew Ammons and a growing congregation from that section— All stood gazing up at the stockade. Two posts had pitched down and in—it was at a point perhaps a rod past the nearest sentry station—and rapidly sentry stations were thronged with more than their usual complement of guards. The two posts had dropped a yard or more, and the third, the tilted one, had dropped at least that far. No one of that immediate crowd except Willie and Lew knew exactly what had happened; but it would not take the guards long to decide, and then of course they would come hunting for the tunnel's mouth.

How high is our tunnel roof, Willie?

A yard and more.

Who was down there, Willie?

Jude. I should have been.

Why, you barely finished. . . .

Lew! Let loose of me, get your claws out of my hide! I'm going down the well, and see—

Twon't do no good.

Or as an hidden untimely birth I had not been; as infants which never saw light.

Willie went scrambling down the old well shaft, he lost his hold and fell the last several feet, landing on his face and knocking out two of his loosened front teeth. He went back into the tunnel as far as he could crawl, and with bleeding mouth he called Jude, Jude, Jude, until more earth came sliding around him as if responding to his cry. He had to snake backward out of there, rapidly, in order to avoid those developing cave-ins. He examined the ragged rope with his hand, on the way out, counting knots; he might have missed one or two. He told his companions, once he was come up to the surface, that he had been able to penetrate the tunnel only to a distance of approximately forty or forty-five feet. Beyond that point the ground had settled, and directly beneath the stockade it must have settled more quickly and tightly than anywhere else. What would one of those pine logs weigh? Maybe a foot to a foot-and-a-half in diameter; and they were said to be twenty feet in length, though but fifteen feet in height showed above the ground.

There the wicked cease from troubling; and there the weary be at rest.

There the prisoners rest together.

Willie Mann and Eri Gaines went down into the well and, working with the speed born of acute necessity, managed to close up the mouth of the tunnel. It was not an especially good job, and would not have defied close scrutiny. Still, the guards never found it. They were too incompetent, too old, too young, too impatient, they moved too rapidly about their search. Eri Gaines would die in Andersonville, Willie Mann would not, Lew Ammons would die in Andersonville, Old Bush would die in Andersonville, Willie Mann would not. Benny Ballentine would live to be eighty-six.

46

. . . Soldier, do you hunger, are you sickened by the bitter fare they give you, the bitter fare withheld? Would you dine again on fresh plucked quail and baked potato? Sit down and place the wooden trencher across your knees, and—mind! the potatoes are very hot, they can burn your fingers; and the birds are scarcely cooler. . . .

So once more Nathan Dreyfoos strayed from Andersonville, and higher, higher he was riding: no more Moorish towns streaked in white along the precipices, no more farms. Stony watercourses (all dry as toast because the upper snows were long since gone, and so the water of snows' melting was gone) enfolded each its treasure of pink and green, the dry hills squeezed their pink and green, the pink oozed luxuriantly from watercourse crevices as if the hand of the hills had pressed it from a tube, and its name was oleanders. A billion oleander blooms to tickle the soul . . . how long, asked the boy, have they grown here? Did Carthaginians plant them, did Phoenicians scatter the seeds? Nay, magpies and nightingales must have let the treasure fall from their beaks when this wild portion of the planet was still cooling.

Out into the path the squat charcoal burner marched, and held up his hand in a manner of defiance, halting Nathan, halting the little *mulo* in his tracks.

Good afternoon.

Good afternoon, friend.

Please, do you have wine with you? My bottle is dry. My wife should have brought me wine yesterday, but she did not appear. I have been drinking water but I fear to become ill because of the water.

That is not true. The water in these mountains is pure. I have been drinking of it for two days.

Ha. You are young. I have thirty-one years, and I have health because I drink much wine.

Friend, I have two liters of wine with me, and I am happy to share with you. Nathan reached into the basket hanging behind him and brought forth a hide bottle which bulged like the udder of an unmilked goat. The eyes of the charcoal burner gleamed with joy, and blackened corners of his mouth twisted, and his sooty eyebrows went on high. God will reward you, he said. He tipped the bottle above his open mouth and the lovely purple stream spurted. He drank, swallow, swallow, long swallow, pause, long swallow, swallow, swallow, swallow. He lowered the bottle, not so bulging now, and said, Ah, in a rapture which echoed along the splintered chasms above.

You dwell here alone?

Through many days. It is necessary, because I am a charcoal burner, and must keep the fires going, and distribute the wood, and remove the *carbón* when it is charred. My wife lives with her father on the road to Gaucín; she cannot live with me here in my hut, because the place is too high for her. You know—women, with their infirmities? Or do you know? You are very young. How many years have you?

Only fifteen.

You are tall, *hombre*—taller than I, by far, and I am twice thy age. May I be permitted to have more wine?

Yes, yes, yes—please.

Again the thin pretty stream curving, the open mouth receiving. The urine of the gods, said the charcoal burner, and he and Nathan laughed at the ancient jest.

Man, what name have you?

Natán. And you?

I am called Pepe. José Romera and Mancera, but of course I am called Pepe. Natán, can you shoot a gun?

Yes, I have skill with guns.

Can you kill birds?

I have killed many birds. In France, doves; also here in Spain. In Scotland I have shot many grouse. In the United States of America I have killed many birds of the name of wild ducks—some are called mallards, some are called teal.

Is that a jest? You have traveled in many nations, and you are so young?

Nathan Dreyfoos felt uncomfortably ashamed, and felt also a sudden discomfort which did not stem from shame. Perhaps Pepe was acquainted with bandits, and would tell them that in these mountains and on this path there traveled a youth who had ranged far and wide through the world, and whose parents must be wealthy without doubt and able to pay a large ransom.

But he felt also that he must not lie to Pepe. He had been taught that there was an infallible virtue in truth for its own sake. Solomon Dreyfoos said that even in business it was not necessary to lie. There were wiser and more diplomatic ways to avoid offending, or to convey an intended meaning; a man should cultivate these methods, and not burden his conscience with untruths. Nathan could not recall himself as telling fibs—not since he was six or seven, and stole comfits and barley-sugar, and denied it, and got a thrashing.

He said, My friend, it is a strange story, too long a story to be related now. But I swear it by the head of my mother.

Natán, I have a gun, also powder and shot. In this upper valley are many *cordonices* but my eyes give me pain and I cannot see as well as I could when I was younger. Perhaps it is because I have filled my eyes with smoke for so many years, as a charcoal burner. I grow weary of baked potatoes. Do you like baked potatoes?

Yes, very much. Especially with salt and butter.

Salt I have, but no butter. But how should you like to dine on baked potatoes, dinner after dinner, luncheon after luncheon? Also for breakfast? I have bread and oil; but my bread is growing dry as a rock; my wife was to bring me fresh bread, and I pray that she is not sick. Natán, why should you not take my gun and shoot some quail? Can you afford to spend the time? I have wasted powder and shot, many times; as I informed you, my eyes are bad. It is early for quail, but certainly the chicks are now large enough to take care of themselves. Please?

For reply Nathan brought his mule off the track and past the smouldering charcoal kilns, and up to the very door of Pepe's hut. It was the usual habitation of shepherds or herdsmen in lonely places—a conical wigwam thatched with pine, floored and based with stones, softened with a thick bed of dry grasses.

Where is your gun? Where is a good spot for Tomás to graze?

I have my gun in my hut, wrapped in a blanket. It has rust but it will serve. Is Tomás the name of your mule? He is a handsome animal. See—below here, immediately beyond those large rocks, there is still some grass—some of the grass is still green or partly green.

I shall remove the saddle.

Natán, allow me to assist you.

. . . High he went along the scar of a stream no longer a stream. He could actually hear birds piping ahead of him. The gun was a smooth-bore flintlock, very old, it had a loose stock, it would not do to load it with a heavy charge. It would be necessary to kill the quail at close range, he would need to shoot quickly as they rose. The gun's lock had proved rusty and stiff, but Pepe used olive oil, working it into the mechanism with his thumb, holding the weapon aloft, turning it, oiling through gravity. Nathan examined the flint, didn't approve of it, requested a fresh flint, which was found. He donned an ammunition belt—a kind of antique bandolier, dry and smelly, with pouches for shot, powder and a special fine priming powder. Nathan rubbed this latter substance in his palm, and sniffed it. Where had such powder ever come from; how had the lonely charcoal burner acquired it? It was fine, silvery, beautifully blended, crushed to infinitesimal particles, finer than the finest English powder; surely it would explode with a flash, instanter.

High he went, there were plants like sage, plants like heather, surely they were sage and heather. Clumps of cobalt live-forever flowers tufted underfoot, the afternoon sun glinted on scraps of marble, two eagles swung challengingly. The first quail came flurrying up with a light roar; Nathan lifted his gun but did not shoot. He wished to grow accustomed to the feel of the weapon, to grow accustomed to the buzzing of quail's wings and the sight of their feathers whirling, their wings blurring. Another bird, more birds . . . next time he would fire. Two feathery little bombshells went bursting up in a single second, and Nathan took the left-hand *cordoniz* of the brace; he longed for his own double-barrel. The fancy powder burnt with the flame of a star, the charge roared with a sullen gasp in the rusty barrel, the shot flew out, the bird came down. Nathan reloaded laboriously before he went to pick up his prize, and it was well that he did so: another bird flew out before he reached the dead one. In Scotland he had known an old gillie who called such a lonely lingering refusing-to-fly-until-the-last-possible-moment bird a *jouck* or *jouk* or *joock*—anyway it was rhymed with *book* or *look*. The jouck died in midair and fell near the other. Far down the glen Tomás brayed in annoyance each time the gun was fired. Nathan wasted but two charges on empty air; also he wounded one bird slightly, crippling it until the poor thing went hobbling into the shrubbery and he had to run after it and dispatch it with a stick. Otherwise he shot to perfection, and came back an hour later, glorying in splashes of oleander pink which burst from creased valleys far below. He lifted his voice in a homemade *flamenco*. His new friend Pepe replied in kind; he sang with a voice far more musical than Nathan's; he confessed that he sang assiduously, beguiling his loneliness all day long and sometimes in nighttimes when he thought of his young wife. He sang now a *saeta* completely out of season. He sang that it was a long and dolorous road which Our Lord was compelled to walk . . . oh, dear Lord, the nails in his hands . . . so heavy the Cross. Pepe had drunk more of the wine and —wineless for two preceding days—was growing slightly tipsy. He had put several fat new potatoes to roast in the ashes of his kiln, and displayed proudly to Nathan a bottle of oil which he said was the best to be had in Andalucia . . . it was refined in Coín, highly refined . . . members of the royal family sent all the way from Madrid and Aranjuez for this same oil.

Nathan came apparently empty-handed, except for the gun from which he now drew the charge for safety's sake.

What? No fortune? No quail? I thought you were an expert.

See, *hombre!* For a trick Nathan had tied the dead birds to a cord slung down the middle of his back. He lifted the loop over his head and twirled the feathery burden to the ground in front of the startled charcoal burner. See. Ten birds. Sufficient? Roast them all and eat all you please, and keep some of them to eat cold at your next *comida!*

Nathan had eaten nothing since early morning except cheese and a wad from a loaf of bread (he preferred crusts to the insides of the loaves, and had eaten the crust from this loaf the day before). He sat on a rock with long arms bent around his knees, watching Pepe at his cookery. It seemed that Pepe could cook birds as well as *carbón.* Pepe had made a long spit of peeled wood and on this spit the quail were impaled, roosting and roasting in a solemn headless gutted row. Someone else must come past this lonely place now and again, for Pepe admitted that he could not shoot birds, yet he had the crotched posts for his spit already cut, old and blackened; and crevices had been prepared to receive them. Yes, someone else came to that place and secured quail.

My friend, you have some other person who provides *cordonices* for your kitchen?

Pepe turned swiftly. His face was so baked by the heat and so dirtied by his occupation that Nathan could not estimate the expression accurately; yet he was certain that Pepe gave him a look of intense suspicion.

No, young sir. No one.

But the posts for the spit? They were prepared.

Oh, once I had a partner. That was long ago. He is dead, he died beneath an avalanche. See? Over on that next mountain. Under that great loose mass of gray stones, he is lying there somewhere, very deep down; it was impossible to dig him out. No, no, *hombre,* this is a lonely place! No one comes.

. . . But now, he cried in another hour, waving a quail breast aloft, this is indeed my afternoon of fortune. You have brought me good fortune, Natán! See: look down at the cleft where the path curves, where the clumps of mullein are growing. Do you not see her? My wife! See, she comes with one basket on her head and another on her arm. She is late in coming, which means that she will spend the night with me. Thanks to God.

Her name was Angelita. She had blue eyes, narrow but dancing, and tumbled brown hair which did not appear too clean. She was nearly as brown as the original Moors who must have been numbered thickly among her ancestors. Her tough legs, her round hips swung with a flourish beneath the layers of colored Andalucian skirts, and caused Nathan much aching later when he lay in bed, in a distant village, and thought of Pepe and Pepe's wife, and how they must be united in that wigwam.

. . . Does the ugliness corrode you, soldier? Would you escape its burning and stain? Then drift once more where holly oaks and stripped cork oaks put down their shade.

He'd spent two days in Ronda. For hours he'd leaned on the bridge across the chasm, staring down at specks which were swallows and pigeons, at larger slower blacker specks which he supposed were crows or rooks. Gypsy children hung about to importune him for money each time he stirred, but he was deaf to their whining and had ears only for the loose rumble of the shrunken stream far below. He wondered how it would have been had he lain as a prisoner in that jail so close at hand—hearing the shrillness of swallows, the hollow eternal vesper song of the river, yet walled away, fettered tight, unable to participate in the beauties of the gorge . . . how would it be, to be a prisoner? Oh, he lamented, that there must be any prisoners, anywhere, in any time.

On the second day following, Nathan became in fact a prisoner—at least he was taken in charge by others, he was commanded to do a thing he had not planned to do. It came about as Tomás paced sedately up a narrow path, a connecting link between the road which led from Ronda to the Cuevas de Becerro and the road which led from Ronda to Burgo. A peasant had told Nathan about this track, he had drawn a map in the dust with a stick. Many miles of traveling would be saved, and the path led through wild and beautiful country (all the country roundabout was wild, it was beautiful . . . a few late poppies shed brilliant blood in the valleys, bees lived above thistles as dainty as orchids). But the peasant had been incorrect about the feasibility of the path for a traveler on muleback. Good enough for black goats with their stiff wiry legs, but a trial for a tall youth whose own knees were scraped by jutting rocks along a dozen keyhole passages. Nathan had to dismount and let Tomás follow him through rising crannies, and for a time he had to carry the baskets, for they were fairly torn from the mule's trappings by the narrowness of the way. Still it was a fair adventure. Once they routed out a wolf which galloped off disdainfully, twice Nathan saw spool-spindled horns of the ibex gleaming on some upper shelf. Over the crest of this range the road turned wider once more, and again Nathan was able to ride.

He sang discordantly, he wished he had his violin. He could not make pleasant music with his voice but the sheer enthusiasm of living youth made him roar. He sang Mendelssohn, sang airs for which there were no words, he invented ohs and ahs and roodle-doodles to support the strain. The path wound down through a gradually widening gorge, and Nathan could see a sparse flock of sheep feeding where grass began once more, and two motionless dots which were the shepherds, watching. Why two shepherds for a mere eight or ten sheep? And there leaped no dog to challenge him as he approached. Nathan left off singing as he approached, and was about to call a greeting when he was treated to an abominable surprise: one of the shepherds reached down behind a boulder and came up with a blunderbuss—truly, one of those bell-barreled relics which you saw in museums. He waved this weapon in Nathan's general direction and ordered him to dismount.

Why do you threaten me with that ugly gun? Is it because I'm such a bad singer?

Bad singer, good singer, it matters not. Get down from that mule! Examine his pockets, Tello.

Nathan stood with his hands in the air, frightened but managing to keep smiling. The armed shepherd was a sour-faced fellow of middle age; he had greasy iron-gray hair curling to the collar of his patched blue jacket. The other man resembled him—perhaps a son or a much younger brother—but was less forbidding in appearance, and wore a yellowish smock. He had been eating food laden with garlic, his breath nearly suffocated Nathan, who liked garlic well enough but not in such nauseous doses.

Behold, he has a pistol, brother. Unloaded.

Take it from him nevertheless.

And a splendid knife.

Take it. And money?

A few coppers only.

He must have more, perhaps concealed. We'll find out later. The Wolf will soon discover whether he has money or no. Young man, where are you bound?

To Burgo, said Nathan, thinking it best to name the nearer town rather than Málaga.

Is your home in Burgo? And what a magnificent mule we have here!

We have no mule, Nathan cried. The mule does not belong to me; he belongs to a friend; his name is Tomás, and back to that friend Tomás goes.

Not if I give you a dose of stones from this weapon of death, *bobo.*

I do not believe that it will shoot.

You'll soon find out if you attempt to flee. Now, march! We go to *El Lobo.* You have heard of him, no doubt.

Is he the wolf I frightened on the trail some kilometers distant? Nathan was terrified, but still he insisted on jeering at his captors. He felt that it was essential for him to put up a bold front. The wolf ran like a *cabrito* the moment I appeared. Will your precious *Lobo* do the same?

You'll see. March! Tello, lead the mule.

Despite his fright, Nathan wondered about the sheep, and whether they would be left to the mercies of predatory beasts. He did not wonder for long. The elder bandit—for such these must be—slid two fingers into his mouth and emitted a whistle as piercing as the blast of a French locomotive. A little boy came bounding down the slope before they'd taken many steps; he did not stare in surprise at Nathan and Tomás, for he had watched the whole performance from his perch on the walls of an ancient fold. He was a ragged dwarfish creature with squinting brown eyes.

Rafaelito, the sheep are in your charge.

Yes, uncle. The boy whipped a sling from his rags and went to assume his duty.

If you harm me or the mule, declared Nathan, soldiers will come into this region and give you a taste of bayonets.

Soldiers? I laugh at the word. *El Lobo* is ruler here.

He'll learn whether he is ruler or whether Queen Isabella is ruler, once those soldiers appear.

I spit at the word. The iron-gray bandit spat. Now you shall march. *Siléncio!*

They prodded Nathan Dreyfoos along for nearly two miles on a side path which might have been fit for kids; it seemed to Nathan that certainly the track was not suited to the travel of adult goats. He slipped and stumbled, Tomás stumbled, the bandits carried Tomás's baskets, the bandits walked cat-footed with the elder man ahead and the younger behind. Finally they reached a chasm choked with bouquets of oleander. The elder man grunted and unfastened the black scarf tied around his neck. This smelly kerchief he folded into small compass and bound tightly across the upper part of Nathan's face. The men took him, one by each arm, and going thus blindfolded he found it easier to travel than before, because the men were practically carrying him. He could not guess where they went: it must have been across a wide field above the chasm's brink . . . throughout most of the journey there was room for the three of them to move abreast, and Tomás squirmed dutifully behind—Nathan could hear him coming. *Urrro,* said Tello again and again, urging the mule. In time Nathan felt a coolness as of shadows, and the captors altered their positions: one was ahead of him, guiding, with Nathan's hands on his shoulders; the other had his hands on the boy's hips. Nathan brushed a raw cliffside, first with one shoulder, then with the other. He lurched, and might have fallen if the bandits had not supported him. Surely they went through the narrowest defile in those mountains. A hand ripped the cloth away from his eyes and he stood blinking. Here was a region of yellow precipices, shallow caves curling darkly beneath the overhang, caves oiled with the woodsmoke of centuries. Hannibal's soldiers might have slept there, and a thousand herdsmen had bedded away from the rain, delighting in the comfort of their fires through the ages which followed.

El Lobo and four of his men were lunching off eggs and roast veal, and where had they got hen's eggs in such a weird place? *El Lobo* was perhaps thirty-five or forty years of age—tall for an Andalucian, not as tall as Nathan. His tanned well-chiseled face carried the marks of smallpox spread thickly, and when he grinned he displayed wide-spaced brownish teeth which were near the size of tushes: doubtless those fangs had given him his name. His blue eyes were intelligent and piercing, but somehow there was madness in his manner. The gods have glowered on me, thought Nathan with dreary humor. Father was right about the bandits, and now they will knock me on the head; and no one will ever know where or how I vanished in these hills.

El Lobo was dressed in baggy black pantaloons and sash and a silk shirt which had once been red but was faded to pink across the shoulders, and discolored otherwise by the ravages of perspiration. He wiped egg off his mouth and arose leisurely to survey the new arrivals. Rocks made the table, rocks made the stove and cellar, and they were paved and upholstered by a collection of colorful and very dirty blankets.

El Lobo sauntered forward with a crust of hot veal in his hand. He stopped immediately in front of Nathan, examined him from head to foot, then offered the meat.

Thank you, said Nathan. I am not hungry.

Because of fear?

I suppose you are The Wolf.

Thus I am called. What name have you?

Natán.

The Wolf stared, rolled up his eyes, and clapped a hand to his close-cropped head. Nátan, Natán, he repeated. Of all travelers who might have chosen to pass this way, to think that it should be you! Why, Natán, your home is in Málaga. And this animal is Tomás. Where did you sleep on Thursday night? At the small inn conducted by Angel Matas and Dorado, the inn known as the House of Gold. You feasted on chicken, cucumbers and *manzanilla.* You paid in gold coin, and it was difficult for Señor Matas to provide the change. Oh, Natán, you have broken my heart today!

How is it that you know these things? asked Nathan.

I know everything which occurs within this region. I have friends, and the news is carried to me promptly. If this were not true I should have been hanged long ago. Even so I was caught and imprisoned—long ago—and have no wish to be caught and imprisoned again. Observe these scars on my wrists. And—here—on my legs. Those came from fetters. Never again shall I be fettered.

He dropped his greasy hands on the surprised boy's shoulders and called him *hombre.*

Nathan inquired dizzily, Why do you greet me in such a manner of friendship? Is this a false thing?

No, no, it is true. You are a friend of the husband of my sister.

It is impossible.

No, no, it is true. How many birds did you shoot for Pepe with his old gun? My sister tells that you are a polite youth with excellent manners, and probably have great wealth in your family, for you have traveled to the ends of the earth. And you gave Pepe your wine, freely, when he said that he had thirst.

This conversation was accompanied by a chorus of exclamation and repetition on the part of the other men clustered around them. He shot birds for Pepe. Pepe cannot see to shoot. Yes, probably great wealth in his family. Very tall for a boy. Pepe said that he had but fifteen years.

Antonio, you and Tello are idiots. Did you not know these things? Could you not recognize Natán from the description?

Antonio, of the greasy iron-gray hair and blue jacket, mumbled something or other.

Antonio, how often have I said that you were an idiot?

Very many times.

¿Es verdad? Now everyone was laughing, and The Wolf had his arm around Nathan. Nathan felt himself enfolded in their primitive childish circle; it was a good and simple warmth he felt; he was still enough of a boy to linger joyfully with the notion of playing bandit.

Suppose, he said, that it were true that my family had wealth. Would you keep me as a captive until much money was paid?

Ah, I have a number of friends who are men with fortunes. I have taken them to hunt the ibex. I did not keep them as captives. No, Natán, you are a friend of my sister's husband and thus you are a friend of mine. Come and enjoy some veal and wine. I fear that the eggs are all devoured. The veal is roasted beautifully; and it was stolen from the herd of Don Miguel Sagasta and Arias, but butchered only yesterday.

At last Nathan knew the identity of that other marksman who fetched quail, sometimes, for the larder of the charcoal burner. . . .

Why, he asked over the veal, does Pepe not give up his work as charcoal burner, and come to live this free-and-easy life with you?

He has fear. Once the soldiers took him and tortured him, hoping to discover where they might seize me. Pepe did not tell them, for the very good reason that he did not know. He does not know, at this moment. He would rather blacken himself with *carbón*, he declares, than risk his neck as we outlaws do. Oh well, one day they may shoot me; but never again shall I be lodged in a dungeon.

Antonio and Tello went back to their sheep, but Nathan remained with The Wolf. Nathan lived blissfully through the dream of that afternoon and the long evening following, and the night. There was a wide moon in this week. A sentinel was on duty each hour through the night, and perhaps more sentinels were posted nearer to the roads. The men took turns at sentry duty, in the manner of soldiers and with almost no bickering. It was hard for Nathan to sleep; he did not rest well, but he did not really wish to sleep at all; he wanted to stay awake, and glory in the enormous blue and silver myth which moonlight made of this region. Valley and shallow caves lost their entity as an actual part of the world's surface—they became legend, along with the storied tinkle of goat bells somewhere in hills below, the wolves which howled on upper pinnacles, the gem made by a lounging sentinel overlooking the crack in the boulders which was the door to this mountain closet. The sentinel stirred, he moved his musket, it took fire from the moon and became a diamond wand, again it was a black stick and part of his bulk as he sat blanket-wrapped against the coolness. One sentinel had a big pipe and perpetually he smoked dried mullein leaves as a treatment for his cough. His pipe would glow and sputter when he came down to put a twig in the low broad fire and light the pipe, the strange tonic odor of charring mullein would penetrate deeply into the nostrils of Nathan Dreyfoos. And with it would come the smell of baked meat, the scent of the campfire itself, the rough sour scent of old perspiration in old stained blankets. Over all—the dry pervading smell of dry Spain itself, Spain and its mountains, the rocks long lived-over, lived-among. . . . I am alone in the hills, sleeping with a gang of outlaws. It will be a memory for me when I am old, so old that I cannot bestride a *burro* but must sit sideways like a woman. What a memory, what a joy. It is more potent than the oldest brandy, the richest wine from Jerez.

They arose at dawn, they ate soon after sunrise, they ate the raw flat ham of the hills, long slices razor-thin. They drank their hot brew of scorched brown oats, and filled their mouths with bread, and laughed. The men were joking with *El Lobo* about some feat of villainy planned for that day; again it concerned Don Miguel Sagasta or some relative of his who did not appear to enjoy the bandits' favor. But Nathan could make nothing of their jests; they seemed to speak in a kind of code, and with sly references which he couldn't follow.

Must you be on your way so soon? asked The Wolf pointedly, and Nathan knew that his visit was to terminate at once.

Tomás was unhobbled and brought from his grazing, and harnessed for the road. Ceremonially *El Lobo* handed back the knife and pistol which Tello had taken from Nathan.

Don't fasten his baskets, ordered The Wolf. The way is too narrow. You, Joselito, and you, Pedro, shall carry the baskets and guide Natán to the outer world. Be sure that his blindfold is tight.

Embraces were exchanged.

I have a small gift for you, my friend The Wolf.

Ha, in most times I select my own gifts. From the purses of callers, or the purses of their relatives. I trust it is not a watch or a ring? I have many, and it is difficult to dispose of them. But I am happy that you have a gift for me, Natán.

It is this: a small penknife. I bought it in Paris several years ago. It does not look like much but—Now, do as I do. Hold it up to the light, and apply your eye to this tiny hole. What see you?

El Lobo bayed with delight. A beautiful woman! And without clothing. And all in color!

The men clustered eagerly to view in their turns.

Natán, this is a hard life for women. I have a woman friend, I have had many others, but they cannot dwell in these chambers of rock for long. It makes them complain, and also their presence causes much dissension among the men. But this woman you have just given me— Ah, she can delight me when I am lonely. Has she a name?

I have never given her one.

Then I shall give her one. I'll call her Belita. I like that name, and never have I had a friend named Belita. There, there, Belita, rest snugly in thy private little pocket.

Adiós. Until a little while.

No, no, Natán. Farewell for ever. I feel that we shall never meet again, but I shall remember thee.

Nathan and Tomás were escorted to the road where he had been taken in charge by the shepherds, but neither they nor their few sheep were in sight. He said goodbye to Pedro and Joselito, and they stood watching as he moved down the long crooked trace, and he waved back at them many times, and they at him.

(*El Lobo* spoke the truth; he and Nathan were not to meet again. In 1859 Nathan read an account of Spanish bandits, in a British magazine. It mentioned *El Lobo,* and told how he had been captured when he visited Ronda in disguise. He was put into a cell while the authorities wrangled about whether or not he should be condemned to death. They wrangled long, and The Wolf was suffering from consumption. He died in his cell. Nathan was pained to learn of this, but he was able to divorce his own recollection of the bandit from the hateful, coughing, damp, expectorating misery of the picture conjured up. He saw *El Lobo* always, in his mind's eye, presiding over rude lunches by hillside fires; he saw him enriched by moonlight, and listening to the wail of his brother wolves even as he slept.)

Being young and thus inclined toward rebellion, sometimes Nathan Dreyfoos doubted the existence of God, and very often he doubted the benevolence of God. But there were no moments of question or refusal as he progressed slowly eastward and southward through the mountains, hearing far away the mule song, seeing new eagles, marveling eventually at wind playing with loose grain on threshing floors near the villages, knowing that the last range of coastal hills would be roasted brutally by dry summer by the time he arrived there; yet he could carry highland poppies, gay blue straw flowers, the chocolate limbs of stripped cork oaks (curved with promise like the legs and arms of beautiful brown women)— He could carry with him whatever beauties he chose; a sad or an ugly thing he should ignore, he should leave behind him.

Men of a village walked out to meet him sternly as he reached the outskirts; he dismounted and removed his hat while they paced in close-packed ragged column, for a flat black box was borne on the shoulders of several. They were bound for the white-walled cemetery on the next windy ridge. The coffin was a small one; it was a child who had died. Now that was a sad thing, and should be left behind . . . never carry it consciously; let the very awareness of death die; abandon it in the hills or wherever else it occurs to provoke.

He passed a troop of gypsies, and one of their women had a wet reddish horror instead of a nose, she was dying of this cancer, and had stuffed a rag into it, and her black eyes, once perhaps as lively as Nathan's own— Her eyes stared and said, This is a horror, I am it, I am the horror, do you see me, how could you avoid seeing the horror which I am? Her claw came out for the coin he gave; and Nathan thought in momentary agony of the Jew whom most of the Jews rejected, and why had not He chosen to walk Andalucia with His healing ways a good eighteen hundred years after He walked Palestine? This was ugliness; forget it, let the hills forget.

Nathan thought of his own mother's voice saying, God go with thee, and thought of the gentle perfection of her soul; and a great fountain of love for mankind and pity for mankind spouted up within him . . . take the beauties along, basket loads of them, bury the miseries beneath clay willing to receive them.

Here and there he found shrines, some no longer in use, unoccupied by Crosses; others wearing small flowers which the peasants had left, and an old woman in black and two sunny freckled little girls knelt in front of one shrine. Nathan thought of the cave of the two altars, and how the felt of moss was blanketing those fallen rocks, cut and squared and beveled so long before. . . . How many sandaled feet had walked this road, how many bare feet, and for how long a time? How many mules had gone tinkling in file, how many whips had snapped, how many weapons of steel had been lugged by the armies, the retainers, the bandits, the youngest soldiers whooping a song of adventure? Each hill was dignified by its own antiquity . . . yes, yes, so it must be throughout the whole Mediterranean area. Sometime he should go to the land of the Moors, sometime to Egypt, sometime to Greece and the land of the Turks. He knew that in all those regions he would find that same impress of centuries to reassure him. It should have been frightening—the visible evidence, the reminder that human beings had been in love or warring hereabouts for thousands of years—but it was not. It was heartening.

At fifteen Nathan was growing tall of spirit as already he had grown lengthy of body. He must study more and more, he must ask Mr. Halliburton to lay out an intensive course of reading, so that he could immerse himself in the great ocean of the past. The common truth now occurred to him for the first time (as in the first discovery of all common truths, it seemed very uncommon indeed, strictly personal, strictly his own attainment in thought): that there was no protection against the ills of the present day, no shield against dangers of the future so infallible as the wisdom which arises from a knowledge of the past. This was true, true! Nathan sang discordantly in celebration of this remarkable thought. So he rode on, singing. Would he serve the world as a philosopher or as an antiquarian? He didn't know, it didn't matter, he would learn and serve.

The sun came hotter each day as he neared Málaga. He had bought Tomás a hat of heavy straw, with slits for his ears to stick through. Nathan decided to ask his mother, with her artistic skill, to draw a pen sketch of Tomás thus decked out, and he could keep it always. In Coín, the bandit areas now far behind, he went shopping. Coín was a bustling town, despite its distance from the sea, and there were many shops; Coín was the second largest city in the province, according to the Atlas of Spain put out by Bachiller. Here Nathan found the woven harness on which he'd set his heart; delighted by ornate medallions and colored tassels he permitted himself extravagance which would have brought a perfunctory groan from Solomon Dreyfoos; but Olmedo the gardener would be proud as a duke. And Tomás—he tossed his head, he brayed seventeen times as soon as the new adornment was put upon him. Nathan bought colored sandals for the *camereras,* a trinket for each of the other servants, a medal of St. Christopher for his tutor, a work basket for his mother, a pill-box of chased silver, very old but with the soft glory of antiquity when it was polished afresh, for his father. On a stifling Sunday evening, just when strolling soldiers and sailors began packing the avenue to smile at girls and whisper compliments if they got a chance, Nathan rode into the courtyard in front of the huge house which they rented from Don Carlos Alessandri. He was home at last, he had wandered for weeks, he had known that he would find delight and the beginnings of maturity in his traveling. He had found them.

These treasures, invested through years, brought to Nathan a perpetual income—an appanage which could not be withheld from him by any lord chamberlain of the future. It accrued in Andersonville when sorely needed.

. . . Soldier, does stench arise in waves? There's honeysuckle tangling on a broken tower above the pale sea. Go and find it.

47

Commonly the Federals believed that a month's furlough was the mandatory prize given to any guard who shot a prisoner. They did not realize how silly this was in its essence. They did not realize that if this were true the mortality from gunshot wounds would have ascended to fantastic heights and that not half the guards would have been left On Parapet, they would have been off enjoying furloughs. A majority of smaller boys among the Reserves were homesick to the point of hysteria, so were many old men. Also the sentry shacks were infested often with nit-brained incompetents who had been rejected by recruiters until this season of Georgia's downfall, and who grew as murderous under one sort of influence as they might have grown tractable under another.

Sharing crowded miseries were several hundred citizens who had been gathered up along with the military during raids and Yankee defeats. Most of these citizens were teamsters employed by the National Government; there were sutlers, some topographical engineers, a few male nurses, a few telegraph operators. One of the latter was shot and killed by Private Mackey Nall of the Fourth Georgia Reserves, late in July. The victim was a nearsighted man named Loughran, a native of Cincinnati, whose specs had been broken before ever he was counted Inside. Loughran's distorted vision could not estimate the fatal breadth of the deadline area, not when a section of scantling had been stolen during the night. Just after sunrise he blundered along the barrier. Mackey Nall screwed his face into a wad and shut his eyes as he fired. Citizen Loughran was dragged away with a ball in his backbone and he died in pain a few hours later, spared the longer pain of a hacking death from the consumption which had thinned him to a mere paring of humanity. Mackey Nall said, I blooded this weapon sure enough, when they stacked their arms on coming Off Parapet. Irby Flincher and Flory Tebbs both felt the tremor of curiosity and envy. How did it feel, to shoot a Yank?

By Jesus, Sojers, did you listen to him holler?

We heard him holler but—

A Yankee ain't but chicken-shit neath my feet! Reckon they all deserve killing.

Flory and Irby wished to know if Captain Wirz had been cross when he interrogated Mackey.

Oh, he wasn't mean about it no way. Just says, Was that prisoner past the deadline, and I said he sure as hell was. Then he says, God damn Yankees ought to stay away from the deadline, or something like that. You know how he talks, foreign like. Can't tell much about what he is speaking, saving when he cusses. Course, that's most of the time.

Some weeks later a dancing skeleton, clad only in dirty drawers which draped his nether portions, trotted within the region surveyed by Irby Flincher, trotted in ever widening circles. Scurvy-bent Yankees fell back to make space for his gyrations. His gray elf-locks waved, he waved great thin hands limply, bending them at the wrists, the hands flapped on high as he held his stiff arms aloft. This wild man's leapings carried him on a course wider and wider, bound to include the deadline if he continued to travel so. Irby cocked his musket. First one voice, then another, then more, took up the warning in a litany of pleas. Don't shoot, hey, don't shoot! He's crazy. Hey, guard, don't shoot, he's crazy, that's a *crazy man. Guard!* Irby lifted the heavy gun and sighted ahead of the crazy man, sighted at the deadline where he thought the man would strike, he waited for the victim to pass beneath his muzzle. The wild man danced ahead, a prisoner grabbed one of his arms, he spun twice around before he broke loose from the Yankee holding him, and then he came on, flapping his hands like fins. Don't shoot! Hey, that fellow's crazy! So Mackey Nall thinks he's Big Injun Chief, was the only thing in Irby's mind. Now you just bet I'll show that Mackey. His buck-and-ball gouged the Yank's ribby chest, front and back; there flew a smoky red spatter.

Oh, you son of a bitch! You son of a bitching little—

Thirty days for you, thirty *days,* you coward!

Give the little fart a furlough!

Joe Brown's Pets! Trundle-bed poops—

You'd break your neck running if anyone ever busted a cap behind you, you knee-high piss-ant!

They're all piss-ants. Think of shooting a crazy man that way!

That's old Weinlund from New Jersey, isn't it?

Yep, deader'n hell. That little cuss up there just shot him!

Only one of the other nearby guards was enraged by this abuse to the point of firing, and his charge made a harmless splash in the marsh beyond. Irby Flincher tried to reload his musket. His body was shaking worse than he had feared it might, he was spilling powder right and left. His jaws ground out the words, Mother-fucking old Yankee mudsills. . . .

That night Nall said, So you went and done it too.

Them was my orders: shoot to kill. I sure as hell kilt.

Their tentmate Duckworth read them a lecture, rambling and vague, based mainly upon Thou Shall Not Kill, but the children gave him little attention. They were bent on putting their equipment to rights in case the sergeant appeared, they were bent on feeding themselves and then proceeding to Uncle Arch Yeoman's store where they might barter some of their stolen sorghum for tobacco (they had sold all of their stolen tobacco to Yanks, except what portion they themselves had chewed).

If Thou Shalt Not Kill, old whiskers, what you a-doing up on that fence with a musket?

I never did want to come to be a soldier no way. I'm of a religious persuasion. They just took and fetched me! The old man let the asthma rock him, shook his tousled head, held his Bible closer to firelight. He could not read the Bible actually; yet lines of text stimulated his memory; his wife could read, he thought of her reading, he thought of verses he had learned or partially learned, they were mixed up, they were addled as his mind was addled. And now his wife was dead, many months dead. Oily tears ran in his wrinkles.

Floral Tebbs felt once more the weakness of the unaccomplished. Irby and Mackey invited him to accompany them through yellow-smelling twilight to Uncle Arch's, but there was a carelessness in the manner of their invitation. It was as if, Oh, shall we ask him? Oh, he might as well come along. Usually when the path to the road narrowed, one of the three had to fall back or go ahead, only two could walk abreast. Usually it was Floral and Irby Flincher who walked abreast, but now it was Irby and Mackey Nall. They Belonged, Flory Tebbs did not Belong. They had each Shot A Mudsill. He had not Shot A Mudsill.

. . . Got me a Yank today, cried Irby with nervous glee, and all the faces came closer through pocked light of tin lanterns. Men with beards, men with mustaches, men with heavy mannish voices— They treated Irby Flincher as a full-fledged adult, as one of note.

Where you shoot that Yankee—in the head or in the body?

Kill him quick, or did he flutter much?

There was a dark-faced young man from Savannah who was said to be of Spanish or French extraction, and who had certainly spent a great deal of time in prison before the drafters got him, for he could tell you every detail of a city prison's interior, sleeping arrangements, menu. I got me two already, declared Looey Blooey, which was what they called him. Always I aim for body, not the head. They wag their heads and you might miss.

I sure didn't miss today! Again attention swung toward Irby Flincher.

Uncle Arch doled out tobacco in payment for the sorghum. Them Yankees steep themselves in wine, he said. Natural born drunkards, and let that be the fate of every drunkard! Oh, I know that some of you military people are engaged in liquor traffic, and as engagers in that traffic you are equally guilty as if them same drops of devil's brew had passed your own lips—

Uncle Arch, cried Irby, where'd a feller be apt to make the raise of a canteen of pine-top around here?

Now you get out from my place, you Irby!—I don't care how many Yanks you done kilt. I got my cattle-whip for protection, and I'll sure take it to you—

Aw, Uncle Arch, I was a-funning.

There hain't no fun in the sight of children with empty bellies, in the sight of women a-selling their virtue along city streets where them saloons are! Irby, you pay heed: doubtless twas the Almighty's own hand that pressed that trigger, not yourn. For them Yankees send ships to tropic ports, and just load them with nothing but rum. Look not upon the wine when tis red in your cup, and them are the words of our dear Lord. But them Yankees look upon the wine, and they sop it up like beasts, that they do.

Someone wished to know, Well, what about Jesus Christ, when He done changed that water into wine, like it says?

Heed me, you all! Twasn't no wine like people got today. Twas a special kind, kind of Bible wine, twouldn't fuddle a man's wits. Kind of grapejuice and tweren't wicked to drink it. But this here wine them Yankees have a-brewed and are a-drinking of, in this day and age— And brandy-peaches too! I mind the day a bunch of Yanks was marching past my little place here, bound for the stockade, and one of them actually had the evil intent to ask me did I have any peaches-in-brandy to sell, and he waved a greenback in my face. Little Irby, you're a good boy, and so is Mackey there, for you were avengers tried and true! If I wasn't so tight run I'd give you each a stick of candy. As tis, I'll give you one stick, and you can divide betwixt the two of you.

Here tis—cinnamon candy. He sniffed. . . . No, this one's a peppermint stick.

Shoot to kill when you got to shoot. Them rum-pots are one and all traffickers with Satan. I hear they got them a round thousand saloons in the great City of New York alone.

Uncle Arch Yeoman's opinion of the Yankees' drinking proclivities was formed during the raiders' heyday; he had not bothered to readjust it. The bulk of prisoners still sane, and with hopes and imagination still active, were much more concerned about the progress of Sherman's army than they were with bartering for pine-top.

A great many fresh fish had come in after the fierce engagements of late July; those battles were indecisive. A spindly but tough young prisoner named John McElroy declared tersely to fellow Illinoisans: Anything short of an absolute success is a disguised defeat. There was a general nodding of heads over this. Leroy Key and Seneca MacBean felt the same way; thus shrewder prisoners refused to entertain an extravagant notion that they might be freed at any moment. They heard of the defeat of Stoneman and his cavalry, they twisted their lips. They heard of the defeat of Union infantry at Etowah Creek; they spat, their silence was a snarl of acceptance of the inevitable. A few maltreated Rebel newspapers found their way Inside; the columns proved conclusively that Sherman's failure was already become history. Prisoners heard later that Sherman had raised the siege of Atlanta and fallen back to the Chattahoochee River. From that moment even men and boys who'd owned the most ardent spirit sat in bitterness.

Through dusk of earliest September, Floral Tebbs walked a beat immediately outside the headquarters of the post commander. While he was there certain momentous tidings penetrated to even his stunted intelligence. He heard a dispatch being read aloud and commented upon. Flory had no idea what Atlanta was like. It was a place. Savannah, Macon, Richmond, Washington, Americus, Albany, Milledgeville: these also were places, he had heard of them. The Government was there, he supposed, in any or all of those places. He had no idea what Sherman was like or how many troops fought under his command . . . Sherman was a Yankee. Flory supposed vaguely that Sherman commanded all the Yankees in the world (in this way there was a confusion of Sherman with Lincoln) but on over-hearing the conversation of officers, and finally paying heed to it, Flory stood aware that Sherman was in Atlanta.

He brooded over this. He said nothing to comrades later, when they were eating bread and bacon, and trying to boil crust coffee in a leaky pail. Flory desisted from spreading the news at this point chiefly because he feared that the rest would not believe him—being jealous, as is humanly common, of the individual who possesses factual information unpossessed by others. Nevertheless Flory desired to cry disaster from his own private housetop. But he would want no one to press him for details, since he was not sure whether Atlanta was the most important city in Georgia or not. He was not sure where Georgia began and ended. He was not sure whether or not Atlanta might be the capital of the whole Confederate States and possibly some Yankee States as well.

Some people had talked jokingly of Sherman's having a tail. Some said that General Sherman had hoofs on his feet, that he galloped on all fours, bore sharp spreading horns, raped every Southern woman he came upon. Some said that he was a Negro in disguise. This might lend credence to the legend of wholesale rape, since all blacks were believed to be lusting secretly after white women (had Flory been certain just what lust might be, and how the deed of rape was practiced, he would have been more comfortable).

After the meager supper there came a change of guards On Parapet; Flory was told off to Post Number Four. He climbed to the platform and stood shivering and a little feverish with a cold which had been irking him. He dreamed of a vast Atlanta studded with domed buildings such as he had seen in the few magazine and newspaper illustrations which came his way, in the fewer books he'd ever peeped into. Through this cartooned ornate metropolis rioted columns of armed Yankees, and at their head loped the rapacious Sherman with six pistols on his belt and a knife clamped in his fangs. Yankees were bursting buildings apart, playing ball with babies tossed from bayonet to bayonet. . . .

The eight o'clock call came droning from stations beyond. It was relayed immediately from Station Number Three on Flory's right. Station Number Three, the guard called, eight o'clock and all's well. Flory stood with feet apart, frail hands clenched around his musket barrel. He put a special agony into the news he squawked abroad: Station Number Four, eight o'clock, and Atlanta's gone to hell!

Bewilderment of the next sentinel on platform Number Five (he was so astonished by Flory's squeal that he failed to respond vocally) went unheeded in the hubbub which burst beyond the deadline. It was as if Floral had jerked the cork out of a bottle from which acid froth, invisible but sputtering, fumed high.

Did you hear that, did you hear that? The guard called it! Yep, I heard. Hell, you can't trust those snot-nosed brats. But— Heard it . . . Atlanta's gone to hell! Must mean Atlanta's fallen to the Federals. . . . Weak cheer here, louder stronger yip in another direction. A deeper manlier yell spread from a hundred nearer shebangs and scraped-out pits, it blended up, spreading wider. It seemed that the entire aggregation, the compressed city-full of depraved tramps, was roaring. Flory might not know it, but he instigated numerous prayers—many spoken, many unvoiced, some pronounced formally and accompanied by hymns, by such people as Frank Ives and his devout circle.

(And by a man named Boston Corbett, who had been captured in Virginia and who entered the stockade on July twelfth. Boston Corbett was as staunch a patriot as he was a religionist. He prayed hourly that he would survive this ordeal because he wished to go on serving the Nation. He did not know that he would survive this ordeal, but he would survive it; again he would walk in blue uniform instead of this sloven's attire which dressed him now; and in a future hour a man would slay the President, and Boston Corbett would slay the man who slew the President. He would become a subject of fame, contradiction, praise, censure, envy, perplexity, abuse. He would stand serene in the same faith which prescribed a Holy prayer when he heard of Atlanta's fall.)

Guards were more suspicious than the men they guarded. Many refused to believe this news until they had checked with sergeants when sergeants appeared on their next rounds . . . even until sergeants checked with officers and came back to report between tobacco spurtings, yep, twas true: the story was all around the camps. Sherman had pounded into Atlanta. The Reserves might be manning these local embrasures any day now. The news was in such general circulation by the time Floral Tebbs came off duty that men forgot the fact that he had been the first to cry those tidings aloud; he was disappointed, tried to brag shrilly, was ignored.

The next day Flory's contingent was ordered On Picket instead of On Parapet; they spent doleful hours shifting about in the rain. It was customary for Sergeant Jester Sinkfield to seek the driest spot possible under these conditions; he apportioned duties to his men, and then went to sleep in the smokehouse on the Bile property, where he had cowed the black caretakers into submission. Once he was vanished the pickets knew that they would be safe from observation for many hours. They left the road and scooted for the trees. Flory, as junior of the lot, was made to walk through rain to a point of roadside vantage every now and then, in case an officer should decide to ride in that direction. Mackey and Irby had been told off into another detail. All of these fellow pickets in this detachment were taller, stouter, older, rougher than Flory Tebbs. Chill of the thick steady rain, slippery clay underfoot, the motionless dripping pines all spooky, and seeming lifeless in their very height and aloofness— These evils increased Flory's sensation of futility, of Not Belonging. He had not felt like this since first he was enlisted, he had not felt like this after gouging and biting his companions and winning the accolade of devil-festered little runt. If a stray Yankee had appeared before him on this day, Flory would have shot the Yankee instanter.

Flory, you go take a look.

Ah, I just took one.

No, I reckon not, not in an hour surely. Officer comes along and we get tromped on in a hurry. Now you go!

So once more down the path, once more scrambling on a short cut to the road's edge and the curve of the hill . . . wet and spineless, knowing he had no spine, not even wishing that he had one. God damn it to hell, those guards On Picket over next the depot got all the hats, fast as any prisoners got off the cars; and nowadays fewer and fewer Northerners came with hats. Here was this saturated ruin of quilted calico dripping its hated streams down Flory's neck, down his front. No longer was there a decent hat within the stockade which might be traded for; they were gone; if you were a baby guard you wore the calico monstrosity which had been given you by the Government, you could get no other. Twice Flory had attempted to steal felt hats from fellow Reserves; once he was detected in the act of thievery, once afterward. He got a beating on both occasions. Anybody could whip Floral Tebbs except Irby and Mackey Nall; and now, since they were exalted beyond him by their recent accomplishments, he feared that they would try to whip him again. Flory's nose was running, the steady bathing of the rain did not help his nose at all. He mourned wordlessly, he wiped his nose on the cuff of his jacket where he had wiped it before.

Got to do it. Got to.

There would be no peace or security for him on earth unless he did.

Whom should he shoot? Where? When?

Next time he went On Parapet—

Donner? Donner was the cook of the late Willie Collins. He it was who'd fetched, in payment for saleratus, the buttons with hens on them which now adorned Flory's makeshift uniform. Donner had not died with the ringleaders, he had been sentenced to the chain gang, had served his sentence, was now become a sniveling beggar, lethargic, dropsical. Once he had been savage, surly, once he had overawed the other prisoners, had preyed upon weak ones. Now he tottered toward his doom unwashed, unfed, unfeared, unloved. Sometimes his wheezing voice reached to the hearing of Floral Tebbs when Flory stood on his platform. Hi . . . guard . . . member me? Donner? Man who got you those buttons . . . you member . . . with eagles, like you wanted? Please . . . give me . . . give me. . . .

Yank, said Flory haughtily, what you got to trade?

Me? I got . . . nothing . . . please . . . give me a gristly bone, maybe? Or you got . . . lard, like?

Can't make no trade less you got something to trade.

Got . . . maybe . . . bacon? One day . . . seen you eating a chunk of pork up there. . . .

Now, listen, you old greasy mechanic you— Get away from here fore I take a pot-shot at you!

The brim of the quilted hat was folded under clogging rainfall, it was like an old woman's sunbonnet, heavier than any old woman's sunbonnet, more grotesque. Distantly Flory heard the creaking of wagons on an adjacent road beyond the trees, the creaking of wagons being hauled up the hill with their loads of dead bodies. Rain seemed thinner now, you could hear things, you couldn't hear the mutter of Andersonville and it seemed good to get loose from it; but you observed the faraway snap of a whip, you heard the driver ordering his team, Now you boys walk off on your tails!

—Donner. Why not shoot Donner, next time he came doddering around?

—Shoot somebody.

—Some damn Yankee, some old bastard Yankee.

—Or just fire at random, maybe somebody would get hit? If Captain Wirz demanded to know why Flory had fired, he could say, Twas an accident. That old hammer just cotched on my clothes, sir. It did.

No! For the other boys had fired deliberately, they had aimed at specific individuals, had picked them out in their sights. They had stood like soldiers defending a barricade (and certainly they were in an act of defense, as sworn to serve. They were defending Georgia against the horde of hated savages within that fence). Mackey and Irby had done a studied purposeful thing; each of them had; they won praise for it. Floral Tebbs might never hold up his head beneath its sagging soaked drippings of calico, he might never claim to be a man until his finger squeezed the trigger and the charge split the air and split an enemy's body. . . .

What you see this time, Flory?

Never saw nothing. Heard some wagons yonder.

Must have been on the graveyard road.

By Jesus God, Norrel, I did think I smelt something for sure!

Hain't you ever been On Picket hereabouts before, Barty? You ought to been here on a hot day like a couple weeks since. By God, them damn Yanks did stink meaner than a bucket of turds.

You know, they ought to plant them deeper.

Sure ought. You hear how them hogs got to rooting?

How I would hate to have a hog of mine feeding off'n Yanks. Twould poison the fat on his back for sure.

O laughter, and rain renewing again, and wind beginning to stroke the tree-tops; the clay slippery as lard beneath your sorry shoes when you walked on it; and awareness of long shallow trenches beyond the pines, and the thought of what lay compressed there.

The storm developed, beat, lifted, went away. Pickets straggled back to their proper station. They lounged, chewing quids until Sergeant Sinkfield appeared headachy and sullen because he had slept too long. Everyone's spirits, except the spirits of Flory Tebbs, rose when they had marched back to camp. Under a dripping tent fly sat that rarest of his species in any army—a paymaster. Several delighted old men assisted him in counting out that portion of the Confederacy's substance which might accrue to this command according to whatever records were kept in the frightened town of Macon.

Major Lonny. The good-natured voice of the colonel. (The colonel was thirty years old. His voice held a drawling yet spirited quality. A pigeon-toed barefooted Afric in a gray jacket with gilt buttons—This proud small servant, whose name was Little Jolly, led the colonel to his desk, led him home, led him to the water closet. There had been a flash, a popping, a quick searing like boiling milk being poured over the colonel's eyeballs— That happened more than one year before, when Captain Charles Whitlow Overcash of the Eleventh Georgia led his company across the Emmetsburg Road in Adams County, Pennsylvania; and now he was promoted, he served in the Georgia Reserves. Aha.) Major Lonny, I think it would be wise for you to take this money at once and pay our troops now on duty at Camp Sumter. Most of them have not been paid since May or June. The general declares (Colonel Overcash laughed lightly, always he laughed easily and lightly; he was glad to be alive, he had not expected to remain alive) that we are not in funds, shouldn't spare a farthing for soldiers' pay, and so on. But he has finally left the matter to my own discretion; and I am informed that additional disciplinary problems will face the commanders of these units unless the men have, very soon, something to chink together in their pockets. Excuse me, Major —did I say chink? Rather I meant something to wad and squeeze together in their pockets. General Sherman might greet us across the breakfast board some fine morning; and it's better that the troops should have this prettily printed currency than that Sherman should. Goodness sakes, Major Lonny, Sherman doesn't need the money! Why, he must be independently wealthy by now—he and all of his bummers. My own Uncle Billy—*not* Uncle Billy Sherman, most emphatically— has a nice place up in Floyd County. I mean to say, sir, he *had* a fine place. And he's standing there in trepidation, watching the bummers go by with all the live-stock, the few remaining head of livestock which the niggers declared they had hidden safe away in the woods, and naturally they hadn't. Uncle Billy is fearing for the safety of his house, when up rides a good-looking Yankee on horseback and says, quick as scat, Insure your house for fifty dollars. Yes or no? . . . I'm afraid the answer must be No, says Uncle Billy, for I haven't fifty dollars handy. Got thirty? says the Yank. You know how they are—very deft at business, most definitely shrewd, able to drive a bargain; unlike we lazy Southrons. Haven't got thirty, says my unfortunate Uncle Billy. I am the proud possessor of sixteen dollars Confederate, and one handsome gold watch, a lady's watch, designed for dangling on her pretty bosom, but now reposing in my vest pocket, sir; and formerly it belonged to my Aunt Jonnie Lee. Will that suffice, Mister Insurance Broker? Entirely adequate, says the Yank. You may now consider your house as fully covered by insurance. Well, that Yank posted two armed men at the front gate and two at the rear, until the bummers were gone from there; and thus they did not burn the house of my Uncle Billy, although they burnt the Izards' and the Witherspoons' and the Foxworths', who were apparently improvident folk with straitened vision which did not permit them to see the wisdom of such a transaction, sir. Ah, where was I, Major Lonny? Digressing again, I fear. Digression is the curse of my life, sir. You will take this cash, proceed to Andersonville, and pay through the last day of the month just past. All ranks. That is an order. My adjutant will provide you with travel orders and, of course, the rolls. I think they are very long rolls indeed. That is a pun, Major, a gentle one. *Long Roll,* you see. I must repeat that to my wife this evening. Little Jolly, where are you?

I's here, said the tiny voice from the floor beside him.

Little Jolly, what are you doing?

I's playing with them big glass marbles you done give me, Mastah Colonel Charley, sir.

At long taw or short taw, Little Jolly?

Sir?

Merely a jest, Little Jolly. The terminology of marbles. That will be all, Major Lonny.

. . . And soon the colonel knew that it was growing late, other people were leaving, he heard the jingle of sword chains, he heard goodbyes given at the end of another work-day, heard feet going out. And soon the black child led him through a door, down three steps, along a cool place where he could feel coolness, down six more steps, across a place, down five more steps; then the colonel felt bricks under his shoes. . . . Horse smell, the voice of Benjamin who served as coachman, the metal step, the metal rail to grasp, the squeak and settling of the decrepit vehicle under the colonel's tall strong weight. Soon the colonel was at home, soon his daughters came to him. He played with their curly hair and he said, It's Patsy.

No, I'm Ginny.

Nothing of the kind, Miss. Possibly you are Linda?

Ha, ha, ha, and gleeful shrieks coming up around him, as if he stood in the middle of a pleasant-smelling and pleasant-sounding bouquet of little girl shrieks. Ha, ha, ha, oh Daddy, we swapped, we changed, Ginny and I changed our ribbons, and Mother did Linda's hair in *pigtails* just to tease you, Daddy.

Then the smell of meat and corn gems, and roasting ears also, and pungent taste of boiled greens, and ripe melons, and hot crust coffee. And chatter, and Sue reading the news to him, and there was so little of good in the news; yet somehow it seemed like good news even when it was bad. Later the yawning, and the saying that tomorrow was another day; and soon the long trip to the chamber, and preparation for retiring. The mutual prayer. At last the lying down in dark together . . . strange way which the blind seem to have, of detecting the difference between daylight and dark.

Sue, pet, is there a moon?

Tis a very new moon. . . .

Captain Sue, I thought as much. Captain Sue, have you employed those horrid curl-papers again?

No, sir, I was under strict orders not to do so.

Delighted to know that you obeyed orders. You may be permitted to approach the Colonel . . . indeed, you may be permitted to approach even closer . . . ah, that's better.

Her body shaking suddenly, her grief wetting his naked arm, her hot wild young wet grief.

Sue . . . after a time . . . don't.

Charley— I—can't—

Is it because I'm—? You said you wouldn't, again.

Tisn't! No, no— Oh, Charley, what if they should come *here?* To Macon? What would they do to *you?* To—to the girls? To—me?

I think we'd all be safe, my dear. Very safe indeed. There are some decent people among them.

And tears to come, and soothing and exploration and then the easy bliss . . . increasing power of bliss, the burning gasping glee of bliss, the ease, the wiping away of hurts of war or any other hurts. Colonel Charles Whitlow Overcash went to sleep.

Major Lonny, acting as paymaster, went to Andersonville.

For some hours the poverty-stricken Reserves edged past the extemporized office consisting of a broken field desk cobbled together by the addition of one leg which wouldn't fold, consisting also of several barrels turned on end— They presented themselves, smooth-chinned or bald-headed, bearded dreamer or young dunce, to the paymaster's extemporized family. They signed for their money or made their marks; there were more marks than names, for some of the signatures were little more than marks although the individuals insisted that they could write, and read too. Fragile scrip was put into their hands, more than three thousand folds of it, when all was done. This distribution had begun when Floral Tebbs and his party were On Picket and was completed by lantern light; thus all contingents of the guards On Picket and On Parapet had an opportunity to draw their pay, excepting those unhappy individuals in the guardhouse. (In the latter cases commanders signed for the men; some of the men would never see their money.) Flory had fifty-two dollars Confed in his pocket. It didn't remain in his pocket for long. He kept taking the money out and looking at it.

You going to wear that money out, you Flory, fore you get a chance to spend it. This from the gangling Mackey, who was scarcely less excited about his own pay.

Aw.

Flory had never owned fifty-two dollars in any kind of currency before; almost he had never owned fifty-two cents. He should have received fifty-four dollars for a part of May, for June, July and August. (Early in June the rate of pay for infantrymen was raised from eleven to eighteen dollars per month.) But fines stood against his name: on two occasions he had been fined one dollar for misuse or abuse of Government equipment. Now he wished that he had been better behaved.

Think I know where, said Mackey in concealed excitement.

Ask that there tall what-you-call-him, said Irby Flincher. You know, Sojer, from Company D. Jim Waller—that's his name. He went there recent, and knows where to go.

Think we could find it in the dark?

Maybe steal a lantern. Twill be dead dark soon. But let's ask that feller Waller.

They spoke in riddles, and Flory Tebbs might not know what was going on, although he clung to his comrades. He talked boastfully of cleaning out Uncle Arch Yeoman's candy jars, and maybe the tobacco box as well; he complained with the others that they were not paid nearly enough, the Government ought to allow them more money now that the purchasing power of Confed had shrunken so badly. He talked of buying a bottle of pine-top, or maybe only half a canteen of it. But Irby Flincher and Mackey Nall continued to dwell apart from him, he could not reach them, they whispered at times, they laughed loudly about some joke in which Flory was not asked to share.

Ah, said old Duckworth, man might know what you was up to. Get off with some idle young strumpet, and act like Sodom and Gomorrah!

Flory wondered who Sodom and Gomorrah might be; certainly they were not in Company E; they might, like the man Waller, be members of Company D.

Duckworth preached at them, but received only nose-thumbings from the unregenerate. Best you should give the bulk of your substance to the Lord, and prepare yourselves for His coming! For He's a-coming, make no doubt of that. And where will you be when we all get called to the Judgment Seat, lined up maybe like we done today in front that paymaster?

Aw, go lay an egg, you old Duck.

Boys, I give no care how you revile me and spit upon me. For well I know I'm Saved; but when the flames of the Devil start a-reaching and a-grabbing after you, then will you regret! Great shall be the lamentation of you all, with wailing and gnashing of teeth!

Irby gnashed his teeth, Mackey combed through his lore of obscenity which was vast though hackneyed. Floral followed the other boys when they left the tent; he fought to hold back tears; he was scorned, undesired, he had not Shot A Mudsill. But, by God, next time he went On Parapet. . . .

Look who's a-coming, said one of them, and they turned and stood challengingly in the gloom. What you want, Flory?

Where you bound, fellers? What's ado?

Hell, Irby, we're done in.

Naw, let him come along.

Bet he couldn't even get it up, and they both laughed loudly.

I could, when I was his age.

Well, bet on it. Bet you a dollar?

Bet! So we might as well take him with us, so's we can see. You got your pay in your pants, Flory?

Got it, cried Flory. He slapped his pocket. Now, please to tell me where we're bound? To Uncle Arch's?

Naw, naw, naw, not to Uncle Arch's. Mackey tried to mimic Flory's treble. And twill cost you at least five dollars Confed, or so tis said. First we're going over here to Company D to find that man Waller.

Irby Flincher added in a whisper, Then we got to get us a lantern, cause we don't know the way around outside the post too well. And we got to get past the sentries.

Ho, cried Flory, hain't no trick to that! Reckon I know every coontrot in this country.

Lanterns were guarded jealously, people were forbidden to remove them from any tent or shack where such illumination was permitted. But Flory Tebbs thought suddenly of the paymaster. That major, he whispered to his companions; and they stood to listen with what amounted almost to respect. Major Lonny had not yet left the camp, they had seen him strolling past with other officers while they cooked their evening meal. There was no northbound train expected during the evening, and if a southbound train arrived with fresh prisoners at this late hour it couldn't depart until all the prisoners had been counted from it. Hence the paymaster must be spending the night, hence a tent must have been made available.

While Irby Flincher sought Private Waller, Flory and Mackey hunted out the paymaster's tent (there was such a tent, indeed) after questioning only a few people. It was called the Visitors' Tent, and stood slightly northeast of their own camp, among pines near the path which led to the soup house. The sentry guarding this region was stationed even farther to the northeast. Flory and Mackey snaked silently among the trees and came up to the Visitors' Tent from the rear, and saw no shadow walking on dirty dark canvas. A faint light glowed. Mackey made cat sounds, then growled like a dog. Nothing moved in the tent. Flory went under the rear canvas and, sure enough the paymaster must be in residence, for there was his desk dumped in the corner, complete with the mended leg sticking up and straps buckled tightly. Flory thought of currency, vast slabs of it, still to be paid to other troops; but doubtless those scabby black bags were now well-guarded at the commander's headquarters. He blew out the lantern, he and Mackey carried it away in triumph, and met Irby Flincher at a pre-arranged rendezvous in the ravine below the fort.

We got to watch sharp. Sentries on the depot road.

Well I know! Stood there often my own self.

You tell me, said Flory, what direction we're bound?

Over towards the car tracks, then left.

Flory had learned Right and Left since he joined the Fourth Reserves; he had never been absolutely certain just which was his right hand, and his left, before. Such designations were not applied at the Widow Tebbs's house. One said, Under there. No, tother side. One said, It hain't on the shelf next that corn. It's nigh that rag lamp alongside the string of dried pumpkin.

Flory said, Left? Then we got to get past the depot and past them quartermaster's offices and stores.

And car tracks go smack betwixt them buildings and the guards' hospital, so's there's bound to be sentries.

Just you leave that to me, said Flory pridefully. He led the way through sloping woodland toward the northeast fork of the Sweetwater branch, but avoided a swamp which spread between the three small forks. They skipped across the ooze and continued west up a fourth miniature fork which began at a slow-rising spring amid hummocks near the railroad. They crossed the tracks and circled warily south and west beyond General Winder's quarters; there were lights burning in the quarters, a dog barked protractedly but the dog did not come close.

You taking us plumb to Alabama, Flory?

Now just you watch. Well do I know this region. Hellfire, Sojers, I was raised here!

He could not guess their destination, or what excitement awaited; it was enough that he moved respected and depended upon. He hadn't shot a prisoner yet, but he would shoot one perhaps tomorrow. Meanwhile he seemed to have regained the stature which he had assumed when he fought his friends, when he bit off a portion of Mackey's ear. He fancied that possibly some of the other older guards had decided to buy a pig with their riches; and Irby and Mackey were invited to partake of this delight at some secret wilderness barbecue, because of their prowess in killing prisoners. Yes, that could be the answer to this puzzle, easily. The bed of fire glowing a welcome, scorched dripping body of the pig held up on its spit, scent of burnt hair and cracklings newly made, the bottles of liquor handed round. Well, pine-top gagged him and burnt his little throat, but once more he might try to drink it. He was a man and a half, by God. Or would be.

Now he ain't a-guiding us to Alabama, Irby. We must be halfway to Egypt or somewheres.

Jesus Mighty!

What is it?

God damn stump. I like to broke my leg! Flory, you get us out this here forest or I'll kick your balls off.

Light the lantern, Sojer.

No, too many guards yonder. Flory, you—

Them lights ahead, said Floral Tebbs, ought to be that quartermaster place. We get around there safe, we can come square out on the railroad.

I think the little bastard's right.

Sure as death I am right.

They were not challenged, no sentinels walked near, they left stores and offices behind them and floundered through vines until they could creep into a low ditch and then up to ties and rails beyond. Reckon I guided you in the right fashion, cried Flory triumphantly.

Reckon you did. Waller says it's just down the tracks past here, then take first road to the right. He says usual you see a lamp a-burning in the house.

Flory stopped so abruptly that the others bumped him. They swore, stepped aside, looked at him through vague damp starlight, for the slice of moon was fallen below the trees. Where we a-going? He added, Sojers, but the word became a gulp and a grunt.

He's scairt.

I said he was too blame small. Couldn't get it up—

Flory, they wanted to know, and spoke jeeringly between their giggles. Flory, did you ever poke a girl?

His voice was shaking. Whwhwhat's that?

You know. Give her a good poking, where it does the most good.

No, I never, he managed to confess through puny bewilderment. Never did.

Aw-haw! I win my dollar.

But—where we—going to do it? Whwhwhat girl?

Oh, she ain't exactly a girl, guess she's a growed-up lady with kids and truck, but Waller says she does take a good poking and likes it right well. Hell, that's where lots the growed-men guards go. Even officers as well.

There's a nigger wench along that road up northwest of the depot, said Mackey. But they say this white lady is better. But you better have that five-dollar shinplaster handy. I still think I'll win that dollar off'n Irby, sure enough.

They started down the tracks. Flory stood fastened to mud and gravel between the ties. After a few minutes he could not make out the slight shapes which were his companions, going on ahead with the tinkling lantern, seeking the lane which led to the Widow Tebbs'. Flory trembled in momentary spasm, a taste of his supper came into his throat. He had a wish to put his head upon his mother's lap and cry and cry and cry. Sometimes he had done that, when he was little, when he was hurt; he had done that when he was bitten by a stray dog, he had done it when he was watching workmen on this railroad and a stone flew from under a pick and hit him on the cheek. When he was hurt, his mother had been kind to him, often. She'd say, Now, you hain't kilt. Just stop that bawling, baby boy, cause twon't get you no place. You want bread-and-lasses? Well, I'm a-going to fix you some right now, and she had been tender if coarse-spoken when her flabby hands lifted her apron or petticoat and wiped his face.

Irby and Mackey were gone ahead into the night. It was not far to the side lane. Once they seemed to halt, as if waiting for Flory. They moved on after calling some taunt intended for his ears. Flory turned toward the north. For a time he tried his old trick of walking on the rail but he kept falling off. He trudged on, and then there were men with guns immediately ahead of him. He toppled into the ditch and lay motionless until the men had vanished. It could have been that these were sentries patrolling the area of stores and offices. No lights in any of the buildings by this time. Even Uncle Arch's store was dark when Flory reached the depot's vicinity. He walked wearily into camp, slipping past guards who were probably asleep. Before he reached the wall tent which was Home he could hear old Duckworth's snores.

Mackey Nall was not so fortunate. When later he and Irby Flincher tried to creep to camp they were challenged. Irby made his escape among trees, but Mackey was seized and a pass was demanded of him. He had no pass; thus he was marched to the guardhouse. . . . Irby crawled into the tent as silently as he could, a few minutes later, and when Flory coughed the other boy could tell by the manner of his coughing that Flory was awake.

You little prick, muttered Irby.

Just bet I ain't. Want me to come over and rub your eye out like I nearly done afore?

Leastways you never have got you a Yank, and I did, by Jesus God.

Irby. Did you—? Whereabouts is Mackey?

He got cotched and jailed. I damn near did too.

Irby, did you—do that—? Poking that lady—?

Hell, we never got no chance. Blame yard was just full of folks a-waiting their turns.

The bulk of their company drew Parapet the next morning and marched straggling along the gummy road toward the east, and deployed by uneven files down the path which led from station ladder to station ladder. When he had climbed in his turn Flory found himself on the platform of Station Number Forty-one, and saw that Irby was a few rods distant on Number Forty-two. Irby Flincher's inherent viciousness had resolved itself into a combined hatred of Yankees, superior officers, comrades. Honestly Irby could have told no one which he loathed the most (because in fact he despised himself most of all; and thus like all who find themselves despicable he turned the weapon of revulsion out and away, waved it blindly, brandished it at God and Nature) but he seemed declaring in each twitch of his moody eyes or his blobber-lip that Flory was less worthy than dung, less to be admired than a maggot. Irby's studied contempt reached along ninety feet of jagged post-tops even when it was unvoiced. When it was voiced it took the form of rusty barbs, fish-hooks twisted through Flory's skin.

—Whyn't you hold your gun proper?

—Hey, you Flory! Lost me a dollar, you did!

—Shouldn't never have bet you could get it up.

Sergeant Sinkfield, swaggering in the path on a round of inspection, looked up and told Irby to shut his trap. This rebuke administered to his tormentor should have delighted Floral Tebbs but he was plunged too deeply into the pitch of despair. His nostrils were raw and dripping, his soul was sodden as the mat of motionless gray clouds overhead, he had had no appetite for breakfast. He gazed stupidly at hobbling currents of prisoners, unable to sense their demented activity or inquire about it, unable to ask a question of himself.

A fresh rumor of exchange had come into the stockade, it had been peddled by Little Red Cap. Promptly this rumor gave birth to many little rumors and they were waved, hugged, embroidered, waved hysterically again, as if no such gossip had ever been voiced to be accepted by the credulous, to poison them in time. New (and therefore vigorous) prisoners talked together volubly, slapped one another on the back, pumped one another by the hand, spoke of Akron and Fort

Dodge and Mattoon and New Haven. Surviving veterans (therefore they were cynical men) who had managed to retain a fair portion of their strength, swallowed momentarily beneficent pills of legend which brought—momentarily again —vitality into frames and minds long clutched by the drug of cynicism. Their eyes shone despite any discipline they tried to impose in order to keep their eyes from shining; they went with briskness to shebangs of friends; they said, Have you heard? Well, I don't believe it— But— Thought I'd tell you— Somebody heard Wirz talking in his office— Ten detachments going out right away. No, seven. No, six. It was a letter to General Winder from the Rebel war department. Everybody who can walk, going to Savannah. No, Charleston. Paroled. No, exchanged. Going to take them on boats to Maryland. They're going to remove all the sick. No, it's just us well ones. Have you heard—? Did you hear about—?

Men who were in the early stages of crippling illness arose and walked as if a gentle Stranger had strolled among their couches of rags and earth and had said, Walk; you can take up your bed if you want to, you can leave it behind. But— Arise and walk. Boys who lay infecting the spirits of the rest with slow or hasty decay— These boys got up on their haunches, they tried to stand and they could not stand but still they tried to stand. Ten detachments going out tonight! No, tomorrow. No, I got it from a feller who got it from a guard. Got it from a baker, got it from Lieutenant Davis, got it from— Going to take out all the cases that have to be carried and take them on a ship to New York— Take them to Philadelphia. Paroled. No, exchanged. Six detachments to be counted out, day after tomorrow.

Going to make an exchange at New Berne, North Carolina! Make an exchange at Norfolk. Cooking extra rations for eight detachments to take along on the cars. Sherman's got too close. Sherman's ten miles away, only thirty miles away, Sherman's only a hundred miles away. Sherman sent a flag of truce and told the sons of bitches that he'd execute every Rebel citizen behind his lines if the Rebs open on this stockade with those damn guns. Lincoln sent a telegram to Richmond and told the Rebs that if they open on this stockade he'll have artillery open on the prison at Rock Island, the prison in Chicago, Sandusky, Elmira, Point Lookout. . . . Five detachments going out tonight, twelve detachments going out tomorrow.

Boys who were crawling got up and hobbled on scurvy-tightened limbs, boys who were motionless began to crawl. It could have been that the dead already deposited in the dead row began to roll away from it . . . there seemed motion and flexing among stiff meager bodies on the hill yonder even as shovels tamped them down. It's true, it's honest. They're going to nail up a notice this afternoon on the North Gate! A Rebel general's coming inside to make the announcement. Two detachments going out every day from now on. Going North on the cars, going North on ships, going to Florida, going to New Orleans. All the sick, all the well.

Alice had been forgotten, Mother had faded into infinity, Etta had become too misty to be remembered, Sister Kate had become meaningless; so had Father, so had Brother Rufus, so had Shep, so had Muggins the cat. So had Home faded, so had ginger cake and cucumber pickles and the thud of the village fire gong and the bubbling laughter of a certain child. Amazingly these glories reappeared as the rumor went firing to the Island in the marsh, as it went banging against the far north wall, bouncing back to be reflected from the old raider area near South Street. Home became not only a long neglected, long vanished prettiness; it became a certainty, alive, resounding, tinted, embellished, you could taste and smell it. Prisoners gathered by dozens where before they had stood by twos and threes. Now they were pushing by hundreds in the wide rutted streets. A man went mad suddenly and ripped the blanket which was the roof of his solitary hovel, he said that he would need it no more; a boy went mad and sailed his precious half-canteen at a guard. Someone cried that an official notice had been posted on the inside of the North Gate, and throngs went loping or tottering to see the notice for themselves; although the gate had not been opened, no Reb of importance or unimportance had come Inside, no notice had been nailed.

To this trotting and outcry the ears of Floral Tebbs might have been sealed, his eyes stared unseeing. He did not comprehend or even observe. A waif conceived in misery, born in misery, chewing misery for a ration, he appeared to shrink within himself while his scrawny structure remained immovable. He was blighted before he began, yet this blight was unrecognizable and so could not be cured; he felt the blight but could not name it. Bruise of stone, no meal in a lean season, dog bite, nail in his foot, Coral's crutch lamming into his back, nose running now, Sinkfield's wide hand slapping and slapping, bellyache from eating green peaches, wet and weak in the rain, not enough cover on a cold night, no pennies for candy when he craved pennies for candy: these had made his life, a life marred in the making. It seemed that his slight rubbery soul left his body with the explorative dash of a rat emerging from its hole—uncertain dash toward the chicken coop, dash toward the swill barrel—ha, is that a step, a threatening sound, a smell? Then dart to the burrow again and hide. But while his soul was free and vibrating aimlessly it looked back and saw Flory's shape upon the sentry station, and noted with disgust how bedraggled was that shape, how leaking the nostrils and hacking the cough, how filthy the hat and coat sleeve . . . ha! Into the rat hole again. Tattered rat soul scooting into tattered rat body.

Irby Flincher twisting every device for torture.

—Hey, you Flory. Want to go a-poking tonight?

—Fraid to get grabbed by the sentries like old Mackey.

—Hell, yes. Reckon you're scairt of your own farts.

—No guts. Never will have.

—Hain't got guts enough to shoot a Yankee.

The voice of some unknown ancestor lifted in strength from the past, rang out from an unknown unmarked grave (or perhaps it was a genteel grave with a good name on it, guarded by marble) and spoke one word to Flory, and he heard. The word was *Assert*. He did not know this word, had never used it, but it commanded him and he obeyed.

His bony pallid left hand tightened around the wood and metal of musket barrel and stock. He lifted steadily with his left hand, and his bony pallid right hand slid down to clamp below the gun's lock. He strained upward with both hands and tilted the barrel until the butt was at his right shoulder; then he pressed it back, tighter and tighter, until he held notion that he was grinding flesh and little sinews there. Pick out a big one, he told himself. By God, yes, biggest damn Yankee in sight. Now his left hand was far forward, the first finger of his right hand curling past the trigger guard. His thumb wrenched on high to heave against the hammer, he saw the cap exposed on the tube, saw the open rear sight. Slice of the front sight moved into its groove in gentle and orderly fashion. Twin sights strolled here and there, settling first on one man, then on another; and Irby Flincher was hullooing from Station Number Forty-two and another guard was hullooing from Station Number Forty. Also prisoners had seen Flory aiming the gun, and they began to run, to duck and dodge. A tall dark-haired prisoner, a very tall very dark-haired prisoner, turned quickly from the group with which he had been conversing and stood rooted in one fatal fractional second of immobility. The sights were roosting on his face, and he was not more than thirty yards away, in a bee-line, in line of bore and line of sight. *Poom.*

48

Oh, ho, ho, ho. Flory was halfway down the ladder when his arms dissolved, seemed to lose connection with his trunk; he fell the rest of the way, he lit on his side but with those useless arms stretched above his head, and so he did not break one of those loose useless arms. His cheek was mashed against the butt of the gun which had drifted from his hands while still he wavered upon the platform and thus he arose with blood upon him. He did not understand, he did not know that it was his own blood, he thought it was blood from the tall prisoner which gushed to that supreme height as thrown by the nozzle of a hose (once he had seen Mr. Claffey spraying fruit trees—the hose stretched out, and two slaves worked the handles of a pump which brought solution from a tank upon a wagon, and another slave dragged at the hose, and the masked Mr. Claffey himself held the nozzle, directing poison against trees. The masked Mr. Claffey was terrifying, utterly. Floral cut for home).

As now he ran.

Yells of other guards, the demons' yells from within the pen, were no deterrent; they were a wind propelling him. He blew before it like a wisp of cotton blowing, forgotten cotton spilled from cart or picking bag in the earlier childhood of Floral Tebbs when cotton was raised in those parts . . . but the long white wisp would soon find lodgment against a weed, Floral lodged nowhere.

Palisades were behind him, rifle pits were behind, the star fort loomed on the left. Someone grabbed at Flory's arm but he tore his arm away. Hey there, Sojer! Bubby, what the devil—? His calico hat was gone. Drip from his nose ran over his blubbering mouth and tasted salty, and went dripping off his chin. Sheds and tents of the south camps lay to the right, a detail of guards marched in the narrow road directly ahead. The boy swung blindly and darted between tents, and then the long shape of the guards' hospital was before him, and the railroad stretched behind it; soon Flory's feet found the ties although he could not feel his feet striking anything, not even when they blundered against the rail and when they were tripped by the rail and when he fell across the rail, and then arose and went jogging. He did not feel his body striking the railroad track when he fell, he did not feel himself getting up and running on. *Oh, ho, ho, ho, ho.*

Close after him bayed every wolf of which he'd ever heard, close crept every rattlesnake and mad dog and varmint of fact or fancy. The tall Yankee trotted in the pack, shooting out his blood at every pace; and there were Irby Flincher, Sergeant Sinkfield, ghosts from a graveyard, gators from the marshes. Woogums trotted there.

When he was very small he'd played with some of the blacks from the Claffey and Bile plantations. Long since they'd all been sold away—Hector and Isaiah and fat brown Brutus and the rest—but terrors they'd contrived were here pursuing, skeletal hands were reaching.

We not go no further down this way, Mass Flory.

Nossuh! Not down them dead trees, all that black water—

Huh, nig? Why not?

Woogums get us sure.

Huh, nig? What's Woogums?

Close they pushed together and the smell of their color was around him as he listened, and as he cried loud scorn and said that there were no such critters as Woogums in the swamp.

. . . Yes, boy! The truth, yes, it the truth, Mass Flory! Woogums all live down there, I hear growed niggers tell bout Woogums— And my old lady, she belong Mistuh Ganwood fore she belong Mistuh Ira Claffey, we both belong Mistuh Ganwood, and she say I not never go down them bog ways, for Woogums get me sure. All the Ganwood niggers tell bout Woogums. They got eyes red like coals' fire, and big long teeth like bobcat, and they hands they come from the grave, all bone, just bone.

. . . Old Woogum he come in cabin at night, he get real hungry, and he like eat baby— Baby girl he like pretty well, but baby boy he relish lot more! He like white meat pretty well, like black meat better! Old Woogums they live in hollow tree yonder, and they got big cave place back behind all that black water; big storehouse like place, all just smack full dead children they keep for they dinner. Woogums they howl in the nighttime, sometime howl all night long. Well, I hear Woogums howl in the daytime too, you Brutus. You hear me, Hec—

. . . Woogums got long nail on they dead bone finger like great big cat claw, and they reach right through and rip out you belly. Hi, that truth! And old Woogum he all gray like death. Death gray color. They keep old buzzard in cage for have cage-bird, and they teach old buzzard how sing like lark.

And Woogums teach old buzzard how howl, too! Like Woogums.

And Woogums grow real tall—

Yes, boy. Yi! And make himself small like mouse, so he get in your cabin; then he get big again. And he eat you, he *pick your bones.*

Out of the dreariness of six long years the mysterious voices talked in Flory's memory; so there were Woogums behind him now, along with the Yankee whom he'd shot, and the other masses of mad Yankees whom he'd guarded . . . ghosts his half-sister had told him about . . . every terror which could creep or dance or gnash its teeth. *Oh, ho, ho, ho, ho.* It would seem that he had no breath left for sobbing, no breath left to feed his body while he ran; yet he sobbed still, he ran.

Ma, he tried to shriek as he staggered into the dooryard past leaning vine-draped palings. Ma . . . he made but a drawn-out M sound, a Mmmmmm, a mumble barely heard. Zoral had gathered mule-apples left by some mule belonging to a customer, and this dung was upon the step. Again Floral slipped and fell. Again he did not feel the hurt; he bobbed up, gasping, went through space, struck the side of the open door with his shoulder. He staggered back against the door and it crashed shut under the impact. Then Flory was in the bedroom. Laurel was not there, Coral was not there, the Widow Tebbs was not there (oh, faintly, distantly tinkled the music box; she was in The Crib). Flory rolled under the wide disordered bed and pushed his way through lint until he lay against the wall, he lay shivering, trying to draw more tightly against the wall. His foot jerked out spasmodically and upset the chamber pot. His ears listened to liquid go trickling away, draining down through cracks of the floor. At last it quit dripping. His ears heard nothing, there was nothing for them to hear but that frenzied explosion of the musket and the squawk of death following.

After a long while there did come another sound: a scratching at the outer door of the cottage, was it wolf, Yank, or Woogum? Something was coming, some small shape approached the bed, trot, trot, trot. No word was spoken through otherwise unyielding silences, no bay went up, there was no snarl of threat or upbraiding. A tiny hand lifted the hanging bedclothing draped over the edge, and Zoral squatted there. He peeped in at his half-brother, and the half-brother turned his head and saw him.

You get out of here, you Zoral, was the thought which crawled in Flory's mind, but he could not speak. Beady eyes looked into Flory's; then the queer pinched face grinned. In that grin was awful understanding—the age-old wisdom of the dwarf, the cretin.

49

Flory was carried back to the camps and put in jail—not for the slaying of the prisoner, but for deserting his post. There had been so many other crimes of similar nature that the stockade did not buzz for long about this topic, though the victim was well known. The stockade buzzed night and day about the matter of exchange. With official stoppage of exchange long before, the weaker people had given up hope, the very strongest had felt their hopes watered, thinned to vanishing. No one was in possession of all the facts, many were in possession of no facts at all. Yet they hated ruthlessly and with catholicity of hate. Alike they hated General Benjamin Butler, General Ulysses Grant and Colonel Robert Ould, the Confederate agent for exchange.

A tale which had survived more than two years of war centered around Howell Cobb, who was quoted as refusing to exchange prisoners on a man-for-man basis, when General Wool suggested it. Accordingly Cobb became despicable. . . . President Davis was said to have written to General Lee in discussing difficulties in the application of the cartel: *Scarcely had that cartel been signed when the military authorities of the United States commenced to practise changing the character of the war from such as becomes civilized nations into a campaign of indiscriminate robbery and murder.*

So we're robbers and murderers, are we?

God damn right. That's why they treat us so. They got us shoved into this one big shit-house, just to keep reminding us that we *are* robbers and murderers!

Charlie, what would you do to that son of a bitch Davis, if you could get your hands on him?

I wish you boys would quit your cursing. *Thou Shalt Not Curse.*

It don't say that in the Bible.

It says not to take the name of the Lord thy God in vain!

Well, Estes, I never did cuss, fore I joined up. Tried not to, out of respect for my mother. Guess I never did cuss much till I came to Andersonville. But, by God, this stink-pot— And when I think of boys I know at home, like Harley

Tatham and that slob of a Jewett—Never did join up, wouldn't be drafted, hired substitutes— And now they're walking around, big as life, walking down Prospect Street, maybe taking girls for a buggy ride, going on pic-nics to Strawberry Point— Here I sit in this— Know what I'd do to Jeff Davis if I could catch him?

Hang him to a sour apple tree?

By God, yes. By his balls!

For my part, I'd like to hang that God damn Stanton from the same limb.

Why, Shroder?

Why? Cause way back two three years ago he cut loose with that General Order to arrest all disloyal male citizens within our lines!

That wasn't the fault of Stanton—

Hell it wasn't—

I *do* wish you boys would cease your blasphemy—

Listen, Estes, the word hell ain't blasphemous—

Well, I do wish—

It was the fault of that damn old Dutch Steinwehr. He arrested some citizens up in Virginia and told them they was going to be put to death. No wonder the Rebs got mad.

Cracky, I remember that! The Rebs said we had violated all the rules of warfare; said we were on a campaign of robbery and murder against unarmed citizens and peaceful tillers of the soil. Or something like that—

If you truly want to know who's at fault: tis all on account of the niggers. Never should have put them in uniform in the first place!

Wirz is real hard on niggers. Up there at the graveyard. Georgie Hudson went out on wood-detail tother day, and they went nigh the cemetery. Wirz was having two of the niggers whipped. Georgie said they fair to beat the Jesus out of them; said you could hear them yelling halfway back to the stockade—

God damn Wirz to hell. He's as bad as General Steinwehr.

Two rotten apples off the same Dutch limb!

Wirz ain't really German: he's a damn Switzer—

I *do* wish you boys—

This was a reflection of general opinion. The exchange of Negro troops had been a problem insurmountable. The Confederates declared that many of the colored soldiers were former slaves (as indeed they were), and armed by the Yankees. Thus the Yankees were, in effect, inciting an insurrection against the civil populace of the South. White officers commanding those black troops were held to be beyond the protection of any military law, and should be punished according to State laws. . . .

That damn Ben Butler. It all started with him—

How do you mean?

You know what happened when he was commanding over in New Orleans: he hung a citizen, said he had been pulling down a National flag—

The hell with the National flag! I'd like to pull the damn thing down myself.

That's treason!

If this be treason, make the most of it.

Yes. *Give me liberty or give me death.*

Likely you'll get death.

You'll get liberty when you die.

Yep. Exchanged.

Yep. *Paroled!*

Get shot by that little snot up there on the fence.

You can take all the Stantons and Jeff Davises you want, and hang them on a sour apple tree. Hang them any way you choose; but just give *me* Grant!

That drunken worthless poop! Enoch, wouldn't I just like to get my hands on him! At least before they rot off. . . .

What's Grant got to do with it?

Twas in all the papers up North. Didn't you see me talking to them fresh fish that came in yesterday? One of them was from the Thirty-first, same as me. He had it on good authority: Colonel Ould—that's the Rebel agent—agreed to a man-for-man exchange a while back, and Grant positively refused. He wept a few crocodile tears; he said it was soooo hard on our men down here in Andersonville, not to exchange them; but it wouldn't be fair to the rest of the dear boys who were left in the ranks still to fight. Just imagine that!

It's God's own truth—or the Devil's. Grant pointed out that every Johnny held by the North would become an active soldier against us, the moment he got exchanged.

And us?

We're worthless, we're dirt.

That drunken skunk!

You know he *was* drunk at Shiloh. That's why the Rebs ran all over us.

Grant said that if they exchanged the Rebs held by the North, it would probably defeat Bill Sherman.

Bill Sherman! He couldn't get us into a scrape that old Pap Thomas couldn't get us out of. . . .

As I just said, Joel, we're not worth blowing up. Not worth the powder and shot to do it! Just look at you and me and the rest: sick, rotten, starved, hungry, bowels running loose, teeth falling out— Oh, wouldn't we just make soldiers once again!

Hell, I couldn't carry a musket fifty foot, let alone my knapsack and forty rounds.

Certain we're worthless. We're poison! Just let us set here in our own filth until we're mildewed—

I'm mildewed already, by God.

If you boys will only stop—

They felt the deadly justice of their universal opinion.

It was to an encampment such as this that Henry Wirz had returned at the end of August. Wirz came thinner, more probed, more scraped and drained. The right arm burned and leaked as it had never burned and leaked before. The surgeon Greenaway was no miracle man.

Wirz accepted records kept by Lieutenant Davis and the clerks, and tried to make sense out of them in his regular report.

Consolidated Return for Confederate States Military Prison, Camp Sumter, Andersonville, Georgia, for the Month of August, 1864.

Prisoners on hand 1st of August, 1864:

In camp	29,985	
In hospital	1,693	31,678
Received from various places during August	3,078	
Recaptured	4	3,082
Total		34,760
Died during the month of August	2,993	

Sent to other parts	23	
Exchanged	21	
Escaped	30	3,067

Remaining on hand		31,693
Of which there are on the 31st of August:		
In camp	29,473	
In hospital	2,220	31,693

The same complaint has been made again against the carelessness and insufficiency of the guard of the thirty prisoners. . . . Perhaps twenty-five more escaped during the month, but were taken up by the dogs before the daily return was made out, and for that reason they are not on the list of escaped nor recaptured.

That only four were recaptured is owing to the fact that neither the guard nor the officers of the guard reported a man escaped. The roll-call in the morning showed the man missing, but he was too far gone to be tracked. As we have no general court-martial here, all such offenses go unpunished, or nearly so.

The worthlessness of the guard forces is on the increase day by day.

H. Wirz,
Captain Commanding Prison.

In Augusta, however, and during the journey south, Wirz had felt that his load might be lightened soon. It was this belief, expressed incautiously to subordinates, which caused the rumors to gush. For several days Henry Wirz had received no orders, no directive of any kind to support this opinion. Nothing in the world could have pleased him more than the withdrawal of the vast plaguing mass. After the fall of Atlanta he was hopelessly certain that a removal could not be accomplished. Yankee columns would go fanning out from the city and slice the railroads, surely. . . . But less than forty-eight hours after the Atlanta news came, Wirz was summoned to Winder's headquarters.

The old general lay on a sagging sofa which had been requisitioned for his purposes from somewhere or other. He lay there frequently nowadays. He did not lift his head from the cushion when Wirz came in and saluted with his left hand. He did not return the salute or invite the superintendent to sit down.

Captain—

Ja, mein General?

Shut the door!

Wirz closed the door and returned to stand beside the sofa, while Winder rambled hoarsely. The general seemed to be excruciatingly tired; he had been traveling; probably now he dwelt in dread of capture by Sherman's cavalry.

We've got to get these God damn prisoners out of here.

Where, sir, do you take them?

Savannah, Charleston—maybe even up to Florence. I had another stockade built at Millen. Designation: Camp Lawton. Not ready for them yet, no facilities—

Wirz wondered drearily what facilities had ever been provided at Andersonville.

Can't bother with the sick; take the well ones. God damn sick can die here as easily as anywhere else. We'll fill up detachments with only those able to walk. Get them out of here as fast as cars are available to carry them out. Use open cars, flat cars—any type—just so they've got wheels on them. Trouble is, half the God damn bastards will go leaping off the cars and running wild all over the countryside. They'll try to join Sherman; and that's just what we don't want. That's where you come in, Captain Wirz. I want you to impress upon these prisoners that they are to be *exchanged* immediately. A good share of them have their time expired anyway, and won't try to join Sherman if they think they're going to be exchanged and sent to the North.

But, *mein* General— Where do they get exchange?

God damn it, I didn't say that they were to *be exchanged!* I said that you were to *tell them that they would be exchanged!* Can't you get that through your thick Swiss skull? You are to *tell* them that there is to be a *general exchange.* Tell them that vessels are waiting in the harbor. Instruct your subordinates to talk exchange, exchange, exchange, where the prisoners will hear it. Drop rumors where they'll do the most good. I don't want these black-hearted Federal sons of bitches to cut for it. I don't want them loose. At least there are some thousands of them over there in the pines that aren't going to trouble anybody further!

Wirz repeated: *Ja.* So I am to tell them they get exchange. But truly they do not get exchange. Then they do not run away.

That's the ticket, Captain. Transportation officer thinks he can get me two or three trains by tomorrow—day after tomorrow at the latest. How many would you say are able to travel?

Upwards from two thousand prisoners we have already by the hospital. In camp maybe thirty thousand we have. Wirz considered slowly. Maybe half from those— No, maybe twenty thousand from those. They could walk—they could walk to the cars.

Then publish that information immediately!

A laugh like a growl sounded deep below the seamed bulging face, deep within old tissues.

I'd like to see their faces when they walk into Camp Lawton, instead of aboard a ship! By God, maybe I will be there to see their faces! Twould be worth the journey.

He dreamed aloud: I am considering removing my headquarters as far as Florence. . . . God damn Sherman. God damn all the Yankees; but God damn Cump Sherman the most. I wish I'd had him in my class at the Point. I'd have made him sweat! But of course he was there years after my time. . . .

Winder hoisted himself suddenly into a sitting position and glared at Wirz as if he had just discovered him in the room. Well, what are you lingering for? Get out, and to the business! Carry out my orders to the letter. I've got to see to it that Sherman isn't reinforced by any prisoners that might be halfway considered as able-bodied. Get along with you. . . .

Ja, mein General. Wirz got along.

Faithfully he drew up an order, and copies were passed along to Wry-necked Smith and the other roll-call sergeants. On the evening of the sixth of September, squads were assembled within the stockade. Wirz's order was read aloud.

Prisoners: I am instructed by General Winder to inform you that a general exchange has been agreed upon. Twenty thousand men will be exchanged immediately at Savannah, where your vessels are now waiting for you. Detachments from One to Ten will prepare to leave early tomorrow morning.

It can't be true.

God. Can't be *true.*

And will I go back, and will I find a pale blue sky in spring—the spring day which meant the most to me, though this is next to autumn now, the heat is cooling. And will I go back into that day, or go ahead to it? . . . Somehow be exchanged, get home, make my way to the day again, and springtime clinging around the day. When that ribbon-blue sky is covered by thin motionless film: more a suggestion of clouds than clouds in fact . . . my shadow elongated, when the sun hangs low, to five times its normal length. I know—I've paced it off. I'm little, I'm but five feet tall; but my shadow was twenty-five feet long on all that fresh grass . . . fresh grass tender as fine minced salad under old weeds. And larks talkative beyond us; frogs in Garnett's marsh trying to talk comfort; a solitary crow reiterating some annoyance a hundred times. And peach blooms, breath-taking in their cream and candied pinkish flesh: fluffy, close-packed, strung out along the twigs and thinner branches . . . broom straw blazing, polished tan like tin, letting the low sun burn it up . . . haze like Indian smoke, a springtime haze, all over the horizon.

God, God, it isn't *true.*

Through all the raw yelling.

. . . But if it were true— What a soldier I would be! Oh, what a cavalryman I would be again! Just take me back, up in that Tennessee valley, and see how fast I travel when the bugle starts to blat Assembly! The orderlies wouldn't have to wear out their patience, trying to get the laggards to fall in for Roll Call. Gad, how glad I'd be for stable duty! And when they blew the Water Call, how glad I'd be to mount my horse and ride him! Let them sound a million Guards or Drills when I get back! Why, great damnation, there'd be music in the Surgeon's Call! *Come— get—your—q-u-i-n-i-n-e. Come, get your quinine; it'll make you sad; it'll make you sick. Come, come.* Let them play Reveille, then Assembly, then Boots and Saddles; let the gunners go to hitching up, let the buglers signal Forward. Let the wheels roll, let me hear Right Turn, Left Turn, as batteries roll away. I'll never be a lazy coffee-cooler again. What a soldier I will be!

Oh, God, I don't *believe* it.

You mean to tell me—God, or Holy Ghost, or Somebody—that all those rumors have come to life and built a thing we can believe? Why, I see Alice now— I'd forgotten her for so long. And Mother comes back in my mind, and Etta is standing here, and Sister Kate has come to have a meaning. Father does mean something now, and so does Brother Rufus. So does Shep; I can even tolerate Muggins the cat! I can taste the ginger cake and cucumber pickles—taste them on my tongue, and I can hear that fire gong a-thudding, and I can hear the laughter of a certain child. . . .

You mean to say there's a *world* within the world?

There's cider to drink?

There's Chicago smoke to smell, instead of these pine smudgings?

You mean to say I can stand with Ma in front of St.-Mark's-In-The-Bouwerie once more, and look up at that facade with its trees and animals a-feeding, and feel good holy thoughts? That I can run my fingernail through moss above old Peter Stuyvesant, and think all sorts of grave and holy thoughts about the past? That now there can be a past, because there is a future?

God, God, oh God Almighty!

Slap me on my sore back, Willie.

Punch me in my sore belly, Herbert.

Swat me on my sore arm, Augustus.

We're a-going home.

You mean to tell me there can be that slough beside the Mississippi, and great big channel cats a-waiting there? That I can walk to Hazel Green, that I can work the dasher churn for Auntie? Mean to say there's hazel nuts in Wilder's brush? You mean to say there's that cold clear good driving honest clean wind coming in across Lake Huron? You mean to tell me there's fresh respectable snow atop the Alleghenies, and we can go a-sledding? Oh, how glad I'll be to cut the wood, to clean the old cow's stable. How glad I'll be to wrench the flinty dry corn ears and thud them up against the bang-board. . . .

How glad I'll be to climb the stairs to Sweet's. And let's see—What'll I have? Why, Uncle Amos—thank you kindly, Unk. I'll take a glass of ale—maybe two glasses, or more, if you give the word. And let's see now: well, these are Long Island oysters, but— Yes, that'll be fine. Thank you, Uncle Amos. And I wouldn't be surprised but what I could eat a dozen, right along with you. . . . Here's the nice fresh lemon juice, and there's pepper sauce in the flask. Yes, thank you. And I'd like to grind off just a few flakes of this good black pepper. A dozen of the oysters, then! No—don't think I'd fancy flounder; but I'll take the broiled halibut, if you don't mind. Broiled halibut? That's good: just the way I like it, in that little crockery baking dish; and kind of sputtering and talking as the darkey brings it to us. And boiled potatoes, too. Yes, I'll take some slaw along with it. And all the good fish market smells coming through the window, and sounds of wheels a-rumbling, and masts a-sticking up along the waterfront like great big weeds, and beer-barrels being rolled across the sidewalk, and—

But tis true, by jumping Jesus Christ!

Well, let me tell you first: twill be good to be back with the boys! If you know anything about the Army of the Cumberland, you remember that we've got just about as good a record as any regiment that trains around Pap Thomas. And you know him: he don't allow no slouches near him! You can bet five hundred dollars to a cent on that. And then offer to give back the cent if you win! Ours is Jim Steedman's old regiment. You know him: you've all heard of old Chickamauga Jim. You remember how he throwed his division—seven thousand fresh men— into the Rebel flank on that second day at Chickamauga. Hell's bells! he made Longstreet wish he'd stayed on the Rappahannock. Hell's bells! he made Long- street wish he'd never tried to get up any little sociable with a gang of Westerners! If I do say it myself: we've got as good a crowd of boys as ever ate a chunk of sow belly. We got all the grunters and weak sisters fanned out the first year; and since then we've been on a real business basis. . . . No, no, we weren't licked, we never were licked! The way I got caught was when we left camp one night and went out about five miles to an old cotton press. A nigger told us there were a lot of nice smoked hams hidden there, and we found them all right, and hitched up a team to take them into camp. Hadn't seen no Johnny signs anywhere, so we set our guns down to help load the meat. And right then a company of Reb cavalry popped up out of the woods and flung themselves on top of us before we could say Scat. You see, they'd heard about the hams, too.

Tis true.

We're going.

That's official!

You heard the Rebel's reading of the orders.

There will be a smell and blush of haws upon the hillside, if I can but survive to reach the hillside. . . .

Brother, I believe a brief service should be held.

A service should be held indeed; but I should say not necessarily *brief,* Brother Frank!

And now Brother Boston has prayed.

And now we shall read: *The wilderness of the solitary place shall be glad for them; and the desert shall rejoice, and blossom as the rose. . . .* And the sound and rumble of response, the muted chant of response, congregational response, all in a lower worshipful key. *It shall blossom abundantly, and rejoice even with joy and singing. . . . And the ransomed of the Lord shall return, and come to Zion with songs and everlasting joy upon their heads: they shall obtain joy and gladness, and sorrow and sighing shall flee away.*

The first detachments were marched out of the stockade on September seventh. Ira Claffey was busy with his Negroes constructing a log bridge across a branch of Little Sweetwater at the farther boundary of the plantation where August storms had left destruction. So he did not see the prisoners go, he did not know that any were leaving definitely, he had heard only rumors.

At midnight his light slumber was disturbed by an unprecedented screaming of engine whistles at the Anderson station, where the side track switch was jammed; a train waiting there could not enter upon the main line until repairs were effected. Ira went to his window. The valley glowed red with those same baleful flames which had shone in February, though tonight flames were fewer. It was one thing to guard prisoners being fetched into Andersonville, quite another thing to watch and guard them on their way to be Exchanged. . . .

Ira put on his clothes and hung a shawl around his shoulders; the night was unseasonably chilly. He went through woods and past the south camps and stood close to watch the exodus, then moved nearer the South Gate.

Some of these were the identical goblins who had marched in their Belle Isle rags half a year earlier. Their rags were worse now: many Yankees were nearly naked, their grimy skeletal limbs were sticks. Ira wished to cry a hosanna because these people were being taken away, yet he could only grieve at their plight. He did not know the men and boys, he did not know their names. They were enemies reduced beyond the point of enmity because suffering made men brothers, and made brutes into men to be pitied. Undoubtedly there were raiders, or their onetime sycophants, in the halting collapsing throng. Starvation they'd shared with the rest. It divested them of monstrosity.

. . . Here marched Eben Dolliver, with one other survivor of the Moon Hotel mess. Here walked the sergeant named Colony, who had once been a member of the same household in which the dead Edward Blamey was numbered. The Wingate brothers lay on the hill toward the north. . . .

A queer shape moved in torchlit gloom beside Ira, and he saw that it was the Confederate sergeant with the twisted neck, whom often Ira had observed on duty.

How many are they taking, Sergeant?

Reckon bout ten detachments left already, Mister. Reckon there's about seven coming out tonight. They're only letting the well ones go.

Would you call these prisoners well?

Leastways they can walk. They won't let no crawlers go. Nobody that has to be carried.

. . . Here moved the wraith named Private Allen who had shared the shebang with Nathan Dreyfoos; and Tyke, the drummer boy who had wept in a crowded box car last spring. There were the Vermonters, Garrett and Appleby, and somewhere ahead of them staggered their neighbor from Maine. In the herd was a soldier named Malachi Plover, and another named Willie Mann (one day, before many months had passed, Willie would press his clipped scarred head into the pink cambric lap of Katrine Christine Ernestine Fiedenbruster). . . .

The boy who'd kept a diary, John Ransom, was just coming through the gate.

Ira did not know him, he knew none of them, yet his heart went out. He thought, Only the well may go, that lad is unwell, he can scarcely walk. Actually he can't walk: that big Indian is holding him. The edged voice of an officer clipped through the shadows: Hold on there. Wait! That man can't walk. He can't go Out—

Such a press of smelly bodies crowding. The officer ran for a few steps on the outskirts of the column, gesticulating. He turned, seeking a guard. The shaggy-haired Indian leered in pine knots' flare, his hard face grinned, his teeth shone. Yes, yes, he walk all right, he go. Still he had his arm wrapped around the sagging bent scurvy-ridden puppet whom he loved and carried. Other prisoners bawled and muttered, they seemed shaking in mass hysteria, a disbelieving delight . . . more pushed out through the gate. The officer had to run back to his post again, he could not prevent this violation.

. . . Here were numbers of the Regulators who had crushed raider bands. Some of them walked crying, there were prayers being said. A weak voice was heard: Annapolis, here we come . . . hellfire, Ned, probably just go to another stockade . . . can't be as bad as this one. . . .

Their weakness claimed Ira Claffey and made him their relative. He turned and limped into darkness. He stumbled against a stump, stumbled again over exposed roots. He could not see because of his tears. Behind him the angular form of the Galena printer, Seneca MacBean, was just strolling through the gate. His friend Nathan Dreyfoos was not with him. The horrid thing which had been Nathan Dreyfoos lay wormy beneath a yard of loose soil on that distant hilltop. The shot fired by Floral Tebbs had drilled his gracious brain.

50

About two o'clock in a white night Ira Claffey was awakened by a persistent pounding at the front door on the gallery below his room. Seldom had he been routed out at unearthly hours except as a prelude to catastrophe. There was the time the quarters burned at the McWhorter place, the time a black child was snake-bitten while walking in her sleep, the time Uncle Arch Yeoman's simple-minded daughter put her right hand into the hot stove because she had stolen money from her father's purse with that right hand, and she recollected a Biblical injunction she'd heard preached. Veronica Claffey walked to doom in nighttime. The news of Moses Claffey's death had come at night. Also a train was wrecked at night on the line north of Anderson with several people killed and many injured. Ira took up no robe but hurried down in his nightshirt. Apprehensively he drew back the two bolts.

Coral Tebbs was poised outside the door, dark eyes glistening in the candle's flame. Nowadays he traveled on two crutches; long ago he had shaped a rude crutch himself to match the one whittled out by Flory.

Mr. Claffey, sir. It's Laurel.

What say, my boy? Ah—your half-sister—

She's took bad. The old lady asked me would I traipse over here and seek that there surgeon.

I fear he's at the prison hospital.

What about Miss Lucy, sir? Hain't she good at tending the sick?

Come into the house, Coral. I'll fetch my daughter. What seems to ail your sister?

Reckon it's a kind of fever. She's clean out of her wits, and talks foolish like. Seems like she's griped in the belly or something. She just keeps a-clutching and a-moaning. Ma's scairt to death.

Ira went up to Lucy; her door was not latched; he tapped and then opened the door and called softly until Lucy sat up in response. He gave her the message and then went down and sent Coral on his way; the lame boy would travel slowly. Ira dressed quickly, and sipped cold okra coffee until Lucy appeared, gowned. She had brought down some necessaries which she fancied might be of use. Most of the things were packed already in a basket which stood always above her wash-stand, ready for emergencies; this was her Florence Nightmare basket, it was traditional in the household. Ira carried the basket as they trudged through moonlight to the Tebbs cottage. They spoke of the moon, of its aloofness, of the drama inherent in its very placidity because of the marvels it had witnessed for so long.

On such a night as this, said Ira.

I know, I know. Did I ever tell you, Poppy? Once I ran away in the moonlight, and no one ever knew that I had gone. I rose—well, I reckon you can guess: to use the vessel—and then I looked out. The night was just plain mad—like this—cream all over everywhere. So I snuck, Poppy, just plain snuck. Mother would have perished.

How did you get out?

Remember the magnolia which used to grow beside my window, and it grew sickly, and you took it down?

Climbing down trees in your night-rail. Ha.

I did get scratched a teentsie. Then I ran and ran and ran. Accompanied by Deuce. Met with no disaster whatsoever, but I felt *wild*. Oh, might the Lord make me young again!

You crone, said Ira. They walked on in silence, chuckling a little, and then growing more serious as the Tebbs place could be seen directly ahead with lights burning in the two rooms; they thought of the sick girl waiting there.

Whatever can be the matter with that child, Poppy?

I trust it's nothing catching.

Don't be selfish and cruel, sir. Poppy, does her mother— Does she still— I mean, do all those men—?

All the time, said Ira shortly. He shuddered within, thinking of how his disturbed lust had nearly sent him into the widow's bed many months before. Am I dried, he thought, dried up and old before my time? At least I feel that I'm commanding myself better than I did. The long sadness has been a disciplining factor.

Coral was just entering the dooryard ahead of them, and the Widow Tebbs hurried out to the stoop on hearing their approach. She was fully dressed, twisting her hands in her apron, her plump face sticky with tears. Did you fetch the surgeon, sonny? Oh, she's bad took—my poor little Laurel—

Ira explained that Harrell Elkins was at the prison hospital. Lucy took her basket and sped into the room beyond, with Mag following her. Before she closed the door Ira had a glimpse of Laurel's face in the low lamplight; she was discolored, her abnormally thin face seemed now abnormally bloated, her lips hung apart, she gave forth alternate grunts and whinnyings.

Coral dragged out a chair for Ira and sat across the table from him.

Mr. Claffey, sir. You got a chaw tobacco on you?

I'm sorry, Coral. I use tobacco but infrequently, and have none now. Sometimes I enjoy a pipe. Ever smoke a pipe?

Little bit, when I was soldiering. Ruther chew.

How does Floral get on with his soldiering?

Little cuss, said Coral. He shot a Yankee, killed him dead. He hadn't no call to go firing like that. God knows I hate Yankees—got good reason to hate them—but I wouldn't go around blasting right and left the way he done.

Oh, he was too young to go for a soldier!

Well, he hain't got sense enough to bell a buzzard. Ma says Flory's daddy was easy-tongued as they come—just a real charmer, so she says—but Flory hain't got cat sense. He's in the calaboose; been there ever since the day he shot the damn Yankee, and I reckon he'll be there sixty days. They come over here and fetched him back, a squad of them.

Coral tittered scornfully. He was under Ma's bed, and little Zoral he pointed him out to the squad.

Where is Baby Zoral now?

Coral jerked his elbow toward the door. Asleep in that old hen-coop out there. Ma said she couldn't have him sleeping in yonder, with Laurel laying sickly, and I was fetched if I'd have him sleeping alongside of me, count of he wets the bed so bad. So he's got a kind of bed in the old chicken-coop. Reckon he likes it tolerable.

Through this conversation there had sounded a murmur of voices in the room beyond, punctuated—to Ira's pain and fears—by the wailing of the sick girl. The door opened and Lucy appeared with her face paler than it had been. Poppy. May I speak with you? Outside.

They went into the wonderland of moonlight which could enrich every object, which enriched even the tumbled dooryard and made each grotesquerie a prettiness.

Oh, Poppy. It's dreadful! You must go for Cousin Harry.

Child, Coz can't be two places at once; he'll feel that the sick need him over there, as indeed they do, and he'll be distraught. Nevertheless I'll try to fetch him. What ails Laurel?

That woman— The widow told me most artlessly. She's such a simpleton! Poppy, I dislike to speak of such matters to you, but know that I'll be forgiven. The girl—Laurel—was going to have a baby. Her mother discovered this when some time had elapsed since the girl asked for— These are womanly matters. But for—cloths. Well, the widow undertook to interrupt the pregnancy; she employed a wooden knitting needle, of all things. And this is the result.

Ira exclaimed sharply and hurried toward the lane, but turned back before he had reached the corner. Lucy, do you go inside and do whatever you can—doubtless there's little you can do—until I get hold of Harry. But Laurel will require constant nursing, constant attendance, if indeed she survives until morning. There's a train at the depot, disgorging prisoners or perhaps taking them to Blackshears—the Lord knows. I mean to send a note to Americus for Mrs. Dillard, by the engine-driver. I've no writing materials in my pockets.

Lucy flew into the cottage. Coral obliged by finding a stub of pencil in the old clock, and a torn envelope of patriotic pattern. (This relic had been discarded by some visitor of Mag's, and depicted an embattled female Confederacy, complete with helmet, sword and flowing robes, who had just given the quietus to a writhing dragon. Mag said, That's right pretty, and pinned the thing upon the wall as a picture to admire; but Coral hated it always and was glad to be rid of it. Coral said that war was no business for a woman; if there was dragon-killing to be done then let the menfolks go do it.) Ira put these things in his shirt pocket and fairly ran toward the tracks; he feared that the train might have started already, possibly he could flag it down. But no, the light still glared dully; the train motionless, it turned out that a gang of blacks was wooding-up the engine's tender. Ira could not actually run because of the tendon which had fastened itself to the femur of his leg, but he hopped along, perspiring, and made very good time. It was odd, he thought . . . now the smell of Andersonville was thick as smoke, yet he and Lucy had forgotten it when they were moving at slower pace through the moon's beauty. It took but the suggestion of an evil and a stink to bring increased evil, more persistent stink.

He found an amiable bearded engineer who was glad to be of service when he heard that a girl was stricken. It was expected that the train would reach Americus in an hour and a half, and Ira had no longer a fast horse on the plantation—nothing but mules and two feeble pensioners.

Are there not ordinarily some niggers about the depot at Americus, even in nighttime?

Sure to be, Mister. There's the wood gang, and usually some of their pickaninnies.

Then give one of them this note I'm scribbling and—here, this bit of currency —and send him to Parson Dillard's with all haste!

Ira crossed the branch and went up through spectral light and shadow to his home. Twice he was challenged by sentries—there were many more of them about since Atlanta fell—but he had no trouble getting past; he was known by sight to practically all the guards except a few recruits newly come.

He awakened Jonas and told him to hitch a mule to a cart. Ira's wounded leg was plaguing him because of unaccustomed exertion, and also he could imagine Elkins's weariness (but it was a steady exhaustion which the younger man would never admit in so many words). Ira started east along what was left of the lane. At this spot once he had scented decay and had held a fear indefinable . . . the battering of a lifetime had slugged against him and his since then. . . . Bordering wild shrubbery was gone, the area was gashed by a thousand heavy wheel-rollings, the lane ended in an embankment with rifle pits strung beside. Out of milk and mist ahead came a lone figure with skull face ashine: if a child had seen it the child would have run squawking. This spook was Surgeon Elkins who had given the shreds of strength remaining to him and was now ordered to bed by the surgeon commanding.

Violets, said Harry distinctly.

Ira Claffey reached through the pale light and put his big hand around Elkins's arm, and shook him slightly. Did you say violets?

I thought of them, not far from here, said the rough high voice. Twas the first time I visited the stockade region. I picked two, for Lucy.

Ah, violets no longer. Naught but exhalations.

The surgeon yielded himself to Ira's support for a moment only, as if he wanted to be a little boy again, to let an adult take over his charge. Then he pulled loose and straightened his shoulders even while he shrugged them, as he were saying, Come, come, I'm well again, I'm adult, strong once more, I'm still a man.

I dislike to add to your burdens, Coz. But would you be able to come to the bedside of a sick child? A young girl, daughter of our neighbor, the Tebbs woman—

Surely. Did you know that there were two kinds of miasma identified by medical writers?

They were nearing the Claffey gate, and Ira could hear crying wheels of the cart as Jonas brought it up from the stables. He said, The girl is in a desperate condition. I've sent to Americus for Mrs. Effie—

Mrs. Prod-Pry! Forever with a question—

You should be flattered, Cousin Harry. Ira tried to laugh about it. She's vastly respectful of your erudition, and means to learn whatever you can teach her—

I shall teach her, said Elkins as they halted at the gate. Two miasmas thus identified. The *kino* and the *ideo*. One consists of exhalations from the human body in a state of disease, the other of exhalations from vegetable decompositions and saturations generally.

Jonas came driving up and leaped from the cart. Bad night air, Mastah. He was firm in the belief that night air was more dangerous than day air, stockade or no stockade.

Then get to your cabin before you catch your death, Jonas. You in your shirt-tail. The slave hastened off, a tatterdemalion under the serene moon. Ira demanded abruptly of Harrell Elkins whether he felt capable of approaching this new responsibility. You, he said, poor thing, with your babble of violets and miasmas.

That was mere relaxation. Harry tried to be spry as an athlete when he pulled his awkward body into the car. Pay strict heed to the professor, sir. *Kino* and *ideo:* we have both varieties at the hospital, together with a few not yet ticketed by those who research into the matter. But I shall ticket them. Now, then, and he lifted his gaunt glassy face to the white light above. Tell me of the patient, sir.

She's fourteen or so. It seems she was in the family way and her mother sought to abort her.

Elkins growled a curse. He swore but seldom, and then it always came as a shock; it was like seeing a parson cut a buck-and-wing behind his pulpit. Is there severe hemorrhage?

I'm not aware. Daughter Lucy is with her. Laurel would appear to be unconscious or in delirium. I believe she's very weak, and in acute pain.

A pox on all abortionists! Good grief, sir, have I my medical kit with me? Harry looked about wildly.

You're clutching it in your hand, said Ira weakly.

He had grave doubts about Elkins's ability to deal with this dangerous baffling case, rubbed to a rag as he was, chanting absurdities. But once arrived at the cottage Harrell Elkins became all physician; you would not have known the depth of his depletion unless you'd looked intently into his bony face. The questions he asked of the widow and Lucy were terse, searching, sane. Elkins opened his kit and withdrew tiny flasks containing his store of drugs, holding them with care to the light as he read the labels, holding them with a hand no longer sunburnt—a wide bony hand that was pale and seemed frail and yet remained unshaking. Have you salt and common loaf sugar? he asked of Mag.

The widow was in such a twitter that she scarcely knew. Yes, she did own salt . . . twas in a box . . . now, where was that salt-box . . . reckoned there was a mite of sugar on the shelf. . . .

I'll go see, whispered Lucy.

No, have your father and the lad make a search. Elkins lowered his voice. And get this woman out of here.

I'm to stay?

I fear I shall need your help. His spectacles were opaque, frightening as he looked down at the girl. In a most intimate way, Madam. He had not addressed her in such fashion since the long ago day of his first arrival.

Coral was of much more help than his mother. Small quantities of salt and sugar were discovered, a pint of soft water was put to simmer upon the fire. The Widow Tebbs huddled, banished to the porch where she mourned for a time and then fell asleep and snored loudly.

Thank Heaven, said Harry Elkins, as if Lucy understood the drugs he mentioned, and their use. I've still a bit of white vitriol in my kit. And sugar of lead—I shall need to scrape the bottle. Attend me, please.

He put into her hands a miniature mortar and pestle. This contains alum. Please to pulverize it finely.

He had rubbed the patient with fever liniment, and was applying cold compresses. Such a paucity of needfuls, Lucy heard him muttering. Always a paucity. Damn it, here's a muslin pillowcase, appears fairly clean. Sacrifice, and she heard the tearing of the muslin. When she looked at Elkins again he was bending tenderly over the smelly moaning invalid with a fresh moist compress. Is the alum well pulverized, Madam? he inquired without turning.

Tis to a powder, sir.

Do you fetch the pot of water that's simmering.

She brought the steaming pot and watched with respect as Elkins stirred in his materials—salt, sugar, the alum she'd powdered, the drugs he'd measured. She found mysterious satisfaction in the steam which rose from the compound, in its whiteness, its odor. Lucy regarded Laurel Tebbs with that affection which a kind person gives to fledglings fallen from their nests, to starved stray dogs and cats. Laurel was a pathetic beast which had been treated cruelly, Lucy agonized with her in sympathy, she hoped that Laurel would not die. But momentarily also she might forget danger and delirium, and see beauty wrought between herself and Harrell Elkins: they had combined to make medicine, she had squeezed the pestle, she was helping him to help another.

Return this to the fire, please.

When she came back he had drawn a syringe from his bag and was inspecting it critically. You know— His abrasive voice seemed to speak from a sad vague past. My uncle was a surgeon, as I've told you. A wicked man, I believe, but I recall some of his theories and adhere to them whenever possible. He believed in professional cleanliness, he thought that disease might be spread by untidiness. I'm but a beginner. But I feel discomfort unless I've washed my instruments— again, whenever possible. Tis impossible to keep them clean over there—

Lucy knew the place he meant when he spoke the last two words.

Take this syringe and cleanse it in a basin. Give it a scrubbing.

In this way they toiled until the window was gray, until the moon sank toward western woods and lost its brightness. Coral slept on his bed, Ira Claffey slept at the table with his head on his arms, the widow had risen and gone to The Crib to resume her slumbers. Once, in the last hour of night, surgeon and nurse heard voices outside; they paid no heed, they were working. Ira told his daughter later, smiling behind his hand, that one of the middle-aged officers from the Reserves had appeared, a man whom Ira knew slightly.

He was more than astonished to find me in the cottage. I fear he was somewhat the worse for drink. The Widow Tebbs sent him packing.

Poppy. If you please!

Well, my dear, I thought it amusing.

Reckon I don't. I find it disgusting!

Yet peculiarly she found no disgust in her experience with Elkins as they bent above the skinny misery in the bedroom. She had never thought to share an intimacy, even a second-handed intimacy, with any man unless she were married to him. She knew that women as nurses went about bathing the sick; they bathed men, but only their hands and faces, perhaps they bathed their hairy chests a mite; male nurses did the rest. She had not believed that in this night or in any night she would be lifting the limbs of another female, opening those limbs, striving to preserve immobility in the sufferer while the man beside her manipulated his syringe, his sponges and compresses. The possibility had never even entered her mind. She was close to being appalled at discovering her lack of abashment.

We are faced with a variety of complications.

Yes, sir.

On the one hand it's essential that we reduce the fever, and in doing so must reduce the pain suffered by the patient; on the other hand there's been butchery; we must treat the local situation— As now.

Yes, sir.

Sometimes Laurel was silent, sometimes she snarled or cried out recognizable pleas, sometimes she tossed her arms wildly while wailing; it was difficult to tend her. Sometimes she made so much noise that Lucy could scarcely hear what Elkins was saying.

. . . Necessary to . . . more quietly . . . you see, I must hold the syringe . . . injection . . . regular female syringe would be preferable but . . . none . . . into the vagina for at least. . . .

The Dillards came driving up behind Blackie two hours after daylight. Laurel was still alive although Elkins had feared that she would die with the sunrise; she'd weakened terribly. But deep within the girl's scrambled inheritance there was a will to live, there was power to be invoked—that tonic contained in bodies and souls of some of the weakest, some of the most wasted.

Effie Dillard bustled furiously to her task, ragged starched cap-frill standing out like sunrays above her pocked yellow face. She took one look at Harrell Elkins and ordered him home. Clean white cloths appeared magically, rough towels were drying and warming in front of the fire. Be off with you, Surgeon, or you'll be lying sickly as this unhappy lass! She set the amazed Coral to picking the chicken she had rushed to decapitate before leaving Americus. If only I can get a wee swallow of broth down the child's throat. Away with you, Surgeon! The dominie can help me as he's helped before. Cousin Harry and the Claffeys rode off in the cart.

Before Harrell Elkins went up to bed he stood gazing fixedly at the bedraggled Lucy. Florence Nightmare, he said, indulging in the family jest as his beloved Sutherland had done often.

Mrs. Dillard fetched everything from febrifuge to Peckham's Cough Balsam, from emenagogue tincture to female laxative and anodyne pills. She must have cleared two shelves of her medicine closet. She shared the concern of Elkins: it appeared that she would lose her patient about four o'clock of the first afternoon. She worked in frenzy to stimulate the child's heart action and circulation. She reported, when Cousin Harry was able to look in the next morning, that Laurel was mending. Harry did not share this hopeful opinion. But when the girl lived still, two days following, he asked Mrs. Dillard what witches' remedies she had employed.

A spicy friendship grew between the voluble Scotswoman and the weary young zealot. They made dreadful jokes about live chickens split with an axe and laid upon a sufferer's wound, about black cats killed in the dark of the moon. When Elkins and Lucy arrived at the cottage in company, they came laden with provisions which Lucy had selected; but Harrell declared the rusks to be English worm cakes, the fresh bacon to be toad ointment. For sprains, strains, lame-back, rheumatism And So Forth, he recommended it. Obtain good-sized live toads, four in number. He described the process. Put into boiling water and cook until very soft. Then take out and boil the water down to one-half pint, and add fresh butter, one pound; and simmer together, and at the last add tincture of arnica. Lucy squealed and covered her ears, Mrs. Dillard regarded Elkins with studied malevolence. Well enough for you to scoff and jeer at wiser elder minds, young man! But I had yon toad ointment from a physician of the old school, and with it I cured two women of caked breasts. She added in meditation, Some folk might think it cruel to the poor toadies. But you could no kill them quicker.

Cato Dillard spent two nights at the Claffeys' and then returned to Americus to keep an engagement with the ruling elder. But Effie remained at the Tebbs place for more than three weeks, sleeping on a sofa which black people brought from the Claffey house, sleeping close to her patient so that she could be alert at the first groan from Laurel. Mag was allowed to occupy the bed in the front room (but only after Coral had been commanded to beat the mattress in hot sunlight for an hour, and after fresh bedclothing had been put upon it). Coral was billeted in The Crib with Zoral; Effie Dillard demanded that he burn the chicken-coop which served previously as Zoral's kennel. Coral undertook to obey, but Zoral witnessed the preparations and set up such a screaming that Coral took pity and dragged the coop behind the ruined stable where Zoral might dwell in it when so minded. The Widow Tebbs's professional life was at a standstill. She sulked because of this, once she had recovered from fright over her daughter, and once she recognized that the girl was recovering, that friends had saved her.

Mrs. Effie preached a violent sermon on the subject of abortion until the widow was in tears. Then Mrs. Effie offered her Georgia version of cockaleekie, and spice cake baked between bedside labors. She won Coral's heart with vinegar pies and with the gift of a miniature brass pocket pistol which had belonged to Effie's own father. Immediately thereafter she sentenced Coral to scrub the front room's floor and to help her in wiping down walls.

She scolded about the state of affairs under the house, and declared that she would fetch one of her own Negroes from Americus some fine day to rake that smelly mess.

Coral said, Taint that which smells mostly. Reckon it's the stockade yonder.

You're daft, lad! A reek arises through the very cracks in the floor. Think you I've no nose upon my face to smell with?

Reckon it's on account of that blame little Zoral. He's fetched by the sight of a dead critter. Always pulling them under the house to play with. Plays like they're a train and he's a engine-driver.

Then I'll work him a poke of yarn balls, the poor mannie, and he shall sport with those.

Reckon Zoral he wouldn't fancy no such pretty-plays. What he likes most is a dead bat. He hain't never had but one, less twas when I was off to the war.

On the second day of her stay she found time to scrub Zoral in a tub of hot water and to clip his shaggy hair. His yells were heard past the boundary of the Claffey plantation. She levied upon Lucy for clothing. Sundry items were extracted from the funereal chests packed by Veronica Claffey; Lucy saw no sense in hoarding all those things, neither did her father. Zoral was provided with underdrawers for the first time in his life, which article of clothing held fascination for him: he was always lifting the skirt of an ancient plaid dress once worn by Sutherland Claffey, and bending over to look at his own drawers. He received a wide-brimmed red straw hat which had belonged to Lucy. The hat vanished, only to reappear later on the head of a very young Reserve private who strolled past the house.

Effie was out of the cottage in a flash. Young man, you've stolen yon hat from the bairn!

Didn't steal nothing, lady. He sold it to me for a polecat I done shot over here on the railroad. We made a trade.

But the bairn's an innocent! Scarce can he speak an intelligible word!

Well, he made out that he wanted my polecat, and he kind of grinned, and he give me the hat. I was tickled a-getting it, for I had none.

Effie's sense of justice compelled her to lecture the youth on his sin in taking advantage of a simple-minded infant, her benevolence compelled her to provide him with a paper of sorghum candy.

Two barrels of whiting had been discovered in one of Ira Claffey's sheds, so from Ira the minister's wife begged a few pounds of this material. She asked her husband to stop by the glue-works at Americus before he drove north on his next visit. Here were essentials for the manufacture of whitewash. Mrs. Dillard presented Coral with the bullet mould and powder flask which should have accompanied the brass pistol. Submitting to this bribery, he worked without resentment at mixing a wash for rooms in the cottage. Even Zoral was taught to carry water in assistance, though he spilled half the water each time in mounting the steps, and managed to fall into whitewash when the vat was full, thus entailing more work for Mrs. Effie, more laundering of Zoral, more roars. Very soon the widow sat sewing carpet-rags in a freshly whitened front room (later she was made to shape the circular rag-rugs themselves: she manufactured two, lumpy and uneven, to present additional hazard to Coral and his crutches. One rug was variegated rosily, the other blue and white. Mag thought them beautiful) and Laurel pursued her convalescence in a freshly whitened bedroom.

Twas sin of the flesh, lass. You're fortunate that God let you live, that you weren't punished by the Devil!

Ma said she'd just have to use that there needle on me, count of I hadn't come round. It hurt terrible, Ma'am.

Tis not that evil to which I refer. I refer to the carnal deed in the first place.

I didn't want to do it; he done it to me. And I was scairt to tell Ma for fear she'd take a stick to me.

Ah, I fear you attempted to emulate your wicked mother!

Don't know what you mean, Ma'am. I wasn't trying to do nothing to Ma. She weren't even here in the cottage when't happened.

I mean you wished to do wicked things, lass. With men, as she does. Which is why she's scarlet! Who was the man?

Twas Sergeant Sinkfield. He said twas just a game we was a-playing like when he worked— With little pigs—Laurel rolled over and buried her face in the pillow, she wept savagely and would tell no more. The alarmed Effie Dillard soothed her gently, blamed herself, blamed some unknown sergeant, blamed the Widow Tebbs. She lured Laurel into sipping a glass of her best scuppernong wine, and sat to read aloud somewhat incongruously from an old copy of the *Temperance Songster.*

> *Come, all ye merry maidens,*
> *Miss Lucy or Miss Poll,*
> *Come pass around the paper,*
> *You're sure to sign them all!*

. . . Cate, the lass shall come to dwell with us.

I feared you'd suggest that, Effie.

And why do you say feared?

For we're old. Punished by age, by the adversities which have befallen our beloved State. Flogged by bereavement. . . .

I'll no leave her here to suffer and to sin!

Then she shall come as you wish.

Such a help as she'll be to me, Cate! I'll teach her to sew, to work my caps. And to read and write: she shall make copies of your sermons before you muddy them up with lead pencil, man. . . .

Laurel's pinched face brightened and beamed at the prospect. She had never been to Americus, she thought it quite a city. There were said to be great glass spheres of colored liquid at the druggist's, and a tin roof on the Masonic Hall or some such place. Coral affirmed that there was an entire case in Kinnett's store filled with nothing but candy, or had been when he last saw the town. Mrs. Roach's carriage was believed to have red wheels. It was told that Judge Ladshaw had a pet monkey which would eat goobers and throw the shells in your face.

And you'll be taught to knit, and be taught the Shorter Catechism. And you're no to greet about it!

Nome.

And I'll clothe you decently as a God-fearing lass should be clothed; and not one soul in the place knows of your trouble, so you're no to cast sheep's eyes at the men.

Nome.

In this way you shall be lifted out of iniquity and in time shall stand Redeemed.

Mag said, Just think on it. My little girl, going clean to Americus and getting new gowns. And maybe a bonnet of her own. Well, I never. Don't you go a-getting yourself in a family way again, Laurel, hear me? You like to died of it.

Twenty-three days after her arrival at the Tebbs cottage, Effie Dillard set out with Laurel for Americus. Only Mag saw them off; tears ran at the thought of her daughter going far away, and for so long—how long? But there was the winning thought that—perhaps—on this very night— If word got around— She might prevail upon Coral to visit Uncle Arch's and remark casually that Mrs. Dillard was no longer in residence at the Tebbs place. I hain't lain with a man for such a while, she thought. I'm nigh dead rusted.

Coral was hunting, Zoral crouched in his hen coop behind the stable. Mag waved happily if tearfully from the stoop. You get holt of any extra ribbons you save them for your Ma, she called. Or glass buttons, like. Blackie drew the two-seated buggy down the lane; the gig would not have been sufficient for the three of them, since Cato Dillard waited at the Claffeys. As wheels lurched over the railway a detail of shabby gray-and-blue jacketed Reserves trailed into the lane from the left. They had guns and wore equipment, they were bound for sentry duty perhaps, bound somewhere.

In the socket beside Mrs. Dillard's right knee sprouted a buggy whip which had never been used. It boasted a long braided lash with a streamer of red silk, though the streamer had now faded through pink nearly to white. This handsome object had been presented to Cato Dillard by its fabricator, who was a member of Cato's flock. The Reverend Mr. Dillard would never have struck Blackie with the thing, not for all the world, but he disliked to offend one of his congregation and so carried the whip displayed.

Mis Dillard, Ma'am, said Laurel's limp voice. Would you please to pull up a second?

Even as Effie drew upon the reins, the girl leaned forward and across her lap and, to Effie Dillard's paralysis, extracted the whip from its socket. Blackie stopped, wheels stopped. A whiny questioning voice requested, Sergeant? A dozen boys turned, and with them turned the bloated pimply face of Sergeant Jester Sinkfield. Laurel shut her eyes tightly and her knuckles turned to white bone; she struck with the force of both arms. She had not much force to muster in her slow-recovering body, yet it seemed she must have been awarded strength from some outer reservoir beyond the reckoning of men. The lash was narrow, limber, tightly braided. It opened up Jester Sinkfield's face across the right cheek and into the chin, it sliced his lips in half. No wound like that would ever mend except as a scar. The bellow of spurting agony sent Blackie forward with a lunge, though the wild-faced Mrs. Dillard tried to hold him.

It's all right, Ma'am, said Laurel. Reckon we can drive on.

51

Ira Claffey received a letter from Lieutenant-Colonel Persons which saddened but did not surprise him.

You may be interested to know, wrote Persons after polite preliminaries, that I am no longer in any position to assist in a reduction of the horror on your doorstep! This came about because of a proceeding to enjoin the authorities from further continuing the prison there at Andersonville. Observe how the legalistic mind seeks to take up the weapons to which it has been trained. In the character of counsel, I drew a bill for an injunction to abate the nuisance. What makes it a nuisance? You should be well aware, and are. The graveyard makes it a nuisance —the military works, fortifications, wretched personnel, etc., make it a nuisance to you property holders there—and the stockade generally is a nuisance, from the intolerable stench, the effluvia, the malaria that it gives out, and things of that sort. After I drew the bill I went to see the judge of the district court. I read my bill to him and asked him for the injunction. He said that he would appoint a day on which he would hear the argument in chambers. This general suggestion of secrecy should have given suspicion and caused me to lose heart, but still I was consumed with fervor. So the judge appointed a day; I made preparations for trial and was about in the act of going to present the argument, when I received an official communication from General Howell Cobb.

Harrell Elkins, to whom Ira was reading this letter, slapped his hands against the table.

General Cobb asked me if that bill was to be charged to me—the bill against my own Government, was the way he termed it. In reply to his communication, I wrote him that indeed I had drawn the bill, and that it could be charged to me. He replied, through his adjutant-general, Major Harrit, that he deemed it inconsistent with my duty as a Confederate officer, to appear in a case like that, presenting, as General Cobb declared, a bill against my Government. The tenor of his communication was unmistakable: it was obvious that I would be treated by court martial or something of that sort. I said to General Cobb that if he deemed what I had done in the matter unofficerlike, I would leave the case. He said that he did deem it that way, and would be glad if I would retire without being driven.

. . . The authorities are responsible. I cannot say who. The great blunder has been the concentration of so many men at one place, without proper preparations. Again and again the authorities were notified of the fact, but to no advantage. I think some of the higher officials are responsible; but who they are I cannot say. A stockade with supposed accommodations for not more than ten thousand prisoners, and there were nearly forty thousand prisoners sent to it! Captain Wirz cannot be blamed for that. No man on earth could have abated the rigors of Andersonville, except the man who wielded the power. I do not know that man. General Winder was in advance of me, and several others are in advance of him. Who is responsible I cannot say. . . .

Poor man, said Ira, poor man. He looked across the table at Elkins. Poor Cousin Harry, he said.

Poor prisoners, said Elkins. Poor Nation.

Ira thought with increased bitterness that it was a very poor Nation. He felt as he might have felt had he possessed an affectionate, vigorous, beautiful sweetheart, and seen her take to drink or narcotics, and thus deteriorate. It seemed that there was some one thing which he should do personally; but he was not aware what it might be, no search seemed to give the answer. Once, in a borderland between waking and sleeping, it even occurred to Ira that he might calmly assassinate General Winder—turn his back on religion and morality, take the law into his own hands, cry that he was invoking a higher law. He sat up in bed, shocked yet still playing with the possibility. But who might then follow Winder? A worse Winder, no doubt; if such there could be.

The population of the stockade was diminished greatly; to what extent it was difficult to tell. There was still a capacity load of some twenty-five hundred sick in the hospital. A list of figures came to Elkins's attention; he copied them down and presented them to Ira without comment. From February twenty-fourth to September twenty-first, there had been recorded nine thousand, four hundred and seventy-nine deaths.

Nearly one-third of the entire number confined, said Harry. My experience leads me to presume that also there were a great many unrecorded deaths.

It was apparent from advices and from observation that Henry Wirz lived in concentrated terror of a prison break, even with the great lessening of the pen's population. He fussed about at the star fort, the thought of Kilpatrick's cavalry hung like a saber above. He was continually fetching orders to the battery's commander regarding ammunition and the alerting of personnel. At any time, if Yankees on the interior gathered in a mob, Wirz demanded that the cannon should open fire. All through September and into October ragged throngs were herded to the station as rapidly as transportation was made available. No longer could they be considered as tractable, because word of Winder's duplicity had inevitably trickled back to Andersonville. There were more attempts to escape than before. Few people had any desire to be removed to Millen or Florence or Charleston, or to be carried south to Blackshears—any of those places might be worse. Since they had been hoodwinked, and since actually no exchange was in effect, men went plunging off the trains at every trip. Many were shot, or were mutilated in the process of their tumbling. A few got away into lonely underbrush and dragged out starved existence until eventually they were picked up by rustic Home Guards. Only a handful were successful in eluding those armed bands who rode piny forest ways in persistent patrol. The region was filled with straggling refugees from upper counties of the State . . . also there were many runaway slaves . . . every dirty-faced vagabond was suspect as an escaped Yankee prisoner, aching to cut a throat. Wirz bristled beside columns of outgoing Federals, revolver ready in his hand. Sometimes he fired the revolver; it was told that he had killed several prisoners; also it was affirmed that he had killed no one, had shot in the air, or had not even drawn his weapon.

Uncertainties of these cooler drying weeks twisted like stray dust-devils through the countryside. Paroles were sundered right and left; sick boys stumbled in the swamps, vanished there. Hounds of Wes Turner, reinforced by a pack tended by another oaf named Ben Harris, went hollering day and night. Wirz yelled, paid out currency to Harris and Turner, fought with them about price per head and numbers of individuals recaptured. Wirz yelled, his arm yelled back at him, he perspired until his clothing was soaked. Wirz caught cold, went riding again in a fever; he meted out stocks-and-chain-gang penalties for the most minor infractions. Wirz yelled. . . .

In a certain lone glade surrounded by tall trees, shovels sank and turned. The naked bodies were rolled, pushed down. Flimsy records were kept. An effort had been made, on the part of stockade prisoners and hospital attendants alike, to record names and regiments of the dead, dates of their dying; but many scraps of paper were torn from corpses in handling. A slab of split pine grew at the head of each grave. But they were not individual graves, they were populous trenches, they had been filled with cold fruit, each appeared to be lined by a single fence, grave-slabs were the palings of the fence. A marker read: Vork C (that was the name of the thing underneath) 5 Mich (that was the regiment) K (the company) Sept 22 (the date). Slabs said, Unknown, Unknown. A slab said, Waiter G 9 Minn H Sept 9. Scrawled penciling: Brewer J S 6 New York B Oct 2. Rough wood with splinters sticking out on the edges: Lickley P 1 New York Cav E Oct 5. Or Hoagler N C 39 Ind E Oct 8. Or Ballinger Geo 87 Penn D Oct 9. Or Unknown, Unknown, Unknown. There were fourteen Joneses and twelve Johnsons from New York State alone, had anyone cared to go stalking and peering and counting, collecting Joneses and Johnsons. Tossed clay made a wide hummocked quilt from edge of forest to edge of forest. Negroes on duty with the burial detail tried to desert in droves. They were dragged back, tied across stumps or logs; whips popped, the shrieks came up. Wirz trotted fiercely to the scene and said, *Ja,* him I know, that tall one. Three times he has tried for escape! Five hundred lashes he must have! Perhaps the flogger took pity and gave only two hundred lashes after Wirz's back was turned.

Within the stockade Wirz had achieved an autumnal triumph: several long open sheds, built again on the North Side near where the first flimsy hospital had existed. Beneath these sheds many of the stockade's sick might be placed; at least they were out of the rain. There were not beds enough, room enough for the sick in the main hospital. Wirz thought that he should be praised for this accomplishment . . . no one praised him. General Winder grunted, growled, departed in a northerly direction. . . . There was space enough now: people reconstructed more commodious shebangs, using rags and twigs, the very louse-ridden earth which had been yielded by comparatively stronger departing throngs. Those were detachments newly told off, containing again only men able to walk.

Inner acres were studded with slow-moving bent figures, no longer a press, but creeping loosely, widely, wandering hunched, wandering forever in a search for scraps of abandoned valuables . . . half-canteen here, a button there, a belt buckle which might be rubbed up and traded to a guard for a collard stalk. It was a poorhouse half denuded, but still the smell rose festering. Winter was on the way, soon the air would be colder, thinner, rarer in a hint of sleet to come.

Another visitor appeared at the Claffey house, escorted one afternoon by Cousin Harry, whose lined face beamed at satisfaction in again meeting with an admired friend. Dr. Joseph Jones had become medical chemist at Augusta while the young civilian Harrell Elkins studied there; Harry was privileged to work as his assistant for a time. During the previous spring exigencies of war had pushed them into contact again, when Cousin Harry toiled in exploration of hospital gangrene. Jones was a brilliant and observing man, some years Harry's elder, but essentially much more the scientist than the soldier. Nevertheless he had served for six months as a private in the ranks during the earlier part of the war. Now belatedly the Confederacy exhibited a tendency to make use of his erudition. . . . Jones declared that he was flabbergasted by Andersonville. He had heard merely of unusual mortality among the Federal prisoners; he had never dreamed of the nature of drainage, water supply and food supply. He had never dreamed that no shelter whatsoever was afforded. He said, I am so appalled by what I see here that I find myself at a loss for words.

This was at an evening meal shared by the three men. (Lucy had withdrawn in order to give them full scope in discussion.)

Another report? asked Ira. Reports have been made to every section of command in the past, and were met with identical silence.

In my innocence I had thought in terms of fevers, said Dr. Jones. In August I had an opportunity to visit Richmond and suggested to Surgeon-General S. P. Moore that conditions at Andersonville might be worth a minute investigation. Indeed! Little did I think that—I was told nothing, nothing! Believe me, sir, not a word was breathed of this horror. I considered only that a large body of men from the Northern portion of the United States, suddenly transported to a warmer Southern climate, and confined upon a small portion of land, would furnish an excellent field for the investigation of the relations of typhus, typhoid and malarial fevers. I received my orders, proceeded here, and walked into—this.

You should have seen the stockade during that same August, Elkins told him. Since then a great many of the Federals have been removed elsewhere.

How many are now confined, Harry?

Perhaps fifteen thousand, all told, stockade and hospital. However, numerous detachments are still being sent forth. It is hoped that the total may be reduced to at least eight thousand or thereabouts by the first of next month.

Have conditions at the hospital been in any way ameliorated by these withdrawals?

Not in the slightest, sir. We are tight run—never tighter than now. There's not an inch of space remaining within the hospital itself. In fact our task has been increased and intensified by these outgoing detachments.

Why on Earth—?

Because many of these prisoners were cared for to some degree by their comrades. The comrades were ordered away and were forbidden to carry the sick along with them. There was a certain amount of subterfuge, naturally; some of the sick did go along with the well. But the greater number were left in what amounted to abandonment. Therefore the increase in the ratio of reported sickness and resulting mortality.

Dr. Jones had produced his Richmond orders, with which Surgeon Isaiah White, in charge of the hospital, was duly impressed. In this way Jones was able to have Elkins transferred from other duties temporarily to serve as his assistant, both in post mortem examinations and the rough draft of his report. The two men drove themselves mercilessly through all hours of daylight in first-hand exploration. At night papers were unrolled upon the Claffey dining table. The plantation's stock of candles suffered, and Lucy was at her wits' end to see that more candles were manufactured immediately. The two surgeons correlated their notes. In tired voices suggestions were made, there was mutual criticism of style and content.

I can't say merely a pile of human excrement, Harry. It does not convey the enormity of the thing; we *must* convey it.

Let us see . . . say, filthy quagmire of human excrements.

Yes, much better.

Alive with working maggots, Elkins added.

More impressive still. And hideously correct!

Lucy tapped at the edge of the open door: would the gentlemen take coffee now? They would indeed. Ninny was sent with the old Bavarian china pot, the chipped delicate cups. Grain coffee was poured, a smidgin of precious cane syrup stirred in.

Where will you go, sir, when you have concluded your investigation here?

Jones said, Doubtless to hospitals connected with the Army of Tennessee, and shall probably be there until November. For the eventual preparation of the final draft, I must await the reception of answers to numerous other inquiries I've made. . . .

Diarrhoea, dysentery, scurvy, and hospital gangrene were the diseases which have been the main cause of this extraordinary mortality. The origin and character of the hospital gangrene which prevailed to so remarkable a degree and with such fatal effects amongst the Federal prisoners, engaged my most serious and earnest consideration. More than 30,000 men, crowded upon twenty-seven acres of land, with little or no shelter from the intense heat of a Southern summer, or from the rain and from the dew of night, with coarse corn bread from which the husk had not been removed, with but scant supplies of fresh meat and vegetables, with little or no attention to hygiene, with festering masses of filth at the very doors of their rude dens and tents, with the greater portion of the banks of the stream flowing through the stockade a filthy quagmire of human excrements alive with working maggots, generated by their own filthy exhalations and excretions, an atmosphere that so deteriorated and contaminated their solids and fluids that the slightest scratch and even the bites of small insects were in some cases followed by such rapid and extensive gangrene as to destroy extremities and even life itself. . . .

Let's see, Harry. Where is August?

August, August. There August lies yonder, under the saucer.

. . . August: fifty-three cases and fifty-three deaths recorded as marasmus.

That was the terminology.

But surely this large number of deaths must have been due to some other morbid state than slow wasting? If they were due to improper and insufficient food, they should have been classified accordingly.

In our hospital, said Harry Elkins slowly, there have been peculiar notions regarding statement of the causes of death.

But, Harry, if due to diarrhoea, dysentery or scurvy, the classification should in like manner have been explicit!

I suggest, sir, that you incorporate that query in your report.

Elkins hoisted his thinning body into a bent but standing position, and beat his hand on the table in a fashion now grown characteristic. Let us take, for example, *vulnus sclopeticum*. A great many deaths have been entered as due to that cause. I am referring to prisoners shot by guards. As you are well aware, sir, that is the technical name for a gunshot wound! Even stranger recordings have been made. I found, when ordered to assemble certain previous reports which had been made at best in fragmetary fashion, that on the eleventh of July, six men died of *as-phyxia*. I was very curious about this. . . . Had the men smothered in their sleep? They had not. It was merely that they were hanged by the neck until dead. Those were the raiders executed by their fellow prisoners. An amusing circumstance, do you not think? He cackled.

Pray sit down, said Joseph Jones sadly. Where were we? Ah, yes: August again. What was the mortality of mean strength, sick and well, in August?

Nine and nine-hundredths per cent.

What was the first month—February or March?

The first prisoners came in a few days before the end of February. Thus the first figures available for a complete month are for March.

And the rate then?

Three and eleven-hundredths per cent of mean strength for March.

Then the rate of mortality has very nearly tripled, for the prisoners as a whole?

That does not approach the rate of hospital mortality, sir.

Ah, I'm well aware of that. But let me have the sum of deaths for September eighteenth. I believe you said that would astound me.

Here it is: one hundred and twenty-seven.

In *one day?*

Correct, sir.

My eyes are swimming, confronted with numerals. Let us put numerals by for a time. . . . Now: have you seen my preliminary description concerning the hospital itself?

They hunted for the papers, found them at last jammed into a worn saddle bag which served as Doctor Jones's literary kit.

The patients and attendants . . . are crowded into this confined space and are but poorly supplied with old and ragged tents. Large numbers of them are without any bunks in the tents, and lie upon the ground, ofttimes without even a blanket. No beds or straw appeared to have been furnished. The tents extend to within a few yards of the small stream, the eastern portion of which, as we have before said, is used as a privy and is loaded with excrements; and I observed a large pile of corn bread, bones, and filth of all kinds, thirty feet in diameter and several feet in height, swarming with myriads of flies, in a vacant space near the pots used for cooking. Millions of flies swarmed over everything and covered the faces of the sleeping patients, and crawled down their open mouths, and deposited their maggots in the gangrenous wounds of the living, and in the mouths of the dead. Mosquitoes in great numbers also infested the tents, and many of the patients were so stung by these pestiferous insects, that they resembled those suffering with a slight attack of measles.

Harry, lad, you've fallen asleep.

Why— So I did, so I did. My apologies—

Ira Claffey wondered without much confidence whether this third effort of a dedicated Confederate would turn the trick. Some people held three to be a lucky number . . . the third time was the charm . . . old saws of that nature. Persons, Chandler, Jones. Would demands of other duties allow Jones to complete his report? Would a sudden onrush of Federals from Atlanta preclude the completion? If the report were completed, what of its reception at Richmond? . . . Harrell Elkins shared Ira's fears, yet he toiled with angry enthusiasm. Joseph Jones made certain that the statistics which he carried away with him were as accurate as might be, despite slovenly bookkeeping at original sources. He turned to the prose body of his report only when eyes and brain refused to accept another statistic. Thus those at the Claffey house might have little idea as to the shape this report would assume eventually, the damning quality of the utterance.

Only an occasional summary relating to a specific fault stood out in something like acceptable form; these Surgeon Jones read to his angrily-impressed small audience the night before his departure. Jones held that there should be nothing secret in his document. He hoped indeed that it would be published in all directions. He felt that he was violating no confidential rule, where his Nation or his superiors were concerned, in including sympathetic citizens in the last candlelit session.

This gigantic mass of human misery calls loudly for relief, not only for the sake of suffering humanity, but also on account of our own brave soldiers now captives in the hands of the Federal government. Strict justice to the gallant men of the Confederate armies, who have been or who may be so unfortunate as to be compelled to surrender in battle, demands that the Confederate government should adopt that course which will best secure their health and comfort in captivity; or at least leave their enemies without a shadow of an excuse for any violation of the rules of civilized warfare in the treatment of prisoners.

It was still October when Dr. Jones went away. As he had foreseen, he was ordered to the hospitals with the Army of Tennessee. Harrell Elkins returned to miscellaneous overwork, the disorganized routine of hospital and stockade gate. He had a special corner of an outbuilding wherein he strove to rid himself of lice and fleas before reëntering the Claffey house after each tour of duty. Despite his best intention, vermin did accompany him. Lucy prowled with coal oil, hunting the sly tiny villains.

She observed that her father was growing more and more detached as the autumn lengthened into November. Ira shirked self-appointed garden tasks . . . sometimes the Negroes were left with nothing to do because no work had been laid out for them. Ira went often with his gun to the uplands but brought back few birds. Sometimes he brought no birds at all—the weapon was unsmudged, had not been fired. I wonder if he thinks he sees the boys, as he murmured that once he saw them a year since? cried Lucy to herself. I wonder. . . .

Ira routed his daughter from her bed one evening, when Elkins was asleep, when a small fire burned on the library hearth. Ira made Lucy don a comforter and sit before this fire.

I am going. Today I decided that I must go. I cannot dwell in harmony with myself unless I try.

Go where?

To Richmond—where else? Did I not tell you what was my thought?

Poppy, you've said nothing. Sakes! Nothing at all. You've gone poking sometimes with your gun, sometimes without it. I declare, I've tried to think what ailed you, and could never decide. I knew it must have to do with the prison. You've changed in such a way since Surgeon Jones was here.

Ira sat staring at the fire, his chin on his fists. Beg pardon for any withdrawal; it was a matter I had to thrash out. But viewing those three men—all doing their best to secure a reformation—our friend Alex Persons; then Chandler; Jones at the last. Indeed we've heard nothing from Jones, there's been no alteration of circumstances. Conditions grow worse steadily at the approach of winter. You've heard Coz say so, and his opinion is to be trusted above others. Gad, it seems the others might have offered their reports as Coz offered his: wafted into flame, directed upwards to the Almighty!

No, no, he cried, and stood up to wave his fists. It cannot continue like this. I'll not let it continue!

But, Poppy— All the way to Richmond? And it's just a trial, traveling these days. Everyone tells that. And such a sight of cash. Poppy, have we—? Do you have sufficient funds?

I shall draw money out of my box, come what may. Daughter, as you know, I was acquainted with President Davis many years ago. But still I knew him, and he knew me. What is a commander? A man with subordinates, many of them appointed directly by that commander. Somewhere along the line of subordinates sits the official who individually might rectify the present, who might benefit the future—I know too well that past months cannot be rectified. Perhaps I was appointed by Fate, because of this acquaintanceship with the Chief Executive! It may be that I have disregarded impassioned summons heretofore. I have been sluggardly, Lucy—weak and sluggardly. A man may not feel he has done everything he can do—not until he has *done* everything he *can* do.

Then God speed you, Poppy.

Lucy. In a tone of equal tenderness. I cannot leave you alone—not with a man in the house to whom in fact we are not related.

She sat in silence.

Early the next morning Ira set out for Americus. There was a fairly good horse left on the Yeoman place, he borrowed that horse. He conferred with Effie Dillard. She came somewhat reluctantly to the plantation on the following day, leaving a long list of admonitions to Laurel Tebbs: tasks which Laurel must perform, comforts and duties essential to the well-being of the Reverend Mr. Cato Dillard.

A grievance, she told her husband.

No grievance, Effie. It's kindness which you must award to friends.

Aye, we dare risk no scandal where our dear lass Lucy is concerned! Bear with it all, Cate. You shall be in my prayers nightly, husband, and in my thoughts each hour.

At the Claffey place Ira was immersed in his own preparations. Lucy stood behind a curtain and watched the round-shouldered Harry striding off to the hospital. Suddenly her cheeks grew hot, she closed her eyes and spread her hands against her cheeks.

52

Fire swept Atlanta on the night of November fifteenth, and rumor held that Sherman was driving on Augusta. Because the entire Southwestern railway line had been taken over by the military, Ira Claffey was compelled to apply for a pass before boarding a train. Permission was granted readily: another contingent labored here since the departure of Winder and his flock. Wirz and Colonel Thurlow survived, together with some members of the surgical staff. Commissary and quartermaster's departments were administered by new people, so was the office of transportation. The transportation officer was a plaintive little grub who had been shot through the throat and could not raise his voice above a whisper. He whispered thanks to Ira. . . . Quantities of yams, cabbages, onions, pumpkins from the Claffey plantation found their way to the officers' mess. Some people considered it possible that Wirz might have given permission for such fare to be carried into stockade and hospital also, had he not feared the slug of a fist thrusting down from Florence or Camp Lawton.

About four o'clock in the afternoon Ira took leave of Lucy and Mrs. Dillard; Harry Elkins was on duty at the hospital. Ira walked to Anderson Station carrying his own carpetbag; there was no meanness about this nowadays; his hands were at work getting winter wood, he did not wish to take one hand from his task. Ira sat on the tailboard of a collapsed wagon almost until dusk: the train had been long delayed between Albany and Americus.

There were other delays to be incurred north of Anderson. A rail sprang from ties, it had to be spiked into place. An engine crew was become a track maintenance crew in these times. . . . In darkness the head-lamp would not operate, it was burned out. For such emergencies an old-fashioned dolly was carried aboard the wood tender; but it lay buried under pine lengths, so there must ensue unloading before the flat little car could be dragged out and secured in front of the engine. Knots were set aflame, the engine sparked mournfully at a mule's pace as if it shoved a gay bonfire unwillingly. Pine flames leaned back against the shield, red glow stole ahead, cars grated, creaked, shoved together in couplings, pulled apart in couplings. The train crept, its ruddy fingers of light closing slowly on the rope of track. Interiors thickened with the smell of woodsmoke and deep-dyed sweat, together with smell of the place where some passenger had been sick. The door of a corner privy banged back and forth; it could not be secured and kept from banging; the wooden privy box shifted and smelled. A bench was built along each side of the car and across the ends, another bench ran down the middle. On this slept, end to end, several youthful soldiers dragged from some port farther south. They were being sent up-State to serve as reinforcements . . . from a hundred other posts such elements were drawn. Reinforcements, reinforcements, said slow rough wheels chewing the rails. Sherman's left Atlanta . . . Sherman's out of Atlanta. . . .

Ira Claffey rested in a front corner of the car, as far from the privy smell as possible. But the bench was narrow, he could not stretch safely upon it as thin boys did. He tried to pillow his head on his bag, tried to secure himself against the tenacious hammering of patched equipment. It was gray sunrise before they reached Macon, and they did not leave Macon on the Georgia Central for many hours. Lucy had prepared a basket of corn sticks, pickled pork, and biscuit sandwiches spread with sorghum, along with an old brandy bottle filled with grain coffee. The five freckled mossy-necked boys in the car had no food. They explained to Ira Claffey that they had been told to draw rations; but rations were refused because of some technicality. Ira divided his store of meat and bread into six portions as equally as possible. Also during the eternity of waiting outside Macon, a stout Negress came along the track offering fish for sale. Ira treated the soldiers to fried catfish.

He thought that he had seen refugees before . . . truly he had not seen them. Oh, there had been visible evidence of distant battles, wickedness of distant campaigns. Stupid frightened black people inched along the railway, along the road past the Claffey plantation. Some of the Negro men had been impressed—captured, as it were—and set to menial tasks in the Andersonville cemetery or around the camps. It was whispered through the neighborhood that some of the more comely Negresses were persuaded to linger for a time, to afford pleasure for men in a tent outside the picket lines. Ira's own pickaninnies had come from play along a weedy fence, fetching a stray child in verminous rags. Scarcely could you tell the sex of the critter. The hair was kinked, the body neglected, eyes rolled

frantically. Only children of its own size could have lured it to the plantation. Lucy gave orders that the thing should be scrubbed and fed. It turned out to be a little girl. Lucy named her Dryad, since she was found in the woods, and for nearly a week the black children enjoyed their new playmate; until Dryad quarreled with little Gracious and ran off, declaring that she was going home to her Mammy. Ira ordered the hands to go searching. They never found her, nor did she return to the plantation again. They heard nothing more of the child. It was feared that she might have been drowned in Little Sweetwater, or perhaps went down into a bog.
. . . Yes, he had seen black people drifting, and some whites. He was accustomed to ragged nomads who glared suspiciously, whose lean yellow faces gave forth little except suspicion and colder resentment. He had seen them in their camps, had watched against their thefts, had given them food in every case when they came to beg. Their starved dogs skulked along with them, forever it seemed that the dogs traveled on three legs.

But here in the Macon region tumbled hordes who had been shunted out of Atlanta and smaller towns in the northwest region where Union brigades came growling and firing. Along the side track sentries were disposed solely for the purpose of restraining these confused tribes. Ira stood in the car door, observing with pity, and hearing reiteration of the guards: no citizen dared board this train without displaying a pass for self and family. This rule was honored in the breach, and Ira surmised that there had been some bribes as well. Benches and floors filled up with strident women, squalling babies, madcap older children who wrestled and ran, making holiday and war dance out of the whole miserable matter.

There came the tall judge with face like dry paper. His eyes were pink-rimmed, he twisted his skinny beard, said that he had had two sons and three grandsons in the army. But all were dead, sir. All were dead . . . and the Yankees had taken over his house, sir, and flung him out to wander and starve, sir. There came a spinster seamstress dragging her mother along. The fat old lady scolded and palpitated; she said that her head was spinning, and where were those aromatic salts, Letty John—where were those salts? There came the small shy pretty woman, large with child, trying to manage two covered baskets and two little boys who owned their mother's cool brown eyes and soft voice and fuzzy brown hair. The woman said that her husband was serving under General Hampton, and wasn't this just the beat? . . . A slobbery fat man, drunk and threatening; he claimed that the Yankees had killed his hogs. He swore that he had escaped barely with his life, and was confident that his wife was ravished by invaders. But he had run off without her; it appeared that he had not waited to see what had befallen her; perhaps he could not bear to witness her ravished condition. . . .

There was the nine-year-old boy who had been separated from grandparents with whom he traveled. He wore a miniature gray uniform with ragged braid on it. He was naughty, he stamped and screeched, slapped at smaller children, yelled that he was hungry. Ira offered him some biscuit and sorghum, but the boy snarled that he didn't want any of that old nigger food: he wanted spice cake. . . . Two meek maidens of teen age; they were not twins, but were dressed in similar shawls and gowns, almost identical bonnets. One of them was doubled with abdominal cramps. She cried quietly, could not refrain from holding her hand against her middle, she buried her face against her sister as she cried. . . .

A grinning servant with a face like crumpled black tin. He said that he was taking care of The Doctor. Yes, sir, he was taking care of The Doctor. And the doctor was every day of eighty, and carried an ear trumpet, and stared hopelessly out of eyes on which the film of cataracts showed. The servant said his own name was Jack and he had belonged to the doctor for forty-four years. He said that he knew his numbers, he could cipher well. It was in 1820 that the doctor bought him, bought him in North Carolina. That was before they moved down here, and —he lowered his voice mysteriously the doctor wasn't deaf then; but he was very deaf now. No sir, old Jack wasn't going to stay to home. He knew what would happen if he fell into hands of the Yankees: he would be worked to death on fortifications, or else would be put out right smack in front of all those soldiers; right in front of the line of battle he would be put, to absorb shot directed at the Yankees. Or else he would be sent to Cuba and sold. And he knew well enough what the Yankees did to old women and young children: they would be drowned like blind puppies or cats. No, sir, he was getting out of there. The Doctor didn't want to come, but he had done persuaded The Doctor. Yes sir, he had done persuaded him. They were going to Savannah, that's where they were going.

Wounded soldiers in the throng . . . boys with bandages. . . . A loud-voiced young woman with brilliantly red cheeks and coils of brassy hair straggling. She made much of rustling her patched silk gown, she giggled when the young soldiers talked to her. She laughed as the ignorant and light-brained laugh. Her laughter went up in a shriek, she could not laugh without shrieking. The shriek would start on a high note, it sounded like ungreased axles of the train itself, it held a protracted *eeeh* at high pitch, it died down only to spout again when something else was said. . . . A very new baby wailed ceaselessly. It said *lah* at regular intervals. Ira began to count the *lahs*. He counted to two hundred with scarce a break, then wearied of counting and became insensitive to the sound . . . heard no more of it, though the hungry mite wailed on, was silenced briefly at its mother's breast, refused the breast, continued *lah*ing.

There sat a small Jewish tailor with fat small wife. The woman cried a little, touching her eyes with a folded cambric handkerchief, but she made no sound. At last she opened a willow basket, brought out lunch: some strange crackery compound, and homemade cheese. The old couple munched stoically. They said that their son and his wife had elected to remain at home. The son had lost his arm in the war. He said that he had no fear of the Yankees, had often traded tobacco for coffee. Actually he had traded with the Yankees when they were fighting at the North! But Mamma here— She would not wait. She thinks the Yankees would kill her. I do not believe it so, but that is what she thinks. But this is not so bad. It is bad, but it is not so bad. When I was a lad— That was many years ago—it was in the Old Country. I remember I fled with my parents, for soldiers were to kill us, and it was cold, much colder than now. . . .

Eventually the car was crammed to suffocation, though some of these runaways grew restless because the train did not move. They pushed their way out, left the car, went perhaps into some other car or back into the town. Once a woman shrieked, Yankee cavalry! There they are! and there was a great pushing and punching as everyone struggled to see. But no Yankee cavalry could be found on the landscape—only some Negro boys leading several head of mules.

Once again in afternoon the rusty splintery worm crawled its course. Engine puffed and shuddered, greaseless axles screamed like caged demons above tortured boxes, loose metal banged and thudded, steam and smoke went coughing. May we get to Savannah, Sherman is loose, Sherman is loose, Sherman is coming. Sherman has left Atlanta, gulp, Sherman has left Atlanta, gulp, Sherman is loose, gasp, Sherman's coming, gasp. In its soiled pink shawl the baby cried. Rustling in soiled silken skirts, the girl with brassy locks still squealed, boy soldiers said funny things to her.

In late afternoon the train stopped dead with a grinding lurch which sent the passengers into convulsions. The jolt was so severe that Ira Claffey supposed a driving-rod must have lashed up into the engine, or that the engine had upset and cars rammed it. Ira was hurled against old Jack on the side bench. He got free from the caterwauling mass of citizens, and carried his carpetbag to the door. . . . It's a wreck! Children clamoring. Ma, we're in a wreck!

The car was upright, there rose no sound of flames, no demonstration of serious injury. I don't believe it's a wreck, said Ira. Now everybody hush!

He pushed open the rickety door and peered out and forward along the left side of the train. Soldier boys ganged around him to peer also, they pushed their heads past Ira, over and under the arm with which he braced himself. The train was halted on a curve, the engineer was getting down, several Negroes had hopped off the tender. Two officers from another car hastened toward the engine.

We ain't allowed to get out, sir, said a youth. We got to stay aboard, less we're ordered to get down.

See if you can quiet these women and children, Ira told him and the other boys. I'll attempt to satisfy our curiosity. He swung from the car, still carrying his bag; it would not do to leave it behind.

The engine-driver stood at the front, rubbing sooty hands against his flanks. Two Confederate officers were with him, and were joined by bearded citizens. Come all the way from Albany, an old man said, just to run into this! The engine was smashed into a barricade of logs and ties. Smaller logs had been sent flying, one had been hurled like a spear to bury itself in the side of the embankment. The train stood in a cut rounding the lower portion of a hill. Heavier substance of the barricade remained, crushed under forward wheels or surmounting the cow-catcher. Two wheels at the left side were pushed from the U-shaped track. We hain't got the power, the engineer said sourly, to lever them back.

Who would have done this? Ira asked.

One officer unfastened a revolver holster and fingered the butt of his weapon. Could be Sherman's folks have got this far. I heard last night they was headed nigh.

You might be captured, Major.

The old major declared emphatically, That's just the rub. But my orders were to take this train. Naught arrived to countermand them.

Ira Claffey pointed. A wisp of smoke blew above trees perhaps one hundred rods to the northwest. It was the light forerunner of a thicker column—twisting, congealing, darkening to black as it climbed.

By Mercy, said the engine-driver. Could be those damn bummers!

I thought twas customary for them to destroy railroads, rather than build barricades.

Hell, mister. They'd do anything!

A younger officer exclaimed nervously. Now that they had moved past the engine other fires loomed ahead, the horizon was layered with smoke.

Reckon I'll take to the woods, the wrinkled major said decisively. Got no wish to be snatched up by Yanks.

Ira walked back beside the cars, trying to decide a wise course. If Yankees had penetrated this region (it was apparent that they had; or at least some accompanying bands of straggling raiders must have done so) they might shoot anyone who seemed anxious to conceal himself. He thought that under these conditions the woodland offered little sanctuary. He considered it unlikely that the frightened freight of refugees would come to harm. He recalled what papers he was carrying. Papers should prove his identity, give evidence that he was not a Confederate soldier in citizen's clothing. Ira reached his own car and spoke one low word to faces studding the doorway. Sherman. Three of the boys came down like jumping jacks, weaponless, not even pausing to secure haversacks. Two others went back for their equipment, then they sprang down as well. One youngster sprinted up the embankment immediately, filling his shoes with ashes as he climbed, and disappeared over the edge. The others stood debating, while there ensued a gush of women and old people and children from the cars. Ira walked away from the train, south around the extremity of the curve, until he was out of sight. He should strike for a road, any road. He had not gone out of earshot, however. A series of yells rose behind him—staccato whoops of challenge or triumph. He walked steadily, glancing occasionally over his shoulder to see if he was being followed. Later he heard shots. He hoped that no one had been hurt, he trusted that the shots were fired merely for intimidation, or in a celebrating spirit. No one pursued him. If a bushwhacking gang was raiding the train they must have come up too late to see his departure.

Ira came to a creek where rails were supported by a trestle; he slid down and crouched beneath the trestle. He had with him nearly three thousand dollars in Confederate currency . . . he did not know how long it would take him to reach Richmond, how long to return. He carried also a letter from Americus authorizing him to draw a draft as necessary. Now he thought it wise to destroy this letter: the practice of holding for ransom might exist. He tore the letter into scraps and scattered them on the water. He left one hundred and eighty dollars in odd certificates, rolled this money and thrust it into his pocket. He was dressed very nearly in his best; no one would believe him if he professed to be penniless. The bulk of the money, together with his watch, he put into his wallet. He disrobed partially and, constructing a belt of handkerchief strings, bound the wallet against his inner thigh. In the carpetbag Ira carried only clothing and a few toilet articles. Again he thought it better not to be empty-handed on meeting free-booters. He put the razor case into his coat pocket, the razor might serve as a weapon. Reclothed, he ascended to the railway, crossed the trestle, found a wagon road a few hundred yards to the south. There were no vehicles in sight—no pedestrians, no animals, not a figure moving.

The train had halted but a few miles beyond Macon if one judged correctly the speed and the time elapsed. Possibly Northern troops were in Macon already or would be immediately. If Macon were captured, Milledgeville also must have been captured, or would be captured soon, or besieged. The reduction of an important military point such as Macon, the reduction of the State capital itself— to be accompanied by wastage and looting—would consume time. If Ira traveled rapidly across country toward Savannah he might reach that port before Yankees did. He thought of counties to the east, reviewing geography involved. He must get across the Oconee. Traveling southeast by way of Reidsville he might keep to the right of the Federal advance, and thus escape stragglers. Perhaps he would still be able to journey by boat from Savannah or by rail from Savannah to Charleston. . . . A horse. Wilkinson County had not yet been raided: he might be able to buy a mount and travel long, and next day trade his horse for a fresh one. . . . How far is Savannah? Perhaps a hundred and fifty miles as the crow flies? . . . Ira was embarked upon a sacred course. His conscience had sent him into this hazard, his conscience must sustain him.

Sun came through low haze and turned the rutted clay road to a brassy streak. Ira halted, looked to the west, flattened his hand, held it out at arm's length with wrist against the horizon. The sun would set in little more than an hour. He resumed his plodding. The way swung slightly to the north, then back south of east. There came a rise, he topped it, he stood on a slight ridge. . . . No smoke ahead, but several separate trunks of smoke twisted at the left. He envisioned them as outskirts of a forest which might thicken. He must avoid that forest, not be tangled in it, not be lost.

Ira saw himself in Richmond, signing for a room at the Spotswood Hotel. Halls were filled with belted officers in gray, with citizens shouldering. Streets were a press and torrent . . . horses bringing down their hoofs, army wagons a-jumble. There were beggars and armless veterans . . . Ira imagined one young man with both legs gone; the fellow pushed himself upon a wheeled platform as Ira had seen another beggar do in a Northern city long ago. This legless man had a cake of solid wood strapped to each hand: with these slabs as motive power he drew himself ahead, bumping, straining on his low cart. These things Ira saw . . . perhaps prostitutes sauntering at entrances of small lanes, the Capitol rising beyond.

He stood eventually in the presence of Mr. Seddon. He had never seen Mr. Seddon, but a friend told him that the Secretary wore habitually a black skull cap. Appropriately beneath that cap his face was a dry corpse-face bereft of vitality. Eyes were pits, the voice mouldered as it spoke. . . . There loomed a repository in the shape of a burial casket, with glass where the face of a dead person might be seen. Therein was contained no body: only the mass of reports sent by inspecting officers and angry surgeons. Pleas of good men like Persons and Chandler and Jones . . . you could witness those reports through glass, each rolled into a little rod, tied tightly with red tape, scratched with chicken tracks which said that those reports had been Noted By Secretary Seddon And Then Filed Away.

No, doubtless he would never stand before James Seddon, he could but try to reach Mr. Seddon's presence. Guards, underlings would hold him back. He would stand instead before some other desk, be greeted tonelessly by a slit-eyed subordinate, be told to go away, just as General Winder had ordered the people of Americus to go away with their vegetables.

Sir, as I have described to you, the place is a menace and disgrace.

But upwards of twenty thousand prisoners have already been removed, Mr. Claffey!

Some of them have been returned, because there seemed no safe place to hold them, either at Savannah or at Blackshears. True, the crowded conditions have lessened, but smell continues. And disease. A higher percentage of hospital patients go to death each day, because they constituted originally the sick and crippled, the unable-to-travel, the weaklings, the rotting outcasts.

Mr. Claffey, the Secretary is engaged. He cannot possibly see you.

Then I shall presume to address myself to President Davis. I knew him— It was during the Mexican War—

Blank formless visage, still formless, still blank, still repellent . . . somehow wearing a supercilious smile. The President knew many people during the late War with Mexico, Mr. Claffey! I doubt that he would recall you. I doubt that he would recall your name.

Then I shall go to—

To whom?

Surgeon Elkins addressed himself in appeal to the Almighty God. Can I not do the same?

God will not see you. He is engaged.

In desperation of anguish. . . .

Oh, please to hear me, please to assist! I plead not solely on behalf of the miserable Yankees who whine and vomit in those several acres of so-called hospital between the creeks! I plead on behalf of my three sons who died boldly, died with honor. I plead on behalf of our dear new Nation, on behalf of whatever tradition shall be suffered to exist when once we have gained the—the—victory, the—unchallenged independence we seek. What matters a chivalrous Lee if we have a Winder? What matters the sacrifice of a Hood, if we have a Captain Wirz? What matters the competence of a Johnston or the spiritual strength of a sickly Stephens, if we have at home only the incompetence of venal surgeons, incompetence of a Seddon, frailty and futility of a sickly Seddon?

You are near to provoking me into issuing an order for your arrest, Mr. Claffey! You are presumptuous, stubborn, ignorant of necessities of war. Go way!

Then nothing can be done?

Nothing. Go way!

I prophesy with all the terrible ardor I can muster: this will be a stench in the nostrils of history.

Those are not my nostrils, nor the nostrils of any living soldier or office-holder. How can I be held responsible, you upstart? Who can be held responsible?

If an individual, it is difficult for me to name him.

Ira Claffey felt the doom of his hope. Still he must progress, win through to Richmond. He felt that Sherman's entire army was on his flank . . . beloved Creator, I must turn that flank. He limped on. How could a mere carpetbag grow so heavy?

Ahead appeared a house and outbuildings on the north side of the road. It was a substantial house; but as Ira came closer he could see that the steps were in bad repair, some windows were broken, there was a scurrying which occurred among outbuildings at the rear. He heard the whinny of a horse. Then, past the next clump of leafless trees, he saw three horses standing riderless in front of the dwelling. Saddles were empty but there were odd-shaped baskets and bundles tied to the saddles. Some hurly-burly was in progress within the farmhouse. Voices raised . . . Ira heard suddenly a scream that started as a squeak, a moan rising in pitch until it pierced walls and roof. The yell was accompanied by a dragging banging sound. Murder, he thought. That is the sound of murder. He dropped his carpetbag at the gate and hurried along a graveled path littered with debris and chicken droppings. He went up five steps to the gallery, felt a board break beneath his weight; he did not fall. The door was a double door, giving on an open hallway which passed directly through the house; a door stood open at the other end. No person was in sight. There were pans, utensils, implements hung along the passageway. A tall chest of drawers stood against one wall, and bundles of seed corn dried from the roof. Banging sound and the continuing shriek filled the first room on the right; Ira blundered there. The scene struck him swiftly: a mussed bed, a gray-haired woman—perhaps an invalid—who sat stiffly in a small rocking chair and held her hands over her eyes as she wailed. A medium-sized man was bending in front of another bureau there. He had pulled out all the drawers and was rummaging, dipping both hands into masses of clothing, bundles of letters. A rag doll was tossed aside, tossed over the man's shoulder, the doll fell at Ira's feet as he entered. The man swung around, straightened. His hand went to his hip as if reaching for a weapon. Ira struck him on the side of the jaw; the man sprawled and lay grunting. His face was stubbly, the beard grown out an inch. Plunging, two other men came across the corridor from some opposite room. Ira whirled, ready with his fists, then he dropped his fists. He saw the muzzle of a carbine. One man was tall, clean-shaven, the other squat. Yes, both carried carbines. Ira thought swiftly that he would be shot, he stood anticipating the blow of bullets against his body. These men were in blue or half in blue. Still they did not look like soldiers.

Where the hell did you come from, Mister?

Ira stood thinking of the combined charge of those carbines, still expecting it. You belong here?

I was passing.

Passing?

Passing by. I heard screams.

Look at Terry, said the taller man. Lowering his carbine, he came past Ira as if he did not exist. Hi, Terry! What you doing on the floor?

Son of a bitch hit me.

Why, Mister, said the taller man. His hair clung matted, straggling under his shapeless colorless hat, dirty silver at the temples. He must be nearly as old as Ira. Mister, you like to killed our partner here. You could get shot for that!

The old lady in the chair had quieted down. She'd lowered her hands, hands bounced up and down upon her dirty aproned lap, her jaws kept twitching spasmodically, her pale eyes gyrated in knots of wrinkles, she appeared to be having a fit.

The man called Terry raised into a sitting position. He sat feeling his face. By God, where'd I put my pistol? I'm going to kill that son of a bitch!

Yes, said the taller older man mockingly, you kill him, we're like to be hung. Come on, Terry, get the rocks out of your ass. Let's move along.

He took Terry's hand and pulled the man to his feet. Terry staggered back against the rifled bureau.

Mr. Secesh, the taller fellow addressed Ira, you got any money?

I have a little money.

Then we'll just take that.

Ira reached for his pocket.

No, no! Right pants pocket? I'll just take that myself. Keep your gun on his head, Lester, he directed the man in the door. For Christ sake don't shoot me if you got to pull trigger. Swiftly his hairy hands slapped around Ira's breast and flanks, feeling for a pistol, but he did not touch the inside of the thigh. One hand struck the razor case in Ira's coat pocket. The razor was produced, the man put it in his own pocket. That'll be for Terry, he said. He needs a good shave—don't you, Terry boy? He found the fold of Ira's bills, counted swiftly, pocketed the money. By all appearances he was the commander; yet his blue coat, torn at one shoulder, bore no insignia of rank. Lester, he ordered the squat fellow with the carbine, go take a look-see. And you, Mister Secesh—he motioned with his own weapon. Go over and set down on that sofy. There was a couch behind. Ira backed off, sat down in obedience. From outside sounded the inarticulate yap of Lester. Then he came stumbling to the door. Critter soldiers, he said breathlessly. Despite his blue jacket he must not be a Yankee born and bred: not if he said critter soldiers.

Whereabouts?—

Two three fields yonder—

They galloping?—

Sort of poking along. We got time to get—

Then let's get! Stay where you be, Mister!—

The rough-bearded Terry had already moved speedily if uncertainly into the passage, and Ira could hear him, with Lester, crossing the gallery, descending the steps. There was a wrenching of rotten wood, the sound of someone falling, a spout of curses and simultaneous laughter from the man who had not fallen. You keep setting, the tall man directed Ira Claffey. He pointed his carbine once more in Ira's general direction. Glad you had some currency on you, even Secesh. Our luck's been skinny all the day. I swear that these folks haven't got nothing to bite

or break. Then he was gone; you could hear pull of leather as the men mounted
. . . quickly the diminishing sound of galloping. Ira stood at the cobwebby eastern window and watched the party moving with speed along the clay road, disappearing behind a bank of chinaberries which might or might not shield another
house. He turned to the old lady who had not left her chair, who still sat shuddering. It's all right, Madam. He doubted if she heard or understood him. There was
a scratching in the passageway. He stepped to the door and found two Negro girls,
aged perhaps nine and eleven, who shrank away from him and then went scurrying toward the rear. They wore crude gowns made of sacking, they looked like
miniature witches in panic, they began yelping in the rear yard. Ira recognized a
jangle of buckles or weapons, a muddle of hoofs outside. He stepped to the
gallery, and counted: six cavalrymen in the mixed blue-gray so common nowadays
among Confederates, yet gray predominated. These were no bushwhackers—not
in the way they sat their horses, not in the way they were poised. They filed
through a gate from the western field. Only one man drew a revolver, though all
were gazing curiously at the stranger who made his way down the ruined steps and
walked to meet them.

Your house? asked a soldier.

No. I was on the road. The Yankees stopped our train.

We saw it, said another. We was watching from the woods. Reckon you hain't
no Yankee?

I come from Sumter County. Ira told briefly of the occurrence at this farmhouse. All six cavalrymen rested quietly, gazing down without comment, unimpressed. Just bummers, they said. Same old story, happens all the while. Did you
say that the old lady was hurted?

I doubt they laid a hand on her. But she seems hysterical, shocked and frightened half to death.

Which way did you say them bummers went?

Due ahead, east. They were galloping: I fear you'd have a hard time catching
up. What is your organization, gentlemen?

We're with Joe Wheeler, said one with tarnished stripes of a sergeant. Then, to
another— What you say, Lilly? Less pick ourselves a bummer or two for supper.
They rode away.

Ira Claffey reclaimed his carpetbag. He found that he was covered with sweat
in spite of chill raw air which blew with increasing sharpness. The hazy sun was
hiding behind western pines. Ira heard someone at the house, he turned to see.
An extremely tall Negress stood above the steps, facing him belligerently. Her
skirts were pinned up raggedly above spindly shanks, she had a faded red cloth
tied around her head, two of the corners stood up from the knot like erect ears of
some animal. Her hands were on her hips, though one hand gripped a wooden
potato masher.

You go long, she ordered Ira distinctly. Done you bother round here, bother
Miss Gracie no more!

Ira grinned. He went along the road to the east, following the little band of
Wheeler's cavalry who were trotting, then loping, who soon disappeared over the
ridge. There stood a new column of black smoke in the north; Ira fancied that he
could see flames at the base of it; a large structure must be burning beyond those
empty fields. He turned to look back at the ramshackle farmhouse. The angular
black woman had come down from the porch and stood in the road, a stiff threat
against the fading sunlight. She turned and went back to the gallery.

Ira marveled, as he had marveled earlier, at the peculiar casual quality of war.
He had a baffled curiosity concerning smaller events which accompanied warfare,

offshoots of the cruel parent plant. He wondered how men might ever conceive tapestries and paintings which they created, presumably to portray battles. He had never traveled abroad, had seen but a few great paintings; yet those he had seen—or engravings in books—never suggested the fact of war. Ira remembered the first man he ever saw struck by a bullet. A column of troops, cooking inside thick blue uniforms, wearing jackets and shirts open at the neck (some mutineers against authority, some bold seekers after comfort, had actually taken their jackets off and flung them away)— The column straggled into the pitted street of a Mexican village, stumbling over red-dusted stones. He remembered a white church on an eminence beyond; he remembered women in black costumes who ran toward that church, some carrying babies, herding children ahead of them. He remembered that some of the children were naked, they looked like sprites. Then a party of guerrillas, or citizens acting as guerrillas, fired from roof-tops ahead. There was a patter of balls pocking into various individuals of the troops or scraping on hard-baked earth and stones, squealing in ricochet. A young man directly ahead of Ira was struck. He was blowing his nose at the moment of impact, blowing his nose into a dirty handkerchief turned brown by grime of the march. The man made a sound like *gah,* he swung out his right hand holding the handkerchief, brought it back again. Adjacent people scattered; orders were being shouted, officers were trying to deploy men off that fatal road, to have them take shelter behind rocks. The man with the handkerchief (Ira couldn't remember his name for a certainty; he thought that it was Bradley) had gone down on one knee in a kneeling posture. His musket, which he had been carrying slung, fell from his shoulder and lay with its barrel across the foot bent behind him. Then he finished blowing his nose. Ira and two others had halted to give him aid. The soldier wiped his nose carefully, and all the time he accomplished this rite, a wet place was spreading down from the hole in his coat. A button turned red, then drops fell from the button and a polished fly buzzed close. The man fell forward and a little to one side. When they turned him over it was amazing to see that he had a mystic grin on his face, as if he were delighted at the whole occurrence.

Oh, Ira cried, it is casual, casual. War and death in war are unstudied, never built in rigid pattern as once I believed that they would be.

So it went forever: a colonel directing troops in battle, his jaw swollen with toothache; the straggler shot behind a fence whilst in the act of evacuation; a bottle lying on the battlefield, a bottle with no label, containing some dark liquid, the neck trimmed off neatly by a bullet . . . still the bulk of the bottle was unshattered. The casualness of war . . . thing without duplication; no several shots ever sounded quite alike, hills gave back different echoes. The song of war was never sung twice in the same way.

As Ira Claffey went on helplessly and hopelessly, with twilight following him and then overtaking him, he perceived the same disordered uncertain quality which had been in his thought. He thought that fog rose to the north and east. It was strange to have fog and smoke mingled, resembling a wall of bad weather rising to threaten. Then he began to smell the fog: it was not fog, it was thick dust. There had been no rain in these parts, fields and roads were unseasonably parched.

What might so disturb the dust?

Vast numbers of wheels and hoofs.

It seemed that he heard them: wide-flung rumble and pushing and treading beyond the ridges.

On an instant he felt earth trembling under his feet, responding to a drumming from behind. He turned and stepped across a ditch for safety's sake. Out of dimness and dust a throng of blue cavalrymen bore down upon him. No Confederates, these: solidly in blue, and a veteran aspect to them, even at first glimpse. There galloped fifty or sixty men in the group. What was the strength of a troop or a squadron?—Ira could not recollect. They poured past, only a few streaked faces turned to regard him. What was a man, a citizen standing beside a fence with a carpetbag in his hand? They had seen many such figures. Then darkening dust was so thick that Ira could not see where the riders had gone. He wondered if they would overtake the half-dozen of Wheeler's men, he wondered if they were seeking them.

He went on aimlessly, grieved by growing awareness that invaders were all around him, ahead of him. He would never reach Savannah, never reach Richmond. Dear Lord, I started too late. I should have gone earlier; but had not dreamt that I could do a particle of good until desperation drove me to believe it. Murky landscape was turned pinkish. As Ira walked he began to identify individual stronger glows which gave forth a solid color: large fires, two to the left, one directly ahead and seeming low and wide as if a valley were lit, another fire ahead and slightly to the right.

Night tightened. Ira passed a stand of forest, mostly oaks—he could see the points of leaves clinging to the starkness, revealed easily against illumination beyond. He passed the last of the trees and stood where the road dipped. Yes, it was a valley. A house was burning, there seemed to be other embers beyond. A figure moved beside the crackling house, some other figures were motionless. Flames burst and stung; it sounded like a vast popping of corn; fleet somersaulting embers made unholy pyrotechnics above the blast. As Ira came near he heard the sound of crying as if dogs howled there. Closer he came limping to the yard fence. There was too much heat, he could not approach the actual blaze nor could the victims whose home was spouting aloft. A woman and a girl—mother and daughter—stood clutched in each other's arms. Tears seemed fairly boiling on their faces, yet they did not dare turn from this ascending horror; they stood hypnotized as they wept. The woman was comely; but her hair was coming down, her wet round cheeks were varnished in reflection; she was young, perhaps not much above thirty. The daughter was old enough to have her skirts long, but she had not put up her brownish hair: it was a mane around her shoulders, and one small ribbon was gilded by glow. The hair became a lovely thing in that light.

A man spoke beside Ira. By God, I never burned that bridge. I never. And look what they done to me!

A few things had been dragged out, but only a few: a barrel had been rolled, a clock stood on the barrel; there were two chairs, a kettle with tongs sticking out, a pile of bed-clothing, a bonnet, a lantern: Ira saw these things. Now a black-and-white cat rushed frantically across the hot open ground, leaped up on the fence beside the two men, gave them a look of fury, spilled herself down into darkness of the road.

Leastways, said the farmer, we got the kittens out. We forgot them; then my girl went back and fetched the basket, and blame near got herself burned up a-doing it. Strangely he gave a weak giggle. First off I thought you was neighbor Barfield from beyond the ridge; now I see you ain't. You ain't one of them bummers? and suddenly he loomed at Ira and lifted his hands as if ready to throttle.

I'm from Sumter County. Claffey's my name.

Name is Keeling, said the bushy-bearded man—a tall fellow, extremely spare of body. Somehow Ira thought of an Andersonville prisoner, and wondered what the resemblance might be. I'm Jim Keeling, said the man again. Always played fair with the Yanks, and reckoned maybe they'd play fair with me if they headed this way. But it didn't come out like that, as you can see. He turned and yelled, Minnie, you and the girl get away from that, now. Sparks liable to set your gowns afire!

Neither the woman nor the girl answered or moved. They were rooted and clutching, still crying.

You got a chaw on you? asked Keeling. No? Well, the surgeons done told me I shouldn't chew tobacco neither, count of my digestion. But it's something to do. . . . He told his story to Ira as flames kept howling. He had been drafted more than two years previously. His wife and the girl and an old grandfather tried to work the farm while he was gone, but now the grandfather was dead. Good thing he didn't live to see this! He'd of had a fit and fell in it. For he built this very house, mostly with his own hands. Well.

Jim Keeling served finally with the Forty-ninth Georgia and had been wounded in Virginia the previous summer. . . . Twas a spent ball, but it nigh knocked the breath out of me. Ever since twas healed, I've had great difficulty keeping my food down. That's how come I lost so many pounds: don't weigh two-thirds my natural self now.

Shortly before sunset the bridge beside that house had been set afire. None of the Keelings saw who started the blaze, they saw no one running from the scene. It was just that suddenly they heard and smelled and saw the fire, and ran into their yard to watch the bridge burning. . . . This ain't exactly a turnpike through here, mister; but it's a good road and I spose valued by the Yanks accordingly. After that bridge fell through, just a while ago, a whole kit and boiling of Yankee cavalry come into this here very yard.

I think I saw them, said Ira. They passed me, beyond that hill. At least fifty of them.

Could have been—they looked like five hundred to me. They said I'd burned that bridge to hold up the Yank advance, and I told them, by God I never. Well, they said I ought to have kept from doing it whoever he was who done it. They said I was big enough; and then they found my gun and they says, See, you could have kept anybody from burning that bridge. So they broke my gun, smashed it gainst the fireplace. I couldn't do nothing to repel them; they was far too many for me. Anyway I'm sickly, as I tolt you. Well. The officer, he said twas retaliation: that was the word he used. Said he'd been ordered to perform such duty, and by that time some of his men had took my sow, and blooded her, and had her up on a horse, like the horse was carrying double. Don't reckon they took much else. But it don't matter now—everything's burning, cept the little bit we got out. They just marched us from the house and cut some sticks of pine from my wood pile and went to torching right and left. When they had her well alight, they rode off. Then we run to get what we could; but, as you see, twasn't much.

It seemed odd to Ira that the Federals had left the low stable and other outbuildings untouched; perhaps they were pressed for time. Thus far a light but steady north wind had turned the drift of flames and embers away from the sheds; but now, as the roof of the house went in with a bright crash, a shift occurred. Blazing little birds traveled to the southeast and still more easterly, settling in profusion upon the sheds. Simultaneously with Keeling, Ira saw this danger, the wife and daughter saw it as well. All went hastening past the furnace. Before they reached the stable new tongues were showing on the dried shakes.

I got a couple buckets here, mister, shouted Keeling. Help us fetch water from the creek!

Ira cried, I've a bad knee; but help me to get up there!

A cart stood near; Ira and the younger man pushed it with desperate strength against the stable. Ira managed to mount from cart to roof, with Keeling shoving at his legs. The man could not help much . . . Ira tore his own clothing . . . in another moment he had scrambled among the jeering flames. He yelled for a broom which he had seen lying in the yard; Keeling passed it to him while the young girl came laboring from the creek, spilling water from two wooden pails. Ira beat savagely with the broom, other naughty embers were flurrying down. Between water and poundings, the flames soon went out.

Best that your womenfolks splash water on those shed roofs too, Ira gasped. . . . So the danger passed as the main body of blaze went lower. They moved like actors on an orange-lighted stage. The area of illumination included the road, where now several horsemen could be seen halted, watching the affair. The stable was saved. . . . Ira had more difficulty getting down than he'd had ascending, until Keeling got his wits about him and fetched a homemade ladder from among his fruit trees. Ira walked across the dooryard toward the road, to find that the watchers were a youngish Federal major accompanied by three soldiers.

It's too bad, said the major.

You should know. Bitterly. Your people did this.

Your house? asked the major.

Ira smelled burning of wool, he found where his coat sleeve was charring, he slapped at this tiny destruction. Not my house. It belongs—or did belong—to the man approaching there—a former soldier, wounded into the bargain.

Jim Keeling came up with no fear and shook his fist at the Northerners; the major's horse shied. You blue-bellied devils, said Jim Keeling. Burnt the roof right off the heads of my family! Does a man's heart good to see you Yanks warring against women and girls!

The Unionist motioned toward the ruined bridge beyond, where posts were glowing still. What of the bridge?

I never put hand to it! But I wish your damn Sherman had stood here and heard my wife and daughter a-crying. We should of marched into the North, God damn it! Would of trained you God damn Yanks how to act decent.

Major Hitchcock, sir! cried one of the privates. You want us to arrest this man? He's abusive.

By no means, Chris. His house has just been burnt; I don't blame him for being abusive, not in the slightest. The frightened cat raced across the roadway once more, and the major's horse began to dance. He brought the animal under control and pulled over against the fence. He asked calmly of Ira, Have any troops passed this way, sir? At the moment I'm looking for some people from Illinois.

Obviously they've passed. They were cavalry.

No, no, and at this closer range Ira could see that Major Hitchcock's face held a great weariness, there was solemn grief in his face. No, I'm seeking infantry. Perhaps they're on the next road north.

He addressed himself directly to Jim Keeling. A word with you, Friend Southerner.

I got no good words for you, said Keeling. And I'm no friend.

I wish to say this: the fortunes of war held your army mainly away from the North; but at least you made no bones about burning Chambersburg, Pennsylvania. And we've had you people planting mines in the roads ahead of us. Citizens —making war! Some of our boys have been killed by those mines, some had their feet blown off. We've discovered you Georgians burning forage and corn along our route. Therefore General Sherman has ordered that houses will be burnt and cotton gins will be burnt to keep them company. Back on Buffalo Creek we found a bridge in ashes. The adjacent house was destroyed. I must admit that I felt impelled to argue with the general about this, and I'll tell you exactly what he said. He said: Let the enemy look to his own people. If the Southerners find that their burning of bridges only destroys their own houses, they'll soon stop it.

His face was tinted to bright copper by diminishing flames. Major Hitchcock closed his eyes in concentration, then leaned toward the people in the yard. He spoke earnestly. That is General Sherman's belief, I heard him say it. He said: In war everything is right that prevents anything. He said that he feels there's nothing to do but to make war so terrible that when peace comes it will *last*.

There was something in his speech. . . . Where were you born? Ira asked. . . . Hitchcock smiled. Alabama. But my parents had come from the North. Oh yes, I was reared in Missouri and in Tennessee, but educated at Yale. I do have, as you might understand, a strong sympathy for the Southern people. Also I hold unalterable devotion to the Union cause. Now we must be on our way. Good evening. And you, he said to the tall thin Keeling— I am sorry for your loss; but I fear it had to be. Abruptly he rode toward the creek, soldiers clattering after him. The Georgians could hear them splashing through the stream, then they vanished.

Ira spent the night beside the embers. It was unhappily warm there, an open refuge from November's chill. The Keelings took the bed-clothing which had escaped destruction and bedded down in the stable. Jim Keeling said that he owned plenty of clean corn-shucks, they were not uncomfortable. The people offered to share their meager supply with Ira, in appreciation for help he had given them, but he refused. He was affected deeply by their gratitude. The man insisted on bringing a piece of canvas, and with this Ira made a rude tent to keep off winds. He lay within the folds, watching the play of light from ruins which still fried. He thought that he was safer here than he might be along avenues traveled by dangerous bands who clung alongside the Federal advance. Men would see that destruction had occurred already; obviously the place was stripped, they would pass by.

There came disturbances through the night: horses passed, men talked; they stopped to discuss the lingering blaze, went on. Once two wagons came also, with hullabaloo about their fording the stream. Soon after sunrise a frightened elderly couple appeared with a basket. These were the Jarells from down the road, and feared to come sooner . . . they had seen the blaze, knew that the Keeling place must have burned, there was nothing else to burn at that point. Mr. Jarell said that his own place had been visited by foragers who took nothing except chickens. They said that Mrs. Keeling and her daughter must sleep in their house for the time being. It appeared that they were distant cousins of the wounded veteran; Ira heard talk about Aunt Mame and Cousin Neddy. The Jarells had fetched bread and side meat . . . Ira ate but sparingly. An extra mouth was a dreadful thing in times like these.

Ira went into the privy and extracted a thousand dollars Confederate from his hoard. He insisted that Jim Keeling should accept this as a loan—to be paid back, without interest, when and if. It may be worth nothing at all, now that the Yanks are come, Ira told the haggard man. Again it may be the only currency in circulation for some time. Do with it as you can. Keeling cried openly.

After Ira stopped to play with the rescued kittens in their basket—with the mother cat no longer terrified but buzzing contentedly as the kittens fed—he went away. He smiled grimly. Literally he did not know which way to turn. From conversation which he'd heard, and rumor reaching the Jarells during the night, he judged that the bulk of the Federal army trod paths to the north and east. There was no point any longer in even considering Savannah.

Freebooters had passed but more might be trailing. A man might remain in danger as long as he remained in this region . . . all people would be in danger. Ira wondered if a talon of the blue iron hand reached toward Andersonville. He might come home to find his own house in ashes; but at least thousands of the prisoners still incarcerated were too weak to do much revengeful harm. Most of the Reserves could not fight, they would run away. He thought of hasty feet trampling in his hall, big shoes pounding the stair, drawers jerked out, tables upset. In his imaginings a hooting bandit dressed himself in Ira's Mexican War uniform and went parading. Ira Claffey thought about his black people. Most of all Lucy was in his thoughts. But he felt that Mrs. Effie Dillard could cope with almost any band of raiders. Also Cousin Harry would be at hand. . . . No, he found no real worry, none worth entertaining. Resolutely he put the unhappy panorama out of his mind.

Beyond the next hill he was confronted by a party of terror-stricken citizens, driving a few head of sheep and a white cow about to come fresh. There were dogs trotting, and children, and an old man being pushed in a hand-cart. They just gave us sut! cried an old woman. My son-in-law, he'd made thirty-two hundred gallons of syrup; twas more than he had casks for, so he'd sunk a tank in the ground, buried it deep, and if those Yanks didn't come along yesterday and help themselves to the whole! . . . They ruint my flower garden, cried a younger woman. They took Pa's watch! screamed a child. Oh, mister, they all cried. You better turn round and go back tother way. . . . Wouldn't even wait for me to give them the keys to the bureau, cried the woman who'd lamented the loss of her garden. They just smashed in the drawers with musket butts. . . . They shot Jed! cried a little boy, as Ira continued doggedly on his way. He speculated drearily who Jed might have been: dog or pig or tomcat, he did not suppose that Jed was a person.

He went on and met the mass of the Union army's right wing: rank and file and furbelow. Long afterward, Ira learned that there had been sixty-odd thousand men in the punishing hordes which slammed from Atlanta to Savannah; but on sight he thought that there were millions. The next northwest-to-southeast road was crammed as he had seen a small hallway in Milledgeville crammed during legislative session. There was not space enough in the road for the people. They would have shoved fences aside but the fences were gone: smoking patches showed where rails burned during the night. At the first intersection a foraging party assembled with their loot. A group of boys stood guarding a heap of smoked hams—a heap which might have filled one of the Claffey wardrobes to capacity and then some. The boys were laughing, not especially in arrogance, but seemingly with sheer spookish joy of living and of plundering. Always Ira would remember one: a hard-faced youngster of seventeen or thereabouts, who stood arrogantly with a cob pipe turned upside down in his mouth, as he would guard it against a rain; but it was not raining now. Whenever in after years someone said Sherman, or Sherman's Invasion, or Sherman's March to the Sea, he would think of that lean boy . . . freckled, beardless, shock-headed, with upside-down pipe. A big wagon came banging, and the boys yelled a question at the wagoner. Thirty-ninth Iowa? The wagoner nodded. He did not pull his four-horse team to a stand. It was impossible for anyone to halt in the road: too many people came swarming on their course. As the wagon continued, the group of youths labored after it with armloads of the hams. They pushed hams up across the tailboard, unseen hands received them apparently, hams vanished into the black-draped interior. Back and forth the soldiers went, hurrying through a distance of perhaps thirty rods before the meat was all put aboard. Them Iowa boys must have found themselves a big butcher, said someone behind Ira Claffey; but he could not even turn to see who was talking, he was agape.

There rode on good horses a noisy herd of wenches (all young, perhaps the youngest was fourteen) dressed in gowns of colored silk stolen undoubtedly from some wealthy house. Crimson and gold of their disheveled costuming fairly hurt the eyes. They were headed by a pompous fat Negro bestriding a dappled stallion; he rode bareback, he kept turning to the chattering mounted bevy behind, holding out his hand, saying sharply, Keep up, you all, keep up, stay together! He wore a gilt-piped coat hanging open, unbuttoned, and a beaver hat too small for his head. Ira supposed the fellow was some officer's servant who had gathered this harem.

Ira stood at the edge of a clump of trees and blackberry vines; still he carried his carpetbag: it had endured through vicissitudes since the train was stopped. But now he felt the bag wrenched from his grasp. A clumsy young man had stepped out of the lounging files, twisted the carpetbag away, and was going off with it coolly. A voice sang sharply, Hi! with an inquiring lift to the cry. A young lieutenant on a bay kicked his horse into a trot along the edge of the field and overtook the robber. He retrieved the carpetbag, whirled his horse, came back to Ira. Here, mister, and he leaned down to deliver the bag. Better drop it out of sight behind that brush. Some of these folks have got the itch, they'll steal anything in sight! He was gone before Ira could thank him.

He tossed the bag behind him into a weed patch. He would have liked to have sat on his haunches. His stiff knee would not permit this, but a little farther on there was a stump; there he sat for a time. Regiments, cattle, black wanderers, wagons from which corn and parlor chairs spilled down, more lounging tough companies—the crowd kept flowing. Ira thought of a celebration he'd seen in New York, with Broadway thronged between its shop fronts, brass bands hallooing. Here there were no bands, although he did see a bass drum carried atop a chaise. It was as if the earth had erupted in the northwest and spewed a strange concentrated lava of people, brown and white, to come rolling down these sluiceways. A Negro woman skipped there, young, waving long bony arms, trying to make screams although her voice was worn from previous screaming. Tildy, cried another black woman, overtaking her and tugging her to the side. Now you quit crying for that baby! He's safe with Jesus. . . . In the wwwater, the other woman kept blubbering. In that old wwwater. Got push off that old bridge. All these soldier folks they push my baby. . . .

More troops coming, herds of ragged blacks keeping them company. Zachary Clark, a voice yelled. Oh, Zach, where are you? and a big laugh sounded ahead, a curly head turned. Zachary Clark was a Yankee soldier, an older man, his ringlets were silver, his fleshy face beamed. Right up here, he called in response. Come along, Archie! . . . What you carrying, Zach? . . . Ladies' pants. . . . And so he was: a queer double bag made from voluminous drawers with each leg tied at the bottom. This strange receptable rode atop his right shoulder, his rifle was slung on his left. . . . What you got in them pants, Zach? Hey, Bob! . . . there was running of feet to catch up with him. . . . I bet you'd just like to know! Voices drifted off into the pounding, striding, hoofing, wheel-turning.

Smoke and dust lay in a compress high over the road and beyond it . . . would Georgia ever rise again? Smudge of the Keelings' house had been but a firefly. Ira thought drearily of what Major Hitchcock, the tired-faced Yankee, had said the night before. Hitchcock spoke of burning cotton gins. Oh, would we have ruined the simple economy of the North, if we instead had made a march? Say that we had gone the length of Indiana. Would we have put their corn into ashes? Perhaps, perhaps. . . . No, no, we would never have done so. I, at least, have a pretention to decency. So have people like Cato Dillard, so has even the crippled Coral Tebbs—a hard warped pride. So have men like the unfortunate Keeling. But would we have done this, what homes might we have looted? In Indiana are no slaves for us to turn loose, but— Ira thought of the vicious Winder. He treated us so. How might he have treated Yankees at the North? Ira got up from his stump, went back and gathered up the carpetbag. Now he did not even care if it were taken from him. So much else had been taken from everyone.

A silver shine came bobbing along the road: yes, it was a helmet, a souvenir perhaps from Napoleonic times. God knew how it had ever come to Georgia. But a boy found it, in press or cupboard, so now he wore it gaily, the old horse-hair plume blew in the wind. *Mooooo* said the cows, great buffalo herds of them, they dropped their dung as they traveled. A thousand feet of men came to tread and skate in slime behind them, wagon wheels came to crease the dung.

But these people were not mere bummers: bummers drifted far on the outskirts of the march. These men were plunderers, they were arsonists, but first they were soldiers. They had the stringy tough weathered look of veterans, they were of the West, there was a pioneer hunter's quality to their marching. They carried blankets rolled, their rifles were well rubbed; very few wore the bulky knapsacks, their haversacks swung as Confederate haversacks swung. Ira thought of what their units might be: Thirty-second Missouri, Ninth Iowa, One Hundred and Eleventh Illinois, Nineteenth Wisconsin, Thirtieth Iowa . . . they looked as if they had risen out of tall grass and unkempt woods. . . . Have we sufficient force to stand against them? Will they be turned back before they reach Savannah? Never, thought Ira. Our power is drained; we cannot halt them, scarcely impede their youthful brutal Western force. Miner, trapper, lumberman, and miner's son and trapper's son and lumberman's son: they come, they possess somehow the quality of Indians, you expect them to whoop as Indians do, some of them whoop so.

Ira Claffey suffered the depression of one who looks at bad weather and knows that he may not restrain it. . . . You cannot subdue a tornado; this shaggy twisting wind has sprung from beyond the horizon. Its thunder is heard, lightning has knived us already, rain comes smashing, our roof is gone.

He was haunted by the absurd delusion that if his sons had been allowed to survive, they might have kept this rabble out of Georgia. But if his sons had been born beside the upper Mississippi, instead of in the county where they were born, they would have helped to make the rabble. He turned and started south stubbornly, resolved to watch no more. He had seen enough, seen too much. These invaders took everything, burned everything, they cut their swath toward the coast. Now Ira Claffey was marooned, and so was Andersonville marooned, unless wild cavalry had gone pushing there. Behind him the jumble of individual identifiable sounds resolved into a low roar, the call and flapping of a million birds. There they traveled, cutting landscape at his back: Forty-seventh Ohio and Fifteenth Michigan and Twelfth Indiana and Fourth Iowa; they'd gathered up the very soil of Georgia, folded it around them, were wearing it as uniforms. . . . Later that day, Ira managed to buy a dinner of sorts, and also a very sorry mule. He rode the mule down into Dooly County where the mule died. Ira walked the rest of the way home.

53

. . . We go the gate again, Surgeon Crumbley. What is your news from Albany? A letter on Thursday, to be sure? I am glad, sir, that Mrs. Crumbley is mending. It must be an ordeal for you to serve so far away during her illness. . . . Paregoric? Fortunate that it was available. I wish that we might have some at this point.

. . . No, no, Surgeon White established no particular pens for any of us today. I observed no such notation on the Duty List. Take any pen you choose—they'll all be filled. There remains but to prescribe formulas and numbers as has been the custom. How many have you on your list? Mine runs up to thirty-odd: Number One is prescribed to serve for diarrhoea; Number Two for dysentery; Number Three for scorbutus, and so on. Is it in accord with your notions of medical procedure to take the discretion entirely away from the prescribing physician himself? I objected to this in my first assignment to such duty, as did you. I felt that I could not prescribe properly for my patients. I looked upon it as utter quackery! Quite so, Surgeon Crumbley. I discovered that the diseases from which our patients were suffering stemmed from want of the proper kind of dieting, remedies, etc. To begin with, I was convinced that I could have done more— indeed yes, I know I could—with proper dieting, than I could have with the medicines available. When first I came here—it must have been for two whole days, not more—I examined each new case, made my diagnosis, wrote out my prescription accordingly. I found that the medicines had not been supplied. I asked the reason, and they informed me that I was not to practice in that way: I must practice according to the numbers and formulas presented. I told them: I know nothing of such formulas and numbers, and care nothing for them. And, gentlemen, I refuse to practice in any such way! . . . What's more, I went my round, diagnosed the cases again, made out a prescription for each case. It was extremely laborious; there were many under my charge, as you will understand, Surgeon Crumbley, as you have had under your charge. I sent up the prescriptions, and once again they were refused. I said to my clerk—a Yankee prisoner, no less, and On Parole, but with some claim to a background embracing pharmacopoeia—I said, What ho, Yank? . . . Surgeon Elkins, he told me, it is quite useless for you to make out such prescriptions.

It would appear that there is a blockade.

It would appear that if President Davis himself were suffering from the pip, perhaps he might be served.

Might the Secretary of War be served properly? Might General Winder? Let us say that is a moot question.

As I recall now, you were overjoyed, Surgeon Crumbley, when a bottle of paregoric was found—a medicament to relieve your wife—in the recesses of some friend's closet in Albany.

Let us not seek narcotic for our senses, sir. 'Twill be unavailable.

For diarrhoea? Red pepper, and decoctions of blackberry root and of pine leaves.

For coughs and lung diseases? A decoction of wild cherry bark.

For chills and fever? A decoction of dogwood bark.

If fever patients seem to crave especially something sour, let us dose them with the weak acid made by fermenting a small quantity of meal in a barrel of water. Vinegar? My flask is empty, I regret to say. My vinegar is a tiny vial of fresh water sprayed into the Sahara sands.

Let us consider gangrenous sores. Ha, ha—here is the specific: peanut oil, no less! May we hope that the hospital orderlies do not steal it for a slosh in which to sop their corn bread! Dear, dear—why be picayunish about the matter? Gangrenous patients will die anyway; the hospital orderlies might live, and not eventually join their fellows amid pine straw, amid oozing holes where stumbling sick have let go their bowels, amid pools where stumbling sick have let go their bladders. What fun if the hospital orderlies were to be tricked—damn Yankees anyway, and Paroles, what's more—and let them have a ration of castor oil instead! What a lark!

How many are you empowered to admit today, Surgeon Crumbley? Five patients? The same for myself, sir. So we shall stand in our rude pens at the gate and observe the flow, the crawling and the carried.

. . . My, my, here is a grand ulcer, to be sure: at least four inches in diameter, on the calf of the leg. . . . What have we here? Necrosis of the jaw. Hold still, patient. Keep him still, friends of the patient; hold the patient, let me make an examination with my fingers. . . . Huzza! Necrosis indeed. A piece of bone nearly an inch long came out attached to my finger.

. . . It is my opinion that the diarrhoea commonly observed hereabouts is an attendant symptom of scurvy, not to be confused with the ordinary camp diarrhoea observed in our own army.

. . . Generally there is an enervation of the nervous system. It runs down in consequence of the dietary condition. Naturally the nervous system must sink under such pressure. I observe the effect manifested in idiocy, dementia and other mental weaknesses.

. . . Yes, yes, I should expect that morally such abject circumstances would produce deep humiliation and resignation. However, the effect seems otherwise: the moral attitude of the prisoners declines, men seem to abandon themselves. The well will steal from the sick, the sick will steal from the dead. Why, by God, it has come under my observation that the sick will nerve themselves to remarkable accomplishments, and steal from the *well!*

. . . That man with the bucket in his mouth, gripping the bail of the bucket as a dog would hold a bone? I have seen him frequently. He crawls for his rations.

. . . Surgeon Crumbley, have you observed the deadhouse in the hospital lately? When first I went there, there were boards forming a shed. Goodness sake —but the boards disappeared. I presume that they were stolen by those inmates of the hospital able to crawl. Lately the dead have lain with no shelter whatsoever, until wagons and mules and niggers came to cart them away.

. . . Did you observe that patient bearing the name of Clayton? Yes, yes, carried away just now . . . but you should have heard him exclaiming how he was put upon! He had a good stout belt—buckle and all—and he contended that the orderly fancied the belt. He said that he woke up; his arm was open and raw, as you remember, and he declared—it was in the night—that the orderly was rubbing gangrenous fluid into his sore. The belt, you see. What matter now? A false accusation, perhaps . . . naturally, yes: the orderly was a Yankee as well.

. . . For the treatment of wounds, ulcers, etc., we have literally nothing except water. The wards, some of them, are filled with gangrene, and we are compelled to fold our arms and look quietly upon its ravages, not even having stimulants to support the system under its depressing influences.

. . . Ulcers are produced from the slightest causes imaginable. A pin scratch, a prick of a splinter, a pustula, an abrasion, or even a mosquito bite are sufficient causes for their production. The surface presents a large ash-colored or greenish-yellow slough, and emits a very offensive odor. After the slough is removed by appropriate treatment, the parts beneath show but little tendency to granulate. Occasionally, however, apparently healthy granulations spring up and progress finely for a time, and again fall into sloughing, and thus, by an alternate process of slough and phagedenic ulceration, large portions of the affected member or large masses of the body are destroyed. In this condition gangrene usually sets in, and if not speedily arrested soon puts an end to the poor sufferer's existence.

. . . On examining the roster I find that twenty-four medical officers are charged to the hospital, and yet but twelve are on duty. The rest either by order of General Brown (at their own request) are off on sick leave or leave of indulgence. In order to attend to the wants of the sick and wounded, not less than thirty efficient medical officers should be on duty in the hospital.

. . . The corn bread received from the bakery, being made up without sifting, is wholly unfit for the use of the sick, and often, as in the last twenty-four hours, upon examination, the inner portion is found to be practically raw. . . . The corn bread cannot be eaten by many, for to do so would be to increase the diseases of the bowels, from which a large majority are suffering, and it is therefore thrown away. All then that is received by way of subsistence is two ounces of boiled beef and a half pint of rice soup per day, and under these circumstances all the skill that can be brought to bear upon their cases by the medical officers will avail nothing.

. . . Surgeon I. H. White, chief surgeon post, informed me that timely requisitions have been made on the quartermaster's department for the necessary materials to make the sick and wounded comfortable, but thus far he has been unable to procure scarcely anything.

. . . Feeling we have done our whole duty, both in the eyes of God and man, we leave the matter to rest with those whose duty it was to furnish supplies and build up a hospital that might have reflected credit on the Government and saved the lives of thousands of our race. . . .

Harrell Elkins believed truly that he had done his duty in the eyes of God and man. But he had not done all his duty; his work would end only with the termination of the hospital, with the last death there, the last removal. He went home in the dark. He had served an hour and a half past his time. Scarcely had he seen Lucy since Ira Claffey left. Harry did not allow himself to think of her when he was at work; but he could not keep her out of his thoughts at other times—especially in those many occasions when he was too tense for sleep, when he could not relax, when he lay taut as a ramrod, feeling thin and hard as a ramrod. Mrs. Effie buzzed about, but discerned soon that the young man was actually too worn to engage in professional discussion. She recognized that Elkins had toil and nuisance thrown in his face in a quantity beyond her accumulated experience. She thought that she might derive benefit from him in the future, if the cyclone of foreseen defeat did not tear him away from this region.

Harry remembered a period of shellfire when missiles came down and burst interminably. He had thought then, along with the rest of the troops, Won't it ever stop? I'm so weary of it. Can't they ever stop firing those shells? Can there be anything else in existence beyond this constant crouching, waiting, fearing, jarring? . . . So battle recurred to him now, in the form of hospital and stockade gate. Will it ever cease? Nay, never. It cannot, cannot, will not, never will cease.

November wind hit him and it was dark, dark; the surface of the lane was so ruptured that he stumbled even though he knew the way. He reached an open area of lawn behind a fence at the corner of the Claffey orchard. A lantern was being carried to the rear shed where Elkins always stopped to brush and examine his clothing. Someone had been watching, someone had made out his approach and was ready with the lantern (for the supply of oil was low: one could not leave a lantern hanging alight indefinitely, one took care, one saved and saved). He went up the drive and into the shed corner. There the lantern waited, hung on its peg; but hands which had carried it and hung it were gone away. He thought he knew whose hands. He took off his jacket, shivering in cold. He shook the jacket, worked over his shirt with the brush he kept in this shed, brushed the jacket, brushed his pants. He felt an itch. He closed the shed door, removed his shoes, took off his pants and shook them violently, turned them inside out, examined the frayed seams. He killed four graybacks, he could find no more. A flea went hopping into space. Harry wiped his shoes with a rag, and then dressed once more and carried the lantern into the rear hall of the house. Reflected gleam of candle-light drifted from the library ahead. He blew out the flame, put the utensil on its shelf, and went hesitatingly to the library door.

You are late, Cousin. Lucy was curled at the end of the sofa in folds of a faded shawl, she held a book.

Yes, late, he said. What have you been reading?

Keats.

I wish that I were not too weary to play the Poetry Game with you.

She came to meet him in the doorway, her voice telling a secret. We are alone.

Alone?

Our neighbor, old Mrs. Bile, is said to be dying. She's been poorly for a long time, and Mrs. Effie was sent for. Jonas took her to the Bile place and fetched back a note saying that Mrs. Bile's condition was grave. Thus Mrs. Dillard must needs spend the night.

Do you think that I might be of service over there?

I doubt it, Harry. She is very old, very frail. I presume twould be merely a case of rest and quiet—mild stimulants perhaps.

Should you be there yourself, Lucy?

She had lowered her face but lifted it quickly. I thought that you would need me, she said.

Suddenly he could not breathe.

No Game for you, sir. No tug and pull upon that tired brain! I had Naomi put by a few necessaries before she went to the quarters. She's left a fire, so now I shall prepare your supper.

Somehow I feel especially soiled tonight. A weak chuckle caught in his throat.

Your pitcher is filled, I trust. But I'll just bring some hot water, Cousin. The large kettle is on—

You will not tote water for me, said Harry firmly. He followed her out to the kitchen. She went ahead, carrying a candle, holding her hand to shield the flame.

Do you go scrub now, she told him when she had filled the pitcher. I'll make ready, and serve you in style upon a tray.

With an apple in my mouth and sausages about my neck?

He heard her quiet, Most assuredly, coming after him. In his room Harry Elkins stood upon the mat and bathed. He owned some clean clothes, for he had been given most of Sutherland's. Certain garments had been a trifle tight for him before, they were tight no longer. The trousers were now too loose. He belted them tightly, put on slippers and jacket, arranged his maroon stock. Maroon might have done for Sutherland Claffey; Harry thought that in his own case maroon was absurd; but still it was the only such scarf he owned. He went down into the library. Lucy had put his supper tray upon a table, and stood rubbing her thumbs against her first fingers in a display of nervousness quite adolescent. Through strained silence Harry could actually hear the pressure and squeezing of flesh upon flesh. Later he could not recall exactly what was said. He remembered an overpowering sense of isolation, and then recognition of a long tortured defeat: it was as if Ira Claffey directed the thought to him across chilly dark miles which separated them. He had a notion that Lucy spoke of ham and warmed-up biscuits, he was not sure. Rising out of knowledge that the two of them were alone, sole alone, alone in the house, alone and unwatched and unguarded, there shafted suddenly an enormous desire. The candle was behind Lucy, so light which shone from it made transparent delicacy around the outer surface of her hair . . . candlelight limned her figure, made it dark and solitary and haloed. Why should stockade and hospital diminish into oblivion now? They had refused to diminish before. Harry's weariness gave desperation, desperation gave strength. He started to say, The morning you kissed me, the other time I held you in my arms. . . . He was shocked at the harshness of his own voice. He could say nothing more, he whirled Lucy against him. God, God, he heard her gasping, before her mouth was smothered by his. The two of them pushed against the table, wrapped close: over went the candle upon the tray, there was a flash and sizzling, the light went out, there was faintest smell rising from an edge of ham newly scorched.

. . . And my darling, my darling Harry, I've never before, as you know, because it's sinful. It's— I shouldn't ask you if you have— No, no, I daren't ask.

But Lucy, I—haven't.

Never before?

Never.

They were in his room; somehow each felt that it would be an additional wickedness to have gone to hers.

Soon as we're married, Lucy whispered, lifting herself up to peer closely at him in gloom— We shall move in here, shan't we? Somehow, my room— It was always mine, my maiden room. Actually this is larger—

He drew her face down into the hair of his chest. You know, he said, and well aware that simple frankness was ridiculous— This is adultery. We've committed adultery, are committing it.

She breathed, Yes, yes, Harry. Will we burn in Hell?

Myself, perhaps yes. No one could burn you, no power of fiends.

But—the Bible— Uncle Dayto, and sermons— All the prayers I've uttered and other folks have uttered. Oh I declare, we're so wicked, aren't we? . . . Why didn't you love me before? Why didn't you let me know that you loved me?

You know.

No, my darling, I don't, I don't. Tis the same old hospital, same old horrid stockade, the same nasty knowledge of men dying, dying, dying, watching them die, smelling them die. It must have been the same today for you.

Harry told her, Not the same now. Suddenly I felt that I must turn to you.

Darling.

There was only their struggle and rapid breathing for a time.

Afterward he was the first to speak. Should you wish to play the Game? he asked.

Yes, yes, yes. . . .

I shall let you into the secret without a Black Mark. Proverbs, Fifth Chapter: *Rejoice with the wife of thy youth. Let her be as the loving hind and pleasant roe; let her breasts satisfy thee at all times; and be thou ravished always with her love.*

Lucy began to whimper. But I'm not your wife, you see.

Do you suppose the Lord will forgive us for being a bit hasty, Lucy? Possibly we could do penance as Catholics do. Just for the sake of a few days?

My love, twill be weeks. There are the banns.

Something else, said Harry. First Corinthians, somewhere or other: *But if they cannot contain, let them marry.* So we shall, Lucy.

She repeated, We shall. And presently she asked as they lay side by side gazing up into dark, What would Suthy think?

He would shoot me, beyond doubt.

He cannot shoot you now.

Again they were silent for a long while, until timidly Lucy began to trace the pattern of his eyebrows with her finger. In turn she pushed down the weary crumpled eyelids and let her hand pass smoothly and coolly over the closed eyes. So odd to see you close, even in dark, without your specs. Harry, you must know I'm very wicked. I suffer lust. Harry, I—I've dreamed of you.

So have I dreamed of you.

In this way they broke the dignity of rearing, cut through the veil of morality in which both had been draped. They were shocked to discover that they did not feel at all depressed about it. They kept reiterating that they should be sunk in remorse, should be praying for forgiveness. The staunch pure code forever applied —and especially in Lucy's case—seemed a shriveled broken hedge behind them. They had crashed through it, had cavorted in Eden.

I wonder, said Harry, when the Fall will occur, Cousin?

Dear Harry, you must call me Cousin no longer. Soon you will say Wife, soon say Mrs. Elkins, Ma'am. She tittered at the thought; then relaxed wide awake and glowing, a little sore in intimate portions; but enriched by joy. She believed that her joy would be perpetual.

Old Mrs. Bile died the next morning, and Mrs. Dillard was driven back to the Claffeys' at noon by a Bile nephew. Effie's mind was filled with recollections of a peaceful passing; she thought of agéd death as a release from all sin and pain, a glorification to be envied; she continued in busy thought, concerning herself also with Heaven, and the notion of her own children and grandchildren revelling there. In this mood she scarcely recollected that Lucy and Harrell Elkins had spent a night to threaten chastity. She presumed that she knew a gentleman when she saw one, and a lady as well. She knew that no gentleman such as Elkins would presume to dishonor a pure young lady, that no pure young lady such as Lucy would presume to desire to be dishonored.

The footsore Ira came trudging up with the dusk—thwarted, charged with dread weight of the invasion he had witnessed, dread knowledge that he had started for Richmond too late. . . . Twould have done no good in the end, Poppy, Lucy soothed him. And God let you come back to us safely through all dangers. When they sat alone later, with Mrs. Effie sleeping, and Elkins not yet come from the hospital, Ira saw the new Lucy. He recognized much, almost he guessed and could imagine more.

His stubbled face broke into a smile. My dear, you appear comely, especially comely.

She came flying, running across the room, dropped down, buried her face in his lap, hugged his legs convulsively.

Is it Cousin Harry?

The fair head nodded violently.

I take it he's declared himself?

Again the furious nodding.

Now, how dared he do so? He has not spoken to me.

Her head was motionless, her face burning against him.

But do you wish me to forgive him?

Once more the nodding, more rapidly than ever.

Are you happy, my dear?

Oh, Poppy, she mumbled.

In that event I shall embrace Cousin Harry with fatherly affection when he appears, and we shall take a glass of wine together.

They did in fact do this; but Elkins suffered the guilt which he had not suffered when lying with Lucy. He spilled his silver cup of wine—Sutherland's cup—before it was half empty, temporarily miserable. He thought that he should confess the enormity of his sin. Almost he struggled to speak awful words, to ask forgiveness of this wronged father; then the whole wide picture of agony near which and in which they had lived, rose before him. It was a persuasive mural in which life and death were elementals and essentials—not the practice of morality or of social or religious custom. He thought, Come, come, don't be a child about this matter. He and Ira shook hands fervently on separating. Harry went to his room and slept with more bliss than he had known in sleep since first he sought duty at Andersonville.

The Reverend Mr. Cato Dillard took delight in publishing the banns according to elderly Scottish procedure; this practice was approved by the presbytery. Cato almost regretted that he might not cry Lucy and Harry indefinitely; but rules said that they were to be cried on three successive Sundays, and that was enough; so he made the most of it. The Dillards approved contentedly of the match. Effie foresaw pleasant future episodes wherein Harrell Elkins might instruct her in medicinal procedures. Even so she rankled a little when she recalled his sport about toad ointment. . . . Cato Dillard gave opinion that each of the young pair was an excellent Christmas present to give to the other, albeit a trifle in advance of the season. Banns were cried on the twenty-seventh of November, on the fourth and eleventh of December. Cousin Harry entered a plea for a wedding on the twelfth, but Lucy said that they must wait until Wednesday the fourteenth. That was her mother's birthday. It would give her the feeling that her mother was somehow part of this solemn joy, that Veronica Claffey was no longer a forlorn shrunken monster to be shuddered away from in thought.

The Dillards arrived at the plantation Tuesday evening, accompanied by Laurel Tebbs, who had acquired the art of blushing whenever spoken to. She carried with pride a puckered bag of black silk, complete with drawstrings. This feminine delight had been given her by one of the neighboring Dennards of Americus, who found it among the effects of a recently deceased aunt. It now contained a pocket handkerchief actually dampened with cologne, and a square looking glass which said on the back: *Compliments of Beglois & Sons, Cotton Brokers, Savannah, Ga.* These things were Laurel's personal property, she would not have parted with them under any circumstances. She had also a pill-box containing seven imitation garnet buttons which had come off an old gown of Mrs. Effie's, and were a present to Laurel's mother. Laurel was driven in style to the Tebbs place. Mrs. Dillard refused to allow her to spend the night there: she was sure that the widow must have retrogressed since October, she said that someone would call for Laurel at eight. . . . With Laurel safely bedded in Moses Claffey's old room, the rest

stayed round the fire a while. Cato Dillard quoted liberally from the Directory
For Worship.

Marriage is of a public nature.

In her heart Lucy did not agree: she thought it rather a private affair.

The welfare of civil society, said Mr. Dillard, fraying his whisker tufts between
his fingers as he beamed, *the happiness of families and the credit of religion are
deeply interested in it.*

Well they should be, his wife agreed.

*Therefore, the purpose of marriage ought to be sufficiently published a proper time
previously to the solemnization of it.*

I think that it has been sufficiently published in our case, Cousin Harry murmured sleepily. Three mortal Sundays.

*It is enjoined on all ministers to be careful that, in this matter, they neither trans-
gress the laws of God nor the laws of the community.*

Cate, said Effie Dillard, you *are* an old blether! Away to bed with you. Away to
bed with all of us.

The wedding day dawned gray, murky, raw. There were to be few guests, there
were few whom the Claffeys wanted for wedding guests. Elkins had been given
leave of indulgence from his hospital duties for two days; he would not request
more leave, though Lucy begged. He said stubbornly that he would not be happy
for longer, he would be thinking of his patients, of what he might do for them. Of
the fellow surgeons he invited only Dr. Crumbley, that slight brown-faced man
with whom he had worked long, and who labored with earnestness approaching
his own—not enforced by external strictness, but of the soul. Two loads of Americus Presbyterians came driving up in midforenoon. These were not people rooted
deeply in affections of the Claffeys: they were merely people whom the Claffeys
had known for long, and so a strong association was imagined if not practiced.
Two of the younger women had gone to the Female Institute along with Lucy.
There ensued a certain amount of embracing and tearful cooing . . . these
social appurtenances were vague, meaningless. Lucy could observe them, they did
not strike deep. She looked beyond the people, saw Harry's luminous eyes smiling
within their glass.

That is all ye need to know, she misquoted gently when they were near each
other again, ignoring the tangle of conversation.

Truth is beauty, said Harry. God bless you.

Bless you!

He did that when He brought me to you.

Shortly before the ceremony was to commence, the party received recruits. Ira
it was who looked first through the window and saw them approaching: the
stuffed rounded figure of a woman in ragged fringed shawl and broken-feathered
bonnet, a woman dragging a small child in a cart which squeaked . . . the sullen
black-haired youth teetering on crutches behind. The Tebbses! Ira whispered.
Whom have we to thank for this?

Lucy peeked with him at the window. I make no doubt, Poppy, that we have
our dear Harry to thank. Remember his ministration to the girl? . . . She hurried out on the gallery.

Miss Lucy, crowed Mag, we done heard about your going to get married! We
do thank you, and the surgeon too, count of you all done so much for poor little
Laurel. We hain't got much to offer, but I made a wreath: wedding wreath, kind
of. Twould be good for Christmas greens as well. . . . You Zoral! Let go that
now!

She snatched up a wreath which the boy had been plucking at. It was quite handsomely made, of dark holly with pine cones attached; the cones were tied with fragments of old ribbons.

And Coral—he went and shot you a coon. They're right good roasted now. Zoral, you yield up that coon, baby boy—tain't yourn, belongs to Miss Lucy! Zoral screamed and struck when she took the dead raccoon from him.

You're much too kind and, oh so thoughtful, Lucy cried. I just naturally love roast coon! And such a pretty wreath! I declare, we've had no time to think of Christmas greens. . . . Ira came to make sure that Coral could negotiate the steps on his crutches. The three were escorted inside to become a portion of the Dearly Beloved Assembled.

54

The first memory which Meriwether Kinsman held was of a crooning. The song was played by a bird which adhered to topmost twigs of a vase-shaped elm which grew against a corner of the Kinsman cottage. The cottage was small, old, white-painted. The elm had grown large during years since the house was built, and swelling of its gray seamed trunk actually had pushed the cottage askew. Lichens were thick upon shingles and on the north side of the elm's trunk—it was hard to tell where trunk left off and shingles began. In this tree, almost a part of the house, the brownish-gray bird gave its fluting. A bird not only gray . . . tints of peach and blue . . . this was a mourning-dove which sang, although Meriwether Kinsman did not know its name, would not know it for years. The bird made promise of peace and strength intermingled; it blew upon an instrument, a wet wooden instrument. The boy was very young at the time, indeed it was his first memory. He was in bed, a ragged colored comforter over him. He remembered . . . he had been playing with the squares of material in the old crazy quilt. He bent and folded the cover in small hands, trying to match red with red, lilac with lilac. Then warbling came from on high.

What is it? he thought. Oh, what is it?

He was in his trundle bed, the quilt had been cut down to size. He rolled over the low edge of bed and ran to the open window, he pushed his tufted yellow head out of the open window, and looked up . . . space between the leaves, Merry could see all the way to the elm's top because one branch had been broken in a recent storm. There lived the bird in earliest morning serenity against light sky. There it fifed its rich low tone. So it was his first memory. So Merry Kinsman would go fifing into Eternity.

His mother was a widow, a bakeress, proud of telling how she was forty-two years old when her son Meriwether was born; she had not expected that she would ever have a child. Merry's father died when the boy was a baby, died because he was drunk and caught his clothing ablaze in the middle of the night when he sought to prepare an oven fire. Promptly Mrs. Kinsman took over the full task of baking in which she had merely assisted before. The child's next memories were of yeast and flour and dough—always dough—and great heat. And aware-ness also that in summer the Kinsmans had more money than in winter, because many wives of the village refused to bake themselves along with their bread; although they preferred to make their own bread in cooler weather.

Merry went to school only until he was eleven. Then Mr. Adams, the miller at the edge of town, refused to let Mrs. Kinsman have any more meal or flour until her debt was paid, and Merry went to help at the mill. . . . There were sacks of grain stored in an upper story of the mill, and the sour-faced Mr. Adams instructed Merry to fetch the grain down to a lower floor, to pile sacks near the hopper. After dragging down only one of the lubberly sacks, and falling on the stairs and nearly breaking his back, the boy began to speculate upon some other method. The water gate was closed, the mill was not turning, Mr. Adams had gone to vote. Merry rigged a competent trough out of smooth-sawn planks and extended this trough on a slope from the upper story to the lower. He arranged an open sack at the bottom end, and began pouring grain into the trough above. By this means the entire burden was conveyed soon to its proper destination. Merry ran down to cord up each bag again when it was filled. Miller Adams returned at the moment the child was tightening the last sack in triumph. He did not praise Merry for his ingenuity. He said that the boy had demonstrated how lazy he was, and Mr. Adams would tolerate no lazybones about the place. He slapped Merry, to make him remember; then ordered him to drag all the sacks up the stair to their original position, and bring them down again, as he had been told to do in the first place. He said that this was a lesson which Meriwether Kinsman would not forget. It was in fact a good lesson: it taught Merry to avoid fiends in human form, such as Mr. Adams, whenever he could.

Mr. Adams was a part of America . . . Merry preferred to forget that portion of America. He thought that America should be constituted of men and objects deserving of veneration. Some children worshipped guns which hung in their homes, and guns were a good thing, they were part of the Nation, a sustaining part; but Merry had something which he adored more. Toby Rambler bragged about his father's rifle with its tawny maple stock, and stars and crescents of brass; and in Micah Jones's house there was a Queen's-arm above the fireplace. But neither these boys nor others owned a fife, and Merry Kinsman had a fife. It had belonged to Aaron Briggs, his mother's father.

He found the fife several years before—he was seven at the time, he was hunting peppermints. His mother had bought him peppermints as a Christmas treat. They were delectable wafers, odd as to shape, but bearing the same pink beauty and same pink taste. She said that Merry must not eat them all at once, he must save some for a rainy day. Well, a January thaw had set in, and this was a rainy day, with dark water drilling steadily into big pocked drifts around the cottage. Mrs. Kinsman was busy over pies, and no one restrained Merry as he explored for mints. Several high shelves hung on brackets in a corner of the parlor, and Merry had observed that often things were put up there to be kept out of his reach. He labored to put a smaller chair upon a larger chair, and then a hassock atop this structure. By such means he could clamber aloft, his seven-year-old eyes and fingers might proceed with their examining. He did not find the mints but he found something else. It was a stained tube of pale brown wood with a peculiarly-shaped hole cut near one end, and six smaller holes piercing the tube farther down. Rims of metal were inlaid at either end of the thing. It was a fascinating object, he did not know what it could be. It seemed that one might play upon it . . . he tried to blow in the end but no sound issued.

Merry teetered on his crazy structure for too long. The hassock began to slide. Merry came down abruptly, chairs and all, in noise and pain. He howled, but the strange implement was unhurt in his hand. His mother rushed to see that he was not killed, then she gave him a spanking. Often she spanked him when still she had flour on her big angular hands; often his breeches were white on the seat, a fresh spanking would dust flour into the air like smoke. Merry roared until punishment was concluded, then forgot it promptly in wonder of the thing he had found.

Ma, what is this?

Tis Pa's fife.

What's a fife?

It makes music. My Pa—your Grandpa—played that when he was fighting gainst the British.

I want to play music on it, Ma.

Well, I don't know how. But you can play *with* the fife, if you mind and keep it careful.

She did indicate the one hole which should be blown upon, but Merry could not sound a note. He had a strange sensation that some utter beauty, some almost religious joy was being withheld from him. Was there no one in the neighborhood, or perhaps in all of Pennsylvania or in America or in the World—no one to show him how? It seemed that there was no one.

The next summer an event of patriotic interest was celebrated in a grove beside the Susquehanna. (Ah, he loved the sound of the river's name, he loved all those names: Wyalusing, Towanda, Mehoopany, Meshoppen. Lovely places, he had heard of them, their Indian sound sent a prickle through his being, they had the accent of America; so did Tunkhannock and Wyoming and Minooka. He thought of feathers and paint, and moccasins made from deer's hide; he thought of birch bark, arrows whistling, a gobbling yell going up. He thought of Grandma Rummer's house on the edge of the village across from the mill. It was the oldest house in town: there were logs under modern siding, and the original door still hung upon its great handforged hinges, a door low and narrow—tall men had to stoop—but thick, strengthened with iron. There was a deep triangular gash driven into this thick wood, and children were fond of gathering on the step and poking their fingers into the cut. Everyone knew the story. Indians had come speeding along that road, long ago . . . just before dawn, it was said, of an autumn day. A tall Indian with a hideous face dashed up the path to the Rummer house and tried to push open the door. When the door would not budge he yelled, he struck with his hatchet. Here was the mark to prove it. Did the Indian run away, did someone shoot him as he threatened on the doorstep? No one knew, least of all Grandma Rummer. She was deaf, aging. . . . Oh, yes, children, she'd say, in answer to questions. Twas in Grandpa's time, but he's long dead. Twas when he was young. That's just where that red Indian hit with his tomahawk. And then the townsfolk banded together and drove the villains off, and I've heard tell some was killed on both sides. . . . This was something to think about, in autumn, in mornings when mists of night still made their curving pattern above the shining Susquehanna. Oh, there were other towns of which men spoke: a place called Blackwalnut, a place called Sugar Run; there were Luther's Mills and Eagle's Mere and Greene's Landing. They were not Indian names; but somehow they sounded like Indians, like America.)

His mother might not attend the patriotic celebration; but she said that Merry could go along with the Rambler family, and she provided him with crullers and pies. Merry might trade with other children, and thus come in for his share of chicken and salad and cold spiced beef. His mother gave him a half-dime. He could buy lemonade if it were being sold.

He rioted round the grove with other boys. Life was not a pic-nic for Meriwether Kinsman; indeed he had seen little of pic-nics, so he enjoyed this one utterly. . . . A cannon which some young men had dragged there . . . when it went off, it sounded like the hills along the Susquehanna falling apart. With throbbing ears and starting eyes Merry Kinsman peered through smoke to see whether indeed the hills were blown apart.

But greater delectation lay ahead, it came marching. Distantly above squall and chatter in the grove sounded a high-pitched round-throated wailing. This wailing was sustained by a grumble: old voices of the past talking together in slamming monotone, talking of wars, talking of something native and peculiar to the landscape on which people stood and stared. A rude platform had been erected to hold speakers and other dignitaries; but the program was not yet commenced, and Merry Kinsman and a troop of other boys trampled on yellow planks, cutting capers. He was on the platform when he heard the distant piping and spasm of drums which came along. Then he was in air, floating through air as he leaped from the platform, floating through space as he ran toward the cart path which wound from the main road into this oak and chestnut wood. A homely procession appeared. People said, My, just look at the old soldiers! There were seven of the old soldiers, marching with a few younger men in blue uniforms. The old soldiers were not in uniform, although Uncle Dan Ellis was among them, and he wore a strange-shaped cap which Merry had never seen him wear in his butcher's shop. Judge Ephraim Knowles was one of the old soldiers; truly he was not so old: there was not a glint of gray in his hair, his luxuriant brown beard bristled with challenge. Seven of the old soldiers walking together . . . they had fought the British, their noses had sniffed powder smoke. Uncle Dan Ellis was glad to show any child the place where a portion of his ear had been shot away, and where an old blue-silver streak raked behind his ear, where thin graying hair would not grow.

More wonderful than their presence, more wonderful than their momentary exultation and enduring fame, was the music coming along with them. A tall man with cottony white hair—a stranger—sustained in his hands a fife very much like the one which Merry had found upon that high shelf at home. It spoke with the crying of hawks, high wild lift of an eagle's shriek. There were two small drums muttering in accompaniment, one larger drum booming at intervals in uninter-rupted cannonade; but Merry had eyes and ears only for the fife, for the fierce-eyed man who played it. The tune was ragged, savage. The old man played it over and over, and Merry Kinsman ran before him, looking up and back. He trotted backward most of the time. Once he fell, in a muddy place where the cart path turned; he got up, trotted on, keeping pace ahead of the martial music. The tune began with a slow and ponderous threat in lower registers. You thought of horses, war horses, parading off somewhere, going in cumbrous decision to engage in a battle. The great decisive powerful horses wore trappings of leather and brass; dragoons bestrode them. Solid shot flew but they kept coming. Above the storm, hawks and eagles began to soar. They were over the trees, far over powder smoke, they carried glinting banners in their beaks. They said, Here we are: ferocious, untrammeled . . . the Conestoga wagons rumble in roads beneath . . . mus-kets are being charged and fired, bayonets find the blood of invaders. But here we are, high and fluting! We have power not possessed by more orchestral flutes, we carry a shot-riddled flag held in many beaks. Our tanned wings are wheeling . . . we are America, embattled America. High, proud, far and high!

Certainly other tunes were played that day; Merry could not remember them. He hummed and whistled and burbled the initial chant, the thing which pierced and tooted ahead of the little throng as they came to display themselves, to be proud with the pride which only soldiers feel, which only men may feel who have risked themselves in a war. The tune had been conceived in such pride and spoke of it. All the way home the boy whistled the tune. He ran into the house whistling it. His mother came, floury as always, cloth tied over her hair, apron dusty. She said, Why, Merry, child. You back so soon? Still he kept trying to rebuild the new tune (which was in fact so old a tune) and imagining that sunburnt drumheads were vibrating alongside him, that the boom of artillery arose.

Child, what are you whistling? What is that song? Her face seemed whitening under smudges of wheat flour.

He cried, They played it at the grove. Uncle Dan Ellis was there and all them old soldiers, and young ones that fit the Mexicans, and— They was an old gentleman with white hair, Ma, and he had a fife thing like—like this.

He ran to find the fife of chocolate-colored wood, to show it to her.

But that tune, child—what is it?

I don't know. His tough small lips began building the delicious sounds once more.

His mother sat down on a stool and began to cry. Pa used to play that, she said between sobs. I don't know the name, but it's mighty old. A martial tune like when he was fighting gainst the redcoats. Pa used to play that.

The boy was haunted throughout the night by weird important melodies, haunted especially by the Tune Which Pa Used To Play. Amid fifing and drumbeats he thought that Indians were running loose, he was being chased by a black bear. In a later dream he shot that same bear with an antique weapon. He had graduated from trundle bed to full-sized cot. . . . He left this cot as a fugitive might have stolen, for fear his mother would not wish him out of bed: she might declare that he should be in bed because it was night, because little boys belonged in bed. He went through darkness until his hand closed upon the favored thing, he took it back into bed with him. Eventually he returned to sleep while lying on the fife, and had another dream approaching nightmare in which his chest was impaled by an Iroquois arrow.

In the morning, since there was no school at this season, he could run errands. First off he was sent to the grocer's shop with a basket of cookies, bearing a note addressed to Mr. Yunke the proprietor. The Widow Kinsman hoped to trade these cookies for cherries from which to make pies. Mr. Yunke had no cherries left this late in the season; he kept the cookies to sell, on shares, or to serve as credit against some future purchase. He gave Meriwether another note to this effect.

Merry did not deliver it, not immediately. Instead he ran to Uncle Dan Ellis's butcher shop and found the elderly man in his ice shed. There meat was kept through the summer. In winter time Uncle Dan and his sons and his daughters' husbands cut ice for future needs, and dragged great chunks of it to the village on an ox-sled. It always smelled cool in the shed. Ice was covered with sawdust, and sometimes in summer Uncle Dan could be persuaded to sell chunks. People made cold drinks; root beer was the favorite.

Uncle Dan was trimming a leg of lamb, his knobby scarred hands directing the sharp knife keenly, surely.

Uncle Dan. Who was that old man? That old soldier?

What say, bubby?

He played that thing yesterday. At the rally, before all them gentlemen started to make speeches. He played the fife—

Oh. Name is Parker. Mr. Abijah Parker. Dwells over to Crow Corners.

Crow Corners was a weary way: six miles. Merry Kinsman went there on that same day. He carried his grandfather's fife. He walked through dust all the way to Church Hollow, then a farmer came along with a team and gave him a ride. At Crow Corners he inquired shyly for the tall cotton-haired Mr. Parker, and was directed to a barnlike structure behind an apple orchard where Abijah Parker pursued his trade of wheelwright. Merry Kinsman could hear ringing tools before he reached the place. Mr. Parker was working alone, pounding a rim upon a hub.

. . . The tune, he said, was called Jefferson and Liberty. Oh yes, twas old; it went all the way back to the Revolution. That was not the war in which Abijah Parker served, but his own father had been a soldier under General John Sullivan. Oh yes, young boy, it was a mighty old tune. And some there were who called it Paul Revere's Ride, but Mr. Parker and his fellow musicians had always called it Jefferson and Liberty. And some there were who called it The Gobby O, he didn't quite know why. He said that sometimes musicians referred to their fifes as gobsticks; again, he didn't know why.

He told Merry Kinsman about the Saranac. Planking had been taken up from a bridge, there were just runners of the bridge, and British tried to cross on those runners. They were brave, young boy! They were brave, they kept a-coming. Mr. Parker believed that some officer should have stopped them but maybe their officers were killed by the first volley. And us Americans behind ramparts on the other side—we made up our minds not to let them British get across, so they never even got to the middle of the bridge. They kept running on them three lines of stringers. They were soldiers, they obeyed, they just kept a-coming. And there wasn't nobody left to give an order to halt. Twas sickening work, young boy. Sickening! Folks talk about the bloody Saranac, and that was the reason: all them bodies gushing out their blood, fast as they fell into that water, turning the stream to red. Twas sad, because war is sad business.

Sun came through apple leaves and lay kindly on the hair of the old man, the gold hair of the child.

Mr. Abijah Parker did not offer to resume his labor with the wheel hub. He and Merry Kinsman sat upon the step beside other leaning wheels against the wall of the building . . . wheels like those had carried wagons forward, had borne supplies, had lugged people into wilderness . . . larger thicker wheels supported the cannon. . . .

His own fife was put away, doubtless on a shelf or in a bureau in the neat brown house beyond; but Mr. Parker held Aaron Briggs's fife. His firm tapering knowledgeable fingers pressed tightly over six holes and rose and rippled as tunes rippled and rolled. This one, he said; we played it. Funny . . . you said your Grandpa was a fifer too, and this here cocoa-wood was his; but I reckon we never met, though I've met many a good fifer in my time, and drummers too. This is the old Eighteen-twelve Stop March. We played it frequent.

His beardless lips caressed the hole into which he must blow. There came a great wisdom thus early to the boy beside him. Merry could see clearly things which he had never seen and might never see. He could have an understanding of matters which factually he might never understand or even witness. But it was as if he held familiarity with them now. . . . You thought not only of guns: you thought of implements, you thought of cauldrons in which maple sap boiled, you thought of late winter woodlands where sap froze to an icicle at the tip of every spout hammered into a maple tree.

This one, he said. We played it. Tis called Charley Over the Water, and maybe was made up about the Bonnie Prince himself. I've heard tell my mother came from Scotland. . . . You thought of bagpipes. You had never seen bagpipes, did not know how they were shaped; nor did you know a claymore, but you saw the blade flashing, and heard young men rushing through heather, and you did not know what heather was, nor how purple it bloomed in August.

This one, said Abijah Parker, is the Cuckoo's Nest. . . . That one I played just then? Tis named the Jaybird. And so you thought of birds again: the gentle bird who'd fifed low-toned for you in first awareness, high on the elm. And hawks once more. All were American birds, flying high.

Another Stop March. Now, notice how I watch my stops. The Old Seventy-six, and I reckon folks played it in the Revolution, when they was fighting Hessians not far away from here. . . . Here's another six-eight, he said. They name it Tattered Jack.

He tried to show Meriwether Kinsman how to spread his fingers among the holes; but Merry's hand was so tiny that his fingers would not reach. This way, Mr. Parker said. Now you take your left hand—so. You put it out in front, put the thumb at the back to help hold. The three middle fingers on the first three holes— so. Now your right hand: it goes down here, and with the thumb to hold the fife likewise. Three middle fingers, bottom three holes. All closed tight for the first note. When you want to take a high octave, you hold up this highest finger. Makes the tone clearer so. Otherwise it's kind of graty.

This one, he said. Two-four, of course. We called it Gilderoy. Reckon it's about a kind of fable. . . . And this, he said. Two-four as well. We called it Adam Bell's March, and it goes clear back. Now this, said Abijah Parker, and his fingers were limber—you would not have known that they were elderly fingers, that joints were stiffening as joints of the aged must. They were so fluid, notes which sped were fluid and oily. . . . Called that one the Turkey Gobbler. So you thought of turkeys running wild, their burnished necks metallic in the woods, spurred feet fleeing. You heard the rifle sound: a man in buckskin clothes had shot a turkey, shot him dead. . . . Haste To The Wedding, said old Mr. Parker. You thought of a frontier wedding, people dancing as fiddles whined.

Abijah Parker's bent little wife came out on the cottage stoop and cried, Hoo-hoo. That, he said, was the signal for dinner. Mother doesn't know we've got company to set down with us, he told Merry Kinsman. But she'll have plenty to eat. Always does. I always did like to set a good table, and somehow managed to do so. He took Merry by the hand and led him to wash at a bench beside the well. Soon the three of them sat at table in the narrow kitchen with its crooked floor, and a bright new step-stove gleaming hotly, squarely in front of the wide fireplace. Mrs. Parker said in a hushed mousy voice, Little boy, and she bowed her head, and then she lifted her eyes again and said, Father, warningly. Old Abijah bowed his head, and Merry bowed his; but he kept stealing glances at this great man. He could not refrain from watching. Abijah Parker had his eyes squeezed shut, his brows were tufted, icy, his forehead cragged. For what we are about to receive, the old man muttered, hold us to be thankful, dear Lord, and love and keep us all. Amen. There were tiny new potatoes boiled in pink jackets; creamed peas, a great bowl of lettuce, a jar crammed with thin young onions, green tops spreading to form a bouquet . . . slice after slice of pungent ham, sliced thinly, with a sugary crust to it; a platter of eggs basted until their tops were white, freckled with pepper. There was berry pie, a big yellow pitcher of milk, pickles and jellies such as Merry had never tasted before. He would dream of them often. In fact he would sit at that table again and again, until the day of hushed voices, the day when, grown a mite taller but still skinny, he would be conducted into the front parlor to see a black coffin placed across chairs. . . .

They said that it was a weary way for young feet to travel. Best to wait by the gate until a neighbor came. The first who passed were only farmers headed for a mile or two beyond, and they drove slow oxen. But soon appeared a swirl of hot dust, with the dappled neck of a big gelding reaching up out of dust, bright wheels flashing, sun flashing on spokes. It was Squire Hart, no less, and he was going all the way to Merry Kinsman's village. So Merry was hoisted up beside the fat squire, who talked unceasingly of things of which the boy had no comprehension. He remembered later that *litigation* was a favorite word of Squire Hart's. All he could do was to sit in blissful daze, listening to those remembered bright notes rolling through the orchard . . . imagined columns of rough soldiers tramping. The Jaybird . . . Adam Bell's March, Tattered Jack; above all, Jefferson and Liberty. He heard them, he heard them when he was set down at the Widow Kinsman's gate; he heard tunes crying above and beyond his own lament as the willow switch struck sharply against his little legs and bottom; heard glorious music after he was put to bed without any supper. But he had his fife. He held Grandpa's fife gripped in damp hands . . . useless fife. His infant fingers could not spread to cover the holes.

. . . Joe Jew came by. As always that was an event of first importance. Merry's mother was removing cakes with her long-handled paddle, she was out at her oven which abutted on the roofed back porch. The boy ran to carry good news.

Ma! Ma, it's Joe Jew! He's stopping at the gate.

Everyone in the region knew this peddler; he had traveled those roads for years. His ill-tempered brown pony, his jolting wagon with oilcloth top and sides: this vehicle was a peripatetic treasure house. No wonder children clustered hopefully at the tailboard in every village. Sometimes Joe Jew was in a generous mood, he passed out sugarplums; sometimes he was grumpy, he pretended not to see the children. His name was Joseph Iscowitz, and people knew him all the way up to Binghamton and over to Elmira in York State. Twice a year the Widow Kinsman stocked up on spices, flavorings and fruit color; necessarily she bought things like these from Joe Jew because of the paucity of such stock for sale locally. . . . Wonderful cases, all secured by straps, hanging in the wagon; and any one of them could be carried by its strap over the little man's shoulder as he made his hunched way to the front door.

First off he fetched his case of spices and candies. Mrs. Kinsman selected for her needs, and brought the ginger jar in which she kept her change.

But I want you should see my threads. Such a beautiful new stock I got, Mrs. Kinsman! . . . He could call her by name: that was a trick of his trade; Joe Jew had the names of thousands of customers salted within his curly head. He could say, Well, well, and look at little Hannah. My, how she is growing!

Smart time I have for fancy sewing, said the widow. I can scarcely catch an hour to do the mending for Merry and me.

Joe Jew insisted, he gave Merry a somewhat crushed caramel to show that his heart was in the right place. He fetched the case containing needles, scissors, yarn and such trifles. As always, the child was fascinated by rich colors, delightful purples and crimsons and tans of tinted thread. Still a packet of pins was all that the widow felt that she should afford. She looked wistfully at other items, but shook her head with discipline.

As Joe Jew was closing the case and sighing—as he always did, no matter how much people bought—there was a light thud. Some shiny black object rolled on the old carpet.

Wrong case, said Joe Jew. Now how did that get in here? He picked up the thing.

Instantly Merry Kinsman's eyes were alight. Oh, please— Oh, Mr. Joe Jew. It's a kind of fife!

No fife, said the peddler. No, little boy, they call this a penny whistle. But the price is a dime.

A tin whistle . . . actually it was not composed of tin: it was made of some heavier metal, perhaps lead. Probably made in the same mould with hundreds of others. . . . Ma! cried Meriwether Kinsman, dancing as he waved the thing in his hand.

You've got along thus far without a whistle, Merry. Guess you can get along still.

But, Ma, *look*. It's just like a fife, cept—see—you blow in the end. It's got six holes, like a fife. Look, Ma, they're real close together! I can reach them with my fingers. I can't reach the holes on Grandpa's fife until I get growed.

The little boy, he loves the whistle, said Joe Jew, wheedling. It would be nice were you to buy it for him?

Can't afford it.

Oh, Ma!

Can't afford it, said the widow sternly. She ushered Joe Jew out of the house and went back to her oven. Merry collapsed on the step in tears.

Joe Jew clambered up into his driver's seat with some difficulty, since he had been more or less crippled for years (some said that the pony ran away with him) and he clucked to brown Sadie. Wheels started to turn; then Joe Jew pulled on his reins and said Whoa. Little boy, you come here.

Merry ran to the edge of the road, wondering.

Tell your Mamma I would settle for apple turnovers.

Merry rushed shrieking through the cottage, then his heart sank into his bare feet as his mother informed him that her stock of apple turnovers was spoken for; he must carry the basket over to Mrs. Doctor Neely's within the hour. But, she said, relenting, I would be willing to give him a sack of cinnamon buns. Last baking didn't sell too well. She made a sack out of newspaper, because manufactured paper sacks were expensive, and Merry carried this poke filled with a dozen buns to the peddler.

Well, said Joe Jew, shrugging. A good apple turnover would be so much better; but I am next door to a beggar, so I cannot be a chooser, and no dinner did I have this noon. Nothing but work, work, work, peddle, peddle, peddle! He complained for a moment more; but he accepted the parcel of buns, and passed the wonderful whistle down to the boy. Merry did not even see him drive away, he did not realize that Joe Jew was gone. He stood graven, caressing the magic tube. He tried to remember what Mr. Abijah Parker had told him; he tried to remember how Mr. Parker's fingers looked on the fife, how he held it. This was different; but it was the same, because there were six holes. And anyone who could learn to play on such a whistle could, Merry was sure, learn to play upon a fife. He sat again on the step, no longer in collapse. He remembered . . . six holes . . . all closed for the first note. Then lift this third finger of the right hand for the next note. Now—up with the second finger as well . . . now up with the first finger. Loose shrill notes crawled softly if uncertainly. Soon Merry was playing the scale. It would not be long . . . oh, mercy and delight . . . it didn't sound like a fife: the music was thinner, more bird-like. But the same tunes could be played, and in the same way.

The next time he could win permission and beg a ride over to Crow Corners to sit at the feet of his idol, Merry was discomfited to find that Abijah Parker rather sniffed at the whistle. Oh, that's not much, the veteran said. Sounds like a sparrow. I mind seeing a gypsy or something, playing such a little toot as this, time I was in Philadelphia. Walked right along the street, squeaking away on it. Had a tin cup hanging on his belt. I guess he expected folks to give him pennies; but I didn't give him none; I couldn't abide the infernal noise he was a-making.

Said Merry Kinsman shyly, I can learn the proper tunes. Then, when my hands get big enough to reach acrost the holes on Grandpa's fife—Well, then I'd know the tunes, wouldn't I, Uncle Bijah?

(Now they had grown to this intimacy.)

Well, maybe that makes sense. I guess you could. You know, I hadn't come across no one else, except for drummers of course, who really cared about my fifing. Not for years and years, not till you come along. Now, set real quiet and I'll play a six-eight for you—an easy one. Oh, Lassie, Art Thou Sleeping Yet—I'll teach you how.

Through the next hawking, eagling, rolling years he taught him. Oh, yes: The Raw Recruit. Oh, yes: The Huntsman Hornpipe. Oh, yes: Granny Will Your Dog Bite? It was as if rough shrilling voices of a hundred deerskin melodists had lain compressed within the tube which Merry Kinsman learned to play; only his weaving fingers might let them loose. When at eleven he was forced to servitude under Miller Adams, it was tragedy worse than the punishment he received in his grain sack episode, far worse than slaps or slavery . . . it was molten agony poured within his being . . . Mr. Adams would *not* tolerate his whistle at the mill. Mr. Adams told him to take that wretched thing home and never bring it back, or he'd fling it clean over the mill race into the Susquehanna. He said that only idle boys would sit around, blowing on a thing like that. (In fact, for Mr. Adams's money, no one except idle folk make any music at all. He held fiddlers in especial scorn, and would not let his daughters go into any home where fiddling and jigging were permitted. Therefore, as so often occurs, both daughters managed to get into trouble, and had to be married; and neither was happy in her enforced matrimony.)

Merry was small for his age: a towhead whose hair deepened only slightly in color as he grew older. His eyes were large, solemn, gray as the river on a cloudy day; but his hands and feet were large out of proportion. He could play Grandpa's fife instead of the tin whistle, by the time he was twelve.

Visits to Abijah Parker were few and far between. Winter time was the only chance usually; and it was a grave chore to get across those six miles through drifts. But Merry did go plodding. Once a storm struck when he was halfway home. Drifts were higher than his head, white hard salt of snow ripped and stung his eyes, worse than the dust of the mill might sting them. Merry Kinsman lost his way, he came near to perishing, he lost a mitten. The right side of his face froze, fingers were frozen on his right hand. It was with difficulty that he was thawed when at last he stumbled upon a house occupied by an old German couple. Still the thawing was not accomplished properly; Merry's fingers swelled and grew discolored, one of them split open. It was thought later that the finger might have to be cut off, and what would that have done to his fifing? But the finger was saved, eventually Merry could use it. Few boys could have been as thankful for anything in the world, as was Meriwether Kinsman for this fortune.

When the war broke out (or, as Uncle Dan Ellis always put it, when the army broke out) Merry longed to go and serve as a fifer. He knew for a certainty that already, even at his tender age, he was a better fifer than might be found among musicians of an entire army corps. Uncle Bijah had said as much. But the Widow Kinsman was not well, she had dizzy spells, sometimes she had to sit down and rest her head upon the bread board. When Joe Jew came by that year, Mrs. Kinsman invested heavily in several remedies which the peddler offered and recommended with enthusiasm; but none of them seemed to help her a great deal.

Merry dreamed almost nightly of cannon fire, the long roll of drums. He dreamed of himself shrilling out garrison calls, winning applause and praise for his skill, as well as for his bravery in thundering battles. He dreamed . . . still he dared not run away and leave his mother. One benefit came, because he was old enough now, at thirteen, to take over a great many baker's tasks: he was allowed to give up his work under the hated Adams.

Mr. Adams flew into rage. He said that Mrs. Kinsman still owed him money; he said that Merry hadn't worked off all the debt as yet; he threatened to sue in a court of law, but nothing came of his bluster. Mr. Adams threatened also that he might refuse to sell any flour at all to Mrs. Kinsman. Merry thought that Adams would reconsider if he, Merry, came with cash in hand.

Good morning, Mr. Adams. I come for some white flour.

Oh. How much you want, Merry?

Two two-dollar sacks.

You won't be able to carry them.

I brung the little wagon that I use when I'm peddling bread and stuff about town. I can haul it all right.

Well, let's see the color of your money.

Carefully Merry counted hard-won dimes and half-dimes, quarter-dollars, broad pennies. He counted coins into Mr. Adams's palm. He knew that the sum was correct, he had counted it at home.

Hain't but three dollars ninety-eight that I can see.

Yes, sir, four dollars!

But the miller had to go through the pile three times before he admitted that the amount was correct. He took out his purse, dumped in the change, dropped the purse back into a deep pocket in the skirts of his white dusty coat. Now, he said, that'll go on the debt your Ma still owes me.

Merry gaped. Oh, the man was so tall, so cruel, he was a giant. He could handle a sack of wheat as if it were a rag doll. He stood there in his grim adult state. He was rich: he owned a farm, he owned two houses in town. And Merry was poor, he was only thirteen, going on fourteen; and skinny.

You mean— He gulped again. You won't give me my flour? Ma's got to have it.

You tell your Ma I'll sell her all the flour she wants, soon as she settles up with me. I figure she still owes me better than seven dollars. Money doesn't grow on trees.

Indeed it did not, and no one knew that fact better than Merry Kinsman. His shocked voice rattled in remonstrance: Mr. Adams! You said you'd credit us a dollar a week, for the time I put in here. We figured it honest, and—leaving out the seasons when you was closed up, and that time you said you didn't need me, you couldn't use me for about five months—and leaving out the time I was sick with my hand— Well, Ma says the debt *is* paid. And more.

Seven dollars and thirty-five cents to go, said Mr. Adams.

Merry wondered what Uncle Bijah Parker would have done at the same age. Abijah had been only a few years older than Merry when he fought the redcoats. With clarity Merry Kinsman saw immediately just what Abijah Parker would have done. Merry walked steadily to the corner where stood Mr. Adams's desk, closed up to keep out as much mill dust as possible; and he knew what stood in that corner behind the desk. Mr. Adams had a persistent fear of two enemies: a rat and a thief. The one would ruin his grain, the other might put a knife to his throat and make off with his money. Mr. Adams considered a loaded shotgun good insurance against either threat. Merry jerked the old tablecloth which hung over the weapon to protect it; flour flew in a cloud. When the cloud settled sufficiently, Mr. Adams was looking into the twin barrels of his own gun. Merry had cocked both hammers.

My little wagon's just outside the door, said Merry.

You young devil. Put down that gun!

You're just a highway robber, said Merry. I come to buy flour, you took my money and then said you wouldn't give me no flour. That's just plain robbery, and robbers ought to get shot. So you take two sacks of flour and put them on my little wagon your own self, or I'll let go with both barrels.

You—you— You're a murderer! You—

Tain't murder to protect yourself against robbers. That's what you always say. That's why you keep this here shotgun loaded, and warned me not to touch it. Mr. Adams, you load that flour, or I'll shoot you here and now.

There was no more dust floating. The miller could see clearly the boy's cold gray gaze, see his finger close to the triggers. Sweating and gasping, Mr. Adams stumbled about the business of loading sacks on the homemade cart with its strong but sagging wheels.

Now, said Merry Kinsman, I've took the caps off both tumblers. That's just so you won't shoot me, Mr. Adams, and maybe claim I stole your flour.

The bearded miller looked down at the boy in utter terror. Never in his life had anyone ever pointed a gun at this man, and told him that he would be shot if he didn't do thus and so; and sincerely he knew that the youth had been ready and willing to kill him.

What do you think the constable'll say, when I tell him that you threatened me with my own gun?

He won't say a thing, sir, cause you ain't going to tell him. Of course Merry was correct again: he knew that Mr. Adams would not tell anything, could not tell anything. He knew that Mr. Adams would never try that trick again, for fear that Merry might kill him in some fashion afterward, whether Mr. Adams's shotgun was put away safely or whether it wasn't. Merry went home with the flour. He held his head up, held his gaze up, he thought the drums were rolling around and behind him. He could hear the scream of Abijah Parker's fife, climbing to the last exultant cheer of Jefferson and Liberty.

One day in the summer of 1862, when Merry was fourteen, Mrs. Kinsman fell flat amid a shower of bread loaves. Merry had been up early to prepare the fire, and was out wielding a hay fork in Mr. McMurchie's field. Thus he did not discover his mother; it remained for customers to do that when they came to the house. A little girl was sent running to the McMurchie place. . . .

The afternoon following his mother's funeral, Merry Kinsman wandered near the warped wharves stretching out across mud flats as the river shrank to its late summer level. He would have liked to have gone fishing; he had even gone to the woodshed and examined a willow pole which he had not had time to ply in two years at least (because there was so little time for him to enjoy the sports of other boys). The fishing line wound about the dry willow was frayed in several places, as if mice had chewed it. So no fishing.

Merry's grief for his mother's departure was not so much grief as a shattering and displacement; and, as people have often mused, the sadness of death was not a sadness at reviewing a death, but a sadness at reviewing the misfortunes of a life. Merry's emotions had stormed as he sat staring silently into space, not hearing prayers and the polite sniffling of neighbor women. His mother had had so little! She was stern . . . truly it was not her fault . . . poverty at times very nearly squeezed her into the shape of a termagant. She had looked longingly at pretty things offered in the cases of Joe Jew, she had not been able to buy them. Merry had seen her eyes brighten, as indeed his own eyes brightened, at seeing beautiful tight little rolls: purple thread, scarlet thread, thread of pea-green. And there were lengths of flowered new calico, itching to be sewn, itching to be made into frilled gay aprons. So must his mother have wished to wear happy aprons of bright-patterned calico, instead of workaday aprons made roughly from flour sacking. . . . There were those gleaming embroidery scissors, snapped tempt-ingly by Joe Jew, and sun starred up from the steel surfaces as he snipped the scissors back and forth. They cost sixty cents, she could not buy them.

But some peace came to Merry later, when they put the Widow Kinsman into the ground, because now she would be in recollection and literally a part of American soil which bold men had enriched. Some of the bold men were her forebears. Merry thought that it would have been appropriate if fifes and drums fluted and banged above her mound, because she was the daughter and the granddaughter and the wife of soldiers. Would ever she be the mother of a soldier? . . . He heard her tight thin voice say, Merry, what tune is that? Pa used to play that. He contrived a scene wherein she was being welcomed by a conclave of Briggses and Kinsmans and their kind . . . bony men in three-cornered 'hats, frontier women in bonnets. Also there seemed to be a few Indians coming out of the woods, with baskets of fish or popcorn, as they had come to the Pilgrim Fathers. Distantly, persistently fifes blended. They were playing Oh, Lassie, Art Thou Sleeping Yet? . . . drums grumbled with spirit. Why, of course that was Uncle Bijah playing—Mr. Abijah Parker. He had been gone nearly a year . . . Mrs. Kinsman would sit on a cabin step beside him, and say, My own Pa—Aaron Briggs—used to play that. Did you know him when you was at the Saranac?

Meriwether Kinsman poked beside the Susquehanna. He had no desire to go back to the house: it was gloomy, with the minister and Squire Hart and several other people sitting around and talking about Merry. Mr. Rothrup held the mort-gage on the house . . . there was the question of who should serve as guardian for Merry, and to whom, perhaps, he should be bound. Someone suggested, Better bind him out to Enoch Adams, since he already knows the mill work. When informed of this, Mr. Adams declared, with a cry which sounded almost like an oath, that he would never take Merry. Then they talked of Farmer McMurchie. He was nothing like so mean as Mr. Adams, but still short-tempered and plagued by rheumatism. His wife had a reputation as a disgusting cook, an incompetent housekeeper.

. . . Sun approaching the nearest hill to the west, the Susquehanna glinted. A flat small barge stopped and anchored at some distance, and its crew of two young men were pulling toward the shore in their skiff.

Hey there, they said to Merry Kinsman. Where can a feller buy tobacco around here?

At the grocer's.

Where's that?

He told them, he pointed up past the first brick house and shading elms. He asked the young men where they were bound.

Harrisburg, they said. That was more than one hundred and fifty miles down the river. It was the State capital . . . oh, how he longed to go there.

We're taking a load of stuff to sell, in the barge, they said, and told him that they were cousins. First we'll sell the load, then the barge and this here skiff. Then we'll join.

Join what?

Why, the army, of course. A great log gate swung open, smoke of battle drifted in . . . or maybe it was the door of Grandma Rummer's house swinging, tomahawk dent and all. . . .

How much would you gentleman charge, to take a passenger along to Harrisburg with you?

How much you got?

There was more talk; it did not take long. Merry went scooting to the grocer's, carrying currency which the young men had given him to buy a pound of tobacco fine cut for the pipe. With this package he hurried home. Mr. Rothrup's horse was still tied outside, still the people were settling Merry's fate. He entered through the back door, hunted out a basket, filled it with what food supplies he could assemble quickly. He observed how cold and dark the oven looked; he wondered who, if anyone, would be baking there again. Merry put the covered basket on the bench behind the woodshed. He emptied jingling contents of the ginger jar into his own pocket, and uncrumpled a few wads of paper currency. His mother had been saving against the mortgage interest. He was lucky to be facing the world with a few dollars, rather than with empty purse.

Merry presented himself in the hot parlor, where all tried to treat him kindly.

The minister put his arm around the boy's shoulder. Merry, lad. We have now decided that you shall go to the McMurchies. That would be better than the Poor House, wouldn't it? Ah yes—far, far better. And twould be so sad and lonely for you to stay here in the night again, so Mr. Rothrup will drive you out to the farm directly, if you'll but get your things together.

Merry bowed his head as if in assent. He could not trust himself to speak. Suddenly he felt impatient with himself for scheming to trick these well-intentioned people, yet trick them he must.

He went upstairs and made a bundle. There wasn't much which he needed to take, there was not much which he could take. He gathered a few keepsakes from the dresser . . . silhouettes of his mother and father when they were young. He took Grandpa Briggs's watch, which the widow would not consider selling in direst season. He slid his fife down into those inner loops of his jacket which Merry's mother had sewn according to specifications. Softly he tore the mosquito-bar from a window above the kitchen roof and went across the roof and down the apple tree—a route he had traveled often since he was six or thereabouts. With basket and bundle he thought of himself as the traditional fugitive of caricature. He thought that he should have had a stick over his shoulder, and the bundle swinging from the end. He climbed across a stone fence and circled through the weedy orchard behind the Striver house. He met only Rudy Banton, who carried a string of suckers; and Rudy Banton was peculiar in the head—he cared only about hunting or fishing, and could not talk plain: it made little difference, meeting him. Once on the river road, Merry hurried to Darwin's Bend, which he had indicated when he spoke with those strangers at the landing. Sure enough there was the barge, anchored off shore—one young man sitting in it, the other concealed in his skiff among drooping willows. A few minutes later Merry was aboard the larger craft; they drifted down the Susquehanna, shadows of hills covered them.

The cousins were named Norton, and they came from Towanda, where their fathers were in partnership, owning a forge. . . . Our line is iron. Born to it. They showed Merry some of the materials included in their cargo: grilles and hinges and such. These they would sell in Harrisburg—part would satisfy certain orders, the rest would have to go on the open market. Merry nodded as if he knew as much about hand-wrought iron as he did about the home baking business.

We're Paul and Silas, the cousins told him. Everybody knows the Nortons, up Towanda way. Born in the same week.

No, said Silas. Nine days apart. Remember that, Paul: I'm still your elder.

And went to the same church and same school, and our fathers are brothers, and what's more than that, our mothers are first cousins. How do you like that, hey? Thicker than thieves, aren't we, Si?

Thicker than fleas, Paul. Yes sir, Mr. Meriwether Kinsman: they don't come any thicker than we two. Just like two fingers on your hand. . . . Why, what are you a-fingering of? What you got there? . . . Well, I swan, it's a fife. Can you play it? . . .

There were obstructions, rapids to be encountered and traveled past. Some of it was heavy work—loading and unloading the barge, beating paths through weeds, lugging ironware. The light tiny skiff was an eggshell: Paul Norton could hike it up on one wide shoulder and carry the thing. But they had a set of rollers on which the barge must be hauled when it was necessary to land it; and Merry's job was to lift out the rear roller as soon as it was exposed by the boat's progression, then carry the thing to the front and insert it there, and repeat successively. There were nights when his body, unaccustomed to such concentrated exertion, ached steadily like a sore tooth. He thought his arms and legs would fall off. But the Cousins Norton praised him for his willingness and, later, aptitude. Merry loved this. Scarcely had he ever been praised by anyone—except Uncle Bijah, when at last Merry mastered the rapid intricacies of a freakish tune called Hell On The Wabash. . . . There were long days, comfortable and lazy, when they dropped smoothly in wide easy current, with only a pole to be thrust down now and then. It was fun to trail a fishline over the side. Soon they had more fish than they could eat, but the Nortons said, Keep fishing, Merry; we can trade for garden truck. The cousins smoked great pipes with curved stems, smoked them perpetually. They said they had cut their pipes from the same block of cherry root, had sent away to the city for proper amber stems, and naturally the two pipes were just alike. Paul and Silas squabbled good-humoredly sometimes; one claimed that the other had taken his pipe—he could tell by the taste of the spit therein.

What's this place? they'd call to a man on shore.

Shickshinny.

And what do you call that, over there?

Mocanaqua.

. . . Drifting down, down the gentle river. Oh, mister, what lies over beyond there?

That, friends, is the great and aggressive city of Wapwallopen.

. . . Farther, farther against the sun: Hey, stranger, what's this place?

Berwick to be sure.

And yonder?

Oh, acrost and up the road you'd come to Nescopeck.

It seemed sometimes as if Indians were all around them in canoes. That week there rode a moon, comforting, serene. Merry watched the great silver whiteness as it freed its surface from eastern hills and pushed higher, higher in clarity . . . half asleep on a blanket he contemplated the moon. Maybe Paradise was up there. Now his mother was there . . . Uncle Bijah played his fife on the moon . . . that was where the gathering of linsey-woolsey Americans was taking place . . . tufts of willow shadowed on a sandbar ahead. Ah, red Indians, Merry thought, advancing in their birch-bark boats. A night bird cried in the sky.

They cooked on the barge; they had a box which they would fill with sand, they could build their small fire. It was fun to cook on a boat. Tender fish would curl and sizzle, salt fat perfume of frying would drift. There were other adventures: Silas Norton encountered a cross bull when he was cutting through a pasture to trade for eggs at a farmhouse. And all three of the voyagers—the broad-shouldered brown-haired cousins, and the skinny blond Merry—were chased out of an orchard by a watchful farmer, when they thought to appropriate a few apples of the Early Harvest variety.

Hey, boy, what's this river flowing in, here on the right?

The Juniata, mister.

Then they could sing and put their hearts in it . . . *Wild roved an Indian girl, bright Alfarata . . . where sweep the waters of the blue Juniata. . . .* Spires of Harrisburg rose before them, there must be a parting. It would take the Nortons some days to dispose of their wares, before they would be ready to enlist. Merry Kinsman could not afford to sit idly; he felt that he dared not spend money at a tavern, because he had so little money with him, so little in the world. Actually he did not care about money, because it seemed now that the mapled world of America belonged to him completely, and the Susquehanna as well, and the fabled fabric of the Juniata. Generously the Nortons offered him a share in proceeds, if he would help them with their delivering and haggling. But Merry said No. He knew that they did this purely out of kindness, and he would be cutting into their profits; he would not really be able to assist, he would have to be shown and told what to do. His strong slender hand disappeared repeatedly in the huge grip of the Nortons. He was presented with a gift to remember them by (as if he needed reminder!): a pipe which the cousins bought for Merry on arriving at Harrisburg. He had admired their manner of smoking pipes, had enjoyed the scent of tobacco, said bashfully that he might wish to try, himself. He felt grown and manly with this untried pipe and a paper of tobacco in his shirt pocket.

After leaving the Nortons he inquired of a few bearded soldiers, asking where he might find the recruiters.

What for? Does your Pa want to join? and there was laughter.

They told him: they said that the best thing for Merry to do was to go out to Camp Curtin. That was a long hot walk but eventually Merry found himself standing under a tent fly. A sergeant with a red face and sunburn peeling all over it— The sergeant said, What might your name be?

Meriwether Kinsman.

Good enough name, but I reckon the ranks of the Boys' Brigade are full up. Again that laughter from the idle and clustering. How old might you be, Meriwether?

Fourteen.

That would be a trick! Is your family hot after you—or maybe the uncle you ran away from?

Sergeant Glisson, ordered a vigorous young captain who had just come stooping under the fly, don't you go to signing up any children! Just mean trouble for us later on. He frowned at Merry accusingly.

Sir, said Merry. Here's the point: there ain't no one chasing me. There ain't nobody *to* chase me, there ain't no one knows where I've gone; I've got no one. He told how he had left the village the very afternoon of his mother's funeral, and who was there now to transport him back up the Susquehanna? Who would want to, anyway, and why? It was so obvious that he was telling the truth that the young captain relented, he put his hand on Merry's sleeve. Glisson, he said, could be that they have need of another drummer in the tiger band. Can you rattle a drumstick, bub?

No, sir, I can do better than that.

Out came the fife. Merry Kinsman played Jefferson and Liberty as he had never played it before; he played it as Abijah Parker might have played it when homespun columns were approaching the Saranac River. Before he finished, the captain was smiling and twisting his thick black mustache with approval. His black eyes danced; and two boys behind the sergeant were beating out a drum accompaniment on cracker boxes.

Oh, go and get our Principal Musician! cried Sergeant Glisson in delight. Go long, one of you, and fetch him. What's his name, what's that new chief musician —Cassidy? Tell him we've got a fine addition to his Sheepskin Battery!

That day Merry Kinsman was sworn in. His age was put down on the rolls as eighteen; that was the practice. Later he encountered a good many boys two or three years older than he; but Merry was said to be the youngest in the regiment, and he was the smallest of all the fifers. In no time at all, after he had learned the strains for regimental and camp duties, he was accounted also the best. Shortly before they prepared to depart for Cockeysville, Maryland, a new company came moving up to take its place alongside Merry Kinsman's company, and there rose a combined roar of recognition. There stood Paul and Silas Norton, side by side in a rank. It was a stout friendship, a valuable one, but all too short. The cousins went out of life together as they had entered life and faced it. Both were killed at Chancellorsville, next May.

. . . Reveille, Second Camp, Third Camp . . . many bars away the fifes silent, drums rolling. Slow Scotch . . . again the roll. The Austrian, and roll, roll. Quick Dutch, The Hessian, Quick Scotch, roll, roll, roll. Drumsticks were like dry bones of the past become hot fresh bones of the present. Sometimes Merry Kinsman thought his fife was the child of the drums, sometimes he thought his fifes fathered the drums. . . . Peas Upon A Trencher. How merry the tooting of the brisk two-four . . . how surprised he was to learn that there was one call for breakfast, an entirely different call for supper. How naked and piercing the notes poured from under his fingers: the Surgeon's Call (Quinine Call, the boys named it) and a dozen different Guard Mounts, and Assembly and Retreat and Tattoo! He wished that Uncle Bijah was there to hear him spraying out the Single Drag. Maybe Uncle Bijah was there.

In ranks of the drum corps (one drummer and one fifer from each of the ten companies, with a regimental bass drummer thrown in) he met musicians of a dozen different communities. Two or three older men had traveled far and learned a lot. All Take Tea, The Squirrel Hunters, Biddy Oats, On the Road To Boston . . . many more he heard for the first time. He learned them. Here's a new one, the Principal Musician said, and here's the way she goes: *When we go down to Washington, when we go down to Washington, I was shot five times in the ankle bone, and once at Manassas Junction.* . . .

This is a hard one, son, said a tall fifer with a whiskey breath. (Yet somehow he reminded Merry of Uncle Bijah.) A clog, and tis hard to do. We call it the Corn Cob. . . . And this here one. His hand went down through firelight and lifted a tin cup: stolen whiskey mixed with water therein. Old Tupley was becoming drunk again, but still he could fife, he said that he could fife better when drunk than when sober, but Merry decided early that this was not true. Now we're heading into another six-eight, Tupley said. One maybe you never heard before. Tis called, Go To the Devil and Shake Yourself.

Meriwether Kinsman drank deeply of Tupley's lore. He did not drink whiskey, he only smoked his pipe and listened, but the tunes squirted into his memory and nothing could dislodge them. It was heartbreaking to participate in the final tragedy surrounding Tupley, but duty decreed that Merry must. During the same battle in which the cousins Norton lost their lives, Tupley disappeared. He was supposed to carry stretchers, he carried none; he was required to assist at a field hospital, he was not there. Later a sergeant discovered the old fellow drunk and quaking. He had hidden himself in a thicket behind an oak tree, had pulled leaves over his head in an effort to conceal himself. He was dragged out, arrested, confined. After the Northern army crossed a flooded Rappahannock in retreat— after the broken regiment was bedded down in a camp, Tupley was drummed out by the very musicians who once had respected his skill. It was a sad day, but they played, they obeyed orders. Shattered companies lined up, musicians massed . . . poor Tupley, coat hanging open, face like a mussel shell, beard dripping with drool as he passed in disgrace with big signs hung upon him, signs saying *Coward* front and back. The Rogues' March shrilled. War was not all a pic-nic, though Merry found it a better pic-nic than most until he was captured.

The Sheepskin Battery became a hospital brigade in every battle. Drums were left behind, fifes put aside. Musicians went out hunting amid thickets and haycocks, hunting for the fallen, and some of them were killed doing this. Merry himself was nicked in the side on the second day of Gettysburg; blood came freely although the wound did not hurt much. He was frightened. Still he recognized that at last he was one of the elect: he had Shed Blood for His Country. . . . He climbed a wall. The countryside was thick with smoke, thicker with noise; but Merry ducked his head, and was bound and determined to go over that wall because someone yelled that young Brinkoff of Company C had tumbled wounded behind it. Merry Kinsman did not find Brinkoff; he found instead a party of crouching men in gray who glared at him, poked guns at him. One of them marshalled him away through mats of smoke to where other lugubrious captives were herded behind a barn. You hurt bad, Baby Yank? asked a Rebel. He ripped Merry's shirt when Merry lifted his torn jacket, he examined the wound. Hell, ain't nothing wrong with you that a good piece of sticking plaster wouldn't cure! Just set here and don't move till the firing stops, else you'll get shot by your own men! That night Merry was taken to the rear of the Rebel lines with others. So he became a captive and remained a captive through the long winter at Belle Isle, and then was taken to Andersonville.

He celebrated his sixteenth birthday by watching the raider chiefs fall and dangle. Because of extreme youth and litheness, he remained in fair shape until August, then went downhill rapidly. Of the several members of his regiment who survived in the stockade at this time, there was only one with whom he had been fairly well acquainted previously: a youth somewhat older than himself, named Stricker. Stricker was captured in the same battle which made Merry Kinsman a prisoner. Stricker had but one hand, he could render little aid to Merry after scurvy began to bend and shrink him. Merry tried to flank out with detachments removed in September, but failed. He was knocked down by Henry Wirz, who became hysterical at seeing invalids trying to pretend that they were sound. Merry Kinsman was turned back Inside and languished alone, since Stricker had become a Parole at the hospital (and later would become a patient).

Merry had recollection of being carried somewhere in a blanket. At this time he was thinking, as he usually thought, of his lost fife. It had remained in his possession through Belle Isle; there he played it to the diversion of fellow prisoners. Also to the pleasure of the Belle Isle superintendent, Lieutenant Boisseau, who often asked Merry to strike up a tune, and once had him to dinner. Lieutenant Boisseau frequently fed Belle Isle prisoners who caught his fancy; but such a thing was unheard of at Andersonville, except among favored Paroles detailed directly under Wirz.

Merry's fife was taken from him by a guard while they journeyed south from the Richmond-Manchester area, so he arrived at Camp Sumter fifeless. Here he met up with a young fellow of his own age who had managed to retain his fife. Occasionally the boy lent it to Merry, but only occasionally, since it turned out that Wabash Davey was jealous because Meriwether Kinsman could play more skillfully than he. Finally the condition of Wabash Davey's mouth was such that he could no longer build a tune. Merry now sought to bargain for the abandoned instrument, but had practically nothing to offer, and Wabash sat upon his fife—a dog in a manger. After he died his mates in the shebang held the fife for a high price. One morning the thing was reported as stolen; at least it disappeared. If some raider had taken it and found that he could make no music, he might have thrown the fife into the marsh. . . . Merry encountered also several musicians, most of them drummers, minus their instruments; during their season of comparative strength they sat in fury whenever they heard bleating across the stockade's rim. There was a single fifer who played camp duties for the Georgia Reserves. He could play but one tune: The Bonnie Blue Flag, and that badly. It was The Bonnie Blue Flag for Guard Mount, Reveille, Mess Call, everything. Federal musicians cursed until severally they lost interest. One by one they died. Only two of the little group straggled out in the autumn, when able prisoners were removed. A freemasonry had held them together because it was the habit of many soldiers to regard musicians patronizingly or even with scorn. The term Sheepskin Battery was somehow derisive when applied by others. But in their own cult fifers and drummers were proud of the name.

. . . Stronger people carried him in a blanket, bent double with scurvy as he was, gums puffed into a wad. On this day, so early in the morning, there loomed a vacancy; Merry Kinsman was conveyed to the hospital. Some attempt had been made to separate types of cases, but exigency decreed that often the gangrenous would lie among scorbutics or those suffering from diarrhoea. Merry emerged from a spell of sodden unconsciousness to listen to wailing on one side of him, to feel the loose splashings of his left-hand neighbor shooting warm against his leg. A face swam above him often during the icy weather . . . he shivered and shook with cold. The face said, Lad, I've brought you a scrap of blanket. Hands pressed the fabric around him, Merry was weakly grateful. Face was attached to the body of a surgeon. Face wore great spectacles. Face brought to him sips of diluted vinegar with a bit of salt added. Once Face even brought him a trickle of some burning fluid which he said was whiskey . . . Merry Kinsman remembered that once there had been an old whiskey drinker named Tupley who was drummed out of camp. . . .

Face said, Here is a bit of raw potato. It would be good for you—raw sweet potato—if you can but get it down. Merry tried to gnaw the fragment, but another of his teeth came out and the contact hurt his mouth. He gave up with a groan. . . . Face had a knife, the knife scraped and scraped: you could hear the dragging sound of that blade on hard substance of potato. Shredded filaments were injected into Merry's mouth; in this fashion he could swallow them. There came a noble keen spicy taste. He hoped that his eyes, though deeply receded in a swollen countenance, could look appreciation.

Once he saw something else clearly. The face had withdrawn mistily, had become a bread board. That bread board stood upon a shelf in the Widow Kinsman's kitchen. The old German lady, who tended Merry when his hand was frozen, had given it to Mrs. Kinsman. It was carved of pale wood—a perfect circle. It was really a plate to be put upon the table, with little flowers and vines growing in carved wood around the edge. The cut-out letters read: *Gib uns heute unser täglich Brod,* and that meant give us our daily bread, or something of the sort. It was the only German which Merry knew. He associated it in his mind because the wooden bread plate was round and the surgeon's wafers of glass before his eyes were round. It was odd to think of scraped sweet potato as being daily bread.

Merry became alert in imagination during his last hours. Because he had poetry in his nature, and the simple selfless courage sometimes evinced by good children who have a love of life, he could depart from personal tragedy and forget utterly the strain which disease put upon his carcass. He saw himself as a symbol of a proud manner of living. . . . Fifes were good, he thought, because of what they taught and the way they sounded. There needed to be no other reason for the existence of such music. . . . It did not occur to him that other boys in other lands had felt the same about their lands. Meriwether Kinsman's honor and his faith were one with those of an Iroquois or a Delaware: he thought that his Nation was the best, that was all there was to it. It was the best because it was the best. Also because it abounded, or had abounded, in moose and wild turkeys, in mountainous wagons rumbling west, in long rifles to guard the wagons.

In this time the world turned into a picture which Merry thought someone should paint, he felt that it would be painted in the future. Perhaps even now somewhere there wandered a young veteran like himself who ached with the same vague unreasonable impractical dream which had occupied Merry Kinsman since first he stood, jumped and ran within that Pennsylvania grove, since first he heard fifes and drums. It was a dream unfounded in necessity (he hated the idea of necessity because necessity had ruled his childhood) and would pay a penny to no one (he hated the idea of pennies because men like Mr. Adams were always counting them). His dream took the form of marching men, old and young, who hammered drumheads and blew upon a fife. One was of the stamp of the dearly recalled Abijah Parker; he was the tallest. There was blood upon a bandage, bright blood shed willingly as Merry had shed his driblets of blood above the soil of his native Pennsylvania. There was smoke of cannon, men came through it. Dead and dying were upon the ground, wreckage of war littered the earth, bullets made their harsh quick *raahhhhh,* screaming off into terrible space. Somewhere sometime an artist might paint this picture; never could he paint the sound; other men and boys would have to fight in other wars, in order to pick up the sound again. Will ever our dear fifes be silent? Merry Kinsman wondered . . . somehow weakly he feared that they would be. Brass bands, he thought. Too many folks like their noise; and also there are the music boxes. . . .

But in distance were desert places and fabled mountains, so still the eagles and the hawks would cling to wild free air. They would hang high, wide of wing, angry of beak, ready to assault any force which came to threaten America. But— Why, he thought, I sought to destroy Americans by bolstering an attack with my melodies! And now, in captivity, Americans have destroyed *me.* I would weep at this awful knowledge, but somehow am too weak to weep. They have destroyed me— Southerners have killed me dead—Southerners, but still Americans. And how many bullets did the One Hundred and Forty-eighth Pennsylvania put into Southerners' skins? Too many, he thought, too many; so they have taken revenge.

He lay quietly, hearing nothing of the mutter and squeal beneath that canvas and sagging scraps of pine, until the surgeon came again.

So you're still with us, the queer voice came down to Merry's ears.

Yes. He could let a whisper steal from his rotting mouth. He wanted to add something about, I'm still here but shan't be for long, but could not find the words, could not summon strength to send forth the words. He felt that familiar solution of vinegar and salt wetting the great black mass of tissue from which his teeth had fallen out. Trickle found its way into his throat, there was a taste, he swallowed, it tasted good. Oh, how good it tasted. Chore name? he asked. It was his way of saying, What is your name? and it was strange to think that he had never asked before, he had never considered that Face might have a name.

My name, lad? Elkins. The surgeon floated away.

Merry Kinsman stood motionless upon a formless plane. Now, he thought, I am removed from the earth, am here with the eagles. He looked down and saw a crowded mass of filthy skeletons, young and old—most of them were young skeletons—with blackened hide drawn tight, hide still trying to cover the bones and not always succeeding, for some of the bones had broken through the hide, and were oozing and raw. Up with the eagles, he said. He heard a rush and snap of their wings. He looked down and saw the surgeon return, saw his own shape lying, saw the surgeon bending, saw him straighten and turn and summon an orderly. Together surgeon and orderly picked up the wisp of Merry Kinsman, a piece of canvas was slid beneath; they carried the wisp out from under the sagging canopy; later two other ragged orderlies carried it still farther; but the watching Merry had lost interest, was turned away, did not care where they carried it.

Jefferson and Liberty, said the unmistakable voice of Abijah Parker beside him.

I hain't forgotten!

Six-eight! The drums'll catch us.

Merry's fife was pressed into his hands, his hands were grown strong again. Uncle Bijah played the first three notes alone, then Merry joined him. They strode off together through the smoke, drums thudding and booming beside and behind them.

55

Late in the autumn of 1864, John Winder had established his headquarters at Millen, Georgia, rather than at Florence, South Carolina. His new title of commissary-general of all prisoners east of the Mississippi brought with it a complete assumption of command, giving him full latitude. As he had told Henry Wirz in early September, the designation of the new prison at Millen was Camp Lawton. Here the superintendent, a lieutenant named Boyce, held some misguided notion that Yankees could make pretension to the estate of Man. In vain did General Winder attempt to dispel this idea: Boyce was a gentleman. John Winder would have loved to remove him, but literally there was not another officer to take the post.

Mortality at Camp Lawton was enormous despite improved internal conditions. Prisoners died of wounds, they died because Andersonville had wounded them. . . . Within the stockade nothing was known concerning Sherman's advance. No fresh fish came to carry news; no fish had come excepting unfresh fish from Andersonville. Winder established grotesque but effective penalties, forbidding the circulation of gossip on the Sherman situation to any of the prisoners. Therefore they were not hard to handle when, at three o'clock of a drizzly morning in late November, the first detachments were routed out and herded to the cars. Within a day or two the entire living population of the stockade had been removed to Savannah. At first it was thought that they could be left there with safety. This was not to be: Sherman aimed at Savannah.

General Winder traveled up to South Carolina as speedily as possible. There, with the Florence superintendent, he arranged for eventual reception of Andersonville-Millen prisoners. Without difficulty he infected red-headed Lieutenant Barrett with his own viciousness. This was simple to accomplish: Barrett had practiced cruel arts since he was a child.

Barrett's latest exhibition of native tolerance and charity concerned a rumored tunnel. The tunnel could not be found, but Barrett was convinced that it was there. General Winder filled his subordinate's ears with mumblings concerning successful tunnels at Andersonville, by which means allegedly hordes of Yankees had crept forth to despoil the Confederacy. Barrett ordered all rations withheld from the stockade's population until the tunnel-makers should voluntarily give themselves up to justice. After several days of enforced starvation (during which many of the more sickly were released from pangs by the most obvious means) sturdier Unionists banded together and selected four tunnel-makers by lot. In the interests of community survival these four marched to the gate and were delivered to the tenderness of the red-haired Lieutenant Barrett. His charity was exemplified promptly: he hung them by their thumbs for only two hours. He might have kept them hanging for five hours, but after two hours even he had become wearied of their yells.

Like Andersonville the prison at Florence was a parallelogram composed of pine trunks. Prisoners declared that the Confederates were the God damnedest people to go around standing logs on end. Fifteen acres of ground were enclosed by the palisade, including the inevitable creek, swamp, deadline area. No sentry stations bloomed atop the fence: there were only platforms for cannon at four corners. Earth had been shoveled against the outside of the pen in a high embankment; along this elevation guards walked their posts, beating a deep path into the mound. It had been difficult for John Winder to hoist himself to the eyries of Andersonville. Here there were easy twisting trails by which he might ascend. So he could stand, top of the stockade breast-high against his thick body . . . he could rest stained hands on the axed ends of logs, and peer down at the seething shivering herd.

Sir. They resemble a bunch of rats, don't they?

A slippery sucking voice had spoken beside him. The general twisted his head, glowered. Who're you?

Excuse me, sir! I'm afraid I shouldn't have intruded on your thoughts. I apologize humbly.

. . . He had the manner of a pawnbroker. Or he was a man with something to sell . . . you did not know what he was selling . . . manner of a pawnbroker. Or else the manner of the weakling who approaches a pawnbroker, trusting to receive more than the pledging of the trophy is worth, knowing that he will never redeem it . . . perhaps he has stolen it. . . .

Here was the man who would bring John Winder to his end.

He was Sammons Kight, native to the Florence region. His miserly father and elder brother kept this incompetent on short fare. Sam Kight was forty-one, he looked older. His shoulders slumped, arms were limp, his belly jutted under the shabby long gray winter coat.

God damn it! Can't you answer with civility? I said—who *are* you?

Captain Kight, sir. Excuse me—I assist your adjutant—

Without saluting or assuming the semblance of military posture, Kight removed his crushed felt hat. You could see his bald tight scalp glistening even in steady wind of February. Tendrils of brown hair lay brushed silkily across his bald head, brushed laboriously. Kight had a flat nose with hollow fuzzy nostrils; he wore a shaggy mustache; his mouth and chin disappeared beneath the mustache. He wore greasy spectacles, glasses cut into flat ellipses within brass frames; the window caging the right eye had been shattered, glued together again.

Captain Kight was married to a wisp of a woman whose father had married her off to him because of his own father's wealth. None of the wealth had come their way. This woman drudged through cares of a numerous household aided only by two bungling Negresses, one of whom was quarter-witted. Rooms of their cavernous home were encrusted with religious mottoes. Bible reading occurred night and morning, Grace was spoken before each meal, Thanks rendered afterward. Agony rose from the Kight place on Sunday afternoons when one child or another was discovered in some activity deemed detrimental to the Sabbath, and was flayed accordingly. Mr. Sammons Kight held an office in the Baptist church, he was superintendent of the Sunday School. He respected the term *Loving Kindness* which he mumbled as a single word. He droned it long, pushed out his small lips under brindled hair whenever he spoke the term.

What you want with me? Hey?

Nothing, General Winder. . . . Nothing at all. . . . I was off duty . . . merely looking . . . at the prisoners.

Kight put his life into his throat.

General, allow me a question? One can see that most of them are villains—shockingly depraved— And yet— Would it be possible for the Word of God to lighten their souls?

He went on eagerly: A service of prayer, perhaps even a sermon attuned to their needs? I would be willing to volunteer! I know of others who—

No God in any of their souls! They haven't *got* any souls! Now you go way!

Yes, General. Yes, yes. Of course—

The captain went gliding along the sentries' path. . . . He had seen Winder many times across the breadth of a room. He had risen, bowed, smirked, had been ignored. Nevertheless he felt fearfully that something was now accomplished. Winder at least knew who he was.

Meat supply dwindled in the Kight family. It was decided to do a certain amount of butchering in mid-winter to supplement sides and hams still remaining from the first butchering of the season. Accordingly six hogs were chased and roped in woodland adjoining the country homestead of Sam Kight's father. A single carcass fell to the share of Sammons Kight.

Even this was enough to awaken excitement in his spindly children when they heard the good news.

Mr. Kight, asked his wife drearily, Is your Pa giving us a whole hog, sure enough?

So he says. Sam drank dregs of grain coffee.

I am glad! All the little ones have just been a-begging and a-begging. We're so shy of meat these days.

A great hope had risen within Sam Kight—a brilliant idea with which he was toying. Through natural inclination and sad experience he had grown to accept the truth: value and importance could not be gained in this world without the coöperation, even the benevolence, of higher stronger authority. Sammons Kight was mightily afraid of God, he believed that other men awarded veneration to God solely because also they were terrified by Him. In turn Sam was afraid of his father. Early in life he had learned that his father would award him no benefit unless he was pleased with him . . . to this office of giving pleasure Sam obtained but rarely.

He had hoped to be a minister. His father would not hear of it. Ministers earned but little money. . . . Sam studied long, he'd studied earnestly if ineffectually for the Law. He had failed each time he was examined. Old Kight roared, thrust him into the small ironmongery which he owned in Florence. Sammons had undertaken later to manage a tobacco farm belonging to his brother. He failed with one crop after another. Until this last winter of the war he failed at everything he undertook, except his superintendency of the Sunday School (in that also he would have been accounted a failure, had anyone been willing to consult the children). In 1862 Sam marched off to war, racked by ordeals awaiting him . . . he fell sick, lay near death. Eventually he was sent home, discharged as an invalid. Now in this fourth winter he was delighted to be addressed as Captain. The bottom of the barrel had been scraped. Sammons Kight was one of the scrapings.

But suppose he reached a higher situation in the military establishment? Suppose he was awarded field grade? . . . Captains were a dime a dozen. There were even captains who could barely read! And he, Sam Kight, had read Law for a time in the office of a man who later went to the Confederate Congress!

Suppose he were to be made a major? Generals had it in their power to award promotions. Suppose that Sam Kight pleased General Winder? He had scarcely been able to please anybody. . . .

As kindling for fire of his plan he could assemble only a few shreds of conversation: laughing and rather scornful conversation which passed between the adjutant and Winder's son, when one day that worthy sat beside the adjutant's desk.

But if the statement which he had heard were true . . . Sam became inattentive to clerical duties, he snapped at his children when they were restless during evening Bible reading at home (he was quartered in his own house, there was no other place for him). Later he took little Ocie into a bed chamber and whipped him with his belt: Ocie had sneezed repeatedly during the long prayer which followed Bible reading. Kight intoned a new prayer over the moaning child, put on his belt, went to the kitchen shanty to inspect a hog's carcass which hung outside the door. It had been fetched, drawn but not quartered, from the senior Kight's homestead that evening. Sam put his pale hand upon the pebbled clammy hide, he inspected the chopped ends of ribs, he thought of General Winder. He looked at scrubbed cloven hoofs, he thought of the Devil, he thought also of General Winder, he thought of pickled pig's-feet.

Captain Sam Kight was up betimes the next day, giving orders to a reluctant wife. He badgered her into acceptance of a task far beyond her strength and beyond the abilities of the two wenches.

He was nervous through the morning, blotting reports which he copied. His hands shook. He dropped a sand-filled bottle which they used as a paper-weight, and broke it . . . the adjutant spoke biting words. With his own hands Sammons Kight swept up the glass and sand; he did not ask a subordinate to do it, though there were two corporals in the office.

Early he had requested an audience with General Winder. The desired permission was slow in coming: Winder wanted to know why the damn captain didn't talk to the adjutant instead, about whatever it was he wanted to talk about. Having progressed through echelons, it was nearly noon when at last Sam was permitted to tap his transparent knuckles against the old man's door, and to be growled at after he had entered and closed the door.

John Winder sat upon the sofa which had been brought by train all the way from Andersonville (there might not be a sofa available in Florence). The general was dosing himself with Harlem oil. This mixture, composed of flowers of sulphur boiled in cottonseed oil, with amber and turpentine added, was accounted to be of great value in strengthening the stomach and kidneys, stimulating liver and lungs, quieting asthmatic complaints and palpitations, dispelling shortness of breath. The formula had been given to the general by a subordinate named Gwenn, who called it Welch medicamentum. Colonel Llewellyn Gwenn was alarmed at symptoms displayed by his superior. Winder started out with a dose of ten drops, now he took twenty-five. His thick breath could be heard.

Damn it, Captain, what you want?

Excuse me, sir. I—I have an invitation—

Invitation? Winder snorted, swallowed down the spoonful of drops, sputtered, wiped his sagging mouth with the back of his hand. From whom?

From myself, sir.

The devil! What kind of invitation do you want to give me?

Sir, it has come to my attention that you are very fond of fresh pork.

Where the devil did you hear that?

Sir, it was—your son—the captain— I chanced to overhear him speaking with Major Crawley—

John Winder said decisively, after belching over the Harlem oil: Hell, yes, I do like fresh pork. Who doesn't? Precious little we've got around here these days.

But, General, a whole hog has come into my possession, and—

Twelve officers, including the trembling Kight, sat down to a pork banquet in the Kight dining room. It was a mid-day meal: Winder insisted that he could accept only if the meal were served at noon on Wednesday, February the eighth. He had to go over to Columbia on the afternoon train.

The drawn-faced Mrs. Kight managed briefly to greet her husband's guests, to be presented to the general; then she staggered back to the kitchen. She had been up most of the night, overseeing groaning black women in the preparation of sausage. Mrs. Kight had done the bulk of the work herself. . . . Penny, the dullard slave, managed to chop up a portion of the best loin, instead of scraps set aside for the purpose. . . . Nevertheless the other loin was roasted. There were patties and chops . . . the roast was garnished with strips of side meat. Appetizers of pickle were ready on the table, with several bottles of tart wine and two bottles of spirits which the desperate Sam had wheedled from his brother in exchange for the Kight mantel clock. There were two bowls of sweet potato pudding, mounds of corn sticks on platters. A private plate of sausages was put before General Winder. The old man gobbled rapidly, never looking at his host, talking only to the aide who sat at his left hand. . . . The general drank but little. He said that he must have a clear head for multitudinous tasks awaiting him.

Scorched and oily smells of roast and fried meat drifted up the staircase to torture a throng of wan children huddling above stairs. The children wondered what was being done with the bones; they wished that the soldiers would leave quickly; the children would like to put their hands on those bent chewed ribs before the wenches got at them. . . .

Less than an hour after they'd trooped in through the unpainted double doors, the guests took their departure. Soon General Winder and his military family stood upon the railway platform, awaiting transportation.

That was a meal, sir, said Captain Peschau.

Too damn greasy. That captain's niggers don't know how to cook. . . . Sammons Kight was not present to hear these words: he was in his house, praying actually and idiotically for a promotion which never came.

Captain Peschau said something or other to the general; the other officers were standing at a distance; later Peschau could not remember exactly what it was that he said. He thought he heard a responsive grunt. It was a strange response. Peschau turned quickly to look at his commander.

The platform of the Florence station was composed of cinders and gravel, tamped down between old splintery ties; it was one of those wide ties upon which Winder beat his swollen face as he fell. Peschau saw him sagging, Peschau tried to hold him, Peschau was a slight man, he could not support the weight. The old man's bulk draped the aide's straining shoulder, swept his arm aside, pitched loose. Other people exclaimed, came diving. They turned John Winder on his back. Eyes glared out of a face slaty blue. People kept exclaiming, crying to the general. They kept calling, General *Win*der, again and again, as men might try to awaken a sleeper.

Cashmyer's tent, said someone.

He referred to the nearby abode of Philip Cashmyer, John Winder's detective officer.

Ralphie, run for the surgeon!

Ralphie was running already.

Five pairs of hands slid beneath the great chunk. Two hands slid under each of the old man's thighs, two hands were straining up under each of his shoulders. Another pair of hands supported the mighty drooping head and helped to support the shoulders as well.

The officers went laboring toward a tent beyond the station. The detective came rushing to hold up the tent fly and admit them. As gently as possible they put the general upon the single cot, saw it sag deeply, weight straining the cords; they heard the crunch of cords against wood. . . . John Winder was breathing. . . . The surgeon came at a dog-trot. A ring of idle ragged troops gathered at a safe distance from the tent.

Inside the tent John Winder gazed at the canvas roof with eyes unmoving, bulbous. Presently he gave an explosive belch; there drooled a trickle from one corner of the open mouth; the massive head swung slightly to one side. The black blood was turning blacker. . . . A little later the surgeon pushed down the crusty eyelids and weighted them with Federal coins.

When Andersonville learned of this demise, they were quick to supply the last words spoken by John Winder (although in fact he was not granted the dramatic gesture of a last utterance): My faith is in Christ. I expect to be saved! Wirz, cut down the Yankees' rations!

Two railroads—the North Eastern, and the Wilmington and Manchester— formed a junction at that insignificant village of Florence. In a gray wintry swamp not far from the intersection of iron paths, straggles of moss clung to empty branches. This was not the luxuriant Spanish moss of more southerly regions: it was a brittle neglected fuzz, a last relic of sub-tropics. It dangled dried and feeble on emaciated boughs, dark as the stuffing of a carriage cushion. Amongst these tatters roosted a convocation of vultures. Solemn in silence they wadded on higher boughs. They had lunched to repletion (as had the officers in the Kight house) but a consumptive cow had been their fare. The buzzards squatted, waiting for a new death, or for the discovery of an older death.

Suddenly they moved, shifting position, some moved to outer limbs. Their wide heavy wings stretched when they hopped; there was the scraping of feathers as they shifted and then draped scalloped black shawls about their bodies again. A raw wrinkled neck twisted, a hooked beak went out and drew back into immobility. It was almost as if another of their kind had come, unseen yet detected, to dwell among them.

56

Coral Tebbs slid his shotgun through the drying leaves, resting its weight in a low crotch of a sweet-gum sapling. He bent lower to sight. The hawk was still there: that was its favorite perch on the stub of a high dead cypress branch. You could tell that it was the hawk's favorite perch, for even at such a distance (he estimated that it might be ten rods) the accumulation of droppings showed like whitewash on a lower limb. The hawk bent forward, disturbed its wings as if for flight, then folded back onto the stub again. Old chicken stealer, thought Coral. I've come a weary way, crutches sticking in soft ground long the edge of this here marsh. Wonder how many other one-footed folks ever try to leg it through woods like these, crutches and all? . . . Chicken stealer! I'm going to spoil your guts.

He had been waiting over two hours for the hawk to return to its perch, and now the hawk had come back, and Coral's bony finger sank slowly against the trigger.

Powder exploded, the boom hurt, the butt crunched into the youth's shoulder. A dust—feathers?—blew loose from the bird. The hawk went forward into space, wings half lifted again, but wings bent under, wings bent under.

Got you, you son of a bitch, cried Coral in his heart with hate like glee. Birdshot'd never carry up there, but a mite of buckshot done the trick. That's a right heavy animal, he thought in continuation, as he heard the body go plunging through cypress twigs and heard stringy streamers of moss ripped loose and saw them waving. Then came a light damp mingled thud and splash as the hawk landed at the edge of some shallow pool which Coral could not see.

He put his dark brows together and rubbed his hairy chin with a speculative hand. Well, now. Hawk must be a hundred and fifty foot over yonder and all sorts of brush and vines in between.

But damn if he wasn't going to get that hawk, if he had to crawl to do it. He'd have a sorry time, hoisting his crutches and wriggling his one sound limb over all those logs and tangles but— By God, he meant to take that hawk home. Tote it all the way home, and maybe his mother would like to have a couple nice big hawk-wing fans for next summer instead of the regular turkey-wing fans that most folks had. Tote it home, dump it down on the stoop and say, Here's one robber ain't going to make off with no more of our fries. Cripple or no cripple! And wouldn't that puny little dragged-out Flory be fetched? Sick at heart, poison sick with the jealousy, Flory would be. Flory couldn't have got this hawk first shot or hundredth.

Coral took a bearing on the hawk's vacant perch, perceiving where the area directly beneath it must lie in the thicket ahead. Tough work, a-crawling and a-climbing, and he'd have to leave the shotgun right here. No help for it; but he could always use a crutch on a snake if he met one. Coral reloaded the gun and hung it in a tree. Then he hitched his way along the damp cypress log and pushed through a layer of vines, looking back constantly to keep to the bee-line he had established. Thorns bit him, but Coral only cursed in spirit monotonously and proceeded on his cautious stubborn path. He fell when his crutches caught on a root; then he cursed aloud. He swore at root, crutches, swamp, hawk, the winter sun overhead; he swore at his own clumsiness, at the Yankees who'd riddled his foot, at the surgeons who had cut it off. He went on, breathing heavily; and from ahead sounded a faint plashing as if some wild animal were molested by his approach. Oh, damn to hell, why hadn't he toted that gun along, somehow or other? Here he might meet up with something else to shoot, and he would have no gun, and—

At last he panted beneath the half dead tree. Surely this was the place—it was open, a small glade higher and drier than the surrounding thickets—yet no hawk could be seen. Yes, yes, here were white spatters of dung on some sodden old cypress knees; this was the place, it had to be. But no hawk.

What was that sound he'd observed as he came? Surely not the beating lunging flopping noise a big bird would make if, not killed as dead as Coral had thought, the creature were still trying to take flight or struggle off through the woods. Then, immediately before his gaze, Coral Tebbs saw footprints in the mould, and those footprints were filling slowly with water.

All right, God damn it, he heard a strange strained churlish voice; it was fearful to recognize that voice as his own. He'd just passed another tupelo tree, and now he found himself backing against that tree, small as it was. All right, God damn you, he said again to the gloom. Got a knife here.

So he had, one made at home, and in a scabbard of his own construction. He'd sewn the bent fold of old leather with toil through several evenings; it contained the honed blade of a butcher knife which, had he but known it, once graced the kitchen of his grandfather Lumpkin. Coral had made a handle for that knife by wrapping the rusty spike with strings of rawhide.

Got a knife here. Come out them bushes, mister.

Sprouts and vines and moss were motionless, then they twitched, then the twitching died and they were motionless again.

Telling you for the last time, come out them bushes.

A figure arose to confront him. It was such a spook as might have sent any field Negro of the region scuttling. It was a spook somewhat smaller than Coral Tebbs, nearly beardless, with a crusted blackened skull for a face, and dressed in scarecrow shreds of flannel and jeans. Coral could not recognize immediately this starveling for what the thing really was. He had never stood aloft on a sentry's perch, rimmed on the stockade; his condition precluded any climbing of ladders. True, he had lurked to watch wagonloads of bodies go past, but usually the dead were naked; often they were bloated, before or after death.

By God, said Coral, that's my hawk you got in your hand.

Sure enough. The creature had the hawk, and the hawk hung limp-winged and bloody.

What you doing with my hawk that I just shot off'n this cypress?

The figure tumbled loosely out of the vines and went down among twisting knees of the swamp: it was half a sitting down, half a falling down. The thing wore a mouldy cap with a corroded clover leaf on the top of it; you could see that the clover leaf had once been red, but the visor of the cap was gone. The thing still held the hawk.

What was you going to do with my bird, you?

Faint weak voice whispered, Eat it.

Well, I hope to shit, said Coral Tebbs. Son of a bitch if you hain't a damn
Yankee!

Yes.

God blast your measly soul to hell!

Guess He's nearly done so.

What you say?

Nearly blasted my soul to hell already.

You got loose from that pen over yonder! Well, I'm going to turn you in.

Go ahead.

Reckon I'll get a reward, too. You got ary weapon about you?

Naw.

What might be your name? You are a measly rat for certain.

Name's Stricker.

What?

Naz Stricker.

What?

Nazareth Stricker.

That's a hell of a name. God damn Yankee name. Where you from?

Hundred and Forty-eighth Pennsylvania.

You mean to say you damn Yankees'll eat a hawk? Hawk ain't fit.

I'd eat anything, said Naz Stricker.

I did hear them trail-dogs in the night. Never did hear the catch-dogs
a-barking. Reckon twas you they was after.

The Yankee swayed, seemed about to fall flat, then caught himself and remained in a hunched sitting position.

Coral Tebbs swung his crutches and his leg, moving closer. What's that red
dingus on your cap, you?

I don't know.

You don't know? Guess you damn Yankees don't know nothing. Worse'n a
pack of niggers.

Yes . . . do know. It's—clover leaf. That means Second Corps. Red because
we were First Division of the Second Corps. . . .

What division was that?

Naz Stricker considered dreamily. The battle was a long time ago, a lifetime
ago. Caldwell's, he said.

When Coral lay on old dry blood-blackened straw in a wagon, while a column
of wounded pitched and screamed and muddied up and down the racking Maryland hills, he had seen prisoners marching alongside, unwounded ones. At Anderson Station he had, many times, watched ranks of fresh prisoners being formed
into squads while Wirz danced and mouthed at them. Thus he had seen many
Yankees close at hand. He had felt the venom fly from his own eyes, it was as if
the Yankees must feel it also, spraying over their skin and burning as it sprayed.
Put the sons of bitches in the pen; let them stink; let them yell; shoot the first
bastard who comes nigh the deadline. If he'd received a lighter wound with no
amputation resulting— Oh, he'd learned that there were plenty of them, wounded
Confederate veterans who were considered unfit for further duty in the field; yet
they had been accepted to help fill up new ranks of the Georgia Reserves. They
were guarding Yanks, and a thousand times Coral Tebbs had wished that he might
stand among the guards. Bet he'd show those blue-bellies who was boss . . . how
he'd show them! A thousand times he had looked at Flory, with his thin little-girl
voice with scarce a rasp in it— Looked at Flory prancing to show Ma what a swell
he was as a soldier, all togged out in Yankee jacket and Yankee breeches too big

for him, and a big calico hat sinking over his ears— Looked at Flory and thought, Devil beat the ass off of me. Look at that: he can pack a musket, and go on guard, and all I can do is crutch myself through the brush— Looked at Flory and hated Flory's guts, silently or aloud.

You going to come along of me.

The Yankee's eyes were shut.

Want I should bust your head with this here crutch?

Go ahead, came the whisper. Bust it.

Hold up your hands, God damn you! So's I can see you hain't got a weapon.

The hawk slid into muck below the cypress knees. The ragamuffin's right hand came wavering up; the left hand came wavering up, except that there was no left hand. Nothing but a tattered sleeve and what appeared to be a grimy bone sticking out of tatters.

Coral made a sound. Oh, by God, his soul was saying, oh, by God, and yet he could not speak a word which sounded like a word.

The escaped prisoner's arms fell back beside him.

Yank. The harsh sound of the word hurt the throat of Coral Tebbs as if that throat were scraped by a dull knife. Yank, what you got there? What befell you? Your hand—

They—took it off. Right at—the wrist.

Who took it off?

Rebel surgeons.

Where'd you get hit?

I was damn near—back home. Just a few counties away—up in Pennsylvania. Twas at—Gettysburg.

A red glare swept Coral's gaze. For a moment he could not see the shriveled youth in rags before him, could not see the shriveled face or the foolish visorless cap, could not see the rotten embroidery of the red clover leaf; nor could he see the barred wings of the hawk he'd shot, or gloom pervading there in loneliness.

What day? . . . God damn it, I *asked* you. What day of the battle?

Second day, I guess it was. Right by that—wheatfield.

Oh, by God. We come against you! I was with the Fifty-third Georgia. I'll be buggered with a cob!

The Yankee sat without moving. Then shudders began to disturb his body as if he suffered an attack of ague. His lips were jelly; he hadn't lost all his teeth, you could hear some of his teeth clattering against each other as he shook.

Look at what you done to my foot! Coral swung his leg forward. Think you're the only one got hit? I'd rather be shy a hand like you than shy a foot like I am!

This shrunken scarecrow spook could be made to say nothing, he could not be made to look up. Coral tore a crutch from beneath his right arm and wrapped his hand around the stem of it. By God, I'm going to bust you . . . but the cudgel remained suspended in air. Coral's breath was burning out of his lungs in blasts, and saliva trickled from the corners of his open mouth. Slowly he lowered the crutch. At last he slid it into his armpit again.

Yank. Come on. Going to take you in!

The boy tried to arise; he seemed to try to arise; again he slid back among cypress knobs.

Catch-dogs ought to have got you and that's a fact. How come they never got you last night?

I held—to—wet places. And used—pepper.

Pepper? Where'd you get pepper?

Bought—it—from a guard.

Come on, you Yank!

Feebly the Northerner shook his head. Can't do it.

You can't move? You claim you can't move?

Naw. Can't—move.

Then I got to knife you or blow the damn head off'n you.

Now fierce tiny blue eyes glinted up from dark sockets of the skull. Blow—damn—head off me? What with?

Why, dad blast it, I got a shotgun back in them bushes! What'd you think I shot that hawk with, anyway? Here—give me my hawk.

The Yankee didn't move, so Coral steadied himself and employed a crutch to work the muddied hawk forward into his own possession. He tied the weight of it to the·cord looped around his neck; yes, it was heavier than anyone might imagine. It was remarkable, how a hawk could look so light and cloudy, wheeling above trees; yet it seemed to weigh as much as a fox when you were carrying it.

—Can't make up my mind, said Coral.

—Can't you make reply? Didn't you hear me tell you I couldn't make up my mind?

—Whether to stick you with this here knife.

—Shotgun's back yonder. Couldn't see you from there, count of all the brush. So I'd have to clamber all the way back here.

—By God. Dirty damn Yankee! Not fit to waste a charge of powder on.

—Yank, what was that name you give me?

—Oh. Nazareth Stricker! Chicken-shit name for certain.

Coral Tebbs toiled back through the canopy of gum branches and stickery vines. In two minutes the mute crouching ragged figure of Naz Stricker was masked from his sight. If Coral had breathed in trumpet blasts before, he was breathing in engine blasts by the time he reached the tree where hung his shotgun.

He owned the loose extravagant imagination common to many primitive people who have dwelt as outcasts, who have dwelt in lonely places. His hates were simple, unreasonable, intense; in time perhaps he might grow to love with as little reason and with as great an intensity. . . . He pictured the Yankee, Nazareth Stricker (somehow it sounded like Bible talk) as struck by his shotgun pellets, bursted and ripped as Coral had seen other boys bursted beside him. Good enough for him; there was nothing good for a Yankee except killing. Pennsylvania . . . so that's where he came from. Funny place, peopled by a herd of foreigners who couldn't even talk like white folks. Coral remembered standing with other shaggy dusty hungry boys outside the door of a brick farmhouse; he recalled the barn which stood beyond; damndest looking stable or what-do-you-want-to-call-it he ever saw. Stable was about as big as a county courthouse, and it stood on a hillside, and part of it was built straight out in the air, and there were cows standing underneath the built-out portion and feeding there (not for long: the foragers herded them away) and there were queer round signs and symbols painted on the barn in color . . . Lieutenant Anglin talked to Captain Tyree, and Coral overheard the lieutenant saying that those queer arrangements had something to do with the Evil Eye. What Evil Eye? Bunch of God damn foreigners and hirelings, like most of the Yankees. . . . He stood there with others, and two fat pink-faced women gazed out at them with swollen eyes gleaming in terror.

Lady. You got some bread to spare us?

Ja. Bread we got. Today was baking.

Meat. You got any meat?

Ja. Pickled pork we got—

Got any beef?

Nein. The beef is all.

Cakes? somebody shouted behind Coral.

Ja. Crullers we got. Today was baking.

Well, the damn Yankee womenfolks could cook like sin. Coral and the rest made themselves a meal, they made themselves a meal under peach trees until they like to popped their bellies open. . . . He saw Naz Stricker as coming from such a house. Except Naz Stricker could talk straighter talk than the rest of those hirelings at the North . . . shooting was too good for him. Because he came from a pinkish-reddish-brick house, and there was the springhouse yonder where were spread wide pans of milk with cream rising slowly, and Coral remembered how he stood with a tin pan of milk held in his quivering hot hands . . . he drank slowly and tenderly and continually until the friend next to him—fellow name of Jo Coppedge—said, Look, Cory, this here's the way to do it. Jo Coppedge put down the pan he was holding, put it on the damp cool stones, and lifted from inside his shirt a big wedge of solid cherry pie, and using that pie as a utensil Jo Coppedge skimmed slowly across the surface of the milk in the pan, he pushed the dripping chunk of thick rosy-crusty pie all the way across the pan. When he took it out it was coated with golden cream, it was dripping with rich cream, and Jo bit deeply into pie and cream, pushed his hot thin dusty face into the mass of pie and cream, and his brown eyes rolled bright above the thick paint he had thus put upon his face, and he said, Oh, Mister! . . . Damn Yankee hirelings . . . shooting too good for them . . . not worth wasting powder and shot . . . Jo Coppedge got killed right in front of that same wheatfield that Coral and the Yank were speaking of.

Nrrrrwhuck.

Dad blast it, *Jo!* Coral reached down and lifted Jo's arm, and gave it a jerk, and then let go, and the arm fell back. The sound of *nrrrrwhuck,* the sound of the bullet's whacking, it resounded in Coral's ears even after the bullet had passed through Jo Coppedge's face and had broken through the softness of his brain and had splintered scraps out of the bones of his head and had gone crooning tenderly into space beyond, and had left the cream of Jo's brain a-dripping . . . white-yellow of cream, red of the cherries, *nrrrrwhuck,* dad blast it, *Jo!* Captain Tyree waving his pistol, pointing his pistol, he was crying an order, but there was too much noise, you couldn't hear a word. *Whoooooo,* said the Fifty-third Georgia and began to stumble forward, and Coral Tebbs was moving with the rest, firing and loading, ramming down another charge, firing into smoke, seeing no Yankees to shoot at, but squeezing the trigger into smoke, until someone dropped a big rock on his left foot and ankle, and it felt numb after the first blow—it felt as if the rock were still lying on top of his foot and ankle, pressing off all feeling. A voice boomed against his ear, saying something about The Rear; so he started picking his smoky way backward, away from the thicker lower newer smoke, using his gun and another gun he had picked up, using the two guns for canes, and he kept putting his wounded foot down upon the earth, taking regular steps with it, but he couldn't feel the ground underneath it each time he pressed it on the ground. . . .

Coral Tebbs took his shotgun from the tree, examined it with a crafty smile playing under tufts of silky black beard which grew longer and less silky, week by week, in weeks when he neglected to shave with his father's old razor. He cocked the shotgun, looked at the swamp from which he'd emerged, thought of Naz Stricker sodden and weak and helpless (all Yankees should be sodden and weak and helpless) and then thought, What a weary way, back through all them logs and brambles, and my crutches sucking down into the marsh the while. He thought of Naz Stricker throwing his arms wide and going over backward or forward as lead wrenched through his body at high speed. He thought, Wish every Yankee in this here world had the shit shot out of him.

It would be a long way, back through those tangles.

Coral Tebbs hated Naz Stricker on principle, and hated him also because he came from Pennsylvania and probably came from a fine brick house, and probably had eaten cherry pie and thick cream all his life. Those foreign Yankees had every damn thing in the world: big houses, and barns built out into the air, and factories to make things, and buttons and shoes and blankets, and medicine if they got sick . . . had everything they needed, except good powder. Secesh powder was a hell of a lot better than Yankee powder . . . Coral had heard that it was foreign, the powder in his own cartridges—heard that it came from England or France or Africa or some such far-off place. Once, in a hospital, he lay for two days on a pallet right betwixt two Yankees . . . he wouldn't talk to them, but he heard their talk. They talked about gunpowder, and how the dirt was so bad in their powder—regular black dirt, right out of the soil, they said, and manufactured so by some thieving contractor in a factory— The dirt was so bad that half the time you couldn't fire at all. Never knew whether your gun was going to shoot or not. He guessed they were laying it on mighty thick, just for his benefit, because they knew he was Secesh. But finally they got taken away to a prison hospital, and then there were just Secesh alongside. That talk about the powder haunted Coral's mind. Finally he asked an older man—a corporal, he was, from the Twelfth South Carolina, and also wounded at Gettysburg—Asked him if twere so. Hell, yes, said the South Carolinian. Once't I was out on the field, a-seeking my young brother after we'd had a mean scrap, and I run smack into a clan of Yankees. Reckon you can believe that I laid low and pretended I was one of the dead. Well, boy, them Yankees wasn't looking for wounded. No, sir, boy, twas powder they was a-seeking. Confederate powder, out of the pouches of us Confederates. They'd open up a pouch, say, Hell, he ain't got none, he's done fired all his cartridges, or words of that nature, and then go on looking for more. I was scairt piss-less they'd come grubbing around for my own pouch, but finally they went tother way.

Ever find your brother, Corporal?

Surely did. He was deader'n hell, and puffed up already. . . .

Slowly Coral Tebbs held his thumb against the hammer, retaining it against pressure of his forefinger applied to the trigger. Slowly he put the hammer down upon the cap.

If he had killed any Yankees in that battle he couldn't know, but certainly he had fired his rifle until it fried his fingers to touch it, so he'd sent a lot of balls flying. If he had killed any Yankees in that battle they were the last ones he'd ever get to kill, on account of his foot being cut off . . . not even fit to serve as a guard on the stockade, like that vile little freak of a Flory. If he didn't go back and shoot Naz Stricker now, he might not have another chance to do it. Because Naz Stricker might run away before he, Coral Tebbs, got back. . . . Oh, reckon not. Too tuckered.

—Come back with some guards from the stockade.

—Not Flory. That'd be a feather in the little stinker's cap that he'd flaunt and pride himself on forever.

—Heard something about a reward.

—*You mean to say you damn Yankees'll eat a hawk? . . . I'd eat anything. . . . They—took it off. Right at—the wrist.*

Twenty-five dollars reward? Maybe thirty? What was it folks said about Turner and Harris getting so much a head for every escaped prisoner that their dogs ran down?

—Twas thirty. That was what folks said, down at Uncle Arch Yeoman's store. Thirty dollars a head. Course, that would be Secesh.

—Why, by Jesus. Here was home. He'd come all this way, toting that hawk, and it was a weary way.

Coral stood examining the house and The Crib and the whole area with suspicion. Couldn't see a mule under the trees. Ma might be entertaining, but he considered it unlikely. She had entertained through practically the entire night; now it was nigh onto noontime, and doubtless she would be asleep. What with Flory messing with the soldiers, and Laurel gone to the Dillards', the Tebbs family was surely eating high on the hog these days. Coral suspected that his mother was suffering in some degree from the Venus' curse, for he had seen her dosing herself out of mysterious bottles. But always she was in good humor; it didn't seem to interfere with her entertaining of visitors. With all the troops in the neighborhood (far less than in previous months, after that big batch of Yanks was taken away in September—but still hundreds and hundreds of those Georgia Reserves) and with citizens traveling in droves, to get away from Bill Sherman— Sure enough! High on the hog. Two less mouths to feed: just Ma and himself and the baby—and the old lady had a sight of shinplasters which he had seen, and he reckoned that she had more tucked away that he hadn't seen. Once in awhile she even gave him money without his asking for it. She said, Coral, sonny, I do feel so shameful bad bout that foot of your'n. Now you take this currency, and go you down to Uncle Arch's and buy yourself a nice plug tobacco.

Coral rolled his chew in his mouth and thought about it. Suddenly he found himself wondering whether that damn Yankee, Naz Stricker, chewed tobacco. Stricker hadn't asked him for any—hadn't said, like most folks you encountered, What's the chance for a chaw? Give me a chaw. Lend me a chaw. Hain't had a chaw all the day.

I'd eat anything.

There was something about that damn Yankee that was important—yes, sir, damn important. Coral's brows squeezed together as he tried to consider what that important element might be, as he pegged and swung his way toward the house with the hawk bumping against him (and he reckoned he'd be chafed sadly from the continual bounce, bounce of the dead hawk). In solitary cogitation of the solitary way he went, Coral had acquired a habit of searching for whys and wherefores. He pried silently, constantly for reasons. The reasons he found were seldom the right ones, the purposes he ascribed were often bizarre, the motives and imagined results were apt to be fantastic. His lonely speculations exceeded the limits of his intelligence, but there was no one to tell him that he might be wrong. He kept pondering.

He froze suddenly, he was motionless for a second or two; an astonished grin widened his mouth. If both hands had not been occupied with crutches and with retaining the shotgun on its homemade sling, he would have slapped himself across his ribby chest. He had found the answer.

Naz Stricker was the first person he had talked to, since he came home, who had lost a foot or a hand in battle! And, by Jesus God, he got wounded on July the second, nigh that same wheatfield where he, Coral, felt his own left foot and ankle crushed and going numb.

—Long way off.

—Like a nigger song. Oh, long, long, long, long way.

—Course, they did give Coral a lot of whiskey before they started cutting. They said, Boy, get yourself drunk fast. They had a big barrel of Pennsylvania whiskey, and it was good whiskey, and you could hear a little firing in the distance, but it was nighttime—there wasn't much firing.

—Would the Secesh surgeons give whiskey to a Yank when they were going to go to slicing and chopping? Well, by God. He ought to ask the Yank about that.

—Boy, get yourself drunk fast. The dipper coming closer, someone holding the dipper, whiskey splashing and Coral swallowing and gagging, and the whiskey burnt like coal oil and it gagged him, and moths and other critters were going like fiends against the big bright lanterns hanging under the tent fly up above . . . surgeon said, Where'll we go on this one, Luce? Articulating surface? Right above the nodule. Single flap or double flap? . . . Farther up. Single; he's got the hide to spare . . . *ahhhh!* And that was his own first fierce scream, coming back to ruin his ears, coming back sometimes in the middle of the night to be echoed again by his own throat, to make the baby wake up and yell in sympathy, to make that rotten little Flory say, Aw, shut your trap and try to act like white folks, you.

—Long way off, Gettysburg place.

—Naz Stricker said that he lived not far away from there.

—But what about the whiskey? Hell no, you could bet on it. Good whiskey was too scarce all over the South; they'd not go to wasting it on some damn Yankee.

—But that was in Pennsylvania, where Stricker got shot, where he got captured. Well, they had plenty whiskey there—wagonloads of it. Stole it in that town yonder, name of Chambersburg—great big kind of warehouse chock full of it. They called it Monongahela or some such foreign name; said they could read it right off'n the barrel label.

—Ought to ask the Yank about that.

Coral Tebbs moved beneath a stunted magnolia tree which twitched its hard papery leaves next to the stoop. Zoral was playing beside the step, playing with a small dead chicken from which a mink had sucked the blood . . . minks got a chance't of chickens nowadays. Coral had sat up two nights with a lantern, trying to intercept the enemy, but always he nodded and went to sleep . . . maybe minks were too smart for him. Zoral wore a jacket which the widow had hacked out of a Federal blanket, with the broad stripe showing, and he had a string tied around the chicken's neck, and he was dragging the chick after him, making train noises. He paid no attention to his half-brother Coral, sometimes he paid no attention to anyone, sometimes not even to his mother. The Widow Tebbs insisted that Zoral had had brain fever when he was just a mite, and like to died of it. Coral regarded this disgusting baby and his disgusting sport with equal disgust, then went jigging up onto the stoop and into the house. His shotgun caught against the tilted post and nearly threw him backward; he cursed in loud fury, and awakened his mother in the bedroom where she slept (she had slept with Laurel when Laurel was at home, and Zoral occupied the foot of their bed) when she was not at The Crib.

What you do, Coral?

Nothing.

What you cussing about?

Nnnnn.

Where you been, Coral?

A-hunting.

What you get?

God damn bastard of a chicken hawk.

Oh, Coral. Such language as you use the while!

Well, look who's a-talking! Maybe you got religion like old Grandad-Blow-His-Bottom-Out that you tolt me about?

No, I hain't got no religion; but I like gentlemanly ways. When menfolks come to me to be entertained, I always ask them, if they be strangers, Will you please act like a gentleman and not cuss?

Well, I got that damn hawk, and I reckon he's the one took so many of our fries.

Where you get him, Coral?

Swamp back of the hill.

Well, I reckon too that he's the one, and I do thank you, sonny. You want to go purchase yourself a plug tobacco?

I still got some.

His mother was in the bedroom, and he could not see her, and suddenly for a special reason he was glad that there was no one else in that one room which served as dining room, kitchen, sitting room, and Coral's bedroom. He dumped the bruised dead hawk upon the hearth and stood looking at it, and for some strange reason mirth came to him. Mirth came so seldom. Coral said loudly, God damn Yankee chicken hawk. He batted the hawk into the cold fireplace with his crutch.

—Like what they call a lodge.

—Freemasons?

—He guessed his daddy hadn't been a Freemason, but he'd heard that his grandfather Tebbs was one.

—Jo Coppedge used to say, When I get growed I'm going to get to be a Mason, sure enough. You can go anywhere and do anything, and you got somebody to help you out. Take Yanks: Suppose you get yourself captured, and you say to a Yank—You give him that secret sign or utter them secret words. Then you got a friend for life.

—A lodge which only those who are shy a hand or a foot can belong to.

—Secret words?

—Secret sign? Tain't no secret. Sign is: you got a leg that comes down, and suddenly there ain't no foot on the end of it. Sign is: you got an arm that just ends short off. Like that damn Yankee Naz Stricker.

Even while he stood in contemplation of the disordered table and shelves, Coral heard his mother snoring in the next room. She snored like a man. The more finicky of her customers had complained about her snoring when sometimes the customer and the Widow Tebbs both fell asleep after their encounter, and then the customer was rudely awakened by the growling roar beside him. Coral had heard Captain Oxford Puckett laughing in The Crib. Hi, Mag, put the lid on it. You sound like a battery of brass Napoleons firing at will.

But now the hoarse throbbing from the next room spelled security for Coral's endeavors. The wicked grin twitched on his thin bearded face. Wouldn't Flory's jaw fall off if he knew about this? Flory would plain fart. Opportunity to catch a Yankee—maybe to shoot him—Opportunity to get thirty dollars, even Secesh! It seemed to Coral that he was visiting a personal spite on Floral by the procedure which he planned. There was nothing in this world which he might enjoy more.

Well, toting the stuff was a problem. But soon his eye roved to his old army haversack, hanging on a peg beside the chimney. It was burdened with dust, soot, scraps of crumbled plaster accumulating during the months which had elapsed since the ministrations of Mrs. Dillard. A Yankee sack, a small one; he'd picked it up in 1863 in the woods near that place—what they call it? It was a hard word to say—Chan-cell-ors-ville. It said *U.S.* but half the belts and canteens and buckles and equipment in the Confederacy said *U.S.* Coral reached up, got the sack, opened it, expelled some mummified remains which turned out to be those of a mouse, and shook the sack vigorously. There.

Fried pork? Hell yes, there was a lot left on that platter. It was good; nice pink stripes in it, and fried just right, even though twas cold. Liberally Coral helped himself to the slabs. Black-eyed peas? Hell yes, a regular hopping John. The mass of peas in the huge brown bowl was studded generously with chunks of hog jowl. (Strangely as occurs, the Widow Tebbs, in her slatternly ways and in her slovenly ignorance, was an excellent cook. If one did not inquire too closely into sanitary conditions. When times were hard, times were hard. But times weren't hard, at present, not for the widow. The menfolks liked a snack, many of them, afterward . . . they'd say, Missis, I could relish a plate of fried potatoes right now. Got any bacon handy? Maybe piece of pie, maybe cup of nice cold milk? I'll pay extry.)

Coral found a torn Macon *Telegraph* and wrapped a mass of peas and hog jowl in that. Cold potatoes—sure enough. Chunk of pone—the Widow Tebbs's pone was always crisp and well salted—when she had meal, when she had salt. Apple pie. Nearly half the pie left, and let Ma think that he'd eaten it all. I declare, she'd say. Coral, you going to eat me out of house and home.

Out in the yard Zoral said, Guh, guh, guh, and still he must be playing train, dragging that miserable chicken. Then a real train came grinding past, and smoke blew all the way to the Tebbs house, for the wind was rising. This week was unseasonably chilly, for March.

Knowledge of that wind posed a new problem for Coral. Loose boards on the roof rattled, it would be cold in the swamp tonight, it would be cold everywhere. Touch and consideration of the haversack brought his comrades back to him. He saw them, lounging in column; far long twisty roads, stones bulging out of clay to hurt you, blackened skillets fastened to the rifles, the spittle rolling in a hard hot ball when you spat into the dust. *Rye whiskey, rye whiskey, rye whiskey so free, you done kilt my Pappy, God damn you, try me.* He began humming as he moved with caution about the room, he was not humming loudly enough to awaken his mother. Which barrel? One over here: that was where she kept stuff. He grubbed around in the barrel, brought out a torn pair of drawers, some old skirts of Zoral's, a gown which Laurel hadn't taken with her. Here, by Jesus God. Union army coat to wear in the rain—one of those kind of oilcloth ones. Some visitor had left it in The Crib the year before; it had part of the cape missing, it wasn't of too much account, but it would serve. And this here old quilt. Coral worked at the table, kneading quilt and raincoat into a familiar roll, passing the roll over his head and shoulder after he had donned the haversack, after he had tied the ends of the roll with raveling twine.

. . . Coral, she'd say some day, what went with that old green and white quilt? Don't know. Hain't seen hide nor hair of it.

He found his old canteen, also *U.S.*, and filled it with milk.

Canteen, blanket roll, haversack. *Foooorward, ha.* Jo Coppedge, Bunny Teasley, Kyle Leftwich, Darius Voyles. Gettysburg, Chancellorsville, South Mountain, little place name of something or other where they camped one night and where Darius Voyles shot himself through the heart because he was careless with his gun and forgot to draw the charge. *Foooorward.*

Once more Coral smiled his shameless smile. He recalled community gossip at Uncle Arch Yeoman's.

—Yes, sir. Put you in jail.

—Worse'n that. Reckon they can hang you or shoot you.

—Says so in the lawbooks. Petey Rooks was a-telling me, and he can read, and he seen it plain in print. They call it giving aid and comfort to the enemy; and him who disobeys that law is liable to get himself hanged by the neck until dead. So Petey says.

So there was a law, was there? . . . Hang him? By God, he was a hero, kind of man senators and such talked about when they were speechifying. . . . He'd say, O.K. (Kind of speech he'd picked up when they was invading against the North: it meant, All right, mister, that's so, that's true, that's right with me, or something of that nature.) O.K. What you mean to do? Hack the other foot off'n me?

Nazareth Stricker. It *did* sound like Bible talk.

Coral, reared in a godless home, if he could have been said to have been reared, and if it could have been called a home— Coral knew naught of the Scriptures. Lot of the boys in the army were mighty Scripturalish. Preacher came around sometimes, a-praying . . . and then, they sang hymns too. Jo Coppedge came from a farm up in Bibb, and he said his old man was a deacon of the church. Jo knew right smart about Saviours and Apostles and Testaments and such. He said, Cory, I'd admire to open the portal for you and make you see the Light. If'n you should go to your doom, Godless and in sin as you dwell, you will suffer in Eternal Torment forever and a day. *Cepting you Believe on Me thou shalt not be Saved.*

Well, now, what about them Yanks? Reckon they Believe?

That hain't the point, Cory. *Him that hearest on the Word and Believeth Not, and Accepteth Not, him also shall be Crucified alongside of Me.* Or something like that. What my Pap always says, and I reckon they don't come no more Godlier than he.

Aw, Jo, go pound salt up your butt.

But that Nazareth was a— Was a— By God. That was it. Nazareth was one of those Apostles or Disciples that Jo Coppedge was always talking about when he got going on religion, dad fetch him.

And there was that boy name of Apostle, got killed— Where? Got killed someplace or other, when they were tearing down that rail fence in front of their lines, acting as skirmishers. Yank shot him with one of those fancy long-range rifles, maybe had a telescope on it. Apostle Epperson. That was his name.

. . . O long dead burnt dried pastures with no herds feeding, O long tall bristly woodlands with winds converging, O dead dark chilly swamp with wind seeming to lift and sustain itself amid higher dignified trees and not coming low enough to riffle the water in solid black pools.

—Hey.

—You still laying here on this log? Them catch-dogs come along, going to grab you sure.

—Hey. God damn Yank! You want some rations?

The voice repeated the word, the voice said dully, Rations, but the wild blue eyes did not open to glimmer at him.

Set up, dad blast you.

Naz Stricker twisted into a sitting position, his eyes opened and he glared about. The first thing he saw was the haversack beside him from which Coral fished a wad of soggy newspaper. The wet paper fell apart, peas and hog jowl splashed in a mass upon the mossy bark of the log. Naz Stricker gave a cry. His single hand came shaking forward, turning itself into a claw as it came. The glinting eyes touched Coral Tebb's face in disbelief and then lowered again.

Well, you said you'd eat anything!

The claw dipped into food, peas and grease were dripping, the claw reached the mouth, a gnarl came from shrunken depths of Stricker's throat even while his jaws clacked together and he made sucking sounds.

Reckon all you damn Yankees eat just like hogs.

Stricker wept while he chewed. Tears drained down over his blackened cheeks, they could not wash the grime coated there, they licked over grime and kept sliding. He blubbered between his bites.

This here canteen's got milk in it.

The Yankee wailed in disbelief. Milk?

I hain't a-storying you.

Stricker tried to remove the cap from the canteen with his one hand. Oh, God, Fumble Buttons, cried Coral in annoyance. He took back the canteen, unscrewed the cap and let it dangle by its rusty chain. He pushed the flask forward and Stricker's dried lips opened trustingly. Coral had a dim thought of a baby seeking its mother's breast . . . he held the canteen, tilting it gradually as the weight lessened, and the Yankee's dark thin neck twitched with contractions of swallowing.

Needn't take it all to once't. It hain't all the milk in the world. Just one canteen-full, you hog.

Nazareth Stricker munched pork, potatoes, pone; he ate the rest of the peas, he scraped them from the log with dancing fingers. Throughout the madness of this meal he kept making little chirrups and moanings. Tears still flowed.

God damndest bawl-baby ever I see. Do all you Yanks bawl like that?

I don't know, mourned Naz Stricker, I don't know. But his shrunken stomach could not accept this load, could not retain it for long. He began to retch, his whole body was torn with the struggle, his shoulders went into spasm, he turned and bent away across the fallen tree, and lost everything while Coral sat scowling.

Too much, said Stricker when he could speak again, too much.

You hadn't no call to go a-wasting it.

Know what?

What?

The Yankee spoke with the astonishing vigor of those stockaders who lay on the boundary of death. Men scarcely able to wiggle their fingers had at times crawled up and belabored each other with clubs; yet within hours they were collapsed, they were cold.

In the stockade there's fellows go around—hunting for the stuff that—other fellows have thrown up. And what's passed—through them. Passed through their bodies.

What they want to do that for?

To eat it, you damn Rebel!

Don't you call me no damn Rebel!

Guess you are—are one, aren't you? Or *were?*

They sat staring; and it was as if the food which Stricker had wolfed and then rejected— The food had, in some odd way and in a matter of minutes— As if it had given him strength. He emerged from the status of a beast into the ranks of humanity.

If they do that, said Coral Tebbs at long last, then they got mighty dirty ways. Like a bunch of birds after horse-apples.

Reb—what's your name?

Coral Tebbs.

Did you say *Coral?*

Yes, I said *Coral.* Hain't I got a right to my own name? Here I go fetching rations to you, and right off you start making mock of me.

I wasn't making mock, Coral. It's—kind of—unusual—for a name.

Well, so's your'n.

'Twas my father's name before me, and my grandfather's.

Coral imagined Naz Stricker's father and grandfather, he saw them as bearded Pennsylvanians peering dumbly from red farmhouses, watching in alarm the Confederates' advance, fearful for safety of their livestock; well might they be fearful.

How's your belly feel, Nazareth Stricker?

Feels better. Might— Could I have some more milk?

Coral offered the canteen, but this time Stricker held it for his own drinking. He stopped suddenly, lowering the canteen and saying, Don't you—want any?

I done made a meal.

Stricker ate again, he ate more slowly, there was painful leisure in his approach to the morsels which remained. He ate half of a boiled potato, two more scraps of the fried pork; he looked at the large chunk of corn pone which was left, then stuffed it inside his shirt.

I got some pie, said Coral.

I can't believe— Ain't any pie on earth.

Oh, yes, there is, and Coral exhibited in triumph the great crushed chunk of it.

Stricker shook his head wearily. Wish I could. But I can't.

Well, keep it safe till you can, said Coral gruffly.

Already, and in this limited acquaintanceship, a meeting of witches, Nazareth Stricker showed himself as a soldier. A thing was there: it was for him, he took it. A thing was not there: he went without. He did not pry and examine, he did not query, he accepted. Coral Tebbs had not summoned him to a Stated Communication of the fierce new Lodge . . . the Lodge went into session, though no gavel fell, and a mystic unseen sentinel gave the requisite number of knocks on the closed door, and announced that there was a Brother who desired permission to approach. The Brother was examined, he gave the Grip (it was a Grip to be managed with but one hand or foot, or perhaps with no hands or no feet); he responded properly to silent questions; he was found to be a Mutilated Militant in Good Standing, or in Good Sitting.

You live around here, Reb?

Out yonder. My old lady's got a little place.

Your wife?

Naw, naw, naw. My Ma! I'm scarce eighteen.

I'm twenty.

Yank, you got the shakes again. Here, I got this blanket roll . . . tain't much of a coat but . . . and this here coverlid for to sleep in.

If I stay, the dogs might pick me up. But I can't move. Yet.

I got to think about some other place for you. I'll reason out a place. . . . Can't take you to the house; Ma gets too many folks come a-calling. And then Flory trots himself over sometimes from the stockade. He's in them Georgia Reserves. He's my half-brother, the little scut. . . . Naz Stricker, I had a funny notion.

Such as?

Oh, spose like that smoke was all around, there by that wheatfield, second day of the battle. We was coming up on you, and you was trying to shove us back—

Guess I had the—same idea, Coral.

What was you a-shooting?

Springfields. Regular bullets, paper-cartridge type.

Reckon that's what hit me. See, you could have fired, I could have fired, did fire, practically the same second.

It's—unlikely.

But it could have happened.

Yes. Could.

Yank, you live in a brick house? When you're to home?

Yes, I do.

Got one of them big funny barns out behind, sticking clean over the hillside?

No, we haven't much of a barn. We—live in a little town. We've only a stable and buggy-shed, and the shop. Out back.

What kind of shop?

Where Father works, and Uncle Asaph.

Asaph? Dad blast these Yankee names!

Father's fond of telling—how Uncle Asaph got his name. Twas a few days after his—birth—and they didn't know what to call him. He was having his didy put on him, and he—kicked out, like babies will. Kicked over a pewter cup, and it—fell on plates and things. So they fell, all—a-clatter. And my grandfather said, It says in—the Book of Chronicles—it says, Asaph made a sound with cymbals. So we shall call him Asaph. You see?

I don't see no way. What they make in that shop?

Coral, I'm—tired. Want to go to sleep.

Then get back in that brush, where you was when the hawk fell down. Here. I'll help you fetch this stuff.

They staggered and mauled their way to the center of the thick-clad little island.

You—asked me something.

Oh, twas just talk.

Asked me what they make in the shop. And I—used to help. I—grew up in the shop. Ask me again, Coral.

Well?

Ask me—again.

I'm a-asking.

They make feet. And legs. Legs and feet.

Coral Tebbs crowed wordlessly.

As God's my witness!

Oh, they do, do they? They make them any hands too?

Usually just—hooks. But Squire Barth lost his hand in a sawmill, and they made him—a hand. Just for show. Twon't work. It's got a glove on it, with the fingers kind of—folded. Natural as life. But twon't work.

Coral Tebbs sat talking with Naz Stricker until the Yankee, a thin bent ragged seed within the pod of coat and comforter, became voiceless. His breath blew out noisily as he slept; Coral watched him; sometimes he gargled and groaned and gave little squeaks; once he said something about Uncle Asaph. Coral watched him for what seemed an hour, it might have been longer. Then Coral made his way home and dropped exhausted upon his bed and found his own sleep, disturbed by nightmares as was Naz Stricker's slumber. One trip into the marsh, a trip home, the trip back to the marsh, laden with haversack and blanket roll, his crutches slipping and catching . . . he had fallen twice, with those burdens . . . the trip back home again.

But in the middle of the night he sat upright, eyes staring into gloom, ears hurtfully alert. Dogs. The dogs were out. That free running pack, bound to hunt Naz Stricker in his lair, the catch-dogs bound to seize him when trail-dogs had smelt their way to the island. Then Coral laughed hoarsely, and lay back, head cradled under his arms. The dogs were over east, winding and tracking and baying across the Claffey plantation. Some other escaped prisoner must be their immediate quarry, not Nazareth. And it sounded as if the dogs were a solid mile and a half away from that sacred island, and going farther all the while. Coral reached out, got this trousers, found his plug, bit off his chew, and worked the spittoon out from under the bed. He propped himself comfortably on the bed, wishing only that his shoulders would not ache so strenuously, gnawed as they were by merciless wooden jaws of those crude crutches. Faintly he heard the music box playing in The Crib, and smiled to hear it, but he could not pick out the air. Those were all old foreign tunes on that spindle—someone had said that they were German tunes—and Coral did not know their names because the list pasted inside the music box lid was long defaced, and anyway the list was printed in a strange higgledy-piggledy script, and anyway he could not read well.

Zoral woke up in the next room and said, Maw.

She ain't here.

Mawwww!

She's over to The Crib, you blame grasshopper!

Jink.

Well, if'n you want a drink you come get it your ownself.

Jink.

You heard what I said, you Zoral. I ain't toting no water to you, not this night. You're big enough to wait on yourself. I hain't your nigger.

It was doubtful whether Zoral understood half of what was said, but finally he came into the room, trotting slowly, and made his way to the water bucket, and drank deeply, squinting over the gourd at his half-brother while he drank. Then trot, trot back through the shadows; and a train went past, and again Zoral started to make train sounds until Coral roared at him to shut up.

Coral considered the swamp, and considered Naz Stricker, and thought of the Union army coat and the green and white comforter, now touched with muck, but covering Naz Stricker, shielding his weak body, helping to keep warm the wizened stump of his left arm. He thought of Flory, and his grin spread. Flory would puke. Thirty dollars a head . . . Turner and his dogs, Harris and his dogs . . . Captain Wirz, sir, I got this here Yankee. Give me thirty dollars, please . . . Coral slept.

. . . But awakened once more (and long after the widow's callers had departed, and after she was bugling in the next room) to take notice of his own confusions, recollections and the hard stolid body of a single ambition which stood like a segment amid these other riffraff. *A foot.* Nazareth Stricker—in awful weakness, but mumbling still the answers which Coral sought—had said that they used special kinds of wood. One kind came from some foreign land, and it was light but strong, not weighty to tote around. It was costly. Couldn't find any wood like that around here. But— Gum, tupelo, oak, pine, magnolia, haw? Sure enough, what about haw? Coral could— No, he couldn't. He couldn't cut down a haw tree by himself. But he might go over to the Claffey place and say, Mr. Claffey, sir, it might be that you're pestered with chicken hawks? Well, I aim to rid you of them hawks. Set out still as a stump until Old Hawk comes, and then blast the daylight through him. But— Mr. Claffey, sir, if'n I'm successful a-doing it, it might be that one of your niggers could cut down a tree for me? Teeny little tree, not much account? That'd be one way to get haw-wood, if haw-wood could serve. Maybe peach, maybe apple? Ma had a rolling pin made of apple.

The rolling pin took him on the trail of a more magnificent idea. He saw a kind of rolling-pin thing, sticking up out of grass. Saw it clearly. But where? . . . It was in dry grass and blackberry spines, over next door on the Granny Rambo place. Granny Rambo's house had burned down, burned to smithereens, the winter before Coral went to the army. Folks thought she must have put hickory in her fireplace, and hickory sparked like mad, and maybe that was what caught the bedclothes afire, and Granny sick beneath them. Black smoke boiling high, and men flocking with yells from the railroad train when they came past and saw the smoke and stopped to fight the fire. There wasn't much use a-fighting it. They dragged Granny out, what was left of her, and got out a few pieces of furniture; then the roof caved in, and the woodshed and old smokehouse burned up too. Nothing left standing on the place except the privy with blackened pines towering sad beside it. . . . It was there that Coral had seen that big kind of rolling-pin-shaped apparatus, sticking up out of the weeds.

And the privy.

Nobody went there; no longer was there a path; the fence was down, hungry whips of berry vines extended over the deserted soil and made new bushes like a barrier. And you couldn't see the privy from the railroad, couldn't see it from the Tebbs place.

You needn't worry about black people straying in that direction, for all of them believed that Granny Rambo walked the jungle which had been her dooryard for twenty-odd years, walked at odd seasons and in odd guise. . . . Saw her in her bonnet. She had that old shawl a-folded across her shoulders. She had a basket on her arm. She walked young as once she had been, with golden curls showing, and in a white gown, and she carried her youngest child in her arms. She walked old, she leaned on her cane, her face was hateful and hating.

To tell the truth, Coral Tebbs had first heard these tales when he returned in the fall of 1863, and had more or less believed them. But his honest memory of Granny Rambo was of a gentle little body who made gingerbread men to give to hungry children when she had the wherewithal. He did not believe that she would actually harm a soul, whether she walked or whether she didn't.

He wondered if Naz Stricker was afraid of ghosts.

Nowadays Coral himself feared few things. Scorn or pity directed at himself: these he feared and resented. And he was afraid of bad dreams, echoes of *nrrrr-whuck* and himself hooting under the knife and saw.

Coral had another nap (brief deep rewarding nap, a soldier's sleep). He went prowling round the yard in the first hollowness of dawn. Maybe it was warmer in the swamp than it was here, warmer where wind could not reach so easily. He searched in ordinary places: in the broken hogshead lying on its side; in a mouldering wagon box; he searched behind sheds and under dry vines, he peeked at nests of leaves and straw and pine straw. No one had gathered eggs the previous evening, or possibly for two previous evenings, so now he found eight eggs. Coral built a tiny quick fire under the kettle and boiled all of the eggs. Zoral awoke and came running out in his shirt, he dripped lather as a dog might drip. Coral gave him an egg, and gave him corn bread. Coral was kind enough to offer milk to this loathsome mite as well, but the milk had turned sour, and Zoral upset his mug on the floor. Coral struck at the child but missed. Zoral fled shrieking to his mother's bed. The Widow Tebbs awakened.

What you doing up so early, Coral?

Going a-hunting.

What you going to hunt?

Just a-hunting.

What you cooking?

Hen-fruit. I collected— He looked into the pot. Collected five. I give one to Zoral. He spilt his milk, the little bastard.

Coral, don't you talk so bout my baby boy. You saving an egg for me, sonny?

Saving two. There was five. I et two.

Well, thank you for a good boy, Coral, she said drowsily, and soon was raucous in her snoring once more.

Again Coral packed the haversack: three boiled eggs for Naz Stricker, more pone, the last of the cold potatoes, the last slab of cooked pork. He shook the empty canteen . . . the balance of that milk was no good, but wasn't there some wine in that keg yonder? He remembered that his mother had bought a cask of wine for future hospitality. Scuppernong wine, but just about the worst ever made. Coral opened the spigot and tasted, and made a face. Sour and muddy into the bargain, but it would be better than nothing for the invalid Yankee, so he filled the canteen. He left the house finally, weighted with shotgun and ammunition. These he hid as soon as he was out of sight, he wasn't going to lug them to the swamp, he had no intention of hunting. In highest excitement he made his way through the forest . . . it seemed that the gray world was grown immaculately bright, promising bounty, promising varieties of wealth. Coral chanted quietly as he went; he could not sing well, but he chanted. Only the few stark birds and field-mice heard him. *O baby, O baby, I've tolt you before, just make me a pallet, I'll lay on the floor.*

Nazareth Stricker had built himself a house; he said that he scratched it to-gether in the late afternoon after he came from stupor. He was not able to tell Coral that he had been nerved as much by unexpected charity from a foe as by the few nourishing juices which strayed into his body; no more would Coral have been able to countenance the thought consciously; yet in secret fashion each youth was aware of the benefit offered, the goodness prevailing and digested, the warm human treasure accruing to the pair of them. Naz Stricker had drawn light twigs and flakes of old moss into a pile amid which he'd nested in the quilt. Overhead hung the cowl of the torn raincoat, held aloft by broken sticks, serving as cape and shelter tent. Naz said that he had been truly cosy for the first time in— For the first time in a long time. He thought that he had never been so cosy before. He remembered—but, again, could not tell Coral—that in sudden frantic awakenings he had felt a horror at the soundlessness, the detachment from that race of noisy monsters amid whom he'd dwelt. And then, throbbing through lone blackness and past a twitch of branches and the night cry spoken by some bird or animal, Nazareth had heard the ticking of the mantel clock in the kitchen-living-room at home. On this first occasion of his long separation from home, he had heard it. He had heard a doctor's buggy rattling away down Lilac Street, he had heard his eldest sister talking in her sleep in the next room as often she talked, he had heard and felt his shepherd dog Buchanan changing position under the bed. He had whispered, Buke. Good Buke. You want to go out? Go to sleep, Buke. Then he himself had gone floating, unhurt, unstarved, master of time and distance, loved.

Nazareth Stricker ate eggs and pone, he said that he would save the potatoes and the bit of meat and the rest of the pone, he drank greedily of sour wine.

Don't you go drinking too much all to once't. Twill put you flat.

I've been drinking this water beside the island.

Swamp water! No good for your innards.

It's better than in the stockade—much better. Cepting for the spring.

You got a spring in there? I mean, you had—?

It busted loose last summer. They said God broke it free of the ground. It was good water, but I only had a little cup—practically doll-sized—and then I'd have to stand in line again.

Yank. You feared of ghosts?

Nazareth Stricker said judiciously, I never met any.

You mind dwelling in a privy?

Would it stink?

No, it's mighty old, no smell left.

Couldn't stink as bad as the—stockade. Whose privy is it?

Next place to our'n, but everything else got burnt; and tis told that Granny Rambo goes walking there, but I hain't never seen her, and I don't reckon she'd hurt a flea. Naz Stricker, you tolt me about that queer kind of wood they used for legs. What might be its name?

I can't remember. It came by ship from some tropic port. Pa couldn't always get hold of it.

Could you make me a foot?

Me with my one hand?

Reckon I could help. Reckon I could hold things, and turn them, and cut, and shave away, if'n I was showed proper.

Stricker meditated on this. Finally he said, It's a question of tools and materials. Up home in Pennsylvania we had everything: Pa and Uncle Asaph have got a turning lathe they work with a treadle, and we've got tools galore. We fill orders from— Oh, New York, Philadelphia, Baltimore, places such as that. Guess Pa and Uncle Asaph are now rushed to death, what with the war and all.

He said later, Guess they think I'm dead.

Well, you hain't.

Guess I could try to make a kind of peg-leg-foot, granted we had the proper wood and some tools. With you helping. Let me see your—leg.

On no other occasion had Coral displayed his stump to anyone as an exhibition, as a deliberate act. His family had seen the thing necessarily in their intimacy . . . his mother crooned about it until Coral shouted for her to keep still. Once the exasperated Flory called him Old Stumpy-Stump, and that time Coral's crutch caught Flory between the shoulders and like to busted his back. Floral was nigh to knocked senseless. He blubbered in bed for a day and a half, and his back was lame for weeks. The Widow Tebbs beat Coral across the head and shoulders until she broke her broom, but he only sat laughing, saying repeatedly that he was glad he had not missed.

The amputation was effected about two inches above the nodule of his ankle bone at the narrowest portion of his left shin. Peel off the sock, you damn Rebel, said Naz Stricker. Meekly Coral obeyed, removing the dirty knitted woolen wrappings so that Naz might examine the stump. The flap had grown into place soundly. Naz Stricker pushed against the stump with his hand. Hurt?

Not too much.

Does it hurt, really? Sometimes my stump feels all a-quiver. Sometimes it feels like my hand—was still there. Then I try to grab something and can't.

Reckon I know. Same way. Oft I feel like I got a left foot.

Ain't it—funny? Both left? Funnier than if it had been me right and you left, or tother way around.

It's just as blame funny as all hell, said Coral Tebbs. The two of them engaged in a tittering laugh; thus they were no longer Entered Apprentices, they had taken the Second Degree of their Lodge. They were Fellow Craftsmen.

Coral, I'm no surgeon. But I've watched Pa fit feet—fit feet, and more often wooden legs. And he's made some of cork-wood, cork-wood that comes all the way from Spain and places. But it has to be braced within.

God damn it, can you make me a foot or can't you?

Guess I—we—could fashion a peg-leg-foot. Granted we had the makings.

Would it work?

Straps—would be hard to manage. The fastenings . . . twould have to be thickly padded where the stump fits in. . . .

I said, Can you or can't you?

We'll see. That was all that Coral Tebbs could get out of him.

That day Nazareth Stricker lived on potatoes, pone, wine and the scrap of fried meat. He regretted the waste of food on the previous day, but was too much of a philosopher to torture himself idly with unhappy contemplations. He kept looking ahead, Coral had made him able to look ahead. Naz had slept well and in comparative warmth. Inside his skeletal frame the values of milk, eggs and other nobilities were enriching him. This night he might sleep with a board roof over his head for the first time since he had been hauled from Richmond to Andersonville (albeit a backhouse roof). His shrunken face turned into a black smile at thought of Granny Rambo's ghost. He had lain amid some thirteen thousand men while they died; many of them he had seen puffed to fierce proportions before they were removed from his sight; he had worked in the hospital, also he had been a patient there; he had worked Outside, he had languished Inside; and he should be afraid of Granny Rambo, he should recoil from fancied odors of an unused latrine? Were he not a philosopher he had never been able to crawl through the reek of the old hospital drain, to worm his cold wet way past shivering trigger-ready guards, to circle the stockade and embrasures so that folks might think he'd escaped to the east instead of to the west, to provide himself with pepper and to scatter it, to flounder in low places where the wet going was hard; and to collapse at last in wilderness, no matter how loudly the dogs sounded in other portions of this boundless Avernus; and then to have the hawk come toppling.

While in the hospital Coral Tebbs had traded a stolen watch for a broken pepperbox revolver and ten dollars in greenbacks. The money was long since spent, but he had managed to repair the revolver, and now it would shoot. Late in the afternoon he fired the revolver three times at a rusty codfish can and missed every time. Mag popped her head out of the house door and cried, You Coral, take care like I bid you if'n you go shooting at a mark, for Zoral's at play in the dooryard. Hell, he told her, I was firing towards the brush. Three revolver shots were the agreed signal for Nazareth Stricker to take up his journey, blanket roll and all. Naz must be established in the old Rambo privy before dark, because Coral could travel through brambles and ruin of the Rambo homestead only by daylight or in the edges of dusk. He could not travel there when it was black-dark.

Painstakingly the Yankee must walk his solitary path as directed: through the swamp to the sweet-gum thicket, off in a left oblique directly toward the tall twin pines which could be seen rising in the east . . . then, when arrived between the pines, he must scrooch down and work south until he reached the remains of a rail fence. That was the most dangerous part of his journey: the woods were open. But Coral had met not so much as a stray Georgia Reserve or a Negro through all his recent trips to the swamp.

Coral thrust the revolver in his belt and crutched leisurely behind a weedy brake as if bent on more target shooting; then he headed for the Rambo ruins as fast as he could travel. It was hard for him to negotiate the last fifty yards because of blackberry coils. He arrived at the privy cursing and scratched. He envisioned misfortunes—he saw Naz forgetting to scatter the last of his pepper, and thus he was pursued by the noisy hounds once more. Would Naz remember to cross the broken rails, and slink behind concealing dried-out vines until he saw the charred chimney on Granny Rambo's cottage site looming before him? Would he have sense enough to lie flat and motionless if he heard voices or the step of an approaching mule?

Coral pushed open the swollen door of the old bleached structure and nearly fell backward. Naz Stricker was lounging upon his rolled quilt.

Jesus God! You scairt the piss out of my bladder.

But ain't this the place? This backhouse—

Sure it's the place, but you ought to waited my signal.

You did shoot.

They had a lively discussion. It seemed that an hour earlier Nazareth Stricker had heard three shots and had started out. They did not know where the shots came from; Coral had not heard them.

Guards at Andersonville, said Naz. Guess they shot three more of our boys. Thirty-day furlough apiece.

They don't get that!

Devil they don't. Every time they shoot one of us.

God damn lie.

Well, said Naz judiciously, we won't get anywhere arguing about it.

Tangles grew high, the railroad was out of sight, so was the Tebbs place, so was any track traveled commonly by slaves of the region. Together the youths dragged an old plank and placed it across the privy holes, and on this the quilt and coat could be arranged.

Couldn't find much to feed you on, said Coral. He produced half a dozen raw turnips from the pockets of his ragged jacket.

These'll be prime, Coral. I'm fairly starved for greenery. Naz started gnawing.

Got anything left to wet your whistle?

I filled the canteen with swamp water on the way.

Reckon there's plenty water in Granny's old well. Tomorrow we can rig you a bucket. Too bad you can't build no fire, but smoke'd give us away.

So easily it became *we* and *us*.

Coral, two things I wish I could have. Strange things.

Like what?

A shawl and a bonnet. An old lady's bonnet. Maybe one of those big wide ones that hides the face?

Coral stared at him blankly until he saw Satan jumping in the splintery gaze of Naz Stricker's deep small eyes. Then their glee rose together. Coral laughed seldom, usually he only grinned when he was sardonically pleased. Now he brayed in a choking anguish which had not overwhelmed him since he was wounded. He said, Granny Rambo! Shawl and bonnet! Well, by Jesus, Yank, you shall have them!

He provided these articles of dress the next day but not without peril. He stole an old shawl which he had not seen his mother wear in years, and found a crushed bonnet in the barrel. The slats were bent, the bonnet was a tatter but it would serve. He was in the act of stuffing the booty into his haversack when he was pounced upon by Mag, who had been watching through the crack of the open bedroom door, and he had thought that she was asleep all the time.

Coral. What you think you're a-doing?

He felt dizzy, he felt his face go hot and then felt strength and color draining. Well, he said, sparring for time.

Set down on that bench. Look at me. Look at your Ma. What you up to, anyway?

Well, he said.

You got my shawl that belonged to Aunt Eliza; and half that ham is gone that was left this morning, and I don't know what's come with all the corn pone and leftovers. Who you giving things to?

Well.

You speak up and confess to your Ma, or I won't give you nary a cent for plug tobacco, not never more. Coral, you selling my property, maybe to buy drink?

Hell, you know I don't scarcely never drink. Makes me puke.

You tell me, or I'll get the lend of a cattle whip off'n somebody.

Well. I'm helping somebody.

Who you helping?

His glance, sly and mournful and shamed, came to meet hers. He looked away quickly. I got me a girl.

A girl? Whereabouts?

Back yonder in the swamp.

What's she doing there?

Living. I come acrost her whilst hunting. Member the day I shot that chicken hawk? Twas then.

Mercy on us. Where she come from?

Up Atlanta way. You know. All these folks wandering here and there, ain't got no home to go to, count of Sherman's army and them Yankee bummers. She tells how they burnt the very roof over her head.

Sakes. You never had you a girl before, did you? My sonny boy, my eldest, never did I think— Astonishingly the Widow Tebbs lifted her dirty frilled poplin apron to her face, then lowered it quickly. When I think of all the menfolks I've done entertained, and how I'm scarlet as they say, but I do love a-doing It— When I think about my own flesh and blood— First little Laurel with the boys a-slathering after her— And now you. Coral, you laying with her?

A mite.

Well, that dirty swamp hain't no place fit for a poor homeless girl. Coral, you go fetch her straight away to this house. She can sleep right here in your bed. Go fetch her as I bid you.

Ma, I can't.

How come you can't?

Cause she's black.

The widow fell upon him with open palms, striking blindly, vociferous but incoherent. Zoral, seated on a small vessel in the room beyond, witnessed the assault through the open door and stretched his throat in a scream. Coral was nearly overcome with amusement at the serious rage with which his fabrication was greeted, but he managed to ward off a few of the slaps, and at last had to slam his mother away from him. His arms had always been powerful if stringy of muscle; they had developed additional power through a year and a half of crutching. He did not wish to hurt Mag, he merely shoved her into a state of collapse on the floor, where she remained sobbing.

He took the haversack with him as he left the house. You know what the old saying is, Ma, he chortled over his shoulder. Man hain't a man till he's run a nigger girl down a cotton row.

Oh, sonny boy, sonny! Keeping a wench! Keeping a black girl—

He left her lamenting, and headed for the swamp, and eventually traversed a half circle through open woodland until he could come unobserved to the Rambo farmstead. You damn Yankee, what I suffer for the sake of you. The old lady caught me with this here truck, and she like to jump down my throat. I had to tell her I was keeping a stray nigger wench back yonder in the brush.

Nazareth's grimy face showed alarm. Think she followed you?

Hell, no, she'd never follow. Just set there and bawl.

Won't that yarn make a deal of trouble for you at home?

Hell, no, she'll just fret. And heap insults upon me, and then turn soft. Naz Stricker, I want to show you something.

Coral toiled away from the privy, manipulating his crutches slowly among vines. He began to circle the scraps of blackened timbers near the chimney. At first his search was unrewarded, but after much hunting he found the object he sought, the rolling-pin-kind-of-shape upon which he had seized in thought two nights earlier. It protruded from the wreckage, doubtless it had not been moved since the day when Granny Rambo died. It was a portion of the bed in which the old woman had been lying in her hour of doom. Foot-post or head-post, Coral knew not which. It was turned from a single length of timber, you could not tell what color the wood had been to begin with, you would know only when you cut it. The knob which had reminded Coral of a rolling-pin handle was about four inches in length, thrusting smoothly out from a larger column. Coral got down on his knees and tried to move the thing; he could not. Naz Stricker came to help him.

You ain't even quarter-witted. Never ought to stir from that privy by daylight.

Coral, you can't manage this alone.

Together they loosened the burned-off post (it was two or three feet long) and Nazareth cradled it until they reached shelter. The privy was only forty-nine inches wide: they would find that out when they came to measure. Naz kept a big broken crock in the corner to put his feet on when he slept; thus he made a bed in an L-shape, thus he slept in a foetal position. He declared that it was better than sleeping in Andersonville.

What say you bout this pole, Naz?

It's gosh-awful heavy.

But we'd only need a teeny mite of the thick part.

You're the one who'd have to lug it around . . . of course the core of it would be reamed out to accommodate your stump . . . it's stout enough . . . that'll cut like iron.

What nature of wood is it?

Could be teak or mahogany.

What's them?

From tropic lands. *From many an ancient river, from many a palmy plain.*

Hain't you smart with your rhymes and truck!

It's a hymn.

Don't care if it's a her. Where'd Granny Rambo ever get such like, to build her bed out of?

Devil knows. Doubtless twas carpentered by someone else, long ago. Take teak —some of the ships load it for ballast in the hold; and I've known Pa to buy bits in Philadelphia, where also he bought that other light stuff I can't remember the name of.

Naz, would this serve?

It'll be a chore. You'd have to get hold of tools some way.

Just you leave that to Granddaddy.

Harness and straps and padding will be a chore even worse, said Naz Stricker gloomily.

He was not at all sanguine about the prospect of success. That night, instead of dreaming about Home or dreaming that he was besieged by starvation and complaints and rotting men who labored after him with outstretched hands and swelling eyeballs, he dreamed he had contrived for Coral Tebbs not one wooden peg but two. Neither of them fitted properly. Coral's face grew darker and darker. He took his revolver and shot his mother—a neat but shrunken little white-haired woman, in Naz's dream. Then he shot Naz. Then he shot himself.

  . . . Mr. Claffey, sir.

Ira Claffey looked pityingly from the verandah, and limped down to shake Coral's hand. Coral, what can I do for you?

Like to beg the lend of some tools off'n you.

You shall have them. You look tired, my boy. Does your limb bother you greatly?

No, sir, I get around pretty peart. But I've studied out a way to make me a peg-foot; but we hain't got the needfuls.

Let one of my hands help you. Jem has learned some carpentry, and we have a work-bench here.

Prefer to go my own gait, said Coral stubbornly, sullenly.

Ira looked into the stern young beetling face, and wondered at the almost infernal intent he recognized. Come along to the implement shed, Coral. He reached for his keys.

Saw, gouges, file, other things which Nazareth had declared they would need. These Coral carried to the Rambo place; he carried the saw slung upon his back. He was eager to begin work immediately in the slight period of daylight remaining, but Stricker looked at his shaking hands and said No. Naz was wiser than Coral. Rome, Nazareth told Coral Tebbs, was not built in a day.

Hell no. Nor Atlanta nor Milledgeville neither. But Atlanta got *burnt* in a day, as you damn Yankees ought well to know.

Oh, pull that ramrod out of your ass, said Naz pleasantly.

Naz gained energy by the hour. When the Tebbs family ate high on the hog, as now, the widow paid old Simeon, the Bile Negro, to bring her a hand-cart load of vegetables from time to time. Yams, cabbages, carrots, kale turned sweetly tender by the frosts: these were piled on the stoops, front and back, in profusion. Naz craved these things even more than he enjoyed the ham which Coral had served to him that morning, and there were plenty of goober peas. In days to come Naz would munch on birds and rabbits which Coral Tebbs sought and roasted for him.

The following morning they set to work in earnest. Coral said that his mother had fussed at him but little . . . there was small opportunity to fuss, for men from the guards' camp appeared at sundown. Jollity ruled in The Crib. A railroad engineer came later, bringing liquor. Mag was sound asleep when Coral went to the Rambo site after breakfasting on ham and eggs; he brought ham and leathery fried eggs and fresh milk to his Fellow Craftsman.

Reckon she thinks I'm plumb silly bout that black wench.

Now, Reb, hush. We must fix a place to saw this post.

(A shame which seemed an unnatural figment of existence, when viewed in the light of his domestic surroundings, and his attitude toward them— The same shame which prevailed upon him in the army was active now when Coral spoke of his mother. He had said simply, She's a widow woman. . . . Guess your Pa left her well off? . . . Not too well. We contrive to get along.)

They broke a saw blade on the solid bed post in the first hour of labor, and Coral must needs visit the Claffey plantation again to express regret and to ask the value of the blade. To Ira Claffey's notion the blade had no value . . . it had a value far in excess of anything which Coral might offer in recompense. The saw's worth was beyond estimation in a land where no saws were manufactured except in some crude smithy. Ira found another heavier saw for Coral and watched the boy inch along homeward. Ira tried to envision his sons moving in the same road. He could not envision them. Sometimes he found it hard to assort their features, the individual characteristics of eyes, ears, hair-tufts. The sons blended together, distant, filmy, without voice, with only a hollow song rising, a mingling of drone and unidentified words as in a Mass heard long before in Mexico.

The peg-leg-foot constructed by Naz Stricker and Coral Tebbs resembled a potato masher with a short thick handle, and twin flat staves protruding from the masher portion. Achieving the necessary hollow space to admit Coral's stump was the work of tiresome hours—Coral holding, Naz gouging with his one hand until the fingers cramped; the peg jammed down between stones in the privy's ledge, Naz steadying, Coral gouging out the hard dry powder, powder of wood like the dust of metal. The thing was cumbersome. It had to be: there must be sufficient space in the socket to admit padding—padding soft but solid, and with an aperture tailored to the exact dimensions of the mutilated leg. It was no mean task for anyone to perform, and materials came to hand only as the fruit of ingenuity and long search . . . raw cotton found in an abandoned picking-sack, and ginned by the boys' own fingers . . . a flannel jacket which had been worn in turn by the Widow Tebbs's babies.

Coral, you might as well go soot your face, said Mag. You spend all your hours with that little black tramp.

She ain't no tramp, poor thing.

Who's she belong to, did she say?

Man by the name of—Puckett.

What? Some kin of Captain Ox?

I reckon not.

Whyn't you spend your sleeping hours at night with her, same as your waking hours?

Ain't really room for me and her in the tent I done made.

You mean to say you built her a tent? Out'n what?

Pine branches and old canvas wagon-cover.

Why, where'd you find canvas?

Corner of the loft of our stable.

Why, there ain't— There wasn't no canvas there!

Yes they was.

Mag found the supposed situation easier to accept than she had thought possible. Throughout her life she had seen innumerable yellow people large and small; there was a slave child in Americus pointed out as the spit and image of Mag's elder brother Claudey; often her callers boasted about their high jinks on the other side of the color line. Only trust, she thought, that the wench don't bear Coral a child here and now.

I low you might fetch her to the house, at that, the widow said reluctantly. Folks might think she was a servant of our'n; and she could help see after Zoral, and keep him off'n the railroad track when I lose sight of him.

Folks know we don't own no niggers.

Somebody could of left her to us, like in a will. Coral, you never did tell me what is her name.

Ah—Nazareth.

Hain't that a queer one.

Her old master was mighty religious, so she says. It's a religious word.

So tis. I recollect that Pa talked of Nazareth constant.

Dimly, when she thought of Nazareth at all, Mag thought of her not as kinky-haired Afric, but as a comely brown-faced girl with a soft voice and round small breasts. When rain boiled coldly against the sloping roof at night and made its *tunk-tunk-tunk* in pans spread around to catch leaks, Mag was glad that Coral had built a hut to shield Nazareth from the elements, and that she was well fed. Poor little critter, said Mag in the ignorant depth of her warm misshapen spirit.

The true Nazareth, doubled on his privy bed, sloped the oilcloth above him to ward off steady streams which raced through wide cracks of the structure. Oh, better than the stockade, he thought. Growing peace, the soundness engendered by unspoiled food and plenty of it . . . he stretched in them luxuriously, turned over on the other side, got himself wet in the process, put his feet where his head had been, his head where his cramped feet had been, readjusted the coat and lay sly and happy. He yielded to creature comfort as to a vice. For he knew, in any serious consideration, that he should be up and gone if he hoped to reach the Union lines in Florida or on the Georgia coast. Catch-dogs, straying past on the trail of some other fugitive, could find him here; they could tear the calf off his leg, as they had torn the calf of a man he knew as Frenchy in Andersonville. Frenchy was an unpleasant sight, brought back all reeking. People said that Wirz took a shot at Frenchy when he was treed but didn't hit him. Frenchy descended under threat of Wirz's gun, and then the dogs grabbed him.

Perhaps most of all Naz Stricker lived in fear that some wayfarer, feeling an ominous qualm of nature as he wandered the ragged fields, might spy that privy and decide to make use of it.

One day—it was a Sunday, and Coral was gone to Uncle Arch Yeoman's for tobacco and news—Nazareth sat with the peg-leg between his thin knees. Laboriously he was repacking wadding in the socket for the tenth time. As yet he and Coral had been unable to combine the necessary comfort and staunch support needed. Naz became aware of voices rising beyond the fence. How long the voices had spoken he did not know. Men's voices, and they were coming closer. Shivering as if with malaria, he peeped out and over a low place in the bushes. He saw two Negroes approaching steadily. One was long-limbed and ruddy, the other blacker, more squat. The taller carried a shotgun in his hands. If they continued on their present course they would reach the privy area within a few minutes. Nazareth could imagine the shotgun's blast directed against him, but was assured that he must act before the blacks came nearer. He arose immediately, snatched the shawl and draped himself, shoved the broken bonnet upon his head. His face was lost in scalloped depths of the bonnet. He dragged open the privy door and took slow step after slow step across the weedy area toward the chimney and blackened house timbers. He had turned his back toward the Negroes; every second he could feel shotgun pellets stinging through his carcass; then he heard a concerted cry and scampering, and knew that he was safe. He did not know how big Granny Rambo had been—that was a prime neglect on his part, not to ask Coral—but Naz concluded that she must have been of average old lady size, so he bent and shrank within the shawl. He reached the chimney and from its shelter he peered at the running Negroes. They were far across the briary field, scampering toward eastern pines south of the Tebbs place; the taller man held his gun on high as he fled silently with ungainly leaps; the shorter man lumbered behind, but neither of them looked back. Naz returned to the privy, removed his costume, and sat sweating in the chilly air. Alternately he was shaken by the quivering collapse of hysterical relief and by sheer youthful mirth. What a thing to tell Coral when he came.

Ira Claffey had considered driving to Americus to hear a sermon by Cato Dillard, but gave up the idea when Lucy took to her bed (she did this rarely, and then only when she was overtired and perhaps had caught cold). Harry, of course, was gone to the hospital. Trays were brought up and Ira ate eggs and fried mush with his daughter. Lucy had discovered a little diary she kept when a child, and she persisted in reading sections of this aloud to Ira; they laughed together, and wept a little in their hearts. Ninny came up and said, That Jem and Coffee ask please to speak with Mastah. She always spoke of her spouse as That Jem. Ira went down to hear their petition. Old Leander had already conducted one of his primitive services for the hands . . . the Claffeys had heard the songs while they breakfasted. Now the two younger slaves asked permission to desecrate the Sabbath with powder and shot. Ira doled ammunition out to them, presented the ancient shotgun which was kept especially for their use, and bade them stay within the requisite two miles of the plantation boundaries.

He returned to Lucy's room and read to her a chapter from the Confession of Faith, according to weekly custom. It chanced to be Chapter Twenty-one, *Of Religious Worship, and the Sabbath Day,* with its indirect castigation of Catholics in Section Two, and this they found dull indeed. Lucy fretted, and Ira read only as far as Section Six. He picked up the Bible, began to read the Twelfth Chapter of Romans, more to the Claffey taste. *Be kindly affectioned one to another with brotherly love . . . rejoicing in hope; patient in tribulation; continuing instant in prayer.* A hullabaloo broke forth among the people below, and looking down through the window Ira saw Coffee and Jem trotting into the yard in a state of excitement, groaning and voluble. Something wrong, he said in interruption. I trust they haven't shot someone's mule. He put the Bible aside and hastened downstairs.

Seed her, Mastah. We seed her!

What is the matter with you, Jem? Speak quietly—

Deed they seed her. Deed they did. Oh, oh, oh, oh— Jesus, Blessed Jesus, save us from the fury! With their eyes they seed her—

Coffee, stop making mischief. What did you see? Did you shoot somebody with that gun?

No, Mastah, never even *shot* the gun. But we seed her walking, like folks say.

Who did you see? I've a great notion to shake you, you lout!

Old Mistress Granny Rambo, a-walking and a-walking.

At her old place where she done burnt up!

Bonnet on her head, she come a-walking!

Mastah, we get down on our marrows and pray to the dear Lord, but she was plain!

They seemed terrorized beyond sanity. Ira reassured them, said that Granny Rambo did not walk, that they must have seen a buzzard flying low, that they must have seen a mule in the bushes. Ira introduced these suggestions firmly. Yet both Coffee and Jem were convinced that they had witnessed the ghost in broad daylight, and that was all there was to it. Ira took the gun from them (finding to his horror that Coffee had somehow managed to cock the weapon while in full flight) and persuaded them that if in fact they had seen Granny Rambo there was nothing baleful about her. She would not follow them home, she would not creep down their chimneys or carry off any children. As the people calmed he ordered Naomi to fetch cakes all round; she had baked a batch on Saturday, using substitutes for this and that, but the cakes were delicious and tasted of caraway and ground sunflower seeds. Soon the rest of the blacks were merry, twitting Coffee and Jem about their scare. The two slaves mumbled stubbornly with their mouths full of cake. In the end Ira was convinced that they had seen something other than an animal or a buzzard. God knew that they were familiar with both; and Ira had never observed them in such panic before.

He was mounting the stair when a thought made him halt, halfway up. Perhaps some dangerous vagabond was encamped on the deserted Rambo premises. Heaven knew that the country was filled with drifters; every town held its wounded; the hordes who had fled from Atlanta and other north central war-torn areas were not all people who could be taken safely to the heart of more fortunate communities. There was the natural modicum of prostitutes, thieves, uncertain and light-fingered wanderers of all sorts. Ira had heard rumors of stabbings, rapes, robberies; he believed that such crimes were an inevitable result of war's upheaval, but was determined to protect his own household and community insofar as he was able. Better have a look at the Rambo place. No telling who might lurk there.

He gave Lucy a description of the occurrence which she greeted with glee, but Ira made no mention of his own disquietude. Lucy thought that the slaves had suffered some infantile delusion. She and her father were out of the mood for Bible reading; Lucy did a little sewing, and sipped a glass of wine; then she said that she felt sleepy, and her father left her to the ministrations of Ninny, who came with a soapstone to place at Lucy's feet. Ira went downstairs, loaded a pistol and put it in his jacket pocket. He strolled idly down the lane, seeing only a few lounging off-duty soldiers along the way. It could be that a guard might have deserted, and was hiding out in the Rambo ruins. No, he would make tracks away from there. So would any prisoner escaped from the stockade. But better go and make sure.

Soon he approached the suspect area under cover of the gloomy chimney, working forward with caution, applying the best of his woodsman's facility to advance in silence. Examining the ground, he saw that weeds had been trampled and fresh vegetable rinds lay exposed. A shred of newspaper blew in the breeze. Edging closer quietly, Ira saw a heap of wood shavings and sawdust in front of the privy. He cocked the pistol; holding it ready in his pocket, he stepped to the door which flew shut with a shaking slam.

Ira said, Come out, or I'll shoot through the door.

Nazareth Stricker emerged, quaking and miserable, turned pale under the pitch which still dyed his skin.

Ira Claffey studied the youth, then took out his pistol and released the hammer. You frightened my people, he said. They thought you were a ghost.

Stricker was wearing his ruin of a cap with its corroded Second Corps badge. . . . After a time Ira asked, When did you escape from the pen?

Week or so ago.

Why didn't you travel farther?

Stricker was silent.

Where did you lose your hand?

Gettysburg.

. . . *It behooves their officers to be nonchalant, even to the point of suicide, in disclaiming any attitude which might suggest that they were not invulnerable to minié balls.* Did Suthy shoot off your hand before he fell? Ira asked it in his soul while his mouth said nothing. You were there. Did you kill my eldest? You were there.

How long have you been at Andersonville?

Came in with one of the first batches from Virginia.

More than a year.

Yes, sir, whispered Nazareth Stricker.

I don't understand why you squatted here.

Well, I was—tuckered. And a fellow gave me rations. And—

Who gave you rations?

A keen blue blaze shot from Stricker's deep eyes. Won't tell, he said.

Ira looked past the youth's legs and saw familiar objects scattered on the privy floor and leaning against the inner wall. Those are my tools. He understood before he spoke the words, he understood still more as he uttered them. . . .

What mockery of battle now remains to be fought? Ira inquired of himself. The *Albemarle* was long since destroyed. It was weeks since the news of Fort Fisher had turned souls to lead. Ira wondered if smoke still drifted from the ruins of Columbia . . . and General Preston, of the Bureau of Conscription, announced that at least one hundred thousand deserters had slid from the ranks of the Secessionist army. Aleck Stephens was said to have crept home to Crawfordville; people said that Early's forces were whipped and scattered; Sherman was striding through North Carolina; it was told that Lee might withdraw the defense of Petersburg at any moment, and retreat toward Lynchburg. A man found his way down from Richmond; he reported troops rattling purposefully about the streets of the capital, impressing every horse they could find. They were impressing horses in order to collect the stores of tobacco: one shred of wealth left to the Confederacy. They would burn that tobacco if the Federals entered Richmond — *When* the Federals entered Richmond—

Well, sir . . . Naz Stricker discoursed in monologue, and why should Ira care to listen to him? Whyn't you get it over with? You got a pistol. Whyn't you march me back where I belong?

In the end Claffey told him, Hold your tongue, my boy. He pushed past Stricker, looked into the little structure, and found what he had expected to find: the peg-leg-foot with cotton protruding from the cavity.

You've been making this for Coral. A hard task, one-handedly.

Oh, God. I must have given him away!

No, no, you didn't give him away. I'm Neighbor Claffey from across the way— I've known Coral since he wore skirts. He borrowed these tools from me.

Nazareth sat down on the privy step, folding his arms across his knees, hiding his face so that Ira could not see him as he cried.

Brace up, lad. You're not going back.

The gaunt face came up, greasy with tears, mouth sagging in disbelief.

Twould be tantamount to murder, said Ira sharply.

He stood for a few minutes, scrutinizing fields and woods to make certain that no one else was near, and then he ordered Naz back into hiding. He took Stricker's place upon the step and sat examining the peg, asking many questions which Stricker answered haltingly, lugubriously. It was obvious to Claffey that the boy must doubt him still. Small wonder. The smell of the stockade flowed around him suddenly, as it had drenched over Claffey acres for so long. Ira closed his eyes and shook his head; and then realized that he had done so, and thought with weak amusement of how Lucy would crow could she see him.

Where did you think to get the harness? he asked of Naz Stricker. The straps?

Coral thought his Ma had some old shawl-straps.

Those would never serve. Tell Coral that I have taken the thing home with me, when he comes. Do you both wait here for me, and keep out of sight. There may be other hunters abroad, for this is the Sabbath.

Ira added with grudging humor, And I should advise no more masquerading as Granny Rambo, in the bonnet and shawl which I saw there. The next person might shoot before he ran away.

He arose heavily and stood turning the contraption in his hands. We are whipped, he told the world.

Nazareth stared from concealment with a veteran's challenge. Guessed that you would be, from the first. You could never beat the Union.

That is now apparent. But all three of my boys died a-trying.

I'm sorry, sir, Naz muttered.

How sorry are you indeed? Ira wondered as he went toward the plantation, carrying the peg-leg. But the enfolding humanity which his own torture had instigated would not be denied; he must perform this charity, perform it in the face of law and military conscience.

It occurred to him before he reached home that Badger or Moses, invalided home from the army instead of turned to bones, might have done the same thing. Suthy . . . no . . . Ira feared that Suthy might have remained stiff-backed to the last.

How far off was—the last?

He went to his work-bench and finished repacking the padding in the socket, conforming carefully to the shape which the fugitive young Yankee had said must be retained. Painstakingly Ira upholstered the broad-headed tacks so that none of them would abrade Coral's hide. He cut strong straps of soft leather, and fastened the buckles into place, and punched the holes . . . one strap encircling the leg immediately below the knee, and fastened firmly to the staves; one attached to soft harness and encircling the leg immediately above the knee. That must be the way of it, Nazareth Stricker had said in his apprentice's erudition. It seemed odd to be performing a service for a wounded Yankee and for a wounded Confederate in the same act and in the same breath. Ira wished that he might make a hand for the Yankee boy; but—God knew—if the youth reached the Union lines safely he might in time acquire a hand of sorts.

There came only Jonas, seeking a whetstone, and he gazed in curiosity. What you do with that thing, please, Mastah?

It's a peg-leg for Coral Tebbs. He's done most of the work himself.

That poor young cripple soldier-boy, said Jonas.

In the afternoon, having disregarded his mid-day meal, Ira carried the artificial limb back to the Rambo site, lugging it in a grain sack. Coral Tebbs, scowling and frightened and sulky, was there with Naz Stricker. Like the other boy he found it difficult to believe that Ira Claffey would award such traitorous benevolence. Coral thought that if he were Ira he should wish to kill all Yankees in wholesale revenge. Ira had not lost a limb, he did not belong to the Lodge, he had not been fighting at that wheatfield place. Ira recognized their mutual attitude but said nothing in explanation, because he could not explain the whole thing, not even to himself. He could not say, Yes, once I too was a soldier. In Mexico. I was wounded painfully; I thought that I would lose my leg; for years I had to tie dressings about the wound each day, and let them fill up, and throw them away; until at last a surgeon's probe brought out the remaining loose bits of bone, and those bits had turned black as coal.

To be frank with himself, this was all beside the point.

Coral sat inert while they strapped the thing.

Don't become too ambitious all at once, mind! Ira added, Your knee is weak, your leg shrunken from disuse. You must go slowly. Use your crutches at first.

On a level patch close to the burnt relics Coral crutched solemnly back and forth, putting the heavy peg down cautiously, lifting it again, resting more and more of his bodily weight upon the stump. It caused him a degree of pain . . . it would all take time, but Naz Stricker had warned him of this again and again. Tentatively Coral slid his crutches out from under his arms and used them as canes to hobble with. Oh, the peg was heavier than he had thought it would be; he hoisted his leg in labor, he perspired, but persisted as in a trance. At last he stood in the lowest weeds, resting his entire weight on his good right foot and on the spindle thrusting down from his left leg. He spread his arms wide, and dropped the crutches from his hand. He stood crutch-less for the first time since he was wounded. His black eyebrows rose up. I'll be dipped in shit, he said.

Ira forgave him the vulgarity, he would have forgiven him anything. He turned away and busied himself with the grain sack he had brought. He produced some of Moses's old clothing: jeans trousers for wear in the forest, a rough brown jacket, a shirt and shoes and socks (the shoes were Badger's; Naz Stricker's feet had appeared to be more the size of Badger's), an old black hat.

I'd get out of this, he told the Yankee, as soon as possible. Wait for dark, then travel the railroad. There were guards at the bridges, but I hear they've been removed. But take care; it might have been false information.

Sir, I don't know how to thank—

Coral and I have our secret . . . it won't be long . . . as I said before, we are whipped. Ira repeated it under his breath. Whipped, whipped, whipped. Beaten down.

He took a fold of currency from his pocket. Fifty dollars Confederate. All I can spare. We are very short of cash these days. But it will help you to secure food.

Sir, God bless you.

Ah. He moves in a mysterious way . . . you know the song?

Yes, sir. Used to sing it up home in Pennsylvania.

Goodbye, my boys.

They mumbled their farewell, they stood united and wondering. Ira went home and found that Lucy was sleeping the afternoon away, she had not rested well during the night. But were she awake she might not have appreciated the texts which Ira pondered over in the library. Ruin was here, but she was young, she had a love.

The field is wasted, the land mourneth; for the corn is wasted: the new wine is dried up, the oil languisheth.

Be ye ashamed, O ye husbandmen; howl, O ye vinedressers, for the wheat and for the barley; because the harvest of the field is perished.

. . . Gird yourselves, and lament, ye priests: howl, ye ministers of the altar: come, lie all night in sackcloth, ye ministers of my God. . . .

Ira had no sackcloth, but he lay down all the same; he lay on the sofa and turned away from his dread past; and thought of the scrawny mixed future, but it was a peril, a bewilderment. He slept; he was lucky in having no dreams. He slept into the dusk.

You can always take to the woods, Coral Tebbs told Naz Stricker.

That's so. But I mean to travel by night solely, unless I come to complete wilderness.

Coral stood beside him in the dark. The two shapes bulked dangerously, some-times teetering close together, sometimes drifting farther apart as if washed by winds, though no wind stirred. It was chilly. A bob-cat made a kill in the distant swamp, and screamed in the process; a few scattered dogs preached their immedi-ate alarm.

Wish you could take this here haversack, but twould attract notice.

Why not? If you want to let me have it, Coral. I could be a Rebel soldier bound for home. Guess that's what I will be, though I don't much talk like it.

Then that saves putting spare rations in your clothes!

Coral passed the sack to Naz, and the Yankee slid the strap over his shoulder. Coral said, Looky, and Nazareth poked his head forward through the gloom to see the other youth poised on his true leg and his false leg, crutches upheld in his hands.

Don't you get too gay, Reb.

Shan't.

Coral.

What?

That Mr. Claffey gave me fifty dollars Confed. I'd like to go halves on that.

Coral Tebbs was strangling. Hell, I got Ma to see after me, and she's got enough and plenty. Right now, anyways. You'll need what little cash you got. Twill be slim pickings along the way, though I reckon niggers might help you. All they got in their heads these days is that cusséd Yankee freedom notion, dad blast them! And fifty Secesh hain't no fortune.

(He would say to his mother when at last he went to the house, Old lady, I fibbed my head off. . . . What you mean, you Coral? . . . Bout that wench. I didn't have no wench, I wasn't a-keeping no nigger girl down a cotton row nor no place else. Twas a Yankee, skun out of that stockade, and I've helped him away; and look what he made for me. . . . Coral! You helped a Yankee. You ought to be blown dead! My own flesh and blood, helping a Yankee! . . . Oh, shut up. Look at the pin he fixed for me! Week hence I'll throw these God damn crutches to the crows.)

Guess I'll get along.

Their hands trailed through the night. Long would Coral feel the clasp on his own hand, long would Naz Stricker poke his way southward, choking as he went.

Look out for Home Guards, you bastard Yankee.

Don't stick that peg of yours down a gopher hole.

Now I just won't.

Very softly, *Foooorward*— They parted.

At first each could hear the crunching pace of the other, going away, soon they could hear nothing. Coral Tebbs toiled homeward. Emotionally he was profiting from war as some wise survivors profit. He had a dim notion of knights. When he was small he had looked long at a picture-book someone gave him, and there was a picture of knights carrying shields, with visors lifted to show their faces; he could not read the story, and no one had read it to him, but he remembered the picture, and it spread before him now in the lone cold black. Naz was a knight, so was he; oddly Ira Claffey joined them, and the dead sons paraded behind; so did Jo Coppedge, Apostle Epperson, Darius Voyles and the rest of the expired Rebels. He thought of the nigh-onto-thirteen-thousand dead who had been buried from the nearby stockade, or so Naz declared . . . they put on their mail and walked in his imaginings, even though they were Yanks and so to be despised. There was something in the concentration of death and peril which had occupied his young years, which quickened his sensitivity to a degree unbelievable. It was as if he walked stripped of flesh, tissues exposed, blood open to the night. No one might understand what he felt, he could not speak of it, there was no one to know.

He was only eighteen, for all the angry barbarous maturity which had become his through suffering. Release from storming emotion came to Coral. Crutches slipped, fell from his open clutch, he lay in burs and pea-vines in his mother's dooryard, kneading crushed little sheaves of wire grass in his large hands, sobbing, momentarily without hope. God damn it, Naz, don't go way. But Naz was gone with not even a star to lessen the night into which he walked.

57

The weather warmed for Lucy. Her father would not have wished that she go dreaming alone, nor would her husband. There were chores to be done . . . she knew that Pet and Extra would laze at tasks she had set them to, perhaps they might ruin the entire batch of summer candles, might forget to put in the beeswax. Lucy felt that she did not care. Again she had become a disobedient child, when in fact in childhood seldom had she been disobedient. Yet with the rest of humankind she found spice in the forbidden.

It was late afternoon. She went past cabins, over the rise and down the long gentle slope toward a steeper ravine of Little Sweetwater. Frogs were crunching in some low place already shadowed permanently, forgotten by the drifting sun. A breeze came; the young woman saw the brushes of each separate pine tuft painting erratically on far sky, never leaving paint to mark the sky. Soon Lucy's small shabby mended shoes were slipping among old cornstalks, stalks of a field now let go to weeds because there was not the strength within this population to work an additional field. The stalks were sad about it. How could corn stems—once firm, containing fluid—become so dispirited, leaning sodden? She wanted to say, Be of better faith, old plants. I feel sure that your descendants will one day push up proudly in this same place. There were relics of ancient cotton in an adjacent field; through all this time they had survived, as exhibits contained in a museum . . . through summers, the mass of rain coming down repeatedly, winter freezing stiff. Still they exhibited themselves amid more perishable reeds, and bitter flakes clung to the dry cotton plants, burnt to wire by age. In a swamp delicate new leaves had come out into the warmth—they were widening, showing red-lipped colors. Leaves on taller trees held the pale tender green of new pea-plants. It was a good season . . . one perspired when active, but grew chilly in breeze if jacket or shawl were removed.

O frogs in the swamp. How odd that there could be endearment and promise in such rocky stuttering. (Lucy's frogs were not of the variety which beleaguered Henry Wirz: frogs which jumped and ached in his miserable arm.) They were like water birds, and in solid dark of evening they would be speaking thin-voiced, high-pitched, their vociferous persistent wail and whistle would be suggestive of robins . . . early the following morning they would be calling still, even after chickens began to call, although the frogs' chorus would be thinner. Forever springs had affected Lucy Claffey, as one time she prayed that the promised beauty of religion might glorify her. Yet she could not find the same provocative majesty in contemplation of the Hereafter, or in God's works apparent. The teachings were favorable, they had value; they did not choke her throat as she was choked when she beheld brown-chocolate pads of water plants motionless on silent pools. . . . She went on beneath pines, down nearer the frogs. She was safe here from insult or intrusion, from any ugliness which her menfolks suggested might result from the proximity of a disordered ignorant undisciplined soldiery. In memory she was reminded of the night when she had flown from her

room, the white long-ago moonlight when she ran with Deuce the setter, and—
yes—she had told her father of that recollection many months before. They
laughed about it, then they went on to the cottage where Laurel Tebbs lay. Remembrance came gasping. Lucy closed her eyes momentarily and put her left
hand against a tree to steady herself, to draw sustaining quality from the ardent
life of that tree. She remembered clearly the dreadful room, the girl with puffed
face, the misery. She remembered how she applied the muscles of her hands to
squeeze alum, with mortar and pestle . . . and there was the business of the
syringe, the tall stooped man with queer face . . . how she had grown to love
that face!—then and there, amid that very intrusion, the shared intimacy. It was
an act symbolic of the dangers and disgust of the act of love when love was
perverted into cruelty. Thus people were made into beasts; some of them might
not wash off the stain. Lucy prayed in her heart that the color of that memory
would be washed in time from Laurel's parched little spirit. Then the young girl
might find such magnificence as overwhelmed Lucy now. It was a magnificence of
soul and body intermingled.

She invoked forces of generosity, she wanted all women to share a joy that
burst within her like the great verdant pain of Nature itself.

Did my mother feel that way when she was carrying me?

Carrying. Odd word, for the mite must be so tiny—but a bare speck, a speck.
Human, and therefore of God.

Of the Heavenly Kingdom. There is a Heavenly Kingdom here on earth. It's
embraced me, it stretches before.

In a thicket a cardinal grosbeak danced amid those twigs which would hold
him. He was wearing mating colors redder than raw flesh, showing zest which was
in him until the eyes hurt beholding as his song came out, sometimes squeezed,
sometimes spilled free and loose, he was aflame with song. He knew every flute
and lute and played them. He piped on intimate pipes other males might not
handle, blew a whistle other males might not know how to blow. You did not need
to remember his song consciously; because it stayed, suspended in air, after he
had whisked to last burning in other thickets.

Magnolias' steady green, back at the place, back at the place.

Before too long our child may run beneath them.

Other children may run.

. . . Am I wrong? She prayed, Am I doing a wicked thing in worshipping the
power of woods and of winds, power of the sexes? Is it disproportionate, my
intense savoring of these matters? Should I not set my mind more acutely upon
the matter of Godliness for my child to come? What am I—pantheist, hedonist?

Her soul laughed even while the original strictness of conventional early teaching was rejected. She had rejected it first in lying with Harry. She could not tell
which she loved the more: the original experience, or the recollection and frequent repetition thereof. A spectacle of bereavement and war stood taunting,
accusing also; but it had been there before, been there long, it was so wide-spread
as to have become meaningless.

. . . What of the South, what of my State? Poppy says we are going down so
fast. Why do I not cringe and cry, give myself up to perpetual weeping because of
the youth I loved as a girl, the brothers I knew and loved and lost, the mother who
went to ruin in dismal fashion? Yet those people are no longer thick around me,
they do not persist. It is almost as if they never existed in fact, but are now become
legend. Duty and respect and affection will cause me to teach them to the children borne in my body, once they are born from my body, once they have their

growing wits, prankish hands, fond eyes turning gladly to me for what sustenance I may give.

It has been so long-drawn a conflict, so degrading and caustic a war.

How many other wars have there been?

I cannot recite history, I do not wish to parrot knowledge previously gained.

I fear there will be more wars.

Yea, but there will be women alive then, as well as men. Strangely they may emerge from doom with lips still able to love, wombs still eager to receive the seed pulsed into them. Yea, I know this to be true.

True as God.

A blinding thought struck her. Perhaps this *is* God. These matters are what *make* God.

She turned and floated back toward the plantation. Feel like I'd been to church, she told herself. And how Uncle Dayto might knit his brows over such an affirmation!

A squeaking undercurrent of tiny unidentifiable birds—warblers, no doubt—hid ahead among mats of vines, danced their way north as she came on. Soon she would reach the black people's cabins, the dark life of blacks flowing. She would pause and appreciate the garden, look at bright lettuce; she would appreciate even crinkled leather of old collards standing tall beyond. There would be her flowers (she had so little time to spend with them). Yet perennials were hearty . . . there would be japonicas to dazzle. She would take a single japonica to put before Harry's plate, and say that she had found not a violet, and hoped that someday he would fetch violets to her.

Here, she thought. Her hand went up to touch the fine-spun hair. He loved me here, loved me and my hair. He has worshipped and gladdened my lips, nostrils. His strong fresh male tongue has played its game with the curl of my ear. My breasts, he has known them, will know them again. Our child will know them, more children to come will know them. And that other holy warm glistening orifice of my body—that province which we women guard as we would guard all—He has known that, occupied it well. He will know it again. Oh, dear God in Heaven—again, again. One day there will be a mighty pain, and the child shall emerge. Then my dear one may know me again . . . know me long, know me while life continues to run.

I have never set myself to be a prophet. Now I burn unseen incense in my ritual, cry my prophecy: this local ugliness shall cease. Shortly the last scarecrow columns will come dragging from the gate; wagons will freight out the last of the dead, wagons freight the last of the living. I'll be given a glory. To me will be awarded power of the conquering rescuing army.

Sakes alive, I shouldn't desire the power of *Yankees!* Yet I shall hold it, and with it release those cords which have bound a burden to the back of my brave dear one: a horny thorny pack of stench and wickedness will slip from his shoulders, twill thud and be forgotten. We'll love and cry and weep for joy and relief when it falls.

Sounds of the ragged forest fell behind her. I must know Nature better, she thought, far better than I do. For there's urgency waiting, the urgency of teaching my children.

Yet she knew that she might love Nature less if she knew her better. For, like the capricious woman Nature was, a portion of her enfolding charm lay in mystery.

Far overhead the pines were saying Hush in a determined admonition whenever long high wind moved against them.

58

Jonas found Ira Claffey in the implement shed and said gently, Mastah, please hear me.

With sinking heart Ira looked into the grave brown face, and noted how afternoon sunlight pierced through the open door and found silver in grubby twists of wool on Jonas's head; ah, there was more silver, more each month; Jonas was aging as Ira was aging, though Jonas was believed to be not more than forty. . . . Twice Ira had come upon the Yeomans' mighty Scooper talking to Claffey people with furtiveness. The second time Scooper made off nonchalantly when Ira approached (as if he had merely stopped to pass the time of day). Scooper was bound to be the trouble-maker in this particular neighborhood, just as there must be trouble-makers, thousands, scattered elsewhere.

What is it, Jonas?

Mastah, we wants to walk off.

Who is we?

Me and Extra, Mastah.

Do Jem and Coffee wish to go as well?

Don't know bout that. Spect maybe so, maybe not.

Ira had assembled the people in front of Leander's door a few hours earlier, after Cato Dillard stopped by to confirm the news of Johnston's surrender. Original impulse and lifetime habit dictated that Ira should cope with any unpleasant task promptly; he should slay or bury that which must be slain or buried; he must not keep a rabid dog on the premises, he must delve with shovel and quicklime when a monstrosity was found with birds above.

He said to the people, Our General Johnston has surrendered to the Yankees, which means that the war is practically over. A few bands of Confederates may hold out until the death; I pray that they will not; we are defeated by the North, by the Federal Government, do you understand? All three of the young masters are dead, as you people know—

Promptly they began to moan, and Old Leander, nearly blind, propped in a cushioned chair beside the door, announced that he had seen the young masters in the night; he spoke of raiment—

Hush, all of you! I am talking, you hear?

When the blacks had fallen silent, Ira continued: Your mistress also is dead. Miss Lucy may be here for a time, but I suspect that soon she'll remove elsewhere; thus I shall be alone. I have little to tempt me to remain here, myself; still it is my home, always has been, and I know not where else to go. Now, as to you people: you have been slaves all of your lives, you were born slaves, I had expected that you would die in bondage. But the Nationals say—and they have won, they have whipped the Secessionists, they have whipped Georgia, whipped *us*—

His voice broke suddenly. All the black women had their faces buried in their aprons except Extra; she was staring fixedly at Ira, eyes bulging, nostrils distended, mouth open and dripping.

He continued, The National Government says that you are free. You belong to no one except yourselves, and to God above. I may no longer order you about except as one man orders another because he is the supervisor, the boss; thus he orders him. But no longer as master and slave.

Naomi burst out with a shrill, But you *is* our mastah—

I *was* your master; no longer; the Federal law says that you are free, and now the Federal law prevails, it rules here. But I can still be your employer, and as my employees you may still live here as you've always done—dwell in the same cabins, eat the same food, live as you have done before. But now I must pay you wages.

There was a general beaming as they began to appreciate this statement. You pay us real money, Mastah? Cash money? We get hard money?

If you work for me, and do your work well, you will receive real money. But if you do not do your work well, done as I wish it done, then I'll get some other people to work for me, to live in the houses where you lived before. You will be turned out. I shall need to employ other people in your stead. . . .

Old Leander was nodding pontifically throughout and he said clearly as Ira paused: My children do work like you bid, Mastah. Yes sir, I *make* them do it. We all belong to you, like it say in Scriptures.

Ira said, I provided for you people, just as I provided for the many we had here before the war. You had no thought of the morrow; I thought of that for you. If you were sick, I doctored you myself; if I could do no good for you, and Miss Lucy could do you no good, then I fetched the doctor, and I paid him money to make you well. As with you, Jonas, when you broke your hip whilst lumbering; as with you, Coffee, when the cotton bale toppled on your foot long ago; as with Naomi and her tumor, and the doctor took it out and healed her. You were clothed and fed, fed better than most black people, even in parlous times. No one has ever gone hungry on my place. Is that not true?

True! It true! You good mastah, Mastah—

But now the law says that you must take charge of yourselves. If I am to pay you wages, then with your wages you must buy food and clothing; for I cannot afford to give you these things if I am to pay you money. If you ask me to give you meat and meal, shoes and stockings, then must I charge them against you. You are to sell me the work you do, and I am to pay you wages; if I give you fruit or corn or bacon or a shawl or a blanket, then I shall write it down in a book, each time, and I must show that book to officers who might come and wish to see it, to make sure that I am paying you wages as the law says. And— And I may not keep you on the place against your will! If one of you wishes to leave, he may go elsewhere. You are free men and women and children.

Old Leander declared feelingly that he didn't want any old Yankee law. He said that all this was none of the Yankees' business.

Ira's heart had gone from him as he spoke. Enough, enough, I can say nothing more; I cannot make them understand this thing which has befallen; indeed, do I understand it myself? I fear not.

He managed to tell them that he would explain further, when and if they wished further explanation; in the meantime he must examine his accounts, find out exactly how much money he had, how much he might reasonably expect to make off the plantation, and thus what wages he could offer; and if he said eight dollars or ten dollars, if he spoke of ninety-six dollars a year, then he would try to explain to them exactly what ninety-six dollars might be and what it would buy.

Ira went to his desk and sat among ledgers until he was half blind, until his head rang each time he moved it. He unlocked his iron cash box and counted currency contained therein. He placed Confederate scrip in one pile, the few bits of gold coin in another, the silver in another; he had no greenbacks, the law had said that he might have none, and he had obeyed as few other individuals obeyed. He owned however a sheaf of bills, some issued by the Central Railroad and Banking Company, more by the Georgia Railroad and Banking Company, and these he had held since before the war began. Thank God that the best of the old Georgia banks had been connected with railroads. Ira knew that in 1861 his own State had a greater mileage of railroads than Alabama and Mississippi put together. He had heard that these bills were selling at the North for from seventy-five to ninety-five per cent of their par value. Thus he was not at the moment penniless; he might be penniless in another year if he did not manage cautiously. He shoved his small riches back into the cash box without counting all of the piles, locked the heavy box and put it in its cupboard, locked the cupboard. He went outside with a swimming head, trying to clear head and spirit in the ministration of sun and garden smells, for the day was fair.

Therefore he was in the implement shed, reassuring his hand with the feel of his favorite knife, and thinking vaguely of plum weevils, when Jonas approached.

So you and Extra are determined to go. To what place?

Mastah? murmured Jonas as in a dream, and his eyes were dreaming also, they were intense within narrowed lids.

I said, where are you going?

Savannah, Mastah.

But you've never been there. Why do you wish—?

Get all our back money, Mastah.

Back money? Damn it, said Ira fiercely (almost never had he allowed himself to curse before his blacks; even more rarely did he curse them directly), you damned idiot, what are you talking about?

Scooper say you owe us wage now, Mastah. All time you own us, you owe us wage every day. You own me how long, Mastah? He inquired as one making a most delicate plea.

So Scooper's at the bottom of this!

Scooper he done gone already.

Gone where?

Savannah. Done left at sun-up, take his woman, take all the children.

What? Had he a mule, a rig?

No, Mastah. They a-walking. Old Miss Barney Yeoman, she say she not give him no cart, no nothing. She say she not owe him no wage. But Atlanta niggers, they come through lass fortnight, they walking on the railroad, and they say all our old mastahs owe us money for every day we work, and they get that money in Savannah.

Jonas, you're my best hand. I don't want to see you believing this silly thing. Tis an untruth from start to finish! No one owes you money not one copper cent—not until now. From this time forth—

Scooper say them Atlanta niggers say white folks ain't got no money give us now. But Linkum got money, and he send folks pay us all them dimes, them dollars!

Jonas, Lincoln is dead. He was murdered at the theatre! He—

Could Jonas appreciate a cruel fact so quickly (even now, after only a fortnight) turned into history? He could not appreciate it. Since he stood in the first sturdiness of young maturity Jonas had been owned by Ira, had been dutiful and obliging, had been able to cope with the complication of more demanding tasks better than most slaves. He had trusted Ira, appealed to him, begged before him, begged to have Extra as his wife, had had her awarded to him as a prize when Extra admitted her willingness. In an exceedingly humble way he had shared the rise and fall of Claffey fortunes as a dog might share: a fine beef bone with meat attached, on occasion—scrawny table scraps when the fare was thin. He lamented honestly when the stroke of death fell, bragged about the prowess of young Claffeys when he saw them in uniform, wept afresh when the stroke came down again, wept sincerely again, remembered with pride how he had pulled the toddler Lucy out of a Sweetwater marsh when she went floundering there, loved to read the time from a plated watch which Ira gave him as tribute for this feat, loved to impress his fellows by reading the time even incorrectly. Jonas had tended Deuce when the puppy was near to dying of distemper, had volunteered with Extra to assume parental duties when little Dick was orphaned—he and Extra had volunteered kindly, they did not have to be ordered to take the charge. Ira had never considered selling Jonas and Extra and their children as he had sold so many when it became necessary. Extra was indigenous to the place, Jonas very nearly so.

Yet he would heed the word of the massive bully Scooper, the word of idle strangers; and solely because they were black words, so now to be considered as gospel.

If old Linkum dead, Scooper say they got other folks give us money—

Jonas, no longer are you a slave. As a master I may no longer forbid you to go. But do you believe I am your friend?

You always good to us, and Jonas began to cry.

Then as your friend I forbid you to go!

Scooper say— Jonas blubbered softly, unintelligibly.

Don't mention Scooper to me again, you hear?

Mastah, we wants to walk off.

Ira cursed savagely. And, I presume, take your children with you? Take Bun and little Gracious—?

Mastah, they our—children. They ain't belong you no more, like you say. They *our'n*.

What of Orphan Dick? He's not your child, you shan't have him.

No—Mastah. Pet and Coffee—they say they—look after Orphan Dick.

So it seemed that Coffee, whose intelligence was less than that of Jonas (at least that portion of intelligence essential to the performance of successful labors)— And Jem, the lightest-brained of the three— They were not going, they would not walk off with their wives. This course gave Jonas grief, but he stood here now as a man, not a chattel; and this very transformation was a grief in itself. It did not kill the soul but it hurt the soul, and the wound was in Jonas's eyes as he cried.

For the last time, I tell you it is nonsense, nigger nonsense, you hear? You couldn't find your way to Savannah! How will you feed Extra and the children, where will you put them at night?

Reckon we sleep out by a fire.

And it rains, it blows, you're all drenched, you have no roof over you, nothing to eat!

But when we *gets* to Savannah—

This is his illusion, try to take it from him, you can't, he adheres to it like a seed in a boll. The shiny table is spread with dollars, dimes, quarters, gold. Linkum or Linkum's ghost or deputy sits behind the table and calls the roll. He says, What your name? and Jonas say Jonas, and Extra say Extra. Yes, Jonas. Certainly, Extra. I got all this hard money here for you! Clinkety-clink in the money bag.

Whole great big bagful money you got now, and never have to work no more. Now you walk in town like white folks, go in the store where once white folks bought Christmas for the black people— But now you are just like white folks, and Freedom done come, this the day of Freedom, Jubilee time! Now you just like white folks, got great big bagful dimes and solid gold, you buy Christmas for yourself any day you wish—

There was nothing left but prayer. Ira heard himself telling the glistening stubborn brown face, I shall go into the house and pray that you do not go. I have appealed to you to no avail. I'll appeal to the Lord.

He did go into the house and immediately encountered Lucy, who was smiling wanly and gesturing with her finger toward her lips; and this reminded Ira of Veronica, naturally, although Lucy did not much resemble her mother in appearance. Poppy, let's be still as mice. My dear Harry is asleep on your sofa. He just came in, and I put him there—and soothed him— Praise be, he's fast asleep! Nineteen hours at a single ssstretch— On this last word her voice was shaking.

Lucy, the Yankees will soon be taken away.

But do the Federals know that many sick are still here?

Of course, child, of course they know. They'll be along soon.

He told her of Jonas and Extra, the weird belief which tempted them. Lucy's eyes snapped and she went flying out across the yard; but when she came back much more slowly, and with heavier steps, she said that it was no use, the people were packing their duds. Extra had clung to her and wet her old gown with tears, but it was no use; these two dreamers were free, they were bound to go dreaming along the byways.

When do they go? At once?

I persuaded them to wait until the morning. I told them they should have baskets of food to tote along. It seemed that, if they slept on it— Don't you think, Poppy, if they slept on it—?

I fear tis no earthly use.

Later Ira had a thought that Leander might prevail upon his daughter Extra to prevail in turn upon her husband— This was senseless: Leander had not enough strength left to persuade or adjure. He had been ailing for years, declining for months, Cousin Harry guessed that he suffered enlargement of the spleen, for the old creature wore an uncomfortable protuberance like pregnancy.

Harry Elkins allayed Ira's perplexity if not his doubts for Jonas and Extra and the two children. Late in the evening the young man awoke from exhausted slumber, and Lucy fed him cold bacon and cabbage salad, and warmed up a pot of soup over blazing twigs in the library's fireplace (no longer was there a drop of oil on the plantation, so she might not use her little lamp). Ira came in from a limping plunging walk; he had watched the crescent moon go down, had wandered nearly to the place where Veronica had babbled in slime; then Ira turned back in sadness if not in terror. He thought that there was no terror left. Of what might he now be afraid?

Daughter Lucy told you of my people, Coz?

She did.

Ah, that stupid Jonas!

You know, came Harrell Elkins's mild grating words, I believe I know why he's bound and determined to leave.

Ira bent closer, frowning. Then tell me.

Because he's the only soul upon the place who's smart enough to realize that he is free! He and Extra, perhaps. She was Lucy's playmate, sometimes even her confidante; think you not that it's possible that her association with Lucy has developed her imagination more than the other wenches'? And often I've heard you say that Jonas was smart as tacks. On certain subjects, pertaining—say—to husbandry? Then, you see—

Elkins's head swayed forward and Lucy pressed her shoulder against his to sustain him.

You see, he *knows* that he is free. The two of them know it. They have—you might say, graduated—into a state of rapture without bound. Thus they may see sights, hear sounds, tread among visions never glimpsed or heard or trod among by the other blacks. The notion of Linkum and the money to be given away— They don't believe it actually. They but pretend to.

Harry was silent for a while, so were Ira and Lucy. It serves as an excuse for this seeming descent into starvation and homelessness, said Elkins at last.

Ira gazed long at the young pair through candlelight. If what you say is true, there might be a hope for the future.

Hope? echoed Lucy. For whom?

For black people. All of them, in every place. I mean education. I had not thought of it in that way before; and regarded folks who preached such education as either vicious or demented. But if our slaves are to be set adrift, might it not be wiser and safer for all—for them, for ourselves—to develop their minds, to aid them in developing whatever power might lie within them? Suddenly I feel that it might.

Ira considered this revolutionary departure until he slept belatedly. He thought of it in many phases and ramifications. Would the National Government establish schools quickly for these dogged capricious beasts now designated as humans? The Government should. Our Government, he said very nearly aloud. No longer is it Their Government. What's in a possessive pronoun? Should I assemble the remaining people tomorrow and set them letters upon slates, and bid them copy? His last conscious thought was a thanks given to Cousin Harry. Son-in-law or not, Ira would always think of him as Cousin Harry.

Some two hours after sunrise Jonas and his family presented themselves at the rear yard gate to speak farewells. Elkins was off to the hospital an hour earlier, but Lucy and Ira came down and stood to receive embraces and handclasps while the rest moaned and muttered beyond the palings.

You will be delayed a trifle, Jonas, in departing.

Jonas's eyes widened and his nostrils twitched. You could see that he rose instantly to the willingness for rebellion.

For you are to harness Tiger to the cart. The two-wheeler which little Bun drives about his work.

Mastah? came the guttural shudder of the Negro's voice.

For you are to take Tiger with you. I'm lending him to you, with the cart. I shan't have children trudging, stone-bruising themselves over the miles. . . .

Also Ira had prepared a paper, he had risen in gray light to prepare it. To Whom It May Concern: This will certify that I, Ira Claffey, citizen of Sumter County, Georgia, in recognizance of the laws of the United States of America now prevailing since the recent surrenders by Confederate States' commanders, have given permission to my former slave, Jonas, now a freedman, to proceed with his wife Extra and children Buncombe and Gracious, also formerly my slaves and now freed, to a destination of their own choosing. Warning is given herewith that no person shall interfere with Jonas and his family so long as they proceed peaceably, or attempt to arrest or persecute them, or offer them bodily harm or threat, under penalty of such retaliation as I shall assuredly bring within a court of law, or, if necessary, outside the law. These people have the protection of whatever law now applies to the State of Georgia, and have my own protection as well. The mule and cart in their possession are my property and must be treated as such. Signed by me on the first day of May, 1865. Ira Claffey. Witness: Harrell Elkins, Surgeon, P.A.C.S.

The paper was folded, pinned within the pocket of Jonas's shirt, and baskets of food were put aboard the cart. Ira gave Jonas an old tobacco bag with strings drawn tight, containing dimes and quarters. He thought that Confederate scrip might suddenly be of no value whatsoever, but feared to have Jonas exhibiting dollars in some wayside store; quickly he might be robbed, indeed probably he would be robbed sooner or later. So goodbye to the Tiger mule and the cart as well. But could Ira sit down to a mid-day meal and think of these people wandering with empty bellies, the children wailing? No, no, his arm must reach to feed them over whatever distance it could reach, his wheels and hoofs should bear them forward.

Bear them to what place? They went squeaking down the lane, the blacks waved and jigged and shouted, Coffee announced that he knew which side of his bread had the grease on it, he wasn't going Savannah or no such place. Orphan Dick tried to run after the cart, and was brought back by Pet and jailed; but still he screamed; he thought that Extra was his mother, he remembered no other mother. . . . Bear them to a gaunt freedom wherein the free were never fed, wherein the free suffered a captivity worse than the worst of slavery itself? Again Ira thought of slums in long-ago New York, he was forced to close his eyes against the thought, fling it out of his brain.

Man in blue coat, he got gold buttons on he coat, ha, ha, ha; he got that jubilee money for every day we slaves. Mistuh Soldier Man, you tell me where I find Linkum, like folks say? Please, Mistuh White Man, sir, this here road take us Savannah? . . . No, I ain't run off—I *walk* off—my own mastah, he Mistuh Ira Claffey, I got paper say so right here.

What protection, what interest, what provender? The storm of May might rage . . . but where would they be when June thunders came booming?

I try not to think of them, said Lucy.

But they would go.

Shouldn't you have held them here?

How?

Of course you could not. . . . Extra tattled to Ninny, Poppy. She told her that if they found short commons, they'd be back. She'd counseled Jonas so.

And would they find the way?

Poppy, let me work with you today. There's much to do within doors as always; but somehow I just naturally can't direct Ninny and Pet and Naomi today. Are you killing plum beetles again? Let me put on my old gown and help you.

Very well. I shall save the fattest *Conotrachelus Nenuphar* for you.

Ugh.

And mind, Miss—excuse me, *Mrs.*—Florence Nightmare, you're not to doctor wounded weevils.

Oh, Poppy, I'll *squash* them.

The sudden departure of his daughter Extra was the finish of Old Leander. He mumbled gloomily about it, refused food, tried to walk down the road in his shirt-tail, was helped back tottering and soon lay unconscious. He died quickly. They buried him in the slaves' plot adjoining the Claffey graveyard, the first free Negro to lie there.

59

Captain Ox Puckett gone, everybody gone; the engines of passing trains operated by strangers who did not know the Widow Tebbs, who sent no jovial whistle toots piercing in salutation through walls of the house. Hulsey gone, Quillian gone, Wingo gone, Camp gone, Isbell gone, all the Confederate soldiers paroled and gone off to their homes. The memory of the Widow Tebbs was confused but it was thronged, her past was a pushing active mingling of male feet kicking high, thin or fleshy male arms gripping, some of them hurting her (her standard objection and warning to such customers as these was, Now, mister, you please to take it more easy. You're a-hurting me, and if you don't quit a-hurting me I'm a-going to kick you, and I surely do know where to kick). She did remember how she used to call Isbell Is-a-belle; it was a joke between them, a small joke which her small mind could enjoy. Middlebrooks gone, Deadwyler gone, Strozier gone, Judge gone. The nameless gone, the ones she addressed merely as Bob, Jo, Fat, Bully, Baby, Frankie, Freck, Goose, Pop, Dick (he liked to have her call him Dick, but she did so with reluctance because the use of the name reminded her of her long-dead husband, Dickwood Tebbs, and she had no jolly memories of Dick Tebbs). Gone and paroled, trudged off with tattered haversacks swinging, gone away gun-less, saying that it was a hundred and seventy miles to Home and by God they surely did wish they could catch a ride on a wagon. Defeat and emptiness and neglect and loneliness and defeat and improvidence and defeat and defeat pounded hard against the ragged landscape, no matter how porcelain blue the sky on some fair days, how tender green the pines.

Listlessly Marget Tebbs stirred at her pot of stockpeas, and she felt a drudgery in even the simple unrewarding task of searching bare or littered shelves, hunting for salt, finding no salt.

I do wish, she said to Coral.

Huh?

Wish we had a chunk of meat to put into this mess of peas. Misfortune that we ate up all the chickens already.

Coral was out on the porch, Flory was gone to the depot to try to beg tobacco from passing Unionists. Flory had learned to chew while he was with the Reserves; now he had no tobacco, and there was no money in the house. Zoral was playing train in the yard. Coral came clump, step, thud, step, clump across the warped flooring and halted in the doorway.

You mean to say all that there fat-back is gone?

Twasn't much left, sonny. Flory and I had it to our breakfast.

Whilst I was a-hunting, and you didn't save me a smidgin!

I did trust, Coral, that you'd fetch home some game.

God damn, I never met up with no game.

I smell something awful, the widow said, wrinkling her plump little nose.

By gum, so do I. Coral went outside to investigate and a moment later hooted with rage and disgust, and there sounded a scream from Zoral. Coral shouted, I'm throwing it over behind them bushes, and don't you dast bring it back! Zoral crawled to his den under the house and lay kicking in fury.

He had him an old possum, Coral reported when he came back. Like he's always hauling them dead chickens around, playing like they're cars and he's a engineer.

Dead possum? The widow clucked, angry yells still rose through the floor boards, and finally she was compelled to stamp heavily to claim the child's attention. You Zoral! You stop that caterwauling right this minute or I'll throw water on you like I done the other day.

Zoral stopped.

Dead possum! Hell, he was fat as a skinned horse two days in the sun. Wish I could have met up with a live possum.

Well, said Mag in resignation, least the meat would be stringy at this season.

Coral said, I swear he's Satan cut to size.

Who, sonny? That there possum?

Possum, hell! That blame Zoral of your'n. Know what he done this very morning? I come out: there he was, big as life, standing on the well-curb, peeing down the well. I give him a lick he won't forget.

Oh, sonny! The widow added musingly, But I'm truly glad you done it, for he might have fell in and drownded himself.

I wasn't agonizing about that no way! I just don't want to drink no Zoral pee.

The Widow Tebbs sighed. Guess we can't blame poor little Zoral too much. You know, sonny, the gentleman caller I always took to be his daddy— He was a queer piece sure enough. I don't mind his name now, but he tolt me he used to work in a circus; and first off I liked that, count of all the red and spangles and solid gold carriages and truck. But guess what he done. He said he bit the heads right off of chickens. It fair to turned my stomach, but he just laughed.

She found a few splintery scraps of cinnamon on a high shelf where they had lain long forgotten behind a dusty bottle half full of castor oil and another of coal oil. She stirred cinnamon among the bubbling cowpeas, it would give the vegetables flavor of a sort.

This was not a fair day, clouds were solid above but creased and rolled, turning from tannish to ugly brown beyond the somber tree-swept horizon. Coral returned to the door and sniffed the breeze darkly. Dad burn, I just fear for a whirlwind, day like this.

Don't talk so, sonny. I mind how a hurricane took the roof plumb off our house when I was a girl.

I said whirlwind. Hain't no hurricanes in Maytime.

Well, maybe twas a whirlwind. I wasn't more'n six at the time.

Hadn't never lain with your first man, said Coral in good humor. Not till you was seven.

Coral, that hain't no way for a young man to address his Ma!

Well, maybe not till you was eight. He said suddenly and in a strictly different tone, Reckon I'll walk over Claffey way.

He loved to say, I'll walk, walk here, walk there. The meager squeezed but determined face of Naz Stricker rose before him each time he said the word walk. He thought of Naz Stricker, laboring doggedly off into black space, into the sky itself, into strange Northern cities and villages, walking solitary on a homeward path past overhanging barns. Maybe one day Naz would write him a letter, and Coral could read a little, maybe he could read the letter. If not, maybe his mother could spell it out for him. If she couldn't, Mr. Claffey would read the letter.

Why you going over to Claffeys', Coral?

Oh, I want to talk some business. I been pondering it.

The widow said, My, I just don't cipher no way what business you could be speaking to Mr. Ira Claffey.

There was a note like eagerness in Coral's voice, that tone usually so disapproving, grim, strung with bitterness. Might as well tell you what I got on my mind. Some of Mr. Claffey's niggers have gone off already, though they might come back; but that leaves him short of hands. And you know Old Leander died, for I tolt you I walked past whilst they was a-burying him. Well. Mr. Claffey's got all that big garden in, like he always has planted, with just plain oceans of collards and carrots and onions and yams and Christ knows what all.

Mag smiled happily at the mere mention of these delectable things. You mean maybe you might ask him for a mite of garden truck?

God damn, old lady, did you hear me say *ask?* By God I'm a man, and by God I hain't no beggar like that little Joe-Brown's-Pet-Snot-Nosed Flory of your'n. I can work for what I fetch home.

Coral! You mean—work on his land? Like one of his niggers been doing all the while?

Reckon I could wield a hoe if'n he showed me what he wanted hoed up or down. And lots of raising of garden truck you got to do hunched on your marrow-bones.

I never! Just like a nigger—

Plenty white folks got to get out and dig, these days. I seen that nephew of the old Biles a-raking and a-digging, and he was a officer in Cobb's Legion.

Mag imagined a good stew, vegetables bouncing and turning in broth, and plenty of salt and pepper; and she thought of vinegar to put on greens, too, for she despised greens without vinegar. You know, Coral, we been faring just like them Yankees what was in the stockade, ever since the soldiers was sent away. Scarcely nothing to bite nor break.

Well I know, old lady.

He sighed, he thought of days of plenty, winter days, he thought of ham. So I reckon I'll walk over and put it to him boldly.

You might even be keeping us—

She sighed. Stead of me a-keeping us. Putting victuals on our table for us, Coral! And Zoral's so puny all the while, just punier and punier.

Mag added brightly, You know, Mr. Ira Claffey is a real gentleman and kindly too. If'n it struck his fancy he might give you a mite of meat to go along with what garden truck you earnt.

If I go to doing a nigger's work on the Claffey place, said Coral ominously, that God damn Flory is going to perform his share of toil. I don't aim to feed him free out of hand.

Reckon Flory'd be willing. But you'd have to set him to the task and keep him to it.

By God. The boy spoke with relish. I'd admire to do that.

He went clump-stepping across the porch, stepping across the yard. Mag stiffened when he was near the railway, for sound of his whistling came floating back to her. Vaguely she was amazed, she thought a stranger must be there, she was not accustomed to hearing Coral whistle. He had whistled constantly, with little birdy warbles, before he went to war. He had whistled a time or two in the winter, when she thought he was keeping a black girl in the woods. She thought, I do love pretty music, and had a wish to go to The Crib and turn on the music box; then she remembered sadly that the music box was broken at last.

Pursley gone, Carden gone, Almond gone, Swancey gone. Mag owned a soiled cloth purse decorated with glass beads and dried melon seeds strung together in a manner she thought beautiful. In this purse she had kept money, hiding the purse in various places about the house during those seasons when she possessed green-backs and scrip. But the ragged bauble mocked her now, empty and cast aside beneath a bed, Zoral had played with it, the beads and seeds were coming off. It was not solely empty purse and destitution which taunted. It was the loneliness, the rust of the machine in which she was dressed, the bones and tissues and fluids surrounding her spirit, the body—so active and abused by over-employment. Yet abuse became a long necessity, and Mag had thrived on the juices (clean or tainted, and so all the clean were tainted eventually) poured within her.

She looked through the open door and saw her youngest child streaking across the yard. Cunningly he had come out from under the house and sought to retrieve the dead possum and resume his freighting, his imaginary railroad play, once Coral was departed. Either Coral was returning without ever having reached the Claffey place, or else a stranger approached; nothing else could have caused Zoral to scoot to refuge with such celerity.

Mag stepped into open air and saw not one stranger but two. They were in uniform, they wore blue pants with yellow stripes, short jackets piped with yellow. They sauntered between wheel ruts, glancing up at threatening clouds; one man was smoking his pipe, one carried a tough green weed in his hand and flicked this switch idly against his leg as he strolled.

The widow wished that she were properly dressed. She wished that she was wearing her poplin gown, her blue one, she wished even that she was wearing her wrapper with torn ribbon bows. Hastily she touched her hair.

Howdy, she said from the doorway when the soldiers were a rod away and still coming closer.

Hello, lady. . . . Good day. . . .

It does look like rain. Maybe like we might get a whirlwind?

The taller of the two was chuckling. He said, Guess we scairt your little boy, lady. He went under your house, hot blocks, minute he saw us coming.

They were slender, tight belted, they were young but not too young, caps were worn at jaunty angles on the close trimmed brown head and the longer-haired yellow head, the men walked with the leisurely grace of assured people enjoying a moment of holiday. They were well fed, well booted, the great flaps of their holsters curled beside their belts, one wore a haversack slung from his shoulder, he had a wide sliced scar on his cheekbone and bending down into his neck, the other man affected a well brushed mustache, they were young, not too young.

Mag let her hand steal across her faded calico bosom. My, I wasn't expecting no company. Would have tidied myself.

Lady, we ain't company. Just a couple of old coffee coolers and blackberry pickers spreeing around for a couple hours!

Said the widow, I do believe you two are Yankees. You talk so queerlike.

Ain't nothing else, lady. Fourth U. S. Cavalry.

What we want, missis—

They said that to put it baldly they were skirmishing for a bottle of liquor. They had been working hard and traveling far, and they didn't have to report to Captain Noyes until five o'clock, and what about a bottle of mountain dew?

Hain't no mountains hereabouts. Mag's loose soft mouth was smiling, and a slow dream began to occupy her eyes.

Oh, call it bog juice, bug juice, bull juice, mule juice, white mule or brown mule or red-eye or forty-rod: it was all the same. But not like we got up in Macon, said the sharp rapid voice of Corporal Nevis, the man with the scar. I vow you could taste the feet of the boy that plowed the corn twas made from. Feet of the boy? repeated Private Ewing with emphasis. Goll, you could taste the feet of the mule that pulled the plow. . . . Nope, nothing like that; but just a little something to smooth the hair on their backs. They'd pay well for it, too. Tried to buy some from that old man down there near the depot, man who ran that little store down there, but great Scott, he gave them a regular Cold Water Army sermon for their pains.

The widow's heart was weakening. I'm just plain sorry but I hain't got ary drop of anything.

But they'd pay well.

But she didn't have a drop of anything. She was mighty sorry. Times were hard, she'd been awful tight run.

They laughed sardonically. Tight run as the prisoners over in that stockade?

I never did know any of those. I heard tell they was mighty sickly. But I knowed some of the men a-guarding them.

Well, well, too bad, can't even get our whiskers wet. Lady, is your respected husband to home?

Hain't got no husband. He's long dead.

Five minutes later the pea pot had been moved from the fire, and water began to heat in its place. From his haversack Private Ewing produced a small sack of coffee, and he offered it to the widow with gallantry; he could get more; what was a little coffee? In the bedroom Mag changed hastily into her wrapper, but she called animated pleasantries to her guests while she changed, while she loosened her hair and rearranged it and pinned it, while she hunted for red candy and moistened the candy and colored her round cheeks. I got a nicer place than this to entertain folks in, she cried. Just over yonder behind the house. Tis called The Crib; and I did have me a music box but it's busted. And I got a real nice soft bed, she concluded with mischief, and felt a glowing pleasure through her flesh as she heard vigorous Yankee laughter which rang when she said that.

It was a good day for every member of the Tebbs clan. Had the others but known it, Laurel received the gift of an apron from Mrs. Dillard in Americus. Coral was engaged as an apprentice gardener by Ira Claffey, and there would be work for Floral as well, if he stood willing to perform it. There were other cavalrymen idling at Anderson Station. From these soldiers Flory was successful in begging more tobacco than he could chew in three days, and he traded some of it to Uncle Arch Yeoman for the last scraps of candy in the horehound jar. Corporal Nevis and Private Ewing matched quarters to see who should first enjoy the favors of the widow; Ewing won. Rain came but lightly, the tornado did not strike, it struck Macon County instead. Mag put not two but four greenbacks into her purse, and her body was blissful, and so was her shallow thin soul, and she planned to send Flory back to Uncle Arch's for salt and pork and many other things as soon as Flory reappeared. Zoral found a freshly dead mole under the house.

60

These were enemies . . . Wirz felt in his pained bones that they had come to take him.

At first hand he had known no uniformed enemies except prisoners. In Paris, in 1863, he had sat alone in a small café, listening idly—then with curiosity, then with bewildered horror and disgust—to the conversation of three men in citizens' dress who were at a table behind him. From their talk he recognized that they were officers of the Federal navy. Wirz's dinner was spoiled, dyspepsia or no dyspepsia. His trembling hand spilled coffee from the cup. He paid hastily, left a gratuity out of all proportion to the cost of the meal, hurried away. From a darkened street he peered back through the smoky pane and saw Them, Them, Them; saw their faces, heard faintly their laughter. Enemies. But they were not in uniform. . . . Frogs imprisoned in his arm hopped desperately that night.

These men at his door in noontime were enemies, with all the gaud of cloth, buttons, belts.

Is your name Wirz?

Ja, I am Henry Wirz.

You have been in command of this place, commanding Rebel troops?

Wirz tried to straighten his sagging shoulders. He lifted his voice, cords tense and visible at his throat. *Nein!* The troops I have not commanded. I have been superintendent of the stockade only.

The man with bars on his shoulder straps said, I am Captain Henry E. Noyes, Fourth United States Cavalry. Acting as aide-de-camp to General Wilson. I regret to inform you that you are under arrest. Will you please instruct me as to your rank, so that I may know how to address you?

Henry said, Of promotion I was informed, before I hear the news of surrender. So now I am a major.

Have you received your commission?

It has not come. It is somewhere. . . .

In that case I shall address you as Captain.

Wirz retreated into the small parlor ahead of Noyes. Noyes called over his shoulder, Where are Ewing and Nevis?

A cavalryman said, At the rear of the house, Captain. We were taking precautions.

It's obvious that we don't need to, Sergeant. . . . Then again, to Henry: Captain Wirz, may I trouble you for your side-arms?

Wirz's glance flicked toward the window, back to the officer's face. He lifted his left hand to tug at the beard around his lips.

Mein arms, they hang in the entry yonder. Also a pepperbox revolver I got. Not truly a pepperbox—but from Europe he was—

I'm supposed to take your arms. Where is the revolver?

In the bed chamber I keep him.

Any other arms, or weapons of any sort?

. . . No, no, no, he had no other weapons.

Is any member of your family in the chamber at this time?

Henry Wirz shook his head violently. It seemed that this fierce shaking might rid him of veils gathering in his fogged weary brain, veils gathering before his eyes. My wife, my girls, they are in the garden. Back. They make the garden there. His voice broke in a hysterical titter.

Which chamber is yours?

It is above us. That revolver— I have hanging by the bed—

Sergeant Howe, go up and get the weapon and remove it with other side-arms to the verandah. Wait there until Nevis and Ewing join you. I trust these troops haven't terrified your family, Captain Wirz.

They would not be afraid, said Wirz. We have so many troops here. I mean prisoners, of the Yankees. Some Paroles. They work for me about the place, they brought wood. *Ja,* very good I treat them: double rations.

His voice rose shriller. Why is it I should be under arrest?

The heavy tread of Sergeant Howe returned down the stair. He carried the revolver in its holster. Already he had unfastened the flap in order to draw the ammunition.

Better do that outside, Sergeant. . . . Captain Wirz, will you invite me to sit down?

Ja, ja. . . . They sat, one at either end of the settee. Wirz was sitting chiefly upon his left buttock turned so far out of the seat that he was in a half-crouching position. Why am I under arrest, Captain Noyes? There has been the surrender. Troops you do not arrest after surrender!

I have my orders directly from General Wilson. There seems to be a feeling at Macon that you are subject to examination of your conduct as prison superintendent.

Henry said dryly, as if to himself: This I do not understand.

His thin face brightened for a moment as he looked up into Noyes's solemn gaze. Captain, is it possible that you speak the German? My English is—

Sorry, no German. However we seem to be getting on tolerably well.

But I do not understand! Again Wirz's voice went near a shriek, a cry which broke in two and seemed to leave a ruptured piece of the sound hanging in air before it fell.

See here, said Noyes. He tried to make his speech as smooth and reassuring as possible. The sum and substance of my conversation with the general can be reported. To begin with, about the first of this month, General Wilson sent me to Alabama on a task concerning our forces at Eufaula. On my way I passed through this village of Andersonville, and the train stopped to wood up. Some of our Federal sick were at the station. I observed you there also, Captain Wirz. Wasn't there some business about trying to parole the Northerners? Some of your troops were there with you, and you were presenting little pieces of paper to those sick men, to sign. You should have known very well, sir, that it was unnecessary for them to sign anything! General Wilson's orders had been that all the sick should be brought to Macon as rapidly as possible, and that was that. . . . I heard a voice, Captain Wirz. It was to this effect: Hurry up; sign these paroles or you'll die here anyhow. I can't swear that you made that remark, Captain. But today I have heard your voice, and I think it was your voice that I heard at the depot. What business had you paroling our sick men, after the surrender? Certainly it would have been impossible for you to hear that the armistice was repudiated!

Wirz was swallowing rapidly. *Nein,* nothing do I hear of that.

Matter of fact, said Noyes, I was on the point of going to remonstrate with you.

Just then the train whistle blew, and I had to get on and travel. But when I returned to Macon I reported the circumstances immediately to my superior, and was ordered to proceed to this destination, and bring you back under arrest. That's the story.

Wirz spoke in a coarse crawling whisper (certainly, mused Captain Noyes, he must be thinking of stocks and chain gangs). What— What should they do to me?

I presume that if General Wilson is satisfied that you have only been performing your duty, and acting in accordance with orders, you will probably be released.

Wirz lifted his china face with eagerness. He began to nod. That is true, Captain. That is what I do, all the times: I carry out orders! They tell me to be superintendent of the stockade, so I serve. I *am* superintendent. I do my duty, Captain. You are a soldier. That you should know.

For a minute or two it was very quiet in the small hot room, with little sound except the breathing of Henry Wirz.

You spoke of giving double rations to men who were paroled to work for you, said Noyes. What about the prisoners who remained in the stockade? Did they receive double rations? Did they receive *any* adequate rations?

Wirz shook his head briskly, put his left hand over his face, pressed his face down toward his knee. Captain—

His voice was forced out between spread fingers.

—I tell you, only my duty I have done! That General Winder, he give me nothing, nothing. I do what I can. That Sid Winder: adjutant, he was. That Dick Winder: quartermaster. He is bad. I think he steal much from the food. I think maybe they steal money, those Winders! No help do I receive from them. I am a poor man.

His face came up again, his hollow eyes tried to implore Captain Noyes, to tell him of woes, to make the captain believe how very poor Henry Wirz was indeed.

In the campaign west, Captain, they take my place. I have a small plantation, I have a house in Louisiana. All is gone. I am ruined. Now we are in defeat! What do I *do*? I ask you that. How feed I *mein* wife and children? Three children I have by this house. I mean, one is ours, the two elder girls are of my wife. . . . See you this arm?

He shook the relic within its sling, and made a face, and squealed again in the shaking.

This I get at Fair Oaks, what you call Seven Pines. It is very bad. The surgeons, they are no good, nothing can they do. So much pain I have. Always, always—

Sorry about your wound, said Noyes. Sorry about the whole blame business, the whole blame war. Who isn't? Thank God it's over now.

Wirz said softly, Is it not odd? I was thinking. My name, it is Henry; and now you come to put me in arrest. And you too—your name is Henry. Is it not odd?

Very odd, said Henry Noyes, and again there was silence. Silence gave way before the racket of a door being opened and closed at the rear of the house . . . spasm of high-pitched voices all a-whisper, the rapid treading of light feet. Pale and glassy of eye, Elizabeth Wirz rushed into the room. She stopped short when she saw the Federal captain with her husband.

Noyes arose quickly, Wirz got up with labor.

Elizabeth's three daughters were behind her; they pushed together, staring with terrified gaze. Susie had a hat of plaited straw (she had plaited it herself) tied on her head. The bonnets of Cornelia and Coralie were hanging on their shoulders. The two elder girls wore old gloves for gardening, but the child's hands were grubby. Elizabeth Wirz herself held a wooden trowel, and somehow to Captain Henry Noyes that whittled implement spoke volumes. He thought of manufactories at the North. The wife of this Southern officer had no trowel such as his own wife might have used in her garden. There it was: cumbersome, stained, the edge worn blunt, a split up the middle; what slave had fashioned it? Or perhaps even Henry Wirz? No, no, certainly not Wirz, with his arm in a sling, and a pyramid of prisoners atop his shoulders.

Husband— Is it true—what those Yankee soldiers told me?

This captain, said Wirz. He has told me that with him now I must go.

But husband— Henry, you've done nothing wrong!

This captain, said Wirz. His name also it is Henry. In the Old Country, Heinrich it would be. Again his weak giggle crept out.

The plump woman came closer, confronting the Union officer. He looked down to observe and identify and contend against the defiance in her gaze.

Have you arrested my husband? Pray on what grounds?

Madam, I'm merely obeying orders! As, no doubt, your husband obeyed orders given to him. As I have just told Captain Wirz: I presume that he will be released, if he but make it clear to General Wilson that he was proceeding according to orders. I mean to say—fulfilling the duties of command.

Where must you take him?

The general is at Macon. I was instructed to fetch your husband there.

Tomorrow night I should be home, said Wirz hopefully.

Little Cora had thrown her arms around his thin body. She cried distinctly over her shoulder, Don't you hurt my Pa!

I shan't hurt your Papa the least bit, Noyes told her. He must soothe these people, he must avoid a display of hysteria. What is your name, my dear?

They chorused her name. Wirz and his wife said Coralie, the girls said Cora.

Noyes reached out with strong tanned fingers. There is something very pretty around your neck. Is it a locket?

No, tis a Bible. . . .

Wirz addressed the child in a stuttering whisper.

No, *sir,* tis a Bible. . . .

Never before did I see a Bible worn around the neck!

Cora murmured, although she feared to look at the man. Made out of bone. A prisoner gave it to me, and he made it his own self, and he said to my Papa, Give it to your baby.

Noyes drew gently on the creased ribbon from which the ornament depended. There was nothing else to do: he wanted no yells when he marched Wirz out of the house. It was a tiny thing: *Bible* carved on one side, a diamond-shaped hole on the other side filled with red sealing-wax. A hole had been drilled in one end to admit the ribbon. What piece of bone? thought Noyes. Recollection of that putrid tenantless stockade was still cold and strong in him. What bone? A piece from a brute, or a piece from a human? *They are neither man nor woman, they are neither brute nor human, they are Ghouls. . . .*

And their king it is who tolls.

Who was king of the Ghouls? Wirz? He was unfit to be a king, he must be a courtier.

Noyes left off examining the queer little gaud and stood stroking the child's hair. Still she would not look at him. Her face was pressed against her father, she had squeezed her eyes shut.

Madam, he said again to the mother. Let me repeat: I know of no particular charges having been filed against your husband—no bill of particulars, so to speak. It is merely that the general wishes to question him concerning his role as superintendent of the prison. Also— He turned back to Wirz. We are to carry along all records in your possession. They must be examined.

Ja. The books, I have them.

And loose papers. All papers. My men brought carpetbags for the purpose.

For many bags it will not be necessary. So few records were kept by me. Many are by the Winders, somewhere— I have copies from my reports—

We have already requested the hospital records, said Noyes, again in the most reassuring tone he could muster. He wrinkled his nose. There is a delicious smell in your house, Madam.

Corn bread, said Wirz behind him. Every day we have him.

Elizabeth's trowel was shaking. She looked down, saw the trowel, saw her hands a-tremble. Gradually their shaking ceased. She had willed that she make it cease. Noyes felt a sudden respect for the woman. She was made of good stuff.

She said, Our repasts are extremely simple, sir, but I believe things are soon going onto the table. Eve has not yet rung the bell. Will you join us?

I'd be delighted, if I shouldn't be putting you out.

No, no, said Elizabeth rapidly. There is a sufficiency—I mean for you. I fear we cannot offer your soldiers—

They have their own rations, said Captain Noyes.

The simple luncheon—mainly corn bread and bacon, with a few green things from the garden—was eaten in silence. There was an undercurrent of sniffling from the daughters. Before the end of the meal, Cornelia jumped up suddenly and ran from the table. She burst into tears in the hall; they could hear her tears; they rattled their forks, broke their bread, pretending not to notice the young girl's departure as she went rushing to the second story.

Wirz felt an inexpressible tenderness for his family. There was nothing now which he could say to Captain Noyes. Oh please, he thought, dear God, do make him understand, make the general understand also, when we arrive in Macon. Make them understand that I am a soldier, I was a soldier. One does one's duty. When the prisoners were bad, they were like naughty children, and naughty children must be punished. So I punished the prisoners. I am not a bad man. Dear God, make the Yankees who have now triumphed over us, make them understand that I am a good man! I am not wicked, I have done nothing wicked. That old General Winder (and dead he is now, and a good thing for all that he is dead), he would not coöperate. He was relentless; he did not wish to have the hospital moved to the Outside, and it was a very wrong thing to have the hospital on the Inside. Very little food could we get for anybody! Yes, the prisoners were crowded. I could not conduct a neat and efficient prison; all the time they kept sending more prisoners—train load after train load. More, more, more! It was wrong of the authorities to do this. Oh, dear God, please to make the Yankees understand how handicapped I was! And my arm: how it pained me constantly; it is paining now, with little hopping monsters therein begging to be freed. I should have let those surgeons lop it off in the first place; but I thought that in time I could be healed; I did not wish to have but one arm, I wished to serve the South. I was kind to many of the prisoners. Yes, yes, I shall tell the general how kind I was to them! They wanted clubs to hunt down the raiders, so I gave them clubs. They wanted to hold a court; they asked to have attorneys, so it would be a proper trial, and I let them hold court, let them appoint attorneys. They wanted lumber for a gallows; I gave them lumber. And what did they do with it? It melted away as the fence melted away—seven hundred and eighty feet of fence, and all in one night. Most of them could not be trusted, so I did not trust them. Many broke their paroles, they ran away. There was no fair play about it! They ran off, and some of them managed even to elude the dogs. They were devils and they were bears, worse than the bears in Bern! This also shall I tell to the Federal officials, and make them understand the scorn and unfair treatment received by me. The Yankees threw mud, they called me evil names. They were recalcitrant, disobedient; so I was compelled to enforce my discipline with the stocks and the chains. They were dreadful prisoners, those Yankees. They would not submit, they would not obey my rules. They were very, very dirty. They even killed each other! And the Northerners must understand the worthlessness of the guards foisted upon me: old men and little boys. They were no fit soldiers; they did not know how to be soldiers. The Northerners must understand that in my heart I am a very kind person! If I were not a kind person, I would not have been kind to Little Red Cap. I was very good to Little Red Cap, and he, at least, could be trusted not to run away. Why, my Ilse even gave him gingerbread! And little Coralie trotted after him when he came here to my house to perform errands. I have seen them sitting together on the bench yonder—there is the very bench, out through that window, beneath the chinaberry tree—and I have heard Little Red Cap teaching a song to my Cora.

It was a song he had learned at the North.

He would sing, *Auralee.*

But he would make it instead *Coralie.* He would sing in his young soft voice—a mere boy's voice, because he was a mere boy— He would sing, *Coralie, Coralie, maid with golden hair. Sunshine comes along with thee. . . .*

Her hair, it is not truly golden—it is light brown. But, yes, I think it has a touch of gold in it. So he was right in calling my Cora a maid with golden hair.

Other songs I would sing myself to my little daughter. I have sung them often. Oh, I wish now that I were merely sitting with my child, singing to her the German! Honestly, I am a kind man. I love the old songs in the German! I love to sing:

> *Muss i denn, muss i denn zum—Städtle hinaus,*
> *Städtle hinaus, und du mein Schatz, bleibst hier!*

. . . Must I then to the city away . . . city away . . . and you, my love, stay here. . . .

. . . When I come, when I come, when I come back again, come back again, I'll return to you, my dear. I cannot always be with you, still you are my only joy. . . . So must I then to Macon away! I am positive that General Wilson will understand. I am *almost* positive. . . .

Whatever Captain Noyes might do in ease of the situation, there were tears and wailing when Henry Wirz left the house. Wirz kept babbling about the hospital records: Dr. Roy, who remained there still, had said that the records were not complete, that the Yankees must send him some clerks in order to complete the records. This Captain Noyes promptly agreed to do. But still Wirz kept babbling about it.

Noyes had spent the previous night in Americus, because of lack of accommodations in the Andersonville region. Two of his men—a corporal and a private— had seemed eager to remain at Anderson. That was odd; but they were trustworthy men in whom Noyes had the utmost confidence, so he yielded to their whim. They seemed suffering from lack of energy on this day, but he could smell no liquor. He wondered idly what they had been up to. Noyes himself, and the remainder of the men, had come to Anderson Station on a freight train. He had arranged for a later train to bear the party to Macon with their prisoner.

Thus they reached Macon a few hours later, and at once Noyes escorted his captive to General Wilson's headquarters. He was glad to be rid of this task; but a much more exasperating one awaited him some days later.

Orders came from Washington, requiring that Henry Wirz be fetched to the capital, bag and baggage, together with the records. General Wilson took advantage of the opportunity to send along a bundle of captured battle flags which he had taken from the Confederates during his recent campaign through Alabama and western Georgia. Captain Noyes was very glad to go to Washington; but was extremely annoyed at being burdened with the flags and with Henry Wirz; and still he did not know what was in store for him.

The trip had to be made through the central South, because of the more direct lines being out of commission. At Atlanta, Noyes permitted his prisoner to take exercise upon the station platform, guarded by Ewing and Nevis. He himself was in a toilet room when an unholy row burst forth on the platform. Noyes heard his soldiers' voices, he adjusted his clothing and hastened to the scene. He found a small riot in progress. Ewing's nose had been bloodied, Nevis's jacket ripped. The young men fought savagely to restrain several purple-faced soldiers who struggled to get at the person of Henry Wirz. Even the sharpest tones of command were ignored. Noyes was compelled to draw his revolver before he could quiet the men.

When the party reached Chattanooga, Noyes concluded to take no further chances.

We'll have to remain here the greater part of the day, Sergeant. There's bound to be a post prison: take the prisoner there at once, because otherwise you'll draw a crowd, and we may have trouble.

Yes, sir.

Guard him carefully. I don't want him to be mobbed. And report back here with the prisoner at four o'clock.

Yes, sir.

When Noyes saw Henry Wirz again the brim of his hat flapped, his coat was gone, his shirt dirtied and ripped; even his trousers appeared to have been half torn from his body. Wirz himself was close to collapse. He jabbered in German, he was talking also about his little daughter, and talking about a little red cap. He didn't even make sense.

What the devil, Sergeant Howe! I told you to guard this prisoner with care!

Well, by God, sir! Excuse me, sir— It's on account of all these damn troops. Some of them were prisoners down there, and they kept yelling, Let's kill the son of a bitch! Excuse me, sir. But that's what they said—exactly what they were yelling. Christ sake, sir—excuse me, sir—but we were almost done in! I got knocked down, and finally had to fire a couple shots in the air!

It happened again at Nashville. For Henry Noyes it was from then on a sleepless journey. By this time, the dilapidated appearance of the captive would have drawn a crowd, even if he had not been recognized as being Henry Wirz. He muttered now about a place in Kentucky called Cadiz. He said that that was where he had met his wife, years before. He thought he had friends in Louisville. Perhaps they would supply him with clothing.

The friends were found at Louisville, and Wirz was garbed in a suit of black and given a beaver hat.

Shave off his beard, said Noyes.

Mein beard, Captain? It is that I do not wish to be shaved! Always I have worn a beard.

Shave off his beard, said Noyes again. Wirz was taken to a barber.

When he returned his family would not have known him. And Noyes thought that his cavalrymen were escorting a stranger—even though he had ordered this alteration.

They had no more trouble after that. Soldiers trooped along the platforms, they passed the open window where Henry Wirz sat in dejection— They passed unheeding, although doubtless there were ex-prisoners from Andersonville here and there in the jingling throngs.

Smoke swished through the car, cinders settled. Wirz complained that his arm gave him anguish, it had been injured when the troops hustled him. He asked for sulphate of morphia, so a surgeon was found to furnish him with drugs, at Cincinnati.

The pain seemed to be somewhat relieved after this. But the freshly shaved mouth kept moving, sometimes soundlessly, sometimes making sounds.

What were you saying, Captain Wirz?

It is a song. It is from the German. I learn it in my youth. It goes—in the German: Must I then, must I then to the city away? . . . When I come, when I come, when I come back again, come back again, I shall return to you, my dear. That is the German: *mein Schatz.* . . . Captain Noyes, I tell you I am not a bad man. They should not wish to kill me! I was but doing my duty. And Little Red Cap: I was good to him. I was a kind man to many prisoners.

Then he fell silent and seemed to be in a stupor; but every now and then his thin hand stole up to clutch lightly at his throat.

61

Around the walls of Ira Claffey's chamber was built a moving frieze. It was like marbles of Mediterranean and Aegean temples, wherein men with horses and chariots made eternal progression out to war. But figments cut in relief beyond the whirl of Ira's vision were parading away from a war.

They proceeded up out of a valley of death . . . they were moving, living. Confederate troops escorted them, first off; then came Federal troops into the picture. They were so fresh out of recent memory that Ira sat up in bed and swept blindly at his own eyes to wake himself, to get rid of the lurch and grinding. He could not drive them off, he wondered how long they would be sculptured before his gaze. Depart beyond recall! he tried to tell them. Yet that was sententious falsehood, truly he did not wish them to vanish, they must be accepted as reminder that some survived, some had been carried home. No chariots in this his frieze; but wagons, wagons, wagons with clean straw filling the beds, stretchers and blankets hoisted up, people saying, Now just hold quiet, old top, this is going to hurt a speck when we lift you. The weak shorn-off scream. Soon wheels jolting, rusty smoking engine waiting on the track beyond, Yankee sentries—*Yankee* sentries—strolling by the station where formerly Georgia Reserves had moved.

He thought he saw a Northern house. He was not sure where it might be situated; he had been in but two private houses at the North, and those were palatial. But small ordinary homes he had seen from the railway carriage—their gables peaked sharply, tiny porches, often the leaning plane of a cellar door to be seen. Ira counted it peculiar to think that there was a subterranean life beneath most Northern houses, and that most Southern houses had no cellars and were built high above the ground. . . . Such a house, then, and what shall we name the people sitting there?

A name came to him, echoed from a long-ago business transaction in New York. The name was Kearns.

The people are named Kearns—father and mother—they sit above the door-step, it is late afternoon. Who comes creeping? A spectre wan, the loose jacket and trousers are too big for him, the head has been shaven, face and head are scarred. Bony hands slide from picket to picket of the white fence, the figure comes along. Who on earth is it? says Mother Kearns, and puts up her hand to shade her eyes against the lowering sun. The fence is perhaps a hundred feet away from the doorstep. Still she does not know, she does not know. . . .

Father Kearns sees blue cloth on the weak creeping figure, and he thinks sadly of Johnny who went off to war and perished there. Johnny vanished, they'd heard no more. Johnny has been dead, they believe, a year or two. Mr. Kearns sees faded cloth and says, Just some poor tramp, Metta, and sickly too; maybe one time he was in the army. Father Kearns fastens his pipe between his teeth and picks up the newspaper.

But Rex is lying on the door-mat, Rex pricks his ears.

Oh sad, sad, thinks Mother Kearns, a-rocking and a-rocking. She will not even lift her apron to cry into it, she has wet so many aprons in the past. . . . But still that stubborn figure worries along the wooden sidewalk, still its hands go from picket top to picket top, holding on. He must not fall again, he fell twice on his way from the depot.

The dog stands, his ears are high. He stretches up, his nostrils work, he begins to whine.

Now, Rex, says Mr. Kearns, don't go to barking, that fellow won't hurt no one. The figure halts at the gate and stares at them. Rex dives from the porch. Johnny, Johnny, they are screeching a moment later. Rex is bounding wilder than any wild animal, jigging on hind legs, leaping, trying to tell them that he knew all the time, from the very first, he knew, he alone. . . .

There was a Johnny in each of those wagons which went shuddering from hospital to depot. There were many Johnnies in mendicant columns which prowled forth from the gates in their last Georgia excursion.

Ira got up and dressed, he could sleep no longer. Silence battered his ears. No rifle shots puncturing the night, no yells from a bottomless pit of gangrene and decay; no burble, no mass of human poultry roosting in hospital or stockade. Ira went down into the library and warmed a bent candle in his hands so that he might straighten it before he lit the candle. He began to read his Bible. He'd tiptoed on the way, no one must waken Cousin Harry. Coz had earned his good long sleep, earned it a thousand times over. . . . In her arms, thought Ira. Oh, long may he deserve such sleep, and in my Lucy's arms, and she in his. I would not be surprised but that she owns a secret. I think the secret shines from her eyes, comes up out of her heart and through her eyes. She has told me nothing. He smiled, then tried to put his attention to Scriptures; but problems of Lucy and Harry seemed to come first. For his part Ira would have been happy to have them make their home permanently at the Claffey plantation. He had never enjoyed a harmony greater than his harmony with Lucy. Nor could he imagine that conten-tion might ever rise between himself and Harrell Elkins, since each bore such respect and affection for the other, since they held a common pride and humor. But he knew that young men and women should make their way, a separate way

ANDERSONVILLE 789

from that of each elder generation, they should have their own roof-trees. As he grew older Ira might not find undiluted contentment in observing his own ways and manners tailored to needs of the young. But he knew that Harry did not have a dime, nothing but a faraway family patch where springtime weeds were tall and window panes were broken out of the house, where shutters were sagging, and steps gone, not a plow or a cart or a Negro or a mule on the place.

It would take doing but there would come a way, in time there would come one.

Again Ira hunted for specific reassurance amid the fine print held before him. He could find nothing at the moment. Vaguely he was reassured by the feel of the Book in his hands, by thought of young strength and intimacy above stairs.

It was almost full daylight at last; he should be out and doing. No Leander left to rouse the hands . . . he himself should ring the bell. *Clong. Clong. Clong.* He heard the notes echoing until they were swaddled in stronger silence rising now like a wall from Andersonville. The silence hurt to excruciation. Its very fact reminded you of the noise which had lived.

Ira put Coffee and Jem to their work. The Tebbs boys had arrived, and Ira instructed them in the art of setting bean poles and planting beans. Then he went off to make sure that Jem was not hoeing too closely to young cornstalks, that Coffee was using only old dried guano at the bottom of the cucumber hills.

Just as he had feared! . . .

No, that must be taken out, Coffee, and done over.

Mastah?

It's my own fault: I neglected to make it plain to you. The dry manure is in the smaller bin, not the larger. Remember when you scraped the floor of the hen house? Now that stuff's been bleaching and drying long enough, and will serve.

Old chicken shit better'n fresh chicken shit? Coffee asked in puzzlement.

Exactly so. With this fresh manure the plants would die out. Get rid of it, and use only old and dry.

As he came back to observe Coral and Floral he heard an altercation in progress. Before he reached the scene he saw the older youth strike at the younger with a bean pole. Dad blast you, you little scut! You won't do half what you're tolt to do.

You ain't my sergeant, yelled Flory in rage.

Let us have no more high words, said Ira sharply. What seems to be the trouble, boys?

Coral explained in indignation: He won't plant them poles nor beans proper. I mind what you said—put them in before planting, stick them deep and firm in the ground so's they're maybe ten foot long. And not more'n five or six beans to be put around each pole, and not more'n an inch and a half deep, neither!

That's exactly the fashion. And, Floral, let me tell you this: Coral *is* your sergeant in this case. I am captain over both. Proceed according to orders. Silence in the ranks, he cried over his shoulder as he went away, and was rewarded by a faint giggle from the two.

Silence in the ranks, silence in the valley, silence in the marsh. All quiet along the Sweetwater branch . . . all quiet along Stockade Creek.

Many hours later Ira walked hesitantly into the pen alone.

He stood in that infrequent but dread state of knowing that he had observed history with his own eyes, even that he had helped to make it or had attempted to unmake it. As a very small child he first became aware of the immutability of inanimate objects. He had looked upon them with grave suspicion because they were such blocks and hulks, unfeeling, uncaring, unknowing, left to sit and stare stupidly after the humans were borne off. There had been one of the numerous deaths in the Claffey family: Ira came into the room where the person had lain sick and finally had died (he could not remember which relative it was, it didn't matter) and there was that dresser near the bed, the dresser on which bottles and glasses had stood, on which pewter spoons had been placed with puddles of unabsorbed medicine congealing in their bowls. This debris was removed, servants were carrying out featherbeds to beat them in the sunlight. But the dresser stood; it was there; same knobs, burns on the scarred oaken surface, the split in the wood where some artisan had poked out a primitive keyhole with too heavy a hand. Ah, and clothing was removed from drawers, hung up, given away; a cousin had the handkerchiefs in her own drawer now, a slave named Aba had been given the stockings, a slave named Esther had filched the tippet. But the dresser stood. The dead person was gone with all her appurtenances. The dresser stood. The same piece of broken crockery lay shoved beneath a leg to fill in a depression in the uneven floor. Did the dresser feel? Nay, nay . . . when wood was alive in trees the wood had felt; trees had sorrowed, chuckled, breathed, dreamed. Ira Claffey squinted his eyes and shook his head, recalling this first shock of particular knowledge, particular realization (which brought enduring pain as all wisdom brings pain because the man who acquires wisdom may only watch and try to understand; he may not select, manage, alter). That was Ira Claffey's name in the original Hebrew. Ira: a watcher.

He stood watching.

Or was he engaged in mere observation, evaluation, estimation? You could watch an occurrence, a happening—you were said to be watching when events moved before your eyes. This place, however ruined and despoiled, was become static. Silence smoked up from the offended earth and struck your ears with force. Birds refused to visit here. They were occupied with family cares, with feeding in woods past the fence . . . Andersonville. They'd have none of it . . . Ira moved his shoe and hoisted a dripping wad on the toe of his shoe and let the wad fall off. Declare it to be blanket, jacket, jeans, shirt, drawers in its origin; it was none of these now, it was reek endeavoring to be made into soil. Try once more. A sandal —someone had constructed it painstakingly—it was carved from leather scraps, the scraps had been stitched together (could it have been fabricated by a middle-aged saddler from Ohio? Somewhere good food was being cooked. Its scent came from the past and titillated Ira Claffey's imagination; yet he had never known a man named Gusset, he had known none of the prisoners excepting Nazareth Stricker). Take a homemade broom and with it throw the queer sandal aside. And why a homemade broom, with shavings cut into a bunch and tied with a thong? What might anyone sweep in this wide wild den, what manner of housekeeping had been carried on? Tin receptacle crude and long and flat—ho, he'd heard of those, Colonel Persons had told him a year earlier. They are very ingenious, Persons said. Like all prisoners in all times and places the Yanks are forced to make do with what they have. Some of them were confined in an old warehouse in Richmond before they came here, and those sheets of tin— Something to do with tobacco presses— They filched them and made them into cooking pans— Serve fairly well, or so the prisoners say. Which is fortunate, since we have no pots or cutlery to give them.

Rags, rags, what had they been? Trampled deeply into clay to spoil there, or lying dried by sun, wetted by many rains, dried by numerous suns again. Whittled ladle and broken cow's horn (powder-horn, drinking horn, horn to blow a blast upon? You couldn't tell: it was a scrap of horn) and half-canteen, and tin fork with one of the tines broken off and one sticking east and one sticking west, and wooden bucket with the bottom splintered out of it. These things wounded Ira not in their ugliness but in their silence and lack of life.

Again: the distressing implacable stubbornness of the inanimate which remained after the animate were gone away.

Oats, flour, rice, meal—something had been kept in that wooden pail in its original time and place. Perhaps Vermont maple sugar, perhaps sugar of the South? Certainly. Flinty cany bits had been weighted up to the brim, and the wooden lid had molded the mound flat when it was pressed on, and a woman or a slave (ha, slaves were become women now; it must not be forgotten) had reached in with smooth wooden scoop or teacup or gourd dipper to lift the sugar out, to bake it in a cake, to stir it in a pudding. Sunlight had come kindly through a window and had found the bucket on a shelf in its accustomed situation, and sunlight had warmed through wood and had made the sugar richer, or so you could imagine; and a little boy had come tiptoeing to steal the sugar . . . the bucket waited in docility upon that shelf when Bet whispered outside the pantry door and told her mother bashfully that she was going to have a baby next April; it stood there in February when the baby came too soon, when the baby was born dead, when Bet died, when the preacher stood in the front room and quoted sepulchrally, *I am the Resurrection and the Life.* It stood there.

Hate the inanimate, expunge it.

Let there be but Resurrection and Life.

Whence, and by what power?

Was God strong enough?

What of the Nation? The Nation was mutilated and crippled, crippled worse than Coral Tebbs, crippled worse than Badger Claffey might have been had he dragged himself homeward instead of contributing to cold loam in fabled mountains.

(Perhaps— No loam in the Chickamauga region? Naught but rocks and the gravelly soil of hills, and clay, and clay again, and bones and skin and young men's lungs and tongues turned into fresher clay?)

Shebangs broken, many others unbroken and brooding in emptiness, yawning pits drilled deep—one must be careful not to fall into them— Crushed metal cups, the sole of a boot, the fold of paper with its more exposed portions flaking, and there were marks of penciling upon soggy inner portions, and it had been a letter written from one human being to another, and for some great purpose, but now it could not be read: it was a letter no longer; its legibility had strayed off into the elements as its original purpose had strayed into space with the boy who'd treasured it—

Trudging solitary through this wasteland, Ira Claffey felt the indefinable disease of old age upon him. He feared that it would not let him move his limbs and respire and keep his blood in motion long enough for him to keep his body in motion, and so walk at last through that open gate yonder, and escape the balefulness which clung to every rotting rag and scrap of charcoal.

Nineteen months ago, he mourned, partridges were here. Nineteen months ago the open pine forest was compassionate. What rare concentrated tragedies will have occurred within another nineteen months—not here, for this place has bred a tragedy greater than any recorded in the Nation's past—but elsewhere, all over the South, through back roads and on wharves and in legislative rooms, in foundries which rust because the fires have gone out?

He prayed wordlessly, felt no answer, heard none. Gone far into his fifty-second year he felt that in fact he was a generation older than that, two generations older. He was ninety, he was a hundred and more. If grief made age then his hair was hoary and his flesh pendulous, his tendons frailer than thread, his eyes sightless.

But finally the sun came out, burned weak clouds apart, the sun said that the half-a-button lying here was a jewel, the piece of buckle over there was another jewel, and dank hovels between were nothing but manure needed by soil to fetch a future growth.

Let my age and my weakness fall away; and in some inverse fashion weakness must decline within the Nation's body as its age increases. . . .

Here was a truth to offer strength and—perhaps, later—courage. This truth: any creed for which men are willing to die achieves an historic dignity, and cannot be shamed, no matter how one hated it. I hated the North, said Ira. Hated the National Government. My sons warred against the Nationals, my sons were killed by the Nationals. Yet the youths who suffered within these walls have given the National Government a greatness it did not possess before; and in time that Government may be embraced, welcomed, respected, worshipped by those who once were unwilling to love it without stint.

A slender stiff stick was trodden up by the weight of one boot and passed between his feet as if to trip him. Ira stepped back and nudged the thing aside, then bent to pick it up. He held a tooled length of hardwood, worn smooth by the dirt and touch of many hands. A branded *C* was visible still, no matter how many centuries of soakings and tribulations the broken fragment had endured since Ira handed out implements to his black people in the home dooryard.

. . . All of you watch these axes and shovels, to make certain they're not stolen. Hear me?

. . . Yes, Mastah, we watch.

. . . May be some dishonest folk among the other laborers. And such implements are valuable. Watch as I bid you.

. . . Yassah.

. . . I wish to pick up my shovels, sir. My hands did not fetch them home last night.

. . . Don't know anything about your God damn shovels! I can't go around guarding every bastard's shovels in the land.

Fist swinging and smashing. He could recollect still his boyish primitive satisfaction in that.

Who had used the broken handle as a crutch, who'd used it as a tent pole, had it been a weapon, was a spongy corpse pried with it?

To what use might it be put at last? Might Coral employ it as a bean pole? Ira moved on toward the gate, his knee suffered because of the uneven terrain; now he had a cane. But first and foremost the shovel-handle suggested agriculture, and agriculture had been a prime necessity of men all the way back to those desert tombs where peas of the past were found drying. Ira felt that his own gardening must proceed indefinitely, though it was assuming a new form.

But if he put mind and heart into the soil where his sons had gone, and where the human wastage of Andersonville had gone, and where that enormous blood-curdling fraction of America's young males had gone, North and South— Eventually the stalks might rise, toughen; beards would dry out, husks turn to parchment; and those hands who'd made his crop might reach in memory to carry him in salute to the crop, the fields, the earth itself.

. . . You had to pretend to be surprised, you did not know that a toting was due. Secretly you arranged for Naomi and the wenches to provide meats, cakes, sweets; these were hid and locked away, and so was the cask of wine; you grew both religious and Masonic in your thought and discussed with yourself the virtues of salt, wine, oil, and corn. You sat with your own white flock upon the evening gallery while a chanting came from cabins spread along their private avenue beyond the outbuildings. Your white children giggled and whispered as black children must be giggling and whispering. You sat aloof, you fanned yourself idly with a newspaper, you pretended not to heed.

Oh, that old moon, way up there.

Ooohhhh. . . .

Where he gone, gone, that old moon?

He gone in corn, that where he gone.

Ooohhhh. . . .

Where he gone, gone, that old moon?

The moon was behind a cloud for a while, but then the cloud shifted with its gilt and blue and suggestion of other rainbow colors, the low moon burned white again, and seemed to blister long sacred fields with its oil and its salt and—God knew—also wine in the moonlight? For the intensity of hardening corn was in the air, it made you think of coons and possums and the yammer of dogs, and pine knots flaring scarlet as Negroes whooped.

They approached slowly, trailing banners of flame, the clattering voices muted as the long troop of them passed under the driveway's magnolias . . . men coming on ahead, the women next with torches enchanting their plain garments, children gyrating as if they danced to drums, twisting and turning and holding little arms aloft for sheer love of the twist and turn.

He gone in corn, he gone in corn.

Ooohhhh. . . .

No, sir, old coon, no sir, old coon. . . .

You never get the Mastah's corn!

We pick that corn, own selves, we pick that corn.

Oooohhhh. . . .

They issued from Nile and Congo and Niger, they had come a long way to grow Ira's corn for him and now to carry him in triumph amidst it. They jigged in orange and black and shadows, with eyes agleam, they came pirouetting, the fierce barbaric rank of strong men in the lead.

Now was the time for the planter to arise and step to the front of the gallery (as a general might have stood, as a Highland chief might have stood when pipes came screaming in the March Past). Silence chopping suddenly, the silence a pain from the second the master arose; and his woman and his children and his visiting aunt and cousin grouped behind, years of error stretching off behind them, years of other error staggering ahead with neither servants nor master able to evaluate them.

Mastah! That was before Leander was bent to helplessness, it was when his voice held the bronze timbre of a plantation bell.

Yes, Leander.

Evening, Mastah.

Good evening to you all.

Mastah, time right! Night all right, moon all right, corn all dry, ready now we pick it—

That is so. Some of you shall start the picking tomorrow. I'll be up early to tell you off.

No, sir, please, Mastah. Not up early. Up late! For tonight—

Why, what about tonight?

This was the ritual. It varied from year to year, yet in truth it never varied until a war loomed to dismember the plantation, dismember the Union, eventually dismember the new Confederacy itself.

Tonight—we wants—to *tote* you!

Yah, yah, yah, and suddenly he was festooned amid their babble, their rich smell came up around him, he loved it as he loved the odor of cows and horses which also were his property and paid the same domestic dividends. His haunch was on Jonas's shoulder, his other buttock sustained by Japeth's big hands, Nestor clutched Ira's ankle, Ira was riding high. Dudley had a cowbell, Putty a tin wash-basin, Putty was thrumming the thing with his knuckles as his grandfather might have stroked a jungle drum.

Toting time, toting time. . . .

Oh, woh, woh, woh, woh!

Tote our Mastah to the corn. . . .

Why we tote him? Corn all ripe!

Ah, wah, wah, wah, wah!

Younger women lifted their skirts as they skipped behind, children scuttled and scooted, and soon were chased out of the first cornfield. This was a rule enforced by Leander: he would not permit women and children to venture past the gate, they did too much damage in dry crowded fields, they tore down stalks and made it difficult to find the ears, they made more work for the menfolks and for themselves. A coon whickered over toward the McWhorter place (in pine woods become extended Hades, pools stirred by evil pitchforks; why, it might have been at this very spot that the coon called) and all the pickaninnies yipped to hear it; the bigger more ornery ones said that it was a Woogum. There was thought of autumn coming on, colder weather, potatoes roasting in ashes; birds whirring up as if they were cranked to the whirring; smell of burnt powder, the smoke blowing free, the setter racing, the setter bringing a bird in his mouth. Thought of cool mornings after cooler whiter nights, and Naomi fetched the biscuits wrapped in a red-checked cloth, and pine flames seethed on many a hearth. It was good to be alive and crush a biscuit and smell a fire. And always there was the thought of corn, and how men and beasts would feed on it, and they would profit from the grain because it was a good thing, made good by the earth and the labor of many hands.

Oh, that old moon stay so high. . . .

Why we tote our Mastah dear?

Corn all ripe. Pick, pick, pick! Corn all ripe.

Oohhhhh. . . .

(Here corn bread had rotted, but most of it was rotted away . . . most of the last prisoners had lain within the hospital enclosure, while the stockade itself took on an air of wide desertion. Ah, here indeed was a scrap of corn bread surviving as a paste! A bug was feeding on it, several bugs. Ira turned from the sight and walked on.)

His black people's song cried from the past, but Ira told himself that also he must listen to their lamentation. He thought that he had not caused them to lament, but others had done so. America owned its own Wilberforces, and *Laus Deo* said the poet whose poem had filtered down from the North. No blacks would ever tote Ira again in a triumphal circuit of the cornfields, no other man would ride on slaves' shoulders, because now there were no slaves (and little corn to triumph about). He must tell himself that the institution of slavery was evil because it had perished. He must persuade himself that a greater good was achieved when a thing vanished. For his own part he saw little difference between a legal slavery and an economic one, and he thought that his own people were better off than sickly whites he'd seen trooping through mill gates at the North.

But perhaps the Claffey place was not the Confederacy, and God knew there must be happier children at the North than bobbin boys.

Here was the hillside, here the spring. Often he'd stood upon that sentry platform yonder and watched the prisoners filing for their drinks, with police of their number standing, clubs at the ready, to keep them in line, to discourage speculators, to give fair opportunities for drink to everyone. Police, he thought, may I have my turn? On an impulse he knelt and scooped up water; he closed his eyes and listened to Lucy talking about a fairy she'd seen among mossy places now not mossy but only littered and tattered. Ira Claffey got up blindly and went down the slope, crossed the narrow rotten cat-walk over the marsh (with its smell lessening but still a smell) and went up toward the South Gate past the place where gallows had stood.

Thought of the gallows brought memory of those specific dead—the giants slaughtered to bring them to time!—and also the recognition of the nigh-onto-fourteen thousand who lay past pines northwest of the stockade. How many other Yankees had gone to their sleep in cars bound for Savannah or Charleston, how many had jittered and then silenced themselves in pens at Millen and Florence because they held the evil of Andersonville in their bodies when they staggered through that gate ahead? Say another thousand, or two, or thousands more? What of the relics who were carried to their homes at last? Would they grow keen and sprightly, unblemished except in spirit?—or would they languish and continue the putrefaction which had begun within these acres? Had Americans ever brought so many Americans to death in such limited acreage before? Ira thought, No great battle was ever waged within the confines of a twenty-eight acre patch. It was said that seven thousand were shot dead at Gettysburg; there they fought over twenty miles of hills and orchards. . . .

He groped for a text and found none. Cato Dillard should be near to provide texts. But a great voice intoned somewhere, and Ira stopped to hear it. *Their memory has escaped the reproaches of men's lips, but they bore instead on their bodies the marks of men's hands.* Thucydides quoting Pericles . . . *their story is not graven only on stone over their native earth, but lives on far away, without visible symbol, woven into the stuff of other men's lives.*

He had a renewed sense of timelessness and its values. The song did not ring for a solitary moment, nor merely to enrich the spirit which had sung it, and to enrich admirers of that spirit; but it went echoing indefinitely. Thus the future became packed with a good accumulation. A vanished Pericles had lived anew when Thucydides counseled the listening Athenians to heed a forgotten funeral oration. Thucydides mixed his own dreams and opinions with those of Pericles; therefore the two became indissoluble, creatures in common, neither holding to his own part of the century. Rather they were the Fifth Century, they made it; so they and other honorable souls had manufactured the millenia.

Ira believed that a new Nation was made. It was one which he had prayed not to see; but here it was. His own fields, were he allowed to retain them, extended to Maine and Texas and to the Oregon country; because granule of soil lay next to granule of soil, and small roots were intertwined, and fences broke down in one patch of woods but rose in the next; and rivers were not bottomless, there were earth and rocks underneath, the rocks touched, it was the land, it was all the American land and the American waters belonging principally to America and not to individual planters, and not to New York or Georgia, as had been so cruelly demonstrated.

And now came the strophic echo of the Grecian past (which was not truly the past, and not solely Grecian), *when you have finished your lamentation, let each of you depart.*

There was no Each Of You about it. He was alone, with stains upon his shoes and the legs of his jeans, alone with the recovered shovel-handle for a cane. He moved toward the great gate with not another living man moving there. *For the battle . . . now to face is . . . against the foe in her own household, the desires and ambitions she herself has nurtured.* The Greek said America instead of Athens, and America was an undreamed wilderness beyond seas the Greeks never sailed; yet still he said America, because of the essential timelessness—once more—of clear thought and valuable deed. *Shall she welcome them in their fullness and seek to furnish them with all they need?*

. . . How are you doing with the final stages of Greek, dear Sutherland?

. . . I must say, Father, that you will hear the valedictory spoken in July—but not by me, sir, oh not by me—but by my beloved classmate, Sidney Lanier. He takes as his topic, The Philosophy of History. . . .

Find the philosophy in history if you can, Ira directed himself.

He passed through that gate and felt the eyes of the dead Yankees watching him as he retreated. Were the bulk of the dead too young or too degraded to concern themselves with desires and ambitions of the America for which they had fought and which in turn had slain them; or did the process of extinction award them wisdom? *Or shall she try to put them from her, lest they corrupt her and wreck her peace?* Ira felt that he himself held no desire or ambition, but this bruised collection of States must hold ambition, else the Nation was not fit for the sun to shine upon it; and the sun was shining. *Or, while she is seeking a middle course, will they lay her glory in the dust?* He went past abandoned earthworks, abandoned camps, going directly to his plantation and into the future, and toward challenges waiting there. When he had nearly reached the lane, birds rose before him like an omen.

16 December, 1953.
25 May, 1955.

BIBLIOGRAPHY

Andersonville is a work of fiction, but is presented as an accurate history of the Andersonville prison insofar as specific details concerning the construction, administration, tenancy and supervision of the stockade, with its guards and inhabitants, are made clear.

Those persons portrayed as civilians of the neighborhood are fictitious. The majority of the prison's officials, with certain officers commanding Confederate troops, are drawn from life to the best of the author's ability; and, in his most earnest opinion, are portraits of individuals who did exist and contribute of their lives to this moment of history, whether with baleful or charitable intent. Captain Henry Wirz, the three Winders, Lieutenant-Colonel Alexander Persons, Father Peter Whelan, Colonel D. T. Chandler, Lieutenant Davis, and many others are of history and are not invented. A number of the prisoners described also existed in fact—such men as the several raider leaders, Chickamauga, John McElroy, John Ransom, Bateese, Leroy Key, Boston Corbett and a few more.

Whatever knowledge of the War for Southern Independence—or the Rebellion, or the Civil War, or whatever term is employed (the author no longer considers that there was a "War Between the States")—is demonstrated in the writing of this book was gained through forty years of general reading on the War and those who fought it. A specific approach to the topic of Andersonville began in 1930, four years previous to the publication of *Long Remember,* and six years previous to the publication of *Arouse and Beware.* Therefore a bibliography relating to the Andersonville prison which did not include titles listed in bibliographies appertaining to the two books mentioned above, would not be complete. The student is referred to those bibliographies. Individuals whose assistance was appreciated in studies relating to the other two books also helped concurrently during first investigations of the Andersonville complex. Mentioned once more should be Mr. William A. Slade and Miss Clara Egli of the Library of Congress, and Mr. Randolph W. Church of the Virginia State Library. The author's thanks are reaffirmed after nearly a quarter of a century.

More recently and more specifically again, relating to *Andersonville,* the author is indebted particularly to the following:

Mr. Edward W. Beattie, Jr.; Mr. Clifford Dowdey; Monsignor C. L. Elslander; Mr. Jerome Fried; Colonel W. A. Ganoe; Dr. Thomas C. Garrett; Mrs. Phyllis Gossling; Mr. Edgar Kimsey; Miss Jean L. McKechnie; Colonel William J. Morton, Jr., historian of the United States Military Academy; the Reverend Father John P. O'Connell, editor of the Catholic Press; Dr. William J. Petersen, superintendent of the Iowa State Historical Society, and Miss Mildred Throne of the same organization; the Reverend Mr. David H. Pottie; Miss Hester Rich of the Maryland State Historical Society, and Mr. Fred Shelley, director of that society; Mrs. Elizabeth Service; Miss Ella May Thornton, formerly State Librarian of Georgia, and now honorary librarian; Mr. F. F. Van de Water; Mr. Sylvester

Vigilante, formerly of the New York Public Library and more recently of the New York Historical Society; and Mrs. Mary Gladys Perrin Watkins, only surviving grandchild of Elizabeth and Henry Wirz.

There are general works, some of them original sources, some not: tried and familiar standbys such as *Battles and Leaders of the Civil War,* edited by Robert Underwood Johnson and Clarence Clough Bull, New York, The Century Company, 1884; the *Photographic History of the Civil War,* edited by Francis Trevelyan Miller, New York, The Review of Reviews Company, 1912; the Official Records, War of the Rebellion; and various executive documents published by various United States Congresses. Excerpts from the reports of Confederate officers contained herein are taken verbatim from Executive Document No. 23, Fortieth Congress, Second Session. There has been no tampering with any of the remarks attributed to Confederate officers such as General Howell Cobb, General John H. Winder, Colonel D. T. Chandler and Captain Henry Wirz, when those remarks appear *solidly italicized* in the text.

A great debt is owed to the diaries of John Ransom and John McElroy especially; to the books of General N. P. Chipman; and to the defense published after the war by a former Confederate Chief Surgeon, R. Randolph Stevenson.

A reasonably complete bibliography, each volume including some material employed by the author in the preparation of *Andersonville,* appears below:

A History of the 117th Regiment N. Y. Volunteers. James A. Mowris. Hartford, Conn. Case, Lockwood & Co. 1866.

A History of Popular Music in America. Sigmund Spaeth. New York. Random House. 1948.

A Journal of Hospital Life in the Confederate Army. Kate Cumming. Louisville, Ky. Morton Printers. 1866.

A List of Union Soldiers Buried at Andersonville. Dorence Atwater. New York. The Tribune Association. 1890.

A Memorial Volume of the Hon. Howell Cobb. Edited by Samuel Boykin. Philadelphia. J. B. Lippincott Co. 1870.

A Narrative of Andersonville. Ambrose Spencer. New York. Harper & Bros. 1866.

A Rebel War Clerk's Diary. J. B. Jones. New York. Old Hickory Bookshop. 1935.

A Yankee in Andersonville. T. H. Mann. New York. The Century Magazine, Vol. 18. 1890.

Adventures of an Escaped Union Prisoner from Andersonville. Thomas H. Howe. San Francisco. H. S. Crocker & Co. 1886.

Adventures of George A. Tod. George A. Tod. Edited by Mildred Throne. Iowa City, Iowa. Iowa Journal of History, Vol. 48, No. 4. 1951.

Andersonville. John W. Elarton. Aurora, Neb. Burr Publishing Co. 1913.

Andersonville. J. Frank Hanly. New York. Eaton and Mains. 1912.

Andersonville. John McElroy. Toledo, Ohio. D. R. Locke. 1879.

Andersonville, an Object Lesson in Protection. Herman A. Braun. Milwaukee, Wis. C. D. Fahsel Publishing Co. 1892.

Andersonville and Other War Prisons. Jefferson Davis. New York. Belford Co. 1890.

Andersonville, and the Trial of Henry Wirz. John Howard Stibbs. Iowa City, Iowa. The Clio Press. 1911.

Andersonville Diary. John L. Ransom. Auburn, N.Y. Published by the author. 1881.

Andersonville Prison Park. Compiled by James P. Averill. Atlanta. Byrd Printing Co. 1899.

Ante Bellum Southern Life As It Was. Mary Lennox. Philadelphia. J. B. Lippincott Co. 1868.

Billy and Dick from Andersonville Prison to the White House. Ralph O. Bates. Santa Cruz, Calif. Press Sentinel Publishing Co. 1910.

Captain Sam Grant. Lloyd Lewis. Boston. Little, Brown & Co. 1950.

The Capture, the Prison Pen, and the Escape. Willard W. Glazier. New York. United States Publishing Co. 1868.

Civil War Prisons. William H. Hesseltine. Columbus, Ohio. Ohio State University Press. 1930.

"Co. Aytch." Samuel R. Watkins. Nashville, Tenn. Cumberland Presbyterian Publishing House. 1882.

Collections of a Coffee Cooler. Samuel Creelman. Pittsburgh, Pa. Photo Engraving Co. 1890.

College Life at Old Oglethorpe. Allen P. Tankersley. Athens, Ga. University of Georgia Press. 1951.

Conscription in the C.S.A., 1862–65. Robert P. Brooks. Bulletin of the University of Georgia. Athens, Ga. 1917.

Contributions Relating to the Causation and Prevention of Disease, and to Camp Diseases. Austin Flint. New York. Published for the U.S. Sanitary Commission by Hurd and Houghton. 1867.

Country Life in Georgia in the Days of My Youth. Rebecca Latimer Felton. Atlanta. Index Printing Co. n.d.

The Demon of Andersonville. Anon. Philadelphia. Barclay & Co. 1865.

Doctor Chase's Recipes. A. W. Chase. Ann Arbor, Mich. Published by the author. 1860.

Escape of a Confederate Officer from Prison. Samuel Boyer Davis. Norfolk, Va. The Landmark Publishing Co. 1892.

Florida Plantation Records. Edited by Ulrich Bonnell Phillips and James David Glunt. St. Louis. Missouri Historical Society. 1927.

From Andersonville to Freedom. Charles M. Smith. Providence, R.I. The Society. 1894.

The Gangs of New York. Herbert Asbury. New York. Alfred A. Knopf. 1928.

Gardening for the South. William N. White. New York. Orange Judd and Co. 1868.

Georgia and State Rights. Ulrich Bonnell Phillips. Published by the American Historical Association. Washington, D.C. Government Printing Office. 1902.

The Gray Book. Published by the Sons of Confederate Veterans. n.p. 1920.

Henry Wirz and the Andersonville Prison. Mildred Lewis Rutherford. Athens, Ga. Published by the United Daughters of the Confederacy. 1921.

Historical Record of Macon and Central Georgia. John C. Butler. Macon, Ga. J. W. Burke & Co. 1878.

History of O'Dea's Famous Picture of Andersonville Prison. Thomas O'Dea. Cohoes, N.Y. Clark & Fister. 1887.

History of the 148th Pennsylvania Volunteers. Edited by J. W. Muffly. Des Moines, Iowa. The Kenyon Co. 1904.

The Horrors of Andersonville Rebel Prison. Norton Parker Chipman. San Francisco. The Bancroft Co. 1891.

The Horrors of Southern Prisons During the War of the Rebellion. Wm. Henry Lightcap. Platteville, Wis. Journal Job Rooms. 1902.

In and Out of Andersonville Prison. Wm. Franklin Lyon. Detroit. G. Harland Company. 1905.

Jefferson Davis at West Point. Walter L. Fleming. Baton Rouge, La. Mississippi Historical Society. 1910.

Letter from an Eyewitness at Andersonville Prison. Edited by Spencer B. King, Jr. Collections of the Georgia Historical Society. Vol. 38, No. 1. 1954.

Letters by Hurieosco Austill. Alabama Historical Quarterly, Vol. 7. Wetumpka, Ala. 1945.

The Life and Adventures of Sergt. G. W. Murray. George W. Murray. Minneapolis. Herald Publishing House. 1872.

Life and Death in Rebel Prisons. Robert H. Kellogg. Hartford, Conn. L. Stebbins. 1866.

Life Struggles in Rebel Prisons. Joseph Ferguson. Philadelphia. Published by the author. 1865.

Little Aleck. E. Ramsay Richardson. Indianapolis. The Bobbs-Merrill Co. 1932.

Major Henry Wirz. Lyon G. Tyler. Williamsburg, Va. The William and Mary College Quarterly, Vol. 27. 1919.

Martyria; or, Andersonville Prison. Augustus Choate Hamlin. Boston. Lee and Shepard. 1866.

The Martyrs Who, etc. Published by the Quartermaster's Dept. Washington, D.C. Government Printing Office. 1866.

The Melvin Memorial. Alfred Seelye Roe. Cambridge, Mass. The Riverside Press. 1910.

The Narrative of Amos E. Stearns. Amos Edward Stearns. Worcester, Mass. F. P. Rice. 1887.

Narrative of the Privations and Sufferings, etc. Printed for the U.S. Sanitary Commission by King and Baird, Ptrs. Philadelphia. 1864.

Necrology: or, Memorials of Deceased Ministers. John S. Wilson. Atlanta, Ga. Franklin Printing House. 1869.

Nineteen Months a Prisoner of War. Anon. Milwaukee, Wis. Starr & Son. 1865.

Out-Post. D. H. Mahan. New York. John Wiley. 1863.

Over the Dead-Line. K. C. Bullard. New York. The Neale Publishing Co. 1909.

Prison Life in Andersonville. John Levi Maile. Los Angeles. Grafton Publishing Co. 1912.

Prison Life in Dixie. John B. Vaughter. Chicago. Central Book Concern. 1880.

Prison Life in the South. A. O. Abbott. New York. Harper & Bros. 1865.

The Prisoner of War, and How Treated. Alva C. Roach. Indianapolis. Railroad City Publishing House. 1865.

Reminiscences of Andersonville and Other Rebel Prisons. M. O'Hara. Lyons, Iowa. J. C. Hopkins. 1880.

Report of an Expedition to Andersonville. Clara Barton. New York. The Tribune Association. 1866.

Secondary Education in Georgia. Elbert W. G. Boogher. Philadelphia. Published by the author(?). 1933.

Seven Months in Prison. David E. Russell. Milwaukee, Wis. Godfrey and Crandall. 1866.

Sherman: Fighting Prophet. Lloyd Lewis. New York. Harcourt, Brace and Co. 1932.

Smith's "Knapsack" of Facts and Figures. Frank W. Smith. Toledo, Ohio. Spear, Johnson & Co. 1884.

The Soldier's Story of His Captivity at Andersonville, etc. Warren Lee Goss. Boston. Lee and Shepard. 1869.

Some Records of the Winder Family of Maryland. Philip D. Laird. Baltimore. Maryland Original Research Society. 1913.

The South: A Tour of Its Battlefields and Ruined Cities. J. T. Trowbridge. Hartford, Conn. L. Stebbins. 1866.

The Southern Side, or Andersonville Prison. R. Randolph Stevenson. Baltimore. Turnbull Bros. 1876.

The Story of Andersonville and Florence. James Newton Miller. Des Moines, Iowa. Welch Printing Co. 1900.

To the Memory of My Brother, Edwin W. Niver. Emogene Niver Marshall. Sandusky, Ohio. Krewson Press. 1932.

The Tragedy of Andersonville. Norton Parker Chipman. San Francisco. Blair-Murdock Printing Co. 1911.

Travels in the Confederate States. E. Merton Coulter. Norman, Okla. University of Oklahoma Press. 1948.

The Trial and Death of Henry Wirz. Sarah W. Ashe. Raleigh, N.C. E. M. Uzzell & Co. 1908.

True History. Henry Hernbaker, Jr. Philadelphia. Merrihew & Son. 1876.

The True Story of Andersonville Prison. J. M. Page and M. J. Haley. New York. Neale Publishing Co. 1908.

Twelve Months in Andersonville. Lessel Long. Huntington, Ind. T. & M. Butler. 1886.

Vocabulum, or, the Rogue's Lexicon. Compiled by George W. Matsell. New York. G. W. Matsell & Co. 1859.

The Red Badge of Courage

by
Stephen Crane

STEPHEN CRANE was born in 1871 in Newark, New Jersey. He was a late child, the fourteenth, in fact, in the family of a Methodist minister. His early years were spent in Port Jarvis, New York, and he briefly attended both Lafayette College and Syracuse University. When he was nineteen, and driven by his creative ambition, he decided to move to New York City to seek his future as a writer.

He found mostly poverty as a free-lancer, but by 1893 had published his first book, *Maggie: A Girl of the Streets.* Not surprisingly, this "grim" novel did not sell widely. It did, however, attract the attention of important contemporary literary figures and helped to solidify the new and exciting literary trend of realism of which Mark Twain was the principal figure.

Publication of *The Red Badge of Courage* in 1895 brought Crane fame and even a measure of fortune, the fame in part because of the fact that this remarkable war novel was written by a man who had never been on the field of battle. Though Crane continued to write both verse and prose with awesome power (his short story "The Open Boat" is one of the best of the genre and much anthologized), his personal life took various bizarre turns. Not the least of these was his marriage to a real-life Maggie, a brothel-keeper in Florida. Crane soon left the United States for good—or for ill—serving as a foreign correspondent in Cuba and Greece.

This tortured young talent died before his time, at age 28, of tuberculosis.

1

The cold passed reluctantly from the earth, and the retiring fogs revealed an army stretched out on the hills, resting. As the landscape changed from brown to green, the army awakened, and began to tremble with eagerness at the noise of rumors. It cast its eyes upon the roads, which were growing from long troughs of liquid mud to proper thoroughfares. A river, amber-tinted in the shadow of its banks, purled at the army's feet; and at night, when the stream had become of a sorrowful blackness, one could see across it the red, eyelike gleam of hostile camp-fires set in the low brows of distant hills.

Once a certain tall soldier developed virtues and went resolutely to wash a shirt. He came flying back from a brook waving his garment bannerlike. He was swelled with a tale he had heard from a reliable friend, who had heard it from a truthful cavalryman, who had heard it from his trustworthy brother, one of the orderlies at division headquarters. He adopted the important air of a herald in red and gold.

"We're goin' t' move t' morrah—sure," he said pompously to a group in the company street. "We're goin' 'way up the river, cut across, an' come around in behint 'em."

To his attentive audience he drew a loud and elaborate plan of a very brilliant campaign. When he had finished, the blue-clothed men scattered into small arguing groups between the rows of squat brown huts. A negro teamster who had been dancing upon a cracker box with the hilarious encouragement of twoscore soldiers was deserted. He sat mournfully down. Smoke drifted lazily from a multitude of quaint chimneys.

"It's a lie! that's all it is—a thunderin' lie!" said another private loudly. His smooth face was flushed, and his hands were thrust sulkily into his trousers' pockets. He took the matter as an affront to him. "I don't believe the derned old army's ever going to move. We're set. I've got ready to move eight times in the last two weeks, and we ain't moved yet."

The tall soldier felt called upon to defend the truth of a rumor he himself had introduced. He and the loud one came near to fighting over it.

A corporal began to swear before the assemblage. He had just put a costly board floor in his house, he said. During the early spring he had refrained from adding extensively to the comfort of his environment because he had felt that the army might start on the march at any moment. Of late, however, he had been impressed that they were in a sort of eternal camp.

Many of the men engaged in a spirited debate. One outlined in a peculiarly lucid manner all the plans of the commanding general. He was opposed by men who advocated that there were other plans of campaign. They clamored at each other, numbers making futile bids for the popular attention. Meanwhile, the soldier who had fetched the rumor bustled about with much importance. He was continually assailed by questions.

"What's up, Jim?"

"Th' army's goin' t' move."

"Ah, what yeh takin' about? How yeh know it is?"

"Well, yeh kin b'lieve me er not, jest as yeh like. I don't care a hang."

There was much food for thought in the manner in which he replied. He came near to convincing them by disdaining to produce proofs. They grew much excited over it.

There was a youthful private who listened with eager ears to the words of the tall soldier and to the varied comments of his comrades. After receiving a fill of discussions concerning marches and attacks, he went to his hut and crawled through an intricate hole that served it as a door. He wished to be alone with some new thoughts that had lately come to him.

He lay down on a wide bunk that stretched across the end of the room. In the other end, cracker boxes were made to serve as furniture. They were grouped about the fireplace. A picture from an illustrated weekly was upon the log walls, and three rifles were paralleled on pegs. Equipments hung on handy projections, and some tin dishes lay upon a small pile of firewood. A folded tent was serving as a roof. The sunlight, without, beating upon it, made it glow a light yellow shade. A small window shot an oblique square of whiter light upon the cluttered floor. The smoke from the fire at times neglected the clay chimney and wreathed into the room, and this flimsy chimney of clay and sticks made endless threats to set ablaze the whole establishment.

The youth was in a little trance of astonishment. So they were at last going to fight. On the morrow, perhaps, there would be a battle, and he would be in it. For a time he was obliged to labor to make himself believe. He could not accept with assurance an omen that he was about to mingle in one of those great affairs of the earth.

He had, of course, dreamed of battles all his life—of vague and bloody conflicts that had thrilled him with their sweep and fire. In visions he had seen himself in many struggles. He had imagined peoples secure in the shadow of his eagle-eyed prowess. But awake he had regarded battles as crimson blotches on the pages of the past. He had put them as things of the bygone with his thought-images of heavy crowns and high castles. There was a portion of the world's history which he had regarded as the time of wars, but it, he thought, had been long gone over the horizon and had disappeared forever.

From his home his youthful eyes had looked upon the war in his own country with distrust. It must be some sort of a play affair. He had long despaired of witnessing a Greeklike struggle. Such would be no more, he had said. Men were better, or more timid. Secular and religious education had effaced the throat-grappling instinct, or else firm finance held in check the passions.

He had burned several times to enlist. Tales of great movements shook the land. They might not be distinctly Homeric, but there seemed to be much glory in them. He had read of marches, sieges, conflicts, and he had longed to see it all. His busy mind had drawn for him large pictures extravagant in color, lurid with breathless deeds.

But his mother had discouraged him. She had affected to look with some contempt upon the quality of his war ardor and patriotism. She could calmly seat herself and with no apparent difficulty give him many hundreds of reasons why he was of vastly more importance on the farm than on the field of battle. She had had certain ways of expression that told him that her statements on the subject came from a deep conviction. Moreover, on her side, was his belief that her ethical motive in the argument was impregnable.

At last, however, he had made firm rebellion against this yellow light thrown upon the color of his ambitions. The newspapers, the gossip of the village, his own picturings, had aroused him to an uncheckable degree. They were in truth fighting finely down there. Almost every day the newspapers printed accounts of a decisive victory.

One night, as he lay in bed, the winds had carried to him the clangoring of the church bell as some enthusiast jerked the rope frantically to tell the twisted news of a great battle. This voice of the people rejoicing in the night had made him shiver in a prolonged ecstasy of excitement. Later, he had gone down to his mother's room and had spoken thus: "Ma, I'm going to enlist."

"Henry, don't you be a fool," his mother had replied. She had then covered her face with the quilt. There was an end to the matter for that night.

Nevertheless, the next morning he had gone to a town that was near his mother's farm and had enlisted in a company that was forming there. When he had returned home his mother was milking the brindle cow. Four others stood waiting. "Ma, I've enlisted," he had said to her diffidently. There was a short silence. "The Lord's will be done, Henry," she had finally replied, and had then continued to milk the brindle cow.

When he had stood in the doorway with his soldier's clothes on his back, and with the light of excitement and expectancy in his eyes almost defeating the glow of regret for the home bonds, he had seen two tears leaving their trails on his mother's scarred cheeks.

Still, she had disappointed him by saying nothing whatever about returning with his shield or on it. He had privately primed himself for a beautiful scene. He had prepared certain sentences which he thought could be used with touching effect. But her words destroyed his plans. She had doggedly peeled potatoes and addressed him as follows: "You watch out, Henry, an' take good care of yerself in this here fighting business—you watch out, an' take good care of yerself. Don't go a-thinkin' you can lick the hull rebel army at the start, because yeh can't. Yer jest one little feller amongst a hull lot of others, and ye've got to keep quiet an' do what they tell yeh. I know how you are, Henry.

"I've knet yeh eight pair of socks, Henry, and I've put in all yer best shirts, because I want my boy to be jest as warm and comf'able as anybody in the army. Whenever they get holes in 'em, I want yeh to send 'em right-away back to me, so's I kin dern 'em.

"An' allus be careful an' choose yer comp'ny. There's lots of bad men in the army, Henry. The army makes 'em wild, and they like nothing better than the job of leading off a young feller like you, as ain't never been away from home much and has allus had a mother, an' a-learning 'em to drink and swear. Keep clear of them folks, Henry. I don't want yeh to ever do any thing, Henry, that yeh would be 'shamed to let me know about. Jest think as if I was a-watchin' yeh. If yeh keep that in yer mind allus, I guess yeh'll come out about right.

"Yeh must allus remember yer father, too, child, an' remember he never drunk a drop of licker in his life, and seldom swore a cross oath.

"I don't know what else to tell yeh, Henry, excepting that yeh must never do no shirking, child, on my account. If so be a time comes when yeh have to be kilt or do a mean thing, why, Henry, don't think of anything 'cept what's right, because there's many a woman has to bear up 'ginst sech things these times, and the Lord 'll take keer of us all.

"Don't forget about the socks and the shirts, child; and I've put a cup of blackberry jam with yer bundle, because I know yeh like it above all things. Good-by, Henry. Watch out, and be a good boy."

He had, of course, been impatient under the ordeal of this speech. It had not been quite what he expected, and he had borne it with an air of irritation. He departed feeling vague relief.

Still, when he had looked back from the gate, he had seen his mother kneeling among the potato parings. Her brown face, upraised, was stained with tears, and her spare form was quivering. He bowed his head and went on, feeling suddenly ashamed of his purposes.

From his home he had gone to the seminary to bid adieu to many schoolmates. They had thronged about him with wonder and admiration. He had felt the gulf now between them and had swelled with calm pride. He and some of his fellows who had donned blue were quite overwhelmed with privileges for all of one afternoon, and it had been a very delicious thing. They had strutted.

A certain light-haired girl had made vivacious fun at his martial spirit, but there was another and darker girl whom he had gazed at steadfastly, and he thought she grew demure and sad at sight of his blue and brass. As he had walked down the path between the rows of oaks, he had turned his head and detected her at a window watching his departure. As he perceived her, she had immediately begun to stare up through the high tree branches at the sky. He had seen a good deal of flurry and haste in her movement as she changed her attitude. He often thought of it.

On the way to Washington his spirit had soared. The regiment was fed and caressed at station after station until the youth had believed that he must be a hero. There was a lavish expenditure of bread and cold meats, coffee, and pickles and cheese. As he basked in the smiles of the girls and was patted and complimented by the old men, he had felt growing within him the strength to do mighty deeds of arms.

After complicated journeyings with many pauses, there had come months of monotonous life in a camp. He had had the belief that real war was a series of death struggles with small time in between for sleep and meals; but since his regiment had come to the field the army had done little but sit still and try to keep warm.

He was brought then gradually back to his old ideas. Greeklike struggles would be no more. Men were better, or more timid. Secular and religious education had effaced the throat-grappling instinct, or else firm finance held in check the passions.

He had grown to regard himself merely as a part of a vast blue demonstration. His province was to look out, as far as he could, for his personal comfort. For recreation he could twiddle his thumbs and speculate on the thoughts which must agitate the minds of the generals. Also, he was drilled and drilled and reviewed, and drilled and drilled and reviewed.

The only foes he had seen were some pickets along the river bank. They were a sun-tanned, philosophical lot, who sometimes shot reflectively at the blue pickets. When reproached for this afterward, they usually expressed sorrow, and swore by their gods that the guns had exploded without their permission. The youth, on guard duty one night, conversed across the stream with one of them. He was a slightly ragged man, who spat skillfully between his shoes and possessed a great fund of bland and infantile assurance. The youth liked him personally.

"Yank," the other had informed him, "yer a right dum good feller." This sentiment, floating to him upon the still air, had made him temporarily regret war.

Various veterans had told him tales. Some talked of gray, bewhiskered hordes who were advancing with relentless curses and chewing tobacco with unspeakable valor; tremendous bodies of fierce soldiery who were sweeping along like the Huns. Others spoke of tattered and eternally hungry men who fired despondent powders. "They'll charge through hell's fire an' brimstone t' git a holt on a haversack, an' sech stomachs ain't a-lastin' long," he was told. From the stories, the youth imagined the red, live bones sticking out through slits in the faded uniforms.

Still, he could not put a whole faith in veterans' tales, for recruits were their prey. They talked much of smoke, fire, and blood, but he could not tell how much might be lies. They persistently yelled "Fresh fish!" at him, and were in no wise to be trusted.

However, he perceived now that it did not greatly matter what kind of soldiers he was going to fight, so long as they fought, which fact no one disputed. There was a more serious problem. He lay in his bunk pondering upon it. He tried to mathematically prove to himself that he would not run from a battle.

Previously he had never felt obliged to wrestle too seriously with this question. In his life he had taken certain things for granted, never challenging his belief in ultimate success, and bothering little about means and roads. But here he was confronted with a thing of moment. It had suddenly appeared to him that perhaps in a battle he might run. He was forced to admit that as far as war was concerned he knew nothing of himself.

A sufficient time before he would have allowed the problem to kick its heels at the outer portals of his mind, but now he felt compelled to give serious attention to it.

A little panic-fear grew in his mind. As his imagination went forward to a fight, he saw hideous possibilities. He contemplated the lurking menaces of the future, and failed in an effort to see himself standing stoutly in the midst of them. He recalled his visions of broken-bladed glory, but in the shadow of the impending tumult he suspected them to be impossible pictures.

He sprang from the bunk and began to pace nervously to and fro. "Good Lord, what's th' matter with me?" he said aloud.

He felt that in this crisis his laws of life were useless. Whatever he had learned of himself was here of no avail. He was an unknown quantity. He saw that he would again be obliged to experiment as he had in early youth. He must accumulate information of himself, and meanwhile he resolved to remain close upon his guard lest those qualities of which he knew nothing should everlastingly disgrace him. "Good Lord!" he repeated in dismay.

After a time the tall soldier slid dexterously through the hole. The loud private followed. They were wrangling.

"That's all right," said the tall soldier as he entered. He waved his hand expressively. "You can believe me or not, jest as you like. All you got to do is to sit down and wait as quiet as you can. Then pretty soon you'll find out I was right."

His comrade grunted stubbornly. For a moment he seemed to be searching for a formidable reply. Finally he said: "Well, you don't know everything in the world, do you?"

"Didn't say I knew everything in the world," retorted the other sharply. He began to stow various articles snugly into his knapsack.

The youth, pausing in his nervous walk, looked down at the busy figure. "Going to be a battle, sure, is there, Jim?" he asked.

"Of course there is," replied the tall soldier. "Of course there is. You jest wait 'til to-morrow, and you'll see one of the biggest battles ever was. You jest wait."

"Thunder!" said the youth.

"Oh, you'll see fighting this time, my boy, what'll be regular out-and-out fighting," added the tall soldier, with the air of a man who is about to exhibit a battle for the benefit of his friends.

"Huh!" said the loud one from a corner.

"Well," remarked the youth, "like as not this story'll turn out jest like them others did."

"Not much it won't," replied the tall soldier, exasperated. "Not much it won't. Didn't the cavalry all start this morning?" He glared about him. No one denied his statement. "The cavalry started this morning," he continued. "They say there ain't hardly any cavalry left in camp. They're going to Richmond, or some place, while we fight all the Johnnies. It's some dodge like that. The regiment's got orders, too. A feller what seen 'em go to headquarters told me a little while ago. And they're raising blazes all over camp—anybody can see that."

"Shucks!" said the loud one.

The youth remained silent for a time. At last he spoke to the tall soldier. "Jim!"

"What?"

"How do you think the reg'ment 'll do?"

"Oh, they'll fight all right, I guess, after they once get into it," said the other with cold judgment. He made a fine use of the third person. "There's been heaps of fun poked at 'em because they're new, of course, and all that; but they'll fight all right, I guess."

"Think any of the boys 'll run?" persisted the youth.

"Oh, there may be a few of 'em run, but there's them kind in every regiment, 'specially when they first goes under fire," said the other in a tolerant way. "Of course it might happen that the hull kit-and-boodle might start and run, if some big fighting came first-off, and then again they might stay and fight like fun. But you can't bet on nothing. Of course they ain't never been under fire yet, and it ain't likely they'll lick the hull rebel army all-to-oncet the first time; but I think they'll fight better than some, if worse than others. That's the way I figger. They call the reg'ment 'Fresh fish' and everything; but the boys come of good stock, and most of 'em 'll fight like sin after they oncet git shootin'," he added, with a mighty emphasis on the last four words.

"Oh, you think you know—" began the loud soldier with scorn.

The other turned savagely upon him. They had a rapid altercation, in which they fastened upon each other various strange epithets.

The youth at last interrupted them. "Did you ever think you might run yourself, Jim?" he asked. On concluding the sentence he laughed as if he had meant to aim a joke. The loud soldier also giggled.

The tall private waved his hand. "Well," said he profoundly, "I've thought it might get too hot for Jim Conklin in some of them scrimmages, and if a whole lot of boys started and run, why, I s'pose I'd start and run. And if I once started to run, I'd run like the devil, and no mistake. But if everybody was a-standing and a-fighting, why, I'd stand and fight. Be jiminey, I would. I'll bet on it."

"Huh!" said the loud one.

The youth of this tale felt gratitude for these words of his comrade. He had feared that all of the untried men possessed a great and correct confidence. He now was in a measure reassured.

2

The next morning the youth discovered that his tall comrade had been the fast-flying messenger of a mistake. There was much scoffing at the latter by those who had yesterday been firm adherents of his views, and there was even a little sneering by men who had never believed the rumor. The tall one fought with a man from Chatfield Corners and beat him severely.

The youth felt, however, that his problem was in no wise lifted from him. There was, on the contrary, an irritating prolongation. The tale had created in him a great concern for himself. Now, with the newborn question in his mind, he was compelled to sink back into his old place as part of a blue demonstration.

For days he made ceaseless calculations, but they were all wondrously unsatisfactory. He found that he could establish nothing. He finally concluded that the only way to prove himself was to go into the blaze, and then figuratively to watch his legs to discover their merits and faults. He reluctantly admitted that he could not sit still and with a mental slate and pencil derive an answer. To gain it, he must have blaze, blood, and danger, even as a chemist requires this, that, and the other. So he fretted for an opportunity.

Meanwhile he continually tried to measure himself by his comrades. The tall soldier, for one, gave him some assurance. This man's serene unconcern dealt him a measure of confidence, for he had known him since childhood, and from his intimate knowledge he did not see how he could be capable of anything that was beyond him, the youth. Still, he thought that his comrade might be mistaken about himself. Or, on the other hand, he might be a man heretofore doomed to peace and obscurity, but, in reality, made to shine in war.

The youth would have liked to have discovered another who suspected himself. A sympathetic comparison of mental notes would have been a joy to him.

He occasionally tried to fathom a comrade with seductive sentences. He looked about to find men in the proper mood. All attempts failed to bring forth any statement which looked in any way like a confession to those doubts which he privately acknowledged in himself. He was afraid to make an open declaration of his concern, because he dreaded to place some unscrupulous confidant upon the high plane of the unconfessed from which elevation he could be derided.

In regard to his companions his mind wavered between two opinions, according to his mood. Sometimes he inclined to believing them all heroes. In fact, he usually admitted in secret the superior development of the higher qualities in others. He could conceive of men going very insignificantly about the world bearing a load of courage unseen, and although he had known many of his comrades through boyhood, he began to fear that his judgment of them had been blind. Then, in other moments, he flouted these theories, and assured himself that his fellows were all privately wondering and quaking.

His emotions made him feel strange in the presence of men who talked excitedly of a prospective battle as of a drama they were about to witness, with nothing but eagerness and curiosity apparent in their faces. It was often that he suspected them to be liars.

He did not pass such thoughts without severe condemnation of himself. He dinned reproaches at times. He was convicted by himself of many shameful crimes against the gods of traditions.

In his great anxiety his heart was continually clamoring at what he considered the intolerable slowness of the generals. They seemed content to perch tranquilly on the river bank, and leave him bowed down by the weight of a great problem. He wanted it settled forthwith. He could not long bear such a load, he said. Sometimes his anger at the commanders reached an acute stage, and he grumbled about the camp like a veteran.

One morning, however, he found himself in the ranks of his prepared regiment. The men were whispering speculations and recounting the old rumors. In the gloom before the break of the day their uniforms glowed a deep purple hue. From across the river the red eyes were still peering. In the eastern sky there was a yellow patch like a rug laid for the feet of the coming sun; and against it, black and patternlike, loomed the gigantic figure of the colonel on a gigantic horse.

From off in the darkness came the trampling of feet. The youth could occasionally see dark shadows that moved like monsters. The regiment stood at rest for what seemed a long time. The youth grew impatient. It was unendurable the way these affairs were managed. He wondered how long they were to be kept waiting.

As he looked all about him and pondered upon the mystic gloom, he began to believe that at any moment the ominous distance might be aflare, and the rolling crashes of an engagement come to his ears. Staring once at the red eyes across the river, he conceived them to be growing larger, as the orbs of a row of dragons advancing. He turned toward the colonel and saw him lift his gigantic arm and calmly stroke his mustache.

At last he heard from along the road at the foot of the hill the clatter of a horse's galloping hoofs. It must be the coming of orders. He bent forward, scarce breathing. The exciting clickety-click, as it grew louder and louder, seemed to be beating upon his soul. Presently a horseman with jangling equipment drew rein before the colonel of the regiment. The two held a short, sharp-worded conversation. The men in the foremost ranks craned their necks.

As the horseman wheeled his animal and galloped away he turned to shout over his shoulder, "Don't forget that box of cigars!" The colonel mumbled in reply. The youth wondered what a box of cigars had to do with war.

A moment later the regiment went swinging off into the darkness. It was now like one of those moving monsters wending with many feet. The air was heavy, and cold with dew. A mass of wet grass, marched upon, rustled like silk.

There was an occasional flash and glimmer of steel from the backs of all these huge crawling reptiles. From the road came creakings and grumblings as some surly guns were dragged away.

The men stumbled along still muttering speculations. There was a subdued debate. Once a man fell down, and as he reached for his rifle a comrade, unseeing, trod upon his hand. He of the injured fingers swore bitterly and aloud. A low, tittering laugh went among his fellows.

Presently they passed into a roadway and marched forward with easy strides. A dark regiment moved before them, and from behind also came the tinkle of equipments on the bodies of marching men.

The rushing yellow of the developing day went on behind their backs. When the sunrays at last struck full and mellowingly upon the earth, the youth saw that the landscape was streaked with two long, thin, black columns which disappeared on the brow of a hill in front and rearward vanished in a wood. They were like two serpents crawling from the cavern of the night.

The river was not in view. The tall soldier burst into praises of what he thought to be his powers of perception.

Some of the tall one's companions cried with emphasis that they, too, had evolved the same thing, and they congratulated themselves upon it. But there were others who said that the tall one's plan was not the true one at all. They persisted with other theories. There was a vigorous discussion.

The youth took no part in them. As he walked along in careless line he was engaged with his own eternal debate. He could not hinder himself from dwelling upon it. He was despondent and sullen, and threw shifting glances about him. He looked ahead, often expecting to hear from the advance the rattle of firing.

But the long serpents crawled slowly from hill to hill without bluster of smoke. A dun-colored cloud of dust floated away to the right. The sky overhead was of a fairy blue.

The youth studied the faces of his companions, ever on the watch to detect kindred emotions. He suffered disappointment. Some ardor of the air which was causing the veteran commands to move with glee—almost with song—had infected the new regiment. The men began to speak of victory as of a thing they knew. Also, the tall soldier received his vindication. They were certainly going to come around in behind the enemy. They expressed commiseration for that part of the army which had been left upon the river bank, felicitating themselves upon being a part of a blasting host.

The youth, considering himself as separated from the others, was saddened by the blithe and merry speeches that went from rank to rank. The company wags all made their best endeavors. The regiment tramped to the tune of laughter.

The blatant soldier often convulsed whole files by his biting sarcasms aimed at the tall one.

And it was not long before all the men seemed to forget their mission. Whole brigades grinned in unison, and regiments laughed.

A rather fat soldier attempted to pilfer a horse from a dooryard. He planned to load his knapsack upon it. He was escaping with his prize when a young girl rushed from the house and grabbed the animal's mane. There followed a wrangle. The young girl, with pink cheeks and shining eyes, stood like a dauntless statue.

The observant regiment, standing at rest in the roadway, whooped at once, and entered whole-souled upon the side of the maiden. The men became so engrossed in this affair that they entirely ceased to remember their own large war. They jeered the piratical private, and called attention to various defects in his personal appearance; and they were wildly enthusiastic in support of the young girl.

To her, from some distance, came bold advice. "Hit him with a stick."

There were crows and catcalls showered upon him when he retreated without the horse. The regiment rejoiced at his downfall. Loud and vociferous congratulations were showered upon the maiden, who stood panting and regarding the troops with defiance.

At nightfall the column broke into regimental pieces, and the fragments went into the fields to camp. Tents sprang up like strange plants. Camp fires, like red, peculiar blossoms, dotted the night.

The youth kept from intercourse with his companions as much as circumstances would allow him. In the evening he wandered a few paces into the gloom. From this little distance the many fires, with the black forms of men passing to and fro before the crimson rays, made weird and satanic effects.

He lay down in the grass. The blades pressed tenderly against his cheek. The moon had been lighted and was hung in a treetop. The liquid stillness of the night enveloping him made him feel vast pity for himself. There was a caress in the soft winds; and the whole mood of the darkness, he thought, was one of sympathy for himself in his distress.

He wished, without reserve, that he was at home again making the endless rounds from the house to the barn, from the barn to the house. He remembered he had often cursed the brindle cow and her mates, and had sometimes flung milking stools. But, from his present point of view, there was a halo of happiness about each of their heads, and he would have sacrificed all the brass buttons on the continent to have been enabled to return to them. He told himself that he was not formed for a soldier. And he mused seriously upon the radical difference between himself and those men who were dodging imp-like around the fires.

As he mused thus he heard the rustle of grass, and, upon turning his head, discovered the loud soldier. He called out, "Oh, Wilson!"

The latter approached and looked down. "Why, hello, Henry; is it you? What you doing here?"

"Oh, thinking," said the youth.

The other sat down and carefully lighted his pipe. "You're getting blue, my boy. You're looking thundering peeked. What the dickens is wrong with you?"

"Oh, nothing," said the youth.

The loud soldier launched then into the subject of the anticipated fight. "Oh, we've got 'em now!" As he spoke his boyish face was wreathed in a gleeful smile, and his voice had an exultant ring. "We've got 'em now. At last, by the eternal thunders, we'll lick 'em good!"

"If the truth was known," he added, more soberly, *"they've* licked *us* about every clip up to now; but this time—this time—we'll lick 'em good!"

"I thought you was objecting to this march a little while ago," said the youth coldly.

"Oh, it wasn't that," explained the other. "I don't mind marching, if there's going to be fighting at the end of it. What I hate is this getting moved here and moved there, with no good coming of it, as far as I can see, excepting sore feet and damned short rations."

"Well, Jim Conklin says we'll get a plenty of fighting this time."

"He's right for once, I guess, though I can't see how it come. This time we're in for a big battle, and we've got the best end of it, certain sure. Gee rod! how we will thump 'em!"

He arose and began to pace to and fro excitedly. The thrill of his enthusiasm made him walk with an elastic step. He was sprightly, vigorous, fiery in his belief in success. He looked into the future with clear, proud eye, and he swore with the air of an old soldier.

The youth watched him for a moment in silence. When he finally spoke his voice was as bitter as dregs. "Oh, you're going to do great things, I s'pose!"

The loud soldier blew a thoughtful cloud of smoke from his pipe. "Oh, I don't know," he remarked with dignity; "I don't know. I s'pose I'll do as well as the rest. I'm going to try like thunder." He evidently complimented himself upon the modesty of this statement.

"How do you know you won't run when the time comes?" asked the youth.

"Run?" said the loud one; "run?—of course not!" He laughed.

"Well," continued the youth, "lots of good-a-'nough men have thought they was going to do great things before the fight, but when the time come they skedaddled."

"Oh, that's all true, I s'pose," replied the other; "but I'm not going to skedaddle. The man that bets on my running will lose his money, that's all." He nodded confidently.

"Oh, shucks!" said the youth. "You ain't the bravest man in the world, are you?"

"No, I ain't," exclaimed the loud soldier indignantly; "and I didn't say I was the bravest man in the world, neither. I said I was going to do my share of fighting— that's what I said. And I am, too. Who are you, anyhow? You talk as if you thought you was Napoleon Bonaparte." He glared at the youth for a moment, and then strode away.

The youth called in a savage voice after his comrade: "Well, you needn't git mad about it!" But the other continued on his way and made no reply.

He felt alone in space when his injured comrade had disappeared. His failure to discover any mite of resemblance in their view points made him more misera- ble than before. No one seemed to be wrestling with such a terrific personal problem. He was a mental outcast.

He went slowly to his tent and stretched himself on a blanket by the side of the snoring tall soldier. In the darkness he saw visions of a thousand-tongued fear that would babble at his back and cause him to flee, while others were going coolly about their country's business. He admitted that he would not be able to cope with this monster. He felt that every nerve in his body would be an ear to hear the voices, while other men would remain stolid and deaf.

And as he sweated with the pain of these thoughts, he could hear low, serene sentences. "I'll bid five." "Make it six." "Seven." "Seven goes."

He stared at the red, shivering reflection of a fire on the white wall of his tent until, exhausted and ill from the monotony of his suffering, he fell asleep.

3

When another night came the columns, changed to purple streaks, filed across two pontoon bridges. A glaring fire wine-tinted the waters of the river. Its rays, shining upon the moving masses of troops, brought forth here and there sudden gleams of silver or gold. Upon the other shore a dark and mysterious range of hills was curved against the sky. The insect voices of the night sang solemnly.

After this crossing the youth assured himself that at any moment they might be suddenly and fearfully assaulted from the caves of the lowering woods. He kept his eyes watchfully upon the darkness.

But his regiment went unmolested to a camping place, and its soldiers slept the brave sleep of wearied men. In the morning they were routed out with early energy, and hustled along a narrow road that led deep into the forest.

It was during this rapid march that the regiment lost many of the marks of a new command.

The men had begun to count the miles upon their fingers, and they grew tired. "Sore feet an' damned short rations, that's all," said the loud soldier. There was perspiration and grumblings. After a time they began to shed their knapsacks. Some tossed them unconcernedly down; others hid them carefully, asserting their plans to return for them at some convenient time. Men extricated themselves from thick shirts. Presently few carried anything but the necessary clothing, blankets, haversacks, canteens, and arms and ammunition. "You can now eat and shoot," said the tall soldier to the youth. "That's all you want to do."

There was sudden change from the ponderous infantry of theory to the light and speedy infantry of practice. The regiment, relieved of a burden, received a new impetus. But there was much loss of valuable knapsacks, and, on the whole, very good shirts.

But the regiment was not yet veteranlike in appearance. Veteran regiments in the army were likely to be very small aggregations of men. Once, when the command had first come to the field, some perambulating veterans, noting the length of their column, had accosted them thus: "Hey, fellers, what brigade is that?" And when the men had replied that they formed a regiment and not a brigade, the older soldiers had laughed, and said, "O Gawd!"

Also, there was too great a similarity in the hats. The hats of a regiment should properly represent the history of headgear for a period of years. And, moreover, there were no letters of faded gold speaking from the colors. They were new and beautiful, and the color bearer habitually oiled the pole.

Presently the army again sat down to think. The odor of the peaceful pines was in the men's nostrils. The sound of monotonous axe blows rang through the forest, and the insects, nodding upon their perches, crooned like old women. The youth returned to his theory of a blue demonstration.

One gray dawn, however, he was kicked in the leg by the tall soldier, and then, before he was entirely awake, he found himself running down a wood road in the midst of men who were panting from the first effects of speed. His canteen banged rhythmically upon his thigh, and his haversack bobbed softly. His musket bounced a trifle from his shoulder at each stride and made his cap feel uncertain upon his head.

He could hear the men whisper jerky sentences: "Say—what's all this— about?" "What th' thunder—we—skedaddlin' this way fer?" "Billie—keep off m' feet. Yeh run—like a cow." And the loud soldier's shrill voice could be heard: "What th' devil they in sich a hurry for?"

The youth thought the damp fog of early morning moved from the rush of a great body of troops. From the distance came a sudden spatter of firing.

He was bewildered. As he ran with his comrades he strenuously tried to think, but all he knew was that if he fell down those coming behind would tread upon him. All his faculties seemed to be needed to guide him over and past obstructions. He felt carried along by a mob.

The sun spread disclosing rays, and, one by one, regiments burst into view like armed men just born on the earth. The youth perceived that the time had come. He was about to be measured. For a moment he felt in the face of his great trial like a babe, and the flesh over his heart seemed very thin. He seized time to look about him calculatingly.

But he instantly saw that it would be impossible for him to escape from the regiment. It inclosed him. And there were iron laws of tradition and law on four sides. He was in a moving box.

As he perceived this fact it occurred to him that he had never wished to come to the war. He had not enlisted of his free will. He had been dragged by the merciless government. And now they were taking him out to be slaughtered.

The regiment slid down a bank and wallowed across a little stream. The mournful current moved slowly on, and from the water, shaded black, some white bubble eyes looked at the men.

As they climbed the hill on the father side artillery began to boom. Here the youth forgot many things as he felt a sudden impulse of curiosity. He scrambled up the bank with a speed that could not be exceeded by a bloodthirsty man.

He expected a battle scene.

There were some little fields girted and squeezed by a forest. Spread over the grass and in among the tree trunks, he could see knots and waving lines of skirmishers who were running hither and thither and firing at the landscape. A dark battle line lay upon a sunstruck clearing that gleamed orange color. A flag fluttered.

Other regiments floundered up the bank. The bridge was formed in line of battle, and after a pause started slowly through the woods in the rear of the receding skirmishers, who were continually melting into the scene to appear again farther on. They were always busy as bees, deeply absorbed in their little combats.

The youth tried to observe everything. He did not use care to avoid trees and branches, and his forgotten feet were constantly knocking against stones or getting entangled in briers. He was aware that these battalions with their commotions were woven red and startling into the gentle fabric of softened greens and browns. It looked to be a wrong place for a battle field.

The skirmishers in advance fascinated him. Their shots into thickets and at distant and prominent trees spoke to him of tragedies—hidden, mysterious, solemn.

Once the line encountered the body of a dead soldier. He lay upon his back staring at the sky. He was dressed in an awkward suit of yellowish brown. The youth could see that the soles of his shoes had been worn to the thinness of writing paper, and from a great rent in one the dead foot projected piteously. And it was as if fate had betrayed the soldier. In death it exposed to his enemies that poverty which in life he had perhaps concealed from his friends.

The ranks opened covertly to avoid the corpse. The invulnerable dead man forced a way for himself. The youth looked keenly at the ashen face. The wind raised the tawny beard. It moved as if a hand were stroking it. He vaguely desired to walk around and around the body and stare; the impulse of the living to try to read in dead eyes the answer of the Question.

During the march the ardor which the youth had acquired when out of view of the field rapidly faded to nothing. His curiosity was quite easily satisfied. If an intense scene had caught him with its wild swing as he came to the top of the bank, he might have gone roaring on. This advance upon Nature was too calm. He had opportunity to reflect. He had time in which to wonder about himself and to attempt to probe his sensations.

Absurd ideas took hold upon him. He thought that he did not relish the landscape. It threatened him. A coldness swept over his back, and it is true that his trousers felt to him that they were no fit for his legs at all.

A house standing placidly in distant fields had to him an ominous look. The shadows of the woods were formidable. He was certain that in this vista there lurked fierce-eyed hosts. The swift thought came to him that the generals did not know what they were about. It was all a trap. Suddenly those close forests would bristle with rifle barrels. Ironlike brigades would appear in the rear. They were all going to be sacrificed. The generals were stupids. The enemy would presently swallow the whole command. He glared about him, expecting to see the stealthy approach of his death.

He thought that he must break from the ranks and harangue his comrades. They must not all be killed like pigs; and he was sure it would come to pass unless they were informed of these dangers. The generals were idiots to send them marching into a regular pen. There was but one pair of eyes in the corps. He would step forth and make a speech. Shrill and passionate words came to his lips.

The line, broken into moving fragments by the ground, went calmly on through fields and woods. The youth looked at the men nearest him, and saw, for the most part, expressions of deep interest, as if they were investigating something that had fascinated them. One or two stepped with overvaliant airs as if they were already plunged into war. Others walked as upon thin ice. The greater part of the untested men appeared quiet and absorbed. They were going to look at war, the red animal—war, the blood-swollen god. And they were deeply engrossed in this march.

As he looked the youth gripped his outcry at his throat. He saw that even if the men were tottering with fear they would laugh at his warning. They would jeer him, and, if practicable, pelt him with missiles. Admitting that he might be wrong, a frenzied declamation of the kind would turn him into a worm.

He assumed, then, the demeanor of one who knows that he is doomed alone to unwritten responsibilities. He lagged, with tragic glances at the sky.

He was surprised presently by the young lieutenant of his company, who began heartily to beat him with a sword, calling out in a loud and insolent voice: "Come, young man, get up into ranks there. No skulking'll do here." He mended his pace with suitable haste. And he hated the lieutenant, who had no appreciation of fine minds. He was a mere brute.

After a time the brigade was halted in the cathedral light of a forest. The busy skirmishers were still popping. Through the aisles of the wood could be seen the floating smoke from their rifles. Sometimes it went up in little balls, white and compact.

During this halt many men in the regiment began erecting tiny hills in front of them. They used stones, sticks, earth, and anything they thought might turn a bullet. Some built comparatively large ones, while others seemed content with little ones.

This procedure caused a discussion among the men. Some wished to fight like duelists, believing it to be correct to stand erect and be, from their feet to their foreheads, a mark. They said they scorned the devices of the cautious. But the others scoffed in reply, and pointed to the veterans on the flanks who were digging at the ground like terriers. In a short time there was quite a barricade along the regimental fronts. Directly, however, they were ordered to withdraw from that place.

This astounded the youth. He forgot his stewing over the advance movement. "Well, then, what did they march us out here for?" he demanded of the soldier. The latter with calm faith began a heavy explanation, although he had been compelled to leave a little protection of stones and dirt to which he had devoted much care and skill.

When the regiment was aligned in another position each man's regard for his safety caused another line of small intrenchments. They ate their noon meal behind a third one. They were moved from this one also. They were marched from place to place with apparent aimlessness.

The youth had been taught that a man became another thing in a battle. He saw his salvation in such a change. Hence this waiting was an ordeal to him. He was in fever of impatience. He considered that there was denoted a lack of purpose on the part of the generals. He began to complain to the tall soldier. "I can't stand this much longer," he cried. "I don't see what good it does to make us wear out our legs for nothin'." He wished to return to camp, knowing that this affair was a blue demonstration; or else to go into a battle and discover that he had been a fool in his doubts, and was, in truth, a man of traditional courage. The strain of present circumstances he felt to be intolerable.

The philosophical tall soldier measured a sandwich of cracker and pork and swallowed it in a nonchalant manner. "Oh, I suppose we must go reconnoitering around the country jest to keep 'em from getting too close, or to develop 'em, or something."

"Huh!" said the loud soldier.

"Well," cried the youth, still fidgeting, "I'd rather do anything 'most than go tramping 'round the country all day doing no good to nobody and jest tiring ourselves out."

"So would I," said the loud soldier. "It ain't right. I tell you if anybody with any sense was a-runnin' this army it—"

"Oh, shut up!" roared the tall private. "You little fool. You little damn' cuss. You ain't had that there coat and them pants on for six months, and yet you talk as if—"

"Well, I wanta do some fighting anyway," interrupted the other. "I didn't come here to walk. I could 'ave walked to home—'round an 'round the barn, if I jest wanted to walk."

The tall one, red-faced, swallowed another sandwich as if taking poison in despair.

But gradually, as he chewed, his face became again quiet and contented. He could not rage in fierce argument in the presence of such sandwiches. During his meals he always wore an air of blissful contemplation of the food he had swallowed. His spirit seemed then to be communing with the viands.

He accepted new environment and circumstance with great coolness, eating from his haversack at every opportunity. On the march he went along with the stride of a hunter, objecting to neither gait nor distance. And he had not raised his voice when he had been ordered away from three little protective piles of earth and stone, each of which had been an engineering feat worthy of being made sacred to the name of his grandmother.

In the afternoon the regiment went out over the same ground it had taken in the morning. The landscape then ceased to threaten the youth. He had been close to it and become familiar with it.

When, however, they began to pass into a new region, his old fears of stupidity and incompetence reassailed him, but this time he doggedly let them babble. He was occupied with his problem, and in his desperation he concluded that the stupidity did not greatly matter.

Once he thought he had concluded that it would be better to get killed directly and end his troubles. Regarding death thus out of the corner of his eye, he conceived it to be nothing but rest, and he was filled with a momentary astonishment that he should have made an extraordinary commotion over the mere matter of getting killed. He would die; he would go to some place where he would be understood. It was useless to expect appreciation of his profound and fine senses from such men as the lieutenant. He must look to the grave for comprehension.

The skirmish fire increased to a long clattering sound. With it was mingled far-away cheering. A battery spoke.

Directly the youth would see the skirmishers running. They were pursued by the sound of musketry fire. After a time the hot, dangerous flashes of the rifles were visible. Smoke clouds went slowly and insolently across the fields like observant phantoms. The din became crescendo, like a roar of an oncoming train.

A brigade ahead of them and on the right went into action with a rending roar. It was as if it had exploded. And thereafter it lay stretched in the distance behind a long gray wall, that one was obliged to look twice at to make sure that it was smoke.

The youth, forgetting his neat plan of getting killed, gazed spell bound. His eyes grew wide and busy with the action of the scene. His mouth was a little ways open.

Of a sudden he felt a heavy and sad hand laid upon his shoulder. Awakening from his trance of observation he turned and beheld the loud soldier.

"It's my first and last battle, old boy," said the latter, with intense gloom. He was quite pale and his girlish lip was trembling.

"Eh?" murmured the youth in great astonishment.

"It's my first and last battle, old boy," continued the loud soldier. "Something tells me—"

"What?"

"I'm a gone coon this first time and—and I w-want you to take these here things—to—my—folks." He ended in a quavering sob of pity for himself. He handed the youth a little packet done up in a yellow envelope.

"Why, what the devil—" began the youth again.

But the other gave him a glance as from the depths of a tomb, and raised his limp hand in a prophetic manner and turned away.

4

The brigade was halted in the fringe of a grove. The men crouched among the trees and pointed their restless guns out at the fields. They tried to look beyond the smoke.

Out of this haze they could see running men. Some shouted information and gestured as they hurried.

The men of the new regiment watched and listened eagerly, while their tongues ran on in gossip of the battle. They mouthed rumors that had flown like birds out of the unknown.

"They say Perry has been driven in with big loss."

"Yes, Carrot went t' th' hospital. He said he was sick. That smart lieutenant is commanding 'G' Company. Th' boys say they won't be under Carrott no more if they all have t' desert. They allus knew he was a—"

"Hannises' batt'ry is took."

"It ain't either. I saw Hannises' batt'ry off on th' left not more'n fifteen minutes ago."

"Well—"

"Th' general, he ses he is goin' t' take th' hull cammand of th' 304th when we go inteh action, an' then he ses we'll do sech fightin' as never another reg'ment done."

"They say we're catchin' it over on th' left. They say th' enemy driv' our line inteh a devil of a swamp an' took Hannises' batt'ry."

"No sech thing. Hannises' batt'ry was 'long here 'bout a minute ago."

"That young Hasbrouck, he makes a good off'cer. He ain't afraid 'a nothin'."

"I met one of th' 148th Maine boys an' he ses his brigade fit th' hull rebel army fer four hours over on th' turnpike road an' killed about five thousand of 'em. He ses one more sech fight as that an' th' war 'll be over."

"Bill wasn't scared either. No, sir! It wasn't that. Bill ain't a-gittin' scared easy. He was jest mad, that's what he was. When that feller trod on his hand, he up an' sed that he was willin' t' give his hand, t' his country, but he be dumbed if he was goin' t' have every dumb bushwhacker in th' kentry walkin' 'round on it. See he went t' th' hospital disregardless of th' fight. Three fingers was crunched. Th' dern doctor wanted t' amputate 'm, an' Bill, he raised a heluva row, I hear. He's a funny feller."

The din in front swelled to a tremendous chorus. The youth and his fellows were frozen to silence. They could see a flag that tossed in the smoke angrily. Near it were the blurred and agitated forms of troops. There came a turbulent stream of men across the fields. A battery changing position at a frantic gallop scattered the stragglers right and left.

A shell screaming like a storm banshee went over the huddled heads of the reserves. It landed in the grove, and exploding redly flung the brown earth. There was a little shower of pine needles.

Bullets began to whistle among the branches and nip at the trees. Twigs and leaves came sailing down. It was as if a thousand axes, wee and invisible, were being wielded. Many of the men were constantly dodging and ducking their heads.

The lieutenant of the youth's company was shot in the hand. He began to swear so wondrously that a nervous laugh went along the regimental line. The officer's profanity sounded conventional. It relieved the tightened senses of the new men. It was as if he had hit his fingers with a tack hammer at home.

He held the wounded member carefully away from his side so that the blood would not drip upon his trousers.

The captain of the company, tucking his sword under his arm, produced a handkerchief and began to bind with it the lieutenant's wound. And they disputed as to how the binding should be done.

The battle flag in the distance jerked about madly. It seemed to be struggling to free itself from an agony. The billowing smoke was filled with horizontal flashes.

Men running swiftly emerged from it. They grew in numbers until it was seen that the whole command was fleeing. The flag suddenly sank down as if dying. Its motion as it fell was a gesture of despair.

Wild yells came from behind the walls of smoke. A sketch in gray and red dissolved into a moblike body of men who galloped like wild horses.

The veteran regiments on the right and left of the 304th immediately began to jeer. With the passionate song of the bullets and the banshee shrieks of shells were mingled loud catcalls and bits of facetious advice concerning places of safety.

But the new regiment was breathless with horror. "Gawd! Saunders's got crushed!" whispered the man at the youth's elbow. They shrank back and crouched as if compelled to await a flood.

The youth shot a swift glance along the blue ranks of the regiment. The profiles were motionless, carven; and afterward he remembered that the color sergeant was standing with his legs apart, as if he expected to be pushed to the ground.

The following throng went whirling around the flank. Here and there were officers carried along on the stream like exasperated chips. They were striking about them with their swords and with their left fists, punching every head they could reach. They cursed like highwaymen.

A mounted officer displayed the furious anger of a spoiled child. He raged with his head, his arms, and his legs.

Another, the commander of the brigade, was galloping about bawling. His hat was gone and his clothes were awry. He resembled a man who has come from bed to go to a fire. The hoofs of his horse often threatened the heads of the running men, but they scampered with singular fortune. In this rush they were apparently all deaf and blind. They heeded not the largest and longest of the oaths that were thrown at them from all directions.

Frequently over this tumult could be heard the grim jokes of the critical veterans; but the retreating men apparently were not even conscious of the presence of an audience.

The battle reflection that shone for an instant in the faces on the mad current made the youth feel that forceful hands from heaven would not have been able to have held him in place if he could have got intelligent control of his legs.

There was an appalling imprint upon these faces. The struggle in the smoke had pictured an exaggeration of itself on the bleached cheeks and in the eyes wild with one desire.

The sight of this stampede exerted a floodlike force that seemed able to drag sticks and stones and men from the ground. They of the reserves had to hold on. They grew pale and firm, and red and quaking.

The youth achieved one little thought in the midst of this chaos. The composite monster which had caused the other troops to flee had not then appeared. He resolved to get a view of it, and then, he thought he might very likely run better than the best of them.

5

There were moments of waiting. The youth thought of the village street at home before the arrival of the circus parade on a day in the spring. He remembered how he had stood, a small, thrillful boy, prepared to follow the dingy lady upon the white horse, or the band in its faded chariot. He saw the yellow road, the lines of expectant people, and the sober houses. He particularly remembered an old fellow who used to sit upon a cracker box in front of the store and feign to despise such exhibitions. A thousand details of color and form surged in his mind. The old fellow upon the cracker box appeared in middle prominence.

Some one cried, "Here they come!"

There was rustling and muttering among the men. They displayed a feverish desire to have every possible cartridge ready to their hands. The boxes were pulled around into various positions, and adjusted with great care. It was as if seven hundred new bonnets were being tried on.

The tall soldier, having prepared his rifle, produced a red handkerchief of some kind. He was engaged in knitting it about his throat with exquisite attention to its position, when the cry was repeated up and down the line in a muffled roar of sound.

"Here they come! Here they come!" Gun locks clicked.

Across the smoke-infested fields came a brown swarm of running men who were giving shrill yells. They came on, stooping and swinging their rifles at all angles. A flag, titled forward, sped near the front.

As he caught sight of them the youth was momentarily startled by a thought that perhaps his gun was not loaded. He stood trying to rally his faltering intellect so that he might recollect the moment when he had loaded, but he could not.

A hatless general pulled his dripping horse to a stand near the colonel of the 304th. He shook his fist in the other's face. "You 've got to hold 'em back!" he shouted, savagely; "you 've got to hold 'em back!"

In his agitation the colonel began to stammer. "A-all r-right, General, all right, by Gawd! We-we'll do our—we-we'll d-d-do—do our best, General." The general made a passionate gesture and galloped away. The colonel, perchance to relieve his feelings, began to scold like a wet parrot. The youth, turning swiftly to make sure that the rear was unmolested, saw the commander regarding his men in a highly resentful manner, as if he regretted above everything his association with them.

The man at the youth's elbow was mumbling, as if to himself: "Oh, we're in for it now! oh, we're in for it now!"

The captain of the company had been pacing excitedly to and fro in the rear. He coaxed in schoolmistress fashion, as to a congregation of boys with primers. His talk was an endless repetition. "Reserve your fire, boys—don't shoot till I tell you—save your fire—wait till they get close up—don't be damned fools—"

Perspiration streamed down the youth's face, which was soiled like that of a weeping urchin. He frequently, with a nervous movement, wiped his eyes with his coat sleeve. His mouth was still a little way open.

He got the one glance at the foe-swarming field in front of him, and instantly ceased to debate the question of his piece being loaded. Before he was ready to begin—before he had announced to himself that he was about to fight—he threw the obedient, well-balanced rifle into position and fired a first wild shot. Directly he was working at his weapon like an automatic affair.

He suddenly lost concern for himself, and forgot to look at a menacing fate. He became not a man but a member. He felt that something of which he was a part—a regiment, an army, a cause, or a country—was in a crisis. He was welded into a common personality which was dominated by a single desire. For some moments he could not flee no more than a little finger can commit a revolution from a hand.

If he had thought the regiment was about to be annihilated perhaps he could have amputated himself from it. But its noise gave him assurance. The regiment was like a firework that, once ignited, proceeds superior to circumstances until its blazing vitality fades. It wheezed and banged with a mighty power. He pictured the ground before it as strewn with the discomfited.

There was a consciousness always of the presence of his comrades about him. He felt the subtle battle brotherhood more potent even than the cause for which they were fighting. It was a mysterious fraternity born of the smoke and danger of death.

He was at a task. He was like a carpenter who has made many boxes, making still another box, only there was furious haste in his movements. He, in his thought, was careering off in other places, even as the carpenter who as he works whistles and thinks of his friend or his enemy, his home or a saloon. And these jolted dreams were never perfect to him afterward, but remained a mass of blurred shapes.

Presently he began to feel the effects of the war atmosphere—a blistering sweat, a sensation that his eyeballs were about to crack like hot stones. A burning roar filled his ears.

Following this came a red rage. He developed the acute exasperation of a pestered animal, a well-meaning cow worried by dogs. He had a mad feeling against his rifle, which could only be used against one life at a time. He wished to rush forward and strangle with his fingers. He craved a power that would enable him to make a world-sweeping gesture and brush all back. His impotency appeared to him, and made his rage into that of a driven beast.

Buried in the smoke of many rifles his anger was directed not so much against the men whom he knew were rushing toward him as against the swirling battle phantoms which were choking him, stuffing their smoke robes down his parched throat. He fought frantically for respite for his senses, for air, as a babe being smothered attacks the deadly blankets.

There was a blare of heated rage mingled with a certain expression of intentness on all faces. Many of the men were making low-toned noises with their mouths, and these subdued cheers, snarls, imprecations, prayers, made a wild, barbaric song that went as an undercurrent of sound, strange and chantlike with the resounding chords of the war march. The man at the youth's elbow was babbling. In it there was something soft and tender like the monologue of a babe. The tall soldier was swearing in a loud voice. From his lips came a black procession of curious oaths. Of a sudden another broke out in a querulous way like a man who has mislaid his hat. "Well, why don't they support us? Why don't they send supports? Do they think—"

The youth in his battle sleep heard this as one who dozes hears.

There was a singular absence of heroic poses. The men bending and surging in their haste and rage were in every impossible attitude. The steel ramrods clanked and clanged with incessant din as the men pounded them furiously into the hot rifle barrels. The flaps of the cartridge boxes were all unfastened, and bobbed idiotically with each movement. The rifles, once loaded, were jerked to the shoulder and fired without apparent aim into the smoke or at one of the blurred and shifting forms which upon the field before the regiment had been growing larger and larger like puppets under a magician's hand.

The officers, at their intervals, rearward, neglected to stand in picturesque attitudes. They were bobbing to and fro roaring directions and encouragements. The dimensions of their howls were extraordinary. They expended their lungs with prodigal wills. And often they nearly stood upon their heads in their anxiety to observe the enemy on the other side of the tumbling smoke.

The lieutenant of the youth's company had encountered a soldier who had fled screaming at the first volley of his comrades. Behind the lines these two were acting a little isolated scene. The man was blubbering and staring with sheeplike eyes at the lieutenant, who had seized him by the collar and was pommeling him. He drove him back into the ranks with many blows. The soldier went mechanically, dully, with his animal-like eyes upon the officer. Perhaps there was to him a divinity expressed in the voice of the other—stern, hard, with no reflection of fear in it. He tried to reload his gun, but his shaking hands prevented. The lieutenant was obliged to assist him.

The men dropped here and there like bundles. The captain of the youth's company had been killed in an early part of the action. His body lay stretched out in the position of a tired man resting, but upon his face there was an astonished and sorrowful look, as if he thought some friend had done him an ill turn. The babbling man was grazed by a shot that made the blood stream widely down his face. He clapped both hands to his head. "Oh!" he said, and ran. Another grunted suddenly as if he had been struck by a club in the stomach. He sat down and gazed ruefully. In his eyes there was mute, indefinite reproach. Farther up the line a man, standing behind a tree, had had his knee joint splintered by a ball. Immediately he had dropped his rifle and gripped the tree with both arms. And there he remained, clinging desperately and crying for assistance that he might withdraw his hold upon the tree.

At last an exultant yell went along the quivering line. The firing dwindled from an uproar to a last vindictive popping. As the smoke slowly eddied away, the youth saw that the charge had been repulsed. The enemy were scattered into reluctant groups. He saw a man climb to the top of the fence, straddle the rail, and fire a parting shot. The waves had receded, leaving bits of dark *débris* upon the ground.

Some in the regiment began to whoop frenziedly. Many were silent. Apparently they were trying to contemplate themselves.

After the fever had left his veins, the youth thought that at last he was going to suffocate. He became aware of the foul atmosphere in which he had been struggling. He was grimy and dripping like a laborer in a foundry. He grasped his canteen and took a long swallow of the warmed water.

A sentence with variations went up and down the line. "Well, we've helt 'em back. We've helt 'em back; derned if we haven't." The men said it blissfully, leering at each other with dirty smiles.

The youth turned to look behind him and off to the right and off to the left. He experienced the joy of a man who at last finds leisure in which to look about him.

Under foot there were a few ghastly forms motionless. They lay twisted in fantastic contortions. Arms were bent and heads were turned in incredible ways. It seemed that the dead men must have fallen from some great height to get into such positions. They looked to be dumped out upon the ground from the sky.

From a position in the rear of the grove a battery was throwing shells over it. The flash of the guns startled the youth at first. He thought they were aimed directly at him. Through the trees he watched the black figures of the gunners as they worked swiftly and intently. Their labor seemed a complicated thing. He wondered how they could remember its formula in the midst of confusion.

The guns squatted in a row like savage chiefs. They argued with abrupt violence. It was a grim pow-wow. Their busy servants ran hither and thither.

A small procession of wounded men were going drearily toward the rear. It was a flow of blood from the torn body of the brigade.

To the right and to the left were the dark lines of other troops. Far in front he thought he could see lighter masses protruding in points from the forest. They were suggestive of unnumbered thousands.

Once he saw a tiny battery go dashing along the line of the horizon. The tiny riders were beating the tiny horses.

From a sloping hill came the sound of cheerings and clashes. Smoke welled slowly through the leaves.

Batteries were speaking with thunderous oratorical effort. Here and there were flags, the red in the stripes dominating. They splashed bits of warm color upon the dark lines of troops.

The youth felt the old thrill at the sight of the emblem. They were like beautiful birds strangely undaunted in a storm.

As he listened to the din from the hillside, to a deep pulsating thunder that came from afar to the left, and to the lesser clamors which came from many directions, it occurred to him that they were fighting, too, over there, and over there, and over there. Heretofore he had supposed that all the battle was directly under his nose.

As he gazed around him the youth felt a flash of astonishment at the blue, pure sky and the sun gleaming on the trees and fields. It was surprising that Nature had gone tranquilly on with her golden process in the midst of so much devilment.

6

The youth awakened slowly. He came gradually back to a position from which he could regard himself. For moments he had been scrutinizing his person in a dazed way as if he had never before seen himself. Then he picked up his cap from the ground. He wriggled in his jacket to make a more comfortable fit, and kneeling replaced his shoe. He thoughtfully mopped his reeking features.

So it was all over at last! The supreme trial had been passed. The red, formidable difficulties of war had been vanquished.

He went into an ecstasy of self-satisfaction. He had the most delightful sensations of his life. Standing as if apart from himself, he viewed that last scene. He perceived that the man who had fought thus was magnificent.

He felt that he was a fine fellow. He saw himself even with those ideals which he had considered as far beyond him. He smiled in deep gratification.

Upon his fellows he beamed tenderness and good will. "Gee! ain't it hot, hey?" he said affably to a man who was polishing his streaming face with his coat sleeves.

"You bet!" said the other, grinning sociably. "I never seen sech dumb hotness." He sprawled out luxuriously on the ground. "Gee, yes! An' I hope we don't have no more fightin' till a week from Monday."

There were some handshakings and deep speeches with men whose features were familiar, but with whom the youth now felt the bonds of tied hearts. He helped a cursing comrade to bind up a wound of the skin.

But, of a sudden, cries of amazement broke out along the ranks of the new regiment. "Here they come ag'in! Here they come ag'in!" The man who had sprawled upon the ground started up and said, "Gosh!"

The youth turned quick eyes upon the field. He discerned forms begin to swell in masses out of a distant wood. He again saw the tilted flag speeding forward.

The shells, which had ceased to trouble the regiment for a time, came swirling again, and exploded in the grass or among the leaves of the trees. They looked to be strange war flowers bursting into fierce bloom.

The men groaned. The luster faded from their eyes. Their smudged countenances now expressed a profound dejection. They moved their stiffened bodies slowly, and watched in sullen mood the frantic approach of the enemy. The slaves toiling in the temple of this god began to feel rebellion at his harsh tasks.

They fretted and complained each to each. "Oh, say, this is too much of a good thing! Why can't somebody send us supports?"

"We ain't never goin' to stand this second banging. I didn't come here to fight the hull damn' rebel army."

There was one who raised a doleful cry. "I wish Bill Smithers had trod on my hand, insteader me treddin' on his'n." The sore joints of the regiment creaked as it painfully floundered into position to repulse.

The youth stared. Surely, he thought, this impossible thing was not about to happen. He waited as if he expected the enemy to suddenly stop, apologize, and retire bowing. It was all a mistake.

But the firing began somewhere on the regimental line and ripped along in both directions. The level sheets of flame developed great clouds of smoke that tumbled and tossed in the mild wind near the ground for a moment, and then rolled through the ranks as through a gate. The clouds were tinged an earthlike yellow in the sunrays and in the shadow were a sorry blue. The flag was sometimes eaten and lost in this mass of vapor, but more often it projected, sun touched, resplendent.

Into the youth's eyes there came a look that one can see in the orbs of a jaded horse. His neck was quivering with nervous weakness and the muscles of his arms felt numb and bloodless. His hands, too, seemed large and awkward as if he was wearing invisible mittens. And there was a great uncertainty about his knee joints.

The words that comrades had uttered previous to the firing began to recur to him. "Oh, say, this is too much of a good thing! What do they take us for—why don't they send supports? I didn't come here to fight the hull damned rebel army."

He began to exaggerate the endurance, the skill, and the valor of those who were coming. Himself reeling from exhaustion, he was astonished beyond measure at such persistency. They must be machines of steel. It was very gloomy struggling against such affairs, wound up perhaps to fight until sundown.

He slowly lifted his rifle and catching a glimpse of the thickspread field he blazed at a cantering cluster. He stopped then and began to peer as best he could through the smoke. He caught changing views of the ground covered with men who were running like pursued imps, and yelling.

To the youth it was an onslaught of redoubtable dragons. He became like the man who lost his legs at the approach of the red and green monster. He waited in a sort of a horrified, listening attitude. He seemed to shut his eyes and wait to be gobbled.

A man near him who up to this time had been working feverishly at his rifle suddenly stopped and ran with howls. A lad whose face had borne an expression of exalted courage, the majesty of he who dares give his life, was, at an instant, smitten abject. He blanched like one who has come to the edge of a cliff at midnight and is suddenly made aware. There was a revelation. He, too, threw down his gun and fled. There was no shame in his face. He ran like a rabbit.

Others began to scamper away through the smoke. The youth turned his head, shaken from his trance by this movement as if the regiment was leaving him behind. He saw the few fleeting forms.

He yelled then with fright and swung about. For a moment, in the great clamor, he was like a proverbial chicken. He lost the direction of safety. Destruction threatened him from all points.

Directly he began to speed toward the rear in great leaps. His rifle and cap were gone. His unbuttoned coat bulged in the wind. The flap of his cartridge box bobbed wildly, and his canteen, by its slender cord, swung out behind. On his face was all the horror of those things which he imagined.

The lieutenant sprang forward bawling. The youth saw his features wrathfully red, and saw him make a dab with his sword. His one thought of the incident was that the lieutenant was a peculiar creature to feel interested in such matters upon this occasion.

He ran like a blind man. Two or three times he fell down. Once he knocked his shoulder so heavily against a tree that he went headlong.

Since he had turned his back upon the fight his fears had been wondrously magnified. Death about to thrust him between the shoulder blades was far more dreadful than death about to smite him between the eyes. When he thought of it later, he conceived the impression that it is better to view the appalling than to be merely within hearing. The noises of the battle were like stones; he believed himself liable to be crushed.

As he ran on he mingled with others. He dimly saw men on his right and on his left, and he heard footsteps behind him. He thought that all the regiment was fleeing, pursued by these ominous crashes.

In his flight the sound of these following footsteps gave him his one meager relief. He felt vaguely that death must make a first choice of the men who were nearest; the initial morsels for the dragons would be then those who were following him. So he displayed the zeal of an insane sprinter in his purpose to keep them in the rear. There was a race.

As he, leading, went across a little field, he found himself in a region of shells. They hurtled over his head with long wild screams. As he listened he imagined them to have rows of cruel teeth that grinned at him. Once one lit before him and the livid lightning of the explosion effectually barred the way in his chosen direction. He groveled on the ground and then springing up went careering off through some bushes.

He experienced a thrill of amazement when he came within view of a battery in action. The men there seemed to be in conventional moods, altogether unaware of the impending annihilation. The battery was disputing with a distant antagonist and the gunners were wrapped in admiration of their shooting. They were continually bending in coaxing postures over the guns. They seemed to be patting them on the back and encouraging them with words. The guns, stolid and undaunted, spoke with dogged valor.

The precise gunners were coolly enthusiastic. They lifted their eyes every chance to the smoke-wreathed hillock from whence the hostile battery addressed them. The youth pitied them as he ran. Methodical idiots! Machine-like fools! The refined joy of planting shells in the midst of the other battery's formation would appear a little thing when the infantry came swooping out of the woods.

The face of a youthful rider, who was jerking his frantic horse with an abandon of temper he might display in a placid barnyard, was impressed deeply upon his mind. He knew that he looked upon a man who would presently be dead.

Too, he felt a pity for the guns, standing, six good comrades, in a bold row.

He saw a brigade going to the relief of its pestered fellows. He scrambled upon a wee hill and watched it sweeping finely, keeping formation in difficult places. The blue of the line was crusted with steel color, and the brilliant flags projected. Officers were shouting.

This sight also filled him with wonder. The brigade was hurrying briskly to be gulped into the infernal mouths of the war god. What manner of men were they, anyhow? Ah, it was some wondrous breed! Or else they didn't comprehend—the fools.

A furious order caused commotion in the artillery. An officer on a bounding horse made maniacal motions with his arms. The teams went swinging up from the rear, the guns were whirled about, and the battery scampered away. The cannon with their noses poked slantingly at the ground grunted and grumbled like stout men, brave but with objections to hurry.

The youth went on, moderating his pace since he had left the place of noises.

Later he came upon a general of division seated upon a horse that pricked its ears in an interested way at the battle. There was a great gleaming of yellow and patent leather about the saddle and bridle. The quiet man astride looked mouse-colored upon such a splendid charger.

A jingling staff was galloping hither and thither. Sometimes the general was surrounded by horsemen and at other times he was quite alone. He looked to be much harassed. He had the appearance of a business man whose market is swinging up and down.

The youth went slinking around this spot. He went as near as he dared trying to overhear words. Perhaps the general, unable to comprehend chaos, might call upon him for information. And he could tell him. He knew all concerning it. Of a surety the force was in a fix, and any fool could see that if they did not retreat while they had opportunity—why—

He felt that he would like to thrash the general, or at least approach and tell him in plain words exactly what he thought him to be. It was criminal to stay calmly in one spot and make no effort to stay destruction. He loitered in a fever of eagerness for the division commander to apply to him.

As he warily moved about, he heard the general call out irritably: "Tompkins, go over an' see Taylor, an' tell him not t' be in such an all-fired hurry; tell him t' halt his brigade in th' edge of th' woods; tell him t' detach a reg'ment—say I think th' center 'll break if we don't help it out some; tell him t' hurry up."

A slim youth on a fine chestnut horse caught these swift words from the mouth of his superior. He made his horse bound into a gallop almost from a walk in his haste to go upon his mission. There was a cloud of dust.

A moment later the youth saw the general bounce excitedly in his saddle.

"Yes, by heavens, they have!" The officer leaned forward. His face was aflame with excitement. "Yes, by heavens, they've held 'im! They've held 'im!"

He began to blithely roar at his staff: "We'll wallop 'im now. We'll wallop 'im now. We've got 'im sure." He turned suddenly upon an aid: "Here—you—Jones —quick—ride after Tompkins—see Taylor—tell him t' go in—everlastingly—like blazes—anything."

As another officer sped his horse after the first messenger, the general beamed upon the earth like a sun. In his eyes was a desire to chant a paean. He kept repeating, "They've held 'em, by heavens!"

His excitement made his horse plunge, and he merrily kicked and swore at it. He held a little carnival of joy on horseback.

7

The youth cringed as if discovered in a crime. By heavens, they had won after all! The imbecile line had remained and become victors. He could hear cheering.

He lifted himself upon his toes and looked in the direction of the fight. A yellow fog lay wallowing on the treetops. From beneath it came the clatter of musketry. Hoarse cries told of an advance.

He turned away amazed and angry. He felt that he had been wronged.

He had fled, he told himself, because annihilation approached. He had done a good part in saving himself, who was a little piece of the army. He had considered the time, he said, to be one in which it was the duty of every little piece to rescue itself if possible. Later the officers could fit the little pieces together again, and make a battle front. If none of the little pieces were wise enough to save themselves from the flurry of death at such a time, why, then, where would be the army? It was all plain that he had proceeded according to very correct and commendable rules. His actions had been sagacious things. They had been full of strategy. They were the work of a master's legs.

Thoughts of his comrades came to him. The brittle blue line had withstood the blows and won. He grew bitter over it. It seemed that the blind ignorance and stupidity of those little pieces had betrayed him. He had been overturned and crushed by their lack of sense in holding the position, when intelligent deliberation would have convinced them that it was impossible. He, the enlightened man who looks afar in the dark, had fled because of his superior perceptions and knowledge. He felt a great anger against his comrades. He knew it could be proved that they had been fools.

He wondered what they would remark when later he appeared in camp. His mind heard howls of derision. Their density would not enable them to understand his sharper point of view.

He began to pity himself acutely. He was ill used. He was trodden beneath the feet of an iron injustice. He had proceeded with wisdom and from the most righteous motives under heaven's blue only to be frustrated by hateful circumstances.

A dull, animal-like rebellion against his fellows, war in the abstract, and fate grew within him. He shambled along with bowed head, his brain in a tumult of agony and despair. When he looked loweringly up, quivering at each sound, his eyes had the expression of those of a criminal who thinks his guilt and his punishment great, and knows that he can find no words.

He went from the fields into a thick wood, as if resolved to bury himself. He wished to get out of hearing of the crackling shots which were to him like voices.

The ground was cluttered with vines and bushes, and the trees grew close and spread out like bouquets. He was obliged to force his way with much noise. The creepers, catching against his legs, cried out harshly as their sprays were torn from the barks of trees. The swishing saplings tried to make known his presence to the world. He could not conciliate the forest. As he made his way, it was always calling out protestations. When he separated embraces of trees and vines the disturbed foliages waved their arms and turned their face leaves toward him. He dreaded lest these noisy motions and cries should bring men to look at him. So he went far, seeking dark and intricate places.

After a time the sound of musketry grew faint and the cannon boomed in the distance. The sun, suddenly apparent, blazed among the trees. The insects were making rhythmical noises. They seemed to be grinding their teeth in unison. A woodpecker stuck his impudent head around the side of a tree. A bird flew on lighthearted wing.

Off was the rumble of death. It seemed now that Nature had no ears.

This landscape gave him assurance. A fair field holding life. It was the religion of peace. It would die if its timid eyes were compelled to see blood. He conceived Nature to be a woman with a deep aversion to tragedy.

He threw a pine cone at a jovial squirrel, and he ran with chattering fear. High in a treetop he stopped, and, poking his head cautiously from behind a branch, looked down with an air of trepidation.

The youth felt triumphant at this exhibition. There was the law, he said. Nature had given him a sign. The squirrel, immediately upon recognizing danger, had taken to his legs without ado. He did not stand stolidly baring his furry belly to the missile, and die with an upward glance at the sympathetic heavens. On the contrary, he had fled as fast as his legs could carry him; and he was but an ordinary squirrel, too—doubtless no philosopher of his race. The youth wended, feeling that Nature was of his mind. She re-enforced his argument with proofs that lived where the sun shone.

Once he found himself almost into a swamp. He was obliged to walk upon bog tufts and watch his feet to keep from the oily mire. Pausing at one time to look about him he saw, out at some black water, a small animal pounce in and emerge directly with a gleaming fish.

The youth went again into the deep thickets. The brushed branches made a noise that drowned the sounds of cannon. He walked on, going from obscurity into promises of a greater obscurity.

At length he reached a place where the high, arching boughs made a chapel. He softly pushed the green doors aside and entered. Pine needles were a gentle brown carpet. There was a religious half light.

Near the threshold he stopped, horror-stricken at the sight of a thing.

He was being looked at by a dead man who was seated with his back against a columnlike tree. The corpse was dressed in a uniform that once had been blue, but was now faded to a melancholy shade of green. The eyes, staring at the youth, had changed to the dull hue to be seen on the side of a dead fish. The mouth was open. Its red had changed to an appalling yellow. Over the gray skin of the face ran little ants. One was trundling some sort of a bundle along the upper lip.

The youth gave a shriek as he confronted the thing. He was for moments turned to stone before it. He remained staring into the liquid-looking eyes. The dead man and the living man exchanged a long look. Then the youth cautiously put one hand behind him and brought it against a tree. Leaning upon this he retreated, step by step, with his face still toward the thing. He feared that if he turned his back the body might spring up and stealthily pursue him.

The branches, pushing against him, threatened to throw him over upon it. His unguided feet, too, caught aggravatingly in brambles; and with it all he received a subtle suggestion to touch the corpse. As he thought of his hand upon it he shuddered profoundly.

At last he burst the bonds which had fastened him to the spot and fled, unheeding the underbrush. He was pursued by a sight of the black ants swarming greedily upon the gray face and venturing horribly near to the eyes.

After a time he paused, and, breathless and panting, listened. He imagined some strange voice would come from the dead throat and squawk after him in horrible menaces.

The trees about the portal of the chapel moved soughingly in a soft wind. A sad silence was upon the little guarding edifice.

8

The trees began softly to sing a hymn of twilight. The sun sank until slanted bronze rays struck the forest. There was a lull in the noises of insects as if they had bowed their beaks and were making a devotional pause. There was silence save for the chanted chorus of the trees.

Then, upon this stillness, there suddenly broke a tremendous clangor of sounds. A crimson roar came from the distance.

The youth stopped. He was transfixed by this terrific medley of all noises. It was as if worlds were being rended. There was the ripping sound of musketry and the breaking crash of the artillery.

His mind flew in all directions. He conceived the two armies to be at each other panther fashion. He listened for a time. Then he began to run in the direction of the battle. He saw that it was an ironical thing for him to be running thus toward that which he had been at such pains to avoid. But he said, in substance, to himself that if the earth and the moon were about to clash, many persons would doubtless plan to get upon the roofs to witness the collision.

As he ran, he became aware that the forest had stopped its music, as if at last becoming capable of hearing the foreign sounds. The trees hushed and stood motionless. Everything seemed to be listening to the crackle and clatter and earshaking thunder. The chorus pealed over the still earth.

It suddenly occurred to the youth that the fight in which he had been was, after all, but perfunctory popping. In the hearing of this present din he was doubtful if he had seen real battle scenes. This uproar explained a celestial battle; it was tumbling hordes a-struggle in the air.

Reflecting, he saw a sort of a humor in the point of view of himself and his fellows during the late encounter. They had taken themselves and the enemy very seriously and had imagined that they were deciding the war. Individuals must have supposed that they were cutting the letters of their names deep into everlasting tablets of brass, or enshrining their reputations forever in the hearts of their countrymen, while, as to fact, the affair would appear in printed reports under a meek and immaterial title. But he saw that it was good, else, he said, in battle every one would surely run save forlorn hopes and their ilk.

He went rapidly on. He wished to come to the edge of the forest that he might peer out.

As he hastened, there passed through his mind pictures of stupendous conflicts. His accumulated thought upon such subjects was used to form scenes. The noise was as the voice of an eloquent being, describing.

Sometimes the brambles formed chains and tried to hold him back. Trees, confronting him, stretched out their arms and forbade him to pass. After its previous hostility this new resistance of the forest filled him with a fine bitterness. It seemed that Nature could not be quite ready to kill him.

But he obstinately took roundabout ways, and presently he was where he could see long gray walls of vapor where lay battle lines. The voices of cannon shook him. The musketry sounded in long irregular surges that played havoc with his ears. He stood regardant for a moment. His eyes had an awestruck expression. He gawked in the direction of the fight.

Presently he proceeded again on his forward way. The battle was like the grinding of an immense and terrible machine to him. Its complexities and powers, its grim processes, fascinated him. He must go close and see it produce corpses.

He came to a fence and clambered over it. On the far side, the ground was littered with clothes and guns. A newspaper, folded up, lay in the dirt. A dead soldier was stretched with his face hidden in his arm. Farther off there was a group of four or five corpses keeping mournful company. A hot sun had blazed upon the spot.

In this place the youth felt that he was an invader. This forgotten part of the battle ground was owned by the dead men, and he hurried, in the vague apprehension that one of the swollen forms would rise and tell him to begone.

He came finally to a road from which he could see in the distance dark and agitated bodies of troops, smoke-fringed. In the lane was a blood-stained crowd streaming to the rear. The wounded men were cursing, groaning, and wailing. In the air, always, was a mighty swell of sound that it seemed could sway the earth. With the courageous words of the artillery and the spiteful sentences of the musketry mingled red cheers. And from this region of noises came the steady current of the maimed.

One of the wounded men had a shoeful of blood. He hopped like a schoolboy in a game. He was laughing hysterically.

One was swearing that he had been shot in the arm through the commanding general's mismanagement of the army. One was marching with an air imitative of some sublime drum major. Upon his features was an unholy mixture of merriment and agony. As he marched he sang a bit of doggerel in a high and quavering voice;

> "Sing a song 'a vic'try,
> A pocketful 'a bullets,
> Five an' twenty dead men
> Baked in a—pie."

Parts of the procession limped and staggered to this tune.

Another had the gray seal of death already upon his face. His lips were curled in hard lines and his teeth were clinched. His hands were bloody from where he had pressed them upon his wound. He seemed to be awaiting the moment when he should pitch headlong. He stalked like the specter of a soldier, his eyes burning with the power of a stare into the unknown.

There were some who proceeded sullenly, full of anger at their wounds, and ready to turn upon anything as an obscure cause.

An officer was carried along by two privates. He was peevish. "Don't joggle so,

Johnson, yeh fool," he cried. "Think m' leg is made of iron? If yeh can't carry me decent, put me down an' let some one else do it."

He bellowed at the tottering crowd who blocked the quick march of his bearers. "Say, make way there, can't yeh? Make way, dickens take it all."

They sulkily parted and went to the roadsides. As he was carried past they made pert remarks to him. When he raged in reply and threatened them, they told him to be damned.

The shoulder of one of the tramping bearers knocked heavily against the spectral soldier who was staring into the unknown.

The youth joined this crowd and marched along with it. The torn bodies expressed the awful machinery in which the men had been entangled.

Orderlies and couriers occasionally broke through the throng in the roadway, scattering wounded men right and left, galloping on followed by howls. The melancholy march was continually disturbed by the messengers, and sometimes by bustling batteries that came swinging and thumping down upon them, the officers shouting orders to clear the way.

There was a tattered man, fouled with dust, blood and powder stain from hair to shoes, who trudged quietly at the youth's side. He was listening with eagerness and much humility to the lurid descriptions of a bearded sergeant. His lean features wore an expression of awe and admiration. He was like a listener in a country store to wondrous tales told among the sugar barrels. He eyed the storyteller with unspeakable wonder. His mouth was agape in yokel fashion.

The sergeant, taking note of this, gave pause to his elaborate history while he administered a sardonic comment. "Be keerful, honey, you'll be a-ketchin' flies," he said.

The tattered man shrank back abashed.

After a time he began to sidle near to the youth, and in a different way try to make him a friend. His voice was gentle as a girl's voice and his eyes were pleading. The youth saw with surprise that the soldier had two wounds, one in the head, bound with a blood-soaked rag, and the other in the arm, making that member dangle like a broken bough.

After they had walked together for some time the tattered man mustered sufficient courage to speak. "Was pretty good fight, wa'n't it?" he timidly said. The youth, deep in thought, glanced up at the bloody and grim figure with its lamblike eyes. "What?"

"Was pretty good fight, wa'n't it?"

"Yes," said the youth shortly. He quickened his pace.

But the other hobbled industriously after him. There was an air of apology in his manner, but he evidently thought that he needed only to talk for a time, and the youth would perceive that he was a good fellow.

"Was pretty good fight, wa'n't it?" he began in a small voice, and then he achieved the fortitude to continue. "Dern me if I ever see fellers fight so. Laws, how they did fight! I knowed th' boys'd like when they onct got square at it. Th' boys ain't had no fair chanct up t' now, but this time they showed what they was. I knowed it'd turn out this way. Yeh can't lick them boys. No, sir! They 're fighters, they be."

He breathed a deep breath of humble admiration. He had looked at the youth for encouragement several times. He received none, but gradually he seemed to get absorbed in his subject.

"I was talkin' 'cross pickets with a boy from Georgie, onct, an' that boy, he ses, 'Your fellers 'll all run like hell when they onct hearn a gun,' he ses. 'Mebbe they will,' I ses, 'but I don't b'lieve none of it,' I ses; 'an' b'jiminey,' I ses back t' 'um, 'mebbe your fellers 'll all run like hell when they onct hearn a gun,' I ses. He larfed. Well, they didn't run t' day, did they, hey? No, sir! They fit, an' fit, an' fit."

His homely face was suffused with a light of love for the army which was to him all things beautiful and powerful.

After a time he turned to the youth. "Where yeh hit, ol' boy?" he asked in a brotherly tone.

The youth felt instant panic at this question, although at first its full import was not borne in upon him.

"What?" he asked.

"Where yeh hit?" repeated the tattered man.

"Why," began the youth, "I—I—that is—why—I—"

He turned away suddenly and slid through the crowd. His brow was heavily flushed, and his fingers were picking nervously at one of his buttons. He bent his head and fastened his eyes studiously upon the button as if it were a little problem.

The tattered man look after him in astonishment.

9

The youth fell back in the procession until the tattered soldier was not in sight. Then he started to walk on with the others.

But he was amid wounds. The mob of men was bleeding. Because of the tattered soldier's question he now felt that his shame could be viewed. He was continually casting sidelong glances to see if the men were contemplating the letters of guilt he felt burned into his brow.

At times he regarded the wounded soldiers in an envious way. He conceived persons with torn bodies to be peculiarly happy. He wished that he, too, had a wound, a red badge of courage.

The spectral soldier was at his side like a stalking reproach. The man's eyes were still fixed in a stare into the unknown. His gray, appalling face had attracted attention in the crowd, and men, slowing to his dreary pace, were walking with him. They were discussing his plight, questioning him and giving him advice. In a dogged way he repelled them, signing to them to go on and leave him alone. The shadows of his face were deepening and his tight lips seemed holding in check the moan of great despair. There could be seen a certain stiffness in the movements of his body, as if he were taking infinite care not to arouse the passion of his wounds. As he went on, he seemed always looking for a place, like one who goes to choose a grave.

Something in the gesture of the man as he waved the bloody and pitying soldiers away made the youth start as if bitten. He yelled in horror. Tottering forward he laid a quivering hand upon the man's arm. As the latter slowly turned his waxlike features toward him, the youth screamed:

"Gawd! Jim Conklin!"

The tall soldier made a little commonplace smile. "Hello, Henry," he said.

The youth swayed on his legs and glared strangely. He stuttered and stammered. "Oh, Jim—oh, Jim—oh, Jim—"

The tall soldier held out his gory hand. There was a curious red and black combination of new blood and old blood upon it. "Where yeh been, Henry?" he asked. He continued in a monotonous voice, "I thought mebbe yeh got keeled over. There's been thunder t' pay t'-day. I was worryin' about it a good deal."

The youth still lamented. "Oh, Jim—oh, Jim—oh, Jim—"

"Yeh know," said the tall soldier, "I was out there." He made a careful gesture. "An', Lord, what a circus! An', b'jiminey, I got shot—I got shot. Yes, b'jiminey, I got shot." He reiterated this fact in a bewildered way, as if he did not know how it came about.

The youth put forth anxious arms to assist him, but the tall soldier went firmly on as if propelled. Since the youth's arrival as a guardian for his friend, the other wounded men had ceased to display much interest. They occupied themselves again in dragging their own tragedies toward the rear.

Suddenly, as the two friends marched on, the tall soldier seemed to be overcome by a terror. His face turned to a semblance of gray paste. He clutched the youth's arm and looked all about him, as if dreading to be overheard. Then he began to speak in a shaking whisper:

"I tell yeh what I'm 'fraid of, Henry—I'll tell yeh what I'm 'fraid of. I'm 'fraid I'll fall down—an' then yeh know—them damned artillery wagons—they like as not 'll run over me. That's what I'm 'fraid of—"

The youth cried out to him hysterically: "I'll take care of yeh, Jim! I'll take care of yeh! I swear t' Gawd I will!"

"Sure—will yeh, Henry?" the tall soldier beseeched.

"Yes—yes—I tell yeh—I'll take care of yeh, Jim!" protested the youth. He could not speak accurately because of the gulping in his throat.

But the tall soldier continued to beg in a lowly way. He now hung babelike to the youth's arm. His eyes rolled in the wildness of his terror. "I was allus a good friend t' yeh, wa'n't I, Henry? I've allus been a pretty good feller, ain't I? An' it ain't much t' ask, is it? Jest t' pull me along outer th' road? I'd do it fer you, wouldn't I, Henry?"

He paused in piteous anxiety to await his friend's reply.

The youth had reached an anguish where the sobs scorched him. He strove to express his loyalty, but he could only make fantastic gestures.

However, the tall soldier seemed suddenly to forget all those fears. He became again the grim, stalking specter of a soldier. He went stonily forward. The youth wished his friend to lean upon him, but the other always shook his head and strangely protested. "No—no—no—leave me be—leave me be—"

His look was fixed again upon the unknown. He moved with mysterious purpose, and all of the youth's offers he brushed aside. "No—no—leave me be— leave me be—"

The youth had to follow.

Presently the latter heard a voice talking softly near his shoulders. Turning he saw that it belonged to the tattered soldier. "Ye'd better take 'im outa th' road, pardner. There's a batt'ry comin' helity-whoop down th' road an' he'll git runned over. He's a goner anyhow in about five minutes—yeh kin see that. Ye'd better take 'im outa th' road. Where th' blazes does he git his stren'th from?"

"Lord knows!" cried the youth. He was shaking his hands helplessly.

He ran forward presently and grasped the tall soldier by the arm. "Jim! Jim!" he coaxed, "come with me."

The tall soldier weakly tried to wrench himself free. "Huh," he said vacantly.

He stared at the youth for a moment. At last he spoke as if dimly comprehending. "Oh! Inteh th' fields? Oh!"

He started blindly through the grass.

The youth turned once to look at the lashing riders and jouncing guns of the battery. He was startled from this view by a shrill outcry from the tattered man.

"Gawd! He's runnin'!"

Turning his head swiftly, the youth saw his friend running in a staggering and stumbling way toward a little clump of bushes. His heart seemed to wrench itself almost free from his body at this sight. He made a noise of pain. He and the tattered man began a pursuit. There was a singular race.

When he overtook the tall soldier he began to plead with all the words he could find. "Jim—Jim —what are you doing—what makes you do this way—you'll hurt yerself."

The same purpose was in the tall soldier's face. He protested in a dulled way, keeping his eyes fastened on the mystic place of his intentions. "No—no—don't tech me—leave me be—leave me be—"

The youth, aghast and filled with wonder at the tall soldier, began quaveringly to question him. "Where yeh goin', Jim? What you thinking about? Where you going? Tell me, won't you, Jim?"

The tall soldier faced about as upon relentless pursuers. In his eyes there was a great appeal. "Leave me be, can't yeh? Leave me be fer a minnit."

The youth recoiled. "Why, Jim," he said, in a dazed way, "what's the matter with you?"

The tall soldier turned and, lurching dangerously, went on. The youth and the tattered soldier followed, sneaking as if whipped, feeling unable to face the stricken man if he should again confront them. They began to have thoughts of a solemn ceremony. There was something ritelike in these movements of the doomed soldier. And there was a resemblance in him to a devotee of a mad religion, blood-sucking, muscle-wrenching, bone-crushing. They were awed and afraid. They hung back lest he have at command a dreadful weapon.

At last, they saw him stop and stand motionless. Hastening up, they perceived that his face wore an expression telling that he had at last found the place for which he had struggled. His spare figure was erect; his bloody hands were quietly at his side. He was waiting with patience for something that he had come to meet. He was at the rendezvous. They paused and stood, expectant.

There was a silence.

Finally, the chest of the doomed soldier began to heave with a strained motion. It increased in violence until it was as if an animal was within and was kicking and tumbling furiously to be free.

This spectacle of gradual strangulation made the youth writhe, and once as his friend rolled his eyes, he saw something in them that made him sink wailing to the ground. He raised his voice in a last supreme call.

"Jim—Jim—Jim—"

The tall soldier opened his lips and spoke. He made a gesture. "Leave me be— don't tech me—leave me be—"

There was another silence while he waited.

Suddenly, his form stiffened and straightened. Then it was shaken by a prolonged ague. He stared into space. To the two watchers there was a curious and profound dignity in the firm lines of his awful face.

He was invaded by a creeping strangeness that slowly enveloped him. For a moment the tremor of his legs caused him to dance a sort of hideous hornpipe. His arms beat wildly about his head in expression of implike enthusiasm.

His tall figure stretched itself to its full height. There was a slight rending sound. Then it began to swing forward, slow and straight, in the manner of a falling tree. A swift muscular contortion made the left shoulder strike the ground first.

The body seemed to bounce a little way from the earth. "God!" said the tattered soldier.

The youth had watched, spellbound, this ceremony at the place of meeting. His face had been twisted into an expression of every agony he had imagined for his friend.

He now sprang to his feet and, going closer, gazed upon the pastelike face. The mouth was open and the teeth showed in a laugh.

As the flap of the blue jacket fell away from the body, he could see that the side looked as if it had been chewed by wolves.

The youth turned, with sudden, livid rage, toward the battlefield. He shook his fist. He seemed about to deliver a philippic.

"Hell—"

The red sun was pasted in the sky like a wafer.

10

The tattered man stood musing.

"Well, he was reg'lar jim-dandy fer nerve, wa'n't he," said he finally in a little awestruck voice. "A reg'lar jim-dandy." He thoughtfully poked one of the docile hands with his foot. "I wonner where he got 'is stren'th from? I never seen a man do like that before. It was a funny thing. Well, he was a reg'lar jim-dandy."

The youth desired to screech out his grief. He was stabbed, but his tongue lay dead in the tomb of his mouth. He threw himself again upon the ground and began to brood.

The tattered man stood musing.

"Look-a-here, pardner," he said, after a time. He regarded the corpse as he spoke. "He's up an' gone, ain't 'e, an' we might as well begin t' look out fer ol' number one. This here thing is all over. He's up an' gone, ain't 'e? An' he's all right here. Nobody won't bother 'im. An' I must say I ain't enjoying any great health m'self these days."

The youth, awakened by the tattered soldier's tone, looked quickly up. He saw that he was swinging uncertainly on his legs and that his face had turned to a shade of blue.

"Good Lord!" he cried, "you ain't goin' t'—not you, too."

The tattered man waved his hand. "Nary die," he said. "All I want is some pea soup an' a good bed. Some pea soup," he repeated dreamfully.

The youth arose from the ground. "I wonder where he came from. I left him over there." He pointed. "And now I find 'im here. And he was coming from over there, too." He indicated a new direction. They both turned toward the body as if to ask of it a question.

"Well," at length spoke the tattered man, "there ain't no use in our stayin' here an' tryin' t' ask him anything."

The youth nodded an assent wearily. They both turned to gaze for a moment at the corpse.

The youth murmured something.

"Well, he was a jim-dandy, wa'n't 'e?" said the tattered man as if in response.

They turned their backs upon it and started away. For a time they stole softly, treading with their toes. It remained laughing there in the grass.

"I'm commencin' t' feel pretty bad," said the tattered man, suddenly breaking one of his little silences. "I'm commencin' t' feel pretty damn' bad."

The youth groaned. "O Lord!" He wondered if he was to be the tortured witness of another grim encounter.

But his companion waved his hand reassuringly. "Oh, I'm not goin' t' die yit! There too much dependin' on me fer me t' die yit. No, sir! Nary die! I *can't!* Ye'd oughta see th' swad a' chil'ren I've got, an' all like that."

The youth glancing at his companion could see by the shadow of a smile that he was making some kind of fun.

As they plodded on the tattered soldier continued to talk. "Besides, if I died, I wouldn't die th' way that feller did. That was th' funniest thing. I'd jest flop down, I would. I never seen a feller die th' way that feller did.

"Yeh know Tom Jamison, he lives next door t' me up home. He's a nice feller, he is, an' we was allus good friends. Smart, too. Smart as a steel trap. Well, when we was a-fightin' this atternoon, all-of-a-sudden he begin t' rip up an' cuss an' beller at me. 'Yer shot, yeh blamed infernal!'—he swear horrible—he ses t' me. I put up m' hand t' m' head an' when I looked at m' fingers, I seen, sure 'nough, I was shot. I give a holler an' begin t' run, but b'fore I could git away another one hit me in th' arm an' whirl' me clean 'round. I got skeared when they was all a-shootin' b'hind me an' I run t' beat all, but I cotch it pretty bad. I've an idee I'd a' been fightin' yit, if 't wasn't fer Tom Jamison."

Then he made a calm announcement: "There's two of 'em—little ones—but they're beginnin' t' have fun with me now. I don't b'lieve I kin walk much furder."

They went slowly on in silence. "Yeh look pretty peek-ed yerself," said the tattered man at last. "I bet yeh've got a worser one than yeh think. Ye'd better take keer of yer hurt. It don't do t' let sech things go. It might be inside mostly, an' them plays thunder. Where is it located?" But he continued his harangue without waiting for a reply. "I see 'a feller git hit plum in th' head when my reg'ment was a-standin' at ease onct. An' everybody yelled out to 'im: Hurt, John? Are yeh hurt much? 'No,' ses he. He looked kinder surprised, an' he went on tellin' 'em how he felt. He sed he didn't feel nothin'. But, by dad, th' first thing that feller knowed he was dead. Yes, he was dead—stone dead. So, yeh wanta watch out. Yeh might have some queer kind 'a hurt yerself. Yeh can't never tell. Where is your'n located?"

The youth had been wriggling since the introduction of this topic. He now gave a cry of exasperation and made a furious motion with his hand. "Oh, don't bother me!" he said. He was enraged against the tattered man, and could have strangled him. His companions seemed ever to play intolerable parts. They were ever upraising the ghost of shame on the stick of their curiosity. He turned toward the tattered man as one at bay. "Now, don't bother me," he repeated with desperate menace.

"Well, Lord knows I don't wanta bother anybody," said the other. There was a little accent of despair in his voice as he replied, "Lord knows I've gota 'nough m' own t' tend to."

The youth, who had been holding a bitter debate with himself and casting glances of hatred and contempt at the tattered man, here spoke in a hard voice. "Good-by," he said.

The tattered man looked at him in gaping amazement. "Why—why, pardner, where yeh goin'?" he asked unsteadily. The youth looking at him, could see that he, too, like that other one, was beginning to act dumb and animal-like. His thoughts seemed to be floundering about in his head. "Now—now—look—a—here, you Tom Jamison—now—I won't have this—this here won't do. Where—where yeh goin'?"

The youth pointed vaguely. "Over there," he replied.

"Well, now look—a—here—now," said the tattered man, rambling on in idiot fashion. His head was hanging forward and his words were slurred. "This thing won't do, now, Tom Jamison. It won't do. I know yeh, yeh pig-headed devil. Yeh wanta go trompin' off with a bad hurt. It ain't right—now—Tom Jamison—it ain't. Yeh wanta leave me take keer of yeh, Tom Jamison. It ain't—right—it ain't—fer yeh t' go—trompin' off—with a bad hurt—it ain't—ain't—ain't right it ain't—"

In reply the youth climbed a fence and started away. He could hear the tattered man bleating plaintively.

Once he faced about angrily. "What?"

"Look—a—here, now, Tom Jamison—now—it ain't—"

The youth went on. Turning at a distance he saw the tattered man wandering about helplessly in the field.

He now thought that he wished he was dead. He believed that he envied those men whose bodies lay strewn over the grass of the fields and on the fallen leaves of the forest.

The simple questions of the tattered man had been knife thrusts to him. They asserted a society that probes pitilessly at secrets until all is apparent. His late companion's chance persistency made him feel that he could not keep his crime concealed in his bosom. It was sure to be brought plain by one of those arrows which cloud the air and are constantly pricking, discovering, proclaiming those things which are willed to be forever hidden. He admitted that he could not defend himself against this agency. It was not within the power of vigilance.

11

He became aware that the furnace roar of the battle was growing louder. Great brown clouds had floated to the still heights of air before him. The noise, too, was approaching. The woods filtered men and the fields became dotted.

As he rounded a hillock, he perceived that the roadway was now a crying mass of wagons, teams, and men. From the heaving tangle issued exhortations, commands, imprecations. Fear was sweeping it all along. The cracking whips bit and horses plunged and tugged. The white-topped wagons strained and stumbled in their exertions like fat sheep.

The youth felt comforted in a measure by this sight. They were all retreating. Perhaps, then, he was not so bad after all. He seated himself and watched the terror-stricken wagons. They fled like soft, ungainly animals. All the roarers and lashers served to help him to magnify the dangers and horrors of the engagement that he might try to prove to himself that the thing with which men could charge him was in truth a symmetrical act. There was an amount of pleasure to him in watching the wild march of this vindication.

Presently the calm head of a forward-going column of infantry appeared in the road. It came swiftly on. Avoiding the obstructions gave it the sinuous movement of a serpent. The men at the head butted mules with their musket stocks. They prodded teamsters indifferent to all howls. The men forced their way through parts of the dense mass by strength. The blunt head of the column pushed. The raving teamsters swore many strange oaths.

The commands to make way had the ring of a great importance in them. The men were going forward to the heart of the din. They were to confront the eager rush of the enemy. They felt the pride of their onward movement when the remainder of the army seemed trying to dribble down this road. They tumbled teams about with a fine feeling that it was no matter so long as their column got to the front in time. This importance made their faces grave and stern. And the backs of the officers were very rigid.

As the youth looked at them the black weight of his woe returned to him. He felt that he was regarding a procession of chosen beings. The separation was as great to him as if they had marched with weapons of flame and banners of sunlight. He could never be like them. He could have wept in his longings.

He searched about in his mind for an adequate malediction for the indefinite cause, the thing upon which men turn the words of final blame. It—whatever it was—was responsible for him, he said. There lay the fault.

The haste of the column to reach the battle seemed to the forlorn young man to be something much finer than stout fighting. Heroes, he thought, could find excuses in that long seething lane. They could retire with perfect self-respect and make excuses to the stars.

He wondered what those men had eaten that they could be in such haste to force their way to grim chances of death. As he watched his envy grew until he thought that he wished to change lives with one of them. He would have liked to have used a tremendous force, he said, throw off himself and become a better. Swift pictures of himself, apart, yet in himself, came to him—a blue desperate figure leading lurid charges with one knee forward and a broken blade high—a blue, determined figure standing before a crimson and steel assault, getting calmly killed on a high place before the eyes of all. He thought of the magnificent pathos of his dead body.

These thoughts uplifted him. He felt the quiver of war desire. In his ears, he heard the ring of victory. He knew the frenzy of a rapid successful charge. The music of the trampling feet, the harp voices, the clanking arms of the column near him made him soar on the red wings of war. For a few moments he was sublime.

He thought that he was about to start for the front. Indeed, he saw a picture of himself, dust-stained, haggard, panting, flying to the front at the proper moment to seize and throttle the dark, leering witch of calamity.

Then the difficulties of the thing began to drag at him. He hesitated, balancing awkwardly on one foot.

He had no rifle; he could not fight with his hands, said he resentfully to his plan. Well, rifles could be had for the picking. They were extraordinarily profuse.

Also, he continued, it would be a miracle if he found his regiment. Well, he could fight with any regiment.

He started forward slowly. He stepped as if he expected to tread upon some explosive thing. Doubts and he were struggling.

He would truly be a worm if any of his comrades should see him returning thus, the marks of his flight upon him. There was a reply that the intent fighters did not care for what happened rearward saving that no hostile bayonets appeared there. In the battle-blur his face would, in a way be hidden, like the face of a cowled man.

But then he said that his tireless fate would bring forth, when the strife lulled for a moment, a man to ask of him an explanation. In imagination he felt the scrutiny of his companions as he painfully labored through some lies.

Eventually, his courage expended itself upon these objections. The debates drained him of his fire.

He was not cast down by this defeat of his plan, for, upon studying the affair carefully, he could not but admit that the objections were very formidable.

Furthermore, various ailments had begun to cry out. In their presence he could not persist in flying high with the wings of war; they rendered it almost impossible for him to see himself in a heroic light. He tumbled headlong.

He discovered that he had a scorching thirst. His face was so dry and grimy that he thought he could feel his skin crackle. Each bone of his body had an ache in it, and seemingly threatened to break with each movement. His feet were like two sores. Also, his body was calling for food. It was more powerful than a direct hunger. There was a dull, weightlike feeling in his stomach, and, when he tried to walk, his head swayed and he tottered. He could not see with distinctness. Small patches of green mist floated before his vision.

While he had been tossed by many emotions, he had not been aware of ailments. Now they beset him and made clamor. As he was at last compelled to pay attention to them, his capacity for self-hate was multiplied. In despair, he declared that he was not like those others. He now conceded it to be impossible that he should ever become a hero. He was a craven loon. Those pictures of glory were piteous things. He groaned from his heart and went staggering off.

A certain mothlike quality within him kept him in the vicinity of the battle. He had a great desire to see, and to get news. He wished to know who was winning.

He told himself that, despite his unprecedented suffering, he had never lost his greed for a victory, yet, he said, in a half-apologetic manner to his conscience, he could not but know that a defeat for the army this time might mean many favorable things for him. The blows of the enemy would splinter regiments into fragments. Thus, many men of courage, he considered, would be obliged to desert the colors and scurry like chickens. He would appear as one of them. They would be sullen brothers in distress, and he could then easily believe he had not run any farther or faster than they. And if he himself could believe in his virtuous perfection, he conceived that there would be small trouble in convincing all others.

He said, as if an excuse for this hope, that previously the army had encountered great defeats and in a few months had shaken off all blood and tradition of them, emerging as bright and valiant as a new one; thrusting out of sight the memory of disaster, and appearing with the valor and confidence of unconquered legions. The shrilling voices of the people at home would pipe dismally for a time, but various generals were usually compelled to listen to these ditties. He of course felt no compunctions for proposing a general as a sacrifice. He could not tell who the chosen for the barbs might be, so he could center no direct sympathy upon him. The people were afar and he did not conceive public opinion to be accurate at long range. It was quite probable they would hit the wrong man who, after he had recovered from his amazement would perhaps spend the rest of his days in writing replies to the songs of his alleged failure. It would be very unfortunate, no doubt, but in this case a general was of no consequence to the youth.

In a defeat there would be a roundabout vindication of himself. He thought it would prove, in a manner, that he had fled early because of his superior powers of perception. A serious prophet upon predicting a flood should be the first man to climb a tree. This would demonstrate that he was indeed a seer.

A moral vindication was regarded by the youth as a very important thing. Without salve, he could not, he thought, wear the sore badge of his dishonor through life. With his heart continually assuring him that he was despicable, he could not exist without making it, through his actions, apparent to all men.

If the army had gone gloriously on he would be lost. If the din meant that now his army's flags were tilted forward he was a condemned wretch. He would be compelled to doom himself to isolation. If the men were advancing, their indifferent feet were trampling upon his chances for a successful life.

As these thoughts went rapidly through his mind, he turned upon them and tried to thrust them away. He denounced himself as a villain. He said that he was the most unutterably selfish man in existence. His mind pictured the soldiers who would place their defiant bodies before the spear of the yelling battle fiend, and as he saw their dripping corpses on an imagined field, he said that he was their murderer.

Again he thought that he wished he was dead. He believed that he envied a corpse. Thinking of the slain, he achieved a great contempt for some of them, as if they were guilty for thus becoming lifeless. They might have been killed by lucky chances, he said, before they had had opportunities to flee or before they had been really tested. Yet they would receive laurels from tradition. He cried out bitterly that their crowns were stolen and their robes of glorious memories were shams. However, he still said that it was a great pity he was not as they.

A defeat of the army had suggested itself to him as a means of escape from the consequences of his fall. He considered, now, however, that it was useless to think of such a possibility. His education had been that success for that mighty blue machine was certain; that it would make victories as a contrivance turns out buttons. He presently discarded all his speculations in the other direction. He returned to the creed of soldiers.

When he perceived again that it was not possible for the army to be defeated, he tried to bethink him of a fine tale which he could take back to his regiment, and with it turn the expected shafts of derision.

But, as he mortally feared these shafts, it became impossible for him to invent a tale he felt he could trust. He experimented with many schemes, but threw them aside one by one as flimsy. He was quick to see vulnerable places in them all.

Furthermore, he was much afraid that some arrow of scorn might lay him mentally low before he could raise his protecting tale.

He imagined the whole regiment saying: "Where's Henry Fleming? He run, didn't 'e? Oh, my!" He recalled various persons who would be quite sure to leave him no peace about it. They would doubtless question him with sneers, and laugh at his stammering hesitation. In the next engagement they would try to keep watch of him to discover when he would run.

Wherever he went in camp, he would encounter insolent and lingeringly cruel stares. As he imagined himself passing near a crowd of comrades, he could hear some one say, "There he goes!"

Then, as if the heads were moved by one muscle, all the faces were turned toward him with wide, derisive grins He seemed to hear some one make a humorous remark in a low tone. At it the others all crowed and cackled. He was a slang phrase.

12

The column that had butted stoutly at the obstacles in the roadway was barely out of the youth's sight before he saw dark waves of men come sweeping out of the woods and down through the fields. He knew at once that the steel fibers had been washed from their hearts. They were bursting from their coats and their equipments as from entanglements. They charged down upon him like terrified buffaloes.

Behind them blue smoke curled and clouded above the treetops, and through the thickets he could sometimes see a distant pink glare. The voices of the cannon were clamoring in interminable chorus.

The youth was horror-stricken. He stared in agony and amazement. He forgot that he was engaged in combating the universe. He threw aside his mental pamphlets on the philosophy of the retreated and rules for the guidance of the damned.

The fight was lost. The dragons were coming with invincible strides. The army, helpless in the matted thickets and blinded by the overhanging night, was going to be swallowed. War, the red animal, war, the blood-swollen god, would have bloated fill.

Within him something bade to cry out. He had the impulse to make a rallying speech, to sing a battle hymn, but he could only get his tongue to call into the air: "Why—why—what—what's th' matter?"

Soon he was in the midst of them. They were leaping and scampering all about him. Their blanched faces shone in the dusk. They seemed, for the most part, to be very burly men. The youth turned from one to another of them as they galloped along. His incoherent questions were lost. They were heedless of his appeals. They did not seem to see him.

They sometimes gabbled insanely. One huge man was asking of the sky: "Say, where de plank road? Where de plank road!" It was as if he had lost a child. He wept in his pain and dismay.

Presently, men were running hither and thither in all ways. The artillery booming, forward, rearward, and on the flanks made jumble of ideas of direction. Landmarks had vanished into the gathered gloom. The youth began to imagine that he had got into the center of the tremendous quarrel, and he could perceive no way out of it. From the mouths of the fleeing men came a thousand wild questions, but no one made answers.

The youth, after rushing about and throwing interrogations at the heedless bands of retreating infantry, finally clutched a man by the arm. They swung around face to face.

"Why—why—" stammered the youth struggling with his balking tongue.

The man screamed: "Let go me! Let go me!" His face was livid and his eyes were rolling uncontrolled. He was heaving and panting. He still grasped his rifle, perhaps having forgotten to release his hold upon it. He tugged frantically, and the youth being compelled to lean forward was dragged several paces.

"Let go me! Let go me!"

"Why—why—" stuttered the youth.

"Well, then!" bawled the man in a lurid rage. He adroitly and fiercely swung his rifle. It crushed upon the youth's head. The man ran on.

The youth's fingers had turned to paste upon the other's arm. The energy was smitten from his muscles. He saw the flaming wings of lightning flash before his vision. There was a deafening rumble of thunder within his head.

Suddenly his legs seemed to die. He sank writhing to the ground. He tried to arise. In his efforts against the numbing pain he was like a man wrestling with a creature of the air.

There was a sinister struggle.

Sometimes he would achieve a position half erect, battle with the air for a moment, and then fall again, grabbing at the grass. His face was of a clammy pallor. Deep groans were wrenched from him.

At last, with a twisting movement, he got upon his hands and knees, and from thence, like a babe trying to walk, to his feet. Pressing his hands to his temples he went lurching over the grass.

He fought an intense battle with his body. His dulled senses wished him to swoon and he opposed them stubbornly, his mind portraying unknown dangers and mutilations if he should fall upon the field. He went tall soldier fashion. He imagined secluded spots where he could fall and be unmolested. To search for one he strove against the tide of his pain.

Once he put his hand to the top of his head and timidly touched the wound. The scratching pain of the contact made him draw a long breath through his clinched teeth. His fingers were dabbled with blood. He regarded them with a fixed stare.

Around him he could hear the grumble of jolted cannon as the scurrying horses were lashed toward the front. Once, a young officer on a besplashed charger nearly ran him down. He turned and watched the mass of guns, men, and horses sweeping in a wide curve toward a gap in a fence. The officer was making excited motions with a gauntleted hand. The guns followed the teams with an air of unwillingness, of being dragged by the heels.

Some officers of the scattered infantry were cursing and railing like fishwives. Their scolding voices could be heard above the din. Into the unspeakable jumble in the roadway rode a squadron of cavalry. The faded yellow of their facings shone bravely. There was a mighty altercation.

The artillery were assembling as if for a conference.

The blue haze of evening was upon the field. The lines of forest were long purple shadows. One cloud lay along the western sky partly smothering the red.

As the youth left the scene behind him, he heard the guns suddenly roar out. He imagined them shaking in black rage. They belched and howled like brass devils guarding a gate. The soft air was filled with the tremendous remonstrance. With it came the shattering peal of opposing infantry. Turning to look behind him, he could see sheets of orange light illumine the shadowy distance. There were subtle and sudden lightnings in the far air. At times he thought he could see heaving masses of men.

He hurried on in the dusk. The day had faded until he could barely distinguish a place for his feet. The purple darkness was filled with men who lectured and jabbered. Sometimes he could see them gesticulating against the blue and somber sky. There seemed to be a great ruck of men and munitions spread about in the forest and in the fields.

The little narrow roadway now lay lifeless. There were overturned wagons like sun-dried bowlders. The bed of the former torrent was choked with the bodies of horses and splintered parts of war machines.

It had come to pass that his wound pained him but little. He was afraid to move rapidly, however, for a dread of disturbing it. He held his head very still and took many precautions against stumbling. He was filled with anxiety, and his face was pinched and drawn in anticipation of the pain of any sudden mistake of his feet in the gloom.

His thoughts, as he walked, fixed intently upon his hurt. There was a cool, liquid feeling about it and he imagined blood moving slowly down under his hair. His head seemed swollen to a size that made him think his neck to be inadequate.

The new silence of his wound made much worriment. The little blistering voices of pain that had called out from his scalp were, he thought, definite in their expression of danger. By them he believed that he could measure his plight. But when they remained ominously silent he became frightened and imagined terrible fingers that clutched into his brain.

Amid it he began to reflect upon various incidents and conditions of the past. He bethought him of certain meals his mother had cooked at home, in which those dishes of which he was particularly fond had occupied prominent positions. He saw the spread table. The pine walls of the kitchen were glowing in the warm light from the stove. Too, he remembered how he and his companions used to go from the schoolhouse to the bank of a shaded pool. He saw his clothes in disorderly array upon the grass of the bank. He felt the swash of the fragrant water upon his body. The leaves of the overhanging maple rustled with melody in the wind of youthful summer.

He was overcome presently by a dragging weariness. His head hung forward and his shoulders were stooped as if he were bearing a great bundle. His feet shuffled along the ground.

He held continuous arguments as to whether he should lie down and sleep at some near spot, or force himself on until he reached a certain haven. He often tried to dismiss the question, but his body persisted in rebellion and his senses nagged at him like pampered babies.

At last he heard a cheery voice near his shoulder: "Yeh seem t' be in a pretty bad way, boy?"

The youth did not look up, but he assented with thick tongue. "Uh!"

The owner of the cheery voice took him firmly by the arm. "Well," he said, with a round laugh, "I'm goin' your way. Th' hull gang is goin' your way. An' I guess I kin give yeh a lift." They began to walk like a drunken man and his friend.

As they went along, the man questioned the youth and assisted him with the replies like one manipulating the mind of a child. Sometimes he interjected anecdotes. "What reg'ment do yeh b'long teh? Eh? What's that? Th' 304th N' York? Why, what corps is that in? Oh, it is? Why, I thought they wasn't engaged t'-day— they're 'way over in th' center. Oh, they was, eh? Well, pretty nearly everybody got their share 'a fightin' t'-day. By dad, I give myself up fer dead any number 'a times. There was shootin' here an' shootin' there, an' hollerin' here an' hollerin' there, in th' damn' darkness, until I couldn't tell t' save m' soul which side I was on. Sometimes I thought I was sure 'nough from Ohier, an, other times I could 'a swore I was from th' bitter end of Florida. It was th' most mixed up dern thing I ever see. An' these here hull woods is a reg'lar mess. It'll be a miracle if we find our reg'ments t'-night. Pretty soon, though, we'll meet a-plenty of guards an' provost-guards, an' one thing an' another. Ho! there they go with an off'cer, I guess. Look at his hand a-draggin'. He 's got all th' war he wants, I bet. He won't be talkin' so big about his reputation an' all when they go t'sawin' off his leg. Poor feller! My brother's got whiskers jest like that. How did yeh git 'way over here, anyhow? Your reg'ment is a long way from here, ain't it? Well, I guess we can find it. Yeh know there was a boy killed in my comp'ny t'-day that I thought th' world an' all of. Jack was a nice feller. By ginger, it hurt like thunder t' see ol' Jack jest git knocked flat. We was a-standin' purty peaceable fer a spell, 'though there was men runnin' ev'ry way all 'round us, an' while we was a-standin' like that, 'long come a big fat feller. He began t' peck at Jack's elbow, an' he ses: 'Say, where's th' road t' th' river?' An' Jack, he never paid no attention, an' th' feller kept on a-peckin' at his elbow an' sayin': 'Say, where's th' road t' th' river?' Jack was a-lookin' ahead all th' time tryin' t' see th' Johnnies comin' through th' woods, an' he never paid no attention t' this big fat feller fer a long time, but at last he turned 'round an' he ses: 'Ah, go t' hell an' find th' road t' th' river!' An' jest then a shot slapped him bang on th' side th' head. He was a sergeant, too. Them was his last words. Thunder, I wish we was sure 'a findin' our reg'ments t'-night. It's goin' t' be long huntin'. But I guess we kin do it."

In the search which followed, the man of the cheery voice seemed to the youth to possess a wand of a magic kind. He threaded the mazes of the tangled forest with a strange fortune. In encounters with guards and patrols he displayed the keenness of a detective and the valor of a gamin. Obstacles fell before him and became of assistance. The youth, with his chin still on his breast, stood woodenly by while his companion beat ways and means out of sullen things.

The forest seemed a vast hive of men buzzing about in frantic circles, but the cheery man conducted the youth without mistakes, until at last he began to chuckle with glee and self-satisfaction. "Ah, there yeh are! See that fire?"

The youth nodded stupidly.

"Well, there's where your reg'ment is. An' now, good-by, ol' boy, good luck t' yeh."

A warm and strong hand clasped the youth's languid fingers for an instant, and then he heard a cheerful and audacious whistling as the man strode away. As he who had so befriended him was thus passing out of his life, it suddenly occurred to the youth that he had not once seen his face.

13

The youth went slowly toward the fire indicated by his departed friend. As he reeled, he bethought him of the welcome his comrades would give him. He had a conviction that he would soon feel in his sore heart the barbed missiles of ridicule. He had no strength to invent a tale; he would be a soft target.

He made vague plans to go off into the deeper darkness and hide, but they were all destroyed by the voices of exhaustion and pain from his body. His ailments, clamoring, forced him to seek the place of food and rest, at whatever cost.

He swung unsteadily toward the fire. He could see the forms of men throwing black shadows in the red light, and as he went nearer it became known to him in some way that the ground was strewn with sleeping men.

Of a sudden he confronted a black and monstrous figure. A rifle barrel caught some glinting beams. "Halt! halt!" He was dismayed for a moment, but he presently thought that he recognized the nervous voice. As he stood tottering before the rifle barrel, he called out: "Why, hello, Wilson, you—you here?"

The rifle was lowered to a position of caution and the loud soldier came slowly forward. He peered into the youth's face. "That you, Henry?"

"Yes, it's—it's me."

"Well, well, ol' boy," said the other, "by ginger, I'm glad t' see yeh! I give yeh up fer a goner. I thought yeh was dead sure enough." There was husky emotion in his voice.

The youth found that now he could barely stand upon his feet. There was a sudden sinking of his forces. He thought he must hasten to produce his tale to protect him from the missiles already at the lips of his redoubtable comrades. So, staggering before the loud soldier, he began: "Yes, yes. I've—I've had an awful time. I've been all over. Way over on th' right. Ter'ble fightin' over there. I had an awful time. I got separated from th' reg'ment. Over on th' right, I got shot. In th' head. I never see sech fightin'. Awful time. I don't see how I could a' got separated from the' reg'ment. I got shot, too."

His friend had stepped forward quickly "What? Got shot? Why didn't yeh say so first? Poor ol' boy, we must—hol' on a minnit; what am I doin'. I'll call Simpson."

Another figure at that moment loomed in the gloom. They could see that it was the corporal. "Who yeh talkin' to, Wilson?" he demanded. His voice was angertoned. "Who yeh talkin' to? Yeh th' derndest sentinel—why—hello, Henry, you here? Why, I thought you was dead four hours ago! Great Jerusalem, they keep turnin' up every ten minutes or so! We thought we'd lost forty-two men by straight count, but if they keep on a-comin' this way, we'll git th' comp'ny all back by mornin' yit. Where was yeh?"

"Over on th' right. I got separated"—began the youth with considerable glibness.

But his friend had interrupted hastily. "Yes, an' he got shot in th' head an' he's in a fix, an' we must see t' him right away." He rested his rifle in the hollow of his left arm and his right around the youth's shoulder.

"Gee, it must hurt like thunder!" he said.

The youth leaned heavily upon his friend. "Yes, it hurts—hurts a good deal," he replied. There was a faltering in his voice.

"Oh," said the corporal. He linked his arm in the youth's and drew him forward. "Come on, Henry. I'll take keer a' yeh."

As they went on together the loud private called out after them: "Put 'im t' sleep in my blanket, Simpson. An'—hol' on a minnit—here's my canteen. It's full a' coffee. Look at his head by th' fire an' see how it looks. Maybe it's a pretty bad un. When I git relieved in a couple 'a minnits, I'll be over an' see t' him."

The youth's senses were so deadened that his friend's voice sounded from afar and he could scarcely feel the pressure of the corporal's arm. He submitted passively to the latter's directing strength. His head was in the old manner hanging forward upon his breast. His knees wobbled.

The corporal led him into the glare of the fire. "Now, Henry," he said, "let's have a look at yer ol' head."

The youth sat down obediently and the corporal, laying aside his rifle, began to fumble in the bushy hair of his comrade. He was obliged to turn the other's head so that the full flush of the fire light would beam upon it. He puckered his mouth with a critical air. He drew back his lips and whistled through his teeth when his fingers came in contact with the splashed blood and the rare wound.

"Ah, here we are!" he said. He awkwardly made further investigations. "Just as I thought," he added presently. "Yeh've been grazed by a ball. It's raised a queer lump jest as if some feller had lammed yeh on th' head with a club. It stopped a-bleedin' long time ago. Th' most about it is that in th' mornin' yeh'll feel that a number ten hat wouldn't fit yeh. An' your head'll be all het up an' feel as dry as burnt pork. An' yeh may git a lot a' other sicknesses, too, by mornin'. Yeh can't never tell. Still, I don't much think so. It's jest a damn' good belt on th' head, an' nothin' more. Now, you jest sit here an' don't move, while I go rout out th' relief. Then I'll send Wilson t' take keer 'a yeh."

The corporal went away. The youth remained on the ground like a parcel. He stared with a vacant look into the fire.

After a time he aroused, for some part, and the things about him began to take form. He saw that the ground in the deep shadows was cluttered with men, sprawling in every conceivable posture. Glancing narrowly into the more distant darkness, he caught occasional glimpses of visages that loomed pallid and ghostly, lit with a phosphorescent glow. These faces expressed in their lines the deep stupor of the tired soldiers. They made them appear like men drunk with wine. This bit of forest might have appeared to an ethereal wanderer as a scene of the result of some frightful debauch.

On the other side of the fire the youth observed an officer asleep, seated bolt upright, with his back against a tree. There was something perilous in his position. Badgered by dreams, perhaps, he swayed with little bounces and starts, like an old, toddy-stricken grandfather in a chimney corner. Dust and stains were upon his face. His lower jaw hung down as if lacking strength to assume its normal position. He was the picture of an exhausted soldier after a feast of war.

He had evidently gone to sleep with his sword in his arms. These two had slumbered in an embrace, but the weapon had been allowed in time to fall unheeded to the ground. The brass-mounted hilt lay in contact with some parts of the fire.

Within the gleam of rose and orange light from the burning sticks were other soldiers, snoring and heaving, or lying deathlike in slumber. A few pairs of legs were stuck forth, rigid and straight. The shoes displayed the mud or dust of marches and bits of rounded trousers, protruding from the blankets, showed rents and tears from hurried pitchings through the dense brambles.

The fire crackled musically. From it swelled light smoke. Overhead the foliage moved softly. The leaves, with their faces turned toward the blaze, were colored shifting hues of silver, often edged with red. Far off to the right, through a window in the forest could be seen a handful of stars lying, like glittering pebbles, on the black level of the night.

Occasionally, in this low-arched hall, a soldier would arouse and turn his body to a new position, the experience of his sleep having taught him of uneven and objectionable places upon the ground under him. Or, perhaps, he would lift himself to a sitting posture, blink at the fire for an unintelligent moment, throw a swift glance at his prostrate companion, and then cuddle down again with a grunt of sleepy content.

The youth sat in a forlorn heap until his friend the loud young soldier came, swinging two canteens by their light strings. "Well, now, Henry, ol' boy," said the latter, "we'll have yeh fixed up in jest about a minnit."

He had the bustling ways of an amateur nurse. He fussed around the fire and stirred the sticks to brilliant exertions. He made his patient drink largely from the canteen that contained the coffee. It was to the youth a delicious draught. He tilted his head afar back and held the canteen long to his lips. The cool mixture went caressingly down his blistered throat. Having finished, he sighed with comfortable delight.

The loud young soldier watched his comrade with an air of satisfaction. He later produced an extensive handkerchief from his pocket. He folded it into a manner of bandage and soused water from the other canteen upon the middle of it. This crude arrangement he bound over the youth's head, tying the ends in a queer knot at the back of the neck.

"There," he said, moving off and surveying his deed, "yeh look like th' devil, but I bet yeh feel better."

The youth contemplated his friend with grateful eyes. Upon his aching and swelling head the cold cloth was like a tender woman's hand.

"Yeh don't holler ner say nothin'," remarked his friend approvingly. "I know I'm a blacksmith at takin' keer 'a sick folks, an' yeh never squeaked. Yer a good un, Henry. Most 'a men would a' been in th' hospital long ago. A shot in th' head ain't foolin' business."

The youth made no reply, but began to fumble with the buttons of his jacket.

"Well, come, now," continued his friend, "come on. I must put yeh t' bed an' see that yeh git a good night's rest."

The other got carefully erect, and the loud young soldier led him among the sleeping forms lying in groups and rows. Presently he stooped and picked up his blankets. He spread the rubber one upon the ground and placed the woolen one about the youth's shoulders.

"There now," he said, "lie down an' git some sleep."

The youth, with his manner of doglike obedience, got carefully down like a crone stooping. He stretched out with a murmur of relief and comfort. The ground felt like the softest couch.

But of a sudden he ejaculated: "Hol' on a minnit! Where you goin' t' sleep?"

His friend waved his hand impatiently. "Right down there by yeh."

"Well, but hol' on a minnit," continued the youth. "What yeh goin' t' sleep in? I've got your—"

The loud young soldier snarled: "Shet up an' go t' sleep. Don't be makin' a damn' fool 'a yerself," he said severely.

After the reproof the youth said no more. An exquisite drowsiness had spread through him. The warm comfort of the blanket enveloped him and made a gentle languor. His head fell forward on his crooked arm and his weighted lids went softly down over his eyes. Hearing a splatter of musketry from the distance, he wondered indifferently if those men sometimes slept. He gave a long sigh, snuggled down into his blanket, and in a moment was like his comrades.

14

When the youth awoke it seemed to him that he had been asleep for a thousand years, and he felt sure that he opened his eyes upon an unexpected world. Gray mists were slowly shifting before the first efforts of the sun rays. A impending splendor could be seen in the eastern sky. An icy dew had chilled his face, and immediately upon arousing he curled farther down into his blanket. He stared for a while at the leaves overhead, moving in a heraldic wind of the day.

The distance was splintering and blaring with the noise of fighting. There was in the sound an expression of a deadly persistency, as if it had not begun and was not to cease.

About him were the rows and groups of men that he had dimly seen the previous night. They were getting a last draught of sleep before the awakening. The gaunt, careworn features and dusty figures were made plain by this quaint light at the dawning, but it dressed the skin of the men in corpselike hues and made the tangled limbs appear pulseless and dead. The youth started up with a little cry when his eyes first swept over this motionless mass of men, thick-spread upon the ground, pallid, and in strange postures. His disordered mind interpreted the hall of the forest as a charnel place. He believed for an instant that he was in the house of the dead, and he did not dare to move lest these corpses start up, squalling and squawking. In a second, however, he achieved his proper mind. He swore a complicated oath at himself. He saw that this somber picture was not a fact of the present, but a mere prophecy.

He heard then the noise of a fire crackling briskly in the cold air, and, turning his head, he saw his friend pottering busily about a small blaze. A few other figures moved in the fog, and he heard the hard cracking of axe blows.

Suddenly there was a hollow rumble of drums. A distant bugle sang faintly. Similar sounds, varying in strength, came from rear and far over the forest. The bugles called to each other like brazen gamecocks. The near thunder of the regimental drums rolled.

The body of men in the woods rustled. There was a general uplifting of heads. A murmuring of voices broke upon the air. In it there was much bass of grumbling oaths. Strange gods were addressed in condemnation of the early hours necessary to correct war. An officer's peremptory tenor rang out and quickened the stiffened movement of the men. The tangled limbs unraveled. The corpse-hued faces were hidden behind fists that twisted slowly in the eye sockets.

The youth sat up and gave vent to an enormous yawn. "Thunder!" he remarked petulantly. He rubbed his eyes, and then putting up his hand felt carefully of the bandage over his wound. His friend, perceiving him to be awake, came from the fire. "Well, Henry, ol' man, how do yeh feel this mornin'?" he demanded.

The youth yawned again. Then he puckered his mouth to a little pucker. His head, in truth, felt precisely like a melon, and there was an unpleasant sensation at his stomach.

"Oh, Lord, I feel pretty bad," he said.

"Thunder!" exclaimed the other. "I hoped ye'd feel all right this mornin'. Let's see th' bandage—I guess it's slipped." He began to tinker at the wound in rather a clumsy way until the youth exploded.

"Gosh-dern it!" he said in sharp irritation; "you're the hangdest man I ever saw! You wear muffs on your hands. Why in good thunderation can't you be more easy? I'd rather you'd stand off an' throw guns at it. Now, go slow, an' don't act as if you was nailing down carpet."

He glared with insolent command at his friend, but the latter answered soothingly. "Well, well, come now, an' git some grub," he said. "Then, maybe, yeh'll feel better."

At the fireside the loud young soldier watched over his comrade's wants with tenderness and care. He was very busy marshaling the little black vagabonds of tin cups and pouring into them the streaming, iron colored mixture from a small and sooty tin pail. He had some fresh meat, which he roasted hurriedly upon a stick. He sat down then and contemplated the youth's appetite with glee.

The youth took note of a remarkable change in his comrade since those days of camp life upon the river bank. He seemed no more to be continually regarding the proportions of his personal prowess. He was not furious at small words that pricked his conceits. He was no more a loud young soldier. There was about him now a fine reliance. He showed a quiet belief in his purposes and his abilities. And this inward confidence evidently enabled him to be indifferent to little words of other men aimed at him.

The youth reflected. He had been used to regarding his comrade as a blatant child with an audacity grown from his inexperience, thoughtless, headstrong, jealous, and filled with a tinsel courage. A swaggering babe accustomed to strut in his own dooryard. The youth wondered where had been born these new eyes; when his comrade had made the great discovery that there were many men who would refuse to be subjected by him. Apparently, the other had now climbed a peak of wisdom from which he could perceive himself as a very wee thing. And the youth saw that ever after it would be easier to live in his friend's neighborhood.

His comrade balanced his ebony coffee-cup on his knee. "Well, Henry," he said, "what d'yeh think th' chances are? D'yeh think we'll wallop 'em?"

The youth considered for a moment. "Day-b'fore-yesterday," he finally replied, with boldness, "you would 'a 'bet you'd lick the hull kit-an'-boodle all by yourself."

His friend looked a trifle amazed. "Would I?" he asked. He pondered. "Well, perhaps I would," he decided at last. He stared humbly at the fire.

The youth was quite disconcerted at this surprising reception of his remarks. "Oh, no, you wouldn't either," he said, hastily trying to retrace.

But the other made a deprecating gesture "Oh, yeh needn't mind, Henry," he said. "I believe I was a pretty big fool in those days." He spoke as after a lapse of years.

There was a little pause.

"All th' officers say we've got th' rebs in a pretty tight box," said the friend, clearing his throat in a commonplace way. "They all seem t' think we've got 'em jest where we want 'em."

"I don't know about that," the youth replied. "What I seen over on th' right makes me think it was th' other way about. From where I was, it looked as if we was gettin' a good poundin' yestirday."

"D'yeh think so?" inquired the friend. "I thought we handled 'em pretty rough yestirday."

"Not a bit," said the youth. "Why, lord, man, you didn't see nothing of the fight. Why!" Then a sudden thought came to him. "Oh! Jim Conklin's dead."

His friend started. "What? Is he? Jim Conklin?"

The youth spoke slowly. "Yes. He's dead. Shot in th' side."

"Yeh don't say so. Jim Conklin. . . . poor cuss!"

All about them were other small fires surrounded by men with their little black utensils. From one of these near came sudden sharp voices in a row. It appeared that two lightfooted soldiers had been teasing a huge, bearded man, causing him to spill coffee upon his blue knees. The man had gone into a rage and had sworn comprehensively. Stung by his language, his tormentors had immediately bristled at him with a great show of resenting unjust oaths. Possibly there was going to be a fight.

The friend arose and went over to them, making pacific motions with his arms. "Oh, here, now, boys, what's th' use?" he said. "We'll be at th' rebs in less'n an hour. What's th' good fightin' 'mong ourselves?"

One of the light-footed soldiers turned upon him red-faced and violent. "Yeh needn't come around here with yer preachin'. I s'pose yeh don't approve 'a fightin' since Charley Morgan licked yeh; but I don't see what business this here is 'a yours or anybody else."

"Well, it ain't," said the friend mildly. "Still I hate t' see—"

There was a tangled argument.

"Well, he—," said the two, indicating their opponent with accusative forefingers.

The huge soldier was quite purple with rage. He pointed at the two soldiers with his great hand, extended clawlike. "Well, they—"

But during this argumentative time the desire to deal blows seemed to pass, although they said much to each other. Finally the friend returned to his old seat. In a short while the three antagonists could be seen together in an amiable bunch.

"Jimmie Rogers ses I'll have t' fight him after th' battle t'-day," announced the friend as he again seated himself. "He ses he don't allow no interferin' in his business. I hate t' see th' boys fightin' 'mong themselves."

The youth laughed. "Yer changed a good bit. Yeh ain't at all like yeh was. I remember when you an' that Irish feller—" He stopped and laughed again.

"No, I didn't use t' be that way," said his friend thoughtfully. "That's true 'nough."

"Well I didn't mean—" began the youth.

The friend made another deprecatory gesture. "Oh, yeh needn't mind, Henry."

There was another little pause.

"Th' reg'ment lost over half th' men yestirday," remarked the friend eventually. "I thought a course they was all dead, but, laws, they kep' a-comin' back last night until it seems, after all, we didn't lose but a few. They'd been scattered all over, wanderin' around in th' woods, fightin' with other reg'ments, an' everything. Jest like you done."

"So?" said the youth.

15

The regiment was standing at order arms at the side of a lane, waiting for the command to march, when suddenly the youth remembered the little packet enwrapped in a faded yellow envelope which the loud young soldier with lugubrious words had intrusted to him. It made him start. He uttered an exclamation and turned toward his comrade.

"Wilson!"

"What?"

His friend, at his side in the ranks, was thoughtfully staring down the road. From some cause his expression was at that moment very meek. The youth, regarding him with sidelong glances, felt impelled to change his purpose. "Oh, nothing," he said.

His friend turned his head in some surprise, "Why, what was yeh goin' t' say?"

"Oh, nothing," repeated the youth.

He resolved not to deal the little blow. It was sufficient that the fact made him glad. It was not necessary to knock his friend on the head with the misguided packet.

He had been possessed of much fear of his friend, for he saw how easily questionings could make holes in his feelings. Lately, he had assured himself that the altered comrade would not tantalize him with a persistent curiosity, but he felt certain that during the first period of leisure his friend would ask him to relate his adventures of the previous day.

He now rejoiced in the possession of a small weapon with which he could prostrate his comrade at the first signs of a cross-examination. He was master. It would now be he who could laugh and shoot the shafts of derision.

The friend had, in a weak hour, spoken with sobs of his own death. He had delivered a melancholy oration previous to his funeral, and had doubtless in the packet of letters, presented various keepsakes to relatives. But he had not died, and thus he had delivered himself into the hands of the youth.

The latter felt immensely superior to his friend, but he inclined to condescension. He adopted toward him an air of patronizing good humor.

His self-pride was now entirely restored. In the shade of its flourishing growth he stood with braced and self-confident legs, and since nothing could now be discovered he did not shrink from an encounter with the eyes of judges, and allowed no thoughts of his own to keep him from an attitude of manfulness. He had performed his mistakes in the dark, so he was still a man.

Indeed, when he remembered his fortunes of yesterday, and looked at them from a distance he began to see something fine there. He had license to be pompous and veteranlike.

His panting agonies of the past he put out of his sight.

In the present, he declared to himself that it was only the doomed and the damned who roared with sincerity at circumstance. Few but they ever did it. A man with a full stomach and the respect of his fellows had no business to scold about anything that he might think to be wrong in the ways of the universe, or even with the ways of society. Let the unfortunates rail; the others may play marbles.

He did not give a great deal of thought to these battles that lay directly before him. It was not essential that he should plan his ways in regard to them. He had been taught that many obligations of a life were easily avoided. The lessons of yesterday had been that retribution was a laggard and blind. With these facts before him he did not deem it necessary that he should become feverish over the possibilities of the ensuing twenty-four hours. He could leave much to chance. Besides, a faith in himself had secretly blossomed. There was a little flower of confidence growing within him. He was now a man of experience. He had been out among the dragons, he said, and he assured himself that they were not so hideous as he had imagined them. Also, they were inaccurate; they did not sting with precision. A stout heart often defied, and defying, escaped.

And, furthermore, how could they kill him who was the chosen of gods and doomed to greatness?

He remembered how some of the men had run from the battle. As he recalled their terror-struck faces he felt a scorn for them. They had surely been more fleet and more wild than was absolutely necessary. They were weak mortals. As for himself, he had fled with discretion and dignity.

He was aroused from this reverie by his friend, who, having hitched about nervously and blinked at the trees for a time, suddenly coughed in an introductory way, and spoke.

"Fleming!"

"What?"

The friend put his hand up to his mouth and coughed again. He fidgeted in his jacket.

"Well," he gulped, at last, "I guess yeh might as well give me back them letters." Dark, prickling blood had flushed into his cheeks and brow.

"All right, Wilson," said the youth. He loosened two buttons of his coat, thrust in his hand, and brought forth the packet. As he extended it to his friend the latter's face was turned from him.

He had been slow in the act of producing the packet because during it he had been trying to invent a remarkable comment upon the affair. He could conjure nothing of sufficient point. He was compelled to allow his friend to escape unmolested with his packet. And for this he took unto himself considerable credit. It was a generous thing.

His friend at his side seemed suffering great shame. As he contemplated him, the youth felt his heart grow more strong and stout. He had never been compelled to blush in such manner for his acts; he was an individual of extraordinary virtues.

He reflected, with condescending pity: "Too bad! Too bad! The poor devil, it makes him feel tough!"

After this incident, and as he reviewed the battle pictures he had seen, he felt quite competent to return home and make the hearts of the people glow with stories of war. He could see himself in a room of warm tints telling tales to listeners. He could exhibit laurels. They were insignificant; still, in a district where laurels were infrequent, they might shine.

He saw his gaping audience picturing him as the central figure in blazing scenes. And he imagined the consternation and the ejaculations of his mother and the young lady at the seminary as they drank his recitals. Their vague feminine formula for beloved ones doing brave deeds on the field of battle without risk of life would be destroyed.

16

A sputtering of musketry was always to be heard. Later, the cannon had entered the dispute. In the fog-filled air their voices made a thudding sound. The reverberations were continued. This part of the world led a strange, battleful existence.

The youth's regiment was marched to relieve a command that had lain long in some damp trenches. The men took positions behind a curving line of rifle pits that had been turned up, like a large furrow, along the line of woods. Before them was a level stretch, peopled with short, deformed stumps. From the woods beyond came the dull popping of the skirmishers and pickets, firing in the fog. From the right came the noise of a terrific fracas.

The men cuddled behind the small embankment and sat in easy attitudes awaiting their turn. Many had their backs to the firing. The youth's friend lay down, buried his face in his arms, and almost instantly, it seemed, he was in a deep sleep.

The youth leaned his breast against the brown dirt and peered over at the woods and up and down the line. Curtains of trees interfered with his ways of vision. He could see the low line of trenches but for a short distance. A few idle flags were perched on the dirt hills. Behind them were rows of dark bodies with a few heads sticking curiously over the top.

Always the noise of skirmishers came from the woods on the front and left, and the din on the right had grown to frightful proportions. The guns were roaring without an instant's pause for breath. It seemed that the cannon had come from all parts and were engaged in a stupendous wrangle. It became impossible to make a sentence heard.

The youth wished to launch a joke—a quotation from newspapers. He desired to say, "All quiet on the Rappahannock," but the guns refused to permit even a comment upon their uproar. He never successfully concluded the sentence. But at last the guns stopped, and among the men in the rifle pits rumors again flew, like birds, but they were now for the most part black creatures who flapped their wings drearily near to the ground and refused to rise on any wings of hope. The men's faces grew doleful from the interpreting of omens. Tales of hesitation and uncertainty on the part of those high in place and responsibility came to their ears. Stories of disaster were borne into their minds with many proofs. This din of musketry on the right, growing like a released genie of sound, expressed and emphasized the army's plight.

The men were disheartened and began to mutter. They made gestures expressive of the sentence: "Ah, what more can we do?" And it could always be seen that they were bewildered by the alleged news and could not fully comprehend a defeat.

Before the gray mists had been totally obliterated by the sun rays, the regiment was marching in a spread column that was retiring carefully through the woods. The disordered, hurrying lines of the enemy could sometimes be seen down through the groves and little fields. They were yelling, shrill and exultant.

At this sight the youth forgot many personal matters and became greatly enraged. He exploded in loud sentences. "B'jiminey, we're generaled by a lot 'a lunkheads."

"More than one feller has said that t'-day," observed a man.

His friend, recently aroused, was still very drowsy. He looked behind him until his mind took in the meaning of the movement. Then he sighed. "Oh, well, I s'pose we got licked," he remarked sadly.

The youth had a thought that it would not be handsome for him to freely condemn other men. He made an attempt to restrain himself, but the words upon his tongue were too bitter. He presently began a long and intricate denunciation of the commander of the forces.

"Mebbe, it wa'n't all his fault—not all together. He did th' best he knowed. It's our luck t' git licked often," said his friend in a weary tone. He was trudging along with stooped shoulder and shifting eyes like a man who has been caned and kicked.

"Well, don't we fight like the devil? Don't we do all that men can?" demanded the youth loudly.

He was secretly dumfounded at this sentiment when it came from his lips. For a moment his face lost its valor and he looked guiltily about him. But no one questioned his right to deal in such words, and presently he recovered his air of courage. He went on to repeat a statement he had heard going from group to group at the camp that morning. "The brigadier said he never saw a new reg'ment fight the way we fought yestirday, didn't he? And we didn't do better than many another reg'ment, did we? Well, then, you can't say it's th' army's fault, can you?"

In his reply, the friend's voice was stern. "'A course not," he said. "No man dare say we don't fight like th' devil. No man will ever dare say it. Th' boys fight like hell-roosters. But still—still, we don't have no luck."

"Well, then, if we fight like the devil an' don't ever whip, it must be the general's fault," said the youth grandly and decisively. "And I don't see any sense in fighting and fighting and fighting, yet always losing through some derned old lunkhead of a general."

A sarcastic man who was tramping at the youth's side, then spoke lazily. "Mebbe yeh think yeh fit th' hull battle yestirday, Fleming," he remarked.

The speech pierced the youth. Inwardly he was reduced to an abject pulp by these chance words. His legs quaked privately. He cast a frightened glance at the sarcastic man.

"Why, no," he hastened to say in a conciliating voice, "I don't think I fought the whole battle yesterday."

But the other seemed innocent of any deeper meaning. Apparently, he had no information. It was merely his habit. "Oh!" he replied in the same tone of calm derision.

The youth, nevertheless, felt a threat. His mind shrank from going near to the danger, and thereafter he was silent. The significance of the sarcastic man's words took from him all loud moods that would make him appear prominent. He became suddenly a modest person.

There was low-toned talk among the troops. The officers were impatient and snappy, their countenances clouded with the tales of misfortune. The troops, sifting through the forest, were sullen. In the youth's company once a man's laugh rang out. A dozen soldiers turned their faces quickly toward him and frowned with vague displeasure.

The noise of firing dogged their footsteps. Sometimes, it seemed to be driven a little way, but it always returned again with increased insolence. The men muttered and cursed, throwing black looks in its direction.

In a clear space the troops were at last halted. Regiments and brigades, broken and detached through their encounters with thickets, grew together again and lines were faced toward the pursuing bark of the enemy's infantry.

This noise, following like the yellings of eager, metallic hounds, increased to a loud and joyous burst, and then, as the sun went serenely up the sky, throwing illuminating rays into the gloomy thickets, it broke forth into prolonged pealings. The woods began to crackle as if afire.

"Whoop-a-dadee," said a man, "here we are! Everybody fightin'. Blood an' destruction."

"I was willin' t' bet they'd attack as soon as th' sun got fairly up," savagely asserted the lieutenant who commanded the youth's company. He jerked without mercy at his little mustache. He strode to and fro with dark dignity in the rear of his men, who were lying down behind whatever protection they had collected.

A battery had trundled into position in the rear and was thoughtfully shelling the distance. The regiment, unmolested as yet, awaited the moment when the gray shadows of the woods before them should be slashed by the lines of flame. There was much growling and swearing.

"Good Gawd," the youth grumbled, "we're always being chased around like rats! It makes me sick. Nobody seems to know where we go or why we go. We just get fired around from pillar to post and get licked here and get licked there, and nobody knows what it's done for. It makes a man feel like a damn' kitten in a bag. Now, I'd like to know what the eternal thunders we was marched into these woods for anyhow, unless it was to give the rebs a regular pot shot at us. We came in here and got our legs all tangled up in these cussed briers, and then we begin to fight and the rebs had an easy time of it. Don't tell me it's just luck! I know better. It's this derned old—"

The friend seemed jaded, but he interrupted his comrade with a voice of calm confidence. "It'll turn out all right in th' end," he said.

"Oh, the devil it will! You always talk like a dog-hanged parson. Don't tell me! I know—"

At this time there was an interposition by the savage-minded lieutenant, who was obliged to vent some of his inward dissatisfaction upon his men. "You boys shut right up! There no need 'a your wastin' your breath in long-winded arguments about this an' that an' th' other. You've been jawin' like a lot 'a old hens. All you've got t' do is to fight, an' you'll get plenty 'a that t' do in about ten minutes. Less talkin' an' more fightin' is what's best for you boys. I never saw sech gabbling jackasses."

He paused, ready to pounce upon any man who might have the temerity to reply. No words being said, he resumed his dignified pacing.

"There's too much chin music an' too little fightin' in this war, anyhow," he said to them, turning his head for a final remark.

The day had grown more white, until the sun shed his full radiance upon the thronged forest. A sort of a gust of battle came sweeping toward that part of the line where lay the youth's regiment. The front shifted a trifle to meet it squarely. There was a wait. In this part of the field there passed slowly the intense moments that precede the tempest.

A single rifle flashed in a thicket before the regiment. In an instant it was joined by many others. There was a mighty song of clashes and crashes that went sweeping through the woods. The guns in the rear, aroused and enraged by shells that had been thrown burr-like at them, suddenly involved themselves in a hideous altercation with another band of guns. The battle roar settled to a rolling thunder, which was a single, long explosion.

In the regiment there was a peculiar kind of hesitation denoted in the attitudes of the men. They were worn, exhausted, having slept but little and labored much. They rolled their eyes toward the advancing battle as they stood awaiting the shock. Some shrank and flinched. They stood as men tied to stakes.

17

This advance of the enemy had seemed to the youth like a ruthless hunting. He began to fume with rage and exasperation. He beat his foot upon the ground, and scowled with hate at the swirling smoke that was approaching like a phantom flood. There was a maddening quality in this seeming resolution of the foe to give him no rest, to give him no time to sit down and think. Yesterday he had fought and had fled rapidly. There had been many adventures. For today he felt that he had earned opportunities for contemplative repose. He could have enjoyed portraying to uninitiated listeners various scenes at which he had been a witness or ably discussing the processes of war with other proved men. Too it was important that he should have time for physical recuperation. He was sore and stiff from his experiences. He had received his fill of all exertions, and he wished to rest.

But those other men seemed never to grow weary; they were fighting with their old speed. He had a wild hate for the relentless foe. Yesterday, when he had imagined the universe to be against him, he had hated it, little gods and big gods; today he hated the army of the foe with the same great hatred. He was not going to be badgered of his life, like a kitten chased by boys, he said. It was not well to drive men into final corners; at those moments they could all develop teeth and claws.

He leaned and spoke into his friend's ear. He menaced the woods with a gesture. "If they keep on chasing us, by Gawd, they'd better watch out. Can't stand *too* much."

The friend twisted his head and made a calm reply. "If they keep on a-chasin' us they'll drive us all inteh th' river."

The youth cried out savagely at this statement. He crouched behind a little tree, with his eyes burning hatefully and his teeth set in a cur-like snarl. The awkward bandage was still about his head, and upon it, over his wound, there was a spot of dry blood. His hair was wondrously tousled, and some straggling, moving locks hung over the cloth of the bandage down toward his forehead. His jacket and shirt were open at the throat, and exposed his young bronzed neck. There could be seen spasmodic gulpings at his throat.

His fingers twined nervously about his rifle. He wished that it was an engine of annihilating power. He felt that he and his companions were being taunted and derided from sincere convictions that they were poor and puny. His knowledge of his inability to take vengeance for it made his rage into a dark and stormy specter, that possessed him and made him dream of abominable cruelties. The tormentors were flies sucking insolently at his blood, and he thought that he would have given his life for a revenge of seeing their faces in pitiful plights.

The winds of battle had swept all about the regiment, until the one rifle, instantly followed by others, flashed in its front. A moment later the regiment roared forth its sudden and valiant retort. A dense wall of smoke settled slowly down. It was furiously slit and slashed by the knifelike fire from the rifles.

To the youth the fighters resembled animals tossed for a death struggle into a dark pit. There was a sensation that he and his fellows, at bay, were pushing back, always pushing fierce onslaughts of creatures who were slippery. Their beams of crimson seemed to get no purchase upon the bodies of their foes; the latter seemed to evade them with ease, and come through, between, around, and about with unopposed skill.

When, in a dream, it occurred to the youth that his rifle was an impotent stick, he lost sense of everything but his hate, his desire to smash into pulp the glittering smile of victory which he could feel upon the faces of his enemies.

The blue smoke-swallowed line curled and writhed like a snake stepped upon. It swung its ends to and fro in an agony of fear and rage.

The youth was not conscious that he was erect upon his feet. He did not know the direction of the ground. Indeed, once he even lost the habit of balance and fell heavily. He was up again immediately. One thought went through the chaos of his brain at the time. He wondered if he had fallen because he had been shot. But the suspicion flew away at once. He did not think more of it.

He had taken up a first position behind the little tree, with a direct determination to hold it against the world. He had not deemed it possible that his army could that day succeed, and from this he felt the ability to fight harder. But the throng had surged in all ways, until he lost directions and locations, save that he knew where lay the enemy.

The flames bit him, and the hot smoke broiled his skin. His rifle barrel grew so hot that ordinarily he could not have borne it upon his palms; but he kept on stuffing cartridges into it, and pounding them with his clanking, bending ramrod. If he aimed at some changing form through the smoke, he pulled his trigger with a fierce grunt, as if he were dealing a blow of the fist with all his strength.

When the enemy seemed falling back before him and his fellows, he went instantly forward, like a dog who, seeing his foes lagging, turns and insists upon being pursued. And when he was compelled to retire again, he did it slowly, sullenly, taking steps of wrathful despair.

Once he, in his intent hate, was almost alone, and was firing, when all those near him had ceased. He was so engrossed in his occupation that he was not aware of a lull.

He was recalled by a hoarse laugh and a sentence that came to his ears in a voice of contempt and amazement. "Yeh infernal fool, don't yeh know enough t' quit when there ain't anything t' shoot at? Good Gawd!"

He turned then and, pausing with his rifle thrown half into position, looked at the blue line of his comrades. During this moment of leisure they seemed all to be engaged in staring with astonishment at him. They had become spectators. Turning to the front again he saw, under the lifted smoke, a deserted ground.

He looked bewildered for a moment. Then there appeared upon the glazed vacancy of his eyes a diamond point of intelligence. "Oh," he said, comprehending.

He returned to his comrades and threw himself upon the ground. He sprawled like a man who had been thrashed. His flesh seemed strangely on fire, and the sounds of the battle continued in his ears. He groped blindly for his canteen.

The lieutenant was crowing. He seemed drunk with fighting. He called out to the youth: "By heavens, if I had ten thousand wild cats like you I could tear th' stomach outa this war in less'n a week!" He puffed out his chest with large dignity as he said it.

Some of the men muttered and looked at the youth in awe-struck ways. It was plain that as he had gone on loading and firing and cursing without the proper intermission, they had found time to regard him. And they now looked upon him as a war devil.

The friend came staggering to him. There was some fright and dismay in his voice. "Are yeh all right, Fleming? Do yeh feel all right? There ain't nothin' th' matter with yeh, Henry, is there?"

"No," said the youth with difficulty. His throat seemed full of knobs and burs.

These incidents made the youth ponder. It was revealed to him that he had been a barbarian, a beast. He had fought like a pagan who defends his religion. Regarding it, he saw that it was fine, wild, and, in some ways, easy. He had been a tremendous figure, no doubt. By this struggle he had overcome obstacles which he had admitted to be mountains. They had fallen like paper peaks, and he was now what he called a hero. And he had not been aware of the process. He had slept and, awakening, found himself a knight.

He lay and basked in the occasional stares of his comrades. Their faces were varied in degrees of blackness from the burned powder. Some were utterly smudged. They were reeking with perspiration, and their breaths came hard and wheezing. And from these soiled expanses they peered at him.

"Hot work! Hot work!" cried the lieutenant deliriously. He walked up and down, restless and eager. Sometimes his voice could be heard in a wild, incomprehensible laugh.

When he had a particularly profound thought upon the science of war he always unconsciously addressed himself to the youth.

There was some grim rejoicing by the men. "By thunder, I bet this army'll never see another new reg'ment like us!"

"You bet!"

"A dog, a woman, an' a walnut tree,
Th' more yeh beat 'em, th' better they be!

That's like us."

"Lost a piler men, they did. If an' ol' woman swep' up th' woods she'd git a dustpanful."

"Yes, an' if she'll come around ag'in in 'bout an' hour she'll git a pile more."

The forest still bore its burden of clamor. From off under the trees came the rolling clatter of the musketry. Each distant thicket seemed a strange porcupine with quills of flame. A cloud of dark smoke, as from smoldering ruins, went up toward the sun now bright and gay in the blue, enameled sky.

18

The ragged line had respite for some minutes, but during its pause the struggle in the forest became magnified until the trees seemed to quiver from the firing and the ground to shake from the rushing of the men. The voices of the cannon were mingled in a long and interminable row. It seemed difficult to live in such an atmosphere. The chests of the men strained for a bit of freshness, and their throats craved water.

There was one shot through the body, who raised a cry of bitter lamentation when came this lull. Perhaps he had been calling out during the fighting also, but at that time no one had heard him. But now the men turned at the woeful complaints of him upon the ground.

"Who is it? Who is it?"

"It's Jimmie Rogers. Jimmie Rogers."

When their eyes first encountered him there was a sudden halt, as if they feared to go near. He was thrashing about in the grass, twisting his shuddering body into many strange postures. He was screaming loudly. This instant's hesitation seemed to fill him with a tremendous, fantastic contempt, and he damned them in shrieked sentences.

The youth's friend had a geographical illusion concerning a stream, and he obtained permission to go for some water. Immediately canteens were showered up him. "Fill mine, will yeh?" "Bring me some, too." "And me, too." He departed, ladened. The youth went with his friend, feeling a desire to throw his heated body onto the stream and, soaking there, drink quarts.

They made a hurried search for the supposed stream, but did not find it. "No water here," said the youth. They turned without delay and began to retrace their steps.

From their position as they again faced toward the place of the fighting, they could of course comprehend a greater amount of the battle than when their visions had been blurred by the hurling smoke of the line. They could see dark stretches winding along the land, and on one cleared space there was a row of guns making gray clouds, which were filled with large flashes of orange-colored flame. Over some foliage they could see the roof of a house. One window, glowing a deep murder red, shone squarely through the leaves. From the edifice a tall leaning tower of smoke went far into the sky.

Looking over their own troops, they saw mixed masses slowly getting into regular form. The sunlight made twinkling points of the bright steel. To the rear there was a glimpse of a distant roadway as it curved over a slope. It was crowded with retreating infantry. From all the interwoven forest arose the smoke and bluster of the battle. The air was always occupied by a blaring.

Near where they stood shells were flip-flapping and hooting. Occasional bullets buzzed in the air and spanged into tree trunks. Wounded men and stragglers were slinking through the woods.

Looking down an aisle of the grove, the youth and his companion saw a jangling general and his staff almost ride upon a wounded man, who was crawling on his hands and knees. The general reined strongly at his charger's opened and foamy mouth and guided it with dexterous horsemanship past the man. The latter scrambled in wild and torturing haste. His strength evidently failed him as he reached a place of safety. One of his arms suddenly weakened, and he fell, sliding over upon his back. He lay stretched out, breathing gently.

A moment later the small, creaking cavalcade was directly in front of the two soldiers. Another officer, riding with the skillful abandon of a cowboy, galloped his horse to a position directly before the general. The two unnoticed foot soldiers made a little show of going on, but they lingered near in the desire to overhear the conversation. Perhaps, they thought, some great inner historical things would be said.

The general, whom the boys knew as the commander of their division, looked at the other officer and spoke coolly, as if he were criticising his clothes. "Th' enemy's formin' over there for another charge," he said. "It'll be directed against Whiterside, an' I fear they'll break through there unless we work like thunder t' stop them."

The other swore at his restive horse, and then cleared his throat. He made a gesture toward his cap. "It'll be hell t' pay stoppin' them," he said shortly.

"I presume so," remarked the general. Then he began to talk rapidly and in a lower tone. He frequently illustrated his words with a pointing finger. The two infantrymen could hear nothing until finally he asked: "What troops can you spare?"

The officer who rode like a cowboy reflected for an instant. "Well," he said, "I had to order in th' 12th to help th' 76th, an' I haven't really got any. But there's th' 304th. They fight like a lot 'a mule drivers. I can spare them best of any."

The youth and his friend exchanged glances of astonishment.

The general spoke sharply. "Get 'em ready, then. I'll watch developments from here, an' send you word when t' start them. It'll happen in five minutes."

As the other officer tossed his fingers toward his cap and wheeling his horse, started away, the general called out to him in a sober voice: "I don't believe many of your mule drivers will get back."

The other shouted something in reply. He smiled.

With scared faces, the youth and his companion hurried back to the line.

These happenings had occupied an incredibly short time, yet the youth felt that in them he had been made aged. New eyes were given to him. And the most startling thing was to learn suddenly that he was very insignificant. The officer spoke of the regiment as if he referred to a broom. Some part of the woods needed sweeping, perhaps, and he merely indicated a broom in a tone properly indifferent to its fate. It was war, no doubt, but it appeared strange.

As the two boys approached the line, the lieutenant perceived them and swelled with wrath. "Fleming—Wilson—how long does it take yeh to git water, anyhow—where yeh been to."

But his oration ceased as he saw their eyes, which were large with great tales. "We're goin' t' charge—we're goin' t' charge!" cried the youth's friend, hastening with his news.

"Charge?" said the lieutenant. "Charge? Well, b'Gawd! Now, this is real fightin'." Over his soiled countenance there went a boastful smile. "Charge? Well, b'Gawd!"

A little group of soldiers surrounded the two youths. "Are we sure 'nough? Well, I'll be derned! Charge? What fer? What at? Wilson, you're lyin'."

"I hope to die," said the youth, pitching his tones to the key of angry remonstrance. "Sure as shooting, I tell you."

And his friend spoke in re-enforcement. "Not by a blame sight, he ain't lyin'. We heard 'em talkin'."

They caught sight of two mounted figures a short distance from them. One was the colonel of the regiment and the other was the officer who had received orders from the commander of the division. They were gesticulating at each other. The soldier, pointing at them, interpreted the scene.

One man had a final objection: "How could yeh hear 'em talkin'?" But the men, for a large part, nodded, admitting that previously the two friends had spoken truth.

They settled back into reposeful attitudes with airs of having accepted the matter. And they mused upon it, with a hundred varieties of expression. It was an engrossing thing to think about. Many tightened their belts carefully and hitched at their trousers.

A moment later the officers began to bustle among the men, pushing them into a more compact mass and into a better alignment. They chased those that straggled and fumed at a few men who seemed to show by their attitudes that they had decided to remain at that spot. They were like critical shepherds struggling with sheep.

Presently, the regiment seemed to draw itself up and heave a deep breath. None of the men's faces were mirrors of large thoughts. The soldiers were bended and stooped like sprinters before a signal. Many pairs of glinting eyes peered from the grimy faces toward the curtains of the deeper woods. They seemed to be engaged in deep calculations of time and distance.

They were surrounded by the noises of the monstrous altercation between the two armies. The world was fully interested in other matters. Apparently, the regiment had its small affair to itself.

The youth, turning, shot a quick, inquiring glance at his friend. The latter returned to him the same manner of look. They were the only ones who possessed an inner knowledge. "Mule drivers —hell t' pay—don't believe many will get back." It was an ironical secret. Still, they saw no hesitation in each other's faces, and they nodded a mute and unprotesting assent when a shaggy man near them said in a meek voice: "We'll git swallowed."

19

The youth stared at the land in front of him. Its foliages now seemed to veil powers and horrors. He was unaware of the machinery of orders that started the charge, although from the corners of his eyes he saw an officer, who looked like a boy a-horseback, come galloping, waving his hat. Suddenly he felt a straining and heaving among the men. The line fell slowly forward like a toppling wall, and, with a convulsive gasp that was intended for a cheer, the regiment began its journey. The youth was pushed and jostled for a moment before he understood the movement at all, but directly he lunged ahead and began to run.

He fixed his eye upon a distant and prominent clump of trees where he had concluded the enemy were to be met, and he ran toward it as toward a goal. He had believed throughout that it was a mere question of getting over an unpleasant matter as quickly as possible, and he ran desperately, as if pursued for a murder. His face was drawn hard and tight with the stress of his endeavor. His eyes were fixed in a lurid glare. And with his soiled and disordered dress, his red and inflamed features surmounted by the dingy rag with its spot of blood, his wildly swinging rifle and banging accouterments, he looked to be an insane soldier.

As the regiment swung from its position out into a cleared space the woods and thickets before it awakened. Yellow flames leaped toward it from many directions. The forest made a tremendous objection.

The line lurched straight for a moment. Then the right wing swung forward; it in turn was surpassed by the left. Afterward the center careered to the front until the regiment was a wedge-shaped mass, but an instant later the opposition of the bushes, trees, and uneven places on the ground split the command and scattered it into detached clusters.

The youth, light-footed, was unconsciously in advance. His eyes still kept note of the clump of trees. From all places near it the clannish yell of the enemy could be heard. The little flames of rifles leaped from it. The song of the bullets was in the air and shells snarled among the tree tops. One tumbled directly into the middle of a hurrying group and exploded in crimson fury. There was an instant's spectacle of a man, almost over it, throwing up his hands to shield his eyes.

Other men, punched by bullets, fell in grotesque agonies. The regiment left a coherent trail of bodies.

They had passed into a clearer atmosphere. There was an effect like a revelation in the new appearance of the landscape. Some men working madly at a battery were plain to them, and the opposing infantry's lines were defined by the gray walls and fringes of smoke.

It seemed to the youth that he saw everything. Each blade of the green grass was bold and clear. He thought that he was aware of every change in the thin, transparent vapor that floated idly in sheets. The brown or gray trunks of the trees showed each roughness of their surfaces. And the men of the regiment, with their starting eyes and sweating faces, running madly, or falling, as if thrown headlong, to queer, heaped-up corpses—all were comprehended. His mind took a mechanical but firm impression, so that afterward everything was pictured and explained to him, save why he himself was there.

But there was a frenzy made from this furious rush. The men, pitching forward insanely, had burst into cheerings, moblike and barbaric, but tuned in strange keys that can arouse the dullard and the stoic. It made a mad enthusiasm that, it seemed, would be incapable of checking itself before granite and brass. There was the delirium that encounters despair and death, and is heedless and blind to the odds. It is a temporary but sublime absence of selfishness. And because it was of this order was the reason, perhaps, why the youth wondered, afterward, what reasons he could have had for being there.

Presently the straining pace ate up the energies of the men. As if by agreement, the leaders began to slacken their speed. The volleys directed against them had had a seeming windlike effect. The regiment snorted and blew. Among some stolid trees it began to falter and hesitate. The men, staring intently, began to wait for some of the distant walls of smoke to move and disclose to them the scene. Since much of their strength and their breath had vanished, they returned to caution. They were become men again.

The youth had a vague belief that he had run miles, and he thought, in a way, that he was now in some new and unknown land.

The moment the regiment ceased its advance the protesting splutter of musketry became a steadied roar. Long and accurate fringes of smoke spread out. From the top of a small hill came level belchings of yellow flame that caused an inhuman whistling in the air.

The men, halted, had opportunity to see some of their comrades dropping with moans and shrieks. A few lay under foot, still or wailing. And now for an instant the men stood, their rifles slack in their hands, and watched the regiment dwindle. They appeared dazed and stupid. This spectacle seemed to paralyze them, overcome them with a fatal fascination. They stared woodenly at the sights, and, lowering their eyes, looked from face to face. It was a strange pause, and a strange silence.

Then, above the sounds of the outside commotion, arose the roar of the lieutenant. He strode suddenly forth, his infantile features black with rage.

"Come on, yeh fools!" he bellowed. "Come on! Yeh can't stay here. Yeh must come on." He said more, but much of it could not be understood.

He started rapidly forward, with his head turned toward the men. "Come on," he was shouting. The men stared with blank and yokel-like eyes at him. He was obliged to halt and retrace his steps. He stood then with his back to the enemy and delivered gigantic curses into the faces of the men. His body vibrated from the weight and force of his imprecations. And he could string oaths with the facility of a maiden who strings beads.

The friend of the youth aroused. Lurching suddenly forward and dropping to his knees, he fired an angry shot at the persistent woods. This action awakened the men. They huddled no more like sheep. They seemed suddenly to bethink them of their weapons, and at once commenced firing. Belabored by their officers, they began to move forward. The regiment, involved like a cart involved in the mud and muddle, started unevenly with many jolts and jerks. The men stopped now every few paces to fire and load, and in this manner moved slowly on from trees to trees.

The flaming opposition in their front grew with their advance until it seemed that all forward ways were barred by the thin leaping tongues, and off to the right an ominous demonstration could sometimes be dimly discerned. The smoke lately generated was in confusing clouds that made it difficult for the regiment to proceed with intelligence. As he passed through each curling mass the youth wondered what would confront him on the farther side.

The command went painfully forward until an open space interposed between them and the lurid lines. Here, crouching and cowering behind some trees, the men clung with desperation, as if threatened by a wave. They looked wild-eyed, and as if amazed at this furious disturbance they had stirred. In the storm there was an ironical expression of their importance. The faces of the men, too, showed a lack of a certain feeling of responsibility for being there. It was as if they had been driven. It was the dominant animal failing to remember in the supreme moments the forceful causes of various superficial qualities. The whole affair seemed incomprehensible to many of them.

As they halted thus the lieutenant again began to bellow profanely. Regardless of the vindictive threats of the bullets, he went about coaxing, berating, and bedamning. His lips, that were habitually in a soft and childlike curve, were now writhed into unholy contortions. He swore by all possible deities.

Once he grabbed the youth by the arm. "Come on, yeh lunkhead!" he roared.

"Come on! We'll all git killed if we stay here. We've on'y got t' go across that lot. An' then"—the remainder of his idea disappeared in a blue haze of curses.

The youth stretched forth his arm. "Cross there?" His mouth was puckered in doubt and awe.

"Certainly. Jest 'cross th' lot! We can't stay here," screamed the lieutenant. He poked his face close to the youth and waved his bandaged hand. "Come on!" Presently he grappled with him as if for a wrestling bout. It was as if he planned to drag the youth by the ear on to the assault.

The private felt a sudden unspeakable indignation against his officer. He wrenched fiercely and shook him off.

"Come on yerself, then," he yelled. There was a bitter challenge in his voice.

They galloped together down the regimental front. The friend scrambled after them. In front of the colors the three men began to bawl: "Come on! come on!" They danced and gyrated like tortured savages.

The flag, obedient to these appeals, bended its glittering form and swept toward them. The men wavered in indecision for a moment, and then with a long, wailful cry the dilapidated regiment surged forward and began its new journey.

Over the field went the scurrying mass. It was a handful of men splattered into the faces of the enemy. Toward it instantly sprang the yellow tongues. A vast quantity of blue smoke hung before them. A mighty banging made ears valueless.

The youth ran like a madman to reach the woods before a bullet could discover him. He ducked his head low, like a football player. In his haste his eyes almost closed, and the scene was a wild blur. Pulsating saliva stood at the corners of his mouth.

Within him, as he hurled himself forward, was born a love, a despairing fondness for this flag which was near him. It was a creation of beauty and invulnerability. It was a goddess, radiant, that bended its form with an imperious gesture to him. It was a woman, red and white, hating and loving, that called him with the voice of his hopes. Because no harm could come to it he endowed it with power. He kept near, as if it could be a saver of lives, and an imploring cry went from his mind.

In the mad scramble he was aware that the color sergeant flinched suddenly, as if struck by a bludgeon. He faltered, and then became motionless, save for his quivering knees.

He made a spring and a clutch at the pole. At the same instant his friend grabbed it from the other side. They jerked at it, stout and furious, but the color sergeant was dead, and the corpse would not relinquish its trust. For a moment there was a grim encounter. The dead man, swinging with bended back, seemed to be obstinately tugging, in ludicrous and awful ways, for the possession of the flag.

It was past in an instant of time. They wrenched the flag furiously from the dead man, and, as they turned again, the corpse swayed forward with bowed head. One arm swung high, and the curved hand fell with heavy protest on the friend's unheeding shoulder.

20

When the two youths turned with the flag they saw that much of the regiment had crumbled away, and the dejected remnant was coming slowly back. The men, having hurled themselves in projectile fashion, had presently expended their forces. They slowly retreated, with their faces still toward the spluttering woods, and their hot rifles still replying to the din. Several officers were giving orders, their voices keyed to screams.

"Where in hell yeh goin'?" the lieutenant was asking in a sarcastic howl. And a red-bearded officer, whose voice of triple brass could plainly be heard, was commanding: "Shoot into 'em! Shoot into 'em, Gawd damn their souls!" There was a *melée* of screeches, in which the men were ordered to do conflicting and impossible things.

The youth and his friend had a small scuffle over the flag. "Give it t' me!" "No, let me keep it!" Each felt satisfied with the other's possession of it, but each felt bound to declare, by an offer to carry the emblem, his willingness to further risk himself. The youth roughly pushed his friend away.

The regiment fell back to the stolid trees. There it halted for a moment to blaze at some dark forms that had begun to steal upon its track. Presently it resumed its march again, curving among the tree trunks. By the time the depleted regiment had again reached the first open space they were receiving a fast and merciless fire. There seemed to be mobs all about them.

The greater part of the men, discouraged, their spirits worn by the turmoil, acted as if stunned. They accepted the pelting of the bullets with bowed and weary heads. It was of no purpose to strive against walls. It was of no use to batter themselves against granite. And from this consciousness that they had attempted to conquer an unconquerable thing there seemed to arise a feeling that they had been betrayed. They glowered with bent brows, but dangerously, upon some of the officers, more particularly upon the red-bearded one with the voice of triple brass.

However, the rear of the regiment was fringed with men, who continued to shoot irritably at the advancing foes. They seemed resolved to make every trouble. The youthful lieutenant was perhaps the last man in the disordered mass. His forgotten back was toward the enemy. He had been shot in the arm. It hung straight and rigid. Occasionally he would cease to remember it, and be about to emphasize an oath with a sweeping gesture. The multiplied pain caused him to swear with incredible power.

The youth went along with slipping, uncertain feet. He kept watchful eyes rearward. A scowl of mortification and rage was upon his face. He had thought of a fine revenge upon the officer who had referred to him and his fellows as mule drivers. But he saw that it could not come to pass. His dreams had collapsed when the mule drivers, dwindling rapidly, had wavered and hesitated on the little clearing, and then had recoiled. And now the retreat of the mule drivers was a march of shame to him.

A dagger-pointed gaze from without his blackened face was held toward the enemy, but his greater hatred was riveted upon the man, who, not knowing him, had called him a mule driver.

When he knew that he and his comrades had failed to do anything in successful ways that might bring the little pangs of a kind of remorse upon the officer, the youth allowed the rage of the baffled to possess him. This cold officer upon a monument, who dropped epithets unconcernedly down, would be finer as a dead man, he thought. So grievous did he think it that he could never possess the secret right to taunt truly in answer.

He had pictured red letters of curious revenge. "We *are* mule drivers, are we?" And now he was compelled to throw them away.

He presently wrapped his heart in the cloak of his pride and kept the flag erect. He harangued his fellows, pushing against their chests with his free hand. To those he knew well he made frantic appeals, beseeching them by name. Between him and the lieutenant, scolding and near to losing his mind with rage, there was felt a subtle fellowhhip and equality. They supported each other in all manner of hoarse, howling protests.

But the regiment was a machine run down. The two men babbled at a forceless thing. The soldiers who had heart to go slowly were continually shaken in their resolves by a knowledge that comrades were slipping with speed back to the lines. It was difficult to think of reputation when others were thinking of skins. Wounded men were left crying on this black journey.

The smoke fringes and flames blustered always. The youth, peering once through a sudden rift in a cloud, saw a brown mass of troops, interwoven and magnified until they appeared to be thousands. A fierce-hued flag flashed before his vision.

Immediately, as if the uplifting of the smoke had been prearranged, the discovered troops burst into a rasping yell, and a hundred flames jetted toward the retreating band. A rolling gray cloud again interposed as the regiment doggedly replied. The youth had to depend again upon his misused ears, which were trembling and buzzing from the *mêlée* of musketry and yells.

The way seemed eternal. In the clouded haze men became panic-striken with the thought that the regiment had lost its path, and was proceeding in a perilous direction. Once the men who headed the wild procession turned and came pushing back against their comrades, screaming that they were being fired upon from points which they had considered to be toward their own lines. At this cry a hysterical fear and dismay beset the troops. A soldier, who heretofore had been ambitious to make the regiment into a wise little band that would proceed calmly amid the huge-appearing difficulties, suddenly sank down and buried his face in his arms with an air of bowing to a doom. From another a shrill lamentation rang out filled with profane illusions to a general. Men ran hither and thither, seeking with their eyes roads of escape. With serene regularity, as if controlled by a schedule, bullets buffed into men.

The youth walked stolidly into the midst of the mob, and with his flag in his hands took a stand as if he expected an attempt to push him into the ground. He unconsciously assumed the attitude of the color bearer in the fight of the preceding day. He passed over his brow a hand that trembled. His breath did not come freely. He was choking during this small wait for the crisis.

His friend came to him. "Well, Henry, I guess this is good-bye—John."

"Oh, shut up, you damned fool!" replied the youth, and he would not look at the other.

The officers labored like politicians to beat the mass into a proper circle to face the menaces. The ground was uneven and torn. The men curled into depressions and fitted themselves snugly behind whatever would frustrate a bullet.

The youth noted with vague surprise that the lieutenant was standing mutely with his legs far apart and his sword held in the manner of a cane. The youth wondered what had happened to his vocal organs that he no more cursed.

There was something curious in this little intent pause of the lieutenant. He was like a babe which, having wept its fill, raises its eyes and fixes them upon a distant toy. He was engrossed in this contemplation, and the soft under lip quivered from self-whispered words.

Some lazy and ignorant smoke curled slowly. The men, hiding from the bullets, waited anxiously for it to lift and disclose the plight of the regiment.

The silent ranks were suddenly thrilled by the eager voice of the youthful lieutenant bawling out: "Here they come! Right onto us, b'Gawd!" His further words were lost in a roar of wicked thunder from the men's rifles.

The youth's eyes had instantly turned in the direction indicated by the awakened and agitated lieutenant, and he had seen the haze of treachery disclosing a body of soldiers of the enemy. They were so near that he could see their features. There was a recognition as he looked at the types of faces. Also he perceived with dim amazement that their uniforms were rather gay in effect, being light gray, accented with a brilliant-hued facing. Moreover, the clothes seemed new.

These troops had apparently been going forward with caution, their rifles held in readiness, when the youthful lieutenant had discovered them and their movement had been interrupted by the volley from the blue regiment. From the moment's glimpse, it was derived that they had been unaware of the proximity of their dark-suited foes or had mistaken the direction. Almost instantly they were shut utterly from the youth's sight by the smoke from the energetic rifles of his companions. He strained his vision to learn the accomplishment of the volley, but the smoke hung before him.

The two bodies of troops exchanged blows in the manner of a pair of boxers. The fast angry firings went back and forth. The men in blue were intent with the despair of their circumstances and they seized upon the revenge to be had at close range. Their thunder swelled loud and valiant. Their curving front bristled with flashes and the place resounded with the clangor of their ramrods. The youth ducked and dodged for a time and achieved a few unsatisfactory views of the enemy. There appeared to be many of them and they were replying swiftly. They seemed to be moving toward the blue regiment, step by step. He seated himself gloomily on the ground with his flag between his knees.

As he noted the vicious, wolflike temper of his comrades he had a sweet thought that if the enemy was about to swallow the regimental broom as a large prisoner, it could at least have the consolation of going down with bristles forward.

But the blows of the antagonist began to grow more weak. Fewer bullets ripped the air, and finally, when the men slackened to learn of the fight, they could see only dark, floating smoke. The regiment lay still and gazed. Presently some chance whim came to the pestering blur, and it began to coil heavily away. The men saw a ground vacant of fighters. It would have been an empty stage if it were not for a few corpses that lay thrown and twisted into fantastic shapes upon the sward.

At sight of this tableau, many of the men in blue sprang from behind their covers and made an ungainly dance of joy. Their eyes burned and a hoarse cheer of elation broke from their dry lips.

It had begun to seem to them that events were trying to prove that they were impotent. These little battles had evidently endeavored to demonstrate that the men could not fight well. When on the verge of submission to these opinions, the small duel had showed them that the proportions were not impossible, and by it they had revenged themselves upon their misgivings and upon the foe.

The impetus of enthusiasm was theirs again. They gazed about them with looks of uplifted pride, feeling new trust in the grim, always confident weapons in their hands. And they were men.

21

Presently they knew that no firing threatened them. All ways seemed once more open to them. The dusty blue lines of their friends were disclosed a short distance away. In the distance there were many colossal noises, but in all this part of the field there was a sudden stillness.

They perceived that they were free. The depleted band drew a long breath of relief and gathered itself into a bunch to complete its trip.

In this last length of journey the men began to show strange emotions. They hurried with nervous fear. Some who had been dark and unfaltering in the grimmest moments now could not conceal an anxiety that made them frantic. It was perhaps that they dreaded to be killed in insignificant ways after the times for proper military deaths had passed. Or, perhaps, they thought it would be too ironical to get killed at the portals of safety. With backward looks of perturbation, they hastened.

As they approached their own lines there was some sarcasm exhibited on the part of a gaunt and bronzed regiment that lay resting in the shade of trees. Questions were wafted to them.

"Where th' hell yeh been?"

"What yeh comin' back fer?"

"Why didn't yeh stay there?"

"Was it warm out there, sonny?"

"Goin' home now, boys?"

One shouted in taunting mimicry: "Oh, mother, come quick an' look at th' sojers!"

There was no reply from the bruised and battered regiment, save that one man made broadcast challenges to fist fights and the red-bearded officer walked rather near and glared in great swashbuckler style at a tall captain in the other regiment. But the lieutenant suppressed the man who wished to fist fight, and the tall captain, flushing at the little fanfare of the red-bearded one, was obliged to look intently at some trees.

The youth's tender flesh was deeply stung by these remarks. From under his creased brows he glowered with hate at the mockers. He meditated upon a few revenges. Still, many in the regiment hung their heads in criminal fashion, so that it came to pass that the men trudged with sudden heaviness, as if they bore upon their bended shoulders the coffin of their honor. And the youthful lieutenant, recollecting himself, began to mutter softly in black curses.

They turned when they arrived at their old position to regard the ground over which they had charged.

The youth in this contemplation was smitten with a large astonishment. He discovered that the distances, as compared with the brilliant measurings of his mind, were trivial and ridiculous. The stolid trees, where much had taken place, seemed incredibly near. The time, too, now that he reflected, he saw to have been short. He wondered at the number of emotions and events that had been crowded into such little spaces. Elfin thoughts must have exaggerated and enlarged everything, he said.

It seemed, then, that there was bitter justice in the speeches of the gaunt and bronzed veterans. He veiled a glance of disdain at his fellows who strewed the ground, choking with dust, red from perspiration, misty-eyed, disheveled.

They were gulping at their canteens, fierce to wring every mite of water from them, and they polished at their swollen and watery features with coat sleeves and bunches of grass.

However, to the youth there was a considerable joy in musing upon his performances during the charge. He had had very little time previously in which to appreciate himself, so that there was now much satisfaction in quietly thinking of his actions. He recalled bits of color that in the flurry had stamped themselves unawares upon his engaged senses.

As the regiment lay heaving from its hot exertions the officer who had named them as mule drivers came galloping along the line. He had lost his cap. His tousled hair streamed wildly, and his face was dark with vexation and wrath. His temper was displayed with more clearness by the way in which he managed his horse. He jerked and wrenched savagely at his bridle, stopping the hard-breathing animal with a furious pull near the colonel of the regiment. He immediately exploded in reproaches which came unbidden to the ears of the men. They were suddenly alert, being always curious about black words between officers.

"Oh, thunder, MacChesnay, what an awful bull you made of this thing!" began the officer. He attempted low tones, but his indignation caused certain of the men to learn the sense of his words. "What an awful mess you made! Good Lord, man, you stopped about a hundred feet this side of a very pretty success! If your men had gone a hundred feet farther you would have made a great charge, but as it is —what a lot of mud diggers you've got anyway!"

The men, listening with bated breath, now turned their curious eyes upon the colonel. They had a ragamuffin interest in this affair.

The colonel was seen to straighten his form and put one hand forth in oratorical fashion. He wore an injured air; it was as if a deacon had been accused of stealing. The men were wiggling in an ecstasy of excitement.

But of a sudden the colonel's manner changed from that of a deacon to that of a Frenchman. He shrugged his shoulders. "Oh, well, general, we went as far as we could," he said calmly.

"As far as you could? Did you, b'Gawd?" snorted the other. "Well, that wasn't very far, was it?" he added, with a glance of cold contempt into the other's eyes. "Not very far, I think. You were intended to make a diversion in favor of Whiterside. How well you succeeded your own ears can now tell you." He wheeled his horse and rode stiffly away.

The colonel, bidden to hear the jarring noises of an engagement in the woods to the left, broke out in vague damnations.

The lieutenant, who had listened with an air of impotent rage to the interview, spoke suddenly in firm and undaunted tones. "I don't care what a man is—

whether he is a general or what—if he says th' boys didn't put up a good fight out there he's a damned fool."

"Lieutenant," began the colonel, severely, "this is my own affair, and I'll trouble you—"

The lieutenant made an obedient gesture. "All right, colonel, all right," he said. He sat down with an air of being content with himself.

The news that the regiment had been reproached went along the line. For a time the men were bewildered by it. "Good thunder!" they ejaculated, staring at the vanishing form of the general. They conceived it to be a huge mistake.

Presently, however, they began to believe that in truth their efforts had been called light. The youth could see this conviction weigh upon the entire regiment until the men were like cuffed and cursed animals, but withal rebellious.

The friend, with a grievance in his eye, went to the youth. "I wonder what he does want," he said. "He must think we went out there an' played marbles! I never see sech a man!"

The youth developed a tranquil philosophy for these moments of irritation. "Oh, well," he rejoined, "he probably didn't see nothing of it at all and got mad as blazes, and concluded we were a lot of sheep, just because we didn't do what he wanted done. It's a pity old Grandpa Henderson got killed yestirday—he'd have known that we did our best and fought good. It's just our awful luck, that's what."

"I should say so," replied the friend. He seemed to be deeply wounded at an injustice. "I should say we did have awful luck! There's no fun in fightin' fer people when everything yeh do—no matter what—ain't done right. I have a notion t' stay behind next time an' let 'em take their ol' charge an' go t' th' devil with it."

The youth spoke soothingly to his comrade. "Well, we both did good. I'd like to see the fool what'd say we both didn't do as good as we could!"

"Of course we did," declared the friend stoutly. "An' I'd break th' feller's neck if he was as big as a church. But we're all right, anyhow, for I heard one feller say that we two fit th' best in th' reg'ment, an' they had a great argument 'bout it. Another feller, 'a course, he had t' up an' say it was a lie—he seen all what was goin' on an' he never seen us from th' beginnin' t' th' end. An' a lot more struck in an' ses it wasn't a lie—we did fight like thunder, an' they give us quite a send-off. But this is what I can't stand—these everlastin' ol' soldiers, titterin' an' laughin', an' then that general, he's crazy."

The youth exclaimed with sudden exasperation: "He's a lunkhead! He makes me mad. I wish he'd come along next time. We'd show 'im what—"

He ceased because several men had come hurrying up. Their faces expressed a bringing of great news.

"O Flem, yeh jest oughta heard!" cried one, eagerly.

"Heard what?" said the youth.

"Yeh jest oughta heard!" repeated the other, and he arranged himself to tell his tidings. The others made an excited circle. "Well, sir, th' colonel met your lieutenant right by us—it was th' damnedest thing I ever heard—an' he ses: 'Ahem! ahem!' he ses. 'Mr. Hasbrouck!' he ses, 'by th' way, who was that lad what carried th' flag?' he ses. There, Flemin', what d' yeh think 'a that? 'Who was th' lad what carried th' flag?' he ses, an' th' lieutenant, he speaks up right away: 'That's Flemin', an' he's a jimhickey,' he ses right away. What? I say he did. 'A jimhickey,' he ses—those 'r his words. He did, too. I say he did. If you kin tell this story better than I kin, go ahead an' tell it. Well, then, keep yer mouth shet. Th' lieutenant, he ses: 'He's a jimhickey,' an' th' colonel, he ses: 'Ahem! ahem! he is, indeed, a very good man t' have, ahem! He kep' th' flag 'way t' th' front. I saw 'im.

He's a good un,' ses th' colonel. 'You bet,' ses th' lieutenant, 'he an' a feller named Wilson was at th' head 'a th' charge, an' howlin' like Indians all th' time,' he ses. 'Head 'a th' charge all th' time,' he ses. 'A feller named Wilson,' he ses. There, Wilson, m'boy, put that in a letter an' send it hum t' yer mother, hay? 'A feller named Wilson,' he ses. An' th' colonel, he ses: 'Were they, indeed? Ahem! ahem! My sakes!' he ses. 'At th' head 'a th' reg'ment?' he ses. 'They were,' ses th' lieutenant. 'My sakes!' ses th' colonel. He ses: 'Well, well, well,' he ses, 'those two babies?' 'They were,' ses th' lieutenant. 'Well, well,' ses th' colonel, 'they deserve t' be major-generals,' he ses. 'They deserve t' be major-generals.'

The youth and his friend had said: "Huh!" "Yer lyin', Thompson." "Oh, go t' blazes!" "He never sed it." "Oh, what a lie!" "Huh!" But despite these youthful scoffings and embarrassments, they knew that their faces were deeply flushing from thrills of pleasure. They exchanged a secret glance of joy and congratulation.

They speedily forgot many things. The past held no pictures of error and disappointment. They were very happy, and their hearts swelled with grateful affection for the colonel and the youthful lieutenant.

22

When the woods again began to pour forth the dark-hued masses of the enemy the youth felt serene self-confidence. He smiled briefly when he saw men dodge and duck at the long screeching of shells that were thrown in giant handfuls over them. He stood, erect and tranquil, watching the attack begin against a part of the line that made a blue curve along the side of an adjacent hill. His vision being unmolested by smoke from the rifles of his companions, he had opportunities to see parts of the hard fight. It was a relief to perceive at last from whence came some of these noises which had been roared into his ears.

Off a short way he saw two regiments fighting a little separate battle with two other regiments. It was in a cleared space, wearing a set-apart look. They were blazing as if upon a wager, giving and taking tremendous blows. The firings were incredibly fierce and rapid. These intent regiments apparently were oblivious of all larger purposes of war, and were slugging each other as if at a matched game.

In another direction he saw a magnificent brigade going with the evident intention of driving the enemy from a wood. They passed in out of sight and presently there was a most awe-inspiring racket in the wood. The noise was unspeakable. Having stirred this prodigious uproar, and, apparently, finding it too prodigious, the brigade, after a little time, came marching airily out again with its fine formation in nowise disturbed. There were no traces of speed in its movements. The brigade was jaunty and seemed to point a proud thumb at the yelling wood.

On a slope to the left there was a long row of guns, gruff and maddened, denouncing the enemy, who, down through the woods, were forming for another attack in the pitiless monotony of conflicts. The round red discharges from the guns made a crimson flare and a high, thick smoke. Occasional glimpses could be caught of groups of the toiling artillerymen. In the rear of this row of guns stood a house, calm and white, amid bursting shells. A congregation of horses, tied to a long railing, were tugging frenziedly at their bridles. Men were running hither and thither.

The detached battle between the four regiments lasted for some time. There chanced to be no interference, and they settled their dispute by themselves. They struck savagely and powerfully at each other for a period of minutes, and then the lighter-hued regiments faltered and drew back, leaving the dark-blue lines shouting. The youth could see the two flags shaking with laughter amid the smoke remnants.

Presently there was a stillness, pregnant with meaning. The blue lines shifted and changed a trifle and stared expectantly at the silent woods and fields before them. The hush was solemn and churchlike, save for a distant battery that, evidently unable to remain quiet, sent a faint rolling thunder over the ground. It irritated, like the noises of unimpressed boys. The men imagined that it would prevent their perched ears from hearing the first words of the new battle.

Of a sudden the guns on the slope roared out a message of warning. A spluttering sound had begun in the woods. It swelled with amazing speed to a profound clamor that involved the earth in noises. The splitting crashes swept along the lines until an interminable roar was developed. To those in the midst of it it became a din fitted to the universe. It was the whirring and thumping of gigantic machinery, complications among the smaller stars. The youth's ears were filled up. They were incapable of hearing more.

On an incline over which a road wound he saw wild and desperate rushes of men perpetually backward and forward in riotous surges. These parts of the opposing armies were two long waves that pitched upon each other madly at dictated points. To and fro they swelled. Sometimes, one side by its yells and cheers would proclaim decisive blows, but a moment later the other side would be all yells and cheers. Once the youth saw a spray of light forms go in houndlike leaps toward the waving blue lines. There was much howling, and presently it went away with a vast mouthful of prisoners. Again, he saw a blue wave dash with such thunderous force against a gray obstruction that it seemed to clear the earth of it and leave nothing but trampled sod. And always in their swift and deadly rushes to and fro the men screamed and yelled like maniacs.

Particular pieces of fence or secure positions behind collections of trees were wrangled over, as gold thrones or pearl bedsteads. There were desperate lunges at these chosen spots seemingly every instant, and most of them were bandied like light toys between the contending forces. The youth could not tell from the battle flags flying like crimson foam in many directions which color of cloth was winning.

His emaciated regiment bustled forth with undiminished fierceness when its time came. When assaulted by bullets, the men burst out in a barbaric cry of rage and pain. They bent their heads in aims of intent hatred behind the projected hammers of their guns. Their ramrods clanged loud with fury as their eager arms pounded the cartridges into the rifle barrels. The front of the regiment was a smoke-wall penetrated by the flashing points of yellow and red.

Wallowing in the fight, they were in an astonishingly short time resmudged. They surpassed in stain and dirt all their previous appearances. Moving to and fro with strained exertion, jabbering the while, they were, with their swaying bodies, black faces, and glowing eyes, like strange and ugly friends jigging heavily in the smoke.

The lieutenant, returning from a tour after a bandage, produced from a hidden receptacle of his mind new and portentous oaths suited to the emergency. Strings of expletives he swung lashlike over the backs of his men, and it was evident that his previous efforts had in nowise impaired his resources.

The youth, still the bearer of the colors, did not feel his idleness. He was deeply absorbed as a spectator. The crash and swing of the great drama made him lean forward, intent-eyed, his face working in small contortions. Sometimes he prattled, words coming unconsciously from him in grotesque exclamations. He did not know that he breathed; that the flag hung silently over him, so absorbed was he.

A formidable line of the enemy came within dangerous range. They could be seen plainly—tall, gaunt men with excited faces running with long strides toward a wandering fence.

At sight of this danger the men suddenly ceased their cursing monotone. There was an instant of strained silence before they threw up their rifles and fired a plumping volley at the foes. There had been no order given; the men, upon recognizing the menace, had immediately let drive their flock of bullets without waiting for word of command.

But the enemy were quick to gain the protection of the wandering line of fence. They slid down behind it with remarkable celerity, and from this position they began briskly to slice up the blue men.

These latter braced their energies for a great struggle. Often, white clinched teeth shone from the dusky faces. Many heads surged to and fro, floating upon a pale sea of smoke. Those behind the fence frequently shouted and yelped in taunts and gibelike cries, but the regiment maintained a stressed silence. Perhaps, at this new assault the men recalled the fact that they had been named mud diggers, and it made their situation thrice bitter. They were breathlessly intent upon keeping the ground and thrusting away the rejoicing body of the enemy. They fought swiftly and with a despairing savageness denoted in their expressions.

The youth had resolved not to budge whatever should happen. Some arrows of scorn that had buried themselves in his heart had generated strange and unspeakable hatred. It was clear to him that his final and absolute revenge was to be achieved by his dead body lying, torn and gluttering, upon the field. This was to be a poignant retaliation upon the officer who had said "mule drivers," and later "mud diggers," for in all the wild graspings of his mind for a unit responsible for his sufferings and commotions he always seized upon the man who had dubbed him wrongly. And it was his idea, vaguely formulated, that his corpse would be for those eyes a great and salt reproach.

The regiment bled extravagantly. Grunting bundles of blue began to drop. The orderly sergeant of the youth's company was shot through the cheeks. Its support being injured, his jaw hung afar down, disclosing in the wide cavern of his mouth a pulsing mass of blood and teeth. And with it all he made attempts to cry out. In his endeavor there was a dreadful earnestness, as if he conceived that one great shriek would make him well.

The youth saw him presently go rearward. His strength seemed in nowise impaired. He ran swiftly, casting wild glances for succor.

Others fell down about the feet of their companions. Some of the wounded crawled out and away, but many lay still, their bodies twisted into impossible shapes.

The youth looked once for his friend. He saw a vehement young man, powder-smeared and frowzled, whom he knew to be him. The lieutenant, also, was unscathed in his position at the rear. He had continued to curse, but it was now with the air of a man who was using his last box of oaths.

For the fire of the regiment had begun to wane and drip. The robust voice, that had come strangely from the thin ranks, was growing rapidly weak.

23

The colonel came running along back of the line. There were other officers following him. "We must charge'm!" they shouted. "We must charge'm!" they cried with resentful voices, as if anticipating a rebellion against this plan by the men.

The youth, upon hearing the shouts, began to study the distance between him and the enemy. He made vague calculations. He saw that to be firm soldiers they must go forward. It would be death to stay in the present place, and with all the circumstances to go backward would exalt too many others. Their hope was to push the galling foes away from the fence.

He expected that his companions, weary and stiffened, would have to be driven to this assault, but as he turned toward them he perceived with a certain surprise that they were giving quick and unqualified expressions of assent. There was an ominous, clanging overture to the charge when the shafts of the bayonets rattled upon the rifle barrels. At the yelled words of command the soldiers sprang forward in eager leaps. There was new and unexpected force in the movement of the regiment. A knowledge of its faded and jaded condition made the charge appear like a paroxysm, a display of strength that comes before a final feebleness. The men scampered in insane fever of haste, racing as if to achieve a sudden success before an exhilarating fluid should leave them. It was a blind and despairing rush by the collection of men in dusty and tattered blue, over a green sward and under a sapphire sky, toward a fence, dimly outlined in smoke, from behind which spluttered the fierce rifles of enemies.

The youth kept the bright colors to the front. He was waving his free arm in furious circles, the while shrieking mad calls and appeals, urging on those that did not need to be urged, for it seemed that the mob of blue men hurling themselves on the dangerous group of rifles were again grown suddenly wild with an enthusiasm of unselfishness. From the many firings starting toward them, it looked as if they would merely succeed in making a great sprinkling of corpses on the grass between their former position and the fence. But they were in a state of frenzy, perhaps because of forgotten vanities, and it made an exhibition of sublime recklessness. There was no obvious questioning, nor figurings, nor diagrams. There was, apparently, no considered loopholes. It appeared that the swift wings of their desires would have shattered against the iron gates of the impossible.

He himself felt the daring spirit of a savage religion-mad. He was capable of profound sacrifices, a tremendous death. He had no time for dissections, but he knew that he thought of the bullets only as things that could prevent him from reaching the place of his endeavor. There were subtle flashings of joy within him that thus should be his mind.

He strained all his strength. His eyesight was shaken and dazzled by the tension of thought and muscle. He did not see anything excepting the mist of smoke gashed by the little knives of fire, but he knew that in it lay the aged fence of a vanished farmer protecting the snuggled bodies of the gray men.

As he ran a thought of the shock of contact gleamed in his mind. He expected a great concussion when the two bodies of troops crashed together. This became a part of his wild battle madness. He could feel the onward swing of the regiment about him and he conceived of a thunderous, crushing blow that would prostrate the resistance and spread consternation and amazement for miles. The flying regiment was going to have a catapultian effect. This dream made him run faster among his comrades, who were giving vent to hoarse and frantic cheers.

But presently he could see that many of the men in gray did not intend to abide the blow. The smoke, rolling, disclosed men who ran, their faces still turned. These grew to a crowd, who retired stubbornly. Individuals wheeled frequently to send a bullet at the blue wave.

But at one part of the line there was a grim and obdurate group that made no movement. They were settled firmly down behind posts and rails. A flag, ruffled and fierce, waved over them and their rifles dinned fiercely.

The blue whirl of men got very near, until it seemed that in truth there would be a close and frightful scuffle. There was an expressed disdain in the opposition of the little group, that changed the meaning of the cheers of the men in blue. They became yells of wrath, directed, personal. The cries of the two parties were now in sound an interchange of scathing insults.

They in blue showed their teeth; their eyes shone all white. They launched themselves as at the throats of those who stood resisting. The space between dwindled to an insignificant distance.

The youth had centered the gaze of his soul upon that other flag. Its possession would be high pride. It would express bloody minglings, near blows. He had a gigantic hatred for those who made great difficulties and complications. They caused it to be as a craved treasure of mythology, hung amid tasks and contrivances of danger.

He plunged like a mad horse at it. He was resolved it should not escape if wild blows and darings of blows could seize it. His own emblem, quivering and aflare, was winging toward the other. It seemed there would shortly be an encounter of strange beaks and claws, as of eagles.

The swirling body of blue men came to a sudden halt at close and disastrous range and roared a swift volley. The group in gray was split and broken by this fire, but its riddled body still fought. The men in blue yelled again and rushed in upon it.

The youth, in his leapings, saw, as through a mist, a picture of four or five men stretched upon the ground or writhing upon their knees with bowed heads as if they had been stricken by bolts from the sky. Tottering among them was the rival color bearer, whom the youth saw had been bitten vitally by the bullets of the last formidable volley. He perceived this man fighting a last struggle, the struggle of one whose legs are grasped by demons. It was a ghastly battle. Over his face was the bleach of death, but set upon it was the dark and hard lines of desperate purpose. With this terrible grin of resolution he hugged his precious flag to him and was stumbling and staggering in his design to go the way that led to safety for it.

But his wounds always made it seem that his feet were retarded, held, and he fought a grim fight, as with invisible ghouls fastened greedily upon his limbs. Those in advance of the scampering blue men, howling cheers, leaped at the fence. The despair of the lost was in his eyes as he glanced back at them.

The youth's friend went over the obstruction in a tumbling heap and sprang at the flag as a panther at prey. He pulled at it and, wrenching it free, swung up its red brilliancy with a mad cry of exultation even as the color bearer, gasping, lurched over in a final throe and, stiffening convulsively, turned his dead face to the ground. There was much blood upon the grass blades.

At the place of success there began more wild clamorings of cheers. The men gesticulated and bellowed in an ecstasy. When they spoke it was as if they considered their listner to be a mile away. What hats and caps were left to them they often slung high in the air.

At one part of the line four men had been swooped upon, and they now sat as prisoners. Some blue men were about them in an eager and curious circle. The soldiers had trapped strange birds, and there was an examination. A flurry of fast questions was in the air.

One of the prisoners was nursing a superficial wound in the foot. He cuddled it, baby-wise, but he looked up from it often to curse with an astonishing utter abandon straight at the noses of his captors. He consigned them to red regions; he called upon the pestilential wrath of strange gods. And with it all he was singularly free from recognition of the finer points of the conduct of prisoners of war. It was as if a clumsy clod had trod upon his toe and he conceived it to be his privilege, his duty, to use deep, resentful oaths.

Another, who was a boy in years, took his plight with great calmness and apparent good nature. He conversed with the men in blue, studying their faces with his bright and keen eyes. They spoke of battles and conditions. There was an acute interest in all their faces during this exchange of view points. It seemed a great satisfaction to hear voices from where all had been darkness and speculation.

The third captive sat with a morose countenance. He preserved a stoical and cold attitude. To all advances he made one reply without variation, "Ah, go t' hell!"

The last of the four was always silent and, for the most part, kept his face turned in unmolested directions. From the views the youth received he seemed to be in a state of absolute dejection. Shame was upon him, and with it profound regret that he was, perhaps, no more to be counted in the ranks of his fellows. The youth could detect no expression that would allow him to believe that the other was giving a thought to his narrow future, the pictured dungeons, perhaps, and starvations and brutalities, liable to the imagination. All to be seen was shame for captivity and regret for the right to antagonize.

After the men had celebrated sufficiently they settled down behind the old rail fence, on the opposite side to the one from which their foes had been driven. A few shot perfunctorily at distant marks.

There was some long grass. The youth nestled in it and rested, making a convenient rail support the flag. His friend, jubilant and glorified, holding his treasure with vanity, came to him there. They sat side by side and congratulated each other.

24

The roarings that had stretched in a long line of sound across the face of the forest began to grow intermittent and weaker. The stentorian speeches of the artillery continued in some distant encounter, but the crashes of the musketry had almost ceased. The youth and his friend of a sudden looked up, feeling a dead-ened form of distress at the waning of these noises, which had become a part of life. They could see changes going on among the troops. There were marchings this way and that way. A battery wheeled leisurely. On the crest of a small hill was the thick gleam of many departing muskets.

The youth arose. "Well, what now, I wonder?" he said. By his tone he seemed to be preparing to resent some new monstrosity in the way of dins and smashes. He shaded his eyes with his grimy hand and gazed over the field.

His friend also arose and stared. "I bet we're goin' t' git along out of this an' back over th' river," said he.

"Well, I swan!" said the youth.

They waited, watching. Within a little while the regiment received orders to retrace its way. The men got up grunting from the grass, regretting the soft repose. They jerked their stiffened legs, and stretched their arms over their heads. One man swore as he rubbed his eyes. They all groaned "O Lord!" They had as many objections to this change as they would have had to a proposal for a new battle.

They trampled slowly back over the field across which they had run in a mad scamper.

The regiment marched until it had joined its fellows. The reformed brigade, in column, aimed through a wood at the road. Directly they were in a mass of dust-covered troops, and were trudging along in a way parallel to the enemy's lines as these had been defined by the previous turmoil.

They passed within view of a stolid white house, and saw in front of it groups of their comrades lying in wait behind a neat breastwork. A row of guns were boom-ing at a distant enemy. Shells thrown in reply were raising clouds of dust and splinters. Horsemen dashed along the line of intrenchments.

At this point of its march the division curved away from the field and went winding off in the direction of the river. When the significance of this movement had impressed itself upon the youth he turned his head and looked over his shoulder toward the trampled and *débris*-strewed ground. He breathed a breath of new satisfaction. He finally nudged his friend. "Well, it's all over," he said to him.

His friend gazed backward. "B'Gawd, it is," he assented. They mused.

For a time the youth was obliged to reflect in a puzzled and uncertain way. His mind was undergoing a subtle change. It took moments for it to cast off its battleful ways and resume its accustomed course of thought. Gradually his brain emerged from the clogged clouds, and at last he was enabled to more closely comprehend himself and circumstance.

He understood then that the existence of shot and counter-shot was in the past. He had dwelt in a land of strange, squalling upheavals and had come forth. He had been where there was red of blood and black of passion, and he was escaped. His first thoughts were given to rejoicings at this fact.

Later he began to study his deeds, his failures, and his achievements. Thus, fresh from scenes where many of his usual machines of reflection had been idle, from where he had proceeded sheeplike, he struggled to marshal all his acts.

At last they marched before him clearly. From this present view point he was enabled to look upon them in spectator fashion and to criticise them with some correctness, for his new condition had already defeated certain sympathies.

Regarding his procession of memory he felt gleeful and unregretting, for in it his public deeds were paraded in great and shining prominence. Those performances which had been witnessed by his fellows marched now in wide purple and gold, having various deflections. They went gayly with music. It was a pleasure to watch these things. He spent delightful minutes viewing the gilded images of memory.

He saw that he was good. He recalled with a thrill of joy the respectful comments of his fellows upon his conduct.

Nevertheless, the ghost of his flight from the first engagement appeared to him and danced. There were small shoutings in his brain about these matters. For a moment he blushed, and the light of his soul flickered with shame.

A specter of reproach came to him. There loomed the dogging memory of the tattered soldier—he who, gored by bullets and faint for blood, had fretted concerning an imagined wound in another; he who had loaned his last of strength and intellect for the tall soldier; he who, blind with weariness and pain, had been deserted in the field.

For an instant a wretched chill of sweat was upon him at the thought that he might be detected in the thing. As he stood persistently before his vision, he gave vent to a cry of sharp irritation and agony.

His friend turned. "What's the matter, Henry?" he demanded. The youth's reply was an outburst of crimson oaths.

As he marched along the little branch-hung roadway among his prattling companions this vision of cruelty brooded over him. It clung near him always and darkened his view of these deeds in purple and gold. Whichever way his thoughts turned they were followed by the somber phantom of the desertion in the fields. He looked stealthily at his companions, feeling sure that they must discern in his face evidences of this pursuit. But they were plodding in ragged array, discussing with quick tongues the accomplishments of the late battle.

"Oh, if a man should come up an' ask me, I'd say we got a dum good lickin'."

"Lickin'—in yer eye! We ain't licked, sonny. We're goin' down here aways, swing aroun', an' comin' in behint—"

"Oh, hush, with your comin' in behint 'em. I've seen all 'a that I wanta. Don't tell me about comin' in behint—"

"Bill Smithers, he ses he'd rather been in ten hundred battles than been in that heluva hospital. He ses they got shootin' in th' nighttime, an' shells dropped plum among 'em in th' hospital. He ses sech hollerin' he never see."

"Hasbrouck? He's th' best off'cer in this here reg'ment. He's a whale."

"Didn't I tell yeh we'd come aroun' in behint 'em? Didn't I tell yeh so? We—"

"Oh, shet yeh mouth!"

For a time this pursuing recollection of the tattered man took all elation from the youth's veins. He saw his vivid error, and he was afraid that it would stand before him all his life. He took no share in the chatter of his comrades, nor did he look at them or know them, save when he felt sudden suspicion that they were seeing his thoughts and scrutinizing each detail of the scene with the tattered soldier.

Yet gradually he mustered force to put the sin at a distance. And at last his eyes seemed to open to some new ways. He found that he could look back upon the brass and bombast of his earlier gospels and see them truly. He was gleeful when he discovered that he now despised them.

With this conviction came a store of assurance. He felt a quiet manhood, nonassertive but of sturdy and strong blood. He knew that he would no more quail before his guides wherever they should point. He had been to touch the great death, and found that after all, it was but the great death. He was a man.

So it came to pass that as he trudged from the place of blood and wrath his soul changed. He came from hot plowshares to prospects of clover tranquilly, and it was as if hot plowshares were not. Scars faded as flowers.

It rained. The procession of weary soldiers became a bedraggled train, despondent and muttering, marching with churning effort in a trough of liquid brown mud under a low, wretched sky. Yet the youth smiled, for he saw that the world was a world for him, though many discovered it to be made of oaths and walking sticks. He had rid himself of the red sickness of battle. The sultry nightmare was in the past. He had been an animal blistered and sweating in the heat and pain of war. He turned now with a lover's thirst to images of tranquil skies, fresh meadows, cool brooks—an existence of soft and eternal peace.

Over the river a golden ray of sun came through the hosts of leaden rain clouds.

ABOUT THE EDITOR

MARC JAFFE has been a student of American history and literature since his undergraduate days at Harvard. His military career in World War II included two major campaigns as a platoon and company commander with the 2nd Battalion, First Marines in the Pacific. Mr. Jaffe was Editorial Director at Bantam Books for nineteen years, and since 1987 has had his own imprint, Marc Jaffe Books, in association with Houghton Mifflin Company.

He lives in Berlin, NY, with his wife Vivienne, also an editor, and their two children, Eva Rachel and Benjamin.